THE APPEAL

Also by John Grisham

JOHN
GRISHAM
THE APPEAL

- Black Mele, Matching
 Chorafew
- P+3 what a take on
 grubbing women
 JG has? & bottom
 of P44.

Century · London

First published in Great Britain in 2008 by
Century
Random House, 20 Vauxhall Bridge Road,
London SW1V 2SA

www.rbooks.co.uk

Addresses for companies within The Random House Group Limited can be found at:
www.randomhouse.co.uk/offices.htm

The Random House Group Limited Reg. No. 954009

A CIP catalogue record for this book
is available from the British Library

HB ISBN 9781844138234
TPB ISBN 9781844138548

The Random House Group Limited supports The Forest Stewardship Council (FSC),
the leading international forest certification organisation. All our titles that are printed
on Greenpeace approved FSC certified paper carry the FSC logo. Our paper
procurement policy can be found at www.rbooks.co.uk/environment

Mixed Sources
Product group from well-managed
forests and other controlled sources
www.fsc.org Cert no. TT-COC-2139
© 1996 Forest Stewardship Council
FSC

Printed and bound in Great Britain by
CPI Mackays, Chatham, ME5 8TD

TO PROFESSOR ROBERT C. KHAYAT

PART ONE

THE
VERDICT

CHAPTER 1

The jury was ready.

After forty-two hours of deliberations that followed seventy-one days of trial that included 530 hours of testimony from four dozen witnesses, and after a lifetime of sitting silently as the lawyers haggled and the judge lectured and the spectators watched like hawks for telltale signs, the jury was ready. Locked away in the jury room, secluded and secure, ten of them proudly signed their names to the verdict while the other two pouted in their corners, detached and miserable in their dissension. There were hugs and smiles and no small measure of self-congratulation because they had survived this little war and could now march proudly back into the arena with a decision they had rescued through sheer determination and the dogged pursuit of compromise. Their ordeal was over; their civic duty complete. They had served above and beyond. They were ready.

The foreman knocked on the door and rustled Uncle Joe from his slumbers. Uncle Joe, the ancient bailiff, had guarded them while he also arranged their meals, heard their complaints, and quietly slipped their messages to the judge. In his younger years, back when his hearing was

better, Uncle Joe was rumored to also eavesdrop on his juries through a flimsy pine door he and he alone had selected and installed. But his listening days were over, and, as he had confided to no one but his wife, after the ordeal of this particular trial he might just hang up his old pistol once and for all. The strain of controlling justice was wearing him down.

He smiled and said, "That's great. I'll get the judge," as if the judge were somewhere in the bowels of the courthouse just waiting for a call from Uncle Joe. Instead, by custom, he found a clerk and passed along the wonderful news. It was truly exciting. The old courthouse had never seen a trial so large and so long. To end it with no decision at all would have been a shame.

The clerk tapped lightly on the judge's door, then took a step inside and proudly announced, "We have a verdict," as if she had personally labored through the negotiations and now was presenting the result as a gift.

The judge closed his eyes and let loose a deep, satisfying sigh. He smiled a happy, nervous smile of enormous relief, almost disbelief, and finally said, "Round up the lawyers."

After almost five days of deliberations, Judge Harrison had resigned himself to the likelihood of a hung jury, his worst nightmare. After four years of bare-knuckle litigation and four months of a hotly contested trial, the prospect of a draw made him ill. He couldn't begin to imagine the prospect of doing it all again.

He stuck his feet into his old penny loafers, jumped from the chair grinning like a little boy, and reached for his robe. It was finally over, the longest trial of his extremely colorful career.

The clerk's first call went to the firm of Payton & Payton, a local husband-and-wife team now operating out of an abandoned dime store in a lesser part of town. A paralegal picked up the phone, listened for a few seconds, hung up, then shouted, "The jury has a verdict!" His voice echoed through the cavernous maze of small, temporary workrooms and jolted his colleagues.

He shouted it again as he ran to The Pit, where the rest of the firm was frantically gathering. Wes Payton was already there, and when his

wife, Mary Grace, rushed in, their eyes met in a split second of unbridled fear and bewilderment. Two paralegals, two secretaries, and a book-keeper gathered at the long, cluttered worktable, where they suddenly froze and gawked at one another, all waiting for someone else to speak.

Could it really be over? After they had waited for an eternity, could it end so suddenly? So abruptly? With just a phone call?

"How about a moment of silent prayer," Wes said, and they held hands in a tight circle and prayed as they had never prayed before. All manner of petitions were lifted up to God Almighty, but the common plea was for victory. Please, dear Lord, after all this time and effort and money and fear and doubt, please, oh please, grant us a divine victory. And deliver us from humiliation, ruin, bankruptcy, and a host of other evils that a bad verdict will bring.

The clerk's second call was to the cell phone of Jared Kurtin, the architect of the defense. Mr. Kurtin was lounging peacefully on a rented leather sofa in his temporary office on Front Street in downtown Hatties-burg, three blocks from the courthouse. He was reading a biography and watching the hours pass at $750 per. He listened calmly, slapped the phone shut, and said, "Let's go. The jury is ready." His dark-suited sol-diers snapped to attention and lined up to escort him down the street in the direction of another crushing victory. They marched away without comment, without prayer.

Other calls went to other lawyers, then to the reporters, and within minutes the word was on the street and spreading rapidly.

Somewhere near the top of a tall building in lower Manhattan, a panic-stricken young man barged into a serious meeting and whispered the ur-gent news to Mr. Carl Trudeau, who immediately lost interest in the issues on the table, stood abruptly, and said, "Looks like the jury has reached a verdict." He marched out of the room and down the hall to a vast corner suite, where he removed his jacket, loosened his tie, walked to a window, and gazed through the early darkness at the Hudson River in the distance. He waited, and as usual asked himself how, exactly, so much

of his empire could rest upon the combined wisdom of twelve average people in backwater Mississippi.

For a man who knew so much, that answer was still elusive.

———

People were hurrying into the courthouse from all directions when the Paytons parked on the street behind it. They stayed in the car for a moment, still holding hands. For four months they had tried not to touch each other anywhere near the courthouse. Someone was always watching. Maybe a juror or a reporter. It was important to be as professional as possible. The novelty of a married legal team surprised people, and the Paytons tried to treat each other as attorneys and not as spouses.

And, during the trial, there had been precious little touching away from the courthouse or anywhere else.

"What are you thinking?" Wes asked without looking at his wife. His heart was racing and his forehead was wet. He still gripped the wheel with his left hand, and he kept telling himself to relax.

Relax. What a joke.

"I have never been so afraid," Mary Grace said.

"Neither have I."

A long pause as they breathed deeply and watched a television van almost slaughter a pedestrian.

"Can we survive a loss?" she said. "That's the question."

"We have to survive; we have no choice. But we're not going to lose."

"Attaboy. Let's go."

They joined the rest of their little firm and entered the courthouse together. Waiting in her usual spot on the first floor by the soft drink machines was their client, the plaintiff, Jeannette Baker, and when she saw her lawyers, she immediately began to cry. Wes took one arm, Mary Grace the other, and they escorted Jeannette up the stairs to the main courtroom on the second floor. They could've carried her. She weighed less than a hundred pounds and had aged five years during the trial. She was depressed, at times delusional, and though not anorexic, she simply

didn't eat. At thirty-four, she had already buried a child and a husband and was now at the end of a horrible trial she secretly wished she had never pursued.

The courtroom was in a state of high alert, as if bombs were coming and the sirens were wailing. Dozens of people milled about, or looked for seats, or chatted nervously with their eyes darting around. When Jared Kurtin and the defense army entered from a side door, everyone gawked as if he might know something they didn't. Day after day for the past four months he had proven that he could see around corners, but at that moment his face revealed nothing. He huddled gravely with his subordinates.

Across the room, just a few feet away, the Paytons and Jeannette settled into their chairs at the plaintiff's table. Same chairs, same positions, same deliberate strategy to impress upon the jurors that this poor widow and her two lonely lawyers were taking on a giant corporation with unlimited resources. Wes Payton glanced at Jared Kurtin, their eyes met, and each offered a polite nod. The miracle of the trial was that the two men were still able to treat each other with a modest dose of civility, even converse when absolutely necessary. It had become a matter of pride. Regardless of how nasty the situation, and there had been so many nasty ones, each was determined to rise above the gutter and offer a hand.

Mary Grace did not look over, and if she had, she would not have nodded or smiled. And it was a good thing that she did not carry a handgun in her purse, or half of the dark suits on the other side wouldn't be there. She arranged a clean legal pad on the table before her, wrote the date, then her name, then could not think of anything else to log in. In seventy-one days of trial she had filled sixty-six legal pads, all the same size and color and now filed in perfect order in a secondhand metal cabinet in The Pit. She handed a tissue to Jeannette. Though she counted virtually everything, Mary Grace had not kept a running tally on the number of tissue boxes Jeannette had used during the trial. Several dozen at least.

The woman cried almost nonstop, and while Mary Grace was profoundly sympathetic, she was also tired of all the damned crying. She was

tired of everything—the exhaustion, the stress, the sleepless nights, the scrutiny, the time away from her children, their run-down apartment, the mountain of unpaid bills, the neglected clients, the cold Chinese food at midnight, the challenge of doing her face and hair every morning so she could be somewhat attractive in front of the jury. It was expected of her.

Stepping into a major trial is like plunging with a weighted belt into a dark and weedy pond. You manage to scramble up for air, but the rest of the world doesn't matter. And you always think you're drowning.

A few rows behind the Paytons, at the end of a bench that was quickly becoming crowded, the Paytons' banker chewed his nails while trying to appear calm. His name was Tom Huff, or Huffy to everyone who knew him. Huffy had dropped in from time to time to watch the trial and offer a silent prayer of his own. The Paytons owed Huffy's bank $400,000, and the only collateral was a tract of farmland in Cary County owned by Mary Grace's father. On a good day it might fetch $100,000, leaving, obviously, a substantial chunk of unsecured debt. If the Paytons lost the case, then Huffy's once promising career as a banker would be over. The bank president had long since stopped yelling at him. Now all the threats were by e-mail.

What had begun innocently enough with a simple $90,000 second-mortgage loan against their lovely suburban home had progressed into a gaping hellhole of red ink and foolish spending. Foolish at least in Huffy's opinion. But the nice home was gone, as was the nice downtown office, and the imported cars, and everything else. The Paytons were risking it all, and Huffy had to admire them. A big verdict, and he was a genius. The wrong verdict, and he'd stand in line behind them at the bankruptcy court.

The moneymen on the other side of the courtroom were not chewing their nails and were not particularly worried about bankruptcy, though it had been discussed. Krane Chemical had plenty of cash and profits and assets, but it also had hundreds of potential plaintiffs waiting like vultures to hear what the world was about to hear. A crazy verdict, and the lawsuits would fly.

But they were a confident bunch at that moment. Jared Kurtin was

the best defense lawyer money could buy. The company's stock had dipped only slightly. Mr. Trudeau, up in New York, seemed to be satisfied.

They couldn't wait to get home.

Thank God the markets had closed for the day.

Uncle Joe yelled, "Keep your seats," and Judge Harrison entered through the door behind his bench. He had long since cut out the silly routine of requiring everyone to stand just so he could assume his throne.

"Good afternoon," he said quickly. It was almost 5:00 p.m. "I have been informed by the jury that a verdict has been reached." He was looking around, making sure the players were present. "I expect decorum at all times. No outbursts. No one leaves until I dismiss the jury. Any questions? Any additional frivolous motions from the defense?"

Jared Kurtin never flinched. He did not acknowledge the judge in any way, but just kept doodling on his legal pad as if he were painting a masterpiece. If Krane Chemical lost, it would appeal with a vengeance, and the cornerstone of its appeal would be the obvious bias of the Honorable Thomas Alsobrook Harrison IV, a former trial lawyer with a proven dislike for all big corporations in general and, now, Krane Chemical in particular.

"Mr. Bailiff, bring in the jury."

The door next to the jury box opened, and somewhere a giant unseen vacuum sucked every ounce of air from the courtroom. Hearts froze. Bodies stiffened. Eyes found objects to fixate on. The only sound was that of the jurors' feet shuffling across well-worn carpet.

Jared Kurtin continued his methodical scribbling. His routine was to never look at the faces of the jurors when they returned with a verdict. After a hundred trials he knew they were impossible to read. And why bother? Their decision would be announced in a matter of seconds anyway. His team had strict instructions to ignore the jurors and show no reaction whatsoever to the verdict.

Of course Jared Kurtin wasn't facing financial and professional ruin. Wes Payton certainly was, and he could not keep his eyes from the eyes of the jurors as they settled into their seats. The dairy operator

looked away, a bad sign. The schoolteacher stared right through Wes, another bad sign. As the foreman handed an envelope to the clerk, the minister's wife glanced at Wes with a look of pity, but then she had been offering the same sad face since the opening statements.

Mary Grace caught the sign, and she wasn't even looking for it. As she handed another tissue to Jeannette Baker, who was practically sobbing now, Mary Grace stole a look at juror number six, the one closest to her, Dr. Leona Rocha, a retired English professor at the university. Dr. Rocha, behind red-framed reading glasses, gave the quickest, prettiest, most sensational wink Mary Grace would ever receive.

"Have you reached a verdict?" Judge Harrison was asking.

"Yes, Your Honor, we have," the foreman said.

"Is it unanimous?"

"No, sir, it is not."

"Do at least nine of you agree on the verdict?"

"Yes, sir. The vote is 10 to 2."

"That's all that matters."

Mary Grace scribbled a note about the wink, but in the fury of the moment she could not read her own handwriting. Try to appear calm, she kept telling herself.

Judge Harrison took the envelope from the clerk, removed a sheet of paper, and began reviewing the verdict—heavy wrinkles burrowing into his forehead, eyes frowning as he pinched the bridge of his nose. After an eternity he said, "It appears to be in order." Not one single twitch or grin or widening of the eyes, nothing to indicate what was written on the sheet of paper.

He looked down and nodded at his court reporter and cleared his throat, thoroughly relishing the moment. Then the wrinkles softened around his eyes, the jaw muscles loosened, the shoulders sagged a bit, and, to Wes anyway, there was suddenly hope that the jury had scorched the defendant.

In a slow, loud voice, Judge Harrison read: "Question number one: 'Do you find, by a preponderance of the evidence, that the groundwater

at issue was contaminated by Krane Chemical Corporation?' " After a treacherous pause that lasted no more than five seconds, he continued, "The answer is 'Yes.' "

One side of the courtroom managed to breathe while the other side began to turn blue.

"Question number two: 'Do you find, by a preponderance of the evidence, that the contamination was the proximate cause of the death or deaths of (*a*) Chad Baker and/or (*b*) Pete Baker?' Answer: 'Yes, for both.' "

Mary Grace managed to pluck tissues from a box and hand them over with her left hand while writing furiously with her right. Wes managed to steal a glance at juror number four, who happened to be glancing at him with a humorous grin that seemed to say, "Now for the good part."

"Question number three: 'For Chad Baker, what amount of money do you award to his mother, Jeannette Baker, as damages for his wrongful death?' Answer: 'Five hundred thousand dollars.' "

Dead children aren't worth much, because they earn nothing, but Chad's impressive award rang like an alarm because it gave a quick preview of what was to come. Wes stared at the clock above the judge and thanked God that bankruptcy had been averted.

"Question number four: 'For Pete Baker, what amount of money do you award to his widow, Jeannette Baker, as damages for his wrongful death?' Answer: 'Two and a half million dollars.' "

There was a rustle from the money boys in the front row behind Jared Kurtin. Krane could certainly handle a $3 million hit, but it was the ripple effect that suddenly terrified them. For his part, Mr. Kurtin had yet to flinch.

Not yet.

Jeannette Baker began to slide out of her chair. She was caught by both of her lawyers, who pulled her up, wrapped arms around her frail shoulders, and whispered to her. She was sobbing, out of control.

There were six questions on the list that the lawyers had hammered

out, and if the jury answered yes to number five, then the whole world would go crazy. Judge Harrison was at that point, reading it slowly, clearing his throat, studying the answer. Then he revealed his mean streak. He did so with a smile. He glanced up a few inches, just above the sheet of paper he was holding, just over the cheap reading glasses perched on his nose, and he looked directly at Wes Payton. The grin was tight, conspiratorial, yet filled with gleeful satisfaction.

"Question number five: 'Do you find, by a preponderance of the evidence, that the actions of Krane Chemical Corporation were either intentional or so grossly negligent as to justify the imposition of punitive damages?' Answer: 'Yes.' "

Mary Grace stopped writing and looked over the bobbing head of her client to her husband, whose gaze was frozen upon her. They had won, and that alone was an exhilarating, almost indescribable rush of euphoria. But how large was their victory? At that crucial split second, both knew it was indeed a landslide.

"Question number six: 'What is the amount of punitive damages?' Answer: 'Thirty-eight million dollars.' "

There were gasps and coughs and soft whistles as the shock waves rattled around the courtroom. Jared Kurtin and his gang were busy writing everything down and trying to appear unfazed by the bomb blast. The honchos from Krane in the front row were trying to recover and breathe normally. Most glared at the jurors and thought vile thoughts that ran along the lines of ignorant people, backwater stupidity, and so on.

Mr. and Mrs. Payton were again both reaching for their client, who was overcome by the sheer weight of the verdict and trying pitifully to sit up. Wes whispered reassurances to Jeannette while repeating to himself the numbers he had just heard. Somehow, he managed to keep his face serious and avoid a goofy smile.

Huffy the banker stopped crunching his nails. In less than thirty seconds he had gone from a disgraced, bankrupt former bank vice president to a rising star with designs on a bigger salary and office. He even felt smarter. Oh, what a marvelous entrance into the bank's boardroom he would choreograph first thing in the morning. The judge was going on

about formalities and thanking the jurors, but Huffy didn't care. He had heard all he needed to hear.

The jurors stood and filed out as Uncle Joe held the door and nodded with approval. He would later tell his wife that he had predicted such a verdict, though she had no memory of it. He claimed he hadn't missed a verdict in the many decades he had worked as a bailiff. When the jurors were gone, Jared Kurtin stood and, with perfect composure, rattled off the usual post-verdict inquiries, which Judge Harrison took with great compassion now that the blood was on the floor. Mary Grace had no response. Mary Grace didn't care. She had what she wanted.

Wes was thinking about the $41 million and fighting his emotions. The firm would survive, as would their marriage, their reputations, everything.

When Judge Harrison finally announced, "We are adjourned," a mob raced from the courtroom. Everyone grabbed a cell phone.

Mr. Trudeau was still standing at the window, watching the last of the sun set far beyond New Jersey. Across the wide room Stu the assistant took the call and ventured forward a few steps before mustering the nerve to say, "Sir, that was from Hattiesburg. Three million in actual damages, thirty-eight in punitive."

From the rear, there was a slight dip in the boss's shoulder, a quiet exhaling in frustration, then a mumbling of obscenities.

Mr. Trudeau slowly turned around and glared at the assistant as if he just might shoot the messenger. "You sure you heard that right?" he asked, and Stu desperately wished he had not.

"Yes, sir."

Behind him the door was open. Bobby Ratzlaff appeared in a rush, out of breath, shocked and scared and looking for Mr. Trudeau. Ratzlaff was the chief in-house lawyer, and his neck would be the first on the chopping block. He was already sweating.

"Get your boys here in five minutes," Mr. Trudeau growled, then turned back to his window.

The press conference materialized on the first floor of the courthouse. In two small groups, Wes and Mary Grace chatted patiently with reporters. Both gave the same answers to the same questions. No, the verdict was not a record for the state of Mississippi. Yes, they felt it was justified. No, it was not expected, not an award that large anyway. Certainly it would be appealed. Wes had great respect for Jared Kurtin, but not for his client. Their firm currently represented thirty other plaintiffs who were suing Krane Chemical. No, they did not expect to settle those cases.

Yes, they were exhausted.

After half an hour they finally begged off, and walked from the Forrest County Circuit Court building hand in hand, each lugging a heavy briefcase. They were photographed getting into their car and driving away.

Alone, they said nothing. Four blocks, five, six. Ten minutes passed without a word. The car, a battered Ford Taurus with a million miles, at least one low tire, and the constant click of a sticking valve, drifted through the streets around the university.

Wes spoke first. "What's one-third of forty-one million?"

"Don't even think about it."

"I'm not thinking about it. Just a joke."

"Just drive."

"Anyplace in particular?"

"No."

The Taurus ventured into the suburbs, going nowhere but certainly not going back to the office. They stayed far away from the neighborhood with the lovely home they had once owned.

Reality slowly settled in as the numbness began to fade. A lawsuit they had reluctantly filed four years earlier had now been decided in a most dramatic fashion. An excruciating marathon was over, and though they had a temporary victory, the costs had been great. The wounds were raw, the battle scars still very fresh.

The gas gauge showed less than a quarter of a tank, something that Wes would have barely noticed two years earlier. Now it was a much more serious matter. Back then he drove a BMW—Mary Grace had a Jaguar—and when he needed fuel, he simply pulled in to his favorite station and filled the tank with a credit card. He never saw the bills; they were handled by his bookkeeper. Now the credit cards were gone, as were the BMW and the Jaguar, and the same bookkeeper was working at half salary and doling out a few dollars in cash to keep the Payton firm just above the waterline.

Mary Grace glanced at the gauge, too, a recently acquired habit. She noticed and remembered the price of everything—a gallon of gas, a loaf of bread, a half gallon of milk. She was the saver and he was the spender, but not too many years ago, when the clients were calling and the cases were settling, she had relaxed a bit too much and enjoyed their success. Saving and investing had not been a priority. They were young, the firm was growing, the future had no limits.

Whatever she had managed to put into mutual funds had long since been devoured by the *Baker* case.

An hour earlier they had been broke, on paper, with ruinous debts far outweighing whatever flimsy assets they might list. Now things were different. The liabilities had not gone away, but the black side of their balance sheet had certainly improved.

Or had it?

When might they see some or all of this wonderful verdict? Might Krane now offer a settlement? How long would the appeal take? How much time could they now devote to the rest of their practice?

Neither wanted to ponder the questions that were haunting both of them. They were simply too tired and too relieved. For an eternity they had talked of little else, and now they talked about nothing. Tomorrow or the next day they could begin the debriefing.

"We're almost out of gas," she said.

No retort came to his weary mind, so Wes said, "What about dinner?"

"Macaroni and cheese with the kids."

The trial had not only drained them of their energy and assets; it had also burned away any excess weight they might have been carrying at the outset. Wes was down at least fifteen pounds, though he didn't know for sure because he hadn't stepped on the scale in months. Nor was he about to inquire into this delicate matter with his wife, but it was obvious she needed to eat. They had skipped many meals—breakfasts when they were scrambling to dress the kids and get them to school, lunches when one argued motions in Harrison's office while the other prepared for the next cross-examination, dinners when they worked until midnight and simply forgot to eat. PowerBars and energy drinks had kept them going.

"Sounds great," he said, and turned left onto a street that would take them home.

———

Ratzlaff and two other lawyers took their seats at the sleek leather table in a corner of Mr. Trudeau's office suite. The walls were all glass and provided magnificent views of skyscrapers packed into the financial district, though no one was in the mood for scenery. Mr. Trudeau was on the phone across the room behind his chrome desk. The lawyers waited nervously. They had talked nonstop to the eyewitnesses down in Mississippi but still had few answers.

The boss finished his phone conversation and strode purposefully across the room. "What happened?" he snapped. "An hour ago you guys were downright cocky. Now we got our asses handed to us. What happened?" He sat down and glared at Ratzlaff.

"Trial by jury. It's full of risks," Ratzlaff said.

"I've been through trials, plenty of them, and I usually win. I thought we were paying the best shysters in the business. The best mouthpieces money can buy. We spared no expense, right?"

"Oh yes. We paid dearly. Still paying."

Mr. Trudeau slapped the table and barked, "What went wrong?!"

Well, Ratzlaff thought to himself and wanted to say aloud except

that he very much treasured his job, let's start with the fact that our company built a pesticide plant in Podunk, Mississippi, because the land and labor were dirt cheap, then we spent the next thirty years dumping chemicals and waste into the ground and into the rivers, quite illegally of course, and we contaminated the drinking water until it tasted like spoiled milk, which, as bad as it was, wasn't the worst part, because then people started dying of cancer and leukemia.

That, Mr. Boss and Mr. CEO and Mr. Corporate Raider, is exactly what went wrong.

"The lawyers feel good about the appeal," Ratzlaff said instead, without much conviction.

"Oh, that's just super. Right now I really trust these lawyers. Where did you find these clowns?"

"They're the best, okay?"

"Sure. And let's just explain to the press that we're ecstatic about our appeal and perhaps our stock won't crash tomorrow. Is that what you're saying?"

"We can spin it," Ratzlaff said. The other two lawyers were glancing at the glass walls. Who wanted to be the first to jump?

One of Mr. Trudeau's cell phones rang and he snatched it off the table. "Hi, honey," he said as he stood and walked away. It was (the third) Mrs. Trudeau, the latest trophy, a deadly young woman whom Ratzlaff and everyone else at the company avoided at all costs. Her husband was whispering, then said goodbye.

He walked to a window near the lawyers and gazed at the sparkling towers around him. "Bobby," he said without looking, "do you have any idea where the jury got the figure of thirty-eight million for punitive damages?"

"Not right offhand."

"Of course you don't. For the first nine months of this year, Krane has averaged thirty-eight million a month in profits. A bunch of ignorant rednecks who collectively couldn't earn a hundred grand a year, and they sit there like gods taking from the rich and giving to the poor."

"We still have the money, Carl," Ratzlaff said. "It'll be years before a dime changes hands, if, in fact, that ever happens."

"Great! Spin that to the wolves tomorrow while our stock goes down the drain."

Ratzlaff shut up and slumped in his chair. The other two lawyers were not about to utter a sound.

Mr. Trudeau was pacing dramatically. "Forty-one million dollars. And there are how many other cases out there, Bobby? Did someone say two hundred, three hundred? Well, if there were three hundred this morning, there will be three thousand tomorrow morning. Every redneck in south Mississippi with a fever blister will now claim to have sipped the magic brew from Bowmore. Every two-bit ambulance chaser with a law degree is driving there now to sign up clients. This wasn't supposed to happen, Bobby. You assured me."

Ratzlaff had a memo under lock and key. It was eight years old and had been prepared under his supervision. It ran for a hundred pages and described in gruesome detail the company's illegal dumping of toxic waste at the Bowmore plant. It summarized the company's elaborate efforts to hide the dumping, to dupe the Environmental Protection Agency, and to buy off the politicians at the local, state, and federal level. It recommended a clandestine but effective cleanup of the waste site, at a cost of some $50 million. It begged anyone who read it to stop the dumping.

And, most important at this critical moment, it predicted a bad verdict someday in a courtroom.

Only luck and a flagrant disregard for the rules of civil procedure had allowed Ratzlaff to keep the memo a secret.

Mr. Trudeau had been given a copy of it eight years earlier, though he now denied he'd ever seen it. Ratzlaff was tempted to dust it off now and read a few selected passages, but, again, he treasured his job.

Mr. Trudeau walked to the table, placed both palms flat on the Italian leather, glared at Bobby Ratzlaff, and said, "I swear to you, it will never happen. Not one dime of our hard-earned profits will ever get into the hands of those trailer park peasants."

The three lawyers stared at their boss, whose eyes were narrow and

glowing. He was breathing fire, and finished by saying, "If I have to bankrupt it or break it into fifteen pieces, I swear to you on my mother's grave that not one dime of Krane's money will ever be touched by those ignorant people."

And with that promise, he walked across the Persian rug, lifted his jacket from a rack, and left the office.

CHAPTER 2

Jeannette Baker was taken by her relatives back to Bowmore, her hometown twenty miles from the courthouse. She was weak from shock and sedated as usual, and she did not want to see a crowd and pretend to celebrate. The numbers represented a victory, but the verdict was also the end of a long, arduous journey. And her husband and little boy were still quite dead.

She lived in an old trailer with Bette, her stepsister, on a gravel road in a forlorn Bowmore neighborhood known as Pine Grove. Other trailers were scattered along other unpaved streets. Most of the cars and trucks parked around the trailers were decades old, unpainted and dented. There were a few homes of the permanent variety, immobile, anchored on slabs fifty years earlier, but they, too, were aging badly and showed signs of obvious neglect. There were few jobs in Bowmore and even fewer in Pine Grove, and a quick stroll along Jeannette's street would depress any visitor.

The news arrived before she did, and a small crowd was gathering when she got home. They put her to bed, then they sat in the cramped

den and whispered about the verdict and speculated about what it all meant.

Forty-one million dollars? How would it affect the other lawsuits? Would Krane be forced to clean up its mess? When could she expect to see some of the money? They were cautious not to dwell on this last question, but it was the dominant thought.

More friends arrived and the crowd spilled out of the trailer and onto a shaky wooden deck, where they pulled up lawn chairs and sat and talked in the cool air of the early evening. They drank bottled water and soft drinks. For a long-suffering people, the victory was sweet. Finally, they had won. Something. They had struck back at Krane, a company they hated with every ounce of energy they could muster, and they had finally landed a retaliatory blow. Maybe the tide was turning. Somewhere out there beyond Bowmore someone had finally listened.

They talked about lawyers and depositions and the Environmental Protection Agency and the latest toxicology and geological reports. Though they were not well educated, they were fluent in the lingo of toxic waste and groundwater contamination and cancer clusters. They were living the nightmare.

Jeannette was awake in her dark bedroom, listening to the muffled conversations around her. She felt secure. These were her people, friends and family and fellow victims. The bonds were tight, the suffering shared. And the money would be, too. If she ever saw a dime, she planned to spread it around.

As she stared at the dark ceiling, she was not overwhelmed by the verdict. Her relief at being finished with the ordeal of the trial far outweighed the thrill of winning. She wanted to sleep for a week and wake up in a brand-new world with her little family intact and everyone happy and healthy. But, for the first time since she heard the verdict, she asked herself what, exactly, she might purchase with the award.

Dignity. A dignified place to live and a dignified place to work. Somewhere else of course. She would move away from Bowmore and Cary County and its polluted rivers and streams and aquifers. Not far,

though, because everyone she loved lived nearby. But she dreamed of a new life in a new house with clean water running through it, water that did not stink and stain and cause sickness and death.

She heard another car door slam shut, and she was grateful for her friends. Perhaps she should fix her hair and venture out to say hello. She stepped into the tiny bathroom next to her bed, turned on the light, turned on the faucet at the sink, then sat on the edge of the tub and stared at the stream of grayish water running into the dark stains of the fake-porcelain bowl.

It was fit for flushing human waste, nothing else. The pumping station that produced the water was owned by the City of Bowmore, and the city itself prohibited the drinking of its own water. Three years earlier the council had passed a resolution urging the citizens to use it only for flushing. Warning signs were posted in every public restroom. "DON'T DRINK THE WATER, by Order of the City Council." Clean water was trucked in from Hattiesburg, and every home in Bowmore, mobile and otherwise, had a five-gallon tank and dispenser. Those who could afford it had hundred-gallon reservoirs mounted on stilts near their back porches. And the nicest homes had cisterns for rainwater.

Water was a daily challenge in Bowmore. Every cup was contemplated, fussed over, and used sparingly because the supply was uncertain. And every drop that entered or touched a human body came from a bottle that came from a source that had been inspected and certified. Drinking and cooking were easy compared with bathing and cleaning. Hygiene was a struggle, and most of the women of Bowmore wore their hair short. Many of the men wore beards.

The water was legendary. Ten years earlier, the city installed an irrigation system for its youth baseball field, only to watch the grass turn brown and die. The city swimming pool was closed when a consultant tried treating the water with massive amounts of chlorine, only to watch it turn brackish and reek like a sewage pit. When the Methodist church burned, the firemen realized, during a losing battle, that the water, pumped from an untreated supply, was having an incendiary effect. Years

before that, some residents of Bowmore suspected the water caused tiny cracks in the paint of their automobiles after a few wash jobs.

And we drank the stuff for years, Jeannette said to herself. We drank it when it started to stink. We drank it when it changed colors. We drank it while we complained bitterly to the city. We drank it after it was tested and the city assured us it was safe. We drank it after we boiled it. We drank it in our coffee and tea, certain the heat would cure it. And when we stopped drinking it, we showered and bathed in it and inhaled its steam.

What were we supposed to do? Gather at the well each morning like the ancient Egyptians and carry it home in pots on our heads? Sink our own wells at $2,000 a hole and find the same putrid mix the city had found? Drive to Hattiesburg and find a spare tap and haul it back in buckets?

She could hear the denials—those from long ago when the experts pointed at their charts and lectured the city council and the mob packed into a crowded boardroom, telling them over and over that the water had been tested and was just fine if properly cleansed with massive doses of chlorine. She could hear the fancy experts Krane Chemical had brought in at trial to tell the jury that, yes, there may have been some minor "leakage" over the years at the Bowmore plant, but not to worry because bichloronylene and other "unauthorized" substances had actually been absorbed by the soil and eventually carried away in an underground stream that posed no threat whatsoever to the town's drinking water. She could hear the government scientists with their lofty vocabularies talk down to the people and assure them that the water they could barely stand to smell was fine to drink.

Denials all around as the body count rose. Cancer struck everywhere in Bowmore, on every street, in almost every family. Four times the national average. Then six times, then ten. At her trial, an expert hired by the Paytons explained to the jury that for the geographical area as defined by the Bowmore city limits, the rate of cancer was fifteen times the national average.

There was so much cancer that they got themselves studied by all manner of public and private researchers. The term "cancer cluster" became common around town, and Bowmore was radioactive. A clever magazine journalist labeled Cary County as Cancer County, U.S.A., and the nickname stuck.

Cancer County, U.S.A. The water placed quite a strain on the Bowmore Chamber of Commerce. Economic development disappeared, and the town began a rapid decline.

Jeannette turned off the tap, but the water was still there, unseen in the pipes that ran unseen through the walls and into the ground somewhere underneath her. It was always there, waiting like a stalker with unlimited patience. Quiet and deadly, pumped from the earth so polluted by Krane Chemical.

She often lay awake at night listening for the water somewhere in the walls.

A dripping faucet was treated like an armed prowler.

She brushed her hair with little purpose, once again tried not to look at herself too long in the mirror, then brushed her teeth with water from a jug that was always on the sink. She flipped on the light to her room, opened the door, forced a smile, then stepped into the cramped den, where her friends were packed around the walls.

It was time for church. *(4 pages Narration)*

Mr. Trudeau's car was a black Bentley with a black chauffeur named Toliver who claimed to be Jamaican, though his immigration documents were as suspicious as his affected Caribbean accent. Toliver had been driving the great man for a decade and could read his moods. This was a bad one, Toliver determined quickly as they fought the traffic along the FDR toward midtown. The first signal had been clearly delivered when Mr. Trudeau slammed the right rear door himself before a lunging Toliver could fulfill his duties.

His boss, he had read, could have nerves of cold steel in the boardroom. Unflappable, decisive, calculating, and so on. But in the solitude of

tried to recreate her new life based on her old one. wildcule guilty,

you have got to find what it takes to get back & write. Or die. You choose.

the backseat, even with the privacy window rolled up as tightly as possible, his real character often emerged. The man was a hothead with a massive ego who hated to lose.

Mil - you are ready. Start NOW!! 4/08 !!

And he had definitely lost this one. He was on the phone back there, not yelling but certainly not whispering. The stock would crash. The lawyers were fools. Everyone had lied to him. Damage control. Toliver caught only pieces of what was being said, but it was obvious whatever happened down there in Mississippi had been disastrous.

His boss was sixty-one years old and, according to *Forbes*, had a net worth of almost $2 billion. Toliver often wondered, how much was enough? What would he do with another billion, then another? Why work so hard when he had more than he could ever spend? Homes, jets, wives, boats, Bentleys, all the toys a real white man could ever want.

But Toliver knew the truth. No amount of money could ever satisfy Mr. Trudeau. There were bigger men in town, and he was running hard to catch them.

Toliver turned west on Sixty-third and inched his way to Fifth, where he turned suddenly and faced a set of thick iron gates that quickly swung back. The Bentley disappeared underground, where it stopped and a security guard stood waiting. He opened the rear door. "We'll leave in an hour," Mr. Trudeau barked in Toliver's general direction, then disappeared, carrying two thick briefcases.

The elevator raced up sixteen levels to the top, where Mr. and Mrs. Trudeau lived in lavish splendor. Their penthouse rambled over the top two floors and looked out from its many giant windows at Central Park. They had purchased the place for $28 million shortly after their momentous wedding six years earlier, then spent another $10 million or so bringing it up to designer-magazine quality. The overhead included two maids, a chef, a butler, his and hers valets, at least one nanny, and of course the obligatory personal assistant to keep Mrs. Trudeau properly organized and at lunch on time.

A valet took his briefcases and overcoat as he flung them off. He bounded up the stairs to the master suite, looking for his wife. He had no real desire to see her at the moment, but their little rituals were expected.

Judith walked Andrew around every nook & cranny of their new apartment

She was in her dressing room, a hairdresser on each side, both working feverishly on her straight blond hair.

"Hello, darling," he said dutifully, more for the benefit of the hairdressers, both young males who seemed not the least bit affected by the fact that she was practically nude.

"Do you like my hair?" Brianna asked, glaring at the mirror as the boys stroked and fussed, all four hands doing something. Not, "How was your day?" Not, "Hello, dear." Not, "What happened with the trial?" Just simply, "Do you like my hair?"

"It's lovely," he said, already backing away. Ritual complete, he was free to go and leave her with her handlers. He stopped at their massive bed and looked at her evening gown—"Valentino," she had already advised him. It was bright red with a plunging neckline that might or might not adequately cover her fantastic new breasts. It was short, almost sheer, probably weighed less than two ounces, and probably cost at least $25,000. It was a size 2, which meant it would sufficiently drape and hang on her emaciated body so the other anorexics at the party would drool in mock admiration at how "fit" she looked. Frankly, Carl was growing weary of her obsessive routines: an hour a day with a trainer ($300 per), an hour of one-on-one yoga ($300 per), an hour a day with a nutritionist ($200 per), all in an effort to burn off every last fat cell in her body and keep her weight between ninety and ninety-five pounds. She was always ready for sex—that was part of the deal—but now he sometimes worried about getting poked with a hip bone or simply crushing her in the pile. She was only thirty-one, but he had noticed a wrinkle or two just above her nose. Surgery could fix the problems, but wasn't she paying a price for all this aggressive starvation?

He had more important things to worry about. A young, gorgeous wife was just one part of his magnificent persona, and Brianna Trudeau could still stop traffic.

They had a child, one that Carl could easily have forgone. He already had six, plenty, he reasoned. Three were older than Brianna. But she insisted, and for obvious reasons. A child was security, and since she was married to a man who loved ladies and adored the institution of

marriage, the child meant family and ties and roots and, left unsaid, legal complications in the event things unraveled. A child was the protection every trophy wife needed.

Brianna delivered a girl and selected the hideous name of Sadler MacGregor Trudeau, MacGregor being Brianna's maiden name and Sadler being pulled from the air. She at first claimed Sadler had been a roguish Scottish relative of some variety, but abandoned that little fiction when Carl stumbled across a book of baby names. He really didn't care. The child was his by DNA only. He had already tried the father bit with prior families and had failed miserably.

Sadler was now five and had virtually been abandoned by both parents. Brianna, once so heroic in her efforts to become a mother, had quickly lost interest in things maternal and had delegated her duties to a series of nannies. The current one was a thick young woman from Russia whose papers were as dubious as Toliver's. Carl could not, at that moment, remember her name. Brianna hired her and was thrilled because she spoke Russian and could perhaps pass on the language to Sadler.

"What language did you expect her to speak?" Carl had asked.

But Brianna had no response.

He stepped into the playroom, swooped up the child as if he couldn't wait to see her, exchanged hugs and kisses, asked how her day had been, and within minutes managed a graceful escape to his office, where he grabbed a phone and began yelling at Bobby Ratzlaff.

After a few fruitless calls, he showered, dried his perfectly dyed hair, half-gray, and got himself into his newest Armani tux. The waistband was a bit snug, probably a 34, up an inch from the early days when Brianna stalked him around the penthouse. As he dressed himself, he cursed the evening ahead and the party and the people he would see there. They would know. At that very moment, the news was racing around the financial world. Phones were buzzing as his rivals roared with laughter and gloated over Krane's misfortune. The Internet was bursting with the latest from Mississippi.

For any other party, he, the great Carl Trudeau, would simply call in sick. Every day of his life he did whatever he damned well pleased, and

if he decided to rudely skip a party at the last minute, what the hell? But this was not just any event.

Brianna had wormed her way onto the board of the Museum of Abstract Art, and tonight was their biggest blowout. There would be designer gowns, tummy tucks and stout new breasts, new chins and perfect tans, diamonds, champagne, foie gras, caviar, dinner by a celebrity chef, a silent auction for the pinch hitters and a live auction for the sluggers. And, most important, there would be cameras on top of cameras, enough to convince the elite guests that they and only they were the center of the world. Oscar night, eat your heart out.

The highlight of the evening, at least for some, would be the auctioning of a work of art. Each year the committee commissioned an "emerging" painter or sculptor to create something just for the event, and usually forked over a million bucks or so for the result. Last year's painting had been a bewildering rendering of a human brain after a gunshot, and it went for six mill. This year's item was a depressing pile of black clay with bronze rods rising into the vague outline of a young girl. It bore the mystifying title *Abused Imelda* and would have sat neglected in a gallery in Duluth if not for the sculptor, a tortured Argentine genius rumored to be on the verge of suicide, a sad fate that would instantly double the value of his creations, something that was not lost on savvy New York art investors. Brianna had left brochures around the penthouse and had dropped several hints to the effect that *Abused Imelda* would be stunning in their foyer, just off the elevator entrance.

Carl knew he was expected to buy the damned thing and was hoping there would not be a frenzy. And if he became its owner, he was already hoping for a quick suicide.

She and Valentino appeared from the dressing room. The hair boys were gone, and she had managed to get into the gown and the jewelry all by herself. "Fabulous," Carl said, and it was indeed true. In spite of the bones and ribs, she was still a beautiful woman. The hair very much resembled what he had seen at six that morning when he kissed her goodbye as she sipped her coffee. Now, a thousand dollars later, he could tell little difference.

Oh, well. He knew very well the price of trophies. The prenuptial gave her $100,000 a month to play with while married and twenty million when they split. She also got Sadler with liberal visitation for the father, if he so chose.

In the Bentley, they hurried from beneath the apartment building and were onto Fifth Avenue when Brianna said, "Oh, my, I forgot to kiss Sadler. What kind of mother am I?"

"She's fine," Carl said, who likewise had failed to say good night to the child.

"I feel awful," Brianna said, feigning disgust. Her full-length black Prada coat was split so that the backseat was dominated by her amazing legs. Legs from the floor up to her armpits. Legs unadorned by hosiery or clothing or anything whatsoever. Legs for Carl to see and admire and touch and fondle and she really didn't care if Toliver had a good look, either. She was on display, as always.

Carl rubbed them because they felt nice, but he wanted to say something like "These things are beginning to resemble broomsticks."

He let it pass.

"Any word from the trial?" she finally asked.

"The jury nailed us," he said.

"I'm so sorry."

"We're fine."

"How much?"

"Forty-one million."

"Those ignorant people."

Carl told her little about the complicated and mysterious world of the Trudeau Group. She had her charities and causes and lunches and trainers, and that kept her busy. He didn't want and didn't tolerate too many questions.

Brianna had checked online and knew exactly what the jury decided. She knew what the lawyers were saying about the appeal, and she knew Krane's stock would take a major hit early the next morning. She did her research and kept her secret notes. She was gorgeous and thin, but she was not stupid. Carl was on the phone.

The MuAb building was a few blocks south, between Fifth and Madison. As the traffic inched closer, they could see the popping flashes of a hundred cameras. Brianna perked up, crunched her perfect abs, brought her new additions to attention, and said, "God, I hate those people."

"Who?"

"All those photographers."

He snickered at the obvious lie. The car stopped and an attendant in a tuxedo opened the door as the cameras swung to the black Bentley. The great Carl Trudeau popped out without a smile, then the legs followed. Brianna knew precisely how to give the photographers, and thus the gossip pages and maybe, just maybe, a fashion magazine or two, what they wanted—miles of sensuous flesh without revealing everything. The right foot landed first, shoed with Jimmy Choo at a hundred bucks per toe, and as she expertly swung around, the coat opened and Valentino cooperated upward and the whole world saw the real benefit of being a billionaire and owning a trophy.

Arm in arm they glided across the red carpet, waving at the photographers and ignoring the handful of reporters, one of whom had the audacity to yell, "Hey, Carl, any comment on the verdict in Mississippi?" Carl of course did not hear, or pretended not to. But his pace quickened slightly and they were soon inside, on somewhat safer turf. He hoped. They were greeted by paid greeters; coats were taken; smiles were offered; friendly cameras appeared; old pals materialized; and they were soon lost in the warm cluster of seriously rich people pretending to enjoy one another's company.

Brianna found her soul mate, another anorexic trophy with the same unusual body—everything superbly starved but the ridiculous breasts. Carl went straight for the bar, and almost made it before he was practically tackled by the one jerk he hoped to avoid. "Carl, ole boy, bad news down south I hear," the man boomed as loudly as possible.

"Yes, very bad," Carl said in a much lower voice as he grabbed a champagne flute and began to drain it.

Pete Flint was number 228 on the *Forbes* list of the 400 richest Americans. Carl was number 310, and each man knew exactly where the other fit on the roster. Numbers 87 and 141 were also in the crowd, along with a host of unranked contenders.

"Thought your boys had things under control," Flint pressed on, slurping a tall glass full of either scotch or bourbon. He somehow managed a frown while working hard to conceal his delight.

"Yes, we thought so, too," Carl said, wishing he could slap the fat jowls twelve inches away.

"What about the appeal?" Flint asked gravely.

"We're in great shape."

At last year's auction, Flint had valiantly hung on to the frenzied end and walked away with the *Brain After Gunshot*, a $6 million artistic waste but one that launched the MuAb's current capital campaign. No doubt he would be in the hunt for tonight's grand prize.

"Good thing we shorted Krane last week," he said.

Carl started to curse him but kept his cool. Flint ran a hedge fund famous for its daring. Had he really shorted Krane Chemical in anticipation of a bad verdict? Carl's puzzled glare concealed nothing.

"Oh yes," Flint went on, pulling on his glass and smacking his lips. "Our man down there said you were screwed."

"We'll never pay a dime," Carl said gamely.

"You'll pay in the morning, ole boy. We're betting Krane's stock drops 20 percent." And with that he turned and walked away, leaving Carl to finish off his drink and lunge for another. Twenty percent? Carl's laser-quick mind did the math. He owned 45 percent of the outstanding common shares of Krane Chemical, a company with a market value of $3.2 billion, based on the day's closing price. A 20 percent decline would cost him $280 million, on paper. No real cash losses, of course, but still a rough day around the office.

Ten percent was more like it, he thought. The boys in finance agreed with him.

Could Flint's hedge fund short a significant chunk of Krane's stock

without Carl knowing about it? He stared at a confused bartender and pondered the question. Yes, it was possible, but not likely. Flint was simply rubbing a little salt.

The museum's director appeared from nowhere, and Carl was delighted to see him. He would never mention the verdict, if he in fact knew about it. He would say only nice things to Carl, and of course he would comment on how fabulous Brianna looked. He would ask about Sadler and inquire into the renovation of their home in the Hamptons.

They chatted about such things as they carried their drinks through the crowded lobby, dodging little pockets of dangerous conversations, and settled themselves before *Abused Imelda*. "Magnificent, isn't it?" the director mused.

"Beautiful," Carl said, glancing to his left as number 141 happened by. "What will it go for?"

"We've been debating that all day around here. Who knows with this crowd. I say at least five million."

"And what's it worth?"

The director smiled as a photographer snapped their picture. "Now, that's an entirely different issue, isn't it? The sculptor's last major work was sold to a Japanese gentleman for around two million. Of course, the Japanese gentleman was not donating large sums of money to our little museum."

Carl took another sip and acknowledged the game. MuAb's campaign goal was $100 million over five years. According to Brianna, they were about halfway there and needed a big boost from the evening's auction.

An art critic with the *Times* introduced himself and joined their conversation. Wonder if he knows about the verdict, Carl thought. The critic and the director discussed the Argentine sculptor and his mental problems as Carl studied *Imelda* and asked himself if he really wanted it permanently situated in the foyer of his luxurious penthouse.

His wife certainly did.

CHAPTER 3

The Paytons' temporary home was a three-bedroom apartment on the second level of an old complex near the university. Wes had lived nearby in his college days and still found it hard to believe he was back in the neighborhood. But there had been so many drastic changes it was difficult to dwell on just one.

How temporary? That was the great question between husband and wife, though the issue hadn't been discussed in weeks, nor would it be discussed now. Maybe in a day or two, when the fatigue and the shock wore off and they could steal a quiet moment and talk about the future. Wes eased the car through the parking lot, passing an overfilled Dumpster with debris littered around it. Mainly beer cans and broken bottles. The college boys humored themselves by hurling their empties from the upper floors, across the lot, above the cars, in the general direction of the Dumpster. When the bottles crashed, the noise boomed through the complex and the students were amused. Others were not. For the two sleep-deprived Paytons, the racket was at times unbearable.

The owner, an old client, was widely considered the worst slumlord in town, by the students anyway. He offered the place to the Paytons, and

their handshake deal called for a thousand bucks a month in rent. They had lived there for seven months, paid for three, and the landlord insisted he was not worried. He was patiently waiting in line with many other creditors. The law firm of Payton & Payton had once proven it could attract clients and generate fees, and its two partners were certainly capable of a dramatic comeback.

Try this comeback, Wes thought as he turned in to a parking place. Is a verdict of $41 million drama enough? For a moment he felt feisty, then he was tired again.

Slaves to a dreadful habit, both got out of the car and grabbed their briefcases in the rear seat. "No," Mary Grace announced suddenly. "We are not working tonight. Leave these in the car."

"Yes, ma'am."

They hustled up the stairs, loud raunchy rap spilling from a window nearby. Mary Grace rattled the keys and unlocked the door, and suddenly they were inside, where both children were watching television with Ramona, their Honduran nanny. Liza, the nine-year-old, rushed forth yelling, "Mommy, we won, we won!" Mary Grace lifted her in the air and clutched her tightly.

"Yes, dear, we won."

"Forty billion!"

"Millions, dear, not billions."

Mack, the five-year-old, ran to his father, who yanked him up, and for a long moment they stood in the narrow foyer and squeezed their children. For the first time since the verdict, Wes saw tears in his wife's eyes.

"We saw you on TV," Liza was saying.

"You looked tired," Mack said.

"I am tired," Wes said.

Ramona watched from a distance, a tight smile barely visible. She wasn't sure what the verdict meant, but she understood enough to be pleased with the news.

Overcoats and shoes were removed, and the little Payton family fell onto the sofa, a very nice thick leather one, where they hugged and tickled and talked about school. Wes and Mary Grace had managed to keep

most of their furnishings, and the shabby apartment was decorated with fine things that not only reminded them of the past but, more important, reminded them of the future. This was just a stop, an unexpected layover.

The den floor was covered with notebooks and papers, clear evidence that the homework had been done before the television was turned on.

"I'm starving," Mack announced as he tried in vain to undo his father's tie.

"Mom says we're having macaroni and cheese," Wes said.

"All right!" Both kids voiced their approval, and Ramona eased into the kitchen.

"Does this mean we get a new house?" Liza asked.

"I thought you liked this place," Wes said.

"I do, but we're still looking for a new house, right?"

"Of course we are."

They had been careful with the children. They had explained the basics of the lawsuit to Liza—a bad company polluted water that harmed many people—and she quickly declared that she didn't like the company, either. And if the family had to move into an apartment to fight the company, then she was all for it.

But leaving their fine new home had been traumatic. Liza's last bedroom was pink and white and had everything a little girl could want. Now she shared a smaller room with her brother, and though she didn't complain, she was curious about how long the arrangement might last. Mack was generally too preoccupied with full-day kindergarten to worry about living quarters.

Both kids missed the old neighborhood, where the homes were large and the backyards had pools and gym sets. Friends were next door or just around the corner. The school was private and secure. Church was a block away and they knew everyone there.

Now they attended a city elementary school where there were far more black faces than white, and they worshipped in a downtown Episcopal church that welcomed everyone.

"We won't move anytime soon," Mary Grace said. "But maybe we can start looking."

"I'm starving," Mack said again.

The topic of housing was routinely avoided when one of the kids raised it, and Mary Grace finally rose to her feet. "Let's go cook," she said to Liza. Wes found the remote and said to Mack, "Let's watch *Sports-Center*." Anything but local news.

"Sure."

Ramona was boiling water and dicing a tomato. Mary Grace hugged her quickly and said, "A good day?" Yes, a good day, she agreed. No problems at school. Homework was already finished. Liza drifted off to her bedroom. She had yet to show any interest in kitchen matters.

"A good day for you?" Ramona asked.

"Yes, very good. Let's use the white cheddar." She found a block of it in the fridge and began grating it.

"You can relax now?" Ramona asked.

"Yes, for a few days anyway." Through a friend at church, they had found Ramona hiding and half-starved in a shelter in Baton Rouge, sleeping on a cot and eating boxed food sent south for hurricane victims. She had survived a harrowing three-month journey from Central America, through Mexico, then Texas, and on to Louisiana, where none of the things she had been promised materialized. No job, no host family, no paperwork, no one to take care of her.

Under normal circumstances, hiring an illegal and unnaturalized nanny had never occurred to the Paytons. They quickly adopted her, taught her to drive but only on a few selected streets, taught her the basics of the cell phone, computer, and kitchen appliances, and pressed her to learn English. She had a good foundation from a Catholic school back home, and she spent her daytime hours holed up in the apartment cleaning and mimicking the voices on television. In eight months, her progress was impressive. She preferred to listen, though, especially to Mary Grace, who needed someone to unload on. During the past four months, on the rare nights when Mary Grace prepared dinner, she chatted nonstop

while Ramona absorbed every word. It was wonderful therapy, especially after a brutal day in a courtroom crowded with high-strung men.

"No trouble with the car?" Mary Grace asked the same question every night. Their second car was an old Honda Accord that Ramona had yet to damage. For many good reasons, they were terrified of turning loose on the streets of Hattiesburg an illegal, unlicensed, and quite uninsured alien in a Honda with a zillion miles and their two happy little children in the rear seat. They had trained Ramona to travel a memorized route through the backstreets, to the school, to the grocery, and, if necessary, to their office. If the police stopped her, they planned to beg the cops, the prosecutor, and the judge. They knew them well.

Wes knew for a fact that the presiding city judge had his own illegal pulling his weeds and cutting his grass.

"A good day," Ramona said. "No problem. Everything is fine."

A good day indeed, Mary Grace thought to herself as she began melting cheese.

The phone rang and Wes reluctantly picked up the receiver. The number was unlisted because a crackpot had made threats. They used their cell phones for virtually everything. He listened, said something, hung up, and walked to the stove to disrupt the cooking.

"Who was it?" Mary Grace asked with concern. Every call to the apartment was greeted with suspicion.

"Sherman, at the office. Says there are some reporters hanging around, looking for the stars." Sherman was one of the paralegals.

"Why is he at the office?" Mary Grace asked.

"Just can't get enough, I guess. Do we have any olives for the salad?"

"No. What did you tell him?"

"I told him to shoot at one of them and the rest'll disappear."

"Toss the salad, please," she said to Ramona.

They huddled over a card table wedged in a corner of the kitchen, all five of them. They held hands as Wes prayed and gave thanks for the good things of life, for family and friends and school. And for the food.

He was also thankful for a wise and generous jury and a fantastic result, but he would save that for later. The salad was passed first, then the macaroni and cheese.

"Hey, Dad, can we camp out?" Mack blurted, after he'd swallowed.

"Of course!" Wes said, his back suddenly aching. Camping out in the apartment meant layering the den floor with blankets and quilts and pillows and sleeping there, usually with the television on late at night, usually on Friday nights. It worked only if Mom and Dad joined the fun. Ramona was always invited but wisely declined.

"Same bedtime, though," Mary Grace said. "This is a school night."

"Ten o'clock," said Liza, the negotiator.

"Nine," said Mary Grace, a thirty-minute add-on that made both kids smile.

Mary Grace was knee to knee with her children, savoring the moment and happy that the fatigue might soon be over. Maybe she could rest now, and take them to school, visit their classes, and eat lunch with them. She longed to be a mother, nothing more, and it would be a gloomy day when she was forced to reenter a courtroom.

———

Wednesday night meant potluck casseroles at the Pine Grove Church, and the turnout was always impressive. The busy church was located in the middle of the neighborhood, and many worshippers simply walked a block or two on Sundays and Wednesdays. The doors were open eighteen hours a day, and the pastor, who lived in a parsonage behind the church, was always there, waiting to minister to his people.

They ate in the fellowship hall, an ugly metal addition stuck to the side of the chapel, where folding tables were covered with all manner of home-cooked recipes. There was a basket of white dinner rolls, a large dispenser of sweet tea, and, of course, lots of bottled water. The crowd would be even larger tonight, and they hoped Jeannette would be there. A celebration was in order.

Pine Grove Church was fiercely independent with not the slightest link to any denomination, a source of quiet pride for its founder, Pastor

Denny Ott. It had been built by Baptists decades earlier, then dried up
like the rest of Bowmore. By the time Ott arrived, the congregation con-
sisted of only a few badly scarred souls. Years of infighting had deci-
mated its membership. Ott cleaned out the rest, opened the doors to the
community, and reached out to the people.

He had not been immediately accepted, primarily because he was
from "up north" and spoke with such a clean, clipped accent. He had
met a Bowmore girl at a Bible college in Nebraska, and she brought him
south. Through a series of misadventures he found himself as the interim
pastor of Second Baptist Church. He wasn't really a Baptist, but with so
few young preachers in the area the church could not afford to be selec-
tive. Six months later all the Baptists were gone and the church had a
new name.

He wore a beard and often preached in flannel shirts and hiking
boots. Neckties were not forbidden but were certainly frowned upon. It
was the people's church, a place where anyone could find peace and so-
lace with no worries about wearing the Sunday best. Pastor Ott got rid
of King James and the old hymnal. He had little use for the mournful
anthems written by ancient pilgrims. Worship services were loosened up,
modernized with guitars and slide shows. He believed and taught that
poverty and injustice were more important social issues than abortion
and gay rights, but he was careful with his politics.

The church grew and prospered, though he cared nothing about
money. A friend from seminary ran a mission in Chicago, and through
this connection Ott maintained a large inventory of used but very usable
clothing in the church's "closet." He badgered the larger congregations
in Hattiesburg and Jackson and with their contributions kept a well-
stocked food bank at one end of the fellowship hall. He pestered drug
companies for their leftovers, and the church's "pharmacy" was filled
with over-the-counter medications.

Denny Ott considered all of Bowmore to be his mission, and no
one would go hungry or homeless or sick if he could possibly prevent it.
Not on his watch, and his watch never ended.

He had conducted sixteen funerals of his own people killed by

Krane Chemical, a company he detested so bitterly that he constantly prayed for forgiveness. He didn't hate the nameless and faceless people who owned Krane, to do so would compromise his faith, but he most certainly hated the corporation itself. Was it a sin to hate a corporation? That furious debate raged in his soul every day, and to be on the safe side, he kept praying.

All sixteen were buried in the small cemetery behind the church. When the weather was warm, he cut the grass around the headstones, and when it was cold, he painted the white picket fence that surrounded the cemetery and kept the deer away. Though he had not planned it, his church had become the hub of anti-Krane activity in Cary County. Almost all of its members had been touched by the illness or death of someone harmed by the company.

His wife's older sister finished Bowmore High with Mary Grace Shelby. Pastor Ott and the Paytons were extremely close. Legal advice was often dispensed in the pastor's study with the door closed and one of the Paytons on the phone. Dozens of depositions had been taken in the fellowship hall, packed with lawyers from big cities. Ott disliked the corporate lawyers almost as much as the corporation itself.

Mary Grace had phoned Pastor Ott often during the trial and had always warned him not to be optimistic. He certainly was not. When she called two hours earlier with the astounding news, Ott grabbed his wife and they danced through the house yelling and laughing. Krane had been nailed, humbled, exposed, brought to justice. Finally.

He was greeting his flock when he saw Jeannette enter with her stepsister Bette and the rest of her entourage. She was immediately engulfed by those who loved her, those who wanted to share in this great moment and offer a quiet word. They sat her in the rear of the room, near an old piano, and a receiving line materialized. She managed to smile a few times and even say thanks, but she looked so weak and frail.

With the casseroles growing colder by the minute, and with a full house, Pastor Ott finally called things to order and launched into a windy prayer of thanks. He finished with a flourish and said, "Let us eat."

As always, the children and old folks lined up first, and dinner was

served. Ott made his way to the back and was soon sitting next to Jean-nette. As the attention shifted away from her and to the food, she whispered to her pastor, "I'd like to go to the cemetery."

He led her through a side door, onto a narrow gravel drive that dipped behind the church and ran for fifty yards to the small graveyard. They walked slowly, silently, in the dark. Ott opened the wooden gate, and they stepped into the cemetery, neat and tidy and well tended to. The headstones were small. These were working people, no monuments or crypts or gaudy tributes to great ones.

Four rows down on the right, Jeannette knelt between two graves. One was Chad's, a sickly child who'd lived only six years before tumors choked him. The other held the remains of Pete, her husband of eight years. Father and son, resting side by side forever. She visited them at least once a week and never failed to wish she could join them. She rubbed both headstones at the same time, then began talking softly. "Hello, boys, it's Mom. You won't believe what happened today."

Pastor Ott slipped away, leaving her alone with her tears and thoughts and quiet words that he did not want to hear. He waited by the gate, and as the minutes passed, he watched the shadows move through the rows of headstones as the moonlight shifted through the clouds. He had already buried Chad and Pete. Sixteen in all, and counting. Sixteen silent victims who perhaps were not so silent anymore. From within the little picket-fenced cemetery at the Pine Grove Church a voice had finally been heard. A loud angry voice that begged to be heard and was demanding justice.

He could see her shadow and hear her talking.

He had prayed with Pete in the minutes before he finally slipped away, and he had kissed the forehead of little Chad in his final hour. He had scraped together money for their caskets and funerals. Then he and two of his deacons had dug the graves. Their burials were eight months apart.

She stood, said her farewells, and began moving. "We need to go inside," Ott said.

"Yes, thank you," she said, wiping her cheeks.

Mr. Trudeau's table cost him $50,000, and since he wrote the check, he could damned well control who sat with him. To his left was Brianna, and next to her was her close friend Sandy, another skeleton who'd just been contractually released from her last marriage and was on the prowl for husband number three. To his right was a retired banker friend and his wife, pleasant folks who preferred to chat about the arts. Carl's urologist sat directly across from him. He and his wife were invited because they said little. The odd man out was a lesser executive at Trudeau Group who simply drew the short straw and was there by coercion.

The celebrity chef had whipped up a tasting menu that began with caviar and champagne, then moved on to a lobster bisque, a splash of sautéed foie gras with trimmings, fresh Scottish game hen for the carnivores, and a seaweed bouquet for the veggies. Dessert was a gorgeous layered gelato creation. Each round required a different wine, including dessert.

Carl cleaned every plate put before him and drank heavily. He spoke only to the banker because the banker had heard the news from down south and appeared to be sympathetic. Brianna and Sandy whispered rudely and, in the course of dinner, hammered every other social climber in the crowd. They managed to push the food around their plates while eating virtually none of it. Carl, half-drunk, almost said something to his wife while she tinkered with her seaweed. "Do you know how much that damned food cost?" he wanted to say, but there was no sense starting a fight.

The celebrity chef, one Carl had never heard of, was introduced and got a standing ovation from the four hundred guests, virtually all of them still hungry after five courses. But the evening wasn't about food. It was about money.

Two quick speeches brought the auctioneer to the front. *Abused Imelda* was rolled into the atrium, hanging dramatically from a small mobile crane, and left to hover twenty feet off the floor for all to see clearly. Concert-style spotlights made it even more exotic. The crowd grew quiet

as the tables were cleared by an army of illegal immigrants in black coats and ties.

The auctioneer rambled on about *Imelda,* and the crowd listened. Then he talked about the artist, and the crowd really listened. Was he truly crazy? Insane? Close to suicide? They wanted details, but the auctioneer held the high ground. He was British and very proper, which would add at least a million bucks to the winning bid.

"I suggest we start the bidding at five million," he said through his nose, and the crowd gasped.

Brianna was suddenly bored with Sandy. She moved closer to Carl, fluttered her eyelashes at him, and placed a hand on his thigh. Carl responded by nodding at the nearest floor assistant, a man he'd already spoken to. The assistant flashed a sign to the podium, and *Imelda* came to life.

"And we have five million," the auctioneer announced. Thunderous applause. "A nice place to start, thank you. And now onward to six."

Six, seven, eight, nine, and Carl nodded at ten. He kept a smile on his face, but his stomach was churning. How much would this abomination cost him? There were at least six billionaires in the room and several more in the making. No shortage of enormous egos, no shortage of cash, but at that moment none of the others needed a headline as desperately as Carl Trudeau.

And Pete Flint understood this.

Two bidders dropped out on the way to eleven million. "How many are left?" Carl whispered to the banker, who was watching the crowd and searching for the competition.

"It's Pete Flint, maybe one more."

That son of a bitch. When Carl nodded at twelve, Brianna practically had her tongue in his ear.

"We have twelve million." The crowd exploded with applause and hoorays, and the auctioneer wisely said, "Let's catch our breath here." Everyone took a sip of something. Carl gulped more wine. Pete Flint was behind him, two tables back, but Carl didn't dare turn around and acknowledge their little battle.

If Flint had really shorted Krane's stock, then he would reap millions from the verdict. Carl, obviously, had just lost millions because of it. It was all on paper, but then wasn't everything?

Imelda was not. It was real, tangible, a work of art that Carl could not lose, not to Pete Flint anyway.

Rounds 13, 14, and 15 were dragged out beautifully by the auctioneer, each ending in rapturous applause. Word had spread quickly, and everyone knew it was Carl Trudeau and Pete Flint. When the applause died, the two heavyweights settled in for more. Carl nodded at sixteen million, then accepted the applause.

"Do we have seventeen million?" boomed the auctioneer, quite excited himself.

A long pause. The tension was electric. "Very well, we have sixteen. Going once, going twice, ah yes—we have seventeen million."

Carl had been making and breaking vows throughout the ordeal, but he was determined not to exceed seventeen million bucks. As the roar died down, he settled back in his seat, cool as any corporate raider with billions in play. He was finished, and quite happy about it. Flint was bluffing, and now Flint was stuck with the old girl for $17 million.

"Dare I ask for eighteen?" More applause. More time for Carl to think. If he was willing to pay seventeen, why not eighteen? And if he jumped at eighteen, then Flint would realize that he, Carl, was staying to the bloody end.

It was worth a try.

"Eighteen?" asked the auctioneer.

"Yes," Carl said, loud enough for many to hear. The strategy worked. Pete Flint retreated to the safety of his unspent cash and watched in amusement as the great Carl Trudeau finished off a lousy deal.

"Sold for eighteen million, to Mr. Carl Trudeau," roared the auctioneer, and the crowd leaped to its feet.

They lowered *Imelda* so her new owners could pose with her. Many others, both envious and proud, gawked at the Trudeaus and their new addition. A band cranked up and it was time to dance. Brianna was in

heat—the money had sent her into a frenzy—and halfway through the first dance Carl gently shoved her back a step. She was hot and lewd and flashing as much skin as possible. Folks were watching and that was fine with her.

"Let's get out of here," Carl said after the second dance.

CHAPTER 4

During the night, Wes had somehow managed to gain the sofa, a much softer resting place, and when he awoke before daylight, Mack was wedged tightly by his side. Mary Grace and Liza were sprawled on the floor beneath them, wrapped in blankets and dead to the world. They had watched television until both kids dropped off, then quietly opened and finished a bottle of cheap champagne they had been saving. The alcohol and the fatigue knocked them out, and they vowed to sleep forever.

Five hours later Wes opened his eyes and could not close them. He was back in the courtroom, sweating and nervous, watching the jurors file in, praying, searching for a sign, then hearing the majestic words of Judge Harrison. Words that would ring in his ears forever.

Today would be a fine day, and Wes couldn't waste any more of it on the sofa.

He eased away from Mack, covered him with a blanket, and moved silently to their cluttered bedroom, where he slipped into his running shorts and shoes and a sweatshirt. During the trial, he tried to run every day, often at midnight, often at five in the morning. A month earlier, he'd found himself six miles from home at 3:00 a.m. The running cleared his

mind and relieved the stress. He plotted strategy, cross-examined witnesses, argued with Jared Kurtin, appealed to the jurors, did a dozen tasks as he pounded the asphalt in the dark.

Perhaps on this run he might concentrate on something, anything, other than the trial. Maybe a vacation. A beach. But the appeal was already bugging him.

Mary Grace did not move as he eased from the apartment and locked the door behind him. It was 5:15.

Without stretching, he took off and was soon on Hardy Street, headed for the campus of the University of Southern Mississippi. He liked the safety of the place. He circled around the dorms where he once lived, around the football stadium where he once played, and after half an hour pulled into Java Werks, his favorite coffee shop, across the street from the campus. He placed four quarters on the counter and took a small cup of the house blend. Four quarters. He almost laughed as he counted them out. He had to plan his coffee and was always looking for quarters.

At the end of the counter was a collection of morning newspapers. The front-page headline of the *Hattiesburg American* screamed: "Krane Chemical Nailed for $41 Million." There was a large, splendid photo of him and Mary Grace leaving the courthouse, tired but happy. And a smaller photo of Jeannette Baker, still crying. Lots of quotes from the lawyers, a few from the jurors, including a windy little speech by Dr. Leona Rocha, who, evidently, had been a force in the jury room. She was quoted as saying, among other gems, "We were angered by Krane's arrogant and calculated abuse of the land, by their disregard for safety, and then their deceit in trying to conceal it."

Wes loved that woman. He devoured the long article while ignoring his coffee. The state's largest paper was the *Clarion-Ledger*, out of Jackson, and its headline was somewhat more restrained, though still impressive: "Jury Faults Krane Chemical—Huge Verdict." More photos, quotes, details of the trial, and after a few minutes Wes caught himself skimming. The *Sun Herald* from Biloxi had the best line so far: "Jury to Krane—Fork It Over."

Front-page news and photos in the big dailies. Not a bad day for the little law firm of Payton & Payton. The comeback was under way, and Wes was ready. The office phones would start ringing with potential clients in need of divorces and bankruptcies and a hundred other nuisances that Wes had no stomach for. He would politely send them away, to other small-timers, of which there was an endless supply, and he would check the nets each morning and look for the big ones. A massive verdict, photos in the paper, the talk of the town, and business was about to increase substantially.

He drained his coffee and hit the street.

CARL — P. O. V

Carl Trudeau also left home before sunrise. He could hide in his penthouse all day and let his communications people deal with the disaster. He could hide behind his lawyers. He could hop on his jet and fly away to his villa on Anguilla or his mansion in Palm Beach. But not Carl. He had never run from a brawl, and he wouldn't start now.

Plus, he wanted to get away from his wife. She'd cost him a fortune last night and he was resenting it.

"Good morning," he said abruptly to Toliver as he scampered into the rear seat of the Bentley.

"Good morning, sir." Toliver wasn't about to ask something stupid, such as "How are you doing, sir?" It was 5:30, not an unusual hour for Mr. Trudeau, but not a customary one, either. They normally left the penthouse an hour later.

"Let's push it," the boss said, and Toliver roared down Fifth Avenue. Twenty minutes later, Carl was in his private elevator with Stu, an assistant whose only job was to be on call 24/7 in case the great man needed something. Stu had been alerted an hour earlier and given instructions: Fix the coffee, toast a wheat bagel, squeeze the orange juice. He was given a list of six newspapers to arrange on Mr. Trudeau's desk, and was in the midst of an Internet search for stories about the verdict. Carl barely acknowledged his presence.

In his office, Stu took his jacket, poured his coffee, and was told to hurry along with the bagel and juice.

Carl settled into his aerodynamic designer chair, cracked his knuckles, rolled himself up to his desk, took a deep breath, and picked up the *New York Times*. Front page, left column. Not front page of the Business section, but the front page of the whole damned paper!! Right up there with a bad war, a scandal in Congress, dead bodies in Gaza.

The front page. "Krane Chemical Held Liable in Toxic Deaths," read the headline, and Carl's clenched jaw began to slacken. Byline, Hattiesburg, Mississippi: "A state court jury awarded a young widow $3 million in actual damages and $38 million in punitive damages in her wrongful-death claims against Krane Chemical." Carl read quickly—he knew the wretched details. The *Times* got most of them right. Every quote from the lawyers was so predictable. Blah, blah, blah.

But why the front page?

He took it as a cheap shot, and was soon hit with another on page 2 of Business, where an analyst of some variety held forth on Krane's other legal problems, to wit, hundreds of potential lawsuits claiming pretty much the same thing Jeannette Baker had claimed. According to the expert, a name Carl had never seen, which was unusual, Krane's exposure could be "several billion" in cash, and since Krane, with its "questionable policies regarding liability insurance," was practically "naked," such exposure could be "catastrophic."

Carl was cursing when Stu hurried in with juice and a bagel. "Anything else, sir?" he asked.

"No, now close the door."

Carl rallied briefly in the Arts section. On the front page beneath the fold there was a story about last night's MuAb event, the highlight of which had been a spirited bidding war, and so on. In the bottom right-hand corner was a decent-sized color photo of Mr. and Mrs. Carl Trudeau posing with their newest acquisition. Brianna, ever photogenic, as she damned well should be, emanated glamour. Carl looked rich, thin, and young, he thought, and *Imelda* was as baffling in print as she was in

person. Was she really a work of art? Or was she just a hodgepodge of bronze and cement thrown together by some confused soul working hard to appear tortured?

The latter, according to a *Times* art critic, the same pleasant gentleman Carl had chatted with before dinner. When asked by the reporter if Mr. Trudeau's $18 million purchase was a prudent investment, the critic answered, "No, but it is certainly a boost for the museum's capital campaign." He then went on to explain that the market for abstract sculpture had been stagnant for over a decade and wasn't likely to improve, at least in his opinion. He saw little future for *Imelda*. The story concluded on page 7 with two paragraphs and a photo of the sculptor, Pablo, smiling at the camera and looking very much alive and, well, sane.

Nevertheless, Carl was pleased, if only for a moment. The story was positive. He appeared unfazed by the verdict, resilient, in command of his universe. The good press was worth something, though he knew its value was somewhere far south of $18 million. He crunched the bagel without tasting it.

Back to the carnage. It was splashed across the front pages of the *Wall Street Journal*, the *Financial Times*, and *USA Today*. After four newspapers, he was tired of reading the same quotes from the lawyers and the same predictions from the experts. He rolled back from his desk, sipped his coffee, and reminded himself of exactly how much he loathed reporters. But he was still alive. The battering by the press was brutal, and it would continue, but he, the great Carl Trudeau, was taking their best shots and still on his feet.

This would be the worst day of his professional life, but tomorrow would be better.

It was 7:00 a.m. The market opened at 9:30. Krane's stock closed at $52.50 the day before, up $1.25 because the jury was taking forever and appeared to be hung. The morning's experts were predicting panic selling, but their damage estimates were all over the board.

He took a call from his communications director and explained that he would not talk to any reporters, journalists, analysts, whatever they called themselves and regardless of how many were calling or camped

out in the lobby. Just stick to the company line—"We are planning a vigorous appeal and expect to prevail." Do not deviate one word.

At 7:15, Bobby Ratzlaff arrived with Felix Bard, the chief financial officer. Neither had slept more than two hours, and both were amazed that their boss had found the time to go partying. They unpacked their thick files, made the obligatory terse greetings, then huddled around the conference table. They would be there for the next twelve hours. There was much to discuss, but the real reason for the meeting was that Mr. Trudeau wanted some company in his bunker when the market opened and all hell broke loose.

Ratzlaff went first. A truckload of post-trial motions would be filed, nothing would change, and the case would move on to the Mississippi Supreme Court. "The court has a history of being plaintiff-friendly, but that's changing. We have reviewed the rulings in big tort cases over the past two years, and the court usually splits 5 to 4 in favor of the plaintiff, but not always."

"How long before the final appeal is over?" Carl asked.

"Eighteen to twenty-four months."

Ratzlaff moved on. A hundred and forty lawsuits were on file against Krane because of the Bowmore mess, about a third of them being death cases. According to an exhaustive and ongoing study by Ratzlaff, his staff, and their lawyers in New York, Atlanta, and Mississippi, there were probably another three hundred to four hundred cases with "legitimate" potential, meaning that they involved either death, probable death, or moderate to severe illness. There could be thousands of cases in which the claimants suffered minor ailments such as skin rashes, lesions, and nagging coughs, but for the time being, these were classified as frivolous.

Because of the difficulty and cost of proving liability, and linking it with an illness, most of the cases on file had not been pushed aggressively. This, of course, was about to change. "I'm sure the plaintiff's lawyers down there are quite hungover this morning," Ratzlaff said, but Carl did not crack a smile. He never did. He was always reading, never looking at the person with the floor, and missed nothing.

"How many cases do the Paytons have?" he asked.

"Around thirty. We're not sure, because they have not actually filed suit in all of them. There's a lot of waiting here."

"One article said that the *Baker* case almost bankrupted them."

"True. They hocked everything."

"Bank loans?"

"Yes, that's the rumor."

"Do we know which banks?"

"I'm not sure if we know that."

"Find out. I want the loan numbers, terms, everything."

"Got it."

There were no good options, Ratzlaff said, working from his outline. The dam has cracked, the flood is coming. The lawyers will attack with a vengeance, and defense costs would quadruple to $100 million a year, easily. The nearest case could be ready for trial in eight months, same courtroom, same judge. Another big verdict, and, well, who knows.

Carl glanced at his watch and mumbled something about making a call. He left the table again, paced around the office, then stopped at the windows looking south. The Trump Building caught his attention. Its address was 40 Wall Street, very near the New York Stock Exchange, where before long the common shares of Krane Chemical would be the talk of the day as investors jumped ship and speculators gawked at the roadkill. How cruel, how ironic, that he, the great Carl Trudeau, a man who had so often watched happily from above as some unfortunate company flamed out, would now be fighting off the vultures. How many times had he engineered the collapse of a stock's price so he could swoop down and buy it for pennies? His legend had been built with such ruthless tactics.

How bad would it be? That was the great question, always followed soon by number two: How long would it last?

He waited.

CHAPTER 5

Tom Huff put on his darkest and finest suit, and after much debate de-
cided to arrive at work at the Second State Bank a few minutes later than
usual. An earlier entry would seem too predictable, perhaps a little too
cocky. And, more important, he wanted everyone in place when he
arrived—the old tellers on the main floor, the cute secretaries on the sec-
ond, and the vice somethings, his rivals, on the third floor. Huffy wanted
a triumphant arrival with as big an audience as possible. He'd gambled
bravely with the Paytons, and the moment belonged to him.

What he got instead was an overall dismissal by the tellers, a collec-
tive cold shoulder from the secretaries, and enough devious grins from his
rivals to make him suspicious. On his desk he found a message marked
"Urgent" to see Mr. Kirkhead. Something was up, and Huffy began to
feel considerably less cocky. So much for a dramatic entrance. What was
the problem?

Mr. Kirkhead was in his office, waiting, with the door open, always
a bad sign. The boss hated open doors, and in fact boasted of a closed-
door management style. He was caustic, rude, cynical, and afraid of his
shadow, and closed doors served him well.

"Sit down," he barked, with no thought of a "Good morning" or a "Hello" or, heaven forbid, a "Congratulations." He was camped behind his pretentious desk, fat hairless head bent low as if he sniffed the spreadsheets as he read them.

"And how are you, Mr. Kirkhead?" Huffy chirped. How badly he wanted to say "Prickhead" because he said it every other time he referred to his boss. Even the old gals on the main floor sometimes used the substitution.

"Swell. Did you bring the Payton file?"

"No, sir. I wasn't asked to bring the Payton file. Something the matter?"

"Two things, actually, now that you mention it. First, we have this disastrous loan to these people, over $400,000, past due of course and horribly under-collateralized. By far the worst loan in the bank's portfolio."

He said "these people" as if Wes and Mary Grace were credit card thieves.

"This is nothing new, sir."

"Mind if I finish? And now we have this obscene jury award, which, as the banker holding the paper, I guess I'm supposed to feel good about, but as a commercial lender and business leader in this community, I think it really sucks. What kind of message do we send to prospective industrial clients with verdicts like this?"

"Don't dump toxic waste in our state?"

Prickhead's fat jowls turned red as he swept away Huffy's retort with the wave of a hand. He cleared his throat, almost gargling with his own saliva.

"This is bad for our business climate," he said. "Front page all over the world this morning. I'm getting phone calls from the home office. A very bad day."

Lots of bad days over in Bowmore, too, Huffy thought. Especially with all those funerals.

"Forty-one million bucks," Prickhead went on. "For a poor woman who lives in a trailer."

"Nothing wrong with trailers, Mr. Kirkhead. Lots of good folks live in them around here. We make the loans."

"You miss the point. It's an obscene amount of money. The whole system has gone crazy. And why here? Why is Mississippi known as a judicial hellhole? Why do trial lawyers love our little state? Just look at some of the surveys. It's bad for business, Huff, for our business."

"Yes, sir, but you must feel better about the Payton loan this morning."

"I want it repaid, and soon."

"So do I."

"Give me a schedule. Get with these people and put together a repayment plan, one that I will approve only when it looks sensible. And do it now."

"Yes, sir, but it might take a few months for them to get back on their feet. They've practically shut down—"

"I don't care about them, Huff. I just want this damned thing off the books."

"Yes, sir. Is that all?"

"Yes. And no more litigation loans, you understand?"

"Don't worry."

——— *Jared Kurtin POV*

Three doors down from the bank, the Honorable Jared Kurtin made a final inspection of the troops before heading back to Atlanta and the icy reception waiting there. Headquarters was a recently renovated old building on Front Street. The well-heeled defense of Krane Chemical had leased it two years earlier, then retrofitted it with an impressive collection of technology and personnel.

The mood was somber, as might be expected, though many of the locals were not troubled by the verdict. After months of working under Kurtin and his arrogant henchmen from Atlanta, they felt a quiet satisfaction in watching them retreat in defeat. And they would be back. The verdict guaranteed new enthusiasm from the victims, more lawsuits, trials, and so on.

On hand to witness the farewell was Frank Sully, local counsel and partner in a Hattiesburg defense firm first hired by Krane and later demoted in favor of a "big firm" from Atlanta. Sully had been given a seat at the rather crowded defense table and had suffered the indignity of sitting through a four-month trial without saying a word in open court. Sully had disagreed with virtually every tactic and strategy employed by Kurtin. So deep was his dislike and distrust of the Atlanta lawyers that he had circulated a secret memo to his partners in which he predicted a huge punitive award. Now he gloated privately.

But he was a professional. He served his client as well as his client would allow, and he never failed to do what Kurtin instructed him to do. And he would gladly do it all over again because Krane Chemical had paid his little firm over a million dollars to date.

He and Kurtin shook hands at the front door. Both knew they would speak by phone before the day was over. Both were quietly thrilled by the departure. Two leased vans hauled Kurtin and ten others to the airport, where a handsome little jet was waiting for the seventy-minute flight, though they were in no hurry. They missed their homes and families, but what could be more humiliating than limping back from Podunk with their tails between their legs?

Carl POV

———

Carl remained safely tucked away on the forty-fifth floor, while on the Street the rumors raged. At 9:15, his banker from Goldman Sachs called, for the third time that morning, and delivered the bad news that the exchange might not open trading with Krane's common shares. It was too volatile. There was too much pressure to sell.

"Looks like a fire sale," he said bluntly, and Carl wanted to curse him.

All POV in Ratt..

The market opened at 9:30 a.m., and Krane's trading was delayed. Carl, Ratzlaff, and Felix Bard were at the conference table, exhausted, sleeves rolled up, elbows deep in papers and debris, phones in each hand, all conversations frantic. The bomb finally landed just after 10:00 a.m., when Krane began trading at $40.00 a share. There were no buyers, and

none at $35.00. The plunge was temporarily reversed at $29.50 when speculators entered the fray and began buying. Up and down it went for the next hour. At noon, it was at $27.25 in heavy trading, and to make matters worse, Krane was the big business story of the morning. For their market updates, the cable shows happily switched to their Wall Street analysts, all of whom gushed about the stunning meltdown of Krane Chemical.

Then back to the headlines. Body count from Iraq. The monthly natural disaster. And Krane Chemical.

Bobby Ratzlaff asked permission to run to his office. He took the stairs, one flight down, and barely made it to the men's room. The stalls were empty. He went to the far one, raised the lid, and vomited violently.

His ninety thousand shares of Krane common had just decreased in value from about $4.5 million to around $2.5 million, and the collapse wasn't over. He used the stock as collateral for all his toys—the small house in the Hamptons, the Porsche Carrera, half interest in a sailboat. Not to mention overhead items such as private school tuition and golf club memberships. Bobby was now unofficially bankrupt.

For the first time in his career, he understood why they jumped from buildings in 1929.

The Paytons had planned to drive to Bowmore together, but a last-minute visit to their office by their banker changed things. Wes decided to stay behind and deal with Huffy. Mary Grace took the Taurus and drove to her hometown.

She went to Pine Grove, then to the church, where Jeannette Baker was waiting along with Pastor Denny Ott and a crowd of other victims represented by the Payton firm. They met privately in the fellowship hall and lunched on sandwiches, one of which was eaten by Jeannette herself, a rarity. She was composed, rested, happy to be away from the courthouse and all its proceedings.

The shock of the verdict was beginning to wear off. The possibility of money changing hands lightened the mood, and it also prompted a

flood of questions. Mary Grace was careful to downplay expectations. She detailed the arduous appeals ahead for the *Baker* verdict. She was not optimistic about a settlement, or a cleanup, or even the next trial. Frankly, she and Wes did not have the funds, nor the energy, to take on Krane in another long trial, though she did not share this with the group.

She was confident and reassuring. Her clients were at the right place; she and Wes had certainly proved that. There would soon be many lawyers sniffing around Bowmore, looking for Krane victims, making promises, offering money perhaps. And not just local lawyers, but the national tort boys who chased cases from coast to coast and often arrived at the crash sites before the fire trucks. Trust no one, she said softly but sternly. Krane will flood the area with investigators, snitches, informants, all looking for things that might be used against you one day in court. Don't talk to reporters, because something said in jest could sound quite different in a trial. Don't sign anything unless it's first reviewed by the Paytons. Don't talk to other lawyers.

She gave them hope. The verdict was echoing through the judicial system. Government regulators had to take note. The chemical industry could no longer ignore them. Krane's stock was crashing at that very moment, and when the stockholders lost enough money, they would demand changes.

When she finished, Denny Ott led them in prayer. Mary Grace hugged her clients, wished them well, promised to see them again in a few days, then walked with Ott to the front of the church for her next appointment.

The journalist's name was Tip Shepard. He had arrived about a month earlier, and after many attempts had gained the confidence of Pastor Ott, who then introduced him to Wes and Mary Grace. Shepard was a freelancer with impressive credentials, several books to his credit, and a Texas twang that neutralized some of Bowmore's distrust of the media. The Paytons had refused to talk to him during the trial, for many reasons. Now that it was over, Mary Grace would do the first interview. If it went well, there might be another.

omni Pov

"**M**r. Kirkhead wants his money," Huffy was saying. He was in Wes's office, a makeshift room with unpainted Sheetrock walls, stained concrete floor, and Army-surplus furniture.

Wes speaks, then JG

"I'm sure he does," Wes shot back. He was already irritated that his banker would arrive just hours after the verdict with signs of attitude. "Tell him to get in line." *tells reader his state of mind*

"We're way past due here, Wes, come on."

"Is Kirkhead stupid? Does he think that the jury gives an award one day and the defendant writes a check the next?"

"Yes, he's stupid, but not that stupid."

"He sent you over here?"

"Yes. He jumped me first thing this morning, and I expect to get jumped for many days to come."

"Couldn't you wait a day, two days, maybe a week? Let us breathe a little, maybe enjoy the moment?"

"He wants a plan. Something in writing. Repayments, stuff like that."

Wes speaks - then JG tells reader his thoughts.

"I'll give him a plan," Wes said, his words trailing off. He did not want to fight with Huffy. Though not exactly friends, they were certainly friendly and enjoyed each other's company. Wes was extremely grateful for Huffy's willingness to roll the dice. Huffy admired the Paytons for losing it all as they risked it all. He had spent hours with them as they surrendered their home, office, cars, retirement accounts. *Then, Huffy's too*

"Let's talk about the next three months," Huffy said. The four legs of his folding chair were uneven and he rocked slightly as he talked. *says How Wes is feeling* Wes took a deep breath, gave a roll of the eyes. He suddenly felt very tired. "Once upon a time, we were grossing fifty thousand a month, clearing thirty, before taxes. Life was good, you remember. It'll take a year to crank up that treadmill, but we can do it. We have no choice. We'll survive until the appeals run their course. If the verdict stands, Kirkhead can take his money and take a hike. We'll retire, time for the

what is coming next .

Tells the reader

sailboat. If the verdict is reversed, we'll go bankrupt and start advertising for quickie divorces."

"Surely the verdict will attract clients."

"Of course, but most of it'll be junk."

By using the word "bankrupt," Wes had gently placed Huffy back in his box, along with old Prickhead and the bank. The verdict could not be classified as an asset, and without it the Paytons' balance sheet looked as bleak as it did a day earlier. They had lost virtually everything already, and to be adjudged bankrupt was a further indignity they were willing to endure. Pile it on.

They would be back.

"I'm not giving you a plan, Huffy. Thanks for asking. Come back in thirty days and we'll talk. Right now I've got clients who've been ignored for months."

"So what do I tell Mr. Prickhead?"

"Simple. Push just a little bit harder, and he can use the paper to wipe with. Ease off, give us some time, and we'll satisfy the debt."

"I'll pass it along."

Scene change

Mary Grace "Remembers" Tool for telling y background

At Babe's Coffee Shop on Main Street, Mary Grace and Tip Shepard sat in a booth near the front windows and talked about the town. She remembered Main Street as a busy place where people shopped and gathered. Bowmore was too small for the large discount stores, so the downtown merchants survived. When she was a kid, traffic was often heavy, parking hard to find. Now half the storefronts were covered with plywood, and the other half were desperate for business.

A teenager with an apron brought two cups of black coffee and left without a word. Mary Grace added sugar while Shepard watched her carefully. "Are you sure the coffee is safe?" he asked.

"Of course. The city finally passed an ordinance forbidding the use of its water in restaurants. Plus, I've known Babe for thirty years. She was one of the first to buy her water."

Shepard took a cautious sip, then arranged his tape recorder and notebook.

"Why did you take the cases?" he asked.

She smiled and shook her head and kept stirring. "I've asked myself that a thousand times, but the answer is really simple. Pete, Jeannette's husband, worked for my uncle. I knew several of the victims. It's a small town, and when so many people became ill, it was obvious there had to be a reason. The cancer came in waves, and there was so much suffering. After attending the first three or four funerals, I realized something had to be done."

He took notes and ignored the pause.

She continued. "Krane was the biggest employer, and for years there had been rumors of dumping around the plant. A lot of folks who worked there got sick. I remember coming home from college after my sophomore year and hearing people talk about how bad the water was. We lived a mile outside of town and had our own well, so it was never a problem for us. But things got worse in town. Over the years, the rumors of dumping grew and grew until everyone came to believe them. At the same time, the water turned into a putrid liquid that was undrinkable. Then the cancer hit—liver, kidney, urinary tract, stomach, bladder, lots of leukemia. I was in church one Sunday with my parents, and I could see four slick, shiny bald heads. Chemo. I thought I was in a horror movie."

"Have you regretted the litigation?"

"No, never. We've lost a lot, but then so has my hometown. Hopefully, the losing is over now. Wes and I are young; we'll survive. But many of these folks are either dead or deathly ill."

"Do you think about the money?"

"What money? The appeal will take eighteen months, and right now that seems like an eternity. You have to see the big picture."

"Which is?"

"Five years from now. In five years, the toxic dump will be cleaned up and gone forever and no one will ever be hurt by it again. There will

be a settlement, one big massive settlement where Krane Chemical, and its insurers, are finally brought to the table with their very deep pockets and are forced to compensate the families they have ruined. Everybody gets their share of damages."

"Including the lawyers."

"Absolutely. If not for the lawyers, Krane would still be here manufacturing pillamar 5 and dumping its by-products in the pits behind the plant, and no one could hold them accountable."

"Instead, they are now in Mexico—"

"Oh yes, manufacturing pillamar 5 and dumping its by-products in the pits behind the plants. And nobody gives a damn. They don't have these trials down there."

"What are your chances on appeal?"

She sipped the stale and heavily sugared coffee and was about to answer when an insurance agent stopped by, shook her hand, hugged her, said thanks several times, and appeared to be on the verge of tears when he walked away. Then Mr. Greenwood, her junior high principal, now retired, spotted her as he entered and practically crushed her in a bear hug. He ignored Shepard while rambling on about how proud he was of her. He thanked her, promised to keep praying for her, asked about her family, and so on. As he withdrew in a windy farewell, Babe, the owner, came over for a hug and another lengthy round of congratulations.

Shepard finally stood and eased out the door. A few minutes later, Mary Grace made her exit. "Sorry about that," she said. "It's a big moment for the town."

"They are very proud."

"Let's go see the plant."

The Krane Chemical Bowmore Plant Number Two, as it was officially known, was in an abandoned industrial park on the east side of the city limits. The plant was a series of flat-roofed cinder-block buildings, connected by massive piping and conveyors. Water towers and storage silos rose behind the buildings. Everything was overgrown with kudzu and weeds. Because of the litigation, the company had secured the facility with miles of twelve-foot chain-link fencing, topped with glistening razor

wire. Heavy gates were chained and padlocked. Like a prison, where bad things happened, the plant shut out the world and kept its secrets buried within.

Mary Grace had visited the plant at least a dozen times during the litigation, but always with a mob—other lawyers, engineers, former Krane employees, security guards, even Judge Harrison. The last visit had been two months earlier when the jurors were given a tour.

She and Shepard stopped at the main gate and examined the padlocks. A large, decaying sign identified the plant and its owner. As they stared through the chain-link fence, Mary Grace said, "Six years ago, when it became apparent that litigation was inevitable, Krane fled to Mexico. The employees were given three days' notice and $500 in severance pay; many of them had worked here for thirty years. It was an incredibly stupid way to leave town, because some of their former workers were our best witnesses during the trial. The bitterness was, and is, astounding. If Krane had any friends in Bowmore, it lost every one of them when it screwed its employees."

A photographer working with Shepard met them at the front gate and began snapping away. They strolled along the fence, with Mary Grace directing the brief tour. "For years, this place was unlocked. It was routinely vandalized. Teenagers hung out here, drinking and doing drugs. Now people stay as far away as possible. The gates and fences are really not needed. No one wants to get near this place."

From the north side, a long row of thick metal cylinders was visible in the midst of the plant. Mary Grace pointed and explained, "That's known as Extraction Unit Two. The bichloronylene was reduced as a by-product and stored in those tanks. From there, some was shipped away for a proper disposal, but most was taken into the woods there, farther back on the property, and simply dumped into a ravine."

"Proctor's Pit?"

"Yes, Mr. Proctor was the supervisor in charge of disposal. He died of cancer before we could subpoena him." They walked twenty yards along the fence. "We really can't see from here, but there are three ravines in there, deep in the woods, where they simply hauled the tanks

and covered them with dirt and mud. Over the years, they began to leak—they were not even sealed properly—and the chemicals soaked into the earth. This went on for years, tons and tons of bichloronylene and cartolyx and aklar and other proven carcinogens. If you can believe our experts, and the jury evidently did, the poisons finally contaminated the aquifer from which Bowmore pumps its water."

A security detail in a golf cart approached on the other side of the fence. Two overweight guards with guns stopped and stared. "Just ignore them," Mary Grace whispered.

"What're you lookin' for?" a guard asked.

"We're on the right side of the fence," she answered.

"What're you lookin' for?" he repeated.

"I'm Mary Grace Payton, one of the attorneys. You boys move along."

Both nodded at once, and then slowly drove away.

She glanced at her watch. "I really need to be going."

"When can we meet again?"

"We'll see. No promises. Things are quite hectic right now."

They drove back to the Pine Grove Church and said goodbye. When Shepard was gone, Mary Grace walked three blocks to Jeannette's trailer. Bette was at work, the place was quiet. For an hour, she sat with her client under a small tree and drank bottled lemonade. No tears, no tissues, just girl talk about life and families and the past four months together in that awful courtroom.

CHAPTER 6

With an hour to go before trading closed, Krane bottomed at $18 a share, then began a rather feeble rally, if it could be called that. It nibbled around $20 a share for half an hour before finding some traction at that price.

To add to the catastrophe, investors for some reason chose to exact revenge on the rest of Carl's empire. His Trudeau Group owned 45 percent of Krane and smaller chunks of six other public companies—three chemical companies, an oil exploration firm, an auto parts maker, and a chain of hotels. Shortly after lunch, the common shares of the other six began slipping as well. It made no sense whatsoever, but then the market often cannot be explained. Misery is contagious on Wall Street. Panic is common and rarely understood.

Mr. Trudeau did not see the chain reaction coming, nor did Felix Bard, his savvy financial wizard. As the minutes dragged by, they watched in horror as a billion dollars in market value slipped away from the Trudeau Group.

Blame was rampant. Obviously, it all went back to the verdict in Mississippi. But many analysts, especially the babbling experts on cable,

made much of the fact that Krane Chemical had for years chosen to go brazenly forward without the benefit of full liability insurance. The company had saved a fortune in premiums, but was now giving it back in spades. Bobby Ratzlaff was listening to one such analyst on a television in a corner when Carl snapped, "Turn that thing off!"

It was almost 4:00 p.m., the magic hour when the exchange closed and the bloodshed ended. Carl was at his desk, phone stuck to his head. Bard was at the conference table watching two monitors and recording the latest stock prices. Ratzlaff was pale and sick and even more bankrupt than before, and he went from window to window as if selecting the one for his final flight.

The other six stocks rallied at the final buzzer, and though they were down significantly, the damage was not ruinous. The companies were solid performers, and their stocks would readjust themselves in due course. Krane, on the other hand, was a train wreck. It closed at $21.25, a full $31.25 collapse since the day before. Its market value had shrunk from $3.2 billion to $1.3 billion. Mr. Trudeau's 45 percent share of the misery was about $850 million. Bard quickly added the declines from the other six companies and computed a one-day loss for his boss at $1.1 billion. Not a record, but probably enough to land Carl on someone's Top Ten list.

After a review of the closing numbers, Carl ordered Bard and Ratzlaff to put on their jackets, straighten their ties, and follow him.

Four floors below, in the corporate offices of Krane Chemical, its top executives were hunkered down in a small dining room reserved exclusively for themselves. The food was notoriously bland, but the view was impressive. Lunch had not been important that day; no one had an appetite. They had been waiting for an hour, shell-shocked and expecting an explosion from above. A mass funeral would have been a livelier event. But Mr. Trudeau managed to brighten up the room. He marched purposefully in, his two minions in tow—Bard with a plastic grin, Ratzlaff green at the gills—and, instead of yelling, thanked the men (all boys) for their hard work and commitment to the company.

A wide smile, and Carl said, "Gentlemen, this is not a very good

day. One which I'm sure we'll remember for a long time." His voice was pleasant, just another friendly little drop-in from the man at the top.

"But today is now over, thankfully, and we are still standing. Tomorrow, we start kicking ass."

A few nervous looks, maybe a smile or two. Most were expecting to be sacked on the spot.

He continued: "I want you to remember three things that I'm about to say on this historic occasion. First, no one in this room is losing his job. Second, Krane Chemical will survive this miscarriage of justice. And third, I do not intend to lose this fight."

He was the epitome of the confident leader, the captain rallying his troops in their foxholes. A victory sign and long cigar and he could've been Churchill in his finest hour. He ordered chins up, backs to the wall, and so on.

Even Bobby Ratzlaff began to feel better.

Change of scene not POV

Two hours later, Ratzlaff and Bard were finally dismissed and sent home. Carl wanted time to reflect, to lick his wounds, to clear his head. To help matters, he fixed himself a scotch and took off his shoes. The sun was setting somewhere beyond New Jersey, and he said good riddance to such an unforgettable day.

He glanced at his computer and checked the day's phone calls. Brianna had called four times, nothing urgent. If she had an important matter, Carl's secretary logged it as "Your Wife" and not "Brianna." He'd call her later. He was in no mood for the summary of her daily workouts.

There were over forty calls, and number twenty-eight caught his attention. Senator Grott had checked in from Washington. Carl barely knew him personally, but every serious corporate player knew of The Senator. Grott had served three terms in the U.S. Senate from New York before he retired, voluntarily, and joined a powerful law firm to make his fortune. He was Mr. Washington, the ultimate insider, the seasoned counselor and adviser with offices on Wall Street, Pennsylvania Avenue, and anywhere else he chose. Senator Grott had more contacts than anyone,

often golfed with whoever happened to occupy the White House, trav-
eled the world in search of more contacts, offered advice only to the pow-
erful, and was generally regarded as the top connection between big
corporate America and big government. If The Senator called, you
called him back, even though you'd just lost a billion dollars. The Sena-
tor knew exactly how much you had lost and was concerned about it.

Carl dialed the private number. After eight rings a gruff voice said,
"Grott."

"Senator Grott, Carl Trudeau here," Carl said politely. He was def-
erential to very few people, but The Senator demanded and deserved re-
spect.

"Oh yes, Carl," came the reply, as if they had played golf many
times. Just a couple of old pals. Carl heard the voice and thought of the
countless times he'd seen The Senator on the news. "How is Amos?" he
asked.

The contact, the name that linked both men to this call. "Great.
Had lunch with him last month." A lie. Amos was the managing partner
of the corporate law firm Carl had been using for a decade. Not The
Senator's firm, not even close. But Amos was a substantial person, cer-
tainly big enough to be mentioned by The Senator.

"Give him my regards."

"Certainly." Now get on with it, Carl was thinking.

"Listen, I know it's been a long day, so I won't keep you." A pause.
"There is a man in Boca Raton that you should see, name is Rinehart,
Barry Rinehart. He's a consultant of sorts, though you'll never find him
in the phone book. His firm specializes in elections."

A long pause, and Carl had to say something. So he said, "Okay.
I'm listening."

"He is extremely competent, smart, discreet, successful, and expen-
sive. And if anyone can fix this verdict, Mr. Rinehart is your man."

"Fix this verdict," Carl repeated.

The Senator continued: "If you're interested, I'll give him a call,
open the door."

"Well, yes, I'd certainly be interested."

Fix this verdict. It was music.

"Good, I'll be in touch."

"Thank you."

And with that the conversation was over. So typical of The Senator. A favor here, the payback there. All contacts running to and fro, everybody's back getting properly scratched. The call was free, but one day The Senator would be paid.

Carl stirred his scotch with a finger and looked at the rest of his calls. Nothing but misery.

Fix this verdict, he kept repeating.

In the center of his immaculate desk was a memo marked "CONFIDENTIAL." Weren't all of his memos confidential? On the cover sheet someone had scrawled with a black marker the name "PAYTON." Carl picked it up, arranged both feet on his desk, and flipped through it. There were photos, the first from yesterday's trial when Mr. and Mrs. Payton were leaving the courthouse, walking hand in hand in glorious triumph. There was an earlier one of Mary Grace from a bar publication, with a quick bio. Born in Bowmore, college at Millsaps, law school at Ole Miss, two years in a federal clerkship, two in a public defender's office, past president of the county bar association, certified trial lawyer, school board, member of the state Democratic Party and a few tree-hugger groups.

From the same publication, a photo and bio of James Wesley Payton. Born in Monroe, Louisiana, lettered in football at Southern Miss, law school at Tulane, three years as an assistant prosecutor, member of all the available trial lawyer groups, Rotary Club, Civitan, and so on.

Two backwater ambulance chasers who had just orchestrated Carl's exit from the Forbes 400 list of the richest Americans.

Two children, an illegal nanny, public schools, Episcopal church, near foreclosures on both home and office, near repossessions of two automobiles, a law practice (no other partners, just support staff) that was now ten years old and was once fairly profitable (by small-town standards) but now sought refuge in an abandoned dime store where the rent was at least three months in arrears. And then the good part—heavy debts, at

least $400,000 to Second State Bank on a line of credit that is basically unsecured. No payments, not even on the interest, in five months. Second State Bank was a local outfit with ten offices in south Mississippi. Four hundred thousand dollars borrowed for the sole purpose of financing the lawsuit against Krane Chemical.

"Four hundred thousand dollars," Carl mumbled. So far he'd paid almost $14 million to defend the damned thing.

Bank accounts are empty. Credit cards no longer in use. Other clients (non-Bowmore variety) rumored to be frustrated by lack of attention.

No other substantial verdicts to speak of. Nothing close to $1 million.

Summary: These people are heavily in debt and hanging on by their fingernails. A little push, and they're over the edge. Strategy: Drag out the appeals, delay, delay. Crank up pressure from the bank. Possible buyout of Second State, then call the loan. Bankruptcy would be the only course. Huge distraction as appeals rage on. Also, Paytons would be unable to pursue their other thirty (or so) cases versus Krane and would probably decline more clients.

Bottom line: this little law firm can be destroyed.

The memo was unsigned, which was no surprise, but Carl knew it was written by one of two hatchet men working in Ratzlaff's office. He'd find out which one and give the boy a raise. Good work.

The great Carl Trudeau had dismantled large conglomerates, taken over hostile boards of directors, fired celebrity CEOs, upset entire industries, fleeced bankers, manipulated stock prices, and destroyed the careers of dozens of his enemies.

He could certainly ruin a garden-variety mom-and-pop law firm in Hattiesburg, Mississippi.

———

Toliver delivered him home shortly after 9:00 p.m., a time selected by Carl because Sadler would be in bed and he would not be forced to dote on a child he had no interest in. The other child could not be avoided. Brianna was waiting, dutifully, for him. They would dine by the fire.

When he walked through the door, he came face-to-face with

Imelda, already permanently ensconced in the foyer and looking more abused than the night before. He couldn't help but gawk at the sculpture. Did the pile of brass rods really resemble a young girl? Where was the torso? Where were the limbs? Where was her head? Had he really paid that much money for such an abstract mess?

And how long might she haunt him in his own penthouse?

As his valet took his coat and briefcase, Carl stared sadly at his masterpiece, then heard the dreaded words "Hello, darling." Brianna swept into the room, a flowing red gown trailing after her. They pecked cheeks.

"Isn't it stunning?" she gushed, flopping an arm at *Imelda*.

"Stunning is the word," he said.

He looked at Brianna, then he looked at *Imelda*, and he wanted to choke both of them. But the moment passed. He could never admit defeat.

"Dinner is ready, darling," she cooed.

"I'm not hungry. Let's have a drink."

"But Claudelle has fixed your favorite—grilled sole."

"No appetite, dear," he said, yanking off his tie and tossing it to his valet.

"Today was awful, I know," she said. "A scotch?"

"Yes."

"Will you tell me about it?" she asked.

"I'd love to."

Brianna's private money manager, a woman unknown to Carl, had called throughout the day with updates on the collapse. Brianna knew the numbers, and she had heard the reports that her husband was down a billion or so.

She dismissed the kitchen staff, then changed into a much more revealing nightgown. They met by the fire and chatted until he fell asleep.

CHAPTER 7

At 10:00 a.m. Friday, two days post-verdict, the Payton firm met in The Pit, a large open space with unpainted Sheetrock walls lined with home-made bookshelves and cluttered with a heavy collage of aerial photos, medical summaries, juror profiles, expert-witness reports, and a hundred other trial documents and exhibits. In the center of the room was a table of sorts—four large pieces of inch-thick plywood mounted on sawhorses and surrounded with a sad collection of metal and wooden chairs, almost all of which were missing a piece or two. The table had obviously been the center of the storm for the past four months, with piles of papers and stacks of law books. Sherman, a paralegal, had spent most of the previous day hauling out coffee cups, pizza boxes, Chinese food containers, and empty water bottles. He'd also swept the concrete floors, though no one could tell.

Their previous office, a three-story building on Main Street, had been beautifully decorated, well-appointed, and spruced up each night by a cleaning service. Appearance and neatness were important back then.

Now they were just trying to survive.

In spite of the dismal surroundings, the mood was light, and for ob-

vious reasons. The marathon was over. The incredible verdict was still hard to believe. United by sweat and hardship, the tight-knit little firm had taken on the beast and won a big one for the good guys.

Mary Grace called the meeting to order. The phones were put on hold because Tabby, the receptionist, was very much a part of the firm and was expected to participate in the discussion. Thankfully, the phones were beginning to ring again.

Sherman and Rusty, the other paralegal, wore jeans, sweatshirts, no socks. Working in what was once a dime store, who could care about a dress code? Tabby and Vicky, the other receptionist, had abandoned nice clothes when both snagged dresses on the hand-me-down furniture. Only Olivia, the matronly bookkeeper, turned herself out each day in proper office attire.

They sat around the plywood table, sipping the same bad coffee they were now addicted to, and listened with smiles as Mary Grace did her recap. "There will be the usual post-trial motions," she was saying. "Judge Harrison has scheduled a hearing in thirty days, but we expect no surprises."

"Here's to Judge Harrison," Sherman said, and they toasted him with their coffee.

It had become a very democratic firm. Everyone present felt like an equal. Anyone could speak whenever he or she felt like it. Only first names were used. Poverty is a great equalizer.

Mary Grace continued: "For the next few months, Sherman and I will handle the *Baker* case as it moves forward, and we will keep the other Bowmore cases current. Wes and Rusty will take everything else and start generating some cash."

Applause.

"Here's to cash," Sherman said, another toast. He possessed a law degree from a night school but had not been able to pass the bar exam. He was now in his mid-forties, a career paralegal who knew more law than most lawyers. Rusty was twenty years younger and contemplating med school.

"While we're on the subject," Mary Grace continued, "Olivia has

given me the latest red-ink summary. Always a pleasure." She picked up a sheet of paper and looked at the numbers. "We are now officially three months behind in rent, for a total of $4,500."

"Oh, please evict us," Rusty said.

"But the landlord is still our client and he's not worried. All other bills are at least two months past due, except, of course, the phones and electricity. Salaries have not been paid in four weeks—"

"Five," Sherman said.

"Are you sure?" she asked.

"As of today. Today is payday, or at least it used to be."

"Sorry, five weeks past due. We should have some cash in a week if we can settle the *Raney* case. We'll try to catch up."

"We're surviving," Tabby said. She was the only single person in the firm. All others had spouses with jobs. Though budgets were painfully tight, they were determined to survive.

"How about the Payton family?" Vicky asked.

"We're fine," Wes said. "I know you're concerned, thank you, but we're getting by just like you. I've said this a hundred times, but I'll say it again. Mary Grace and I will pay you as soon as we possibly can. Things are about to improve."

"We're more concerned about you," Mary Grace added.

No one was leaving. No one was threatening.

A deal had been struck long ago, though it was not in writing. If and when the Bowmore cases paid off, the money would be shared by the entire firm. Maybe not equally, but everyone present knew they would be rewarded.

"How about the bank?" Rusty asked. There were no secrets now. They knew Huffy had stopped by the day before, and they knew how much Second State Bank was owed.

"I stiff-armed the bank," Wes said. "If they push a little more, then we'll file Chapter 11 and screw 'em."

"I vote to screw the bank," Sherman said.

It seemed to be unanimous around the room that the bank should get screwed, though everyone knew the truth. The lawsuit would not

have been possible without Huffy's lobbying on their behalf and convincing Mr. Prickhead to raise the line of credit. They also knew that the Paytons would not rest until the bank was paid.

"We should clear twelve thousand from the *Raney* case," Mary Grace said. "And another ten thousand from the dog bite."

"Maybe fifteen," Wes said.

"Then what? Where is the next settlement?" Mary Grace threw this on the table for all to consider.

"Geeter," Sherman said. It was more of a suggestion.

Wes looked at Mary Grace. Both gave blank looks to Sherman. "Who's Geeter?"

"Geeter happens to be a client. Slip and fall at the Kroger store. Came in about eight months ago." There were some odd glances around the table. It was obvious that the two lawyers had forgotten one of their clients.

"I don't recall that one," Wes admitted.

"What's the potential?" Mary Grace asked.

"Not much. Shaky liability. Maybe twenty thousand. I'll review the file with you on Monday."

"Good idea," Mary Grace said and quickly moved on to something else. "I know the phones are ringing, and we are definitely broke, but we are not about to start taking a bunch of junk. No real estate or bankruptcies. No criminal cases unless they can pay the freight. No contested divorces—we'll do the quickies for a thousand bucks, but everything must be agreed on. This is a personal injury firm, and if we get loaded down with the small stuff, we won't have time for the good cases. Any questions?"

"There's a lot of weird stuff coming in by phone," Tabby said. "And from all over the country."

"Just stick to the basics," Wes said. "We can't handle cases in Florida or Seattle. We need quick settlements here at home, at least for the next twelve months."

"How long will the appeals take?" Vicky asked.

"Eighteen to twenty-four months," Mary Grace answered. "And

there's not much we can do to push things along. It's a process, and that's why it's important to hunker down now and generate some fees elsewhere."

"Which brings up another point," Wes said. "The verdict changes the landscape dramatically. First, expectations are through the roof right now, and our other Bowmore clients will soon be pestering us. They want their day in court, their big verdict. We must be patient, but we can't let these people drive us crazy. Second, the vultures are descending on Bowmore. Lawyers will be chasing one another looking for clients. It will be a free-for-all. Any contact from another attorney is to be reported immediately. Third, the verdict places even greater pressure on Krane. Their dirty tricks will get even dirtier. They have people watching us. Trust no one. Speak to no one. Nothing leaves this office. All papers are shredded. As soon as we can afford it, we'll hire nighttime security. Bottom line—watch everyone and watch your backs."

"This is fun," Vicky said. "Like a movie."

"Any questions?"

"Yes," Rusty said. "Can Sherman and I start chasing ambulances again? It's been four months, you know, since the beginning of the trial. I really miss the excitement."

"I haven't seen the inside of an ER in weeks," Sherman added. "And I miss the sounds of the sirens."

It wasn't clear if they were joking or not, but the moment was humorous and good for a laugh. Mary Grace finally said, "I really don't care what you do; I just don't want to know everything."

"Meeting adjourned," Wes said. "And it's Friday. Everyone has to leave at noon. We're locking the doors. See you Monday."

They picked up Mack and Liza from school, and after fast food for lunch they headed south through the countryside for an hour, until they saw the first sign for Lake Garland. The roads narrowed before finally turning to gravel. The cabin was at the dead end of a dirt trail, perched above the

water on stilts and wedged into a tight spot where the woods met the
shoreline. A short pier ran from the porch into the water, and beyond it
the vast lake seemed to stretch for miles. There was no other sign of hu-
man activity, either on the lake or anywhere around it.

The cabin was owned by a lawyer friend in Hattiesburg, a man Wes
had once worked for and who had declined to get involved in the Bow-
more mess. That decision had seemed a wise one, until about forty-eight
hours ago. Now there was considerable doubt.

The original idea had been to drive a few more hours to Destin and
have a long weekend on the beach. But they simply couldn't afford it.

They unloaded the car as they roamed through the spacious cabin,
an A-frame with a huge loft, which Mack surveyed and declared perfect
for another night of "camping out."

"We'll see," Wes said. There were three small bedrooms on the
main level, and he planned to find a comfortable bed. Serious sleep was
the goal for the weekend. Sleep and time with the kids.

As promised, the fishing gear was in a storage room under the
porch. The boat was winched at the end of the pier, and the children
watched with anticipation as Wes lowered it into the water. Mary Grace
fiddled with the life jackets and made sure both kids were properly se-
cured. An hour after they arrived, she was tucked away comfortably un-
der a quilt in a lounge chair on the porch, book in hand, watching the
rest of her family inch across the blue horizon of Lake Garland, three
small silhouettes in search of bream and crappie.

It was mid-November, and red and yellow leaves were falling, twist-
ing in the breeze, and covering the cabin, the pier, and the water around
it. There were no sounds. The small boat motor was too far away. The
wind was too soft. The birds and wildlife were elsewhere for the moment.
Perfect stillness, a rare event in any life but one that she especially trea-
sured now. She closed the book, closed her eyes, and tried to think of
something unrelated to the past few months.

Where would they be in five years? She concentrated on the future
because the past was thoroughly consumed by the *Baker* case. They would

certainly be in a house, though never again would they hock their future with a fat mortgage on a showy little castle in the suburbs. She wanted a home, nothing more. She no longer cared about imported cars and an expensive office and all the other toys that once seemed so important. She wanted to be a mother to her children, and she wanted a home to raise them in.

Family and assets aside, she wanted more lawyers. Their firm would be larger and full of smart and talented lawyers who did nothing but pursue the creators of toxic dumps and bad drugs and defective products. One day Payton & Payton would be known not for the cases it won but for the crooks it hauled into court for judgment.

She was forty-one years old, and she was tired. But the fatigue would pass. The old dreams of full-time motherhood and a cushy retirement were forever forgotten. Krane Chemical had converted her into a radical and a crusader. After the last four months, she would never be the same.

Enough. Her eyes were wide open.

Every thought took her back to the case, to Jeannette Baker, the trial, Krane Chemical. She would not spend this quiet and lovely weekend dwelling on such matters. She opened her book and started to read.

———

For dinner, they roasted hot dogs and marshmallows over a stone pit near the water, then sat on the pier in the darkness and watched the stars. The air was clear and cool, and they huddled together under a quilt. A distant light flickered on the horizon, and after some discussion it was agreed upon that it was just a boat.

"Dad, tell us a story," Mack said. He was squeezed between his sister and his mother.

"What kind of story?"

"A ghost story. A scary one."

His first thought was about the dogs of Bowmore. For years a pack of stray dogs had roamed the outskirts of the town. Often, in the dead of night, they shrieked and yelped and made more noise than a pack of coy-

otes. Legend held that the dogs were rabid and had been driven crazy be-
cause they drank the water.

But he'd had enough of Bowmore. He remembered one about a
ghost who walked on water in the night, looking for his beloved wife,
who'd drowned. He began to tell it, and the children squeezed closer to
their parents.

The last para/scene is a
sort of 'collective POV' ending
in Wes's head.

7.12.09
Can everything that
culminated in seeing Zodiac
really come to nothing?
Is it possible?

CHAPTER 8

A uniformed guard opened the gates to the mansion, then nodded smartly to the driver as the long black Mercedes rushed by, in a hurry as always. Mr. Carl Trudeau had the rear seat, alone, already lost in the morning's papers. It was 7:30 a.m., too early for golf or tennis and too early for Saturday morning traffic in Palm Beach. Within minutes, the car was on Interstate 95, racing south.

Carl ignored the market reports. Thank God the week was finally over. Krane closed at $19.50 the day before and showed no signs of finding a permanent floor. Though he would be forever known as one of the very few men who'd lost a billion dollars in a day, he was already plotting his next legend. Give him a year and he'd have his billion back. In two years, he'd double all of it.

Forty minutes later he was in Boca Raton, crossing the waterway, headed for the clusters of high-rise condos and hotels packed along the beach. The office building was a shiny glass cylinder ten floors tall with a gate and a guard and not one word posted on a sign of any type. The Mercedes was waved through and stopped under a portico. A stern-faced

young man in a black suit opened the rear door and said, "Good morning, Mr. Trudeau."

"Good morning," Carl said, climbing out.

"This way, sir."

———

According to Carl's hasty research, the firm of Troy-Hogan worked very hard at not being seen. It had no Web site, brochure, advertisements, listed phone number, or anything else that might attract clients. It was not a law firm, because it was not registered with the State of Florida, or any other state for that matter. It had no registered lobbyists. It was a corporation, not a limited partnership or some other variety of association. It was unclear where the name originated because there was no record of anyone named Troy or Hogan. The firm was known to provide marketing and consulting services, but there was no clue as to the nature of this business. It was domiciled in Bermuda and had been registered in Florida for eight years. Its domestic agent was a law firm in Miami. It was privately owned, and no one knew who owned it.

The less Carl learned about the firm, the more he admired it.

The principal was one Barry Rinehart, and here the trail grew somewhat warmer. According to friends and contacts in Washington, Rinehart had passed through D.C. twenty years earlier without leaving a fingerprint. He had worked for a congressman, the Pentagon, and a couple of midsized lobbying outfits—the typical résumé of a million others. He left town for no apparent reason in 1990 and surfaced in Minnesota, where he ran the successful campaign of a political unknown who got elected to Congress. Then he went to Oregon, where he worked his magic in a Senate race. As his reputation began to rise, he abruptly quit doing campaigns and disappeared altogether. End of trail.

Rinehart was forty-eight years old, married and divorced twice, no children, no criminal record, no professional associations, no civic clubs. He had a degree in political science from the University of Maryland and a law degree from the University of Nevada.

No one seemed to know what he was doing now, but he was certainly doing it well. His suite on the top floor of the cylinder was beautifully decorated with minimalist contemporary art and furniture. Carl, who spared no expense with his own office, was impressed.

Barry was waiting at the door of his office. The two shook hands and exchanged the usual pleasantries as they took in the details of the other's suit, shirt, tie, shoes. Nothing off-the-rack. No detail left undone, even though it was a Saturday morning in south Florida. Impressions were crucial, especially to Barry, who was thrilled at the prospect of snaring a new and substantial client.

Carl had half-expected a slick car salesman with a bad suit, but he was pleasantly surprised. Mr. Rinehart was dignified, soft-spoken, well-groomed, and very much at ease in the presence of such a powerful man. He was certainly not an equal, but he seemed to be comfortable with this.

A secretary asked about coffee as they stepped inside and met the ocean. From the tenth floor, beachside, the Atlantic stretched forever. Carl, who gazed at the Hudson River several times a day, was envious. "Beautiful," he said, staring from the row of ten-foot glass windows.

"Not a bad place to work," Barry said.

They settled into beige leather chairs as the coffee arrived. The secretary closed the door behind her, giving the place a nice secure feel.

"I appreciate you meeting me on a Saturday morning and with such short notice," Carl said.

"The pleasure is mine," Barry said. "It's been a rough week."

"I've had better. I take it you've spoken personally with Senator Grott."

"Oh yes. We chat occasionally."

"He was very vague about your firm and what you do."

Barry laughed and crossed his legs. "We do campaigns. Have a look." He picked up a remote and pushed the button, and a large white screen dropped from the ceiling and covered most of a wall, then the entire nation appeared. Most of the states were in green, the rest were in a soft yellow. "Thirty-one states elect their appellate and supreme court

judges. They are in green. The yellow ones have the good sense to appoint their courts. We make our living in the green ones."

"Judicial elections."

"Yes. That's all we do, and we do it very quietly. When our clients need help, we target a supreme court justice who is not particularly friendly, and we take him, or her, out of the picture."

"Just like that."

"Just like that."

"Who are your clients?"

"I can't give you the names, but they're all on your side of the street. Big companies in energy, insurance, pharmaceuticals, chemicals, timber, all types of manufacturers, plus doctors, hospitals, nursing homes, banks. We raise tons of money and hire the people on the ground to run aggressive campaigns."

"Have you worked in Mississippi?"

"Not yet." Barry punched another button and America was back. The green states slowly turned black. "The darker states are the ones we've worked in. As you can see, they're coast-to-coast. We maintain a presence in all thirty-nine."

Carl took some coffee, and nodded as if he wanted Barry to keep talking.

"We employ about fifty people here, the entire building is ours, and we accumulate enormous amounts of data. Information is power, and we know everything. We review every appellate decision in the green states. We know every appellate judge, their backgrounds, families, prior careers, divorces, bankruptcies, all the dirt. We review every decision and can predict the outcome of almost every case on appeal. We track every legislature and keep up with bills that might affect civil justice. We also monitor important civil trials."

"How about the one in Hattiesburg?"

"Oh yes. We were not at all surprised at the verdict."

"Then why were my lawyers surprised?"

"Your lawyers were good but not great. Plus, the plaintiff has a bet-

ter case. I've studied a lot of toxic dumps, and Bowmore is one of the worst."

"So we'll lose again?"

"That's my prediction. The flood is coming."

Carl glanced at the ocean and drank some more coffee. "What happens on appeal?"

"Depends on who's on the Mississippi Supreme Court. Right now, there's a very good chance the verdict will be affirmed in a 5-to-4 decision. The state has been notoriously sympathetic to plaintiffs for the past two decades and, as you probably know, has a well-earned reputation as a hotbed of litigation. Asbestos, tobacco, fen-phen, all sorts of crazy class actions. Tort lawyers love the place."

"So I'll lose by one vote?"

"More or less. The court is not entirely predictable, but, yes, it's usually a 5-to-4 split."

"So all we need is a friendly judge?"

"Yes."

Carl placed his cup on a table and shot to his feet. He slid out of his jacket, hung it over a chair, then walked to the windows and stared at the ocean. A cargo ship inched along a mile out, and he watched it for several minutes. Barry slowly sipped his coffee.

"Do you have a judge in mind?" Carl finally asked.

Barry hit the remote. The screen went blank, then disappeared into the ceiling. He stretched as if he had a sore back, then said, "Perhaps we should talk business first."

Carl nodded and took his chair. "Let's hear it."

"Our proposal goes something like this. You hire our firm, the money gets wired into the proper accounts, then I will give you a plan for restructuring the Supreme Court of Mississippi."

"How much?"

"There are two fees. First, a million as a retainer. This is all properly reported. You officially become our client, and we provide consulting services in the area of government relations, a wonderfully vague term that covers just about anything. The second fee is seven million

bucks, and we take it offshore. Some of this will be used to fund the campaign, but most will be preserved. Only the first fee goes on the books."

Carl was nodding, understanding. "For eight million, I can buy myself a supreme court justice."

"That's the plan."

"And this judge earns how much a year?"

"Hundred and ten thousand."

"A hundred and ten thousand dollars," Carl repeated.

"It's all relative. Your mayor in New York City spent seventy-five million to get elected to a job that pays a tiny fraction of that. It's politics."

"Politics," Carl said as if he wanted to spit. He sighed heavily and slumped an inch or two in his chair. "I guess it's cheaper than a verdict."

"Much cheaper, and there will be more verdicts. Eight million is a bargain."

"You make it sound so easy."

"It's not. These are bruising campaigns, but we know how to win them."

"I want to know how the money is spent. I want the basic plan."

Barry walked over and replenished his coffee from a silver thermos. Then he walked to his magnificent windows and gazed out at the Atlantic. Carl glanced at his watch. He had a 12:30 tee time at the Palm Beach Country Club; not that it mattered that much. He was a social golfer who played because he was expected to play.

Rinehart drained his cup and returned to his chair. "The truth, Mr. Trudeau, is that you really don't want to know how the money is spent. You want to win. You want a friendly face on the supreme court so that when *Baker versus Krane Chemical* is decided in eighteen months, you'll be certain of the outcome. That's what you want. That's what we deliver."

"For eight million bucks I would certainly hope so."

You blew eighteen on a bad piece of sculpture three nights ago, Barry thought but wouldn't dare say. You have three jets that cost forty million each. Your "renovation" in the Hamptons will set you back at least ten million. And these are just a few of your toys. We're talking busi-

ness here, not toys. Barry's file on Carl was much thicker than Carl's file on Barry. But then, in fairness, Mr. Rinehart worked hard to avoid attention, while Mr. Trudeau worked even harder to attract it.

It was time to close the deal, so Barry quietly pressed on. "Mississippi has its judicial elections a year from now, next November. We have plenty of time, but none to waste. Your timing is convenient and lucky. As we slug it out through the election next year, the case plods along through the appellate process. Our new man will take office a year from January, and about four months later will come face-to-face with *Baker versus Krane Chemical.*"

For the first time, Carl saw a flash of the car salesman, and it didn't bother him at all. Politics was a dirty business where the winners were not always the cleanest guys in town. One had to be a bit of a thug to survive.

"My name cannot be at risk," he said sternly.

Barry knew he had just collected another handsome fee. "It's impossible," he said with a fake smile. "We have fire walls everywhere. If one of our operatives gets out of line, does something wrong, we make sure another guy takes the fall. Troy-Hogan has never been even remotely tarnished. And if they can't catch us, they damned sure can't find you."

"No paperwork."

"Only for the initial fee. We are, after all, a legitimate consulting and government relations firm. We will have an official relationship with you: consulting, marketing, communications—all those wonderfully nebulous words that hide everything else. But the offshore arrangement is completely confidential."

Carl thought for a long time, then smiled and said, "I like it. I like it a lot."

equation descri "eqnadictory contrast"

Grisham is a master of contradictory descriptive comment:

ie. Reinhardt worked hard to avoid attention while Carl worked harder to attract it" "contra descriptive?

CHAPTER 9

"We have plenty of time but none to waste"

contra (Eqnadictory descriptive)

The law office of F. Clyde Hardin & Associates had no associates. It was just Clyde and Miriam, his feeble secretary who outranked him because she had been there for over forty years, far longer than Clyde. She had typed deeds and wills for his father, who came home from the Second War without a leg and was famous for removing his wooden one in front of juries to distract them. The old man was gone now, long gone, and he had bequeathed his old office and old furniture and old secretary to his only child, Clyde, who was fifty-four and very old himself.

The Hardin law office had been a fixture on Main Street in Bowmore for over sixty years. It had survived wars, depressions, recessions, sit-ins, boycotts, and desegregation, but Clyde wasn't so sure it could survive Krane Chemical. The town was drying up around him. The nickname Cancer County was simply too much to overcome. From his ringside seat, he had watched merchants and cafés and country lawyers and country doctors throw in the towel and abandon the town.

Clyde never wanted to be a lawyer, but his father gave him no choice. And though he survived on deeds and wills and divorces, and

though he managed to appear reasonably happy and colorful with his seersucker suits, paisley bow ties, and straw hats, he silently loathed the law and the small-town practice of it. He despised the daily grind of dealing with people too poor to pay him, of hassling with other deadbeat lawyers trying to steal said clients, of bickering with judges and clerks and just about everybody else who crossed his path. There were only six lawyers left in Bowmore, and Clyde was the youngest. He dreamed of retiring to a lake or a beach, anywhere, but those dreams would never come true. *E-D* .

Clyde had sugared coffee and one fried egg at 8:30 every morning at Babe's, seven doors to the right of his office, and a grilled cheese and iced tea every noon at Bob's Burgers, seven doors to the left. At five every afternoon, as soon as Miriam tidied up her desk and said goodbye, Clyde pulled out the office bottle and had a vodka on the rocks. He normally did this alone, in the solitude of the day, his finest hour. He cherished the stillness of his own little happy hour. Often the only sounds were the swishing of a ceiling fan and the rattling of his ice cubes.

He'd had two sips, gulps really, and the booze was beginning to glow somewhere in his brain when there was a rather aggressive knock on his door. No one was expected. Downtown was deserted by five every afternoon, but there was the occasional client looking for a lawyer. Clyde was too broke to ignore the traffic. He placed his tumbler on a bookshelf and walked to the front. A well-dressed gentleman was waiting. He introduced himself as Sterling Bitch or something of that order. Clyde looked at his business card. Bintz. Sterling Bintz. Attorney-at-Law. From Philadelphia, PA.

Mr. Bintz was about forty years old, short and thin, intense, with the smugness that Yankees can't help but exude when they venture into decaying towns of the Deep South.

How could anyone live like this? their smirks seemed to ask.

Clyde disliked him immediately, but he also wanted to return to his vodka, so he offered Sterling a cocktail. Sure, why not?

They settled around Clyde's desk and began to drink. After a few minutes of boring chitchat, Clyde said, "Why don't you get to the point?"

"Certainly." The accent was sharp and crisp and oh so grating. "My firm specializes in class actions for mass torts. That's all we do."

"And you're suddenly interested in our little town. What a surprise."

"Yes, we are interested. Our research tells us that there may be over a thousand potential cases around here, and we'd like to sign up as many as possible. But we need local counsel."

"You're a bit late, bud. The ambulance chasers have been combing this place for the past five years."

"Yes, I understand that most of the death cases have been secured, but there are many other types. We'd like to find those victims with liver and kidney problems, stomach lesions, colon trouble, skin diseases, as many as a dozen other afflictions, all caused, of course, by Krane Chemical. We screen them with our doctors, and when we have a few dozen, we hit Krane with a class action. This is our specialty. We do it all the time. The settlement could be huge."

Clyde was listening but pretending to be bored. "Go on," he said.

"Krane's been kicked in the crotch. They cannot continue to litigate, so they'll eventually be forced to settle. If we have the first class action, we're in the driver's seat."

"We?"

"Yes. My firm would like to associate with your firm."

"You're looking at my firm."

"We'll do all the work. We need your name as local counsel, and your contacts and presence here in Bowmore."

"How much?" Clyde was known to be rather blunt. No sense mincing words with this little shyster from up north.

"Five hundred bucks per client, then 5 percent of the fees when we settle. Again, we do all the work."

Clyde rattled his ice cubes and tried to do the math.

Sterling pressed on. "The building next door is vacant. I—"

"Oh yes, there are many vacant buildings here in Bowmore."

"Who owns the one next door?"

"I do. It's part of this building. My grandfather bought it a thousand years ago. And I got one across the street, too. Empty."

"The office next door is the perfect place for a screening clinic. We fix it up, give it a medical ambience, bring in our doctors, then advertise like hell for anyone who thinks he or she might be sick. They'll flock in. We sign them up, get the numbers, then file a massive action in federal court."

It had the distinct ring of something fraudulent, but Clyde had heard enough about mass torts to know that Sterling here knew what he was talking about. Five hundred clients, at $500 a pop, plus 5 percent when they won the lottery. He reached for the office bottle and refilled both glasses.

"Intriguing," Clyde said.

"It could be very profitable."

"But I don't work in federal court."

Sterling sipped the near-lethal serving and offered a smile. He knew perfectly well the limitations of this small-town blowhard. Clyde would have trouble defending a shoplifting case in city court. "Like I said. We do all the work. We're hardball litigators."

"Nothing unethical or illegal," Clyde said.

"Of course not. We've been winning class action in mass tort cases for twenty years. Check us out."

"I'll do that."

"And do it quick. This verdict is attracting attention. From now on, it's a race to find the clients and file the first class action."

———

After he left, Clyde had a third vodka, his limit, and near the end of it found the courage to tell all the locals to go to hell. Oh, how they would love to criticize him! Advertising for victims/clients in the county's weekly paper, turning his office into a cheap clinic for assembly-line diagnoses, crawling into bed with some slimy lawyers from up north, profiting from the misery of his people. The list would be long and the gossip would consume Bowmore, and the more he drank, the more determined he became to throw caution to the wind and, for once, try to make some money.

For a character with such a blustery personality, Clyde was secretly afraid of the courtroom. He had faced a few juries years earlier and had been so stricken with fear that he could hardly talk. He had settled into a safe and comfortable office practice that paid the bills but kept him away from the frightening battles where the real money was made and lost.

For once, why not take a chance?

And wouldn't he be helping his people? Every dime taken from Krane Chemical and deposited somewhere in Bowmore was a victory. He poured a fourth drink, swore it was the last, and decided that, yes, damn it, he would hold hands with Sterling and his gang of class action thieves and strike a mighty blow for justice.

Two days later, a subcontractor Clyde had represented in at least three divorces arrived early with a crew of carpenters, painters, and gofers, all desperate for work, and began a quick renovation of the office next door.

Twice a month Clyde played poker with the owner of the *Bowmore News*, the county's only paper. Like the town itself, the weekly was declining and trying to hang on. In its next edition, the front page was dominated by news about the verdict over in Hattiesburg, but there was also a generous story about Lawyer Hardin's association with a major national law firm from Philadelphia. Inside was a full-page ad that practically begged every citizen of Cary County to drop by the new "diagnostic facility" on Main Street for screening that was absolutely free.

Clyde enjoyed the crowd and the attention and was already counting his money.

It was 4:00 a.m., cold and dark with a threat of rain, when Buck Burleson parked his truck in the small employees' lot at the Hattiesburg pumping station. He collected his thermos of coffee, a cold biscuit with ham, and a 9-millimeter automatic pistol and carried it all to an eighteen-wheel rig with unmarked doors and a ten-thousand-gallon tanker as its payload. He started the engine and checked the gauges, tires, and fuel.

The night supervisor heard the diesel and walked out of the second-floor monitoring room. "Hello, Buck," he called down.

"Mornin', Jake," Buck said with a nod. "She loaded?"

"Ready to go."

That part of the conversation had not changed in five years. There was usually an exchange about the weather, then a farewell. But on this morning, Jake decided to add a wrinkle to their dialogue, one he'd been contemplating for a few days. "Those folks any happier over in Bowmore?"

"Damned if I know. I don't hang around."

And that was it. Buck opened the driver's door, gave his usual "See you later," and closed himself inside. Jake watched the tanker ease along the drive, turn left at the street, and finally disappear, the only vehicle moving at that lonesome hour.

On the highway, Buck carefully poured coffee from the thermos into its plastic screw-on cup. He glanced at his pistol on the passenger's seat. He decided to wait on the biscuit. When he saw the sign announcing Cary County, he glanced at his gun again.

He made the trip three times a day, four days a week. Another driver handled the other three days. They swapped up frequently to cover vacations and holidays. It was not the career Buck had envisioned. For seventeen years he'd been a foreman at Krane Chemical in Bowmore, earning three times what they now paid him to haul water to his old town.

It was ironic that one of the men who'd done so much to pollute Bowmore's water now hauled in fresh supplies of it. But irony was lost on Buck. He was bitter at the company for fleeing and taking his job with it. And he hated Bowmore because Bowmore hated him.

Buck was a liar. This had been proven several times, but never in a more spectacular fashion than during a brutal cross-examination a month earlier. Mary Grace Payton had gently fed him enough rope, then watched him hang himself in front of the jury.

For years, Buck and most of the supervisors at Krane had flatly denied any chemical dumping whatsoever. They were ordered to do so by

their bosses. They denied it in company memos. They denied it when talking to company lawyers. They denied it in affidavits. And they certainly denied it when the plant was investigated by the Environmental Protection Agency and the U.S. Attorney's Office. Then the litigation began. After denying it for so long and so fervently, how could they suddenly flip their stories and tell the truth? Krane, after fiercely promoting the lying for so long, vanished. It escaped one weekend and found a new home in Mexico. No doubt some tortilla-eating jackass down there was doing Buck's job for $5 a day. He swore as he sipped his coffee.

A few of the managers came clean and told the truth. Most clung to their lies. It didn't matter, really, because they all looked like fools at trial, at least those who testified. Some tried to hide. Earl Crouch, perhaps the biggest liar of all, had been relocated to a Krane plant near Galveston. There was a rumor that he had disappeared under mysterious circumstances.

Buck again glanced at the 9-millimeter.

So far, he had received only one threatening phone call. He wasn't sure about the other managers. All had left Bowmore, and they did not keep in touch.

Mary Grace Payton. If he'd had the pistol during his cross-examination, he might have shot her, her husband, and a few of the lawyers for Krane, and he would have saved one bullet for himself. For four devastating hours, she had exposed one lie after another. Some of the lies were safe, he'd been told. Some were hidden away in memos and affidavits that Krane kept buried. But Ms. Payton had all the memos and all the affidavits and much more.

When the ordeal was almost over, when Buck was bleeding and the jury was furious and Judge Harrison was saying something about perjury, Buck almost snapped. He was exhausted, humiliated, half-delirious, and he almost jumped to his feet, looked at the jurors, and said, "You want the truth, I'll give it to you. We dumped so much shit into those ravines it's a wonder the whole town didn't explode. We dumped gallons every day—BCL and cartolyx and aklar, all class-1 carcinogens—hundreds of gallons of toxic stuff directly into the ground. We dumped it from vats

and buckets and barrels and drums. We dumped it at night and in broad daylight. Oh sure, we stored a lot of it in sealed green drums and paid a fortune to a specialty firm to haul it away. Krane complied with the law. They kissed the EPA's ass. You've seen the paperwork, everything nice and proper. Real legal like. While the starched shirts in the front office were filling out forms, we were out back in the pits burying the poison. It was much easier and much cheaper to dump it. And you know what? Those same assholes up front knew exactly what we were doing out back." Here he would point a deadly finger at the Krane executives and their lawyers. "They covered it up! And they're lying to you now. Everybody's lying."

Buck gave this speech out loud as he drove, though not every morning. It was oddly comforting to do so, to think about what he should have said instead of what he did. A piece of his soul and most of his manhood had been left behind in that courtroom. Lashing out in the privacy of his big truck was therapeutic.

Driving to Bowmore, however, was not. He was not from there and had never liked the town. When he lost his job, he had no choice but to leave.

As the highway became Main Street, he turned right and drove for four blocks. The distribution point had been given the nickname the "city tank." It was directly below the old water tower, an unused and decayed relic whose metal panels had been eaten from the inside by the city's water. A large aluminum reservoir now served the town. Buck pulled his tanker onto an elevated platform, killed the engine, stuffed the pistol into his pocket, and got out of the truck. He went about his business of unloading his cargo into the reservoir, a discharge that took thirty minutes.

From the reservoir, the water would go to the town's schools, businesses, and churches, and though it was safe enough to drink in Hattiesburg, it was still greatly feared in Bowmore. The pipes that carried it along were, for the most part, the same pipes that had supplied the old water.

Throughout the day, a constant stream of traffic arrived at the

reservoir. The people pulled out all manner of plastic jugs and metal cans and small drums, filled them, then took them home.

Those who could afford to contracted with private suppliers. Water was a daily challenge in Bowmore.

It was still dark as Buck waited for his tank to empty. He sat in the cab with the heater on, door locked, pistol close by. There were two families in Pine Grove that he thought about each morning as he waited. Tough families, with men who'd served time. Big families with uncles and cousins. Each had lost a kid to leukemia. Each was now suing.

And Buck was a well-known liar.

———————

Eight days before Christmas, the combatants gathered for the last time in Judge Harrison's courtroom. The hearing was to wrap up all loose ends, and especially to argue the post-trial motions.

Jared Kurtin looked fit and tanned after two weeks of golf in Mexico. He greeted Wes warmly and even managed to smile at Mary Grace. She ignored him by talking to Jeannette, who still looked gaunt and worried but at least wasn't crying.

Kurtin's pack of subordinates shuffled papers at hundreds of dollars an hour each, while Frank Sully, the local counsel, watched them smugly. It was all for show. Harrison wasn't about to grant any relief to Krane Chemical, and everybody knew it.

Others were watching. Huffy held his usual spot, curious as always, still worried about the loan and his future. There were several reporters, and even a courtroom artist, the same one who'd covered the trial and sketched faces that no one could recognize. Several plaintiffs' lawyers were there to observe and to monitor the progress of the case. They were dreaming of a massive settlement that would allow them to become rich while avoiding the type of brutal trial the Paytons had just endured.

Judge Harrison called things to order and charged ahead. "So nice to see everyone again," he said drily. "There are a total of fourteen motions that have been filed—twelve by the defense, two by the plaintiff—

and we are going to dispose of all of them before noon." He glared at
Jared Kurtin, as if daring him to utter one superfluous word.

He continued: "I've read all the motions and all the briefs, so please
don't tell me anything that you've already put in writing. Mr. Kurtin, you
may proceed."

The first motion was for a new trial. Kurtin quickly went through
all the reasons his client got screwed, beginning with a couple of jurors
he wanted to bounce, but Harrison refused. Kurtin's team had conjured
up a total of twenty-two errors they deemed grave enough to complain
about, but Harrison felt otherwise. After listening to the lawyers argue for
an hour, the judge ruled against the motion for a new trial.

Jared Kurtin would have been shocked at any other ruling. These
were routine matters now, the battle had been lost, but not the war.

The other motions followed. After a few minutes of uninspired ar-
gument on each one, Judge Harrison said, "Overruled."

When the lawyers finished talking, and as papers were being gath-
ered and briefcases were being closed, Jared Kurtin addressed the court
and said, "Your Honor, it's been a pleasure. I'm sure we'll do the whole
thing over in about three years."

"Court's adjourned," His Honor said rudely, then rapped his gavel
loudly.

———

Two days after Christmas, late on a raw, windy afternoon, Jeannette
Baker walked from her trailer through Pine Grove to the church and to
the cemetery behind it. She kissed the small headstone at Chad's grave,
then sat down and leaned against her husband Pete's. This was the day
he died, five years earlier.

In five years she had learned to dwell on the good memories,
though she couldn't get rid of the bad ones. Pete, a big man, down to 120
pounds, unable to eat, finally unable to force water through the tumors
in his throat and esophagus. Pete, thirty years old and as gaunt and pale
as a dying man twice that age. Pete, the tough guy, crying at the unrelent-
ing pain and begging her for more morphine. Pete, the big talker and

spinner of big tales, unable to emit anything but a pitiful groan. Pete, begging her to help him end it all.

Chad's final days had been relatively calm. Pete's had been horrific. She had seen so much.

Enough of the bad memories. She was there to talk about their life together, their romance, their first apartment in Hattiesburg, the birth of Chad, the plans for more children and a larger house, and all the dreams they once laughed about. Little Chad with a fishing pole and an impressive string of bream from her uncle's pond. Little Chad in his first T-ball uniform with Coach Pete by his side. Christmas and Thanksgiving, a vacation at Disney World when they were both sick and dying.

She stayed until after dark, as she always did.

Denny Ott watched her from the kitchen window of the parsonage. The little cemetery he maintained so carefully was getting more than its share of traffic these days.

CHAPTER 10

The New Year began with another funeral. Miss Inez Perdue died after a lengthy and painful deterioration of her kidneys. She was sixty-one years old, a widow, with two adult children who'd luckily left Bowmore as soon as they were old enough. Uninsured, she died in her small home on the outskirts of town, surrounded by friends and her pastor, Denny Ott. After he left her, Pastor Ott went to the cemetery behind the Pine Grove Church and, with the help of another deacon, began digging her grave, number seventeen.

As soon as the crowd thinned, the body of Miss Inez was loaded into an ambulance and taken directly to the morgue at the Forrest County Medical Center in Hattiesburg. There, a doctor hired by the Payton law firm spent three hours removing tissue and blood and conducting an autopsy. Miss Inez had agreed to this somber procedure when she signed a contract with the Paytons a year earlier. A probe of her organs and an examination of her tissue might produce evidence that one day would be crucial in court.

Eight hours after her death, she was back in Bowmore, in a cheap

casket tucked away for the night in the sanctuary of the Pine Grove Church.

Pastor Ott had long since convinced his flock that once the body is dead and the spirit ascends into heaven, the earthly rituals are silly and of little significance. Funerals, wakes, embalming, flowers, expensive caskets—all were a waste of time and money. Ashes to ashes, dust to dust. God sent us into the world naked and that's how we should leave.

The following day he conducted Miss Inez's service before a full house that included Wes and Mary Grace, as well as a couple of other lawyers looking on with curiosity. During these services, and he was certainly becoming accomplished, Pastor Ott strove to make the occasion uplifting, at times even humorous. Miss Inez was the backup piano player for the church, and though she played with heavy hands and great enthusiasm, she usually missed about half the notes. And since she was practically deaf, she had no idea how bad she sounded. Recollections of her performances lightened the mood.

It would be easy to bash Krane Chemical and its multitude of sins, but Pastor Ott never mentioned the company. She was dead and nothing could change that. Everybody knew who killed her.

After a one-hour service, the pallbearers lifted her wooden casket onto Mr. Earl Mangram's authentic buckboard, the only one left in the county. Mr. Mangram had been an early victim of Krane, burial number three in Denny Ott's career, and he specifically requested that his casket be hauled away from the church and to the cemetery on his grandfather's buckboard with his ancient mare, Blaze, under tack. The short procession had been such a hit that it became an instant tradition at Pine Grove.

When Miss Inez's casket was placed on the carriage, Pastor Ott, standing next to Blaze, pulled her bridle and the old quarter horse began lumbering along, leading the little parade away from the front of the church, down the side road, and back to the cemetery.

———

Holding fast to the southern tradition, her farewell was followed by a potluck get-together in the fellowship hall. For a people so accustomed to dying, the post-burial meal allowed the mourners to lean on one another and share their tears. Pastor Ott made the rounds, chatting with everyone, praying with some.

The great question at these dark moments was, who was next? In many ways, they felt like prisoners. Isolated, suffering, not sure which one would be chosen by the executioner. Rory Walker was a fourteen-year-old who was losing ground fast in his decadelong battle with leukemia. He was probably next. He was at school and missed the Perdue service, but his mother and grandmother were there.

The Paytons huddled in a corner with Jeannette Baker and talked about everything but the case. Over paper plates sparsely covered with a broccoli-and-cheese casserole, they learned that she was now working as a night clerk in a convenience store and had her eye on a nicer trailer. She and Bette were fighting. Bette had a new boyfriend who slept over often and seemed much too interested in Jeannette's legal situation.

Jeannette looked stronger and her mind was sharper. She had gained a few pounds and said she was no longer taking all those antidepressants. People were treating her differently. She explained in a very low voice as she watched the others: "For a while these people were really proud. We struck back. We won. Finally, somebody on the outside had listened to us, all these poor little people in this poor little town. Everybody circled around me and said sweet things. They cooked for me, cleaned the trailer, somebody was always stopping by. Anything for poor little Jeannette. But as the days went by, I started hearing the money talk. How long will the appeal take? When will the money come in? What was I planning to do with it? And on and on. Bette's younger brother stayed over one night, drank too much, and tried to borrow a thousand dollars. We got into a fight and he said everybody in town knew that I'd already received some of the money. I was shocked. People were talking. All kinds of rumors. Twenty million this and twenty million that. How much will I give away? What kind of new car am I going to get? Where will I build my big new house? They watch everything I buy now, which isn't much.

And the men—every tomcat in four counties is calling, wanting to stop by and say hello or take me to the movies. I know for a fact that two of them are not even divorced yet. Bette knows their cousins. I couldn't care less about men."

Wes glanced away.

"Are you talking to Denny?" Mary Grace asked.

"Some. And he's wonderful. He tells me to keep praying for those who gossip about me. I pray for them all right. I really do. But I get the feeling that they're praying harder for me and the money." She looked around suspiciously.

Dessert was banana pudding. It was also an excuse to drift away from Jeannette. The Paytons had several other clients present, and each needed to be given some attention. When Pastor Ott and his wife began clearing the tables, the mourners finally headed for the door.

Wes and Mary Grace met with Denny in his study next to the sanctuary. It was time for the post-burial legal update. Who had fallen ill? What were the new diagnoses? Who in Pine Grove had hired another law firm?

"This Clyde Hardin thing is out of control," Denny said. "They're advertising on the radio and once a week in the paper, full page. They're almost guaranteeing money. People are flocking in."

———

Wes and Mary Grace had walked down Main Street prior to the service for Miss Inez. They wanted to see firsthand the new screening clinic next to F. Clyde's office. On the sidewalk, there were two large coolers filled with bottled water and packed with ice. A teenager with a Bintz & Bintz T-shirt handed them a bottle each. The label read: "Pure Spring Water. Compliments of Bintz & Bintz, Attorneys." There was a toll-free number.

"Where does the water come from?" Wes had asked the kid.

"Not from Bowmore," came the quick retort.

As Mary Grace chatted up the boy, Wes stepped inside, where he joined three other potential clients who were waiting to get themselves screened. None gave any indication of being ill. Wes was greeted by a

comely young lady of no more than eighteen, who handed him a bro-
chure, a form on a clipboard, and a pen and instructed him to fill out
both front and back. The brochure was professionally done and gave the
basics of the allegations against Krane Chemical, a company now
"proven in court" to have contaminated the drinking water of Bowmore
and Cary County. All inquiries were directed to the firm of Bintz & Bintz
in Philadelphia, Pennsylvania. The questions on the form were all back-
ground and medical, except for the last two: (1) Who referred you to this
office? and (2) Do you know anyone else who might be a potential victim
of Krane Chemical? If so, list names and phone numbers. As Wes was
scribbling on the form, the doctor entered the waiting room from some-
where in the rear and called for the next patient. He wore a white physi-
cian's office jacket, complete with a stethoscope around his neck. He was
either Indian or Pakistani and looked no older than thirty.

After a few minutes inside, Wes excused himself and left.

"It's small-time stuff," Wes said to Denny. "They'll sign up a few hundred
cases, most of them frivolous. Then they'll file a class action in federal
court. If they're lucky, it'll be settled years from now for a few thousand
bucks each. The lawyers will skim off some nice fees. But there's a better
chance that Krane will never settle, and if that happens, then all those
new clients get nothing and Clyde Hardin will be forced to go back to
drafting deeds."

"How many from your church have signed up?" Mary Grace asked.

"I don't know. They don't tell me everything."

"We're not worried about it," Wes said. "Frankly, we have enough
of these cases to keep us busy for a long time."

"Did I see a couple of spies at the service today?" Mary Grace
asked.

"Yes. One was a lawyer named Crandell, from Jackson. He's been
hanging around since the trial. He's actually stopped by here to say hello.
Just a hustler."

"I've heard of him," Wes said. "Has he hooked any cases?"

"Not from this church."

They discussed the lawyers for a while, then had their usual conversation about Jeannette and the new pressures she was facing. Ott was spending time with her and was confident she was listening to him.

After an hour they wrapped up their meeting. The Paytons drove back to Hattiesburg, another client in the ground, another injury case now converted into a wrongful-death suit.

————

The preliminary paperwork arrived at the Mississippi Supreme Court in the first week of January. The trial transcript, 16,200 pages, was finalized by the court reporters, and copies were sent to the clerk of the court and to the lawyers. An order was entered giving Krane Chemical, the appellant, ninety days to file its brief. Sixty days after that, the Paytons would file their rebuttal.

In Atlanta, Jared Kurtin passed the file to the firm's appellate unit, the "eggheads," as they were known, brilliant legal scholars who functioned poorly in normal circles and were best kept in the library. Two partners, four associates, and four paralegals were already hard at work on the appeal when the massive transcript arrived and they had their first look at every word that was recorded at trial. They would dissect it and find dozens of reasons for a reversal.

In a lesser section of Hattiesburg, the transcript was plopped on the plywood table in The Pit. Mary Grace and Sherman gawked at it in disbelief, almost afraid to touch it. Mary Grace had once tried a case that went on for ten full days. Its transcript had been twelve hundred pages long, and she read it so many times that the sight of it made her ill. Now this.

If they had an advantage, it was because they had been in the courtroom throughout the entire trial and knew most of what was in the transcript. Indeed, Mary Grace appeared on more pages than any other participant.

But it would be read many times, and procrastination was not an option. The trial and its verdict would be cleverly and savagely attacked

by Krane's lawyers. Jeannette Baker's lawyers had to match them argument for argument, word for word.

In the heady days after the verdict, the plan had been for Mary Grace to concentrate on the Bowmore cases while Wes worked the other files to generate income. The publicity had been priceless; the phones rang incessantly. Every nutcase in the Southeast suddenly needed the Paytons. Lawyers mired in hopeless lawsuits called for help. Family members who'd lost loved ones to cancer saw the verdict as a hopeful sign. And the usual assortment of criminal defendants, divorcing spouses, battered women, bankrupt businesses, slip-and-fall hustlers, and fired employees called or even stopped by in pursuit of these famous lawyers. Very few could pay a decent fee.

Legitimate personal injury cases, however, had proven scarce. The "Big One," the perfect case with clear liability and a defendant with deep pockets, the case upon which retirement dreams often rest, had not yet found its way to the Payton law firm. There were a few more car wrecks and workers' compensation cases, but nothing worth a trial.

Wes worked feverishly to close as many files as possible, and with some success. The rent was now current, at least at the office. All past-due wages had been paid. Huffy and the bank were still on edge but afraid to push harder. No payments had been made, either on principal or on interest.

CHAPTER 11

They settled on a man named Ron Fisk, a lawyer unknown outside of his small town of Brookhaven, Mississippi, an hour south of Jackson, two hours west of Hattiesburg, and fifty miles north of the Louisiana state line. He was selected from a pool of similar résumés, though none of those considered had the slightest hint that their names and backgrounds were being so carefully evaluated. Young white male, one marriage, three children, reasonably handsome, reasonably well dressed, conservative, devout Baptist, Ole Miss law school, no ethical glitches in the law career, not a hint of criminal trouble beyond a speeding ticket, no affiliation with any trial lawyer group, no controversial cases, no experience whatsoever on the bench.

There was no reason anyone outside of Brookhaven would ever have heard the name of Ron Fisk, and that was exactly what made him their ideal candidate. They picked Fisk because he was just old enough to cross their low threshold of legal experience, but still young enough to have ambitions.

He was thirty-nine years old, a junior partner in a five-man firm that specialized in defending lawsuits involving car wrecks, arson, injured

workers, and a myriad of other routine liability claims. The firm's clients were insurance companies who paid by the hour, thus allowing the five partners to earn comfortable but not lucrative salaries. As a junior partner, Fisk made $92,000 the year before. A far cry from Wall Street but not bad money in small-town Mississippi.

A supreme court justice was currently earning $110,000.

Fisk's wife, Doreen, earned $41,000 as the assistant director of a privately owned mental health clinic. Everything was mortgaged—home, both cars, even some furniture. But the Fisks had a perfect credit rating. They vacationed once a year with their children in Florida, where they rented a condo in a high-rise for a thousand bucks a week. There were no trust funds and nothing significant to be expected from their parents' estates.

The Fisks were squeaky-clean. There was nothing to dig up in the heat of a nasty campaign. Absolutely nothing, they were certain of that.

———

Tony Zachary entered the building at five minutes before 2:00 p.m. and stated his business. "I have an appointment with Mr. Fisk," he said politely, and a secretary disappeared. As he waited, he examined the place. Sagging bookshelves laden with dusty tomes. Worn carpet. The musty smell of a fine old building in need of some work. A door opened, and a handsome young man stuck out a hand. "Mr. Zachary, Ron Fisk," he said warmly, as he probably did to all new clients.

"A pleasure."

"This is my office," Fisk said, sweeping his hand at the door. They walked through it, closed it, then settled around a large busy desk. Zachary declined coffee, water, a soda. "I'm fine, thanks," he said.

Fisk had his sleeves rolled up and his tie loosened, as if he'd been performing manual labor. Zachary liked the image immediately. Nice teeth, just a touch of gray above the ears, strong chin. This guy was definitely marketable.

They played Who-do-you-know? for a few minutes, with Zachary claiming to be a longtime resident of Jackson, where he'd spent most of

his career in government relations, whatever that meant. Since he knew that Fisk had no history of political involvement, he had little fear of being exposed. In truth, he'd lived in Jackson less than three years and until very recently had worked as a lobbyist for an association of asphalt contractors. There was a state senator from Brookhaven they both knew, and they chatted about him for a few minutes, anything to pass the time.

When things were comfortable, Zachary said, "Let me apologize, I'm really not a new client. I'm here on some much more important business."

Fisk frowned and nodded. Keep talking, sir.

"Have you ever heard of a group called Judicial Vision?"

"No."

Few people had. In the murky world of lobbying and consulting, Judicial Vision was a newcomer.

Zachary moved on. "I'm the executive director for the state of Mississippi. It's a national group. Our sole purpose is to elect quality people to the appellate courts. By quality, I mean conservative, business oriented, temperate, highly moral, intelligent, and ambitious young judges who can literally, Mr. Fisk, and this is the core of what we believe, change the judicial landscape of this country. And if we can do that, then we can protect the rights of the unborn, restrict the cultural garbage that is consumed by our children, honor the sanctity of marriage, keep homosexuals out of our classrooms, fight off the gun-control advocates, seal our borders, and protect the true American way of life."

Both took a deep breath.

Fisk wasn't sure where he fit into this raging war, but his pulse was definitely up ten beats per minute. "Yes, well, sounds like an interesting group," he said.

"We're committed," Zachary said firmly. "And we're also determined to bring sanity back to our civil litigation system. Runaway verdicts and hungry trial lawyers are robbing us of economic advancement. We're scaring companies away from Mississippi, not attracting them."

"There's no doubt about that," Fisk said, and Zachary wanted to shout for joy.

"You see all the frivolous stuff they file. We work hand in hand with the national tort-reform groups."

"That's good. And why are you in Brookhaven?"

"Are you politically ambitious, Mr. Fisk? Ever thought about tossing your hat in the ring for elective office?"

"Not really."

"Well, we've done our research, and we think you'd be an excellent candidate for the supreme court."

Fisk instinctively laughed at such foolishness, but it was the sort of nervous laugh that leads you to believe that whatever is supposed to be humorous is really not. It's serious. It can be pursued.

"Research?" he said.

"Oh yes. We spend a lot of time looking for candidates who (*a*) we like and (*b*) can win. We study the opponents, the races, the demographics, the politics, everything, really. Our data bank is unmatched, as is our ability to generate serious funds. Care to hear more?"

Fisk kicked back in his reclining rocker, put his feet on his desk and his hands behind his head, and said, "Sure. Tell me why you're here."

"I'm here to recruit you to run against Justice Sheila McCarthy this November in the southern district of Mississippi," he announced confidently. "She is very beatable. We don't like her or her record. We have analyzed every decision she's made in her nine years on the bench, and we think she's a raging liberal who manages to hide her true colors, most of the time. Do you know her?"

Fisk was almost afraid to say yes. "We met once, just in passing. I don't really know her."

Actually, according to their research, Justice McCarthy had participated in three rulings in cases involving Ron Fisk's law firm, and each time she had ruled the other way. Fisk had argued one of the cases, a hotly disputed arson mess involving a warehouse. His client lost on a 5-to-4 vote. It was quite likely that he had little use for Mississippi's only female justice.

"She is very vulnerable," Zachary said.

"What makes you think I can beat her?"

"Because you are a clean-cut conservative who believes in family values. Because of our expertise in running blitzkrieg campaigns. Because we have the money."

"We do?"

"Oh yes. Unlimited. We partner with some powerful people, Mr. Fisk."

"Please call me Ron."

It'll be Ronny Boy before you know it. "Yes, Ron, we coordinate the fund-raising with groups that represent banks, insurance companies, energy companies, big business, I'm talking serious cash here, Ron. Then we expand the umbrella to include the groups that are dearest to us—the conservative Christian folks, who, by the way, can produce huge sums of money in the heat of a campaign. Plus, they turn out the vote."

"You make it sound easy."

"It's never easy, Ron, but we seldom lose. We've honed our skills in a dozen or so races around the country, and we're making a habit of pulling off victories that surprise a lot of people."

"I've never sat on the bench."

"We know that, and that's why we like you. Sitting judges make tough decisions. Tough decisions are sometimes controversial. They leave trails, records that opponents can use against them. The best candidates, we have learned, are bright young guys like yourself who don't carry the baggage of prior decisions."

Inexperience had never sounded so good.

There was a long pause as Fisk tried to gather his thoughts. Zachary stood and walked to the Wall of Respect, this one covered in diplomas, Rotary Club citations, golfing photos, and lots of candid shots of the family. Lovely wife Doreen. Ten-year-old Josh in a baseball uniform. Seven-year-old Zeke with a fish almost as big as himself. Five-year-old Clarissa dressed for soccer. "Beautiful family," Zachary said, as if he knew nothing about them.

"Thanks," Fisk said, truly beaming.

"Gorgeous kids."

"Good genes from their mother."

"First wife?" Zachary asked, offhanded and innocent.

"Oh yes. Met her in college."

Zachary knew that, and much more. He returned to his seat and resumed his position.

"I haven't checked recently," Fisk said, somewhat awkwardly, "but what does the job pay now?"

"One ten," Tony said and suppressed a smile. He was making more progress than he realized.

Fisk grimaced slightly as if he couldn't afford such a drastic cut in pay. His mind was racing, though, dizzy with the possibilities. "So you're recruiting candidates for the supreme court," he said, almost in a daze.

"Not for every seat. We have some good judges here, and we'll support them if they draw opponents. But McCarthy has got to go. She is a feminist who's soft on crime. We're going to take her out. I hope it's with you."

"And if I say no?"

"Then we'll go to the next name on our list. You're number one."

Fisk shook his head, bewildered. "I don't know," he said. "It would be hard to leave my firm."

But at least he was thinking about leaving the firm. The bait was in the water, and the fish was watching it. Zachary nodded in agreement. Completely sympathetic. The firm was a collection of worn-out paper pushers who spent their time deposing drunk drivers and settling fender benders the day before trial. For fourteen years, Fisk had been doing the same thing over and over. Each file was the same.

———

They took a booth in a pastry shop and ordered ice cream sundaes. "What is a blitzkrieg campaign?" Fisk asked. They were alone. All other booths were empty.

"It's basically an ambush," Zachary replied, warming up to his favorite subject. "Right now Judge McCarthy has no idea she has an opponent. She's thinking, hoping, actually confident, that no one will

challenge her. She has six thousand bucks in her campaign account, and she won't raise another dime if she doesn't have to. Let's say you decide to run. The qualifying deadline is four months away, and we'll wait until the last minute to announce your candidacy. However, we get busy right now. We put your team together. We get the money in the bank. We print all the yard signs, bumper stickers, brochures, direct mail materials. We cut your television ads, hire the consultants, pollsters, and the like. When you announce, we flood the district with direct mail. The first wave is the friendly stuff—you, your family, your minister, Rotary Club, Boy Scouts. The second wave is a hard but honest look at her record. You start campaigning like a madman. Ten speeches a day, every day, all over the district. We'll buzz you around in private planes. She won't know where to begin. She will be overwhelmed from the first day. On June 30, you'll report a million bucks in your campaign fund. She won't have ten thousand. The trial lawyers will scramble and raise some money for her, but it'll be a drop in the bucket. After Labor Day, we start hitting hard with television ads. She's soft on crime. Soft on gays. Soft on guns. Against the death penalty. She'll never recover."

The sundaes arrived and they began eating. "How much will this cost?" Fisk asked.

"Three million bucks."

"Three million bucks! For a supreme court race?"

"Only if you want to win."

"And you can raise that much money?"

"Judicial Vision already has the commitments. And if we need more, we'll get more."

Ron took a mouthful of ice cream and, for the first time, asked himself why an organization was willing to spend a fortune to unseat a supreme court justice who had little impact on the social issues of the day. The Mississippi courts rarely were drawn into cases involving abortion, gay rights, guns, immigration. They dealt with the death penalty all the time, but were never expected to abolish it. The weightier matters were always in federal court.

Perhaps the social issues were important, but something else was at work here. "This is about liability, isn't it?" Fisk asked.

"It's a package, Ron, with several elements. But, yes, limiting liability is a huge priority of our organization and its affiliated groups. We're going to find a horse for this race—hope it's you, but if not, then we'll go to the next guy—and when we find our man, we will expect a firm commitment to limit liability in civil litigation. The trial lawyers must be stopped."

———————

Doreen brewed decaf coffee late that night. The kids were asleep, but the adults definitely were not. Nor would they be anytime soon. Ron had called her from the office after Mr. Zachary left, and since then they had thought of nothing but the supreme court.

Issue number one: They had three young children. Jackson, home of the supreme court, was an hour away, and the family was not leaving Brookhaven. Ron thought he would need to spend only two nights a week in Jackson, at most. He could commute; it was an easy drive. And he could work from home. Secretly, to him, the idea of getting away from Brookhaven for a couple of nights each week was not altogether unappealing. Secretly, to her, the idea of having the house to herself occasionally was refreshing.

Issue number two: The campaign. How could he play politics for the rest of the year while continuing to practice law? His firm would be supportive, he thought, but it would not be easy. But then, nothing worthwhile is without sacrifice.

Issue number three: Money, though this was not a significant concern. The increase in pay was obvious. His net from the law firm's profits rose slightly each year, but no big bonuses were likely. Judicial salaries in Mississippi were increased periodically by the legislature. Plus, the state had a better retirement plan and health coverage.

Issue number four: His career. After fourteen years of doing the same thing, with no break in sight, he found the idea of a sudden career

change exhilarating. The mere thought of leaving the ranks of thousands to become only one of nine was thrilling. Jumping from the county court-house to the pinnacle of the state's legal system in one boisterous somer-sault was so exciting that it made him laugh. Doreen was not laughing, though she was very amused and engaged.

Issue number five: Failure. What if he lost? In a landslide? Would they be humiliated? This was a humbling thought, but he kept repeating what Tony Zachary had said. "Three million bucks will win the race, and we'll get the money."

Which brought up the rather large issue of who exactly was Tony Zachary, and could they believe him? Ron had spent an hour online tracking down Judicial Vision and Mr. Zachary. Everything looked le-gitimate. He called a friend from law school, a career man with the at-torney general's office in Jackson, and, without revealing his motives, nibbled around the edges of Judicial Vision. The friend had heard of them, he thought, but didn't know much about them. And besides, he dealt with offshore oil rights and stayed away from politics.

Ron had called the Judicial Vision office in Jackson and was routed through a maze back to Mr. Zachary's secretary, who informed him that her boss was traveling in south Mississippi. After she hung up, she called Tony and reported the contact.

The Fisks met Tony for lunch the following day at the Dixie Springs Café, a small restaurant near a lake ten miles south of Brookhaven, far away from potential eavesdroppers in the town's restaurants.

For the occasion, Zachary adopted a slightly different posture. To-day he was the man with other options. Here's the deal—take it or leave it because my list is long and I have other young white Protestant male lawyers to talk to. He was gentle and perfectly charming, especially to Doreen, who began the lunch with suspicion but was soon won over.

At some point during the sleepless night, both Mr. and Mrs. Fisk had independently arrived at the same conclusion. Life would be much

fuller, much richer in their little town if Lawyer Fisk became Justice Fisk. Their status would be elevated magnificently. No one could touch them, and while they didn't seek power or notoriety, the allure was irresistible.

"What's your principal concern?" Tony asked after fifteen minutes of worthless chatter.

"Well, it's January," Ron began. "And for the next eleven months I will do little else but plan and execute the campaign. Naturally, I'm worried about my law practice."

"Here's one solution," Tony said without hesitation. He had solutions for everything. "Judicial Vision is a well-coordinated and concerted effort. We have lots of friends and supporters. We can arrange for some legal work to be shifted to your firm. Timber, energy, natural gas, big clients with interests in this part of the state. Your firm might want to add a lawyer or two to handle things while you're busy elsewhere, but that should ease the strain. If you choose to run, you will not suffer financially. Quite the opposite."

The Fisks couldn't help but look at each other. Tony buttered a saltine and took a large bite.

"Legitimate clients?" Doreen asked, then wished she'd kept her mouth shut.

Tony frowned as he chewed, then when he could speak he said, rather sternly, "Everything we do, Doreen, is legitimate. We are completely ethical to begin with—our ultimate mission is to clean up the court, not trash it. And everything we do will be scrutinized. This race will become heated and attract a lot of attention. We do not stumble."

Chastised, she lifted her knife and went for a roll.

Tony continued: "No one can question legitimate legal work and fair fees paid by clients, whether big or small."

"Of course," Ron said. He was already thinking about the wonderful conversation with his partners as they anticipated this infusion of new business.

"I can't see myself as a political wife," Doreen said. "You know, out on the campaign trail giving speeches. I've never even thought about it."

Tony smiled and exuded charm. He even offered a quick laugh.

"You can do as much or as little as you like. With three young children, I would guess that you'll be pretty busy on the home front."

Over catfish and hush puppies, they agreed to meet again in a few days when Tony was passing through. They would have another lunch, and a final decision would be made. November was far away, but there was so much work to do.

CHAPTER 12

She once laughed at herself when she went through the dreaded ritual of crawling onto her stationary bike at dawn and pedaling away, going nowhere as the sun crept up and lightened her little gym. For a woman whose public veneer was a somber face behind an intimidating black robe, she was amused at what people would think if they could see her on the bike, in old sweats, hair a mess, eyes swollen, face unadorned with cosmetics. But that was a long time ago. Now she just went through the routine with little thought of how she looked or what anyone might think. Of particular concern now was the fact that she had gained five pounds over the holidays, eleven since her divorce. The gaining had to be stopped before the losing could commence. At fifty-one, the pounds were clinging now, refusing to burn away as quickly as when she was younger.

Sheila McCarthy was not a morning person. She hated mornings, hated getting out of bed before her sleep was finished, hated the cheery voices on television, hated the traffic on the way to the office. She didn't eat breakfast, because she hated breakfast food. She hated coffee. She had always secretly loathed those who reveled in their early morning exploits—the joggers, yoga nuts, workaholics, hyperactive soccer moms. As

a young circuit court judge in Biloxi, she had often scheduled trials for 10:00 a.m., a scandalous hour. But it was her court and she made the rules.

Now she was one of nine, and the tribunal on which she served clung desperately to its traditions. On certain days she could roll in at noon and work until midnight, her preferred schedule, but most of the time she was expected by 9:00 a.m.

She was sweating after one mile. Eighty-four calories burned. Less than a cup of Häagen-Dazs chocolate chip mint, her most serious temptation. A television hung from a rack above the bike, and she watched and listened as the locals gushed over the latest car wrecks and murders. Then the weatherman was back for the third time in twelve minutes, clucking on about snow in the Rockies because there wasn't a single cloud at home to analyze.

After two miles, and down 161 calories, Sheila stopped for water and a towel, then crawled onto the treadmill for more work. She switched to CNN for a quick review of the national gossip. When she had burned 250 calories, Sheila quit and went to the shower. An hour later, she left her two-story condo on the reservoir, got into her bright red BMW convertible sports car, and headed to work.

————

The Mississippi Supreme Court is divided into three neat districts—northern, central, and southern—with three justices elected from each. A term is eight years, with no limit. Judicial elections take place in the off years, those quiet ones in which there are no races for local, legislative, or other statewide positions. Once obtained, a seat on the court lasts for a long time, usually until death or voluntary retirement.

The elections are nonpartisan, with all candidates running as independents. Campaign finance laws limit contributions from individuals at $5,000 each, and $2,500 from organizations, including political action committees and corporations.

Sheila McCarthy was appointed to the bench nine years earlier by a friendly governor, following the death of her predecessor. She ran un-

opposed once and was certainly planning on another easy victory. There was not the faintest whiff of a rumor that someone out there had designs on her seat.

With nine years' experience, she outranked only three others, and was still considered by most members of the state bar to be a relative newcomer. Tracking her written opinions and her voting record baffled liberals and conservatives alike. She was a moderate, a consensus builder, neither a strict constructionist nor a judicial activist, but more or less a practical fence straddler who, some said, decided the best outcome first, then found enough law to support it. As such, she was an influential member of the court. She could broker a deal between the hard right-wingers, of which there were always automatically four in number, and the liberals, of which there were two on most days and none on others. Four on the right and two on the left meant Sheila had two comrades in the center, though this simplistic analysis had burned many a lawyer trying to predict an outcome. Most cases on the docket defied categorization. Where's the liberal or conservative side in a big messy divorce, or a boundary line dispute between two timber companies? Many cases were decided 9–0.

The supreme court does its work in the Carroll Gartin Justice Building in downtown Jackson, across the street from the state capitol. Sheila parked in her reserved space underneath the building. She rode the elevator to the fourth floor alone and stepped into her suite at exactly 8:45. Paul, her chief clerk, a strikingly handsome twenty-eight-year-old single straight male of whom she was extremely fond, walked into her office seconds after she did.

"Good morning," Paul said. He had long dark curly hair and a small diamond in his ear, and he somehow managed to maintain a perfect growth of three days' worth of stubble. Hazel eyes. She often expected to see Paul modeling Armani suits in the fashion magazines stacked around her condo. Paul had more to do with her gym time than she cared to admit.

"Good morning," she said coolly, as if she had barely noticed him.

"You have the *Sturdivant* hearing at nine."

"I know that," she said, glancing at his rear end as he walked across her office. Faded jeans. The ass of a model.

He walked out, her eyes following every step.

Her secretary took his place. She locked the door and pulled out a small makeup kit, and when Justice McCarthy was ready, the touch-up was done quickly. The hair—short, almost above the ear, half sandy blond and half gray, and now carefully colored twice a month at $400 a pop—was fussed into place, then sprayed.

"What are my chances with Paul?" Sheila asked with her eyes closed.

"A bit young, don't you think?"

The secretary was older than her boss and had been doing the touch-ups for almost nine years. She kept powdering.

"Of course he's young. That's the point."

"I don't know. I hear he's awfully busy with that redhead in Albritton's office."

Sheila had heard the rumors, too. A gorgeous new clerk from Stanford was getting plenty of attention down the hall, and Paul usually had his pick.

"Have you read the *Sturdivant* briefs?" Sheila asked, standing as she prepared to be robed.

"Yes." The secretary carefully draped the black robe over her shoulders. The zipper ran down the front. Both ladies tugged and fussed until the bulky garment was perfect.

"Who killed the cop?" Sheila asked, gently pulling the zipper.

"It wasn't Sturdivant."

"I agree." She stepped before a full-length mirror, and both ladies inspected the presentation. "Can you tell I've gained weight?" Sheila asked.

"No." Same answer to the same question.

"Well, I have. And that's why I love these things. They can hide twenty pounds."

"You love it for another reason, dear, and we both know it. You're the only girl out there with eight boys, and none of them are as tough or as smart as you."

"And sexy. Don't forget sexy."

The secretary laughed at the idea. "No competition, dear. Those old goats can only dream about sex."

And they went off, out of the office, down the hall, where they met Paul again. He rattled off some key points in the *Sturdivant* case as they rode the elevator to the third floor, where the courtroom was located. One lawyer might argue this, and the other might possibly argue that. Here are some questions to trip both of them.

————

Three blocks away from where Justice McCarthy assumed her position on the bench, a group of rather intense men and (two) women gathered to discuss her demise. They met in a windowless conference room in a nondescript building, one of many clustered near the state capitol where countless civil servants and lobbyists ground out the work of running Mississippi.

The meeting was hosted by Tony Zachary and Judicial Vision. The guests were the directors of other like-minded "government relations" firms, some with vague names that deflected categorization—Freedom Network, Market Partnership, Commerce Council, Enterprise Advocacy. Other names got right to the point—Citizens Opposed to Lawsuit Tyranny (COLT), Fair Litigation Association, Jury Watch, Tort Reform Committee of Mississippi. And the old guard was there, the associations representing the interests of banks, insurance, oil, medicine, manufacturing, retail, commerce, trade, and the best of our American way of life.

In the murky world of legislative manipulation, where loyalties shift overnight and a friend can become an enemy by noon, the people in the room were known, at least to Tony Zachary, to be worthy of trust.

"Ladies and gentlemen," Tony began, standing with a half-eaten croissant on the plate before him, "the purpose of this meeting is to inform you that we will remove Sheila McCarthy from the supreme court

in November and her replacement will be a young justice committed to economic growth and limited liability."

There was light applause around the table. Everyone else was seated, all curious and listening. No one was certain who was behind Judicial Vision. Zachary had been around a few years and had a fair reputation, but he had no personal money. Nor did his group have much of a membership. Nor had he ever shown much interest in the civil justice system. His newfound passion for changing liability laws seemed to spring from nowhere.

But there was no doubt that Zachary and Judicial Vision were well funded. And in their game, that meant everything.

"We have the initial financing on the table, with more committed down the road," he said proudly. "More, of course, will be needed from you. We have a campaign plan, a strategy, and we, Judicial Vision, will be running the show."

More applause. The biggest obstacle was always coordination. There were so many groups, so many issues, so many egos. Raising the money was easy, from their side of the street anyway, but spending it wisely was often the challenge. The fact that Tony had, rather aggressively, assumed control was wonderful news. The rest of them were more than content to write the checks and turn out the voters.

"What about a candidate?" someone asked.

Tony smiled and said, "You'll love him. Can't give you his name right now, but you'll love him. Made for television." Ron Fisk had not yet said yes to the campaign, but Tony knew that he would. And if, for some reason, he did not, there were more names on the list. They would indeed have themselves a candidate, and soon, even if it took sackfuls of cash.

"Shall we talk money?" Tony asked, then plunged headlong into the issue before anyone could respond. "We have a million bucks on the table. I want to spend more than both candidates spent in the last contested race. That was two years ago, and I don't need to remind you that your boy in that race came up short. My boy in this race will not lose. To guarantee this, I need two million from you and your members."

Three million for such a race was a shock. In the last governor's race, a race that covered all eighty-two counties and not just a third of them, the winner spent $7 million and the loser spent half that. And a good governor's race was always a major spectacle, the centerpiece of state politics. Passions were high, turnouts even higher.

A race for a seat on the supreme court, when one did occur, seldom drew more than a third of the registered voters.

"How do you plan to spend $3 million?" someone asked. It was telling that the question was not about raising so much money. It was assumed they had access to pockets deep enough.

"Television, television, television," Tony responded. This was partly true. Tony would never reveal his entire strategy. He and Mr. Rinehart planned to spend a lot more than three million, but many of their expenditures would be either in cash or carefully hidden out of state.

An assistant popped up and began passing around thick folders. "This is what we've done in other states," Tony was saying. "Please take it with you and read it at your leisure."

There were questions about his plan, and more about his candidate. Tony revealed little, but continually emphasized his need for their financial commitments, the sooner the better. The only blip in the meeting came when the director of COLT informed them that his group had been actively recruiting candidates to run against McCarthy and that he himself had a plan to take her out. COLT advertised eight thousand members, though that number was dubious. Most of its activists were ex-litigants who'd been burned in a lawsuit of some variety. The organization had credibility, but it did not have a million dollars. After a brief but tense flare-up, Tony invited the COLT guy to go run his own campaign, at which time he backed down quickly and rejoined ranks.

Before adjourning, Tony urged secrecy, a vital element of the campaign. "If the trial lawyers find out now that we have a horse in the race, they will crank up their fund-raising machine. They beat you the last time."

They were irked by this second reference to "their" loss in the last race, as if they would've won if only they'd had Tony. But everyone let it

pass. The mere mention of the trial lawyers immediately refocused their attention.

They were too excited about the race to bicker.

————

The class action claimed to include "over three hundred" victims injured in various ways by the gross negligence of Krane Chemical at its Bowmore plant. Only twenty were named as plaintiffs, and of these twenty perhaps half had significant afflictions. Whether their ailments were linked to polluted groundwater would be a question for another day.

It was filed in Hattiesburg at the federal courthouse, a good stone's throw from the Forrest County Circuit Court building, where Dr. Leona Rocha and her jury had rendered its verdict barely two months earlier. Lawyers Sterling Bintz of Philadelphia and F. Clyde Hardin of Bowmore were on hand to do the filing, and also to chat with any reporters who'd responded to their prefiling press alert. Sadly, there were no television cameras, only a couple of green print reporters. At least for F. Clyde, though, it was an adventure. He hadn't been near a federal courthouse in over thirty years.

For Mr. Bintz, the pathetic lack of recognition was appalling. He had dreamed of huge headlines and long stories with splendid photographs. He had filed many important class actions and had usually managed to get them adequately covered by the media. What was wrong with the rural Mississippians?

F. Clyde hurried back to Bowmore, to his office, where Miriam was lingering to see how things went. "What channel?" she asked.

"None."

"What?" It was without a doubt the biggest day in the history of the firm of F. Clyde Hardin & Associates, and Miriam couldn't wait to watch it all on television.

"We decided not to deal with those reporters. Can't trust them," F. Clyde explained as he glanced at his watch. It was a quarter after five, past time for Miriam to leave the office. "No need to stick around," he said, flinging his jacket. "I've got things under control here."

She quickly left, disappointed, and F. Clyde went straight for the office bottle. The chilled, thick vodka soothed him immediately, and he began to replay his big day. With a bit of luck, the Hattiesburg paper would include his photo.

Bintz was claiming three hundred clients. At $500 each, F. Clyde was due a nice referral fee. So far he'd been paid only $3,500, most of which he used for back taxes.

He poured a second drink and said what the hell. Bintz wouldn't screw him, because he needed him. He, F. Clyde Hardin, was now an attorney of record in one of the most important class action cases in the country. All roads ran through Bowmore, and F. Clyde was the man.

CHAPTER 13

It was explained to his firm that Mr. Fisk would be in Jackson for the entire day, something to do with personal business. In other words, don't ask. As a partner he had earned the right to come and go as he pleased, though Fisk was so disciplined and organized that anyone in the firm could usually find him within five minutes.

He left Doreen on the front steps at dawn. She was invited to make the trip, but with a job and three kids it simply wasn't possible, not with such short notice. Ron left the house without breakfast, not that time was a factor. Tony Zachary had said, "We'll eat on the plane," and this was enough to entice Ron to skip his bran flakes.

The Brookhaven airstrip was too small for the jet, so Ron happily agreed to rush off to the airport in Jackson. He had never been within a hundred yards of a private jet, and had never given much thought to flying on one. Tony Zachary was waiting at the general aviation terminal with a hearty handshake and a vigorous "Good morning, Your Honor." They walked purposefully across the tarmac, past a few old turboprops and pistons—smaller, inferior vessels. Waiting in the distance was a magnificent carrier, as sleek and exotic as a spaceship. Its navigation lights

were flickering. Its handsome stairway was extended down, a splendid invitation to its special passengers. Ron followed Tony up the steps to the landing, where a pretty flight attendant in a short skirt welcomed them aboard, took their jackets, and showed them their selection of seats.

"Ever been on a Gulfstream before?" Tony asked as they settled in. One of the pilots said hello as he pushed a button to retract the stairway.

"No," Ron said, gawking at the polished mahogany and soft leather and gold trimmings.

"This is a G5, the Mercedes of private jets. This one could take us to Paris, nonstop."

Then let's go to Paris instead of Washington, Ron thought as he leaned into the aisle to absorb the length and size of the airplane. A quick count revealed seating for at least a dozen pampered folks. "It's beautiful," he said. He wanted to ask who owned it. Who was paying for the trip? Who was behind this gold-plated recruitment? But to inquire would be rude, he told himself. Just relax, enjoy the trip, enjoy the day, and remember all the details because Doreen will want to hear them.

The flight attendant was back. She explained emergency procedures, then asked what they might like for breakfast. Tony wanted scrambled eggs, bacon, and hash browns. Ron ordered the same.

"Bathroom and kitchen are in the back," Tony said, as if he traveled by G5 every day. "The sofa pulls out if you need a nap." Coffee arrived as they began to taxi. The flight attendant offered a variety of newspapers. Tony grabbed one, yanked it open, waited a few seconds, then asked, "You keeping up with that Bowmore litigation?"

Ron pretended to look at a newspaper as he continued to soak in the luxury of the jet. "Somewhat," he said.

"They filed a class action yesterday," Tony said in disgust. "One of those national tort firms out of Philadelphia. I guess the vultures have arrived." It was his first comment to Ron on the subject, but it definitely would not be his last.

The G5 took off. It was one of three owned by various entities controlled by the Trudeau Group, and leased through a separate charter

company that made it impossible to track the true owner. Ron watched the city of Jackson disappear below him. Minutes later, when they leveled off at forty-one thousand feet, he could smell the rich aroma of bacon in the skillet.

———

At Dulles general aviation, they were whisked into the rear of a long black limo, and forty minutes later they were in the District, on K Street. Tony explained en route that they had a 10:00 a.m. meeting with one group of potential backers, then a quiet lunch, then a 2:00 p.m. meeting with another group. Ron would be home in time for dinner. He was almost dizzy from the excitement of such luxurious travel and feeling so important.

On the seventh floor of a new building, they stepped into the rather plain lobby of the American Family Alliance and spoke to an even plainer receptionist. Tony's summary on the jet had been: "This group is perhaps the most powerful of all the conservative Christian advocates. Lots of members, lots of cash, lots of clout. The Washington politicians love them and fear them. Run by a man named Walter Utley, a former congressman who got fed up with all the liberals in Congress and left to form his own group."

Fisk had heard of Walter Utley and his American Family Alliance.

They were escorted into a large conference room where Mr. Utley himself was waiting with a warm smile and handshake and several introductions to other men, all of whom had been included in Tony's briefing on the jet. They represented such groups as Prayer Partnership, Global Light, Family Roundtable, Evangelical Initiative, and a few others. All significant players in national politics, according to Tony.

They settled around the table, behind notepads and briefing papers, as if they were about to place Mr. Fisk under oath and take his deposition. Tony led off with a summary of the Supreme Court of Mississippi and kept his comments generally positive. Most of the judges were good men with solid voting records. But, of course, there was the matter of Jus-

tice Sheila McCarthy and her closet liberalism. She couldn't be trusted on the issues. She was divorced. She was rumored to have loose morals, but Tony stopped without going into specifics.

To challenge her, they needed Ron here to step forward and answer the bell. Tony ran through a quick biography of their man and, in doing so, did not offer a single fact that was not already known by those present. He handed off to Ron, who cleared his throat and thanked them for the invitation. He began talking about his life, education, upbringing, parents, wife, and kids. He was a devout Christian, a deacon in St. Luke's Baptist Church, a Sunday school teacher. Rotary Club, Ducks Unlimited, youth league baseball coach. He stretched his résumé as far as he could, then shrugged as if to say, "There's nothing else."

He and his wife had been praying about this decision. They had even met with their pastor for yet more prayer, hopefully at a higher level. They were comfortable. They were ready.

Everyone was still warm, friendly, delighted he was there. They asked about his background—was there anything back there that could haunt him? An affair, a DUI, a stupid fraternity prank in college? Any ethics complaints? First and only marriage? Yes, good, we thought so. Any claims of sexual harassment from your staff? Anything like that? Anything whatsoever to do with sex because sex is the killer in a hot campaign? And while they were on the subject, what about gays? Gay marriage? Absolutely not! Civil unions? No, sir, not in Mississippi. Gays adopting children? No, sir.

Abortion? Opposed. All abortions? Opposed.

Death penalty? Very much in favor.

No one seemed to grasp the contradiction between the two.

Guns, the Second Amendment, the right to bear arms, and so on? Ron loved his guns, but was curious for a second about why these religious men were concerned about weapons. Then it hit him—it's all about politics and getting elected. His lifetime of hunting pleased them mightily, and he dragged it out as much as possible. No animal seemed safe.

Then the squeaky-voiced director of the Family Roundtable pursued a line of questions dealing with the separation of church and state,

and everybody seemed to nod off. Ron held his ground, answering thoughtfully, and seemed to satisfy those few who were listening. He also began to realize that it was all a show. Their minds had been made up long before he left Brookhaven that morning. He was their man, and at the moment he was simply preaching to the choir.

The next round of questions dealt with freedom of speech, especially religious speech. "Should a small-town judge be allowed to hang the Ten Commandments in his courtroom?" was the question. Ron sensed that this issue intrigued them, and he was at first inclined to be perfectly honest and say no. The U.S. Supreme Court has ruled that it's a violation of the separation of church and state, and Ron happened to agree. He did not, however, want to upset the party, so he said, "One of my heroes is my local circuit court judge in Brookhaven." He began to bob and weave. "A great man. He's had the Ten Commandments hanging on his wall for thirty years, and I've always admired him."

A slick nonanswer that they recognized for what it was. They also recognized that it was a fine example of slickness that could help Mr. Fisk survive a heated campaign. So there was no follow-up, no objection. They were, after all, battle-tested political operatives, and they could appreciate a savvy nonresponse when they heard one.

After an hour, Walter Utley glanced at his watch and announced that he was a bit behind schedule. The day held many more important meetings. He concluded the little meet and greet with a declaration that he was very impressed with Ron Fisk and saw no reason why his American Family Alliance could not only endorse him but hit the ground running down there and get some votes. Everyone nodded around the table, and Tony Zachary seemed as proud as a new father.

———

"There's been a change in our lunch plans," he said when they were once again tucked away in the limo. "Senator Rudd would like to see you."

"Senator Rudd?" Fisk asked in disbelief.

"You got it," Tony said proudly.

Myers Rudd was halfway through his seventh term (thirty-nine

years) in the U.S. Senate, and for at least the last three elections he had
scared away all opposition. He was despised by at least 40 percent of the
people and loved by at least 60 percent, and he had perfected the art of
helping those on his side of the street and dismissing all others. He was a
legend in Mississippi politics, the fixer, the inveterate meddler in local
races, the king who picked his candidates, the assassin who slaughtered
those who ran against his candidates, the bank who could finance any
race and funnel hoards of cash, the wise old man who led his party, and
the thug who destroyed the others.

"Senator Rudd has an interest in this case?" Fisk asked, so inno-
cently.

Tony gave him a wary look. How naive can one be? "Of course he
does. Senator Rudd is very close to those folks you just met. He maintains
a perfect voting record in their score books. Perfect, mind you. Not 95
percent, but perfect. One of only three in the Senate, and the other two
are rookies."

What will Doreen say about this? Ron thought to himself. Lunch
with Senator Rudd, in Washington! They were somewhere near the
Capitol when the limo ducked into a one-way street. "Let's jump out
here," Tony said before the driver could get out. They headed for a nar-
row door next to an old hotel called the Mercury. An ancient doorman
in a green uniform frowned as they approached. "To see Senator Rudd,"
Tony said abruptly, and the frown lessened somewhat. Inside, they were
led along the edge of an empty and gloomy dining room and down a pas-
sageway. "It's The Senator's private quarters," Tony said quietly. Ron was
greatly impressed. Ron was noticing the worn carpet and peeling paint,
but the old building had a strong dose of shabby elegance. It had a his-
tory. How many deals have been put together inside these walls? he asked
himself.

At the end of the hallway, they walked into a small private dining
room where all manner of serious power was on display. Senator Rudd
was seated at the small table, cell phone stuck to his head. Ron had never
met him, but he certainly looked familiar. Dark suit, red tie, thick shiny
gray hair plastered to the left and held in place with no small amount of

spray, large round face that seemed to grow thicker each year. No fewer than four of his minders and handlers were hovering like bees, all engaged in urgent cell phone chats, probably with one another.

Tony and Fisk waited, watching the show. Government in action.

Suddenly The Senator slapped his phone shut, and the other four conversations were instantly concluded. "Clear out," the great man grunted, and his minions fled like mice. "How are you, Zachary?" he said, standing behind the table. Introductions were made, small talk pursued for a moment. Rudd seemed to know everyone back home in Brookhaven, an aunt once lived there, and he was honored to meet this Mr. Fisk that he'd heard so much about. At some predetermined point, Tony said, "I'll be back in an hour," and vanished. He was replaced by a waiter in a tuxedo.

"Sit down," Rudd insisted. "The food's not much, but the privacy is great. I eat here five times a week." The waiter ignored the comment and handed over menus.

"It's lovely," Ron said, looking around at the walls lined with books that had been neither read nor dusted in a hundred years. They were dining in a small library. No wonder it's so private. They ordered soup and grilled swordfish. The waiter closed the door when he left.

"I have a meeting at one," Rudd said, "so let's talk fast." He began pouring sugar into his iced tea and stirring it with a soupspoon.

"Certainly."

"You can win this race, Ron, and God knows we need you."

Words from the king, and hours later Ron would quote them over and over to Doreen. It was a guarantee from a man who'd never lost, and from that opening volley Ron Fisk was a candidate.

"As you know," Rudd continued because he really wasn't accustomed to listening, especially in conversations with small-time politicians from back home, "I don't get involved in local races." Fisk's first impulse was to laugh, and loudly, but he quickly realized that The Senator was dead serious.

"However, this race is too important. I'll do what I can, which is nothing to sneeze at, you know?"

"Of course."

"I've made some powerful friends in this business, and they will be happy to support your campaign. Just takes a phone call from me."

Ron was nodding politely. Two months earlier, *Newsweek* ran a cover story on the mountains of special-interest cash in Washington and the politicians who took it. Rudd topped the list. He had over $11 million in his campaign war chest, yet had no foreseeable race. The notion of a viable opponent was too ridiculous to even consider. Big business owned him—banks, insurance, oil, coal, media, defense, pharmaceuticals—no segment of corporate America had escaped the tentacles of his fundraising machine.

"Thank you," Ron said because he felt obligated.

"My folks can put together a lot of money. Plus, I know the people in the trenches. The governor, the legislators, the mayors. Ever hear of Willie Tate Ferris?"

"No, sir."

"He's a supervisor, beat four, Adams County, in your district. I kept his brother out of prison, twice. Willie Tate will walk the streets for me. And he is the most powerful politician in those parts. One phone call from me, and you got Adams County." He snapped his fingers. Just like that the votes were falling in place.

"Ever hear of Link Kyzer? Sheriff in Wayne County?"

"Maybe."

"Link's an old friend. Two years ago he needed new patrol cars, new radios, new bulletproof vests and guns and everything. County wouldn't give him crap, so he calls me. I go to Homeland Security, talk to some friends, twist some arms, and Wayne County suddenly gets six million bucks to fight terrorism. They got more patrol cars than they got cops to drive them. Their radio system is better than the navy's. And, lo and behold, the terrorists have decided to stay the hell out of Wayne County." He laughed at his own punch line, and Ron was obliged to guffaw along with him. Nothing like wasting a few more million tax dollars.

"You need Link, you got Link, and Wayne County," Rudd promised as he slugged down some tea.

With two counties under his belt, Ron began contemplating the other twenty-five in the southern district. Would the next hour be spent listening to war stories from all of them? He rather hoped not. The soup arrived.

"This gal, McCarthy," Rudd said between slurps. "She's never been on board." Which Ron took as an indictment on the grounds of not supporting Senator Rudd. "She's too liberal, plus, between us boys, she just ain't cut out for the black robe. Know what I mean?"

Ron nodded slightly as he studied his soup. Little wonder The Senator preferred dining in private. He doesn't know her first name, Ron said to himself. He knows very little about her, except that she is indeed female and, in his opinion, out of place.

To ease things away from the good ole white boy talk, Ron decided to interject a semi-intelligent question. "What about the Gulf Coast? I have very few contacts down there."

Predictably, Rudd scoffed at the question. No problem. "My wife's from Bay St. Louis," he said, as if that alone could guarantee a landslide for his chosen one. "You got those defense contractors, naval shipyards, NASA, hell, I own those people."

And they probably own you, Ron thought. Sort of a joint ownership.

A cell phone hummed next to The Senator's tea glass. He glanced at it, frowned, and said, "Gotta take this. It's the White House." He gave the impression of being quite irritated.

"Should I step outside?" Ron asked, at once impressed beyond words but also horrified that he might eavesdrop on some crucial matter.

"No, no," Rudd said as he waved him down. Fisk tried to concentrate on his soup, and tea, and roll, and though it was a lunch he would never forget, he suddenly wished it would quickly come to an end. The phone call did not. Rudd grunted and mumbled and gave no clue as to which crisis he was averting. The waiter returned with the swordfish, which sizzled a bit at first but soon cooled off. The white beets beside it were swimming in a large pool of butter.

When the world was safe again, Rudd hung up and stuck a fork into

the center of his swordfish. "Sorry about that," he said. "Damned Russians. Anyway, I want you to run, Ron. It's important to the state. We have got to get our court in line."

"Yes, sir, but—"

"And you have my complete support. Nothing public, mind you, but I'll work my ass off in the background. I'll raise serious cash. I'll crack the whip, break some arms, the usual routine down there. It's my game, son, trust me."

"What if—"

"No one beats me in Mississippi. Just ask the governor. He was twenty points down with two months to go, and was trying to do it himself. Didn't need my help. I flew down, had a prayer meeting, the boy got converted, and he won in a landslide. I don't like to get involved down there, but I will. And this race is that important. Can you do it?"

"I think so."

"Don't be silly, Ron. This is a onetime chance to do something great. Think of it, you, at the age of, uh—"

"Thirty-nine."

"Thirty-nine, damned young, but you're on the Supreme Court of Mississippi. And once we get you there, you'll never leave. Just think about it."

"I'm thinking very hard, sir."

"Good."

The phone hummed again, probably the president. "Sorry," Rudd said as he stuck it in his ear and took a huge bite of fish.

———

The third and final stop on the tour was at the office of the Tort Reform Network on Connecticut Avenue. With Tony back in charge, they blitzed through the introductions and short speeches. Fisk answered a few benign questions, much lighter fare than what had been served up by the religious boys that morning. Once again, he was overwhelmed by the impression that everyone was going through the motions. It was important for them to touch and hear their candidate, but there seemed to be little

interest in a serious evaluation. They were relying on Tony, and since he'd found his man, then so had they.

Unknown to Ron Fisk, the entire forty-minute meeting was captured by a hidden camera and sent upstairs to a small media room where Barry Rinehart was watching carefully. He had a thick file on Fisk, one with photos and various summaries, but he was anxious to hear his voice, watch his eyes and hands, listen to his answers. Was he photogenic, telegenic, well dressed, handsome enough? Was his voice reassuring, trustworthy? Did he sound intelligent or dull? Was he nervous in front of such a group, or calm and confident? Could he be packaged and properly marketed?

After fifteen minutes, Barry was convinced. The only negative was a hint of nervousness, but then that was to be expected. Yank a man out of Brookhaven and thrust him before a strange crowd in a strange city and he's likely to stutter a few times. Nice voice, nice face, decent suit. Barry had certainly worked with less.

He would never meet Ron Fisk, and, as in all of Barry's campaigns, the candidate would never have the slightest clue about who was pulling the strings.

every section always ends with an astute JG point/ observation. Like ... "already spending it"

Flying home, Tony ordered a whiskey sour and tried to force a drink on Ron, who declined and stuck with coffee. It was the perfect setting for a drink—aboard a luxurious jet, with a gorgeous young lady as the bartender, at the end of a long and stressful day, with no one in the world watching and knowing.

"Just coffee," Ron said. Regardless of the setting, he knew he was still being evaluated. Plus, he was a teetotaler anyway. The decision was easy.

Not that Tony was much of a drinker. He took a few sips of his cocktail, loosened his tie, settled deep into his seat, and eventually said, "Rumor has it that this McCarthy gal hits the booze pretty hard."

Ron simply shrugged. The rumor had not made its way to Brookhaven. He figured that at least 50 percent of the people there couldn't

name any of the three justices from the southern district, let alone their habits, good or bad.

Another sip, and Tony kept going. "Both of her parents were heavy drinkers. Of course, they're from the Coast, so that's not unexpected. Her favorite hangout is a club called Tuesday's, near the reservoir. Ever hear of it?"

"No."

"Kind of a meat market for the middle-aged swingers, so I hear. Never been there myself."

Fisk refused to take the bait. Such low gossip seemed to bore him. This didn't bother Tony. In fact, he found it admirable. Let the candidate keep the high ground. The mud would be slung by others.

"How long have you known Senator Rudd?" Fisk asked, changing the subject.

"A long time." And for the remainder of the short trip they talked about their great senator and his colorful career.

———

Ron raced home, still floating from such a heady encounter with power and its trappings. Doreen was waiting for the details. They ate warmed-up spaghetti while the kids finished homework and prepared for bed.

She had many questions, and Ron struggled with some of the answers. Why were so many diverse groups willing to spend so much on an unknown and thoroughly inexperienced politician? Because they were committed. Because they preferred bright, clean-cut young men with the right beliefs and without the baggage of prior service. And if Ron said no, they would find another candidate just like him. They were determined to win, to clean up the court. It was a national movement, and a critical one.

The fact that her husband had dined alone with Senator Myers Rudd was the clincher. They would take a dramatic plunge into the unknown world of politics, and they would conquer.

CHAPTER 14

Barry Rinehart took the shuttle to LaGuardia, and from there a private car to the Mercer hotel in SoHo. He checked in, showered, and changed into a heavier wool suit because snow was expected. He picked up a fax at the front desk, then walked eight blocks to a tiny Vietnamese restaurant near the Village, one that had yet to appear in the travel guides. Mr. Trudeau preferred it for discreet meetings. It was empty and he was early, so Barry settled himself onto a bar stool and ordered a drink.

F. Clyde Hardin's cheap class action may have been small news in Mississippi, but it was a far better story in New York. The daily financial publications ran with it, and the battered shares of Krane's common stock took another drubbing.

Mr. Trudeau had spent the day working the phones and yelling at Bobby Ratzlaff. Krane's stock had been trading between $18.00 and $20.00, but the class action knocked it back a few bucks. It closed at $14.50, a new low, and Carl pretended to be upset. Ratzlaff, who had

borrowed a million bucks from his retirement fund, seemed even more depressed.

The lower the better. Carl wanted the stock to fall as far as possible. He'd already lost a billion on paper and he could lose more, because one day it would all come roaring back. Unknown to anyone, except two bankers in Zurich, Carl was already buying Krane's stock through a wonderfully nebulous company in Panama. He was carefully gathering shares in small lots so that his buying would not upset the downward trend. Five thousand shares on a slow day and twenty thousand on a busy one, but nothing that would draw attention. Fourth-quarter earnings were due soon, and Carl had been cooking the books since Christmas. The stock would continue to slide. Carl would continue to buy.

He sent Ratzlaff away after dark, then returned a few calls. At seven, he crawled into the backseat of his Bentley and Toliver drove him to the Vietnamese place.

Carl had not seen Rinehart since their first meeting in Boca Raton, back in November, three days after the verdict. They did not use regular mail, e-mail, faxes, overnight parcels, landlines, or standard cell phones. Each had a secure smart phone that was linked solely to the other, and once a week, when Carl had the time, he called for an update.

They were led through a bamboo curtain to a dimly lit side room with one table. A waiter brought drinks. Carl was going through the motions of cursing class actions and the lawyers who bring them. "We're down to nosebleeds and skin rashes," he said. "Every redneck who ever drove by the plant down there is suddenly a plaintiff. No one remembers the good old days when we paid the highest wages in south Mississippi. Now the lawyers have created a stampede and it's a race to the courthouse."

"It could get worse," Barry said. "We know of another group of lawyers who are rounding up clients. If they file, then their class will be added to the first one. I wouldn't sweat it."

"You wouldn't sweat it? You're not burning cash in legal fees."

"You're going to get it back, Carl. Relax." It was now Carl and Barry, first names and lots of familiarity.

"Relax. Krane closed today at $14.50. If you owned twenty-five million shares, you might find it hard to relax."

"I would be relaxed, and I would be buying."

Carl knocked back his scotch. "You're getting pretty cocky."

"I saw our boy today. He made the rounds in Washington. Nice-looking fella, so clean-cut it's frightening. Smart, good speaker, handles himself well. Everybody was impressed."

"Has he signed on?"

"He will tomorrow. He had lunch with Senator Rudd, and the ole boy knows how to twist arms."

"Myers Rudd," Carl said, shaking his head. "What a fool."

"Indeed, but he can always be bought."

"They can all be bought. I spent over four million last year in Washington. Sprinkled it around like Christmas candy."

"And I'm sure Rudd got his share. You and I know he's a moron, but the people in Mississippi don't. He's the king and they worship him down there. If he wants our boy to run, then the race is on."

Carl squirmed out of his jacket and flung it across a chair. He removed his cuff links, rolled up his sleeves, and, with no one to watch, loosened his tie and slouched in his chair. He sipped his scotch. "Do you know the story about Senator Rudd and the EPA?" he asked, with full knowledge that fewer than five people knew the details.

"No," Barry said, tugging at his own tie.

"Seven, maybe eight years ago, before the lawsuits started, the EPA came to Bowmore and started their mischief. The locals there had been complaining for years, but EPA is not known for swift action. They poked around, ran some tests, became somewhat alarmed, then got pretty agitated. We were watching all this very closely. We had people all over the place. Hell, we have people inside the EPA. Maybe we cut some corners with our waste, I don't know, but the bureaucrats really became aggressive. They were talking about criminal investigations, calling in the U.S. attorney, bad stuff, but still kept internal. They were on the verge of going public with all sorts of demands—a zillion-dollar cleanup, horrendous fines, maybe even a shutdown. A man named Gabbard was CEO

of Krane at the time; he's gone now, but a decent sort who knew how to persuade. I sent Gabbard to Washington with a blank check. Several blank checks. He got with our lobbyists and set up a new PAC, another one that supposedly worked to further the interests of chemical and plastics manufacturers. They mapped out a plan, the key to which was getting Senator Rudd on our side. They're scared of him down there, and if he wants the EPA to get lost, then you can forget the EPA. Rudd's been on the Appropriations Committee for a hundred years, and if EPA threatens to buck him, then he simply threatens to cut their funding. It's complicated, but it's also very simple. Plus, this is Mississippi, Rudd's backyard, and he had more contacts and clout than anyone else. So our boys at the new PAC wined and dined Rudd, and he knew exactly what was happening. He's a simpleton, but he's played the game for so long he's written most of the rules."

Platters of shrimp and noodles arrived and were casually ignored. Another round of drinks.

"Rudd finally decided that he needed a million bucks for his campaign account, and we agreed to route it through all the dummy corporations and fronts that you guys use to hide it. Congress has made it legal, but it would otherwise be known as bribery. Then Rudd wanted something else. Turns out he's got this slightly retarded grandson who has some weird fixation on elephants. Kid loves elephants. Got pictures all over his walls. Watches wildlife videos. And so on. And what The Senator would really like is one of those first-class, four-star African safaris so he can take his grandson to see a bunch of elephants. No problem. Then he decides that the entire family would enjoy such a trip, so our lobbyists arrange the damned thing. Twenty-eight people, two private jets, fifteen days in the African bush drinking Dom Pérignon, eating lobster and steak, and, of course, gawking at a thousand elephants. The bill was close to three hundred grand and he never had a clue it was paid for by me."

"A bargain."

"An absolute bargain. He buried the EPA and they fled Bowmore. They couldn't touch us. And, as a side benefit, Senator Rudd is now an expert on all issues dealing with Africa. AIDS, genocide, famine, human

rights abuses—you name it and he's an expert because he spent two weeks in the Kenyan outback watching wild game from the back of a Land Rover."

They shared a laugh and made the first advance upon the noodles. "Did you ever contact him when the lawsuits started?" Barry asked.

"No. The lawyers took over with a vengeance. I remember one conversation with Gabbard about Rudd, but it was the combined wisdom back then that politics would not mix with the litigation. We were pretty confident. How wrong we were."

They ate for a few minutes, but neither seemed thrilled with the food.

"Our boy's name is Ron Fisk," Barry said as he handed over a large manila envelope. "Here are the basics. Some photos, a background check, no more than eight pages, at your request."

"Fisk?"

"That's him."

———

Brianna's mother was in the area, her twice-yearly drop-in, and for such visits Carl insisted that they use the mansion in the Hamptons and leave him alone in the city. Her mother was two years younger than Carl and fancied herself attractive enough to catch his eye. He spent less than an hour a year in her presence, and each time caught himself practically praying that Brianna had a different set of genes. He loathed the woman. The mother of a trophy wife is not automatically a trophy mother-in-law, and she is usually much too enamored with the topic of money. Carl had loathed each of his mothers-in-law. He detested the very notion that he had a mother-in-law in the first place.

So they were gone. The Fifth Avenue penthouse was all his. Brianna had loaded up Sadler MacGregor, the Russian nanny, her assistant, her nutritionist, and a maid or two and headed out in a small caravan to the island, where she could invade their fine home up there and abuse the staff.

Carl stepped from his private elevator, came face-to-face with

Abused Imelda, cursed at the sight of her, ignored his valet, dismissed the rest of the staff, and when he was finally alone in the wonderful privacy of his bedroom, he put on his pajamas, a bathrobe, and heavy wool socks. He found a cigar, poured a single malt, and stepped out onto the small terrace overlooking Fifth Avenue and Central Park. The air was raw and windy, perfect.

Rinehart had cautioned him against fretting the details of the campaign. "You don't want to know everything," he said more than once. "Trust me. This is my profession, and I'm very good at what I do."

But Rinehart had never lost a billion dollars. According to one newspaper article, about Carl no less, only six other men had ever lost a billion dollars in one day. Barry would never know the humiliation of falling so fast and so hard in this city. Friends become harder to find. Carl's jokes were not funny. Certain portions of the social circuit seemed to be closed (though he knew this was ever so temporary). Even his wife seemed a bit colder and less fawning. Not to mention the cold shoulders from those who really mattered—the bankers, fund managers, investment gurus, the elite of Wall Street.

As the wind reddened his cheeks, he looked slowly around at the buildings up and down Fifth Avenue. Billionaires everywhere. Did anyone feel sorry for him, or were they delighted at his fall? He knew the answer because he had taken so much delight when others had stumbled.

Keep laughing, boys, he said with a long pull on the malt. Laugh your asses off, because I, Carl Trudeau, now have a new secret weapon. His name is Ron Fisk, a nice, gullible young man purchased (offshore) by me for chump change.

Three blocks to the north, at the top of a building Carl could barely see, was the penthouse of Pete Flint, one of his many enemies. Two weeks earlier, Pete had made the cover of *Hedge Fund Reports*, dressed in an ill-fitting designer suit. He was obviously gaining weight. The story raved about Pete and his fund and, in particular, a spectacular final quarter last year, thanks almost solely to his shrewd shorting of Krane Chemical. Pete claimed to have made a half-billion dollars on Krane because of his brilliant prediction that the trial would end badly. Carl's name

wasn't mentioned; it wasn't necessary. It was common knowledge that he'd lost a billion, and there was Pete Flint claiming to have raked in half of it. The humiliation was beyond painful.

Mr. Flint knew nothing about Mr. Fisk. By the time he heard his name, it would be too late and Carl would have his money back. Plus a lot more.

CHAPTER 15

The winter meeting of the Mississippi Trial Advocates (MTA) was held each year in Jackson, in early February while the legislature was still in session. It was usually a weekend affair with speeches, seminars, political updates, and the like. Because the Paytons currently had the hottest verdict in the state, the trial lawyers wanted to hear from them. Mary Grace demurred. She was an active member, but it wasn't her scene. The gatherings typically included long cocktail hours and war stories from the trenches. Girls were not excluded, but they didn't exactly fit in, either. And someone needed to stay home with Mack and Liza.

Wes reluctantly volunteered. He, too, was an active member, but the winter meetings were usually boring. The summer conventions at the beach were more fun and family oriented, and the Payton clan had attended two of them.

Wes drove to Jackson on a Saturday morning and found the mini-convention at a downtown hotel. He parked far away so none of his fellow trial lawyers would see what he was driving these days. They were noted for their flashy cars and other toys, and Wes, at the moment, was embarrassed by the ragged Taurus that had survived the trip from Hat-

tiesburg. He would not spend the night, because he could not afford a hundred bucks for a room. It could be argued that he was a millionaire, in someone's calculation, but three months after the verdict he was still squeezing every dime. Any payday from the Bowmore mess was a distant dream. Even with the verdict, he still questioned his sanity in getting involved with the litigation.

Lunch was in the grand ballroom with seating for two hundred, an impressive crowd. As the preliminaries dragged on, Wes, from his seat on the dais, studied the crowd.

Trial lawyers, always a colorful and eclectic bunch. Cowboys, rogues, radicals, longhairs, corporate suits, flamboyant mavericks, bikers, deacons, good ole boys, street hustlers, pure ambulance chasers, faces from billboards and yellow pages and early morning television. They were anything but boring. They fought among themselves like a violent family, yet they had the ability to stop bickering, circle the wagons, and attack their enemies. They came from the cities, where they feuded over cases and clients, and they came from the small towns, where they honed their skills before simple jurors reluctant to part with anyone's money. Some had jets and buzzed around the country piecing together the latest class action in the latest mass tort. Others were repulsed by the mass tort game and clung proudly to the tradition of trying legitimate cases one at a time. The new breed were entrepreneurs who filed cases in bulk and settled them that way, rarely facing a jury. Others lived for the thrill of the courtroom. A few did their work in firms where they pooled money and talent, but firms of trial lawyers were notoriously difficult to keep together. Most were lone gunmen too eccentric to keep much of a staff. Some made millions each year, others scraped by, most were in the $250,000 range. A few were broke at the moment. Many were up one year and down the next, always on the roller coaster and always willing to roll the dice.

If they shared anything, it was a streak of fierce independence and the thrill of representing David against Goliath.

On the political right, there is the establishment, the money, and big business and the myriad groups it finances. On the left, there are the mi-

norities, labor unions, schoolteachers, and the trial lawyers. Only the trial
lawyers have money, and it's pocket change compared with big business.

Though there were times when Wes wanted to choke them as a
whole, he felt at home here. These were his colleagues, his fellow war-
riors, and he admired them. They could be arrogant, bullish, dogmatic,
and they were often their own worst enemies. But no one fought as hard
for the little guy.

As they lunched on cold chicken and even colder broccoli, the
chairman of the legislative affairs committee delivered a rather bleak up-
date on various bills that were still alive over at the capitol. The tort re-
formers were back and pushing hard to enact measures designed to
curtail liability and close courthouse doors. He was followed by the chair-
man of political affairs, who was more upbeat. Judicial elections were in
November, and though it was too early in the year to be sure, it appeared
as though their "good" judges at both the trial and the appellate levels
would not draw serious opposition.

After frozen pie and coffee, Wes Payton was introduced and re-
ceived a rousing welcome. He began by apologizing for the absence of
his co-counsel, the real brains behind the Bowmore litigation. She hated
to miss the event but believed she was needed more at home with the
kids. Wes then launched into a long recap of the *Baker* trial, the verdict,
and the current state of other lawsuits against Krane Chemical. Among
such a crowd, a $41 million verdict was a much-revered trophy, and they
could have listened for hours to the man who obtained it. Only a few had
felt firsthand the thrill of such a victory, and all of them had swallowed
the bitter pill of a bad verdict.

When he finished, there was another round of boisterous applause,
then an impromptu question-and-answer session. Which experts had
been effective? How much were the litigation expenses? (Wes politely re-
fused to give the amount. Even in a room of big spenders, the sum was
too painful to discuss.) What was the status of settlement talks, if any?
How would the class action affect the defendant? What about the appeal?
Wes could have talked for hours and kept his audience.

Later that afternoon, during an early cocktail hour, he held court

again, answering more questions, deflecting more gossip. A group that was circling a toxic dump in the northern part of the state descended on him and wheedled advice. Would he take a look at their file? Recommend some experts? Come visit the site? He finally escaped by going to the bar, and there he bumped into Barbara Mellinger, the savvy and battle-weary executive director of the MTA and its chief lobbyist.

"Got a minute?" she asked, and they retreated to a corner where no one could hear them.

"I've picked up a frightening rumor," she said, sipping gin and watching the crowd. Mellinger had spent twenty years in the halls of the capitol and could read the terrain like no other. And she was not prone to gossip. She heard more than anyone, but when she passed along a rumor, it was usually more than just that.

"They're coming after McCarthy," she said.

"They?" Wes was standing next to her, also watching the crowd.

"The usual suspects—Commerce Council and that group of thugs."

"They can't beat McCarthy."

"Well, they can certainly try."

"Does she know it?" Wes had lost interest in his diet soda.

"I don't think so. No one knows it."

"Do they have a candidate?"

"If they do, I don't know who it is. But they have a knack for finding people to run."

What, exactly, was Wes supposed to say or do? Campaign funding was the only defense, and he couldn't contribute a dime.

"Do these guys know?" he asked, nodding at the little pockets of conversation.

"Not yet. We're lying low right now, waiting. McCarthy, typically, has no money in the bank. The Supremes think they're invincible, above politics and all that, and by the time an opponent pops up, they've been lulled to sleep."

"You got a plan?"

"No. It's wait and see for now. And pray that it's only a rumor. Two

years ago, in the McElwayne race, they waited until the last minute to an-
nounce, and by then they had a million plus in the bank."

"But we won that race."

"Indeed. But tell me you were not terrified."

"Beyond terrified."

An aging hippie with a ponytail lurched forward and boomed,
"Y'all kicked their asses down there." His opening gave every impression
that he would consume at least the next half hour of Wes's life. Barbara
began her escape. "To be continued," she whispered.

———

Driving home, Wes savored the occasion for a few miles, then slipped
into a dark funk over the McCarthy rumor. He kept nothing from Mary
Grace, and after dinner that night they slipped out of the apartment and
went for a long walk. Ramona and the children were watching an old
movie.

Like all good lawyers, they had always watched the supreme court
carefully. They read and discussed every opinion, a habit they started
when their partnership began and one they clung to with conviction. In
the old days, membership on the court changed little. Openings were cre-
ated by deaths, and the temporary appointments usually became perma-
nent. Over the years, the governors had wisely chosen the fill-ins, and the
court was respected. Noisy campaigns were unheard-of. The court took
pride in keeping politics out of its agenda and rulings. But the genteel
days were changing.

"But we beat them with McElwayne," she said more than once.

"By three thousand votes."

"It's a win."

Two years earlier, when Justice Jimmy McElwayne got himself am-
bushed, the Paytons had been too mired in the Bowmore litigation to
contribute financially. Instead, they had devoted what little spare time
they had to a local committee. They had even worked the polls on Elec-
tion Day.

"We've won the trial, Wes, and we're not losing the appeal," she said.

"Agreed."

"It's probably just a rumor."

The following Monday afternoon, Ron and Doreen Fisk sneaked away from Brookhaven and drove to Jackson for a late meeting with Tony Zachary. There were some people they needed to meet.

It had been agreed that Tony would serve as the official director of the campaign. The first person he brought into the conference room was the proposed director of finance, a sharply dressed young man with a long history of statewide campaigns, in a dozen states no less. His name was Vancona, and he quickly, and confidently, laid out the basic structure of their financial plan. He used a laptop and a projector and everything was flashed against a white screen, in vivid color. On the income side, the coalition of supporters would contribute $2.5 million. Many of these were the folks Ron had met in Washington, and for good measure Vancona presented a long list of groups. The names were a blur, but the sheer number was impressive. They could expect another $500,000 from individual donors around the district, moneys that would be generated when Ron hit the stump and began to win friends and impress folks.

"I know how to raise the money," Vancona said more than once, but without being offensive. Three million dollars was the magic number, and it virtually guaranteed a win. Ron and Doreen were overwhelmed.

Tony watched them carefully. They weren't stupid. They were just as easily misled as anyone else would be under the circumstances. They asked a few questions, but only because they had to.

On the expense side, Vancona had all the numbers. Television, radio, and newspaper ads, direct mail, travel, salaries (his would be $90,000 for the venture), office rental, all the way down to bumper stickers, yard signs, billboards, and rental cars. His grand total was $2.8 million, which left some wiggle room.

Tony slid over two thick binders, each majestically labeled: "SU-PREME COURT, SOUTHERN DISTRICT, RON FISK VERSUS SHEILA MCCARTHY. CONFIDENTIAL."

"It's all in there," he said.

Ron flipped some pages, asked a few benign questions.

Tony nodded gravely as if his boy had genuine insight.

The next visitor—Vancona stayed in the room, a member of the team now—was a saucy sixty-year-old woman from D.C. whose specialty was advertising. She introduced herself as Kat something or other. Ron had to glance at his notebook to confirm—Broussard. Next to her name was her title: Director of Advertising.

Where had Tony found all these people?

Kat was filled with big-city hyperactivity. Her firm specialized in state races and had worked in over a hundred.

What's your winning percentage? Ron wanted to ask, but Kat left few openings for questions. She adored his face and voice and felt confident they would put together the "visuals" that would adequately convey his depth and sincerity. Wisely, she spent most of her time looking at Doreen as she talked, and the girls connected. Kat took a seat.

Communications would be handled by a Jackson firm. Its boss was another fast-talking lady named Candace Grume, and, not surprisingly, she had vast experience in these matters. She explained that a successful campaign must coordinate in communications at all times. "Loose lips sink ships," she chirped. "They also lose elections." The current governor was a client, and she saved the best for last. Her firm had represented Senator Rudd for over a decade. Enough said.

She yielded the floor to the pollster, a brainy statistician named Tedford who managed to claim, in less than five minutes, that he had correctly predicted the outcome of virtually every race in recent history. He was from Atlanta. If you're from the big city of Atlanta and you find yourself in the outback, then it's important to remind everyone there that you are indeed from Atlanta. After twenty minutes they were tired of Tedford.

The field coordinator was not from Atlanta but from Jackson. His

name was Hobbs, and Hobbs looked vaguely familiar, at least to Ron. He boasted that he had been running successful campaigns in the state— sometimes out front, sometimes in the background—for fifteen years. He threw out the names of his winners without a thought of mentioning his losers. He preached about the necessity of local organization, grassroots democracy, knocking on doors, turning out the vote, and so on. He had an oily voice, and at times his eyes glowed with the fervor of a street preacher. Ron disliked him immediately. Later, Doreen would admit she found him charming.

Two hours after the parade began, Doreen was almost catatonic, and Ron's notepad was bristling with the drivel he wrote in an effort to remain engaged.

The team was now complete. Five well-paid professionals. Six including Tony, but his salary would be covered by Judicial Vision. Ron, poring through his notebook while Hobbs was ranting, found the column that projected "professional salaries" at $200,000 and "consultants" at $175,000. He made a note to quiz Tony about these amounts later. They seemed much too high, but then what did he know about the ins and outs of a high-powered campaign?

They broke for coffee, and Tony herded the others out of the room. They left with warm farewells, excitement about the thrilling race ahead, and promises to meet again as soon as possible.

When Tony was alone again with his clients, he suddenly looked tired. "Look, I know this is a lot. Forgive me, but everybody is busy and time is crucial. I thought one big meeting would work better than a bunch of smaller ones."

"No problem," Ron managed to say. The coffee was working.

"Remember, this is your campaign," Tony continued, straight-faced.

"Are you sure about that?" Doreen asked. "Doesn't really feel like it."

"Oh yes, Doreen. I've assembled the best team available, but you can cut any one of them right now. Just say the word, and I'll be on the phone finding a replacement. Someone you don't like?"

"No, it's just that—"

"It's overwhelming," Ron admitted. "That's all."

"Of course it is. It's a major campaign."

"Major campaigns don't have to be overwhelming. I realize I'm a novice here, but I'm not naive. Two years ago in the McElwayne race, the challenger raised and spent about two million dollars and ran a great race. Now we're tossing around numbers that are far more than that. Where is the money coming from?"

Tony snapped on his reading glasses and reached for a binder. "Well, I thought we covered that," he said. "Vancona went over the numbers."

"I can read, Tony," Ron shot across the table. "I see the names and amounts. That's not the question. I want to know why these people are willing to pony up three million bucks to support someone they've never heard of."

Tony slowly peeled off his reading glasses with an air of exasperation. "Ron, haven't we covered this a dozen times? Last year, Judicial Vision spent almost four million to elect a guy in Illinois. We spent close to six million in Texas. These numbers are outrageous, but winning has become very expensive. Who's writing the checks? The folks you met in Washington. The economic development movement. The conservative Christians. Doctors who are being abused by the system. These are people who are demanding change, and they are willing to pay for it."

Ron drank some more coffee and looked at Doreen. A long, silent moment passed.

Tony re-shifted, cleared his throat, and said softly, "Look, if you want out, then just say the word. It's not too late."

"I'm not quitting, Tony," Ron said. "But this is too much for one day. All these professional consultants and—"

"I'll handle these people. That's my job. Yours is to hit the stump and convince the voters you're the man. The voters, Ron and Doreen, will never see these people. They will never see me, thank God. You are the candidate. It's your face, your ideas, your youth and enthusiasm that will convince them. Not me. Not a bunch of staff members."

Fatigue overcame them and the conversation lagged. Ron and

Doreen gathered up the bulky notebooks and said their goodbyes. The drive home was quiet, but not unpleasant. By the time they drove through an empty downtown Brookhaven, they were once again excited by the challenge.

The Honorable Ronald M. Fisk, Justice, Mississippi Supreme Court.

CHAPTER 16

Justice McCarthy eased into her office late Saturday morning and found it deserted. She flipped through her mail as she turned on her computer. Online, at her official e-mail address, there was the usual court business. At her personal address, there was a note from her daughter confirming dinner that night at her home in Biloxi. There were notes from two men, one she'd been dating and one who was still a possibility.

She wore jeans, sneakers, and a brown tweed riding jacket her ex-husband gave her many years ago. There was no weekend dress code at the supreme court because only the clerks showed up.

Her chief clerk, Paul, materialized without a sound and said, "Good morning."

"What are you doing here?" she asked.

"The usual. Reading briefs."

"Anything of interest?"

"No." He tossed a magazine on her desk and said, "This one is on the way. Could be fun."

"What is it?"

"The big verdict from Cancer County. Forty-one million dollars. Bowmore."

"Oh yes," she said, picking up the magazine. Every lawyer and judge in the state claimed to know someone who knew something about the *Baker* verdict. The coverage had been extensive, during the trial and especially afterward. It was often discussed by Paul and the other clerks. They were already watching it, anticipating the arrival in a few months of the appellate briefs.

The article covered all aspects of the Bowmore waste site and the litigation it created. There were photos of the town, desolate and boarded up; photos of Mary Grace peering at the razor wire outside the Krane plant and sitting with Jeannette Baker under a shade tree, each holding a bottle of water; photos of twenty of the alleged victims— blacks, whites, kids, and old folks. The central character, though, was Mary Grace, and her importance grew as the paragraphs flew by. It was her case, her cause. Bowmore was her town and her friends were dying.

Sheila finished the article and was suddenly bored with the office. The drive to Biloxi would take three hours. She left without seeing another person and headed south, in no particular hurry. She stopped for gas in Hattiesburg and, on a whim, turned east, suddenly curious about Cancer County.

———

When she presided over trials, Judge McCarthy often sneaked to the scene of the dispute for a furtive firsthand look at the site. The murky details of a tanker collision on a busy bridge became much clearer after she spent an hour on the bridge, alone, at night, at the precise moment of the accident. In a murder case, the defendant's claim of self-defense was discounted by her after she ventured into the alleyway where the body was found. A light from a warehouse window glared down, illuminating the spot. During the trial of a wrongful death at a railroad crossing, she drove the street night and day, twice stopping for trains, and became convinced the driver was at fault. She kept these opinions to herself, of course. The

jury was the trier of fact, not the judge, but a strange curiosity often attracted her to the scene. She wanted to know the truth.

Bowmore was as bleak as the article said. She parked behind a church two blocks from Main Street and took a walk. It was unlikely that she would see another red BMW convertible in the town, and the last thing she wanted was attention.

Even for a Saturday, traffic and commerce were slow. Half the storefronts were boarded up, and only a few of the survivors were open. A pharmacy, a discount store, a few other retail merchants. She paused at the office of F. Clyde Hardin & Associates. He was mentioned in the article.

As was Babe's Coffee Shop, where Sheila took a stool at the counter in anticipation of learning something about the case. She would not be disappointed.

It was almost 2:00 p.m. and no one else was at the counter. Two mechanics from the Chevrolet place were having a late lunch in a front booth. The diner was quiet, dusty, in need of paint and refinished floors, and apparently hadn't changed much in decades. The walls were covered with football schedules dating back to 1961, class pictures, old newspaper articles, anything anybody wanted to display. A large sign announced: "We Use Only Bottled Water."

Babe appeared across the counter and began with a friendly "What would you like, dear?" She wore a starched white uniform, spotless burgundy apron with "Babe" embroidered in pink, white hose, and white shoes, and could have stepped from a 1950s movie. She had probably been around that long, though her teased hair was still aggressively colored. It almost matched her apron. She had the wrinkled eyes of a smoker, but the wrinkles were no match for the thick layer of foundation Babe caulked on every morning.

"Just some water," Sheila said. She was curious about the water.

Babe performed most of her tasks while gazing forlornly at the street through the large windows. She grabbed a bottle and said, "You're not from around here."

"Just passing through," Sheila said. "I have some kinfolks over in

Jones County." And it was true. A distant aunt, one she thought might still be alive, had always lived next door in Jones County.

In front of her, Babe placed a six-ounce bottle of water with the simple label "Bottled for Bowmore." She explained that she, too, had kin-folks in Jones County. Before they went too far down the genealogical road, Sheila hastily changed subjects. In Mississippi, sooner or later, everyone is related.

"What's this?" she asked, holding the bottle.

"Water," Babe said with a puzzled look.

Sheila held it closer, allowing Babe to take charge of the conversation. "All our water here in Bowmore is bottled. Trucked in from Hatties-burg. Can't drink the stuff they pump here. It's contaminated. Where you from?"

"The Coast."

"You ain't heard about the Bowmore water?"

"Sorry." Sheila unscrewed the cap and took a swig. "Tastes like water," she said.

"You oughta taste the other stuff."

"What's wrong with it?"

"Good Lord, honey," Babe said and glanced around to see if anyone else had heard this shocking question. There was no one else, so Babe popped the top on a diet soda and sidled up the counter. "You ever heard of Cancer County?"

"No."

Another look of disbelief. "That's us. This county has the highest rate of cancer in the country because the drinking water is polluted. There used to be a chemical plant here, Krane Chemical, buncha smart boys from New York. For many years—twenty, thirty, forty, depending on who you believe—they dumped all kinds of toxic crap—pardon my lan-guage—into some ravines behind the plant. Barrels and barrels, drums and drums, tons and tons of the crap went into the pit, and it eventually filtered into an underground aquifer that the city—run by some real dunces, mind you—built a pump over back in the late eighties. The drinking water went from clear to light gray to light yellow. Now it's

brown. It began smelling funny, then it began stinking. We fought with the city for years to clean it up, but they stonewalled us. Boy, did they ever. Anyway, the water became a huge fight, and then, honey, the bad stuff started. Folks started dying. Cancer hit like the plague around here. Folks were dying right and left. Still are. Inez Perdue succumbed in January. I think she was number sixty-five. Something like that. It all came out in the trial." She paused to examine two pedestrians who were strolling along the sidewalk.

Sheila carefully sipped the water. "There was a trial?" she asked.

"You ain't heard of the trial either?"

Sheila gave an innocent shrug and said again, "I'm from the Coast."

"Oh, boy." Babe switched elbows and leaned on the right one. "For years there was talk about lawsuits. I get all the lawyers in here for their little coffee chats and no one taught those boys how to whisper. I heard it all. Still hearing it. Big talk for a long time. They're gonna sue Krane Chemical for this and for that, but nothing happened. I think that the suit was just too big, plus you're taking on a big chemical company with lots of money and lots of slick lawyers. The talk died down, but the cancer didn't. Kids were dying of leukemia. Folks with tumors in their kidneys, liver, bladder, stomach, and, honey, it's been awful. Krane made a fortune off a pesticide called pillamar 5, which was outlawed twenty years ago. Outlawed here, but not down in Guatemala and places like that. So they kept making pillamar 5 here, shipping it off to the banana republics, where they sprayed it on their fruits and vegetables and then shipped 'em all back here for us to eat. That came out in the trial, too, and they tell me it really ticked off the jury. Something sure ticked 'em off."

"Where was the trial?"

"You sure you don't have any kinfolks here?"

"I'm sure."

"Any friends here in Bowmore?"

"None."

"And you ain't no reporter, are you?"

"Nope. I'm just passing through."

Satisfied with her audience, Babe took a deep breath and plunged on. "They moved it out of Bowmore, which was a smart move because any jury here would've handed down a death penalty for Krane and the crooks who run it, and they tried the case over in Hattiesburg. Judge Harrison, one of my favorites. Cary County is in his district, and he's been eating here for many years. He likes the ladies, but that's okay. I like the men. Anyway, for a long time the lawyers just talked, but no one would dare take on Krane. Then a local girl, a young woman, mind you, one of our own, said to hell with it and filed a massive suit. Mary Grace Payton, grew up a mile out of town. Bowmore High School class valedictorian. I remember when she was a kid. Her daddy, Mr. Truman Shelby, still comes in from time to time. I love that girl. Her husband is a lawyer, too, they practice together in Hattiesburg. They sued for Jeannette Baker, sweet girl, whose husband and little boy died of cancer eight months apart. Krane fought like hell, had a hundred lawyers, according to the traffic. The trial lasted for months and damned near broke the Paytons, from what I hear. But they won. Jury threw the book at Krane. Forty-one million dollars. I can't believe you missed it. How could anyone miss it? It put Bowmore on the map. You want something to eat, honey?"

"How about a grilled cheese?"

"You got it." Babe threw two pieces of white bread on the grill without missing a beat. "Case is on appeal, and I pray every night that the Paytons'll win. And the lawyers are back, sniffing around, looking for new victims. Ever hear of Clyde Hardin?"

"Never met him."

"He's seven doors down, on the left, been here forever. A member of my eight-thirty coffee club, a bunch of blowhards. He's okay, but his wife's a snot. Clyde is afraid of the courtroom, so he hooked up with some real shysters from Philadelphia—Pennsylvania, not Mississippi— and they've filed a class action on behalf of a bunch of deadbeats who are trying to join the parade. Rumor has it that some of their so-called clients don't even live here. They're just looking for a check." She unwrapped two slices of processed cheddar and placed them on the hot bread. "Mayonnaise?"

"No."

"How about some fries?"

"No thanks."

"Anyway, the town's split worse than ever. The folks who are really sick are angry at these new victims who are just claiming to be. Funny what money does to some folks. Always looking for a handout. Some of the lawyers think Krane'll finally give in and make a big settlement. Folks'll get rich. Lawyers'll get even richer. But others are convinced Krane will never admit any wrongdoing. They never have. Six years ago, when the lawsuit talk was hot, they simply folded up one weekend and fled to Mexico, where I'm sure they're free to dump and pollute all they want to. Probably killing Mexicans right and left. It's criminal what that company did. It killed this town."

When the bread was almost black, she put the sandwich together, sliced it in two, and served it with a slice of dill pickle.

"What happened to the Krane employees?"

"Got screwed. No surprises there. A lot of them left the area to find work. Ain't much in the way of jobs around here. Some were nice folks, others knew what was happening and kept quiet. If they squealed, they'd get fired. Mary Grace found some of them and hauled them back for the trial. Some told the truth. Some lied, and Mary Grace ripped them to pieces, according to what I hear. I never watched the trial, but I got reports almost daily. The whole town was on pins and needles. There was a man named Earl Crouch who ran the plant for many years. Made good money, and rumor has it that Krane bought him off when they tucked tail. Crouch knew all about the dumping, but during his deposition he denied everything. Lied like a dog. That was two years ago. They say that Crouch has disappeared under mysterious circumstances. Mary Grace couldn't find him to come testify at trial. He's gone. AWOL. Not even Krane could find him."

She let this rich little nugget hang in the air for a moment as she sauntered over to check on the Chevrolet mechanics. Sheila chewed on the first bite of the sandwich and pretended to have little interest in the story.

"How's the grilled cheese?" Babe asked when she was back.

"Great." Sheila took a sip of water and waited for the narrative to continue. Babe leaned in closer and lowered her voice.

"There's a family over in Pine Grove, the Stones. Tough bunch. In and out of prison for stealing cars and such. Not the kinda folks you'd want to start a fight with. Four, maybe five years ago, one of the little Stone boys caught cancer and died quick. They hired the Paytons and their suit is still pending. What I hear is that the Stones found Mr. Earl Crouch somewhere out in Texas and got their revenge. Just a rumor, and folks here ain't talking about it. Wouldn't surprise me, though. Nobody messes with the Stones. Feelings are raw, very raw. You mention Krane Chemical around here people want to fight."

Sheila wasn't about to mention it. Nor was she about to pry much deeper. The mechanics stood, stretched, went for the toothpicks, and headed for the cash register. Babe met them there and insulted them as she took their money, about $4 each. Why were they working on a Saturday? What did their boss think he was accomplishing? Sheila managed to choke down half the sandwich.

"You want another one?" Babe asked when she returned to her stool.

"No thanks. I need to be going." Two teenagers ambled in and settled at a table.

Sheila paid her bill, thanked Babe for the conversation, promised to stop in again. She walked to her car, then spent half an hour crisscrossing the town. The magazine article mentioned Pine Grove and Pastor Denny Ott. She drove slowly through the neighborhood around the church and was struck by its depressed state. The article had been kind. She found the abandoned industrial park, then the Krane plant, gloomy and haunted but protected behind the razor wire.

After two hours in Bowmore, Sheila left, hopefully never to return. She understood the anger that led to the verdict, but judicial reasoning must exclude all emotions. There was little doubt Krane Chemical had done bad things, but the issue was whether their waste actually caused the cancers. The jury certainly thought so.

It would soon be the job of Justice McCarthy and her eight colleagues to settle the matter.

————

They tracked her movements to the Coast, to her home three blocks off the Bay of Biloxi. She was there for sixty-five minutes, then drove a mile to her daughter's home on Howard Street. After a long dinner with her daughter, son-in-law, and two small grandchildren, she returned to her home and spent the night, apparently alone. At ten on Sunday morning, she had brunch at the Grand Casino with a female acquaintance. A quick check of license plates revealed this person to be a well-known local divorce lawyer, probably an old friend. After brunch, McCarthy returned to her home, changed into blue jeans, and left with her overnight bag. She drove nonstop to her condo in north Jackson, arriving at 4:10. Three hours later, a man by the name of Keith Christian (white male, age forty-four, divorced, history professor) showed up with what appeared to be a generous supply of take-out Chinese food. He did not leave the McCarthy condo until seven the following morning.

Tony Zachary summarized these reports himself, pecking away at a laptop he still despised. He'd been a terrible typist long before the Internet, and his skills had improved only marginally. But the details could be trusted to no one—no assistant, no secretary. The matter demanded the utmost secrecy. Nor could his summaries be e-mailed or faxed. Mr. Rinehart insisted that they be sent by overnight letter via Federal Express.

PART TWO

THE
CAMPAIGN

CHAPTER 17

In the old town of Natchez there is a slice of land below a bluff, near the river, known as Under-the-Hill. It has a long and colorful history that begins with the earliest days of steamboat traffic on the Mississippi. It attracted all the characters—the merchants, traders, boat captains, speculators, and gamblers—headed to New Orleans. Because money was changing hands, it also attracted ruffians, vagabonds, swindlers, bootleggers, gunrunners, whores, and every imaginable misfit from the underworld. Natchez was rich with cotton, most of which was shipped and traded through its port, Under-the-Hill. Easy money created the need for bars, gambling dens, brothels, and flophouses. A young Mark Twain was a regular during his days as a steamboat pilot. Then the Civil War killed river traffic. It also wiped out the fortunes in Natchez, and most of its nightlife. Under-the-Hill suffered a long period of decline.

In 1990, the Mississippi legislature approved a bill that allowed riverboat gambling, the idea being that a handful of fake paddle wheelers would churn up and down the river while their cargo of retirees played bingo and blackjack. Along the Mississippi River, businessmen rushed to establish these floating casinos. Remarkably, once the legislation was ac-

tually read and analyzed, it was discovered that the boats would not be required to physically leave the shore. Nor were they required to be equipped with any type of engine to propel them. As long as they touched the river, or any of its chutes, sloughs, oxbow lakes, man-made canals, or backwaters, the structures qualified as riverboats under the legislation. Under-the-Hill made a brief comeback.

Unfortunately, upon further analysis, the legislation accidentally approved full-fledged Vegas-style casino gambling, and within a few years this roaring new industry had settled itself along the Gulf Coast and in Tunica County, near Memphis. Natchez and the other river towns missed the boom, but did manage to hang on to a few of their engineless, stationary casinos.

One such establishment was the Lucky Jack. There, at his favorite blackjack table with his favorite dealer, Clete Coley sat hunched over a stack of $25 chips and sipped a rum and soda. He was up $1,800 and it was time to quit. He watched the door, waiting on his appointment.

Coley was a member of the bar. He had a degree, a license, a name in the yellow pages, an office with the word "Attorney" on the door, a secretary who answered the occasional phone call with an unenthusiastic "Law Office," and business cards with all the necessary data. But Clete Coley wasn't a real lawyer. He had few clients to speak of. He wouldn't draft a will, or a deed, or a contract, at gunpoint. He didn't hang around the courthouse, and he disliked most of the other lawyers in Natchez. Clete was simply a rogue, a big, loud, hard-drinking rogue of a lawyer who made more money at the casinos than he did at the office. He'd once dabbled in politics, and barely missed an indictment. He'd dabbled in government contracts, and dodged another one. In his early years, after college, he'd done some pot smuggling, but abruptly abandoned that career when a partner was found dead. In fact, his conversion was so complete that he became an undercover narcotics officer. He went to law school at night and finally passed the bar exam on his fourth attempt.

He doubled-down on an eight and a three, drew a jack, and collected another $100. His favorite cocktail waitress brought him another drink. No one spent as much time in the Lucky Jack as Mr. Coley. Anything for Mr. Coley. He watched the door, checked his watch, and kept gambling.

"You expecting someone?" asked Ivan, the dealer.

"Would I tell you?"

"Reckon not."

The man he was expecting had also escaped a few indictments. They went back almost twenty years, though they were anything but friends. This would be their second meeting. The first had gone well enough to lead to this one.

Ivan was showing fourteen when he drew a queen and went bust. Another $100 for Clete. He had his rules. When he won $2,000 he quit, and when he lost $500 he quit. Anything between those limits and he would play and drink all night. The IRS would never know it, but he was up eighty grand for the year. Plus, all the rum was free.

He flipped two chips to Ivan and began the elaborate task of freeing his massive body from the elevated chair.

"Thanks, Mr. Coley," Ivan said.

"Always a pleasure." Clete stuffed the rest of the chips into the pockets of his light brown suit. Always brown, always a suit, always with shiny Lucchese cowboy boots. At six feet four, he weighed at least 280, though no one knew for sure, but he was more thick than fat. He lumbered away toward the bar, where his appointment had arrived. Marlin was taking a seat at a corner table, one with a view of the floor. No greetings of any sort, no eye contact. Clete dropped into a chair and pulled out a pack of cigarettes. A waitress brought them drinks.

"I have the money," Marlin said, finally.

"How much?"

"Same deal, Clete. Nothing's changed. We're just waiting on you to say yes or no."

"And I'll ask you again. Who is 'we'?"

"It's not me. I'm an independent contractor, paid a fee for a job well done. I'm on no one's payroll. I've been hired to recruit you for the race, and if you say no, then I might be hired to recruit someone else."

"Who's paying you?"

"That's confidential, Clete. I explained this a dozen times last week."

"You did. Maybe I'm a little dense. Or maybe I'm just a little nervous. Perhaps I want answers. Otherwise, I'm not in."

Based on their first meeting, Marlin was doubtful that Clete Coley would eventually say no to $100,000 in cash in unmarked bills. Marlin had virtually put it on the table. A hundred grand to get in the race and stir things up. Coley would make a beautiful candidate—loud, outrageous, colorful, able to say anything with no concern about the fallout. An anti-politician the press would follow like ants.

"Here's what I can tell you," Marlin said, with a rare eyeball-to-eyeball glance at Clete. "Fifteen years ago, in a county far away from here, a young man and his young family returned home from church one night. They didn't know it, but two black punks were in the house, a very nice house, and they were burglarizing the hell out of it. The punks were hopped up on crack, pistols in every pocket, nasty characters. When the young family came home and surprised them, things got out of control. The girls got raped. Everybody got a bullet in the head, then the punks set the house on fire. Cops caught them the next day. Full confessions, DNA, the works. They've been on death row at Parchman ever since. Turns out the young man's family has serious money. His father had a nervous breakdown, went insane, poor guy. But he's back and he's pissed. He's furious that the punks are still alive. He's livid that his beloved state never executes anybody. He hates the judicial system, and he especially hates the nine honorable members of the supreme court. He, Clete, is where the money is coming from."

It was all a lie, but lying was a part of the job.

"I like that story," Clete said, nodding.

"The money is peanuts to him. It's yours if you jump in the race and talk about nothing but the death penalty. Hell, it's a natural. The

people here love the death penalty. We got polls that show almost 70 percent believe in it and more than that are upset because we don't use it enough in Mississippi. You can blame it on the supreme court. It's a perfect issue."

Clete was still nodding. For a week he'd thought of little else. It was indeed the perfect issue, and the court was the perfect target. A race would be a hell of a lot of fun.

"You mentioned a couple of groups," he said, slugging his double rum.

"There are several, but two in particular. One is Victims Watching, a tough bunch who've lost loved ones and been chewed up by the system. They don't have a lot of members, but they are committed. Between me and you, Mr. X is also secretly funding this group. The other is the Law Enforcement Coalition, a very legitimate law-and-order group with some clout. Both of these will jump on board."

Clete was nodding, grinning, watching a cocktail waitress glide by with a tray loaded with drinks. "Such balance," he said, just loud enough to be heard.

"I really have nothing else to add," Marlin said without pushing.

"Where's the money?"

Marlin took a deep breath and couldn't conceal a smile. "In the trunk of my car. Half of it, fifty grand. Take that now, and the day you officially announce, you get the other fifty."

"Fair enough."

They shook hands, then both grabbed their drinks. Marlin pulled keys out of a pocket. "My car is a green Mustang with a black top, on your left when you leave. Take the keys, take the car, take the money, I don't want to see it. I'll sit here and play blackjack until you return."

Clete grabbed the keys, struggled to his feet, then strutted across the casino floor and out the door.

———

Marlin waited for fifteen minutes, then called the cell phone of Tony Zachary. "Looks like we've hooked us one," he said.

"He took the money?" Tony asked.

"The deal is going down now, but, yes, you'll never see that money again. I suspect that the Lucky Jack will get its share, but, regardless, he's in."

"Excellent."

"This guy is going to be a scream, you know? The cameras will love him."

"Let's hope so. I'll see you tomorrow."

Marlin found a spot at a $5 table and managed to lose a hundred bucks in half an hour.

Clete was back, grinning, the happiest man in Natchez. Marlin was certain that his trunk was now empty.

They returned to the bar and drank until midnight.

———

Two weeks later, Ron Fisk was leaving baseball practice when his cell phone rang. He was the head coach of his son Josh's Little League team, the Raiders, and the first game was a week away. Josh was in the backseat with two of his teammates, sweaty and dirty and very happy.

At first, Ron ignored the phone, then glanced at the caller ID. It was Tony Zachary. They talked at least twice a day. "Hello, Tony," he said.

"Ron, you got a minute?" Tony always asked this, as if he were willing to call back later. Ron had learned that Tony was never willing to call back later. Every call was urgent.

"Sure."

"A bit of a wrinkle, I'm afraid. Looks like the race might be more crowded than we thought. Are you there?"

"Yes."

"Just got it from a good source that some crackpot named Clete Coley, from Natchez, I believe, will announce tomorrow that he is running against Judge McCarthy."

Ron took a deep breath, then pulled onto the street next to the city's baseball complex. "Okay, I'm listening."

"Ever heard of him?"

"No." Ron knew several lawyers in Natchez, but not this one.

"Me neither. We're doing a background check now. The preliminary stuff is not too impressive. Sole practitioner, not much of a reputation, at least as a lawyer. Got his license suspended eight years ago for six months, something to do with neglecting clients. Two divorces. No bankruptcies. One DUI but no other criminal record. That's about all we know, but we're digging."

"Where does this fit?"

"Don't know. Let's wait and see. I'll call when I hear more."

Ron dropped off Josh's friends, then rushed home to tell Doreen. They fretted over dinner, then stayed up late tossing around scenarios.

———

At ten the following morning, Clete Coley wheeled to a stop at the edge of High Street, directly in front of the Carroll Gartin Justice Building. Two rented vans were behind him. All three vehicles were parked illegally, but then their drivers were looking for trouble. A half-dozen volunteers quickly spilled out of the vans and began carrying large posters up a few steps to the sweeping concrete terrace that surrounded the building. Another volunteer hauled up a makeshift podium.

A capitol policeman noticed this activity and strolled over to inquire.

"I'm announcing my candidacy for the supreme court," Clete explained at full volume. He was flanked by two beefy young men in dark suits, one white, one black, both almost as large as Clete himself.

"You got a permit?" the officer asked.

"Yep. Got it from the attorney general's office."

The cop disappeared, in no particular hurry. The display was put together rapidly, and when it was complete, it stood twenty feet high, thirty feet long, and was nothing but faces. High school graduation portraits, candid snapshots, family photos, all enlarged and in color. The faces of the dead.

As the volunteers scurried about, the reporters began arriving. Cameras were mounted on tripods. Microphones were mounted on the

podium. Photographers began snapping away, and Clete was ecstatic. More volunteers arrived, some with homemade posters with proclamations such as "Vote the Liberals Out," "Support the Death Penalty," and "Victims Have Voices."

The cop was back. "I can't seem to find anyone who knows anything about your permit," he said to Clete.

"Well, you found me, and I'm telling you that I have permission."

"From who?"

"One of those assistant attorney generals in there."

"You got a name?"

"Oswalt."

The cop left to go find Mr. Oswalt.

The commotion attracted the attention of those inside the building, and work came to a halt. Rumors flew, and when word reached the fourth floor that someone was about to announce a campaign for a seat on the court, three of its justices dropped everything and hustled to a window. The other six, those whose terms expired in later years, likewise ventured over out of curiosity.

Sheila McCarthy's office faced High Street, and it was soon filled with her clerks and staff, all suddenly alarmed. She whispered to Paul, "Why don't you go down there and see what's up?"

Others, from the court and from the attorney general's office, eased down, too, and Clete was thrilled with the mob that was quickly gathering in front of his podium. The cop returned with reinforcements, and just as Clete was about to give his speech, he was confronted by the officers. "Sir, we're gonna have to ask you to leave."

"Hang on, boys, I'll be through in ten minutes."

"No, sir. This is an illegal gathering. Disband it now, or else."

Clete stepped forward, chest to chest with the much smaller officer, and said, "Don't show your ass, okay? You got four television cameras watching everything. Just be cool, and I'll be outta here before you know it."

"Sorry."

With that, Clete strode to the podium, and a wall of volunteers

closed ranks behind him. He smiled at the cameras and said, "Good morning, and thanks for coming. My name is Clete Coley. I'm a lawyer from Natchez, and I'm announcing my candidacy for the supreme court. My opponent is Judge Sheila McCarthy, without a doubt the most liberal member of this criminal-coddling, do-nothing supreme court." The volunteers roared with approval. The reporters smiled at their good fortune. A few almost laughed.

Paul swallowed hard at this unbelievable volley. The man was loud, fearless, and colorful and was loving every second of the attention.

And he was just warming up. "Behind me you see the faces of one hundred and eighty-three people. Black, white, grandmothers, babies, educated, illiterate, from all over the state and from all walks of life. All innocent, all dead, all murdered. Their killers are, as we speak, preparing for lunch up at Parchman, on death row. All duly convicted by juries in this state, all properly sent to death row to be executed." He paused and grandly waved at the faces of the innocents.

"In Mississippi, we have sixty-eight men and two women on death row. They're safe there, because this state refuses to execute them. Other states do not. Other states are serious about following their laws. Since 1978, Texas has executed 334 killers. Virginia, 81; Oklahoma, 76; Florida, 55; North Carolina, 41; Georgia, 37; Alabama, 32; and Arkansas, 24. Even northern states like Missouri, Ohio, and Indiana. Hell, Delaware has executed 14 killers. Where is Mississippi? Currently in nineteenth place. We have executed only 8 killers, and that, my friends, is why I'm running for the supreme court."

The capitol police now numbered almost a dozen, but they seemed content to watch and listen. Riot control was not a specialty, and besides, the man was sounding pretty good.

"Why don't we execute?" Clete yelled at the crowd. "I'll tell you why. It's because our supreme court pampers these thugs and allows their appeals to drag on forever. Bobby Ray Root killed two people in cold blood during the robbery of a liquor store. Twenty-seven years ago. He's still on death row, getting three meals a day, seeing his mother once a month, with no execution date in sight. Willis Briley murdered his four-

year-old stepdaughter." He stopped and pointed to the photo of a little black girl at the top of the display. "That's her, cute little thing in the pink dress. She'd be thirty years old now. Her murderer, a man she trusted, has been on death row for twenty-four years. I could go on and on, but the point is well made. It's time to shake up this court and show all of those who have committed murder or who might do so that, in this state, we're serious about enforcing our laws."

He paused for another boisterous round of applause, one that obviously inspired him.

"Justice Sheila McCarthy has voted to reverse more murder convictions than any other member of the court. Her opinions are filled with legalistic nit-pickings that warm the soul of every criminal defense lawyer in the state. The ACLU loves her. Her opinions drip with sympathy for these murderers. They give hope to the thugs on death row. It is time, ladies and gentlemen, to take away her robe, her pen, her vote, her power to trample the rights of the victims."

Paul considered scribbling down some of this, but he was too petrified to move. He wasn't sure his boss voted so often in favor of capital defendants, but he was certain that virtually all of their convictions were affirmed. Regardless of shoddy police work, racism, malice by prosecutors, stacked juries, and boneheaded rulings by presiding judges, regardless of how horribly defective the trial was, the supreme court rarely reversed a conviction. Paul found it sickening. The split was usually 6–3, with Sheila leading a vocal but overmatched minority. Two of the justices had never voted to reverse a capital conviction. One had never voted to reverse a criminal conviction.

Paul knew that privately his boss was opposed to capital punishment, but she was also committed to upholding the laws of the state. A great deal of her time was spent on death cases, and he had never once seen her substitute her personal beliefs for a strict following of the law. If the trial record was clean, she did not hesitate to join the majority and affirm a conviction.

Clete did not yield to the temptation of speaking too long. He'd made his points. His announcement was a fabulous success. He lowered

his voice, grew more sincere, and finished by saying: "I urge all Mississippians who care about law and order, all who are sick of random, senseless crimes, to join with me in turning this court upside down. Thank you." More applause.

Two of the larger officers moved in close to the podium. The reporters began to throw questions. "Have you ever served as a judge? How much financial support do you have? Who are these volunteers? Do you have specific proposals to shorten the appeals?"

Clete was about to begin with his answers when an officer grabbed his arm and said, "That's it, sir. Party's over."

"Go to hell," Clete said as he yanked his arm away. The rest of the police contingent scurried forward, jostling through the volunteers, many of whom began yelling at them.

"Let's go, buddy," the officer said.

"Get lost." Then to the cameras he boomed, "Look at this. Soft on crime but to hell with the freedom of speech."

"You're under arrest."

"Arrest! You're arresting me because I'm making a speech." As he said this, he gently, and voluntarily, placed both hands behind his back.

"You don't have a permit, sir," one officer said as two more slapped on the handcuffs.

"Look at these supreme court guards, sent down from the fourth floor by the very people I'm running against."

"Let's go, sir."

As he moved from the podium, Clete kept yelling, "I won't be in jail long, and when I get out, I'll hit the streets telling the truth about these liberal bastards. You can count on that."

Sheila watched the spectacle from the safety of her window. Another clerk, standing near the reporters, relayed the news via cell phone.

That nut down there had chosen her.

———

Paul lingered until the display was removed and the crowd drifted away, then he raced up the steps to Sheila's office. She was at her desk, with the

other clerk and Justice McElwayne. The air was heavy, the mood somber. They looked at Paul as if he might by chance have some good news.

"This guy's crazy," he said. They nodded their agreement.

"He doesn't appear to be a pawn for big business," McElwayne said.

"I've never heard of him," Sheila said softly. She appeared to be in shock. "I guess an easy year just became very complicated."

The idea of starting a campaign from scratch was overwhelming.

"How much did your race cost?" Paul asked. He had just joined the court two years earlier, when Justice McElwayne was under assault.

"One point four million."

Sheila grunted and laughed. "I have $6,000 in my campaign account. It's been there for years."

"But I had a legitimate opponent," McElwayne added. "This guy is a nut."

"Nuts get elected."

———

Twenty minutes later, Tony Zachary watched the show in his locked office, four blocks away. Marlin had captured it all on video, and was more than pleased to see it again.

"We've created a monster," Tony said, laughing.

"He's good."

"Maybe too good."

"Anybody else you want in the race?"

"No, I think the ballot is complete at this point. Nice work."

Marlin left, and Tony punched the number for Ron Fisk. Not surprisingly, the busy lawyer answered after the first ring. "I'm afraid it's true," Tony said gravely, then recounted the announcement and the arrest.

"The guy must be crazy," Ron said.

"Definitely. My first impression is that this is not all bad. In fact, it could help us. This clown will generate a lot of coverage, and he seems perfectly willing to take a hatchet to McCarthy."

"Why do I have a knot in my stomach?"

"Politics is a rough game, Ron, something you're about to learn. I'm not worried, not right now. We stick to our game plan, nothing changes."

"It seems to me that a crowded field only helps the incumbent," Ron observed. And he was right, as a general rule.

"Not necessarily. There's no reason to panic. Besides, we can't do anything about others who jump in. Stay focused. Let's sleep on it and talk tomorrow."

CHAPTER 18

Clete Coley's colorful launch landed with perfect timing. There was not another interesting story throughout the entire state. The press seized Coley's announcement and beat it like a drum. And who could blame them? How often does the public get to see vivid footage of a lawyer getting handcuffed and dragged away while yelling about those "liberal bastards." And such a loud, large lawyer at that? His haunting display of dead faces was irresistible. His volunteers, especially the relatives of the victims, were more than happy to chat with the reporters and tell their stories. His gall in holding the rally directly under the noses of the supreme court was humorous, even admirable.

He was rushed downtown to central headquarters, and there he was booked, fingerprinted, and photographed. He assumed, correctly, that his mug shot would find its way to the press in short order, and so he had a few moments to think about its message. An angry scowl might confirm the suspicion that this guy was a bit off his rocker. A goofy smile might lead to questions about his sincerity—who smiles when he's just arrived at the jail? He settled on a simple blank face, with just a trace of a curious glare, as if to say, "Why are they picking on me?"

Procedures called for every inmate to strip, shower, and change into an orange jumpsuit, and this usually happened before the mug shot. But Clete would have none of it. The charge was simple trespass, with a maximum fine of $250. Bail was twice that, and Clete, his pockets bulging with $100 bills, flashed enough money around to let the authorities know he was on his way out of jail, not the other way around. So they skipped the shower and the jumpsuit, and Clete was photographed in his nicest brown suit, starched white shirt, paisley silk tie in a perfect knot. His long, graying hair was in place.

The process took less than an hour, and when he emerged a free man, he was thrilled to see that most of the reporters had followed him. On a city sidewalk, he answered their questions until they finally grew weary.

On the evening news, he was the lead story, with all the drama of the day. On the late night news, he was back. He watched it all on a wide-screen TV in a bikers' bar in south Jackson, where he was holed up for the night, buying drinks for everyone who could get in the door. His tab was over $1,400. A campaign expense.

The bikers loved him and promised to turn out in droves to get him elected. Of course, not a single one was a registered voter. When the bar closed, Clete was driven away in a bright red Cadillac Escalade, just leased by the campaign at a thousand dollars a month. Behind the wheel was one of his new bodyguards, the white one, a young man only slightly more sober than his boss. They made it to the motel without further arrest.

———

At the offices of the Mississippi Trial Advocates on State Street, Barbara Mellinger, executive director and chief lobbyist, met for an early round of coffee with her assistant, Skip Sanchez. For the first cup, they mulled over the morning newspapers. They had copies of four of the dailies from the southern district—Biloxi, Hattiesburg, Laurel, and Natchez—and Mr. Coley's face was on the front page of all four. The Jackson paper reported little else. The *Times-Picayune* out of New Orleans had a

readership along the Coast, and it ran an AP story, with photo (hand-cuffs) on page 4.

"Perhaps we should advise all our candidates to get themselves arrested when they do their announcements," Barbara said drily and with no attempt at humor. She hadn't smiled in twenty-four hours. She drained her first cup and went for more.

"Who the hell is Clete Coley?" Sanchez asked, staring at the various photos of the man. Jackson and Biloxi had the mug shot—the look of a man who would throw a punch and ask questions after it landed.

"I called Walter last night, down in Natchez," she was saying. "He says Coley has been around for years, always on the edge of something shady but smart enough not to get caught. He thinks that at one time he did oil and gas work. There was a bad deal with some small business loans. Now he fancies himself a gambler. Never been seen within six blocks of the courthouse. He's unknown."

"Not anymore."

Barbara got up and moved slowly around the office. She refilled the cups, then sat down and resumed her study of the newspapers.

"He's not a tort reformer," Skip said, though not without some doubt. "He doesn't fit their mold. He's got too much baggage for a hard campaign. There's at least one DUI, at least two divorces."

"I think I agree, but if he's never been involved before, then why is he suddenly screaming about the death penalty? Where does this conviction come from? This passion? Plus, his show yesterday was well organized. He's got people. Where do they come from?"

"Do we really care? Sheila McCarthy beats him two to one. We should be thrilled he is what he is—a buffoon who, we think, is not being financed by the Commerce Council and all the corporate boys. Why aren't we happy?"

"Because we're trial lawyers."

Skip turned gloomy again.

"Should we arrange a meeting with Judge McCarthy?" Barbara asked after a long, heavy pause.

"In a couple of days. Let the dust settle."

Judge McCarthy was up early, and why not? She certainly couldn't sleep. At 7:30 she was seen leaving her condo. She was trailed to the Belhaven section of Jackson, an older neighborhood. She parked in the driveway of the Honorable Justice James Henry McElwayne.

Tony was hardly surprised by this little get-together.

Mrs. McElwayne greeted her warmly and invited her inside, through the den and kitchen and all the way back to his study. Jimmy, as he was known to his friends, was just finishing the morning papers.

McElwayne and McCarthy. Big Mac and Little Mac, as they were sometimes referred to. They spent a few minutes chatting about Mr. Coley and his astounding press coverage, then got down to business.

"Last night, I went through my campaign files," McElwayne said as he handed over a folder an inch thick. "The first section is a list of contributors, beginning with the heavy hitters and going south. All the big checks were written by trial lawyers."

The next section summarized his campaign's expenses, numbers that Sheila found hard to believe. After that there were reports from consultants, sample ads, poll results, a dozen other campaign-related reports.

"This brings back bad memories," he said.

"Sorry. This is not what I wanted, believe me."

"You have my sympathy."

"Who's behind this guy?"

"I thought about it all night. He could be a decoy. He's definitely a nut. Whatever he is, you can't take him lightly. If he's your only opponent, sooner or later the bad guys will find their way into his camp. They'll bring their money. And this guy with a fat checkbook could really be frightening."

McElwayne had once been a state senator, then an elected chancery court judge. He'd fought the political wars. Two years earlier, Sheila watched helplessly as he was savaged and abused in a bitter campaign. At its lowest point, when his opponent's television ads (later known to be financed by the American Rifle Association) accused him of being

in favor of gun control (there is no greater sin in Mississippi), she had told herself that she would never, under any circumstances, allow herself to be so degraded. It wasn't worth it. She would scamper back to Biloxi, open a little boutique firm, and see her grandchildren every other day. Someone else could have the job.

Now she wasn't so sure. She was angered by Coley's attacks. Her blood was not yet boiling, but it wouldn't take much more. At fifty-one, she was too young to quit and too old to start over.

They talked politics for over an hour. McElwayne spun yarns of old elections and colorful politicians, and Sheila gently nudged him back to the battles she now faced. His campaign had been expertly run by a young lawyer who took a leave of absence from a large Jackson firm. McElwayne promised to call him later in the day and check his pulse. He promised to call the big donors and the local operatives. He knew the editors of the newspapers. He would do whatever he could to protect her seat on the bench.

Sheila left at 9:14, drove nonstop to the Gartin building, and parked.

————

The Coley announcement was noted at Payton & Payton, but little was said. On April 18, the day after, three important events occurred, and the firm had no interest in other news. The first event was well received. The others were not.

The good news was that a young lawyer from the tiny town of Bogue Chitto stopped by and cut a deal with Wes. The lawyer, an office practitioner with no personal injury experience, had somehow managed to become the attorney for the survivors of a pulpwood cutter who'd been killed in a horrible accident on Interstate 55 near the Louisiana line. According to the highway patrol, the accident had been caused by the recklessness of the driver of an eighteen-wheeler owned by a large company. An eyewitness was already on record stating that the truck passed her in a wild rush, and she was doing "around" seventy miles per hour. The lawyer had a contingency agreement that would give him 30 percent

of any recovery. He and Wes agreed to equally split it. The pulpwood cutter was thirty-six years old and earned about $40,000 a year. The math was easy. A million-dollar settlement was quite possible. Wes drew up a lawsuit in less than an hour and was ready to file. The case was especially gratifying because the young lawyer chose the Payton firm on account of its recent reputation. The *Baker* verdict had finally attracted a worthwhile client.

The depressing news was the arrival of Krane's appellant brief. It was 102 pages long—twice the limit—and gave every impression of being beautifully researched and written by an entire team of very bright lawyers. It was too long and two months late, but the concessions had been granted by the court. Jared Kurtin and his men had been very persuasive in their arguments for more time and more pages. It was, obviously, not a routine case.

Mary Grace would have sixty days to respond. After the brief was gawked at by the rest of the firm, she hauled it to her desk for the first reading. Krane was claiming a grand total of twenty-four errors at trial, each worthy of correction on appeal. It began pleasantly enough with an exhaustive review of all the comments and rulings by Judge Harrison that allegedly revealed his intense bias against the defendant. Then it challenged the selection of the jury. It attacked the experts called on behalf of Jeannette Baker: the toxicologist who testified as to the near-record levels of BCL and cartolyx and aklar in Bowmore's drinking water; the pathologist who described the highly carcinogenic nature of these chemicals; the medical researcher who described the record rate of cancer in and around Bowmore; the geologist who tracked the toxic wastes through the ground and into the aquifer under the town's well; the driller who drilled the test holes; the doctors who performed the autopsies on both Chad and Pete Baker; the scientist who studied pesticides and said ghastly things about pillamar 5; and the most crucial expert, the medical researcher who linked BCL and cartolyx to the cancerous cells found in the bodies. The Paytons had used fourteen expert witnesses, and each was criticized at length and declared unqualified. Three were described as charlatans. Judge Harrison was wrong time and again for allowing

them to testify. Their reports, entered into evidence after lengthy fights, were picked apart, condemned in scholarly language, and labeled as "junk science." The verdict itself was against the overwhelming weight of the evidence and a clear indication of undue sympathy on the part of the jury. Harsh but skillful words were used to attack the punitive element. The plaintiff fell far short in her efforts to prove that Krane had contaminated the drinking water either by gross negligence or by outright intent. Finally, the brief ended with a strident plea for a reversal and new trial, or, better yet, an outright dismissal by the supreme court. "This outrageous and unjustified verdict should be reversed and rendered," it read in closing. In other words, throw it out forever.

The brief was well written, well reasoned, and persuasive, and after two hours of nonstop reading Mary Grace finished it with a splitting headache. She took three Advil, then gave it to Sherman, who eyed it with all the caution he would have given a rattlesnake.

The third event, and the most alarming news, came in a phone call from Pastor Denny Ott. Wes took it after dark, then walked to his wife's office and closed the door.

"That was Denny," he said.

As Mary Grace looked at her husband's face, her first thought was that another client had passed away. There had been so many sad phone calls from Bowmore that she could almost anticipate one. "What is it?"

"He talked to the sheriff. Mr. Leon Gatewood is missing."

Though they had no affection whatsoever for the man, the news was still troubling. Gatewood was an industrial engineer who had worked at the Krane plant in Bowmore for thirty-four years. A company man to the core, he had retired when Krane fled to Mexico, and had admitted, in deposition and on cross-examination at trial, that the company had given him a termination package worth three years' salary, or about $190,000. Krane was not known for such generosity. The Paytons had found no other employee with such a sweet deal.

Gatewood had retired to a little sheep farm in the southwest corner of Cary County, about as far from Bowmore and its water as one could possibly get and still reside in the county. During his three-day deposition, he steadfastly denied any dumping at the plant. At trial, with a stack of documents, Wes had grilled him without mercy. Gatewood called the other Krane employees liars. He refused to believe records that showed tons of toxic by-products had, in fact, not been hauled away from the plant, but had simply gone missing. He laughed at incriminating photographs of some of the six hundred decomposed BCL drums dug up from the ravine behind the plant. "You doctored those," he shot back at Wes. His testimony was so blatantly fabricated that Judge Harrison talked openly, in chambers, of perjury charges. Gatewood was arrogant, belligerent, and short-tempered and made the jury despise Krane Chemical. He was a powerful witness for the plaintiff, though he testified only after being dragged to court by a subpoena. Jared Kurtin could have choked him.

"When did this happen?" she asked.

"He went fishing alone two days ago. His wife is still waiting."

The disappearance of Earl Crouch in Texas two years earlier was still an unsolved mystery. Crouch had been Gatewood's boss. Both had vehemently defended Krane and denied what had become obvious. Both had complained of harassment, even death threats. And they weren't alone. Many of the people who worked there, who made the pesticides and dumped the poisons, had been threatened. Most had drifted away from Bowmore, to escape the drinking water, to look for other jobs, and to avoid getting sucked into the coming storm of litigation. At least four had died of cancer.

Others had testified and told the truth. Others, including Crouch, Gatewood, and Buck Burleson, had testified and lied. Each group hated the other, and collectively they were hated by the remainder of Cary County.

"I guess the Stones are at it again," Wes said.

"You don't know that."

"No one will ever know. I'm just happy they're our clients."

"Our clients are restless down there," she said. "It's time for a meeting."

"It's time for dinner. Who's cooking?"

"Ramona."

"Tortillas or enchiladas?"

"Spaghetti."

"Let's go find a bar and have a drink, just the two of us. We need to celebrate, dear. This little case from Bogue Chitto might just be a quick million-dollar settlement."

"I'll drink to that."

CHAPTER 19

After ten performances, Coley's Faces of the Dead Tour came to an end. It ran out of gas in Pascagoula, the last of the big towns in the southern district. Though he tried desperately along the way, Clete was unable to get himself arrested again. He did, however, manage to generate quite a buzz at every stop. The reporters loved him. Admirers grabbed his brochures and began writing checks, albeit small ones. The local cops watched his announcements with silent approval.

But after ten days, Clete needed a break. He returned to Natchez and was soon at the Lucky Jack taking cards from Ivan. He had no real campaign strategy, no plan. He'd left nothing behind in the places he stopped, except for some fleeting publicity. There was no organization, except for a few volunteers that he would soon ignore. Frankly, he wasn't about to spend the time or the money necessary to rev up a campaign of respectable size. He wasn't about to touch the cash Marlin had given him, not for campaign expenses anyway. He would spend whatever contributions trickled in, but he had no plans to lose money on this adventure. The attention was addictive and he would show up when necessary to make a speech, attack his opponent, and attack liberal judges of all

stripes, but his priority was gambling and drinking. Clete had no dreams of winning. Hell, he wouldn't take the job if they handed it to him. He had always hated those thick law books.

———

Tony Zachary flew to Boca Raton and was picked up by a chauffeur-driven car. He had been to Mr. Rinehart's office once before and looked forward to the return. They would spend most of the next two days together.

Over a splendid lunch with a beautiful view of the ocean, they had a great time reviewing the antics of their stooge, Clete Coley. Barry Rinehart had read every press clipping and seen every TV news report. They were quite pleased with their decoy.

Next, they analyzed the results of their first major poll. It covered five hundred registered voters in the twenty-seven counties of the southern district and had been conducted the day after Coley's tour ended. Not surprisingly, at least to Barry Rinehart, 66 percent could not name any of the three supreme court judges from the southern district. Sixty-nine percent were unaware that the voters actually elected the members of the supreme court.

"And this is a state where they elect highway commissioners, public service commissioners, the state treasurer, state commissioners of insurance and agriculture, county tax collectors, county coroners, everybody but the dogcatcher," Barry said.

"They vote every year," Tony said, peering over his reading glasses. He had stopped eating and was looking at some graphs.

"Every single year. Whether it's municipal, judicial, state and local, or federal, they go to the polls every year. Such a waste. Small wonder turnout is low. Hell, the voters are sick of politics."

Of the 34 percent who could name a supreme court justice, only half mentioned Sheila McCarthy. If the election were held today, 18 percent would vote for her, 15 percent would vote for Clete Coley, and the rest either were undecided or simply wouldn't vote because they didn't know anyone in the race.

After some initial straightforward questions, the poll began to reveal

its slant. Would you vote for a supreme court candidate who is opposed to the death penalty? Seventy-three percent said they would not.

Would you vote for a candidate who supports the legal marriage of two homosexuals? Eighty-eight percent said no.

Would you vote for a candidate who is in favor of tougher gun-control laws? Eight-five percent said no.

Do you own at least one gun? Ninety-six percent said yes.

The questions had multiple parts and follow-ups, and were obviously designed to walk the voter down a path lined with hot-button issues. No effort was made to explain that the supreme court was not a legislative body; it did not have the responsibility or jurisdiction to make laws dealing with these issues. No effort was made to keep the field level. Like many polls, Rinehart's skillfully shifted into a subtle attack.

Would you support a liberal candidate for the supreme court? Seventy percent would not.

Are you aware that Justice Sheila McCarthy is considered the most liberal member of the Mississippi Supreme Court? Eighty-four percent said no.

If she is the most liberal member of the court, will you vote for her? Sixty-five percent said no, but most of those being polled didn't like the question. If? Was she or wasn't she the most liberal? Anyway, Barry considered the question useless. The promising part was how little name recognition Sheila McCarthy had after nine years on the bench, though, in his experience, this was not unusual. He could argue with anyone, privately, that this was another perfect reason why state supreme court judges shouldn't be elected in the first place. They should not be politicians. Their names should not be well-known.

The poll then shifted away from the supreme court and settled onto the individual participants. There were questions about religious faith, belief in God, church attendance, financial support of the church, and so on. And there were questions about certain issues—where do you stand on abortion, stem cell research, et cetera?

The poll wrapped up with the basics—race, marital status, number of children, if any, approximate income status, and voting history.

The overall results confirmed what Barry suspected. The voters were conservative, middle-class, and white (78 percent) and could easily be turned against a liberal judge. The trick, of course, was to convert Sheila McCarthy from the sensible moderate she was into the raging liberal they needed her to be. Barry's researchers were analyzing every word she had ever written in a legal ruling, both at the circuit court level and on the supreme court. She could not escape her words; no judge could ever do that. And Barry planned to hang her with her own words.

After lunch, they moved to the conference table, where Barry had a display of the initial mock-ups of Ron Fisk's campaign literature. There were hundreds of new photographs of the Fisk family in all its wholesomeness—walking into church, on the front porch, at the baseball park, the parents together, alone, dripping with love and affection.

The first soft ads were still being edited, but Barry wanted to share them anyway. They had been filmed by a crew sent from Washington to Mississippi. The first was of Fisk standing by a Civil War monument at the Vicksburg battlefield, gazing off into the distance as if listening to distant cannons. His soft, richly accented voice played over: "I'm Ron Fisk. My great-great-grandfather was killed on this spot in July of 1863. He was a lawyer, a judge, and a member of the state legislature. His dream was to serve on the supreme court. That's my dream today. I am a seventh-generation Mississippian, and I ask for your support."

Tony was surprised. "The Civil War?"

"Oh yes. They love it."

"What about the black vote?"

"We'll get 30 percent of it, from the churches. That's all we need."

The next ad was shot in Ron's office. Jacket off, sleeves rolled up, desk arranged in a careful clutter. Looking sincerely at the camera, Ron talked about his love of the law, the pursuit of truth, the demands of fairness from those who sit on the bench. It was a fairly bland effort, but it did convey warmth and intelligence.

There were a total of six ads. "Just the soft ones," Barry promised. A couple would not survive editing, and there was a good chance the camera crew would be sent back for more.

"What about the nasty ones?" Tony asked.

"Still in the writing stage. We won't need them until after Labor Day."

"How much have we spent so far?"

"Quarter of a million. A drop in the bucket."

They spent two hours with an Internet consultant whose firm did nothing but raise money for political races. So far, he had put together an e-mail bank with just over forty thousand names—individuals with a history of contributing, members of the associations and groups already on board, known political activists at the local level, and a smaller number of people outside of Mississippi who would feel sympathetic enough to send a check. He guessed that the list would grow by another ten thousand, and he projected total contributions at somewhere in the range of $500,000. Most important, his list was ready and waiting. When given the green light, he simply pushed a button, the solicitation flew out, and the checks started coming.

The green light was the principal topic over a long dinner that night. The deadline to qualify was a month away. Though there were the usual rumors, Tony firmly believed that the race would attract no one else. "There will be only three horses," he said. "And we own two of them."

"What's McCarthy doing?" Barry asked. He received daily updates on her movements, which so far had revealed little.

"Not much. She appears to be shell-shocked. One day she's unopposed; the next day she's got some crazy cowboy named Coley calling her a liberal convict lover and the newspapers are printing everything he says. I'm sure she's getting advice from McElwayne, her sidekick, but she has yet to put together a staff for the campaign."

"Is she raising money?"

"The trial lawyers issued one of their standard panic e-mails last week, begging for money from the membership. I have no idea how that's going."

"Sex?"

"Just the usual boyfriend. You've got the report. No real dirt yet."

Shortly after opening the second bottle of a fine Oregon pinot noir, they decided to launch Fisk in two weeks. The boy was ready, straining at the leash, desperate to hit the trail. Everything was in place. He was taking a six-month leave from his firm, and his partners were happy. And well they should be. They had just picked up five new clients—two large timber companies, a pipeline contractor from Houston, and two natural gas firms. The vast coalition of lobbying groups was on board, ready with cash and foot soldiers. McCarthy was afraid of her shadow and apparently hoping Clete Coley would simply go away or self-destruct.

They touched glasses and toasted the eve of an exciting campaign.

He is a master of the one-liner that summarizes a situation, closes it off & sets the reader up for part 2.

As always, the meeting was held in the fellowship hall of the Pine Grove Church. And as usual, several non-clients tried to wiggle their way in to hear the latest. They were politely escorted out by Pastor Ott, who explained that this was a very confidential meeting between the lawyers and their clients.

Other than the *Baker* case, the Paytons had thirty Bowmore cases. Eighteen involved people who were already dead. The other twelve involved people with cancer in various stages. Four years earlier, the Paytons had made the tactical decision to take their best case—Jeannette Baker's—and try it first. It would be far cheaper than trying all thirty-one at one time. Jeannette was the most sympathetic, having lost her entire family in the span of eight months. That decision now looked brilliant.

Wes and Mary Grace hated these meetings. A sadder, more tragic group of people could not be found anywhere. They had lost children, husbands, and wives. They were terminally ill and living with incredible pain. They asked questions that could not be answered, over and over, in slightly different variations because no two cases were identical. Some wanted to quit, and others wanted to fight forever. Some wanted money, and others just wanted Krane to be held accountable. There were always tears, and harsh words, and for this reason Pastor Ott was there as a calming influence.

Now, with the *Baker* verdict legendary, the Paytons knew the rest of their clients had much higher expectations. Six months after the verdict, the clients were more anxious than ever. They called the office more often. They sent more letters and e-mails.

The meeting had the extra tension caused by the funeral, three days earlier, of Leon Gatewood, a man they all despised. His body was found in a pile of brush three miles downriver from his capsized fishing boat. There was no evidence of foul play, but everyone suspected it. The sheriff was busy with an investigation.

All thirty families were represented. The notepad Wes passed around had sixty-two names on it, names he knew well, including that of Frank Stone, a caustic bricklayer who usually said little during these meetings. It was assumed, without a shred of evidence, that if Leon Gatewood's death had been caused by someone else, then Frank Stone knew something about it.

Mary Grace began with a warm hello. She thanked them for coming, and for their patience. She talked about the *Baker* appeal, and for a little dramatic effect she hoisted the thick brief filed by Krane's lawyers as evidence that many hours were being spent on the appellate front. All briefs would be in by September, then the supreme court would decide how to handle the case. It had the option of passing it off to a lower court, the court of appeals, for an initial review, or it could simply keep it. A case of this magnitude would eventually be decided by the supreme court, and she and Wes were of the opinion that it would bypass the lower court. If that happened, oral arguments would be scheduled for later in the year, or perhaps early next year. Her best guess was a final ruling in about a year.

If the court affirmed the verdict, there were several possible scenarios. Krane would be under enormous pressure to settle the remaining claims, which, of course, would be a highly favored result. If Krane refused to settle, she was of the opinion that Judge Harrison would consolidate the other cases and try them in one huge trial. In that event, their firm would have the resources to fight on. She confided in the clients that

they had spent borrowed funds in excess of $400,000 to get the *Baker* case to a jury, and they simply could not do it again unless the first verdict was upheld.

As poor as the clients were, they were not nearly as broke as their lawyers.

"What if the *Baker* verdict is rejected by the court?" asked Eileen Johnson. Her head was bare from chemo, and she weighed less than a hundred pounds. Her husband held her hand throughout the meeting.

"That's a possibility," Mary Grace admitted. "But we are confident it won't happen." She said this with more assurance than she possessed. The Paytons felt good about the appeal, but any rational lawyer would be nervous. "But if it happens, the court will send it back for another trial. It could be on all issues, or simply on damages. It's hard to predict."

She moved on, anxious to get away from more talk about losing. She assured them that their cases were still receiving the full attention of their firm. Hundreds of documents were being processed each week and filed away. Other experts were being sought. They were in a holding pattern, but still working hard.

"What about this class action?" asked Curtis Knight, the father of a teenage boy who'd died four years earlier. The question seemed to arouse the crowd. Others, less deserving, were encroaching on their territory.

"Forget about it," she said. "Those plaintiffs are at the bottom of the pile. They win only if there's a settlement, and any settlement must first satisfy your claims. We control the settlement. You are not competing with those people."

Her answer seemed good enough.

Wes took over with cautionary words. Because of the verdict, the pressure on Krane Chemical was greater than ever. They probably had investigators in the area, watching the plaintiffs, trying to gather information that might be damaging. Be careful who you talk to. Be wary of strangers. Report anything even remotely unusual.

For a long-suffering people, this was not welcome news. They had enough to worry about.

The questions continued and went on for over an hour. The Paytons worked hard to reassure, to show compassion and confidence, to give hope. But the tougher challenge was keeping a lid on expectations.

If anyone in the room was concerned about a supreme court race, it was never mentioned.

CHAPTER 20

When he stepped forward and gazed at the large congregation on Sunday morning, Ron Fisk had no idea how many pulpits he would visit over the next six months. Nor did he realize that the pulpit would become a symbol of his campaign.

He thanked his minister for the opportunity, then thanked his congregation, his fellow members of St. Luke's Baptist Church, for their indulgence. "Tomorrow, down the street at the Lincoln County Courthouse, I will announce my candidacy for the Mississippi Supreme Court. Doreen and I have been struggling with and praying about this for several months now. We have counseled with Pastor Rose. We have discussed it with our children, our families, and our friends. And we are finally at peace with our decision and want to share it with you before the announcement tomorrow."

He glanced at his notes, looked a little nervous, then continued.

"I have no background in politics. Frankly, I've never had the stomach for it. Doreen and I have established a happy life here in Brookhaven, raising our kids, worshipping here with you, taking part in our commu-

nity. We are blessed, and we thank God every day for his goodness. We thank God for this church and for friends like you. You are our family."

Another nervous pause.

"I seek to serve on the supreme court because I cherish the values that we share. Values based on the Bible and our faith in Christ. The sanctity of the family—man and woman. The sanctity of life. The freedom to enjoy life without fear of crime and government intervention. Like you, I am frustrated by the erosion of our values. They are under attack by our society, by our depraved culture, and by many of our politicians. Yes, also by our courts. I offer my candidacy as one man's fight against liberal judges. With your help, I can win. Thank you."

Mercifully brief—another long-winded sermon was surely coming next—Ron's words were so well received that a polite round of applause rippled through the sanctuary as he returned to his seat and sat with his family.

Two hours later, while the white churchgoers in Brookhaven were having lunch and the black ones were just getting cranked up, Ron bounded up red-carpeted steps to the massive podium of the Mount Pisgah Church of God in Christ on the west side of town and delivered a lengthier version of the morning's comments. (He omitted the word "liberal.") Until two days earlier, he had never met the reverend of the town's largest black congregation. A friend pulled some strings and manipulated an invitation.

That night, in the middle of a rowdy Pentecostal holy hour, he grabbed the pulpit, waited for the racket to die down, then introduced himself and made his appeal. He ignored his notes and spoke longer. He went after the liberals again.

Driving home afterward, he was struck by how few people he actually knew in his small town. His clients were insurance companies, not people. He rarely ventured outside the security of his neighborhood, his church, his social circle. Frankly, he preferred to stay there.

At nine Monday morning he gathered on the steps of the courthouse with Doreen and the kids, his law firm, a large group of friends,

[handwritten note at bottom of page] Grisham is a master at contradictory colour in his language — this is just ONE example

courthouse employees and regulars, and most of his Rotary Club, and he announced his candidacy to the rest of the state. It was not planned as a media event. Only a few reporters and cameras showed up.

Barry Rinehart subscribed to the strategy of peaking on Election Day, not when the announcement is made.

Ron delivered his carefully worded and rehearsed remarks for fifteen minutes, with lots of applause thrown in. He answered every question the reporters had, then moved inside to a small, empty courtroom, where he happily gave a thirty-minute exclusive to one of the political reporters for the Jackson newspaper.

The party then moved three blocks down the street, where Ron cut the ribbon across the door of his official campaign headquarters in an old building that had been freshly painted and covered with campaign propaganda. Over coffee and biscuits, he chatted with friends, posed for pictures, and sat for another interview, this one with a newspaper he'd never heard of. Tony Zachary was there, supervising the festivities and watching the clock.

Simultaneously, a press release of his announcement was sent to every newspaper in the state and to the major dailies throughout the Southeast. One was also e-mailed to each member of the supreme court, each member of the legislature, every other elected official in the state, every registered lobbyist, thousands of state employees, every doctor with a license, and every lawyer admitted to the bar. There were 390,000 registered voters in the southern district. Rinehart's Internet consultants had found e-mail addresses for about a fourth of them, and these lucky folks received the news online while Ron was still at the courthouse making his speech. A total of 120,000 e-mails went out in one blast.

Forty-two thousand solicitations for money were sent by e-mail, along with a message that touted the virtues of Ron Fisk while attacking the social evils caused by "liberal, left-leaning judges who substitute their own agendas for those of the people."

From a rented warehouse in south Jackson, a building Ron Fisk did not know about and would never lay eyes on, 390,000 stuffed envelopes

were removed and taken to the central post office. Inside each was a campaign brochure with lots of endearing photos, a warm letter from Ron himself, a smaller envelope if one wished to send back a check, and a complimentary bumper sticker. The colors were red, white, and blue, and the artwork was obviously done by professionals. Every detail in the mailing was of the highest quality.

At 11:00 a.m., Tony moved the show south to McComb, the eleventh-largest city in the district. (Brookhaven ranked fourteenth with a population of 10,800.) Traveling in a newly leased Chevrolet Suburban, with a volunteer named Guy at the wheel, with his new but already indispensable first assistant, Monte, in the front seat and on the phone, and with Doreen sitting by his side on the rather spacious middle bench of the SUV, Ron Fisk smiled smugly at the countryside flying by him. It was a moment to be savored. His first foray into politics, and in such grand style. All those supporters, their enthusiasm, the press and the cameras, the heady challenge of the job ahead, the thrill of winning, all in just the first two hours of the campaign. The strong rush of adrenaline was only a sample of what was coming. He imagined a great victory in November. He could see himself springing from the mundane anonymity of a small-town law practice to the prestige of the supreme court. It all lay before him.

Fisk P.O.V.

Tony followed closely behind, relaying a quick update to Barry Rinehart.

At the City Hall in McComb, Ron announced again. The crowd was small but loud. There were a few friends but the rest were total strangers. After two quick interviews, with photos, he was driven to the McComb airstrip, where he boarded a Lear 55, a handsome little jet built like a rocket, although, as Ron couldn't help but notice, much smaller than the G5 that had whisked him to Washington. Doreen barely managed to suppress her excitement at her first encounter with a private jet. Tony joined the flight. Guy raced ahead with the SUV.

Fifteen minutes later they landed in Hattiesburg, population forty-eight thousand, the third-largest city in the district. At 1:00 p.m., Ron

and Doreen were the guests at a Prayer Lunch thrown together by a loose coalition of fundamentalist pastors. The setting was an old Holiday Inn. Tony waited in the bar.

Over badly fried chicken and butter beans, Ron did more listening than talking. Several of the preachers, evidently still inspired by their Sunday labors, felt the need to bless him with their views on various issues and evils. Hollywood, rap music, celebrity culture, rampant pornography, the Internet, underage drinking, underage sex, and on and on. Ron nodded sincerely and was soon ready to escape. When he did say a few words, he chose all the right ones. He and Doreen had prayed about this race and felt the Lord's hand in it. Laws created by man should strive to emulate the laws of God. Only men of clear moral vision should judge the problems of others. And so on. He was unequivocally endorsed on the spot.

Freed from the meeting, Ron addressed a group of two dozen supporters outside the Forrest County Circuit Court building. The event was covered by the Hattiesburg TV station. After a few questions, he walked along Main Street, shaking hands with any and all, passing out his slick brochures, and ducking into every law office for a quick heyhowdy. At 3:30, the Lear 55 took off and headed to the Coast. At eight thousand feet and climbing, it flew over the southwest corner of Cancer County.

Guy was waiting with the Suburban at the Gulfport-Biloxi Regional Airport. Ron kissed Doreen goodbye, and the plane took her back to McComb. Another driver there would take her to Brookhaven. At the Harrison County Courthouse, Ron announced again, answered the same questions, then sat down for a long interview with the *Sun Herald*.

Biloxi was the home of Sheila McCarthy. It was adjacent to Gulfport, the largest city in the southern district, with a population of sixty-five thousand. Biloxi and Gulfport were the center of the Coast region, a three-county area along the Gulf with 60 percent of the votes. To the east was Ocean Springs, Gautier, Moss Point, Pascagoula, and then Mobile. To the west was Pass Christian, Long Beach, Waveland, Bay St. Louis, then New Orleans.

Tony planned for Ron to spend at least half of his time there dur-

ing the campaign. At 6:00 p.m., the candidate was introduced to his
Coast office, a renovated fast-food franchise on Highway 90, the heavily
traveled four-lane at the beach. Brightly colored campaign signs blan-
keted the area around the headquarters, and a large crowd gathered to
hear and meet their candidate. Ron knew none of them. Nor did Tony.
Virtually all were employees of some of the companies indirectly financ-
ing the campaign. Half worked in the regional office of a national auto
insurance company. When Ron arrived and saw his headquarters, its
decorations, and the crowd, he marveled at the organizational skills of
Tony Zachary. This might be easier than he thought.

The Gulf Coast's economy is now fueled by casinos, so he throttled
back his high moral comments and dwelled on his conservative approach
to judicial thought. He talked about himself, his family, his son Josh's un-
defeated Little League team. And for the first time, he voiced concern
over the state's crime rate and its seeming indifference to executing con-
demned killers.

Clete Coley would've been proud.

Dinner that night was a fancy fund-raiser at the Biloxi Yacht Club,
a thousand dollars a plate. The crowd was a mix of corporate suits,
bankers, doctors, and insurance defense lawyers. Tony counted eighty-
four present.

Late that night, with Ron asleep in the room next door, Tony called
Barry Rinehart with a summary of the great day. It wasn't as colorful as
Clete's dramatic entrance, but it was far more productive. Their candi-
date had handled himself well.

Day two began with a 7:30 Prayer Breakfast at a hotel in the shadows of
the casinos. It was sponsored by a newly organized group known as the
Brotherhood Coalition. Most of those in attendance were fundamental-
ist pastors from a dozen strains of Christianity. Ron was quickly learning
the strategy of adapting to his audience, and he felt at home talking
about his faith and how it would shape his decisions on the supreme
court. He emphasized his long service to the Lord as a deacon and Sun-

day school teacher, and almost choked up when he recalled the story of his son's baptism. Again, he was endorsed on the spot.

At least half the state awoke to morning newspapers with full-page ads for candidate Ron Fisk. The ad in Jackson's *Clarion-Ledger* had a handsome photograph above the bold caption "Judicial Reform." Smaller print gave Ron's pertinent biographical data, with emphasis on his membership in his church, civic organizations, and the American Rifle Association. Still smaller print listed an impressive collection of endorsements: family groups, conservative Christian activists, panels of ministers, and associations that seemed to represent the rest of humanity; doctors, nurses, hospitals, dentists, nursing homes, pharmacists, retail merchants, real estate agents, banks, savings and loans, finance companies, brokerage firms, mortgage banks, insurance companies (health, life, medical, fire, casualty, malpractice), highway contractors, architects, energy companies, natural gas producers, and three "legislative relations" groups that represented the manufacturers of virtually every product to be found in any store.

In other words, everyone who might get sued and therefore paid insurance premiums as protection. The list reeked of money and proclaimed that Ron Fisk, heretofore unknown, was now in the race as a serious player.

The ad cost $12,000 in the Jackson *Clarion-Ledger*, $9,000 in the Biloxi *Sun Herald*, and $5,000 in the *Hattiesburg American*.

The two-day cost of the Fisk rollout was roughly $450,000, which did not include travel expenses, the jet, and the Internet assault. The bulk of the money was spent on direct mail.

Ron spent the rest of Tuesday and Wednesday on the Coast, with every minute planned with precision. Campaigns habitually run late, but not with Tony in charge. They announced at the courthouses in Jackson and Hancock counties, prayed with preachers, stopped at dozens of law offices, worked a few busy streets handing out brochures, and shook hands. Ron even kissed his first baby. And it was all recorded by a film crew.

On Thursday, Ron made six more stops throughout south Missis-

sippi, then hurried back to Brookhaven for a quick change of clothes. The game began at six. Doreen was already there with the kids. The Raiders were warming up, and Josh was pitching. The team was in the dugout listening to an assistant when Coach Fisk hustled in and took charge.

There was a nice crowd at the game. Ron already felt like a celebrity.

————

Rather than researching law, Sheila's two clerks spent the day collecting press accounts of the Ron Fisk rollout. They gathered copies of the full-page ads from the different newspapers. They tracked the news online. As the file grew thicker, their moods sank.

Sheila tried gamely to go about her job as if nothing was happening. The sky was falling, but she pretended to ignore it. Privately, and this usually meant a closed-door session with Big Mac, she was stunned and thoroughly overwhelmed. Fisk was spending what looked like a million dollars, and she had raised virtually nothing.

Clete Coley had convinced her she had light opposition. The Fisk ambush was so brilliantly executed she felt as though she'd been killed in battle.

————

The board of directors of the Mississippi Trial Advocates met in an emergency meeting late Thursday afternoon in Jackson. Its current president was Bobby Neal, a veteran trial lawyer with many verdicts under his belt and a long history of service to the MTA. Eighteen of the twenty directors were present, the highest number in many years.

The board, by its very nature, was a collection of high-strung and highly opinionated lawyers who worked by their own rules. Few had ever had a boss. Most had clawed their way up through the lower rungs of the profession to reach a level of great respectability, at least in their opinions. To them, no calling was higher than that of representing the poor, the injured, the unwanted, the troubled.

Typically, each gathering was long and loud and usually began with everyone present demanding the floor. And that was a normal meeting. Place the same group in an urgent setting with their backs pinned to the wall by the sudden and imminent threat of losing one of their most trusted allies on the supreme court, and all eighteen began arguing at once. Each had all the answers. Barbara Mellinger and Skip Sanchez sat in one corner, silent. No alcohol was being served. No caffeine. Only water.

After a raucous half hour, Bobby Neal managed to bring the meeting into some semblance of order. He got their attention when he informed them that he had spent an hour with Justice McCarthy earlier in the day. "She is in great spirits," he said with a smile, one of the few around the table that afternoon. "She is hard at work doing her job and really doesn't want to get sidetracked. However, she understands politics and said more than once that she will run a hard campaign and has every intention of winning. I promised our unwavering support."

He paused, shifted gears. "However, I found the meeting a bit discouraging. Clete Coley announced four weeks ago, and Sheila still doesn't even have a campaign manager. She has raised a few bucks, but she wouldn't say how much. I got the impression that she settled down after the Coley thing and convinced herself he was simply a nut with no credibility. She thought she could slide. Her thoughts have now changed dramatically. She's been asleep, and now she's running to catch up. As we know from experience, there is very little money on our side of the street, except ours."

"It'll take a million bucks to beat this guy," someone said, and the comment was rapidly drowned out in a wave of ridicule. A million wasn't close. The tort reformers spent two million against Judge McElwayne, and they lost by three thousand votes. They'll spend more than that this time around because they're better organized and really ticked off. And the guy who ran against McElwayne was a reprobate who'd never tried a lawsuit and had spent the last ten years teaching political science at a junior college. This guy Fisk is a real lawyer.

So they talked about Fisk for a while, at least four different conversations boiling at any given moment.

Tapping his water glass, Bobby Neal slowly dragged them back to his agenda. "There are twenty of us on this board. If we commit ten thousand each, right now, Sheila's campaign can at least get organized."

Instant silence. Deep breaths were taken. Water was gulped. Eyes darted here and there, searching for other eyes that might agree or disagree with this bold proposition.

Someone at the far end of the table barked, "That's ridiculous." The lights flickered. The AC vents went silent. Everyone gawked at Willy Benton, a fiery little Irish brawler from Biloxi. Benton rose slowly and spread his hands. They had heard his passionate summations before, and they settled in for another. Juries found him irresistible.

"Gentlemen, and lady, this is the beginning of the end. We can't fool ourselves. The forces of evil who want to slam the courthouse doors and deny our clients their rights, the same pro-business lobby that has slowly, methodically marched across this country and purchased one supreme court seat after another, that same bunch of assholes is here, banging on our door. You saw their names in those ads Fisk ran. It's a confederation of dunces, but they have the money. We have what I believe is a consistent one-vote majority on the supreme court, and here we sit, the only group who can fight these thugs, and we argue about how much we should give. I'll tell you what we should give. Everything! Because if we don't, then the practice of law as we know it will quickly fade away. We won't take cases anymore, because we won't be able to win them. The next generation of trial lawyers will not exist.

"I gave a hundred thousand dollars to Judge McElwayne, and it was a stretch. I'll do the same for Judge McCarthy. I don't have an airplane. I don't handle the mass torts and rake in outrageous fees. Y'all know me. I'm from the old school, one case at a time, one trial after another. But I'll sacrifice again. So should you. We all have our toys. If you can't pledge fifty thousand each, then get off this board and go home. You know you can afford it. Sell a condo, a car, a boat, skip a couple of vaca-

tions. Hock your wife's diamonds. You pay your secretaries fifty grand a year. Sheila McCarthy is far more important than any secretary or any associate."

"The limit is five thousand per person, Willy," someone said.

"Well aren't you a smart son of a bitch," he fired back. "I have a wife and four children. That's thirty grand right there. I also have two secretaries and some satisfied clients. I'll raise a hundred thousand bucks by the end of the week, and everyone here can do the same."

He sat down, his face red. After a long pause, Bobby Neal looked at Barbara Mellinger and asked, "How much did we give Judge Mc-Elwayne?"

"One point two, from about three hundred trial lawyers."

"How much did he raise?"

"One point four."

"How much would you guess McCarthy will need to win?"

It was a subject Barbara and Skip Sanchez had discussed for three days. "Two million," she said without hesitation.

Bobby Neal frowned and recalled the fund-raising efforts two years earlier on behalf of Jimmy McElwayne. Pulling teeth without anesthesia would have been easier.

"Then we have to raise two million bucks," he said with confidence. They nodded gravely and seemed to agree on that figure. They returned to the challenge on the table, and a fierce debate erupted about how much each should commit. The ones who earned a lot also spent a lot. Those who were struggling were afraid to commit. One admitted he'd lost his last three jury trials and was effectively broke at the moment. Another, a mass tort star with his own jet, promised $150,000.

They adjourned without agreeing on a fixed amount, which surprised no one.

C H A P T E R 2 1

The qualifying deadline passed with no other fireworks. Justice Calligan from the central district and Justice Bateman from the northern escaped opposition and were safe for another eight years. Both had a history of showing little sympathy for accident victims, consumers, and criminal defendants, and thus were greatly admired by the business community. At the local level, only two of the state's circuit court judges drew opposition.

One, though, was Judge Thomas Alsobrook Harrison IV. An hour before the deadline passed, a Hattiesburg real estate lawyer named Joy Hoover filed the necessary papers and fired a few shots in a press release. She was a local political activist, well regarded and well-known in the county. Her husband was a popular pediatrician who operated a free clinic for poor mothers as a hobby.

Hoover was recruited by Tony Zachary and Judicial Vision. She was a gift from Barry Rinehart to Carl Trudeau, who, on several occasions in quiet conversations with Rinehart, had voiced his strong feelings against the judge who presided over the *Baker* trial. That judge now had his hands full and would be unable to meddle, as he was prone to do, in

other races. For a mere $100,000, the legitimate, above-the-table commitment to Hoover, Judge Harrison now had much more serious matters on his hands.

———

Rinehart was scheming on several fronts. He picked a quiet day in late June to fire his next salvo.

Two gay men, Al Meyerchec and Billy Spano, had quietly arrived in Jackson three months earlier. They rented a small apartment near Millsaps College, registered to vote, and obtained Mississippi driver's licenses. Their old ones were from Illinois. They claimed to be self-employed illustrators who worked at home. They kept to themselves and met no one.

On June 24, they walked into the offices of the Hinds County Circuit Clerk and requested the necessary forms to apply for a license to be married. The clerk balked and attempted to explain that the laws under which she operated did not allow same-sex marriages. Things grew tense, heated words were offered by Meyerchec and Spano, and they finally left. They called a reporter from the *Clarion-Ledger* and gave their side of the story.

The following day, with the reporter and a photographer, they returned to the clerk's office and again requested the paperwork. When it was denied, they began shouting and threatening to sue. The next day the story was front-page news, complete with a photograph of the two men as they berated the hapless clerk. They retained a radical lawyer, paid him $10,000, and made good on their pledge to litigate the matter. The new lawsuit also made the front page.

It was shocking news. Stories of attempts by gay people to legally marry were common in places like New York, Massachusetts, and California but were unheard-of in Mississippi. What was the world coming to?

A follow-up story revealed that the two men were new to the area, were unknown in the gay community, and had no apparent ties to any business, any family, or anything else in the state. Graphic condemna-

tions were offered by those who could be expected to say such things. A local state senator explained that these matters were governed by state laws and said laws were not about to be changed, not while he was running the legislature. Meyerchec and Spano were unavailable for comment. Their lawyer said they traveled extensively on business. In truth, they were back in Chicago, where one worked as an interior designer and the other owned a bar. They would retain their legal residence in Mississippi and return only when their lawsuit required it.

Jackson was then rocked by another brutal crime. Three gang members, all armed with assault weapons, invaded a rented duplex occupied by twenty or so illegal immigrants from Mexico. The Mexicans were known to work eighteen hours a day, save every dime, then send it all home once a month. Such home invasions were not uncommon in Jackson and other southern cities. In the chaos of the crime, with the Mexicans scrambling about pulling cash from floors and walls and shrieking hysterically in Spanish as the gunmen screamed in very plain English, one of the Mexicans produced a pistol and fired some shots, hitting no one. The gunfire was returned, and a frantic scene turned even more horrific. When the shooting stopped, four of the Mexicans were dead, three were injured, and the gang members had retreated into the night. Their haul was estimated at about $800, though the police would never be certain.

Barry Rinehart could not claim the event as one of his creations, but he was nonetheless pleased to hear about it.

A week later, at a forum sponsored by a law-enforcement association, Clete Coley seized the crime with zeal and hammered away at his usual themes of violence running unchecked and aided by a liberal court that was stifling executions in Mississippi. He pointed at Sheila McCarthy, onstage next to Ron Fisk, and harshly blamed her for the court's unwillingness to use the death chamber up at Parchman. The crowd loved him.

Ron Fisk was not to be outdone. He railed against gangs and drugs and lawlessness, and he criticized the supreme court, though in softer language. He then unveiled a five-step plan to streamline capital murder ap-

peals, and his staff handed out the specific proposals as he spoke. It was an impressive showing, and Tony, seated in the rear, was delighted at the performance.

By the time Justice McCarthy rose to speak, the crowd was ready to throw stones. She calmly explained the complexities of death penalty appeals and said that a great deal of the court's time was devoted solely to these difficult cases. She stressed the need to be careful and thorough and make sure each defendant's rights were properly guarded. The law knows no greater burden than protecting the legal rights of those society has decided to execute. She reminded the crowd that at least 120 men and women condemned to death row had later been completely exonerated, including two in Mississippi. Some of these people had spent twenty years waiting to die. In the nine years she had served on the court, she had participated in forty-eight death penalty cases. Of those, she had voted with the majority twenty-seven times to affirm the convictions, but only after being certain that fair trials had been conducted. In the other cases, she had voted to reverse the convictions and send the cases back for retrials. She did not regret a single vote. She did not consider herself a liberal, a conservative, or a moderate. She was a supreme court justice, sworn to fairly review her cases and uphold the law. Yes, she was personally opposed to the death penalty, but she had never substituted her convictions for the laws of the state.

When she finished, there was a scattering of light applause, but only of the polite variety. It was difficult not to admire her bluntness and courage. Few, if any, would vote for her, but the lady knew what she was talking about.

It was the first time all three candidates had appeared together, and the first time Tony had watched her under pressure. "She will not be a pushover," he reported to Barry Rinehart. "She knows her stuff and sticks to her guns."

"Yes, but she's broke," Barry said with a laugh. "This is a campaign, and it's all about money."

———

McCarthy wasn't exactly broke, but her campaign was off to a miserable start. She had no campaign manager, no one to coordinate the fifty things that needed to be done immediately while coordinating a thousand details for later. She had offered the job to three people. The first two declined after considering it for twenty-four hours. The third said yes, then a week later said no.

A campaign is a small, frantic business thrown together under great pressure and with the knowledge that it will have a very short life. The full-time staff works brutal hours for low pay. The volunteers are invaluable but not always dependable. A forceful and decisive campaign manager is crucial.

Six weeks after Fisk's announcement, Justice McCarthy had managed to open a campaign office in Jackson, near her condo, and one in Biloxi, near her home. Both were run by longtime friends, volunteers, who stayed busy recruiting more staff and calling potential donors. There were piles of bumper stickers and yard signs, but the campaign had been unable to secure a decent firm to put together the ads, direct mail, and, hopefully, television spots. There was a very basic Web site, but no other Internet activity. Sheila had received $320,000 in contributions, all but $30,000 of it coming from trial lawyers. Bobby Neal and the board had promised her, in writing, that the MTA members would donate at least $1 million, and she did not doubt that they would. But making promises was much easier than writing checks.

Getting organized was made more difficult by the fact that she had a demanding job that could not simply be ignored. The court's docket was backed up for a mile with cases that should have been decided months earlier. There was the constant strain of never catching up. The appeals would never stop. And lives were in the balance: men and women on death row; children pulled back and forth in messy divorces; horribly injured workers waiting on a final ruling that, hopefully, would bring relief. Some of her colleagues were professional enough to detach themselves from the real people behind the cases they considered, but Sheila had never been able to.

But it was summertime, and the schedule was less taxing. She was

taking off Fridays and spending long weekends on the road, visiting her district. She worked hard Monday through Thursday, then became the candidate. She planned to spend the month getting her campaign organized and on track.

Her first opponent, Mr. Coley, generally loafed Monday through Friday, resting himself for the rigors of the blackjack table. He gambled only at night, and thus had plenty of time to campaign, if he wanted to. Generally he did not. He showed up at a few county fairs and delivered colorful speeches to enthusiastic crowds. If his volunteers from Jackson were in the mood, they would drive down and erect the Faces of the Dead display, and Clete raised the volume. Every town has a dozen civic clubs, most of which are always looking for speakers. Word spread that candidate Coley could liven up the lunch, and he received an invitation or two each week. Depending on the drive, and the severity of his hangover, he would entertain the idea. By late July, his campaign had received $27,000 in donations, more than enough to cover the costs of his leased SUV and his part-time bodyguards. He'd also spent $6,000 on brochures. Every politician must have something to hand out.

Sheila's second opponent, though, was leading a campaign that ran like a well-tuned engine. Ron Fisk worked hard at his desk on Mondays and Tuesdays, then hit the road with a detailed schedule that left only the tiniest of towns untouched. Using both the Lear 55 and a King Air, he and his traveling staff quickly circled the district. By mid-July, there was an organized committee in each of the twenty-seven counties, and Ron had given at least one speech in all of them. He spoke to civic clubs, volunteer fire departments, library teas, county bar associations, motorcycle clubs, bluegrass festivals, county fairs, and churches, churches, and churches. At least half of his speeches were in pulpits.

On July 18, Josh played his final baseball game of the season, and his father was free to campaign even more. Coach Fisk did not miss a game, though the team fell apart after he announced his candidacy. Most parents agreed that the two were not related.

In the rural areas, Ron's message never varied. Because of liberal judges, our values are under attack from those who support gay marriage,

gun control, abortion, and unrestricted access to Internet pornography. Those judges must be replaced. His first loyalty was to the Bible. Laws made by men came next, but as a supreme court justice he would manage to reconcile both when necessary. He began each speech with a short prayer.

In the less rural areas, depending on the audience, he would often move a little from the far right and dwell on the death penalty. Ron found that audiences were captivated by graphic stories of brutal crimes committed by men who were sentenced to die twenty years ago. He worked a couple of these into his routine.

But regardless of where he was, the evil-liberal-judge theme dominated every speech. After a hundred or so, Ron himself believed that Sheila McCarthy was a raging leftist who'd caused many of the state's social problems.

On the money front, with Barry Rinehart quietly pulling the strings, contributions were arriving at a steady rate and managed to keep pace with expenses. By June 30, the first deadline to file financial reports, the Fisk campaign had received $510,000 from twenty-two hundred people. Of his contributors, only thirty-five gave the maximum of $5,000, and every one of these was a Mississippi resident. Ninety percent of donors were from within the state.

Barry knew the trial lawyers would scrutinize the contributors in the hope that out-of-state money was pouring in from big business interests. It had been a troublesome campaign issue before, and he would avoid it in the Fisk race. He was confident he would raise huge sums of money from out of state, but these donations would pour in at the chosen moment, late in the campaign when the state's benign reporting laws protected it from being an issue. In contrast, McCarthy's reports revealed that she was being financed by the trial lawyers, and Barry knew precisely how to wield this as an issue in his favor.

Barry also had the results of his latest poll, one that he would not share with the candidate. As of June 25, half the registered voters were now aware that there was a race. Of that number, 24 percent favored Ron Fisk, 16 percent Sheila McCarthy, and 10 percent Clete Coley.

Those numbers were exciting. In less than two months, Barry had packaged an unknown lawyer who'd never worn a black robe and thrust him ahead of an opponent with nine years of experience.

And they had yet to run a single ad on television.

———

On July 1, the Second State Bank was purchased by New Vista Bank, a regional chain based in Dallas. Huffy called Wes Payton with the news and was generally upbeat. The Hattiesburg office had been assured that nothing would change but the name. His loan portfolio had been reviewed by the new owners. They had quizzed him about the Paytons, and seemed content with Huffy's promises that the loan would eventually be satisfied.

For the fourth straight month, the Paytons sent Huffy a check for $2,000.

CHAPTER 22

In another life, Nathaniel Lester had been a flamboyant criminal defense lawyer with an uncanny knack for winning murder trials. At one point, two decades earlier, he had put together a streak of twelve consecutive not-guilty verdicts, virtually all in small towns throughout Mississippi, the types of places where those accused of heinous crimes are generally presumed guilty the moment they are arrested. His notoriety attracted clients from the civil side, and his country law office in the town of Mendenhall prospered nicely.

Nat won big verdicts and negotiated even larger settlements. His specialty became catastrophic personal injuries on the offshore oil rigs where many local men went for high-paying jobs. He was active in various trial lawyer groups, gave huge sums to political candidates, built the biggest house in town, went through a series of wives, and began drinking heavily. The booze, along with a string of ethics complaints and legal skirmishes, finally slowed him down, and when he was ultimately boxed in, he surrendered his law license to avoid a prison sentence. He left Mendenhall, found a new wife, sobered up, and resurfaced in Jackson, where he embraced Buddhism, yoga, vegetarianism, and a simpler life-

style. One of the few smart decisions he'd made during his heyday was to bury some of his money.

During the first week of August, he pestered Sheila McCarthy until she agreed to a quick lunch. Every lawyer in the state knew something of his colorful history, and she was understandably nervous. Over tofu and sprouts, he offered to run her campaign, at no cost. He would devote his considerable energies to nothing else for the next three months. She was apprehensive. His long gray hair fell to his shoulders. He had matching diamond earrings, and though they were quite small, they were still visible. He displayed one tattoo, on his left arm, and she didn't want to think of the others and where they might be. He wore jeans and sandals and a collection of bright leather bracelets on each wrist.

But Nat had not been a successful courtroom lawyer because he was dull and unpersuasive. He most definitely was not. He knew the district, its towns and courthouses and the people who ran them. He had a passionate hatred of big business and the influence it bought, and he was bored and looking for a war.

She caved in and invited him to join hers. Driving away from the restaurant, she questioned her sanity, but she also had a gut feeling that Nathaniel Lester could be the spark her campaign so badly needed. Her own poll showed her trailing Fisk by five points, and a sense of desperation was settling in.

They met again that night at her Jackson headquarters, and in a four-hour meeting Nat assumed control. With a combination of wit, charm, and castigation, he whipped her ragtag staff into a near frenzy of excitement. To prove his mettle, he called three Jackson trial lawyers, at home, and, after a few pleasantries, asked them why in the hell they had not yet sent money to the McCarthy campaign. Using a speakerphone, he shamed them, cajoled them, berated them, and refused to hang up until each had promised significant contributions from themselves and their families, clients, and friends. Don't mail the checks, he said—he would personally drive over before noon tomorrow and get the money himself. The three commitments totaled $70,000. From that moment, Nat was in charge.

The following day he picked up the checks and began the process of calling every trial lawyer in the state. He contacted labor groups and black leaders. He fired one staff member and hired two others. By the end of the week, Sheila was getting a morning printout of Nat's version of her daily schedule. She haggled a little, but not much. He was already working sixteen hours a day and expected that from the candidate and everyone else.

————

In Hattiesburg, Wes stopped by the home of Judge Harrison for a quiet lunch. With thirty Bowmore cases on his docket, it would be unwise to be seen in public. Though they had no intention of discussing pending business, the coziness would seem inappropriate. Tom Harrison had extended the invitation to Wes and Mary Grace, whenever they had the time. Mary Grace was out of town and sent her regrets.

The subject was politics. Tom's circuit court district covered Hattiesburg and Forrest County and the three rural counties of Cary, Lamar, and Perry. Almost 80 percent of the registered voters were in Hattiesburg, his home and also that of Joy Hoover, his opponent. She would do well in certain precincts in the city, but Judge Harrison was confident he would do even better. Nor was he worried about the smaller counties. In fact, he seemed generally unconcerned about losing. Hoover appeared to be well financed, probably with outside money, but Judge Harrison knew his district and enjoyed its politics.

Cary County had the smallest population of the four, and it was continuing to decline with no small measure of help from Krane Chemical and its toxic history. They avoided that topic and discussed various politicians in and around Bowmore. Wes assured him that the Paytons, as well as their clients, friends, Pastor Denny Ott, and Mary Grace's family, would do everything possible to reelect Judge Harrison.

Conversation shifted to other races, primarily that of Sheila McCarthy. She had passed through Hattiesburg two weeks earlier and spent half an hour at the Payton firm, where she awkwardly managed to avoid mentioning the Bowmore litigation while rounding up votes. The Pay-

tons admitted they had no money to contribute but promised to work overtime to get her reelected. A truckload of yard signs and other campaign materials had been delivered to the office the following day.

Judge Harrison lamented the politicization of the supreme court. "It's unseemly," he was saying, "how they are forced to grovel for votes. You, as a lawyer representing a client in a pending case, should have no contact whatsoever with a supreme court justice. But because of the system, one comes to your office seeking money and support. Why? Because some special interests with plenty of money have decided they would like to own her seat on the court. They're spending money to purchase a seat. She responds by raising money from her side of the street. It's a rotten system, Wes."

"How do you fix it?"

"Either take away the private money and finance the races with public funds or switch to appointments. Eleven other states have figured out how to make the appointment system work. I'm not sure their courts are vastly superior to ours in terms of legal talent, but at least the special interests don't control them."

"Do you know Fisk?" Wes asked.

"He's been in my courtroom a couple of times. Nice fella, green as hell. Looks nice in a suit, typical insurance defense routine. Opens his files, files his motions, settles, closes his files, never gets his hands dirty. He's never heard a case, mediated one, tried one, and he's never shown any interest in being a judge. Think about it, Wes. Every small town needs lawyers occasionally to serve as city judges or assistant magistrates or traffic court referees, and we all felt the obligation to step in when we were younger. Not this guy. Every small county needs lawyers to pinch-hit with youth court and drug court and the like, and those of us who aspired to be real judges volunteered. I mean, you gotta start somewhere. Not this guy. I'll bet he's never been to city court in Brookhaven or youth court in Lincoln County. He wakes up one day, decides he's suddenly passionate about the judiciary and, what the hell, he'll just start at the top. It's an insult to those of us who toil in the system and make it work."

"I doubt if running was his idea."

"No, he was recruited. That makes it even more shameful. They look around, pick some greenhorn with a nice smile and no record to attack, and package him with their slick marketing. That's politics. But it shouldn't contaminate the judiciary."

"We beat them two years ago with McElwayne."

"So you're optimistic?"

"No, Judge, I'm terrified. I haven't slept well since Fisk announced, and I won't sleep well until he's defeated. We're broke and in debt, so we can't write a check, but every member of our firm has agreed to spend one hour a day knocking on doors, passing out brochures, putting up yard signs, and making phone calls. We've written letters to our clients. We're leaning on our friends. We've organized Bowmore. We're doing everything possible because if we lose the *Baker* case there is no tomorrow."

"Where is the appeal?"

"All the briefs are in. Everything is nice and tidy and waiting on the court to tell us when, and if, it wants oral argument. Probably early next year."

"No chance of a decision before the election?"

"None whatsoever. It's the most important case on the docket, but then every lawyer feels this way. As you know, the court works on its own schedule. No one can push it."

They had iced coffee as they inspected the judge's small vegetable garden. The temperature was a hundred degrees and Wes was ready to go. They finally shook hands on the front porch. As Wes drove away, he couldn't help but worry about him. Judge Harrison was much more concerned about the McCarthy race than his own.

The hearing was on a motion to dismiss filed by Hinds County. The courtroom belonged to Chancellor Phil Shingleton. It was a small, busy, efficient courtroom with oak walls and the obligatory faded portraits of long-forgotten judges. There was no box for the jurors because jury trials did not occur in chancery court. Crowds were rare, but for this hearing every seat was taken.

Meyerchec and Spano, back from Chicago, sat with their radical lawyer at one table. At the other were two young women representing the county. Chancellor Shingleton called things to order, welcomed the crowd, noted the interest from the media, and looked at the file. Two courtroom artists worked on Meyerchec and Spano. Everyone waited anxiously as Shingleton flipped through paperwork as if he'd never seen it. In fact, he'd read it many times and had already written his ruling.

"Just curious," he said without looking up. "Why did you file this thing in chancery court?"

The radical lawyer stood and said, "It's a matter of equity, Your Honor. And we knew we could expect a fair trial here." If it was intended as humor, it missed its mark.

The reason it was filed in chancery court was to get it dismissed as soon as possible. A hearing in circuit court would take even longer. A federal lawsuit would go off in the wrong direction.

"Proceed," Shingleton said.

The radical lawyer was soon railing against the county and the state and society in general. His words came in short, rapid bursts, much too loud for the small room and much too shrill to listen to for more than ten minutes. He went on and on. The laws of the state were backward and unfair and discriminated against his clients because they couldn't marry each other. Why shouldn't two mature and consenting gay adults who are in love and want all the responsibilities and obligations and commitments and duties of matrimony be allowed the same privileges and legal rights as two heterosexuals? He managed to ask this question at least eight different ways.

The reason, explained one of the young ladies for the county, is that the laws of the state do not permit it. Plain and simple. The state's constitution grants to the legislature the right to make laws regarding marriage, divorce, and so on, and no one else has this authority. If and when the legislature approves same-sex marriage, then Mr. Meyerchec and Mr. Spano will be free to pursue their desires.

"Do you expect the legislature to do this anytime soon?" Shingleton deadpanned.

"No," was the quick reply, and it was good for some light laughter.

The radical lawyer rebutted with the strenuous argument that the legislature, especially "our" legislature, passed laws every year that are struck down by the courts. That is the role of the judiciary! After making this point loud and clear, he devised several ways to present it in slightly different formats.

After an hour, Shingleton was fed up. Without a recess, and glancing at his notes, he gave a ruling that was rather succinct. His job was to follow the laws of the state, and if the laws prohibited marriage between two men or two women, or two men and one woman, or whatever combination, anything other than one man and one woman, then he, as a chancellor, had no choice but to dismiss the case.

Outside the courthouse, with Meyerchec on one side and Spano on the other, the radical lawyer continued his screeching for the press. He was aggrieved. His clients were aggrieved, though it was noted by a few that both looked quite bored with it all.

They were appealing immediately to the Mississippi Supreme Court. That's where they were headed, and that's where they wanted to be. And with the shadowy firm of Troy-Hogan paying the bills from Boca Raton, that's exactly where they were going.

CHAPTER 23

During its first four months, the race between Sheila McCarthy and Ron Fisk had been markedly civil. Clete Coley had thrown his share of mud, but his general appearance and unruly personality made it difficult for voters to see him as a supreme court justice. Though he still received around 10 percent in Rinehart's polls, he was campaigning less and less. Nat Lester's poll gave him 5 percent, but that poll was not as detailed as Rinehart's.

After Labor Day, with the election two months away and the homestretch of the race at hand, Fisk's campaign took its first ugly step toward the gutter. Once on that course, it would not and could not turn back.

The tactic was one Barry Rinehart had perfected in other races. A mass mailing was sent to all registered voters from an outfit called Lawsuit Victims for Truth. It screamed the question "Why Are the Trial Lawyers Financing Sheila McCarthy?" The four-page diatribe that followed did not attempt to answer the question. Instead, it excoriated trial lawyers.

First, it used the family doctor, claiming that trial lawyers and the frivolous lawsuits they bring are responsible for many of the problems in

our health-care system. Doctors, laboring under the fear of lawsuit abuse, are forced to perform expensive tests and diagnoses that drive up the cost of medical care. Doctors must pay exorbitant premiums for malpractice insurance to protect themselves from bogus lawsuits. In some states, doctors have been driven out, leaving their patients without care. One doctor (no residence given) was quoted as saying, "I couldn't afford the premiums, and I was tired of spending hours in depositions and trials. So I simply quit. I still worry about my patients." A hospital in West Virginia was forced to close after getting hit with an outrageous verdict. A greedy trial lawyer was at fault.

Next, it hit the checkbook. Rampant litigation costs the average household $1,800 a year, according to one study. This expense is a direct result of higher insurance premiums on automobiles and homes, plus higher prices for a thousand household products whose makers are constantly being sued. Medications, both prescription and over-the-counter, are a perfect example. They would be 15 percent cheaper if the trial lawyers didn't hammer their manufacturers with massive class action cases.

Then it shocked the reader with a collection of some of the country's zaniest verdicts, a well-used and trusted list that always sparked outrage. Three million dollars against a fast-food chain for hot coffee that was spilled; $110 million against a carmaker for a defective paint job; $15 million against the owner of a swimming pool that was fenced and padlocked. The infuriating list went on and on. The world is going crazy and being led by devious trial lawyers.

After breathing fire for three pages, it finished with a bang. Five years earlier, Mississippi had been labeled by a pro-business group as a "judicial hellhole." Only four other states shared this distinction, and the entire process would have been overlooked but for the Commerce Council. It seized the news and splashed it around in newspaper ads. Now the issue was worthy of being used again. According to the Lawsuit Victims for Truth, the trial lawyers have so abused the court system in Mississippi that the state is now a dumping ground for all sorts of major lawsuits. Some of the plaintiffs live elsewhere. Many of the trial lawyers live else-

where. They forum-shop until they find a friendly county with a friendly judge, and there they file their cases. Huge verdicts are the result. The state has earned a shady reputation, and because of this many businesses avoid Mississippi. Dozens of factories have packed up and left. Thousands of jobs are gone.

All thanks to the trial lawyers, who of course adore Sheila McCarthy and her pro-plaintiff leanings and will spend anything to keep her on the court.

The mailing ended with a plea for sanity. It never mentioned Ron Fisk.

An e-mail blast then sent the ad to sixty-five thousand addresses in the district. Within hours, it had been picked up by the trial lawyers and sent to all of the MTA's eight hundred members.

———

Nat Lester was thrilled with the ad. As campaign manager, he preferred broad-based support from many groups, but the reality was that the only major donors to McCarthy were the trial lawyers. He wanted them angry, spitting nails, frothing at the mouth, ready for an old-fashioned bare-knuckle brawl. So far, they had given just under $600,000. Nat needed twice that, and the only way to get it was by throwing grenades.

He sent an e-mail to every trial lawyer, and in it he explained the urgent necessity of answering the propaganda as quickly as possible. Negative ads, both in print and on television, must be responded to immediately. Direct mail is expensive, but very effective. He estimated the cost of the Lawsuit Victims for Truth mailing at $300,000 (actual cost: $320,000). Since he planned to use direct mail more than once, he demanded an immediate infusion of $500,000, and he insisted on commitments by return e-mail. His coded e-mail address would publish a running total of new contributions from trial lawyers, and until it reached the goal of $500,000, the campaign would remain virtually hamstrung. His tactic bordered on extortion, but then he was still, at heart, a trial lawyer, and he knew the breed. The mailing jolted their blood pressure

to near-lethal levels. They loved to fight anyway, and the commitments would pour in.

While he manipulated them, he met with Sheila and tried to calm her. She had never been attacked before in such a manner. She was upset, but also angry. The gloves were off, and Mr. Nathaniel Lester was relishing the fight. Within two hours, he had designed and written a response, met with the printer, and ordered the necessary supplies. Twenty-four hours after the Lawsuit Victims for Truth's plea was sent by e-mail, 330 trial lawyers had committed $515,000.

Nat also went after the Trial Lawyers of America, several of whose members had made fortunes in Mississippi. He e-mailed the Lawsuit Victims for Truth's fulmination to fourteen thousand of its members.

———

Three days later, Sheila McCarthy counterpunched. Refusing to hide behind some silly group organized just to send propaganda, she (Nat) decided to send the correspondence from her own campaign. It was in the form of a letter, with a flattering photo of her at the top. She thanked each voter for his or her support, and quickly ran through her experience and qualifications. She claimed to have nothing but respect for her opponents, but neither had ever worn the black robe. Neither, frankly, had ever shown any interest in the judiciary.

Then she posed the question: "Why Is Big Business Financing Ron Fisk?" Because, she explained in detail, big business is currently in the business of buying seats on supreme courts all over the country. They target justices like herself, compassionate jurists who strive for the common ground and are sympathetic to the rights of workers, consumers, victims injured by the negligence of others, the poor, and the accused. The law's greatest responsibility is to protect the weakest members of our society. Rich people can usually take care of themselves.

Big business, through its myriad support groups and associations, is successfully coordinating a grand conspiracy to drastically change our court system. Why? To protect its own interests. How? By blocking the

courthouse door; by limiting liability for companies that make defective products, for negligent doctors, for abusive nursing homes, for arrogant insurance companies. The sad list went on.

She finished with a folksy paragraph asking the voters not to be fooled by slick marketing. The typical campaign run by big business in these races gets very ugly. Mud is their favorite tool. The attack ads would soon begin, and they would be relentless. Big business would spend millions to defeat her, but she had faith in the voters.

————

Barry Rinehart was impressed with the response. He was also delighted to see the trial lawyers rally so quickly and spend so much money. He wanted them to burn money. The high end of his projection was $2 million for the McCarthy camp, with 90 percent from the trial lawyers.

His boy Fisk could easily double that.

His next ad, again by direct mail, was a sucker punch that would quickly dominate the rest of the campaign. He waited a week, time for the dust to settle from the first exchange of jabs.

The letter came straight from Ron Fisk himself, on his campaign letterhead, with a photo at the top of the handsome Fisk family. Its ominous headline announced: "Mississippi Supreme Court to Rule on Gay Marriage."

After a warm greeting, Ron wasted no time in launching into the issue at hand. The case of *Meyerchec and Spano v. Hinds County* involved two gay men who wanted to get married, and it would be decided the following year by the supreme court. Ron Fisk—Christian, husband, father, lawyer—was adamantly opposed to same-sex marriages, and he would take this unshakable belief to the supreme court. He condemned such unions as abnormal, sinful, against the clear teachings of the Bible, and detrimental to society on many levels.

Halfway through the letter, he introduced to the fray the well-known voice of the Reverend David Wilfong, a national loudmouth with a huge radio following. Wilfong decried such efforts to pervert our laws and bend, yet again, to the desires of an immoral few. He denounced lib-

eral judges who insert their own beliefs into their rulings. He called upon the decent and God-fearing people of Mississippi, "the heart and soul of the Bible Belt," to embrace men like Ron Fisk and, in doing so, protect their state's sacred laws.

The liberal-judge theme continued to the end of the letter. Fisk signed off with another promise to serve as a conservative, commonsense voice of the people.

––––––––––

Sheila McCarthy read the letter with Nat, and neither knew what the next step should be. Her name was never mentioned, but then it really wasn't necessary. Fisk certainly wasn't accusing Clete Coley of being a liberal.

"This is deadly," Nat said, exasperated. "He has claimed this issue as his own, and to take it back, or even to share it, you have to pulverize homosexuals worse than he does."

"I'm not doing that."

"I know you're not."

"It is so improper for a member of the court, or one who aspires to be, to state how he or she will decide a future case. It's horrible."

"This is just the beginning, dear."

They were in the cramped storage room that Nat called his office. The door was shut, no one was listening. A dozen volunteers were busy in the adjacent room. Phones rang constantly.

"I'm not sure we answer this," Nat said.

"Why not?"

"What are you going to say? 'Ron Fisk is being mean.' 'Ron Fisk is saying things he shouldn't.' You'll come off looking bitchy, which is okay for a male candidate, but not for a female."

"That's not fair."

"The only response is a denial of your support for same-sex marriages. You would have to take a position, which—"

"Which I'm not going to do. I'm not in favor of these marriages, but we need some type of civil union arrangement. It's a ridiculous de-

bate, though, because the legislature is in charge of making laws. Not the court."

Nat was on his fourth wife. Sheila was looking for husband number two. "And besides," she said, "how could homosexuals possibly screw up the sanctity of marriage any worse than heterosexuals?"

"Promise me you'll never say that in public. Please."

"You know I won't."

He rubbed his hands together, then ran his fingers through his long gray hair. Indecisiveness was not one of his shortcomings. "We have to make a decision, here and now," he said. "We can't waste time. The smartest route is to answer by direct mail."

"What's the cost?"

"We can scale back some. I'd say two hundred thousand."

"Can we afford it?"

"As of today, I would say no. Let's revisit it in ten days."

"Agreed, but can't we do an e-mail blast and at least respond?"

"I've already written it."

The response was a two-paragraph message sent that day to forty-eight thousand e-mail addresses. Justice McCarthy issued a strong rebuke to Ron Fisk for pledging his vote on a case he was far away from hearing. Had he been a member of the court, he would have been chastised. Dignity demands that the justices keep matters confidential and refrain from any comment whatsoever about pending cases. In the one he mentioned, no briefs had been filed in the appeal. No arguments heard. Nothing was before the court as of this date. Without knowing the facts or the law, how could Mr. Fisk, or anyone else for that matter, possibly decide on a final ruling?

Sadly, it was just another example of Mr. Fisk's woeful inexperience in judicial matters.

————

Clete Coley's losses were piling up at the Lucky Jack, and he confided this to Marlin late one night in a saloon in Under-the-Hill. Marlin was

passing through, checking on the candidate, who seemed to have forgotten about the race.

"I have a great idea," Marlin said, warming up to the real reason for his visit. "There are fourteen casinos on the Gulf Coast, big, beautiful, Vegas-style—"

"I've seen them."

"Right. I know the guy who owns Pirate's Cove. He'll put you up three nights a week for the next month, penthouse suite, great view of the Gulf. Meals are on the house. You can play cards all night, and during the day you can do a bit of campaigning. Folks down there need to hear your message. Hell, that's where the votes are. I can line up some audiences. You do the politicking. You've got a great speech and people love it."

Clete was visibly taken with the idea. "Three nights a week, huh?"

"More if you want it. You gotta be tired of this place."

"Only when I'm losing."

"Do it, Clete. Look, the folks who put up the money would like to see more activity. They know it's a long shot, but they are serious about their message."

Clete admitted it was a great idea. He ordered more rum and began thinking of those beautiful new casinos down there.

is this acceptable ms. for dialogue?
a) an acceptable
b) would the reader view it as such?

CHAPTER 24

Mary Grace and Wes stepped off the elevator on the twenty-sixth floor of the tallest building in Mississippi, and into the plush reception suite of the state's largest law firm. She immediately noticed the wallpaper, the fine furniture, the flowers, things that had once mattered.

The well-dressed woman at the desk was sufficiently polite. An associate in the standard-issue navy suit and black shoes escorted them to a conference room, where a secretary asked if they wanted something to drink. No, they did not. The large windows looked down at the rest of Jackson. The dome of the capitol dominated the view. To its left was the Gartin building, and somewhere in there on someone's desk was the case of *Jeannette Baker v. Krane Chemical*.

The door opened and Alan York appeared with a big smile and warm handshake. He was in his late fifties, short and heavy and a bit sloppy—wrinkled shirt, no jacket, scuffed shoes—unusual for a partner in such a hidebound firm. The same associate was back, carrying two large expandable files. After greetings and small talk they took their places around the table.

The lawsuit the Paytons filed in April on behalf of the family of the

The degree of courtesy just adequate

deceased pulpwood cutter had sped through the early rounds of discovery. No trial date was set, and that possibility was at least a year away. Liability was clear—the truck driver who caused the accident had been speeding, at least fifteen miles per hour over the limit. Two eyewitnesses had been deposed and provided detailed and damning testimony about the speed and recklessness of the truck driver. In his deposition, the driver admitted to a long history of moving violations. Before taking to the road, he worked as a pipe fitter but had been fired for smoking pot on the job. Wes had found at least two old DUIs, and the driver thought there might be another one, but he couldn't remember.

In short, the case wouldn't get anywhere near a jury. It would be settled, and after four months of vigorous discovery Mr. Alan York was ready to begin the negotiations. According to him, his client, Littun Casualty, was anxious to close the file.

Wes began by describing the family, a thirty-three-year-old widow and mother with a high school education and no real job skills and three young children, the oldest being twelve. Needless to say, the loss was ruinous in every way.

As he talked, York took notes and kept glancing at Mary Grace. They had spoken on the phone but never met. Wes was handling the case, but York knew she was not there simply because she was pleasant to look at. One of his close friends was Frank Sully, the Hattiesburg lawyer hired by Krane Chemical to add bodies to the defense table. Sully had been pushed to the rear by Jared Kurtin and was still bitter about it. He had passed along to York many stories about the *Baker* trial, and it was Sully's opinion that the Payton tag team worked best when Mary Grace was chatting with the jury. She was tough on cross-examination, very quick on her feet, but her strength was connecting with people. Her closing argument was brilliant, powerful, and, obviously, very persuasive.

York had been defending insurance companies for thirty-one years. He won more than he lost, but there had been a few of those awful moments when juries failed to see the case his way and nailed him for big verdicts. It was part of the business. He had never, though, been in the neighborhood of a $41 million award. It was now a legend in the state's

legal circles. Add the drama of the Paytons risking everything, losing their home, office, cars, and borrowing heavily to sustain a four-month trial, and the legend kept growing. Their fate was well-known and much discussed at bar meetings and golf tournaments and cocktail parties. If the verdict stood, they would be primed to rake in huge fees. A reversal, and their survival was seriously in doubt.

As Wes went on, York couldn't help but admire them.

After a brief review of the liability, Wes summed up the damages, added a chunk for the carelessness of the trucking company, and said, "We think two million is a fair settlement."

"I bet you do," York said, managing the customary defense lawyer reaction of shock and dismay. Eyebrows arched in disbelief. Head shaking slowly in bewilderment. He grabbed his face with his hand and squeezed his cheeks, frowning. His quick smile was long gone.

Wes and Mary Grace managed to convey apathy while their hearts were frozen.

"To get two million," York said, studying his notes, "you have to factor in some element of punitive damages, and, frankly, my client is simply not willing to pay these."

"Oh yes," Mary Grace said coolly. "Your client will pay whatever the jury tells it to pay." Such blustering was also part of the business. York had heard it a thousand times, but it did indeed sound more ominous coming from a woman who, during her last trial, extracted a huge punitive award.

"A trial is at least twelve months away," York said as he looked at his associate for confirmation, as if anyone could project a trial date so far in the future. The associate dutifully confirmed what his boss had already said.

In other words, if this goes to trial, it will be months before you receive a dime in fees. It's no secret that your little firm is drowning in debt and struggling to survive, and everyone knows that you need a big settlement, and quick.

"Your client can't wait that long," York said.

"We've given you a number, Alan," Wes replied. "Do you have a counteroffer?"

York suddenly slapped his file shut, gave a forced grin, and said, "Look, this is really simple. Littun Casualty is very good at cutting its losses, and this case is a loser. My authority to settle is $1 million. Not a penny more. I have a million bucks, and my client told me not to come back for more. One million dollars, take it or leave it."

The referring lawyer would get half of the 30 percent contingency contract. The Paytons would get the other half. Fifteen percent was $150,000, a dream.

They looked at each other, both frowning, both wanting to leap across the table and begin kissing Alan York. Then Wes shook his head, and Mary Grace wrote something on a legal pad.

"We have to call our client," Wes said.

"Of course." York bolted from the room, his associate racing to keep up.

"Well," Wes said softly, as if the room might be bugged.

"I'm trying not to cry," she said.

"Don't cry. Don't laugh. Let's squeeze him a little."

When York was back, Wes said gravely, "We talked to Mrs. Nolan. Her bottom line is one point two million."

York exhaled as his shoulders drooped and his face sagged. "I don't have it, Wes," he said. "I'm being perfectly candid with you."

"You can always ask for more. If your client will pay a million, then they can kick in another $200,000. At trial, this case is worth twice that."

"Littun is a tough bunch, Wes."

"One phone call. Give it a try. What's there to lose?"

York left again, and ten minutes later burst back into the room with a happy face. "You got it! Congratulations."

———

The shock of the settlement left them numb. Negotiations usually dragged on for weeks or months, with both sides bickering and posturing

and playing little games. They had hoped to leave York's office with a general idea of where the settlement might be headed. Instead, they left in a daze and for fifteen minutes roamed the streets of downtown Jackson, saying little. For a moment they stopped in front of the Capitol Grill, a restaurant known more for its clientele than for its food. Lobbyists liked to be seen there, picking up tabs for fine meals with heavyweight politicians. Governors had always favored the place.

Why not splurge and eat with the big boys?

Instead, they ducked into a small deli two doors down and ordered iced tea. Neither had an appetite at the moment. Wes finally addressed the obvious. "Did we just earn $180,000?"

"Uh-huh," she said while sipping tea through a straw.

"I thought so."

"A third goes for taxes," she said.

"Are you trying to kill the party?"

"No, just being practical."

On a white paper napkin, she wrote down the sum of $180,000.

"Are we spending it already?" Wes asked.

"No, we're dividing it. Sixty thousand for taxes?"

"Fifty."

"Income, state and federal. Employee withholding, Social Security, unemployment, I don't know what else but it's at least a third."

"Fifty-five," he said, and she wrote down $60,000.

"Bonuses?"

"What about a new car?" he asked.

"Nope. Bonuses, for all five employees. They have not had a raise in three years."

"Five thousand each."

She wrote down $25,000, then said, "The bank."

"A new car."

"The bank? Half the fee is already gone."

"Two hundred dollars."

"Come on, Wes. We won't have a life until the bank is off our backs."

"I've tried to forget about the loan."

"How much?"

"I don't know. I'm sure you have a figure."

"Fifty thousand for Huffy, and ten thousand for Sheila McCarthy. That leaves us with thirty-five thousand." Which, at that moment, seemed like a fortune. They stared at the napkin, both recasting the numbers and rearranging the priorities, but neither willing to suggest a change. Mary Grace signed her name at the bottom, then Wes did likewise. She put the napkin in her purse.

"Can I at least get a new suit out of the deal?" he asked.

"Depends on what's on sale. I guess we should call the office."

"They're sitting by the phone."

Three hours later, the Paytons walked into their office, and the party started. The front door was locked, the phones were unplugged, the champagne began to flow. Sherman and Rusty, the law clerks, proposed lengthy toasts they had hurriedly put together. Tabby and Vicky, the receptionists, were tipsy after two glasses. Even Olivia, the ancient bookkeeper, kicked up her heels and was soon laughing at everything. The money was spent, re-spent, overspent, until everyone was rich.

When the champagne was gone, the office closed and everyone left. The Paytons, their cheeks warm from the bubbly, went to their apartment, changed into casual clothes, then drove to the school to fetch Mack and Liza. They had earned a night of fun, though the children were too young to understand the settlement. It would never be mentioned.

Mack and Liza were expecting Ramona, and when they saw both parents in the school pickup line, a long day instantly became brighter. Wes explained that they simply got tired of working and decided to play. The first stop was Baskin-Robbins for ice cream. Next, they went to a shopping mall, where a shoe store attracted their attention. Each Payton picked out a pair, at 50 percent off, with Mack being the boldest with a pair of Marine combat boots. In the center of the mall was a four-screen cinema. They caught the 6:00 p.m. showing of the latest Harry Potter.

Dinner was at a family pizzeria with an indoor playground and a rowdy atmosphere. They finally made it home around ten, where Ramona was watching television and enjoying the quiet. The kids handed her leftover pizza, and both talked at once about the movie. They promised to finish their homework in the morning. Mary Grace relented, and the entire family settled onto the sofa and watched a reality rescue show. Bedtime was pushed back to eleven.

When the apartment was quiet and the kids tucked in, Wes and Mary Grace lay on the sofa, heads on opposite ends, legs tangled together, minds drifting far away. For the past four years, as their finances had spiraled downward, with one loss after another, one humiliation following the last, fear had become a daily companion. Fear of losing the home, then the office, then the autos. Fear of not being able to provide for their children. Fear of a serious medical emergency that exceeded their insurance. Fear of losing the *Baker* trial. Fear of bankruptcy if the bank pushed too hard.

Since the verdict, the fear had become more of a nuisance than a constant threat. It was always there, but they had slowly gained control of it. For six straight months now, they had paid the bank $2,000 a month, hard-earned moneys that were left over after all other bills and expenses. It barely covered the interest, and it reminded them of how insurmountable their debt was. But it was symbolic. They were digging out from the rubble and could see the light.

Now, for the first time in years, there was a cushion, a safety net, something to catch them if they fell even deeper. They would take their share of today's settlement and hide it, and when they were afraid again, they would be comforted by their buried treasure.

———

At ten the following morning, Wes dropped by the bank and found Huffy at his desk. He swore him to silence, then whispered the good news. Huffy almost hugged him. Mr. Prickhead was on his back from nine to five, demanding action.

"The money should be here in a couple of weeks," Wes said proudly. "I'll call as soon as it lands."

"Fifty grand, Wes?" Huffy repeated, as if his job had just been saved.

"You got it."

From there Wes drove to his office. Tabby handed him a phone message from Alan York. Just routine stuff, probably some details to nail down.

But York's voice lacked its usual warmth. "Wes, there's a new wrinkle," he said slowly, as if searching for words.

"What's the matter?" Wes asked. A knot was already forming in his stomach.

"I don't know, Wes, I'm really frustrated, and confused. This has never happened to me, but, well, anyway, Littun Casualty has flipped on the settlement. It's off the table, all of it. They're yanking it. Some tough A-holes. I've been yelling at them all morning. They yell back. This firm has represented the company for eighteen years, never had a problem like this. But, as of one hour ago, they are looking for another firm. I've fired the client. I gave you my word, and now my client has hung me out to dry. I'm sorry, Wes. Don't know what else to say."

Wes pinched the bridge of his nose and tried not to groan. After a false start, he said, "Well, Alan, this is a shock."

"Damned right it is, but in all fairness it does no harm to the lawsuit. I'm just glad this didn't happen the day before the trial or something crazy like that. Some real bad boys up there."

"They won't be so tough at trial."

"Damned right, Wes. I hope you nail these guys for another huge verdict."

"We will."

"I'm sorry, Wes."

"It's not your fault, Alan. We'll survive and push for a trial."

"You do that."

"We'll talk later."

"Sure. Say, Wes, is your cell phone nearby?"

"It's right here."

"Here's my cell number. Hang up and call me back."

When both men were off the landlines, York said, "You didn't hear this from me, okay?"

"Okay."

"The chief in-house lawyer for Littun Casualty is a guy named Ed Larrimore. For twenty years he was a partner in a New York law firm called Bradley & Backstrom. His brother is also a partner at that firm. Bradley & Backstrom does the blue-chip thing, and one of its clients is KDN, the oil exploration firm whose biggest shareholder is Carl Trudeau. That's the connection. I have never talked to Ed Larrimore, there's no reason to. But the supervising attorney I deal with whispered to me that a decision was made at the very top to stiff this settlement."

"A little retribution, huh?"

"Smells like it. It's nothing illegal or unethical. The insurance company decides not to settle and goes to trial. Happens every day. There's nothing you can do about it, except burn them at trial. Littun Casualty has assets of twenty billion, so they aren't worried about a jury in Pike County, Mississippi. My guess is they'll drag it out until you get to trial, then try to settle."

"I'm not sure what to say, Alan."

"I'm sorry this happened, Wes. I'm out of the picture now, and you didn't get this from me."

"Sure."

Wes stared at the wall for a long time, then mustered the energy to stand, walk, leave his office, and go look for his wife.

CHAPTER 25

Like clockwork, Ron Fisk kissed Doreen goodbye at the front door at six o'clock on a Wednesday morning, then handed his overnight bag and briefcase to Monte. Guy was waiting in the SUV. Both assistants waved to Doreen, then they sped away. It was the last Wednesday in September, week twenty-one of his campaign, and the twenty-first consecutive Wednesday that he had kissed his wife goodbye at 6:00 a.m. Tony Zachary could not have found a more disciplined candidate.

In the rear seat, Monte handed Ron his daily briefing. One of Tony's deputies in Jackson prepared it during the night and e-mailed it to Monte at exactly five each morning. Page 1 was the schedule. Page 2 was a summary of the three groups he would address that day, along with the names of the important people who would attend.

Page 3 had updates from his opponents' campaigns. It was all mainly gossip but still his favorite part of the briefing. Clete Coley was last seen addressing a small group of sheriffs' deputies in Hancock County, then retiring to the blackjack tables at Pirate's Cove. Today, McCarthy is expected to be at work and has no campaign events.

Page 4 was the financial summary. Contributions so far totaled $1.7

million, with 75 percent coming from within the state. Expenditures of
$1.8 million. The deficit was of no concern. Tony Zachary knew the
heavy money would arrive in October. McCarthy had received $1.4 million, virtually all from trial lawyers. She had spent half of it. The prevailing thought in the Fisk camp was that the trial lawyers were tapped out.

They were at the airport. The King Air lifted off at 6:30, and at
that moment Fisk was on the phone to Tony in Jackson. It was their first
chat of the day. Everything was running smoothly. Fisk had already
reached the point of believing that all campaigns were so effortless. He
was always prompt, fresh, prepared, rested, well financed, and ready to
move on to the next event. He had little contact with the two dozen people under Tony's thumb who sweated the details.

————————

Justice McCarthy's version of the daily briefing was a glass of fruit juice
with Nat Lester at her Jackson headquarters. She aimed for 8:30 each
morning, and was fairly prompt. By then, Nat had put in two hours and
was yelling at people.

They had no interest in the whereabouts of her two opponents.
They spent little time with poll numbers. Their data showed her running
even with Fisk, and that was troubling enough. They quickly reviewed
the latest fund-raising schemes and talked about potential donors.

"I may have a new problem," she said that morning.

"Only one?"

"Do you remember the Frankie Hightower case?"

"Not at this moment, no."

"State trooper was gunned down in Grenada County five years ago.
He stopped a car for speeding. Inside the car were three black men and
a black teenager, Frankie Hightower. Someone opened fire with an assault weapon, and the trooper got hit eight times. Left him in the middle
of Highway 51."

"Let me guess. The court has reached a decision."

"The court is getting close. Six of my colleagues are ready to affirm
the conviction."

"Let me guess. You would like to dissent."

"I'm going to dissent. The kid had inadequate counsel. His defense lawyer was some jackass with no experience and apparently very little intelligence. The trial was a joke. The other three thugs pled for life and pointed the finger at Hightower, who was sixteen years old and sitting in the backseat, without a gun. Yes, I'm going to dissent."

Nat's sandals hit the floor and he began to pace. Arguing the merits of the case was a waste of time. Arguing the politics of it would take some skill. "Coley will go ballistic."

"I don't care about Coley. He's a clown."

"Clowns get votes."

"He's not a factor."

"Fisk will receive it as a wonderful gift from God. More proof that his campaign is divinely inspired. Manna from heaven. I can see the ads now."

"I'm dissenting, Nat. It's that simple."

"It's never that simple. Some of the voters might understand what you're doing and admire your courage. Perhaps three or four of them. The rest will see the Fisk ad with the smiling face of that handsome young state trooper next to the mug shot of Frankie whatever his name is."

"Hightower."

"Thank you. The ad will refer to liberal judges at least ten times, and it will probably show your face. Powerful stuff. You might as well quit now."

His words trailed off but were bitter nonetheless. For a long time they said nothing. Sheila broke the silence by saying, "That's not a bad idea. Quitting. I've caught myself reading the briefs and asking, 'What will the voters think if I rule this way or that?' I'm not a judge anymore, Nat, I'm a politician."

"You're a great judge, Sheila. One of the three we have left."

"It's all about politics now."

"You're not quitting. Have you written your dissent?"

"I'm working on it."

"Look, Sheila, the election is five weeks away. How slow can you

write? Hell, the court is famous for taking its sweet time. Surely to God you can sit on this thing until after the election. What's five weeks? It's nothing. The murder was five years ago." He was stomping around, arms flailing.

"We do have a schedule."

"Bullshit. You can manipulate it."

"For politics."

"Damned right, Sheila. Give me a break here. We're busting our asses for you and you act like you're too good for the dirty work. This is a filthy business, okay?"

"Lower your voice."

He lowered it several octaves but kept pacing. Three steps to one wall, then three steps to the other. "Your dissent is not going to change a damned thing. The court will run over you again 6 to 3, maybe even 7 to 2, perhaps even 8 to 1. The numbers don't really matter. The conviction is affirmed, and Frankie Whoever will stay exactly where he is right now and where he'll be ten years from now. Don't be stupid, Sheila."

She finished her fruit juice and did not respond.

"I don't like that smirk," Nat said. He pointed a long bony finger at her. "Listen to me. If you file a dissent before the election, I'm walking out the door."

"Don't threaten me."

"I'm not threatening. I'm promising. You know ten different ways to sit on that case for another five weeks. Hell, you could bury it for six months."

She stood and said, "I'm going to work."

"I'm not kidding!" he yelled. "I'll quit!"

She yanked open the door and said, "Go find us some money."

———

Three days later, the skillfully coordinated avalanche began. Only a handful of people knew what was coming.

Ron Fisk himself did not comprehend the scope of his own saturation. He had performed for the cameras, changed into various outfits,

worked his way through the scripts, dragged in his family and some friends, and he was aware of the budget and the media buys and the market shares of the various television stations in south Mississippi. And, in a normal campaign, he would have worried about financing such expensive marketing.

But the machine that bore his name had many parts he knew nothing about.

The first ads were the soft ones—warm little vignettes to open the doors and let this fine young man into the homes. Ron as a Boy Scout, with the richly accented old voice of an actor playing the role of his scoutmaster in the background. "One of the finest Boy Scouts we ever had. He made it to Eagle in less than three years." Ron in a robe at high school graduation, a star student. Ron with Doreen and the kids and his own voice saying, "Families are our greatest asset." After thirty seconds, the ad signed off with the slogan, in a deep, heavenly voice, "Ron Fisk, a judge with our values."

A second ad, a series of black-and-white still photos, began with Ron on the steps of his church, in a fine dark suit, chatting with his pastor, who narrated, "Ron Fisk was ordained as a deacon in this church twelve years ago." Ron with his jacket off, teaching Sunday school. Ron holding his Bible as he makes a point to a group of teenagers under a shade tree. "Thank God for men like Ron Fisk." Ron and Doreen greeting people at the church's door. And the same farewell: "Ron Fisk, a judge with our values."

There was not the slightest hint of conflict, nothing about the campaign, not a trace of mud, no indication of the savagery that would follow. Just a charming hello from an incredibly wholesome young deacon.

The ads blanketed south Mississippi, and central as well because Tony Zachary was paying the steep prices charged by the Jackson outlets.

September 30 was a crucial date on Barry Rinehart's calendar. All contributions made in the month of October would not be reported until November 10, six days after the election. The flood of out-of-state money

he was about to unleash would go undetected until it was too late. The losers would scream, but that was all they could do.

On September 30, Rinehart and company kicked into high gear. They began with their A-list: tort-reform groups, right-wing religious organizations, business lobbyists, business PACs, and hundreds of conservative organizations ranging from the well-known American Rifle Association to the obscure Zero Future Tax, a small gang dedicated to abolishing the Internal Revenue Service. Eleven hundred and forty groups in all fifty states. Rinehart sent each a detailed memo and request for an immediate donation to the Fisk campaign in the amount of $2,500, the maximum for an organized entity. From this collection, his goal was $500,000.

For the individuals—$5,000 maximum gift—Rinehart had a list of a thousand corporate executives and senior managers of companies in industries that attracted litigation from trial lawyers. Chief among these were insurance companies, and he would collect a million dollars from his contacts there. Carl Trudeau had given him the names of two hundred executives of companies controlled by the Trudeau Group, though no one from Krane Chemical would write a check. If the Fisk campaign took money from Krane, then a front-page story was likely. Fisk might feel compelled to recuse himself, a disaster Rinehart couldn't begin to contemplate.

He expected $1 million from Carl's boys, though it would not go directly into the Fisk campaign. To keep their names away from nosy reporters, and to make sure no one ever knew of Mr. Trudeau's involvement, Rinehart routed their money into the bank accounts for Lawsuit Victims for Truth and Gunowners United Now (GUN).

His B-list contained a thousand names of donors with proven records of supporting pro-business candidates, though not at the $5,000 level. He expected another $500,000.

Three million dollars was his goal, and he was not at all concerned about reaching it.

CHAPTER 26

In the excitement of the moment, Huffy had made a dreadful mistake. The expectation of a meaningful payment, coupled with the constant pressure from Mr. Prickhead, had caused a lapse in judgment.

Not long after Wes stopped by with the promise of $50,000, Huffy marched into the big office and proudly informed his boss that the Paytons' debt was about to be reduced. When he got the bad news two days later that it was not, he was too afraid to tell anyone.

After losing sleep for almost a week, he finally forced himself to confront the devil again. He stepped in front of the massive desk, swallowed hard, and said, "Some bad news, sir."

"Where's the money?" Mr. Kirkhead demanded.

"It's not going to happen, sir. Their settlement fell through."

Forgoing curse words, Mr. Prickhead said, "We're calling the loan. Do it now."

"What?"

"You heard me."

"We can't do that. They've been paying two thousand a month."

"Super. That doesn't even cover the interest. Call the loan. Now."

"But why?"

"Just a couple of small reasons, Huffy. Number one, it's been in default for at least a year. Number two, it's grossly under-collateralized. As a banker, certainly you can understand these small problems."

"But they're trying."

"Call the loan. Do it now, and if you don't, then you'll be either reassigned or dismissed."

"That's obscene."

"I don't care what you think." Then he relented a bit and said, "It's not my decision, Huffy. We have new ownership, and I have been ordered to call the loan."

"But why?"

Kirkhead picked up the phone and offered it. "You want to call the man in Dallas?"

"This will bankrupt them."

"They've been bankrupt for a long time. Now they can make it official."

"Son of a bitch."

"Talking to me, son?"

Huffy glared at the fat hairless head, then said, "Not really. More to that son of a bitch in Dallas."

"We'll keep that here, okay?"

Huffy returned to his office, slammed the door, and watched the walls while an hour passed. Prickhead would stop by soon for the follow-up.

———

Wes was in a deposition downtown. Mary Grace was at her desk and took the call.

She admired Huffy for his bravery in extending much more credit than anyone had thought possible, but the sound of his voice always rattled her. "Good morning, Tom," she said pleasantly.

"It's not a good morning, Mary Grace," he began. "It's a bad morning, an awful morning, one of the worst ever."

A heavy pause. "I'm listening."

"The bank, not the bank you've been dealing with but another bank now, one owned by some people I've met only once and never care to see again, has decided that it can no longer wait to be paid. The bank, not me, is calling the loan."

Mary Grace emitted a strange guttural sound that could have passed for an expletive but really wasn't a word at all. Her first thought was of her father. Other than the Paytons' signatures, the only security for the loan was a two-hundred-acre tract of farmland her father had owned for many years. It was near Bowmore, and it did not include the forty acres and family home. The bank would foreclose on the property.

"Any particular reason, Huffy?" she asked coolly.

"None whatsoever. The decision was not made in Hattiesburg. Second State sold out to the devil, if you will recall."

"This doesn't make sense."

"I agree."

"You'll force us into bankruptcy, and the bank will get nothing."

"Except for the farm."

"So you'll foreclose on the farm?"

"Someone will. I hope not me."

"Smart move, Huffy, because when they foreclose on the courthouse steps in Bowmore there might be a killing."

"Maybe they'll get ole Prickhead."

"Are you in your office?"

"Yes, with the door locked."

"Wes is downtown. He'll be there in fifteen minutes. Unlock the door."

"No."

———

Fifteen minutes later, Wes charged into Huffy's office, his cheeks red with anger, his hands ready to strangle. "Where's Prickhead?" he demanded.

Huffy jumped to his feet behind his desk and placed both hands in the air. "Be cool, Wes."

"Where's Prickhead?"

"Right now he's in his car, driving to an urgent meeting, one that suddenly materialized ten minutes ago. Sit down, Wes."

Wes took a deep breath, then slowly eased into a chair. Huffy watched him, then returned to his own chair. "It's not his fault, Wes," Huffy said. "Technically, the loan has been in default for almost two years. He could have done this months ago, but he didn't. I know you don't like him. I don't like him. His wife doesn't like him. But he's been very patient. This was a decision made in the home office."

"Give me a name at the home office."

Huffy slid across a letter he'd received by fax. It was addressed to the Paytons, on New Vista Bank letterhead, and signed by a Mr. F. Patterson Duvall, vice president. "This arrived thirty minutes ago," Huffy said. "I don't know Mr. Duvall. I've called his office twice, but he's in a very important meeting, one that I'm sure will last until we stop calling. It's a waste of time, Wes."

The letter demanded payment in full of $414,656.22, with daily interest kicking in at $83.50. Pursuant to the terms of the loan agreement, the Paytons had forty-eight hours to pay, or collection and foreclosure proceedings would commence. Of course, the resulting attorneys' fees and court costs would also be tacked on to the amount due.

Wes read it slowly as he continued to cool down. He placed it back on the desk. "Mary Grace and I talk about this loan every day, Huffy. It's a part of our marriage. We talk about the kids, the office, the debt to the bank, what's for dinner. It's always there, and we've busted our asses to pay off all other obligations so we can bust our asses to pay off the bank. We came very close to giving you fifty thousand last week. We vowed to work ourselves ragged until this bank is out of our lives. Now this stunt. Now some moron in Dallas has decided he's tired of seeing this past-due loan on his daily rap sheet, and he wants to get rid of it. You know what, Huffy—"

"What?"

"The bank just screwed itself. We'll file for bankruptcy, and when

you try to foreclose on my father-in-law's property, I'll put him in bankruptcy. And when we work our way out of bankruptcy, and we're back on our feet, guess who ain't getting paid."

"The moron in Dallas?"

"You got it. The bank gets nothing. It'll be wonderful. We can keep the $400,000 when we earn it."

———

Late that afternoon, Wes and Mary Grace called a firm meeting in The Pit. Other than the humiliation of filing for bankruptcy, which seemed to bother no one, there was little to worry about. In fact, the bank's actions would give the firm some breathing room. The $2,000 monthly payments would cease, and the cash could certainly be used elsewhere.

The concern, of course, was the land owned by Mr. Shelby, Mary Grace's father. Wes had a plan. He would find a friendly buyer who would appear at the foreclosure and write a check. Title would pass, and it would be held in "a handshake trust" until the Paytons could buy it back, hopefully within a year. Neither Wes nor Mary Grace could stomach the idea of asking her father to join them at the bankruptcy court.

Forty-eight hours passed with no payment. Sticking to its word, the bank filed suit. Its lawyer, a local gentleman the Paytons knew well, called ahead of time and apologized. He'd represented the bank for years and could not afford to lose it as a client. Mary Grace accepted his apology and gave him her blessing to sue them.

The next day the Paytons filed for bankruptcy, both individually and as Payton & Payton, Attorneys-at-Law. They listed combined assets of $35,000—two old cars, furniture, office equipment—all of which was protected. They listed debts of $420,000. The filing effectively stayed the lawsuit, and would eventually render it useless. The *Hattiesburg American* reported it on its second page the following day.

Carl Trudeau read about it online and laughed out loud. "Sue me again," he said with great satisfaction.

Within a week, three Hattiesburg law firms informed ole Prickhead

that they were withdrawing their funds, closing their accounts, and moving their business down the street. There were at least eight other banks in town.

A wealthy trial lawyer named Jim McMay called Wes and offered assistance. The two had been friends for many years and had collaborated twice on product liability cases. McMay represented four Bowmore families in the Krane litigation, but had not pushed the cases aggressively. Like the other trial lawyers suing Krane, he was waiting for the outcome of *Baker* and hoping to hit the jackpot if and when there was a settlement.

They met for breakfast at Nanny's, and over biscuits and country ham McMay readily agreed to rescue the two hundred acres at foreclosure and keep the title until the Paytons could buy it back. Farmland in Cancer County wasn't exactly selling at a premium, and Wes speculated that the Shelby property would fetch around $100,000, the only money the bank would collect from its foolish maneuver.

Sheila McCarthy was enduring the morning's torture on the treadmill when she hit the stop button and gawked at the television in disbelief. The ad ran at 7:29, smack in the middle of the local news. It began with the provocative sight of two well-dressed young men kissing passionately while a minister of some variety smiled behind them. A husky voice-over announced, "Same-sex marriages are sweeping the country. In places like Massachusetts, New York, and California, laws are being challenged. Advocates of gay and lesbian marriages are pushing hard to force their lifestyles on the rest of our society." A still photo of a wedding couple—male and female—at the altar was suddenly desecrated with a bold black X. "Liberal judges are sympathetic to the rights of same-sex marriages." The photo was replaced with a video of a group of happy lesbians waiting to tie the knot in a mass ceremony. "Our families are under attack from homosexual activists and the liberal judges who support them." Next was a quick video of a mob burning an American flag. The voice said, "Liberal judges have approved the burning of our flag." Then a quick shot of a magazine rack lined with copies of *Hustler*. "Liberal judges see nothing wrong with pornography." Then a photo of a smiling

family, mother and father and four children. "Will liberal judges destroy our families?" the narrator inquired ominously, leaving little doubt that they would if given half a chance. The family photo was ripped apart into two jagged pieces. Suddenly the handsome but serious face of Ron Fisk appeared. He looked sincerely at the camera and said, "Not in Mississippi. One man. One woman. I'm Ron Fisk, candidate for the supreme court. And I approved this ad."

Dripping with sweat, her heart pounding even faster, Sheila sat on the floor and tried to think. The weatherman was prattling on, but she didn't hear him. She lay down on her back, stretched out her arms and legs, and took deep breaths.

Gay marriage was a dead issue in Mississippi and would remain so forever. No one with an audience or a following had dared to suggest that the laws be changed to allow it. Every member of the state legislature could be expected to rail against it. Only one judge in the entire state— Phil Shingleton—had addressed it, and he had dismissed the Meyerchec/ Spano lawsuit in record speed. The supreme court would probably deal with that case in a year or so, but Sheila expected a rather terse review followed by a quick 9–0 vote affirming Judge Shingleton.

How, exactly, had she now been cast as a liberal judge who supported gay marriage?

The room was spinning. At a commercial break, she tensed and waited for another assault, but there was nothing but the squawking of a car dealer and frantic urgings of a discount-furniture retailer.

Fifteen minutes later, though, the ad was back. She lifted her head and watched in disbelief as the same images followed the same voice.

Her phone was ringing. Caller ID told her not to answer. She showered and dressed in a hurry and at 8:30 walked into her headquarters with a wide smile and warm "Good morning." The four volunteers were subdued. Three televisions were running three different programs. Nat was in his office yelling at someone on the phone. He slammed the phone down, waved her inside, then closed the door behind her.

"You've seen it?" he said.

"Twice," she said softly. On the surface, she seemed unfazed. Everyone else was rattled, and it was important to at least try to appear calm.

"Total saturation," he said. "Jackson, Gulf Coast, Hattiesburg, Laurel, every fifteen minutes on all stations. Plus radio."

"What kind of juice do you have?"

"Carrot," he said and opened his small refrigerator. "They're burning money, which, of course, means they're raking it in by the truckload. Typical ambush. Wait until October 1, then push the button and start printing cash. They did it last year in Illinois and Alabama. Two years ago in Ohio and Texas." He poured two cups as he spoke.

"Sit down and relax, Nat," she said. He did not.

"Attack ads must be answered in kind," he said. "And quickly."

"I'm not sure this is an attack ad. He never mentions my name."

"He doesn't have to. How many liberal judges are running against Mr. Fisk?"

"None that I know of."

"As of this morning, dear, you are now officially a liberal judge."

"Really? I don't feel any different."

"We have to answer this, Sheila."

"I'm not getting dragged into a mudslinging fight over gay marriage."

Nat finally wiggled himself into his chair and shut up. He drank his juice, stared at the floor, and waited for his breathing to relax.

She took a sip of carrot juice, then said with a smile, "This is deadly, isn't it?"

"The juice?"

"The ad."

"Potentially, yes. But I'm working on something." He reached into a pile of rubble next to his desk and pulled out a thin file. He opened it and lifted three sheets of paper clipped together. "Listen to this. Mr. Meyerchec and Mr. Spano leased an apartment on April 1 of this year. We have a copy of the lease. They waited thirty days, as required by law, then registered to vote. The next day, May 2, they applied for Mississippi

driver's licenses, took the exam, and passed. The Department of Public Safety issued licenses on May 4. A couple of months passed, during which there is no record of employment, business licenses, nothing official to indicate they were working here. Remember, they claim to be self-employed illustrators, whatever the hell that is." He was riffling through the papers, checking facts here and there. "A survey of the illustrators who advertise various services in the yellow pages revealed that no one knows Meyerchec or Spano. Their apartment is in a big complex, lots of units, lots of neighbors, none of whom can remember seeing them. In gay circles, not a single person who was contacted has ever met them."

"Contacted by whom?"

"Hang on. Then they try to get a marriage license, and the rest of the story has been in the newspapers."

"Contacted by whom?"

Nat arranged the papers in the file and closed it. "This is where it gets interesting. Last week I received a call from a young man who described himself as a gay law student here in Jackson. He gave me his name and the name of his partner, another law student. They're not in the closet, but not exactly ready for the Gay Pride Parade. They were intrigued by the Meyerchec/Spano case, and when it exploded into a campaign issue, they, like a few other folks with brains, began to get suspicious. They know a lot of the gays here in town, and they began to ask about Meyerchec and Spano. No one knows them. In fact, the gay community was suspicious from the day the lawsuit was filed. Who are these guys? Where did they come from? The law students decided to find the answers. They've called the Meyerchec/Spano phone number five times a day, at different hours, and never gotten an answer. For thirty-six days now, they've made their calls. No answer. They've talked to the neighbors. Never a sighting. No one saw them move in. They've knocked on the door, peeked in the windows. The apartment is barely furnished, nothing on the walls. To make themselves real citizens, Meyerchec and Spano paid $3,000 for a used Saab, titled in both names like a real married couple, then bought Mississippi car tags. The Saab is parked in front of their apartment and hasn't moved in thirty-six days."

"Where might this be going?" she asked.

"I'm getting there. Now, our two law students have found them, in Chicago, where Meyerchec owns a gay bar and Spano works as an interior designer. The students are willing, for a little cash, to fly to Chicago, spend a few days, hang out in the bar, infiltrate, gather information."

"Information for what?"

"Information that, hopefully, will prove that they are not residents of this state; that their presence here was a sham; that someone is using them to exploit the gay marriage issue; and maybe that they are not even a couple in Chicago. If we can prove that, then I'll go to the *Clarion-Ledger*, the Biloxi *Sun Herald*, and every other newspaper in the state and deliver the goods. We can't win a fight on this issue, dear, but we can damned sure fight back."

She drained her glass and shook her head in disbelief. "Do you think Fisk is this smart?"

"Fisk is a pawn, but, yes, his handlers are this smart. It's a cynical scheme, and it's brilliant. No one thinks about gay marriage here because it will never happen, then, suddenly, everybody's talking about it. Front-page news. Everybody's scared. Mothers are hiding their children. Politicians are blathering."

"But why use two gay men from Chicago?"

"I'm not sure you can find two gay men in Mississippi who want this kind of publicity. Plus, gays here who are committed to tolerance understand the backlash from the straight world. The worst thing they could do is exactly what Meyerchec and Spano have done."

"If Meyerchec and Spano are gay, why would they do something to hurt the cause?"

"Two reasons. First, they don't live here. Second, money. Someone's paying the bills—the apartment lease, the used car, the lawyer, and a few thousand bucks to Meyerchec and Spano for their time and trouble."

Sheila had heard enough. She glanced at her watch and said, "How much do they need?"

"Expense money—airfare, hotel, the basics. Two thousand."

"Do we have it?" she asked with a laugh.

"It's out of my pocket. We'll keep it off the books. I just want you to know what we're doing."

"You have my approval."

"And the Frankie Hightower dissent?"

"I'm hard at work. Should take me another two months."

"Now you're talking like a real supreme court justice."

————

Denny Ott received a left-handed invitation to the meeting when a fellow preacher mentioned it to him over coffee one morning at Babe's. Not every minister in town was invited. Two from the Methodist churches and the Presbyterian pastor were specifically excluded, but it appeared as if all others were welcome. There was no Episcopal church in Bowmore, and if the town had a single Catholic, he or she had yet to come forward.

It was held on a Thursday afternoon in the fellowship hall of a fundamentalist congregation called Harvest Tabernacle. The moderator was the church's pastor, a fiery young man who was generally known as Brother Ted. After a quick prayer, he welcomed his fellow ministers, sixteen in number, including three black ministers. He cast a wary eye at Denny Ott, but said nothing about his presence.

Brother Ted quickly got down to business. He had joined the Brotherhood Coalition, a newly formed collection of fundamentalist preachers throughout south Mississippi. It was their purpose to quietly and methodically do everything possible, within the Lord's will, to elect Ron Fisk and thus kill off any chance of same-sex marriages occurring in Mississippi. He ranted on about the evils of homosexuality and its growing acceptability in American society. He quoted the Bible when appropriate, his voice rising with indignation when necessary. He stressed the urgency of electing godly men to all public positions and promised that the Brotherhood would be a force for years to come.

Denny listened with a straight face but growing alarm. He'd had several conversations with the Paytons and knew the real issues behind the race. The manipulation and marketing of Fisk made him sick. He

glanced at the other ministers and wondered how many funerals they had held for people killed by Krane Chemical. Cary County should be the last place to embrace the candidacy of someone like Ron Fisk.

Brother Ted grew sufficiently pious when he moved to the subject of Sheila McCarthy. She was a Catholic from the Coast, which in rural Christian circles meant she was a woman of loose morals. She was divorced. She liked to party, and there were rumors of boyfriends. She was a hopeless liberal, opposed to the death penalty, and could not be trusted when faced with decisions dealing with gay marriage and illegal immigration and the like.

When he finished his sermon, someone suggested that perhaps churches should not become so involved in politics. This was met with general disapproval. Brother Ted jumped in with a brief lecture about the culture wars and the courage they should have to fight for God. It's time for Christians to get off the sidelines and charge into the arena. This led to a fervent discussion about the erosion of values. Blame was placed on television, Hollywood, the Internet. The list grew long and ugly.

What was their strategy? someone asked.

Organization! Church folk outnumbered the heathen in south Mississippi, and the troops must be mobilized. Campaign workers, door knockers, poll watchers. Spread the message from church to church, house to house. The election was only three weeks away. Their movement was spreading like wildfire.

After an hour, Denny Ott could take no more. He excused himself, drove to his office at the church, and called Mary Grace.

The MTA directors met in an emergency session two days after the Fisk campaign launched its waves of anti-gay-marriage ads. The mood was somber. The question was obvious: How did such an issue take center stage? And what could the McCarthy campaign do to counter the attack?

Nat Lester was present and gave a summary of their plans for the final three weeks. McCarthy had $700,000 to fight with, much less than Fisk. Half of her budget was already committed to television ads that

would begin running in twenty-four hours. The remainder was for direct mail and some last-minute radio and TV spots. After that, they were out of money. Small donations were coming from labor, conservationists, good-government groups, and a few of the more moderate lobbying organizations, but 92 percent of McCarthy's funds were mailed in by trial lawyers.

Nat then summarized the latest poll. The race was a dead heat with the two front-runners at 30 percent, with the same number of voters still undecided. Coley remained around 10 percent. However, the poll was conducted the week before and did not reflect any shift due to the gay marriage ads. Because of those ads, Nat would begin polling over the weekend.

Not surprisingly, the trial lawyers had wild and varied opinions about what to do. All of their ideas were expensive, Nat continually reminded them. He listened to them argue. Some had sensible ideas, others were radical. Most assumed they knew more about campaigns than the others, and all of them took for granted that whatever course of action they finally agreed on would be immediately embraced by the McCarthy campaign.

Nat did not share with them some depressing gossip. A reporter from the Biloxi newspaper had called that morning with a few questions. He was exploring a story about the raging new issue of same-sex marriages. During the course of a ten-minute interview, he told Nat that the largest television station on the Coast had sold $1 million in prime airtime to the Fisk campaign for the remaining three weeks. It was believed to be the largest sale ever in a political race.

One million dollars on the Coast meant at least that much for the rest of the markets.

The news was so distressing that Nat was debating whether to tell Sheila. At that moment, he was leaning toward keeping it to himself. And he certainly wouldn't share it with the trial lawyers. Such sums were so staggering that it might demoralize Sheila's base.

The MTA president, Bobby Neal, finally hammered out a plan, one that would cost little. He would send to their eight hundred members an

urgent e-mail detailing the dire situation and begging for action. Each trial lawyer would be instructed to (1) make a list of at least ten clients who were willing and able to write a check for $100, and (2) make another list of clients and friends who could be motivated to campaign door-to-door and work the polls on Election Day. Grassroots support was critical.

As the meeting began to break up, Willy Benton stood at the far end of the table and got everyone's attention. He was holding a sheet of paper with small print front and back. "This is a promissory note on a line of credit at the Gulf Bank in Pascagoula," he announced, and more than one lawyer considered diving under the table. Benton was no small thinker, and he was known for drama. "Half a million dollars," he said slowly, the numbers booming around the room. "In favor of the campaign to reelect Sheila McCarthy. I've already signed it, and I'm going to pass it around this table. There are twelve of us here. It requires ten signatures to become effective. Each will be liable for fifty thousand."

Dead silence. Eyes were darting from face to face. Some had already contributed more than $50,000, others much less. Some would spend $50,000 on jet fuel next month, others were bickering with their creditors. Regardless of their bank balances at the moment, each and every one wanted to strangle the little bastard.

Benton handed the note to the unlucky stiff to his left, one without a jet. Fortunately, such moments in a career are rare. Sign it and you're a tough guy who can roll the dice. Pass it along unsigned and you might as well quit and go home and do real estate.

All twelve signed.

CHAPTER 28

The pervert's name was Darrel Sackett. When last seen, he was thirty-seven years old and housed in a county jail awaiting a new trial on charges of molesting small children. He certainly looked guilty: long sloping forehead, vapid bug eyes enlarged by thick glasses, splotchy stubble from a week's growth, a thick scar stuck to his chin—the type of face that would alarm any parent, or anyone else for that matter. A career pedophile, he was first arrested at age sixteen. Many other arrests followed, and he'd been convicted at least four times in four different states.

Sackett, with his frightening face and disgusting rap sheet, was introduced to the registered voters of south Mississippi in a snazzy direct mailing from another new organization, this one calling itself Victims Rising. The two-page letter was both a bio of a pathetic criminal and a summary of the miserable failures of the judicial system.

"Why Is This Man Free?" the letter screamed. Answer: Because Justice Sheila McCarthy overturned his conviction on sixteen counts of child molestation. Eight years earlier, a jury convicted Sackett, and the judge sentenced him to life without parole. His lawyer—one paid by taxpayers—appealed his case to the supreme court, and "there Darrel Sack-

ett found the sympathetic embrace of Justice Sheila McCarthy." McCarthy condemned the honest and hardworking detectives who extracted a full confession from Sackett. She chastised them for what she saw as their faulty search-and-seizure methods. She hammered the trial judge, who was highly respected and tough on crime, for admitting into evidence the confession and materials taken from Sackett's apartment. (The jury was visibly shaken when forced to view Sackett's stash of child porn, seized by the cops during a "valid" search.) She claimed distaste for the defendant, but begged off by saying that she had no choice but to reverse his conviction and send his case back for a new trial.

Sackett was moved from the state prison back to the Lauderdale County jail, where he escaped one week later. He had not been heard from since. He was out there, "a free man," no doubt continuing his violence against innocent children.

The last paragraph ended with the usual rant against liberal judges. The fine print gave the standard approval by Ron Fisk.

Certain relevant facts were conveniently omitted. First, the court voted 8 to 1 to reverse the Sackett conviction and send it back for a new trial. The actions of the police were so egregious that four other justices wrote concurring opinions that were even more scathing in their condemnation of the forced confession and warrantless, unconstitutional search. The lone dissenter, Justice Romano, was a misguided soul who had never voted to reverse a criminal conviction, and privately vowed that he would never do so.

Second, Sackett was dead. Four years earlier he'd been killed in a bar fight in Alaska. The news of his passing barely made it to Mississippi, and when his file was retired in Lauderdale County, not a single reporter noticed. Barry Rinehart's exhaustive research discovered the truth, for what little it mattered.

The Fisk campaign was far beyond the truth now. The candidate was too busy to sweat the details, and he had placed his complete trust in Tony Zachary. The race had become a crusade, a calling of the highest order, and if facts were slightly bent or even ignored, then it was justified because of the importance of his candidacy. Besides, it was politics, a

Isn't this so true of the fundamentally dishonest?

dirty game, and you could rest assured the other side wasn't playing fair, either.

Barry Rinehart had never been shackled by the truth. His only concern was not getting caught in his lies. If a madman like Darrel Sackett was out there, on the loose, very much alive and doing his filthy deeds, then his story was more shocking. A dead Sackett was a pleasant thought, but Rinehart preferred the power of fear. And he knew that McCarthy couldn't respond. She had reversed his conviction, plain and simple. Any effort to explain why would be futile in the world of thirty-second ads and snappy sound bites.

After the shock of the ad, she would try to erase Sackett from her mind.

———

After the shock, though, she had to at least revisit the case. She saw the ad online, at the Victims Rising Web site, after receiving a frantic call from Nat Lester. Paul, her clerk, found the reported case, and they read it in silence. She vaguely remembered it. In the eight years since, she had read a thousand briefs and written hundreds of opinions.

"You got it right," Paul said when he finished.

"Yes, but why does it look so wrong now?" she said. She'd been hard at work, her desk covered with memos from half a dozen cases. She was stunned, bewildered.

He didn't answer.

"I wonder what's next," she said, closing her eyes.

"Probably a death penalty case. And they'll cherry-pick the facts again."

"Thanks. Anything else?"

"Sure. There's lots of material in these books. You're a judge. Every time you make a decision someone loses. These guys don't care about the truth, so they can make anything sound bad."

"Please shut up."

———

Her first ads began, and they lightened the mood somewhat. Nat chose to begin with a straightforward piece with Sheila in a black robe sitting at the bench, smiling earnestly at the camera. She talked about her experience—eight years as a trial judge in Harrison County, nine years on the supreme court. She hated to pat her own back, but twice in the past five years she had received the highest rating in the state bar's annual review of all appellate judges. She was not a liberal judge, nor a conservative one. She refused to be labeled. Her commitment was simply to follow the laws of Mississippi, not to make new ones. The best judges are those without agendas, without preconceived notions of how they might rule. The best judges are those with experience. Neither of her opponents had ever presided over a trial, or issued a ruling, or studied complicated briefs, or listened to oral arguments, or written a final opinion. Until now, neither of her opponents had shown the slightest interest in sitting as a judge. Yet they are asking the voters to jump-start their judicial careers at the very top. She finished by saying, without the smile, "I was appointed to this position by the governor nine years ago, then I was reelected by you, the people. I am a judge, not a politician, and I don't have the money that some are spending to purchase this seat. I ask you, the voters, to help send the message that a seat on the Mississippi Supreme Court cannot be bought by big business. Thank you."

Nat spent little money at the Jackson stations and much more on the Coast. McCarthy would never be able to saturate like Fisk. Nat speculated that Fisk and all those wealthy folks behind him were burning $200,000 a week on the anti-gay-marriage ads alone.

Sheila's first round was about half of that, and the response was lukewarm. The ad was called "uncreative" by her coordinator in Jackson County. A noisy trial lawyer, no doubt an expert in all things political, sent an angry e-mail in which he blasted Nat for such a soft approach. You gotta fight fire with fire and answer the attack ads with more of the same. He reminded Nat that his firm had contributed $30,000 and might forgo any more if McCarthy didn't take off the gloves.

Women seemed to like the ad. Men were more critical. After reading a few dozen e-mails, Nat realized he was wasting his time.

———

Barry Rinehart had been waiting impatiently for some television from the McCarthy strategists. When he finally saw her first ad, he laughed out loud. What an old-fashioned, out-of-date, pathetically lame effort—judge in black robe, at a bench, thick law books as props, even a gavel for good measure. She looked sincere, but she was a judge, not a television presence. Her eyes moved as she read from the teleprompter. Her head was as rigid as a deer in headlights.

A weak response indeed, but it had to be answered. It had to be buried. Rinehart reached into his video library, his arsenal, and selected his next grenade.

Ten hours after McCarthy began running her ad, she was blown off the television by an attack ad that stunned even the most jaded political junkies. It began with the sharp crack of a rifle shot, then a black-and-white photo of Justice McCarthy, one from the court's official Web site. A powerful, barbed voice announced, "Justice Sheila McCarthy does not like hunters. Seven years ago she wrote, 'The hunters of this state have a poor record on safety.' " This quote was splashed across her face. The photo changed to one from a newspaper story with Sheila shaking hands at a rally. The voice continued, "And Justice Sheila McCarthy does not like gun owners. Five years ago she wrote, 'The ever vigilant gun lobby can always be expected to attack any statute that might in any way restrict the use of handguns in vulnerable areas. Regardless of how sensible a proposed statute might be, the gun lobby will descend upon it with a vengeance.' " This, too, was printed rapidly, word for word, across the screen. Then there was another blast, this one from a shotgun firing at a blue sky. Ron Fisk appeared, decked out like the real hunter he was. He lowered his shotgun and chatted with the voters for a few seconds. Memories of his grandfather, hunting in these woods as a child, love of nature, a vow to protect the sacred rights of hunters and gun owners. It ended with Ron walking along the edge of the woods, a pack of frisky dogs behind him.

Some small, quick print at the end of the ad gave credit to an organization called Gunowners United Now (GUN).

The truth: The first case mentioned in the ad involved the acciden-
tal shooting death of a deer hunter. His widow sued the man who shot
him, a nasty trial ensued, and the jury in Calhoun County awarded her
$600,000, the highest ever in that courtroom. The trial was as sordid as
a divorce, with allegations of drinking and pot smoking and bad behav-
ior. The two men were members of a hunting club and had been at deer
camp for a week. During the trial, a contentious issue was safety, and sev-
eral experts testified about gun laws and hunter education. Though the
evidence was hotly disputed, it appeared, from the record, that the bulk
of the testimony proved that the state's record on safety lagged behind
others'.

In the second case, the City of Tupelo, in response to a schoolyard
shooting that killed none but injured four, passed an ordinance banning
the possession of a firearm within a hundred yards of any public school.
Gun advocates sued, and the American Rifle Association wedged itself
into the picture by filing a portentous and overblown friend-of-the-court
brief. The court struck down the ordinance on Second Amendment
grounds, but Sheila dissented. In doing so, she couldn't resist the tempta-
tion to take a swipe at the ARA.

Now the swipe was back. She watched Fisk's latest ad in her office,
alone and with the sinking feeling that her chances were fading. On the
stump, she had the time to explain her votes and point out the unfairness
of taking her words out of context. But on television, she had thirty sec-
onds. It was impossible, and the clever handlers of Ron Fisk knew it.

———

After a month at Pirate's Cove, Clete Coley had overstayed his welcome.
The owner was fed up with giving away a penthouse suite, and he was
fed up with feeding Coley's astounding appetite. The candidate was get-
ting three meals a day, many of them sent to his room. At the blackjack
tables, he drank rum like it was water and got hammered every night. He
badgered the dealers, insulted the other players, and groped the cocktail
waitresses. The casino had pocketed about $20,000 from Coley, but his
expenses were at least that much.

Marlin found him at the bar early one evening, having a drink and limbering up for another long night at the tables. After small talk, Marlin cut to the chase. "We'd like for you to drop out of the race," he said. "And while you're leaving, endorse Ron Fisk."

Clete's eyes narrowed. Deep wrinkles tightened around his forehead. "Say what?"

"You heard me."

"I'm not so sure I did."

"We're asking you to withdraw and endorse Fisk. It's simple."

Coley gulped the rum without taking his eyes off Marlin. "Keep talking," he said.

"There's not much to say. You're a long shot, to put it mildly. You've done a good job of stirring things up, attacking McCarthy, but it's time to bail out and help elect Fisk."

"What if I don't like Fisk?"

"I'm sure he doesn't like you. It's immaterial. The party's over. You've had your jollies, gotten some headlines, met lots of interesting folks along the way, but you've made your last speech."

"The ballots have been printed. My name is on them."

"That means that a handful of your fans won't hear the news. Big deal."

Another long pull on the rum, and Coley said, "Okay, a hundred thousand to get in, how much to get out?"

"Fifty."

He shook his head and glanced at the blackjack tables in the distance. "That's not enough."

"I'm not here to negotiate. It's fifty thousand cash. Same suitcase as before, just not as heavy."

"Sorry. My figure is a hundred."

"I'll be here tomorrow, same time, same place." And with that, Marlin disappeared.

At nine the next morning, two FBI agents banged on the door to the penthouse suite. Eventually, Clete staggered to the door and demanded, "Who the hell is it?"

"FBI. Open up."

Clete cracked the door and peered over the chain. Twins. Dark suits. Same barber. "What do you want?"

"We'd like to ask you some questions, and we prefer not to do it from this side of the door."

Clete opened it and waved them in. He was wearing a T-shirt and a pair of NBA-style shorts that fell to his knees and sagged halfway down his ass. As he watched them sit at the small dining table, he racked his muddled brain for some recollection of which law he'd broken. Nothing recent sprang to mind, but then nothing would at this miserable time of the day. He maneuvered his cumbersome stomach—how much weight had he gained in the last month?—into a chair and glanced at their badges.

"Does the name Mick Runyun ring a bell?" one asked.

It did, but he wasn't ready to admit anything. "Maybe."

"Meth dealer. You represented him three years ago in federal court. Pled to ten years, cooperated with the government, real nice boy."

"Oh, that Mick Runyun."

"Yes, that one. Did he pay you a fee?"

"My records are at the office in Natchez."

"Great. We have a warrant for them. Can we meet there tomorrow?"

"Love to."

"Anyway, we're betting that your records don't tell us too much about the fees paid by Mr. Runyun. We have a real good source telling us that he paid you in cash, twenty thousand bucks, and that this was never reported."

"Do tell."

"And if this is true, then it's a violation of RICO and a few other federal statutes."

"Good ole RICO. You boys wouldn't be in business without it."

"What time tomorrow?"

"I was planning on campaigning tomorrow. The election is in two weeks."

They looked at this bleary-eyed, wild-haired, hungover beast and found it comical that he was a candidate for the supreme court.

"We'll be at your office in Natchez at noon tomorrow. If you don't show, then we'll have a warrant for your arrest. That should impress the voters."

They marched out of the room and slammed the door behind them.

Late that afternoon, Marlin appeared, as promised. He ordered coffee, which he didn't touch. Clete ordered rum and soda and smelled as though it was not the first one of the day.

"Can we agree on fifty, Clete?" Marlin asked after a long spell of gazing at the cocktail waitresses scurrying about.

"I'm still thinking."

"Were those two Fibbies nice to you this morning?"

Clete absorbed this without a flinch, without the slightest twitch to indicate his surprise. In fact, he wasn't surprised at all. "Nice boys," he said. "The way I figure it, Senator Rudd is meddling again. He wants Fisk to win because they're from the same tribe. Of course we know that Rudd is the uncle of the U.S. attorney down here, a real imbecile who got the job only because of his connections. Damned sure couldn't find a job anywhere else. Rudd leans on his nephew, who brings in the FBI to twist my arm. I drop out while singing the praises of Ron Fisk, and he squeaks out a great victory. He's happy. Rudd's happy. Big business is happy. Ain't life grand?"

"You're very close," Marlin said. "And you also took a $20,000 cash fee from a drug dealer and didn't report it. Pretty stupid, but not the end of the world. Nothing that can't be fixed by The Senator. You play along now, take your cash, bow out gracefully, and you'll never hear from the Fibbies again. Case closed."

Clete's red eyes settled on Marlin's blue ones. "You swear?"

"I swear. We shake hands now, you can forget the meeting at noon tomorrow in Natchez."

"Where's the money?"

"Outside, to the right. Same green Mustang." Marlin gently laid his keys on the bar. Clete grabbed them and disappeared.

CHAPTER 29

With only fifteen days left before the election, Barry Rinehart was invited to dinner at the Vietnamese hole-in-the-wall on Bleecker Street. Mr. Trudeau wanted an update.

On the flight from Boca, Barry gloated over his latest poll. Fisk was sixteen points ahead, a lead that could not be lost. The gay marriage issue had bumped him four points. The GUN attacks on McCarthy added three more. Clete Coley's rather lame farewell added another three. The campaign itself was running smoothly. Ron Fisk was a workhorse who did exactly what Tony Zachary told him to do. There was plenty of money. Their television ads were hitting all markets with perfect regularity. The responses from their direct mail were nothing short of astonishing. The campaign had raised $320,000 from small donors who were upset about gays and guns. McCarthy was running hard to catch up and falling further behind.

Mr. Trudeau looked lean and tanned, and he was thrilled with the latest summaries. The sixteen-point lead dominated the dinner conversation. Carl quizzed Rinehart relentlessly about the numbers. Could they be trusted? How were they arrived at? How did they compare with

Barry's other races? What would it take to blow the lead? Had Barry ever seen such a big lead evaporate?

Barry all but guaranteed a win.

For the first three quarters of the year, Krane Chemical reported dismal sales and weak earnings. The company was racked with production problems in Texas and Indonesia. Three plants shut down for major, unscheduled repairs. A plant in Brazil closed for undisclosed reasons, leaving its two thousand employees out of work. Huge orders were unfilled. Longtime customers left in frustration. The sales force could not get product. Competitors cut prices and poached business. Morale was down and there were rumors of major cutbacks and layoffs.

Behind the chaos, Carl Trudeau was skillfully pulling all the strings. He did nothing illegal, but cooking the books was an art he'd mastered many years ago. When one of his companies needed bad numbers, Carl could deliver them. During the year, Krane wrote off huge chunks of research and development, shifted unusually large sums of money into legal reserves, borrowed heavily on its credit lines, stifled sales by sabotaging production, bloated expenses, sold two profitable divisions, and managed to alienate many of its customers. Through it all, Carl coordinated enough leaks to float a printing press. Since the verdict, Krane had been on the radar of business reporters, and all bad news got plenty of ink. Of course, every story referred to the massive legal problems the company was facing. The possibility of bankruptcy had been mentioned several times, after careful plants by Carl.

The stock began the year at $17.00. Nine months later, it was $12.50. With the election just two weeks away, Carl was ready for one last assault on the battered common shares of Krane Chemical Corporation.

The phone call from Jared Kurtin seemed like a dream. Wes listened to the words and closed his eyes. It could not be true.

Kurtin explained that he had been instructed by his client to ex-

plore the possibilities of settling the Bowmore litigation. Krane Chemical was a mess, and until the lawsuits went away, it could not regain its focus and compete effectively. His proposal was to gather all the attorneys in one room at one time and start the process. It would be complicated because there were so many plaintiffs with so many issues. It would be difficult because there were so many lawyers to control. He insisted that Wes and Mary Grace act as lead counsel for the plaintiffs' lawyers, but they could work out those details at the first meeting. Time was suddenly crucial. Kurtin had already reserved a convention room at a hotel in Hattiesburg, and he wanted the meeting to begin on Friday and run through the weekend, if necessary.

"Today is Tuesday," Wes said, gripping the phone with white knuckles.

"Yes, I know. As I said, my client is anxious to begin this process. It could take weeks or months to complete, but we're ready to sit down."

Wes was ready, too. He had a deposition set for Friday, something that was easily postponed. "What are the rules?" he asked.

Kurtin had the benefit of hours of planning. Wes was reacting out of shock and excitement. Plus, Kurtin had been around the block a few more times than Wes. He had negotiated mass settlements on several occasions. Wes could only dream of one.

"I'm sending a letter to all known plaintiffs' attorneys," Kurtin said. "Look over the list and see if I'm missing anyone. As you know, they're still popping up. All lawyers are invited, but the easiest way to screw up a settlement conference like this is to give the trial lawyers the microphones. You and Mary Grace will talk for the plaintiffs. I'll talk for Krane. The first challenge is to identify all persons who are making any sort of claim. Our records show about six hundred, and these range from dead bodies to nosebleeds. In my letters, I'm asking the lawyers to submit the names of clients, whether they have filed suit or not. Once we know who expects a piece of the pie, the next challenge will be to classify the claims. Unlike some mass tort settlements with ten thousand plaintiffs, this one will be manageable in that we can talk about individual claims. Our current numbers show 68 dead, 143 wounded and probably

dying, and the rest with various afflictions that, in all probability, are not life threatening."

Kurtin ticked off the numbers like a war correspondent reporting from battle. Wes couldn't help but grimace, nor could he suppress another vile thought about Krane Chemical.

"Anyway, we'll start the process of going through these numbers. The goal is to arrive at one figure, then compare it with the cash my client is willing to spend."

"And what might that number be?" Wes asked with a desperate laugh.

"Not now, Wes, maybe later. I'm asking each lawyer to fill out a standardized form for each client. If we can get these back before Friday, we'll have a head start. I'm bringing a full team, Wes. My litigators, support staff, experts, number crunchers, and I'll even have a guy with some spine from Krane. Plus, of course, the usual crew from the insurance companies. You might want to reserve a large room for your support people."

Reserve with what? Wes almost asked. Surely Kurtin knew about the bankruptcy.

"Good idea," he said.

"And, Wes, my client is really concerned about secrecy. There is no reason for this to be publicized. If word gets out, then the plaintiffs and their lawyers and the whole town of Bowmore will get excited. What happens then if the negotiations go nowhere? Let's keep a lid on this."

"Sure." How ridiculous. Kurtin was about to send his letter to no fewer than twenty law firms. Babe at the coffee shop in Bowmore would know about the settlement conference before she began serving lunch.

———

The following morning the *Wall Street Journal* ran a front-page story about Krane Chemical's settlement overtures. An anonymous source who worked for the company confirmed the truth of the rumors. Experts chimed in with varying opinions, but it was generally regarded as a pos-

itive step for the company. Large settlements can be calculated. Liabilities can be contained. Wall Street understands hard numbers, and it hates unpredictability. There is a long history of battered companies shoring up their financial futures with massive settlements that, while costly, were effective in cleaning up litigation.

Krane opened at $12.75 and advanced $2.75 in heavy trading.

By midafternoon Wednesday, the phones were ringing nonstop at Payton & Payton, and many other law firms as well. Word of a settlement was out there, on the street and flying around the Internet.

Denny Ott called and talked to Mary Grace. A group of Pine Grove residents had gathered at the church to offer prayers, exchange gossip, and wait for a miracle. It was like a vigil, he said. Not surprisingly, there were different versions of the truth. A settlement had already been negotiated, and money was on the way. No, the settlement would take place on Friday, but there was no doubt that it would happen. No, there was no settlement at all, just a meeting of the lawyers. Mary Grace explained what was happening and asked Denny to pass along the truth. It quickly became apparent that either she or Wes would need to hustle over to the church and meet with their clients.

Babe's was packed with spirited coffee drinkers, all looking for the latest word. Would Krane be required to clean up its toxic dump? Someone claiming authority answered yes, that would be a condition of the settlement. How much would the death claims be worth? Someone else had heard the figure of $5 million each. Arguments raged. Experts rose up and were soon shouted down.

F. Clyde Hardin walked over from his law office and immediately took center stage. His class action had been ridiculed by many of the locals who felt he was just riding the Paytons' coattails with a bunch of opportunistic clients. He and his good pal Sterling Bintz from Philadelphia were claiming almost three hundred "severely and permanently injured" members of their class action. Since its filing in January, it had gone nowhere. Now, however, F. Clyde had instantly gained stature. Any settlement had to include "his people." He would have a seat at the table on

Friday, he explained to the silent crowd. He would be sitting there along-side Wes and Mary Grace Payton.

Jeannette Baker was behind the counter of a convenience store at the south edge of Bowmore when she received the call from Mary Grace. "Do not get excited," her lawyer warned, rather sternly. "This could be a lengthy process, and the possibility of a settlement is remote." Jeannette had questions but did not know where to begin. Mary Grace would be at the Pine Grove Church at 7:00 p.m. for a full discussion with all of her clients. Jeannette promised to be there.

With a $41 million verdict attached to it, Jeannette Baker's case would be the first one on the table.

The settlement news was too much for Bowmore to handle. In the small offices downtown the secretaries and Realtors and insurance agents talked of nothing else. The languid human commerce along Main Street stopped dead as friends and neighbors found it impossible to pass one another without comparing gossip. The clerks in the Cary County Court-house collected rumors, amended them, embellished some, and reduced some, then passed them along. In the schools the teachers gathered in their coffee rooms and exchanged the latest news. Pine Grove wasn't the only church where the faithful and the hopeful met for prayer and coun-seling. Many of the town's pastors spent the afternoon on the phone lis-tening to the victims of Krane Chemical.

A settlement would close the town's ugliest chapter, and allow it to begin again. The infusion of money would compensate those who had suffered. The cash would be spent and re-spent and boost the dying economy. Krane would certainly be required to clean up its pollution, and once it was finally gone, perhaps the water would become safe again. Bowmore with clean water—a dream almost impossible to believe. The community could finally shake off the nickname Cancer County.

A settlement was a fast and final end to the nightmare. No one in the town wanted litigation that would be prolonged and ugly. No one wanted another trial like Jeannette Baker's.

————

Nat Lester had been pestering newspaper editors and reporters for a month. He was furious at the misleading advertising that had drenched south Mississippi, and even angrier at the editors for not railing against it. He put together a report in which he took the Fisk ads—print, direct mail, radio, Internet, and television—and dissected them, pointing out every lie, half-truth, and manipulated word. He also estimated, based on direct mail media buys, the amount of cash that was pouring into the Fisk campaign. His figure was at least $3 million, and he predicted that the vast majority was coming from out of state. There was no way to verify this until after the election. His report was e-mailed and sent overnight to every newspaper in the district, then followed up with aggressive phone calls. He updated it every day, then re-sent it and grew even more obnoxious on the phone. It finally paid off.

To his amazement, and great satisfaction, the three largest papers in the district informed him, separately and off the record of course, that they planned to run stinging editorials on the Fisk campaign in the upcoming Sunday editions.

And Nat's luck continued. The same-sex marriage issue caught the attention of the *New York Times*, and a reporter arrived in Jackson to poke around. His name was Gilbert, and he soon made his way to the McCarthy campaign office, where Nat gave him an earful, off the record. He also gave Gilbert the phone numbers of the two gay law students who were stalking Meyerchec and Spano.

Speaking off the record, they told Gilbert everything and showed him their file. They had spent four days in Chicago and learned a lot. They met Meyerchec in his bar near Evanston, told him they were new to the city and looking for friends. They spent hours in the place, got roaring drunk with the regulars, and never once heard anyone mention anything about a lawsuit in Mississippi. In the photos in the Jackson paper, Meyerchec had blond hair and funky eyeglasses. In Chicago, the hair was darker and there was no eyewear. His smiling face was in one of the group photos they had taken at the bar. As for Spano, they visited the design center where he worked as a consultant for lower-end home buyers. They pretended to be new residents in an old building nearby, and they

spent two hours with him. Noticing their accents, Spano at one point asked where they were from. When they answered Jackson, Mississippi, he had no reaction to the place.

"Ever been there?" one of them asked.

"I've passed through a couple of times," Spano said. This, from a registered voter, a licensed driver, and a current appellant before the state's supreme court. Though Spano was never seen at Meyerchec's bar, it appeared as if the two men were indeed a couple. They shared the same address, a bungalow on Clark Street.

The law students had continued to call and visit the near empty apartment in Jackson, with no response. Forty-one days earlier, while knocking on the door, they stuck a piece of junk mail into a small gap near the doorknob. It was still there; the door had not been opened. The old Saab had not been moved. One tire was flat.

Gilbert became captivated by the story and pursued it doggedly. The attempt to get married in Mississippi smelled like a cynical ploy to thrust the same-sex marriage issue to the forefront of the McCarthy-Fisk race. And only McCarthy was getting hurt.

Gilbert badgered the radical lawyer who represented Meyerchec and Spano, but got nowhere. He dogged Tony Zachary for two days but couldn't get a word. His phone calls to Ron Fisk and his campaign head-quarters went unanswered. He spoke to both Meyerchec and Spano by phone, but was quickly cut off when he pressed them on their ties to Mississippi. He gathered a few choice quotes from Nat Lester, and he verified the facts dug up by the law students.

Gilbert finished his report and sent it in.

CHAPTER 30

The first fight was over the question of who would be allowed in the room. On the defense side, Jared Kurtin had full command of his battalion and there were no problems. The brawl was on the other side.

Sterling Bintz arrived early and loudly with an entourage that included young men who appeared to be lawyers and others who appeared to be leg breakers. He claimed to represent over half of the Bowmore victims, and therefore deserved a lead role in the negotiations. He spoke with a clipped nasal voice and in an accent quite foreign to south Mississippi, and he was instantly despised by everyone there. Wes settled him down, but only for a moment. F. Clyde Hardin watched from the safety of a corner, crunching a biscuit, enjoying the argument, and praying for a quick settlement. The IRS was now sending registered letters.

A national toxic tort star from Melbourne Beach, Florida, arrived with his support staff and joined in the debate. He, too, claimed to represent hundreds of injured people, and, since he was a veteran of mass tort settlement, he figured he should handle things from the plaintiffs' side.

The two class action lawyers were soon bickering over stolen clients.

There were seventeen other law firms jockeying for position. A few were reputable personal injury firms, but most were small-town car-wreck lawyers who had picked up a case or two while sniffing around Bowmore.

Tensions were high hours before the meeting began, and once the yelling started, there was the real possibility of a punch being thrown. When the voices were sharpest, Jared Kurtin calmly got their attention and announced that Wes and Mary Grace Payton would decide who sat where. If anyone had a problem with that, then he and his client and its insurance company would walk out the door with all the money. This calmed things down.

Then there was the issue of the press. At least three reporters were on hand to cover this "secret" meeting, and when asked to leave, they were quite reluctant. Fortunately, Kurtin had arranged for some armed security. The reporters were eventually escorted out of the hotel.

Kurtin had also suggested, and offered to pay for, a referee, a disinterested person well versed in litigation and settlements. Wes had agreed, and Kurtin found a retired federal judge in Fort Worth who worked part-time as a mediator. Judge Rosenthal quietly assumed control after the trial lawyers had settled down. It took him an hour to negotiate the seating. He would have the chair at the end of the long table. To his right, halfway down and in the center, would be Mr. Kurtin, flanked by his partners, associates, Frank Sully from Hattiesburg, two suits from Krane, and one from its liability insurance carrier. A total of eleven at the table for the defense, with another twenty packed behind them.

To his left, the Paytons sat in the center, opposite Jared Kurtin. They were flanked by Jim McMay, the Hattiesburg trial lawyer with four death cases out of Bowmore. McMay had made a fortune on the fen-phen diet pill litigation and had participated in several mass settlement conferences. He was joined by a lawyer from Gulfport who had similar experience. The other chairs were taken by Mississippi lawyers who had legitimate cases from Bowmore. The class action boys were shoved into

the background. Sterling Bintz voiced his objection to his placement in the room, and Wes angrily told him to shut up. When the leg breakers reacted badly, Jared Kurtin announced that the class actions were the lowest priority on Krane's list, and if he, Bintz, hoped to collect a dime, then he should keep quiet and stay out of the way.

"This ain't Philadelphia," Judge Rosenthal said. "Are those bodyguards or lawyers?"

"Both," Bintz snapped back.

"Keep them under control."

Bintz sat down, mumbling and cursing.

It was 10:00 a.m., and Wes was already exhausted. His wife, though, was ready to begin.

———

For three hours nonstop they shuffled papers. Judge Rosenthal directed traffic as client summaries were produced, copied next door, reviewed, then classified according to the judge's arbitrary rating system: death was Class One, confirmed cancer was Class Two, all others were Class Three.

A stalemate occurred when Mary Grace suggested that Jeannette Baker be given first priority, and thus more money, because she had actually gone to trial. Why is her case worth more than the other death cases? a trial lawyer asked.

"Because she went to trial," Mary Grace shot back with a hard gaze. In other words, Baker's lawyers had the guts to take on Krane while the other lawyers chose to sit back and watch. In the months before the trial, the Paytons had approached at least five of the other trial lawyers present, including Jim McMay, and practically begged them for help. All declined.

"We will concede that the *Baker* case is worth more," Jared Kurtin said. "Frankly, I'm unable to ignore a $41 million verdict." And for the first time in years, Mary Grace actually smiled at the man. She could have hugged him.

At one, they broke for a two-hour lunch. The Paytons and Jim Mc-May hid away in a corner of the hotel restaurant and tried to analyze the meeting so far. Going in, they were consumed with the question of Krane's intent. Was it serious about a settlement? Or was it a stunt to push along the company's agenda? The fact that the national business papers knew so much about the secret settlement talks made the lawyers suspicious. But so far Mr. Kurtin had given every indication that he was a man on a mission. There had been no smiles from the Krane suits or the insurance boys, perhaps a sign that they were about to part with their money.

———

At 3:00 p.m. in New York, Carl Trudeau leaked the word that the negotiations were progressing nicely down in Mississippi. Krane was optimistic about a settlement.

Its stock closed the week at $16.50, up $4.00.

At 3:00 p.m. in Hattiesburg, the negotiators reassumed their positions, and Judge Rosenthal started the paper mill again. Three hours later, the initial accounting was complete. On the table were the claims of 704 people. Sixty-eight had died of cancer, and their families were blaming Krane. A hundred and forty-three were now suffering from cancer. The rest had a wide range of lesser illnesses and afflictions that were allegedly caused by the contaminated drinking water from the Bowmore pumping station.

Judge Rosenthal congratulated both sides on a hard and productive day, and adjourned the meeting until nine o'clock Saturday morning.

Wes and Mary Grace drove straight to the office and reported to the firm. Sherman had been in the negotiating room all day and shared his observations. They agreed that Jared Kurtin had returned to Hattiesburg with the goal of settling the Bowmore litigation and that his client seemed committed to that end. Wes cautioned that it was much too early to celebrate. They had managed only to identify the parties. The first dollar was nowhere near the table.

Mack and Liza begged them to go to the movies. Halfway through the eight o'clock show, Wes began to nod off. Mary Grace stared blankly at the screen, munching on popcorn and mentally crunching numbers related to medical expenses, pain and suffering, loss of companionship, loss of wages, loss of everything. She did not dare entertain thoughts of calculating attorneys' fees.

There were fewer suits and ties at the table Saturday morning. Even Judge Rosenthal looked quite casual in a black polo shirt under a sport coat. When the restless lawyers were in place and things were quiet, he said, with a great old voice that must have dominated many trials, "I suggest we start with the death cases and walk through them all."

No two death cases were the same from a settlement standpoint. Children were worth much less than adults because they have no record of earning power. Young fathers were worth more because of the loss of future wages. Some of the dead folks suffered for years, others went quickly. Everyone had a different figure for medical bills. Judge Rosenthal presented another scale, arbitrary but at least a starting point, in which each case would be rated based on its value. The highest cases would get a 5, and the cheapest (children) would get a 1. Time-out was called several times as the plaintiffs' lawyers haggled over this. When it was finally agreed upon, they began with Jeannette Baker. She was given a 10. The next case involved a fifty-four-year-old woman who worked part-time in a bakery and died after a three-year battle with leukemia. She was given a 3.

As they plowed through the list, each lawyer was allowed to present his particular case and plead for a higher rating. Through it all, there was no indication from Jared Kurtin of how much he was willing to pay for any of the death cases. Mary Grace watched him carefully when the other lawyers were talking. His face and actions revealed nothing but deep concentration.

At 2:30, they finished with Class One and moved to the longer list

of those claimants who were still alive but battling cancer. Rating their cases was trickier. No one could know how long each would survive or how much each would suffer. No one could predict the likelihood of death. The lucky ones would live and become cancer-free. The discussion disintegrated into several heated arguments, and at times Judge Rosenthal was flustered and unable to suggest a compromise. Late in the day, Jared Kurtin began to show signs of strain and frustration.

As 7:00 p.m. approached and the session was mercifully winding down, Sterling Bintz could not restrain himself. "I'm not sure how much longer I can sit here and watch this little exercise," he announced rudely as he approached the table at the far end, away from Judge Rosenthal. "I mean, I've been here for two days and I haven't been allowed to speak. Which, of course, means my clients have been ignored. Enough is enough. I represent a class action of over three hundred injured people, and you all seem determined to screw them."

Wes started a rebuke, but thought better of it. Let him ramble. They were about to adjourn anyway.

"My clients are not going to be ignored," he practically shouted, and everyone grew still. There was a hint of madness in his voice and certainly in his eyes, and perhaps it was best to let him rant a little. "My clients have suffered greatly, and are still suffering. And you people are not concerned with them. I can't hang around here forever. I'm due in San Francisco tomorrow afternoon for another settlement. I got eight thousand cases against Schmeltzer for their laxative pills. So, since everyone here seems quite content to chat about everything but money, let me tell you where I am."

He had their attention. Jared Kurtin and the money boys perked up and stiffened a bit. Mary Grace watched every wrinkle in Kurtin's face. If this nut was about to throw a figure on the table, she wanted her adversary's reaction.

"I'm not settling my cases for less than a hundred thousand each," Bintz said with a sneer. "Maybe more, depending on each client."

Kurtin's face was frozen, but then it usually was. One of his asso-

ciates shook his head, another one smiled a silly smile of amusement. The two Krane executives frowned and shifted as they dismissed this as absurd.

As the notion of $30 million floated around the room, Wes did the simple math. Bintz would probably take a third, throw a few crumbs at F. Clyde Hardin, then quickly move on to the next mass tort bonanza.

F. Clyde was cowering in a far corner, the same spot he'd occupied for many hours now. The paper cup in his hand was filled with orange juice, crushed ice, and four ounces of vodka. It was, after all, almost 7:00 p.m. on a Saturday. The math was so simple he could do it in his sleep. His cut was 5 percent of the total fees, or $500,000 under the rather reasonable scheme being so boldly suggested by his co-counsel. Their arrangement also paid F. Clyde $500 per client, and with three hundred clients he should have already received $150,000. He had not. Bintz had passed along about a third of that, but seemed disinclined to discuss the rest. He was a very busy lawyer and hard to get on the phone. Surely, he would come through as promised.

F. Clyde gulped his drink as Bintz's declaration rattled around the room.

Bintz continued. "We're not taking peanuts and going home," he threatened. "At some point in these negotiations, and the sooner the better, I want my clients' cases on the table."

"Tomorrow morning at nine," Judge Rosenthal suddenly barked. "As for now, we are adjourned."

———

"A Pathetic Campaign" was the title of the lead editorial in Sunday's *Clarion-Ledger* out of Jackson. Using a page out of Nat Lester's report, the editors damned the Ron Fisk campaign for its sleazy advertising. They accused Fisk of taking millions from big business and using it to mislead the public. His ads were filled with half-truths and statements taken wholly out of context. Fear was his weapon—fear of homosexuals, fear of gun control, fear of sexual predators. He was condemned for labeling

Sheila McCarthy a "liberal" when in fact her body of work, which the editors had studied, could only be considered quite moderate. They blasted Fisk for promising to vote this way or that on cases he had yet to review as a member of the court.

The editorial also decried the entire process. So much money was being raised and spent, by both candidates, that fair and unbiased decision making was in jeopardy. How could Sheila McCarthy, who had so far received over $1.5 million from trial lawyers, be expected to ignore this money when those same lawyers appeared before the supreme court?

It finished with a call to abolish judicial elections and have the judges appointed based on merit by a nonpartisan panel.

The *Sun Herald* from Biloxi was even nastier. It accused the Fisk campaign of outright deceit and used the Darrel Sackett mailing as its prime example. Sackett was dead, not loose and on the prowl. He'd been dead for four years, something Nat Lester had learned with a couple of quick phone calls.

The *Hattiesburg American* challenged the Fisk campaign to retract its negative and misleading ads and to disclose, before Election Day, its contributions from big donors outside the state. It urged both candidates to clean up the race and honor the dignity of the supreme court.

On page 3 of section A of the *New York Times*, Gilbert's exposé ran with photos of Meyerchec and Spano, as well as Fisk and McCarthy. It covered the race in general, then focused on the gay marriage issue created and injected into the race by the two men from Illinois. Gilbert did a thorough job of accumulating evidence that the two men were longtime residents of Chicago and had virtually no ties to Mississippi. He did not speculate that they were being used by conservative political operatives to sabotage McCarthy. He didn't have to. The punch line was delivered in the final paragraph. Nat Lester was quoted as saying: "These guys are a couple of stooges being used by Ron Fisk and his backers to create an issue that does not exist. Their goal is to fire up the right-wing Christians and march them down to the polls."

Ron and Doreen Fisk were at the kitchen table, ignoring their early cof-
fee, rereading the Jackson editorial, and fuming. The campaign had gone
so smoothly. They were ahead in all the polls. Nine days to go and they
could see the victory. Why, then, was Ron suddenly being described as
"deceitful" and "dishonest" by the state's largest newspaper? It was a
painful, humiliating slap, one that they had no idea was coming. And it
was certainly not deserved. They were honest, upstanding, clean-cut
Christian people. Why this?

The phone rang and Ron grabbed it. Tony's tired voice said, "Have
you seen the Jackson paper?"

"Yes, we're looking at it now."

"Have you seen the one from Hattiesburg and the *Sun Herald*?"

"No. Why?"

"Do you read the *New York Times*?"

"No."

"Check them out online. Call me in an hour."

"Is it bad?"

"Yes."

They read and fumed for another hour, then decided to skip
church. Ron felt betrayed and embarrassed and was in no mood to leave
the house. According to the latest numbers from his pollster in Atlanta,
he had a comfortable lead. Now, though, he felt defeat was certain. No
candidate could survive such a thrashing. He blamed the liberal press. He
blamed Tony Zachary and those who controlled the campaign. And he
blamed himself for being so naive. Why did he place so much trust in
people he barely knew?

Doreen assured him it was not his fault. He had thrown himself so
completely into the campaigning that he'd had little time to watch every-
thing else. Any campaign is chaotic. No one can monitor the actions of
all the workers and volunteers.

Ron unloaded on Tony during a lengthy and tense phone conver-
sation. "You've embarrassed me," Ron said. "You've humiliated me and
my family to the point that I really don't want to leave the house. I'm
thinking about quitting."

"You can't quit, Ron, you have too much invested," Tony replied, trying to control his panic and reassure his boy.

"That's the problem, Tony. I've allowed you guys to generate too much cash, and you cannot handle it. Stop all television ads right now."

"That's impossible, Ron. They're already in the pipeline."

"So I'm not in control of my own campaign, is that what you're telling me, Tony?"

"It's not that simple."

"I'm not leaving the house, Tony. Pull all the ads right now. Stop everything, and I'm calling the editors of these newspapers. I'm admitting my mistakes."

"Ron, come on."

"I'm the boss, Tony, it's my campaign."

"Yes, and you've got the race won. Don't screw it up with only nine days to go."

"Did you know that Darrel Sackett was dead?"

"Well, I really can't—"

"Answer the question, Tony. Did you know he was dead?"

"I'm not sure."

"You knew he was dead and you deliberately ran a false ad, didn't you?"

"No, I—"

"You're fired, Tony. You're fired and I quit."

"Don't overreact, Ron. Settle down."

"You're fired."

"I'll be down in an hour."

"You do that, Tony. You get down here as quick as possible, and until then you're fired."

"I'm leaving now. Don't do anything until I get there."

"I'm calling the editors right now."

"Don't do that, Ron. Please. Wait until I get there."

The lawyers had little time for newspapers on Sunday morning. By eight o'clock they were gathering at the hotel for what would surely be the most important day yet. There had been no indication from Jared Kurtin as to how long he might negotiate before heading back to Atlanta, but it was assumed that round one would be over on Sunday afternoon. Other than the $30 million suggestion made by Sterling Bintz the evening before, there had been no talk of money. That had to change on Sunday. Wes and Mary Grace were determined to leave that day with a general idea of how much the Class One and Class Two cases were worth.

By 8:30 all the plaintiffs' lawyers were in place, most of them huddled in serious conversations, all of them ignoring Sterling Bintz, who in turn ignored them. His entourage was still intact. He was not speaking to the other class action lawyer from Melbourne Beach. Judge Rosenthal arrived at 8:45 and commented on the absence of everyone on the defense side. The trial lawyers finally noticed this. There was not a soul sitting opposite them. Wes punched in the number of Jared Kurtin's cell phone, but listened to his recording.

"We did agree on 9:00 a.m., didn't we?" asked Rosenthal, five minutes before the hour. It was unanimously agreed that nine was the magic hour. They waited, and time suddenly moved much slower.

At 9:02, Frank Sully, local counsel for Krane, walked into the room and said, somewhat sheepishly, almost in embarrassment, "My client has decided to recess these negotiations until further notice. I've very sorry for the inconvenience."

"Where's Jared Kurtin?" Judge Rosenthal demanded.

"He's flying back to Atlanta right now."

"When did your client make this decision?"

"I don't know. I was informed about an hour ago. I'm very sorry, Judge. I apologize to everyone here."

The room seemed to tilt as one side sank under the weight of this sudden turn of events. Lawyers giddy in anticipation of finally slicing up the pie dropped their pens and pencils and gaped at one another in

shock. Great gasps of air were discharged. Curses were mumbled just loud enough to be heard. Shoulders sagged. They wanted to throw something at Sully, but he was just the local and they had learned a long time ago that he had no clout.

F. Clyde Hardin wiped sweat from his wet face and tried valiantly not to throw up.

There was a sudden rush to leave, to clear out. It was maddening to sit there and stare at the empty chairs, chairs once occupied by men who just might have made them rich. The trial lawyers quickly gathered stacks of papers, restuffed their briefcases, and offered brusque goodbyes.

Wes and Mary Grace said nothing as they drove to their apartment.

CHAPTER 31

Monday morning, the *Wall Street Journal* broke the news of the collapse of the settlement negotiations down in Hattiesburg. The story, on page 2, was written by a reporter with some very good sources inside Krane Chemical, one of whom blamed the plaintiffs' lawyers. "Their demands were just too unrealistic. We went in in good faith, and got nowhere." Another anonymous source said, "It's hopeless. Because of the verdict, every trial lawyer thinks his case is worth forty million bucks." Mr. Watts, Krane's CEO, said, "We are very disappointed. We wanted to get this litigation behind us and move on. Now our future is quite uncertain."

Carl Trudeau read the story online at 4:30 in the morning in his penthouse. He laughed and rubbed his hands together in anticipation of a very profitable week.

Wes called Jared Kurtin throughout the morning, but the great man was traveling and could not be reached. His cell phone was stuck on voice mail. His secretary eventually became rude, but then so was Wes. He and Mary Grace seriously doubted if the wild demands by Sterling Bintz had frightened Krane away. In relative terms, his suggestion of $30 million would be a fraction of any workable settlement.

When the news finally arrived in Bowmore, it was received like another plague.

———

At McCarthy headquarters, Nat Lester had worked through the night and was still wired when Sheila arrived at 8:30, her usual time. He had e-mailed the *Times* story to every newspaper in the district and was calling reporters and editors when she walked in with a well-rested smile and asked for a pineapple juice.

"We've got these clowns on the run!" he announced jubilantly. "Their dirty tricks have caught up with them."

"Congratulations. It's beautiful."

"We're sending the editorials and the *Times* story to every registered voter."

"How much does that cost?"

"Who cares? With a week to go, we can't pinch pennies. Are you ready?"

"I leave in an hour."

The next seven days would take her to thirty-four stops in twenty counties, all made possible by the use of a King Air on loan from one trial lawyer and a small jet from another. The blitz had been coordinated by Nat and would take place with the help of schoolteachers, labor bosses, black leaders, and, of course, trial lawyers. She would not return to Jackson until after the election. While she was on the stump, her last round of television ads would flood the district.

By the time the votes were counted, her campaign would not have one dime. She was praying that it would not be in debt.

———

Ron Fisk finally left the house on Monday morning, but he did not make his usual trip to the office. Instead, he and Doreen drove to Jackson, to the offices of Judicial Vision for another long and stressful meeting with Tony Zachary. They had slugged their way through a four-hour ordeal

on Sunday afternoon in the den of the Fisk home, and they had resolved little. Ron was suspending all campaign activities until he could repair his good name. He had fired Tony at least four times, but they were still talking.

Throughout the day and into Sunday night, Tedford in Atlanta had been polling furiously, and by late Monday morning there were some results. In spite of the barrage of condemnation, Ron Fisk was still three points ahead of Sheila McCarthy. The gay marriage issue had captivated the voters, most of whom still favored the more conservative candidate.

Ron wasn't sure if he could believe anyone who worked for his campaign, but the new poll did lighten his mood somewhat. "You've got this thing won, Ron," Tony said again and again. "Don't blow it."

They finally reached an understanding, one that Ron insisted they sign as if they had negotiated a contract. First, Ron would stay in the race. Second, Tony would keep his job as campaign manager. Third, Ron would meet with the newspaper editors, admit his mistakes, and promise a clean race for the remaining eight days. Fourth, no campaign literature, ads, TV spots, direct mail, radio commercials, nothing would be used until it was first approved by Ron.

When they were pals again, they enjoyed a quick lunch at the Capitol Grill, then Ron and Doreen drove home. They were proud that they had held their ground, and anxious to resume the campaign. They could smell the victory.

––––––––

Barry Rinehart arrived in Jackson at noon on Monday and established his base in the largest suite of a downtown hotel. He would not leave Mississippi until after the election.

He waited impatiently for Tony to arrive with the news that they still had a horse in the race. For a man who took great pride in staying cool regardless of the pressure, the past twenty-four hours had been nerve-racking. Barry had slept little. If Fisk quit, then Rinehart's career would be severely damaged, if not outright ruined.

Tony walked into the suite with a huge smile, and both men were able to laugh. They were soon reviewing their media buys and advertising plans. They had the cash to saturate the district with TV ads, and if Mr. Fisk wanted only positive ones, then so be it.

————

The market's reaction to the settlement news was swift and ugly. Krane opened at $15.25 and by noon was trading at $12.75. Carl Trudeau watched the fall gleefully, his net worth shrinking by the minute. To add to the fear and frenzy, he organized a meeting between the top Krane executives and the company's bankruptcy attorneys, then leaked this news to a reporter.

On Tuesday morning, the Business section of the *New York Times* ran a story in which an in-house lawyer for the company said, "We'll probably file for bankruptcy protection this week." For the first time in twenty years, the stock fell through the $10.00 floor and traded around $9.50.

At midday on Tuesday, Meyerchec and Spano arrived in Jackson by private jet. They were picked up by a car with a driver and taken to the office of their attorney, where they met a reporter with the Jackson *Clarion-Ledger*. In a one-hour interview, they rebuked the story by Gilbert, reaffirmed their citizenship in their new state, and talked at length about the importance of their lawsuit now pending before the Mississippi Supreme Court. They held hands throughout the entire interview and posed for a photographer from the newspaper.

While this was happening, Barry Rinehart and Tony Zachary pored over the findings from their latest poll. Fisk's sixteen-point lead had been reduced to five, the most dramatic seventy-two-hour drop Barry had ever seen. But he was too seasoned to panic. Tony, however, was a nervous wreck.

They decided to reshuffle the television ads. They discarded the Darrel Sackett attack piece and one showing illegal aliens crossing the border. For the next three days, they would stick to gay marriage and the glory of guns. Over the weekend, they would shift to the comfort ads

and leave the voters with warm and fuzzy feelings about Ron Fisk and his wholesomeness.

Meanwhile, the weary mail carriers in south Mississippi would deliver several tons of Fisk propaganda each day until the campaign was mercifully over.

All to be done with Mr. Fisk's approval, of course.

Denny Ott finished his letter after several drafts and asked his wife to read it. When she approved, he took it to the post office. It read:

Dear Brother Ted:

I have listened to a recording of your sermon last Sunday, broadcast on radio station WBMR during your worship hour. I hesitate to call it a sermon. It was more along the lines of a stump speech. I'm sure your condemnation of homosexuals is standard fare from your pulpit, and I will not comment on it. However, your attack on liberal judges, nine days before the election, was nothing but a diatribe against Sheila McCarthy, who, of course, was never called by name. By attacking her, you obviously endorsed her opponent.

Such political speech is expressly forbidden by law, and specifically forbidden by Internal Revenue Service regulations. As a 501 (C) (3) nonprofit organization, Harvest Tabernacle cannot engage in political activity. To do so is to risk losing its nonprofit status, a catastrophic event for any church.

I have heard from good sources that other local pastors, all members of your Brotherhood Coalition, are involving themselves and their churches in this campaign. I'm sure this is part of a well-coordinated effort to help elect Ron Fisk, and I have no doubt that this Sunday you and the others will use the pulpit to urge your members to vote for him.

Mr. Fisk is being used by a conspiracy of big business interests to stack our supreme court with judges who will protect corporate wrongdoers by limiting their liability. Only the little folks will suffer— your people and mine.

> *Be warned that I will be watching and listening this Sunday. And I*
> *will not hesitate to notify the Internal Revenue Service if you continue*
> *your illegal activities.*
>
> *Yours in Christ,*
>
> *Denny Ott*

At noon Thursday, the Payton law firm met for a quick lunch and final review of its last-minute campaigning. On a Sheetrock wall in The Pit, Sherman had arranged, in chronological order, the print ads used so far by Ron Fisk. There were six full-page solicitations from newspapers and five direct mailings. The collection was now being updated daily because the Fisk printing presses were working overtime.

It was an impressive, and quite depressing, lineup.

Using a street map of Hattiesburg and a list of registered voters, Sherman assigned neighborhoods near the university. Walking door-to-door, he would go with Tabby, Rusty with Vicky, Wes with Mary Grace. They had two thousand doors to cover during the next five days. Olivia agreed to stay behind and answer the phone. She was a bit too arthritic to hit the streets.

Other teams, many of them from the offices of local trial lawyers, would canvass the rest of Hattiesburg and its outlying suburbs. In addition to handing out McCarthy materials, most of these volunteers would distribute brochures for Judge Thomas Harrison.

The prospect of knocking on hundreds of doors was actually quite welcome, at least to Wes and Mary Grace. The mood at the office had been funereal since Monday. The settlement fiasco had drained their spirits. The constant chatter about Krane filing Chapter 11 frightened them. They were distracted and edgy, and both needed a few days off.

The final push was orchestrated by Nat Lester. Every precinct in all twenty-seven counties had someone assigned to it, and Nat had the cell phone number of every volunteer. He started calling them Thursday afternoon, and he would hound them until late Monday night.

The letter from Brother Ted was hand delivered to Pine Grove Church. It read:

Dear Pastor Ott:

I'm touched by your concern, and I'm also delighted you have taken an interest in my sermons. Listen to them carefully, and one day you may come to know Jesus Christ as your personal savior. Until then, I will continue to pray for you and all those you are leading astray.

God built our house of worship fourteen years ago, then He paid off the mortgage. He led me to the pulpit there, and each week He speaks to His beloved flock through my words.

When preparing my sermons, I listen to no one but Him. He condemns homosexuality, those who practice it, and those who support it. It's in the Bible, which I suggest you spend more time reading.

And you can stop wasting your time worrying about me and my church. Surely, you have enough on your plate in Pine Grove.

I shall preach whatever I choose. Send in the federal government. With God on my side, I have nothing to fear.

Praise be to Him,

Brother Ted

CHAPTER 32

By noon Friday, Barry Rinehart had propped up his poll numbers to the point where he felt confident enough to call Mr. Trudeau. Fisk was seven points ahead and seemed to have regained momentum. Barry had no qualms about rounding the numbers up a bit to make the great man feel better. He'd been lying all week anyway. Mr. Trudeau would never know they had almost blown a sixteen-point lead.

"We're up by ten points," Barry said confidently from his hotel suite.

"Then it's over?"

"I know of no election in which the front-runner has dropped ten points over the last weekend. And, with all the money we're spending on media, I think we're gaining."

"Nice job, Barry," Carl said, and closed his phone.

As Wall Street waited for the news that Krane Chemical would file for bankruptcy, Carl Trudeau purchased five million shares of the company's stock in a private transaction. The seller was a fund manager who handled the retirement portfolio of the public employees of Minnesota. Carl had been stalking the stock for months, and the manager was finally

convinced that Krane was hopeless. He dumped the stock for $11 a share and considered himself lucky.

Carl then launched a plan to purchase another five million shares as soon as the market opened. His identity as the buyer would not be disclosed until he filed with the SEC ten days later.

By then, of course, the election would be over.

In the year since the verdict, he had secretly and methodically increased his stake in the company. Using offshore trusts, Panamanian banks, two dummy corporations based in Singapore, and the expert advice of a Swiss banker, the Trudeau Group now owned 60 percent of Krane. The sudden grab for ten million more shares would raise Carl's ownership to 77 percent.

At 2:30 p.m. Friday, Krane issued a brief press release announcing that "a bankruptcy filing has been indefinitely postponed."

———

Barry Rinehart was not following the news on Wall Street. He had little interest in Krane Chemical and its financial dealings. There were at least three dozen important matters to monitor during the next seventy-two hours, and none could be overlooked. However, after five days in the hotel suite, he needed to move.

With Tony driving, they left Jackson and went to Hattiesburg, where Barry got a quick tour of the important sights: the Forrest County Circuit Court building, where the verdict started it all, the semi-abandoned shopping center that the Paytons called their office—Kenny's Karate on one side and a whiskey store on the other—and a couple of neighborhoods where Ron Fisk yard signs outnumbered Sheila McCarthy's two to one. They had dinner in a downtown restaurant called 206 Front Street and at 7:00 p.m. parked outside Reed Green Coliseum on the campus of Southern Miss. They sat in the car for thirty minutes and watched the crowd arrive, in vans and converted school buses and fancy coaches, each one with the name of its church painted boldly along the sides. They were from Purvis, Poplarville, Lumberton, Bowmore, Collins, Mount Olive, Brooklyn, and Sand Hill.

"Some of those towns are an hour from here," Tony said with satisfaction.

The worshippers poured into the parking lots around the coliseum and hurried inside. Many carried identical blue and white signs that said, "Save the Family."

"Where did you get the signs?" Tony asked.

"Vietnam."

"Vietnam?"

"Got 'em for a buck ten, fifty thousand total. The Chinese company wanted a buck thirty."

"So nice to hear we're saving money."

At 7:30, Rinehart and Zachary entered the coliseum and hustled up to the nosebleed seats, as far away as possible from the excited mob below. A stage was set up at one end, with huge "Save the Family" banners hanging behind it. A well-known white gospel quartet ($4,500 for the night, $15,000 for the weekend) was warming up the crowd. The floor was covered with neat rows of folding chairs, thousands of them, all filled with folks in a joyous mood.

"What's the seating capacity?" Barry asked.

"Eight thousand for basketball," Tony said glancing around the arena. A few sections behind the stage were empty. "With the seats on the floor, I'd say we're close to nine thousand."

Barry seemed satisfied.

The master of ceremonies was a local preacher who quieted the crowd with a long prayer, toward the end of which many of his people began waving their hands upward, as if reaching for heaven. There was a fair amount of mumbling and whispering as they prayed fervently. Barry and Tony just watched, content in their prayerlessness.

The quartet fired them up with another song, then a black gospel group ($500 for the night) rocked the place with a rowdy rendition of "Born to Worship." The first speaker was Walter Utley, from the American Family Alliance in Washington, and when he assumed the podium, Tony recalled their first meeting ten months earlier when Ron Fisk made the rounds. It seemed like years ago. Utley was not a preacher, nor was

he much of a speaker. He dulled the crowd with a frightening list of all the evils being proposed in Washington. He railed against the courts and politicians and a host of other bad people. When he finished, the crowd applauded and waved their signs.

More music. Another prayer. The star of the rally was David Wilfong, a Christian activist with a knack for wedging himself into every high-profile dispute involving God. Twenty million people listened to his radio show every day. Many sent him money. Many bought his books and tapes. He was an educated, ordained minister with a fiery, frantic voice, and within five minutes he had the crowd jumping up in a standing ovation. He condemned immorality on every front, but he saved his heavy stuff for gays and lesbians who wanted to get married. The crowd could not sit still or remain quiet. It was their chance to verbally express their opposition, and to do so in a very public manner. After every third sentence, Wilfong had to wait for the applause to die down.

He was being paid $50,000 for the weekend, money that had originated months earlier from somewhere in the mysterious depths of the Trudeau Group. But no human could trace it.

Twenty minutes into his performance, Wilfong stopped for a special introduction. When Ron and Doreen Fisk stepped onto the stage, the arena seemed to shake. Ron spoke for five minutes. He asked for their votes come Tuesday, and for their prayers. He and Doreen walked across the stage to a thunderous standing ovation. They waved and shook their fists in triumph, then walked to the other side of the stage as the mob stomped its feet.

Barry Rinehart managed to contain his amusement. Of all his creations, Ron Fisk was the most perfect.

————

Families were saved throughout south Mississippi the following day and into Sunday. Utley and Wilfong drew huge crowds, and of course the crowds adored Ron and Doreen Fisk.

Those who chose not to take a church bus to a rally were bombarded with relentless advertising on television. And the mailman was al-

ways close by, hauling to the besieged homes yet more campaign propaganda.

While publicly the campaign raced on in a numbing frenzy, a darker side came together over the weekend. Under Marlin's direction, a dozen operatives fanned out through the district and hooked up with old contacts. They visited rural supervisors on their farms, and black preachers in their churches, and county ward bosses in their hunting cabins. Voter registration rolls were reviewed. Numbers were agreed upon. Sacks of cash changed hands. The tariff was $25 per vote. Some called it "gas money," as if it could be justified as a legitimate expense.

The operatives were working for Ron Fisk, though he would never know of their activities. Suspicions would be raised after the votes were counted, after Fisk received an astounding number of votes in black precincts, but Tony would assure him that it was simply a case of some wise people understanding the issues.

On November 4, two-thirds of those registered in the southern district cast their votes.

When the polls closed at 7:00 p.m., Sheila McCarthy drove straight to the Biloxi Riviera Casino, where her volunteers were preparing for a party. No reporters were allowed. The first results were somewhat satisfying. She carried Harrison County, her home, with 55 percent of the vote.

When Nat Lester saw this figure in Jackson, at the McCarthy headquarters, he knew they were dead. Fisk got almost half the votes in the most laid-back county in the district. It soon got much worse.

Ron and Doreen were eating pizza at the crowded campaign office in downtown Brookhaven. The Lincoln County votes were being tallied just down the street, and when the news came that his neighbors had turned out in big numbers and given him 75 percent of the vote, the party began. In Pike County, next door, Fisk received 64 percent.

When Sheila lost Hancock County on the Coast, her night was

over, as was her career on the supreme court. In one ten-minute span, she then lost Forrest County (Hattiesburg), Jones County (Laurel), and Adams County (Natchez).

All precincts were in by 11:00 p.m. Ron Fisk won easily with 53 percent of the vote. Sheila McCarthy received 44 percent, and Clete Coley retained enough admirers to give him the remaining 3 percent. It was a solid thrashing, with Fisk losing only Harrison and Stone counties.

He even beat McCarthy in Cancer County, though not in the four precincts within the city limits of Bowmore. In the rural areas, though, where the Brotherhood ministers toiled in the fields, Ron Fisk took almost 80 percent of the vote.

Mary Grace wept when she saw the final numbers from Cary County: Fisk, 2,238; McCarthy, 1,870; Coley, 55.

The only good news was that Judge Thomas Harrison had survived, but barely.

————

The dust settled in the week that followed. In several interviews, Sheila McCarthy presented the face of a graceful loser. She did, however, say, "It will be interesting to see how much money Mr. Fisk raised and spent."

Justice Jimmy McElwayne was less gracious. In several articles, he was quoted as saying, "I'm not too keen to serve with a man who paid three million for a seat on the court."

When the reports were filed, though, three million looked rather cheap. The Fisk campaign reported total receipts of $4.1 million, with a staggering $2.9 million collected in the thirty-one days of October. Ninety-one percent of this money flooded in from out of state. The report did not list any contributions from or expenses paid to such groups as Lawsuit Victims for Truth, Victims Rising, and GUN. Ron Fisk signed the report, as required by law, but had many questions about the financing. He pressed Tony for answers about his fund-raising methods, and when the answers were vague, they exchanged heated words. Fisk accused him of hiding money and of taking advantage of his inexperience.

Tony responded hotly that Fisk had been promised unlimited funds, and it wasn't fair to complain after the fact. "You should be thanking me, not bitching about the money," he yelled during a long, contentious meeting.

Soon, though, they would be attacked by reporters and forced to present a united front.

The McCarthy campaign raised $1.9 million and spent every penny of it. The $500,000 note produced by Willy Benton and signed by twelve of the MTA directors would take years to satisfy.

Once the final numbers were available, a storm erupted in the media. A team of investigative journalists with the *Clarion-Ledger* went after Tony Zachary, Judicial Vision, Ron Fisk, and many of the out-of-state donors who'd sent $5,000 checks. The business groups and the trial lawyers exchanged heated words through the various newspaper stories. Editorials raged about the need for reform. The secretary of state pursued Lawsuit Victims for Truth, Victims Rising, and GUN for such details as the names of members and total amounts spent on advertising. But the inquiries were met with stiff resistance by Washington lawyers with wide experience in election issues.

Barry Rinehart watched it from the safety of his splendid office in Boca Raton. Such postgame antics were the rule, not the exception. The losers always squawked about the lack of fairness. In a couple of months, Justice Fisk would be on the big bench and most folks would forget the campaign that put him there.

Barry was moving on, negotiating with other clients. An appellate judge in Illinois had been ruling against the insurance industry for many years, and it was time to take him out. But they were haggling over Barry's fees, which had jumped dramatically after the Fisk victory.

Of the $8 million funneled through various routes by Carl Trudeau to Barry and his related "units," almost $7 million was still intact, still hidden.

Thank God for democracy, Barry said to himself many times a day. "Let the people vote!"

PART THREE

THE
OPINION

CHAPTER 33

Ron Fisk was sworn in as associate justice of the Supreme Court of Mississippi during the first week of January. It was a short, quiet ceremony attended by Doreen and the three children, a few friends from Brookhaven, Tony Zachary, and the other eight members of the court and some of the staff. The chief justice, the most senior member, gave a short welcoming speech, then everybody had punch and cookies. Justice Jimmy McElwayne skipped the refreshments and returned to his office. He had not expected to like Ron Fisk, and so far he had not been disappointed. Fisk stumbled badly when he summarily fired Sheila's law clerks and secretary without the courtesy of first meeting them. He stumbled again when he showed up in early December and began pestering the chief justice to see the docket and have a look at some of the upcoming cases. At forty years of age, Fisk was by far the youngest member of the court, and his eager-beaver enthusiasm had already rankled some of his brethren.

Once sworn in, Fisk had the right to participate in every case not yet decided, regardless of how long the matter had been before the court. He plunged into the work and was soon putting in long hours. Ten days

after arriving, he voted with a seven-member majority (including McElwayne) to reverse a zoning case out of DeSoto County, and he dissented with three others in a wetlands dispute in Pearl River County. He just voted, without comment.

In each case, every judge can write his own opinion, either concurring with the majority or dissenting from it. Ron was itching to write something, but he wisely kept quiet. It was best not to rush things.

The people of Mississippi got their first glimpse of the new, post-McCarthy court in late January. The case involved an eighty-year-old woman with Alzheimer's who was found under her nursing home bed, naked and filthy. She was found there by her son, who went ballistic and eventually sued the nursing home on her behalf. Though accounts varied and records were incomplete, testimony at trial proved that the woman had been completely neglected for at least six hours. She had not been fed for nine. The nursing home was a low-end facility, one of many owned by a company from Florida, and its history of safety and sanitation violations was long and pathetic. The jury, in the rural county of Covington, awarded actual damages of $250,000, though it was difficult to gauge the extent of the physical injuries. There were bruises on her forehead, but the poor lady had lost her mind a decade earlier. The interesting part of the case was the punitive award of $2 million, a record for Covington County.

Justice Calligan had been assigned the case. He rounded up his other three votes and wrote an opinion that reversed the $250,000 and sent it back for another trial. More proof was needed on the issue of damages. As for the punitive award, it "shocked the conscience of the court" and was reversed and rendered—thrown out once and for all. Judge McElwayne wrote an opinion in which he upheld the entire verdict. He went to great lengths to spell out the wretched history of the nursing home—lack of staff, untrained staff, unsanitary rooms and bed linens and towels, poisonous food, inadequate air-conditioning, overcrowded rooms, and so on. His opinion was joined by three others, so the old court was equally divided. The new man would be the swing vote.

Justice Fisk did not hesitate. He, too, found the medical proof inadequate, and claimed to be shocked by the punitive award. As an insurance defense lawyer, he had spent fourteen years fighting off the wild claims of punitive damages so carelessly thrown about by the plaintiffs' bar. At least half the lawsuits he defended had included a bogus plea for an exorbitant sum of money because of the defendant's "outrageous and reckless conduct."

By a vote of 5–4, the court announced its new course and sent the case back to Covington County in much worse shape than when it left.

The elderly victim's son was a fifty-six-year-old cattle farmer. He was also a deacon in a country church a few miles outside the town of Mount Olive. He and his wife had been strong supporters of Ron Fisk because they viewed him as a godly man who shared their values and would protect their grandchildren.

Why would Mr. Fisk now rule in favor of some outlaw corporation from another state?

———

Each case accepted for review by the supreme court is assigned by the clerk to one of the nine judges, who have no control over the process. Each one knows that every ninth case will land on his or her desk. They work on three-judge panels for six weeks, then the little teams are reshuffled.

In almost all cases before the supreme court, the lawyers request an oral argument, but these are rarely granted. The panels listen to the lawyers in less than 5 percent of the appeals.

Because of the size of the verdict, the case of *Jeannette Baker v. Krane Chemical Corporation* was deemed important enough to allow the attorneys an audience with its three-judge panel. On February 7, they gathered—Jared Kurtin and his mob, and the entire firm of Payton & Payton.

The case had been assigned to Justice Albritton months earlier. Ron Fisk had no business in the courtroom that day and was not there. Tony Zachary stopped by out of curiosity, but sat in the back row and did not

speak to anyone. He took notes and would call Barry Rinehart as soon as the hearing ended. A vice president for Krane also sat in the back row and took notes.

Each side was allowed twenty minutes, and a digital timer clicked off the seconds. Warnings were given by a clerk. Long-winded lawyers were not tolerated. Jared Kurtin went first and quickly cut to the heart of his client's appeal. Krane had always argued that there was no credible, reasonable medical link between the BCL and cartolyx found on its property and the cancers that afflicted so many of Bowmore's residents. Krane would never concede that illegal dumping had occurred, but, hypothetically speaking, even if you assumed toxic wastes were emitted into the soil and found their way into the water, there was "no medically causal connection" between the chemicals and the cancers. Oh, there was lots of speculation all right. Look at the rate of cancer in Bowmore. Look at the cancer clusters. But cancer rates vary widely from region to region. And, most important, there are thousands of carcinogens in the air, food, beverages, household products, the list goes on and on. Who can say that the cancer that killed little Chad Baker came from the water, and not the air? How do you rule out the carcinogens found in the highly processed foods Ms. Baker admitted they had eaten for years? It's impossible.

Kurtin was on his game, and the three judges left him alone for ten minutes. Two were already with him. Justice Albritton was not, and he finally asked, "Mr. Kurtin, excuse me, but were there any other factories or plants in this general area that manufactured pesticides or insecticides?"

"Not to my knowledge, Your Honor."

"Does that mean something other than 'No'?"

"The answer is no, Your Honor. There were no other manufacturers in Cary County."

"Thank you. And with all of your experts did you find any other factory or plant where bichloronylene, cartolyx, or aklar was processed and/or disposed of?"

"No, Your Honor."

"Thank you. And when you argue that other areas of the country

have seen very high rates of cancer, you're not suggesting that any of these other places are fifteen times above the national average, are you?"

"No, I'm not suggesting that, but we do dispute the ratio of fifteen."

"Fine, then will you stipulate to a rate of cancer twelve times the national average?"

"I'm not sure—"

"That was what your expert said at trial, Mr. Kurtin. Bowmore's rate is twelve times the national average."

"Yes, I believe you are correct, Your Honor."

"Thank you."

There were no more interruptions, and Kurtin finished a few seconds after his buzzer.

Mary Grace looked spectacular. The boys might be limited by their black and navy suits, white shirts, dull ties, and black wing tips, the usual boring everyday getup, but the girls had no rules. Mary Grace wore a bright dress that fell just above the knees and a matching jacket with sleeves that stopped at the elbows. Black stiletto heels. Plenty of leg, though none visible to the three justices once she assumed the podium.

Picking up where Justice Albritton left off, she launched into an attack on Krane's defense. For at least twenty years the company had illegally dumped tons of class-1 carcinogens into the ground. As a direct cause of this dumping, Bowmore's drinking water was polluted with these same carcinogens, none of which were produced or dumped or even found in significant quantities anywhere else in the county. The people of Bowmore drank the water, the same way that each member of the panel had drunk water that very morning. "You shaved, brushed your teeth, showered, used the city's water in your coffee or tea. You drank it at home and you drank it here at work. Did you question the water? Where did it come from? Is it safe? Did you for one second this morning ask yourself if your water contained carcinogens? Probably not. The people of Bowmore were no different."

As a direct result of drinking the water, the people got sick. The town was hit with a wave of cancer never before seen in this country.

And, as always, this fine, upstanding New York corporation—and

here she turned and waved a hand at Jared Kurtin—denied everything. Denied the dumping, the cover-up, denied the lying, even denied its own denials. And, most important, denied any causation between its carcinogens and the cancer. Instead, as we've heard here today, Krane Chemical blames it on the air, the sun, the environment, even the peanut butter and sliced turkey Jeannette Baker used to feed her family. "The jury really loved that part of the trial," she said to a hushed crowd. "Krane dumped tons of toxic chemicals into our ground and our water, but, hey, let's blame it on Jif peanut butter."

Maybe it was out of respect for the lady, or maybe it was their reluctance to interrupt such an impassioned plea, but, whatever the reason, the three judges said nothing.

Mary Grace finished with a quick lecture on the law. The law did not require them to prove that the BCL found in the tissue cells of Pete Baker came directly from the Krane facility. To do so would elevate the standard of proof to clear and convincing evidence. The law only required proof by a preponderance of the evidence, a lower standard.

When her time was up, she sat down next to her husband. The judges thanked the lawyers, then called the next case.

————

The midwinter meeting of the MTA was a somber affair. Attendance was up sharply. The trial lawyers were anxious, deeply concerned, even frightened. The new court had reversed the first two plaintiffs' verdicts on its docket for the year. Could this be the beginning of some horrible streak? Was it time to panic, or was it already too late?

A lawyer from Georgia helped darken the mood with a summary of the sorry state of things in his state. The Supreme Court of Georgia also had nine members, eight of whom were loyal to big business and consistently rejected verdicts for injured or dead plaintiffs. Twenty-two of the last twenty-five verdicts had been reversed. As a result, insurance companies were no longer willing to settle, and why should they? They were not afraid of juries anymore, because they owned the supreme court.

Once upon a time, most cases were settled before trial. For a trial lawyer, this meant a caseload that was manageable. Now nothing got settled, and the plaintiff's lawyer had to take every case to trial. And even if he got a verdict, it wouldn't stand on appeal. The fallout is that lawyers are taking fewer cases and fewer injured folks with legitimate claims are being compensated. "The courthouse doors are closing rapidly," he said as he finished.

Though it was only 10:00 a.m., many in the crowd were looking for a bar.

The next speaker lightened the mood, if only a little. Former Justice Sheila McCarthy was introduced and greeted warmly. She thanked the trial lawyers for their unwavering support and hinted that she might not be finished with politics. She railed against those who had conspired to defeat her. And as she was winding down, she brought them to their feet when she announced that since she was now in private practice, she had paid her dues and was a proud member of the Mississippi Trial Advocates.

———

The Mississippi Supreme Court decides, on average, about 250 cases each year. Most are uncomplicated, fairly routine disputes. Some involve novel issues the court has never seen before. Virtually all are disposed of in an orderly, almost genteel fashion. Occasionally, though, one starts a war.

The case involved a large commercial grass cutter commonly known as a bush hog. The one in question was being pulled behind a John Deere tractor when it struck an abandoned manhole cover hidden in the weeds of a vacant lot. A four-inch piece of jagged steel was launched from the swirling blades of the bush hog. Once airborne, it traveled 238 feet before striking a six-year-old boy in the left temple. The boy's name was Aaron, and he was holding his mother's hand as they walked into a branch bank office in the town of Horn Lake. Aaron was grievously injured, almost died on several occasions, and in the four years

since the accident had undergone eleven operations. His medical bills were well over the cap of $500,000 on the family's health insurance policy. Expenses for his future care were estimated at $750,000.

Aaron's lawyers had determined that the bush hog was fifteen years old and not equipped with side rail guards, debris chains, or any other safety feature used by most of the industry for at least thirty years. They sued. A jury in DeSoto County awarded Aaron $750,000. Afterward, the trial judge increased the award to include the medical expenses. He reasoned that if the jury found liability, then Aaron should be entitled to more damages.

The supreme court was faced with several options: (1) affirm the jury's award of $750,000; (2) affirm the judge's increased award of $1.3 million; (3) reverse on either liability or damages and send it back for a new trial; or (4) reverse and render and kill the lawsuit. Liability appeared to be clear, so the question was more about the money.

The case was assigned to Judge McElwayne. His preliminary memo agreed with the trial judge and pushed for the higher award. If given the chance, he would have advocated for even more money. There was nothing in either amount to compensate the child for the excruciating pain he had endured and would continue to face in the future. Nor was there any award for the loss of future earning capacity. The child, while actually holding hands with his mother, had been crippled for life by an inherently dangerous product that was carelessly manufactured.

Justice Romano from the central district saw it differently. He rarely saw a big verdict he couldn't attack, but this one proved to be a challenge. He decided that the bush hog was, in fact, reasonably designed and properly assembled at the factory, but in the intervening years its safety features and devices had been removed by its various owners. Indeed, the chain of ownership was not clear. Such is the nature of products like bush hogs. They are not clean, neat, safe products. Instead, they are designed to do one thing—cut down thick grass and brush through the use of a series of sharp blades rotating at high speeds. They are extremely dangerous products, but they are nonetheless efficient and necessary.

Justice McElwayne eventually picked up three votes. Justice Ro-

mano worked on his brethren for several weeks before getting his three. Once again, it would be decided by the new guy.

Justice Fisk wrestled with the case. He read the briefs shortly after being sworn in, and changed his mind from day to day. He found it easy to believe that the manufacturer could reasonably expect its product to be modified over time, especially in light of the violent nature of a bush hog. But the record wasn't entirely clear as to whether the manufacturer had complied with all federal regulations at the factory. Ron had great sympathy for the child, but would not allow his emotions to become a factor.

On the other hand, he had been elected on a platform of limiting liability. He had been attacked by trial lawyers and supported by the people they loved to sue.

The court was waiting; a decision was needed. Ron flip-flopped so many times he became hopelessly confused. When he finally cast his vote with Romano, he had no appetite and left the office early.

Justice McElwayne revised his opinion, and in a scathing dissent accused the majority of rewriting facts, changing legal standards, and circumventing the jury process, all in an effort to impose its own brand of tort reform. Several in the majority fired back (Ron did not), and when the opinion was finally published, it spoke more to the internal upheaval in the supreme court than to the plight of little Aaron.

Such nastiness among civilized jurists was extremely rare, but the bruised egos and hurt feelings only deepened the rift between the two sides. There was no middle ground, no room for compromise.

When a case involved a substantial verdict, the insurance companies could now relax.

CHAPTER 34

Justice McElwayne's bitter dissents continued into the spring. But after the sixth loss in a row, another 5–4 split, he lost some of his spunk. The case involved gross negligence on the part of an incompetent doctor, and when the court took away the verdict, McElwayne knew that his brethren had shifted so far to the right that they would never return.

An orthopedic surgeon in Jackson botched a routine surgery to repair a herniated disk. His patient was rendered a paraplegic, and eventually filed suit. The doctor had been sued five times previously, had lost his medical license in two other states, and had been treated on at least three occasions for addiction to painkillers. The jury awarded the paraplegic $1.8 million for actual damages, then slapped the doctor and the hospital with $5 million in punitive damages.

Justice Fisk, in his first written opinion for the majority, declared the actual damages to be excessive and the punitive award unconscionable. The decision sent the case back for a new trial on actual damages only. Forget punitive.

Justice McElwayne was apoplectic. His dissent bristled with vague allegations that special interests of the state now had more influence on

the supreme court than did four of its own members. The final sentence of his initial draft was almost libelous: "The author of the majority opinion feigns shock at the amount of the punitive award. However, he should be rather comfortable with the sum of $5 million. That was the price of the seat he now occupies." To get a laugh, he e-mailed a copy of the draft to Sheila McCarthy. She indeed laughed, then begged him to remove the last sentence. Eventually, he did.

McElwayne's dissent raged for four pages. Albritton concurred with another three. They wondered privately if they could find happiness in writing useless dissents for the rest of their careers.

———————

Their useless dissents were beautiful music to Barry Rinehart. He was carefully reading every decision out of Mississippi. His staff was analyzing the opinions, the pending cases, and the recent jury trials that might one day send a verdict to the high court. As always, Barry was watching closely.

Electing a friendly judge was indeed a victory, but it wasn't complete until the payoff. So far, Justice Fisk had a perfect voting record. *Baker v. Krane Chemical* was ripe for a decision.

On a flight to New York to see Mr. Trudeau, Barry decided that their boy needed some reassurance.

———————

The dinner was at the University Club, on the top floor of Jackson's tallest building. It was a quiet event, almost secret, by invitation only and the invitations were not printed. A phone network had rounded up the eighty or so guests. The evening was in honor of Justice Ron Fisk. Doreen was there and had the high honor of sitting next to Senator Myers Rudd, who'd just flown in from Washington. Steak and lobster were served. The first speaker was the president of the state medical association, a dignified surgeon from Natchez who at times seemed near tears as he talked about the enormous sense of relief in the medical community. For years, the doctors had labored under the fear of litigation. They had

paid enormous insurance premiums. They had been subjected to frivo-
lous lawsuits. They had been abused in depositions and during trials. But
now everything had changed. Because of the new direction of the su-
preme court, they could properly treat their patients without looking over
their shoulders. He thanked Ron Fisk for his courage, his wisdom, and his
commitment to protecting the doctors and nurses and hospitals of the
state of Mississippi.

Senator Rudd was on his third scotch, and the host knew from ex-
perience that the fourth one meant trouble. He called on The Senator to
say a few words. Thirty minutes later, after fighting battles around the
world and settling everything but the conflict in the Middle East, Rudd
finally remembered why he was there. He never used notes, never
planned a speech, never wasted time on forethought. His presence alone
was enough to thrill everyone. Oh yes, Ron Fisk. He recounted their first
meeting in Washington a year earlier. He called him "Ronny" at least
three times. When he saw the host point at his watch, he finally sat down
and demanded scotch number four.

The next speaker was the executive director of the Commerce
Council, a veteran of many bruising battles with the trial lawyers. He
spoke eloquently about the drastic change in the state's economic devel-
opment environment. Companies young and old were suddenly making
bold plans, no longer afraid to take risks that might lead to litigation. For-
eign firms were now interested in locating facilities in the state. Thank
you, Ron Fisk.

Mississippi's reputation as a judicial hellhole, as a dumping ground
for thousands of frivolous lawsuits, as a haven for reckless trial lawyers,
had changed almost overnight. Thank you, Ron Fisk.

Many firms were beginning to see the first signs of stabilized rates
for liability insurance protection. Nothing definite yet, but things looked
promising. Thank you, Ron Fisk.

After Justice Fisk had been showered with praise, almost to the
point of embarrassment, he was asked to say a few words himself. He
thanked everyone for their support during his campaign. He was pleased
with his first three months on the court, and he was certain that the ma-

jority there would hold together on the issues of liability and damages. (Heavy applause.) His colleagues were bright and hardworking, and he claimed to be enamored with the intellectual challenge of the cases. He did not feel the least bit disadvantaged because of his inexperience.

On behalf of Doreen, he thanked them for a wonderful evening.

It was a Friday night, and they drove home to Brookhaven still floating on the accolades and admiration. The kids were asleep when they arrived at midnight.

Ron slept six hours and awoke in a panic over where to find a catcher. Baseball season was beginning. Tryouts were at 9:00 a.m. for the eleven- and twelve-year-olds. Josh, eleven, was moving up and would be one of the highest-ranked newcomers to the league. Because of his demanding job, Ron could not commit to a head coaching position. He could not make all the practices, but he was determined not to miss a single game. He would handle the pitchers and catchers. One of his former law partners would handle the rest and call himself the head coach. Another father would organize the practices.

It was the first Saturday in April, a chilly morning throughout the state. A nervous bunch of players and parents and especially coaches gathered at the city park for the beginning of the season. The nine- and ten-year-olds were sent to one field, the elevens and twelves to another. All players would be evaluated, then ranked, then placed in the draft.

The coaches met behind home plate to get organized. There was the usual nervous chatter and cheap shots and lighthearted insults. Most of them had coached in the same league the year before. Ron, back then, had been a popular coach, just another young father who would spend hours on the field from April to July. Now, though, he felt a bit elevated. He had put together a brilliant campaign and won an important political race with a record vote. That made him unique among his peers. There was, after all, only one supreme court justice in the town of Brookhaven. There was a certain detachment that he did not particularly like, though he wasn't sure if he disliked it, either.

There were already calling him "Judge."

Judge Fisk pulled a name out of the hat. His team was the Rockies.

———

The apartment was so cramped during the week they had to escape on Saturdays.

The Paytons coaxed Mack and Liza out of bed with the suggestion of breakfast at a nearby pancake house. Afterward, they left Hattiesburg and arrived in Bowmore before 10:00 a.m. Mrs. Shelby, Mary Grace's mother, had promised a long lunch under an oak tree—catfish followed by homemade ice cream. Mr. Shelby had the boat ready. He and Wes took the kids to a small lake where the crappie were biting.

Mary Grace and her mother sat on the porch for an hour, covering the usual topics, avoiding anything remotely related to the law. Family news, church gossip, weddings, and funerals, but they stayed away from cancer, which for years had dominated the chatter in Cary County.

Long before lunch, Mary Grace drove to town, to Pine Grove, where she met with Denny Ott. She passed along her latest thoughts on the new supreme court, a rather sad summary. Not for the first time she warned Denny that they would probably lose. He was preparing his people. He knew they would survive. They had lost everything else.

She drove two blocks and parked in the gravel driveway of Jeannette's trailer. They sat outside, under a shade tree, sipping bottled water and talking about men. Jeannette's current boyfriend was a fifty-five-year-old widower with a nice job and a nice home and little interest in her lawsuit—not that the lawsuit was attracting the attention it once commanded. The verdict was now seventeen months old. Not a dime had changed hands, and none was anticipated.

"We expect a ruling this month," Mary Grace said. "And it will be a miracle if we win."

"I'm praying for a miracle," Jeannette said, "but I'm ready for whatever happens. I just want it to be over."

After a long chat and a quick hug, Mary Grace left. She drove the

streets of her hometown, past the high school and the homes of child-
hood friends, past the stores on Main Street, then into the countryside.
She stopped at Treadway's Grocery, where she bought a soda and said
hello to a lady she had known her entire life.

Driving back to her parents' home, she passed the Barrysville Vol-
unteer Fire Department, a small metal building with an old pumper that
the boys rolled out and washed on election days. The station also served
as a precinct, where, five months earlier, 74 percent of the fine folks of
Barrysville voted for God and guns and against gays and liberals. Barely
five miles from the Bowmore town limits, Ron Fisk had convinced these
people that he was their protector.

Perhaps he was. Perhaps his mere presence on the court was too intimi-
dating for some.

The Meyerchec and Spano appeal was dismissed by the clerk for a
lack of prosecution. They failed to file the required briefs, and after the
usual warnings from the clerk their lawyer said they had no desire to go
forward. They were not available for comment, and their lawyer did not
return phone calls from reporters.

On the day of the dismissal, the supreme court reached a new low
in its movement to drastically limit corporate exposure. A privately held
pharmaceutical company called Bosk had made and widely marketed a
strong painkiller called Rybadell. It proved to be horribly addictive, and
within a few years Bosk was getting hammered with lawsuits. During one
of the first trials, Bosk executives were caught lying. A U.S. attorney in
Pennsylvania opened an investigation, and there were allegations that the
company had known about Rybadell's addictive propensities but had
tried to bury this information. The drug was extremely profitable.

A former Jackson cop named Dillman was injured in a motorcycle
accident, and in the course of his recovery became addicted to Rybadell.
He battled the addiction for two years, during which time his health and
the rest of his life disintegrated. He was arrested twice for shoplifting. He

eventually sued Bosk in the Circuit Court of Rankin County. The jury found the company liable and awarded Dillman $275,000, the lowest Rybadell verdict in the country.

On appeal, the supreme court reversed, 5–4. The principal reason, set forth in the majority opinion by Justice Romano, was that Dillman should not be awarded damages because he was a drug addict.

In a rancorous dissent, Justice Albritton begged the majority to step forward and produce any scintilla of proof that the plaintiff was a drug addict "before his introduction to Rybadell."

Three days after the decision, four Bosk executives pled guilty to withholding information from the Food and Drug Administration, and to lying to federal investigators.

CHAPTER 35

Krane Chemical's first-quarter earnings were much better than expected. In fact, they astounded the analysts, who had been expecting about $1.25 per share on the high end. When Krane reported $2.05 per share, the company and its amazing comeback attracted even more interest from financial publications.

All fourteen plants were running at full throttle. Prices had been cut to recapture market share. The sales force was working overtime to fill orders. Debt had been slashed. Most of the problems that had dogged the company throughout the preceding year were suddenly gone.

The stock had made a steady and impressive climb from single digits, and was trading around $24 when the earnings news hit. It jumped to $30. When last seen at that price, the stock was free-falling the day after the verdict in Hattiesburg.

The Trudeau Group now owned 80 percent of Krane, or around forty-eight million shares. Since the rumors of bankruptcy just before the election back in November, Mr. Trudeau's net worth had increased by $800 million. And he was quite anxious to double that.

Before a final decision is handed down by the supreme court, the justices spend weeks reading one another's memos and preliminary opinions. They sometimes argue, privately. They lobby for votes to support their positions. They lean on their clerks for useful gossip from down the hall. Occasionally, there are deadlocks that take months to resolve.

The last thing Justice Fisk read late Friday afternoon was McElwayne's dissent in the case of *Jeannette Baker v. Krane Chemical Corporation*. It was widely assumed to be a dissent with three others concurring. The majority opinion was written by Justice Calligan. Romano was working on a concurring opinion, and there was a chance that Albritton would write a dissent of his own. Though the details were not complete, there was little doubt that the final decision would be a 5–4 reversal of the verdict.

Fisk read the dissent, scoffed at it, and decided to concur with Calligan first thing Monday morning. Then Justice Fisk changed clothes and became Coach Fisk. It was time for a game.

The Rockies opened their season with a weekend jamboree in the delta town of Russburg, an hour northwest of Jackson. They would play one game on Friday night, at least two on Saturday, and maybe one on Sunday. The games were only four innings long, and every player was encouraged to pitch and play different positions. There were no trophies and no championships—just a loosely competitive round-robin to start the season. Thirty teams signed up in the eleven- and twelve-year-old division, including two others from Brookhaven.

The Rockies' first opponent was a team from the small town of Rolling Fork. The night was cool, the air clear, the sports complex filled with players and parents and the excitement of five games going at once.

Doreen was in Brookhaven with Clarissa and Zeke, who had a game at nine on Saturday morning.

In the first inning, Josh played second base, and when he came to bat, his father was coaching at third. When he struck out on four pitches,

his father yelled encouragement and reminded him that he could not hit the ball if he kept the bat on his shoulder. In the second inning, Josh went to the mound and promptly struck out the first two batters he faced. The third hitter was a stocky twelve-year-old, the catcher, batting in the seven hole. He yanked the first pitch foul but very hard.

"Keep it low and away," Ron yelled from the dugout.

The second pitch was not low and away. It was a fastball right down the middle of the plate, and the hitter ripped it hard. The ball shot off the barrel of the aluminum bat and left the plate much faster than it had arrived. For a split second, Josh was frozen, and by the time he began to react, the ball was in his face. He jerked just slightly as the ball hit him square in the right temple. The ball then careened over the shortstop and rolled into left field.

Josh's eyes were open when his father reached him. He was lying in a heap at the base of the mound, stunned and groaning.

"Say something, Josh," Ron said as he gently touched the wound.

"Where's the ball?" Josh asked.

"Don't worry about it. Can you see me all right?"

"I think so." Tears were leaking from his eyes, and he clenched his teeth to keep from crying. The skin had been scraped, and there was a little blood in his hair. The swelling had already started.

"Get some ice," someone said.

"Call the EMTs."

The other coaches and umpires hovered around. The kid who hit the line drive stood nearby, ready to cry himself.

"Don't close your eyes," Ron said.

"Okay, okay," Josh said, still breathing rapidly.

"Who plays third base for the Braves?"

"Chipper."

"And center field?"

"Andruw."

"Attaboy."

After a few minutes, Josh sat up and the fans applauded. Then he

stood and walked with his father's help to the dugout, where he stretched out on the bench. Ron, his heart still hammering away, gently placed a bag of ice on the knot on Josh's temple. The game slowly picked up again.

A medic arrived and examined Josh, who seemed perfectly responsive. He could see, hear, remember details, and even mentioned returning to the game. The medic said no, as did Coach Fisk. "Maybe tomorrow," Ron said, but only to comfort his son. Ron had a knot of his own, stuck firmly in his throat, and he was just beginning to calm down. He planned to take him home after the game.

"He looks fine," the medic said. "But you might want to get him x-rayed."

"Now?" Ron asked.

"No rush, but I'd do it tonight."

By the end of the third inning, Josh was sitting up and joking with his teammates. Ron returned to the third-base coach's box and was whispering to a runner when one of the Rockies yelled from the dugout, "Josh is throwing up!"

The umpires stopped the game again, and the coaches cleared the Rockies' dugout. Josh was dizzy, sweating profusely, and violently nauseous. The medic was nearby, and within minutes a stretcher arrived with two emergency medical technicians. Ron held his son's hand as they rolled him to the parking lot. "Don't close your eyes," Ron said over and over. And, "Talk to me, Josh."

"My head hurts, Dad."

"You're okay. Just don't close your eyes."

They lifted the stretcher into the ambulance, locked it down, and allowed Ron to squat beside his son. Five minutes later, they wheeled him into the emergency room entrance at Henry County General Hospital. Josh was alert and had not vomited since leaving the ballpark.

A three-car smashup had occurred an hour earlier, and the emergency room was in a frenzy. The first doctor to examine Josh ordered a CT scan and explained to Ron that he would not be allowed to go farther into the hospital. "I think he's fine," the doctor said, and Ron found

a chair in the cluttered waiting room. He called Doreen and managed to get through that difficult conversation. Time virtually stopped as the minutes dragged on.

The Rockies' head coach, Ron's former law partner, arrived in a rush and coaxed Ron outside. He had something to show him. From the backseat of his car he produced an aluminum bat. "This is it," he said gravely. It was a Screamer, a popular bat manufactured by Win Rite Sporting Goods, one of a dozen to be found in any ballpark in the country.

"Look at this," the coach said, rubbing the barrel where someone had tried to sand off part of the label. "It's a minus seven, outlawed years ago."

Minus seven referred to the differential between the weight and the length of the bat. It was twenty-nine inches long but weighed only twenty-two ounces, much easier to swing without yielding any of the force upon contact with the ball. Current rules prohibited a differential greater than four. The bat was at least five years old.

Ron gawked at it as if it were a smoking gun. "How'd you get it?"

"I checked it when the kid came to the plate again. I showed it to the ump, who threw it out and went after the coach. I went after him, too, but, to be honest, he didn't have a clue. He gave me the damned thing."

More of the Rockies' parents arrived, then some of the players. They huddled around a bench near the emergency exit and waited. An hour passed before the doctor returned to brief Ron.

"CT scan's negative," the doctor said. "I think he's okay, just a mild concussion."

"Thank God."

"Where do you live?"

"Brookhaven."

"You can take him home, but he needs to be very still for the next few days. No sports of any kind. If he experiences dizziness, headaches, double vision, blurred vision, dilated pupils, ringing in his ears, bad taste in his mouth, moodiness, or drowsiness, then you get him to your local doctor."

Ron nodded and wanted to take notes.

"I'll put all this in a discharge report, along with the CT scan."

"Fine, sure."

The doctor paused, looked at Ron a bit closer, then said, "What do you do for a living?"

"I'm a judge, supreme court."

The doctor smiled, offered a hand to shake. "I sent you a check last year. Thank you for what you're doing down there."

"Thanks, Doc."

An hour later, ten minutes before midnight, they left Russburg. Josh sat in the front seat with an ice pack stuck to his head and listened to the Braves-Dodgers game on the radio. Ron glanced at him every ten seconds, ready to pounce on the first warning sign. There were none, until they entered the outskirts of Brookhaven and Josh said, "Dad, my head hurts a little."

"The nurse said a small headache is okay. But a bad one means trouble. On a scale of one to ten, where is it?"

"Three."

"Okay, when it gets to five, I want to know."

Doreen was waiting at the door with a dozen questions. She read the discharge summary at the kitchen table while Ron and Josh ate a sandwich. After two bites, Josh said he was not hungry. He'd been starving when they left Russburg. He was suddenly irritable, but it was hours past his bedtime. When Doreen began her version of a physical exam, he barked at her and went to use the bathroom.

"What do you think?" Ron asked.

"He appears to be fine," she replied. "Just a little cranky and sleepy."

They had a huge fight over the sleeping arrangements. Josh was eleven years old and wasn't about to sleep with his mother. Ron explained to him, rather firmly, that on this particular night, and under these unusual circumstances, he would indeed go to sleep with his mother at his side. Ron would be napping in a chair next to the bed.

Under the steady gaze of both parents, he fell asleep quickly. Then Ron nodded off in the chair, and at some point around 3:30 a.m. Doreen finally closed her eyes.

She opened them an hour later when Josh screamed. He had vomited again, and his head was splitting. He was dizzy, incoherent, and crying and said everything looked blurry.

The family doctor was a close friend named Calvin Treet. Ron called him while Doreen ran next door to fetch a neighbor. In less than ten minutes, they were walking into the ER at the Brookhaven hospital. Ron was carrying Josh, and Doreen had the discharge papers and the CT scan. The ER physician did a quick exam, and everything was wrong—slow heart rate, unequal pupils, drowsiness. Dr. Treet arrived and took over while the ER physician examined the discharge summary.

"Who read the scan?" Treet asked.

"The doctor in Russburg," Ron said.

"When?"

"About eight o'clock last night."

"Eight hours ago?"

"Something like that."

"It doesn't show much," he said. "Let's do a scan here."

The ER doctor and a nurse took Josh to an exam room. Treet said to the Fisks, "You need to wait out there. I'll be right back."

They sleepwalked to the ER waiting room, too numb and too terrified to say anything for a few moments. The room was empty but gave the impression of having survived a rough night—empty soda cans, newspapers on the floor, candy wrappers on the tables. How many others had sat here in a daze waiting for the doctors to appear and deliver bad news?

They held hands and prayed for a long time, silently at first, then back and forth in short soft sentences, and when the praying was over, they felt some relief. Doreen called home, talked to the neighbor who was babysitting, and promised to call again when they knew something.

When Calvin Treet walked into the room, they knew things were

not going well. He sat down and faced them. "Josh has a fracture of the skull, according to our CT scan. The scan you brought from Russburg is not very helpful because it belongs to another patient."

"What the hell!" Ron said.

"The doctor there looked at the wrong CT scan. The patient's name is barely readable at the bottom, but it ain't Josh Fisk."

"This can't be true," Doreen said.

"It is, but we'll worry about it later. Listen carefully; here's where we are. The ball hit Josh right here," he said, pointing to his right temple. "It's the thinnest part of the skull, known as the temporal bone. The crack is called a linear fracture, and it's about two inches long. Just inside the skull is a membrane that encases the brain, and feeding it is the middle meningeal artery. This artery goes through the bone, and when the bone was cracked, the artery was lacerated, causing blood to accumulate between the bone and the membrane. This compressed the brain. The blood clot, known as an epidural hematoma, grew and increased the pressure inside the skull. The only treatment now is a craniotomy, which is a removal of the hematoma by opening the brain."

"Oh, my God," Doreen said and covered her eyes.

"Please listen," Treet went on. "We need to get him to Jackson, to the trauma unit at University Medical Center. I suggest we call their air ambulance and get him there in a helicopter."

The ER physician arrived in a hurry and said to Dr. Treet, "The patient is deteriorating. You need to take a look."

As Dr. Treet started to walk away, Ron stood, grabbed his arm, and said, "Talk to me, Calvin. How serious is this?"

"It's very serious, Ron. It could be life threatening."

———

Josh was boarded onto the helicopter and whisked away. Doreen and Calvin Treet rode with him while Ron raced home, checked on Zeke and Clarissa, and threw a few necessities in an overnight bag. Then he sped north on Interstate 55, driving a hundred miles per hour and daring any

cop to stop him. When he wasn't plea-bargaining with God, he was curs-
ing the doctor in Russburg who studied the wrong CT scan. And occa-
sionally, he turned around and glanced at the defectively designed and
unreasonably dangerous product in the rear seat.

He had never liked aluminum bats.

CHAPTER 36

At ten minutes after eight on Saturday morning, some thirteen hours after being struck by the baseball, Josh underwent surgery at the University of Mississippi Medical Center in Jackson.

Ron and Doreen waited in the hospital's chapel with friends who were arriving from Brookhaven. Their pastor was with them. Back at St. Luke's, a prayer vigil was under way in the church's sanctuary. Ron's brother arrived at noon with Zeke and Clarissa, both as frightened and shell-shocked as their parents. Hours passed with no word from the surgeons. Dr. Treet disappeared from time to time to check on things, but seldom brought back any useful news. As some of their friends left, others came to replace them. Grandparents and uncles and aunts and cousins arrived, and waited, and prayed, and then left to roam around the sprawling hospital.

Four hours after the Fisks last saw their son, the chief surgeon appeared and motioned for them to follow him. Dr. Treet joined the conversation as they walked down a hallway, away from the crowd. They stopped near a door to a restroom. Ron and Doreen clutched each other, bracing for the worst. The surgeon spoke in a grave and weary voice:

"He has survived the surgery and is doing as well as can be expected. We removed a large hematoma compressing the brain. The pressure inside the skull has been reduced. But there was a lot of brain swelling, an extraordinary amount to be honest. There will likely be some permanent damage."

"Life" and "death" are easily understood, but "damage" conveys fears that are not readily defined.

"He's not going to die," Doreen said.

"As of right now, he's alive and his vital signs are good. He has a 90 percent chance of survival. The next seventy-two hours will be crucial."

"How much damage?" Ron asked, getting to the point.

"There's no way to tell right now. Some of the damage might be reversible with time and therapy, but that's really a conversation for another day. Right now, let's just continue to pray that he improves over the next three days."

————

Late Saturday night, Josh was in the ICU. Ron and Doreen were allowed to see him for ten minutes, though he was in a drug-induced coma. They didn't manage to maintain their composure when they first saw him. His head was wrapped like a mummy, and a breathing tube ran from his mouth. He was hooked to a ventilator. Doreen was afraid to touch any part of his body, even his foot.

A sympathetic nurse agreed to move a chair to a spot outside his room and allow one parent to sit there throughout the night. Ron and Doreen sent their support team back to Brookhaven, then began alternating between the ICU and the waiting room. Sleep was out of the question, and they walked the halls until sunrise Sunday morning.

The doctors were pleased with Josh's first night. After an early morning review, Ron and Doreen found a motel nearby. They showered and managed a quick nap before reassuming their positions at the hospital. The waiting rituals began again, as did the prayer vigils at home. The flow of visitors coming and going soon became an ordeal in itself. Ron and Doreen just wanted to be alone in the room with their son.

Late Sunday night, when Doreen was in the ICU and the crowd had left, Ron strolled the corridors of the hospital, stretching his legs and trying to stay awake. He found another waiting room, one for the families of noncritical patients. It was much more inviting, with nicer furniture and a wider selection of vending machines. Dinner was a diet soda and a bag of pretzels, and as he crunched on them mindlessly, a small boy walked by and seemed ready to touch his knee.

"Aaron," his mother barked from across the room. "Come here."

"He's fine," Ron said, smiling at the child, who quickly drifted away.

Aaron. The name brought back a memory. Aaron was the boy struck in the head by the piece of metal thrown by the bush hog. A brain injury, permanent disability, financial ruin for the family. The jury found the manufacturer liable. The trial had a clean record. At that moment, Justice Fisk could not remember why he had so easily voted with the majority in reversing the verdict.

Back then, barely two months ago, he had never felt the pain of a parent with a severely injured child. Or the fear of losing the child.

Now, in the middle of this nightmare, he remembered Aaron in a different way. When he read the medical summaries in the case, he had done so in the comfort of his office, far removed from reality. The kid was severely injured, which was a pity, but accidents happen in everyday life. Could the accident have been prevented? He thought so then, and he certainly thought so now.

Little Aaron was back, staring at the bag of pretzels. It was shaking.

"Aaron, leave that man alone," the mother yelled.

Ron stared at the shaking pretzels.

The accident could have been prevented, and should have been. If the manufacturer had followed established regulations, then the bush hog would have been much safer. Why had he been so eager to protect its manufacturer?

The case was gone, forever dismissed by five supposedly wise men, none of whom had ever shown much sympathy for those who suffer. He had to wonder if the other four—Calligan, Romano, Bateman, and

Ross—had ever roamed the tomb-like halls of a hospital at all hours of the day and night waiting for a child to live or die.

No, they had not. Otherwise, they wouldn't be what they are today.

———

Sunday slowly yielded to Monday. Another week began, though it was far different from any one before. Ron and Doreen refused to leave the hospital for more than an hour or two. Josh was not responding well, and they were afraid that each visit to his bed might be their last glimpse of him alive. Friends brought clothes and food and newspapers, and they offered to sit and wait if the Fisks would like to go home for a few hours. But Ron and Doreen stood fast and plowed on with a fixed determination, zombielike in their belief that Josh would do better if they stayed close by. Tired and haggard, they lost patience with the parade of visitors from home and began to hide in various places around the hospital.

Ron called his office and told his secretary he had no idea when he might return. Doreen told her boss she was taking a leave of absence. When the boss explained, delicately, that their policies did not grant such leaves, she politely informed him it was time to change said policies. He agreed to do so immediately.

The hospital was fifteen minutes from the Gartin building, and early Tuesday Ron stopped by for a quick look at his desk. It had accumulated several new piles of paperwork. His chief clerk ran down the list of all pending cases, but Ron was distracted. "I'm thinking about a leave of absence. Run it by the chief," he instructed the clerk. "For thirty days, maybe sixty. I can't concentrate on this stuff right now."

"Sure, will do. You were planning to concur this morning on *Baker versus Krane*."

"It can wait. Everything can wait."

He managed to leave the building without seeing another member of the court.

———

Tuesday's edition of the *Clarion-Ledger* ran a story about Josh and his injury. Justice Fisk could not be reached for comment, but an unidentified source got most of the facts right. The doctors had removed a large blood clot that had been pressing on his brain. His life was no longer in danger. It was too soon to speculate about long-term problems. There was no mention of the doctor who read the wrong CT scan.

However, the online chatter soon filled in the gaps. There was gossip about an illegal baseball bat involved in the accident, and speculation about severe brain damage, and an account from someone inside the Henry County General Hospital who claimed to know that the doctors there had screwed up. There were a couple of wild theories that Justice Fisk had undergone a dramatic conversion in his judicial philosophy. One rumor declared that he was about to resign.

Wes Payton watched it carefully from his office. His wife did not. She was working hard to distract herself with other cases, but Wes was consumed with the story about Josh. As the father of young children, he could not imagine the horror the Fisks were enduring. And he could not avoid wondering how the tragedy might affect the *Baker* case. He did not expect a sudden about-face by Ron Fisk, but the possibility was there.

They had only one prayer left, and that was for a miracle. Could this be it?

They waited. The decision was due any day now.

———

By early Tuesday afternoon, Josh was beginning to show signs of improvement. He was awake, alert, and following commands. He couldn't talk, because of the breathing tube, but he seemed fidgety, which was a good sign. The pressure on his brain had been reduced to almost normal levels. The doctors had explained several times that it would take days, maybe weeks to determine a long-term prognosis.

With Josh awake, the Fisks decided to spend the night at home. This was greatly encouraged by the doctors and nurses. Doreen's sister agreed to sit in the ICU, within fifteen feet of her nephew's bed.

They left Jackson, relieved to be away from the hospital and anx-

ious to see Zeke and Clarissa. Their conversation was about home-cooked food, long showers, and their comfortable bed. They vowed to savor the next ten hours, because their ordeal was just beginning.

But it would be difficult to relax. On the outskirts of Jackson, Ron's cell phone rang. It was Justice Calligan, and he began the conversation with a long-winded inquiry into Josh's condition. He conveyed condolences from everyone at the court. He promised to stop by the hospital as soon as possible. Ron was thankful, but soon had the feeling there was a business angle to the call.

"Just a couple of matters, Ron," Calligan said, "and I know you're preoccupied right now."

"I am indeed."

"There's nothing terribly urgent here, except for two cases. It looks as though that Bowmore toxic case is split 4 to 4. No surprise there, I guess. I was hoping you would concur with me on this one."

"I thought Romano was writing, too."

"He is, and he's finished, as is Albritton. All opinions are ready, and we need your concurrence."

"Let me sleep on it."

"Fine. The other is that nursing home case out of Webster County. Another 4–4 split."

"That's a very ugly case," Ron said, almost in disgust. In yet another nursing home case, a patient was basically abandoned by the staff and eventually found unfed, lying in his own waste, covered in bedsores, unmedicated, and delirious. The company that owned the facility had reported huge profits, which came as a surprise to the jury when it was proven just how little was spent on patient care. Nursing home abuse was so rampant Ron was already sick of reading about it.

"Yes, it is. Very tragic," Calligan said, as if he were capable of sympathy.

"And I guess you want to reverse?"

"I don't see the liability, and the damages are exorbitant."

In the three and a half months Ron had been on the court, Justice Calligan had never managed to see liability in any death or injury case.

He believed jurors were stupid and easily led astray by slick trial lawyers. And he believed that it was his solemn responsibility to correct every miscarriage of justice (plaintiff's verdict) from the comfort of his detached environment.

"Let me sleep on it," Ron said again. Doreen was becoming irritated with the phone call.

"Yes, always a good idea. If we could finish these two cases, Ron, then a short leave of absence might work."

A short leave of absence, or a long one for that matter, was solely within the discretion of each justice. Ron did not need Calligan to approve it. He thanked him anyway and hung up.

The Fisks' kitchen was filled with food from friends, mainly cakes and pies and casseroles. A buffet was arranged on one counter, and they ate with Zeke, Clarissa, two neighbors, and Doreen's parents. They slept six hours, then drove back to the hospital.

When they arrived, Josh was in the midst of a prolonged seizure, the second in the past hour. It passed and his vital signs improved, but it was a setback in his slow recovery. Thursday morning, he was alert again, but irritable, restless, unable to concentrate, unable to remember anything about the accident, and highly agitated. One of the doctors explained that his condition was symptomatic of post-concussion syndrome.

Thursday night, the Rockies' coach, Ron's former law partner, drove to Jackson for another visit. He and Ron had dinner in the hospital canteen, and over soup and salad he pulled out his notes. "I've done some research," the coach said. "Win Rite stopped making the lighter bats six years ago, probably in response to complaints about injuries. In fact, the entire industry went to minus four and nothing higher. Over the years, the aluminum alloys got lighter but also stronger. The barrel of the bat wall actually absorbs the ball upon contact, then launches it when the wall pops back into its original position. The result is a lighter bat, but also a much more dangerous one. Safety advocates have been bitching about these bats for a decade, and lots of studies have been done. In one test, a pitching machine threw a fastball at 90 miles an hour, and the ball

came off the bat at 120. Two fatalities on record, one in high school, one in college, but hundreds of injuries in all age-groups. So, Little League and some of the other youth organizations got together and banned anything above a minus four.

"But the problem is obvious. Win Rite and the other bat makers have a million of the old bats still out there, still being used, and we finally saw one in the game last Friday."

"There was never a recall?" Ron asked.

"None whatsoever. And they know the damned things are dangerous. Their own tests prove it."

Ron was nibbling on a saltine, certain of where this was going and unwilling to help it get there.

"The Rolling Fork team is probably liable, but it's not worth the trouble. The City of Russburg could be held liable because the umpire, a city employee by the way, failed to check the equipment. And the big tuna is, of course, Win Rite. Assets of two billion. Tons of insurance coverage. Very good case of liability. Damages undetermined but substantial. All in all a strong case, except for one small problem. Our supreme court."

"You sound like a trial lawyer."

"They're not always wrong. If you ask me, I say you should consider filing a product case."

"I don't recall asking you, and I can't file a lawsuit. I'd be laughed out of the state."

"What about the next kid, Ron? What about the next family that will go through the same nightmare? Litigation has cleaned up a lot of bad products and protected a lot of people."

"There's no way."

"And why should you and the State of Mississippi get stuck with a million bucks in medical bills? Win Rite is worth billions. They made a lousy product; make them pay."

"You are a trial lawyer."

"No. I'm your former partner. We practiced together for fourteen

years, and the Ron Fisk I remember had great respect for the law. Justice Fisk seems determined to change all of it."

"Okay, okay. I've heard enough."

"I'm sorry, Ron. I shouldn't have—"

"It's okay. Let's go check on Josh."

———

Tony Zachary returned to Jackson on Friday and heard the news about Josh Fisk. He went straight to the hospital and eventually found Ron napping on a waiting room sofa. They talked for an hour about the accident, about the surgery, and also about Tony's fishing expedition down in Belize.

Tony was deeply concerned about young Josh. He certainly hoped the child would make a quick and complete recovery. But what he wanted to know, but couldn't bring himself to ask, was, "When might you finish up with the *Krane* appeal?"

As soon as he was in his car, he called Barry Rinehart with the disturbing news.

———

A week after he arrived at the hospital, Josh was moved from the ICU to a private room, one that was immediately inundated with flowers, stuffed animals, cards from his fifth-grade classmates, balloons, and enough candy to feed an entire elementary school. A cot was arranged so that one of his parents could sleep next to his bed.

While the room at first gave the impression of a lighter mood, things turned gloomy almost immediately. The team of neurologists began extensive evaluations. There was no paralysis, but a definite decline in motor skills and coordination, along with severe memory loss and an inability to concentrate. Josh was easily distracted and slow to recognize objects. The tubes were gone, but his speech was noticeably slower. Some recovery was likely in the months to come, but there was a good chance of permanent damage.

The thick head bandages were replaced with much smaller ones. Josh was allowed to walk to the restroom, a heartbreaking sight as he shuffled awkwardly forward, one clumsy step after another. Ron helped him, and fought back tears.

His little baseball star had played his final game.

CHAPTER 37

Dr. Calvin Treet drove to Russburg and arranged a meeting with the ER physician who had read the wrong CT scan. After they examined the two scans, Josh's and the other patient's, they argued briefly before the doctor admitted that the emergency room that night had been chaotic and understaffed, and, yes, mistakes were made. The fact that he'd botched the treatment of the son of a supreme court justice was overwhelming. "Will the family file suit?" he asked, clearly shaken.

"I don't know, but you should notify your insurance company."

Treet took the file to Jackson and discussed it with Ron and Doreen. He walked them through standard CT scan procedure, then recounted his conversation with the ER doctor.

"What should've been done?" Doreen asked.

Treet knew the question was coming. He knew he would be asked by his friends to pass judgment on the performance of another doctor. He had decided days ago to be as honest as possible. "They should've brought him here immediately and removed the blood clot. It's brain surgery, but it's not a complicated procedure. Josh would have been home two days after surgery, completely healed with no damage whatsoever."

"This CT scan was taken at eight o'clock Friday night," Ron said. "You saw Josh in Brookhaven about nine hours later, right?"

"Something like that."

"So for nine hours the pressure continued to build inside his skull?"

"Yes."

"And the compression of the brain by the blood clot damages the brain?"

"Yes."

There was a long silence as they danced around the obvious conclusion. Ron finally asked, "Calvin, what would you do if it were your kid?"

"Sue the bastard. It's gross negligence."

"I can't sue, Calvin. I'd make a mockery out of myself."

After a game of squash, a shower, and a massage in the Senate gym, Myers Rudd ducked into a limo and suffered through the late afternoon traffic like everyone else. An hour later, he arrived at the general aviation terminal at Dulles, and there he boarded a Gulfstream 5, the newest in the fleet owned by Mr. Carl Trudeau. The Senator did not know who owned the jet, nor had he ever met Mr. Trudeau, which in most cultures would seem odd since Rudd had taken so much money from the man. But in Washington, money arrives through a myriad of strange and nebulous conduits. Often those taking it have only a vague idea of where it's coming from; often they have no clue. In most democracies, the transference of so much cash would be considered outright corruption, but in Washington the corruption has been legalized. Senator Rudd didn't know and didn't care that he was owned by other people. He had over $11 million in the bank, money he could eventually keep if not forced to waste it on some frivolous campaign. In return for such an investment, Rudd had a perfect voting record on all matters dealing with pharmaceuticals, chemicals, oil, energy, insurance, banks, and on and on.

But he was a man of the people.

He traveled alone on this night. The two flight attendants served him cocktails, lobster, and wine, and the meal was hardly over when the

Gulfstream began its descent into Jackson International. Another limo was waiting, and twenty minutes after landing, The Senator was dropped off at a side entrance of the University Medical Center. In a room on the third floor, he found Ron and Doreen staring blankly at a television while their son slept. "How's the boy?" he asked with great warmth as they scrambled to get to their feet and look somewhat presentable. They were stunned to see the great man himself suddenly appearing from nowhere at 9:30 on a Tuesday night. Doreen couldn't find her shoes.

They chatted softly about Josh and his progress. The Senator claimed to be in town on business, just passing through on his way back to Washington, but he'd heard the news and felt compelled to drop in for a quick hello. They were touched by his presence. In fact, they were rattled and found it hard to believe.

A nurse broke things up and declared it was time to turn off the lights. The Senator hugged Doreen, pecked her cheek, squeezed her hands, promised to do anything within his power to help, then left the room with Ron, who was startled to see no signs of an entourage hovering in the hallway. Not a single staffer, gofer, bodyguard, driver. No one.

The Senator had come to visit, all by himself. The gesture meant even more to Ron.

As they walked down the hall, Rudd offered the same quick "Howdy" and the same plastic grin to everyone they passed. These were his people, and he knew that they adored him. He was blathering on about some mundane fight in Congress, and Ron was trying to appear captivated while suddenly wishing the man would just wrap things up and leave. At the exit doors, Rudd wished him well, promised to pray for the family, and extended offers to help on any front.

As they shook hands, The Senator, almost as an afterthought, said, "By the way, Judge, it'd be nice to finish that *Krane* appeal."

Ron's hand went limp and his jaw dropped. He tried to think of a response. As he treaded water, The Senator gave his parting shot. "I know you'll do the right thing. These verdicts are killing our state."

Rudd grabbed his shoulder, blessed him with another plastic grin, then walked through the doors and disappeared.

Back in the limo, Rudd ordered the driver to the suburbs north of town. There he would spend the night with his Jackson mistress, then hustle back to D.C. on the Gulfstream early in the morning.

———

Ron lay on the cot and tried to settle himself in for another long night. Josh's sleep patterns had become so erratic that every night was a new adventure. When the nurse made the rounds at midnight, both father and son were wide awake. Doreen, thankfully, was at the motel, fast asleep thanks to little green pills the nurses were sneaking to them. Ron took another one, and the nurse gave Josh his own sedative.

In the awful darkness of the room, Ron grappled with the visit by Senator Rudd. Was it a simple matter of an arrogant politician stepping over the line to help a big donor? Rudd relentlessly took money from anyone who wanted to hand it out, legally, so it would be no surprise if he'd taken a bundle from Krane.

Or was it more complicated than that? Krane had not contributed one dime to the Fisk campaign. Ron had combed through the records after the election when he, too, had been shocked at the cash raised and spent. He had argued and fought with Tony Zachary about where the money came from. It's all right there in the reports, Tony said over and over. And Ron had studied the reports. His donors were corporate executives and doctors and defense lawyers and lobbying groups, all dedicated to limiting liability. He knew that when his campaign began.

He smelled a conspiracy, but fatigue finally engulfed him.

———

Somewhere in the deep murkiness of a chemical-induced sleep, Ron heard the steady clicking of something he couldn't identify. Click, click, click, click, the same sound over and over and very rapid. It was near him.

He reached through the darkness and felt Josh's bed, then he bolted to his feet. In the dim light from the bathroom, he could see his son in the grips of a grotesque seizure. His entire body was shaking violently. His face contorted, his mouth open, his eyes wild. The clicking and rattling

got louder. Ron pushed the button to call the nurses, then he grabbed Josh by the shoulders and tried to settle him. He was astounded at the ferocity of the attack. Two nurses swept in and took charge. A third was right behind them, then a doctor. There was little to be done except stick a depressor in Josh's mouth to prevent an injury to his tongue.

When Ron couldn't watch any longer, he backed away, into a corner, and looked at the surreal image of his badly damaged son lost in a crowd of helping hands while the bed still shook and rails still clicked. The seizure finally relented, and the nurses were soon washing his face with cool water and speaking in childlike voices. Ron eased from the room for another mindless hike through the corridors.

The seizures continued off and on for twenty-four hours, then abruptly stopped. By that time, Ron and Doreen were too weary and frazzled to do anything but stare at their son and pray that he remained still and calm. Other doctors arrived, all grim faced and uttering incomprehensible words among themselves. More tests were ordered, and Josh was taken away for hours, then brought back.

Days passed and blurred together. Time meant nothing.

———

On a Saturday morning, Ron sneaked into his office at the Gartin building. Both clerks were there, at his request. There were twelve cases to decide, and Ron had read their brief summaries and recommendations. The clerks had their own little docket prepared and were ready for the roll call.

A rape conviction from Rankin County. Affirmed, with a unanimous court.

An election dispute from Bolivar County. Affirmed, with seven others.

An extremely dull secured-transaction brouhaha from Panola County. Affirmed, with a unanimous court.

And so on. With Ron preoccupied and showing little interest in the work, the first ten cases were disposed of in twenty minutes.

"*Baker versus Krane Chemical,*" a clerk said.

"What's the buzz?" Ron asked.

"Four–four split, with everybody throwing knives. Calligan and company are quite nervous about you. McElwayne and his side are curious. Everybody's watching, waiting."

"They think I've cracked up?"

"No one's sure. They think you're under a great deal of stress, and there's speculation about some great cathartic flip-flop because of what's happened."

"Let 'em speculate. I'll wait on *Baker* and that nursing home case."

"Are you considering a vote to uphold the verdicts?" the other clerk asked.

Ron had already learned that most of the court's gossip was created and spread by the network of clerks, all of them.

"I don't know," he said. Thirty minutes later, he was back at the hospital.

CHAPTER 38

Eight days later, on a rainy Sunday morning, Josh Fisk was loaded into an ambulance for the drive to Brookhaven. Once there, he would be placed in a room at the hospital five minutes from home. He would be watched closely for a week or so, then, hopefully, released.

Doreen rode with him in the ambulance.

Ron drove to the Gartin building and went to his office on the fourth floor. There was no sign of anyone there, which was precisely what he wanted. For the third or fourth time, he read Calligan's opinion reversing the verdict in *Baker v. Krane Chemical*, and though he had once agreed with it completely, he now had doubts. It could have been written by Jared Kurtin himself. Calligan found fault with virtually all of *Baker's* expert testimony. He criticized Judge Harrison for admitting most of it. His sharpest language condemned the expert who linked the carcinogenic by-products to the actual cancers, calling it "speculative at best." He imposed an impossible standard that would require clear proof that the toxins in the Bowmore water caused the cancers that killed Pete and Chad Baker. As always, he caterwauled at the sheer size of the shocking verdict, and blamed it

on the undue passion created by Baker's attorneys that inflamed the jurors.

Ron read again the opinion by McElwayne, and it, too, sounded much different.

It was time to vote, to make his decision, and he simply had no stomach for it. He was tired of the case, tired of the pressure, tired of the anger at being used like a pawn by powerful forces he should have recognized. He was exhausted from Josh's ordeal and just wanted to go home. He had no confidence in his ability to do what was right, and he wasn't sure what that was anymore. He had prayed until he was tired of praying. He had tried to explain his misgivings to Doreen, but she was as distracted and unstable as he was.

If he reversed the verdict, he would betray his true feelings. But his feelings were changing, were they not? How could he, as a detached jurist, suddenly swap sides because of his family's tragedy?

If he upheld the verdict, he would betray those who had elected him. Fifty-three percent of the people had voted for Ron Fisk because they believed in his platform. Or did they? Perhaps they had voted for him because he was so well marketed.

Would it be fair to all the Aarons out there for Ron to selfishly change his judicial philosophy because of his own son?

He hated these questions. They exhausted him even more. He paced around his office, more confused than ever, and he thought of leaving again. Just run, he told himself. But he was tired of running and pacing and talking to the walls.

He typed his opinion: "I concur and agree with Justice Calligan, but I do so with grave misgivings. This court, with my complicity and especially because of my presence, has rapidly become a blind protector of those who wish to severely restrict liability in all areas of personal injury law. It is a dangerous course."

In the nursing home case, he typed his second opinion: "I concur with Justice Albritton and uphold the verdict rendered in the Circuit Court of Webster County. The actions of the nursing home fall far short of the standard of care our laws require."

Then he typed a memo to the court that read: "For the next thirty days, I will be on a leave of absence from the court's business. I am needed at home."

The Supreme Court of Mississippi posts its rulings on its Web site each Thursday at noon.

And each Thursday at noon quite a few lawyers either sat before their computers in nervous anticipation or made sure someone did so for them. Jared Kurtin kept an associate on guard. Sterling Bintz watched his smart phone at that precise hour, regardless of where in the world he happened to be. F. Clyde Hardin, still a caveman with technology, sat in the darkness of his locked office, drank his lunch, and waited. Every trial lawyer with a Bowmore case kept watch.

The anticipation was shared by a few nonlawyers as well. Tony Zachary and Barry Rinehart made it a point to be on the phone with each other when the opinions came down. Carl Trudeau counted the minutes each week. In lower and mid-Manhattan dozens of securities analysts monitored the Web site. Denny Ott had a sandwich with his wife in the office at the church. The parsonage next door did not have a computer.

And nowhere was the magical hour more dreaded and anticipated than within the shabby confines of Payton & Payton. The entire firm gathered in The Pit, at the always cluttered worktable, and had lunch as Sherman stared at his laptop. On the first Thursday in May, at 12:15, he announced, "Here it is." Food was shoved aside. The air grew thinner, and breathing became more difficult. Wes refused to look at Mary Grace, and she refused to look at him. Indeed, no one in the room made eye contact with anyone else.

"The opinion is written by Justice Arlon Calligan," Sherman continued. "I'll just skim along here. Five pages, ten pages, fifteen pages, let's see, a majority opinion that's twenty-one pages long, joined by Romano, Bateman, Ross, Fisk. Reversed and rendered. Final judgment entered for the defendant, Krane Chemical."

Sherman continued: "Romano concurs with four pages of his usual drivel. Fisk concurs briefly." A pause as he kept scrolling. "And then a twelve-page dissent by McElwayne with Albritton concurring. That's all I need to know. I won't read this piece of shit for at least a month." He stood and left the room.

"It's not exactly a surprise," Wes said. No one responded.

———

F. Clyde Hardin wept at his desk. This disaster had been looming for months, but it still crushed him. His one chance to strike it rich was gone, and with it all of his dreams. He cursed Sterling Bintz and his hare-brained class action. He cursed Ron Fisk and the other four clowns in his majority. He cursed the blind sheep in Cary County and throughout the rest of south Mississippi who had been hoodwinked into voting against Sheila McCarthy. He fixed another vodka, then cursed and drank and cursed and drank until he passed out with his head on his desk.

Seven doors down, Babe took a phone call and got the news. Her coffee shop was soon packed with the Main Street crowd looking for answers and gossip and support. For many, the news was incomprehensible. There would be no cleanup, no recovery, no compensation, no apologies. Krane Chemical was walking free and thumbing its nose at the town and its victims.

Denny Ott received a call from Mary Grace. She gave a quick summary and stressed that the litigation was over. They had no viable options. The only avenue left was an appeal to the U.S. Supreme Court, and they would, of course, file the obligatory paperwork. But there was no chance that the Court would agree to consider such a case. She and Wes would be down in a few days to meet with their clients.

Denny and his wife opened the fellowship hall, pulled out some cookies and bottled water, and waited for their people to arrive for consoling.

———

Late in the afternoon, Mary Grace walked into Wes's office and closed the door. She had two sheets of paper, and she handed one to him. It was a letter to their Bowmore clients. "Take a look," she said, and sat down to read it herself. It read:

> *Dear Client:*
>
> Today the Supreme Court of Mississippi ruled in favor of Krane Chemical. Jeannette Baker's appeal was reversed and rendered, which means that it cannot be retried or re-filed. We intend to ask the court for a rehearing, which is customary, but also a waste of time. We will also appeal her case to the U.S. Supreme Court, but this, too, is a mere formality. That Court rarely considers state court cases such as this.
>
> Today's ruling, and we will send you a full copy next week, makes it impossible to proceed with your case against Krane. The court applied a standard of proof that makes it impossible to pin liability on the company. And it's painfully obvious what would happen to another verdict when presented to the same court.
>
> Words cannot express our disappointment and frustration. We have fought this battle for five years against enormous odds, and we have lost in many ways.
>
> But our losses are nothing compared to yours. We will continue to think of you, pray for you, and talk to you whenever you need us. We have been honored by your trust. God bless you.

"Very nice," Wes said. "Let's get 'em in the mail."

Krane Chemical roared to life in the afternoon's trading. It gained $4.75 a share and closed at $38.50. Mr. Trudeau had now regained the billion he lost, and more was on the way.

He gathered Bobby Ratzlaff, Felix Bard, and two other confidants in his office for a little party. They sipped Cristal champagne, smoked Cuban cigars, and congratulated themselves on their stunning turnaround. They now considered Carl a true genius, a visionary. Even in the

darkest days, he never wavered. His mantra had been "Buy the stock. Buy the stock."

He reminded Bobby of his promise on the day of the verdict. Not one dime of his hard-earned profits would ever be handed over to those ignorant people and their slimy lawyers.

CHAPTER 39

The guests ranged from hard-core Wall Street types like Carl himself all the way down to Brianna's hair colorist and two semi-employed Broadway actors. There were bankers with their aging though nicely sculpted wives, and moguls with their superbly starved trophies. There were Trudeau Group executives who would rather have been anywhere else, and struggling painters from the MuAb crowd who were thrilled at the rare chance to mingle with the jet set. There were a few models, number 388 on the Forbes 400 list, a running back who played for the Jets, a reporter from the *Times* along with a photographer to record it all, and a reporter from the *Journal* who would report none of it but didn't want to miss the party. About a hundred guests, all in all a very rich crowd, but no one at the party had ever seen a yacht like the *Brianna*.

It was docked on the Hudson at the Chelsea Piers, and the only vessel larger at that moment was a mothballed aircraft carrier a quarter of a mile to the north. In the rarefied world of obscenely expensive boating, the *Brianna* was classified as a mega-yacht, which was larger than a super-yacht but not in the same league as a giga-yacht. The latter, so far, had

been the exclusive domain of a handful of software zillionaires, Saudi princes, and Russian oil thugs.

The invitation read: "Please join Mr. and Mrs. Carl Trudeau on the maiden voyage of their mega-yacht, *Brianna*, on Wednesday, May 26, at 6 p.m., at Pier 60."

It was 192 feet long, which ranked it number twenty-one on the list of the largest yachts registered in America. Carl paid $60 million for it two weeks after Ron Fisk was elected, then spent another $15 million on renovations, upgrades, and toys.

Now it was time to show it off, and to display one of the more dramatic comebacks in recent corporate history. The crew of eighteen gave tours as the guests arrived and took their glasses of champagne. With four decks above water, the ship could comfortably accommodate thirty pampered friends for a month at sea, not that Carl ever intended to have that many people living so close to him. Those lucky enough to be chosen for an extended cruise would have access to a gym with a trainer, a spa with a masseuse, six Jacuzzis, and a chef on call around the clock. They would dine at one of four tables scattered throughout the boat, the smallest with ten seats and the largest with forty. When they felt like playing, there was scuba gear, clear-bottom kayaks, a thirty-foot catamaran, Jet Skis, and fishing gear, and, of course, no mega-yacht is complete without a helicopter. Other luxuries included a movie theater, four fireplaces, a sky lounge, heated tile floors in the bathrooms, a private pool for nude sunbathing, and miles of mahogany and brass and Italian marble. The Trudeaus' stateroom was larger than their bedroom back on land. And, in the formal dining room on the third level, Carl had finally found the permanent place for *Abused Imelda*.

Never again would she greet him in the foyer of his penthouse after a hard day at the office.

As a string quartet played on the main deck, the *Brianna* shoved off and turned south on the Hudson. It was dusk, a beautiful sunset, and the view of lower Manhattan from the river was breathtaking. The city shook with its frenetic energy, which was fascinating to watch from the deck of

such a fine boat. The champagne and caviar also helped the view. Those on ferries and smaller vessels couldn't help but gawk as *Brianna* moved by, her twin 2,000-horsepower Caterpillar diesels churning a quiet wake.

A small army of black-tied waiters moved deftly about the decks, hauling drinks on silver trays and finger food too pretty to eat. Carl ignored most of his guests and spent his time with those he controlled, one way or another. Brianna was the perfect hostess, gliding from group to group, kissing all the men and all the women, making sure everyone got the chance to see her.

The captain circled wide so the guests could have a nice view of Ellis Island and the Statue of Liberty, then turned north in the direction of the Battery, at the southern tip of Manhattan. It was dark now, and the rows of skyscrapers lit up the financial district. Under the Brooklyn Bridge, under the Manhattan Bridge, under the Williamsburg Bridge, the *Brianna* sailed up the East River in all its majesty. The string quartet retired, and the best of Billy Joel boomed through the ship's elaborate sound system. Dancing erupted on the second-level deck. Someone got shoved into a pool. Others followed, and clothing soon became optional. It was the younger crowd.

As per Carl's instructions, the captain turned around at the United Nations building and increased speed, though it was not noticed. Carl, at that moment, was giving an interview in his sweeping office on the third deck.

At precisely 10:30, on schedule, the *Brianna* docked at Pier 60, and the guests began their slow departures. Mr. and Mrs. Trudeau saw them off, hugging, kissing, waving, wishing they would all hurry along now. A midnight dinner was waiting. Fourteen remained behind, seven lucky couples who would cruise south to Palm Beach for a few days. They changed into more casual clothing and met in the formal dining room for yet another drink while the chef finalized the first course.

Carl whispered to the first mate that it was now time to leave, and fifteen minutes later the *Brianna* pushed off again from Pier 60. While the guests were being charmed by his wife, he excused himself for a few minutes. He climbed the steps to the fourth level, and on a small elevated

deck found his favorite spot on this fabulous new toy of his. It was an observation post, the ship's highest point above the water.

As the cool wind blew his hair, he gripped the brass railing and stared at the mammoth towers in the financial district. He caught a glimpse of his building, and his office, forty-five floors up.

Everything was up. Krane common stock was just under $50 a share. Its earnings were through the roof. His net worth was over $3 billion and rising steadily.

Some of those idiots out there had been laughing eighteen months earlier. Krane is finished. Trudeau is a fool. How can a man lose a billion dollars in one day? they howled.

Where was their laughter now?

Where were all those experts now?

The great Carl Trudeau had outfoxed them again. He'd cleaned up the Bowmore mess and saved his company. He'd driven its stock into the ground, bought it cheap at a fire sale, and now owned virtually all of it. It was making him even richer.

He was destined to move up the Forbes 400 list, and as Carl sailed along the Hudson at the very top of his extraordinary ship, and gazed with smug satisfaction at the gleaming towers packed around Wall Street, he admitted to himself that nothing else mattered.

Now that he had three billion, he really wanted six.

AUTHOR'S NOTE

I am compelled to defend my native state, and do so with this flurry of disclaimers. All characters herein are purely fictional. Any similarity to a real person is coincidental. There is no Cary County, no town of Bowmore, no Krane Chemical, and no product such as pillamar 5. Bichloronylene, aklar, and cartolyx do not exist, as far as I know. The Mississippi Supreme Court has nine elected members, none of whom were used as models or inspiration for anyone mentioned or described in the preceding pages. None of the organizations, associations, groups, nonprofits, think tanks, churches, casinos, or corporations are real. I just made them up. Some of the towns and cities can be found on a map, others cannot. The campaign is a figment of my imagination. The lawsuit is borrowed from several actual cases. A few of the buildings really do exist, but I'm not altogether sure which ones.

In another life, I served as a member of the Mississippi House of Representatives, and in that capacity had a role in making laws. In this book, some of those laws have been amended, modified, ignored, and even outright butchered. Writing fiction sometimes requires this.

A few of the laws, especially those dealing with casino gambling, survive without tampering on my part.

Now that I have impugned my own work, I must say that there is a lot of truth in this story. As long as private money is allowed in judicial elections we will see competing interests fight for seats on the bench. The issues are fairly common. Most of the warring factions are adequately described. The tactics are all too familiar. The results are not far off the mark.

As always, I leaned on others for advice and expertise. Thanks to Mark Lee, Jim Craig, Neal Kassell, Bobby Moak, David Gernert, Mike Ratliff, Ty, Bert Colley, and John Sherman. Stephen Rubin published this book, Doubleday's twentieth, and the gang there—John Fontana, Rebecca Holland, John Pitts, Kathy Trager, Alison Rich, and Suzanne Herz—again made it happen.

And thanks to Renee for her usual patience and abundance of editorial comments.

<div style="text-align: right">

John Grisham
October 1, 2007

</div>

MANAGEMENT AND ORGANISATIONAL BEHAVIOUR

Visit the *Management and Organisational Behaviour,* Eighth Edition Companion Website with Grade Tracker at **www.pearsoned.co.uk/mullins** to find valuable **student** learning material including:

● Multiple choice questions with Grade Tracker function to test your learning and monitor your progress

● Interactive exercises to reinforce your knowledge

● Annotated links to relevant sites on the web

● An online glossary to explain key terms

● Flashcards to test your knowledge of key terms

About the author

Laurie Mullins was formerly principal lecturer at the University of Portsmouth Business School. Before taking early retirement, Laurie specialised in managerial and organisational behaviour, and managing people at work, and was subject leader for the behavioural and human resource management group.

Laurie has experience of business, local government and university administration and human resource management. For a number of years he was also a member of, and an instructor in, the Territorial Army.

He has undertaken a range of consultancy work including with the United Nations Association International Service (UNAIS); served as a visiting selector for Voluntary Service Overseas (VSO); acted as adviser and tutor for a number of professional and educational bodies including UNISON Education; and served as an external examiner for university degree and postgraduate courses, and for professional organisations.

Laurie has undertaken a year's academic exchange in the Management Department, University of Wisconsin, USA, and a visiting fellowship at the School of Management, Royal Melbourne Institute of Technology (RMIT) University, Australia, and given invited lectures in The Netherlands and South Africa. Laurie is also author of *Hospitality Management and Organisational Behaviour* and *Essentials of Organisational Behaviour* both published by Pearson Education.

About the contributors

Gill Christy is principal lecturer in the Department of Human Resource and Marketing Management at the University of Portsmouth Business School.

Linda Carter is a Chartered Occupational Psychologist who specialises in management development and coaching with her consultancy 'Zest for Change'.

Peter Scott is senior lecturer in the Department of Human Resource and Marketing Management at the University of Portsmouth Business School.

EIGHTH EDITION
MANAGEMENT AND ORGANISATIONAL BEHAVIOUR
LAURIE J. MULLINS

Formerly, Principal Lecturer, The Business School, University of Portsmouth

FT Prentice Hall
FINANCIAL TIMES

An imprint of **Pearson Education**

Harlow, England • London • New York • Boston • San Francisco • Toronto • Sydney • Singapore • Hong Kong
Tokyo • Seoul • Taipei • New Delhi • Cape Town • Madrid • Mexico City • Amsterdam • Munich • Paris • Milan

Pearson Education Limited
Edinburgh Gate
Harlow
Essex CM20 2JE
England

and Associated Companies throughout the world

Visit us on the World Wide Web at:
www.pearsoned.co.uk

First published in 1985 in Great Britain under the Pitman imprint
Fifth edition published in 1999 by Financial Times Pitman Publishing imprint
Seventh edition 2005
Eighth edition 2007

© Laurie J. Mullins 1985, 1989, 1993, 1996, 1999, 2002, 2005, 2007
Chapters 4, 6 © Linda Carter and Laurie J. Mullins 1993, 1996, 1999, 2002, 2005, 2007
Chapter 5 © Linda Carter 1993, 1996, 1999, 2002, 2005, 2007
Chapter 17 © David Preece 1999, 2002, 2005

ISBN 978-0-273-70888-9

British Library Cataloguing-in-Publication Data
A catalogue record for this book is available from the British Library

Library of Congress Cataloging-in-Publication Data
A catalog record for this book is available from the Library of Congress

10 9 8 7 6 5 4 3 2 1
11 10 09 08 07

Typeset in Giovanni Book 9.5/12pt by 30
Printed and bound by Mateu Cromo Artes Graficas, Spain

The publisher's policy is to use paper manufactured from sustainable forests.

To my wife Pamela
and Kelvin, Kerrie, Tracey, Paul

SUPPORTING RESOURCES

Visit **www.pearsoned.co.uk/mullins** to find valuable online resources

Companion Website with Grade Tracker for students
- Multiple choice questions with Grade Tracker function to test your learning and monitor your progress
- Interactive exercises to reinforce your knowledge
- Annotated links to relevant sites on the web
- An online glossary to explain key terms
- Flashcards to test your knowledge of key terms

Also: The Companion Website provides the following features:
- Search tool to help locate specific items of content
- Online help and support to assist with website usage and troubleshooting

For instructors
- Complete, downloadable Instructor's Manual, which includes teaching tips and solutions/examples to discussion and other questions
- Testbank of question material
- Downloadable PowerPoint slides of section summaries and figures in the book

Note: A CD-ROM version of the Instructor's Manual and PowerPoint slides is also available free to adopters of *Management and Organisational Behaviour*, Eighth Edition. Please contact your local sales representative, whose details can be located on our website **www.pearsoned.co.uk**

For more information please contact your local Pearson Education sales representative or visit **www.pearsoned.co.uk/mullins**

CONTENTS IN BRIEF

CONTENTS IN DETAIL

Part 4
THE NATURE OF MANAGEMENT

MANAGEMENT IN THE NEWS and CASE STUDIES

Chapter	Page no.	Type of case	Title	Subject	Organisation/ business person	Country/ region
Chapter 1 The Nature of Organisational Behaviour	31	Management in the News	How global strategy can get lost in translation	Organisations, strategy and culture		Global
	34	Case Study	Virgin Atlantic and Ryanair	How two similar organisations develop very different organisational cultures	Virgin Atlantic Airways, Richard Branson and Ryanair, Michael O'Leary	UK/Ireland
Chapter 2 Approaches to Organisation and Management	65	Management in the News	Problem with perform-ance-managing professionals	Professionalism: what does the term 'professional' mean today?		UK
	69	Case Study	Dell Computers: the world at your fingertips	From small business to global giant, Dell Computers mobilises workers on three continents to get your new PC to you	Dell Computers, Michael Dell	USA/ Global
Chapter 3 The Nature and Context of Organisations	107	Management in the News	A spun-out tale of two corporate cultures	Crossing continents: even for top managers, adapting to culture-shock can be difficult	Lanxess, Bayer, Liu Zhengrong	Germany/ China
	111	Case Study	Grameen Bank: a case of applied business ethics	How ingenuity coupled with enterprise can present an alternative to charity and government aid as a route out of poverty	Grameen Bank, Mohammed Yunus	Bangladesh
Part 1 Case Study	116	Longer Case Study	Cadbury: organisation, culture and history	The historical context may change organisational practices, but doesn't necessarily change core values	Cadbury	UK
Chapter 4 Individual Differences and Diversity	157	Management in the News	Norway shatters the glass ceiling – but will it promote women's cause?	Women on the board: promoting equal opportunities for women in the corporate world		Norway/UK
	161	Case Study	B&Q: The business case for diversity	Diversity in the workforce as a way to grow a business	B&Q	UK
Chapter 5 The Nature of Learning	199	Management in the News	Online learning comes of age	Innovation in e-learning tools		Global
	202	Case Study	Managing knowledge for 'e-government' in the UK	People's expectations about online shopping are having a big impact on public sector organisations	Public sector organisations	UK
Chapter 6 Perception and Communications	240	Management in the News	Tough at the top	Despite media images of tough-talking bosses, a positive style is often what can produce results	Cable & Wireless, John Pluthero	UK
	245	Case Study	What you say is what you get . . .?	Gender differences in communication may partly explain the 'glass ceiling', but not everywhere	Female managers in France, UK, Germany and China	Global
Chapter 7 Work Motivation and Job Satisfaction	284	Management in the News	Microsoft plans perks to retain staff	Towels and talent: company strategies to attract and retain staff	Microsoft and Google	USA
	287	Case Study	Don't get mad, get online!	Blogging may open a new window on organisational life, but it can get you fired	Ellen Simonetti, Queen of the Sky; IBM	UK/USA/ France
Part 2 Case Study	292	Longer Case Study	Philanthropy: the resur-gence of personal social responsibility	It was big in the 19th century, but is there a resurgence in philanthropy as a new form of ethical behaviour by business leaders?	Bill Gates, Warren Buffet and Anita Roddick	Global

Chapter	Page no.	Type of case	Title	Subject	Organisation/ business person	Country/ region
Chapter 15 Organisation Structure and Design	592	Management in the News	Can Google's random genius last?	Freewheeling at Google: can its organisation meet the potential of its business model?	Google	USA
	596	Case Study	Zara: a dedicated follower of fashion	The demands of the retail fashion industry lead to some innovative organisational structures	Zara	Spain/ Global
Chapter 16 Patterns of Structure and Work Organisation	626	Management in the News	Another side to a McJob	Dead end or turning point: is there more to a 'McJob' than previously thought?	McDonald's	UK
	629	Case Study	John Lewis, Waitrose and Ocado; distinctively successful	An unusual organisational structure leads to a very particular culture and style of organisational behaviour	John Lewis, Waitrose and Ocado	UK
Chapter 17 Technology and Organisations	659	Management in the News	Clockwork radios: not all tech is hi-tech	We tend to think of technology in terms of IT, but sometimes simple solutions are the best	Trevor Baylis	Africa/UK
	663	Case Study	Accessible technology: Tesco's accessible website	How technical advances can change people's quality of life	Tesco, RNIB	UK
Part 5 Case Study	669	Longer Case Study	Co-operatives	Invented in the 19th century, co-operatives are still going strong	Rochdale Equitable Pioneers Society, Mondragón Cooperative Corporation	Global
Chapter 18 Organisational Control and Power	709	Management in the News	Vodafone faces grilling at annual meeting	Boardroom battles	Vodafone	Global
	713	Case Study	Turbulence in the tulip fields	A controversial politician exercises her power and influence in the Dutch parliament	Hirsi Ali, Rita Verdonk	The Netherlands
Chapter 19 Organisation Development, Culture and Change	744	Management in the News	The business of doing good	Being charitable: the organisational culture of a charitable organisation is not necessarily a relaxed one		UK
	750	Case Study	The Haier Corporation	Chinese business organisations are entering the world market in a big way, so how do they adapt to local cultures?	Haier	China/USA
Chapter 20 Organisational Performance and Effectiveness	784	Management in the News	Why most managers are plagiarists	Writing the unwritten rules of management	William Swanson, Raytheon	USA
	790	Case Study	Who says business is boring? M&S's roller-coaster ride	How Marks & Spencer went from takeover target to the toast of the stock exchange	Marks & Spencer, Stuart Rose	UK
Part 6 Case Study	794	Longer Case Study	Enron: the fall of a giant	The convergence of factors that led to the collapse of the company	Enron	USA

ABOUT THIS BOOK

The concepts and ideas presented in this book provide a basis for the appraisal of contrasting perspectives on the structure, operation and management of organisations, and interactions among people who work in them. It is hoped that this will encourage a greater level of awareness of, and sensitivity to, the organisational factors and management processes influencing the behaviour and performance of people at work. The underlying theme of the book is the need for organisational effectiveness, the importance of an understanding of organisational behaviour and the role of management as an integrating activity.

The aims of this book

The **aims of this book** are to:

- relate the study of organisational behaviour to that of management;
- provide an integrated view embracing both theory and practice;
- point out applications of social science within work organisations and implications for management action;
- indicate ways in which organisational performance may be improved through better use of human resources and the effective management of people.

The book is written with a minimum of technical terminology and the format is clearly structured. Each chapter is supported with illustrations and contains:

- a short introduction and learning outcomes;
- critical reflections throughout the text;
- a synopsis of key points;
- review and discussion questions;
- personal awareness and skills exercise;
- assignment(s);
- a practical example of management in the news;
- a case study;
- detailed notes and references.

The comprehensive coverage and progressive presentation of contents will appeal to students at undergraduate, graduate or post-experience level in business or management, or on related professional courses. It is also hoped that the book will appeal not only to those aspiring to managerial positions but to practising managers and supervisors who wish to expand their views and knowledge of the subject area.

The scope of this book

No single book could hope to cover adequately all aspects of what is a wide and essentially multidisciplinary field of inquiry and it is not the intention to attempt to cover all aspects of individual or social behaviour. In order to attain a reasonable depth, this book concentrates on selected topics of particular relevance to organisational behaviour and the management of people in work situations, and which meet the needs of the intended audience.

The behaviour and actions of people at work and the activities of an organisation are directed towards the achievement of certain goals. The study of organisational behaviour should not therefore be considered in a vacuum but should be related to the process of management and to the wider organisational context and environment. **Broadening the**

scope of the subject matter beyond the concerns of traditional organisational behaviour texts is a distinctive feature of this book.

Main sections are identified clearly within each chapter and there are detailed headings and sub-headings.

> *A significant feature of this book is that it is especially suitable across a range of different but related modules, including both single or double semester units, and will help to provide an integrated approach to the course of study. Although there is a logical flow to the sequencing of topic areas, each part and each chapter of the book is self-contained, with appropriate cross-referencing to other chapters. This provides a flexible approach. The selection and ordering of chapters can be varied to suit the demands of particular courses of study or individual interests.*

The eighth edition

It is now 20 years since the first edition of *Management and Organisational Behaviour*, during which time the book has successfully developed and evolved. The continuing complimentary and supportive comments from reviewers and users of previous editions are very much appreciated. This eighth edition retains the same underlying aims and approach that have been a hallmark of the success of the book, but recognition has been given to the helpful feedback that now indicates a need to reduce the size. Accordingly, every effort has been made to achieve the balance of a smaller text yet with the inclusion of new material and maintaining the positive characteristics of the book. This has demanded difficult choices and it is regrettable but inevitable that some topics are excluded or given limited coverage. I hope that readers familiar with previous editions will accept my apology if it has not been possible to cover fully your favoured contents.

We have taken the opportunity to undertake a thorough review and reordering of the overall plan of contents, restructuring within and between chapters, and the sequencing of all material to give added clarity. Main changes include:

- the reduction from eight to six interrelated parts – *see* Figure A.1 on page xx – and from 23 to 20 chapters;
- a new section on globalisation and the international context (Chapter 1), with greater attention to international issues and cultural differences throughout the text;
- conflict and stress moved earlier in the contents to Chapter 3;
- the addition of a major new section on diversity management (Chapter 4);
- expanded coverage of values and ethics with an international theme (Chapter 14);
- complete rewriting of technology and organisations (Chapter 17);
- deletion of the chapter on job satisfaction and work performance with the most relevant material integrated elsewhere through the text;
- deletion of the chapter on resourcing the organisation as this material is more appropriately covered in specialised books on human resource management;
- for every chapter a new contemporary opening quotation;
- for every chapter a set of critical reflections throughout the text in the form of self-analysis questions;
- for every chapter a completely new management in the news and case study;
- the addition of a section case study at the end of each part of the book.

Attention continues to be given to design features and the overall layout and appearance. **These changes provide a more manageable and attractive text with a sharper more concise focus of attention as well as enhanced readability.**

Figure A.1

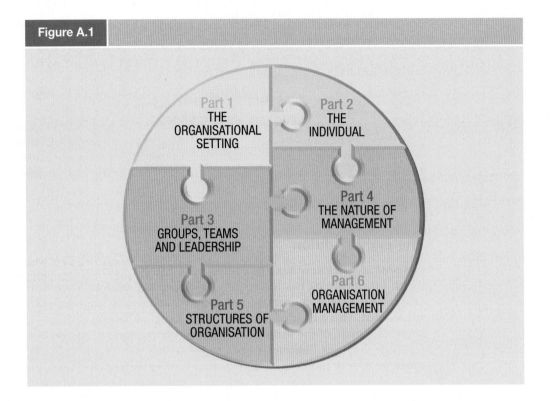

Your study of the book

This book adopts an applied approach to the study of management and organisational behaviour. The objective analysis of organisations is supported, where appropriate, by a more prescriptive stance. For example, the underlying need to establish a framework of order and system of command by which the work of the organisation is undertaken demands attention be given to certain basic principles and consideration of organisation and management.

You are invited to test your knowledge and understanding of the contents by attempting the review and discussion questions at the end of each chapter. These questions provide a basis for revision and review of progress. The management in the news, discussion questions, assignment(s), personal awareness and skills exercise and case study tasks at the end of each chapter provide an opportunity to relate ideas, principles and practices to specific work situations, to think and talk about major issues, and to discuss and compare views with colleagues. In order to help relate the contents of the chapters to real-life situations, many of the questions ask you to support your discussion with examples from your own organisation. **This can, of course, be your college or university. Alternatively, you may have work experience, even part-time or casual employment, in other organisations that you may draw upon.**

The notes and references given at the end of each chapter are to encourage you to pursue further any issues of particular interest. You are encouraged to complement your reading by drawing upon your experience of work organisations. Search for both good and bad examples of management and organisational behaviour. Consider the manner in which concepts, ideas and examples presented in this book can best be applied in particular work situations. Contemporary examples from your own observations should help illustrate real-life applications and further your interest in the subject area.

I hope you will find satisfaction, and even some measure of enjoyment, from the book.

Laurie J. Mullins

GUIDED TOUR

Navigation and setting the scene

The book is divided into six **parts**, each of which opens with a list of chapters and a light-hearted cartoon.

Quotes from today's managers and management thinkers immediately demonstrate the relevance of the chapter to real world management.

Chapter introductions provide a brief introduction to the key themes of the chapter.

Learning outcomes enable you to focus on what you should have achieved by the end of the chapter.

Follow the **Refresh icon** in the main text to activities on the Companion Website to check your understanding of the topics covered.

Organisational behaviour in context

The brand new **Management in the news** feature provides interesting journalistic comment on relevant, current issues and companies.

Discussion questions and **Tasks** encourage you to relate the Management in the News and Case studies to theories covered in the chapter.

New, engaging **Case studies** conclude each chapter and each part, providing insight into organisational behaviour in a wide variety of contemporary UK and international organisations.

Aiding your understanding

Management quotes provide insight into managerial thinking.

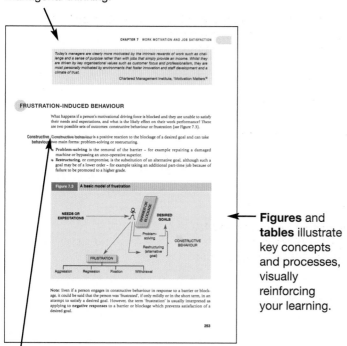

Synopsis brings together the key concepts of the chapter to aid your understanding.

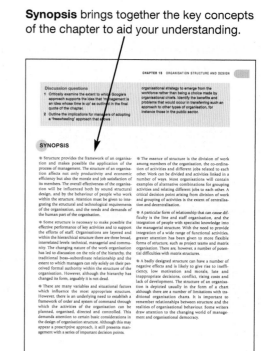

Figures and **tables** illustrate key concepts and processes, visually reinforcing your learning.

Key terms are highlighted in the text when they first appear. These terms are also included in the **Glossary** at the end of the book and on the Companion Website. You can test your knowledge of these key terms using **flashcards** on the website.

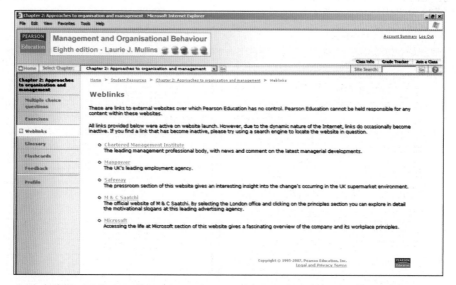

Annotated weblinks allow you to develop your understanding of relevant organisations.

Reinforcing your knowledge and thinking critically

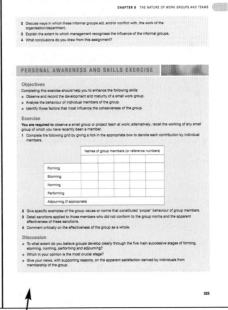

Critical reflections are controversial statements to inspire critical thinking about the areas you have just read.

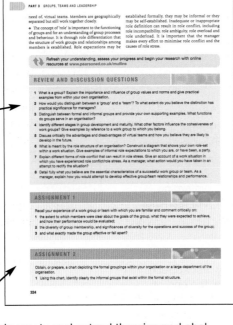

Review and discussion questions help you to check your understanding of the topic, stimulate further investigation and encourage debate.

Assignments help you to understand theories and challenge your assumptions by applying ideas and analysis to your own experiences.

Personal awareness and skills exercises develop your interpersonal and work-based skills.

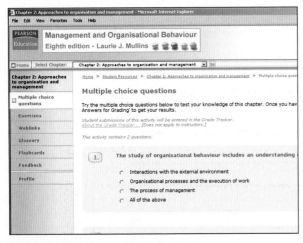

Multiple choice questions on the Companion Website test your learning and monitor your progress.

Interactive exercises on the Companion Website reinforce your knowledge.

IN ACKNOWLEDGEMENT AND APPRECIATION

A warm and special tribute is paid to my wife Pamela and family for their love, constant support and encouragement for this eighth edition.

A particular acknowledgement and thank you is due for the contribution from my friends and colleagues Gill Christy, Linda Carter and Peter Scott.

Thanks and gratitude also to:

Richard Christy, Ray French, Karen Meudell, Christine Paterson, Amanda Stevens, Lynn Thomson;

Managers who gave permission to reproduce material from their own organisations;

The team at Pearson Education including Simon Lake, Matthew Walker, Hetty Reid, Joe Vella, Colin Reed, and members in design, marketing and sales;

Those who in a variety of ways through their friendship and support have helped in the completion of this eighth edition, including: Brigitte Bjorn, Di and Mike Blyth, Christina and Barry Croad, Valerie and Peter Hallam, Jenny and Tony Hart, Lynn and Wayne Miller.

Reviewers

A debt of thanks and appreciation to the following reviewers, approached by the publishers, for their insightful and constructive comments that have helped shape the contents of this eighth edition:

Pawan Budhwar, Professor of International Human Resource Management, Aston University

Dr Whyeda Gill McLure, University of Derby

Mr Brian Good, University of Surrey

Dr Tina Harness, Senior Lecturer in Human Resource Management, Leeds Business School, Leeds Metropolitan University

Dr Anders Hytter, School of Management and Economics, Vaxjo University

Dr Deborah Knowles, University of Westminster, London, UK

Dr Steve Lyne, Head of School of Economics, Finance and Management, University of Bristol.

Dr Julian Randall, Aberdeen Business School

Dr Koos J. Swanink, MBA, The Hague University of Professional Education

Dr Theo van Dellen, University of Groningen, Department of Adult Education

Dr. Antonie van Nistelrooij, Faculty of Social Sciences, Vrije Universiteit

Jouni Virtaharju, M.Sc. (Tech.), Helsinki University of Technology

Gordon Weller, Head of Work Based Learning and Senior Lecturer in Human Resource Management, Bedfordshire Business School, University of Bedfordshire

Dr Pamela Yeow, Lecturer in Human Resource Management, Kent Business School, University of Kent.

Laurie J. Mullins

PUBLISHER'S ACKNOWLEDGEMENTS

We are grateful to the following for permission to reproduce copyright material:

Figures and Illustrations: Figure 1.6: From Brooks, I., *Organisational Behaviour: Individuals, Groups and Organisation*, Third Edition, Financial Times Prentice Hall (2006), p. 272. Reproduced by permission of Pearson Education Ltd; Figures 1.7, 3.10, 5.7, 6.13, 7.15, 8.2, 9.9, 10.8, 12.8, 13.3, 14.3, 15.11, 18.7, 19.2 and 20.4: Concept maps for education and training: key skills, management, business and the environment, courtesy of Training Learning Consultancy Ltd, Bristol, England (tlcltd@aol.com). Reproduced with permission; Figure 1.8: Hellreigel, D., Jackson, S.E. and Slocum, J. W., Jr., *Management*, Eighth Edition, Southwestern Publishing (1998), p. 6. Reprinted with permission of South-Western, a division of Thomson Learning; Figure 3.7: Adapted from Lynch, R., *Corporate Strategy*, Fourth Edition, Financial Times Prentice Hall (2006), p. 84. Reprinted by permission of Pearson Education Ltd; Figure 3.9: Lysons, K., 'Organisational analysis,' supplement to *Manager, The British Journal of Administrative Management*, No. 18, March/April (1997). Reproduced with permission The Institute of Administrative Management; Figure 3.11: Health and Safety Executive, *Work-related Stress: A Short Guide*, (INDG281Rev1) (2003). © Crown Copyright 2003. Crown copyright material is reproduced with permission of the Controller of Her Majesty's Stationery Office (HMSO) under terms of the click-use licence; Figure 4.3: Briggs-Myers, Isabel, *Introduction to Type*, Sixth Edition, CPP, Inc. (1998). Copyright © 1998 by Peter B. Myers and Katharine D. Myers, Inc. All rights reserved. Modified and reproduced by special permission of the Publisher, CPP, Inc., Palo Alto, CA 94303. Further reproduction is prohibited without the Publisher's written consent; Figure 4.4: Adapted from Vernon, P. E., 'The hierarchy of abilities' in Wiseman, S. (ed.) *Intelligence and Ability* (first published 1967, reprinted 1968, Second Edition 1973). This selection copyright © the Estate of Stephen Wiseman 1967, 1973. Reproduced by permission of Penguin Books Ltd.; Figure 4.5: From Guilford, J. P., 'Three faces of intellect' in Wiseman, S. (ed.) *Intelligence and Ability* (first published 1967, reprinted 1968, 2nd edition 1973). This selection copyright © the Estate of Stephen Wiseman 1967, 1973. Reproduced by permission of Penguin Books Ltd. Figure 4.6: From Emotional Competence Inventory, Version 2. Copyright © 2002 Hay Acquisition Company 1, Inc. All rights reserved. Reproduced with permission; Figure 5.5: Adapted from Thornhill, A., Lewis, P., Millmore, M. and Saunders, M., *Managing Change: A Human Resource Strategy Approach*, Financial Times Prentice Hall (2000), p. 289. Reproduced with permission from Pearson Education Ltd; Figure 5.6: From Atkins, M. J., Beattie, J. and Dockrell, W. B., *Assessment Issues in Higher Education*, Department of Employment (October 1993), p. 51. Crown copyright material is reproduced with permission of the Controller of Her Majesty's Stationery Office (HMSO) under terms of the click-use licence; Figure 6.7: From King, R., *Introduction to Psychology*, Third Edition, McGraw-Hill (1996). Reproduced with permission from the author, Professor Richard King, University of South Carolina and the McGraw-Hill Companies, Inc.; Figure 6.11: From Gregory, R. L., *Odd Perceptions*, Metheun (1986), p. 71. Reprinted by permission of the publishers, Routledge, a division of Taylor & Francis, Ltd; Figure 6.12: Adapted from Guirdham, M., *Interactive Behaviour at Work*, Third Edition, Financial Times Prentice Hall (2002), p. 162. Reproduced with permission from Pearson Education Ltd; Figure 7.13: Reproduced with permission from Tampoe, M., 'Knowledge workers – the new management challenge', *Professional Manager*, Chartered Management Institute, November 1994, p. 13; Figure 7.14: Hackman, J. R. and Oldham, G. R., *Work Redesign*, Addison-Wesley Publishing Company, Inc. (1980), Figure 4.6, p. 90. Reproduced with permission from Pearson Education, Inc.; Figure 8.1: Belbin, R. M., *Beyond the Team*,

Butterworth-Heinemann, (2000). Copyright © 2000, reproduced with permission from Elsevier Ltd; Figure 9.2: Greenberg, J. and Baron, R. A., *Behavior in Organizations*, Sixth Edition, Prentice-Hall (1995), p. 306. Reproduced with permission from Pearson Education, Inc.; Figure 9.7: Bishop, S. and Taylor, D., *Developing Your Staff*, Pitman Publishing / Longman Training (1994). Reproduced with permission from Pearson Education Ltd; Figure 10.2: Adair, J., *Action-Centred Leadership*, Gower Press (1979), p. 10. Reproduced with permission from Gower Publishing Ltd; Figure 10.4: Tannenbaum, R. and Schmidt, W. H., 'How to choose a leadership pattern' *Harvard Business Review*, May/June 1973, p.167. Copyright © 1973 by Harvard Business School Publishing Corporation; all rights reserved. Reprinted by permission; Figure 10.5: Adapted from Fielder, F. E., *A Theory of Leadership Effectiveness*, McGraw-Hill (1967), p. 146. Reproduced with permission from the McGraw-Hill Companies, Inc.; Figure 10.7: From Hersey, P., *The Situational Leader*, Center for Leadership Studies, Inc. (1984) p. 63. Copyright 1984 Leadership Studies, Inc. Situational Leadership is a registered trademark of the Center for Leadership Studies. Reproduced with permission. All rights reserved. Figure 10.9: With thanks to AIM Scholars: Munshi, N., Oke, A., Stafylarakis, M., Puranam, P., Towells, S., Möslein, K. and Neely, A., *Leadership for Innovation: The Impact of Leadership on Innovation*, Advanced Institute of Management Research (AIM) (2005), Figure 5, p. 18. Reproduced with permission from the Advanced Institute of Management Research; Figure 10.10: Reproduced from Cutler, A., 'A good fit is essential', *Professional Manager*, Vol. 15, No. 3, May 2005, p. 38. Published by the Chartered Management Institute with permission from Alan Cutler; Figure 11.1: Watson, T. J., *Management, Organisation and Employment Strategy*, Routledge & Kegan Paul (1986), p. 29. Reproduced by permission of the publisher, Routledge, a division of Taylor & Francis, Ltd; Figure 11.3: From Moorcroft, R., 'Managing in the 21st century', *Manager, The British Journal of Administrative Management*, January/February 2000, p. 10. Reproduced with permission from the Institute of Administrative Management; Figure 11.6: Mintzberg, H., 'The manager's job: folklore and fact', *Harvard Business Review Classic*, March–April 1990, p. 168. Copyright © 1990 by Harvard Business School Publishing Corporation; all rights reserved. Reprinted by permission of the Harvard Business Review; Figure 11.8: Mabey, C., 'Management development works: the evidence', *Professional Manager*, Vol. 14, No. 2, March 2005, p. 4 Reproduced with permission from the Chartered Management Institute; Figure 12.1: Blake, R. R. and McCanse, A. A., *Leadership Dilemmas – Grid Solutions*, Gulf Publishing Company (1991), grid figure, p. 29, paternalism figure, p. 30, opportunism figure, p. 31. Reproduced by permission of Grid International, Inc., Houston, Texas; Figure 12.2: Likert, R., *The Human Organization*, McGraw-Hill (1967), p. 137. Reproduced with permission from the McGraw-Hill Companies Inc.; Figure 13.2: Reproduced with permission from Kermally, S., 'Appraising employee performance', *Professional Manager*, July 2002, p. 31. Published by the Chartered Management Institute; Figure 15.12: Gray. J. L. and Starke. F. A., *Organisational Behaviour: Concepts and Applications*, Fourth Edition. Merrill Publishing Company (1988), p. 431. Reproduced with permission from Pearson Education, Inc.; Figure 16.1: Adapted from Lynch, R., *Corporate Strategy*, Fourth Edition, Financial Times Prentice Hall (2006), p. 582. Reprinted by permission of Pearson Education Ltd; Figure 16.4: Birkinshaw, J., 'The structures behind global companies', in Pickford, J. (ed.) *Mastering Management* 2.0, Financial Times Prentice Hall (2001), p. 76. Reproduced with permission from Pearson Education Ltd; Figure 16.5: Adapted from Perrow, C., *Organisational Analysis: A Sociological View*, Tavistock Publications (1970), p. 78. and Mitchell, T. R., *People in Organisations*, Second Edition, McGraw-Hill (1982), p. 32. Reproduced with permission from the McGraw-Hill Companies Inc.; Figure 16.6: Copyright © Reed Business Information Ltd, reprinted with permission; Figure 17.1: Adapted from Preece, D. A., *Organisations and Technical Change: Strategy, Objectives and Involvement*, Routledge/ITBP (1995), p. 3. Reproduced with permission of the publisher, Routledge, a divison of Taylor & Francis, Ltd; Figure 17.2: Preece, D. A., *Organisations and Technical Change: Strategy, Objectives and Involvement*, Routledge/ITBP (1995), p. 7. Reproduced with permission of the publisher,

Routledge, a divison of Taylor & Francis, Ltd; Figure 18.3: Child, J., *Organization: Contemporary Principles and Practice*, Blackwell Publishing (2005), p. 121. Reproduced with permission from Blackwell Publishing Ltd; Figure 18.4: Etzioni, A., *A Comparative Analysis of Complex Organizations*, Revised Edition, Free Press (1975), p. 12. Copyright © 1975 by Amitai Etzioni. All rights reserved. Reprinted with the permission from The Free Press, a Division of Simon & Schuster Adult Publishing Group; Figure 19.1: Johnson, G., Scholes, K. and Whittington, R., *Exploring Corporate Strategy*, Seventh Edition, Financial Times Prentice Hall (2005), p. 202. Reproduced with permission from Pearson Education Ltd; Figure 19.3: Adapted from French, W. L., Kast, F. E. and Rosenzweig, J. E., *Understanding Human Behaviour in Organizations*, Harper and Row (1985), p. 9. Reproduced with permission from Pearson Education Ltd; Figure 20.1: From Handy, C. B., *Understanding Organizations*, Fourth Edition, Penguin Books (1993), p. 15. Copyright © Charles Handy, 1976, 1981, 1985, 1993, 1999. Reproduced by permission from Penguin Books Ltd; Figure 20.3: Adapted from Gratton, L., *The Democratic Enterprise*, Financial Times Prentice Hall, (2004), p. 35. Reproduced with permission from Pearson Education Ltd; Figure 20.5: From *The Leadership and Management Model*, Investors in People UK (2006, pp. 5–7. Copyright © 2006. Reproduced with kind permission of Investors in People (www.investorsinpeople.co.uk); Figure 20.6: EFQM. Copyright © 1999 EFQM. The Model is a registered trademark of the EFQM. Reproduced with permission; Figure 20.7: Gratton, L., *Living Strategy: Putting People at the Heart of Corporate Purpose*, Financial Times Prentice Hall (2000), p. 101. Reproduced with permission from Pearson Education Ltd.

Tables: Table 1.1: Source: Bouchikhi, H. and Kimberly, J. R., 'The customized workplace', in Chowdhury, S. (ed.) *Management 21C*, Financial Times Prentice Hall (2000), p. 215. Reproduced with permission from Pearson Education Ltd; Table 3.1: Macdonald, J., 'Service is different', *The TQM Magazine*, vol. 6, no. 1, 1994, p. 6. Reproduced with permission from Emerald Publishing Group Limited; Table 3.2: Adapted from Gray, J. L. and Starke, F. A., *Organizational Behavior: Concepts and Applications*, Fourth Edition, Merrill Publishing Company (1988), p. 432. Reproduced with permission from Pearson Education Inc.; Table 4.4: Adapted from Erikson, E. H., *Identity and the Life Cycle*, W. W. Norton & Company, Inc. (1980), worksheet table appendix. Copyright © 1980 by W. W. Norton & Company, Inc. Copyright © 1959 by International Universities Press, Inc. Reproduced by permission of W. W. Norton & Company, Inc.; Table 5.1: Burgoyne, J., Cunningham, I., Garratt, B., Honey, P., Mayo, A., Mumford, A., Pearn, M. and Pedler, M., 'The debate starts here' in *People Management in Perspective: A Collection of Key Articles Published in the Last Year on Training and Development*, IPD, April 1999, pp. 16–17. Reproduced with permission from Chartered Institute of Personnel and Development (CIPD); Table 6.1: Adapted from Wilson, P. R., 'Perceptual distortion of height as a function of ascribed academic status', *Journal of Social Psychology*, No. 74, 1968, pp. 97–102. Reproduced with permission of the Helen Dwight Reid Educational Foundation. Published by Heldref Publications, 1319 Eighteenth Street NW, Washington, DC 20036-1802. Copyright © 1968; Table 7.3: Mumford, E., 'Job satisfaction: a method of analysis', *Personnel Review*, Vol. 20, No. 3, 1991, p. 14. Reproduced with permission from Emerald Group Publishing Limited; Table 9.1: Belbin, R. M., *Team Roles at Work*, Butterworth-Heinemann, a division of Reed Elsevier UK Ltd and Belbin Associates (1993), p. 23. Reproduced with permission. (www.belbin.com); Table 12.1: Blake, R. R. and McCanse, A. A., *Leadership Dilemmas – Grid Solutions*, Gulf Publishing Company (1991), p. 29. Reproduced with permission from Grid International, Inc., Houston, Texas; Table 12.2: From the Management Standards Centre (www.management-standards.org) I am grateful to Dr Kion Ahadi, Policy and Projects Manager, Management Standards Centre for providing this information; Table 16.1: Woodward, J., *Industrial Organization: Theory and Practice*, Second Edition, Oxford University Press (1980), p. 128. Reproduced with permission from Oxford University Press; Table 16.2: From Litterer, J. A., *The Analysis of Organisations*, Second Edition, Wiley (1973), p. 339. Reproduced with permission from the estate of Joseph A. Litterer;

Table 18.1: Woodward, J., *Industrial Organisation: Theory and Practice*, Second Edition, Oxford University Press (1980) p. xxi. Reproduced with permission from Oxford University Press; Table 20.1: Mabey, C. and Ramirez, M., 'Developing managers: a European Perspective', *Chartered Management Institute report*, May 2004, p. 6. Reproduced with permission from the Chartered Management Institute.

Photos and cartoons: Page 1: Scott Adams, 29 August 2003 / © 2003 United Feature Syndicate, Inc. Agent in UK and Ireland: Peter Knight, Knight Features; 35 (left): Empics / Associated Press; 35 (right): EMPICS Sports Photo Agency; 66: Isopix / Rex Features; 70: Rex Features; 112: AP Photo / Pavel Rahman / Empics; 116: Fox Photos / Getty Images; 121: Scott Adams, 15 August 1998 / © 1998 United Feature Syndicate, Inc. Agent in UK and Ireland: Peter Knight, Knight Features; 157: Veuve Clicquot Award Business Woman of the Year; 162: George Sweeney / Rex Features; 203: PA / EMPICS; 245: Royalty-Free / Corbis; 288: www.petiteanglaise.com / Catherine Sanderson; 293: Empics / Associated Press; 294: Empics / AP Photo / Seth Wenig; 295: Empics / Jean / allactiondigital.com; 297: Scott Adams, 11 August 1995 / © 1995 United Feature Syndicate, Inc. Agent in UK and Ireland: Peter Knight, Knight Features; 322: www.markwhittakerphotography.com; 326: Nick Hanna / Alamy; 354: Neil Tingle / actionplus; 358: Innocent Drinks; 400: Empics / Associated Press; 404: Jon Arnold Images / Alamy; 409: Scott Adams, 5 March 1998 / © 1998 United Feature Syndicate, Inc. Agent in UK and Ireland: Peter Knight, Knight Features; 438: Paul Ridsdale / Photofusion; 476: Empics / PA WIRE; 517: Larry Lilac / Alamy; 522: Kim Myung Jung Kim / PA / Empics; 527: © Scott Adams, 3 March 2003 / Distributed by United Feature Syndicate, Inc. Agent in UK and Ireland: Peter Knight, Knight Features; 555: Neil Setchfield / Alamy; 559: EMPICS Sports Photo Agency; 592: Screenshot © Google Inc. is reproduced with permission; 597: Kevin Foy / Alamy; 626: Empics / Associated Press; 630: Roger Bamber / Alamy; 660: Hugh Threlfall / Alamy; 663: Courtesy of Tesco Ltd; 669: 2000 Credit:Topham Picturepoint; 675: © Scott Adams, 11 September 2003 / Distributed by United Feature Syndicate, Inc. Agent in UK and Ireland: Peter Knight, Knight Features; 709: Empics / PA WIRE; 713: Fred Ernst / AP / Empics; 744: Digital Vision / Photolibrary Group Ltd; 750: Lou Linwei / Alamy; 790: PA / PA / Empics; 794: Empics / Associated Press.

Text: Page 34: Personal Awareness and Skills Exercise (Chapter 1): 'So what's your work ethic?' *Professional Manager*, Chartered Management Institute, May 2003, p. 38 and Walmsley, C. J., *Your Future Looks Bright*, Preston Beach (2002), p.98; Reproduced with permission; 68: Assignment (Chapter 2): DuBrin, A. J., *Human Relations: A Job-Oriented Approach*, Reston Publishing/Prentice Hall/ Pearson Education (1978), pp. 296–7. Reproduced with permission; 110: Assignment 1 (Chapter 3): Kast, F. E. and Rosenzweig, J. E., 'Our organizational society: your association with organizations', in *Experimental Exercises and Cases in Management*, McGraw-Hill (1976), pp. 13–15. Reproduced with permission from the McGraw-Hill Companies; 134: Extract (Chapter 4): Briner, R., 'Feeling and smiling', *The Psychologist*, Vol. 12, No. 1, January 1999, pp. 16–19. Reproduced with permission from the British Psychology Society; 151: Extract (Chapter 4): Lloyds TSB, Equality and Diversity Team, reproduced with permission; 157: Management in the News (Chapter 4): Susie Mesure, 'Norway shatters the glass ceiling – but will it promote women's cause?', *The Independent*, 8 March 2006. Copyright © 2006 Independent News and Media Limited, reproduced with permission; 187: Extract (Chapter 5): Judith Jones and Carol Batterson, Iyengar Yoga Teachers, Hampshire. Reprinted with permission; 233: Extract (Chapter 6): 'Hospitals set to play it by ethnic book', in *The News*, Portsmouth, 16 February 1999. Reprinted courtesy of *The News*; 240: Management in the News (Chapter 6): Sally Bibb, 'Tough at the top', *The Guardian*, 4 March 2006. Copyright © 2006 The Guardian News and Media Limited, reproduced with permission; 313: Extract (Chapter 8): 'Remote team working at Prudential' *Manager, The British Journal of Administrative Management*, March/April 2002, pp. 30–31 and with the permission of Murray Blair; 321: Extract (Chapter 8): Heller, R., *In Search of*

European Excellence, Profile Books (1997), p. 231. Reproduced with permission; 322: Management in the News (Chapter 8): Watts, R. 'No men please, we're cabbies', *Daily Telegraph*, 5 January 2006. © Copyright of Telegraph Group Limited 2006, reproduced with permission; 395: Management in the news (Chapter 10): Richard Donkin, 'Leadership: ways to instil those elusive qualities', *Financial Times*, 13 November 2005. Copyright © Richard Donkin, author of *Blood, Sweat and Tears: The Evolution of Work*, published by Texere, www.richarddonkin.com. Reproduced with permission; 397: Assignment (Chapter 10): From Schermerhorn, J. R., Jr., Hunt, J. G. and Osborn R. N., *Managing Organizational Behavior*, Fourth Edition, John Wiley & Sons (1991), p. 484. Reproduced with permission from John Wiley & Sons Inc.; 398: Personal Awareness and Skills Exercise (Chapter 10): *The Path to Leadership: Developing a Sustainable Model within Organisations*, CBI (in association with Harvey Nash), September 2005. Reproduced with permission from CBI; 473: Assignment (Chapter 12): Adapted from Myers, M. S., *Every Employee a Manager*, McGraw-Hill (1970). Reproduced with permission from the McGraw-Hill Companies. Inc.; 474: Personal Awareness and Skills Exercise (Chapter 12): From Bibb, S. and Kourdi, J., 'Do people trust you?', *Professional Manager*, Volume 14, July 2004, p. 32. A Chartered Management Institute publication, reproduced with permission. Bibb and Kourdi are the authors of *A Question of Trust – The Crucial Nature of Trust in Business, Work and Life – and How to Build It* (Cyan / Marshall Cavendish); 495: Extract (Chapter 13): Simon Fitzgerald, Development and Training Manager, Autoglass Limited, the UK's leading vehicle glass repair and replacement business. Reproduced with permission; 510: Management in the News (Chapter 13): Daniel Thomas, 'Fattism is the last bastion of employee discrimination', *Personnel Today*, 25 October 2006. Copyright © 2006 Reed Business Information Limited, reproduced with permission; 515: Appendix (Chapter 13): The Standard Overview from www.iipuk.co.uk. Copyright © 2004 Investor in People UK. Reproduced with permission; 554: Management in the news (Chapter 14): Tom Lester, 'The cost of not caring for your customers', *Financial Times*, 29 January 2006. Copyright © Tom Lester. Reproduced with permission; 576: Personal Awareness and Skills Exercise (Chapter 14): Misselhorn, A., *The Head and Heart of Management*, Organization Development Consultants (SA) (2003), p. 36. Reproduced with permission from Organization Development Consultants; 595: Assignment 2 (Chapter 15): From Child, J., *Organization: Contemporary Principles and Practice*, Blackwell Publishing (2004), p. 22. Reproduced with permission from Blackwell Publishing Ltd; 623: Extract (Chapter 16): Eatherden, R., 'Home alone stir crazy', *Management Today*, March 2005, p. 75. Reproduced with permission from Haymarket Publishing Ltd; 712: Assignment 1 (Chapter 18): Osland, J., Kolb, D., and Rubin, R., Organisational *Behaviour: An Experimental Approach*, Seventh Edition, Prentice Hall (2001). Reproduced with permission from Pearson Education, Inc.; 749: Assignment (Chapter 19): Stewart, T. A., 'Rate your readiness to change', *Fortune*, 7 February 1994, pp. 63–4, Copyright © 1994 Time Inc. All rights reserved. Reproduced with permission; 788: Personal Awareness and Skills Exercise (Chapter 20): Bourn, John for a UNISON distance learning course and is used with permission of the education officer.

We are also grateful to the Financial Times Limited for permission to reprint the following material:

Page 31: Management in the news (Chapter 1): Stefan Stern, 'How global strategy can get lost in translation', *Financial Times*, 31 July 2006. Copyright © 2006 The Financial Times Limited. Reproduced with permission; 65: Management in the news (Chapter 2): Stefan Stern, 'Problem with performance-managing professionals', *Financial Times*, 10 July 2006. Copyright © 2006 The Financial Times Limited. Reproduced with permission; 107: Management in the news (Chapter 3): Geoff Dyer, 'A spun-out tale of two corporate cultures', *Financial Times*, 22 May 2006. Copyright © 2006 The Financial Times Limited. Reproduced with permission; 199: Management in the news (Chapter 5): Linda Anderson,

'Online learning comes of age', *Financial Times*, 20 March 2006. Copyright © 2006 The Financial Times Limited. Reproduced with permission; 284: Management in the news (Chapter 7): Richard Waters, 'Microsoft plans perks to retain staff', *Financial Times*, 20 May 2006. Copyright © 2006 The Financial Times Limited. Reproduced with permission; 354: Management in the news (Chapter 9): John Kay, 'Football's example can help companies score', *Financial Times*, 10 July 2006. Copyright © 2006 The Financial Times Limited. Reproduced with permission; 433: Management in the news (Chapter 11): Lucy Kellaway, 'Managers who want to get up close and personal', *Financial Times*, 25 June 2006. Copyright © 2006 The Financial Times Limited. Reproduced with permission; 471: Management in the news (Chapter 12): Alison Maitland, 'Bosses with "no time to be nice"', *Financial Times*, 11 May 2006. Copyright © 2006 The Financial Times Limited. Reproduced with permission; 592: Management in the news (Chapter 15): Simon London, 'Can Google's random genius last?', *Financial Times*, 31 January 2006. Copyright © 2006 The Financial Times Limited. Reproduced with permission; 709: Management in the news (Chapter 18): Kate Burgess and Andrew Parker, 'Vodafone faces grilling at annual meeting', *Financial Times*, 22 July 2006. Copyright © 2006 The Financial Times Limited. Reproduced with permission; 744: Management in the news (Chapter 19): Sathnam Sanghera, 'The business of doing good', *Financial Times*, 25 May 2006. Copyright © 2006 The Financial Times Limited. Reproduced with permission; 784: Management in the news (Chapter 20): Lucy Kellaway, 'Why most managers are plagiarists', *Financial Times*, 7 May 2006. Copyright © 2006 The Financial Times Limited. Reproduced with permission.

In some instances we have been unable to trace the owners of copyright material, and we would appreciate any information that would enable us to do so.

> **Knowledge is of two kinds.
> We know a subject ourselves,
> or we know where we can
> find information about it.**
>
> **Samuel Johnson** (1709–84)
> Renowned essayist, journalist and lexicographer

Part ① ○ ○ ○ ○ ○

THE ORGANISATIONAL SETTING

THE NATURE OF ORGANISATIONAL BEHAVIOUR

> **When people are engaged and committed they are more likely to behave in the interests of the company and they have less need to be controlled and measured. In essence, engaged people can be trusted to behave in the interests of the company, in part because they perceived their interests to be the same as, or aligned with, the interests of the company.**

Lynda Gratton – global authority on the people implications of strategy

The Democratic Enterprise, Financial Times Prentice Hall (2004), p. 208

The scope for the examination of behaviour in organisations is very wide. There is a multiplicity of interrelated factors that influence the behaviour and performance of people as members of a work organisation. It is important to recognise the role of management as an integrating activity and the increasingly global business environment. People and organisations need each other. The manager needs to understand the main influences on behaviour in work organisations and the nature of the people–organisation relationship.

Learning outcomes

After completing this chapter you should be able to:

- explain the meaning and nature of organisational behaviour;
- detail main interrelated influences on behaviour in work organisations;
- outline contrasting perspectives of organisations and different orientations to work;
- explain the importance of management as an integrating activity;
- assess the nature and importance of the new psychological contract;
- recognise the need for a global context to management and organisational behaviour;
- review the changing nature of work organisations.

Critical reflection

Although a commonly used term, organisational behaviour is a misnomer: rarely do all members act collectively in such a way as to represent the behaviour of the organisation as a whole. In practice, we are talking about the attitudes and actions of individuals or small group within the organisation.

Do you agree? What term would you suggest best explains this subject area?

THE MEANING OF ORGANISATIONAL BEHAVIOUR

We live in an organisational world. Organisations of one form or another are a necessary part of our society and serve many important needs. The decisions and actions of management in organisations have an increasing impact on individuals, other organisations and the community. It is important, therefore, to understand how organisations function and the pervasive influences which they exercise over the behaviour of people.[1]

Organisational behaviour is concerned with the study of the behaviour of people within an organisational setting. It involves the understanding, prediction and control of human behaviour.[2] Common definitions of organisational behaviour (OB) are generally along the lines of: **the study and understanding of individual and group behaviour and patterns of structure in order to help improve organisational performance and effectiveness**.[3]

However much of a cliché it may sound, it is still an inescapable fact that people are the main resource of any organisation. Without its members, an organisation is nothing; an organisation is only as good as the people who work within it. In today's increasingly global and competitive environment the effective management of people is even more important for organisational survival and success.

There is a close relationship between organisational behaviour and management theory and practice. Some writers seem to suggest that organisational behaviour and management are synonymous, but this is something of an over-simplification because there are many broader facets to management. Organisational behaviour does not encompass the whole of management; it is more accurately described in the narrower interpretation of providing a behavioural approach to management.

THE STUDY OF ORGANISATIONAL BEHAVIOUR

The use of separate topic areas is a recognised academic means of aiding study and explanation of the subject. In practice, however, the activities of an organisation and the job of management cannot be isolated neatly into discrete categories. The majority of actions are likely to involve a number of simultaneous functions that relate to the total processes within an organisation.[4]

Consider, for example, a manager briefing departmental staff on an unexpected, important and urgent task that has to be undertaken quickly. Such a briefing is likely to include consideration of goals and objectives, organisation structure, management system, process of delegation and empowerment, systems of communication, leadership style, motivation and control systems. The behaviour of the staff will be influenced by a combination of individual, group, organisational and environmental factors.

Topic studies in organisational behaviour should not be regarded, therefore, as entirely free-standing. Any study inevitably covers several aspects and is used to a greater or lesser extent to confirm generalisations made about particular topic areas. The use of the

same studies to illustrate different aspects of management and organisational behaviour serves as useful revision and reinforcement and helps to bring about a greater awareness and understanding of the subject.

The relevance of theory

In the study of management and organisational behaviour you will come across many theories. However, you should not be put off by the use of the word 'theory'. Most rational decisions are based on some form of theory. Theory contains a message on how managers might behave. This will influence attitudes towards management practice and lead to changes in actual patterns of behaviour. **Theory helps in building generalised models applicable to a range of organisations or situations. It further provides a conceptual framework and gives a perspective for the practical study of the subject.** Thus theory and practice are inseparable. Together they lead to a better understanding of factors influencing patterns of behaviour in work organisations and applications of the process of management.[5]

However, to be of any help to the practising manager, theory has to be appropriate. For example, *Lee* refers to:

> *... the danger of adopting theories because they are teachable, rather than because they are effective ... [however] without appropriate theory, there would be very little communication of the insights of scientific theory to practising managers.*[6]

Although it is not always easy to establish their exact origins, ideas do percolate through to best practice.[7]

Patching suggests that all managers who think about what they do are practical students of organisational theory.

> *Theory is not something unique to academics, but something we all work with in arriving at our attitudes, beliefs and decisions as managers. It seems obvious to most of us that some theories are better than others. Many managerial discussions which we undertake in meetings focus upon trying to agree upon which theory will be best for a particular decision.*[8]

Alternative approaches

There is a number of alternative approaches to the study of organisational behaviour. For example, in addition to a managerialist approach, *Drummond* refers to two other intellectual standpoints, interpretative and critical.

The interpretative standpoint views ambiguity, paradox and contradictions as part of the natural experiences of organisations, with an emphasis upon understanding the subtleties and dynamics of organisational life. The critical standpoint believes that reality is very real and people have only a marginal amount of freedom, and regards management science as bogus, a means of legitimising economic exploitation.[9]

While acknowledging the existence and potential contributions of both these standpoints, **the main thrust of this book is to present a managerial approach to organisational behaviour.** It is concerned with interactions among the structure and operation of organisations, the process of management and the behaviour of people at work. The underlying theme of the book is the need for organisational effectiveness and the importance of the role of management as an integrating activity.

A FRAMEWORK OF STUDY

The behaviour of people, however, cannot be studied in isolation. It is necessary to understand interrelationships with other variables that together comprise the total organisation. This involves consideration of interactions among the formal structure, the tasks to be

undertaken, the technology employed and methods of carrying out work, the process of management and the external environment.

The study of organisational behaviour embraces therefore an understanding of:

- the behaviour of people;
- the process of management;
- the organisational context in which the process of management takes place;
- organisational processes and the execution of work; and
- interactions with the external environment of which the organisation is part.

This provides us with a basic, but convenient, framework of analysis (*see* Figure 1.1).

> *Organisational Behaviour is one of the most complex and perhaps least understood academic elements of modern general management, but since it concerns the behaviour of people within organisations it is also one of the most central ... its concern with individual and group patterns of behaviour makes it an essential element in dealing with the complex behavioural issues thrown up in the modern business world.*
>
> Financial Times Mastering Management Series[10]

Wilson, however, suggests that the meaning of the term organisational behaviour is far from clear. She challenges what constitutes organisational behaviour and questions whether we should be interested only in behaviour that happens within organisations. There is a reciprocal relationship in what happens within and outside organisations. Wilson suggests that we also look outside of what are normally thought of as organisations and how we usually think of work. We can also gain insight into organisational life and behaviour by looking at what happens in rest and play; considering emotion and feeling; considering the context in which work is defined as men's or women's work; and looking at less organised work, for example work on the fiddle and the meaning of work for the unemployed.[11] These suggestions arguably add an extra dimension to the meaning and understanding of organisational behaviour.

Refresh your understanding

Activity 1A
www.pearsoned.co.uk/mullins

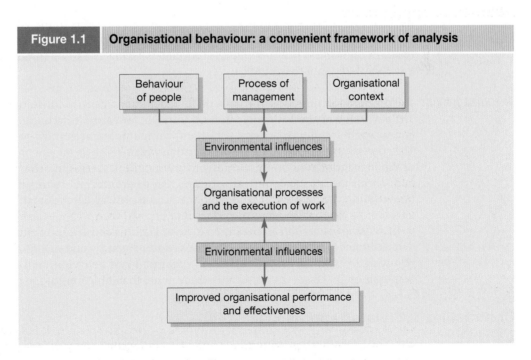

Figure 1.1 **Organisational behaviour: a convenient framework of analysis**

INFLUENCES ON BEHAVIOUR

The variables outlined above provide parameters within which a number of interrelated dimensions can be identified – the individual, the group, the organisation and the environment – which collectively influence behaviour in work organisations.

The individual Organisations are made up of their individual members. The individual is a central feature of organisational behaviour, whether acting in isolation or as part of a group, in response to expectations of the organisation, or as a result of the influences of the external environment. Where the needs of the individual and the demands of the organisation are incompatible, this can result in frustration and conflict. It is the task of management to integrate the individual and the organisation and to provide a working environment that permits the satisfaction of individual needs as well as the attainment of organisational goals.

The group Groups exist in all organisations and are essential to their working and performance. The organisation comprises groups of people and almost everyone in an organisation will be a member of one or more groups. Informal groups arise from the social needs of people within the organisation. People in groups influence each other in many ways and groups may develop their own hierarchies and leaders. Group pressures can have a major influence over the behaviour and performance of individual members. An understanding of group structure and behaviour complements a knowledge of individual behaviour and adds a further dimension to organisational behaviour.

The organisation Individuals and groups interact within the structure of the formal organisation. Structure is created by management to establish relationships between individuals and groups, to provide order and systems and to direct the efforts of the organisation into goal-seeking activities. It is through the formal structure that people carry out their organisational activities in order to achieve aims and objectives. Behaviour is affected by patterns of organisation structure, technology, styles of leadership and systems of management through which organisational processes are planned, directed and controlled. The focus of attention, therefore, is on the impact of organisation structure and design, and patterns of management, on the behaviour of people within the organisation. *McPhee* refers to the growth in the nature and importance of organisational structures and their essence, and for greater emphasis on business-to-business (B2B) depth or group interviewing as part of an insight into business and organisational behaviour.[12]

The environment The organisation functions as part of the broader external environment of which it is a part. The environment affects the organisation through, for example, technological and scientific development, economic activity, social and cultural influences and governmental actions. The effects of the operation of the organisation within its environment are reflected in terms of the management of opportunities and risks and the successful achievement of its aims and objectives. The increasing rate of change in environmental factors has highlighted the need to study the total organisation and the processes by which the organisation attempts to adapt to the external demands placed upon it.

Increasing globalisation means that organisations must respond to different market demands and local requirements. 'In globalization, strategy and organisation are inextricably twined.'[13] Globalisation impacts on organisational behaviour and has placed greater emphasis on processes within organisations rather than functions of the organisation.

Contrasting but related approaches

These different dimensions provide contrasting but related approaches to the understanding of human behaviour in organisations. They present a number of alternative pathways for

the study of the subject and level of analysis. It is possible, for example, to adopt a **psychological** approach with the main emphasis on the individuals of which the organisation is comprised. Psychological aspects are important but by themselves provide too narrow an approach for the understanding of management and organisational behaviour. Our main concern is not with the complex detail of individual differences and attributes *per se* but with the behaviour and management of people within an organisational setting.

It is also possible to adopt a **sociological** approach concerned with a broader emphasis on human behaviour in society. Sociological aspects can be important. A number of sociology writers seem set on the purpose of criticising traditional views of organisation and management. Many of the criticisms and limitations to which such writers refer are justified and help promote healthy academic debate. Unfortunately, however, much of the argument tends to be presented in the abstract and is lacking in constructive ideas on how, in practical terms, action can be taken to improve organisational performance.

A MULTIDISCIPLINARY APPROACH

Whatever the approach, the study of organisational behaviour cannot be undertaken entirely in terms of a single discipline. It is necessary to provide a multidisciplinary, behavioural science perspective (*see* Figure 1.2). Although there are areas of overlap among the various social sciences, their sub-divisions and related disciplines such as economics and political science, the study of behaviour can be viewed in terms of three main disciplines – **psychology, sociology** and **anthropology**. All three disciplines have made an important contribution to the field of organisational behaviour.

- **Psychologists** are concerned, broadly speaking, with the study of human behaviour, with traits of the individual and membership of small social groups. The main focus of attention is on the individual as a whole person, or what can be termed the 'personality system', including, for example, perception, attitudes and motives.

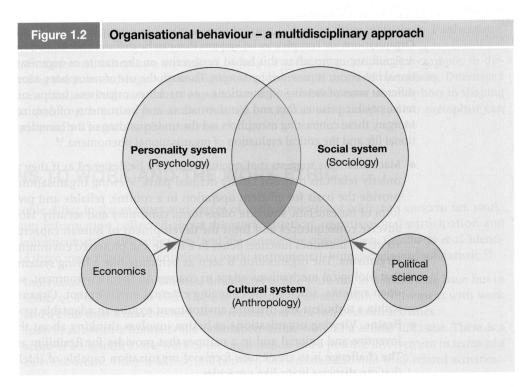

Figure 1.2	Organisational behaviour – a multidisciplinary approach

Personality system
(Psychology)

Social system
(Sociology)

Economics

Political science

Cultural system
(Anthropology)

- Individuals with a solidaristic orientation define the work situation in terms of group activities. There is an ego involvement with work groups rather than with the organisation itself. Work is more than just a means to an end. Non-work activities are linked to work relationships.

Different work situations Some people may well have a set motivation to work, whatever the nature of the work environment. However, different work situations may also influence the individual's orientation to work. For example, the lack of opportunities for team work and the satisfaction of social expectations may result in an instrumental orientation to work and a primary concern for economic interests such as pay and security. In other situations where there are greater opportunities to satisfy social needs, membership of work groups may be very important and individuals may have a more solidaristic orientation to work.

According to *Herman*, the work ethic has been deeply challenged by two trends – the division of labour and the destruction of continuity in employment. Work has been fractured in task and sub-divided into specialised sub-tasks or branches, creating new kinds of work altogether. The division of labour has generated tens of thousands of discrete functions in the workplace. A more recent trend is the destruction of continuity in employment, with many employees likely to re-enter the job market multiple times. This discourages the development of bonds of loyalty or employees investing themselves in their work with the hope of long-term employment.[17]

Knights and Willmott contend that most management textbooks do not make the connection between managing and everyday life. By drawing on a number of contemporary novels they attempt to 'bring to life' what they see as the reality of managing and organising, and dimensions of human experience at work and elsewhere. They explore, in an interesting way, the changing meaning of work and orientations to it, and how different kinds of work are meaningful to some people and not to others.[18]

International and cultural influences

National culture is also a significant influence on orientations to work. For example, *Reeves* comments on the importance of conversation for effective organisational relationships but how this is resisted in the British work culture.

> *The Protestant version of the work ethic prevails, implying heads-down work, focused agendas, punctuality, efficiency. In French and Spanish offices, it takes the first hour to kiss everyone, the second to discuss local gossip and the third to pop out for a coffee and croissant. In Britain, these activities would count as sexual harassment, time-wasting and absenteeism. Many firms have built cafés or break out areas and then discovered people are too scared to use them for fear of looking work-shy.[19]*

As another example, the author experienced for himself how in parts of Australia work-related activities could often be undertaken comfortably in local coffee houses without concern about 'presenteeism' or being seen as being away from the place of work.

Cartwright comments on the psychological process of culture that has the power and authority not only to determine lifestyle but also to form individual personality traits, behaviours and attitudes.

> *It is the cultural environment that motivates people to do their best and to give of their best, often irrespective of or even in spite of their working or living environment. In this respect we make a clear distinction between social conditions and the cultural environment. In the same way that a first-class system does not guarantee first-class results, good living and working conditions do not, in themselves, guarantee high morale and motivation. People in the best working and living conditions can still have low morale and motivation without the benefit of a supportive culture.[20]*

Work/life balance Popular newspaper articles often suggest that work is still a large component of what gives meaning to people's lives and give examples of lottery or pools winners staying in work and often in their same old job. Other surveys and reports suggest that the workplace is no longer a central feature of social activity. For a majority of people the main reason for work remains the need for money to fulfil the necessities of life. However, much still appears to depend on the extent of an individual's social contacts and activities outside of the work situation.

From a survey conducted among subscribers to *Management Today*, the majority of Britain's managers are engaged in a perpetual juggling act with the work/life balance and in meeting both personal and work commitments. For many of those surveyed, however, work remains a huge source of satisfaction.[21] The work/life balance is discussed more fully in Chapter 3.

MANAGEMENT AS AN INTEGRATING ACTIVITY

Whatever the individual's orientations to work or cultural influences, it is through the process of management that the efforts of members of the organisation are co-ordinated, directed and guided towards the achievement of organisational goals. Management is the cornerstone of organisational effectiveness (*see* Figure 1.3).

Patterns of human behaviour It is the responsibility of management to manage. But organisations can achieve their aims and objectives only through the co-ordinated efforts of their members. This involves the effective management of human resources. However, it is important always to remember that it is people who are being managed and people should be considered in human terms.

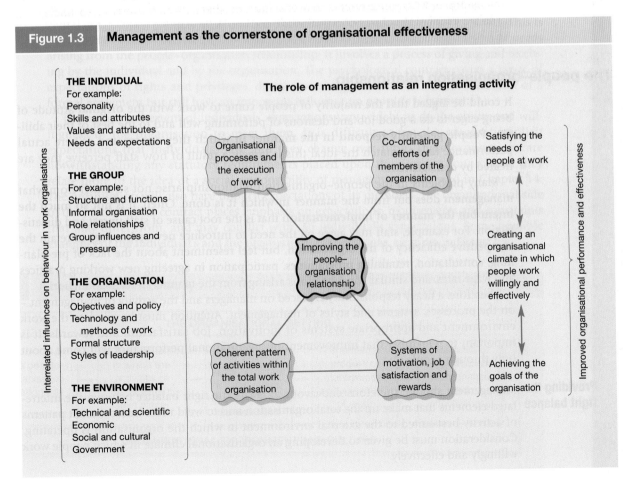

| Figure 1.3 | Management as the cornerstone of organisational effectiveness |

THE INDIVIDUAL
For example:
Personality
Skills and attributes
Values and attributes
Needs and expectations

THE GROUP
For example:
Structure and functions
Informal organisation
Role relationships
Group influences and
 pressure

THE ORGANISATION
For example:
Objectives and policy
Technology and
 methods of work
Formal structure
Styles of leadership

THE ENVIRONMENT
For example:
Technical and scientific
Economic
Social and cultural
Government

Interrelated influences on behaviour in work organisations

The role of management as an integrating activity

Organisational processes and the execution of work

Co-ordinating efforts of members of the organisation

Improving the people–organisation relationship

Coherent pattern of activities within the total work organisation

Systems of motivation, job satisfaction and rewards

Satisfying the needs of people at work

Creating an organisational climate in which people work willingly and effectively

Achieving the goals of the organisation

Improved organisational performance and effectiveness

Figure 1.5	The psychological contract: possible examples of individual and organisational expectations

INDIVIDUALS' EXPECTATIONS OF THE ORGANISATION

- Provide safe and hygienic working conditions.
- Make every reasonable effort to provide job security.
- Attempt to provide challenging and satisfying jobs, and reduce alienating aspects of work.
- Adopt equitable human resource management policies and procedures.
- Respect the role of trade union officials and staff representatives.
- Consult fully with staff and allow genuine participation in decisions which affect them.
- Implement best practice in equal opportunity policies and procedures.
- Reward all staff fairly according to their contribution and performance.
- Provide reasonable opportunities for personal development and career progression.
- Treat members of staff with respect.
- Demonstrate an understanding and considerate attitude towards personal problems of staff.

ORGANISATIONAL EXPECTATIONS OF THE INDIVIDUAL

- Uphold the ideology of the organisation and the corporate image.
- Work diligently in pursuit of organisational objectives.
- Adhere to the rules, policies and procedures of the organisation.
- Respect the reasonable authority of senior members of staff.
- Not take advantage of goodwill shown by management.
- Be responsive to leadership influence.
- Demonstrate loyalty and not betray positions of trust.
- Maintain harmonious relationships with work colleagues.
- Not abuse organisational facilities such as email or Internet access.
- Observe reasonable and acceptable standards of dress and appearance.
- Show respect and consolidation to customers and suppliers.

Implications for organisational strategy

The Chartered Institute of Personnel and Development (CIPD) suggests that the psychological contract may have implications for organisational strategy in a number of areas, for example:

- **process fairness** – people want to know their interests will be taken into account, treated with respect and consulted about change;
- **communications** – an effective two-way dialogue between employer and employee;
- **management style** – adopting a more 'bottom-up' style and drawing on the strategic knowledge of employees;
- **managing expectations** – making clear what new recruits can expect and distinguishing rhetoric from reality;

- **measuring employees' attitudes** – regular monitoring of employee attitudes and acting on the results.[28]

Process of balancing It is unlikely that all expectations of the individual or of the organisation will be met fully. There is a continual process of balancing, and explicit and implicit bargaining. The nature of these expectations is not defined formally and although the individual member and the organisation may not be consciously aware of them, they still affect relationships between them and have an influence on behaviour.

The psychological contract is a useful concept in examining the socialisation of new members of staff to the organisation. According to *Kotter*, early experiences have a major effect on an individual's subsequent career in an organisation and influence job satisfaction, attitude and level of productivity. The extent of the matches between individual and organisational expectations also influences the willingness of people to stay with the organisation and of the organisation to continue to employ them.[29]

Stalker suggests that successful companies are those that have the ability to balance the unwritten needs of their employees with the needs of the company. Such companies use a simple formula of Caring, Communicating, Listening, Knowing and Rewarding:

- **Caring** – demonstrating genuine concern for individuals working in the organisation.
- **Communicating** – really talking about what the company is hoping to achieve.
- **Listening** – hearing not only the words but also what lies behind the words.
- **Knowing** – the individuals who work for you, their families, personal wishes, desires and ambitions.
- **Rewarding** – money is not always necessary; a genuine thank-you or public recognition can raise morale.[30]

The significance of the psychological contract depends on the extent to which it is perceived as fair by both the individual and the organisation, and will be respected by both sides. *Cartwright*, refers to mutuality as the basic principle of the psychological contract:

> A psychological contract is not only measured in monetary value or in the exchange of goods or services, it is in essence the exchange or sharing of beliefs and values, expectations and satisfactions. Mutuality is the basic principle of the psychological contract and consensus or mutual understanding is the basis of mutuality. Ideally therefore self-interest should be balanced with common interest in a 'win–win' arrangement.[31]

The nature of the employer–employee relationship is clearly a central feature of the psychological contract. *Emmott* points out that good people-management practices are the basis for a positive psychological contract and this means managers having to deal with the 'soft stuff'. Properly managed, the psychological contract delivers hard, bottom-line results and improved business performance.

> Managers at all levels can have an influence on employees' perceptions of the psychological contract. It is, however, the **relationship between individual employees and their line manager** that is likely to have most influence in framing and managing employees' expectations.[32]

News that Barclay would be off-shoring 1,800 jobs subjected the bank to intense scrutiny from government, trade unions, shareholders, customers and, of course, employees. The bank recognised it needed to do something to strengthen the 'psychological contract' it had with its employees if it was to redeploy them elsewhere within the organisation.

Management Today [33]

CHANGING NATURE OF THE PSYCHOLOGICAL CONTRACT

The changing nature of organisations has placed increasing emphasis on the importance of effective human resource management, including the importance of the psychological contract within the employment relationship. From a review of research, *McBain* maintains that human resource management plays a key role in ensuring the promotion of business success and managing change. This involves paying attention to the psychological contract and the establishment of expectations and obligations with all groups of employees within the organisation.[34] The Institute of Administrative Management has introduced a new module on 'The Individual and the Organisation in Context' that has come about because of the need to keep abreast of changes affecting the individual at work.

> There is a need for managers to be aware of the new psychological contracts the individual members of their teams are bringing to work. Managers will have to consider alternative management styles to meet this new need and to use new skills to motivate and train their staff. People no longer come to work to be 'told what to do', but are aspiring to be part of the whole, with a real role as stakeholders in the success of 'their' organisation. Wise managers will harness this commitment for the benefit of everyone concerned.[35]

Hiltrop suggests that the increasing pressure for organisations to change has prompted growing disillusionment with the traditional psychological contract based on lifetime employment and steady promotion from within. Companies must develop new ways to increase the loyalty and commitment of employees. This includes attention to reward strategies based on recognition of contribution rather than status or position; systematic training and development including the skills for working in cross-functional teams; and the training of managers in counselling, coaching and leadership skills.[36]

According to CIPD, changes currently affecting the workplace have persuaded people to take the psychological contract seriously. These changes include more employees on part-time and temporary contracts and more jobs outsourced; delayering and 'leanness' of organisations; more demanding customers and improved quality and service standards; the increasing importance of human capital as a source of competitive advantage; and more fluid organisation structures. The effect of these changes is that employees are increasingly recognised as the key business drivers. The psychological contract offers a framework for monitoring employee attitudes and priorities.[37]

Performance management *Stiles et al.* also draw attention to how new competitive conditions and dynamic environments have brought performance management to centre stage as a major element in the changing nature of the psychological contract. From an examination of three large UK organisations, the authors explore 'how performance management processes are being used to support moves from the traditional contract of job security and clear career paths, while attempting to maintain commitment and morale'. The authors conclude that there are two main areas of difficulty in changing the psychological contract so that it focuses on performance management. The presence of mixed messages from employers is undermining the employment relationship and changes are being driven in a top-down manner with a lack of consultation. There is also disenchantment and concern about the accuracy and fairness of performance management processes, with employees expressing scepticism towards managerial attempts to implement change.[38]

A new moral contract

The changing nature of organisations and individuals at work has placed increasing pressures on the awareness and importance of new psychological contracts. *Ghosal et al.* suggest that in a changing social context the law of masters and servants that underlies the old psychological contract is no longer acceptable to many people. Forces of global competition and turbulent

change make employment guarantees unfeasible and also enhance the need for levels of trust and teamwork. The new management philosophy needs to be grounded in a very different moral contract with people. Rather than seeing people as a corporate asset from which value can be appropriated, people are seen as a responsibility and a resource to be added to. The new moral contract also demands much from employees, who need to abandon the stability of lifetime employment and embrace the concept of continuous learning and personal development.[39]

However, *Furnham and Taylor* assert that despite the importance of the psychological contract, as many as two-thirds of employees believe their employers 'patently violated' this understanding.[40]

ORGANISATIONAL PRACTICES

It is convenient, here, to consider two sets of observations on the nature of human behaviour and what may actually happen, in practice, in organisations: the Peter Principle and Parkinson's Law. Although these observations are presented in a satirical manner, they nevertheless make a serious and significant point about the management and functioning of organisations and the actual nature and practice of organisational behaviour.

THE PETER PRINCIPLE

This is concerned with the study of occupational incompetence and the study of hierarchies. The analysis of hundreds of cases of occupational incompetence led to the formulation of the 'Peter Principle', which is:

In a hierarchy every employee tends to rise to their level of incompetence.[41]

Employees competent in their position are promoted and competence in each new position qualifies for promotion to the next highest position until a position of incompetence is reached. The principle is based on perceived incompetence at all levels of every hierarchy – political, legal, educational and industrial – and ways in which employees move upwards through a hierarchy and what happens to them after promotion.

Among the many examples quoted by Peter are those from the teaching occupation. *A* is a competent and conforming college student who becomes a teacher following the textbook, curriculum guide and timetable schedule, and who works well except when there is no rule or precedent available. *A* never breaks a rule or disobeys an order but will not gain promotion because, although competent as a student, *A* has reached a level of incompetence as a classroom teacher.

B, a competent student and inspiring teacher, although not good with paperwork, is promoted to head of the science department because of success as a teacher. The head of science is responsible for ordering all science supplies and keeping extensive records and *B*'s incompetence becomes evident.

C, a competent student, teacher and head of department, is promoted to assistant principal and being intellectually competent is further promoted to principal. *C* is now required to work directly with higher officials. By working so hard at running the school, however, *C* misses important meetings with superiors and has no energy to become involved with community organisations. *C* thus becomes regarded as an incompetent principal.

Means of promotion Peter suggests two main means by which a person can affect their promotion rate, 'Pull' and 'Push'.

- Pull is an employee's relationship – by blood, marriage or acquaintance – with a person above the employee in the hierarchy.

● Push is sometimes manifested by an abnormal interest in study, vocational training and self-improvement.

In small hierarchies, Push may have a marginal effect in accelerating promotion; in larger hierarchies the effect is minimal. Pull is, therefore, likely to be more effective than Push.

Never stand when you can sit; never walk when you can ride; never Push when you can Pull.[42]

PARKINSON'S LAW

A major feature of **Parkinson's Law** is that of the 'rising pyramid', that is, 'Work expands so as to fill the time available for its completion'.[43] General recognition of this is illustrated in the proverb, 'It is the busiest person who has time to spare.' There is little, if any, relationship between the quantity of work to be done and the number of staff doing it. Underlying this general tendency are two almost axiomatic statements:

● An official wants to multiply subordinates, not rivals.
● Officials make work for each other.

Parkinson goes on to give the following example. If a civil servant, A, believes he is over-worked, there are three possible remedies: (i) resignation; (ii) ask to halve the work by having it shared with a colleague, B; or (iii) seek the assistance of two subordinates, C and D. The first two options are unlikely. Resignation would involve loss of pension rights, while sharing work with a colleague on the same level would only bring in a rival for promotion. So A would prefer the appointment of two junior members of staff, C and D. This would increase A's status. There must be at least two subordinates, so that by dividing work between C and D, A will be the only person to understand the work of them both. Furthermore, each subordinate is kept in order by fear of the other's promotion.

When, in turn, C complains of overwork, A, with the agreement of C, will advise the appointment of two assistants, E and F. However, as D's position is much the same and to avoid internal friction, two assistants, G and H, will also be recommended to help D. There are now seven people, A, C, D, E, F, G, H, doing what one person did before, and A's promotion is almost certain.

People making work for each other
With the seven people now employed, the second stage comes into operation. The seven people make so much work for each other that they are all fully occupied and A is actually working harder than ever. For example, an incoming document comes before each of them in turn. E decides it is F's concern; F places a draft reply for C, who makes drastic amendments before consulting with D, who asks G to action it. But then G goes on leave and hands the file to H, who drafts a minute signed by D and returned to C, who revises the first draft and puts the new version before A. What does A do? A could find many excuses for signing C's draft unread. However, being a conscientious person, and although beset with problems created by subordinates both for A and for themselves, A reads through the draft carefully, deletes the fussy paragraphs added by C and H and restores it to the format presented in the first instance by F.

Among other features of organisational practice that Parkinson discusses are principles of personnel selection; the nature of committees; personality screen; high finance – and the 'Law of Triviality', which means in a committee that the time spent on any agenda item will be in inverse proportion to the sum involved; layout of the organisation's administration block; and 'injelitis' – the disease of induced inferiority.

Relevance of observations
Despite the light vein of Parkinson's writing, the relevance of his observations can be gauged from comments in the Introduction by HRH The Duke of Edinburgh.

The most important point about this book for serious students of management and administration is that it illustrates the gulf that exists between the rational/intellectual approach to human organisation and the frequent irrational facts of human nature … The law should be compulsory reading at all business schools and for all management consultants. Management structures solve nothing if they do not take the facts of human nature into proper consideration, and one of the most important facts is that no one really likes having to make decisions. Consequently structures may generate a lot of activity but little or no useful work.[44]

Refresh your understanding

Activity 1C

www.pearsoned.co.uk/mullins

I first read Parkinson's Law when studying for Economics A-level. Many of the laws are just as relevant today as they were then. They include: how to 'manage' a meeting, and how time spent in meetings is inversely proportional to the importance of each issue – his example is a short discussion on a £10 million power plant followed by a lengthy debate over a £350 bicycle shed. Ever been there? … Parkinson's most famous law is that 'work expands to fill the time available – as we all make work for one another'. This is still true today.

Iain Herbertson, Managing Director of Manpower [45]

THE CHANGING NATURE OF WORK ORGANISATION

The effective management of people takes place in the context of the wider environmental setting, including the changing patterns of organisations and attitudes to work. It is frequently documented that a global economy, increased business competitiveness, the move towards more customer-driven markets, and advances in scientific knowledge, especially telecommunications and office automation, have led to a period of constant change and the need for greater organisational flexibility.

The power and influence of private and public organisations, the rapid spread of new technology and the impact of various socio-economic and political factors have attracted increasing attention to the concept of corporate social responsibilities and business ethics. Increasing attention is also being focused on the ethical behaviour that underlies the decisions and actions of managers and staff; many responsible organisations and professional bodies now choose to publish a Code of Ethics.

The changing nature of organisations and individuals at work has placed growing pressure on the awareness and importance of new psychological contracts. Forces of global competition and turbulent change make employment guarantees unfeasible and demand a new management philosophy based on trust and teamwork. People are seen as a responsibility and a resource to be added to. Employees need to abandon the stability of lifetime employment and embrace the concept of continuous learning and personal development.[46]

According to an Economic and Social Research Council (ESRC) publication, in any analysis of the transformation of Britain's employment relations we cannot neglect the changing nature of work. The influence of technological innovation, work restructuring and job redesign are all helping to reshape shopfloor attitudes among managers, unions and workers.[47]

In their discussion of the 21st-century organisation, *Bouchikhi and Kimberly* refer to the customised workplace that represents a radical departure from commonly accepted management principles and techniques. They summarise the main differences between 19th-, 20th- and 21st-century management – *see* Table 1.1.[48]

New approaches to management and organisational behaviour

In discussing new approaches to management practices for the next decade, *Muzyka* suggests that: 'Organisational behavior has moved from an emphasis on the structural aspects of functional and cross-functional organisations to more flexible models, including enhanced consideration of short-term, high performance teams.'

Table 1.1	Contrasting the paradigms		
	19th century	**20th century**	**21st century**
Theory of personhood	Interchangeable muscle and energy	A subordinate with a hierarchy of needs	Autonomous and reflexive individual
Information and knowledge	The province of management alone	Management-dominated and shared on a limited basis	Widely diffused
The purpose of work	Survival	Accumulation of wealth and social status	Part of a strategic life plan
Identification	With the firm and/ or with the working class	With a social group and/or the firm	The disenfranchised self
Conflict	Disruptive and to be avoided	Disruptive but tolerated and can be settled through collective bargaining	A normal part of life
Division of labour	Managers decide, employees execute	Managers decide, employees execute thoughtfully	Employees and managers decide and execute
Power	Concentrated at the top	Limited, functional sharing/empowerment	Diffused and shared

Source: Bouchikhi, H. and Kimberly, J. R., 'The customized workplace', in Chowdhury, S. (ed.) *Management 21C*, Financial Times Prentice Hall (2000), p. 215. Reproduced with permission from Pearson Education Ltd.

New ideas of how to motivate and deploy people have developed. A new contract is evolving that involves the exchange of value. Individuals need to be encouraged and permitted to achieve: to perform to their highest potential, for their benefit and that of the employer. Organisations are encouraging staff to craft more flexible, value-laden, and specific rules governing their relationships.[49]

Cloke and Goldsmith refer to the age of traditional management coming to an end and the decline of hierarchical, bureaucratic, autocratic management. They contend that management is an idea whose time is up and organisations that do not recognise the need to share power and responsibility with all their workers will lose them.[50]

GLOBALISATION AND THE INTERNATIONAL CONTEXT

One major challenge facing managers in the early 21st century arises from what many commentators have identified as an increasingly international or **global** business environment. The following factors are frequently cited as potential explanatory factors underlying this trend:

- improvements in international communication facilities leading to an increased consciousness of differences in workplace attitudes and behaviour in other societies;
- international competitive pressure – for example, the emergence of newly industrialised and/or free-market nations (the Far East region and former communist bloc countries are often viewed as examples of this phenomenon);
- the spread of production methods and other business processes *across* nations and regions;

● international business activity, for example: overseas franchising or licensing agreements; outsourcing of business units to other countries (call centres provide a topical example); direct foreign investment and the activities of multinational corporations which, by definition, operate outside national boundaries.

In broad terms, globalisation refers to organisations integrating, operating and competing in a worldwide economy. The organisations' activities are more independent across the world rather than confined nationally. Globalisation will also impact on the nature of business ethics and international corporate social responsibilities, discussed in Chapter 14. With globalisation, strategy and structure are inextricably linked. As organisations, and especially large business organisations, adopt a more global perspective this will have a significant effect on the broader context of management and organisational behaviour.

For example, *Francesco and Gold* refer to the globalisation of the economy that has created new types of structures such as the 'boundaryless organisation' which breaks the traditional demarcations of authority and task specialisation associated with bureaucracies and other structures. 'Features of a boundaryless organization include a widespread use of project teams, interfunctional teams, networks, and similar structural mechanisms, thus reducing boundaries that typically separate organizational functions and hierarchical levels.' A key management challenge is the socialisation and training of members of the organisation away from the effects of the bureaucratic mentality. Although there is still some form of authority structure, and task and political boundaries, such boundaries are flexible and unlike the rigid horizontal and vertical dimensions of traditional organisations.[51]

However, according to *McLean*, globalisation has ultimately and importantly altered the terms of reference and resulted in a paradigm shift for the way organisations are managed.

> *It has altered the way we work, via, for example, sophisticated systems and procedures aimed at streamlining and 'internationalising' business activities and practices. It has brought companies closer together through opening up new markets and through technological innovations, such as e-business and e-commerce via the World Wide Web. It has increased competition, the speed of innovation, the ubiquity of change and environmental complexity and uncertainty.*[52]

However, although national action may be informed by global thinking, an underlying guideline for multinational organisations is to 'think globally; act locally'. Consider the area of strategic human resource management (HRM). To what extent do differences in, for example, legislation, social security provisions, the philosophy of employment relations, arrangements for collective bargaining, management practices, regulation of the employment contract, the informal organisation, as well as communications over long distances and different time zones, demand attention to HRM at primarily a national level?

The future of globalisation Globalisation has been subjected to much criticism in part at least due to lack of clarity as to its exact meaning and to the confusion about organisations that are very large-scale (such as Walmart in the USA) but have only a small proportion of their operations on a global basis. Globalisation has also become the source of demonstrations and has been blamed for escalating inequalities in the developing world and endangering regional cultures. There appears to be a return to strong nationalistic tendencies in countries such as America and France. *Rugman* refers to the illusion of the global company and maintains that there is no trend towards globalisation but strong evidence of a hardening of triad blocs and regional groups of the EU, USA and Japan.[53] *Saul* dates the rise of globalisation from 1971 but contends that its heyday was in the mid-1990s and it is now in retreat.[54]

According to *Child*, globalisation is a complex phenomenon and the term is used in so many different ways it is in danger of losing any useful purpose. Globalisation is a trend rather than a condition that necessarily already exists, it is not spreading evenly across the

world and many unsubstantiated and sweeping claims have been made. 'The trend towards globalisation is a strong one, but it remains to be seen how far and how fast it will spread. It has powerful opponents.'[55]

Meanwhile, *McLean* maintains that globalisation is here to stay – it won't go away and if anything will get worse. 'We must face the realism that the world, and indeed organisations and the way they are managed, will never be the same. We must encompass these changes and harness the opportunities they present.'[56]

Whatever the extent of globalisation, there are clear implications for organisational behaviour in accommodating international dimensions of management and cultural differences.

Cultural environment

The importance of people in business understanding cultural differences is illustrated by IBM which publishes for members of staff a comprehensive guide to main dimensions of culture and business, and an introduction to concepts, tips, resources and tools for building cross-cultural competencies across national, organisational, team and interpersonal barriers.

Within the global civilisation there are of course many differences in cultural values and attitudes. According to *Dana*, it is essential for people in business to understand cultural differences, but this is not just a matter of noting different ways but rather rooting out the reasons behind these differences. 'Complex cultural environments require fluency not only in words, but more importantly in understanding what is not said – and this takes time, patience and dedication.' For example, the Japanese believe in sharing and the concept of harmony (*wa*) and will often ponder and think through responses as part of a conciliatory relationship and to avoid conflict. Other cultures may find the periodic silence awkward and a sign of mistrust.[57]

In America, there is a strong commitment to the organisation (the corporation) and work and career are taken very seriously (as the author has experienced for himself). Hard work is accepted as part of the American way of life and good timekeeping is important. It is a long-hours culture and generally there is little concern for the work/life balance. There is a strong emphasis on political correctness and little banter or humour at work (again as the author found out to his cost), especially not in formal meetings. Americans do not like self-deprecation and find it strange that the British are prepared to laugh at themselves.[58]

In China there is an enormous bureaucracy and the hierarchy is an important indication of authority. In the business world you may need to deal with several ascending levels of management before reaching the senior manager. There can be an apparent lack of courtesy – and rather than given, respect and trust have to be earned. There is a strong superior–subordinate relationship, with staff often undertaking menial tasks for their boss.[59]

In Japan and Korea, where society tends to be male dominated, in the business world men are more likely to be taking the main role in setting agendas, communications and decision-making.

Cross-cultural approach to management
One rationale for taking a cross-cultural approach to management lies in the potential benefits to be gained in performance terms. *Schneider and Barsoux*, in advocating cultural awareness of one's **own** society, note:

> *Each country has its unique institutional and cultural characteristics, which can provide sources of competitive advantage at one point, only to become liabilities when the environment changes. Managers therefore need to evaluate the extent to which national culture can interfere with their company's efforts to respond to strategic requirements, now and in the future.'*[60]

In addition to practically based benefits in considering our own 'home' culture, there has been a long tradition of looking to other cultures for examples of 'successful' practice which could be transplanted into work organisations in different societies. Different models may be dominant at different times. *Thompson and McHugh* note: 'In the post-war period the

giant US corporations transferred work organisation and managerial techniques across capitalist countries.'[61] However, in subsequent eras Scandinavian autonomous work group arrangements and Japanese management techniques were examined by and, to some extent, implemented in, organisations across the world. Such a search for good practice in other countries is, of course, ongoing and an awareness of how other cultures organise work and manage people is likely to be of continuing benefit in the future.

It is not only businesses that choose to operate in more than one country or import foreign business and management techniques that are affected by cross-cultural concerns. *Tayeb* reported United States Department of Labor statistics indicating that in the period from 1985 to 2000, only 15 per cent of new entrants to the workforce in the USA were white males.[62] This highlights the importance of managing diversity in workforces *within* national boundaries. The management of diversity is discussed in Chapter 4.

Managing people from different cultures Another advantage of adopting a cross-cultural approach to the study of organisational behaviour, and to the management of people more generally, lies in the recognition of variations in workplace attitudes and behaviour between individuals and groups in different cultural contexts. *Brooks* notes: 'Differences in national culture may have a bearing on how organisations deal with each other and also on behaviour within organisations which comprise a mix of nationalities.'[63] If we accept this fundamental point then it follows that key topics within the subject area of organisational behaviour may be influenced by national culture and that we should therefore re-evaluate models and concepts when applying them to other societies.

One leading writer in the field of cross-cultural studies, *Trompenaars*, commenting on his own work, suggests: 'It helped managers to structure their experiences and provided new insights for them and their organisations into the real source of problems faced when managing across cultures or dealing with diversity.'[64] In examining the centrally important topic of motivation, *Francesco and Gold* inform their readers: 'Managers must develop organisational systems that are flexible enough to take into account the meaning of work and the relative value of rewards within the range of cultures where they operate.'[65] A practical example of the impact of cultural diversity in the organisational behaviour area is provided in the recollections of an international human resource manager cited in *Schneider and Barsoux*: 'Indonesians manage their culture by a group process, and everyone is linked together as a team. Distributing money differently among the team did not go over all that well; so we've come to the conclusion that pay for performance is not suitable for Indonesia.'[66] It may be extremely useful therefore to examine academic frameworks and research findings within the field of organisational behaviour to indicate the extent to which they are applicable worldwide or, alternatively, subject to meaningful variation in different cultural contexts.

Critical reflection

To what extent do you support the suggestion that national culture is not only an explanation of human beliefs, values and actions but arguably the most significant feature in the study of organisational behaviour? What examples can you give in support of your view?

IS ORGANISATIONAL BEHAVIOUR CULTURE-BOUND?

While it can be valuable to apply organisational behaviour concepts to diverse cultural settings, it should also be borne in mind that some **universal** theories and models may, in reality, contain important culturally derived assumptions. When examining classical frame-

Evaluation of Hofstede's work

Extremely influential, the seminal work of Hofstede has been criticised from certain quarters. In common with other writers in this area there is a focus on the national rather than the regional level. The variations within certain countries, for example Spain, can be more or less significant. Again in common with other contributors Hofstede's classifications include medium categories which may be difficult to operationalise, accurate though they may be. Some may also find the masculinity/femininity dimension unconvincing and itself stereotypical. Other writers have questioned whether Hofstede's findings remain current. *Holden* summarises this view: 'How many people have ever thought that many of Hofstede's informants of three decades ago are now dead? Do their children and grandchildren really have the same values?'[73]

Ultimately, readers can assess the value of his work in the light of their own experiences and interpretations of the business world. Hofstede in his extensive research has attempted to locate the essence of work-related differences across the world and to relate these to preferred management styles.

CULTURAL DIVERSITY: THE CONTRIBUTION OF TROMPENAARS

Another significant contributor to this area of study is *Fons Trompenaars* whose later work is co-authored with *Charles Hampden-Turner*.[74] Trompenaars's original research spanned 15 years, resulting in a database of 50,000 participants from 50 countries. It was supported by cases and anecdotes from 900 cross-cultural training programmes. A questionnaire method comprised a significant part of the study which involved requiring participants to consider their underlying norms, values and attitudes. The resultant framework identifies seven areas in which cultural differences may affect aspects of organisational behaviour.

- Relationships and rules. Here societies may be more or less **universal**, in which case there is relative rigidity in respect of rule-based behaviour, or **particular**, in which case the importance of relationships may lead to flexibility in the interpretation of situations.
- Societies may be more oriented to the **individual** or **collective**. The collective may take different forms: the corporation in Japan, the family in Italy or the Catholic Church in the Republic of Ireland. There may be implications here for such matters as individual responsibility or payment systems.
- It may also be true that societies differ to the extent it is thought appropriate for members to show emotion in public. **Neutral** societies favour the 'stiff upper lip', while overt displays of feeling are more likely in **emotional** societies. Trompenaars cites a survey in which 80 employees in each of various societies were asked whether they would think it wrong to express upset openly at work. The numbers who thought it wrong were 80 in Japan, 75 in Germany, 71 in the UK, 55 in Hong Kong, 40 in the USA and 29 in Italy.
- In **diffuse** cultures, the whole person would be involved in a business relationship and it would take time to build such relationships. In a **specific** culture, such as the USA, the basic relationship would be limited to the contractual. This distinction clearly has implications for those seeking to develop new international links.
- **Achievement**-based societies value recent success or an overall record of accomplishment. In contrast, in societies relying more on **ascription**, status could be bestowed on you through such factors as age, gender or educational record.
- Trompenaars suggests that societies view **time** in different ways which may in turn influence business activities. The American dream is the French nightmare. Americans generally start from zero and what matters is their present performance and their plan to 'make it' in the future. This is 'nouveau riche' for the French, who prefer the 'ancien pauvre'; they have an enormous sense of the past.

● Finally it is suggested that there are differences with regard to attitudes to the **environment**. In Western societies, individuals are typically masters of their fate. In other parts of the world, however, the world is more powerful than individuals.

Trompenaars' work is based on lengthy academic and field research. It is potentially useful in linking the dimensions of culture to aspects of organisational behaviour which are of direct relevance, particularly to people approaching a new culture for the first time.

The high- and low-context cultures framework

This framework for understanding cultural difference has been formulated by Ed Hall; his work is in part co-authored with Mildred Reed Hall.[75] *Hall* conceptualises culture as comprising a series of 'languages', in particular:

● language of time;
● language of space;
● language of things;
● language of friendships;
● language of agreements.

In this model of culture Hall suggests that these 'languages', which resemble shared attitudes to the issues in question, are communicated in very different ways according to whether a society is classified as 'high' or 'low' context.

The features of 'high' context societies, which incorporate Asian, African and Latin American countries, include:

● a high proportion of information is 'uncoded' and internalised by the individual;
● indirect communication styles … words are less important;
● shared group understandings;
● importance attached to the past and tradition;
● 'diffuse' culture stressing importance of trust and personal relationships in business.

'Low' context societies, which include the USA, Australia, Britain and the Scandinavian countries, exhibit contrasting features including:

● a high proportion of communication is 'coded' and expressed;
● direct communication styles … words are paramount;
● past context is less important;
● 'specific' culture stressing importance of rules and contracts.

Other countries, for example France, Spain, Greece and several Middle Eastern societies, are classified as 'medium' context.

To take one example as an illustration: American managers visiting China may find that a business transaction in that country will take more time than at home. They may find it difficult to interpret the true feelings of their Chinese host and may need to decode non-verbal communication and other signals. They may seek to negotiate a rules-based contract whereas their Chinese counterpart may lay greater stress upon building a mutually beneficial reciprocal relationship. There is scope for potential miscommunication between the two cultures and interesting differences in interpersonal perception. In so far as much of the management literature canon originates from the Anglo-American context, there is again considerable merit in adopting a cross-cultural perspective.

A concept map of some issues for discussion on cross-cultural organisational differences is set out in Figure 1.7.

Figure 1.7 Concept map of cross-cultural organisational differences

CROSS-CULTURAL ORGANISATIONAL DIFFERENCES
(– some issues for discussion)

- FEATURES OF CULTURES
- 4 DIMENSIONAL SPECTRA OF NATIONAL CULTURES

- MASCULINITY v FEMININITY
 – Identified in the dominant values of the society

- UNCERTAINTY AVOIDANCE
 – Low U.A. suggests a culture of risk takers; a concern with performance and doing something to satisfy needs as suggested by Maslow

- POWER DISTANCE
 dimension relates to people as subordinates and their attitude to superiors. Large power distance mean superiors are held in awe as inaccessible (probably autocratic) persons/leaders

- COLLECTIVIST ENVIRONMENT
 local employees need ties with the organisation for mutual loyalty and emotional dependence. Emphasises 'belonging' (prefers non-capitalist order)

IMPLICATIONS FOR TRAINING MANAGERS (INTL)
If destined to work abroad, they need a thorough familiarisation with the new culture using:–
- Specialised cross-cultural training institutes, or
- Host country personnel to advise them

CULTURE is a collective mental programming of the people of/in a particular environment – encompassing a number of people conditioned by the same education and life experiences
GEERT HOFSTEDE 1980

MASCULINITY
concerned with:
– Assertiveness
– Acquisition of wealth and things
– Live to work
– Clear sex roles, leading to male dominance

FEMININITY
concerned with:
– Quality of life
– Working to live
– Fluid sex roles, leading to equality

– Having a powerful superior whom one can blame (and praise) satisfies the need to avoid uncertainty
– Cultures with strong uncertainty avoidance trends don't take risks and don't conform to Maslow's perception of a hierarchy of human needs (Western)

– Leadership complements subordinateship/followership
– Small power distances relate to more participative leadership styles
– What is feasible depends on the cultural conditioning of subordinates
– Western leadership theories advocate participation in decision making by subordinates
– Medium power distances (USA/UK) initiatives taken by the manager
– Larger power distances initiatives taken by the leader

– Capitalism more associated with 'individualist' cultures e.g. US and UK
– Individualism is characterised by a society where people care for themselves and immediate family. Any involvement with the organisation is calculative, we seek autonomy and financial security

FEATURES
- *They are difficult to change. Any change is usually very slow (years) and is resisted.*
- *Cultures may be identified in diverse groupings e.g. family; organisations; nations; etc.*

– USA/UK e.g. place Esteem > Social Needs > Security
– Other value systems Security > Social Needs > Esteem and achievement (belonging)

– Initiatives taken by subordinates

COMPANY POLICY IMPLICATIONS
- *If differences in environmental cultures are obvious, Western management theories are constrained*
- *If culture matters, policies are less effective in different cultural environments*
- *Identical personnel policies may have differing effects in different countries*
- *Also perceptions of absenteeism; financial incentives; performance; quality costs; grievance procedures; labour turnover; etc.*

Source: Training Learning Consultancy Ltd, Bristol, England. Reproduced with permission.

CONVERGENCE OR CULTURE-SPECIFIC ORGANISATIONAL BEHAVIOUR

There is evidence of a narrowing or even increasing elimination of cultural differences in business. *Grint* sees both positive and negative consequences of aspects of globalisation. While noting that 'at last we are approaching an era when what is common between people transcends that which is different; where we can choose our identity rather than have it thrust upon us by accident of birth', the same author goes on to suggest: 'We are heading for global convergence where national, ethnic and local cultures and identities are swamped by the McDonaldization ... and/or Microsoftization of the world.'[76]

There is an undoubted narrowing of cultural differences in work organisations and such narrowing may apply to individual and group behaviour at work. *Thompson and McHugh* note, 'Russia is now experiencing rampant individualism and uncertainty following the collapse of the old solidaristic norms', thus implying convergence of work values.[77] For the most part, however, it is argued here that growing similarity and harmonisation relate more often to production, IT and quality systems which are more likely to converge due to best-practice comparisons and universal computer standards. Human resource management is, contrastingly, less likely to converge due to national institutional frameworks and culturally derived preferences. Recent significantly different responses to the need for greater workplace 'flexibility' in Britain and France illustrate this point. Above all, those aspects of organisational behaviour which focus on individual differences, groups and managing people are the most clearly affected by culture and it is argued strongly here that it is and is likely to remain essential to take a cross-cultural approach to the subject.

THE IMPORTANCE OF PEOPLE AND ORGANISATIONAL BEHAVIOUR

However one looks at the nature or disciplines of organisational behaviour it is important to remember, as *Morgan* reminds us, that 'the reality of organisational life usually comprises numerous different realities.'[78]

Hellriegel, Slocum and Woodman suggest:

> ... *One way to recognise why people behave as they do at work is to view an organisation as an iceberg. What sinks ships isn't always what sailors can see, but what they can't see.*[79]

The overt, formal aspects focus only on the tip of the iceberg (organisation). It is just as important to focus on what you can't see – the covert, behavioural aspects (*see* Figure 1.8).

As part of the *Financial Times Mastering Management* series, *Wood*, in his discussion of the nature of organisational behaviour, suggests that in its concern for the way people behave in an organisational context, organisational behaviour can be regarded as the key to the whole area of management.

> *Is the study of behaviour in organisations important? I think it is vital. What the social sciences, humanities and the arts are to university education, OB is to business school education. The more technical a manager's training, the more important organisational behaviour becomes. It is arguably the one area that can carry the burden of bringing the collective wisdom of human history into the decision-making calculus of developing managers. And this is no trivial task.*[80]

In the foreword to Cloke and Goldsmith's thought-provoking book *The End of Management*, *Bennis* claims that a distinct and dramatic change is taking place in the philosophy underlying organisational behaviour, calling forth a new concept of humanity.

Figure 1.8	The organisational iceberg

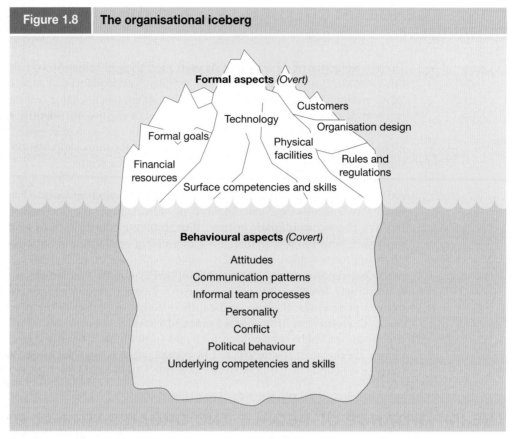

Source: Hellriegel, D., Jackson, S.E. and Slocum, J. W., Jr., *Management*, Eighth Edition, South-Western Publishing (1998), p. 6. Reprinted with the permission of South-Western, a division of Thomson Learning (www.thomsonrights.com / Fax: 800-730-2215).

This new concept is based on expanded knowledge of our complex and shifting needs, replacing an oversimplified, innocent, push-button idea of humanity. This philosophical shift calls for a new concept of organisational depersonalized, mechanistic value system of bureaucracy. With it comes a new concept of power, based on collaboration and reason, replacing a model based on coercion and threat ... The real push for these changes stems from the need not only to humanize organisations, but to use them as crucibles for personal growth and self-realization.[81]

Refresh your understanding

Activity 1E

www.pearsoned.co.uk/mullins

Critical reflection

'The study of organisational behaviour is really an art that pretends it is a science and produces some spurious research findings in a vain attempt to try to prove the point.' How far do you agree with this statement? Do you think the study of organisational behaviour is too subjective ever to be a science?

MANAGEMENT IN THE NEWS

Organisations, strategy and culture

How global strategy can get lost in translation

Stefan Stern

Business leaders pull levers, issue uplifting statements, announce eye-catching initiatives ... and then what? Not even the most hyperactive executive team can be everywhere at all times to monitor what is going on in the furthest reaches of the organisation. The actions of managers and staff on the ground will determine whether quarterly targets are hit and whether grand strategies are realised. Knowing this does not make it any less frustrating when carefully thought-out plans fail to deliver or seem to be simply ignored out in the field. An imposing corporate headquarters may impress visitors, but managers in distant time zones are unlikely to be so easily intimidated. As the old Chinese proverb has it: 'The mountains are high and the emperor is far away.'

Irritation at the persistent failure of managers lower down the corporate ladder to perform partly explains the huge popularity of the hottest management buzzword of the early 21st century – execution. 'There is nothing wrong with our strategy,' senior management teams can console themselves. 'What we lack is the ability to execute it.' It is not only CEOs who suffer while trying to change vast organisations. As Philip Stephens reported in the *Financial Times* last week, Tony Blair, the British prime minister, is exasperated at his lack of success in reforming the UK's public sector. For almost a decade now the prime minister has been giving roughly the same speech, every three to six months, on the need for painful and radical reform. Every time the speech is delivered, front-line public sector managers look up wearily from their desks with a mixture of incomprehension and despair.

When strategy and culture are at odds, it is said, culture always wins. Large organisations are complex. A great deal can get lost in translation between the brilliant PowerPoint presentation to the board and the daily hand-to-hand combat of the marketplace. We use the misleadingly simple term 'globalisation' to describe how the largest corporations do business internationally, as though there is only one way of behaving. But trading across borders inevitably means running up against cultural differences. As the consultant and guru Fons Trompenaars has pointed

out, culture can be a very slippery customer. So, understand the vagaries of the different cultures you are dealing with and all will be well with your global corporate strategy, right? Sadly, no. Indeed, blaming 'cultural differences' has become an easy excuse for business leaders who have failed either to devise the right strategy in the first place or to appreciate how to put it into effect.

Andrew Kakabadse, a professor at Cranfield University's school of management in the UK, argues that cultural issues are often a red herring when international businesses are struggling to perform.

In the best-run companies the culture of individual countries makes no difference to the performance of the business. The company creates its own powerful culture which supersedes the country culture.

Business leaders need to mind the gap between head office and the rest of the company. Communicating strategy effectively will take longer, much longer, than you imagine. And 'communication' should mean a frank and unhurried two-way exchange of views, not simply a lavish print run of gleaming corporate brochures.

'What about the workers?' was the traditional cry of organised labour in the last century. Before launching your next big strategic move, spare a moment to ask: what about the managers?

Source: Stern, S., 'How global strategy can get lost in translation', *Financial Times*, 31 July 2006. Copyright © 2006 The Financial Times Limited, reproduced with permission.

Discussion questions

1 Analyse the content of this article using the framework for organisational behaviour given in Figure 1.1. What can we learn from it about the nature of organisational behaviour?

2 Discuss and explain why Trompenaars and Kakabadse might seem to have different views about the relative importance of cultural factors and communication systems in the achievement of organisational goals. Can these views be reconciled?

SYNOPSIS

● Organisations play a major and continuing role in the lives of us all, especially with the growth of large-scale business organisations. It is important, therefore, to understand how organisations function and the pervasive influences they exercise over the behaviour of people. Organisational behaviour is broadly concerned with the study of the behaviour of people within an organisational setting. It is also necessary to understand interrelationships with other variables that together comprise the total organisation.

● The behaviour of people in work organisations can be viewed in terms of multirelated dimensions concerning the individual, the group, the organisation and the environment. The study of organisational behaviour cannot be understood fully in terms of a single discipline. It is necessary to provide a behavioural science approach drawing on selected aspects of the three main disciplines of psychology, sociology and anthropology together with related disciplines and influences.

● Organisations are complex social systems that can be defined and studied in a number of ways. One approach is to view organisations in terms of contrasting metaphors. Gauging the effectiveness or success of an organisation is not an easy task, however, although one central element is the importance of achieving productivity through the effective management of people. People differ in the manner and extent of their involvement with, and concern for, work. Different situations influence the individual's orientation to work and work ethic. A major concern for people today is balancing work and personal commitments.

● It is through the process of management that efforts of members of the organisation are co-ordinated, directed and guided towards the achievement of organisational objectives. It is essentially an integrating activity and concerned with arrangements for the carrying out of organisational processes and the execution of work. How managers exercise the responsibility for, and duties of, management is important. Attention should be focused on improving the people–organisation relationship.

● One particular aspect of the relationship between the individual and the organisation is the concept of the psychological contract. This is not a formal, written document but implies a series of mutual expectations and satisfaction of needs arising from the people–organisation relationship. There is a continual process of explicit and implicit bargaining. The nature of expectations has an important influence on the employment relationship and behaviour in work organisations. The changing nature of organisations and individuals at work has placed increasing focus on the awareness and importance of a different moral contract with people.

● A major challenge facing managers today arises from an increasingly international or global business environment. This highlights the need for a cross-cultural approach to the study of organisational behaviour and the management of people. In an increasingly global context, managers need to recognise and understand the impact of national culture. However, culture is a multifaceted concept and notoriously difficult to pin down. But it has important repercussions for the effective management of people and the study and understanding of workplace behaviour.

 Refresh your understanding, assess your progress and begin your research with online resources at **www.pearsoned.co.uk/mullins**

REVIEW AND DISCUSSION QUESTIONS

1 Discuss critically what you believe are the main factors to bear in mind with, and particular difficulties presented by, the study of organisational behaviour.

2 Suggest main headings under which interrelated factors that influence behaviour in work organisations can best be identified. Where possible, give practical examples based on your experience.

3 Discuss how organisations may be viewed in terms of contrasting metaphors. Explain how you would apply these metaphors to an understanding of your own organisation.

4 Discuss the role of management as an integrating activity. Give your views on the responsibility of management and the manner in which you believe this responsibility should be exercised.

5 Explain the nature of the people–organisation relationship. Why is it important to distinguish between the 'intent' and the 'implementation' of management decisions and actions?

6 Discuss with supporting examples the changing nature of the psychological contract. List (i) the personal expectations you have of your own organisation and (ii) what you believe to be the expectations of the organisation.

7 Why is it increasingly important for managers to adopt an international approach? Discuss critically the likely longer-term impact of Britain's membership of the European Union.

8 Debate fully the importance of national culture to the study of management and organisational behaviour. Where possible, give your own actual examples.

ASSIGNMENT 1

Five figures are shown below.

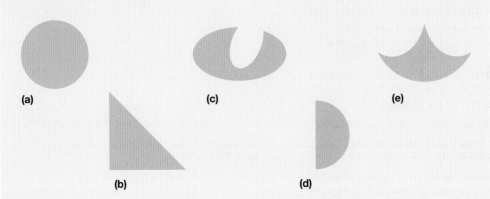

(a)

(c)

(e)

(b)

(d)

You are required to:

1 Select the one that is different from all the others.

2 Discuss in small groups reasons for the individual selections and be prepared to justify your own decision.

3 See whether you can reach a consensus on a single group answer.

Discussion

● To what extent did members of the group understand the thought processes of others?

● If you were persuaded to change your mind, on what basis was this decision made?

● What conclusions do you draw from this exercise?

ASSIGNMENT 2

Provide for classroom discussion short descriptions (suitably disguised if necessary) to illustrate the practical application of:

1 The Peter Principle.

2 Parkinson's Law.

Include in your descriptions what you believe to be the relevance of each of these sets of observations and the effects on other members of staff.

PERSONAL AWARENESS AND SKILLS EXERCISE

Objectives

Completing this exercise should help you to enhance the following skills:

● Obtain a clearer picture of your own and other people's work ethic.

● Explore the importance of work to you and your fixed attitudes about work.

● Recognise the significance of individuals' orientations to work within an organisation.

Exercise

You are required to start by asking yourself this question: is it a good thing to be a worker? Then think carefully about your responses to the following questions.

How do you feel ...

● when you hear the word 'work'?

● as you get ready for work?

● when you know the day is over?

● about the work you've accomplished?

● about someone who chooses not to work?

● about taking time off?

● when you hear the word 'management'?

● about taking control of your career?

Compare your responses with those of your colleagues. What conclusions do you draw about the work ethic?

Source: 'So what's your work ethic?' *Professional Manager*, May 2003, p. 38. Reproduced with permission from the Chartered Management Institute; and Walmsley, C.J., *Your Future Looks Bright*, Preston Beach (2002), p. 98.

Discussion

● What do you see as the character traits of a person with a healthy work ethic?

● To what extent do you agree with the contention that 'we are employed for our skills but valued for our attitude'?

● What effect might different orientations to work have within an organisation and how might they all be accommodated?

CASE STUDY

Virgin Atlantic and Ryanair

This case examines two organisations that have many similarities as well as a number of significant differences. The essential technology and systems behind each organisation may be very similar, but the nature and style of management and its consequent impact on the way people working in these organisations think, feel and behave have created very different organisational cultures. So what are the similarities and what are the differences?

The most obvious similarity is that both Virgin Atlantic and Ryanair operate in the UK passenger air transport industry. Both are relatively recent creations and might be seen as new entrants to the sector: Virgin's air transport business was founded by Richard Branson in 1984[82] and Michael O'Leary took over as Chief Executive at Ryanair, a small Irish airline which had been founded as Guinness Peat Aviation in 1985.[83] Both started life in competition with major national flag-

Michael O'Leary (left) and Richard Branson (right) have both created very successful airline companies, but their organisational cultures and values are very different from each other.

carrier airlines (British Airways and Aer Lingus respectively) and grew to be major challengers to these established companies. As they grew, their scale of operations brought them into competition with a much larger number and range of airlines operating from the UK: Branson's Virgin Atlantic competes with some major US and other intercontinental companies such as American Airlines and United Airlines; O'Leary competes with the likes of Flybe and EasyJet in the short-haul market. Both Branson, who was born in 1950, and O'Leary, who is ten years younger, are individuals with strong and distinctive personalities, who have a relentless appetite for media presence and who make extensive use of themselves in their frequent marketing communications. They engage in advertising stunts, readily appear on the news media in relation to stories about the industry, and their faces and personalities are easily associated with their companies.

Charting different courses

There are, however, some major differences. First, they differ in their choice of markets. Virgin's air transport business originated in the long-haul, mainly transatlantic market which might be highly profitable but is also extremely competitive. As the business grew, offshoots were founded as independent companies; for instance, Virgin Blue in Australia and Virgin Express which has its hub in Brussels and serves European destinations outside the UK and does not compete directly with Ryanair. Ryanair started as a short-haul carrier and has remained so, focusing on European destinations from a small number of airports in the UK and Eire. The two companies' competitive positioning is also very different. Ryanair is well known as 'The Low Cost Airline'; the first thing that hits you in its publicity material is the price[84] and this is very clearly the core of its business strategy. The 'no frills' approach means just that: even the in-flight food is limited to sandwiches and costs extra. Virgin, by contrast, attracts passengers by offering a superior experience and is firmly positioned at

the quality end of the market. Publicity material emphasises style and comfort, and there is a range of in-flight extras which, even at the economy end of the price range, includes in-flight food and drinks and packs of 'amenities' such as flight socks, eye shades and lip balm.

As was noted, both men love publicity stunts and often use humour in their public communications. Branson is usually smiling and in poses which indicate fun and a desire to show close links with his staff and popularity with employees, customers and the public in general. O'Leary is much more likely to be acerbic, critical and uses what might euphemistically be called 'colourful' language in his public statements. He seems to care little about public opinion of him as an individual and has been in trouble with the advertising standards authorities in the UK and Eire on more than one occasion for 'offensive' adverts that have upset people from British Airways (who were accused of being 'Expensive ba****ds' in an *Evening Standard* advert in 1999) and the Catholic Church (the 'Fourth Secret of Fatima' advert of 2000 featured the Pope).[85]

The brand values are also very different. Virgin as a collection of businesses does everything from running trains to manufacturing contraceptives via cosmetics and financial services. All these enterprises are linked by the single powerful central image of the founder and the characteristic red livery. Ryanair does one thing and one thing only, but in doing so sets an almost buccaneering tone, readily taking on authorities such as the European Union over competition policy and the British Airports Authorities over charging practices. Branson has certainly had his conflicts with British Airways, notably over the 'dirty tricks' affair of the early 1990s, but is not likely to challenge governments.

Virgin tries hard to build customer loyalty and gain repeat business through brand-related service values; Ryanair's repeat business (and for some customers the Ryanair experience is one which inspires the thought 'never again') is on price, not loyalty to the brand. These differences have a significant effect on the nature of

employment relations and the psychological contract between the two companies and their employees.

Working for Richard and Michael

Each company's brand image and treatment of customers have a bearing on the nature of organisational relationship with staff, and vice versa. Aspects of organisational behaviour therefore show through in a variety of interconnected ways to create consistent and very different cultures.

At Virgin Atlantic, cabin crew are there to be helpful and welcoming; they are important projectors of the brand image and their job is partly to encourage the all-important customer loyalty which generates continuing profit. The importance of staff as carriers of company values is clearly reflected in the recruitment material and other statements about the nature of work at Virgin Atlantic.

> *Virgin Atlantic brings together all manner of people in all manner of roles, all playing a crucial role in the smooth running of a very complex operation. But whoever you are and wherever you join us, you'll never stop thinking of our customers and what we can do for them. From frontline cabin crew to IT analysts, everyone here plays a role in delivering the Virgin brand. That means using initiative, taking responsibility for your actions and being ready to support those around you at all times. Similarly, you'll play your part in maintaining the friendly, unconventional professionalism that makes Virgin Atlantic such a unique place of work.*[86]

The recruitment process is lengthy and includes a group interview which acts as a filter for further tests before job offers are made. Training programmes for cabin crew and other staff are run from a dedicated training centre, and there is a wide range of benefits for full-time staff including seven free flights a year, private pensions and medical schemes and discounted goods and services across the Virgin group.

At Ryanair, the cabin crew work for a supplier organisation called Crewlink. You can discover whether you qualify to apply for a job by answering a series of 11 online questions. Successful applicants for cabin crew posts are trained at one of Crewlink's centres and are expected to pay an up-front charge of €1,200 for the five-week course (or with a €400 deposit it can be offset against initial year's salary at a total cost of €1,300). Students are not paid to attend the course; successful graduates get a three-year contract with Crewlink to work on Ryanair flights on a shift-work basis. Ryanair crew are not expected to make overnight stops at its destinations. Post-tax starting salary is listed as being £1,100 per month (£13,200 pa); Crewlink suggests that after the initial three years, and subject to satisfactory performance, a permanent job with Ryanair itself might be available at a salary of up to £25,000 pa. Staff must be flexible in terms of their work location across the 15 European centres and Crewlink does not guarantee work if individuals specify a preferred work location.[87]

By comparison with long haul, a short-haul operation involves very tight turnaround times and Ryanair aims for 20 minutes. This creates a very different pace and set of pressures on the workforce compared with those at Virgin, which is likely to have higher staffing levels and to give crew longer rest breaks in the destination locations between flights. The nature of customer relations, by contrast, might be more demanding at Virgin than at Ryanair – staff and customers are together for longer and the brand image must be maintained.

Complaints and horror stories can be found about work at both organisations; however, Ryanair is subject to a more systematic and organised campaign of criticism for its employment practices by trade union organisations. In particular, the International Transport Workers' Federation[88] has run a major campaign on its website since 2004 called 'Ryan-be-fair', the purpose of which is to pressurise the management at Ryanair into accepting the role of trade unions in representing the workforce. It collects comments from disgruntled crew and former workers which give a flavour of the operational stresses and organisational culture.

Both organisations have been successful – Ryanair has turned in significant profits for several years in a sector which is prone to disruption and financial loss and which has seen a number of brands disappear[89] (Buzz, Go and Debonair). Virgin also continues to go from strength to strength commercially.[90] But the cultures and values which get them off the ground could hardly be more different.

Your tasks

1 Using the organisational metaphors of Morgan given on (p. 8) identify two which you think might be applied appropriately to Virgin Atlantic and two to Ryanair. How would you justify your choices?

2 Critically evaluate both organisations in terms of one or more of the descriptions of the psychological contract given in the chapter (for instance that of Stalker, Cartwright or Emmott) (p. 15).

3 Identify the different demands which might be made of managers to achieve organisational effectiveness in each business (you could use Figure 1.3 as a framework). What are the implications for the role and development of managers in each case?

Notes and references

1 A summary of some merits in understanding organisational behaviour theory and the role of management is given in Mullins, L. J. 'The Organisation and the Individual', *Administrator*, vol. 7, no. 4, April 1987, pp. 11–14.

2 See, for example: Luthans, F. *Organisational Behaviour*, Seventh Edition, McGraw-Hill (1995).

3 See, for example: Robbins, S. P. and Judge, T. A. *Organisational Behavior*, Twelfth edition, Pearson Prentice Hall (2007).

4 A similar view is taken by Watson, T. J. *Organising and Managing Work: organisational, managerial and strategic behaviour in theory and practice*, Financial Times Prentice Hall (2002).

5 See, for example: Billsberry, J. (ed.) 'There's Nothing So Practical as a Good Theory: how can theory help managers become more effective?', in *The Effective Manager: perspectives and illustrations*, Sage Publications (1996), pp. 1–27; and Naylor, J. *Management*, Financial Times Pitman Publishing (1999), pp. 18–20.

6 Lee, R. A. 'There Is Nothing so Useful as an Appropriate Theory', in Wilson, D. C. and Rosenfeld, R. H. *Managing Organisations: text, readings and cases*, McGraw-Hill (1990), p. 31.

7 Crainer, S. 'The Rise of Guru Scepticism', *Management Today*, March 1996, pp. 48–52.

8 Patching, K. *Management and Organisation Development*, Macmillan Business (1999), p. 11.

9 Drummond, H. *Introduction to Organisational Behaviour*, Oxford University Press (2000).

10 'Introduction to Module 6, Organisational Behaviour', *Financial Times Mastering Management*, FT Pitman Publishing (1997), p. 216.

11 Wilson, F. M. *Organisational Behaviour and Work: a critical introduction*, Second edition, Oxford University Press (2004), pp. 1–2.

12 McPhee, N. 'Gaining Insight on Business and Organisational Behaviour: the Qualitative Dimension', *International Journal of Market Research*, vol. 44, Winter 2002, pp. 53–72.

13 Yip, G. S. 'Global Strategy in the Twenty-first Century', in Crainer, S. and Dearlove, D. (eds) *Financial Times Handbook of Management*, Second edition, Financial Times Prentice Hall (2001), p. 151.

14 Morgan, G. *Creative Organisation Theory*, Sage Publications (1989), p. 26.

15 Drummond, H. *Introduction to Organisational Behaviour*, Oxford University Press (2000).

16 Goldthorpe, J. H., Lockwood, D., Bechofer, F. and Platt, J. *The Affluent Worker*, Cambridge University Press (1968).

17 Herman, S. W. 'How Work Gains Meaning in Contractual Time: a narrative model for reconstructing the work ethic', *Journal of Business Ethics*, vol. 38, no. 1–2, June 2002, pp. 65–79.

18 Knights, D. and Willmott, H. *Management Lives: power and identity in work organisations*, Sage Publications (1999).

19 Reeves, R. 'Reality Bites', *Management Today*, March 2003, p. 35.

20 Cartwright, J. *Cultural Transformation*, Financial Times Prentice Hall (1999), p. 27.

21 Oliver, J. 'Losing Control', *Management Today*, June 1998, pp. 32–8.

22 See, for example: Argyris, C. *Integrating the Individual and the Organisation*, John Wiley & Sons (1964).

23 Egan, G. 'The Shadow Side', *Management Today*, September 1993, pp. 33–8.

24 Bassett, G. 'The Case Against Job Satisfaction', *Business Horizons*, vol. 37, no. 3, May–June 1994, pp. 62, 63.

25 See, for example: Robinson, G. 'Improving Performance Through People', *The British Journal of Administrative Management*, September/October 1999, pp. 4–5.

26 Chowdhury, S. *Management 21C*, Financial Times Prentice Hall (2000), p. 119.

27 See, for example: Schein, E. H. *Organisational Psychology*, Third Edition, Prentice Hall (1988).

28 CIPD, *Managing the Psychological Contract*, Chartered Institute of Personnel and Development, December 2004.

29 Kotter, J. P. 'The Psychological Contract: managing the joining-up process', *California Management Review*, vol. 15, no. 3, 1973, pp. 91–9.

30 Stalker, K. 'The Individual, the Organisation and the Psychological Contract', *The Institute of Administrative Management*, July/August 2000, pp. 28, 34.

31 Cartwright, J. *Cultural Transformation*, Financial Times Prentice Hall (1999), p. 39.

32 Emmott, M. 'The Psychological Contract: Managers Do Make a Difference', *Manager, The British Journal of Administrative Management*, September/October 2001, p. 15.

33 M.C.A. Awards, *Management Today*, April 2005, p. xix.

34 McBain, R. 'The Role of Human Resource Management and the Psychological Contract', *Manager Update*, vol. 8, no. 4, Summer 1997, pp. 22–31.

35 Stalker, K. 'The Individual and the Organisation', *Student Adviser*, no. 51, The Institute of Administrative Management, Spring 2003.

36 Hiltrop, J. M. 'Managing the Changing Psychological Contract', *Employee Relations*, vol. 18, no. 1, 1996, pp. 36–49.

37 CIPD, *Managing the Psychological Contract*, Chartered Institute of Personnel and Development, December 2004.

38 Stiles, P., Gratton, L., Truss, C., Hope-Hailey, V. and McGovern, P. 'Performance Management and the Psychological Contract', *Human Resource Management Journal*, vol. 7, no. 1, 1997, pp. 57–66.

39 Ghoshal, S., Bartlett, C. A. and Moran, P. 'Value Creation: the new millennium management manifesto', in Chowdhury, S. *Management 21C*, Financial Times Prentice Hall (2000), pp. 121–40.

40 Furnham, A. and Taylor, J. *The Dark Side of Behaviour at Work*, Palgrave Macmillan (2004).

41 Peter, L. J. and Hull, R. *The Peter Principle*, Pan Books (1970), p. 22.

42 Ibid., p. 56.

43 Parkinson, C. N. *Parkinson's Law*, Penguin Modern Classics (2002), p. 14.

44 HRH The Duke of Edinburgh, 'Introduction' to Parkinson, C. N. *Parkinson's Law*, Penguin Modern Classics (2002), pp. 9–10.

45 Herbertson, I. 'Books', *Management Today*, May 2000, p. 4.

46 Ghoshal, S., Bartlett, C. A. and Moran, P. 'Value Creation: the new millennium management manifesto', in Chowdhury, S. *Management 21C*, Financial Times Prentice Hall (2000), pp. 121–40.

THE CLASSICAL APPROACH

The classical writers thought of the organisation in terms of its purpose and formal structure. They placed emphasis on the planning of work, the technical requirements of the organisation, principles of management, and the assumption of rational and logical behaviour. The analysis of organisation in this manner is associated with work carried out initially in the early part of the last century, by such writers as *Taylor, Fayol, Urwick, Mooney and Reiley*, and *Brech*. Such writers were laying the foundation for a comprehensive theory of management.

A clear understanding of the purpose of an organisation is seen as essential to understanding how the organisation works and how its methods of working can be improved. Identification of general objectives would lead to the clarification of purposes and responsibilities at all levels of the organisation and to the most effective structure. Attention is given to the division of work, the clear definition of duties and responsibilities, and maintaining specialisation and co-ordination. Emphasis is on a hierarchy of management and formal organisational relationships.

Sets of principles The classical writers (also variously known as the formal or scientific management writers – although scientific management is really only a part of the classical approach) were concerned with improving the organisation structure as a means of increasing efficiency. They emphasised the importance of principles for the design of a logical structure of organisation. Their writings were in a normative style and they saw these principles as a set of 'rules' offering general solutions to common problems of organisation and management.

Most classical writers had their own set of principles but among the most publicised are those of *Fayol* and *Urwick*. Fayol recognised there was no limit to the principles of management but in his writing advocated 14.[9] Urwick originally specified eight principles, but these were revised to ten in his later writing.[10] (*See* Chapters 11 and 15.)

Mooney and Reiley set out a number of common principles which relate to all types of organisations. They place particular attention on:

- **the principle of co-ordination** – the need for people to act together with unity of action, the exercise of authority and the need for discipline;
- **the scalar principle** – the hierarchy of organisation, the grading of duties and the process of delegation; and
- **the functional principle** – specialisation and the distinction between different kinds of duties.[11]

Brech attempts to provide a practical approach to organisation structure based on tried general principles as opposed to the concentration on specific cases or complex generalisations of little value to the practising manager. He sets out the various functions in the organisation and the definition of formal organisational relationships.[12] Although clearly a strong supporter of the formal approach in some of his views such as, for example, on the principle of span of control, Brech is less definite than other classical writers and recognises a degree of flexibility according to the particular situation.

Brech does place great emphasis, however, on the need for written definition of responsibilities and the value of job descriptions as an aid to effective organisation and delegation. This work builds on the ideas of earlier writers, such as Urwick, and therefore provides a comprehensive view of the classical approach to organisation and management.

Evaluation of the classical approach

The classical writers have been criticised generally for not taking sufficient account of personality factors and for creating an organisation structure in which people can exercise only limited control over their work environment. The idea of sets of principles to guide managerial action has also been subject to much criticism. For example, *Simon* writes:

Organisational design is not unlike architectural design. It involves creating large, complex systems having multiple goals. It is illusory to suppose that good designs can be created by using the so-called principles of classical organisation theory.[13]

Research studies have also expressed doubt about the effectiveness of these principles when applied in practice.[14] However, the classical approach prompted the start of a more scientific view of management and attempted to provide some common principles applicable to all organisations. These principles are still of relevance in that they offer a useful starting point in attempting to analyse the effectiveness of the design of organisation structure. The application of these principles must take full account of:

- the particular situational variables of each individual organisation; and
- the psychological and social factors relating to members of the organisation.

Major sub-groupings Two major 'sub-groupings' of the classical approach are:

1 scientific management, and
2 bureaucracy.

SCIENTIFIC MANAGEMENT

Many of the classical writers were concerned with the improvement of management as a means of increasing productivity. At this time emphasis was on the problem of obtaining increased productivity from individual workers through the technical structuring of the work organisation and the provision of monetary incentives as the motivator for higher levels of output. A major contributor to this approach was *F. W. Taylor* (1856–1917), the 'father' of scientific management.[15] Taylor believed that in the same way that there is a best machine for each job, so there is a best working method by which people should undertake their jobs. He considered that all work processes could be analysed into discrete tasks and that by scientific method it was possible to find the 'one best way' to perform each task. Each job was broken down into component parts, each part timed and the parts rearranged into the most efficient method of working.

Principles to guide management

Taylor was a believer in the rational–economic needs concept of motivation. He believed that if management acted on his ideas, work would become more satisfying and profitable for all concerned. Workers would be motivated by obtaining the highest possible wages through working in the most efficient and productive way. Taylor was concerned with finding more efficient methods and procedures for co-ordination and control of work. He set out a number of principles to guide management. These principles are usually summarised as:

- the development of a true science for each person's work;
- the scientific selection, training and development of the workers;
- co-operation with the workers to ensure work is carried out in the prescribed way;
- the division of work and responsibility between management and the workers.

In his famous studies at the Bethlehem Steel Corporation, Taylor, who was appointed as a management consultant, applied his ideas on scientific management to the handling of pig iron. A group of 75 men were loading an average of $12\frac{1}{2}$ tons per man per day. Taylor selected a Dutch labourer, called Schmidt, whom he reported to be a 'high-priced' man with a reputation for placing a high value on money, and a man of limited mental ability. By following detailed instructions on when to pick up the pig iron and walk, and when to sit and rest, and with no back talk, Schmidt increased his output to $47\frac{1}{2}$ tons per day. He main-

- higher wages from increased output;
- the removal of physical strain from doing work the wrong way;
- development of the workers and the opportunity for them to undertake tasks they were capable of doing; and
- elimination of the 'boss' and the duty of management to help workers.

Drucker also suggests that Taylor's idea of functional foremen can be related to what is now known as matrix organisation (matrix organisation is discussed in Chapter 15). Support for Drucker's views appears to come from *Locke* who asserts that much of the criticism of Taylor is based on a misunderstanding of the precepts and that many of his ideas are accepted by present-day managers.[21]

Impetus to management thinking Whatever the opinions on scientific management, Taylor and his disciples have left to modern management the legacy of such practices as work study, organisation and methods, payment by results, management by exception and production control. The development of mass assembly line work, invented by Henry Ford in 1913 ('Fordism') and which dominated production methods in Western economies, can be seen to have many common links with the ideas of scientific management.[22]

The principles of Taylor's scientific approach to management appear still to have relevance today. We can see examples of Taylorism alive and well, and management practices based on the philosophy of his ideas. As an example, Figure 2.2 shows a 'Hanger Insertion Programme' for a large American department store. Large hotel organisations often make use of standard recipes and performance standard manuals and it is common for housekeeping staff to have a prescribed layout for each room, with training based on detailed procedures and the one best way. Staff may be expected to clean a given number of rooms per shift with financial incentives for additional rooms.

Whatever else Taylor did, at least he gave a major impetus to the development of management thinking and the later development of organisational behaviour. For example, *Crainer and Dearlove* suggest that although Taylor's theories are now largely outdated, they still had a profound impact throughout the world and his mark can be seen on much of the subsequent management literature.[23] And *Stern* goes a stage further:

> The 'scientific management' of Frederick Taylor … shaped the first coherent school of thought with application to the industrialised world. He was our first professional guru and Taylorism – with its twin goals of productivity and efficiency – still influences management thinking 100 years on.[24]

It is difficult to argue against the general line of Taylor's principles but they are subject to misuse. What is important is the context and manner in which such principles are put into effect. There is arguably one best way *technically* to perform a job, particularly, for example, with factory assembly line production. However, account needs to be taken of human behaviour. People tend to have their preferred way of working and the need for variety and more interesting or challenging tasks. Provided work is carried out safely and to a satisfactory standard and completed on time, to what extent should management *insist* on the 'one best way'?

It seems that Taylor did not so much ignore (as is often suggested) but was more unaware of the complexity of human behaviour in organisations and the importance of the individual's feelings and sentiments, group working, managerial behaviour and the work environment. However, we now have greater knowledge about social effects within the work organisation and about the value of money, incentives, motivation, and job satisfaction and performance.

Figure 2.2	Hanger Insertion Programme: an example of scientific management

KEY IDEAS

Hanger Insertion

- The new programme involving the process of hanging merchandise on hangers efficiently and effectively.

The purposes of this new programme:

- To assist the stores in better customer service – by having the merchandise ready to go on the floor, saving space in the stockroom, and creating customer goodwill.
- To increase the units per hour produced.
- To perform the job duties as efficiently and effectively as possible.

TECHNIQUES

- Keep the necessary items needed in your range. All supplies should be within arm's reach. For example, place the trash bin next to you, have your hanger supply near you. You should not need to take any steps.
- For ANY prepack, Unpack merchandise in the prepack or unpack enough of the prepack in the amount to be placed on the trolley, tearing the plastic off of the entire group.
 Lay the merchandise out on the unpack table, and if applies, unfold each piece, removing tissue, etc.
 Insert the hangers and hang the *entire group* of merchandise at once.
- When removing hangers from the merchandise, have the merchandise in a group on the unpack table; remove these hangers working from the front to the back.
- When inserting hangers, as a group, insert working from the back to the front of the group on the unpack table. Hang pieces as a group.
- If merchandise is bulky, Leave merchandise folded, **remove all of the plastic at once**,
 insert hangers for merchandise unpacked, hang all pieces on the
 trolley, then remove at the same time all excess plastic, clips, etc.
- When possible, it is more efficient to remove all the plastic at once after the merchandise is hung.
- When hanging pants, skirts, etc., slip the hanger over both sides of the piece of merchandise and push metal clips down at the same time. This will alleviate additional steps.
- When pants are in plastic and hangers have to be removed, hang them first, take pants off hangers, lay on table, throw away plastic, insert hangers.
- When having to button pants, skirts, etc., take the top of the button through the hole first. This makes the process flow easier and more efficient.
- Put your supply of hangers in the cover of a tote and place on the table next to you.

BUREAUCRACY

A form of structure to be found in many large-scale organisations is bureaucracy. Its importance in the development of organisation theory means that it is often regarded as a sub-division under the classical heading and studied as a separate approach to management and the organisation of work. The ideas and principles of the classical writers were derived mainly from practical experience. Writers on bureaucracy, however, tend to take a more theoretical view.

Weber, a German sociologist, showed particular concern for what he called 'bureaucratic structures', although his work in this area came almost as a side issue to his main study on power and authority.[25] He suggested that 'the decisive reason for the advance of bureaucratic

Organisational solutions

As organisations face increasing global competitiveness and complex demands of the information and technological age, the need arises for alternative forms of corporate structure and systems. For example, *Ridderstrale* points out that in the past century the hallmark of a large company was hierarchy, which rests on principles at odds with the new strategic requirements. 'Bureaucracies allowed people with knowledge to control ignorant workers. Now, new structures are needed as knowledge spreads.' Ridderstrale suggests four specific ways in which high-performing organisations have responded to increasingly complex knowledge systems by developing organisational solutions which depart from the traditional bureaucratic model:

● more decentralised and flatter structures in order that quick decisions can be taken near to where the critical knowledge resides. Flatter structures can be achieved by increasing the span of control and reducing layers from the top or removing layers of middle management;

● the use of more than a single structure in order that knowledge may be assembled across the boundaries of a traditional organisation chart. If people have less permanent places in the hierarchy they are more readily able to move across functional and geographical borders;

● converting companies into learning organisations and giving every employee the same level of familiarity with personnel and capabilities. Successful companies develop a detailed inventory of core competencies. In order to fully exploit current knowledge, managers need to know what the company knows;

● the broader sharing of expertise and knowledge, which may be located in the periphery where little formal authority resides. Managers need to share principles to ensure co-ordination, encourage 'lowest common denominators' and the development of 'tribal' qualities through shared ownership and rewards, common norms, culture and values.[33]

Public sector organisations In the case of public sector organisations, in particular, there is a demand for uniformity of treatment, regularity of procedures and accountability for their operations. This leads to adherence to specified rules and procedures which limit the degree of discretion exercised by management, and to the keeping of detailed records. For example, *Green* argues that, although bureaucracies are becoming less and less the first-choice format for organisational shape, there is still a place for bureaucracy in parts of most organisations and especially public sector organisations such as local authorities and universities. The use and implementation of tried and tested rules and procedures help to ensure essential values and ethics, and that necessary functions are run on a consistent and fair basis.[34]

New forms of information technology such as electronic transactions processed from home or public access terminals are likely to change processes of government service delivery, administrative workloads and the nature of bureaucracy.[35]

Relevance today By their very nature, bureaucracies are likely to attract criticism. For example, there appears to be a particular dilemma for management in personal service industries. The underlying characteristics of bureaucracy would seem to restrict personal service delivery which requires a flexible approach, responsiveness to individual requirements and the need for initiative and inventiveness.[36] Much of this criticism is valid, but much also appears unfair comment.

Stewart suggests that more organisations today contain mainly or a considerable number of professionals. Such organisations will still have bureaucratic features although there is more reliance on professional discretion and self-regulation than on control through rules and regulations.[37] However, despite new forms of organisation which have emerged, many writers suggest that bureaucracy is still as relevant today as a major form of organisation structure.[38]

STRUCTURALISM

Sometimes Weber's work is associated with the ideas of writers such as Karl Marx under the sub-heading of the **structuralism** approach, which is a synthesis of the classical (or formal) school and the human relations (or informal) school.[39] A major line of thought was that the earlier approaches were incomplete and lacked adequate theoretical assumptions and background. The structuralism approach provides a radical perspective of social and organisational behaviour.[40] Greater attention should be given to the relationship between the formal and informal aspects of the organisation, and the study of conflict between the needs of the individual and the organisation, and between workers and management. (*See also* the discussion on conflict in Chapter 19.) Structuralism is sometimes associated as part of a broader human relations approach, which is discussed below.

Refresh your understanding

Activity 2B
www.pearsoned.co.uk/ mullins

THE HUMAN RELATIONS APPROACH

The main emphasis of the classical writers was on structure and the formal organisation, but during the 1920s, the years of the Great Depression, greater attention began to be paid to the social factors at work and to the behaviour of employees within an organisation – that is, to **human relations**.

The Hawthorne experiments

The turning point in the development of the human relations movement ('behavioural' and 'informal' are alternative headings sometimes given to this approach) came with the famous Hawthorne experiments at the Western Electric Company in America (1924–32) and the subsequent publication of the research findings.[41] Among the people who wrote about the Hawthorne experiments was *Elton Mayo* (1880–1949), who is often quoted as having been a leader of the researchers. However, there appears to be some doubt as to the extent to which Mayo was actually involved in conducting the experiments and his exact contribution to the human relations movement.[42]

There were four main phases to the Hawthorne experiments:

● the illumination experiments;
● the relay assembly test room;
● the interviewing programme;
● the bank wiring observation room.

The illumination experiments The original investigation was conducted on the lines of the classical approach and was concerned, in typical scientific management style, with the effects of the intensity of lighting upon the workers' productivity. The workers were divided into two groups, an experimental group and a control group. The results of these tests were inconclusive as production in the

experimental group varied with no apparent relationship to the level of lighting, but actually increased when conditions were made much worse. Production also increased in the control group although the lighting remained unchanged. The level of production was influenced, clearly, by factors other than changes in physical conditions of work. This prompted a series of other experiments investigating factors of worker productivity.

The relay assembly test room

In the relay assembly test room the work was boring and repetitive. It involved assembling telephone relays by putting together a number of small parts. Six women workers were transferred from their normal departments to a separate area. The researchers selected two assemblers who were friends with each other. They then chose three other assemblers and a layout operator. The experiment was divided into 13 periods during which the workers were subjected to a series of planned and controlled changes to their conditions of work, such as hours of work, rest pauses and provision of refreshments. The general environmental conditions of the test room were similar to those of the normal assembly line.

During the experiment the observer adopted a friendly manner, consulting the workers, listening to their complaints and keeping them informed of the experiment. Following all but one of the changes (when operators complained too many breaks made them lose their work rhythm) there was a continuous increase in the level of production. The researchers formed the conclusion that the extra attention given to the workers, and the apparent interest in them shown by management, were the main reasons for the higher productivity.

The interviewing programme

Another significant phase of the experiments was the interviewing programme. The lighting experiment and the relay assembly test room drew attention to the form of supervision as a contributory factor to the workers' level of production. In an attempt to find out more about the workers' feelings towards their supervisors and their general conditions of work, a large interviewing programme was introduced. More than 20,000 interviews were conducted before the work was ended because of the depression.

Initially, the interviewers approached their task with a set of prepared questions, relating mainly to how the workers felt about their jobs. However, this method produced only limited information. The workers regarded a number of the questions as irrelevant; also they wanted to talk about issues other than just supervision and immediate working conditions. As a result, the style of interviewing was changed to become more non-directive and open-ended. There was no set list of questions and the workers were free to talk about any aspect of their work.

The interviewers set out to be friendly and sympathetic. They adopted an impartial, non-judgemental approach and concentrated on listening.

Using this approach, the interviewers found out far more about the workers' true feelings and attitudes. They gained information not just about supervision and working conditions but also about the company itself, management, work group relations and matters outside of work such as family life and views on society in general. Many workers appeared to welcome the opportunity to have someone to talk to about their feelings and problems and to be able to 'let off steam' in a friendly atmosphere. The interviewing programme was significant in giving an impetus to present-day personnel management and the use of counselling interviews, and highlighting the need for management to listen to workers' feelings and problems.

Being a good listener is arguably even more important for managers in today's work organisations and it is a skill which needs to be encouraged and developed.[43]

The bank wiring observation room

Another experiment involved the observation of a group of 14 men working in the bank wiring room. It was noted that the men formed their own informal organisation with sub-groups or cliques, and with natural leaders emerging with the consent of the members. The group developed its own pattern of informal social relations and 'norms' of what constituted 'proper' behaviour. Despite a financial incentive scheme where the workers could receive more money the more work produced, the group decided on a level of output well below the level they were capable of producing.

Group pressures on individual workers were stronger than financial incentives offered by management. The group believed that if they increased their output, management would raise the standard level of piece rates. The importance of group 'norms' and informal social relations are discussed in Chapter 8.

EVALUATION OF THE HUMAN RELATIONS APPROACH

The human relations approach has been subjected to severe criticism. The Hawthorne experiments have been criticised, for example, on methodology and on failure of the investigators to take sufficient account of environmental factors – although much of this criticism is with the value of hindsight. The human relations writers have been criticised generally for the adoption of a management perspective, their 'unitary frame of reference' and their over-simplified theories.[44]

Other criticisms of the human relations approach are that it is insufficiently scientific and that it takes too narrow a view. It ignores the role of the organisation itself in how society operates.

Sex power differential There are a number of interpretations of the results of the Hawthorne experiments, including the possible implications of the 'sex power differential' between the two groups. In the relay assembly room where output increased, the group was all female, while in the bank wiring room where output was restricted, the group was all male. The workers in the relay assembly test room were all young unmarried women. All except one were living at home with traditional families of immigrant background. In the work environment of the factory the women had been subjected to frequent contact with male supervisors and therefore 'the sex power hierarchies in the home and in the factory were congruent'. It is suggested, therefore, that it was only to be expected that the women agreed readily to participate with management in the relay assembly test room experiment.[45]

Importance of the Hawthorne experiments

Whatever the interpretation of the results of the Hawthorne experiments, they did generate new ideas concerning the importance of work groups and leadership, communications, output restrictions, motivation and job design. They placed emphasis on the importance of personnel management and gave impetus to the work of the human relations writers. The Hawthorne experiments undoubtedly marked a significant step forward in providing further insight into human behaviour at work and the development of management thinking. The Hawthorne experiments are regarded as one of the most important of all social science investigations and are recognised as probably the single most important foundation of the human relations approach to management and the development of organisational behaviour.

In a review of humane approaches to management, *Crainer* asserts: 'The Hawthorne Studies were important because they showed that views of how managers behaved were a vital aspect of motivation and improved performance. Also, the research revealed the importance of informal work groups.'[46]

Humanisation of the work organisation Whereas supporters of the classical approach sought to increase production by rationalisation of the work organisation, the human relations movement has led to ideas on increasing production by humanising the work organisation. The classical approach adopted more of a managerial perspective, while the human relations approach strove for a greater understanding of people's psychological and social needs at work as well as improving the process of management. It is usually regarded as the first major approach to organisation and management to show concern for industrial sociology.

The human relations approach recognised the importance of the informal organisation which will always be present within the formal structure. This informal organisation will influence the motivation of employees who will view the organisation for which they work through the values and attitudes of their colleagues. Their view of the organisation determines their approach to work and the extent of their motivation to work well or otherwise.

Human relations writers demonstrated that people go to work to satisfy a complexity of needs and not simply for monetary reward. They emphasised the importance of the wider social needs of individuals and gave recognition to the work organisation as a social organisation and the importance of the group, and group values and norms, in influencing individual behaviour at work. It has been commented that the classical school was concerned about 'organisations without people' and the human relations school about 'people without organisations'.

NEO-HUMAN RELATIONS

Certainly there were shortcomings in the human relations approach and assumptions which evolved from such studies as the Hawthorne experiments were not necessarily supported by empirical evidence.

For example, the contention that a satisfied worker is a productive worker was not always found to be valid. However, the results of the Hawthorne experiments and the subsequent attention given to the social organisation and to theories of individual motivation gave rise to the work of those writers in the 1950s and 1960s who adopted a more psychological orientation. New ideas on management theory arose and a major focus of concern was the personal adjustment of the individual within the work organisation and the effects of group relationships and leadership styles. This group of writers is often (and more correctly) categorised separately under the heading of 'neo-human relations'. The works of these writers are examined in more detail in subsequent chapters but are summarised broadly here.

The work of Maslow A major impetus for the neo-human relations approach was the work of *Maslow* who, in 1943, put forward a theoretical framework of individual personality development and motivation based on a hierarchy of human needs.[47] The hierarchy ranges through five levels from, at the lowest level, physiological needs, through safety needs, love needs, esteem needs, to the need for self-actualisation at the highest level. Individuals advance up the hierarchy only as each lower-level need is satisfied. Although Maslow did not originally intend this need hierarchy to be applied necessarily to the work situation it has, nevertheless, had a significant impact on management approaches to motivation and the design of work organisation to meet individual needs. The work of Maslow provides a link with the earlier human relations approach.

Some leading contributors Among the best-known contributors to the neo-human relations approach are *Herzberg* and *McGregor*. Herzberg isolated two different sets of factors affecting motivation and satisfaction at work. One set of factors comprises those which, if absent, cause dissatisfaction. These are 'hygiene' or 'maintenance' factors which are concerned basically with job environment. However, to motivate workers to give of their best, proper attention must be given to a different set of factors, the 'motivators' or 'growth' factors. These are concerned with job content.[48]

McGregor argued that the style of management adopted is a function of the manager's attitudes towards human nature and behaviour at work. He put forward two suppositions called Theory X and Theory Y which are based on popular assumptions about work and people.[49]

Other major contributors to the neo-human relations approach are *Likert*, whose work includes research into different systems of management;[50] *McClelland*, with ideas on achievement motivation;[51] and *Argyris*, who considered the effects of the formal organisa-

tion on the individual and psychological growth in the process of self-actualisation.[52] Argyris' major contributions include his work on organisational learning and on effective leadership.[53]

The neo-human relations approach has generated a prolific amount of writing and research not only from original propounders but also from others seeking to establish the validity, or otherwise, of their ideas. This has led to continuing attention being given to such matters as organisation structuring, group dynamics, job satisfaction, communication and participation, leadership styles and motivation. It has also led to greater attention to the importance of interpersonal interactions, the causes of conflict and recognition of 'industrial relations' problems.

THE SYSTEMS APPROACH

More recently, attention has been focused on the analysis of organisations as 'systems' with a number of interrelated sub-systems.

The classical approach emphasised the technical requirements of the organisation and its needs – 'organisations without people'; the human relations approaches emphasised the psychological and social aspects, and the consideration of human needs – 'people without organisations'.

The **systems approach** attempts to reconcile these two earlier approaches and the work of the formal and the informal writers. Attention is focused on the total work organisation and the interrelationships of structure and behaviour, and the range of variables within the organisation. This approach can be contrasted with a view of the organisation as separate parts. The systems approach encourages managers to view the organisation both as a whole and as part of a larger environment. The idea is that any part of an organisation's activities affects all other parts.

Systems theory Systems theory is not new and has been used in the natural and physical sciences for a number of years. One of the founders of this approach was the biologist *Ludwig von Bertalanffy* who used the term 'systems theory' in an article published in 1951 and who is generally credited with having developed the outline of General Systems Theory.[54] The systems approach to organisation has arisen, at least in part, therefore, from the work of biologists, and *Miller and Rice* have likened the commercial and industrial organisation to the biological organism.[55]

Using a General Systems Theory (GST) approach, *Boulding* classified nine levels of systems of increasing complexity according to the state of development and knowledge about each level.[56] Organisations are complex social systems and are more open to change than lower-level simple dynamic or cybernetic systems. Boulding felt there were large gaps in both theoretical and empirical knowledge of the human level and the social organisations level of systems, although some progress has now been made with recent theories of organisational behaviour.

The business organisation as an open system

The business organisation is an open system. There is continual interaction with the broader external environment of which it is part. The systems approach views the organisation within its total environment and emphasises the importance of multiple channels of interaction. Criticisms of earlier approaches to organisation are based in part on the attempt to study the activities and problems of the organisation solely in terms of the internal environment. The view of the organisation as an open system is examined in Chapter 3.

The systems approach views the organisation as a whole and involves the study of the organisation in terms of the relationship between technical and social variables within the system. Changes in one part, technical or social, will affect other parts and thus the whole system.

Longwall coal-mining study
The idea of socio-technical systems arose from the work of *Trist* and others, of the Tavistock Institute of Human Relations, in their study of the effects of changing technology in the coal-mining industry in the 1940s.[57] The increasing use of mechanisation and the introduction of coal-cutters and mechanical conveyors enabled coal to be extracted on a 'longwall' method.

Shift working was introduced, with each shift specialising in one stage of the operation – preparation, cutting or loading. However, the new method meant a change in the previous system of working where a small, self-selecting group of miners worked together, as an independent team, on one part of the coalface – the 'single place' or 'shortwall' method.

Technological change had brought about changes in the social groupings of the miners. It disrupted the integration of small groups and the psychological and sociological properties of the old method of working. There was a lack of co-operation between different shifts and within each shift, an increase in absenteeism, scapegoating and signs of greater social stress. The 'longwall' method was socially disruptive and did not prove as economically efficient as it could have been with the new technology.

The researchers saw the need for a socio-technical approach in which an appropriate social system could be developed in keeping with the new technical system. The result was the 'composite longwall' method with more responsibility to the team as a whole and shifts carrying out composite tasks, the reintroduction of multiskilled roles and a reduction in specialisation. The composite method was psychologically and socially more rewarding and economically more efficient than the 'longwall' method.

The socio-technical system

The concept of the organisation as a 'socio-technical' system directs attention to the transformation or conversion process itself, to the series of activities through which the organisation attempts to achieve its objectives. The **socio-technical system** is concerned with the interactions between the psychological and social factors and the needs and demands of the human part of the organisation, and its structural and technological requirements.

Recognition of the socio-technical approach is of particular importance today. People must be considered as at least an equal priority along with investment in technology. For example, *Lane et al.* point out that major technological change has brought about dramatic changes in worker behaviour and requirements. It is people who unlock the benefits and opportunities of information communication technology.[58]

Technology determinism
The concept of socio-technical systems provides a link between the systems approach and a sub-division, sometimes adopted – the **technology approach**. Writers under the technology heading attempt to restrict generalisations about organisations and management and emphasise the effects of varying technologies on organisation structure, work groups and individual performance and job satisfaction. This is in contrast with the socio-technical approach which did not regard technology, *per se*, as a determinant of behaviour.

Under the heading of the technology approach could be included the work of such writers as *Walker and Guest* (effects of the assembly-line production method on employee behaviour);[59] *Sayles* (relationship between technology and the nature of work groups);[60] and *Blauner* (problems of 'alienation' in relation to different work technologies).[61] Technological determinism is discussed more fully in Chapter 17.

THE CONTINGENCY APPROACH

The classical approach suggested one best form of structure and placed emphasis on general sets of principles while the human relations approach gave little attention at all to structure. In contrast the **contingency approach** showed renewed concern with the importance of structure as a significant influence on organisational performance. The contingency approach, which can be seen as an extension of the systems approach, highlights possible means of differentiating among alternative forms of organisation structures and systems of management. There is no one optimum state. For example, the structure of the organisation and its 'success' are dependent, that is contingent upon, the nature of tasks with which it is designed to deal and the nature of environmental influences.

The most appropriate structure and system of management is therefore dependent upon the contingencies of the situation for each particular organisation. The contingency approach implies that organisation theory should not seek to suggest one best way to structure or manage organisations but should provide insights into the situational and contextual factors which influence management decisions. Contingency models of organisation and management are discussed in Chapter 16.

Refresh your understanding

Activity 2C

www.pearsoned.co.uk/mullins

OTHER APPROACHES TO THE STUDY OF ORGANISATIONS

The four-fold framework of classical, human relations, systems and contingency approaches provides a helpful, although rather simplistic, categorisation. The study of organisations, their structure and management is a broad field of inquiry. Depending on the views and preferences of the writer, other possible main approaches include decision-making and social action.

THE DECISION-MAKING APPROACH

The systems approach involves the isolation of those functions most directly concerned with the achievement of objectives and the identification of main decision areas or sub-systems. Viewing the organisation as a system emphasises the need for good information and channels of communication in order to assist effective decision-making in the organisation. Recognition of the need for decision-making and the attainment of goals draws attention to a sub-division of the systems approach, or a separate category, that of the **decision-making (or decision theory) approach**. Here the focus of attention is on managerial decision-making and how organisations process and use information in making decisions.

Successful management lies in responding to internal and external change. This involves the clarification of objectives, the specification of problems and the search for and implementation of solutions. The organisation is seen as an information processing network with numerous decision points. An understanding of how decisions are made helps in understanding behaviour in the organisation. Decision-making writers seek to explain the mechanisms by which conflict is resolved and choices are made.

Some leading writers Leading writers of the decision-making approach include *Barnard*, *Simon* and *Cyert and March*. The scope of the decision-making approach, however, is wide and it is possible to identify contributions from engineers, mathematicians and operational research specialists in addition to the work of economists, psychologists and writers on management and organisation.

Barnard stressed the need for co-operative action in organisations. He believed that people's ability to communicate, and their commitment and contribution to the achievement of a common purpose, were necessary for the existence of a co-operative system.[62]

These ideas were developed further by Simon. He sees management as meaning decision-making and his concern is with how decisions are made and how decision-making can be improved. Simon is critical of the implication of man as completely rational and proposes a model of 'administrative man' who, unlike 'economic man', 'satisfices' rather than maximises. Administrative decision-making is the achievement of satisfactory rather than optimal results in solving problems.[63]

Economic models of decision-making, based on the assumption of rational behaviour in choosing from known alternatives in order to maximise objectives, can be contrasted with behavioural models based not so much on maximisation of objectives as on short-term expediency where a choice is made to avoid conflict and to stay within limiting constraints. Managers are more concerned with avoiding uncertainties than with the prediction of uncertainties.[64]

SOCIAL ACTION

Social action represents a contribution from sociologists to the study of organisations. Social action writers attempt to view the organisation from the standpoint of individual members (actors) who will each have their own goals and interpretation of their work situation in terms of the satisfaction sought and the meaning that work has for them. The goals of the individual, and the means selected and actions taken to achieve these goals, are affected by the individual's perception of the situation. Social action looks to the individual's own definition of the situation as a basis for explaining behaviour. Conflict of interests is seen as normal behaviour and part of organisational life. According to *Silverman*:

> The action approach … does not, in itself, provide a theory of organisations. It is instead best understood as a method of analysing social relations within organisations.[65]

Criticisms of earlier approaches A main thrust of social action is the criticism of earlier approaches to organisation and management and of what is claimed to be their failure to provide a satisfactory basis for the explanation or prediction of individual behaviour. For example, criticism is directed at approaches which focused on the goals and needs of the organisation rather than on considerations of the effectiveness of an organisation in meeting the needs of its individual members.

The human relations approaches have been criticised because of their focus on generalised theories of good management, group psychology and the suggestion of needs common to all individuals at work. The technology approach has been criticised for attributing feelings of alienation to the nature of technology and the status of work groups rather than an analysis which focused on concern for the individual's expectations of, and reactions to, work. The systems approach has been criticised for failure to examine the orientation of individual members to the organisation, the different expectations people have of their work or ways in which the environment influences expectations of work.

Unitary or pluralistic view Important contributors to a social action approach include *Goldthorpe* (industrial attitudes and behaviour patterns of manual workers)[66] and *Fox*. In a research paper written for the Royal Commission on Trade Unions and Employers' Associations (the Donovan Report), Fox suggests two major ways of perceiving an industrial organisation – a 'unitary' approach and a 'pluralistic' approach.[67]

With the unitary approach the organisation is viewed as a team with a common source of loyalty, one focus of effort and one accepted leader. The pluralistic approach views the organisation as made up of competing sub-groups with their own loyalties, goals and leaders. These competing sub-groups are almost certain to come into conflict.

The unitary and pluralistic perspectives of the organisation are discussed in Chapter 13.

Action theory

A theory of human behaviour from an 'action approach' is presented by *Bowey*.[68] She suggests that action theory, systems theory and contingency theory are not necessarily incompatible approaches to the understanding of behaviour in organisations. It would be possible to take the best parts of the different approaches and combine them into a theory that would model empirical behaviour and also facilitate the analysis of large numbers of people in organisations. Bowey goes on to present such a theory as a particular form of an action theory approach. According to Bowey, action theory is not capable of dealing with the analysis of the behaviour of a large number of people in organisations. Her theory is based, therefore, on three essential principles of action theory, augmented by four additional concepts taken from systems theory.

The three essential principles of action theory can be summarised as below:

● Sociology is concerned not just with behaviour but with 'meaningful action'.
● Particular meanings persist through reaffirmation in actions.
● Actions can also lead to changes in meanings.

Additional concepts Bowey suggests that these three principles apply mainly to explanations of individual, or small-scale, behaviour. She gives four additional concepts, taken from systems theory, on which analysis of large-scale behaviour can be based. These concepts are redefined in accordance with an action approach.

● **Role**. This is needed for the analysis of behaviour in organisations. It explains the similar action of different people in similar situations within the organisation and the expectations held by other people.
● **Relationships**. This is needed to explain the patterns of interaction among people and the behaviours displayed towards one another.
● **Structure**. The relationships among members of an organisation give rise to patterns of action which can be identified as a 'transitory social structure'. The social factors, and non-social factors such as payment systems, methods of production and physical layout, together form the behavioural structure.
● **Process**. Human behaviour can be analysed in terms of processes, defined as 'continuous interdependent sequences of actions'. The concept of process is necessary to account for the manner in which organisations exhibit changes in structure.

The three principles of action theory, together with the four additional concepts from systems theory, provide an action approach to the analysis of behaviour in organisations. Bowey goes on to illustrate her theory with case studies of five different types of organisations, all in the restaurant industry.

A NUMBER OF APPROACHES

We can now see that within the broad four-fold classification of classical, human relations, systems and contingency approaches it is possible to identify a number of other approaches or at least sub-divisions of approaches, although there is no consensus on the categorisation of these different approaches or on the identification of the various contributors to one particular approach. So far we have established a possible nine-fold classification: classical (including scientific management); bureaucracy; human relations; neo-human relations; systems; technology; contingency; decision-making; and social action – and if structuralism is included, we have a ten-fold classification. This classification could be extended still further. For example, another more recent categorisation sometimes identified as a separate approach is management science – with emphasis on quantitative analysis, mathematical models, operational research and computer technology (*see* Figure 2.3.).

| Figure 2.3 | An outline of developments of approaches to organisation and management |

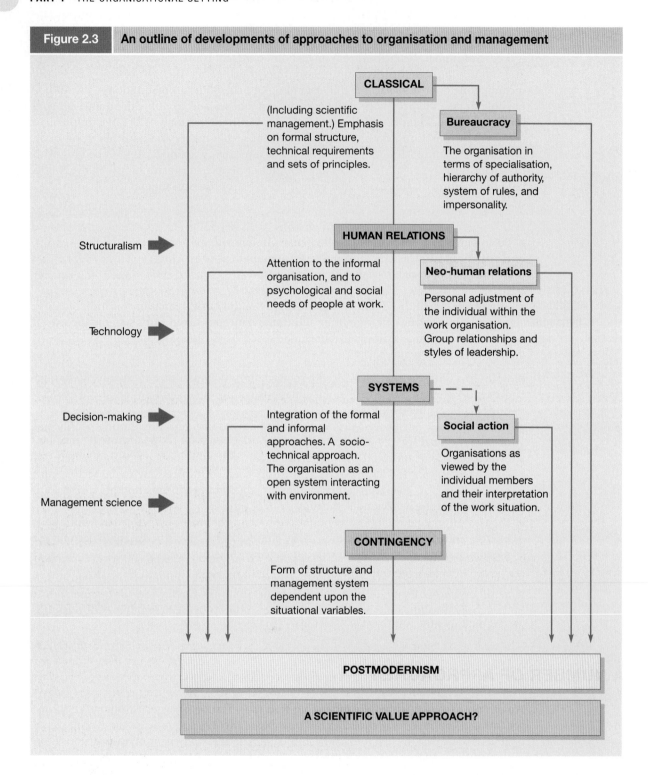

POSTMODERNISM

The work of contemporary writers discussed above together with the achievements of practitioners such as Alfred P. Sloan Jr (1875–1966, Chief Executive and Honorary Chairman of General Motors) gave rise to the so-called 'modern organisation'.[69] With the development of the information and technological age a more recent view of organisations and management is the idea of **postmodernism**. In the 1990s, writers such as *Clegg* described the postmodern organisation in terms of the influence of technological determinism, structural flexibility, premised on niches, multiskilled jobs marked by a lack of demarcation, and more complex employment relationships including subcontracting and networking.[70]

Postmodernism rejects a rational systems approach to our understanding of organisations and management and to accepted explanations of society and behaviour. Highly flexible, free-flowing and fluid structures with the ability to change quickly to meet present demands form the basis of the new organisation. For example, *Watson* suggests that the modernism inherent in the systems-control approach to understanding work organisations and their management is naïve and unrealistic. The possibility of any kind of complete and coherent body of management knowledge has increasingly been brought into question.

> *To enable us to move toward a more realistic or pragmatically reasonable way of 'framing' work organisation and its management, a shift has first to be made in our deeper assumptions about the social world. These are the modernist assumptions which inevitably underpin the whole edifice of work organisation and management thinking.*[71]

By contrast, postmodernism places greater attention on the use of language and attempts to portray a particular set of assumptions or versions of the 'truth'. Watson defines postmodernism as:

> *A way of looking at the world that rejects attempts to build systematic (or 'foundationalist') explanations of history and society and which, instead, concentrates on the ways in which human beings 'invent' their words, especially through the use of language or 'discourse'.*[72]

The idea of postmodernism is, however, not easy to explain fully in clear and simple terms. It is arguably more of a generalised sociological concept rather than a specific approach to organisation and management. There is even some discussion of two connotations, and theories or philosophies of the concept depending on whether the term is hyphenated or not.[73] Perhaps understandably therefore the concept of postmodernism appears to have little interest or appeal to the practical manager.

Indeed Watson, for example, questions the value of labelling more flexible forms of bureaucratic structure and culture as postmodern or post-bureaucratic and differentiating these from the modernist bureaucratic organisation.

> *There is no postmodern or post-bureaucratic organisational form available to us that is essentially different from the modernist bureaucratic organisation. We are indeed seeing different mixes of direct and indirect management control attempts as the world changes. But the world was always changing. Probably from the very beginning of industrialisation there has been a mixing of direct and indirect controls with emphases in one direction and then the other being made at different times.*[74]

Nevertheless, postmodernist organisation can arguably be seen as a healthy challenge to more traditional approaches. It puts forward alternative interpretations of rationality, credibility and ambiguity; a thoughtful critical perspective on disorders in work organisations; and reminds us of the complexities in our understanding of management and organisational behaviour.

Refresh your understanding
Activity 2D
www.pearsoned.co.uk/ mullins

Critical reflection

????

The majority of research and writing on approaches to organisations and management has originated from North America or Western Europe. Do you think that this results in a culturally biased view of organisational behaviour and managerial theory that has only limited value or relevance anywhere else?

RELEVANCE TO MANAGEMENT AND ORGANISATIONAL BEHAVIOUR

The different possible categorisations are not necessarily a bad thing; they illustrate the discursive and complex nature of management. The possible sub-divisions and cross-groupings help illustrate the many factors relevant to the study and practice of management and organisational behaviour. Discussion on the various categorisations of approaches and the identification of individual writers within a particular approach can provide a useful insight into the subject.

Positive advantages Whatever form of categorisation is adopted, the division of writers on organisation and management into various approaches offers a number of positive advantages.

- It is helpful to students in the arrangement and study of their material.
- It provides a setting in which to view the field of management and to consider the contribution of individual writers.
- It traces the major lines of argument developed by writers seeking to advise practising managers on how they might improve performance.
- It provides a framework in which the principles enunciated can be set and against which comparisons with management practice can be made.
- It helps in organisational analysis and in the identification of problem areas. For example, is the problem one of structure, of human relations or of the socio-technical process?
- It enables the manager to take from the different approaches those ideas which best suit the particular requirements of the job. For example, in dealing with a problem of structure, the ideas of the classical writers or of contingency theory might be adopted. When there is a problem relating to personnel management, ideas from the human relations movement might be of most value. If the problem is one of environmental influence, insights from the systems approach might prove most helpful. For problems of a more quantitative nature, ideas from the decision-making approach or from management science might be applicable.

Caveats to be noted There are, however, a number of important caveats that should be noted.

- The various approaches represent a progression of ideas, each building on from the other and adding to it. Together they provide a pattern of complementary studies into the development of management thinking. The different approaches are not in competition with each other and no one approach should be viewed as if it were the only approach, replacing or superseding earlier contributions. Many ideas of earlier writers are still of relevance today and of continuing importance in modern management practice.
- Any categorisation of individual writers into specific approaches is inevitably somewhat arbitrary and not all writers can be neatly arranged in this manner. This is only to be expected. Such writers are expounding their current thoughts and ideas in keeping with the continual development of management theory and changes in management practice. The comment made about some management writers that they are saying different things at different times might therefore be taken more as a compliment than as a criticism.

- Even when there is agreement on the nature of the contribution from different writers, the actual division into varying approaches may take a number of forms. In other words, while there might be acceptance of the need for a framework, there is no agreement on its shape. Different authors have adopted different formats in which to set out the developments in management thinking.

- Some of the literature categorises management thinkers into divisions called 'schools'. The use of this term suggests a clarity of distinction between each division and a uniformity of beliefs within each division. This is perhaps an exaggeration. The distinction between these so-called schools is not clear-cut and there is not necessarily a consistency of thinking among the various contributors in each division. The term 'approaches' to management is more indicative of the obscure lines between the different categorisations and, paradoxically, it is the suggestion of vagueness that, arguably, makes it a more appropriate term to use.

> *Of course, management theories have often been the subject of discourse and criticism. Some critics see organisational philosophies as management fads that will be replaced by new ones as other theories are proposed. That may well be the case, but it is good for management theories to evolve, because organisations change, the environment changes, and as a result, management practices and techniques change ... Theories provide us with valuable insights into how we can be more understanding, influential and ultimately more successful in managing organisations and the turbulent dynamic environments in which they operate ... you of course, may have a different view!*
>
> Jacqueline McLean [75]

The importance of cultural contexts A major criticism of the attempt to define generalised models of management theory is the assumption of national culture. *Schneider and Barsoux* draw attention to how the different theories on how to organise all reflect societal concerns of the times as well as the cultural backgrounds of the individuals. Different approaches reflect different cultural assumptions regarding, for example, human nature and the importance of task and relationships.[76]

Cheng, Sculli and Chan also question the universality of theories of management and organisational behaviour on the ground that they have not adequately addressed the factor of culture. 'Traditionally, the greatest aspiration of researchers is to discover objective, universalistic principles of behaviour. The tacit assumption behind this is that these principles may be discovered without reference to cultural contexts.' They conclude that while there may be some universality to organisation structures, for example the need for some form of hierarchy whatever its shape may be, different national cultures frequently give those structures different meanings.[77]

In a review of management theory and practice, *Heller* contrasts British and American thinking with methods employed by the Japanese. In the 1960s, Western managements showed a total lack of curiosity about competition from Japan; British and European managers were still obsessed by the American example. The Japanese built hugely on what they had borrowed from the USA. However, the Japanese also practised and perfected what management scientists often only preached.[78]

Although British management has failed to live up to Japanese standards, professional standards among managers in Britain have improved greatly over the past 25 years. The potential of a widening Europe and the Japanese penchant for locating more plants in Britain provide the best reasons for brighter prospects.

TOWARDS A SCIENTIFIC VALUE APPROACH?

It might be that the study of organisations, their structure and management is moving towards a more scientific approach. Management science can assist managers in the analysis of complex problems that are subject to quantitative constraints and in the optimisation of decisions in such problems. It may also assist in the establishment of broad theory. However, many operational problems in organisations relate to the nature of human behaviour and the people–organisation relationship and do not lend themselves to the application of a scientific answer.

There are no definitive or final solutions to the problems of organisations. The nature of work organisations and the environment in which they operate is becoming increasingly complex and subject to continual change. However, at least we do understand more about the dynamics of management and organisational behaviour as a basis for the analysis of human behaviour in organisations.[79]

> *It is obvious from even a cursory glance at the history of management science that science and technology are considered to be key instruments in solving workplace problems and in controlling workplaces … While Taylorist scientific management may have its academic critics, management science is thriving. It is itself a large business, providing employment for management consultants whose sole concern is solving workplace problems of other corporations.*[80]

Balance between philosophy and science *Miner*, however, suggests that although the degree of commitment to the scientific value system is increasing, as yet there is insufficient research to move the field entirely into science, completely divorced from philosophy. At present management theory is clearly in the 'schools' phase. As discussed earlier, it is possible to argue over the use of the term 'schools'. However, whatever terminology is used, and whatever the state of our knowledge, the message from Miner is clear:

> *… schools of management thought are very much a reality, and the management student who approaches the field without at least a minimal understanding of them does so at some risk.*[81]

According to *Crainer*, management is active, not theoretical. But management is nothing without ideas.

> *Ideas drive management as surely as the immediate problems which land on managers' desks or which arrive via their email. Decisions have to be based on ideas, as well as instinct. Without ideas managers flit desperately from crisis to crisis. They cannot know where they are going, why they are doing something or what they will achieve, without the fuel of ideas.*[82]

BENEFITS TO THE MANAGER

Whatever the balance between philosophy and science, a knowledge and understanding of management theory will help with the complexities of management in modern work organisations. No single approach to organisation and management provides all the answers. It is the comparative study of different approaches which will yield benefits to the manager.[83] There is, of course, no shortage of new ideas on organisational behaviour and management thinking. To what extent, however, do these ideas lead to improved organisational performance?

There is undoubtedly much scepticism about and criticism of management gurus. For example, according to *Crainer*, the past 30 years have seen management thinking in a state of perpetual flux with a relentless quest for new ideas, such as corporate strategy, the nature of management, culture, quality and the Japanese approach, excellence, the re-emergence of leadership, competitive advantage, empowerment and re-engineering. Crainer believes that

this is what managers have been doing all along, but how well they have succeeded is a matter of debate.

> *Comparing past and present is diverting, but provides more questions than answers. What can be said is that managers remain open to new lights and that over 30 years the sheer profusion of ideas has, at times, been overwhelming.*[84]

Crainer also suggests that as one idea after another fails to translate into sustainable practice, there is a growing disillusionment with the pedlars of managerial wisdom.

> *Yet, the desire for instant solutions which tackle all managerial problems in one fell swoop remains strong … Amid the hard sell, the quick fixes and organisational placebos, it is true to say that there is little that's original. But, without gurus, managers would lose a rich source of inspiration, information and controversy.*[85]

Reporting on a 12-year study of the knowledge and use of management concepts in technical organisations, *Flores and Utley* suggest that a look back at the theories and principles that have been taught in the past could give an indication of the success of any new approach and help prepare today's and tomorrow's managers for the future.[86] And *Stern* has this to say: 'Management thinkers still have a lot to tell us. You don't have to believe everything they say, but they may at least offer stimulation; they might provoke senior managers into abandoning complacency and trying to see problems in a new light.'[87]

There are, then, many aspects to management. There are no simple solutions, no one best way to manage. However, the study of organisations, their structure and management is still important for the manager and remains an indispensable part of the job.

Refresh your understanding

Activity 2E
www.pearsoned.co.uk/
mullins

Critical reflection

'The study of different approaches to organisation and management and the development of organisation theory have no practical relevance for today's managers. It is really no more than a luxury for students and the time could be spent better on more important topic areas.' How would you present a *counter* argument?

MANAGEMENT IN THE NEWS

Professionalism

Problem with performance-managing professionals

Stefan Stern

When our first child was born last spring my wife and I indulged in that traditional speculation practised by many new parents: what did we want the dear girl to do when she grew up? I instinctively veered towards the conventional. She would, of course, pursue a brilliant professional career, achieving both financial security and social respectability. Put your trust in the professions and you can't go wrong. My wife, less hidebound than me, was more pragmatic. 'I bet she'd make a good plumber,' she said.

At only 15 months, my daughter has not yet had to face the literacy and numeracy tests that will soon be coming her way from the UK's Department for Education and Skills. It is therefore too early to say in which direction she is headed – although, to judge b' her talent for destroying order, plumbing may indee turn out to be a favoured option.

But Mrs Stern's scepticism does provoke other, immediate, questions. What does it mean to be a professional today? Where in the past the term c'

Management in the news – continued

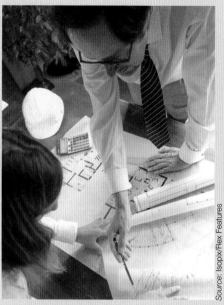

Source: Isopix/Rex Features

What does it mean to be a professional today? Is dedication to your craft being undermined by a need to meet targets?

the established disciplines of law, medicine or accountancy, today it is used to cover even the work done by security guards or contract cleaners. Has the term 'professional' been devalued through its ever wider application to ever more lines of work? And what implications does the changing nature of professionalism have for both employees and their organisations?

One afternoon last month, Demos, a London-based think-tank, gathered together a selection of professional people and gave them a few minutes to describe the challenges they face doing their jobs. The effect was remarkable. In both the public and private sectors, managers are agonising over similar things. In this age of targets, monitoring and performance management, professional people wonder how much autonomy they retain over how they go about their work. They had originally entered a profession because of a vocation, a calling. Now they found themselves pursuing a managerial agenda set remotely by bosses who often did not share the same personal commitment to the work in hand that they do. Richard Sennett, a professor at the London School of Economics, argues that many professional people have lost 'a sense of craft' in their day-to-day work. They are being judged according to their position in an

occupational hierarchy, not by what it is about their work that makes them feel professional: their dedication to their craft.

> We have misunderstood the idea of quality, and how people go about doing quality work. A most important motivator for professionals is being able to do a good job for its own sake, rather than just to meet a target. If you take that ability away from professionals they get very unhappy.

Sometimes, of course, professionalism is in the eye of the beholder. This is a theme film-maker Quentin Tarantino explores in his 1992 crime thriller, *Reservoir Dogs*. Professionalism is the film's leitmotif. A gang of armed robbers collapses into violent disarray as a planned heist goes wrong. Appalled by a colleague's displays of brutality, Mr White, played by Harvey Keitel, issues the most damning criticism imaginable.

> What you're supposed to do is act like a f****** professional. A psychopath is not a professional. You can't work with a psychopath, 'cause ya don't know what those sick assholes are gonna do next.

I have wandered a little from this column's usual territory. How unprofessional. But that is my point. The early 21st-century version of professionalism risks becoming narrow and impoverished. The under-40s coming up through the ranks seek variety and autonomy in their work, as well as financial rewards. They do not want their true professionalism to be performance-managed out of them.

Source: Stern, S., 'Problem with performance-managing professionals', *Financial Times*, 10 July 2006. Copyright © 2006 The Financial Times Limited, reproduced with permission.

Discussion questions

1 Identify and review the arguments for and against regarding management as another 'profession' like law and medicine. How far can the different approaches be seen as a conflict between the 'classical' and 'human relations' approaches to organisation and management?

2 The author of the article suggests that people today seek autonomy and variety in their work. Using the concept of social action theory, discuss the implications for the way in which organisations might be structured and managed in the 21st century.

SYNOPSIS

● The study of organisational behaviour has to proceed on a broad front. A central part of this study is the development of management thinking and what might be termed management theory. In order to help identify main trends in the development of organisational behaviour, it is usual to categorise the work of leading writers into various 'approaches' based on their views of organisations, their structure and management. This provides a simplistic framework on which to direct study and focus attention.

● The classical writers placed emphasis on purpose and structure, on the technical requirements of the organisation, and on the assumption of rational and logical behaviour. The human relations writers emphasised the importance of the informal organisation and the psychological and social needs of people at work. The systems approach focuses attention on the interactions between technical and social variables. The organisation is seen in continual interaction with the external environment. Contingency theory highlights possible means of differentiating between alternative forms of structures and systems of management.

● This four-fold categorisation provides a useful starting point for the identification of main trends in the development of management thinking. Within this framework, however, it is possible to identify a number of other approaches or sub-divisions of approaches. The decision-making approach emphasises the need for good information and channels of communication. Social action writers attempt to view the organisation from the position of individual members who will each have their own interpretation of the work situation in terms of the satisfaction sought and the meaning that work has for them.

● With the development of the information and technological age the need arises for alternative forms of corporate structure and systems. A more recent view is the idea of postmodernism. This rejects a rational systems approach to our understanding of organisations and management, and to accepted explanations of society and behaviour. Postmodernism is arguably more of a generalised sociological concept rather than a specific approach to organisation and management. Nevertheless, postmodernist organisation can arguably be seen as a healthy challenge to more traditional approaches and reminds us of the complexities in our understanding of management and organisational behaviour.

● Whatever form of categorisation is adopted, the division of writers on organisation and management into various approaches offers a number of advantages. It helps in organisational analysis and the identification of problem areas. It enables the manager to take from the different approaches those ideas that suit best the particular requirements of the job. There are, however, a number of caveats that should also be noted, including the significance of cultural contexts. In more recent years attention has been given to potential applications of Japanese management.

● It might be that the study of organisations is moving towards a more scientific value approach. However, whatever the balance between philosophy and science, a knowledge of management theory will help with the complexities of management in modern work organisations. There is much scepticism and criticism of management gurus but the study of organisation theory is an indispensable part of the job. Ideas are as important to management decisions as is instinct. It is necessary to view the interrelationships among the development of theory, behaviour in organisations and management practice.

 Refresh your understanding, assess your progress and begin your research with online resources at **www.pearsoned.co.uk/mullins**

REVIEW AND DISCUSSION QUESTIONS

1 Assess critically the relevance of scientific management to present-day organisations. Illustrate your answer with reference to your own organisation.

2 To what extent is there anything positive to be said for bureaucratic structures? Select a large-scale organisation of your choice and suggest ways in which it displays characteristics of a bureaucracy.

3 What are the main conclusions that can be drawn from the Hawthorne experiments? Discuss critically the relevance of these experiments for management and organisational behaviour today.

Figure 3.1	Common factors in organisations

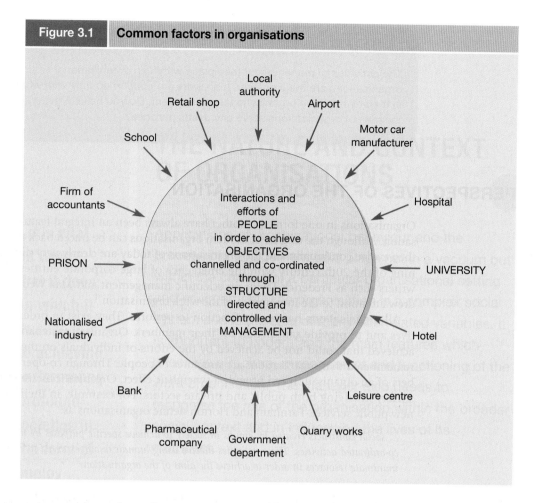

Among the variety of approaches to organisation theory, *Watson* refers to one which stresses three common aspects of organisational life:

- the importance of the creative, critical and situation-defining characteristics of the individuals who make up the organisation;
- the varieties of interests and goals among individuals and groups in the organisation, and the emphasis on conflict and political behaviour; and
- the interactions between the organisation and the general environment, and recognition that organisations make their environment as much as it makes them.[4]

Differences in applications

Despite these common factors, the structure, management and functioning of these organisations will all vary because of differences in the nature and type of the organisation, their respective goals and objectives, and the behaviour of the people who work in them. Let us now consider just two types of organisations towards the opposite ends of a possible continuum – say a maximum security prison and a university largely concerned with research – as a framework on which to focus attention. We can appreciate readily that although both types of organisation will be concerned with the basic activities of organisation and management, their goals and objectives, actual procedures and methods of operation, structure, systems and style of management, and orientation and behaviour of members will differ considerably (*see* Figure 3.2).

Figure 3.2 **The nature of organisations**

THE FORMAL ORGANISATION

The formal organisation can be distinguished from the informal organisation (which is discussed later in this chapter) – the difference between them is a feature of the degree to which they are structured.

A **formal organisation** has been defined by *Schein* as:

> *the planned co-ordination of the activities of a number of people for the achievement of some common, explicit purpose or goal, through division of labor and function, and through a hierarchy of authority and responsibility.*[5]

An organisation is a pattern of roles and a blueprint for their co-ordination. The object of co-ordination is activities, not people. The formal organisation can exist independently of the membership of particular individuals.

The formal organisation is:

- deliberately planned and created;
- concerned with the co-ordination of activities;
- hierarchically structured with stated objectives; and
- based on certain principles such as the specification of tasks, and defined relationships of authority and responsibility.

An organisation chart, for example, gives a representation of the formal structure. Other examples of the formal organisation are rules and regulations, policy manuals, standing orders and job descriptions (*see* Figure 3.9 on p. 91).

The organisation as a coalition The formal organisation can be seen as a coalition of individuals with a number of sub-coalitions.[6] Membership of the coalition will be dependent upon the type of organisation but could include, for example, managers, administrators, workers, elected representatives, appointed officials, volunteers, shareholders, suppliers, trade union officials, leaders of interest groups, customers, clients, patrons, donors, specialists, consultants and representatives of external agencies.

It is difficult to define specific, permanent boundaries for an organisational coalition. However, by focusing on participants over a given period, or participants concerned with particular decision-making processes, it is possible to identify the main members of a coalition. Strategies adopted by particular sectional interests or sub-coalitions will sometimes be

part of the formal organisation structure – for instance, in the pursuit of manifest managerial goals – and will sometimes be related to the informal structure – for example, heads of department vying with each other for limited resources, or workers indulging in restrictive practices.

BASIC COMPONENTS OF AN ORGANISATION

Any organisation can be described, broadly, in terms of an operating component and an administrative component.[7]

- The **operating component** comprises the people who actually undertake the work of producing the products or providing the services.
- The **administrative component** comprises managers and analysts and is concerned with supervision and co-ordination.

Developing this description, we can analyse the work organisation in terms of five basic components: the operational core, operational support, organisational support, top management and middle management (*see* Figure 3.3.).

- The **operational core** is concerned with direct performance of the technical or productive operations and the carrying out of actual task activities of the organisation – for example, people putting together parts on an assembly line, teaching in a classroom, treating a patient, cooking meals in a hotel, serving in a bank, repairing a hole in the road.
- **Operational support** is concerned indirectly with the technical or productive process but closely related to the actual flow of operational work – for example, people working in quality control, work study, progress planning, storekeeping, works maintenance, technical services.
- **Organisational support** is concerned with provision of services for the whole organisation, including the operational core, but which are usually outside the actual flow of operational work – for example, people working in personnel, medical services, canteen, management accounting, office services.

| Figure 3.3 | **Five basic components of an organisation** |

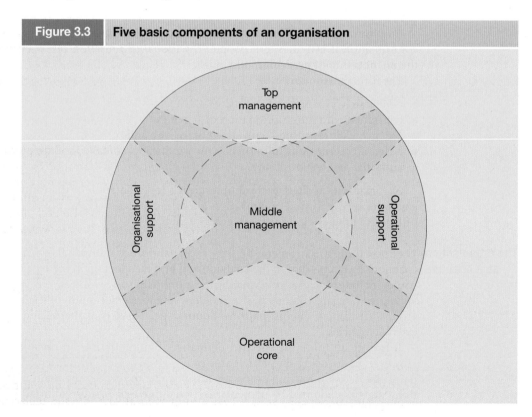

- **Top management** is concerned with broad objectives and policy, strategic decisions, the work of the organisation as a whole and interactions with the external environment – for example, managing director, governors, management team, chief executive, board of directors, council members.
- **Middle management** is concerned with co-ordination and integration of activities and providing links with operational support staff and organisational support staff, and between the operational core and top management.

PRIVATE AND PUBLIC SECTOR ORGANISATIONS

Organisations can, traditionally, be distinguished in terms of two generic groups:

- private enterprise organisations; and
- public sector organisations.

The distinction can be made on the basis of ownership and finance, and the profit motive. **Private enterprise organisations** are owned and financed by individuals, partners or shareholders in a joint stock company and are accountable to their owners or members. They vary widely in nature and size, and the type and scope of goods and services provided. The main aim is of a *commercial* nature such as profit, return on capital employed, market standing or sales level.

Public sector organisations are created by government and include, for example, municipal undertakings and central government departments, which do not have profit as their goal. Municipal undertakings such as local authorities are 'owned' by the council tax payers and ratepayers and financed by council taxes, rates, government grants, loans and charges for certain services. Central government departments are 'state owned' and financed by funds granted by parliament. Public sector organisations have political purposes and do not distribute profits. Any surplus of revenue over expenditure may be reallocated through improved services or reduced charges. The main aim is a *service* to and the *well-being of the community*.

> How well our public services are operating, how effectively they are meeting the needs of those they serve, and how they are delivering those services are all questions that we need to ask. We all need to be confident that public money, our money, is being well spent and is achieving the results that we, the public, require.
>
> Robert Coffey, 'The Service Principle'[8]

Privatisation

The extent of the state ownership of public sector operations, or of their '**privatisation**', and the balance between commercial and social interests is determined by the government of the day. In recent years there has been a vigorous policy of creating freedom from state control and the transfer of business undertakings to private hands (privatisation).

There are other public sector organisations whose aims involve both a commercial interest and a service interest. Nationalised industries such as the postal service at present run as public corporations with autonomy on day-to-day management, a degree of commercial freedom but with ultimate government control in the national interest. These public corporations are required to make efficient use of their resources by ensuring a given minimum rate of return on their investments and to charge prices based on the actual cost of supplying goods or services to certain groups of consumers. However, provision may also be made for certain activities to be undertaken on social grounds as a service to the community even though these activities might be run at a financial loss.

There have been increasing moves to encourage contracting-out of certain local authority services and putting them to compulsory competitive tender (CCT) and a greater degree of competition has also been introduced. The exposure to competition and demands for economical and high-quality service have prompted local authorities to replace administration

TYPES OF AUTHORITY AND ORGANISATIONS

In one of the earliest studies of formal organisations, *Weber* distinguished three types of authority: **traditional**, **charismatic** and **legal–rational**.[18] These types of authority are based on the form of control regarded as legitimate by subordinates and their acceptance of the power of superiors. The three types of authority relate to different types of organisations.

- In traditional organisations, authority is legitimised by custom and a longstanding belief in the natural right to rule, or is possessed by traditional ('proper') procedure. Examples would be the authority of the Pope, kings or queens or a paternalistic employer.
- In charismatic organisations, authority is legitimised by belief in the personal qualities of the leader; authority is based on the leader's strength of personality and inspiration. Winston Churchill might be quoted as an example. The practical need for some routine, for procedures and systems and for economic support means that if the movement is to continue it must become organised. On the impending demise of the charismatic leader the movement might collapse unless a 'legitimate' heir is found. This process tends to transform a charismatic organisation into either a traditional organisation or a bureaucratic organisation.
- In **bureaucratic organisations**, authority is based on the acceptance of the law of formal rules and procedures, and on impersonal principles. There is a legal–rational authority which stems from hierarchical position in the organisation and not from personality. Examples are the armed forces and the authority of government ministers or a college principal.

The concept of legal–rational authority is of most interest to us because most business organisations, particularly large-scale ones, tend to be of the bureaucratic type of structure, although there are variations in degree. Bureaucracy, as applying to certain structural features of organisation, is the most dominant type of formal organisation.

THE CLASSIFICATION OF ORGANISATIONS

In order to relate the study of management and organisational behaviour to one particular type of organisation as distinct from another, it is necessary to group similar types of organisations together. This enables generalisations to be made on the basis of certain characteristic features of organisations within a particular grouping. Organisations can be distinguished by, for example, their nature and type, goods or services provided, size, aims and objectives, and the people who are employed by or who work in them. Organisations can, therefore, be classified in a number of ways and different writers have emphasised particular features of organisations.

Classification by major purpose A common classification of organisations is by their major purpose. This leads to a distinction between, for example:

- business firms (**economic organisations**);
- armies, trade unions and police forces (**protective organisations**);
- clubs and societies (**associative organisations**);

- local authorities and hospitals (**public service organisations**); and
- churches (**religious organisations**).

Further distinctions could be made, for example, into political organisations, educational organisations, military organisations and voluntary organisations.

Such a distinction tends to lack refinement and not all organisations fit simply into one classification. Many universities combine research with teaching. Some hospitals are concerned as much with training and/or research as with treatment of patients. One could debate the main purpose of a prison: is it, for example, corrective, protective, penal or educational? The main purpose of a trade union is seen, presumably, as protection of the interests of its members through their wages and working conditions, but many trade unions also have strong social, educational and political interests.

Many organisations serve more than one goal, but although they are multi-purpose organisations it is usually possible to identify one predominant goal (or purpose) by which the organisation can be classified, however crude this classification may be. It is of interest, however, to note the comment by *Etzioni* that:

> *To the extent that such things can be measured, it appears that many multi-purpose organisations tend to serve each of their goals separately and all of them together more effectively and efficiently than single-purpose organisations of the same category.*[19]

PRIME BENEFICIARY OF THE ORGANISATION

Blau and Scott propose a classification on the basis of the prime beneficiary.[20] Four groups of people involved in a relationship with any organisation are categorised into:

- the members, or rank-and-file participants;
- the owner or managers of the organisation;
- the clients or, more generally, the 'public-in-contact' who are technically 'outside' the organisation yet have regular direct contact with it;
- the public at large – that is, the members of the society in which the organisation operates.

Organisations are then classified on the basis of who benefits – that is, which of the four categories is the prime beneficiary of its operations. Four types of organisation are identified on this basis:

- **mutual-benefit associations**, where the prime beneficiary is the membership, such as political parties, trade unions and professional associations;
- **business concerns**, where the owners are the prime beneficiaries, such as industrial and other firms privately owned and operated for profit;
- **service organisations**, where the client group is the main beneficiary, such as hospitals, schools and welfare agencies;
- **commonweal organisations**, where the prime beneficiary is the public at large, such as central government departments, the armed services and the police.

Problems associated with each type of organisation It is emphasised that the prime beneficiary is not necessarily the only beneficiary. Each of the various groups which make a contribution to an organisation do so only in return for certain benefits received.

Blau and Scott suggest that special problems are associated with each type of organisation.

- In **mutual-benefit organisations** the main problem is that of providing for participation and control by the membership and of maintaining internal democracy.
- In **business concerns** the central problem is that of maximising operational efficiency in a competitive environment.
- In **service organisations** the problem is reconciling conflict between professional service to clients and administrative procedures.
- In **commonweal organisations** the important problem is ensuring democratic procedures by which they are held accountable to the public for their actions.

Figure 3.5	An example of the open systems model

ENVIRONMENTAL INFLUENCES
- General economic health of national industry
- Opportunity of stricter pollution control legislation
- Threat of same legislation
- Competition
- Shareholders
- Culture

INPUTS
- Company products
- Factored products
- Staff
- Technology
- Management/sales/ technical expertise
- Finance
- Subcontractors for installation, wiring, commissioning
- **Customers**

TRANSFORMATION OR CONVERSION PROCESS
- Comfortable and safe environments for customer businesses
- Design of system
- Selling of systems expertise
- Provide customer with quality service
- Staff development
- Project management of customer order
- Site presence
- Innovation
- Internal and external communication
- Management commitment to customers and staff
- Provide solutions to customer problems

OUTPUTS
- Invoiced sales
- Satisfied and committed staff
- Reputation for excellence Installations that are fit for purpose
- **Satisfy customers**

ORGANISATIONAL GOALS
- Market leadership
- Growth
- Profitability
- To be the best in our field
- To invest in our people and view them as our greatest asset
- To be professional and honest in our business dealings
- **Delighted customers**

MEASURES OF ACHIEVEMENT
- Repeat business
- Customer questionnaires
- Budgets (expenditure, cash flow, profit, etc.)
- Margin performance
- Staff appraisal and general feedback
- Free of charge work
- Volume of work (sales)
- Relationship with specifiers (architects/consultants) and government agencies (environmental health/fire officers); support from group board

PESTEL analysis Organisational performance and effectiveness will be dependent upon the successful management of the opportunities, challenges and risks presented by changes in the external environment. One popular technique for analysing the general environment is a **PESTEL** analysis – that is, Political, Economic, Socio-cultural, Technological, Environmental and Legal influences. As an example, *Lynch* presents the main issues that might be considered when undertaking a PESTEL analysis (*see* Figure 3.7).[24]

Figure 3.6	Environmental influences on the organisation

External influences are almost infinite in number and variety and no study could hope to consider them all. For students of business and for managers alike, the requirement is to recognise the complexity of the external environment and to pay greater attention to those influences which appear the most pertinent and pressing for the organisation in question, rather than to attempt to consider all possible contingencies.

I. Worthington and C. Britton, *The Business Environment*[25]

THE COMPARATIVE STUDY OF ORGANISATIONS

All organisations need clear aims and objectives that will determine the nature of inputs, the series of activities to achieve outputs and the realisation of organisational goals. Feedback about the performance of the system, and the effects of its operation on the environment, are measured in terms of achieving the aims and objectives.

Basic principles of organisation and management apply in any series of activities in any organisation. For example:

- attention must be given to the design of a suitable structure;
- the common elements of management – clarification of objectives, planning, organising, directing and control – apply to a greater or lesser extent in all cases;
- essential financial, legal, personnel and administrative functions must be carried out in all types of organisation.

These common features make possible the application of general principles of management and organisational behaviour (including, for example, in both a prison or a university) and the meaningful study of organisation theory.

While general principles and prescriptions apply to all organisations, differences in their aims and objectives, organisational goals and environmental influences will result in differences in the input–conversion–output process and in the series of activities involved in this process. The nature of inputs, the throughputs and the form of the outputs will emphasise

- **Structure** – patterns of organisation, lines of authority, formal relationships and channels of communication among members. The division of work and co-ordination of tasks by which the series of activities is carried out.
- **People** – the nature of the members undertaking the series of activities. For example, their attitudes, skills and attributes; needs and expectations; interpersonal relations and patterns of behaviour; group functioning and behaviour; informal organisation and styles of leadership.
- **Management** – co-ordination of task, technology, structure and people, and policies and procedures for the execution of work. Corporate strategy, direction of the activities of the organisation as a whole and its interactions with the external environment.

A broader view of the organisation's activities The study of organisations as open systems serves to indicate both the common features and the main distinguishing features between different types of organisations. It provides a useful framework for the comparative study of organisations. The systems view of organisations enables managers to view their own organisation in perspective and to compare it in meaningful terms with other types of organisations. Managers cannot afford to take a narrow, blinkered view; they need to adopt a broader view and recognise the interrelationships between various activities and the effects that their actions and decisions have on other activities. The above framework of five main interrelated sub-systems – task, technology, structure, people and management – provides a useful basis for the analysis of organisational performance and effectiveness. Attention should be focused on the total work organisation and on the interrelationships between the range of variables which affect organisational performance.

Critical reflection

The traditional analysis of an organisation is usually based upon the departmental structure and whether individual departments are operating efficiently. Do you think this form of analysis is still relevant or does it lead only to blinkered sectional interests rather than to the interrelationships and co-ordination of sub-systems of the organisation as an integrated whole?

CONTINGENCY MODELS OF ORGANISATION

The analysis of organisational effectiveness requires an understanding of relationships within the organisation's structure, the interrelated sub-systems and the nature of its external environment.

Irrespective of the identification of sub-systems, the nature and scale of the series of activities involved in converting inputs to outputs will differ from one organisation to another in terms of the interrelationships between technology, structure, methods of operation and the nature of environmental influences. 'Contingency' models of organisation highlight these interrelationships and provide a further possible means of differentiation between alternative forms of organisation and management.

The contingency approach takes the view that there is no one best, universal form of organisation. There is a large number of variables, or situational factors, that influence organisational performance. Contingency models can be seen as an 'if–then' form of relationship. *If* certain situational factors exist, *then* certain organisational and managerial variables are most appropriate. Managers can utilise these models to compare the structure and functioning of their own organisation. Contingency models are examined in Chapter 16.

THE INFORMAL ORGANISATION

Whatever the type or nature of an organisation or its formal structure, an informal organisation will always be present (*see* Figure 3.9). The informal organisation arises from the interaction of people working in the organisation, their psychological and social needs, and the development of groups with their own relationships and norms of behaviour, irrespective of those defined within the formal structure.

- The informal organisation is flexible and loosely structured.
- Relationships may be left undefined.
- Membership is spontaneous and with varying degrees of involvement.

Group relationships and norms of behaviour exist outside the official structure and the informal organisation may, therefore, be in conflict with the aims of the formal organisation. A summary of differences between the formal and the informal organisation is given in Table 3.2.

Functions of the informal organisation

The informal organisation can serve a number of important functions.

- It provides satisfaction of members' social needs and a sense of personal identity and belonging.
- It provides for additional channels of communication – for example, through the 'grapevine', information of importance to particular members is communicated quickly.

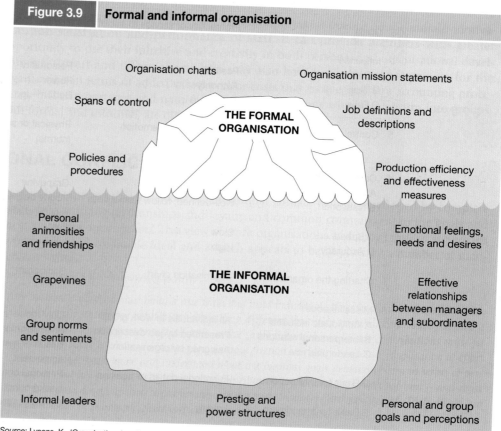

Figure 3.9 Formal and informal organisation

Source: Lysons, K., 'Organisational analysis', supplement to *Manager, The British Journal of Administrative Management*, no. 18, March/April (1997). Reproduced with permission of The Institute of Administrative Management.

dysfunctional outc
sonality clashes or
social action writers
flict among compe
feature of organisa
pluralistic manage
handling and atter

The radical perspective The radical persp
structuralist appr
lenges the traditi
power and contr
means of bringir
in a system stacl
design of organi
part of the strug

According to
tems and the
control within
between the f
between the r
and managem

CONTRASTING VIEW

Most of us w
aware of its
a term that
conflict as
Conflict is
can be viev
term 'orgar
supposed t
able beha
side or the

Comm
tions wh
traditiona
tive and
and char
even tra
formano

Positive and negative outcomes Conflic
certain
an aid
decisio
nal ch
influe
Fro
20 pe
positi

THE

- **Clarification of goals and objectives**. The clarification and continual refinement of goals and objectives, role definitions and performance standards will help to avoid misunderstandings and conflict. Focusing attention on superordinate goals, that are shared by the parties in conflict, may help to defuse hostility and lead to more co-operative behaviour.
- **Resource distribution**. Although it may not always be possible for managers to increase their allocated share of resources, they may be able to use imagination and initiative to help overcome conflict situations – for example, making a special case to higher management; greater flexibility to transfer funds between budget headings; delaying staff appointments in one area to provide more money for another area.
- **Human resource management policies and procedures**. Careful and detailed attention to just and equitable HRM policies and procedures may help to reduce areas of conflict. Examples are job analysis, recruitment and selection; systems of reward and punishment; appeals, grievance and disciplinary procedures; arbitration and mediation; recognition of trade unions and their officials.
- **Non-monetary rewards**. Where financial resources are limited, it may be possible to pay greater attention to non-monetary rewards. Examples are job design; more interesting, challenging or responsible work; increased delegation or empowerment; improved equipment; flexible working hours; attendance at courses or conferences; unofficial perks or more relaxed working conditions.
- **Development of interpersonal/group process skills**. This may help to encourage a better understanding of one's own behaviour, the other person's point of view, communication processes and problem-solving. It may also encourage people to work through conflict situations in a constructive manner.
- **Group activities**. Attention to the composition of groups and to factors which affect group cohesiveness may reduce dysfunctional conflict. Overlapping group membership with a 'linking-pin' process, and the careful selection of project teams or task forces for problems affecting more than one group, may also be beneficial.
- **Leadership and management**. A more participative and supportive style of leadership and managerial behaviour is likely to assist in conflict management – for example, showing an attitude of respect and trust; encouraging personal self-development; creating a work environment in which staff can work co-operatively. A participative approach to leadership and management may also help to create greater employee commitment.
- **Organisational processes**. Conflict situations may be reduced by attention to such features as the nature of the authority structure; work organisation; patterns of communication and sharing of information; democratic functioning of the organisation; unnecessary adherence to bureaucratic procedures, and official rules and regulations.
- **Socio-technical approach**. Viewing the organisation as a socio-technical system, in which psychological and social factors are developed in keeping with structural and technical requirements, will help in reducing dysfunctional conflict.

A summary of conflict management is given in the concept map in Figure 3.10.

THE ORGANISATION OF THE FUTURE

We have looked at the nature and type of organisations and their components. It is, however, important to remember that organisations are living organisms and evolving constantly. The changing nature of work organisations and the social context has led to a climate of constant change and the need for greater organisational flexibility. Managers need to be aware of new psychological contracts and to adopt alternative styles of management.

As *Chowdhury* points out: 'The organization of the 21st century will be characterized by unprecedented complexity and will require a different breed of leader.'[41] *Ulrich* also suggests that with the changing and dynamic contextual factors:

Figure 3.10 Concept map of conflict management

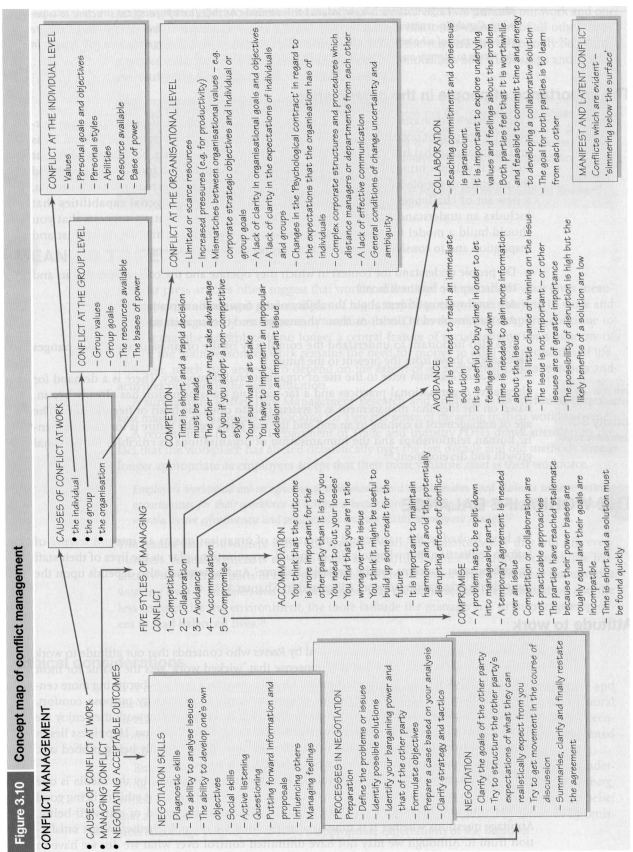

CONFLICT MANAGEMENT

• CAUSES OF CONFLICT AT WORK
• MANAGING CONFLICT
• NEGOTIATING ACCEPTABLE OUTCOMES

Source: Training Learning Consultancy Ltd, Bristol, England. Reproduced with permission.

Notes and references

1 For an account of developments in organisations see: Peters, G. 'Creating the Modern Organization', in Crainer, S. and Dearlove, D. (eds) *Financial Times Handbook of Management*, Second edition, Financial Times Prentice Hall (2001), pp. 24–45.

2 Farnham, D. and Horton, S. (eds) *Managing the New Public Services*, Second edition, Macmillan (1996), p. 26.

3 Schneider, S. C. and Barsoux, J. *Managing Across Cultures*, Second edition, Financial Times Prentice Hall (2003).

4 Watson, T. J. *Management Organisation and Employment Strategy*, Routledge and Kegan Paul (1986).

5 Schein, E. H. *Organizational Psychology*, Third edition, Prentice-Hall (1988), p. 15.

6 Cyert, R. M. and March, J. G. *A Behavioral Theory of the Firm*, Second edition, Blackwell (1992).

7 Mintzberg, H. *The Structuring of Organizations*, Prentice-Hall (1979).

8 Coffey, R. 'The Service Principle', *Chartered Secretary*, March 2005, p. 26.

9 See, for example: Dodds, O. 'Implications of Change for Local Government Managers', *Professional Manager*, November 1995, pp. 15–17.

10 Arnott, J. 'Cause and Ethics', *Chartered Secretary*, December 2002, pp. 22–4.

11 Smith, D. 'Crossing the Private–Public Divide', *Management Today*, August 1998, pp. 26–30.

12 Rose, A. and Lawton, A. *Public Services Management*, Financial Times Prentice Hall (1999), p. 74.

13 Wright, Sir David 'In My Opinion', *Management Today*, March 2003, p. 14.

14 Fitzsimmons, J. A. and Sullivan, R. S. *Service Operations Management*, McGraw-Hill (1982).

15 Levitt, T. 'Production-Line Approach to Service', *Harvard Business Review*, September–October 1972, p. 41.

16 Macdonald, J. 'Service is Different', *The TQM Magazine*, vol. 6, no. 1, 1994, p. 5.

17 For a discussion on the nature of service industries, see, for example: Mullins, L. J. *Hospitality Management and Organisational Behaviour*, Fourth edition, Longman (2001).

18 Weber, M. *The Theory of Social and Economic Organization*, Collier Macmillan (1964).

19 Etzioni, A. *Modern Organizations*, Prentice-Hall (1964), p. 14.

20 Blau, P. M. and Scott, W. R. *Formal Organizations*, Routledge and Kegan Paul (1966).

21 Katz, D. and Khan, R. L. *The Social Psychology of Organizations*, Second edition, Wiley (1978).

22 See, for example: Mullins, L. J. 'The Hotel and the Open Systems Model of Organisational Analysis', *The Services Industry Journal*, vol. 13, no. 1, January 1993, pp. 1–16.

23 For a more detailed discussion of environmental influences, see, for example: Worthington, I. and Britton, C. *The Business Environment*, Fifth edition, Financial Times Prentice Hall (2006).

24 Lynch, R. *Corporate Strategy*, Fourth edition, Financial Times Prentice Hall (2006).

25 Worthington, I and Britton, C. *The Business Environment*, Fifth edition, Financial Times Prentice Hall (2006), p. 13.

26 Law, S. 'Beyond the Water Cooler', *Professional Manager*, January 2005, p. 26.

27 Stewart, R. *The Reality of Management*, Third edition, Butterworth-Heinemann (1999), p. 125.

28 For a fuller discussion, see: Sadler, P. *Designing Organisations: The Foundation for Excellence*, Mercury (1991).

29 Egan, G. 'The Shadow Side', *Management Today*, September 1993, pp. 33–8.

30 Drucker, P. F. *The Practice of Management*, Heinemann Professional (1989), p. 119.

31 For an account of the Marxist critique, see, for example: Johnston, R. 'Hidden Capital', in Barry, J., Chandler, J., Clark, H., Johnston, R. and Needle, D. (eds), *Organization and Management: A Critical Text*, International Thomson Business Press (2000), pp. 16–35.

32 Salaman, G. *Class and Corporation*, Fontana (1981).

33 Ackroyd, S. and Thompson, P. *Organizational Misbehaviour*, Sage Publications (1999).

34 Schmidt, W. H. 'Conflict: A Powerful Process for (Good or Bad) Change', *Management Review*, Issue 63, December 1974, pp. 4–10.

35 Townsend, R. *Further Up the Organisation*, Coronet Books (1985), p. 39.

36 See, for example: Robbins, S. P. *Organizational Behavior: Concepts, Controversies, Applications*, Eighth edition, Prentice-Hall (1998).

37 Irvine, L. 'Conflicts of Interest', *The British Journal of Administrative Management*, March/April 1998, pp. 8–10.

38 Woodward, J. *Industrial Organization: Theory and Practice*, Second edition, Oxford University Press (1980), p. 113.

39 See, for example: James, J. *Body Talk at Work*, Judy Piatkus Limited (2001).

40 Hart, J. 'Mind the Gap', *Professional Manager*, November 2002, pp. 22–3.

41 Chowdhury, S. *Management 21C*, Financial Times Prentice Hall (2000), p. 205.

42 Ulrich, D. 'Context, Capability amd Response', in Chowdhury, S. *Management 21C*, Financial Times Prentice Hall (2000), p. 240.

43 Gratton, L. *Living Strategy: Putting People at the Heart of Corporate Purpose*, Financial Times Prentice Hall (2000).

44 Cloke, K. and Goldsmith, J. *The End of Management and the Rise of Organizational Democracy*, Jossey-Bass (2002).

45 Reeves, R. 'The Joy of Work', *Management Today*, May 2001, pp. 60–3.

46 Armitage, K. 'Can We Really Achieve a Life/Work Balance?' *The British Journal of Administrative Management*, July/August 2001, pp. 14–15.

47 'Work–life Balance: evidence from across the UK', *European Industrial Relations Review*, Issue 380, September 2005, p. 27.

48 Hoar, R. 'Work with Meaning', *Management Today*, May 2004, pp. 45–53.

49 'Work–Life Balance: The Business Case', Department of Trade and Industry, September 2001, p. 3.

50 Rice, M. 'Balancing Acts', *Management Today*, September 2002, pp. 52–9.

51 Summers, J. and Nowicki, M. 'Achievement and Balance: What do Managers Really Want?', *Healthcare Financial Management*, vol. 56, no. 3, March 2003, pp. 80–4.

52 Sternberg, E. *Just Business: Business Ethics in Action*, Second edition, Oxford University Press (2000), pp. 124–5.

53 Browning, G. 'The Search for Meaning', *People Management*, 29 December 2005.

54 'Improving the World of Work', ACAS, August 2005, p. 16.

PERSONALITY

Personality may be viewed as consisting of stable characteristics that explain why a person behaves in a particular way. So, for instance, independence, conscientiousness, agreeableness, self-control would be examples of these personality characteristics. However, it is only when we see/hear/observe a person that we can gain an understanding of their personality. For example, a person who is independent may show that characteristic by displaying a strong sense of self-sufficiency. We would expect him or her to take the initiative and not to depend on other people. Furthermore, if the characteristic is 'stable' we can rely on this being a consistent part of the person's behaviour. We would be surprised if the person one day demonstrated autonomy and initiative and the next withdrew and delayed any decisions. We anticipate that individuals are generally consistent in the way in which they respond to situations.

There are times when we might be surprised by somebody's behaviour and we may feel they are 'acting out of character'. Of course this would be known only if we had an understanding of their 'typical behaviour' in the first place. Individuals may exaggerate or suppress certain personality traits, for example if they are under stress or influenced by drink/drugs. It is self-evident that managers need to learn the art of 'reading' people's behaviour in order to manage relationships effectively.

NOMOTHETIC AND IDIOGRAPHIC APPROACHES

Broadly speaking, personality studies can be divided into two main approaches, labelled as nomothetic and idiographic.

The **nomothetic approach** is a measurable and specific perspective that looks at the identification of traits and personality as a collection of characteristics. These characteristics are ones that can be described, identified and measured and therefore can be subjected to observation and tests. This perspective is especially helpful for managers when they are involved in the selection, training and development of individuals.

Nomothetic approaches tend to view environmental and social influences as minimal and view personality as consistent, largely inherited and resistant to change. Although they would not diminish the difficulties that measuring personality brings, nomothetic approaches would claim that it is possible to measure and predict the ways in which personality types would behave given certain circumstances.

Nomothetic researchers closely align themselves to studies that are 'scientific' in a positivistic sense. (The term positivism refers to the branch of science that is exclusively based on the objective collection of observable data – data that are beyond question.) Such an approach transfers methods used in natural sciences to the social world. Some psychologists are interested in describing and measuring characteristics and comparing individuals' scores. Does this person exhibit more or less than 'average' of this particular trait? Being able to predict behaviour is a major aim and outcome of this approach.

The **idiographic approach** is a holistic and dynamic perspective which insists that managers take into account a 'whole' understanding of the individual at work. This may also require going beyond the study of pure psychology to an understanding of the societal context in which the person lives. These are called idiographic approaches and are particularly pertinent in understanding motivation, career development and team relationships.

Idiographic approaches are concerned with understanding the uniqueness of individuals and the development of the self-concept. They regard personality development as a process that is open to change. They regard individuals as responding to the environment and people around them and see the dynamics of the interactions as playing a critical part in shaping personality. The measurement of traits is seen as largely inappropriate in that one person's responses may not be comparable to another's. They suggest that personality

assessment is not a valid method of understanding the unique ways in which a person understands and responds to the world. The depth and richness of a person's personality cannot be revealed in superficial paper-and-pencil questionnaires. Furthermore, the categories defined by psychologists are too narrow in scope and depth.

Theory and the world of work

The application of theory to the world of work is not always easy and some find the process confusing when theory does not match with their experiences. Psychological investigations emphasise the complexity and variety of individual behaviour and insist that simple answers and explanations are generally inadequate. The study of personality provides an excellent example of some of the complexities involved in applying psychological theory in practice.

Consider two individuals who share similar characteristics. They are both 24 years old and have lived in the same area; both have a first-class honours degree in pharmacy and they have identical personality assessment profiles. However, we would still predict differences with regard to their attitude and performance in the workplace. In addition, differences would be predicted in the ways they interact with others. If one of the pharmacists was male and/or African, a further set of assumptions might be made. It is not only the features themselves which identify individuals as being different, it is also their interaction which leads to a unique pattern of behaviour. The complexities of the process pose a number of questions that interest psychologists and evoke different response (*see* Tables 4.1 and 4.2).

Figure 4.1 identifies the links between the dynamics of personality and life's experiences.

Uniqueness and similarities

Tables 4.1 and 4.2 focus on two major issues of prime importance in the study of personality. First, is personality a constant throughout our lifetime, which remains resistant to change and circumstances? Second, to what extent can we measure and compare individuals on the basis of their personality? This second question assumes that it is possible to distinguish personality characteristics in the first place. Trying to make sense of the nature of personality has resulted in a prolific number of theories, with some psychologists focusing solely on the unique make-up of individuals, others drawing comparisons between individuals or looking for broad similarities in aspirations and goals. Table 4.3 charts these differences as series of 'levels'.

In a work context we tend to be more interested in understanding 'what' an individual's personality is rather than why it is as it is. Furthermore, it is important to understand how various personality characteristics relate to performance at work. The nomothetic approach explores the 'what' of personality and the idiographic approach enriches our understanding of 'why'.

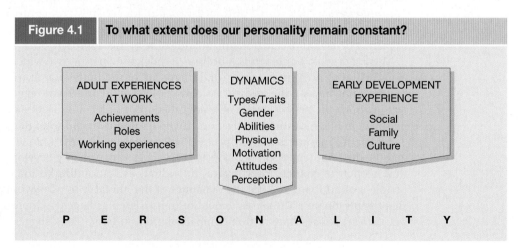

Figure 4.1	To what extent does our personality remain constant?

ADULT EXPERIENCES AT WORK

Achievements
Roles
Working experiences

DYNAMICS

Types/Traits
Gender
Abilities
Physique
Motivation
Attitudes
Perception

EARLY DEVELOPMENT EXPERIENCE

Social
Family
Culture

P E R S O N A L I T Y

Table 4.1	The role of early experiences – what is its impact?

Environment is significant	Inherited characteristics are significant
Approach taken by idiographic approaches	*Approach taken by nomothetic theorists*
The personalities of the two pharmacists described above are the culmination of experiences. Their personalities have been shaped by the people around them from their very earliest years. Early family life – the relationship between family members, the size of the family, the rewards and punishments exercised by parents – would have had an influence on the type of person each is now. In other words, the environment and early learning experiences have significantly contributed to their personality development.	The pharmacists inherited a genetic make-up which would remain core and would be resistant to change. Early experiences, while they may shape the person to a certain extent, do not alter the inherited make-up. Intelligence, physical appearances, physiological reactions are 'wired' in from birth – the 'core' of the individual is a 'given'.

Table 4.2	Is it possible to 'measure' an individual's personality?

No, personality is unique	Yes, there are identifiable traits
Approach taken by idiographic approaches	*Approach taken by nomothetic theorists*
Idiographic approaches do not believe it is possible to put personal characteristics to the test. Our very uniqueness makes comparisons difficult, if not impossible. Is it appropriate to consider the 'strength' of a trait? Our pharmacists may not always reveal their true 'self' – at times circumstances may force them to 'mask' their preferred ways of behaving. Our pharmacists may not reliably report on their own behaviour or there may be a real difference between what they say and what others see. Critics of questionnaires believe answering 'set' questions is 'forcing' responses to questions that may not be relevant. Instead it may be more appropriate to use open-ended techniques. This ensures that individuals use their own definitions and allows for greater understanding about their motivations and causes of behaviour.	Identifying an individual's personality typically refers to distinguishing traits or types. Personality traits are usually identified by what people do, the behaviour they exhibit, e.g. sociable. Psychologists have designed questionnaires which ask people to respond to a series of questions. They assert that asking a person to report on the way they feel or behave is a legitimate way of assessing personality. These self-reporting questionnaires would then be subject to quantitative methods. It is therefore possible to quantify the strength of a person's trait and to enable comparisons to be made with others. Such information then becomes a basis for prediction. For example, if a person has a high score on extroversion, it would be possible to predict the way in which the individual might behave in a given situation.

Table 4.3	Different levels of personality research

Level	Psychologists' research interests
LEVEL 3 ☺ ☺ ☺ ☺ ☺ ☺ ☺ ☺ ☺ ☺ ☺ ☺ Universal human features	Common human aspirations
LEVEL 2 ☺ ☺ ☺ ☺ ☺ ☺ ☺ ☺ Some shared features – gender; ability	Identification, measurements, comparison (nomothetic)
LEVEL 1 ☺ Unique combination of features	'Self' – unique interaction with the world (idiographic)

THE BIG FIVE

Identifying personality traits has been the dominant subject of personality research in the UK and the USA. There is now a body of evidence which suggests that five dimensions capture distinct differences between people. These traits, known as the Big Five,[5] are:

- extraversion/introversion
- agreeableness/hostility
- conscientiousness/heedlessness
- emotional stability/instability
- openness or intellect/closed-mindedness.

Results from a wide number of studies have shown that these factors can be identified as being significant in measuring the variation between people.[6] Of these, conscientiousness is linked to high levels of job knowledge and performance across a range of occupations. The strength and value of the Big Five model has been extolled in a review by *Lord and Rust*. They conclude that:

> *Indeed, the five factor model has become the linchpin that holds personality assessment together, at least within the work context. Without it, how would we generalize with confidence from the validity of one work-based instrument to that of another? Furthermore, the model links the study of assessment instruments within the HR field to research in personality and related areas carried out within clinical and mainstream psychology fields in which the Big Five have also become dominant.*[7]

However, some researchers are critical of the descriptors used.[8] *Bentall*[9] suggests they are 'tainted by the investigators' values' and continues: 'I suspect that most people will have a pretty clear idea of where they would like to find themselves on the dimensions of neuroticism, extraversion, openness, agreeableness and conscientiousness.' He questions the ethical and political nature of the scales.

Gurus in nomothetic personality theories

Eysenck *Hans Eysenck* believed that personality was largely inherited and that we are born with differing physiological tendencies. He identified two major individual differences – *see* Figure 4.2.

Eysenck's approach was influenced by the positivistic tradition with his research findings grounded in robust research. His aim was to produce objective evidence of personality differences using large samples of the population.[10] The two dimensions define four distinct personality types:

- stable extroverts (sanguine) with traits such as talkative, responsive, easygoing, lively, carefree;
- unstable extroverts (choleric) with traits such as impulsive, changeable, excitable, restless;
- stable introverts (phlegmatic) with traits such as calm, even tempered, peaceful, thoughtful;
- unstable introverts (melancholic) with traits such as anxious, moody, reserved, pessimistic.

Figure 4.2	Eysenck's personality dimensions

Individuals in Eysenck's theory could, therefore, be one of four main personality types. The type would lead to a predisposition of traits that would, itself, lead to the likelihood of certain behaviours. For instance, a person typed as an extrovert would predictably talk over things with someone to help them think it through, while an introvert would prefer to mull it over before talking about the issue. Eysenck developed an instrument to measure personality type called EPQ (Eysenck's Personality Questionnaire).

Supporting research evidence Although Eysenck's theory appears simplistic, his theory has an impressive amount of supporting research evidence. His approach has immediate appeal to managers in organisations who are concerned with predicting the future behaviour of their employees, either for selection or promotion. Given the evidence that personality is a useful predictor of behaviour, it is not surprising that the use of psychometric tests has grown substantially over the past decade and that the majority of large companies use occupational tests.[11] (Further information about testing is given later in this chapter.)

Cattell *Cattell's* work resembles Eysenck's in the methods used to study personality. He used quantitative, objective techniques in order to analyse his data and followed traditional scientific procedures in order to understand the basic dimensions of personality.[12] He identified two main types of personality traits:

- **surface traits** – that seem to cluster together consistently and are observable in behaviour such as assertiveness;
- **source traits** – such as self-discipline that can only be inferred and seem to underlie and determine the traits which are likely to 'surface' into behaviour.

Refresh your understanding
Activity 4A
www.pearsoned.co.uk/ mullins

Unlike Eysenck, Cattell did not 'type' individuals but used 'traits' as his main personality descriptor. They also differed with regard to the determinants of personality: Eysenck viewed the inherited physiological basis as the main determinant, whereas Cattell was more interested in taking social factors into account when understanding an individual's personality. Both theorists have contributed to a lively debate about personality structure and its measurement and in doing so have advanced the selection techniques available to managers.[13]

THEORETICAL APPROACHES: IDIOGRAPHIC

Idiographic approaches emphasise the development of the individual and of individuals' views of themselves – their self-concept. Supporters of idiographic approaches are critical of the nomothetic approach that attempts to categorise individuals on the basis of group data. They argue that the techniques used to collate the group data are questionable and the outcome inappropriate to an understanding of personality. For the idiographic researchers, personality is expressed through the experiences and development of the individual. It cannot be understood outside a social context and has to be studied in the light of individuals' own perceptions of their world.

Idiographic researchers would always take into account the social circumstances of the person and in particular the relationships with others, family life and social conditions. In early childhood strong personal relationships and unconditional love are essential for later fulfilment and psychological growth. *Carl Rogers'* theory claims that personality is embedded within personal relationships. The process of becoming an adult requires the ability to give and receive unconditional regard – the warmth and respect for the *person*, who they *are*, regardless of how they behave.[14] The phrase 'the looking-glass self' was first discussed by *Cooley* – by this he meant that we come to know ourselves through our relationship with others and their reactions to us.[15]

Table 4.4	Erikson's eight stages of personality development			
Stage 1	Trust	v	Mistrust	1st year
Stage 2	Autonomy	v	Doubt	2–3 years
Stage 3	Initiative	v	Guilt	4–5 years
Stage 4	Industry	v	Inferiority	6–11 years
Stage 5	Identity	v	Role confusion	12–18 years
Stage 6	Intimacy	v	Isolation	Young adult
Stage 7	Generativity	v	Self-absorption	Middle age
Stage 8	Integrity	v	Despair	Old age

Source: Adapted from Erikson, E. H., *Identity and the Life Cycle*, Norton (1980) worksheet table appendix. Copyright © 1980 by W. W. Norton & Company, Inc. Copyright © 1959 by International Universities Press, Inc. Reproduced with permission from W. W. Norton & Company Inc.

Gurus in idiographic approaches: Erikson

Erik Erikson's theory is a good example of the idiographic approach. He viewed personality development as continuing throughout life. He was interested in the effect of experiences on the development of the self-concept and how different individuals resolved personal conflicts.[16]

He recognised the importance of early childhood in establishing certain basic concepts of trust, autonomy and initiative, but also claimed that all stages of life produce different tensions and conflicts.

Tensions and conflicts For Erikson, there are eight distinct stages of life, each of which produces different tensions and conflicts that have to be resolved (*see* Table 4.4). Successful resolution of these conflicts produces a healthy personality, whereas difficulties in earlier stages may produce problems later on. Erikson's theory not only makes considerable sense in terms of face validity (i.e. 'it feels right' factor), it also links with other research indicating that managers' motivations and goals change with age (see *Hunt*, who identified nine different career/life stages).[17]

Complementary approaches Some researchers do not fit easily into either of the two broad approaches of nomothetic or idiographic and have their own theories and models of personality development, for example the work of Carl Jung and the cognitive approach of George Kelly.

Carl Jung *Carl Jung's* theory is of particular significance in that it bridges the psychoanalytic approach (of writers such as Sigmund Freud) with modern approaches of personality test design. His theory identifies life energy as concerned with hopes and goals of the future and not just of the past. Jung describes three levels of personality:

- a conscious level (daily reality);
- an unconscious level (contains our unique complexes);
- a collective unconscious level (store of universal and evolutionary experiences).

Jung identified four universal aspects of everyone's personality that he referred to as archetypes; for example he claimed we all strive for self-actualisation; have a darker self, have both masculine and feminine qualities, and have a persona – a role we can play.[18]

The Myers–Briggs Type Indicator (MBTI) Jung is probably best known for his constructs that form the foundation for the MBTI personality indicator. The **Myers–Briggs Type Indicator (MBTI)** was designed by *Isabel Briggs-Myers* and *Katherine Briggs* who applied the rigours of systematic testing to Jung's personality functions and attitudes.[19] Jung identified differences between individuals in terms of their libidinal energy that could flow outwards to the external world (extrovert) or inwards to their inner world (introvert). Personality differences would also be manifest through differing cognitive functions of thinking, feeling, sensation and intuition. Myers–Briggs added a further dimension of style of living. The personality types are shown in Figure 4.3.

Figure 4.3 The Myers–Briggs Type Indicator showing characteristics frequently associated with particular personality types

	Sensing types		Intuitive types	
Introverts	**ISTJ** Quiet, serious, earn success by thoroughness and dependability. Practical, matter-of-fact, realistic and responsible. Decide logically what should be done and work towards it steadily, regardless of distractions. Take pleasure in making everything orderly and organised – their work, their home, their life. Value traditions and loyalty.	**ISFJ** Quiet, friendly, responsible, and conscientious. Committed and steady in meeting their obligations. Thorough, painstaking and accurate. Loyal, considerate, notice and remember specifics about people who are important to them, concerned with how others feel. Strive to create an orderly and harmonious environment at work and at home.	**INFJ** Seek meaning and connection in ideas, relationships and material possessions. Want to understand what motivates people and are insightful about others. Conscientious and committed to their firm values. Develop a clear vision about how best to serve the common good. Organised and decisive in implementing their vision.	**INTJ** Have original minds and great drive for implementing their ideas and achieving their goals. Quickly see patterns in external events and develop long-range explanatory perspectives. When committed, organise a job and carry it through. Sceptical and independent, have high standards of competence and performance – for themselves and others.
	ISTP Tolerant and flexible, quiet observers until a problem appears, then act quickly to find workable solutions. Analyse what makes things work and readily get through large amounts of data to isolate the core of practical problems. Interested in cause and effect, organise facts using logical principles, value efficiency.	**ISFP** Quiet, friendly, sensitive and kind. Enjoy the present moment, what's going on around them. Like to have their own space and to work within their own time frame. Loyal and committed to their values and to people who are important to them. Dislike disagreements and conflicts, do not force their opinions or values on others.	**INFP** Idealistic, loyal to their values and to people who are important to them. Want an external life that is congruent with their values. Curious, quick to see possibilities, can be catalysts for implementing ideas. Seek to understand people and to help them fulfil their potential. Adaptable, flexible and accepting unless a value is threatened.	**INTP** Seek to develop logical explanations for everything that interests them. Theoretical and abstract, interested more in ideas than in social interaction. Quiet, contained, flexible and adaptable. Have unusual ability to focus in depth to solve problems in their area of interest. Sceptical, sometimes critical, always analytical.
Extroverts	**ESTP** Flexible and tolerant, they take a pragmatic approach focused on immediate results. Theories and conceptual explanations bore them – they want to act energetically to solve the problem. Focus on the here-and-now, spontaneous, enjoy each moment that they can be active with others. Enjoy material comforts and style. Learn best through doing.	**ESFP** Outgoing, friendly and accepting. Exuberant lovers of life, people and material comforts. Enjoy working with others to make things happen. Bring common sense and a realistic approach to their work, and make work fun. Flexible and spontaneous, adapt readily to new people and environments. Learn best by trying a new skill with other people.	**ENFP** Warmly enthusiastic and imaginative. See life as full of possibilities. Make connections between events and information very quickly, and confidently proceed based on the patterns they see. Want a lot of affirmation from others, and readily give appreciation and support. Spontaneous and flexible, often rely on their ability to improvise and their verbal fluency.	**ENTP** Quick, ingenious, stimulating, alert and outspoken. Resourceful in solving new and challenging problems. Adept at generating conceptual possibilities and then analysing them strategically. Good at reading other people. Bored by routine, will seldom do the same thing the same way, apt to turn to one new interest after another.
	ESTJ Practical, realistic, matter-of-fact. Decisive, quickly move to implement decisions. Organise projects and people to get things done, focus on getting results in the most efficient way possible. Take care of routine details. Have a clear set of logical standards, systematically follow them and want others to also. Forceful in implementing their plans.	**ESFJ** Warm-hearted, conscientious and cooperative. Want harmony in their environment, work with determination to establish it. Like to work with others to complete tasks accurately and on time. Loyal, follow through even in small matters. Notice what others need in their day-to-day lives and try to provide it. Want to be appreciated for who they are and for what they contribute.	**ENFJ** Warm, empathetic, responsive and responsible. Highly attuned to the emotions, needs and motivations of others. Find potential in everyone, want to help others fulfil their potential. May act as catalysts for individual and group growth. Loyal, responsive to praise and criticism. Sociable, facilitate others in a group, and provide inspiring leadership.	**ENTJ** Frank, decisive, assume leadership readily. Quickly see illogical and inefficient procedures and policies, develop and implement comprehensive systems to solve organisational problems. Enjoy long-term planning and goal setting. Usually well informed, well read, enjoy expanding their knowledge and passing it on to others. Forceful in presenting their ideas.

Source: Briggs-Myers, I., *Introduction to Type*, Sixth Edition, CPP, Inc. (1998). Copyright © 1998 by Peter B. Myers and Katharine D. Myers, Inc. All rights reserved. Modified and reproduced by special permission of the Publisher, CPP, Inc., Palo Alto, CA 94303. Further reproduction is prohibited without the publisher's written consent.

The MBTI has promoted considerable research interest, particularly with regard to the correlation between personality type, occupations and management style – *see* Table 4.5. Myers-Briggs asserts that people tend to be attracted to and have the most satisfaction in work that allows them to express and use their psychological type preferences. Such a match enables them to handle their tasks more effectively and generates more energy. Confidence is a likely outcome of this process. The Myers-Briggs instrument is an affirmatory tool and knowledge gained through using the MBTI can lead to recognition and respect for differences between people and appreciation for the value such differences bring.[20]

Table 4.5	Leadership types and the Myers–Briggs		
ISTJ Salt of the earth	**ISFJ** Behind-the-scenes leader	**INFJ** Oracle for people	**INTJ** Designer of the future
ISTP Walking encyclopedia	**ISFP** Gentle spirit	**INFP** Values crusader	**INTP** Blueprinter of ideas
ESTP Self starter	**ESFP** Everyone's friend	**ENFP** Spark of energy	**ENTP** Classic entrepreneur
ESTJ Take-charge leader	**ESFJ** Servant leader	**ENFJ** Values spokesperson	**ENTJ** Grand scale organiser

Critical reflection

?????

The MBTI has been in and out of fashion over the years and there is constant debate about its continuing relevance and usefulness. What value you do believe the MBTI has as a tool for measuring people's personality type? Can you give a specific example of where it might be used with advantage?

KELLY'S PERSONAL CONSTRUCT THEORY

Kelly's theory of personal constructs does not just consider personality development; it considers the whole person in terms of their perceptions, attitudes and goals. For Kelly, personality is the individual's way of construing and experimenting with their world. Kelly was critical of separating the study of personality apart from the 'whole' person:

> The castrating effect of separating personality off as a mini-psychology in its own right is perhaps best seen in the curiously named study of 'individual differences', which in fact turns out to be the study of group sameness. As a result we have focused on the establishment of general dimensions, at some point along which all individuals can be placed, rather than on a study of the dimensions which each individual develops in order to organise his own world.[21]

For Kelly it was critical to take data from one individual person (idiography) and to employ a technique that could cope with the qualitative nature of the data to be collected. He developed the Repertory Grid that was able to measure an individual's construct of the world. Kelly was thus able to employ a clear and valid measure within an idiographic approach. This was an important advance in idiographic techniques and the repertory technique has become increasingly important as a research tool. It enables the person to use their own constructions of the world but in such a way that they are comparable and measurable.

APPLICATIONS WITHIN THE WORK ORGANISATION

Recruitment and selection It would be rare for organisations not to take the personality of a candidate into consideration at a selection interview. For some organisations, personality is a major criterion for selection or rejection. The hospitality industry, for example, is replete with research studies demonstrating the potency of personality.[22] So, how do organisations assess a candidate's personality?

The interview remains the most usual method of selection, but there is an increasing use of objective psychometric measures. Such growth in psychometric testing is significant and a number of studies have demonstrated its growing popularity.[23] Concern has been expressed about the use and misuse of psychological instruments and there is a continuing debate within psychological circles with regard to the validity of these measures.[24] (That is, do they actually measure what they claim to measure?) Testing is discussed in detail in the next section. There are controversies and sensitivities surrounding the use of any psychological test, but tests of typical performance are especially problematic in certain circumstances. As *Anastasi* has stated:

> The construction and use of personality inventories are beset with special difficulties over and above common problems encountered in all psychological testing. The question of faking and malingering is far more acute in personality measurement than in aptitude testing.[25]

Critics have accused consultants and practitioners of inappropriate use of personality assessments and claim low validity between non-work-related personality assessments and work performance.[26] *Goss* suggests that the use of personality assessments not only is an infringement of the individual's privacy but also leads to unfortunate organisational consequences, with 'cloning' as an outcome. Such techniques can be perceived as a form of social engineering and an insidious form of organisational control.[27] Aware of these problems, the British Psychological Society has produced guidelines and codes of practice for users of psychometric tests. Furthermore, evidence is emerging to show that where personality questionnaires have been specifically designed and related to work characteristics, prediction and validity scores are much higher.[28]

Personal development and teamworking Personality questionnaires can be particularly valuable if individuals complete them for their personal development or if they are used within team building and development programmes. Here, they can initiate discussion about individual differences, the importance of diversity in teamworking and the strengths that each personality type can bring to the working situation. The notion of judgement is therefore out of the equation. Personality questionnaires can thus be a valuable diagnostic tool at the start of a coaching session or as a preliminary to a team-building process – an audit of strengths and weaknesses. At these times a discussion can be held to look at a balanced team with complementary personalities, skills and abilities. This could be followed by group training exercises designed to develop strengths and balance the weaknesses of the team. An effective team at work should be aware of the division of their strengths and weaknesses.

None of us is perfect; but a group of people, whose strengths and talents complement each other, can be.[29]

Culture and personality Although personality is a powerful determinant of a manager's effectiveness, account must also be taken of the social rules and expectations within the workplace. People learn the behaviour that is expected of them and may mask their true preferences. For instance, an introverted academic lecturer may prefer to be reflective and have time to think but will be required to 'perform' in front of 200 undergraduate students and be expected to respond immediately to questions. We can respond in ways that are not 'true to type' and we may be

required to take on roles at work that may run counter to our preferences. We have to learn coping strategies and adaptive skills, but for some people stress may result. Furthermore, different temperaments may be rewarded at different times depending on whether they are going through a period of growth or retrenchment. Whereas a manager may be recognised for exciting promotional activity and product development in one situation, other personality characteristics may be needed if there is a period of slow-down and attention to detail and costs. *Gray* contends that researchers will never to able to solve and develop accurate, valid and reliable performance measures. 'Many jobs or critical aspects of them, cannot be quantified. Performance measures are often justifiably subjective, vague and contradictory.'[30]

Refresh your understanding

Activity 4B

www.pearsoned.co.uk/mullins

EMOTIONS AT WORK

Until recently workplaces were seen as rational, logical places where emotions were excluded or seen in a negative light. *Hochschild's*[31] research describes the way in which some jobs require a display of certain emotions, especially those in the service industries, where customer care is inextricably linked with making people feel good. Such work has been labelled as emotional labour and distinguishes between surface acting – displaying emotion without experiencing it – and deep acting – involving thinking, visualising to induce the emotion in the situation. *Briner* challenges psychologists to broaden research to throw light on the complexities of emotions in the workplace. He notes that organisations specify the emotions they would like their employees to feel in the mission statements and in more subtle ways in terms of the rewards and career enhancements people receive when they display appropriate emotions. However, he suggests that little is known about the incidence of emotion at work and the part it plays in work behaviours. The illustration he gives below, although simplistic, plots a possible sequence of events and the power of rewards (or not) and psychological well-being (or not).

A sequence of work emotions, thought and behavior

- Jane is asked to carry out a difficult project, usually given only to more experienced colleagues. She feels valued, flattered and trusted – also a little worried.

- While working hard on the project her emotions range from excitement and elation to fear and frustration.

- She completes the task well and feels proud and relieved.

- Jane tells her boss and shows her completed work.

- Boss gives no thanks or praise and picks out a trivial error.

- Jane then feels resentful and angry and thinks that she will never again 'put herself out' for her boss. Also feels exploited.

- Thinks about looking for another job.

- Doesn't volunteer to do additional tasks any more.

- Starts to feel sad and disappointed.

- Updates her CV and regularly starts looking at job advertisements.

Source: Briner, R., 'Feeling and smiling', *The Psychologist*, vol. 12, no. 1, January 1999 pp. 16–19.
Reproduced with permission from the British Psychological Society.

A classic study by *La Piere* illustrates this point. Visiting American hotels and restaurants with a Chinese couple, *La Piere* found no sign of prejudiced attitudes in the face-to-face situation, but there were marked racist attitudes in the follow-up attitude survey. He found complete contradictions between public and private attitudes.[54]

These findings have important implications for the study of attitudes and reveal two important issues for the psychologist and manager.

1 Attitudes cannot be seen; they can only be inferred.

Given that the attitudes employees hold are important for morale and the effectiveness of organisations, it is important that there is confidence in the measurement techniques used to assess the strength of attitudes. As attitudes are inferred, heavy reliance is placed therefore on the accuracy of assessment. Although there are a number of techniques that could be used to measure attitudes, the two most common are **direct observation** and **self-reporting techniques**.

All of us observe others and assess attitudes on the basis of communication style (both verbal and non-verbal) and behaviour. This is an example of an informal approach – unsystematic, spontaneous and based on our understanding of social cues. We may be wrong in our judgement. Students who turn up late for classes, slouch on their seat and do not ask questions may still hold very positive attitudes towards the subject. Managers may also be erroneous in their assumptions and beliefs about their colleagues (both subordinates and superiors). Their beliefs may never have been tested out – merely assumed to be correct.

Serious mistakes can be made when dealing with people across different cultures. For instance, eye contact in Western countries is normally associated with confidence, politeness and attentiveness but in some African countries may be seen as rude and disrespectful. Bulgarians nod when they mean 'no' and shake their heads when they mean 'yes', while the Greeks nod upwards or raise their eyebrows for 'no' and shake the head side to side or tilt it to say 'yes'. A lack of 'cultural literacy' can lead to incorrect assumptions, poor relationships and a failure to make useful business connections.[55]

Organisations that assess their employees' attitudes by using attitude questionnaires (self-reporting techniques) are attempting to systematically gauge and measure these assumptions. Attitude questionnaires are time-consuming to design and administer. The questions asked, their relevance, style and length are all important variables in the validity of the questionnaire. So, too, is the honest completion of questionnaires. Making public people's private attitudes may also have its dangers as expectations of change may be envisaged. If these do not occur, disappointment and low morale may be the result.[56] (*See also* the discussion on the Johari window in Chapter 9.) Attitude questionnaires are used by many companies as a barometer for the attitudinal climate of organisations and as such enable managers to be in touch with employees' views and feelings (*see* Table 4.6).

2 Attitudes are often shared within organisations and as such are embodied in the culture of organisations.

Classic research has shown the influence of the wider community in the formation of orientations towards work. Differences in class/orientation may elicit a range of loyalties and possibly produce opposing perceptions of commitment, loyalty and co-operation. Attitudes are not just individually formed but arise out of interaction with others. They are often 'locked-in', often regarded as obvious, mere common sense, and are so much taken for granted that they may be overlooked. Sharing the belief system of others also has affective outcomes. If people feel that they belong and are included, it enables them to feel good about working in an organisation. If, however, people do not feel part of the organisation – if they feel that they do not share the dominant attitudes and beliefs – negative emotional consequences are likely to result.

Researchers of organisational culture suggest that it is the shared perceptions of daily practices that are at the core of organisational cultures.[57] 'The reality of everyday life is taken for granted as reality.'[58] (Organisational culture is explored in more detail in Chapter 19.)

143

In recent years greater attention has been given to the management of diversity. Reasons for this include:

- demographic changes in the workforce;
- equal employment opportunities legislation;
- programmes of affirmative action and positive discrimination;
- increasing number of women entering the workforce;
- changing social attitudes;
- a more global environment and increasing internationalisation.

However, valuing differences is easier said than done. It means relating and working with people who hold different perspectives and views, bringing different qualities to the workplace, having different aspirations and having different customs and traditions. Differences are challenging; they question people's views, perceptions and attitudes and require individuals to see things from a different frame of reference. Managing diversity does not mean that managers champion their own values and try to shift other people's values to conform and match their own!

The Chartered Management Institute provides the following definition of diversity:

The concept of diversity encompasses any sort of difference between two or more people. Differences might exist in terms of race, age, gender, disability, geographic origin, family status, education, social background – in fact, anything that can affect workplace relationships and achievement. The management of diversity involves the implementation of strategies through which a network of varied individuals are knitted together into a dynamic workforce.[63]

Dimensions of diversity Diversity embraces a wide range of characteristics unique to each individual. *Hellriegel, Slocum and Woodman* distinguish between common primary categories of diversity and secondary categories of diversity that together influence organisational behaviour.[64] The primary categories are genetic characteristics that affect a person's self-image and socialisation and over which the individual has relatively little influence.

- age
- race
- ethnicity
- gender
- physical abilities and qualities
- sexual orientation.

The secondary categories are learned characteristics that a person acquires and modifies throughout life and over which the individual has relatively more influence.

- education
- marital status
- parental status
- work experience

- religious beliefs
- personal style
- income
- geographical location.

From equal opportunities to managing diversity

The management of diversity complements and further develops initiatives on equal opportunities. Future demographic patterns present new challenges for managers. Equality Direct (part of ACAS) predicts that by the year 2010, 40 per cent of the labour force will be over 45 years of age.[65] Alterations to the identity that individuals hold have also been apparent over the last decade. Devolution and regionalisation have increased and paradoxically so too has the trend towards greater integration into multinational groupings (in terms of both company mergers and political agendas). A complex range of possible identities and affiliations results.

Consider a Scottish national living in the United States, working for a Japanese company and directing European markets: such a manager will have a diverse set of allegiances which may in turn affect motivation and morale. The growth of the portfolio worker and contract worker may result in an employment relationship that is short term, instrumental and driven by outcomes and performance. Loyalty to the organisation and commitment to mission statements do not enter into such a partnership. The rise of consumerism in and out of the workplace has led to greater understanding and expectations of 'rights' and redress of perceived injustice. It is not only morally and socially acceptable to treat all people fairly in the workplace; legislation insists that managers do so.

The government is committed to protect individuals at work against discrimination in employment on the basis of gender, disability or race. For example, under the Race Relations Amendment Act 2000 there is a positive duty on public authorities to promote racial equality in the provision of services and to improve equal opportunities in employment. One of the specific duties required by public authorities is to prepare and publish a race equality scheme and assess, monitor and control functions and policies that have a bearing on race equality. Encouraging a diverse workforce is high on the government's agenda and the reluctant employer is having their hand forced by statutory obligations. There are also new anti-discrimination laws on religion, sexual orientation and age.

Among those who believe that equal opportunities policies and training, though important, are not by themselves enough to secure the positive value of individual contributions is *Guirdham*. Only where an organisation has fully embraced diversity, trained its staff accordingly and inculcated its principles in every way will the barriers to good work communications between subgroups be lowered.

> *Some organisations 'champion' diversity, valuing the positive contribution that diverse individuals can bring, others tolerate it, merely following equal opportunities precepts, and others again treat it as a problem. These different policies and practices significantly affect the climate in which men and women, people of different ethnicities and so on conduct their work-based interactions.*[66]

THE BUSINESS CASE FOR DIVERSITY

All these changes amount to a picture in which the white, Protestant male will no longer dominate. Instead, we can anticipate a complex pattern where, ideally, individual differences will be valued and celebrated and, at the very least, equal opportunities practice will be observed. Personal qualities and characteristics that may have been downgraded, ignored or regarded as nuisance factors will be perceived as adding value. In the longer term, an effective policy on diversity should arguably eliminate the need for affirmative action or positive discrimination.

Embracing individual differences As part of the creative process within organisations, *Hill* refers to the need to embrace individual differences while pursuing collective identity and goals.

> *The creative process demands a mix of diverse individuals. For the collective to benefit from this diversity by drawing on each individual's talents there needs to be a process that allows for varied perspectives, priorities and styles. The only way these voices can be expressed and heard is to treat people fairly, which means to treat people differently … If member diversity is to be acknowledged and differences of opinion encouraged, the collective must develop a culture of trust in which members will want to support one another.*[67]

Organisations that embrace difference and diversity as opposed to those which are merely compliant will, it is claimed, succeed in a fiercely competitive climate. As J. M. Barry Gibson, (then) Chief Executive of Littlewoods, has stated:

- increasing the awareness and value of diversity;
- education in understanding the culture and values of members of a diverse workforce;
- the ability to communicate effectively with all members of staff – and also customers and suppliers;
- developing the skills of effective diversity management;
- addressing biases, prejudices and stereotypes.

Business in the Community (BITC) is one of the agencies that help businesses to embrace a culture of inclusiveness by helping them to look at the competitive case for diversity. Current activities focus on labour market discrimination, religious beliefs, sexual orientation, and general diversity and equality.[76] As another example, ACAS draws attention to managing disability and to the importance of line managers' contribution to organisational culture and managing performance. Training managers in effective people management skills and developing a culture of inclusion are crucial.[77] Attention to top management is also required. *Arkin* suggests that in company headquarters the chances are that the people will be overwhelmingly white, male, able-bodied and of a certain age. There is little joined-up thinking between activities under the diversity agenda and the nurturing of top talent.[78]

The effective management of diversity will also entail a review of organisational processes and the execution of work. For example, not everyone:

- shares the same work ethic or seeks the same goals and objectives;
- responds in the same way to working in a bureaucratic structure;
- works better in a self-managed group or with a more participative style of management;
- will fit the same psychometric profile;
- is motivated in the same way;
- reacts the same way to different forms of control.

Diversity and stereotyping Diversity also challenges many traditional stereotypes (discussed in Chapter 6). Stereotyping infers that people within a particular perceived category are assumed to share the same traits or characteristics. Stereotypes are a means of making simplified judgements of other people instead of coping with a range of individual stimuli. Stereotyping attributes to all individuals the characteristics or tendencies of the categorisation as a whole. An important feature of managing diversity is an awareness of, and training in, overcoming inaccurate stereotyped perceptions and attributions.

Managers' attitudes, values and beliefs If they are to be successful in managing diversity, managers need to have greater reserves of emotional intelligence. In turn this suggests that managers need to have an awareness of, and be able to get in touch with, their own attitudes, values and beliefs – what they are and where they come from. *Clements and Jones* recognise that the process can be uncomfortable:

> A model of good diversity training will recognize that when people engage in an exploration of their attitudes, values, beliefs and prejudices, this may be an uncomfortable process. Some will find out things about themselves that will cause them emotional pain, and often the tension in learners will relate to how they should respond.[79]

TOP PERFORMING ORGANISATIONS

An increasing number of organisations appear to recognise the business case for diversity. In the private sector, Lloyds TSB has been praised for its approach, while the Department of Trade and Industry (DTI) is among top public-sector performers.

Lloyds TSB provides strong organisational commitment to diversity. The Board and Group Executive Committee agree the diversity programme and its delivery is overseen by the Diversity Council of ten managing directors from across the group. This, coupled with a

Research conducted by *Alimo-Metcalfe* supports the view that the modern style of leadership required for organisations is one that embraces vision, individual consideration, strengthening participation and nurtures growth and self-esteem. Alimo-Metcalfe was positive that women managers were bringing with them real qualities of 'warmth, consideration for others, nurturance of self-esteem and above all, integrity'.[92] In a later article leadership is described as not about being a wonder woman (or man) but as someone who:

● values the individuality of their staff;
● encourages individuals to challenge the status quo;
● possesses integrity and humility.

Alimo-Metcalfe claims that myths of leadership are dangerous because they suggest that leadership is rare, found mainly at the top of organisations and is about being superhuman.[93] This, she claims, distinguishes her study from those from the USA that tend to focus on 'distant leaders'. The characteristics of the distant leader may be different to those valued in 'nearby leaders – the immediate line manager'. Although vision, charisma, courage are qualities that are ascribed to the distant leader, subordinates seek qualities in their nearby leader such as being sociable, open and considerate. These were rated more highly in the research and it was found that women scored higher than men in 11 out of the 14 characteristics.

A push to maintaining status quo: male as leader The interest in 'New Leadership' research and transformational leadership in particular has focused on 'heroes' and the nature of charisma. Many studies have focused on public figures, notably men. *Goffee and Jones* claim that inspirational leaders share four unexpected qualities:

● they selectively show their weaknesses;
● they rely heavily on intuition to gauge the appropriate timing and course of their actions;
● they manage employees with tough empathy;
● they reveal their differences; they capitalise on what is unique about them.

However, Goffee and Jones suggest that gender differences can lead to stereotyping and to a double bind situation. They suggest that women may opt to 'play into' their stereotype and make themselves invisible 'by being more like the men' or deliberately play the role of nurturer or set themselves apart by campaigning for rights in the workplace. Whichever route is chosen, females are playing into a negative stereotype. Goffee and Jones ask the question: 'Can female leaders be true to themselves?'[94]

POSITIVE APPROACHES

Reviews and articles explaining the position and status of women typically conclude with exhortations to organisations to introduce and promote schemes that would positively help and support women. The logic of introducing such schemes is based on good business sense in that women represent an untapped human resource. There has been considerable media hype about the progress of women at work and yet this is not revealed in the latest statistics. Improving the 'lot' of women can also provoke resentment from men.

Perhaps the most positive approach to take is for an organisation to acknowledge the changing working pattern of all employees and to consider the best working practices for managing a diverse workforce as a whole. This should not be done mechanically but by analysis of the organisation and its workforce. Organisations need to analyse, consciously debate and question their unwritten assumptions and expectations in order to reveal prejudices inherent in the culture of their organisations. Analysis of the way in which culture is expressed in all its trivial detail would lead to an understanding of perceptions and attitudes. Until a full analysis is completed it remains doubtful whether more egalitarian practices will develop.

A number of agencies see work/life balance as key to equality for women and men. Equality Direct's appeal is to the 'bottom line':

Businesses prosper if they make the best use of their most valuable resource: the ability and skills of their people. And these people, in turn, will flourish if they can strike a proper balance between work and the rest of their lives.[95]

The new focus on equality has moved from one that is focusing only on women's needs to one of inclusiveness. It is a compelling idea as it avoids the difficulties of hostility and resentment potentially caused by the selective focus on women's needs. Rather than being a 'women's issue' it suggests that gender should be 'mainstreamed'; it should be a core practice of the business. The Equal Opportunites Commission identifies that mainstreaming requires rethinking the traditional roles of men and women in society:

Simply, the gender mainstreaming approach means challenging our assumptions and stereotypes about men and women, and their roles in society and the economy. It means making evidence-based policy. This is simply good sense. Well-targeted policy which takes account of the different ways men and women may organise their time, or relate to goods and services, means better use of resources and better outcomes in terms of achieving policy objectives. In the process social and economic inequalities will be challenged.[96]

Approaches to gender equality: a comparison

A study conducted in Australia explored the link between different EO policies and the number of women in management positions. This identified four types of approaches:

- classical disparity – equal treatment practised but gendered roles assumed;
- anti-discrimination – equal outcomes encouraged;
- affirmative action – assistance for disadvantaged groups and specific actions taken (women's groups/networks/mentoring programme for women, formal mechanisms exist with women);
- gender diversity – compensate for disadvantages through a change in culture and organisational systems – flexible systems encouraged – but specific treatment for one group discouraged, for example job sharing, part-time work.

The study found that those organisations that took an **affirmative action** approach had significantly higher numbers of women in all management tiers. Organisations classified as gender diverse did not see such significant increases. *French* states: 'One possible explanation as to why this might be involves the fact that broad application of diversity strategies results in limited practical outcomes. That is, in trying to do everything, nothing substantive is achieved. Another explanation is that the diversity approach to substantive equity may take up to 25 years because of the slow pace of cultural and structural change without the use of direct affirmative action strategies.'[97]

There still seems to be some way to go before flexible working practices become part of our 'normal way of life'. In reality it would seem that the political and cultural nature of the organisation is a major factor in choosing working practices. It appears there is a stigma

IBM – united by diversity

When IBM decided men and women should be paid equally for doing the same job, and should have equal responsibilities and career opportunities, it made headline news. Not surprisingly – it was in 1935. This early recognition of the importance of an inclusive workplace laid the foundation for today's focus on diversity, where every employee is encouraged to perform at their best, and where different opinions are both welcomed and appreciated.

IBM Corporation[98]

attached to employees who choose to work part-time and people fear if they choose to work at home they may miss promotion opportunities. So, even if the opportunities are open to all, in reality the political and cultural nature of the organisation prevents career-hungry individuals from choosing such options. (Cultural processes in organisations are discussed more fully in Chapter 19.)

Refresh your understanding

Activity 4E

www.pearsoned.co.uk/ mullins

Critical reflection

We know that every person is an individual in their own right, but many theories and models of organisational behaviour still appear to apply to people in general. What do you believe is the value of these theories or models? Rather than looking at similarities among people, should we be more concerned with the study of differences among individuals?

MANAGEMENT IN THE NEWS

Women on the board

Norway shatters the glass ceiling – but will it promote women's cause?

Susie Mesure

First Norway, now France. The long arm of the law is feeling its way into boardrooms across Europe as governments come to the rescue of women denied senior company roles because of their sex. Norway is two months into a new regime that could see public companies broken up for failing to hit government-imposed quotas for the number of females on their boards by the end of next year. Women must hold 40 per cent of boardroom positions in groups listed on the Oslo bourse by the end of 2007 or the company will have to delist. Last month, the French government took a similar step to improve the lot of the country's businesswomen by imposing a similar 20 per cent target by 2011. Meanwhile, Spanish politicians are working on a draft bill to ban sex discrimination at work. The sound of glass ceilings cracking is echoing across the Continent.

This noise is resonating badly in Norwegian business circles. The Confederation of Norwegian Enterprise (NHO) estimates Norway's 500 listed blue chips will have to conjure up 600 women to meet the designated quotas. A recent survey of company bosses found a majority felt there was already lack of suitable candidates. The legislative upheaval continues a long tradition of gender equality in Norway, which has a population of 4.5 million. One-third of its MPs are women, as are nine of its 19 cabinet ministers.

So where does this leave Britain? This year we have had a warning from the Equal Opportunities

Veuve Clicquot Business Woman of the Year 2006, Vivienne Cox, has made it to the boardroom of FTSE 100 company BP. Should governments set quotas to help other woman get to the top?

Source: Veuve Clicquot Award

Management in the news – continued

Commission that it will take 40 years for women to have the same sway in FTSE 100 companies as men. The Fawcett Society, which campaigns for greater opportunities for women, has predicted it will take twice as long – 80 years – for women to close the full-time pay gap with men. Is legislation the answer?

Ffion Hague, the wife of the former Conservative leader who works for the recruitment consultancy Hanson Green, said: 'I wouldn't go down that [the legislative] route because we haven't lost the argument yet for appointment on merit. We've got a great pool of potential women candidates if people just stop the lazy tendency of looking at the same circle of people for their appointments.'

One solution that is reaping rewards is a mentoring scheme that seeks to bypass the traditional 'old boys' networks' that still dominate City life. The scheme seeks to create a bond between the predominantly male bosses at the top of FTSE 100 companies and women holding lesser roles in other blue-chip firms. HSBC, Astra Zeneca and Scottish Power are among those that have signed up. While the statistics may look depressing – only 11 per cent of FTSE 100 company directors are women – many high-flying female executives see chinks of light. Once ensconced in the workplace, companies are making it easier for women to leave when nature calls – and, crucially, to

return. Lehman Brothers, the US investment bank, is among those firms keen to ease new mums back into more senior roles than have traditionally been on offer after maternity leave is up.

Britain is a long way off following Norway's legislative example. As Peninah Thomson, the co-author of *A Woman's Place is in the Boardroom*, with Jacey Graham, puts it: 'The combination of Government exhortation and the example set by our captains of industry in the FTSE 100 is proving to be an efficient stimulus for change. We don't need the heavy hand of the State intervening.'

Source: Mesure, S. 'Norway shatters the glass ceiling – but will it promote women's cause?' *The Independent*, 8 March 2006. Copyright © 2006 Independent News and Media Limited, reproduced with permission.

Discussion questions

1 Discuss critically the extent to which the legislative approach described here assumes that men and women are similar or different in what they want from work.

2 What are the arguments for and against quota setting of the sort described here? You might like to consider two main types of argument: the ethical and the practical ones.

SYNOPSIS

● One of the essential requirements of organisations is the development and encouragement of individuality within a work atmosphere in which common goals and aims are achieved. A distinguishing factor of successful managers is their ability to bring out the best in the people who work with and report to them, and to emphasise individual differences and value diversity. Managing relationships well depends on an understanding and awareness of the staff and of their talents, abilities, interests and motives. It is also dependent upon effective social skills and emotional intelligence.

● Recognising and improving individual talent and potential is critical to ensure that the many roles and functions of an organisation are achieved effectively. However, differences between individuals can also be the source of problems and conflict. Personality clashes may occur; differences of attitudes and values may lead to polarisation and discrimination. Although psycholo-

gists do not agree in terms of the relative importance of certain factors, there is much to be gained from both nomothetic and idiographic approaches.

● A major influencing factor affecting work performance is the ability of the employee. Different occupations require different skills, competencies and abilities. Arguments rage over the nature of intelligence and the extent to which it is inherited. Ensuring that the right people are selected for work and are able to use their intelligence effectively is a critical human resource process, now helped by the appropriate use of psychological tests. However, tests are not a panacea and can, if used inappropriately, lead to a sense of false security.

● There are no limits to the attitudes people hold. Attitudes and motives are interlinked and serve a number of important functions. Assessment of attitudes is vital in selecting potential employees and future managers. Given the difficulties of attitude

measurement and doubts associated with predicting behaviour, such assessment is fraught with problems. Attitudes can take on a permanency that is maintained by the culture of the organisation and thus be very resistant to change. Moreover, the power of attitudes should be recognised, particularly with regard to influencing newer members of the organisation and their development.

● An integral and essential feature of individual differences is the concept of diversity. People are not homogeneous and diversity embraces a wide range of characteristics unique to each individual. However, valuing differences is easier said than done. The management of diversity complements and further develops initiatives on equal opportunities. The focus is on the multiplicity of differences among people. An increasing number of organisations appear to recognise the business case for diversity as part of the creative process.

● An understanding of diversity demands a work climate that respects individual differences and treats all members of staff with dignity and mutual respect. Diversity challenges many traditional stereotypes and organisations need to manage diversity in a manner that benefits the well-being of all members of staff. One of the most significant aspects of managing diversity is that of gender equality and the participation of men and women in the workforce. Despite the potential benefits from managing diversity, there are a number of potential criticisms and perceived limitations.

 Refresh your understanding, assess your progress and begin your research with online resources at **www.pearsoned.co.uk/mullins**

REVIEW AND DISCUSSION QUESTIONS

1 What do you see as the main issues relating to the effective management of relationships at work?

2 Discuss the major ways in which individual differences are demonstrated at work.

3 You are required to interview one person from your work or study group to produce an assessment of their personality. What questions will you ask and how accurate do you feel your assessment will be?

4 Why are attitudes difficult to measure and change? Design a simple questionnaire to administer to your colleagues on attitudes towards stress at work.

5 To what extent do you see a clear differentiation between equal opportunities and the effective management of diversity?

6 Discuss critically the contention that too much attention is given to the advantages for business from the management of diversity rather than to broader moral or social issues.

7 How would you plan and implement a training programme intended to overcome inaccurate stereotyped perceptions and attributes?

8 Prepare a discussion document on organisational behaviour, gender and experiences at work.

ASSIGNMENT

Constructing your own Repertory Grid

At the top of each column write in the name of a significant person, starting with yourself, then mother, father, spouse, boyfriend, girlfriend, best friend.

We've put some suggested headings here, but you can add your own. It's up to you how many you include.

Assignment – continued

Row	Self	Mother	Father Spouse/partner	Brother/sister	Ex boy/girl friend	Rejecting person	Threatening person	Constructs
1	O	O	X	O	X	O	X	Shy (x) vs outgoing (o)
2								
3								
4								
5								
6								

Then take three people from the grid and decide in what way two of them differ from the third. For example, perhaps you think that you and your father are shy, while your mother isn't. This is your first *construct*. Write this in the column on the right. Ignore the crosses at the moment.

Choose another combination of three people and do the same again. Put the second construct in the next row below the first.

You can carry on with as many combinations as you want to, but here are some suggestions for relationships which psychologists using Kelly's methods in the past have found particularly useful. It's up to you how many constructs you want to find, but six is a good number to start with. These constructs show you the categories you use to look at the world.

You can stop here, but if you want to take it a step further, start on the left side of the chart with construct 1 and decide whether the left-hand side of the construct describes each person, e.g. is each person shy or not – put crosses for yes and circles for no.

When you've rated everyone for each construct, you can look and see where the ticks match up. The table above helps you to do this. Look at rows 1 and 2 first of all and count the number of times a cross appears in both rows for one person and the number of times a circle appears in both rows for one person. Add these numbers together and this gives you your number of matches to put in the chart. Then do this for all the matches listed and see which has the biggest number. For example, if rows 2 and 6 have the highest number of matches, then the people who could be described by the adjective in construct 2 are, in your view, also described by the adjective in construct 6. So in your view of the world these two constructs are related. This could be because they're similar adjectives, for example you'd expect everyone who was rated as kind to be rated as generous, but sometimes the results can be surprising, showing that you view the world in a slightly different way from the way you'd thought.

We'd be interested to know what constructs you came up with and whether there were any surprises. You can email the programme to: allinthemind@bbc.co.uk

Source: From *All in the Mind*, BBC Radio 4 website (www.bbc.co.uk/radio4/science/allinthemind_20021009.shtnl).

PERSONAL AWARENESS AND SKILLS EXERCISE

Objective

Completing this exercise should help you to enhance the following skills:

- Explore the meaning, dimensions and impact of diversity.
- Develop greater empathy towards other people.
- Reflect on your attitudes and behaviours towards individual differences.

Exercise

For each of the following ten statements you are required to indicate *honestly and fully* the extent to which you:

1 Believe in managing diversity for moral and social reasons.

2 Are happy mixing with people from different cultures.

3 Resist stereotyping or profiling individuals into general categories of people.

4 Show patience and understanding when dealing with people whose English language is limited.

5 Accept that positive discrimination can sometimes be fully justified.

6 View diversity as distinctly different from political correctness.

7 Enjoy learning about different cultures and values.

8 Believe that diversity enriches the working lives of all employees.

9 Feel comfortable working closely with a colleague who has a different sexual orientation.

10 Are prepared to take orders from someone much younger or much older than yourself, or from the opposite gender.

Discussion

After completing the questionnaire, pair with a colleague – where possible with a different ethnicity, culture, gender or age group – and compare and discuss critically both sets of responses.

- What does this exercise say about your awareness of, and adaptability, to diversity?
- To what extent were you surprised by the responses or comments from your colleague?
- What conclusions have you drawn from this exercise?

CASE STUDY

B&Q: the business case for diversity

B&Q is the UK's largest do-it-yourself chain of stores, selling materials and equipment for the home improvement and domestic gardening market. The founders, Richard Block and David Quayle, opened their first store in Southampton in 1969; after nearly 20 years of growth the company was acquired by FW Woolworth and is presently part of the Kingfisher Group. Kingfisher also owns the Brico, Castorama and Hornbach DIY stores which give it significant market presence in France, Spain, Italy, Poland and Russia. B&Q presently has stores throughout the UK and in Ireland, and its headquarters remain in Hampshire.

The business has always sourced some of its products from Chinese manufacturers (China is now the largest source of its DIY products) and so had strong links in the Far East from the outset. These links have helped the company to expand its sales business into the Far East, and in 1996 it opened a store in Taiwan. In 1999 it moved into mainland China with an outlet in Shanghai and is now well established in the Chinese market with six stores, including its largest, B&Q Beijing, which also sells furniture and furnishing materials. The nature of the Chinese property market has also made it viable for the company to offer a fitting and decorating service for

customers moving into newly built apartments, thereby expanding its business opportunities through a strategy of vertical integration.

In 2006 it employed over 38,000 people in more than 300 stores across the UK. However, in March 2006 the company reported a 50.4 per cent drop in pre-tax profits in the UK for the year ending 28 January 2006, largely as the result of a significant downturn in consumer spending on DIY during 2005.[99]

B&Q and the 'demographic time bomb'

As we noted at the start of this chapter, the UK population is ageing and the impact of this so-called 'demographic time bomb' began to generate particular concerns during the late 1980s. Some businesses, like B&Q, took a critical look at their employment practices as a result of predicted shortages in certain parts of the labour market and the consequent fear of intensified competition between employers for younger workers. This was particularly important for a growing company like B&Q, which might find its expansion plans seriously harmed by labour shortages. In 1989, therefore, B&Q management reviewed its workforce and noted that not only did it have a predominantly young age profile (the majority of staff were aged 16–26) but that staff turnover costs were particularly high in the 18–20-year-old category. They also noted positive customer feedback about their older staff, who appeared to deliver better customer service, partly because of their knowledge of DIY.

The company management decided to tackle the problem by challenging widely held views about the disadvantages and problems of employing older workers. Initially, the B&Q Board expressed some concerns about the proposal to target older people in the labour market and were naturally cautious about unproven claims of their effectiveness. 'In 1990 it seemed to make good common sense to employ older people but a number of stereotypes and issues were raised. Answers were needed to explode these myths.'[100]

The concerns and myths about older workers reflected findings in other studies on the subject such as that reported in 1993 to the Institute of Personnel Management (now the CIPD).[101] These included both positive and negative features; for instance, older workers were seen as more reliable, loyal, conscientious and hard working than younger ones; at the same time they were viewed as less adaptable, especially to new technology, as well as being less able and less motivated to learn or be trained. Other studies have shown that stereotypical views about older workers tend to cluster under general headings of poor performance (including those related to assumptions about age-related physical impairment), absenteeism and turnover.[102] There were also concerns about the relationship between younger and older workers and particularly those between young managers and older staff members.

Source: George Sweeney/Rex Features

Is diversity in the workplace simply political correctness? B&Q recognised the value of diversity after a new store staffed by over-50s outperformed its other stores.

So B&Q managers decided that it would be important to collect some hard evidence if they were to gain the backing of the business owners. In 1990 they opened a new store in Macclesfield, staffed wholly by workers over 50. The experiment was monitored by a research team from Warwick University, who carried out a study to benchmark the Macclesfield store's performance against a selection of four similar stores during its first year of operation. The results were significant – the Warwick team reported that the Macclesfield store had higher profits, substantially reduced staff turnover, over a third less absenteeism and almost two-thirds less 'shrinkage' (loss to stock as the result of damage or pilfering by staff and customers).[103] Many of the Board's concerns had clearly been put to rest; the business case for diversifying the workforce had been supported by the evidence. B&Q therefore began to adopt a positive approach towards the recruitment and employment of an age-diverse workforce. This was more than ten years before legislation on the subject came into operation in the UK. Further research in 1995 confirmed the initial results, leading the company to reaffirm its commitment to increasing the age diversity of its workforce. There were clear indications that the policy was about good business in all senses of the word. In 2000 the company became one of the founding members of the Employers Forum on Age (EFA),[104] an independent group of over 200 UK employers that sets out to campaign for and support the cause of employing an age-diverse workforce.

Diversity at B&Q: the growing agenda

Having been successful with its approach to employing the over 50s, B&Q also recognises the value of a broader approach to diversity. The company website includes

substantial information about its current approach to social responsibility, including respect for the diversity of people:

> We believe that a diverse workforce creates a mix of talents that makes us a successful business. We want B&Q to be a 'great place to work and shop'. It is our policy to implement procedures to eliminate discrimination and promote equality of opportunity in employment so that age, gender, colour, ethnic or national origin, culture, religion, disability, marital status, political affiliation or sexual orientation are not barriers for anybody who wants to work and shop at B&Q.[105]

B&Q's Diversity Manager reports directly to the company Chief Executive, and the Board now takes an active interest in the diversity strategy. Today, this strategy includes a strong commitment to cultural diversity and to people with disabilities. The company seeks to reflects all this in its advertising and publicity material as well as its personnel and management policies, thus making diversity an important part of the business's brand values and public image.

The disability policy was formulated in 1998 and, like the age policy, it links the importance of understanding and integrating disability issues into the business strategy. The twin goals are to remove barriers that make working and shopping at B&Q difficult for disabled people. Similarly, the cultural diversity strategy at B&Q goes beyond simple compliance measures to ensure that the company does not breach the law. In 2001 the company discovered that over 1,000 of its staff were bilingual and that between them they spoke over 60 languages other than English, including British Sign Language. Staff are actively encouraged to use languages other than English where this can help to understand and respond to customer needs and many wear language badges to indicate this. The company produces a cultural diversity information pack for use in stores, together with a calendar of religious and cultural festivals which not only helps staff to understand customers but assists managers with work scheduling.

What next for B&Q?

As noted above, B&Q in the UK suffered a significant setback during 2005 which has caused it to review its business strategy. With profits falling in its retail business, the Chief Executive announced in March 2006 that it would begin a push to offer more services such as painting and decorating (it already installs kitchens and bathrooms), in a move which mirrors the vertical integration strategy it has adopted in China. The stumbling block to this development is a UK skills shortage, which the company is proposing to solve by looking east to Poland, with the aim of recruiting large numbers of painters and decorators who would be able to work in the UK.[106]

Your tasks

1 Why did B&Q adopt its present approach to diversity? How far do you agree or disagree with these reasons for its action and why?

2 Review B&Q's approach in the light of theories about personality. Which of the theoretical approaches do you think might best explain the company's approach to its staff and customers?

3 How might the B&Q approach to diversity encourage individuals (both staff and customers) to contribute to the organisation's performance?

4 B&Q operates in a very specific sector: retail DIY building and gardening materials and equipment. Would its approach to diversity translate to other types of organisation, for example an online or telephone retail insurance company (for example, selling for motor, travel or home insurance), a carmaker, or a state-run school or hospital?

Main sources

B&Q company website – http://www.diy.com. You can read about its diversity policies in the 'About Us' and 'Social Responsibility' sections.

The Employers Forum on Age (EFA): – http://www.efa.org.uk – is an independent group of over 200 UK employers, including many major companies, which sets out to campaign for and support the cause of employing an age-diverse workforce.

Kingfisher Group – http://www.kingfisher.co.uk

BBC News: website – http://news.bbc.co.uk

Age Positive; website address http://www.agepositive.gov.uk – Government team within the Department for Work and Pensions which is responsible for promoting the cause of the employment of older people in the labour market. Information about the campaign, together with a number of case studies including that of B&Q, can be found on the website.

Department of Trade and Industry – http://www.dti.gov.uk – is responsible for disseminating details about the Employment Equality (Age) Regulations which came into force on 1 October 2006. Full details of the regulations, together with reports based on consultation exercises in the run-up to October 2006, can be accessed here.

Notes and references

1 Social Trends 36, 2006 edition http://www.statistics.gov.uk.

2 Turner, B. *Exploring the Industrial Sub-culture*, Macmillan (1977).

3 Salaman, G. 'Organisations as Constructions of Social Reality', in Salaman, G. and Thompson, K. (eds) *Control and Ideology in Organisations*, MIT Press (1983).

4 Video 'Management Revolution and Corporate Reinvention', BBC for Business (1993).

5 McCrae, R. R. and Costa, P. T. 'More Reasons to Adopt the Five-Factor Model', *American Psychologist*, vol. 44, no. 2, 1989, pp. 451–2.

6 Bayne, R. 'The Big Five versus the Myers-Briggs', *The Psychologist*, January 1994, pp. 14–17.

7 Lord, W. and Rust, J. 'The Big Five Revisited: Where are we now? A brief review of the relevance of the Big Five for Occupational Assessment', *Selection and Development Review*, vol. 19, no. 4, August 2003, pp. 15–18.

8 Mount, M. K., Barrick, M. R. and Strauss, J. P. 'Validity of Observer Ratings of the Big Five Personality Factors', *Journal of Applied Psychology*, April 1994, p. 272.

9 Bentall, R. P. 'Personality Traits May Be Alive, They May Even Be Well, but Are They Really Useful?', *The Psychologist*, July 1993, p. 307.

10 Eysenck, H. J. *Eysenck on Extroversion*, Crosby, Lockwood Staples (1973).

11 Mabey, B. 'The Majority of Large Companies Use Occupational Tests', *Guidance and Assessment Review*, vol. 5, no. 3, 1989.

12 Personality tests have been debated by: Bartram, D. 'Addressing the Abuse of Personality Tests', *Personnel Management*, April 1991, pp. 34–9; and Fletcher, C. 'Personality Tests: The Great Debate', *Personnel Management*, September 1991, pp. 38–42.

13 Howarth, E. 'A Source of Independent Variation: Convergence and Divergence in the Work of Cattell and Eysenck', in Dreger, R. M. (ed.) *Multivariate Personality Research*, Claiton (1972).

14 Rogers, C. *A Way of Being*, Houghton Mifflin (1980).

15 Cooley, C. 'The Social Self', in Parsons, T., Shils, E., Naegele, K. D. and Pitts, J. R. (eds) *Theories of Society*, The Free Press, New York (1965).

16 Erikson, E. H. *Identity and Life Cycle*, Norton (1980).

17 Hunt, J. W. *Managing People at Work: A Manager's Guide to Behaviour in Organisations*, Third edition, McGraw-Hill (1992).

18 Jung, C. G. *Analytical Psychology: Its Theory and Practice*, Routledge and Kegan Paul (1968). See also: Jacobi, J. *Psychology of C. G. Jung*, Seventh edition, Routledge and Kegan Paul (1968).

19 Myers, Isabel Briggs *Introduction to Type*, Sixth edition, Consulting Psychologists Press (2000); and Myers, K. D. and Kirby, L. K. *Introduction to Type Dynamics and Development*, Second edition, Consulting Psychologists Press (2000).

20 Hirsh, S. K. and Kise, J. *Introduction to Type and Coaching a Dynamic Guide for Individual Development*, Consulting Psychologists Press Inc (1994).

21 Kelly's theory as described by Bannister, D. and Fansella, F., in *Inquiring Mind: The Theory of Personal Constructs*, Penguin (1971), pp. 50–1.

22 Stone, G. 'Personality and Effective Hospitality Management', Paper presented at the International Association of Hotel Management Schools Symposium, Leeds Polytechnic, Autumn 1988; and Worsfold, P. A. 'Personality Profile of the Hotel Manager', *International Journal of Hospitality Management*, vol. 8, no. 1, 1989, pp. 55–62.

23 Bartram, D. 'Addressing the Abuse of Psychological Tests', *Personnel Management*, April 1991, pp. 34–9; Newell, S. and Shackleton, V. 'Management Selection: A Comparative Survey of Methods Used in Top British and French Companies', *Journal of Occupational Psychology*, vol. 64, 1991, p. 23.

24 Kline, P. 'The Big Five and Beyond', Conference Paper given at the British Psychological Society Occupational Psychology Conference, University of Warwick, January 1995.

25 Anastasi, A. *Psychological Testing*, Macmillan (1988), p. 560.

26 Blinkhorn, S. and Johnson, C. 'The Insignificance of Personality Testing', *Nature*, 348, 1990, pp. 671–2.

27 Goss, D. *Principles of Human Resource Management*, Routledge (1994).

28 Gibbons, P., Baron, H., Nyfield, G. and Robertson, I. 'The Managerial Performance and Competences', Conference Paper given at the British Psychological Society Occupational Psychology Conference, University of Warwick, January 1995.

29 Platt, S. with Piepe, R. and Smythe, J. *'Teams': A Game to Develop Group Skills*, Gower (1988).

30 Gray, M. J. 'Personality and Performance', *Selection and Development Review*, vol. 19, no. 1, February 2003, p. 4.

31 Hochschild, A.R. *The Managed Heart: Commericialization of Human Feeling*, University of California Press (1983).

32 Friedman, M and Rosenman, R. *Type A Behavior and Your Heart*, Knopf (1974).

33 Rosenmann, R., Friedman, F. and Straus, R. 'A Predictive Study of CHD', *Journal of the American Medical Association*, vol. 89, 1964, pp. 15–22; and in Warr, P. and Wall, T. *Work and Well Being*, Penguin (1975).

34 Cooper, C. 'Papering over the cracks: individual strategies or organizational intervention in dealing with stress at work', Conference paper given at the British Psychological Society Occupational Psychology conference, University of Warwick, January 1995.

35 http://www.equalitydirect.org.uk. Accessed 3 September 2003.

36 Howe, M. J. A. 'Can IQ Change?', *The Psychologist*, February 1998, pp. 69–72.

37 Spearman, C. *The Abilities of Man*, Macmillan (1927).

38 Vernon, P. E. 'The Hierarchy of Abilities', in Wiseman, S. (ed.) *Intelligence and Ability*, Second edition, Penguin (1973).

39 Thurstone, L. L. 'Primary Mental Abilities', *Psychometric Monographs*, no. 1, 1938.

40 Guilford, J. P. 'Three Faces of Intellect', in Wiseman, S. (ed.) *Intelligence and Ability*, Penguin (1959).

41 Gardner, H. *Frames of Mind*, Second edition, Fontana (1993).

42 Goleman, D. *Emotional Intelligence*, Bloomsbury (1996), p. 34.

43 Goleman, D. *Working with Emotional Intelligence*, Bantam Books, New York (1998).

44 Boyatzis, R., Goleman, D. and Hay/McBer, *Emotional Competence Inventory Feedback Report*, Hay Group (1999).

45 Freely, M. 'Love one another is the first lesson', *The Observer*, Sunday 31 August 2003.

46 Anastasia, A. *Psychological Testing*, Macmillan Publishing (1988), p. 23.

47 Jackson, C. *Understanding Psychological Testing*, BPS Books (1996).

48 Feltham, R., Baron, H. and Smith, P. 'Developing Fair Tests', *The Psychologist*, January 1994, pp. 23–5.

49 Inman, M. *Participants' Perceptions of Assessment Centres*, Unpublished MSc Personnel Management dissertation, University of Portsmouth (1996).

50 Ribeaux, P. and Poppleton, S. E. *Psychology and Work*, Macmillan (1978).

51 Gross, R. D. *Psychology: The Science of Mind and Behaviour*, Edward Arnold (1987).

52 Hofstede, G. *Culture's Consequences: International Differences in Work-Related Values*, Sage (1980).

53 Katz, D. 'The Functional Approach to the Study of Attitudes', *Public Opinion Quarterly*, Issue 21, 1960, pp. 163–204.

54 La Piere, R. T. 'Attitudes versus Action', *Social Forces*, Issue 13, 1934, pp. 230–7.

55 Gidoomal, R., Mahtani, D. and Porter, D. *The British and How to Deal With Them*, Middlesex University Press (2001).

56 Sykes, A. J. M. 'The Effect of a Supervisory Training Course in Changing Supervisors' Perceptions and Expectations of the Role of Management', *Human Relations*, 15, 1962, pp. 227–43.

57 Hofstede, G., Nevijan, B., Dhayu, D. D. and Sanders, G. 'Measuring Organisational Cultures: a qualitative and quantitative study across 20 cases', *Administrative Science Quarterly*, vol. 35, 1990, pp. 286–316.

58 Berger, P. L. and Luckmann, T. *The Social Construction of Reality*, Penguin (1966) p. 37.

59 MacPherson, Sir William *The Stephen Lawrence Inquiry*, The Stationery Office, February 1999.

60 Heider, F. 'Attitudes and Cognitive Organization', *Journal of Psychology*, vol. 21, 1946, pp. 107–12.

61 Festinger, L. A. *A Theory of Cognitive Dissonance*, Row, Peterson and Co. (1957); Reissued by Stanford University Press and Tavistock Publications (1962).

62 Kandola, R. and Fullerton, J. *Managing the Mosaic Diversity in Action*, IPD (1994), p. 19.

63 'Implementing a Diversity Management Programme' Checklist 152, Chartered Management Institute, July 2005.

64 Hellriegel, D., Slocum, J. W. and Woodman, R. W. *Organizational Behavior*, Ninth edition (2001).

65 Equality direct can be found at http://equalitydirect.org.uk.

66 Guirdham, M. *Interactive Behaviour at Work*, Third edition, Financial Times Prentice Hall (2002), p. 67.

67 Hill, L. A. 'Leadership As Collective Genius', in Chowdhury, S. *Management 21C*, Financial Times Prentice Hall (2000), p. 53.

68 'Littlewoods: Increasing diversity, Increasing profits' *Equal Opportunities Review*, no. 81, September/October 1998, pp. 20–7.

69 Nordström, K. and Ridderstråle, J, 'Funky Inc.,' in Crainer, S. and Dearlove, D. (eds), *Financial Times Handbook of Management*, Second edition, Financial Times Prentice Hall, (2001), p. 63.

70 Kirton, G. and Greene, A-M. *The Dynamics of Managing Diversity*, Butterworth Heinemann (2000).

71 Liff, S. and Cameron, I. 'Changing Equality Cultures to Move Beyond Women's Problems', *Gender, Work and Organization*, vol. 4, no. 1, January 1997, pp. 35–46.

72 'Managing Diversity: Linking Theory and Practice to Business Performance' CIPD, May 2005.

73 'Building Better Boards', DTI, December 2004.

74 Reproduced with permission of the Copyright Department, ONS.

75 http://hiltonworldwide.hilton.com. Accessed 1 March 2006.

76 Information on BITC can be found at http://www.bitc.org.uk.

77 'Managing Diversity' *Employment Relations Matters*, ACAS, Issue 3, Spring 2005.

78 Arkin, A. 'Hidden Talents' *People Management*, vol. 11, no. 14, 14 July 2005, p.26.

79 Clements, P. and Jones, J. *The Diversity Training Handbook*, Kogan Page (2002), p. 45.

80 Information kindly provided by the Equality and Diversity Team at Lloyds TSB.

81 'Public Sector: Diversity', *Personnel Today*, 8 March 2005, p. 32.

82 Francesco, A. M. and Gold, B. A. *International Organizational Behavior*, Prentice Hall (1998), p. 236.

83 'Implementing a Diversity Management Programme' Checklist 152, Chartered Management Institute, July 2005.

84 Opportunity Now awards 2003, Opportunity Now London. Can also be accessed http://www.opportunitynow.org.uk.

85 Liff, S. and Cameron, I. 'Changing Equality Cultures to Move Beyond Women's Problems', *Gender, Work and Organization*, vol. 4, no. 1, January 1997, pp. 35–46.

86 'Setting up an EU institute for gender equality', *Social Agenda*, The European Commission's magazine on employment and social affairs, Issue 11, May 2005.

87 'Tackling demographic change', *Social Agenda*, Issue 12, The European Commission, October 2005.

88 Alvesson, Mats and Due Billing, Yvonne *Understanding Gender and Organization*, Sage Publications (1997).

89 Ibid.

90 Walsh, J. 'Myths and counter-myths: an analysis of part-time female employees and their orientation to work and working hours', *Work, Employment and Society*, vol. 3, no. 2, June 1999, pp. 179–204.

91 Alvesson, Mats and Due Billing, Yvonne *Understanding Gender and Organization*, Sage Publications (1997).

92 Alimo-Metcalfe, Beverley 'Leadership and assessment', in Susan Vinnicombe and Nina L. Colwill (eds) *The Essence of Women in Management*, Prentice Hall (1995).

93 Alimo-Metcalfe, Beverley and Alban-Metcalfe, John, ' The Great and the Good', *People Management*, no. 10, January 2002.

94 Goffee, R. and Jones, G. 'Why Should Anyone be Led by You?' *Harvard Business Review*, September–October 2000, pp. 62–70.

95 http://www.equalitydirect.org.uk.

96 EOC Examples of mainstreaming in practice, http://www.eoc.org.uk/EOCeng/EOCcs/Accessed 5 September 2003.

97 French, E. 'Approaches to Equity Management and their Relationship to Women in Management', *British Journal of Management*, vol. 12, 2001, pp. 267–85.

98 'IBM IN THE UK 2005, IBM Corporation, 2005, p. 41.

99 Rigby, L. *B&Q weighs down Kingfisher*, The Financial Times 22 March 2006.

100 B&Q Is *Age a Barrier to Employment? Equality and Diversity; Achieving a Balanced Workforce* available in pdf format from the B&Q website, www.diy.co.uk and accessed 25 March 2006.

101 Warr, P. and Pennington, J. *Views about Age Discrimination and Older Workers*, Institute of Personnel Management (1993).

102 Stoney. C. and Roberts, M 2003 *The case for the older worker at Tesco: An examination of attitudes, assumptions and attributes*. Carleton University School of Public Policy and Administration Working Paper No. 53. available in pdf format from the Internet at www.carleton.ca/spa/Publication

103 B&Q Is *Age a Barrier to Employment? Equality and Diversity; Achieving a Balanced Workforce* available in pdf format from the B&Q website, www.diy.co.uk [accessed 25 March 2006].

104 The Employers Forum on Age can be found at www.efa.org.uk

105 B&Q Statement of Social Responsibility, www.diy.com [accessed 25 March 2006].

106 Wallop, H. *B&Q may bring over thousands of Poles* The Daily Telegraph on-line www.telegraph.co.uk 25 March 2006.

THE NATURE OF LEARNING

Linda Carter

Learning is part of the human condition and is a familiar process to us all. Managers must continually develop their skills to cope with the changing and growing demands of the market place. Technologies have not only impacted upon the way that businesses work but have opened up new ways of accessing, retrieving and sharing knowledge. To be effective leaders need to be able to manage the complexity and paradoxes implicit in organisational life. They need to develop their personal awareness of who they are and the values they hold, and how they align their personal development aspirations with organisational goals.

Learning outcomes

After completing this chapter you should be able to:

- explain the significance of learning in organisational behaviour and in managing others;
- outline and critically discuss knowledge management and the impact new technologies are having on learning and development;
- define the learning organisation and evaluate the difficulties associated with the term;
- develop understanding about individual differences and how people learn, including classical theories of learning and action enquiry approaches;
- apply learning to self-development and the development of others;
- assess the significance of creativity in the learning process.

> When learning is work it is ineffective – look at all the executives 'forced' to go on training courses. The learning that sticks has a joy of discovery, playfulness. Many executives have been to brainstorming seminars where an atmosphere of deliberate playfulness often stimulates high levels of executive learning for an hour or so. Corporations of the future are going to need to find ways to extend that hour to cover the entire working day.

Stuart Crainer and Des Dearlove – contributors to business publications world-wide and columns to *The Times*
Financial Times Handbook of Management, Third Edition, Pearson Education (2004), p. 750

Critical reflection ?????

'However important the skills or knowledge of an individual, the motivation and ability to learn is arguably of even greater importance.' What do you think? Without learning individuals will not be able to cope with change and organisations will not survive. What does learning mean to you and how do you learn best?

THE MEANING AND NATURE OF LEARNING

Learning means change, but change of a relatively permanent kind. Individuals may behave differently because of short-term factors such as tiredness or alcohol; these temporary changes are of a different nature to those associated with the process of learning. Imagine these scenarios:

- a student attending an action learning set;
- a manager completing a learning portfolio;
- a nurse measuring blood pressure for the first time;
- a trainee watching the manager deal with an irate customer;
- a child attempting to beat a score playing a computer game;

These scenarios all share the common feature that learning has taken or is about to take place. They demonstrate that a discussion of learning involves not only knowledge and skills but also attitudes and social behaviour. Learning implies a different internal state which may result in **new behaviours and actions** (for example, a new skill such as taking blood pressure) or **new understanding and knowledge** (for example, a new subject area such as finance). Sometimes behaviour and knowledge coincide (for example, learning a language, becoming IT literate); at other times people will learn to act in certain ways without an underlying understanding of the reasons why (for example, driving a car without an understanding of mechanics). Learning can be a deliberate and formal process or an unintentional outcome of natural progression.

Learning as a formal process When individuals consciously 'learn' and 'study', assessments take place to test the level and depth of their understanding and skills. Such 'formal' learning situations will test, grade and award qualifications on the basis of whether the individual has reached an agreed and measurable standard. Tests will frequently be based on 'what' the individual has learned and not on the 'why' or 'how' a person has learned. Testing 'what' has been learned is ingrained in our society and largely accounts for the ways in which individuals are compared and judged.

Learning as a spontaneous process But much of what we learn takes place without any necessary deliberations or any assessments. Learning can be seen to be a continuous and automatic process, often taking place in a social context. The spontaneous nature of learning can be observed in the young children's play as they imitate and model their behaviour and attitudes on the people around them. Learning has an active and dynamic nature. As active participants, we engage and relate to the people around us. It is a function central to our very humanity. We know that animals can learn, but the complexities of human learning have no parallel in the animal world. Learning would also seem to be irrepressible for some individuals despite their horrific circumstances. (Read, for example, Jean-Dominique Bauby's moving account of him re-learning to communicate with the outside world after suffering a massive stroke –

The Diving Bell and the Butterfly, Fourth Estate, 1997.) Our ability to learn will be affected by both our innate potential and our social experiences. We are not just vessels to be filled with knowledge; we are active participants who interact and relate to the world around us.

Learning, therefore, links the individual to the social world and is both a personal and a social experience. Often learning is an event that is shared with others. The process may be a deliberate sharing of information or guiding behaviour – as, for example, in the parent–child relationship when parents are attempting to socialise the child into acceptable ways of behaving or in organisations where employees are taught opening phrases when answering the telephone. At other times it is the actual sharing of the learning experience – going through the same learning process – which makes the process challenging and valuable. It is through the support of others that individuals can find both strength and rewards.

Incidental learning Learning occurs at many levels and in many ways; information or skills may be imparted quite explicitly and at the same time the values and attitudes of the trainer will also be implicitly communicated. Learning is a rich experience. At times we may be learning 'incidentally' as we acquire, process and remember information automatically. (Playing games like 'Who wants to be a millionaire?' illustrates the extent of our incidental learning.)

It is surprising to observe that in some organisations learning is left to chance. The individual employee is expected to 'pick up' behaviour, attitudes and skills. Until recently, it was unusual to have job descriptions or training for lecturers in universities. It was somehow expected that academics would 'know' what was expected of them in their teaching role and in their administrative tasks, such as course leader or personal tutor. Leadership development is now being taken seriously within universities and the Leadership Foundation for Higher Education, launched in 2004, aims to deliver a significant and visible contribution towards the practice of excellence in leadership. It actively champions examples of excellent leadership, governance and management and develops, commissions and delivers high-quality programmes.[1]

Learning and emotions

Learning implies that an individual has experienced 'something', has stored that experience and is able to refer to and/or use it at a later time. Learning and memory are inextricably linked. There are many factors that influence both the rate and enjoyment of learning (*see* Figure 5.1). The rewards and punishments levelled at us in the past will affect our motivation and attitudes towards learning in the present and the future. Expectations of others and the climate that surrounds us will determine our readiness to learn.

Feelings generated by the process of learning are very powerful and *tend* to be pleasurable. A sense of achievement that often accompanies the completion of a learning process can lead to an enhancement of an individual's self-worth and esteem. However, learning can also be an uncomfortable experience; it can 'shake an individual's comfort zones'; it can provide new and alarming perceptions and can be disruptive and anxiety provoking. An illustration of this has been noted by trainers in diversity who need to challenge individuals' attitudes and perceptions when there is evidence of prejudice: 'learning to learn about diversity can be, and may even have to be, a painful process. It is not a comfortable experience to learn that we have prejudices we need to deal with. It is not comfortable to find that our own view of the world is just one of many and those other views are equally valid.'[2]

The significance of learning Learning inevitably involves an examination of how change takes place. Current organisational literature provides advice for organisations in coping with turbulence and change and the role of learning is central to these discussions. The first part of this chapter will examine the ways in which organisations are managing this process. A critical review will follow of the ways in which knowledge is managed and the concept and reality of the learning organisation.

Figure 5.1	Factors influencing the learning process

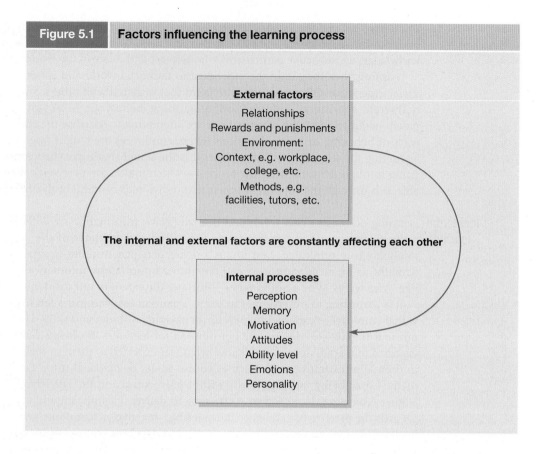

An understanding of how people learn provides insight into vital aspects of our humanity – the process of growth, development and deterioration. Learning is a highly significant area for psychologists to study and has been of continual interest in the development of psychology as a science. It provides a series of challenges in the selection of suitable methods and techniques for studying such a complex process. Learning is a function of the inner workings of our mind and its invisibility has created a number of methodological difficulties. The ways in which psychologists have studied the process will be examined in the second part of this chapter. Individuals differ in their learning capabilities, their style and their creative responses. This chapter will also consider the ways in which learning theories can be applied to the management of individuals at work.

A declaration on learning Eight distinguished scholars on learning in organisations launched a declaration summarising their collective thoughts on the nature of learning, its benefits and what should be done about learning.[3] They singled out learning as a key process for individuals, organisations and for society as a whole for the 21st century. They believe that it is too easy to take learning for granted and treat it as an automatic part of the human condition. They claim that individuals frequently do not organise or plan their learning and they leave the evaluation of learning to chance. Typically individuals fail to check what exactly they can do better or differently as a result of the learning experience. Two parts of the declaration are shown in Table 5.1.

Table 5.1	A declaration on learning: John Burgoyne, Ian Cunningham, Bob Garratt, Peter Honey, Andrew Mayo, Alan Mumford, Michael Pearn, Mike Pedler

Learning: the central issue for the 21st century

Learning is the most powerful, engaging, rewarding and enjoyable aspect of our personal and collective experience. The ability to learn about learning and become masters of the learning process is the critical issue for the next century.

Our understanding of learning has generally been restricted to formal teaching and training. It is often seen as unrelated to daily life and work. Systems of accreditation are sometimes used as a way of unfairly discriminating between individuals and are often felt to be irrelevant to real needs. The biggest missed opportunity for policy-makers and leaders is the failure to capitalise on the collective learning ability of people.

Organisational leaders need to harness relevant knowledge and experience so that the organisation as a whole and the people who comprise it can learn more effectively. The same principle applies at community, national and international levels. Every person, team and organisation both survives and progresses through the ability to internalise and act upon this fundamental truth.

This declaration does not contain all there is to say on the subject of learning. It does, however, reflect the thinking of the eight signatories. The declaration is designed to stimulate and encourage dialogue.

The benefits

The following benefits assume that the learning in question has both morally acceptable intent and outcome:

For individuals

- Learning is the key to developing a person's potential
- Learning to learn is the key to effective learning
- Learning enables the individual to meet the demands of change
- The capacity to learn is an asset that never becomes obsolete
- Embracing learning helps the individual to acknowledge that learning is more than formal education and training

For organisations

- Learning increases everyone's capacity to contribute to the success of organisations
- Learning enables the organisation to be more effective in meeting its goals
- Learning emancipates the organisation through clarification of purpose, vision, values and behaviour
- A focus on learning, planned and unplanned, formal and informal, produces a wider range of solutions to organisational issues
- Learning helps to achieve a better balance between long-term organisational effectiveness and short-term organisational efficiency

For society

- Society survives and thrives through learning
- A focus on capturing and sharing learning contributes to a more cohesive society
- Individual and collective learning reinforces the informed, conscious and discriminating choices that underpin democracy
- Learning helps to enhance the capacity of individuals to create a more fulfilled society

Source: Burgoyne, J., *et al.*, 'The debate starts here', in *People Management in Perspective: A Collection of Key Articles Published in the Last Year on Training and Development*, IPD, April 1999, pp. 16–17. Reproduced with permission from Chartered Institute of Personnel and Development (CIPD).

ORGANISATIONS AND THE MANAGEMENT OF LEARNING

If learning can result in the benefits outlined by *Burgoyne et al.* in Table 5.1, how do organisations achieve these outcomes? Clearly it is in the organisation's best interest to ensure it utilises the knowledge and skills of all its employees and yet in a report published by the Economic and Social Research Council (ESRC) the researchers found that formal education and training provided only a small part of what is learned at work.[4] Most learning arose out of the 'natural demands' of work – solving problems, interacting with colleagues, clients, etc. – and was described as learning achieved through experience. This experiential learning was given very little recognition or appreciation and led the researchers to note that:

One of the key tricks therefore is for organisations to know how to share knowledge and to learn from the experiences of others. Various interests and routes have drawn different organisations to knowledge management; diversity in actual practices is broad. A holistic approach towards KM research is taken in the aerospace industry. Kerr explains that it is necessary to complement social with technological solutions for managing knowledge in the engineering design process – not only the **know-why** (design rationale and reasoning – best practice) but the **know-who** (mapping expertise and skills) and **know-how** (promoting communities of practice for learning in a dynamic context). The Business Processes Resource Centre at Warwick University has distinguished four different types of knowledge management practices:

- valuing knowledge: seeing knowledge as intellectual capital and recognising its worth;
- exploiting intellectual property: organisations that have a strong research and development base may look for new and unconventional ways of using their existing knowledge base;
- capturing project-based learning: ensuring that knowledge gained from working on one project is captured and made available for others to use;
- managing knowledge workers: recognising the needs of knowledge workers and identifying new ways of managing to release creativity and positive outcomes.[18] (See Chapter 7 for more details on motivating knowledge workers.)

Particular attention has been drawn to the use of information systems for capturing knowledge and helping to multiply its effects.

Enablers facilitating knowledge management Key enablers facilitating KM practices include expert systems, knowledge bases, help desk tools as well as content management systems, wikis, blogs and other technologies. Growth will continue as more collaborative IT applications become available. *McElroy*[19] suggests that KM needs a second generation, one that focuses on knowledge creation. He points out that knowledge sharing alone does not lead to innovative thinking, instead a more fluid proactive approach is required which allows people to share, analyse and revise ideas. Collaborative software solutions allowing messaging, forums, etc., are more akin to addressing knowledge required for the future.

The term **communities of practice (CoP)** refers to groups of people who nurture new knowledge, stimulate innovation and share tacit knowledge. They work effectively when people have a common interest and are able to collaborate over a period of time to share ideas, find and develop solutions. *Wenger's*[20] work focused on learning as social participation, in other words it was only when individuals were connected with others and participating in their learning communities that their own identity was constructed.

Refresh your understanding

Activity 5A

www.pearsoned.co.uk/mullins

EMERGING TECHNOLOGIES AND LEARNING

Modern working environments are sending strong messages for change to our education systems in the way children learn and the ways they are assessed. *Järvelä* asks what kind of knowledge future learning and work situations will require and argues that personalisation of learning has become imperative. She believes that developing a personalised learning approach strengthens self-regulation skills and demonstrates the value of learning in order to understand. It is therefore an approach in educational policy whereby every student matters. Järvelä sees advanced technical infrastructures as helpful in developing collaborative learning:

> *By combining the ideas of collaborative learning and networked technology, these approaches aim at turning classrooms of students into communities of learners and learning situations into challenging and interesting projects with authentic problems. Such inquiry activities provide a valuable context for learners to acquire, clarify, and apply an understanding of concepts in different domains.*[21]

Järvelä predicts the growing use of mobile devices and wireless networks for education and that the pedagogical use of such devices will be a future challenge.

In a review of how technology is changing learning the British Educational Communications and Technology Agency, (BECTA)[22] argues that 'we are moving from being consumers of media to becoming creators and producers'. Illustrations such as war blogs by Iraqi citizens and mobile phone films of the London bombs indicate that people have seized the opportunity of becoming digital producers. Mobile learning can generate intense benefits, from podcasting to satellite-based systems, especially in terms of access in contexts not easy to reach. Learning can be enhanced by allowing devices to come together and communicate among themselves – Bluetooth and ZigBee are two examples of this.

The power of this connectivity allows people to create and explore new environments. So it is possible, for example, to create in a classroom an environment down to the sights, sounds and smells, with handheld computers, headphones and special sensors. Human computer interaction is becoming increasingly sophisticated, with multimodal interaction – where computers respond to human sense, mood and voice tones – from using pressure pads and sensors.

As enabling technologies become ever more sophisticated, our dependency on technology increases and our expectations grow. Referring to the attack on the twin towers (11 September 2001), *Peters* illustrates forcefully the necessity for effective, fast connectedness:

> *The FBI, the CIA, a kiloton of tanks and an ocean of aircraft carriers and nuclear subs were no match for passionate focus, coordinated communication and a few box cutters. The terrorists conceived the ultimate 'virtual organisation' – fast, wily, flexible, determined. And then, despite numerous slip-ups, said terrorists use satellite phones and encrypted email, US gatekeepers stand armed against them with pencils and paperwork, and archaic computer systems that don't talk to each other.*[23]

Intelligent networking is producing exciting visions of the future where 'smart objects' are networked and will be able to process data and communicate with other objects. It is speculated that in the future 'we'll have vehicles filling up with not only gasoline but also new data …. stop at the gas station and your car will automatically log on to the local server via a WLAN or similar system. Vehicles will network with one another and exchange information on traffic conditions and potential hazards'.[24]

E-learning in the future

Predicting how future technology might impact upon learning and learners was the focus of attention by a panel of experts and strategists in 2004. The Edinburgh Scenarios[25] as they are now known, were an outcome of the world summit organised by eLearn International in February 2004 where delegates considered what e-learning might be like in ten years' time. They used the techniques of scenario planning to explore the key uncertainties of the future and how the future might impact upon us all. The panel of experts identified two most uncertain and most important issues facing e-learning – these became the two axes. They then considered the kinds of pictures that could occur given these potentially challenging yet plausible possibilities. The four scenarios are described in Table 5.2.

Making use of knowledge Web technology has changed the way in which people communicate and their expectations of the scope, nature and type of knowledge and information. As *Cohen* has said:

> *Information no longer filters from the top down; it branches out into every imaginable direction and it flows away from the information creators and towards information users. Employees can now access information that was once only available to a few key people.*[26]

Networked companies are able to form linkages with partners and to have transparency about processes which would not have been conceivable a decade ago. Changes in the way knowledge is shared often comes hand in hand with other changes in the organisation. In the Royal Mail, traditional functional line structures were replaced with a spider's web

THE LEARNING ORGANISATION

So what does the term **learning organisation** mean? *Peter Senge* defined it as a place:

> *where people continually expand their capacity to create the results they truly desire, where new and expansive patterns of thinking are nurtured, where collective aspiration is set free, and where people are continually learning how to learn together.*[37]

Pedler, Boydell and Burgoyne's definition is the one most often quoted:

> *an organisation which facilitates the learning of all its members and continuously transforms itself.*[38]

The learning organisation sounds ideal – the kind of company in which we might all like to work. The picture that is painted is of an organisation that is ultimately highly flexible and open-ended. It is able to continually transform itself and learn from experience and thus always be ready to take advantage of changing external conditions. Such an organisation values individual development, open communication and trust. It lends itself to flat, open and networked structures. (*See* Chapter 15 for more information about the impact of organisation structures on behaviour at work.) Rather than occurring as separate and sometimes accidental activities, learning is a deliberate and central process in the learning organisation. *Joseph Lampel* has identified five basic principles:

1 Learning organisations can learn as much, if not more, from failure as from success.
2 A learning organisation rejects the adage 'if it ain't broke, don't fix it' as it is constantly scrutinising the way things are done.
3 Learning organisations assume that the managers and workers closest to the design, manufacturing, distribution and sale of the product often know more about these activities than their superiors.
4 A learning organisation actively seeks to move knowledge from one part of the organisation to another, to ensure that relevant knowledge finds its way to the organisational unit that needs it most.
5 Learning organisations spend a lot of energy looking outside their boundaries for knowledge.

Rather than claiming to **be** learning organisations, many suggest that they are working towards **becoming** a learning organisation.[39]

The outcome of the learning organisation is generally discussed as being positive, indeed in some texts as being almost utopian. *Garratt*,[40] for example, views learning organisations as essentially liberating and energising and as crucial for organisational survival and growth. *Burgoyne* suggests that the learning company offers a new focus for organisations and in particular identifies agenda items for HRM as a key contributor of corporate strategic planning. He believes there are four new roles:

● to continue to manage the employee stakeholder – but to view employees as customers and partners;
● to look for new stakeholders and develop new links and alignments, particularly with regard to development processes;
● to be the focus of new organisation development (OD) initiatives and the source of collective learning processes;
● to inform policy formation and the implementation of strategy for the employee stakeholder.[41]

The learning organisation as a feature of OD is discussed in Chapter 20.

There is a growing body of literature that describes the 'journey to become a learning organisation'. The three examples given in Table 5.3 are typical. Initially explaining some of the difficulties different companies had in defining and measuring a learning organisation, their 'travel log' then describes the decisions they made in pushing forward their agenda for change. All produce qualitative and quantitative evidence to support their decisions and to identify positive changes in their organisational culture.

Table 5.3	Learning experiences of different companies	
Organisation	**Steps taken**	**Outcomes**
Club 24[42]	Stairway initiative: experiential learning programme for the 'Collection Department'	Morale higher Attendance and efficiency improvement Change in culture
English Nature[43]	Benchmarking	Raised awareness of different methods of learning Introduction of range of programmes designed to strengthen the links between learning and action Reviewed support given to projects and funding
Hay Management Consultants[44]	Cultural audit	Strengthened focus on clients Increase in teamwork

If learning organisations help in the repositioning of HRM into a central strategic position, the concept is, without doubt, to be welcomed by personnel professionals. In these turbulent days, organisations are going to seize any practical help in coping with continual change. It is therefore no wonder that this concept is gaining increasing attention.

Difficulties with the learning organisation concept

Some academics are concerned that the learning organisation concept has a number of troublesome features in terms of application and rigour. For *Garvin*,[45] effective implementation will need the resolution of three critical issues:

- meaning (or definition);
- management (or practical operational advice);
- measurement (tools for assessment).

Although he believes that the learning organisations 'offer many benefits', he raises concerns about unanswered questions:

- How, for example, will managers know when their companies have become learning organisations?
- What concrete changes in behaviour are required?
- What policies and programmes must be in place?
- How do you get from here to there?

Harrison[46] also critically comments on the 'looseness' of the learning organisation concept and points out that the sum of the learning of individuals does not necessarily equal organisational learning. Processes and systems are required to effectively utilise individual learning. *Mumford* suggests that it is:

> *impossible to conceive of a learning organisation, however defined, which exists without individual learners. The learning organisation depends absolutely on the skills, approaches and commitment of individuals to their own learning.*[47]

Politics and control Furthermore he contends that individuals are empowered to take control of their personal destiny by being given opportunities to learn. Although empowerment may occur for some, Harrison argues that control of learning and the power base of organisation is still

reliability and **validity**. A school of psychology called **behaviourism** developed out of these early research studies. As the name suggests, researchers were interested in the study of behaviour and those actions that could be observed, measured and controlled. Ideas and thoughts in people's minds were considered inaccessible to objective, scientific measurement and were therefore excluded from study.

Exercise and association
J. B. Watson developed the **law of exercise and association**. This refers to the process that occurs when two responses are connected and repeatedly exercised. Watson was particularly interested in the study of fixed habits and routines.[56] In organisational life we can see evidence of this in the habits and routines at work. These behaviours can become 'locked-in', believed to be 'the only way' of completing certain tasks – a part of cultural life; it is as if they are fixed into beds of concrete. Speech is a further illustration of our routine habits. The predictability of a greeting provides acknowledgement of our existence – when people say 'How are you?' they do not expect to be given a rundown of your medical history. The rhetorical question is really saying, 'Hello – I see, acknowledge and recognise you.'

Classical conditioning

Pavlov,[57] working in Russia, developed a theory called **classical conditioning**. His laboratory experiments demonstrated how instinctive reflexes, such as salivation, could be 'conditioned' to respond to a new situation and a new stimulus (*see* Figure 5.2). Pavlov, through his repeated experimental studies, showed the power and strength of association. How can we

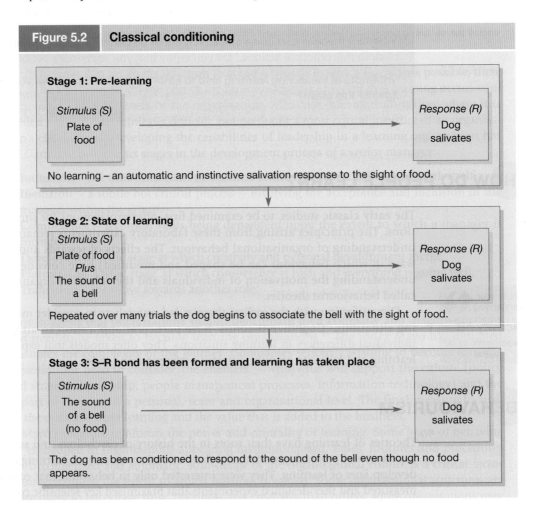

Figure 5.2	Classical conditioning

Stage 1: Pre-learning

Stimulus (S)
Plate of food
→
Response (R)
Dog salivates

No learning – an automatic and instinctive salivation response to the sight of food.

Stage 2: State of learning

Stimulus (S)
Plate of food
Plus
The sound of a bell
→
Response (R)
Dog salivates

Repeated over many trials the dog begins to associate the bell with the sight of food.

Stage 3: S–R bond has been formed and learning has taken place

Stimulus (S)
The sound of a bell
(no food)
→
Response (R)
Dog salivates

The dog has been conditioned to respond to the sound of the bell even though no food appears.

relate these experiments on dogs to behaviour at work? There are times when our body responds more quickly than our mind. We may have an initial panic reaction to a situation without necessarily realising why. Physiological reactions may be appropriate in times of stressful situations – our body may be in a state of readiness to run (fight or flight reaction).[58]

At other times our reactions may be 'conditioned' because of previous associations of pain, guilt or fear. Smells and sounds are particularly evocative and may release physiological reactions akin to the Pavlovian experiments. Thus sitting in a waiting room at the dentist's and hearing the sound of the drill may invoke an increase in our blood pressure or heart rate – nothing to do with any *actual pain we may be experiencing*. Returning to school for a parents' evening may invoke feelings of 'dread' or 'pleasure' depending on our own childhood experiences of school and its associations. Training for some occupations may depend upon learned associations and automatic reactions such as initial military training. If fire drills are to be successful, immediate reaction to the bell or siren is essential.

THE OUTCOMES OF LEARNING

Thorndike's work drew attention to the outcomes of learning – **the Law of Effect**.[59] He watched animals in new situations and noted how they learned to successfully adapt to the environment. He noted that in his experiments there were no flashes of insight shown but learning would occur by **trial and error**. Over time these correct responses were 'stamped in'. If an action was successful and led to a reward, the behaviour was more likely to be repeated.

OPERANT CONDITIONING

Skinner advanced the ideas of Thorndike and produced a thesis of **operant conditioning**.[60] Skinner's experiments on animals showed the effects of reward and punishment on animal learning. Unlike classical conditioning, learning was rewarded after the response had occurred. He proved that a response would be learned when the animal associated the behavioural response with a reward (or reinforcement) and could be broken with punishment (*see* Figure 5.3).

Once the rat had learned that pressing the lever equalled the onset of food, the rat responded to the lever consistently. The rat had been 'conditioned' to act in a particular kind of way. Sometimes the rat learned superfluous actions, such as turning round before pressing the lever, and these actions too would be repeated. Skinner called these responses 'superstitious' as the animal had acted as though such behaviour had produced the reward.

Skinner experimented with the reinforcement process:

- What would happen if the animal was not rewarded in each trial?
- What effect would partial reinforcement have on the rate of learning?

He found that partial reinforcement strengthened the stimulus–response bond and the behaviour was more resistant to extinction. The reward seemed to hold even greater importance when it was given intermittently.

Negative reinforcement was also shown to be powerful. These experiments demonstrated the importance of the stimulus–response bond, but the reward was the prevention of something painful or nasty occurring. The rat learned to associate the stimulus (perhaps a light) with something nasty happening (perhaps an electric shock) and runs (response) to prevent the painful situation. **Not** being shocked is the reward in such experiments. Thus the rat was conditioned to respond to a stimulus and the S–R bond was formed. Negative reinforcement is *not* punishment. **Punishment** is trying to break the S–R bond. For instance, if the animal pressed the lever and received an electric shock it would quickly learn not to press the lever and the S–R bond would be broken.

SOCIAL LEARNING

People learn by watching others. The term 'modelling' was coined by *Miller and Dollard*[63] to explain learning by imitating others and 'role models' as a label for those individuals who are held up as examples of good practice. So, the trainee watching how a car is repaired or the trainee chef learning how to prepare a soufflé will imitate the actions of their role model. Interpersonal skills can also be learned by observation and the new recruit by watching others will 'pick up' the habits and techniques of those around him/her. Miller and Dollard's research brought attention to cognitive functions of thinking, perception, attention and memory in addition to behavioural responses. So, for instance, a trainee watching a supervisor deal with a customer complaint would need to attend to the customer's emotions, note the reaction of the supervisor and learn how the 'lessons' of this interaction could be applied to another situation. This process relies on complex cognitive processes including attention, recall and understanding. Individual intelligence and judgement will play a part in their decision to repeat the behaviour – they may decide that the way in which the supervisor dealt with a customer complaint is an illustration of how they would **not** behave. Such decisions rely on an individual's intellect and thinking skills and the extent to which the consequences are 'fair'.

LIMITATIONS OF THE BEHAVIOURIST SCHOOL

Focusing only on behaviour is useful but limited. The inner mind has particular relevance to understanding how, what and why people learn. Personality, perceptions, motivations and attitudes will all play their part in helping or hindering the learning process. *Gallwey*, in his 'inner game' books, discusses the impact that the inner world of ego personalities has on performance:

> Once I became aware of Self 1, it grew increasingly obvious that this judgmental little voice barking away like a drill sergeant inside my head was not the best thing for my tennis game. Self 1 was more of a hindrance than the great help he wanted me to think he was. Thereafter I began looking for ways to decrease the interference of Self 1 and to see what happened if I trusted the potential of Self 2.[64]

Refresh your understanding

Activity 5C

www.pearsoned.co.uk/mullins

Account of cognitive factors Behaviourism cannot easily explain the natural curiosity that humans have, the great desire to learn, to make sense of their environment and to feel competent in activities. Neither can it explain the extent of incidental learning that takes place. Observing changes in behaviour is only part of the learning process. To understand how and why people learn, attention must be given to myriad individual factors including plans, ambitions, goals, etc.

COGNITIVE THEORIES

Research conducted in the middle of the last century highlighted the fact that the process of learning was more complex than simple stimulus–response associations. *Kohler* demonstrated the use of insight in animals solving problems.[65] *Tolman* showed that rats were capable of learning an image of the maze (a cognitive map) that they would use at a later time.[66] It was a Swiss psychologist, *Piaget*,[67] who demonstrated that the simple behaviourist school could not explain learning observed in children's development. He identified four major stages of intellectual growth, which could be observed in all children. Piaget's theory offers a tight coherent perspective of the maturation of intellectual thought and development. His studies introduced the notion of the **cyclical nature of learning** and the ways in which children and adults adjust and accommodate to their environment.

For many cognitive theorists learning is viewed as a sequence, a sequence which processes information in three distinct stages:

Learning new skills: the importance of feedback

Yoga is one of the six systems of Indian philosophy. There are a number of different interpretations of yoga and one of these is taught by Yogacharya B. K. S. Iyengar.[68]

Learning a physical skill such as Iyengar yoga provides a good illustration of:

- the continual cycle of learning;
- the importance of stages in learning;
- the significance of information and feedback;
- the importance of support structures – physical, social and mental.

The yoga poses are challenging and require the complete involvement of the senses and total concentration of the mind. Otherwise a fall to the floor is likely. The teacher provides clear information about the positioning of the body and the class tries to assimilate this information and imitate the teacher. Initially it is hard to connect to muscles that have been lying dormant for some considerable time!

The final pose is reached after a series of 'sub poses' have been practised. Each sub pose is gradually developed and becomes more complex. At each stage students have to remember 'what it felt like' in the previous sub pose to be sure that they are building on what has already been learnt and progressing to more challenging postures. Learning the poses therefore requires active perception and attention to the teacher as well as attention to internal feedback about the positioning of the body.

Striving for excellence and gaining the benefits from each posture is the goal of Iyengar yoga for all students. Therefore no matter the physical limitations of the body or the inflexibility of the limbs all students are able to achieve maximum gain from each posture with the help of physical supports. Perhaps a belt to support the legs, perhaps a chair to support the back. Each student develops **at their own pace**, and with their own props. A teacher will also provide information about whether a student's posture needs modifying; perhaps a brick under the hand will get the posture closer to perfection. Creativity will be used in identifying the particular needs of certain students. A learning environment is created in which the group supports individuals, information at critical times is provided, individuals are totally engaged in their pursuit of perfection and the teacher encourages, supports and leads by example.

Source: Judith Jones and Carol Batterson, Iyengar Yoga Teachers, Hampshire. Reprinted with permission.

- an active perception stage which gives attention to stimuli from the environment;
- a second mentally active stage which makes sense of the information;
- finally, a restructuring and storage phase.

Although it is beyond the scope of this book to consider the relationship between thinking and learning, some researchers have shed light on the mental constructs that may form. *Glaser*,[69] for instance, has described these as 'scaffolds'. This metaphor suggests that the framework is capable of development and would be built in an individual way. It also suggests strength and support. The different ways in which individuals learn may in part be due to their 'scaffold' as well as other personal qualities.

The learning cycle

Some cognitive theorists have emphasised the cyclical nature of learning and its active nature. *Davis*[70] claims that 'experiential learning is an integration and alteration of thinking and doing'. *Kolb's* learning cycle (*see* Figure 5.4) is typical of this approach and is the one that is most frequently used in the management literature.[71] It provides useful insights into the nature of learning:

| Figure 5.4 | Kolb's learning cycle |

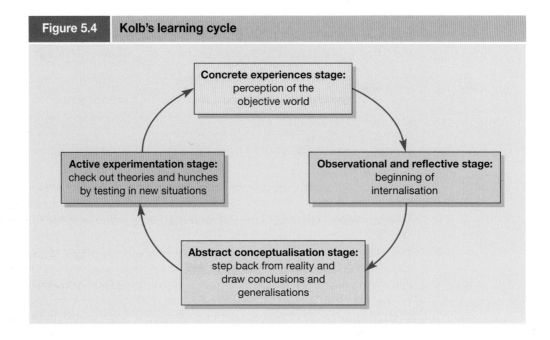

- It demonstrates that there is no end to learning but only another turn of the cycle.
- Learners are not passive recipients but need to actively explore and test the environment.
- It identifies the importance of reflection and internalisation.
- It is a useful way of identifying problems in the learning process.

The approach emphasises the importance of the synthesis between an individual's behaviour and the evaluation of their actions. Reflection of what has been learned in order to experiment with new situations and to become aware of new possibilities is a vital part of the learning process. This is the very essence of action learning; going though the cycle that learners are exposed to applying, reflecting and testing out their learning. This encourages individuals in habits compatible with the notion of lifelong learning. It is therefore no surprise that Kolb addresses his ideas to managers and suggests that experiential learning will enable managers to cope with change and complexity. He has suggested that:

> *A key function of strategic management development ... is to provide managers with access to knowledge and relationship networks that can help them become life-long learners and cope with the issues on their continually changing agendas.*[72]

Kolb and his colleagues suggest that partnerships between education and industry should create feedback loops which enable interactions between ideas and action – certainly ideas which fit well into a learning organisation framework and into the new concept of knowledge management considered earlier in this chapter.

There are other important links that can be made from this model of learning to organisational behaviour. Of late there have been exhortations for organisations to develop employees as 'thinking performers', thus emphasising the important relationship between thinking and action. Focus on thinking has been at the core of work completed by *Nancy Kline*. By mastering what Kline calls a Thinking Environment, people are able to enrich their lives and their relationships. She argues that organisations are able to produce better ideas in less time with better business outcomes. She describes a Thinking Environment as having the following ten components:

- attention – listening with respect, interest and fascination;
- incisive questions – removing assumptions that limit ideas;

- equality – treating each other as thinking peers and giving equal turns and attention. Keeping agreements and boundaries;
- appreciation – practising a five-to-one ratio of appreciation to criticism;
- ease – offering freedom from rush or urgency;
- encouragement – moving beyond competition;
- feelings – allowing sufficient emotional release to restore thinking;
- information – providing a full and accurate picture of reality;
- place – creating a physical environment that says back to people, 'You matter';
- diversity – adding quality because of the differences between us.[73]

Kline believes that employees need to relearn how to think for themselves in an environment which genuinely listens and gives people time to say what they think. As a consequence she argues that more productive meetings and stronger relationships result.

The importance of reflection in aiding the learning process is also demanding attention. Portfolio assessments are becoming more commonplace, both in terms of qualifications and for showing evidence of continuing professional development. At such time individuals are asked to 'reflect' upon their learning experiences. What have they learned? What are they going to learn next? The reflective process demands they place themselves centre stage and it reinforces the circular process of learning. It does not see learning as an end result, as some kind of 'product', but as an ongoing process that never finishes. Becoming a reflective practitioner is seen as essential for managing change and 'of paramount importance for learning and growth'.[74] But reflection is not easy as it insists that individuals challenge their mindsets and see situations in new ways. It leads to individuals redefining their current perspective to develop new ways of thinking and behaving. One of the ways in which this process can be enhanced is through action learning sets.

What are action learning sets?

Action learning is explicitly focused on action and promoting change. *Coghlan and Brannick*[75] note that 'the purpose of (action) research and discourse is not just to describe, understand and explain the world but also to change it' by the effort of data gathering, discussion, action planning, action, reflection and review.

Action learning sets comprise a small group of five to six people, all of whom wish to develop themselves through tackling a live issue. The set will provide an opportunity for each individual to report in turn on their actions and reflect on the progress they have made. Set members will help the presenter to clarify and decide on next actions by asking challenging questions and creating a supportive climate.

Benefits of action learning have been identified by Weinstein as:

- resolves real business problems;
- improves social processes;
- empowers people;
- improves leadership qualities;
- improves coping with change.

But in addition to these organisational benefits, participants report valuable learning that they did not anticipate at the outset. *Weinstein* comments: 'This unanticipated learning was often a shift away from the learning focused on skills, behaviours and knowledge into learning based around values, beliefs and awareness.'[76] Helping others, listening, using the spaces to think and reflect are all identified as important learning moments.

The action research can be portrayed as a spiral of learning and action (*see* Figure 5.5).[77]

Figure 5.5	Action research spiral

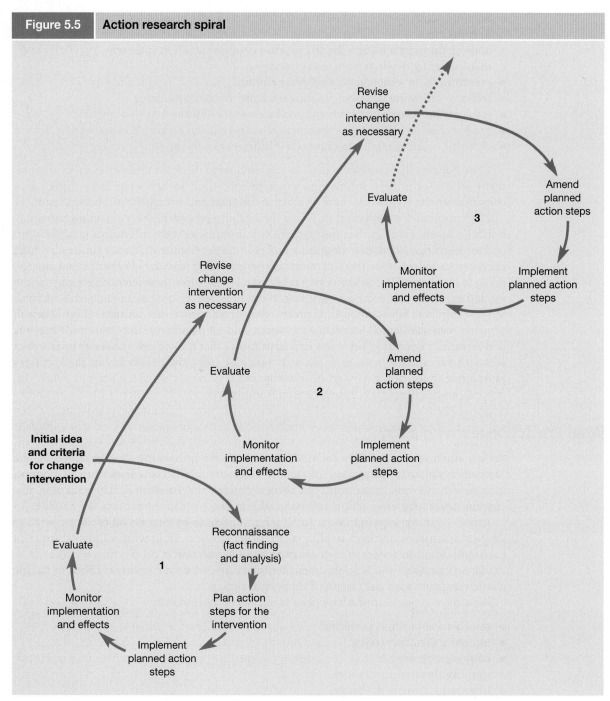

Source: From Thornhill, A., *et al.*, *Managing Change: A Human Resource Strategy Approach*, Financial Times Prentice Hall (2000), p. 289. Reproduced with permission from Pearson Education Ltd.

LEARNING STYLES

When applying the learning cycle to the study of individual differences, Kolb demonstrated that individuals may have a preference for one of the key stages and therein lies their learning style. His work, developed by *Honey and Mumford*,[78] has been applied to managerial behaviour. Kolb identified four different styles of learning:

- **accommodative** – strong preference for concrete experiences and active experimentation (hands on);
- **divergent** – preference for concrete experiences, but to reflect on these from different perspectives;
- **assimilative** – prefers to swing between reflection and conceptualisation and will use inductive reasoning to develop new theory;
- **convergent** – prefers to apply ideas, will take an idea and test it out in practice.

Honey and Mumford simplified Kolb's learning cycle and refined his learning style questionnaire. The result is that managers can identify whether they are predominantly:

Activist What's new? I'm game for anything.
Reflector I'd like time to think about this.
Theorist How does this relate to that?
Pragmatist How can I apply this in practice?[79]

The researchers claim that an understanding of one's learning style will enhance learning effectiveness, whether as a trainee or as a tutor. An integrated and effective learner will be equipped to manage all four styles even though they may have a preference for one.

Other studies have also shown links between personality and learning and have found, for example, that introverts and extroverts differ with respect to punishment and reward. Whereas introverts are more likely to be affected by punishment than extroverts, extroverts' performance is enhanced by reward.[80] They also differ with respect to their retention of short- and long-term material; extroverts tend to have a better performance at short-term intervals whereas the reverse is true for introverts.

Studies using the Myers–Briggs Type Indicator also reveal differences in learning preferences for the 16 personality types. Such differences indicate that introverts work best if they can think before participating or ask questions before completing tasks or exercises, whereas extroverts work best if they can interact in a small group and/or talk the lesson over with other individuals. However, some of the interesting research has been completed on the interaction between trainer and trainee. Thus, an extroverted trainer who is also high on 'sensing' (*see* Chapter 4 for description of the different MBTI categories) may positively evaluate students who are active, energetic and practical, but may overlook the thoughtful introspective and conceptual students.[81] Such studies highlight the necessity for trainers not only to be sensitive to the personality needs of the group of trainees but also to be aware of the impact their own personality has on the learning experience.

Mayo suggests that organisations need to recognise the simple fact that different people learn in different ways and should take the following actions:

- give people the opportunity to discover their most natural learning style;
- offer learning opportunities that suit people with different learning styles;
- recognise the need to complete the full learning cycle;
- help people to translate the learning cycle into an upwards continuous spiral of learning.[82]

COMPLEX MODELS OF LEARNING

So, given the complexity of learning, how can managers make sense of the theories, concepts and frameworks? Models of learning such as that shown in Figure 5.6 are inevitably complex. However, the model might stimulate questions and could help in the preparation and design of learning programmes. Has there been sufficient consideration of past experiences, of the employees' abilities, of the learning styles, the context, the methods and style to be used?[83]

Figure 5.6	A cognitive model of learning

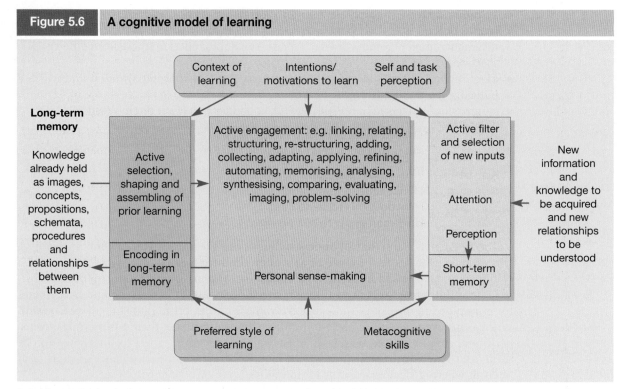

Source: From Atkins, M. J., Beattie, J. and Dockrell, W. B., *Assessment Issues in Higher Education*, Department of Employment (October 1993) p. 51. © Crown Copyright 1993. Crown copyright material is reproduced with the permission of the Controller of Her Majesty's Stationery Office (HMSO).

CREATIVITY

The importance of creativity as a management ability has been creeping onto the management education agenda over the past decade, lending a so-called soft edge to the business literature. *Morgan*'s paper, in which he prophesied that six new competencies would be required by managers to lead their organisations into the next millennium, included the ability to be innovative and initiate change.[84] Other research, indicating that the reality of what managers actually do is unlike the conventional wisdom of what they are supposed to do, in fact, managers are already engaging in activities which are, if not creative, certainly intuitive.[85]

For organisations to be innovative, creative solutions are required. Such a statement is in total harmony with the research on learning organisations. *West* could be speaking about learning organisations when he says:

> *Organisations and teams which practise reflexivity and are prepared to continually challenge and re-define their organisational roles, goals and paradigms, via processes of innovation, develop a more comprehensive and penetrating intellectual representation of their role. They better anticipate and manage problems, and they deal with conflict as a valuable process asset within the organisation, encouraging effectiveness, growth and development. The most reflexive organisations are those within which there is a maelstrom of activity, debate, argument, innovation and a real sense of involvement of all employees.*[86]

So, what is creativity? *Creativity is the application of imaginative thought which results in innovative solutions to many problems.*[87]

Imaginative thought may lead to new ways of seeing things that may be novel for the person or completely novel in time. (*Boden* distinguishes such novel ideas as either P-creative (novel to the person) or H-creative (fundamentally novel to the whole of human

history).[88] An air of mystique surrounds the study of creativity, as if the flash of insight or inspiration indicates some special powers or gift. However, *Boden*[89] suggests that:

> *creativity draws crucially on our ordinary abilities. Noticing, remembering, seeing, speaking, hearing, understanding language and recognising analogies; all these talents of Everyman are important.*

The fascination for Boden is understanding these everyday cognitive functionings.

Given the notion that all individuals have a capacity for creativity, why is it that some generate more ideas than others? *Henry* identified a number of traits found in creative individuals: tolerance for ambiguity, sensitivity, independent thinking, imagination and a reasonable level of intelligence.[90] *Goodman* suggests that:

> *Actively creative people have a talent for getting to the heart of a problem. They are not confused by detail and by the need to invoke standard approaches.*[91]

There is a consensus in the literature that suggests such individuals have a desire for originality, non-conformity and the opportunity to experiment and express new ideas. A difference can also be drawn between those people who are productive in terms of the number of ideas they can create and those individuals who have entrepreneurial capabilities and are able to bring the ideas to the marketplace.

Stages of creative process

Four stages have emerged in the creative thinking process.[92]

1 *Preparation stage* – conscious attempt to understand and absorb information.
2 *Incubation stage* – conscious mind is focused elsewhere but below the level of consciousness the ideas are being continually combined.
3 *Illumination* – solution appears suddenly – flash of insight.
4 *Verification* – solution is tested in a conscious and deliberate way.

Understanding these stages of creativity is acknowledged by many psychologists as being an essential start to understanding and appreciating one's own creativity. *West*[93] reveals that managers lack confidence in their ability to be creative and organisations may set up a vast number of potential inhibitors. It is therefore understandable that creativity is suppressed and devalued. Learning to be creative is encouraged by many writers through exercises and activities designed to stretch the imagination in wild and novel ways (see the personal awareness and skills exercise at the end of this chapter).

Blocks to creativity *Goodman*[94] suggests six common blocks to personal creativity:

- **Perceptual** – habitual responses, stereotyping and reliance on past instructions and experiences.
- **Emotional** – Fear, anxiety about looking foolish in front of others or making errors.
- **Process** – Lack of technique or skills in process; a quick grasp at a solution.
- **Communication** – Style, method or skills unsuitable for dealing with problems.
- **Environmental** – Facilities, stress factors, mind-sets of others which inhibit responses.
- **Cultural** – Culture and attitudes not facilitative; too risky and open-ended.

A distinction can be made in Goodman's list between the first four features that are aspects of the individual's psyche and repertoire of skills and the last two that are functions of the culture of the organisation. Unless there is a culture of creativity and interest in reconstruction, it is more likely that individuals will use their creativity and resourcefulness outside the organisation or against the organisation rather than for the organisation.

These blocks to creativity could also be generalised to many learning situations and not just those that require a creative response. Students embarking on a new educational course, particularly if they have had a break from studies, will frequently report concerns that could

be categorised under the six headings. In addition, many will note that the relationships outside the academic environment are important too; the change process has an impact not only on the student but frequently on the family and partnerships too.

Creating a culture of creativity

Strategic management writers are now suggesting that managers will be required to go beyond rational/logical thinking and use their senses of feeling, creativity and intuition to create businesses for the future. The Creative Model of Management (CM) is:

> built on the philosophical assumption that the real world which surrounds the organisation is a dynamic construct enacted by the members of the organisation over time ... they will require a diverse group of senior managers able to perceive the world differently, yet able to participate in a process that transcends these different views to enact a complex organisational reality.[95]

Such a view suggests that personality, sensitivity, creativity and communication skills are going to be the requirements of managers in the next millennium. (For more information on management strategy and resistance to change, *see* Chapter 19.)

It also requires managers to be proactive in their search for root causes to problems and be imaginative in solving them. *Argyris*[96] usefully distinguished between **single-loop** and **double-loop** learning in organisational strategy and change. Single-loop learning concentrates on the symptoms of problems whereas double-loop learning tries to seek out the deep causes. Differences exist in terms of strategies used to solve problems. Whereas the devices used to tackle surface issues typically involve tightening control, double-loop strategies require a questioning approach. Such investigations may lead to a challenge of the status quo and for Argyris, this open enquiry is a way forward for solving business problems. This enquiring attitude is in line with work on learning organisations and the philosophy of the Creative Management school.

There is a growing interest in drawing the arts and creativity into management programmes. Although innovation is seen as essential for organisations, engaging with creativity and developing creativity is often put on the back burner. At ?What If![97] they believe that organisations need to 'navigate' between the traditional business world of analysis and the world of creativity to generate innovation. Without this they suggest that business growth is compromised, personal growth undermined and feelings of fulfilment are reduced. Interest in developing creativity has blossomed in a range of alternative development offerings from preparing stage productions, developing music projects, to story telling and poetry writing workshops. It is claimed that such activities provide:

- rich learning about the creative process and ways in which creativity can be nurtured or stifled;
- ways to develop 'soft skills' alongside 'hard skills';
- powerful metaphors to facilitate organisational analysis;
- multi-sensory and right-brain approaches that balance left-brain thinking, different learning styles and experiential learning.[98]

A summary of how people learn is given in the concept map in Figure 5.7.

Refresh your understanding

Activity 5D
www.pearsoned.co.uk/
mullins

Critical reflection ?????

Coaching claims to do so much for the person and the organisation – from improving productivity to enhancing relationships and quality of life. It also boasts that people completing coaching are more flexible and adapt to change more easily. Can talking to a trained coach really do so much or is the evaluation evidence too difficult to collect?

Figure 5.7 **Concept map of how people learn**

HOW PEOPLE LEARN

- WHAT IS LEARNING?
- THE THEORIES OF LEARNING
- WHAT CHANGES ARE WE SEEKING?
- WHY DO PEOPLE CHANGE?
- HOW CAN WE CHANGE THEM?
- WHAT MAKES ADULTS WANT TO LEARN?
- WHAT CAN YOU DO?

WHAT IS LEARNING?
- Acquiring or developing
 - knowledge
 - skill
- Increased competence to deal with the environment
- Changing attitudes and behaviour

THEORIES OF LEARNING
Behaviourist theory:
 - people learn to behave in certain ways trying to avoid pain

Cognitive theory:
 - individuals think and form ideas and, as a result of success of those ideas, change their behaviour

WHAT CHANGES ARE WE SEEKING?
- Show more initiative
- Be more creative
- Confront their problems
- Question what is happening

WHY DO PEOPLE CHANGE?
- If they have the ability to change
- If the system allows or encourages them to
- If they are forced or coerced to
- If they want to

HOW CAN WE CHANGE THEM?
- By motivation – with rewards
 e.g. – NVQs certificates, diplomas, opening up promotion opportunities
- By helping them want to learn

WHAT CAN YOU DO?
- Create an atmosphere of openness and confidentiality
- Make people aware of their problems by asking questions
- Make people aware of different interpretations of situations
- Encourage exploration of ideas
- Encourage people to think and feel and to think around the subject
- Get people actively doing things

WHAT MAKES ADULTS WANT TO LEARN?
They must see the relevance and value of what they are learning and know what goals are set
They must be doing something
When they can relate what they are doing to past experiences

KOLB'S MODEL

CONCRETE EXPERIENCES → OBSERVATION AND REFLECTION → FORMATION OF ABSTRACT CONCEPTS LESSONS AND GENERALISATIONS → TEST IMPLICATIONS OF CONCEPTS IN NEW SITUATIONS → (cycle)

CONCRETE EXPERIENCES → FORM STEREOTYPES AND GENERALISATIONS
(more commonly)
Difficult for people with closed minds
E.G.
- Pride and self image
- Lack of confidence
- Lack of interest and commitment

ADULTS
- Have a lot of experience and some will learn from it
- Have set habits
- Are proud
- Like to see themselves as independent
- Have things to lose
- Do not like choice or ambiguity
- Have other preoccupations than learning
- Can change
- May find it hard to change
- Have, something to contribute
- Fear going back to school
- Fear falling behind or being replaced

BARRIERS TO LEARNING
- Pride and self image
- Lack of confidence
- Lack of interest and commitment

ADULT LEARNING
- A move from dependence to independence

PROJECT WORK	INDEPENDENCE
SYNDICATE WORK	INTERDEPENDENCE
LECTURE	DEPENDENCE

Source: Training Learning Consultancy Ltd. Bristol, England. Reproduced with permission.

FACILITATING LEARNING

Organisations need to offer development opportunities which simultaneously challenge and support and they need effective systems and processes that enable people to harness their potential. This requires creativity and courage to emotionally engage and motivate people to operate at their limits. So, how are managers to learn and acquire the skills that are necessary for them to be effective managers? Two current methods of management development that are being advocated are the skills of **mentoring** and **coaching**. One of the joys of managing others is to know that you have helped others develop and grow. Managers have always been informal mentors and coaches – some relishing this role with the required portfolio of skills, some being more hesitant and others having a negative influence and acting as a 'block' rather than a steer to their subordinates.

Recent literature is drawing attention to the skills required to be an effective mentor and coach and research on this topic is to be welcomed. Certainly the concepts fit in well with the idea of a 'learning organisation' and they fit comfortably with principles of learning which extol the virtues of action learning and self-development. The concepts are based on the assumption that the trainee recognises their training needs and has the desire to be a willing and active participant in the process. As *Clutterbuck and Wynne* suggest:

> *Mentoring and coaching … represent an increasing trend towards helping the individual take charge of his or her learning: the primary driver of the acquisition of knowledge and skill becomes the employee; the coach or mentor is available to give guidance, insight and encouragement in the learning process.*[99]

Coaching and mentoring

There is considerable confusion and differences of opinion among individuals within organisations about the interpretation of these two concepts. '**Coaching**' is a supportive relationship aimed at creating understanding, direction and action. It is both facilitative and challenging. A coach does not 'fix' someone or solve their problems or assume an 'expert's' position; rather they try to draw out the wisdom from within. The relationship involved in '**mentoring**' is equally supportive and challenging, but the mentor is typically an expert in an area or is a leader within an organisation. They are able to offer advice, guidance and support. A mentor may choose to use coaching techniques within the mentoring relationship. Rapport is essential for either relationship to work effectively.

In line with these working definitions, the similarities and differences between coaching and mentoring can be highlighted.

Coaching

- It uses deductive techniques.
- The coach does not have to be an expert in the subject.
- Usually coaching sessions are planned and organised over a set period of time, e.g. 6 coaching sessions over 12 months.

Mentoring

- It uses a mixture of inductive and deductive techniques.
- The mentor must be an expert in the subject.
- Mentoring sessions may be on an ad hoc basis.
- Respect for the mentor's knowledge of the subject is essential.

MacLennan[100] reiterates the benefit of an organisation developing a coaching culture and he believes that coaching can have an important and revitalising effect on organisations. *Kalinauckas and King* also suggest that organisations which wish to grow in the future should invest in one-to-one coaching of the directors:

It is essential, if companies wish to keep ahead of their competitors, that there is a strategy for continuous, constant improvement in terms of both employee and business development. This will of necessity involve some coaching.[101]

The trend of having a personal coach has grown over the last few years. *Hardingham*[102] believes the act of talking to a supportive outsider can help managers. It gives them space and time to work out and understand mixed messages they may be hearing in the workplace. The example she uses is a situation where a manager has been explicitly asked to collaborate with other managers and yet the culture is competitive and there are no teambuilding opportunities. She suggests that there is a lack of clarity in the roles that managers are expected to play and speculates that they have lagged behind the complex structures, causing 'double-bind' 'no-win situations' where 'you are damned if you do and damned if you don't'.

Coaching is used to help a person move forward. It is about change and focuses on results. It is therefore no surprise that many organisations are turning to coaching. *Starr*[103] asserts that coaches work from a set of common principles:

- Maintain a commitment to support the individual.
- Build the coaching relationship on truth, openness and trust.
- The coachee is responsible for the results they are generating.
- The coachee is capable of much better results than they are currently generating.
- Focus on what the coachee thinks and experiences.
- Coachees can generate perfect solutions.
- The conversation is based on equality.

Listening is an essential skill and Starr describes different levels of listening, from cosmetic (it looks as if I am listening, but actually I am someplace else) to deep (more focused on you than me – getting a sense of who you are). Asking questions, giving supportive feedback and using intuition are all part of the coach's tool kit. Most coaches use a framework for the session. A common model is the GROW model:[104]

- **Goals** – What does the coachee want to achieve? How do they want to feel afterwards?
- **Reality** – What is the scenario? What is the context? What are the problems? How have they been handled?
- **Options** – What are the possible actions? Which are the most attractive? What has worked in the past?
- **Wrap-up** – What actions are needed? What does success look like? What if things get in the way?

It is easy for managers to slip into habitual ways of thinking and behaving. Some problems take the person relentlessly around the same cycle of thoughts. Powerful questions can stop the circle and help the person to move forward. Coaching can be a helpful mechanism to engage in change. *Grant and Greene* conclude:

Coaching teaches us to monitor our progress and change direction when necessary. As we reach milestones on the way we need to take time to celebrate our successes. The key to it all is action, continuous and delibrate action.[105]

Coaching has also caught the attention of critics who charge it as an 'unregulated, unstructured and (potentially) unethical process' unless the process is evidence based.[106] *Chapman*[107] in her article urges psychologists to empirically test the contribution that coaching can make in performance and behaviour.

Mentoring requires a set of skills that includes the role of a coach. *Clutterbuck and Wynne*[108] define four roles – counsellor, networker, facilitator and coach – and say that 'at its simplest the mentor is there to help the mentee to learn'. However, research into mentoring illustrates that organisations need to be fully committed to the idea and ensure that the individuals are fully prepared for the programme to prevent the onset of problems. Benefits to be gained are obvious and include managerial effectiveness, communication improvements, the promotion of equal opportunities and self-learning.

LEARNING THEORY APPLIED TO STUDY SKILLS

There are three fundamental features of effective study skills:

- good organisation;
- active planned sessions; and
- psychological preparation.

Organisation Material is more easily learned when it is associated and organised in as many ways as possible. In addition to your written and organised notes, use other senses such as visual sense (draw maps, plans and posters) and auditory sense (make and play back revision cassette tapes). Using resources effectively (time, library, tutors) is self-evident, essential, but frequently forgotten.

Active planned sessions Learning is enhanced when you distribute your working sessions and avoid cramming. It is sensible to allow reasonable time breaks and recall sessions. Being constantly active in your learning – that is, ensuring that you understand the material and that you are not passively rewriting notes without thinking them through – is also critical. Constantly testing your knowledge and reviewing material are also good practice.

Psychological preparation Setting targets and goals is important for readiness to learn and cutting down procrastination time. Setting your own psychological contract, by aiming to achieve a goal, being clear about what you are planning to learn and then rewarding yourself when you have reached the target has also proved successful. The environment also promotes this readiness to learn and sitting in the same room or at the same desk can encourage a positive learning attitude. Being positive, getting rid of anxiety and emotional factors may be the most difficult but is probably the most important part of this preparation process.

APPLICATIONS OF LEARNING THEORY TO ORGANISATIONS

The list below is not exhaustive but identifies some of the major areas where it is possible to apply the theories of learning.

1 **Self-development**
 - Learning what to 'do' (for example, skills and knowledge).
 - Learning how to 'be' (role behaviour).
 - Learning the ropes (socialisation process and culture) and the social rules (norms and attitudes).
2 **Development of others**
 - Personal development – training others and developing their potential (including skills of mentoring, assessing, advising and coaching).
 - Development of planned learning events.
3 **Development of learning culture**
 - Policy development – developing policies for 'learning organisations'; coping with changes and development; enabling 'loose', creative and lateral thinking.

Refresh your understanding
Activity 5E
www.pearsoned.co.uk/mullins

Critical reflection ?????

'Less attention should be given to the examination of subject knowledge and more to a stronger focus on the appreciation of life skills, personal development, the use of technology and the ability to adapt to change.' Do you think the way in which students are assessed is outdated? What form of assessment would you recommend?

MANAGEMENT IN THE NEWS

Learning online

Online learning comes of age

Linda Anderson

New technology allows institutions to take the distance out of remote learning, comments Ray Irving, head of learning resources for the MBA at Warwick Business School in the UK.

Certainly innovation means that e-learning tools make distance learning a viable – and for some a preferable – alternative to more traditional face-to-face, classroom-based learning. There is already a huge market potential for e-learning in Asia, and distance/e-learning is also thriving in the US. The research report 'Growing by Degrees: Online Education in the US 2005', published last November, gives a very positive outlook on online education. It says that online enrolment in the US increased from 1.98m in 2003 to 2.35m a year later, a growth rate more than 10 times that predicted by the National Center for Education Statistics for the general post-secondary student population. Elaine Allen, professor of statistics and entrepreneurship at Babson College, who conducted the research with Jeff Seaman, believes that the reason for the success of online education lies in the Internet. 'We truly are becoming a global community, so we are able to pull students from all over the place. And it is an untapped market, even for established universities,' she adds.

Richard Straub, president of the European eLearning Industry Group, also sees a change in the market. Initially, he says, e-learning resembled a classroom on a CD-Rom, it was a very rigid format. 'But e-learning has moved from this formal information to a much more informal, integrated type of learning,' he adds. As technology has improved, demand has increased. The flexibility of the technology now on offer, from synchronous and asynchronous video conferencing to blogs and instant messaging, has allowed schools to flex their imaginations when it comes to creating and designing distance-learning programmes. At Warwick, for example, podcasts allow audio interviews with academics to be delivered online so that participants can download them on to portable players.

Meanwhile, Spain's Instituto de Empresa has launched a Global Communities MBA, a blended programme pitched at young professionals unwilling to interrupt their careers. The programme can be followed from anywhere in the world. However, it is its innovative use of virtual communities that its creators believe give it the edge on other distance-learning programmes. These communities – comprising IE alumni and executives from the corporate world – are focused on specific regions, sectors, functions or other areas of interest. Students can join as many communities as they wish and benefit from mentors and advisers from around the world. The communities interact using technologies such as weblogs and videoconferences and students remain members of the communities even after completing the programme. This in turn means that IE students can benefit from life-long learning.

For those companies which cannot or do not wish to rely on institutions for their learning and training programmes, corporate universities – inhouse training – remain popular. Schlomo Ben-Hur, chief learning officer at Daimler-Chrysler Financial Services, says the company's corporate academy is thriving. When he took on the role in 2000, the academy more closely resembled a training area. 'We tried to consolidate. We need to align the development and learning initiatives with the needs of the individual.'

Although working closely with business schools, it became clear to the company that it could not outsource initiatives in areas such as leadership, succession planning and organisational development. However, business schools continue to play a key role and co-operation rather than rivalry between schools and corporate universities is the way forward.

Source: Anderson, L., 'Online learning comes of age', *Financial Times*, 20 March 2006. Copyright © 2006 The Financial Times Limited, reproduced with permission.

Discussion questions

1 What are the strengths and shortcomings of e-learning in an organisational setting? Is it only appropriate for management learning such as that described in the article or does it have other applications?

2 Is e-learning anything more than classical conditioning? Evaluate e-learning initiatives such as these in the light of some of the theories of learning outlined in the chapter – for instance, Kolb's model of the learning cycle (Figure 5.4).

SELECTIVITY IN ATTENTION AND PERCEPTION

It is not possible to have an understanding of perception without taking into account its sensory basis. We are not able to attend to everything in our environment; our sensory systems have limits. The physical limits therefore insist that we are selective in our attention and perception. Early pioneer work by psychologists has resulted in an understanding of universal laws that underlie the perceptual process. It seems that we cannot help but search for meaning and understanding in our environment. The way in which we categorise and organise this sensory information is based on a range of factors including the present situation, our emotional state and any experiences of the same or a similar event.

Some information may be considered highly important to us and may result in immediate action or speech; in other instances, the information may be simply 'parked' or assimilated in other ideas and thoughts. The link between perception and memory processes becomes obvious. Some of our 'parked' material may be forgotten or, indeed, changed and reconstructed over time.[1]

We should be aware of the assumptions that are made throughout the perceptual process, below our conscious threshold. We have learned to take for granted certain constants in our environment. We assume that features of our world will stay the same and thus we do not need to spend our time and energy seeing things afresh and anew. We make a number of inferences throughout the entire perceptual process. Although these inferences may save time and speed up the process, they may also lead to distortions and inaccuracies.

Perception as information processing It is common to see the stages of perception described as an information-processing system: (top–down) information (stimuli) (Box A) is selected at one end of the process (Box B), then interpreted (Box C), and translated (Box D), resulting in action or thought patterns (Box E), as shown in Figure 6.1. However, it is important to note that such a model simplifies the process and although it makes it easy to understand (and will be used to structure this chapter), it does not do justice to the complexity and dynamics of the process. In certain circumstances, we may select information out of the environment because of the way we categorise the world. The dotted line illustrates this 'bottom–up' process.

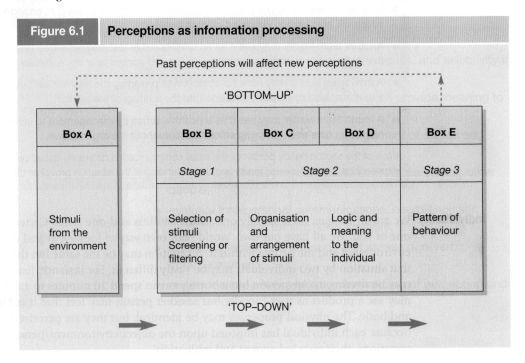

| Figure 6.1 | Perceptions as information processing |

For instance, if a manager has been advised by colleagues that a particular trainee has managerial potential, the manager may be specifically looking for confirmation that those views are correct. This process has been known as 'top down' because the cognitive processes are influencing the perceptual readiness of the individual to select certain information. This emphasises the active nature of the perceptual process. We do not passively digest the information from our senses, but we actively attend and indeed, at times, seek out certain information.

Meaning to the individual

The process of perception explains the manner in which information (stimuli) from the environment around us is selected and organised to provide meaning for the individual. Perception is the mental function of giving significance to stimuli such as shapes, colours, movement, taste, sounds, touch, smells, pain, pressures and feelings. Perception gives rise to individual behavioural responses to particular situations.

Despite the fact that a group of people may 'physically see' the same thing, they each have their own version of what is seen – their perceived view of reality. Consider, for example, the image (published by W. E. Hill in *Puck*, 6 November 1915) shown in Figure 6.2. What do you see? Do you see a young, attractive, well-dressed woman? Or do you see an older, poor woman? Or can you now see both? **And who can say with certainty that there is just the one, 'correct' answer?**

Internal and external factors The first stage in the process of perception is selection and attention. Why do we attend to certain stimuli and not to others? There are two important factors to consider in this discussion: first, internal factors relating to the state of the individual; second, the environment and influences external to the individual. The process of perceptual selection is based, therefore, on both internal and external factors.

Figure 6.2

INTERNAL FACTORS

Our sensory systems have limits – we are not able to see for 'miles and miles' or hear very low or very high-pitched sounds. All our senses have specialist nerves that respond differently to the forms of energy that are received. For instance, our eyes receive and convert light waves into electrical signals that are transmitted to the visual cortex of the brain and translated into meaning.

Our sensory system is geared to respond to changes in the environment. This has particular implications for the way in which we perceive the world and it explains why we are able to ignore the humming of the central heating system but notice instantly a telephone ringing. The term used to describe the way in which we disregard the familiar is 'habituation'.

Sensory limits or thresholds As individuals we may differ in terms of our sensory limits or thresholds. Without eye glasses some people would not be able to read a car's number plate at the distance required for safety. People differ not only in their absolute thresholds but also in their ability to discriminate between stimuli. For instance, it may not be possible for the untrained to distinguish between different grades of tea but this would be an everyday event for the trained tea taster. We are able to learn to discriminate and are able to train our senses to recognise small differences between stimuli. It is also possible for us to adapt to unnatural environments and learn to cope.[2]

We may also differ in terms of the amount of sensory information we need to reach our own comfortable equilibrium. Some individuals would find loud music at a party or gig uncomfortable and unpleasant, whereas for others the intensity of the music is part of the total enjoyment. Likewise, if we are deprived of sensory information for too long this can lead to feelings of discomfort and fatigue. Indeed, research has shown that if the brain is deprived of sensory information then it will manufacture its own and subjects will hallucinate.[3] It is possible to conclude therefore that the perceptual process is rooted to the sensory limitations of the individual.

Psychological factors

Psychological factors will also affect what is perceived. These internal factors, such as personality, learning and motives, will give rise to an inclination to perceive certain stimuli with a readiness to respond in certain ways. This has been called an individual's perceptual set (*see* Figure 6.3). Differences in the ways individuals acquire information have been used as one of four scales in the Myers–Briggs Type Indicator (discussed in Chapter 4). They distinguish individuals who 'tend to accept and work with what is given in the here-and-now,

| Figure 6.3 | Factors affecting an individual's perceptual set |

and thus become realistic and practical' (sensing types) from others who go beyond the information from the senses and look at the possible patterns, meanings and relationships. These 'intuitive types' 'grow expert at seeing new possibilities and new ways of doing things'. Myers and Briggs stress the value of both types and emphasise the importance of complementary skills and variety in any successful enterprise or relationship.[4]

Personality and perception have also been examined in the classic experiments by *Witkin et al.* on field dependence/independence. Field-dependent individuals were found to be reliant on the context of the stimuli, the cues given in the situation, whereas field-independent subjects relied mainly on their internal bodily cues and less on the environment. These experiments led Witkin to generalise to other settings outside the psychological laboratory and to suggest that individuals use, and need, different information from the environment to make sense of their world.[5]

The needs of an individual

The needs of an individual will affect their perceptions. For example, a manager deeply engrossed in preparing an urgent report may screen out ringing telephones, the sound of computers, people talking and furniture being moved in the next office, but will respond readily to the smell of coffee brewing. The most desirable and urgent needs will almost certainly affect an individual perceptual process.

The 'Pollyanna Principle' claims that pleasant stimuli will be processed more quickly and remembered more precisely than unpleasant stimuli. However, it must be noted that intense internal drives may lead to perceptual distortions of situations (or people) and an unwillingness to absorb certain painful information. This will be considered later in this chapter.

Learning from experiences has a critical effect throughout all the stages of the perceptual process. It will affect the stimuli perceived in the first instance, and then the ways in which those stimuli are understood and processed, and finally the response which is given. For example, it is likely that a maintenance engineer visiting a school for the first time will notice different things about it than will a teacher attending an interview or a child arriving on the first day. The learning gained from experiences colours what is seen and processed.

The importance of language

Our language plays an important role in the way we perceive the world. Our language not only labels and distinguishes the environment for us but also structures and guides our thinking patterns. Even if we are proficient skiers, we do not have many words we can use to describe the different texture of snow; we would be reliant on using layers of adjectives. The Inuit, however, have 13 words for snow in their language. Our language is part of the culture we experience and learn to take for granted. Culture differences are relevant because they emphasise the impact of social learning on the perception of people and their surroundings.

So, language not only reflects our experience but also shapes whether and what we experience. It influences our relationships with others and with the environment. Consider a situation where a student is using a library in a UK university for the first time. The student is from South Asia where the word 'please' is incorporated in the verb and in intonation; a separate word is not used. When the student requests help, the assistant may consider the student rude because they did not use the word 'please'. By causing offence the student has quite innocently affected the library assistant's perceptions.

Much is communicated in how words are said and in the silences between words. In the UK speech is suggestive and idiomatic speech is common:

'Make no bones about it' (means get straight to the point).
'Sent to Coventry' (means to be socially isolated).

And action is implied rather than always stated:

'I hope you won't mind if' (means 'I am going to').
'I'm afraid I really can't see my way to ...' (means 'no').

Cultural differences

The ways in which people interact are also subject to cultural differences and such differences may be misconstrued. Embarrassment and discomfort can occur when emotional lines are broken. This was demonstrated in an American study that researched the experience of Japanese students visiting the USA for the first time. The researchers felt that the Japanese students faced considerable challenges in adapting to the new culture. Some of the surprises that the students reported related to social interaction:

> Casual visits and frequent phone calls at midnight to the host room-mate were a new experience to them. The sight of opposite-sex partners holding hands or kissing in public places also surprised them … That males do cooking and shopping in the household or by themselves, that fathers would play with children, and that there was frequent intimacy displayed between couples were all never-heard-of in their own experiences at home.[6]

The ways in which words are used and the assumptions made about shared understanding are dependent upon an individual's culture and upbringing. In cultures where it is 'normal' to explain all details clearly, explicitly and directly (such as the USA), other cultures may find the 'spelling out' of all the details unnecessary and embarrassing. In France, ambiguity and subtlety are expected and much is communicated by what is **not** said. *Hall* distinguished low-context cultures (direct, explicit communication) from high-context cultures (meaning assumed and non-verbal signs significant).[7]

> *Those organizations that can create a culture that challenges unhelpful perceptual processes (stemming, say, from ignorance, prejudice or arrogance) will, in our view, be more able to absorb new information and respond intelligently to change. Broadening our mind, however, is much easier said than done. To understand why this is so, it is worth looking at influences on our perceptual processes. At the most fundamental level lie our values and beliefs. These also colour what we see and how we interpret events. Given this, it is important we reflect on how our own values influence the decisions we make.*
>
> P. Dainty and M. Anderson, 'Mindset for Managers'[8]

EXTERNAL FACTORS

The knowledge of, familiarity with or expectations about a given situation or previous experiences will influence perception. External factors refer to the nature and characteristics of the stimuli. There is usually a tendency to give more attention to stimuli which are, for example:

- large
- moving
- intense
- loud
- contrasted
- bright
- novel
- repeated or
- stand out from the background.

Any number of these factors may be present at a given time or in a given situation. It is therefore the **total pattern** of the stimuli together with the **context** in which they occur that influence perception. For example, it is usually a novel or unfamiliar stimulus that is more noticeable, but a person is more likely to perceive the familiar face of a friend among a group of people all dressed in the same-style uniform (*see* Figure 6.4).[9] The sight of a fork-lift truck on the factory floor of a manufacturing organisation is likely to be perceived quite

Figure 6.4	Is everybody happy?

Source: Block, R. J. and Yuker, H. E., *Can You Believe Your Eyes?*, Robson Books (2002), p. 163.

differently from one in the corridor of a university. The word 'terminal' is likely to be perceived differently in the context of: (i) a hospital, (ii) an airport or (iii) a computer firm. Consumer psychologists and marketing experts apply these perceptual principles with extraordinary success for some of their products.

Refresh your understanding

Activity 6A

www.pearsoned.co.uk/mullins

Critical reflection

We often mask what we really feel, act in ways that cover our true emotions and speak words that we don't really mean – so in our dealings with other people we need to look beyond what is seen and heard and delve beneath the surface. How do you think we can best judge the true beliefs and intentions of other people?

ORGANISATION AND ARRANGEMENT OF STIMULI

The Gestalt School of Psychology led by Max Wertheimer claimed that the process of perception is innately organised and patterned. It described the process as one that has built-in field effects. In other words, the brain can act like a dynamic, physical field in which interaction among elements is an intrinsic part. The Gestalt School produced a series of principles, which are still readily applicable today. Some of the most significant include the following:

- figure and ground
- grouping and
- closure.

Figure and ground

The figure–ground principle states that figures are seen against a background. The figure does not have to be an object; it could be merely a geometrical pattern. Many textiles are perceived as figure–ground relationships. These relationships are often reversible, as in the popular example shown in Figure 6.5. What do you see? Do you see a white chalice (or small stand shape) in the centre of the frame? Or do you see the dark profiles of twins facing each other on the edge of the frame? Now look again. Can you see the other shape?

The figure–ground principle has applications in all occupational situations. It is important that employees know and are able to attend to the significant aspects (the figure) and treat other elements of the job as context (background). Early training sessions aim to identify and focus on the significant aspects of a task. Managerial effectiveness can also be judged in terms of chosen priorities (the figure). Stress could certainly occur for those employees who are uncertain about their priorities and are unable to distinguish between the significant and less significant tasks. They feel overwhelmed by the 'whole' picture.

Figure 6.5

Grouping

The grouping principle refers to the tendency to organise shapes and patterns instantly into meaningful groupings or patterns on the basis of their proximity or similarity. Parts that are close in time or space tend to be perceived together. For example, in Figure 6.6(a), the workers are more likely to be perceived as nine independent people, but in Figure 6.6(b), because of the proximity principle, the workers may be perceived as three distinct groups of people.

Taxi firms often use the idea of grouping to display their telephone number. In the example below, which of the following numbers – (a), (b) or (c) – is most likely to be remembered easily?

Figure 6.6

(a) (b)

347 474	347474	34 74 74
(a)	(b)	(c)

Similar parts tend to be seen together as forming a familiar group. In the following example there is a tendency to see alternate lines of characters – crosses and noughts (or circles). This is because the horizontal similarity is usually greater than the vertical similarity. However, if the page is turned sideways the figure may be perceived as alternate noughts and crosses in each line.

```
×   ×   ×   ×   ×   ×   ×   ×
○   ○   ○   ○   ○   ○   ○   ○
×   ×   ×   ×   ×   ×   ×   ×
○   ○   ○   ○   ○   ○   ○   ○
```

It is also interesting to note that when asked to describe this pattern many people refer to alternate lines of noughts and crosses – rather than crosses and noughts.

There is also an example here of the impact of cultural differences, mentioned earlier. One of the authors undertook a teaching exchange in the USA and gave this exercise to a class of American students. Almost without exception the students described the horizontal pattern correctly as alternate rows of crosses and noughts (or zeros). The explanation appears to be that Americans do not know the game of 'noughts and crosses' but refer to this as 'tic-tac-toe'.

Closure There is also a tendency to complete an incomplete figure – to (mentally) fill in the gaps and to perceive the figure as a whole. This creates an overall and meaningful image rather than an unconnected series of lines or blobs.

In the example in Figure 6.7 most people are likely to see the blobs as either the letter B or the number 13, possibly depending on whether at the time they had been more concerned with written material or dealing in numbers. However, for some people, the figure may remain just a series of 11 discrete blobs or may be perceived as some other (to them) meaningful pattern/object. According to Gestalt theory, perceptual organisation is instant and spontaneous. We cannot stop ourselves making meaningful assumptions about our environment. The Gestaltists emphasised the ways in which the elements interact and claimed that the new pattern or structure perceived had a character of its own, hence the famous phrase 'the whole is more than the sum of its parts'.

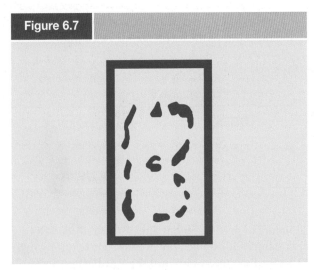

Figure 6.7

Source: King, R., *Introduction to Psychology,* Third Edition, McGraw-Hill (1996) Reproduced with permission from the author, Professor Richard King, University of South Carolina and the McGraw-Hill Companies, Inc.

PERCEPTUAL ILLUSIONS

Here are some examples to help you judge your perceptive skills.

In Figure 6.8 try reading aloud the four words. It is possible that you find yourself 'caught' in a perceptual set that means that you tend to pronounce 'machinery' as if it too were a Scottish surname.

In Figure 6.9, which of the centre blue circles is the larger – A or B? Although you may have guessed that the two centre circles are in fact the same size, the circle on the right (B) may well **appear** larger because it is framed by smaller circles. The centre circle on the left (A) may well **appear** smaller because it is framed by larger circles.

Figure 6.8	

M – A – C – D – O – N – A – L – D
M – A – C – P – H – E – R – S – O – N
M – A – C – D – O – U – G – A – L – L
M – A – C – H – I – N – E – R – Y

Figure 6.9	

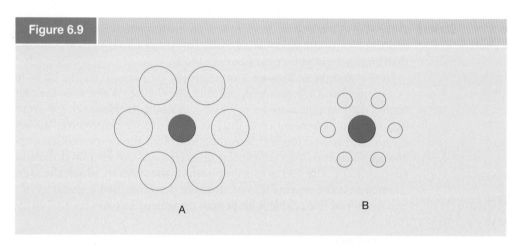

A B

In Figure 6.10 try saying the *colour* of the word, *not* the word itself.

Figure 6.10	

BLUE	GREY	YELLOW	MAUVE
BLACK	ORANGE	GREEN	RED
WHITE	PURPLE	BLUE	BROWN

The physiological nature of perception has already been discussed briefly but it is of relevance here in the discussion of illusions. Why does the circle on the right in Figure 6.9 look bigger? Why is it difficult to say the colour, not the word? These examples demonstrate the way our brain can be fooled. Indeed, we make assumptions about our world that go beyond the pure sensations our brain receives.

Beyond reality Perception goes beyond the sensory information and converts these patterns to a three-dimensional reality that we understand. This conversion process, as we can see, is easily tricked. We may not be aware of the inferences we are making as they are part of our conditioning and learning. The Stroop experiment illustrates this perfectly.[11] (See Assignment 1 at the end of this chapter.) An illustration of the way in which we react automatically to stimuli is the illusion of the impossible triangle (*see* Figure 6.11).

Even when we know the triangle is impossible we still cannot stop ourselves from completing the triangle and attempting to make it meaningful. We thus go beyond what is given and make assumptions about the world, which in certain instances are wildly incorrect. Psychologists and designers may make positive use of these assumptions to project positive images of a product or the environment. For instance, colours may be used to induce certain atmospheres in buildings; designs of wallpaper or texture of curtains may be used to create feelings of spaciousness or cosiness. Packaging of products may tempt us to see something as bigger or perhaps more precious.

Figure 6.11	

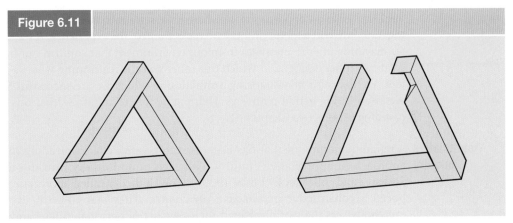

Source: Gregory, R. L., *Odd Perceptions*, Methuen (1986) p. 71. Reprinted by permission of the publishers, Routledge, a division of Taylor & Francis Ltd.

CONNECTION OF THE CONSCIOUS, UNCONSCIOUS AND PHYSIOLOGY

Perceptual processes demonstrate the integration of our conscious self, our unconscious self and our physiology.

- Conscious self – this means our immediate awareness of what is around us. The state of mind we are in when we are making decisions to act and the meaning we place on the world.
- Unconscious self – this relates to the way we carry out tasks with no active thinking taking place; the way we habitually do things automatically – our autopilot. These habits allow the conscious mind to be free to assess new and novel decisions. Habits are very important to us as we do not want to think about everything we do, but habits can get in the way when we want to change habits. In neurolinguistic programming, 'anchors' keep habits in place.[12]

Anchors can be visual, like people, clothes and cars. They can be auditory, like a particular piece of music, an advertising jingle or the voice of a dear friend. They can be kinaesthetic, like the feel of your favourite clothes, sitting in your armchair or the warmth of a hot bath. They can be olfactory or gustatory, like the smell of a hospital (why do they all smell the same?) or the taste of coffee or chocolate (Lindt!). Words can be anchors because they evoke ideas; your name is a powerful anchor for your identity. Anchors evoke emotional states and most of the time we do not notice the anchors, only the states. Some anchors are neutral. Some put us into good states. Others put us into bad states.[13]

- Physiology – the interconnectedness with physiology has already been explained and there is growing evidence for using research identifying the mind–body connections. *Spitzer* explains that:

The human brain contains in the order of 100 billion (10^{11}) neurons and each neuron has up to 10 thousand connections of which less than ten are to the same neuron, such that each neuron is connected with a thousand other neurons. So there are approximately 100 trillion connections (10^{14}).[14]

Each thought and activity corresponds to a pattern of neuron activity – so by repeating the same thought or action we strengthen the associated neural connection. Thus automatically connecting the conscious and unconscious mind with physiology, each aspect influences the other and our emotions operate in all.

Framing The term framing is used to explain how we interpret particular circumstances. Rather like a picture frame, we place into the frame our particular perspective, focus and colour on things. So if we are feeling happy our experience is being 'framed' in a positive way. What is in the 'frame' will depend on what is filtered in or out. Whether we look at a difficult situation as a 'problem' or as an opportunity, or whether we see a mistake as a terrible failure or as a learning moment, will depend on how we have 'framed' the experience. If we are in a good mood we may only filter in messages from our environment that confirm our happy state, we may create an inner dialogue in which our inner voice is reaffirming why we are feeling so content. We may also be visualising a situation in which we are successful and these thoughts are establishing neural pathways. Helping people to reframe situations can be part of the coaching process (*see* Chapter 4).

Appreciative enquiry A reframing technique that has been used to positive effect in leading change has been the approach of appreciative enquiry. This technique initially introduced by Cooperrider, Srivestva and colleagues[15] in the 1980s created a theory called appreciative enquiry that proposed a constructive perspective on change. They started with the proposition that everybody sees the world through their own set of personal 'filters' and that sharing these could be helpful – thus differences should be valued. For every organisation, team or individual something works well, which is worth building on and extending. That which we understand to be reality arises from what we focus on and reality is created in the moment.

They emphasised the importance of language as the way we create our reality and therefore we can use it to create many realities. Asking questions of an organisation, the group, the individual means they are influenced in some way and that people have more confidence to progress to the future when they take with them what has been most helpful and of value from the past. It is important to value difference because we see the world through our own set of personal filters that is often different from a shared set of reality. So, in their approach, teams of people are faced with a different frame, a different mind-set in which to analyse and evaluate change.

Hammond[16] describes the different steps to solving an organisational problem:

Refresh your understanding

Activity 6B

www.pearsoned.co.uk/mullins

Traditional problem-solving approach	Appreciative enquiry approach
- 'felt need' – identification of problem	- appreciating/valuing the best of 'what is'
- analysis of causes	- envisioning 'what might be'
- analysis of possible solutions	- dialoguing 'what should be'
- action planning	- innovating 'what will be'

It is the author's experience that teams of individuals who experience appreciative enquiry techniques find them to be empowering and creative.

PERCEIVING OTHER PEOPLE

Is it any wonder that conflicts and differences of opinion occur when we perceive others? The way we see others, the habits we have formed, the associations we have made and the assumptions we make lead us to make errors and distortions when we are perceiving others. The focus of the following section is to examine the perception of people and to consider the impact this has on the management and development of people at work.

The principles and examples of perceptual differences explained earlier apply to the way we perceive others. Some examples might be as follows:

- **Grouping** – the way in which a manager may think of a number of staff – for example, either working in close proximity; or with some common feature such as all IT technicians, all graduate trainees or all black workers; as a homogeneous group rather than a collection of individuals, each with their own separate identity and characteristics.
- **Figure and ground** – a manager may notice a new recruit and set them apart from the group because of particular characteristics such as appearance or physical features.
- **Closure** – the degree to which unanimity is perceived and decisions made or action taken in the belief that there is full agreement with staff when, in fact, a number of staff may be opposed to the decision or action.

A manager's perception of the workforce will influence attitudes in dealing with people and the style of managerial behaviour adopted. The way in which managers approach the performance of their jobs and the behaviour they display towards subordinate staff are likely to be conditioned by predispositions about people, human nature and work. An example of this is the style of management adopted on the basis of McGregor's Theory X and Theory Y suppositions, discussed in Chapter 12. In making judgements about other people it is important to try to perceive their underlying intent and motivation, not *just* the resultant behaviour or actions.

The perception of people's performance can be affected by the organisation of stimuli. In employment interviews, for example, interviewers are susceptible to contrast effects and the perception of a candidate is influenced by the rating given to immediately preceding candidates. Average candidates may be rated highly if they follow people with low qualifications, but rated lower when following people with higher qualifications.[17]

Testing assumptions Recognising the assumptions held and testing these out requires a heightened level of critical reflection. Many leadership and management development courses start with a 'self-awareness and diagnostic' module intended to help their participants understand and recognise their style and preferences and the impact their style has on others. Courses which take a more challenging stance will encourage managers to question their existing frames of mind and challenge them to constantly re-evaluate their purpose, strategies and action. Such courses take an action enquiry approach[18] and Testing Out Leadership courses typically start with an awareness of self.

Testing out assumptions[19]

Action enquiry: widening our attention

Making unconscious assumptions can limit learning. Failure is perhaps the most common way we become aware that they are only assumptions – at least the erroneous ones – not facts, as we may have previously believed. The later in life we wait to discover our erroneous assumptions in this manner, the more painful the consequences of the failure – divorce, job-loss, etc.

→

Testing out assumptions – continued

We cannot be aware of all our assumptions and cannot help but act out of our assumptions, but it is profoundly important that we learn to test our assumptions in the midst of action. By doing so we create a climate in which others:

1 in the organisation become more aware that they too are making assumptions;

2 become more willing to help us test our own assumptions (sometimes even before we are aware that we are making assumptions);

3 gradually become more willing to test their own assumptions as well.

Once formed, assumptions can blind us to the need for enquiry. We therefore need to behave in a way that reveals the unknown in the midst of action. Cultivating ongoing self-awareness and consciousness is an essential part of action inquiry and self or organisational transformation – a lifetime practice. Acting in such a way and being visibly committed to such a course of action places you in a stronger position to influence others to do the same.

Our attention, perceptions and actions are limited by our untested assumptions.

● Our attention does not register a great deal of what occurs – it is selective and limited by our frame of attention at any given time.

● Our language, mind-sets, frame of reference tend to highlight and emphasise some aspects of our experience and dispose us to see things in a certain way – personal bias.

● Our actions generate much of what we know but we are often unaware of how our actions skew what we know by the impact they have on others and their response.

● Data we have about the world are ordinarily about the past rather than the present, are drastically unsystematic and incomplete and rarely tested for validity on the spot. Scientific method can only disconfirm not confirm a proposition. We often therefore rely on assumptions to simplify matters.

Not all assumptions will be tested or tested well. Many assumptions will be tested and generate learning, subsequent success and higher morale, while minimising failure and accompanying lower morale. An organisation that cultivates courageous, intelligent, competent testing of assumptions will have an enormous competitive advantage over those in the same field which do not.

The dynamics of interpersonal perception

Unlike the perception of an object that just exists, another individual will react to you and be affected by your behaviour – the dynamics are all-important. This interaction is illustrated in the following quotation:

> You are a pain in the neck and to stop you giving me a pain in the neck I protect my neck by tightening my neck muscles, which gives me the pain in the neck you are.[20]

The interaction of individuals thus provides an additional layer of interpretation and complexity. The cue that we may attend to, the expectation we may have, the assumptions we may make, the response pattern that occurs, leave more scope for errors and distortions. We are not only perceiving the stimulus (that is, the other person), we are also processing their reactions to us at the same time that they are processing our reactions to them.

Thus person perception differs from the perception of objects because:

● it is a continually dynamic and changing process; and

● the perceiver is a part of this process who will influence and be influenced by the other people in the situation (*see* Figure 6.12).[21]

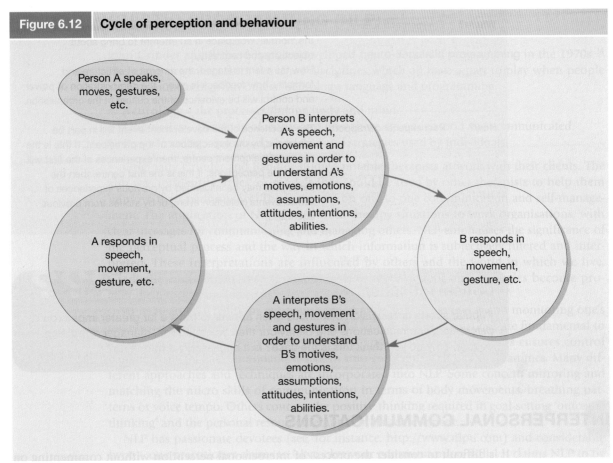

| Figure 6.12 | Cycle of perception and behaviour |

Person A speaks, moves, gestures, etc.

Person B interprets A's speech, movement and gestures in order to understand A's motives, emotions, assumptions, attitudes, intentions, abilities.

B responds in speech, movement, gesture, etc.

A responds in speech, movement, gesture, etc.

A interprets B's speech, movement and gestures in order to understand B's motives, emotions, assumptions, attitudes, intentions, abilities.

Source: From Guirdham, M., *Interactive Behaviour at Work*, Third Edition, Financial Times Prentice Hall (2002), p. 162. Reproduced with permission from Pearson Education Ltd.

Setting and environment

Person perception will also be affected by the setting, and the environment may play a critical part in establishing rapport. For example, next time you are involved in a formal meeting, consider the following factors that will all influence the perceptual process.

For example, attending an in-house development centre:

Why?	Purpose of and motives for meeting	Likely to be an important event for the participant, may be a catalyst for promotion and may signal new and relevant development opportunities. Chance to be visible and demonstrate skills and abilities. Opportunity to network with other managers. Thus high emotional cost to participant.
Who?	Status/role/age/gender/ ethnic group/appearance/ personality/interests/attitudes	How participant prepares for the event will be influenced by factors listed opposite and previous history and encounters of all parties.
When?	Time, date of meeting	The timing of the event might be particularly affected by events outside of the workplace. So if the participant has dependants or responsibilities, the timing of this event may become significant. If the participant is asked to attend in the middle of a religious festival, then again the relevance of time is critical.

Berne identified and labelled the ego states as follows:

- **Child ego state** – behaviour that demonstrates the feelings we remember as a child. This state may be associated with having fun, playing, impulsiveness, rebelliousness, spontaneous behaviour and emotional responses.
- **Adult ego state** – behaviour that concerns our thought processes and the processing of facts and information. In this state we may be objective, rational, reasonable – seeking information and receiving facts.
- **Parent ego state** – behaviour that concerns the attitudes, feelings and behaviour incorporated from external sources, primarily our parents. This state refers to feelings about right and wrong and how to care for other people.

He claimed that the three ego states were universal, but the content of the ego states would be unique to each person. We may be unaware which ego state we are operating in and may shift from one to another. All people are said to behave in each of these states at different times. The three ego states exist simultaneously within each individual, although at any particular time any one state many dominate the other two.

Preferred ego state We all have a preferred ego state which we may revert to: some individuals may continually advise and criticise others (the constant Parents); some may analyse, live only with facts and distrust feelings (the constant Adult); some operate with strong feelings all the time, consumed with anger or constantly clowning (the constant Child). Berne emphasised that the states should not be judged as superior or inferior but as different. Analysis of ego states may reveal why communication breaks down or why individuals may feel manipulated or used.

Berne insists that it is possible to identify the ego state from the words, voice, gestures, and attitude of the person communicating. For example, it would be possible to discern the ego state of a manager if they said the following:

'Pass me the file on the latest sales figures.'
'How do you think we could improve our safety record?'
(**Adult ego state**)

'Let me help you with that – I can see you are struggling.'
'Look, this is the way it should be done; how many more times do I have to tell you?'
(**Parent ego state**)

'Great, it's Friday. Who's coming to the pub for a quick half?'
'That's a terrific idea – let's go for it!'
(**Child ego state**)

A dialogue can be analysed in terms not only of the ego state but also whether the transaction produced a **complementary reaction** or a **crossed reaction**. Complementary means whether the ego state was an expected and preferred response, so for instance if we look at the first statement, 'Pass me the file on the latest sales figures', the subordinate could respond: 'Certainly – I have it here' (Adult ego state) or 'Can't you look for it yourself? I only gave it to you an hour ago' (Parent ego state).

The first response was complementary whereas the second was a crossed transaction. Sometimes it may be important to 'cross' a transaction. Take the example 'Let me help you with that – I can see you are struggling' (Parent ego state). The manager may have a habit of always helping in a condescending way, making the subordinate resentful. If the subordinate meekly accepts the help with a thankful reply, this will only reinforce the manager's perception and attitude, whereas if the subordinate were to respond with 'I can manage perfectly well. Why did you think I was struggling?', it might encourage the manager to respond from the Adult ego state and thus move their ego position.

Understanding of human behaviour

Knowledge of TA can be of benefit to employees who are dealing with potentially difficult situations.[29] In the majority of work situations the Adult–Adult transactions are likely to be the norm. Where work colleagues perceive and respond by adopting the Adult ego state, such a transaction is more likely to encourage a rational, problem-solving approach and reduce the possibility of emotional conflict.

If only the world of work was always of the rational logical kind! Communications at work as elsewhere are sometimes unclear, confused and can leave the individual with 'bad feelings' and uncertainty. Berne describes a further dysfunctional transaction, which can occur when a message is sent to two ego states at the same time. For instance, an individual may say 'I passed that article to you last week, have you read it yet?'. This appears to be an adult-to-adult transaction and yet the tone of voice, the facial expressions **imply** a second ego state is involved. The underlying message says, 'Haven't you even read that yet ... you know how busy I am and yet I had time to read it!' The critical parent is addressing the Child ego state. In such 'ulterior transactions' the social message is typically Adult to Adult and the ulterior, psychological message is directed either Parent–Child or Child–Parent.

Given the incidence of stress in the workplace, analysis of communication may be one way of understanding such conflict. By focusing on the interactions occurring within the workplace, TA can aid the understanding of human behaviour. It can help to improve communication skills by assisting in interpreting a person's ego state and which form of state is likely to produce the most appropriate response. This should lead to an improvement in both customer relations and management–subordinate relations. Therefore TA can be seen as a valuable tool to aid our understanding of social situations and the games that people play both in and outside work organisations.

TA emphasises the strong links between perception and communication and illustrates the way in which they affect each other. However, it does not answer how we construct our social world in the first place, what we attend to and why, or why we have positive perceptions about some people and not others. To answer these questions we can concentrate on the stages of the perceptual process – both selection and attention, and organisation and judgement – and apply these to the perception of people.[30]

Refresh your understanding

Activity 6C

www.pearsoned.co.uk/mullins

SELECTION AND ATTENTION

What information do we select and why? The social situation consists of both verbal and non-verbal signals. The non-verbal signals include:

- bodily contact
- proximity
- orientation
- head nods
- facial expression
- gestures
- posture
- direction of gaze
- dress and appearance
- non-verbal aspects of speech.

Verbal and non-verbal signals are co-ordinated into regular sequences, often without the awareness of the parties. The mirroring of actions has been researched and is called 'postural echoing'.[31] There is considerable evidence to indicate that each person is constantly influencing the other and being influenced.[32]

Cook has suggested that in any social encounter there are two kinds of information that can be distinguished:

- **static information** – information which will not change during the encounter – for example colour, gender, height and age; and
- **dynamic information** – information which is subject to change – for example mood, posture, gestures and expression.[33]

Culture and socialisation The meanings we ascribe to these non-verbal signals are rooted in our culture and early socialisation. Thus it is no surprise that there are significant differences in the way we perceive such signals. For instance, dress codes differ in degrees of formality. *Schneider and Barsoux* summarise some interesting cultural differences:

> *Northern European managers tend to dress more informally than their Latin counterparts. At conferences, it is not unlikely for the Scandinavian managers to be wearing casual clothing, while their French counterparts are reluctant to remove their ties and jackets. For the Latin managers, personal style is important, while Anglo and Asian managers do not want to stand out or attract attention in their dress. French women managers are more likely to be dressed in ways that Anglo women managers might think inappropriate for the office. The French, in turn, think it strange that American businesswomen dress in 'man-like' business suits (sometimes with running shoes).*[34]

Impression management

In some situations we all attempt to project our attitudes, personality and competence by paying particular attention to our appearance and the impact this may have on others. This has been labelled 'impression management'[35] and the selection interview is an obvious illustration. Some information is given more weight than other information when an impression is formed. It would seem that there are central traits that are more important than others in determining our perceptions.

One of these central traits is the degree of warmth or coldness shown by an individual.[36] The timing of information also seems to be critical in the impressions we form. For example, information heard first tends to be resistant to later contradictory information. In other words, the saying 'first impressions count' is supported by research and is called '**the primacy effect**'.[37] It has also been shown that a negative first impression is more resistant to change than a positive one.[38] However, if there is a break in time we are more likely to remember the most recent information – '**the recency effect**'.

Dealings with other people

There are a number of well-documented problems that arise when perceiving other people. Many of these problems occur because of our limitations in selecting and attending to information. This selectivity may occur because:

- we already know what we are looking for and are therefore 'set' to receive only the information which confirms our initial thoughts; or
- previous training and experience have led us to short-cut and see only a certain range of behaviours; or
- we may group features together and make assumptions about their similarities.

The Gestalt principles apply equally well to the perception of people as to the perception of objects. Thus we can see, for example, that if people live in the same geographical area, assumptions may be made about not only their wealth and type of accommodation but also their attitudes, their political views and even their type of personality.

To interact effectively (present ourselves and communicate appropriately, influence others, work with them in relationships and groups or lead them) we must have a grasp of what others are thinking and feeling, including their motives, beliefs, attitudes and intentions. In social perception, accuracy and differentiation are essential but difficult. Achieving them may be linked to the complexity of a person's system of cognitive constructs.

Maureen Guirdham, *Interactive Behaviour at Work*[39]

ORGANISATION AND JUDGEMENT

The way in which we organise and make judgements about what we have perceived is to a large extent based on our previous experiences and learning. It is also important at this point to be aware of the inferences and assumptions we make which go beyond the information given. We may not always be aware of our pre-set assumptions but they will guide the way in which we interpret the behaviour of others. There has been much research into the impact of implicit personality theory.[40] In the same way that we make assumptions about the world of objects and go beyond the information provided, we also make critical inferences about people's characteristics and possible likely behaviours.

A manager might well know more about the 'type of person' A – a member of staff who has become or was already a good friend, who is seen in a variety of social situations and with whom there is a close relationship – than about B – another member of staff, in the same section as A and undertaking similar duties, but with whom there is only a formal work relationship and a limited social acquaintance. These differences in relationship, information and interaction might well influence the manager's perception if asked, for example, to evaluate the work performance of A and B.

Judgement of other people can also be influenced by perceptions of such stimuli as:

- role or status;
- occupation;
- physical factors and appearance; and
- non-verbal communication and body language.

Physical characteristics and appearance

In a discussion on managing people and management style, *Green* raises the question of how managers make judgements on those for whom they are responsible including positive and negative messages.

In my personal research people have admitted, under pressure, that certain physical characteristics tend to convey a positive or negative message. For example, some people find red hair, earrings for men, certain scents and odours, someone too tall or too short; a disability; a member of a particular ethnic group and countless other items as negative ... Similarly there will be positive factors such as appropriate hairstyle or dress for the occasion ... which may influence in a positive way.[41]

Related characteristic A person may tend to organise perception of another person in terms of the 'whole' mental picture of that person. Perceptual judgement is influenced by reference to related characteristics associated with the person and the attempt to place that person in a complete environment. In one example, an unknown visitor was introduced by the course director to 110 American students, divided into five equal groups.[42] The visitor was described differently to each group as:

1 Mr England, a student from Cambridge;
2 Mr England, demonstrator in psychology from Cambridge;
3 Mr England, lecturer in psychology from Cambridge;
4 Dr England, senior lecturer from Cambridge;
5 Professor England from Cambridge.

After being introduced to each group, the visitor left. Each group of students was then asked to estimate his height to the nearest half inch. They were also asked to estimate the height of the course director after he too had left the room. The mean estimated height of the course director, who had the same status for all groups, did not change significantly among groups. However, the estimated height of the visitor varied with perceived status: as ascribed academic status increased, so did the estimate of height (*see* Table 6.1).

Table 6.1	Estimated height according to ascribed academic status	
Group	**Ascribed academic status**	**Average estimated height**
1	Student	5' 9.9"
2	Demonstrator	5' 10.14"
3	Lecturer	5' 10.9"
4	Senior lecturer	5' 11.6"
5	Professor	6' 0.3"

Source: Adapted from Wilson, P. R., 'Perceptual distortion of height as a function of ascribed academic status', *Journal of Social Psychology*, no. 74, 1968, pp. 97–102. Reproduced with permission from Helen Dwight Reid Educational Foundation, Published by Heldref Publications, 1319 Eighteenth Street NW, Washington DC 20036–1802. Copyright © 1968.

Several popular surveys and newspaper articles appear to support the suggestion that tall men are more likely to be successful professionally and earn higher salaries than short men. (We leave you to make your own judgement about this claim!)

NON-VERBAL COMMUNICATIONS AND BODY LANGUAGE

We have referred previously to the significance of non-verbal communication and body language. This includes inferences drawn from posture, gestures, touch, invasions of personal space, extent of eye contact, tone of voice or facial expression. People are the only animals that speak, laugh and weep. Actions are more cogent than speech and humans rely heavily on body language to convey their true feelings and meanings.[43] It is interesting to note how emotions are woven creatively into email messages. Using keyboard signs in new combinations has led to a new e-language – to signal pleasure :), or unhappiness :–c, or send a rose @>---> encapsulate feelings as well as words. The growth of this practice has led to an upsurge of web pages replete with examples.

According to *Mehrabian*, in our face-to-face communication with other people the messages about our feelings and attitudes come only 7 per cent from the words we use, 38 per cent from our voice and 55 per cent from body language, including facial expressions. Significantly, when body language such as gestures and tone of voice conflicts with the words, greater emphasis is likely to be placed on the non-verbal message.[44]

Although actual percentages may vary, there appears to be general support for this contention. According to *Pivcevic*: 'It is commonly agreed that 80 per cent of communication is non-verbal; it is carried in your posture and gestures, and in the tone, pace and energy behind what you say.'[45] *McGuire* suggests when verbal and non-verbal messages are in conflict: 'Accepted wisdom from the experts is that the non-verbal signals should be the ones to rely on, and that what is not said is frequently louder than what is said, revealing attitudes and feelings in a way words can't express.'[46]

James suggests that in a sense, we are all experts on body language already and this is part of the survival instinct:

Even in a 'safe' environment like an office or meeting room you will feel a pull on your gaze each time someone new enters the room. And whether you want to or not, you will start to form opinions about a person in as little as three seconds. You can try to be fair and objective in your evaluation, but you will have little choice. This is an area where the subconscious mind bullies the conscious into submission. Like, dislike, trust, love or lust can all be promoted in as long as it takes to clear your throat. In fact most of these responses will be based on your perception of how the person looks.[47]

In our perceptions and judgement of others it is important therefore to watch and take careful note of their non-verbal communication. However, although body language may be a guide to personality, errors can easily arise if too much is inferred from a single message rather than a related cluster of actions. According to *Fletcher*: 'You won't learn to interpret people's body language accurately, and use your own to maximum effect, without working at it. If you consciously spend half an hour a day analysing people's subconscious movements, you'll soon learn how to do it – almost unconsciously.'[48] However, as *Mann* points out, with a little knowledge about the subject it is all too easy to become body conscious. Posture and gesture can unmask deceivers, but it would be dangerous to assume that everyone who avoids eye contact or rubs their nose is a fibber. Nevertheless an understanding of non-verbal communication is essential for managers and other professions where good communication skills are essential.[49]

Cultural differences

There are many cultural variations in non-verbal communications, the extent of physical contact and differences in the way body language is perceived and interpreted. Italians and South Americans tend to show their feelings through intense body language, while Japanese tend to hide their feelings and have largely eliminated overt body language from interpersonal communication. When talking to another person, the British tend to look away spasmodically, but Norwegians typically look people steadily in the eyes without altering their gaze. In South Korea, women refrain from shaking hands. Japanese often have a weak handshake whereas in Britain a firm handshake is encouraged. When the Dutch point a forefinger at their temples this is likely to be a sign of congratulations for a good idea, but with other cultures the gesture has a less complimentary implication.

In many European countries it is customary to greet people with three or four kisses on the cheek and pulling the head away may be taken as a sign of impoliteness. All cultures have specific values related to personal space and 'comfort zone'. Arabs tend to stand very close when speaking to another person but most Americans when introduced to a new person will, after shaking hands, move backwards a couple of steps to place a comfortable space between themselves and the person they have just met.[50]

A concept map of interacting with other people is set out in Figure 6.13.

Figure 6.13 Concept map of interacting with people

INTERACTING WITH PEOPLE

- DEFINITION
- FACTORS CONTRIBUTING TO RAPPORT

FACTORS
- Proxemics
- Orientation
- Environmental characteristics
- Non-verbal signs
- Other spoken communication
- Dominance roles and rituals

DEFINITION
- An interview is a conversation with a purpose usually 1:1
 Tx – THE TRANSMITTER OF THE COMMUNICATION
 Rx – THE RECEIVER OF THE COMM'N
 (there may be many Rx's)

'PURPOSE-LESS CONVERSATION'
- a form of 'social grooming' e.g. about the weather
- often with casual or unknown contacts 'Good morning, how are you?'
- ritualisation of everyday contact prior to important communications (not to do this in the UK is often considered impolite)

PROXEMICS
The closeness of the Tx to the Rx'(s)
- Consider closeness but be aware of cultural differences and taboos, especially between strangers
- With closeness note mirroring of body movements
- Including touching the Rx

ORIENTATION
Relative positions
- Side-by-side can imply friendliness, intimacy, helpfulness, etc.
- Face-to-face can imply competition, confrontation, etc.
- Territorially – on whose ground will the interview/meeting take place? (theirs/yours/neutral?)

GRAMMATICAL GIMMICKS
Superfluous and meaningless e.g.
- 'you know'
- 'whatever'
- 'I mean',
- 'really'
- and also grunts, snorts, etc.

ENVIRONMENTAL CHARACTERISTICS
- In a large space, Rx's group ... to hear better?
- In a small space Rx's separate ... maintain personal space?
- Furniture, e.g. tables ... could form psychological barriers
- No furnishings ... Rx feels exposed and vulnerable
- Ambient noise too high ... may hinder communication flow
- Distances too great
- Atmospheric conditions (heating/lighting/ventilation)

DOMINANCE ROLES AND RITUALS
Rituals of greetings and farewells
- handshake, kiss, hug, bow, salute, curtsy, raised hat, etc.

BETWEEN SEXES
- strokes, holds, pats ... friendly
- hits ... less friendly
- handshake – ritual touching for reassurance

NON-VERBAL SIGNALS

GAZE direct mutual gaze implies intimacy
 emotions perceived from eyes e.g.
 anger, pleasure, surprise

GESTURES position of fingers/hands/arms the
 same gesture may have different meanings
 across cultures

MOUTH a smile encourages and reassures
 – communicates emotional state
 – controlled or uncontrolled

TOUCH hands – fingers open, closed, fist formed
 fingers – relaxed, pointed ...
 limbs – open or closed
 hands – moving or positioned

EYEBROWS raised rapidly – greeting, flirting, etc.
 furrowed – puzzled, angry, etc.

CLOTHES indicate something of a person's values
 status and authority, or just bodily
 adornment

TONE soft/friendly – loud/assertive (of voice)
 pitch, stress and timing imply mood
 and emphasis

HEAD – nods, shakes indicative of
MOVEMENTS and tilts emotional
 states or
 moods

POSTURE lean forward – confidentially, intimacy, etc. may imply ...
 lean back – relaxed, easy, less concerned, etc. – aggressive intent
 – defensive reaction
 – submissive attitude
 etc.

Source: Training Learning Consultancy Ltd Bristol, England. Reproduced with permission.

Hospitals set to play it by ethnic book

Staff receive guide to help them tend people from different cultures, writes Tanya Johnson

Touching a patient to comfort them would be one of the most natural gestures for a nurse. But being touched by a nurse of the opposite sex could offend an orthodox Jew because being comforted like that is not welcome in Judaism. Similarly, touching or removing a Sikh's turban could also cause offence because it has deep spiritual and moral significance.

Now a book has been produced to help staff at Portsmouth hospitals understand the differences between ethnic minority groups and avoid unwittingly offending them. Called the *Ethnic Minority Handbook*, it contains all the information doctors and nurses need when dealing with patients of different religious persuasions.

It was completed by Florise Elliott, Portsmouth Hospitals NHS Trust's ethnic health coordinator, who said: 'It's always important for people to be aware of other people's cultures. 'This makes staff aware of other cultures and differences in ways of living.'

The book has sections for Buddhists, Chinese people, Christians, Mormons, Hindus, Jehovah's Witnesses, Jews, Muslims, Sikhs and spiritualism and was compiled with help from representatives from each culture.

As well as guidance on diet, language, cultures, death and post-mortems, each section contains contacts hospital medical staff can ring if they need advice. One is Jewish spokesman Julius Klein, a member of the Portsmouth and Southsea Hebrew Congregation, who welcomed the book. He said: 'It's excellent. One of the difficulties when people go into hospital is trying to put over certain things about their culture and life that the hospital needs to know. Anything that helps inform the nursing staff about minorities must be a good thing.'

Each ward at Queen Alexandra Hospital, Cosham, and St Mary's Hospital, Milton, will have a copy of the book that was started by the hospital's service planning manager Petronella Mwasandube. About 1,500 of the 37,500 annual cases the hospitals deal with are people from ethnic minority groups; that does not include emergencies.

Source: 'Hospitals set to play it by ethnic book', *The News*, Portsmouth, 16 February 1999. Reproduced courtesy of *The News*.

Critical reflection ????

There are so many forms of non-verbal communication cues, either intentional or unintentional, that can be interpreted in a number of ways. There are also wide variations in cultural norms that influence the essential meaning and context of interactions. Do you believe therefore that attempting to make valid inferences from body language is of little real value and its use should be discouraged?

ATTRIBUTION THEORY

It seems, therefore, that part of the process of perceiving other people is to attribute characteristics to them. We judge their behaviour and their intentions on past knowledge and in comparison with other people we know. It is our way of making sense of their behaviour. This is known as attribution theory.

Attribution is the process by which people interpret the perceived causes of behaviour. The initiator of **attribution theory** is generally recognised as *Heider*, who suggests that behaviour is determined by a combination of **perceived** internal forces and external forces.[51]

● **Internal forces** relate to personal attributes such as ability, skill, amount of effort or fatigue.
● **External forces** relate to environmental factors such as organisational rules and policies, the manner of superiors, or the weather.

Behaviour at work may be explained by the locus of control, that is whether the individual perceives outcomes as controlled by themselves or by external factors. Judgements made about other people will also be influenced strongly by whether the cause is seen as internal or external.

Basic criteria in making attributions

In making attributions and determining whether an internal or external attribution is chosen, *Kelley* suggests three basic criteria: distinctiveness, consensus and consistency.[52]

● **Distinctiveness.** How distinctive or different was the behaviour or action in this particular task or situation compared with behaviour or action in other tasks or situations?
● **Consensus.** Is the behaviour or action different from, or in keeping with, that displayed by most other people in the same situation?
● **Consistency.** Is the behaviour or action associated with an enduring personality or motivational characteristic over time, or an unusual one-off situation caused by external factors?

Kelley hypothesised that people attribute behaviour to internal forces or personal factors when they perceive **low distinctiveness, low consensus** and **high consistency**. Behaviour is attributed to external forces or environmental factors when people perceived **high distinctiveness, high consensus** and **low consistency** (*see* Figure 6.14).

An example of these criteria related to a student who fails a mid-sessional examination in a particular subject is given in Table 6.2.

Table 6.2	Example of criteria in making attributions		
	Distinctiveness	**Consensus**	**Consistency**
Internal attribution	Student fails all mid-sessional examinations	Student is the only one to fail	Student also fails final examination
External attribution	Student gains high marks in other mid-sessional examinations	All students in the class get low marks	Student obtains a good mark in final examination

Source: Adapted from Mitchell, T. R., *People in Organisations*, Second Edition, McGraw-Hill (1982), p. 104.

Figure 6.14	Representation of attribution theory

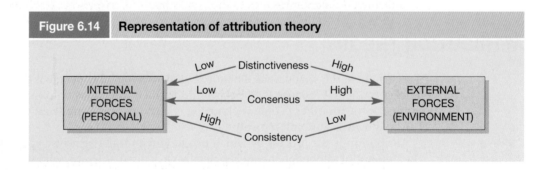

An additional consideration in the evaluation of task performance within an organisational setting is whether the cause of behaviour was due to 'stable' or 'unstable' factors:

● **stable factors** are ability, or the ease or difficulty of the task;
● **unstable factors** are the exertion of effort, or luck.[53]

The combination of internal and external attributions, and stable and unstable characteristics, results in four possible interpretations of a person's task performance (*see* Table 6.3).

Table 6.3	Classification of possible attributions for performance	
	Internal attributions	**External attributions**
Stable factors	ABILITY	TASK DIFFICULTY
Unstable factors	EFFORT	LUCK

Implications of attribution theory
Employees with an internal control orientation are more likely to believe that they can influence their level of performance through their own abilities, skills or efforts. Employees with an external control orientation are more likely to believe that their level of performance is determined by external factors beyond their influence.

Studies appear to support the idea that staff with an internal control orientation are generally more satisfied with their jobs, are more likely to be in managerial positions and are more satisfied with a participatory style of management than staff with an external control orientation.[54] As a generalisation it might be implied that internally controlled managers are more effective than those who are externally controlled. However, this does not appear to be always the case.[55]

People with a high achievement motivation may perceive that successful performance is caused by their own internal forces and their ability and effort rather than by the nature of the task or by luck. If members of staff fail to perform well on their tasks they may believe that external factors are the cause and as a result may reduce the level of future effort. However, if staff perform well but the manager perceives this as due to an easy task or to luck, the appropriate recognition and reward may not be given. If the staff perceive that good performance was due to ability and/or effort, the lack of recognition and reward may well have a demotivating effect.

PERCEPTUAL DISTORTIONS AND ERRORS

We have seen that differences in perception result in different people seeing different things and attaching different meanings to the same stimuli. Every person sees things in their own way and as perceptions become a person's reality this can lead to misunderstandings. The accuracy of interpersonal perception and the judgements made about other people are influenced by:

● the nature of the relationship between the perceiver and the other person;
● the amount of information available to the perceiver and the order in which information is received;
● the nature and extent of interaction between the two people.

There are five main features that can create particular difficulties and give rise to perceptual problems, bias or distortions in our dealings with other people. These are:

- stereotyping
- the halo effect
- perceptual defence
- projection
- self-fulfilling prophecy.

The perceptual paradox

These problems with people perception arise because of the selectivity which exists in the perceptual process. We do not enjoy living in a world where uncertainty abounds and our perceptual system works to minimise our energy consumption. We do not have to start every day afresh – we have our store of memories and experiences to guide us.

The paradox is that this process is also our downfall. Errors and bias are inherent in such a system. Although exhortations can be made for us to become more aware of our own biases and to take more time in making judgements, we are working against our normal quick-fire perceptual system.

Refresh your understanding
Activity 6D
www.pearsoned.co.uk/mullins

STEREOTYPING

This is the tendency to ascribe positive or negative characteristics to a person on the basis of a general categorisation and perceived similarities. The perception of that person may be based more on certain expected characteristics than on the recognition of that person as an individual. It is a form of typecasting. **Stereotyping** is a means of simplifying the process of perception, making sense of the world and making judgements of other people instead of dealing with a range of complex and alternative stimuli. It occurs when an individual is judged on the basis of the group to which it is perceived that person belongs. When we see all people belonging to a particular group as having the same characteristics, we are stereotyping individuals. Pre-judgements are therefore made about an individual without ever really knowing whether such judgements are accurate; they may be wildly wrong.

Examples of common stereotyping may be based on:

- **nationality**, for example all Germans are orderly and industrious, all Australians like cricket;
- **occupation**, for example all accountants are boring, all librarians are serious and undemonstrative;
- **age**, for example all young people are unreliable, no old person wants to consider new ideas;
- **physical**, for example all people with red hair have a fiery temperament; all fat people are lazy;
- **education**, for example all graduates are intelligent;
- **social**, for example all unemployed people are lazy; immigrants do not want to learn English;
- **politics**, for example all Labour voters favour strong trade unions, all Conservative voters support privatisation.

Although stereotyping condenses the amount of information that we need to know and thus enables us to cope with a vast information flow, the consequences of attributing incorrect characteristics are extremely negative.

Social implications

Stereotyping infers that all people within a particular perceived category are assumed to share the same traits or characteristics. A significant social implication of stereotyping is therefore the perception held about particular groups of people based on, for example:

- gender
- race
- sexual orientation

- disability
- religious belief
- age.

A major danger of stereotyping is that it can block out accurate perception of the individual or individual situation. Stereotyping may lead to potential situations of prejudice or discrimination. An example might be the perception of people with HIV or AIDS.[56] Stereotyping may work either negatively or favourably for a particular group of people. For example, a sizeable number of employers still appear to maintain negative and inaccurate stereotypes about the capabilities and training of older workers. However, some firms, such as B&Q, the home-improvement chain, have a policy of staffing certain stores with people over 50 years of age.

THE HALO EFFECT

The Halo Effect is the process by which the perception of a person is formulated on the basis of a single favourable or unfavourable trait or impression. The **halo effect** tends to shut out other relevant characteristics of that person. Some examples might be as follows:

- A candidate for employment who arrives punctually, is smart in appearance and friendly may well influence the perception of the selectors, who then place less emphasis on the candidate's technical ability, qualifications or experience for the job.
- A new member of staff who performs well in a first major assignment may be perceived as a likely person for promotion, even though that assignment is not typical of the usual duties the member of staff is expected to undertake.
- A single trait, such as good attendance and time-keeping, may become the main emphasis for judgement of overall competence and performance rather than other considerations such as the quantity, quality and accuracy of work.

A particular danger with the halo effect is that where quick judgements are made on the basis of readily available stimuli, the perceiver may become 'perceptually blind' to subsequent stimuli at variance with the original perception and (often subconsciously) notice only those characteristics that support the original judgement.

The rusty halo effect The process may also work in reverse: **the rusty halo effect**. This is where general judgements about a person are formulated from the perception of a negative characteristic. For example, a candidate is seen arriving late for an interview. There may be a very good reason for this and it may be completely out of character. But on the basis of that one particular event the person may be perceived as a poor time-keeper and unreliable. Another example may be a new member of staff who performs poorly in a first major assignment. This may have been due to an unusual set of circumstances and not typical behaviour, but the person may still be perceived as a bad appointment.

PERCEPTUAL DEFENCE

Perceptual defence is the tendency to avoid or screen out certain stimuli that are perceptually disturbing or threatening. People may tend to select information that is supportive of their point of view and choose not to acknowledge contrary information. For example, a manager who has decided recently to promote a member of staff against the advice of colleagues may select only favourable information which supports that decision and ignore less favourable information which questions that decision.

PROJECTION

Attributing, or projecting, one's own feelings, motives or characteristics to other people is a further distortion which can occur in the perception of other people. Judgements of other people may be more favourable when they have characteristics largely in common with, and easily recognised by, the perceiver. **Projection** may also result in people exaggerating undesirable traits in others that they fail to recognise in themselves.

Perception is distorted by feelings and emotions. For example, a manager who is concerned about possible redundancy may perceive other managers to be even more concerned. People have a tendency to perceive others less favourably by projecting certain of their own feelings or characteristics on to them. As another example, supervisors may complain that their manager did not work hard enough to secure additional resources for the department when in fact the supervisors failed to provide the manager with all the relevant information and statistics.

Discussed by Freud in his description of defence mechanisms, projection is a way in which we protect ourselves from acknowledging that we may possess undesirable traits and assign them in exaggerated amounts to other people. For instance, a manager who considers all subordinates as insincere may be projecting one of the manager's own characteristics. Perception of 'self' and how people see and think of themselves, and evaluate themselves, are discussed in Chapter 9.

SELF-FULFILLING PROPHECY

A common feature of social interaction is the concept of the **self-fulfilling prophecy** (sometimes known as the Pygmalion effect), a term that is usually attributed to *Merton*.[57] The essence of the prophecy is that simply because it has been made, this will cause it to happen. People strive to validate their perceptions irrespective of the actual reality. People's beliefs or expectations influence their actions and behaviour in such a way as to make the beliefs or expectations more likely to come true. If staff belive a rumour (prophecy) that there will be no promotions or bonuses for the foreseeable future, they are likely to behave in such a way that their performance would not justify promotion or bonuses (even if the rumour were not true).

Rosenthal and Jacobsen undertook a study of American school students in which psychological tests were claimed to predict levels of achievement. The researches informed teachers that certain named students had been identified as 'fast developers' when, in reality, students were assigned at random to both the high-potential and control groups. At the end of the academic year those students designated with high potential achieved noticeably greater increased IQ scores and reading ability than the control group of students.[58]

The expectation of managers has a powerful influence on the behaviour and performance of staff. If a manager expects only minimal performance from staff, they are not likely to perform to the best of their abilities. Therefore, managers need to establish an organisational framework and supportive culture that reinforces positive performance expectations at all levels of the organisation. Staff should also be encouraged to have high self-expectations of performance through working towards common goals.

UNDERSTANDING THE ORGANISATIONAL PROCESS

The process of perception has been outlined as selective and subjective: we perceive the world in our own terms and expect the world to 'fit' into our constructs. Throughout our development we have learned to distinguish what is important and significant (figure) from information that is additional and contextual (ground). This process is repeated when we

join new organisations or take a new job within the same organisation. Fitting into the organisation involves selecting information that is necessary from that which is less significant. At times, the process can be distorted and we can also be 'tricked' into seeing the world in particular ways.

Although some organisations may discriminate, it is the view of the authors that stereotyped perceptions are not always calculated: they are often made automatically and without conscious thought – in much the same way as we may be tricked by visual illusions. In fact, perceptual illusions are a very appropriate way of understanding the organisational setting, including for example the processes affecting women. The 'Ames Room' is relevant for this purpose.[59] This is a room of an irregular size with one of the far corners at a greater distance than the other, although the room is arranged and decorated so that it gives the appearance of being rectangular. If two people of the same size stand in diagonally opposite corners, one in the furthest corner and the other in the near corner, a visual illusion occurs whereby our perception of depth is 'tricked' to see the furthest away looking dramatically smaller (*see* Figure 6.15).

By analogy it is possible to see the room as representing the culture of the organisation surrounded by beliefs and traditions, rather like pictures on the wall. They seem reasonable, logical and appropriate. The individual standing at the furthest corner of the room could, for example, be seen as the female, the nearest the male. Both people are in the room surrounded by the culture, but one, the male, is nearest and most visible. He is perceived differently and advantageously, whereas the woman is perceived in a relatively inconsequential way. If the

Figure 6.15 | **The Ames Room**

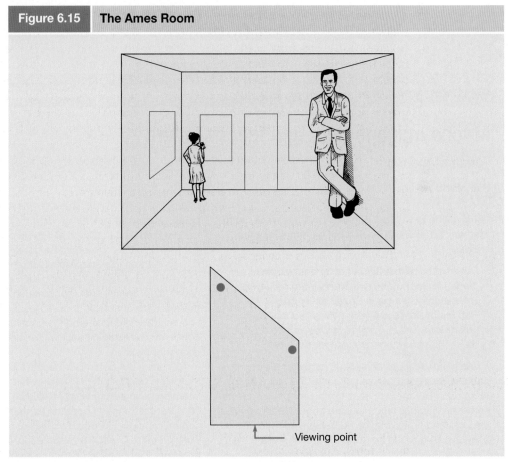

Viewing point

Source: Hicks, L., 'Gender and culture: a study of the attitudes displayed by managers in the hotel world', unpublished doctoral thesis, University of Surrey, 1991, p. 303.

woman stays at the back of the room in an ancillary position or leaves the room altogether, she is reinforcing the beliefs around the walls.

Some women, however, do become managers and these exceptional women would then join the male corner and would seem to become larger and more visible. However, the perceptual distortion is complete because the lone woman could legitimately be viewed as a 'trick', as an illusion. For the males, their position fits and they have only to prove their merit for a management post and not that they are different from the norm. Their success will feed back into the system and reaffirm the beliefs that are held.

For any organisation to be effective it is imperative that the staff are competent to do their work and satisfy the 'psychological contract' (discussed in Chapter 2). One part of the role of managers is to select and train those people whom they predict will perform successfully on the job, and then to monitor and assess their competence for promotion. Accordingly, it clearly seems important for managers to be aware of their own prejudices and assumptions. By opening channels and encouraging and developing all staff, trust might be fed back into the system from which equity could begin and stereotypes might end.

Refresh your understanding
Activity 6E
www.pearsoned.co.uk/
mullins

Critical reflection ?????

Many people do not take the time to think about the person with whom they are interacting. They translate their model of the world and assume that others are working from the same model. But often there is not enough time to see the world from so many perspectives. To what extent therefore do you think it is more effective to trust in your own judgement?

MANAGEMENT IN THE NEWS

Macho management and fear of failure

Tough at the top

Sally Bibb

In his memo to Cable & Wireless staff this week, John Pluthero, head of its UK division, did not mince his words.

As we reduce the number of customers we serve, fix some of our problems, strip out layers of management, we will need fewer people to run the business ... If you are worried that it all sounds very hard, it's time for you to step off the bus. This is no longer a place for the timid.

He needs to fix some serious problems. Fair enough. Many companies cut costs and make people redundant. But the way he is talking about it suggests someone who has much to learn about leading people through hard times. Maybe he thought adopting such a macho style would be good PR and impress the City. Like Alan Sugar on the BBC's *The Apprentice*, he

comes across as lacking in empathy. It is hard to believe men as successful as Pluthero and Sugar have got to where they are without a good understanding of how to lead people successfully through change. The ability to empathise is key. Empathy is not just nice to have – it's a crucial and sophisticated skill for business. It's simple. Without it, we diminish our ability to influence, to gain support; we create needless conflict and resistance and we certainly don't engender loyalty.

So, given the potentially negative consequences of Pluthero's comments this week, what could his intention be in saying what he said? Maybe he did not consider the range of possible approaches to the communication. He would do well to read Jim Collins' book *Good to Great*. The author sets out to answer the question: 'Can a good company become a great

company, and if so, how?' He and his research team examined 1,435 Fortune 500 companies and synthesised the results to identify the drivers of good-to-great transformations. They uncovered the key factors that allowed these companies to achieve cumulative stock returns 6.9 times the stock market over a 15-year period. Among their findings, they discovered that a certain type of leader ran these companies – one who displayed a blend of 'extreme personal humility with intense professional good will'. Collins cites the example of Colman Mockler, chief executive of Gillette from 1975 to 1991. During Mockler's tenure, Gillette faced three takeover bids that threatened to destroy the company's opportunity for greatness. Mockler stuck to his guns and fought for his company. But he did it in a civilised and effective way. He reached out to thousands of individual investors, speaking to many of them on the phone, gained their support and won the battle. Collins describes him as 'a quiet and reserved man, always courteous ... Mockler had the reputation of a gracious, almost patrician gentleman'. Yet he was clearly no pushover. He succeeded by knowing how to gain support from people who mattered.

Would managers like we see in *The Apprentice* get better results faster if they dropped the bully-boy tactics? They would certainly create more loyalty and attract talented, independent-minded people who want to work for people they like and respect. Some people are motivated by fear. But it's the promise of success that makes truly great, impressive, improbable things happen, not the fear of failure.

Source: Bibb, S. 'Tough at the top', *The Guardian*, 4 March 2006. Copyright © 2006 The Guardian News and Media Limited, reproduced with permission.

Discussion questions

1 Critically review John Pluthero's message and explain how it might be subject to perceptual distortion and errors as described in the chapter.

2 Discuss and interpret the main message of this article using the 'Cycle of perception and behaviour' model in Figure 6.12. How far do you agree with the concluding comments and what evidence could you provide that might contradict them?

SYNOPSIS

● The process of perception connects our physiology with our conscious thoughts and actions as well as our unconscious habits and assumptions. By understanding how we see the world and sharing our thoughts with others, we share the same social world. Although we all see the world through our own 'coloured spectacles', by understanding others' perspectives and by widening our understanding of how others may see the world, depth and variety is encouraged and problems of bias and distortion become minimised. Perception is the root of all organisational behaviour and any situation can be analysed in terms of its perceptual connotations.

● For managers, an understanding of perception is essential to ensure that they are aware of the problems that can arise from the process of perceptual attention and selectivity. The process of perception is innately organised and patterned in order to provide meaning for the individual. The process of perception is based on both internal and external factors. The organisation and arrangement of stimuli is influenced by three important factors: figure and ground, grouping and closure. It is important to be aware of potential perceptual illusions.

● Part of the process of perceiving other people is to attribute characteristics to them. We judge their behaviour and intentions on past knowledge and in comparison with other people we know. Perception gives rise to individual behavioural responses in given situations. The principles of perceptual differences reflect the way we perceive other people and are the source of many organisational problems. In the work situation, the process of perception and selection of stimuli can influence a manager's relationship with other staff.

● The importance of communication and the way we interact with others cannot be overestimated, as our well-being and morale can be affected by the nature of these social experiences. Communication and perception are inextricably bound. Two major approaches to interpersonal communications are Neuro-Linguistic Programming (NLP), which can illuminate areas of understanding and help to improve communication skills, and Transactional Analysis (TA), which is a theory that encompasses personality, perception and communication.

● The ways in which we organise and make judgements about what we have perceived are to a large extent based on previous experiences and learning. It is also important to be aware that there are inferences and assumptions that go beyond the information given. Judgements of other people can also be influenced by such stimuli as role or status, occupation, physical factors and appearance, non-verbal communications and body language. The social situation consists of both verbal and non-verbal signals. It is necessary to be aware of cultural differences in non-verbal communications.

● Part of the process of perceiving other people is to attribute characteristics to them. Attribution is the process by which people interpret the perceived causes of behaviour. There are a number of potential difficulties that arise with interpersonal perception. Five main features which may give rise to perceptual distortions or errors are stereotyping, the halo effect, perceptual defence, projection and self-fulfilling prophecy. The perceptual process is selective and subjective. In the work situation, perceptual differences reflect the way we perceive other people. It is important to understand the organisational process.

 Refresh your understanding, assess your progress and begin your research with online resources at **www.pearsoned.co.uk/mullins**

REVIEW AND DISCUSSION QUESTIONS

1 Explain fully why the study of perception is important in the study of management and organisational behaviour.

2 Discuss those factors that affect selection and attention in the process of perception. Give your own examples of the importance of language and cultural differences.

3 Explain the most significant principles that influence the organisation and arrangement of stimuli. Provide your own example of each of these principles.

4 What do you understand by the dynamics of interpersonal perception? Explain the main distortions or errors that can occur in perceiving other people and support your answer with practical examples.

5 Discuss the importance of effective interpersonal communications and perception. What do *you* see as the practical benefits of Neuro-Linguistic Programming (NLP) and Transactional Analysis (TA)?

6 Discuss critically the amount of attention that you believe should be given to non-verbal communications and body language.

7 Explain the principles of attribution theory and its importance to, and implications for, management. Apply the principles to your *own* working life.

8 What do you believe are the main causes and implications of perceptual distortions and errors?

ASSIGNMENT 1

Stroop – illustrative experiment

(This is a development of Figure 6.10 and provides a further opportunity to review possible perceptual illusion.)

a Write two vertical lists of 20 colour names in felt tip pen. For the first list, use the correct colour pen for the colour word you are writing (for example, blue pen for the word blue). Repeat some of the colours but place them in random order.

b For the second list, use different colour pens for the colour word (for example, use a red pen for the word blue).

c Now ask a colleague to read out loud the colour that the word is written in (not the word itself). Compare the amount of time it takes your colleague to read out the two lists. The second list probably not only took longer but had more mistakes and more hesitations.

William Stroop, who first conducted this experiment, noted that the task interferes with expected behaviour. It is difficult to stop yourself from reading the word (the result of our early learning), which in this case directly impairs performance.

ASSIGNMENT 2

Form small groups and then undertake, individually, the following exercise.

COMMUNICATION

1 Read everything before you do anything.

2 Put your name in the upper right-hand corner of the paper, in the space provided.

3 Circle the word 'name' in the second sentence, above.

4 Draw five small squares in the upper left-hand corner of this paper.

5 Put an X in each of the five small squares you have drawn.

6 Put a circle around each of those five small squares above.

7 Sign your name, under and to the left of the title above.

8 Draw a circle, in pen, around sentences 6 and 7 above.

9 Multiply 70 × 30 and write the result on the reverse side.

10 Draw a circle around the word 'paper' in sentence 4, above.

11 Please now call out your first name, loudly.

12 If you feel that you have carefully followed these directions, call out, loudly: 'I have carefully followed directions!'

13 Add 107 and 278, and write the sum on the reverse, immediately under the first figure that you wrote there.

14 Circle that figure on the reverse.

15 In a normal voice, count aloud from 1–10.

16 If no one else has said it, say now, 'I am the leader!'

17 Now that you have read all of the foregoing, very carefully, please complete ONLY sentences 1 and 2.

What conclusions do you draw from this exercise?

PERSONAL AWARENESS AND SKILLS EXERCISE

Objectives

Completing this exercise should help you to enhance the following skills:

- Distinguish between facts and assumptions or inferences.
- Examine the basis upon which you make judgements.
- Review the nature of your communication and decision-making processes.

Personal awareness and skills exercise – continued

Exercise

After reading the following story you are required to:

1 Read the 15 statements about the story and check each to indicate whether you consider it to be true, false or ?

'T' means that the statement is definitely true on the basis of the information presented in the story.
'F' means that it is definitely false.
'?' means that it may be either true or false and that you cannot be certain of which on the basis of the information presented in the story. If any part of a statement is doubtful, mark it '?'.

Answer each statement in turn. You may refer to the story as often as needed but do not go back to change any answer later and do not re-read any statements after you have answered them.

2 After you have checked all 15 statements, work in small groups of three to five and discuss your individual answers. How much agreement is there among members of your group? *Do not change any of your first individual answers. However, if as a result of your group discussion you would now give a different answer to any of the statements, note this alongside your original answer.*

The story

A businessman had just turned off the lights in the store when a man appeared and demanded money. The owner opened a cash register. The contents of the cash register were scooped up and the man sped away. A member of the police force was notified promptly.

Statements about the story

	T	F	?
1 A man appeared after the owner had turned off his store lights.	T	F	?
2 The robber was a man.	T	F	?
3 The man who appeared did not demand money.	T	F	?
4 The man who opened the cash register was the owner.	T	F	?
5 The storeowner scooped up the contents of the cash register and ran away.	T	F	?
6 Someone opened a cash register.	T	F	?
7 After the man who demanded the money scooped up the contents of the cash register, he ran away.	T	F	?
8 While the cash register contained money, the story does not state how much.	T	F	?
9 The robber demanded money of the owner.	T	F	?
10 A businessman had just turned off the lights when a man appeared in the store.	T	F	?
11 It was broad daylight when the man appeared.	T	F	?
12 The man who appeared opened the cash register.	T	F	?
13 No one demanded money.	T	F	?
14 The story concerns a series of events in which only three persons are referred to: the owner of the store, a man who demanded money and a member of the police force.	T	F	?
15 The following events occurred: someone demanded money, a cash register was opened, its contents were scooped up and a man dashed out of the store.	T	F	?

Source: From Hanley, W. V., *Communications and Interpersonal Relations, Texts and Cases*, Sixth Edition, Irwin (1992), p. 213.

Discussion

● How would you explain differences in individual perceptions of the same statement?
● On what basis did members of your group give different answers and how did their perception of the statements about the story differ?
● To what extent can you be absolutely certain about anything?

CASE STUDY

What you say is what you get…?

The issues surrounding perception and communication are clearly complex and varied. What we see and hear is very often mediated by a whole range of cultural and individual factors which distort and vary our understanding of what is happening and therefore affect our reactions to it. The way in which people in organisations communicate and how those communications are perceived and acted upon can, therefore, have a major impact on individual success, team performance and personal career paths. One way in which this question repeatedly makes its way into both academic management texts and media reports of managerial life is via the differential career paths and success rates which appear to exist between men and women. While questions of perception and communication may not tell the whole story about the position of women in organisational life, they do tell part of it. Many women may not be able, or even wish, to challenge the dominant masculine model of society in general and work organisations in particular (this dominance of a male paradigm is often termed patriarchy). Nevertheless, information about gender-related differences in matters of perception and communication can help individuals, both men and women, to become more effective in their working lives.

Diafora and the European Professional Women's Network

In August 2006 Alison Maitland, writing for the *Financial Times*, reported on a training event held for a group of 20 high-ranking female executives at a venue just outside Paris.[60] The course was run by a Paris-based training consultancy called Diafora,[61] which has links to the European Professional Women's Network[62] via one of its founding partners, Avivah Wittenberg-Cox. At the session described, the women were practising saying 'no' in a language which would get the message across clearly to a bullying male boss who was trying to offload his unfinished work. They were learning to speak 'masculine'. The session was addressing a problem which stems from the tendency for women and men to learn different ways of speaking which reflect differing assumptions about the purpose of communication. Women, it has been discovered, tend to communicate in order to make people feel at ease, to include people and to create a sense of harmony. Men tend to communicate as a means of getting a point across or making an argument. This is part of the socialisation process and is based on common

Coming to a boardroom near you; women learn the language of business leadership.

conventions about the role of women and men in society. It results in differences both in the language used and the linguistic structures and habits employed. Deborah Tannen, an American professor of linguistics, who has researched and written extensively on the nature of communication patterns between men and women, notes that women tend to use more 'tag' questions at the end of sentences as a way of attempting to draw the other party into further discussion.[63] Men tend to make statements or express opinions without these mechanisms for encouraging further discussion. For instance, where a woman might say:

> 'I thought the report John gave into the problems at the Zurich office was very clear, didn't you? Should we act on his recommendations?'

A man might simply state:

> 'John's Zurich report was very clear. We'll do what he suggested.'

Both might actually wish to convey the same message: that the report was clear and the recommendations sound. However, the 'female' version, which aims to elicit an opinion or confirm agreement, contains what to the 'male' listener sounds like uncertainty or hesitancy. By contrast, to the female listener, the 'male' version might seem abrupt or arrogant and convey an impression that her views on the subject were irrelevant. Either way, the unconscious message behind the speech pattern can be damaging to the image of the speaker in the eyes of their colleague.

Tannen also noted that women were much more likely to use 'weak' words and phrases in their conversation.

A woman manager might say to her secretary, 'Could you do me a favor and type this letter right away?' knowing that her secretary is going to type the letter. But her male boss, on hearing this, might conclude she doesn't feel she deserves the authority she has.[64]

Another illustration is the phrase 'I'm sorry', which women often use to smooth conversation or to express regret that something has happened and to minimise it, not as an admission of error. For men, 'I'm sorry' is often used to mean something much tougher; it equates to admitting a mistake and apologising for it. Women who are 'always apologising' thus give an impression of incompetence.

Learning to make an impression

Training women to say no to an unreasonable demand is only part of the agenda addressed by the Diafora programmes. Beefing up their language to avoid weak phrases such as 'as soon as possible' or 'I don't know but ...' or 'I guess I could ...' might help women limit some of the day-to-day perceptual damage, but there are other more fundamental problems to consider. One of them is the issue of women's self-promotion and their approach to achieving career success. From her consulting and career experience, Wittenberg-Cox has written about the unconscious bias in many companies caused by a focus on the notion of competence as a fair basis for promotion.

Competence is complicated by perception. We have all been taught to believe that men and women are equal and should be treated the same. So that is what managers do. They treat everybody the same and expect everyone to behave similarly. But women often behave differently from the norm established in a century of male-dominated corporations.[65]

Wittenberg-Cox finds that many young men have already learned what is known as the 80/20 rule of power politics by the time they embark on their careers: that you should spend 80 per cent of your time at work actually working and 20 per cent communicating your achievements and gaining visibility.

This appears to be news to the women on the (Diafora) course, but may be more familiar to their male colleagues back at the office. Guys have told me this rule as if they were fed it with their mother's milk.[66]

These anecdotal findings are supported by those of senior academic researcher Dr Val Singh, working at Cranfield's Centre for Developing Women Business Leaders, which also has links with the European Professional Women's Network. Writing about the question of impression management (IM), she reports that the young men in one of her research samples had learned to use IM at a younger age than their female counterparts and might therefore be getting a head start

on the career ladder.[67] For instance, 60 per cent of the junior males in her sample actively sought out key people for the purpose of networking whereas very few junior females did so.

Some men and women trust the formal HRM systems to provide career opportunities, underestimating the importance of informal networks ...

Women tended to adopt IM strategies later in their careers, usually having noticed their equally capable male colleagues achieving more and more rapid promotions. Cranfield identifies three types of IM: self-focused (which is to do with packaging and 'branding' oneself), manager-focused (which is about building and maintaining relationships in a fairly instrumental way) and job-focused (which is about delivering extra levels of job performance). Men appear to be readier to engage in manager-focused IM, even if they don't like it much, than women. Also, according to research done internally for Hewlett-Packard, men apply earlier for promotion.

... women apply for open job positions if they think they respond to 100 per cent of the criteria listed, while men respond as soon as they feel that they cover 60 per cent of the requirements. Worse though, she noted, is that hiring managers do the same. They recruit women if they respond to 100 per cent of the criteria, but they are ready to recruit men as long as they respond to 60 per cent (and women recruiters are tougher on women candidates than men are).[68]

Women managers and cultural difference

Diafora as an organisation suggests that the cultural difference between men and women is as tangible as that between different nationalities and should be treated as such. The group hopes to encourage and train not only women but also men to become 'gender bilingual' in the search for managerial talent and business success. And indeed national cultural difference itself should not be forgotten as something which might affect perceptions and behaviours, not necessarily to the detriment of women. Some research into both managerial effectiveness and the perception of what makes a good manager is beginning to reveal different levels of sex stereotyping in different cultures. A study by Chow[69] seems to indicate that in Hong Kong financial and telecommunications businesses, the perceptions of both men and women about the characteristics of an effective business leader are substantially gender neutral.

A less assertive and more individualist, more gender egalitarian culture may offer a favourable and women-friendly culture toward female leaders in management positions in Hong Kong organisations in the future, especially if women aspiring to become leaders demonstrate the attributes that subordinates seek. (p. 228)

On a lighter note, Wittenberg-Cox recently perceived a difference between French female managers and those from the US or the UK in relation to the way in which they assert femininity. In an article celebrating the apparent return of high heels to businesswomen's wardrobes at a conference involving the CEOs of some very substantial companies, she observed that they no longer signified the 'dumb-blond plaything of yesteryear' but power. But only, so, far, for French women:

American women have been forced to adapt too much to the male model in their rise to power ... Frenchwomen, in particular, were never asked, like their unfortunate Anglo-Saxon sisters, to choose between family and career, and between femininity and power. Despite the supposed macho nature of Latin men, France has created one of the world's only societies where women work full-time (80 per cent of women between 25 and 50), have lots of children (the highest birth rate in Europe after Ireland) and still look, sound – and are loved – for being women.[70]

Your tasks

1 Analyse the issues raised in this case using the concepts of attribution theory and stereotyping as outlined in the text (pp. 233–7).

2 What light can the notion of the perceptual set (Figure 6.3) shed on the potential differences between men and women's behaviour in the working environment as described in the case study?

3 Discuss reasons for and against organisations using the type of women-focused training offered by Diafora and the Cranfield Centre for Developing Women Business Leaders. How else might organisations ensure fair opportunities for career enhancement and why might this be important for organisational effectiveness?

Notes and references

1 Bartlett, F. C. *Remembering Cambridge*, Cambridge University Press (1932).

2 Kohler, I. 'The Formation and Transformation of the Visual World', *Psychological Issues*, vol. 3, 1964, pp. 28–46, 116–33.

3 Bexton, W., Heron, W. and Scott, T. 'Effects of Decreased Variation in the Sensory Environment', *Canadian Journal of Psychology*, vol. 8, 1954, pp. 70–6.

4 Briggs-Myers, I. *Introduction to Type*, Oxford Psychologists Press (1987).

5 Witkin, H. A., Lewis, H. B., Hertzman, M., Machover, K., Meissner, P. P. and Wapner, S. S. *Personality Through Perception*, Harper & Row (1954).

6 Ling, C. and Masako, I. 'Intercultural Communication and Cultural Learning: the experience of visiting Japanese students in the US', *The Howard Journal of Communications*, vol. 14, 2003, pp. 75–96.

7 Hall E. T. 'The Silent Language of Overseas Business', *Harvard Business Review*, vol. 38, no. 3, 1960, pp. 85–7.

8 Dainty, P. and Anderson, M. 'Mindset for Managers', in Chowdhury, S. *Management 21C*, Financial Times Prentice Hall (2000), pp. 109–10.

9 Block, J. R. and Yuker, H. E. *Can You Believe Your Eyes?*, Robson Books (2002).

10 Morgan, C. T. and King, R. A. *Introduction to Psychology*, Third edition, McGraw-Hill (1966), p. 343.

11 Stroop, J. R. 'Studies of Interference in Serial Verbal Reactions', *Journal of Experimental Psychology*, vol. 4, no. 18, 1935, pp. 643–62; and Penrose, L. S. and Penrose, R.

'Impossible Objects: A Special Type of Illusion', *British Journal of Psychology*, part 1, February 1958.

12 O'Connor, Joseph and Lages, Andrea, Coaching with NLP Element 2004.

13 Ibid., pp. 114–15.

14 Spitzer, M. 'Brain Research and Learning over the Life Cycle in Personalising Education' OECD (2006).

15 Cooperrider, D. l., Srivestva S., An invitation to Organizational Wisdom and Executive Courage, in I. S. Srivastva and D. L. Cooperrrider (eds) *Organisational Wisdom and Executive Courage* (1998) San Francisco, CA, the New Lexington Press.

16 Hammond, S. A. *The Thin Book of Appreciative Inquiry*, Second edition, Thin Book Publishing Company, (1998).

17 Wexley, K. N., Yukl, G. A., Kovacs, S. Z. and Sanders, R. E. 'Importance of Contrast Effects in Employment Interviews', *Journal of Applied Psychology*, vol. 56, 1972, pp. 45–8.

18 See for instance www.lhfe.ac.uk for senior leadership courses using action enquiry.

19 Torbert, W. R. *Managing the Corporate Dream*, McGraw-Hill (1987) See also Breakthrough Consultancy www.breakthrough.ie.

20 Laing, R. D. *Knots*, Penguin (1971), p. 30.

21 Guirdham, M. *Interactive Behaviour at Work*, Third edition, Financial Times Prentice Hall (2002).

22 Fitzherbert, N. 'Magic tricks in communication', *Professional Manager*, vol. 14, no. 5, September 2005, pp. 32–3 and www.fitzgerald.co.uk (reproduced with permission).

23 See, for example: Pivcevic, P. 'Taming the Boss', *Management Today*, March 1999, pp. 68–72.

24 Bandler, R., Grinder, J., Dilts, R. and Delozier, J. *Neuro Linguistic Programming Volume I: The study of the structure of subject experience*, Meta Publications (1980).

25 Leading Edge Communications Ltd. *How to become an irresistible and hypnotic communicator*, p. 2. http://www.nlpandhypnosis.com [accessed 1 December 2003].

26 McCann, D. *How to Influence Others at Work*, Second edition, Butterworth Heinemann (1993).

27 Stone, K. 'Influential People', *Manager: The British Journal of Administrative Management*, June/July 2005, pp. 22–3.

28 Berne, E. *Games People Play*, Penguin (1966).

29 See, for example: Stewart, I. and Jaines, V. *TA today: A New Introduction to Transactional Analysis*, Life Space Publishing (1987).

30 For a summary of NLP, TA, and other thoughts on business psychology, see: Butcher, D. 'Buyer's Guide to Business Psychology', *Management Today*, May 2005, pp. 54–7.

31 Kendon, A. 'Some Functions of Gaze Direction in Social Interaction', *Acta Psychologica*, vol. 26, 1967, pp. 22–63.

32 Mehrabian, A. *Nonverbal Communication*, Aldine Atherton (1972).

33 Cook, M. *Interpersonal Perception*, Penguin (1971).

34 Schneider, S. C. and Barsoux, J. *Managing Across Cultures*, Second edition, Financial Times Prentice Hall (2003), p. 29.

35 Goffman, E. *The Presentation of Self in Everyday Life*, Penguin (1971).

36 Asch, S. E. 'Forming Impressions on Personality', *Journal of Abnormal and Social Psychology*, vol. 41, 1946, pp. 258–90.

37 Miller, N. and Campbell, D. T. 'Recency and Primacy in Persuasion as a Function of the Timing of Speeches and Measurements', *Journal of Abnormal and Social Psychology*, vol. 59, 1959, pp. 1–9.

38 Hodges, B. 'Effect of Volume on Relative Weighting in Impression Formation', *Journal of Personality and Social Psychology*, vol. 30, 1974, pp. 378–81.

39 Guirdham, M. *Interactive Behaviour at Work*, Third edition, Financial Times Prentice Hall (2002) p. 161.

40 Gahagan, J. *Interpersonal and Group Behaviour*, Methuen (1975).

41 Green, J. 'When Was Your Management Style Last Applauded?', *Chartered Secretary*, December 1998, p. 28.

42 Wilson, P. R. 'Perceptual Distortion of Height as a Function of Ascribed Academic Status', *Journal of Social Psychology*, no. 74, 1968, pp. 97–102.

43 See, for example: Torrington, D. *Face-to-Face in Management*, Prentice-Hall (1982).

44 Mehrabian, A. *Tactics of Social Influence*, Prentice-Hall (1970).

45 Pivcevic, P. 'Taming the Boss', *Management Today*, March 1999, p. 70.

46 McGuire, T. 'Don't Just Listen', *Chartered Secretary*, September 1998, p. 24.

47 James, J. *Body Talk at Work*, Judy Piatkus (2001), p. 3.

48 Fletcher, W. 'Let Your Body Do The Talking', *Management Today*, March 2000, p. 30.

49 Mann, S. 'Message in a Body', *Professional Manager*, November 2000, pp. 32–3; and Ribbens, G. and Thompson, R. *Understanding Body Language in a Week*, Institute of Management and Hodder & Stoughton (2000).

50 For other examples of cultural differences, see Schneider S. C. and Barsoux, J. *Managing Across Cultures*, Second edition, Financial Times Prentice Hall (2003).

51 Heider, F. *The Psychology of Interpersonal Relations*, John Wiley and Sons (1958).

52 Kelley, H. H. 'The Process of Causal Attribution', *American Psychologist*, February 1973, pp. 107–28.

53 Bartunek, J. M. 'Why Did You Do That? Attribution Theory in Organizations', *Business Horizons*, September–October 1981, pp. 66–71.

54 Mitchell, T. R., Smyser, C. M. and Weed, S. E. 'Locus of Control: Supervision and Work Satisfaction', *Academy of Management Journal*, September 1975, pp. 623–31.

55 Durand, D. E. and Nord, W. R. 'Perceived Leader Behaviour as a Function of Personality Characteristics of Supervisors and Subordinates', *Academy of Management Journal*, September 1976, pp. 427–38.

56 Goss, D. and Adam-Smith, D. *Organizing Aids*, Taylor & Francis (1995).

57 Merton, R. K. *Social Theory and Social Structure*, Free Press (1957)

58 Rosenthal, R. and Jacobson, L. *Pygmalion in the Classroom*, Holt, Rinehart and Winston (1968).

59 Ames, A. 'Visual Perception and the Rotating Trapezoidal Window', *Psychological Monographs*, vol. 65, no. 7, 1951.

60 Maitland, A. 2006 'Learn the masculine imperative', FT.com, 1 August 2006.

61 www.diaforaconsulting.com.

62 www.europeanpwn.net.

63 Tannen, D. *Talking from 9 to 5: Women and Men at Work*, HarperCollins (2001).

64 Tannen, D. 'The Talk of the Sandbox; How Johnny and Suzy's Playground Chatter Prepares The for Life at the Office' *The Washington Post*, 11 December 1994.

65 Wittenberg-Cox, A. *Women in Leadership: A Business Issue Not a Women's Issue Diafora* Newsletter editorial Winter 2006 www.diaforaconsulting.com [accessed 10 August 2006].

66 Maitland, A. 'Learn the masculine imperative' FT.com, 1 August 2006.

67 Singh, V. *Impression Management* from Cranfield Centre for Developing Women Leaders (2000).

68 Wittenberg-Cox, A. *Europe Wakes Up to Women* Diafora Editorial, Fall 2005 www.diaforaconsulting.com [accessed 10 August 2006].

69 Chow, I. Gender differences in perceived leadership effectiveness in Hong Kong *Women in Management Review* vol. 20 no. 4, 2005, pp. 216–33.

70 Wittenberg-Cox, A. 2005 High heels scale new heights European Professional Women's Network www.europeanpwn.net/tht_wob/articles/new_heights.html [accessed 10 August 2006].

WORK MOTIVATION AND JOB SATISFACTION

The relationship between the organisation and its members is influenced by what motivates them to work and the rewards and fulfilment they derive from it. The work organisation, and the design and content of jobs, can have a significant effect on the satisfaction of staff and their levels of performance. The manager needs to know how best to elicit the co-operation of staff and direct their efforts to achieving the goals and objectives of the organisation.

Learning outcomes

After completing this chapter you should be able to:

- explain the meaning and underlying concept of motivation;
- detail main types of needs and expectations of people at work;
- explain frustration-induced behaviour and possible reactions to frustration at work;
- examine main theories of motivation and evaluate their relevance to particular work situations;
- assess the meaning, nature and dimensions of job satisfaction;
- review broader approaches to job design;
- evaluate the relationship between motivation, job satisfaction and work performance.

> **If your staff do something good, tell them. And then tell them again. And again. Keep it up. Put it in writing. Send them a memo – something they can keep. Put in the company newsletter. Add a note to their file. Whatever, but make it widely known they did good. This is a quick and cheap method of praising and motivating your team and it lets everyone know you are monitoring, praising, motivating.**

Richard Templar – bestselling author of the popular rules books
The Rules of Management, Pearson Prentice Hall (2005), p. 66

THE MEANING OF MOTIVATION

The study of **motivation** is concerned, basically, with why people behave in a certain way. The basic underlying question is, 'Why do people do what they do?'[1] In general terms, motivation can be described as the direction and persistence of action. It is concerned with why people choose a particular course of action in preference to others, and why they continue with a chosen action, often over a long period and in the face of difficulties and problems.[2]

From a review of motivation theory, *Mitchell* identifies four common characteristics which underlie the definition of motivation:[3]

- **Motivation is typified as an individual phenomenon**. Every person is unique and all the major theories of motivation allow for this uniqueness to be demonstrated in one way or another.
- **Motivation is described, usually, as intentional**. Motivation is assumed to be under the worker's control, and behaviours that are influenced by motivation, such as effort expended, are seen as choices of action.
- **Motivation is multifaceted**. The two factors of greatest importance are: (i) what gets people activated (arousal) and (ii) the force of an individual to engage in desired behaviour (direction or choice of behaviour).
- **The purpose of motivational theories is to predict behaviour**. Motivation is not the behaviour itself and it is not performance. Motivation concerns action and the internal and external forces which influence a person's choice of action.

On the basis of these characteristics, Mitchell defines motivation as 'the degree to which an individual wants and chooses to engage in certain specified behaviours'.

Underlying concept of motivation

The underlying concept of motivation is some driving force within individuals by which they attempt to achieve some goal in order to fulfil some need or expectation. This concept gives rise to the basic motivational model, which is illustrated in Figure 7.1.

People's behaviour is determined by what motivates them. Their performance is a product of both ability level and motivation.

$$\text{Performance} = \text{function (ability} \rightarrow \text{motivation)}$$

Kreitner et al. suggest that although motivation is a necessary contributor for job performance, it is not the only one. Along with ability, motivation is also a combination of level of skill, knowledge about how to complete the task, feelings and emotions, and facilitating and inhibiting conditions not under the individual's control.[4] However, what is clearly evident is that if the manager is to improve the work of the organisation, attention must be given to the level of motivation of its members. The manager must also encourage staff to direct their efforts (their driving force) towards the successful attainment of the goals and objectives of the organisation.

Figure 7.1 **A simplified illustration of the basic motivational model**

NEEDS AND EXPECTATIONS AT WORK

But what is this driving force? What are people's needs and expectations and how do they influence behaviour and performance at work? Motivation is a complex subject, it is a very personal thing, and it is influenced by many variables. *Farren* reminds us of the 12 human needs that have been around since the beginning of recorded history: family, health and well-being, work/career, economic, learning, home/shelter, social relationships, spirituality, community, leisure, mobility, and environment/safety. 'Work and private life in the new millennium will continue to revolve around the 12 human needs.'[5]

The various needs and expectations at work can be categorised in a number of ways – for example the simple divisions into physiological and social motives or into intrinsic and extrinsic motivation.

Extrinsic motivation is related to 'tangible' rewards such as salary and fringe benefits, security, promotion, contract of service, the work environment and conditions of work. Such tangible rewards are often determined at the organisational level and may be largely outside the control of individual managers.

Intrinsic motivation is related to 'psychological' rewards such as the opportunity to use one's ability, a sense of challenge and achievement, receiving appreciation, positive recognition and being treated in a caring and considerate manner. The psychological rewards are those that can usually be determined by the actions and behaviour of individual managers.[6]

Higher set of motivational needs

According to *Kets de Vries*, the best-performing companies possess a set of values that creates the right conditions for high performance; he questions whether in such best companies there is something more going on that touches upon a deeper layer of human functioning, causing people to make an extra effort. The emphasis is on widening choice that enables people to choose more freely, instead of being led by forces of which they are unaware; and it is a motivational needs system on which such choice is based. Kets de Vries suggests that in addition to the motivation needs system for physiological needs, sensual and enjoyment needs, and the need to respond to threatening situations, companies that get the best out of their people are characterised by a higher set of motivational needs system:

● **attachment/affiliation** – concerning the need for engagement and sharing, a feeling of community and a sense of belonging to the company; and

- **exploration/assertion** – concerning the ability to play and work, a sense of fun and enjoyment, the need for self-assertion and the ability to choose.[7]

Broad classification for motivation to work

Given the complex and variable nature of needs and expectations, the following is a simplistic but useful, broad three-fold classification as a starting point for reviewing the motivation to work (*see* Figure 7.2):

- **Economic rewards** – such as pay, fringe benefits, pension rights, material goods and security. This is an **instrumental** orientation to work and concerned with 'other things'.
- **Intrinsic satisfaction** – derived from the nature of the work itself, interest in the job, and personal growth and development. This is a **personal** orientation to work and concerned with 'oneself'.
- **Social relationships** – such as friendships, group working and the desire for affiliation, status and dependency. This is a **relational** orientation to work and concerned with 'other people'.

A person's motivation, job satisfaction and work performance will be determined by the comparative strength of these sets of needs and expectations and the extent to which they are fulfilled. For example, some people may make a deliberate choice to forgo intrinsic satisfaction and social relationships (particularly in the short term or in the earlier years of their working life) in return for high economic rewards. Other people are happy to accept comparatively lower economic rewards in favour of a job that has high intrinsic satisfaction and/or social relationships. Social relationships would appear to be an important feature for many people, especially, for example, for those working in the hospitality industry where interactions with other people and the importance of supportive working relationships and good teamwork can be strong motivators at work.[8]

Broader concerns

Popular press reports appear to indicate that many people are increasingly motivated by broader concerns such as their work/life balance, opportunities for flexible working, career advancement and personal development and growth, and a feeling of identification with the values of the organisation. The motivation to work is also influenced by the changing nature of the work environment and the concept of the 'psychological contract', which was discussed in Chapter 1.

Figure 7.2	Needs and expectations of people at work

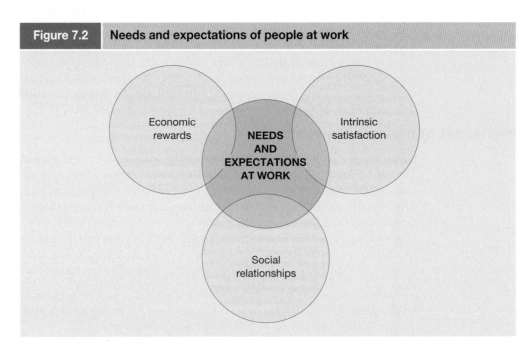

*Today's managers are clearly more motivated by the intrinsic rewards of work such as chal-
lenge and a sense of purpose rather than with jobs that simply provide an income. Whilst they
are driven by key organisational values such as customer focus and professionalism, they are
most personally motivated by environments that foster innovation and staff development and a
climate of trust.*

Chartered Management Institute, 'Motivation Matters'[9]

FRUSTRATION-INDUCED BEHAVIOUR

What happens if a person's motivational driving force is blocked and they are unable to satisfy
their needs and expectations, and what is the likely effect on their work performance? There
are two possible sets of outcomes: constructive behaviour or frustration (*see* Figure 7.3).

**Constructive
behaviour**
Constructive behaviour is a positive reaction to the blockage of a desired goal and can take
two main forms: problem-solving or restructuring.

- **Problem-solving** is the removal of the barrier – for example repairing a damaged
 machine or bypassing an unco-operative superior.
- **Restructuring**, or compromise, is the substitution of an alternative goal, although such a
 goal may be of a lower order – for example taking an additional part-time job because of
 failure to be promoted to a higher grade.

Figure 7.3	A basic model of frustration

Note: Even if a person engages in constructive behaviour in response to a barrier or block-
age, it could be said that the person was 'frustrated', if only mildly or in the short term, in an
attempt to satisfy a desired goal. However, the term 'frustration' is usually interpreted as
applying to **negative responses** to a barrier or blockage which prevents satisfaction of a
desired goal.

Frustration (negative responses) Frustration is a negative response to the blockage of a desired goal and results in a defensive form of behaviour. There are many possible reactions to frustration caused by the failure to achieve a desired goal. These can be summarised under four broad headings: aggression, regression, fixation, and withdrawal.[10] However, these categories are not mutually exclusive. Most forms of frustration-induced behaviour at work are a combination of aggression, regression and fixation.

Aggression is a physical or verbal attack on some person or object, for example striking a supervisor, rage or abusive language, destruction of equipment or documents, malicious gossip about a superior. This form of behaviour may be directed against the person or object that is perceived as the source of frustration, that is the actual barrier or blocking agent. However, where such a direct attack cannot be made, because, for example, the source of frustration is not clear or not specific, or where the source is feared, such as a powerful superior, aggression may be displaced towards some other person or object.

With **displaced aggression** the person may find an easier, safer person or object as a scapegoat for the outlet of frustration – for example picking arguments with colleagues, being short-tempered with subordinates, shouting at the cleaners or kicking the waste-paper bin. A more constructive form of displaced aggression is working off frustrated feelings through demanding physical work or sport, or perhaps by shouting/cursing when alone or in the company of an understanding colleague.

Regression is reverting to a childish or more primitive form of behaviour – for example sulking, crying, tantrums or kicking a broken machine or piece of equipment.

Fixation is persisting in a form of behaviour which has no adaptive value and continuing to repeat actions which have no positive results – for example the inability to accept change or new ideas, repeatedly trying a machine which clearly will not work, insisting on applying for promotion even though not qualified for the job.

Withdrawal is apathy, giving up or resignation – for example arriving at work late and leaving early, sickness and absenteeism, refusal to accept responsibility, avoiding decision-making, passing work over to colleagues or leaving the job altogether.

Factors influencing frustration

Among the factors which determine an individual's reaction to frustration are the:

- level and potency of need (*see*, for example, Maslow's theory of motivation, discussed below);
- degree of attachment to the desired goal;
- strength of motivation;
- perceived nature of the barrier or blocking agent; and
- personality characteristics of the individual.

It is important that managers attempt to reduce potential frustration, for example, through:

- effective recruitment, selection and socialisation;
- training and development;
- job design and work organisation;
- equitable personnel policies;
- recognition and rewards;
- effective communications;
- participative styles of management;
- attempting to understand the individual's perception of the situation.

Proper attention to motivation and to the needs and expectations of people at work will help overcome boredom and frustration-induced behaviour.

MONEY AS A MOTIVATOR

Earlier writers, such as F. W. Taylor, believed in economic needs motivation. Workers wou be motivated by obtaining the highest possible wages through working in the most efficient and productive way. Performance was limited by physiological fatigue. For Taylor, motivation was a comparatively simple issue – what the workers wanted from their employers more than anything else was high wages. This approach is the **rational–economic concept of motivation**. The ideas of F. W. Taylor and his 'rational–economic needs' concept of motivation (discussed in Chapter 2) and subsequent approaches to motivation at work have fuelled the continuing debate about financial rewards as a motivator and their influence on productivity.

Where there is little pleasure in the work itself or the job offers little opportunity for career advancement, personal challenge or growth, many people may appear to be motivated primarily, if not exclusively, by money. Weaver suggests that for many hourly workers in the hospitality industry, such as dishwashers, waiting or housekeeping staff, the work does not change much among different companies and there is little attachment to a particular company. For such staff, Weaver proposes a 'Theory M' programme of motivation based on direct cash rewards for above-average performance. A percentage base is calculated from the average performance of workers on the staff.[11]

Yet we frequently see pronouncements from prominent business figures that motivation is about much more than money.

> *Work is about letting people know they are important, their hard work and efforts matter, and they're doing a good job. And this kind of recognition, in fact, can sometimes be more important than money.*
>
> Gary Kusin, CEO, FedEx Kinko's[12]

The short answer appears to be that for the vast majority of people, money is clearly important and a motivator at work **but** to what extent and **how** important depends upon their personal circumstances and the other satisfactions they derive from work. The bottom line is surely the extent to which money motivates people to work **well** and to the best of their abilities. Although pay may still make people tick, there are now a number of other important influences on motivation. For many people, the feeling of being recognised and valued appears more important than money in motivating them to stay in a particular job. (*See* Herzberg's two-factor theory of motivation, discussed below.)

Motivation other than by money

As *Grayson and Hodges* point out, historically loyalty was bought and employers offered gradual progression up the hierarchy, a decent salary and job security in return for a hard day's work. 'Increasingly, motivation is based on values rather than purely on financial reward.'[13] A similar point is made by *Saunders*:

> *If the 1980s were all about money, and people were only as good as their last bonus, in more recent years time has become the new money, and quality-of-life issues have come to the fore. Benefits that replenish the psychological contract are becoming the most valuable. So holiday arrangements, career breaks and potential for flexible hours and homeworking are now on the agenda.*[14]

A recent study from the Economic & Social Research Council analysed the influences on employee behaviour and productivity and raises the question: What if employees are guided not only by monetary incentives but also by social norms? Social norms interact with economic incentives and may have a large effect upon organisational performance.[15]

Critical reflection ????

'Whatever people may say or would like us to believe, in the real world money is the most potent need and strongest motivator.' Do you agree?

'All the ideas and theories that abound around motivation at work are redundant when it comes to basic issues.' Do you believe that you can motivate employees to do anything as long as they feel their job is under threat?

THEORIES OF MOTIVATION

There are many competing theories that attempt to explain the nature of motivation. These theories may all be at least partially true and help to explain the behaviour of certain people at certain times. It is often most acute for younger people starting on their career, for people at mid-career positions or for those who find limited opportunities for promotion or further advancement. For employers there may be difficulties in motivating staff both in the longer term as well as in the short run. It is because of the complexity of motivation and the fact that there is no ready-made solution or single answer to what motivates people to work well that the different theories are important to the manager. They show there are many motives that influence people's behaviour and performance. Collectively, the different theories provide a framework within which to direct attention to the problem of how best to motivate staff to work willingly and effectively.

Criticisms and reservations It is important to emphasise, however, that these various theories are not conclusive. They all have their critics (this is particularly true of the content theories of motivation) or have been subject to alternative findings that purport to contradict original ideas. Many of these theories were not intended, initially to have the significance that some writers have subsequently placed upon them. It is always easy to quote an example that appears to contradict any generalised observation on what motivates people to work. Despite these reservations the different theories provide a basis for study and discussion, and for review of the most effective motivational style (*see* Figure 7.4).

> *You don't motivate individuals. You provide them with an environment to be self-motivated. It is a personal decision, but it's management's job to provide the right environment.*
>
> Kathy Schofield, Director of Human Resources, HFC Bank[16]

The manager, therefore, must judge the relevance of these different theories, how best to draw upon them, and how they might effectively be applied in particular work situations. The manager should be aware of at least the main theories of motivation.

Content theories and process theories The usual approach to the study of motivation is through an understanding of internal cognitive processes – that is, what people feel and how they think. This understanding should help the manager to predict likely behaviour of staff in given situations. These different cognitive theories of motivation are usually divided into two contrasting approaches: content theories and process theories.

- **Content theories** attempt to explain those specific things that actually motivate the individual at work. These theories are concerned with identifying people's needs and their relative strengths, and the goals they pursue in order to satisfy these needs. Content theories place emphasis on the nature of needs and **what motivates**.

| Figure 7.4 | An overview of main theories of work motivation |

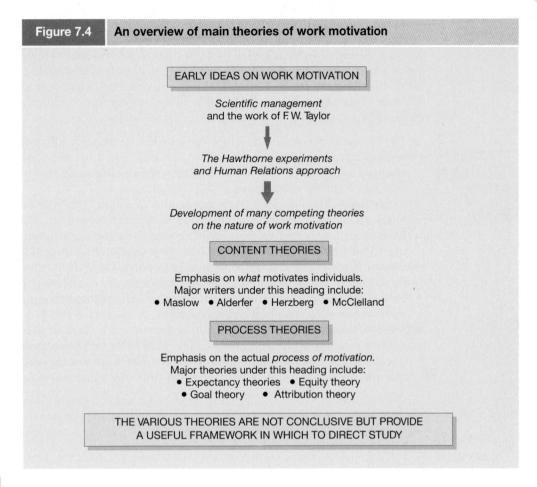

EARLY IDEAS ON WORK MOTIVATION

*Scientific management
and the work of F. W. Taylor*

*The Hawthorne experiments
and Human Relations approach*

*Development of many competing theories
on the nature of work motivation*

CONTENT THEORIES

Emphasis on *what* motivates individuals.
Major writers under this heading include:
● Maslow ● Alderfer ● Herzberg ● McClelland

PROCESS THEORIES

Emphasis on the actual *process of motivation.*
Major theories under this heading include:
● Expectancy theories ● Equity theory
● Goal theory ● Attribution theory

**THE VARIOUS THEORIES ARE NOT CONCLUSIVE BUT PROVIDE
A USEFUL FRAMEWORK IN WHICH TO DIRECT STUDY**

Refresh your
understanding

Activity 7A
www.pearsoned.co.uk/
mullins

● **Process theories** attempt to identify the relationship among the dynamic variables that make up motivation. These theories are concerned more with how behaviour is initiated, directed and sustained. Process theories place emphasis on the **actual process of motivation**. These theories are discussed later in this chapter.

CONTENT THEORIES OF MOTIVATION

Major content theories of motivation include:

● *Maslow's* hierarchy of needs model;
● *Alderfer's* modified need hierarchy model;
● *Herzberg's* two-factor theory;
● *McClelland's* achievement motivation theory.

MASLOW'S HIERARCHY OF NEEDS THEORY

A useful starting point is the work of *Maslow* and his theory of individual development and motivation, published originally in 1943.[17] Maslow's basic proposition is that people are wanting beings, they always want more, and what they want depends on what they already have. He suggests that human needs are arranged in a series of levels, a hierarchy of importance.

Maslow identified eight innate needs, including the need to know and understand, aesthetic needs and the need for transcendence. However, the hierarchy is usually shown as ranging through five main levels, from, at the lowest level, physiological needs, through safety needs, love needs and esteem needs, to the need for self-actualisation at the highest level. The hierarchy of needs may be shown as a series of steps but is usually displayed in the form of a pyramid (Figure 7.5). This is an appropriate form of illustration as it implies a thinning out of needs as people progress up the hierarchy.

- **Physiological needs.** These include homeostasis (the body's automatic efforts to retain normal functioning) such as satisfaction of hunger and thirst, the need for oxygen and to maintain temperature regulation. Also sleep, sensory pleasures, activity, maternal behaviour and, arguably, sexual desire.
- **Safety needs.** These include safety and security, freedom from pain or threat of physical attack, protection from danger or deprivation, the need for predictability and orderliness.
- **Love needs** (often referred to as social needs). These include affection, sense of belonging, social activities, friendships, and both the giving and receiving of love.
- **Esteem needs** (sometimes referred to as ego needs). These include both self-respect and the esteem of others. Self-respect involves the desire for confidence, strength, independence and freedom, and achievement. Esteem of others involves reputation or prestige, status, recognition, attention and appreciation.
- **Self-actualisation needs.** This is the development and realisation of one's full potential. Maslow sees this as 'What humans can be, they must be' or 'becoming everything that one is capable of becoming'. Self-actualisation needs are not necessarily a creative urge and may take many forms which vary widely from one individual to another.

Once a lower need has been satisfied, it no longer acts as a strong motivator. The needs of the next higher level in the hierarchy demand satisfaction and become the motivating influence. Only unsatisfied needs motivate a person. Thus Maslow asserts that '*a satisfied need is no longer a motivator*'.

Not necessarily a fixed order Although Maslow suggests that most people have these basic needs in about the order indicated, he also makes it clear that **the hierarchy is not necessarily a fixed order**. There will be a number of exceptions to the order indicated. For some people there will be a reversal of the hierarchy, for example:

- Self-esteem may seem to be more important than love to some people. This is the most common reversal of the hierarchy. It is often based on the belief that the person most

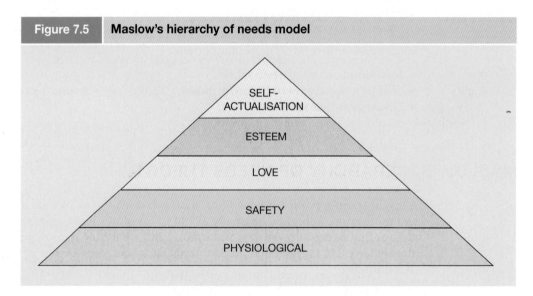

| Figure 7.5 | **Maslow's hierarchy of needs model** |

loved is strong, confident or inspires respect. People seeking love try to put on a show of aggressive, confident behaviour. They are not really seeking self-esteem as an end in itself but for the sake of love needs.

- For some innately creative people the drive for creativity and self-actualisation may arise despite lack of satisfaction of more basic needs.
- Higher-level needs may be lost in some people who will continue to be satisfied at lower levels only: for example, a person who has experienced chronic unemployment.
- Some people who have been deprived of love in early childhood may experience the permanent loss of love needs.
- A need which has continued to be satisfied over a long period of time may be undervalued. For example, people who have never suffered from chronic hunger may tend to underestimate its effects, and regard food as rather an unimportant thing. Where people are dominated by a higher-level need this may assume greater importance than more basic needs.
- People with high ideals or values may become martyrs and give up everything else for the sake of their beliefs.

Maslow claims that the hierarchy is relatively universal among different cultures, but he recognises that there are differences in an individual's motivational content in a particular culture.

Degrees of satisfaction Maslow points out that a false impression may be given that a need must be satisfied fully before a subsequent need arises. **He suggests that a more realistic description is in terms of decreasing percentages of satisfaction along levels of the hierarchy.** For example, arbitrary figures for the average person may be: satisfied 85 per cent in physiological needs; 70 per cent in safety needs; 50 per cent in love needs; 40 per cent in esteem needs; and 10 per cent in self-actualisation needs. There is a gradual emergence of a higher-level need as lower-level needs become more satisfied. The relative importance of these needs changes during the psychological development of the individual. Maslow subsequently modified his views by noting that satisfaction of self-actualisation needs by growth-motivated individuals can actually enhance these needs rather than reduce them. Furthermore, he accepted that some higher-level needs may still emerge after long deprivation of lower-level needs rather than only after their satisfaction.

Evaluation of Maslow's theory

Based on Maslow's theory, once lower-level needs have been satisfied (say at the physiological and safety levels), giving more of the same does not provide motivation. Individuals advance up the hierarchy as each lower-level need becomes satisfied. Therefore, to provide motivation for a change in behaviour, the manager must direct attention to the next higher level of needs (in this case, love or social needs) that seek satisfaction.

Applications to the work situation There are a number of problems in relating Maslow's theory to the work situation. These include the following:

- People do not necessarily satisfy their needs, especially higher-level needs, just through the work situation; they satisfy them through other areas of their life as well. Therefore the manager would need to have a complete understanding of people's private and social lives, not just their behaviour at work.
- There is doubt about the time that elapses between the satisfaction of a lower-level need and the emergence of a higher-level need.
- Individual differences mean that people place different values on the same need. For example, some people prefer what they might see as the comparative safety of working in a bureaucratic organisation to a more highly paid and higher status position, but with less job security, in a different organisation.

- Some rewards or outcomes at work satisfy more than one need. Higher salary or promotion, for example, can be applied to all levels of the hierarchy.
- Even for people within the same level of the hierarchy, the motivating factors will not be the same. There are many different ways in which people may seek satisfaction of, for example, their esteem needs.
- Maslow viewed satisfaction as the main motivational outcome of behaviour. But job satisfaction does not necessarily lead to improved work performance.

A useful basis for evaluation Although Maslow did not originally intend that the need hierarchy should necessarily be applied to the work situation, it remains popular as a theory of motivation at work. Despite criticisms and doubts about its limitations, the theory has had a significant impact on management approaches to motivation and the design of organisations to meet individual needs. It is a convenient framework for viewing the different needs and expectations that people have, where they are in the hierarchy, and the different motivators that might be applied to people at different levels.

The work of Maslow has drawn attention to a number of motivators and stimulated study and research. The need hierarchy model provides a useful base for the evaluation of motivation at work. For example, *Steers and Porter* suggest a list of general rewards and organisational factors used to satisfy different needs (*see* Table 7.1).[18]

Saunders contends that despite the time that has elapsed, Maslow's theory remains watertight.

When prehistoric man first took shelter in a cave and lit a fire, he was satisfying his lowest – physiological and safety needs. When a Buddhist achieves a state of nirvana, she is satisfying the fifth and highest – self-actualisation ... The cave these days might be a three-bedroom semi with garden and off-street parking, but the fact remains that once we've got enough to feed, clothe and house our families money is a low-level motivator for most people. The dash for cash is soon replaced by the desire for recognition, status and ultimately (although Maslow reckoned that a lot of us never get this far) the need to express yourself through your work.[19]

Table 7.1	Applying Maslow's need hierarchy	
Needs levels	**General rewards**	**Organisational factors**
1 Physiological	Food, water, sex, sleep	**a** Pay **b** Pleasant working conditions **c** Cafeteria
2 Safety	Safety, security, stability, protection	**a** Safe working conditions **b** Company benefits **c** Job security
3 Social	Love, affection, belongingness	**a** Cohesive work group **b** Friendly supervision **c** Professional associations
4 Esteem	Self-esteem, self-respect, prestige, status	**a** Social recognition **b** Job title **c** High-status job **d** Feedback from the job itself
5 Self-actualisation	Growth, advancement, creativity	**a** Challenging job **b** Opportunities for creativity **c** Achievement in work **d** Advancement in the organisation

Source: Steers, R. M. and Porter, L. W., *Motivation and Work Behaviour*, Fifth Edition, McGraw-Hill (1991), p. 35.

ALDERFER'S MODIFIED NEED HIERARCHY MODEL

A modified need hierarchy model has been presented by *Alderfer*.[20] This model condenses Maslow's five levels of need into only three levels based on the core needs of existence, relatedness and growth (ERG theory) (*see* Table 7.2. p. 263).

- **Existence needs** are concerned with sustaining human existence and survival and cover physiological and safety needs of a material nature.
- **Relatedness needs** are concerned with relationships to the social environment and cover love or belonging, affiliation and meaningful interpersonal relationships of a safety or esteem nature.
- **Growth needs** are concerned with the development of potential and cover self-esteem and self-actualisation.

A continuum of needs Like Maslow, Alderfer suggests that individuals progress through the hierarchy from existence needs to relatedness needs to growth needs as the lower-level needs become satisfied. However, Alderfer suggests these needs are more a continuum than hierarchical levels. More than one need may be activated at the same time. Individuals may also progress down the hierarchy. There is a frustration–regression process. For example, if an individual is continually frustrated in attempting to satisfy growth needs, relatedness needs may reassume most importance. The lower-level needs become the main focus of the individual's efforts.

Alderfer proposed a number of basic propositions relating to the three need relationships. Some of these propositions followed Maslow's theory, some were the reverse of the theory. A number of studies were undertaken to test these propositions across different samples of people in different types of organisations. Results from the studies were mixed. For example, the proposition that the less existence needs are satisfied the more they will be desired received constant support from all six samples. However, the proposition that satisfaction of existence needs activates desire for relatedness needs was not supported in any of the six samples.

Satisfaction of needs Unlike Maslow's theory, the results of Alderfer's work suggest that lower-level needs do not have to be satisfied before a higher-level need emerges as a motivating influence. The results, however, do support the idea that lower-level needs decrease in strength as they become satisfied. ERG theory states that an individual is motivated to satisfy one or more basic sets of needs. Therefore if a person's needs at a particular level are blocked, attention should be focused on the satisfaction of needs at the other levels. For example, if a subordinate's growth needs are blocked because the job does not allow sufficient opportunity for personal development, the manager should attempt to provide greater opportunities for the subordinate to satisfy existence and relatedness needs.

HERZBERG'S TWO-FACTOR THEORY

Herzberg's original study consisted of interviews with 203 accountants and engineers, chosen because of their growing importance in the business world, from different industries in the Pittsburgh area of America.[21] He used the critical incident method. Subjects were asked to relate times when they felt exceptionally good or exceptionally bad about their present job or any previous job. They were asked to give reasons and a description of the sequence of events giving rise to that feeling. Responses to the interviews were generally consistent and revealed that there were two different sets of factors affecting motivation and work. **This led to the two-factor theory of motivation and job satisfaction.**

Hygiene and motivating factors

One set of factors are those which, if absent, cause dissatisfaction. These factors are related to job context, they are concerned with job environment and extrinsic to the job itself. These factors are the **'hygiene' or 'maintenance' factors** ('hygiene' being used as analogous to the medical term meaning preventive and environmental). They serve to prevent dissatisfaction. The other set of factors are those that, if present, serve to motivate the individual to superior effort and performance. These factors are related to job content of the work itself. They are the **'motivators' or growth factors**. The strength of these factors will affect feelings of satisfaction or no satisfaction, but not dissatisfaction. **The opposite of dissatisfaction is not satisfaction but, simply, no dissatisfaction** (*see* Figure 7.6).

The hygiene factors can be related roughly to Maslow's lower-level needs and the motivators to Maslow's higher-level needs (*see* Table 7.2, p. 263). To motivate workers to give of their best, the manager must give proper attention to the motivators or growth factors. Herzberg emphasises that hygiene factors are not a 'second-class citizen system'. They are as important as the motivators, but for different reasons. Hygiene factors are necessary to avoid unpleasantness at work and to deny unfair treatment. 'Management should never deny

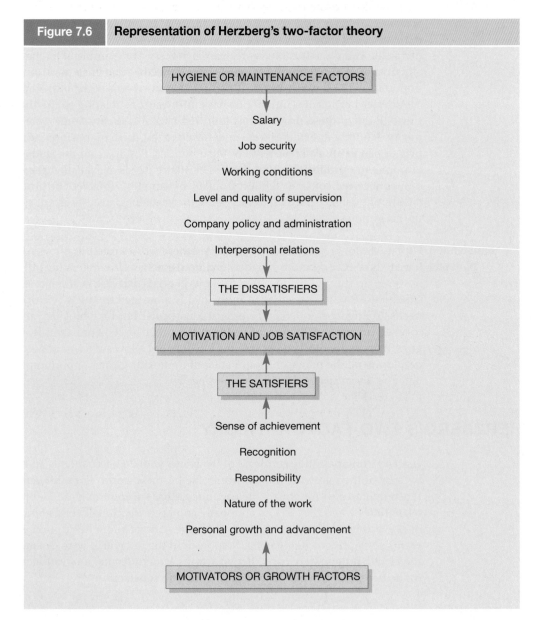

| Figure 7.6 | **Representation of Herzberg's two-factor theory** |

HYGIENE OR MAINTENANCE FACTORS

Salary

Job security

Working conditions

Level and quality of supervision

Company policy and administration

Interpersonal relations

THE DISSATISFIERS

MOTIVATION AND JOB SATISFACTION

THE SATISFIERS

Sense of achievement

Recognition

Responsibility

Nature of the work

Personal growth and advancement

MOTIVATORS OR GROWTH FACTORS

people proper treatment at work.' The motivators relate to what people are allowed to do and the quality of human experience at work. They are the variables which actually motivate people. The work of Herzberg indicates that it is more likely good performance leads to job satisfaction rather than the reverse.

Evaluation of Herzberg's work

Herzberg's theory is, however, a source of frequent debate. There have been many other studies to test the theory. The conclusions have been mixed. Some studies provide support for the theory. However, it has also been attacked by a number of writers. There are two common general criticisms of Herzberg's theory. One is that the theory has only limited application to 'manual' workers. The other is that the theory is 'methodologically bound'.

It is often claimed that the theory applies least to people with largely unskilled jobs or whose work is uninteresting, repetitive and monotonous, and limited in scope. Yet these are the people who often present management with the biggest problem of motivation. Some workers do not seem greatly interested in the job content of their work or with the motivators or growth factors.

A second, general criticism concerns methodology. It is claimed that the critical incident method, and the description of events giving rise to good or bad feelings, influences the results. People are more likely to attribute satisfying incidents at work, that is the motivators, as a favourable reflection on their own performance. The dissatisfying incidents that is the hygiene factors, are more likely to be attributed to external influences and the efforts of other people. Descriptions from the respondents had to be interpreted by the interviewers. This gives rise to the difficulty of distinguishing clearly between the different dimensions and to the risk of possible interviewer bias.

Despite such criticisms, there is still evidence of support for the continuing relevance of the theory. According to *Crainer and Dearlove*:

> *Herzberg's work has had a considerable effect on the rewards and remuneration packages offered by corporations. Increasingly, there is a trend towards 'cafeteria' benefits in which people can choose from a range of options. In effect, they can select the elements they recognise as providing their own motivation to work. Similarly, the current emphasis on self-development, career management and self-managed learning can be seen as having evolved from Herzberg's insights.*[22]

Whatever the validity of the two-factor theory, much of the criticism is with the benefit of hindsight, and *Herzberg* did at least attempt an empirical approach to the study of motivation at work and job satisfaction. Furthermore, his work has drawn attention to the importance of job design in the 'quality of work life'.

Table 7.2	Linking Maslow's, Alderfer's and Herzberg's theories of motivation	
Maslow's hierarchy of needs	**Alderfer's ERG theory**	**Herzberg's two-factor theory**
PHYSIOLOGICAL	EXISTENCE	HYGIENE FACTORS
SAFETY		
LOVE	RELATEDNESS	
ESTEEM	GROWTH	MOTIVATORS
SELF-ACTUALISATION		

McCLELLAND'S ACHIEVEMENT MOTIVATION THEORY

McClelland's work originated from investigations into the relationship between hunger needs and the extent to which imagery of food dominated thought processes. From subsequent research McClelland identified four main arousal-based, and socially developed, motives:

- the Achievement motive;
- the Power motive;
- the Affiliative motive;
- the Avoidance motive.[23]

The first three motives correspond, roughly, to Maslow's self-actualisation, esteem and love needs. The relative intensity of these motives varies between individuals. It also tends to vary between different occupations. Managers appear to be higher in achievement motivation than in affiliation motivation. McClelland saw the achievement need (n-Ach) as the most critical for the country's economic growth and success. The need to achieve is linked to entrepreneurial spirit and the development of available resources.

Use of projective tests Research studies by McClelland use a series of projective 'tests' – Thematic Apperception Test (TAT) – to gauge an individual's motivation. For example, individuals are shown a number of pictures in which some activity is depicted. Respondents are asked to look briefly (10–15 seconds) at the pictures and then to describe what they think is happening, what the people in the picture are thinking and what events have led to the situation depicted.[24] An example of a picture used in a projective test is given in Assignment 1 at the end of this chapter. The descriptions are used as a basis for analysing the strength of the individual's motives.

People with high achievement needs

Despite the apparent subjective nature of the judgements, research studies tend to support the validity of TAT as an indicator of the need for achievement.[25] McClelland has, over years of empirical research, identified four characteristics of people with a strong achievement need (n-Ach): a preference for moderate task difficulty, personal responsibility for performance, the need for feedback, and innovativeness.

- They prefer **moderate task difficulty** and goals as an achievement incentive. This provides the best opportunity of proving they can do better. If the task is too difficult or too risky, it would reduce the chances of success and of gaining need satisfaction. If the course of action is too easy or too safe, there is little challenge in accomplishing the task and little satisfaction from success.
- They prefer **personal responsibility for performance**. They like to attain success through the focus of their own abilities and efforts rather than by teamwork or chance factors outside their control. Personal satisfaction is derived from the accomplishment of the task and recognition need not come from other people.
- They have the need for **clear and unambiguous feedback** on how well they are performing. A knowledge of results within a reasonable time is necessary for self-evaluation. Feedback enables them to determine success or failure in the accomplishment of their goals and to derive satisfaction from their activities.
- They are **more innovative**. As they always seek moderately challenging tasks they tend always to be moving on to something a little more challenging. In seeking short cuts they are more likely to cheat. There is a constant search for variety and for information to find new ways of doing things. They are more restless and avoid routine and also tend to travel more.

Characteristics of achievement motivation The extent of achievement motivation varies between individuals. Some people rate very highly in achievement motivation. They are challenged by opportunities and work hard to achieve a goal. Money is not an incentive but may serve as a means of giving feedback on performance. High achievers seem unlikely to remain long with an organisation that does not pay them well for good performance. Money may seem to be important to high achievers, but they value it more as symbolising successful task performance and goal achievement.

McClelland's research has attempted to understand the characteristics of high achievers. He suggests that n-Ach is not hereditary but results from environmental influences and he has investigated the possibility of training people to develop a greater motivation to achieve.[26] McClelland suggests four steps in attempting to develop achievement drive:

- Striving to attain feedback on performance. Reinforcement of success serves to strengthen the desire to attain higher performance.
- Developing models of achievement by seeking to emulate people who have performed well.
- Attempting to modify their self-image and to see themselves as needing challenges and success.
- Controlling day-dreaming and thinking about themselves in more positive terms.

McClelland was concerned with economic growth in underdeveloped countries. He has designed training programmes intended to increase the achievement motivation and entrepreneurial activity of managers.

Refresh your understanding
Activity 7B
www.pearsoned.co.uk/mullins

McClelland has also suggested that as effective managers need to be successful leaders and to influence other people, they should possess a high need for power.[27] However, the effective manager also scores high on inhibition. Power is directed more towards the organisation and concern for group goals and is exercised on behalf of other people. This is 'socialised' power. It is distinguished from 'personalised' power that is characterised by satisfaction from exercising dominance over other people, and personal aggrandisement.

PROCESS THEORIES OF MOTIVATION

Process theories, or extrinsic theories, attempt to identify the relationships among the dynamic variables that make up motivation and the actions required to influence behaviour and actions. They provide a further contribution to our understanding of the complex nature of work motivation. Many of the process theories cannot be linked to a single writer, but major approaches and leading writers under this heading include:

- expectancy-based models – *Vroom*, and *Porter and Lawler*;
- equity theory – *Adams*;
- goal theory – *Locke*;
- attribution theory – *Heider* and *Kelley* (this was discussed in Chapter 6).

Expectancy theories of motivation The underlying basis of **expectancy theory** is that people are influenced by the expected results of their actions. Motivation is a function of the relationship between:

1 effort expended and perceived level of performance; and

2 the expectation that rewards (desired outcomes) will be related to performance.

There must also be:

3 the expectation that rewards (desired outcomes) are available.

These relationships determine the strength of the 'motivational link' (*see* Figure 7.7).

| Figure 7.7 | Expectancy theory: the motivational link |

Performance therefore depends upon the perceived expectation regarding effort expended and achieving the desired outcome. For example, the desire for promotion will result in high performance only if the person believes there is a strong expectation that this will lead to promotion. If, however, the person believes promotion to be based solely on age and length of service, there is no motivation to achieve high performance. A person's behaviour reflects a conscious choice between the comparative evaluation of alternative behaviours. **The choice of behaviour is based on the expectancy of the most favourable consequences.**

Expectancy theory is a generic theory of motivation and cannot be linked to a single individual writer. There are a number of versions and some of the models are rather complex. More recent approaches to expectancy theory have been associated with the work of *Vroom* and of *Porter and Lawler*.

VROOM'S EXPECTANCY THEORY

Vroom was the first person to propose an expectancy theory aimed specifically at work motivation.[28] His model is based on three key variables: **valence**, **instrumentality** and **expectancy** (VIE theory or expectancy/valence theory). The theory is founded on the idea that people prefer certain outcomes from their behaviour over others. They anticipate feelings of satisfaction should the preferred outcome be achieved.

Valence The feeling about specific outcomes is termed **valence**. **This is the attractiveness of, or preference for, a particular outcome to the individual**. *Vroom* distinguishes valence from value. A person may desire an object but then gain little satisfaction from obtaining it. Alternatively, a person may strive to avoid an object but find, subsequently, that it provides satisfaction. **Valence is the anticipated satisfaction from an outcome**. This may differ substantially from value, which is the actual satisfaction provided by an outcome.

The valence of certain outcomes may be derived in their own right, but more usually they are derived from the other outcomes to which they are expected to lead. An obvious example is money. Some people may see money as having an intrinsic worth and derive satisfaction from the actual accumulation of wealth. Most people, however, see money in terms of the many satisfying outcomes to which it can lead.

Instrumentality The valence of outcomes derives, therefore, from their instrumentality. This leads to a distinction between first-level outcomes and second-level outcomes.

- **The first-level outcomes are performance-related.** They refer to the quantity of output or to the comparative level of performance. Some people may seek to perform well 'for its own sake' and without thought to expected consequences of their actions. Usually, however, performance outcomes acquire valence because of the expectation that they will lead to other outcomes as an anticipated source of satisfaction – second-level outcomes.
- **The second-level outcomes are need-related.** They are derived through achievement of first-level outcomes – that is, through achieving high performance. Many need-related outcomes are dependent upon actual performance rather than effort expended. People generally receive rewards for what they have achieved rather than for effort alone or through trying hard.

On the basis of *Vroom's* expectancy theory it is possible to depict a general model of behaviour (*see* Figure 7.8).

Expectancy When a person chooses between alternative behaviours which have uncertain outcomes, the choice is affected not only by the preference for a particular outcome but also by the probability that such an outcome will be achieved. People develop a **perception** of the degree of probability that the choice of a particular action will actually lead to the desired outcome. This is **expectancy**. It is the relationship between a chosen course of action and its predicted outcome. Expectancy relates effort expended to the achievement of first-level outcomes. Its value ranges between 0, indicating zero probability that an action will be followed by the outcome, and 1, indicating certainty that an action will result in the outcome.

Motivational force

The combination of valence and expectancy determines the person's motivation for a given form of behaviour. This is the **motivational force**. The force of an action is unaffected by outcomes which have no valence or by outcomes that are regarded as unlikely to result from a course of action. Expressed as an equation, motivation (M) is the sum of the products of the valences of all outcomes (V), times the strength of expectancies that action will result in

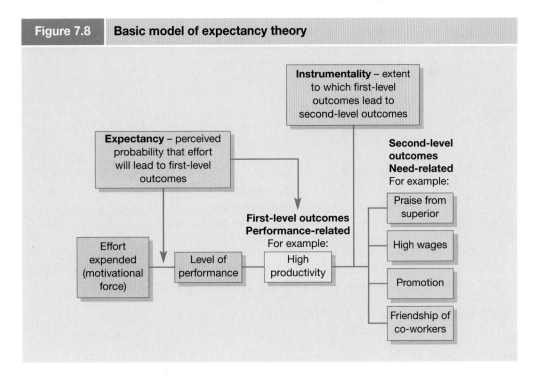

| Figure 7.8 | **Basic model of expectancy theory** |

achieving these outcomes (E). Therefore, if either, or both, valence or expectancy is zero, then motivation is zero. The choice between alternative behaviours is indicated by the highest attractiveness score.

$$M = \overset{n}{\Sigma} E \cdot V$$

There are likely to be a number of outcomes expected for a given action. Therefore, the measure of $E \cdot V$ is summed across the total number of possible outcomes to arrive at a single figure indicating the attractiveness for the contemplated choice of behaviour.

THE PORTER AND LAWLER EXPECTANCY MODEL

Vroom's expectancy/valence theory has been developed by *Porter* and *Lawler*.[29] Their model goes beyond motivational force and considers performance as a whole. They point out that effort expended (motivational force) does not lead directly to performance. It is mediated by individual abilities and traits, and by the person's role perceptions. They also introduce rewards as an intervening variable. Porter and Lawler see motivation, satisfaction and performance as separate variables and attempt to explain the complex relationships among them. Their model recognises that job satisfaction is more dependent upon performance, than performance is upon satisfaction.

Explanation of relationships These relationships are expressed diagrammatically (Figure 7.9) rather than mathematically. In contrast to the human relations approach which tended to assume that job satisfaction leads to improved performance, Porter and Lawler suggest that satisfaction is an effect rather than a cause of performance. It is performance that leads to job satisfaction.

- **Value of reward** (Box 1) is similar to valence in Vroom's model. People desire various outcomes (rewards) which they hope to achieve from work. The value placed on a reward depends on the strength of its desirability.

Figure 7.9	The Porter and Lawler motivation model

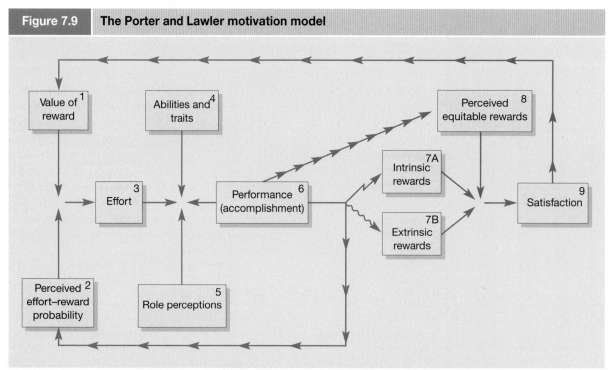

Source: From Porter, I. W. and Lawler, E. E., *Managerial Attitudes and Performance*. Copyright © Richard D. Irwin Inc. (1968) p. 165.

- **Perceived effort–reward probability** (Box 2) is similar to expectancy. It refers to a person's expectation that certain outcomes (rewards) are dependent upon a given amount of effort.
- **Effort** (Box 3) is how hard the person tries, the amount of energy a person exerts on a given activity. It does not relate to how successful a person is in carrying out an activity. The amount of energy exerted is dependent upon the interaction of the input variables of value of reward and perception of the effort–reward relationship.
- **Abilities and traits** (Box 4). Porter and Lawler suggest that effort does not lead directly to performance but is influenced by individual characteristics. Factors such as intelligence, skills, knowledge, training and personality affect the ability to perform a given activity.
- **Role perceptions** (Box 5) refer to the way in which individuals view their work and the role they should adopt. This influences the type of effort exerted. Role perceptions will influence the direction and level of action which is believed to be necessary for effective performance.
- **Performance** (Box 6) depends not only on the amount of effort exerted but also on the intervening influences of the person's abilities and traits, and their role perceptions. If the person lacks the right ability or personality, or has an inaccurate role perception of what is required, then the exertion of a large amount of energy may still result in a low level of performance or task accomplishment.
- **Rewards** (Boxes 7A and 7B) are desirable outcomes. Intrinsic rewards derive from the individuals themselves and include a sense of achievement, a feeling of responsibility and recognition (for example Herzberg's motivators). Extrinsic rewards derive from the organisation and the actions of others and include salary, working conditions and supervision (for example Herzberg's hygiene factors). The relationship between performance and intrinsic rewards is shown as a jagged line. This is because the extent of the relationship depends upon the nature of the job. If the design of the job permits variety and challenge, so that people feel able to reward themselves for good performance, there is a direct relationship. Where job design does not involve variety and challenge, there is no direct relationship between good performance and intrinsic rewards. The wavy line between performance and extrinsic rewards indicates that such rewards do not often provide a direct link to performance.
- **Perceived equitable rewards** (Box 8). This is the level of rewards people feel they should fairly receive for a given standard of performance. Most people have an implicit perception about the level of rewards they should receive commensurate with the requirements and demands of the job, and the contribution expected of them. Self-rating of performance links directly with the perceived equitable reward variable. Higher levels of self-rated performance are associated with higher levels of expected equitable rewards. The heavily arrowed line indicates a relationship from the self-rated part of performance to perceived equitable rewards.
- **Satisfaction** (Box 9). This is not the same as motivation. It is an attitude, an individual's internal state. Satisfaction is determined by both actual rewards received and perceived level of rewards from the organisation for a given standard of performance. If perceived equitable rewards are greater than actual rewards received, the person experiences dissatisfaction. The experience of satisfaction derives from actual rewards that meet or exceed the perceived equitable rewards.

LAWLER'S REVISED EXPECTANCY MODEL

Following the original Porter and Lawler model, further work was undertaken by *Lawler* (*see* Figure 7.10).[30] He suggests that in deciding on the attractiveness of alternative behaviours, there are two types of expectancies to be considered: effort–performance expectancies (E → P) and performance–outcome expectancies (P → O).

The first expectancy (E → P) is the person's perception of the probability that a given amount of effort will result in achieving an intended level of performance. It is measured on a scale between 0 and 1. The closer the perceived relationship between effort and performance, the higher the E → P expectancy score.

The second expectancy (P → O) is the person's perception of the probability that a given level of performance will actually lead to particular need-related outcomes. This is measured also on a scale between 0 and 1. The closer the perceived relationship between performance and outcome, the higher the P → O expectancy score.

Motivational force to perform The multiplicative combination of the two types of expectancies, E → P and the sum of the products P → O, determines expectancy. The motivational force to perform (effort expended) is determined by multiplying E → P and P → O by the strength of outcome valence (V).

$$E(\text{Effort}) = (E \rightarrow P) \times \Sigma \, [(P \rightarrow O) \quad V]$$

The distinction between the two types of expectancies arises because they are determined by different conditions. E → P expectancy is determined in part by the person's ability and self-confidence, past experience and the difficulty of the task. P → O expectancy is determined by the attractiveness of the outcomes and the belief about who controls the outcomes, the person him/herself or other people.

Figure 7.10	An illustration of the Lawler expectancy model

IMPLICATIONS FOR MANAGERS OF EXPECTANCY THEORIES

There are a number of versions of expectancy theory. The main elements tend to be very similar, however, and this suggests the development of a generally accepted approach. Expectancy models are not always easy to understand, or to apply. There are many variables which affect behaviour at work. A problem can arise in attempting to include a large

number of variables or in identifying those variables which are most appropriate in particular situations.

Expectancy theory does, however, draw attention to the complexities of work motivation. It provides further information in helping to explain the nature of behaviour and motivation in the work situation, and helps to identify problems in performance. Expectancy theory indicates that managers should give attention to a number of factors, including the following:

- Use rewards appropriate in terms of individual performance. Outcomes with high valence should be used as an incentive for improved performance.
- Attempt to establish clear relationships between effort–performance and rewards, as perceived by the individual.
- Establish clear procedures for the evaluation of individual levels of performance.
- Pay attention to intervening variables such as abilities and traits, role perceptions, organisational procedures and support facilities, which, although not necessarily direct motivational factors, may still affect performance.
- Minimise undesirable outcomes which may be perceived to result from a high level of performance, such as industrial accidents or sanctions from co-workers, or to result despite a high level of performance, such as short-time working or layoffs.

Porter and Lawler also emphasise that the expectancy model is just a model and that expectancy theory applies only to behaviours which are under the voluntary control of the individual. The two general types of choices over which individuals have voluntary control of work performance in organisations are:

1 the amount of effort and energy expended; and
2 the manner in which they go about performing their work.

> *There is always a choice about the way you do your work, even if there is not a choice about the work itself. You always have a choice about the attitude you bring to the job.*
>
> World famous Pike Place Fish Market, Seattle[31]

Refresh your understanding

Activity 7C
www.pearsoned.co.uk/
mullins

Critical reflection

????

'Expectancy theories of motivation appear to make sense in the classroom and form the basis of an interesting academic debate, but it is unlikely the practising manager will be impressed or take much notice.' What do you think? How would you explain the potential benefits of expectancy theory to a sceptical manager?

EQUITY THEORY OF MOTIVATION

One of the major variables of satisfaction in the Porter and Lawler expectancy model is perceived equitable rewards. This leads to consideration of another process theory of motivation – **equity theory**. Applied to the work situation, equity theory is usually associated with the work of *Adams*.[32]

Equity theory focuses on people's feelings of how fairly they have been treated in comparison with the treatment received by others. It is based on exchange theory. Social relationships involve an exchange process. For example, a person may expect promotion as

an outcome of a high level of contribution (input) in helping to achieve an important organisational objective. People also compare their own position with that of others. They determine the perceived equity of their own position. Their feelings about the equity of the exchange are affected by the treatment they receive when compared with what happens to other people. Most exchanges involve a number of inputs and outcomes. According to equity theory, people place a weighting on these various inputs and outcomes according to how they perceive their importance. When there is an unequal comparison of ratios the person experiences a sense of **inequity**.

Behaviour as a consequence of inequity

A feeling of inequity causes tension, which is an unpleasant experience. The presence of inequity therefore motivates the person to remove or to reduce the level of tension and the perceived inequity. The magnitude of perceived inequity determines the level of tension. The level of tension created determines the strength of motivation. Adams identifies six broad types of possible behaviour as consequences of inequity (*see* Figure 7.11):

- **Changes to inputs**. A person may increase or decrease the level of their inputs, for example through the amount or quality of work, absenteeism, or working additional hours without pay.
- **Changes to outcomes**. A person may attempt to change outcomes such as pay, working conditions, status and recognition, without changes to inputs.
- **Cognitive distortion of inputs and outcomes**. In contrast to actual changes, people may distort, cognitively, their inputs or outcomes to achieve the same results. Adams suggests that although it is difficult for people to distort facts about themselves, it is possible, within limits, to distort the utility of those facts: for example, the belief about how hard they are really working, the relevance of a particular qualification, or what they can or cannot obtain with a given level of pay.

Figure 7.11	An illustration of Adams's equity theory of motivation

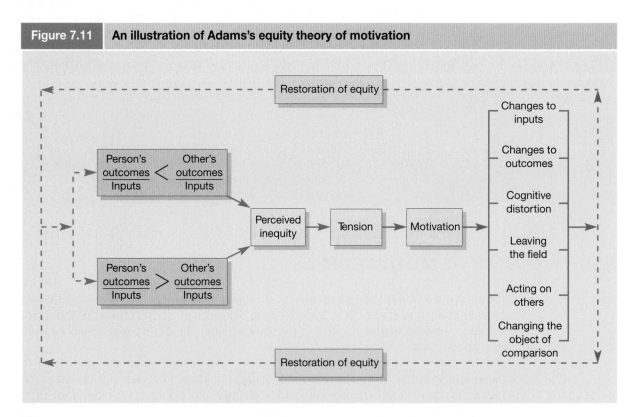

- **Leaving the field**. A person may try to find a new situation with a more favourable balance, for example by absenteeism, request for a transfer, resigning from a job or from the organisation altogether.
- **Acting on others**. A person may attempt to bring about changes in others, for example to lower their inputs or accept greater outcomes. Or the person may cognitively distort the inputs and outcomes of others. Alternatively, a person may try to force others to leave the field.
- **Changing the object of comparison**. This involves changing the reference group with whom comparison is made. For example, where another person with a previously similar outcome–input ratio receives greater outcomes without any apparent increase in contribution, that other person may be perceived as now belonging to a different level in the organisation structure. The comparison need not necessarily be made with people who have the same inputs and outcomes. The important thing is a similar ratio of outcomes to inputs.

Under the control of the manager The manager may seek to remove or reduce tension and perceived inequity among staff by influencing these types of behaviour – for example by attempting to change a person's inputs or encouraging a different object of comparison. However, there are likely to be only two courses of action under the direct control of the manager. Outcomes can be changed by, for example, increased pay, additional perks or improved working conditions, or by instigating a person leaving the field through transfer, resignation or, as an extreme measure, dismissal.

GOAL THEORY

Another theory usually considered under the heading of motivation to work is **goal theory**, or the theory of goal-setting (*see* Figure 7.12). This theory is based mainly on the work of *Locke*.[33] The basic premise of goal theory is that people's goals or intentions play an important part in determining behaviour. Locke accepts the importance of perceived value, as indicated in expectancy theories of motivation, and suggests that these values give rise to the experience of emotions and desires. People strive to achieve goals in order to satisfy their emotions and desires. Goals guide people's responses and actions. Goals direct work behaviour and performance and lead to certain consequences or feedback. Locke subsequently pointed out that 'goal-setting is more appropriately viewed as a motivational technique rather than as a formal theory of motivation.'[34]

Figure 7.12	An illustration of Locke's theory of goal-setting

A climate of creativity

Lucas draws attention to skills shortages as one of the biggest challenges facing employers in the new millennium. In order to attract and keep talented individuals, the so-called knowledge workers, organisations cannot rely simply on a pay rise or cash bonus but have to be more creative about the way they structure remuneration packages. Individual performance-related pay is still the most widely used reward strategy, but attention is also given to employee share ownership, competence-related pay and team reward – and also to non-cash incentives such as gift vouchers. However, Lucas points out that employees, especially high flyers, rank challenging and interesting work and freedom higher on their motivational list than money and performance-related pay. 'Research suggests that most organisations haven't recognised the need to identify and tap into their employees' personal motivators.'[41]

A report from the *Chartered Institute of Personnel and Development* draws attention to the management of knowledge workers, highlighting the importance of autonomy, challenging work and sharing in the creation of organisational values. With the development of new technology it is important to motivate employees to capture, share and transfer knowledge.[42]

Whitmore suggests that in order to create a climate for creativity among employees, recognition must be given to the importance of two human needs that rise above all others and exist independent of race, creed and culture – the need for self-belief and the development of emotional intelligence; and the ever-present need that every human being has for a sense of meaning and purpose in their lives. 'Self-belief and meaningful work are the fundamental bedrocks that underlie business performance. Of course, pay and conditions are important too, but we know that. It is these two others that are barely recognised ... but business leaders ignore them at their peril.'[43]

CROSS-CULTURAL DIMENSIONS OF MOTIVATION

Whatever the popularity of different theories of motivation, doubts are raised about their universality on the ground that they have not adequately addressed the factor of culture.[44] Are theories of motivation universally applicable or are there meaningful differences in motivation at work, or in life more generally, in different societies? Many readers may feel able to recognise perceived variations in extrinsic, intrinsic and relational aspects of motivation as a result of experience of foreign cultures. Do similarities in workplace attitudes and behaviour outweigh differences? A number of writers have questioned whether motivational theories and models originating in one culture are amenable to transference to other parts of the world. *Francesco and Gold* devote a substantial proportion of a discussion of motivation to examining the extent to which American motivation theories are applicable outside the United States.

When discussing Maslow's contribution to this topic and, in particular, the concept of a hierarchy of needs, Francesco and Gold suggest: 'In an international context the circumstances and values of a particular culture can influence the ordering and importance of needs. The values of individualism and collectivism can make the hierarchy more or less relevant.'[45] In evaluating McClelland's work, Francesco and Gold question whether the meaning of an underlying concept, in this case achievement, can even be understood worldwide in the sense it was intended: 'Another concern with Learning Needs Theory is that the concept of achievement is difficult, if not impossible, to translate into languages other than English.'[46]

It has already been suggested that one criticism of content theories of motivation centres on its relative applicability in different circumstances and the suggestion that there may be variations across cultures falls within this line of reasoning. However, perhaps less obviously, process theories of motivation have also been criticised for being culture-bound. As they focus on process rather than content, such theories may appear to be more applicable in diverse cultural contexts. Nonetheless it has been suggested that process theories of motivation contain certain inbuilt assumptions that are themselves culturally derived.

Refresh your
understanding

Activity 7D
www.pearsoned.co.uk/
mullins

Adler reminds us that expectancy models of motivation assume that individuals believe that they can, to some extent, control their environment and influence their fate. If, as in the cases of more fatalistic cultures such as China, people do not have the same sense of internal attribution, the expectancy model may have less force and therefore applicability. When Adams's equity theory is applied across the world, differences in interpretation have been recorded.[47] *Chen* suggests that while individualistic cultures place a high regard on equity, collectivist cultures value equality more than equity. Again we see here the possibility that while a theory of motivation may be essentially valid in principle, it is legitimate to think about the ways in which national culture can intervene in terms of its interpretation in different societies.[48]

THE MEANING AND NATURE OF JOB SATISFACTION

Attempting to understand the nature of job satisfaction and its effects on work performance is not easy. Job satisfaction is a complex and multifaceted concept, which can mean different things to different people. It is usually linked with motivation, but the nature of this relationship is not clear. Satisfaction is not the same as motivation. **Job satisfaction** is more of an attitude, an internal state. It could, for example, be associated with a personal feeling of achievement, either quantitative or qualitative.

It is often suggested that job satisfaction is necessary in order to achieve a high level of motivation and performance. However, although the level of job satisfaction may well affect strength of motivation, this is not always the case. The relationship between job satisfaction and performance is an issue of continuing debate and controversy. One view, associated with the early human relations approach, is that satisfaction leads to performance. An alternative view is that performance leads to satisfaction. *Reeves* draws attention to the relationship between accomplishment at work and the need to 'work harder'.

> *All this busy-ness and stress is creating more heat than light. It is a sign not of work being too hard but too shallow. Human nature is driven by a desire to accomplish things, and so the fewer opportunities for accomplishment a job contains, the more likely we are to fill the void by tearing around in a frenzy in an effort to persuade ourselves and others that our work has a purpose, that it is important.*[49]

DIMENSIONS OF JOB SATISFACTION

There is some doubt whether job satisfaction consists of a single dimension or a number of separate dimensions. Some workers may be satisfied with certain aspects of their work and dissatisfied with other aspects. Job satisfaction is itself a complex concept and difficult to measure objectively. The level of job satisfaction is affected by a wide range of variables relating to individual, social, cultural, organisational and environmental factors.

- **Individual factors** include personality, education and qualifications, intelligence and abilities, age, marital status, orientation to work.
- **Social factors** include relationships with co-workers, group working and norms, opportunities for interaction, informal organisation.
- **Cultural factors** include underlying attitudes, beliefs and values.
- **Organisational factors** include nature and size, formal structure, HR policies and procedures, employee relations, nature of the work, technology and work organisation, supervision and styles of leadership, management systems, working conditions.
- **Environmental factors** include economic, social, technical and governmental influences.

These different factors all affect the job satisfaction of certain individuals in a given set of circumstances but not necessarily in others.

Five contractual areas

Mumford examines job satisfaction in two ways:

1 in terms of the fit between what the organisation requires and what the employee is seeking; and
2 in terms of the fit between what the employee is seeking and what they are actually receiving.

On the basis of various schools of thought on job satisfaction, Mumford identifies five contractual areas by which this organisational/employee relationship can be examined: the knowledge contract, the psychological contract, the efficiency/reward contract, the ethical contract and the task structure contract (*see* Table 7.3).[50]

The work environment

An increasingly important issue affecting job satisfaction and efficiency is the nature of the work environment and workplace facilities. *Handy* argues that an inspired workplace will result in inspired workers and draws attention to the importance for work performance of the atmosphere, quality and style of buildings and offices.[51]

A 2003 study by the Chartered Management Institute reports on UK managers' attitudes to and experiences of their physical working environment. The study was undertaken among a random sample of 4,000 managers across all levels and sectors and size of organisation. Topics addressed included hours worked, commuting and travel, flexible working, the existing and preferred layout of offices and the use of new technologies. Concerns were expressed about the need for more quiet areas, under-equipped meeting rooms, lack of adequate meeting space, and their offices not making a good impression on clients and visitors. Nearly half of those surveyed would relinquish one week's annual leave for a better office and sizeable numbers would forgo £1,000 in salary or private medical insurance for a significantly upgraded workspace. And even if the role, salary and benefits were no better, 45 per cent would contemplate changing companies in return for an improved work environment.[52, 53]

Table 7.3	Five contractual areas relating to job satisfaction	
	The firm	**The employee**
The knowledge contract	Needs a certain level of skill and knowledge in its employees if it is to function efficiently	Wishes the skills and knowledge they bring with them to be used and developed
The psychological contract	Needs employees who are motivated to look after its interests	Seeks to further interests private to self, e.g. to secure: achievement, recognition, responsibility, status
The efficiency/rewards contract	Needs to implement generalised output, quality standards and reward systems	Seeks a personal, equitable effort–reward bargain and controls, including supervisory ones, which are perceived as acceptable
The ethical (social value) contract	Needs employees who will accept the firm's ethos and values	Seeks to work for an employer whose values do not contravene their own
The task structure contract	Needs employees who will accept technical and other constraints which produce task specificity or task differentiation	Seeks a set of tasks which meets their requirements for task differentiation, e.g. which incorporate variety, interests, targets, feedback, task identity and autonomy

Source: Mumford, E., 'Job satisfaction: a method of analysis', *Personnel Review*, vol. 20, no. 3, 1991, p. 14. Reproduced with permission from Emerald Group Publishing Limited.

> *More than any other element, fun is the secret of Virgin's success. I am aware that the idea of business being fun and creative goes right against the grain of convention, and it's certainly not how they teach it at some of those business schools, where business means hard grind and lots of 'discounted cash flows' and 'net present values' ... For us, our employees matter most. It just seems common sense to me that, if you start off with a happy, well motivated workforce, you're much more likely to have happy customers. And in due course the resulting profits will make your shareholders happy.*
>
> Richard Branson, *Losing My Virginity*[54]

Alienation at work One main approach to job satisfaction is in terms of frustration and alienation at work. Job satisfaction can be seen as the obverse of frustration at work (discussed above). Alienation refers to the detachment of the person from their work role. The concept of alienation at work is associated originally with the views of **Marx**.[55] He saw the division of labour in pursuit of profit, and exploitation by employers, as a denial of the workers' need for self-expression. Workers become estranged from the product of their work. Work no longer provided a satisfying experience in itself, but represented a means of satisfying other external demands. The concept of alienation has been extended by *Blauner*.[56] He describes alienation in terms of four dimensions: powerlessness, meaninglessness, isolation and self-estrangement.

- **Powerlessness** denotes the workers' lack of control over management policy, immediate work processes, or conditions of employment.
- **Meaninglessness** stems from standardisation and division of labour. It denotes the inability to see the purpose of work done or to identify with the total production process or finished product.
- **Isolation** is not belonging to an integrated work group or to the social work organisation and not being guided by group norms of behaviour.
- **Self-estrangement** is the failure to see work as an end in itself or as a central life issue. Workers experience a depersonalised detachment and work is seen solely as a means to an end.

In recent years attention to job satisfaction has also become more closely associated with broader approaches to improved job design and work organisation, and the quality of working life movement, and with stress and the work/life balance (discussed in Chapter 3).

Critical reflection

Job satisfaction is very subjective. It is affected by many variables including unknown domestic situations and personal relationships outside of work. Management models of job satisfaction appear to be a complete waste of time. Do you agree? What do you think are the most powerful influences on job satisfaction?

BROADER APPROACHES TO JOB SATISFACTION

Broader approaches to job satisfaction aim to give the person improved empowerment and job enrichment through greater autonomy and authority over the planning, execution and control of their work. It focuses attention on intrinsic satisfaction. Job enrichment increases the complexity of the work. It should provide the person with a more meaningful and challenging job and offer greater opportunities for psychological growth.

The main methods of achieving job enrichment include the following:

- permitting workers greater freedom and control over the scheduling and pacing of their work as opposed to machine pacing;
- allowing workers to undertake a full task cycle, build or assemble a complete product or component, or deliver a complete service;
- providing workers with tasks or jobs which challenge their abilities and make fuller use of their training, expertise and skills;
- giving workers greater freedom to work in self-managing teams with greater responsibility for monitoring their own performance and the minimum of direct supervision; and
- providing workers with the opportunity to have greater direct contact with clients, consumers or users of the product or service.

> *In an organisation, empowerment means that each staff member is responsible for creating that organisation's culture. There aren't many motivating forces more potent than giving your staff an opportunity to exercise and express their idealism.*
>
> Anita Roddick, *Business As Unusual*[57]

A COMPREHENSIVE MODEL OF JOB ENRICHMENT

Attempts to improve intrinsic motivation must not only include considerations of job characteristics but also take account of individual differences and attributes, and people's orientation to work. A popular and comprehensive model of job enrichment has been developed by *Hackman and Oldham* (*see* Figure 7.14).[58] The model views job enrichment in terms of increasing five core job dimensions: skill variety, task identity, task significance, autonomy and feedback. These core job characteristics create three psychological states:

- experienced meaningfulness of the work;
- experienced responsibility for the outcomes of the work; and
- knowledge of the actual results of the work activities.

Figure 7.14	A job characteristics model of work motivation

Source: Hackman, J. R. and Oldham, G. R., *Work Redesign*, Addison-Wesley Publishing Company, Inc. (1980), Figure 4.6, p. 90. Reproduced with permission from Pearson Education, Inc.

Five core dimensions

The five core job dimensions can be summarised as follows:

- **skill variety** – the extent to which a job entails different activities and involves a range of skills and talents;
- **task identity** – the extent to which a job involves completion of a whole piece of work with a visible outcome;
- **task significance** – the extent to which a job has a meaningful impact on other people, either inside or outside the organisation;
- **autonomy** – the extent to which a job provides freedom, independence and discretion in planning the work and determining how to undertake it;
- **feedback** – the extent to which work activities result in direct and clear information on the effectiveness of job performance.

An example of a job with little enrichment could be that of a production assembly line worker or a kitchen porter, where all five core characteristics are likely to score low. An example of an enriched job could be that of a parish priest who draws upon a wide range of social skills and talents, who can usually identify with the whole task and whose job has clear and important meaning and significance. There is a very high level of autonomy and likely to be direct and clear feedback.

Motivating potential score From these five core job dimensions, Hackman and Oldham have developed an equation which gives a single index of a person's job profile. By answering a questionnaire – the Job Diagnostic Survey (JDS) – and by giving a score (between 1 and 7) to each job dimension, the person can calculate an overall measure of job enrichment, called the motivating potential score (MPS).

Examples of questions from the JDS are:

- How much variety is there in your job?
- To what extent does your job involve doing a whole and identifiable piece of work?
- In general, how significant or important is your job?
- How much autonomy is there in your job?
- To what extent does doing the job itself provide you with information about your work performance?

$$MPS = \frac{\{skill\ variety + Task\ variety + Task\ significance\}}{3} \times Autonomy \times Feedback$$

The first three job dimensions of skill variety, task identity and task significance are averaged, since it is the combination of these dimensions which contributes to experienced meaningfulness of work. The remaining two job dimensions, autonomy and feedback, stand on their own. Since scores for skill variety, task identity and task significance are additive, this means that the absence of one dimension can be partially offset by the presence of the other dimensions. However, if either autonomy or feedback is absent then, because of the multiplicative relationship, the MPS would be zero. The job would offer no potential to motivate the person.

Empirical support for the model

Empirical support for the model is mixed. From their studies, Hackman and Oldham claim that people with enriched jobs and high score levels on the Job Diagnostic Survey experienced more satisfaction and internal motivation. The core job dimensions of skill variety, task identity and task significance combined to predict the level of experienced meaningfulness of the work. The core dimensions of autonomy and feedback did not relate so clearly to experienced responsibility and knowledge of results. Some of the other dimensions were as good, or better, in predicting these psychological conditions. In general, however, the results of their studies showed that jobs that scored high on the core dimensions were associated with high levels of personal and work outcomes.

In a study of a sample of six hotels (with between 35 and 65 bedrooms) in Great Yarmouth, *Lee-Ross* undertook an examination of the reliability of the JDS among seasonal workers. From an analysis of 163 questionnaires, Lee-Ross concludes that in general, reliability scores were compatible with those of Hackman and Oldham. The JDS appears to hold just as well for hotel workers as for workers in other industries.[59]

Based on integrating Hackman and Oldham's job characteristics model with Maslow's hierarchy of needs, *Roe et al.* propose a general model of work motivation, tested with Bulgarian, Hungarian and Dutch workers. The model indicates that situational characteristics lead to critical psychological factors, inducing two main motivational factors – **job involvement** and **organisational commitment** – which in turn lead to two proximal outcomes of work motivation – **effort** and **job satisfaction** – which affect **performance**, **stress** and **tendency to leave the organisation**. Although there were some differences that draw attention to cultural variables, there was also a large degree of similarity in results across the three countries.[60]

FLEXIBLE WORKING ARRANGEMENTS

An increasingly significant aspect of motivation and job satisfaction is flexible working. According to CIPD: 'This relates to an organisation's working arrangements in terms of working time, working location and the pattern of working.'[61] Moves towards greater flexibility may afford opportunities for employees to have more freedom and control over their working arrangements and have noticeable effects on their job satisfaction and performance. Flexible working arrangements are discussed in Chapter 16.

CONTEXTUAL FACTORS IN JOB DESIGN

The different methods of job design are not necessarily separate approaches. They are interrelated and there is some overlapping among them. For example, goal-setting is sometimes viewed as another approach to job design. Goal-setting involves building goals, feedback and incentives into the structure of the job. In addition, there are many other associated (contextual) factors which affect job design, including, for example: organisational culture, structure, systems of management and style of leadership, trade unions, HR policies and procedures, communications, group norms, ergonomics, the management of change, and the working environment.

Management style and culture The potential benefits of improved job design are unlikely to be realised if attention is focused on the content of jobs alone. Of equal, if not more, importance is the process by which redesign is carried out. This has led to recognition of the importance of management style and, increasingly, of organisation culture.[62] Central to improving the quality of working life is a participative, open style of management involving employees in decisions that affect them, including the design or choice of technology. Management should attempt to develop a relationship of trust among all members and sections of the organisation and a meaningful partnership approach with trade unions.

Job satisfaction and HRM Theories of work motivation and job satisfaction have influenced management systems and styles of leadership, and developments in HR policies and procedures. The human resource management function is centred on people's needs while working in an organisation and ways in which their work promotes or frustrates the fulfilment of these needs.[63] The practice of modern human resource management is directed towards providing conditions under which people work willingly and effectively, and contribute to the success of the organisation. This involves concern for employee motivation and job satisfaction.

A concept map of job satisfaction is set out in Figure 7.15.

Refresh your understanding
Activity 7E
www.pearsoned.co.uk/
mullins

Figure 7.15 Concept map of job satisfaction

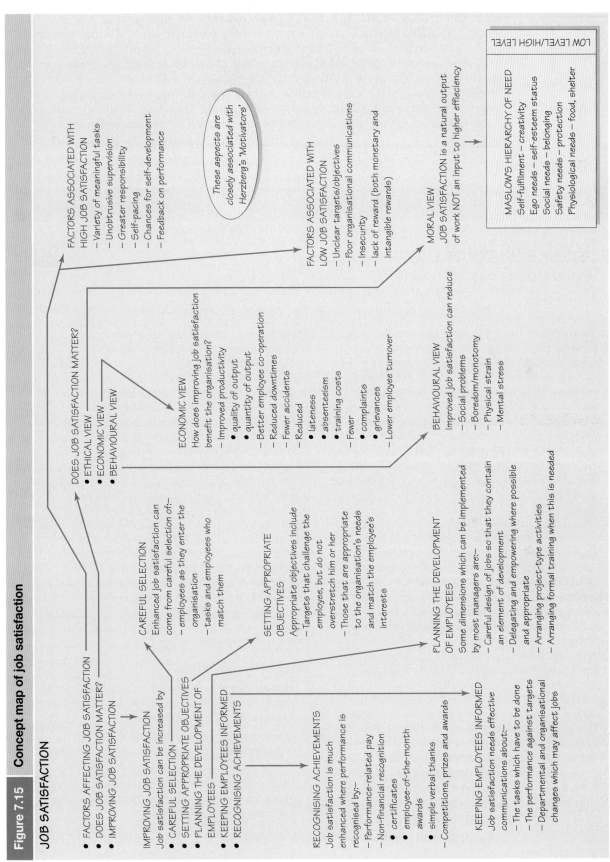

Source: Training Learning Consultancy Ltd, Bristol, England. Reproduced with permission.

Critical reflection

Motivation varies over time and according to circumstances. Individuals have a variety of changing, and often conflicting, needs and expectations which they attempt to satisfy in a number of ways. How do you think your motivation will change in five years' time? Do you agree that the search for a generalised theory of motivation at work is a vain quest and all these competing theories are just a waste of time?

MANAGEMENT IN THE NEWS

Towels and talent

FT

Microsoft plans perks to retain staff

Richard Waters

Microsoft said it would supply free towels in company showers, better food in staff canteens and on-site laundry service in an effort to boost employee morale as it battles for talent with Google and other recent start-ups. The outbreak of the internet 'perks war' is the latest sign of Microsoft's attempt to keep some of the trappings of a fast-growing Silicon Valley start-up as it takes on more of the characteristics of other large, slower-growing blue chip companies.

Google has become the most visible exponent of Silicon Valley's entitlement culture, using the free food in its highly rated cafeteria, along with the availability at its campus of services ranging from massages to automobile oil changes, to help attract and retain workers. The tech companies defend the on-site perks as a way to reward employees who often work long hours and who would otherwise have to leave the premises, making them less efficient.

Microsoft's decision to offer new employee perks, initially only at its headquarters campus near Seattle but eventually also in other sites around the world, marks a reversal of an earlier, unpopular cost-cutting policy. A decision to scrap the free towel service two years ago became a lightening rod for employee dissatisfaction. Under Ken DiPietro, who was hired as head of human resources from Dell, a technology company renowned for its low-cost ways, Microsoft abandoned a number of perks, echoing a wider attempt at the time to bring a new and more stringent financial discipline to the software company.

Mr DiPietro was replaced a year ago by Lisa Brummel, an internal appointment that signalled the company's desire to repair some of the damage to morale. In an internal email to staff earlier this week,

Ms Brummel unveiled a number of changes to Microsoft's compensation system and other management systems. They include adding 15 per cent to the amount of restricted stock that Microsoft sets aside each year to reward employees. Its decision recently to abandon stock options, a form of compensation that had famously created thousands of 'Microsoft Millionaires', has left it at a disadvantage to Google and other fast-growing companies, which use the incentives liberally to attract talent.

Ms Brummel also said Microsoft would scrap a system that had forced managers to rate a certain number of workers as sub-standard each year, and that it would adjust its compensation system to keep 'top talent' at the company. The new perks, which include a grocery delivery service and 'dinners to go from Wolfgang Puck', a celebrity chef who runs a catering service, 'are designed to ease the burden given the hectic pace of life', Ms Brummel wrote.

Source: Waters, R., 'Microsoft plans perks to retain staff', *Financial Times*, 20 May 2006. Copyright © 2006 The Financial Times Limited, reproduced with permission.

Discussion questions

1 With reference to Figure 7.2, assess the extent to which you think Microsoft meets the needs and expectations of its employees.

2 Discuss the extent to which you think that organisational success is the *cause* or the *effect* of meeting employee needs and expectations.

3 What does the experience of Microsoft reveal about the 'psychological contract' between the company and its employees?

SYNOPSIS

● The study of motivation is concerned, basically, with why people behave in a certain way. The underlying concept of motivation is some driving force within individuals by which they attempt to achieve some goal in order to fulfil some need or expectation. Individuals have a variety of changing, and often competing, needs and expectations which they attempt to satisfy in a number of ways. If a person's motivational driving force is blocked and they are unable to satisfy their needs and expectations, this may result either in constructive, problem-solving behaviour or in frustration-induced behaviour.

● There are many competing theories that attempt to explain motivation at work. The different theories may be divided into two contrasting groups: content theories and process theories. Content theories place emphasis on what motivates and are concerned with identifying people's needs and their relative strengths, and the goals they pursue in order to satisfy these needs. Main content theories include Maslow's hierarchy of needs model, Alderfer's modified need hierarchy model, Herzberg's two-factor theory and McClelland's achievement motivation theory.

● Process theories place emphasis on the actual process of motivation. These theories are concerned with the relationships among the dynamic variables that make up motivation, and with how behaviour is initiated, directed and sustained. Many of the process theories cannot be linked to a single writer, but major approaches under this heading include expectancy-based models, equity theory, goal theory and attribution theory.

● These different theories are not conclusive. However, it is because of the complexity of motiva-

tion that these different theories are important to the manager and many writers still expound their relevance today. They help demonstrate the many motives that influence people's behaviour at work. They provide a framework within which to direct attention for how best to motivate and reward staff to work willingly and effectively. One major doubt concerning the different theories of motivation is about their universality, on the grounds that they do not adequately address the factor of culture.

● Attempting to understand the nature of job satisfaction and links with work performance is not easy. Although the level of job satisfaction may well affect the strength of motivation, this is not always the case. Job satisfaction is more of an internal state and could be associated, for example, with a feeling of personal achievement. Job satisfaction is a complex concept and difficult to measure objectively. The level of job satisfaction is affected by a wide range of individual, social, organisational and cultural variables.

● Broader approaches to satisfaction aim to give the person improved empowerment and job enrichment through greater autonomy and control over their work. Attention has also been given to a comprehensive model of job enrichment and five core dimensions. Moves towards greater flexibility may have noticeable effects on job satisfaction and performance of staff. Despite many theories and studies there are still doubts as to how best to manage an organisation so that staff have both high job satisfaction and productivity. Account must also be taken of contextual factors, including management style and culture, and developments in human resource management.

 Refresh your understanding, assess your progress and begin your research with online resources at **www.pearsoned.co.uk/mullins**

REVIEW AND DISCUSSION QUESTIONS

1 Explain what you understand by the underlying concept of motivation. Summarise the main needs and expectations to be taken into account in considering the motivation of people at work.

2 What do you understand by frustration-induced behaviour? Give a practical example, preferably from your work experience, of each of the main forms of this behaviour.

3 Critically assess the practical value of Maslow's hierarchy of needs model to improving the motivation of people at work. Give examples of the extent to which the theory could meaningfully be applied to staff in your own organisation.

Review and discussion questions – continued

4 Discuss critically the validity of the contention that the motivation for staff to work well depends on more than a high salary and good working conditions.

5 Explain your understanding of expectancy-based theories of motivation. Use a simple diagram to help explain an expectancy theory of your choice. What implications do expectancy theories of motivation have for the manager?

6 Give practical examples of situations in which each of the following theories of motivation might be appropriate: (i) achievement motivation; (ii) equity theory; (iii) goal theory.

7 What exactly do you understand by job satisfaction? What are the main dimensions of job satisfaction? Give specific examples of causes of job dissatisfaction that you have experienced.

8 Evaluate critically the relationship between motivation, job satisfaction and effective work performance. Give reasons in support of your views.

ASSIGNMENT 1

a List, as far as possible in rank order, the specific needs and expectations that are most important **to you as an individual**. (Do *not* include basic physiological needs such as to satisfy thirst or hunger, or a *minimal* standard of accommodation.)

b Explain, briefly, to what extent these needs and expectations are met currently by your present work situation and/or to what extent you anticipate they will be met by your future career ambitions.

c Think of any work experience that you have had – even a short-term, vacation or part-time job. Briefly describe those aspects of the job and/or experiences that:

(i) motivated you to work well and to the best of your ability; and

(ii) had a demotivating influence on your behaviour and performance.

Be prepared to share your feelings and comments as part of a class discussion.

ASSIGNMENT 2

a Write a brief description of what you think is happening to the people in the picture and what you think will happen to them in the future.

b After you have written your description, compare your response with those of your colleagues.

PERSONAL AWARENESS AND SKILLS EXERCISE

Objectives

Completing this exercise should help you to enhance the following skills:

● Analyse and review what determines your motivation to work.

● Reflect upon your perceptions about the motives of other people.

● Take account of individual needs and expectations at work.

Exercise

1 Put in writing as openly and precisely as possible, and in rank order, those factors that have the strongest influence on your own motivation and job satisfaction. *Exchange accounts with a partner before proceeding further.*

2 Now assume you are the newly appointed general manager of a 50-room hotel with restaurant. You have been brought in as a trouble shooter and at interview you were informed there is serious concern about the generally poor level of work performance, that morale is low and there is a disturbing high level of staff turnover.

● Detail fully the likely actions you would take to help overcome the present situation.

● Indicate clearly the priorities you would have in mind.

● Make clear any necessary, reasonable assumptions.

● Explain how you might draw upon those theories/studies you consider relevant.

3 Write, fully and honestly, the extent to which there is disparity between your own motives and, based on the above, motivating other people. How would you explain and rationalise differences?

4 Compare and discuss critically accounts with your partner, and be prepared to explain and justify your views.

Discussion

● How far did you avoid generalisations about what motivates other people?

● What assumptions did you make about the work ethic of staff at the hotel?

● To what extent where you able to distance your own motivations?

● What conclusions do you draw from this exercise?

CASE STUDY

Don't get mad, get online!

In 2005 the word 'blog', meaning an on-line journal or web log which is regularly updated by the author, entered the *Oxford English Dictionary* for the first time. Figures collected by academic researchers and other internet monitoring organisations suggest that by the time the word made it into the dictionary there were about 30 million blogs in existence, and the numbers were increasing at the rate of about 70,000 per day.[64] Not all blogs are about work, but the fact that life in the office or workplace is a significant part of many people's lives means that many blogs include references to work, bosses, colleagues and customers alongside other normal daily experiences, opinions about news events and so on. A number of blogs are specifically about work and these are the ones which tend to hit the headlines, usually when an employee gets into trouble for airing their opinions about the organisation they work for in the blogosphere.

Why do individuals blog about work? At one level, blogging is no different from gossip. Many bloggers expect to have small audiences, possibly of like-minded people who have similar experiences to discuss; the content of blogs may be much like the discussions with colleagues that are routinely held in the round the water

cooler or coffee machine; or with friends in a pub or bar after work. Most blogs include opportunities for email and on-line discussion and so become a lively mix of intimate diary items and chat-room style comments. For some authors the aim is to give an insight into their working life, perhaps discussing the type of job which many people know about but few really understand. In the UK, at least one chief police constable and a number of ambulance service workers are known to blog primarily about their work.[65] However, many see it is a way of letting off steam about aspects of their work which enrage them, be it the organisation, their individual managers, their annoying colleagues and often the absurd behaviour of members of the general public and customers in particular.[66] This can make blogging a particularly risky activity, at least if the blogger wishes to keep their job.

Careless blogging can get you dooced

In 2004 Ellen Simonetti hit the headlines[67] when she was sacked by her employer, the American Delta Airlines, essentially for identifying it as the company about which she was blogging on her 'Queen of the Sky' website.[68] The offence which got her sacked was not the blog itself but the fact that by posting photographs of herself draped across the seats of an aircraft in her uniform (pictures which were described by the company as 'inappropriate'), she identified the organisation itself and therefore was considered to have brought it into disrepute. In January

2005, in a similar British case, Joe Gordon, an employee of 11 years' standing at Waterstones book shop in Edinburgh, was dismissed for gross misconduct[69] after 'bringing the company into disrepute' by complaining about his 'evil boss' at the fictionalised but nevertheless sufficiently recognisable bookstore 'Bastardones' in his blog 'The Wolamaloo Gazette.'[70]

The term 'doocing' has since been used to describe the phenomenon of being sacked for blogging, a fate which also befell Catherine Sanderson or 'La Petite Anglaise', who was dismissed from the Parisian branch of British accounting firm Dixon Wilson in July 2006 for committing the 'real and serious' offence of blogging mischievously but anonymously about her boss and colleagues.[71] As with Simonetti, it was when she posted photographs of herself on the site that the company decided that she, and therefore it, could be identified and that it had to act against its employee.

Learning to love bloggers

Not every organisation has reacted with hostility to bloggers. The Chief Constable and the ambulance workers mentioned above are at least tolerated and at best supported by their employers (the Chief Constable's blog is hosted by the North Wales Police website). The same was also true for Robert Scoble, at Microsoft, whose blog (Scobleizer) not only turned him into a cyber-celebrity but also acted to help humanise the previously monolithic corporate face of the company.[72]

Is it acceptable to blog about your company? Catherine Sanderson, "La Petite Anglaise" was sacked for her light-hearted (but anonymous) online account of events in her workplace.

Other organisations have actively embraced blog culture and sought to use it to their advantage. In the UK, Cadbury Schweppes decided to use blogging as a tool in its graduate recruitment programme and in 2005 enabled new graduates to blog their work experiences as a way of communicating to potential applicants about working life with the company.[73] Dell, the US computer giant, has also created its own blog (one2one) as a means of engaging with customer criticism. Yet other businesses have developed on the back of the blogging bandwagon. Market Sentinel offers an internet monitoring service (much like that of a press agency) to companies which want to know what is being blogged about them and be alerted to potential threats posed to their brand image in the blogosphere.

However, the blogging community is not entirely comfortable with attempts by 'corporates' to colonise this corner of cyberspace. Some companies, for example Wal-Mart, which used its public relations agency Edelman to 'feed' positive stories to well-known bloggers, have come in for criticism.[74] Other organisations have recognised the impossibility of controlling employees' private blogs, but have offered guidance and codes of practice for their workforce as a means of establishing out company policy and thereby establishing boundaries of acceptable behaviour. IBM, for example, has developed a set of 11 guidelines for its staff, some of which are summarised below:[75]

- Know and follow IBM's Business Conduct Guidelines.
- IBMers are personally responsible for their posts.
- You must make it clear that you are speaking for yourself and not on behalf of IBM.
- Respect copyright, fair use and financial disclosure laws.
- Don't provide IBM's or another's confidential or other proprietary information.
- Don't use ethnic slurs, personal insults, obscenity, etc. and show proper consideration for others' privacy and topics that may be considered objectionable or inflammatory, such as politics and religion.
- Don't pick fights, be the first to correct your own mistakes and don't alter previous posts without indicating that you have done so.
- Try to add value. Provide worthwhile information and perspective.

Organisational consequences: possibilities and challenges

IBM's approach, the development of guidelines for employees, is increasingly being seen as the way forward for organisations which are concerned about blogging. It prevents them from appearing heavyhanded, avoids the adverse publicity that can sometimes be stirred up by a sacking, and might also preclude legal challenges, for instance on the grounds of unfair dismissal or as an attempt to curtail freedom of speech. Simonetti, Gordon

and Sanderson all challenged their dismissals using employment tribunals or their equivalents, opening the question of the validity of dismissal for blogging. The existence of company guidelines which have clearly been breached by a blogger is likely to support an employer's case for dismissal.

The UK Chartered Institute of Personnel and Development considers that there are occasions when blogging might be easily identifiable as a disciplinary offence but would not necessarily support a dismissal; for instance, the abuse of company equipment and time by workers 'blogging on the job' might not be deemed to warrant dismissal by an employment tribunal unless the blog additionally caused harm to the organisation's reputation and interests.[76] Yet disclosure of confidential information might well breach company data protection policies, and dismissal for libellous or defamatory comments might stand up to the test of a tribunal. Similarly, it seems possible that if employees are using blogs to air their work grievances rather than using the more normal (and in the UK statutorily required) grievance procedures, they might well be risking fair dismissal. However, it is also worth considering how far disgruntled employees' blogs indicate that organisational grievance procedures or other employee feedback mechanisms (such as attitude surveys) are not operating very successfully and that important information about employee morale and job dissatisfaction is being overlooked.

Finally, it might also be necessary to consider how far blogs are acceptable as a form of whistleblowing and whether employees who use blogs in this way would be protected by relevant legislation such as the Public Interest Disclosure Act (PIDA) of 1998 in the UK. The PIDA extends protection to whistleblowers, but normally on the basis that they have already exhausted internal organisational methods of raising their concerns before going public. Here again, blogs might be of enormous value to senior managers within an organisation whose ability to monitor the reality of working life in relation to aims regarding (for example) employee morale or issues of corporate social responsibility is limited.

The last word should perhaps go to an anonymous blogger who reported to *Personnel Today* magazine:

Blogging, with its potential audience of millions, is an easy way to exercise my creativity and make my views heard. I'm dissatisfied with my job and unhappy with the way recent restructuring and management decisions have led to low morale, although I do not have an 'evil boss' like the Waterstone's employee. Most of my work-related moans on my blog are minor, everyday niggles about annoying colleagues or the dull nature of my employment, but I am not afraid to occasionally pull out the big guns over issues I feel passionately about.[77]

Your tasks

1 Using a basic model of expectancy theory such as that in Figure 7.8 or of goal setting theory such as Locke's (Figure 7.12), assess the various motivational forces which might be operating when employees blog about their employer.

2 It seems that for some people, blogging about work can be viewed as a form of frustration-induced behaviour. Critically review the process of blogging as a method of expressing job dissatisfaction. How do you think managers should respond to cases of work-related blogging by frustrated employees?

3 Organisational responses to employee blogs outlined in the case study might be categorised as either hostile (sack and sue), accepting (control and monitor) or creative (encourage and use). For each of these approaches, identify some basic guidelines for handling cases such as those of Simonetti, Gordon and Sanderson, bearing in mind the motivational effects that your proposals might have on both bloggers and other employees.

Notes and references

1 See, for example: Pate, L. E. 'Understanding Human Behaviour', *Management Decisions*, vol. 26, no. 1, 1998, pp. 58–64.

2 Krech, D., Crutchfield, R. S. and Ballachey, E. L. *Individual in Society*, McGraw-Hill (1962).

3 Mitchell, T. R. 'Motivation: New Directions for Theory, Research, and Practice', *Academy of Management Review*, vol. 7, no. 1, January 1982, pp. 80–8.

4 Kreitner, R., Kinicki, A. and Buelens, M. *Organizational Behaviour*, First European edition, McGraw-Hill (1999).

5 Farren, C. 'Mastery: The Critical Advantage' in Chowdhury, S. *Management 21C*, Financial Times Prentice Hall (2000), p. 95.

6 See, for example: Rudolph, P. A. and Kleiner, B. H. 'The Art of Motivating Employees', *Journal of Managerial Psychology*, vol. 4, no. 5, 1989, pp. i–iv.

7 Kets de Vries, M. 'Beyond Sloan: trust is at the core of corporate values' in Pickford, J. (ed.) *Financial Times Mastering Management 2.0*, Financial Times Prentice Hall (2001), pp. 267–70.

8 For a fuller discussion, see: Mullins, L. J. *Hospitality Management and Organisational Behaviour*, Fourth edition, Longman (2001).

9 Cook, P. and Jackson, N. 'Motivation Matters', Chartered Management Institute, October 2005, p. 11.

10 See, for example: Brown, J. A. C. *The Social Psychology of Industry*, Penguin (1954 and 1986).

11 Weaver, T. 'Theory M: Motivating with Money', *Cornell HRA Quarterly*, vol. 29, no. 3, November 1988, pp. 40–5.

12 Kusin, G. 'A 360-Degree Spin', *Hemisphere United*, October 2005, p. 76

13 Grayson, D. and Hodges, A. *Everybody's Business: Managing risks and opportunities in today's global society*, Financial Times (2001), p. 76.

14 Saunders, A. 'Keep Staff Sweet', *Management Today*, June 2003, p. 73.

15 Huck, S., Kubler, D. and Weibull, J. 'Social Norms and Economic Incentives in Firms', Economic & Social Research Council, 5 March 2003.

16 Cited in Crainer, S. 'Re-engineering the Carrot', *Management Today*, December 1995, p. 66.

17 Maslow, A. H. 'A Theory of Human Motivation', *Psychological Review*, 50, July 1943, pp. 370–96 and Maslow, A. H. *Motivation and Personality*, Third edition, Harper and Row (1987).

18 Steers, R. M. and Porter, L. W. *Motivation and Work Behaviour*, Fifth edition, McGraw-Hill (1991).

19 Saunders A, 'Keep Staff Sweet', *Management Today*, June 2003, p. 75.

20 Alderfer, C. P. *Existence, Relatedness and Growth*, Collier Macmillan (1972).

21 Herzberg, F., Mausner, B. and Snyderman, B. B. *The Motivation to Work*, Second edition, Chapman and Hall (1959).

22 Crainer, S and Dearlove, D. (eds) *Financial Times Handbook of Management*, Second edition, Financial Times Prentice Hall (2001), p. 361.

23 McClelland, D. C. *Human Motivation*, Cambridge University Press (1988).

24 For examples of pictures, see: Osland, J. S., Kolb, D. A. and Rubin, I. M. *Organizational Behaviour: An experimental approach*, Seventh edition, Prentice Hall (2001).

25 See, for example: Spangler, W. D. 'Validity of Questionnaire and TAT Measures of Need for Achievement Two Meta-Analyses', *Psychological Bulletin*, July 1992, pp. 140–54.

26 McClelland, D. C. 'Business Drive and National Achievement' *Harvard Business Review*, vol. 40, July–August 1962, pp. 99–112.

27 McClelland, D. C. and Burnham, D. H. 'Power is the Great Motivation', *Harvard Business Review*, vol. 54, March–April 1976, pp. 100–10.

28 Vroom, V.H. *Work and Motivation*, Wiley (1964) Also published by Krieger (1982).

29 Porter, L. W. and Lawler, E. E. *Managerial Attitudes and Performance*, Irwin (1968).

30 Lawler, E. E. *Motivation in Work Organizations*, Brooks/Cole (1973).

31 Lundin, S, Paul, H and Christensen, *Fish: A Remarkable Way to Boost Morale and Improve Results*, Hyperion Press (2001), p. 37.

32 Adams, J. S. 'Injustice in Social Exchange', in Berkowitz, L. (ed) *Advances in Experimental and Social Psychology*, Academic Press (1965). Abridged in Steers, R. M. and Porter, L. W. *Motivation and Work Behavior*, Second edition, McGraw-Hill (1979), pp. 107–24.

33 Locke, E. A. 'Towards a Theory of Task Motivation and Incentives', *Organizational Behavior and Human Performance*, vol. 3, 1968, pp. 157–89.

34 Locke, E. A. 'Personal Attitudes and Motivation', *Annual Review of Psychology*, vol. 26, 1975, pp. 457–80.

35 Gratton, L. *Living Strategy: Putting people at the heart of corporate purpose*, Financial Times Prentice Hall (2000), p. 193.

36 Hannagan, T. *Management*, Fourth edition, Financial Times Prentice Hall (2005), p. 363.

37 Reis, D. and Pena, L. 'Reengineering the Motivation to Work', *Management Decision*, vol. 39, no. 8, (2001), pp. 666–75.

38 'Motivating Your Staff in a Time of Change', *Management Checklist 068*, Chartered Management Institute, 2001.

39 Flores, G. N. and Utley, R. 'Management Concepts in Use – a 12-year perspective', *Engineering Management Journal*, vol. 12, no. 3, September 2000, pp. 11–17.

40 Tampoe, M. 'Knowledge Workers – The New Management Challenge', *Professional Manager*, November 1994, pp. 12–13.

41 Lucas, E. 'Turning on the Knowledge Workers', *Professional Manager*, May 1999, pp. 10–12.

42 'Managing Knowledge Workers: the HR dimension', Chartered Institute of Personnel and Development, January 2002.

43 Whitmore, Sir John 'Breaking Down the Barriers to Management Creativity', *Manager, The British Journal of Administrative Management*, May/June 2002, pp. 24–6.

44 See, for example: Cheng, T., Sculli, D. and Chan, F. S. 'Relationship Dominance – Rethinking management theories from the perspective of methodological relationalism', *Journal of Managerial Psychology*, vol. 16, no. 2, 2001, pp. 97–105.

45 Francesco, A. M. and Gold, B. A. *International Organizational Behavior*, Second edition, Pearson Prentice Hall (2005), p. 126.

46 Ibid., p. 129.

47 Adler, N. J. *International Aspects of Organizational Behaviour*, Third edition, South Western College Publishing (1997).

48 Chen, C. C. 'New Trends in Reward Allocation Preferences: A Sino-US Comparison', *The Academy of Management Journal*, vol. 38, no. 2, 1995, pp. 402–28.

49 Reeves, R. 'Reality Bites', *Management Today*, May 2003, p. 37.

50 Mumford, E. 'Job Satisfaction: A Method of Analysis', *Personal Review*, vol. 20, no. 3, 1991, pp. 11–19.

51 Handy, C. 'Boring Workplace, Boring Worker', *Management Today*, November 1997, p. 29.

52 'The Workplace Survey', Chartered Management Institute, March 2003.

53 Myerson, J. 'Workspace Heaven?', *Management Today*, June 2003, pp. 53–61.

54 Branson, R. *Losing My Virginity*, Virgin Publishing (1998), pp. 431, 444.

55 Marx, K. 'The Notion of Alienation', in Coser, L. A. and Rosenburg, B. *Sociological Theory*, Collier Macmillan (1969), pp. 505–10.

56 Blauner, R. *Alienation and Freedom*, University of Chicago Press (1964).

57 Roddick, A. *Business As Unusual*, Thorsons (2000), p. 70.

58 Hackman, J. R. and Oldham, G. R. *Work Redesign*, Addison-Wesley (1980).

59 Lee-Ross, D. 'The Reliability and Rationale of Hackman and Oldham's Job Diagnostic Survey and Job Characteristics Model among Seasonal Hotel Workers', *International Journal of Hospitality Management*, 17, 1998, pp. 391–406.

60 Roe, R. A., Zinovieva, I. L., Dienes, E. and Ten Horn, L. A., 'A Comparison of Work Motivation in Bulgaria, Hungary and the Netherlands: Test of a model', *Applied Psychology: An International Review*, vol. 49, 2000, pp. 658–87.

61 'Flexible Working: The Implementation Challenge', CIPD, October 2005, p.6.

62 See, for example: Cartwright, J. *Cultural Transformation*, Financial Times Prentice Hall (1999).

63 See, for example: Torrington, D., Hall, L. and Taylor, S. *Human Resource Management*, Sixth edition, Financial Times Prentice Hall (2005).

64 Personnel Today 2006 'Blogging: Waste of time or corporate tool?' published 21 March 2006 and available at www.personneltoday.com [accessed 26 July 2006].

65 Richard Brunstrom, Chief Constable of North Wales at http://www.north-wales.police.uk/nwp/public/en/blogs/; and two blogs by members of the London Ambulance service Random Acts of Reality (www.randomreality.blogware.com) and Nee Naw (www.neenaw.co.uk).

66 E.g. waiterrant.net, youareworthmore.org (Wal-Mart employees).

67 BBC News website 2004 'US Blogger fired by her airline' at http://news.bbc.co.uk dated 3 November 2004 [accessed 26 July 2006].

68 Queen of the Sky; Journal of a (fired) Flight Attendant http://queenofsky.journalspace.com.

69 Personnel Today 2005 'Don't blog your way into trouble' published 17 January 2005 available at www.personneltoday.com [accessed 26 July 2006].

70 The Wolamaloo Gazette, www.wolamaloo.org.uk.

71 Smith-Spark, L. 2006 'How to Blog and keep your job' BBC news website http://news.bbc.co.uk published 20 July 2006 [accessed 26 July 2006].

72 Watkins, D. 2006 'How big business barged in on the bloggers' *The Guardian* 20 March 2006.

73 Paton, N. 2006 'This is what I did at work today...' *Daily Mail*, 29 January 2006.

74 Watkins, D. 2006 'How big business barged in on the bloggers' *The Guardian*, 20 March 2006.

75 For the full guidelines and discussion about how they should be managed, visit the IBM website http://www-128.ibm.com/developerworks/blogs/dw_blog_comments.jspa?blog=351&entry=81328.

76 Spencer, S. 2005 'Illegal blogging', *People Management*, 27 January 2005.

77 Personnel Today 2005 'Don't blog your way into trouble' 17 January 2005 available at www.personneltoday.com [accessed 26 July 2006].

Philanthropy: the resurgance of personal social responsibility

Something rather spectacular happened on 26 June 2006: Warren Buffett, the world's second wealthiest man, announced that he intended to give 85 per cent of his fortune to the Bill and Melinda Gates Foundation (BMGF). There, it will join the billions that Bill Gates, the world's wealthiest man, has already pledged, to make an enormous sum of money to support good works around the world. A few months earlier, Anita Roddick, who founded and built up Body Shop International, announced her intention to give away half of her fortune. Philanthropy has long been a noble and admirable part of the capitalist tradition and now seems to be back in the news.

Why is this sort of philanthropy of interest to students of organisational behaviour? Several reasons can be suggested:

- Firstly, of course, the wealth that is given away is often the result of setting up and running an organisation that successfully fulfils its purpose over a long period: the profits that flow to the owner result from customers choosing and paying for its output.
- Also, the generosity of wealthy individuals makes an interesting contrast with the more familiar concept of 'corporate social responsibility', which sometimes involves donations of company, rather than personal, money.
- The charitable foundations, together with their external relationships, are of interest in their own right.

The word philanthropy is derived from the Greek and is defined as 'love of humankind; the disposition or effort to promote the happiness of and well-being of one's fellow-people'.[1] The practice of philanthropy was well established before that of capitalism, of course, but the early stages of the growth of the American economy saw a significant surge in the social custom of philanthropy. Although it may have been no part of their aim, the names of some of America's most significant philanthropists are as well-known for their giving as for the business careers that made the money. Two celebrated examples from the same era provide a view of the way a philanthropic life can be lived.

From Carnegie and Rockefeller to Bill and Melinda Gates
Andrew Carnegie (1835–1919) was born in Dunfermline, Scotland. He was the son of a weaver and the family emigrated to the United States in 1848. Like many at that time, Carnegie started work at the age of 13 doing a number of jobs until 1865, when he started his own business. This was to become the foundation of the steel industry in Pittsburgh and the origin of Carnegie's fortune. At the turn of the new century, Carnegie sold the business for $480 million and spent the rest of his life devoted to his philanthropic interests. These were diverse, but centred around the theme of the provision of public libraries and education.[2] Over his life, Carnegie gave away more than $350 million (multiply by about 20 for today's values). Some of the quotes attributed to him show the combination of hard-nosed business acumen and the strong sense of social duty that characterises this type of philanthropist:[3]

And while the law of competition may be sometimes hard for the individual, it is best for the race, because it ensures the survival of the fittest in every department.

Surplus wealth is a sacred trust which its possessor is bound to administer in his lifetime for the good of the community.

I would as soon leave my son a curse as the almighty dollar.

As will be seen, similar sentiments and values continue to motivate today's philanthropists.

John D. Rockefeller (1839–1937) was born in the United States to a farming family. In his business career, he founded and developed the Standard Oil Company which became the leading force in the fast-growing oil industry. At the age of 57, Rockefeller decided that he should step aside from the day-to-day leadership of Standard Oil and devote himself to philanthropy. This had been important to him from his early life, but also because of his religious convictions and his approach to finance:

I believe it is every man's religious duty to get all he can honestly and to give all he can.

Like Carnegie, his philanthropic interests centred on education, with substantial donations to found and develop universities and research institutes, as well as the establishment of trusts and foundations for the improvement of education at all levels. Over his life, he gave away some $540 million.[4] Again, some of the quotes attributed to the man show a mixture of hard-headedness and generosity that is far from sentimental:[5]

Charity is injurious unless it helps the recipient to become independent of it.

Bill Gates and his wife set up the Bill and Melinda Gates Foundation with part of the personal fortune he had earned from the success of Microsoft.

I believe that every right implies a responsibility; every opportunity, an obligation; every possession, a duty.

The emerging philanthropists of the 21st century have often made their money through businesses that were not even heard of in the lifetimes of Carnegie and Rockefeller. Bill Gates, for example, is one of the founders of the enormously successful Microsoft Corporation, whose information products are about as far from steel and oil as can be imagined. This case is mainly concerned with the Bill and Melinda Gates Foundation which was established in 1994 with an initial gift of about $94 million from the two founders.[6] It grew rapidly from 1999 to a value of $29.2bn by 2005, by which time a cumulative total of $10.2 billion had been awarded. In 2006, it had 270 employees in three offices (Seattle, Washington and Delhi).

The organisation is built around its three main priorities, which are: global development, global health, and US programmes. In a letter published on the Foundation's website, Bill and Melinda Gates explain their aims in respect of global health, pointing out that health is fundamental to economic development:[7]

When health takes hold, life improves by all measures. Conversely, poor health aggravates poverty, poverty deepens disease, and nations trapped in this spiral will not escape without the world's help. In Africa, the cost of malaria in terms of treatment and lost productivity is estimated to be $12 billion a year. The continent's gross domestic product could be $100 billion higher today if malaria had been eliminated in the 1960s. And if HIV infection rates continue at their present levels, the world will likely see 45 million new infections by 2010 and lose nearly 70 million

people by 2020. That's 70 million of the most productive members of society – health workers, educators, and parents.

Therefore, the foundation's Global Health program works to ensure that lifesaving advances in health are created and shared with those who need them most. Our primary focus areas are HIV/AIDS, TB, malaria, child survival and childhood immunization, and maternal and reproductive health.

*To begin, we invest heavily in research to help **discover** new and better products, particularly vaccines. The foundation also supports work to **develop** products that can be manufactured and distributed. Then, once a product is developed, we work to make sure that there are systems in place to **adopt** and **sustain** these new drugs as they become available. The foundation is a major supporter of the Global Alliance for Vaccines and Immunization (GAVI). This alliance has provided basic immunizations to over 8 million children who would not otherwise have been immunized. As a result, GAVI has already saved an estimated 500,000 children's lives.*

In the world of business, as opposed to philanthropic foundations, there has been growing interest in recent years in the subject of corporate governance: what the business is aiming to do and how it can be sure that its actions are consistent with those aims. It has been common for wealthy individuals to adopt a corporate format in making good works happen, often by setting up and then directing a dedicated foundation to look after both the strategic and operational aspects of the task. This seems to acknowledge the benefits of the corporate approach in terms of efficiency and the ability to recruit and apply specialist skills, while still retaining control by the founder or the founding family. It is also easy to appreciate how focused and effective such an organisation can be in pursuing the goals of the founder, and to acknowledge the possibility that an effective philanthropic foundation may be at least as effective as, say, a government or international agency.

As will already be clear, some of the world's philanthropic foundations have multinational corporation-sized (even government-sized) budgets, meaning that the issue of governance is rightly of some concern to the society within which these organisations operate. One does not need to be a fan of James Bond movies to appreciate that very rich individuals using their wealth to pursue their private aims is not in itself guaranteed to be in the general interest.

In fact, foundations often go to some lengths to communicate their values and aims publicly. BMGF has adopted two key values:

- All lives – no matter where they are being led – have equal value.
- To whom much has been given, much is expected.

These values are the basis for 15 principles that guide BMGF in its operations.[8] As can be seen, these principles relate to the foundation in its external dealings (with other agencies, for example, with the public in general or with its 'grantees', i.e. recipients of aid), but also in its internal relationships (ethical behaviour, respect and professional standards). BMGF is also committed in these principles to communicating clearly what it is aiming to do and what it has achieved.

- This is a family foundation driven by the interests and passions of the Gates family.
- Philanthropy plays an important but limited role.
- Science and technology have great potential to improve lives around the world.
- We are funders and shapers – we rely on others to act and implement.
- Our focus is clear – and limited – and prioritizes some of the most neglected issues.
- We identify a specific point of intervention and apply our efforts against a theory of change.
- We take risks, make big bets, and move with urgency. We are in it for the long haul.
- We advocate – vigorously but responsibly – in our areas of focus.
- We must be humble and mindful in our actions and words. We seek and heed the counsel of outside voices.
- We treat our grantees as valued partners, and we treat the ultimate beneficiaries of our work with respect.
- Delivering results with the resources we have been given is of the utmost importance – and we seek and share information about those results.
- We demand ethical behavior of ourselves.
- We treat each other as valued colleagues.
- Meeting our mission – to increase opportunity and equity for those most in need – requires great stewardship of the money we have available.
- We leave room for growth and change.

Something of the founder's sense of responsibility was evident in the comments that Bill Gates made at the announcement of Warren Buffett's donation to the Foundation. Gates joked that there was something more scary about the possibility of making a mistake with Buffett's money than with his own.[9] These are not sentiments that politicians are often heard to express, making an interesting contrast with the mainstream government-funded approach to social projects that has come to dominate the past 50 years.

Warren Buffett and Anita Roddick

Warren Buffett's fortune was made through the Berkshire Hathaway organisation, which for many years has been very successful in providing investment management services for its clients. Buffett himself is famously moderate in his lifestyle, with a liking for a diet of

Source: Empics/AP Photo/Seth Wenig

The world's most generous man? In 2006 Warren Buffet, the world's second wealthiest man, promised to give 85 per cent of his fortune to support good works around the world.

burgers and Cherry Coke. His extraordinary wealth was recently augmented by his firm decision not to get involved in the late-1990s dotcom boom and subsequent bust: his policy has always been to concentrate on business fundamentals and to invest for the long term. He also has a long-standing reputation for pithy quotes and one attributed remark seemed to sum up the chaos caused by the collapse of rapid stock market growth and the series of corporate scandals that followed:

It's only when the tide goes out that you can see who's been swimming without their trunks on.

From remarks made by Buffett at the announcement of his association with the Gates Foundation, it seems clear that he had been thinking about an involvement in philanthropy for some time.[10] Some of his motivation is bound up with the American tradition of philanthropy by wealthy individuals, including the notion that there is something problematic ('almost un-American' as he put it[11]) about the idea that huge wealth should result from accidents of birth. Children should be left wealthy enough to do anything, but not enough to do nothing. He had also become very impressed by the approach taken by BMGF and by Bill and Melinda themselves: the announcement coincided with that of the succession plans for Gates' leadership of Microsoft, which will allow Gates to devote more time to the Foundation. Buffett has become a trustee of the Foundation and jokingly promised at the launch not to assess Gates' efforts more than once a day. At the same meeting, both

men acknowledged the inspirational value that the news of the donation could have: one questioner suggested that the success of organisations like BMGF could do much to improve public confidence in charitable donation in general and perhaps increase the willingness of a far wider spectrum of people to give.

The decision by the UK entrepreneur Anita Roddick to join the ranks of business-based philanthropists adds some interesting features to the discussion. Roddick has been something of a business celebrity for much of her career, having founded and built up the very successful Body Shop International, a business whose market appeal was always strongly centred on the values of its founder. Its campaigns against animal testing of cosmetics and in favour of fair trade, for example, became prominent during the 1990s. Explaining that she did not want to die rich, Roddick announced at the end of 2005 that she intended to give away half her £100 million fortune, much of which resulted from the sale of her business to L'Oréal. This extraordinarily generous act does not register very far up the world league table of philanthropy, but nonetheless represents a significant step for the UK.

Anita Roddick has often been sharply critical of some aspects of business life in the UK, especially where attitudes have assessed her as being selfish and short-termist. But, in her view, the rich have to look after the poor, and: 'I don't think in our society we have any understanding of that.'

A BBC article commented at the time that personal philanthropy was less prominent in the UK than in America, possibly because people in the UK regard it as a government responsibility to look after the poor, with projects financed from general taxation and with additional contributions from companies under the heading of 'corporate social responsibility'.[12] This is not to suggest that government programmes and corporate donations are by any means unimportant in the United States, but rather to emphasise how unusual personal philanthropy has been in the UK. The article suggested that personal philanthropy might be assuming greater prominence in the UK because of a growing belief that the state is no longer providing an adequate safety net. Whatever the truth of this suggestion, the prospect of more significant philanthropic foundations in the UK will raise some interesting questions of how public and private agencies can learn to work together in identifying priorities and designing programmes of action to address social problems.

Corporate versus personal philanthropy

Many large businesses in the UK have made significant donations to charity from corporate funds, which may be partly motivated by a desire for approval from some stakeholder groups. However, alongside the well-known company names have been some large donations from less prominent companies. One report in 2006, for example, suggested that TCI, a leading hedge fund business, had become one of the most generous UK donors to charity, despite the very limited public awareness of the hedge fund sector among the UK public.[13] TCI seems to have been designed by its founder to generate funds for charity in this way, but other corporate donations are made from company profits. As such, corporate philanthropy – and corporate social responsibility in general – has come in for criticism from some quarters, on the basis that it amounts to acts of generosity using other peoples' money (specifically, that of the shareholders, who own the company). The economist Milton Friedman has been forcefully suggesting for some decades that business should get on with the business of business: making money for its owners through successfully marketing products and services within the law. From this point of view, donations to charity by individuals making choices about their own funds are more desirable than acts of corporate generosity using other peoples' funds. In reality, public opinion seems to be sympathetic towards the idea of corporate donations to charity, whatever scepticism may sometimes be expressed about motives. However, from any reasonable point of view, there remains an important difference between giving personally and approving corporate gifts: the difference perhaps, between signing your own, rather than a company, cheque.

At the BMGF conference mentioned above, Bill Gates alluded to the celebrated work of Adam Smith, the Scottish economist who first explained the general benefits of free markets in identifying and providing for needs effectively and efficiently. From these ideas have

Anita Roddick, founder of the Body Shop, who built a business based on caring values, is giving half of her wealth away.

Source: Empics/Jean/allactiondigital.com

8

THE NATURE OF
WORK GROUPS AND TEAMS

Groups and teams are a major feature of organisational life. The work organisation and its sub-units are made up of groups of people. Most activities of the organisation require at least some degree of co-ordination through the operation of groups and teamwork. An understanding of the nature of groups is vital if the manager is to influence the behaviour of people in the work situation. The manager must be aware of the impact of groups and teams and their effects on organisational performance.

Learning outcomes

After completing this chapter you should be able to:

- explain the meaning and importance of work groups and teams;
- distinguish between groups and teams, and between formal and informal groups;
- explain the main reasons for the formation of groups and teams;
- examine factors which influence group cohesiveness and performance;
- review the characteristics of an effective work group;
- analyse the nature of role relationships and role conflict;
- evaluate the importance of groups and teams for effective organisational performance.

> To build good teams you need a wide pool of staff with different talents to draw upon ... Good managers should delight in the diversity and excellence of their staff and know that one of their main jobs is to manage the problems that come with any diverse group of talented people. In any group of talented people you will naturally get interpersonal tensions. It is important that you show you respect all the different skills and personalities in your team.

Nic Peeling – frontline manager with QinetiQ
Brilliant Manager: What the Best Managers Know, Do and Say, Pearson Prentice Hall (2005), pp. 129–30

Critical reflection

'Groups are an essential part of the structure of an organisation but "teamworking" is no more than a fashionable term used by management to give workers an exaggerated feeling of importance and empowerment. In reality, however, an emphasis on teamworking is only likely to lead to more work, less freedom and even closer control from other team members.' How far do you agree with this comment? What is your experience of teamworking?

THE MEANING AND IMPORTANCE OF GROUPS AND TEAMS

Groups are an essential feature of any organisation. Individuals seldom work in isolation from others. Work is a group-based activity and if the organisation is to function effectively it requires collaboration and co-operation among its members Although there is no single accepted definition, most people will readily understand what constitutes a group. The essential feature is that its members regard themselves as belonging to the group. A popular definition defines the group in psychological terms as:

any number of people who (1) interact with one another; (2) are psychologically aware of one another; and (3) perceive themselves to be a group.[1]

Another useful way of defining a work group is a collection of people who share most, if not all, of the following characteristics:

- a definable membership
- group consciousness
- a sense of shared purpose
- interdependence
- interaction
- ability to act in a unitary manner.[2]

Essential features of work organisations

Groups are a characteristic of all social situations and almost everyone in an organisation will be a member of one or more groups. The working of groups and the influence they exert over their membership is an essential feature of human behaviour and of organisational performance. Members of a group must co-operate in order for work to be carried out, and managers themselves will work within these groups. People in groups influence each other in many ways and groups may develop their own hierarchies and leaders. Group pressures can have a major influence over the behaviour of individual members and their work performance.

DIFFERENCES BETWEEN GROUPS AND TEAMS

In common usage and literature, including to some extent in this book, there is a tendency for the terms 'groups' and 'teams' to be used interchangeably. It is not easy to distinguish clearly between a group and a team. *Guzzo and Dickson*, for example, go so far as to suggest that it is probably pointless and in any case more or less impossible to distinguish groups from teams.[3]

According to *Holpp*, while many people are still paying homage to teams, teamwork, empowerment and self-management, others have become disillusioned. Holpp poses the question: What are teams? 'It's a simple enough question, but one that's seldom asked. We all think we know intuitively what teams are. Guess again. Here are some questions to help define team configurations.'

● Are teams going to be natural work groups, or project-and-task oriented?
● Will they be self-managed or directed?
● How many people will be on the teams; who's in charge?
● How will the teams fit into the organisation's structure if it shows only boxes and not circles or other new organisational forms?

Holpp also poses the question: Why do you want teams? If teams are just a convenient way to group under one manager a lot of people who used to work for several downsized supervisors, don't bother. But if teams can truly take ownership of work areas and provide the kind of up-close knowledge that's unavailable elsewhere, then full speed ahead.[4]

Teamwork a fashionable term

The use of the word 'teams' has become increasingly fashionable in recent years. *Crainer* refers to the use of 'teamworking' as a side effect of increasing concentration on working across functional divides and fits neatly with the trend towards empowerment. However, despite the extensive literature about teams and teamworking, the basic dynamics of teamworking often remain clouded and uncertain.

> *Teams occur when a number of people have a common goal and recognise that their personal success is dependent on the success of others. They are all interdependent. In practice, this means that in most teams people will contribute individual skills many of which will be different. It also means that the full tensions and counter-balance of human behaviour will need to be demonstrated in the team.*[5]

Cane suggests that organisations are sometimes unsure whether they have teams or simply groups of people working together.

> *It is certainly true to say that any group of people who do not know they are a team cannot be one. To become a team, a group of individuals needs to have a strong common purpose and to work towards that purpose rather than individually. They need also to believe that they will achieve more by co-operation than working individually.*[6]

Whereas all teams are, by definition, groups, it does not necessarily follow that all groups are teams.

Belbin points out that to the extent that teamwork was becoming a fashionable term, it began to replace the more usual reference to groups and every activity was now being described as 'teamwork'. He questions whether it matters whether one is talking about groups or teams and maintains that the confusion in vocabulary should be addressed if the principles of good teamwork are to be retained. Belbin suggests there are several factors that characterise the difference between groups and teams (*see* Figure 8.1). The best differentiator is size: groups can comprise any number of people but teams are smaller with a membership between (ideally) four and six. The quintessential feature of a small, well-balanced team is that leadership is shared or rotates whereas large groups typically throw up solo leaders.[7]

While acknowledging the work of Belbin it appears that the term 'group' is often used in a more general sense and 'team' in a more specific context. We continue to refer to 'group' or 'team' according to the particular focus of attention and the vocabulary of the quoted authors.

Figure 8.1	Differences between a team and a group

	Team	Group
Size	Limited	Medium or Large
Selection	Crucial	Immaterial
Leadership	Shared or rotating	Solo
Perception	Mutual knowledge understanding	Focus on leader
Style	Role spread co-ordination	Convergence conformism
Spirit	Dynamic interaction	Togetherness persecution of opponents

Source: Belbin, R. M., *Beyond the Team*, Butterworth-Heinemann, (2000). Copyright © 2000, reproduced with permission from Elsevier Ltd.

Another possible distinction is based on the development and maturity of the 'group'. For example, in terms of Tuckman's model (discussed on p. 310), not until a group proceeds beyond the stages of forming, norming and storming and successfully reaches the performing stage does it become a team.

GROUP VALUES AND NORMS

The classical approach to organisation and management tended to ignore the importance of groups and the social factors at work. The ideas of people such as F. W. Taylor popularised the concept of the 'rabble hypothesis' and the assumption that people carried out their work, and could be motivated, as solitary individuals unaffected by others. The human relations approach, however (discussed in Chapter 2), gave recognition to the work organisation as a social organisation and to the importance of the group, and group values and norms, in influencing behaviour at work.

One experiment involved the observation of a group of 14 men working in the bank wiring room. The men formed their own sub-groups or cliques, with natural leaders emerging with the consent of the members. Despite a financial incentive scheme where workers could receive more money the more work they did, the group decided on 6,000 units a day as a fair level of output. This was well below the level they were capable of producing. Group pressures on individual workers were stronger than financial incentives offered by management.

Informal social relations

The group developed its own pattern of informal social relations and codes and practices ('norms') of what constituted proper group behaviour.

- **Not to be a 'rate buster'** – not to produce at too high a rate of output compared with other members or to exceed the production restriction of the group.

Figure 8.2 Concept map of group norms

GROUP NORMS

- **DEFINITIONS OF NORMS**
- **EVOLUTION OF NORMS**
- **CHANGING NORMS**
- **THE VALUE OF NORMS**

Norms are an observable aspect of any group, in or out of the work setting. New group members are alert to signals of acceptance or rejection as they seek to clarify expectations. They find them in formal and informal contacts.

DEFINITION

A group norm is an assumption or expectation held by group members concerning what kind of behaviour is
- right or wrong
- good or bad
- allowed or not allowed
- appropriate or not appropriate.

EVOLUTION OF NORMS

They may evolve through ...
- modelling behaviour on another 'prestigious' group
- accidental discovery of advantageous behaviour
- witnessing repeated acts
- unintended consequences of formal decisions.

Group norms may evolve over a long period of time. This can lead to them becoming
- rigid
- anachronistic
- irrelevant for current situations.

TYPICAL NORM STATEMENTS
- Around here we always ...
- It doesn't do to ...
- We never ...
- When that happens we ...

IDENTIFYING NORMS

By observation, interview or question you discover
- behaviour which gets reinforced or rewarded
- behaviour which gets discouraged or penalised

CHANGING NORMS

A group is often reluctant to change its norms, so for change to take place ...
- Get group consensus to change
- Generate support for change
- Address as many factors as possible which will help the change.

Management's wishes on their own are sometimes not sufficiently strong to have enough influence to change norms.

Individual changes are rarely, if ever, effective in changing the norms of a group.

THE VALUE OF NORMS
- Counteracts anonymity
- Supports small-group identity
- Are legitimate to group members
- May not support organisation's formal goals
- Provides order
- Provides standards
- Influences behaviour
- Embodies the informal 'shadow' organisation

Not necessarily pro- or anti-management

Predictability desirable, avoids chaos

Enables the group to evaluate and control group behaviour

Often implicit

Language, dress, openness/secrecy, competitiveness, productivity

Expresses unwritten sometimes unspoken rules → May encourage 'we–they' attitudes

PROCESS FOR IMPLEMENTING NORM CHANGES (LEWIN'S CHANGE MODEL)

STAGE 1 UNFREEZING
STAGE 2 CHANGING
STAGE 3 REFREEZING

UNFREEZING

Develop an awareness of
- the nature of the change needed
- the methods planned to achieve the change
- the needs of those affected
- the ways that progress will be planned and monitored.

CHANGING
- Defining problems
- Identifying solutions
- Implementing solution

REFREEZING
- Stabilising the situation
- Building and rebuilding relationships
- Consolidating the systems

Source: Training Learning Consultancy Ltd, Bristol, England. Reproduced with permission.

- **Not to be a 'chiseller'** – not to shirk production or to produce at too low a rate of output compared with other members of the group.
- **Not to be a 'squealer'** – not to say anything to the supervisor or management which might be harmful to other members of the group.
- **Not to be 'officious'** – people with authority over members of the group, for example inspectors, should not take advantage of their seniority or maintain a social distance from the group.

The group had their own system of sanctions including sarcasm, damaging completed work, hiding tools, playing tricks on the inspectors and ostracising those members who did not conform with the **group norms**. Threats of physical violence were also made and the group developed a system of punishing offenders by 'binging' that involved striking someone a fairly hard blow on the upper part of the arm. This process of binging also became a recognised method of controlling conflict within the group.

Team performance According to *Riches*, one way to improve team performance is to establish agreed norms or rules for how the team is to operate and rigorously stick to them. Norms could address the obligations of individual members to the team, how it will assess its performance, how it will work together, what motivation systems will be used, how it will relate to customers, and the mechanisms to facilitate an honest exchange about the team norms and behaviour.[8]

A 2003 study by the *Economic & Social Research Council* draws attention to the importance of social norms among employees and questions whether employees are guided not only by monetary incentives but also by peer pressure towards social efficiency for the workers as a group. 'Intuitively, social norms among workers must be important if they work in teams where bonuses are dependent on group rather than individual effort.'[9] (You may see some similarity here with the bank wiring room experiment, discussed above.)

A concept map of group norms is set out in Figure 8.2.

FORMAL AND INFORMAL GROUPS

Groups are deliberately planned and created by management as part of the formal organisation structure. However, groups will also arise from social processes and the informal organisation that was discussed in Chapter 3. The informal organisation arises from the interaction of people working within the organisation and the development of groups with their own relationships and norms of behaviour, irrespective of those defined within the formal structure. This leads to a major distinction between formal and informal groups.

Formal groups Groups are formed as a consequence of the pattern of organisation structure and arrangements for the division of work, for example the grouping together of common activities into sections. Groups may result from the nature of technology employed and the way in which work is carried out, for example the bringing together of a number of people to carry out a sequence of operations on an assembly line. Groups may also develop when a number of people of the same level or status within the organisation see themselves as a group, for example departmental heads of an industrial organisation or chief officers of a local authority. **Formal groups** are created to achieve specific organisational objectives and are concerned with the **co-ordination of work activities**. People are brought together on the basis of defined roles within the structure of the organisation. The nature of the tasks to be undertaken is a predominant feature of the formal group. Goals are identified by management, and certain rules, relationships and norms of behaviour established.

Formal groups tend to be relatively permanent, although there may be changes in actual membership. However, temporary formal groups may also be created by management, for example the use of project teams in a matrix organisation. Formal work groups can be

differentiated in a number of ways, for example on the basis of membership, the task to be performed, the nature of technology, or position within the organisation structure.

Virtuoso teams *Boynton and Fischer* draw attention to **'virtuoso teams'** that are formed specifically for big change in organisations. They are comprised of individual superstars or virtuosos with a single clear, ambitious mandate and not to remain together over multiple initiatives or projects. Virtuoso teams require a special kind of leadership and to be managed in a manner that unleashes the maximum contribution from each individual superstar. Although most organisations rarely form such teams, they are required for radical change opportunities that represent a significant departure from prior practice and/or how an organisation conducts its business. Examples of big changes that represented a virtuoso team are the Manhattan Project, Thomas Edison's inventory factory and Roald Amundsen's polar expedition.[10]

Informal groups

The formal structure of the organisation, and system of role relationships, rules and procedures, will always be augmented by interpretation and development at the informal level. **Informal groups** are based more on personal relationships and agreement of group members than on defined role relationships. They serve to satisfy psychological and social needs not related necessarily to the tasks to be undertaken. Groups may devise ways of attempting to satisfy members' affiliation and other social motivations lacking in the work situation. Membership of informal groups can cut across the formal structure. They may comprise individuals from different parts of the organisation and/or from different levels of the organisation, both vertically and diagonally, as well as from the same horizontal level. An informal group could also be the same as the formal group, or it might comprise a part only of the formal group (*see* Figure 8.3).

Members of an informal group may appoint their own leader who exercises authority by the consent of the members themselves. The informal leader may be chosen as the person who reflects the attitudes and values of the members, helps to resolve conflict, leads the group in satisfying its goals, or liaises with management or other people outside the group. The informal leader may often change according to the particular situation facing the group.

Figure 8.3	Examples of informal groups within the formal structure of an organisation

Although not usually the case, it is possible for the informal leader to be the same person as the formal leader appointed officially by management.

Major functions of informal groups

Lysons suggests four main reasons for informal groups.

- **The perpetuation of the informal group 'culture'.** Culture in this context means a set of values, norms and beliefs which form a guide to group acceptance and group behaviour. Unless you broadly subscribe to the group culture, you will not belong and will be an 'outsider' or 'isolate'.
- **The maintenance of a communication system.** Groups want all the information that affects their welfare, either negatively or positively. If groups are not apprised of policies and motives behind actions, they will seek to tap into formal communication channels and spread information among group members.
- **The implementation of social control.** Conformity to group culture is enforced by such techniques as ridicule, ostracism and violence. This is illustrated, for example, by the enforcement of group norms in the bank wiring room discussed above.
- **The provision of interest and fun in work life.** Many jobs are monotonous and fail to hold workers' attention. Work may also offer few prospects. Workers may try to compensate by interpersonal relations provided by the group and in such activities as time wasting by talking, gambling, practical joking and drinking. [11]

> *We humans are a gregarious lot. We like to gather together and establish our own social networks, which are often the real key to creativity and innovation in organisations ... But many managers are unaware that seemingly pointless social networking does in fact play a crucial part in the way people interact with each other and get work done.*
>
> Sue Law, 'Beyond the Water Cooler'[12]

An example of informal groups

A lack of direction and clear information flow within the formal structure can give rise to uncertainty and suspicion. In the absence of specific knowledge, the grapevine takes on an important role, rumours start and the informal part of the organisation is highlighted, often with negative results. A typical example concerned an industrial organisation in a highly competitive market and experiencing a drop in sales. Two top managers had suddenly lost their jobs without any apparent explanation and there were board meetings seemingly every other day. Although there was no specific information or statements from top management, the general feeling among the staff was that whatever was about to happen was most unlikely to be good news.

At lunchtime three junior members of staff, one female and two male, each from different departments, were having a chat. With a half smile the female member said to the others that she could well be seeing a lot more of both or at least one of them before long. She said that she had heard, unofficially, from her manager that the department was about to be awarded a very profitable order. She surmised that other departments, which she had also heard had lost their parts of the same contracts and not had many orders recently, would have to integrate into the successful department with the possible loss of certain jobs. The other two members both believed this and talked about it within their own departments as if it were a fact. The result? Even more uncertainty throughout the organisation, increased gloom and distraction from the task. In fact, no such integration did take place, only a minor restructuring of the organisation with no direct loss of jobs other than through voluntary early retirement. However, it proved very difficult for top management to effectively quash the rumour and restore trust and morale.

Refresh your understanding
Activity 8A
www.pearsoned.co.uk/
mullins

Critical reflection ?????

Given the obvious importance of social networks for both the morale and job satisfaction of staff and their levels of work performance, do you think that the main focus in the study of organisational behaviour should be on the operations and effective management of the informal organisation?

REASONS FOR FORMATION OF GROUPS OR TEAMS

Individuals will form into groups or teams, both formal and informal, for a number of reasons.

- **Certain tasks can be performed only through the combined efforts of a number of individuals working together.** The variety of experience and expertise among members provides a synergetic effect that can be applied to the increasingly complex problems of modern organisations.
- **Collusion between members** in order to modify formal working arrangements more to their liking – for example, by sharing or rotating unpopular tasks. Membership therefore provides the individual with opportunities for initiative and creativity.
- **Companionship and a source of mutual understanding and support from colleagues.** This can help in solving work problems and also to militate against stressful or demanding working conditions.
- **Membership provides the individual with a sense of belonging.** It provides a feeling of identity and the chance to acquire role recognition and status within the group or team.
- **Guidelines on generally acceptable behaviour.** It helps to clarify ambiguous situations such as the extent to which official rules and regulations are expected to be adhered to in practice, the rules of the game and what is seen as the correct actual behaviour. The informal organisation may put pressure on members to resist demands from management on such matters as higher output or changes in working methods. Allegiance to the group or team can serve as a means of control over individual behaviour and individuals who contravene the norms are disciplined – for example, the process of 'binging' in the bank wiring room, mentioned above.
- **Protection for its membership.** Group or team members collaborate to protect their interests from outside pressures or threats.

Expectations of group membership Individuals have varying expectations of the benefits from group membership, relating to both work performance and social processes. However, working in groups may mean that members spend too much time talking among themselves rather than doing. Groups may also compete against each other in a non-productive manner. It is a question of balance. It is important, therefore, that the manager understands the reasons for the formation of groups and is able to recognise likely advantageous or adverse consequences for the organisation.

GROUP COHESIVENESS AND PERFORMANCE

Social interaction is a natural feature of human behaviour but ensuring harmonious working relationships and effective teamwork is not an easy task. The manager's main concern is that members of a work group co-operate in order to achieve the results expected of them. Co-operation among members is likely to be greater in a united, cohesive group. Membership of a cohesive group can be a rewarding experience for the individual, can contribute to the promotion of morale and aid the release of creativity and energy. Members of

a high-morale group are more likely to think of themselves as a group and work together effectively. Strong and cohesive work groups can, therefore, have beneficial effects for the organisation. There are many factors which affect **group cohesiveness** and performance that can be summarised under four broad headings, as shown in Figure 8.4.

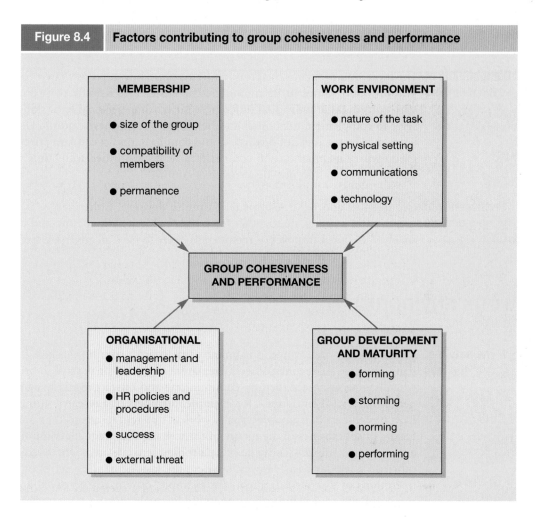

Figure 8.4 Factors contributing to group cohesiveness and performance

MEMBERSHIP
- size of the group
- compatibility of members
- permanence

WORK ENVIRONMENT
- nature of the task
- physical setting
- communications
- technology

GROUP COHESIVENESS AND PERFORMANCE

ORGANISATIONAL
- management and leadership
- HR policies and procedures
- success
- external threat

GROUP DEVELOPMENT AND MATURITY
- forming
- storming
- norming
- performing

MEMBERSHIP

Size of the group As a group increases in size, problems arise with communications and co-ordination. Large groups are more difficult to handle and require a higher level of supervision. Absenteeism also tends to be higher in larger groups. When a group becomes too large it may split into smaller units and friction may develop between the sub-groups.

It is difficult to put a precise figure on the ideal size of a work group and there are many conflicting studies and reports. Much will depend upon other variables, but it seems to be generally accepted that cohesiveness becomes more difficult to achieve when a group exceeds 10–12 members.[13] Beyond this size the group tends to split into sub-groups. A figure of between five and seven is often quoted as an apparent optimum size for full participation within the group. Many readers will be familiar with the classic 1957 movie *Twelve Angry Men* in which one juror persuades the other 11 to change their minds over a murder verdict. This drew attention to a range of intra-group conflicts and the difficulty in groups of more than ten people attempting to reach consensus.

Cane asks the question: how many people should be in a team?

The answers from different organisations as to what is the perfect number vary from between four and fifteen depending on a whole range of variables. Fifteen is about the maximum number of people anyone can communicate with without having to raise their voice significantly and any less than four has a restriction in the amount of creativity and variety that can be produced. It is interesting to note that these figures range between the maximum and minimum numbers of sports teams – perhaps less of a coincidence than it seems.[14]

Compatibility of the members The more homogeneous the group in terms of such features as shared backgrounds, intests, attitudes and values of its members, the easier it is usually to promote cohesiveness. Variations in other individual differences, such as the personality or skills of members, may serve to complement each other and help make for a cohesive group. However, such differences may be the cause of disruption and conflict. Conflict can also arise in a homogeneous group where members are in competition with each other. Individual incentive payment schemes, for example, may be a source of conflict.

Permanence of group members Group spirit and relationships take time to develop. Cohesiveness is more likely when members of a group are together for a reasonable length of time and changes occur only slowly. A frequent turnover of members is likely to have an adverse effect on morale and on the cohesiveness of the group.

WORK ENVIRONMENT

The nature of the task Where workers are involved in similar work, share a common task or face the same problems, this may assist cohesiveness. The nature of the task may serve to bring people together when it is necessary for them to communicate and interact regularly with each other in the performance of their duties – for example, members of a research and development team. Even if members of a group normally work at different locations they may still experience a feeling of cohesiveness if the nature of the task requires frequent communication and interaction – for example, security guards patrolling separate areas who need to check with each other on a regular basis. However, where the task demands a series of relatively separate operations or discrete activities – for example, on a machine-paced assembly line – it is more difficult to develop cohesiveness. Individuals may have interactions with colleagues on either side of them but little opportunity to develop a common group feeling.

Physical setting Where members of a group work in the same location or in close physical proximity to each other this will generally help cohesiveness. However, this is not always the case. For example, in large open-plan offices staff often tend to segregate themselves from colleagues and create barriers through the strategic siting of such items as filing cabinets, bookcases or indoor plants. The size of the office and the number of staff in it are, of course, important considerations in this case. Isolation from other groups of workers will also tend to build cohesiveness. This often applies to a smaller number of workers on a night shift.

Communications The more easily members can communicate freely with each other, the greater the likelihood of group cohesiveness. Communications are affected by the work environment, by the nature of the task and by technology. For example, difficulties in communication can arise with production systems where workers are stationed continuously at a particular point with limited freedom of movement. Even when opportunities exist for interaction with colleagues, physical conditions may limit effective communication. For example, the technological layout and high level of noise with some assembly line work can limit contact

between workers. Restrictions on opportunities for social interaction can hamper internal group unity.

Technology We can see that the nature of technology and the manner in which work is carried out have an important effect on cohesiveness and relate closely to the nature of the task, physical setting and communications. Where the nature of the work process involves a craft or skill-based 'technology' there is a higher likelihood of group cohesiveness. However, with machine-paced assembly line work it is more difficult to develop cohesiveness. Technology also has wider implications for the operation and behaviour of groups and therefore is considered in a separate section later.

ORGANISATIONAL FACTORS

Management and leadership The form of management and style of leadership adopted will influence the relationship between the group and the organisation and are major determinants of group cohesiveness. In general terms, cohesiveness will be affected by such things as the manner in which the manager gives guidance and encouragement to the group, offers help and support, provides opportunities for participation, attempts to resolve conflicts and gives attention to both employee relations and task problems. *McKenna and Maister* draw attention to the importance of the group leader establishing a level of trust among the group by helping them understand the behaviours that build trust. 'The job of the group leader is to encourage people to earn the trust of others in their group and then show them how it can translate into greater commitment, greater creativity, greater professional satisfaction, and better performance.'[15]

HR policies and procedures Harmony and cohesiveness within the group are more likely to be achieved if HR policies and procedures are well developed and perceived to be equitable, with fair treatment for all members. Attention should be given to the effects that appraisal systems, discipline, promotion and rewards, and opportunities for personal development have on members of the group.

Success The more successful the group, the more cohesive it is likely to be, and cohesive groups are more likely to be successful. Success is usually a strong motivational influence on the level of work performance. Success or reward as a positive motivator can be perceived by group members in a number of ways, for example the satisfactory completion of a task through co-operative action, praise from management, a feeling of high status, achievement in competition with other groups, benefits gained, such as high wage payments from a group bonus incentive scheme.

External threat Cohesiveness may be enhanced by members co-operating with one another when faced with a common external threat, such as changes in their method of work or the appointment of a new manager. Even if the threat is subsequently removed, the group may continue to have a greater degree of cohesiveness than before the threat arose. Conflict between groups will also tend to increase the cohesiveness of each group and the boundaries of the group become drawn more clearly.

Refresh your understanding

Activity 8B
www.pearsoned.co.uk/
mullins

GROUP DEVELOPMENT AND MATURITY

The degree of cohesiveness is affected also by the manner in which groups progress through the various stages of development and maturity before getting down to the real tasks in hand. This process can take time and is often traumatic for the members. *Bass and Ryterband* identify four distinct stages in group development:

- mutual acceptance and membership;
- communication and decision-making;
- motivation and productivity; and
- control and organisation.[16]

An alternative, and more popular, model by *Tuckman* identifies five main successive stages of group development and relationships: **forming, storming, norming, performing** and **adjourning**.[17]

- **Stage 1 – forming.** The initial formation of the group and the bringing together of a number of individuals who identify, tentatively, the purpose of the group, its composition and terms of reference. At this stage consideration is given to hierarchical structure of the group, pattern of leadership, individual roles and responsibilities, and codes of conduct. There is likely to be considerable anxiety as members attempt to create an impression, to test each other and to establish their personal identity within the group.
- **Stage 2 – storming.** As members of the group get to know each other better they will put forward their views more openly and forcefully. Disagreements will be expressed and challenges offered on the nature of the task and arrangements made in the earlier stage of development. This may lead to conflict and hostility. The storming stage is important because, if successful, there will be discussions on reforming arrangements for the working and operation of the group, and agreement on more meaningful structures and procedures.
- **Stage 3 – norming.** As conflict and hostility start to be controlled, members of the group will establish guidelines and standards and develop their own norms of acceptable behaviour. The norming stage is important in establishing the need for members to co-operate in order to plan, agree standards of performance and fulfil the purpose of the group.
- **Stage 4 – performing.** When the group has progressed successfully through the three earlier stages of development it will have created structure and cohesiveness to work effectively as a team. At this stage the group can concentrate on the attainment of its purpose and performance of the common task is likely to be at its most effective.
- **Stage 5 – adjourning.** This refers to the adjourning or disbanding of the group because of, for example, completion of the task, members leaving the organisation or moving on to other tasks. Some members may feel a compelling sense of loss at the end of a major or lengthy group project and their return to independence is characterised by sadness and anxiety. Managers may need to prepare for future group tasks and engendering team effort.

Another writer suggests that new groups go through the following stages:

- the polite stage;
- the why are we here, what are we doing stage;
- the power stage, which dominant will emerge;
- the constructive stage when sharing begins; and
- the unity stage – this often takes weeks, eating together, talking together.[18]

POTENTIAL DISADVANTAGES OF STRONG, COHESIVE GROUPS

Although there are potential disadvantages of cohesive groups (discussed below) they may result in greater interaction between members, mutual help and social satisfaction, lower turnover and absenteeism, and often higher production.[19]

If the manager is to develop effective work groups, attention should be given to those factors that influence the creation of group identity and cohesiveness. However, strong and cohesive groups also present potential disadvantages for management. Cohesive groups do not necessarily produce a higher level of output. Performance varies with the extent to which the group accepts or rejects the goals of the organisation. Furthermore, with a very high level of cohesiveness and attention to social activities, there may even be a fall in

output. The level of production is likely to conform to a standard acceptable as a norm by the group. It may be remembered that in the bank wiring room experiment of the Hawthorne studies, group norms imposed a restriction on the workers' level of output.

Once a group has become fully developed and created cohesiveness, it is more difficult for the manager successfully to change the attitudes and behaviour of the group. It is important that the manager should attempt to influence the group during the norming stage when members are establishing guidelines and standards and their own norms of acceptable behaviour. When a group has become fully developed and established its own culture it is more difficult to change the attitudes and behaviour of its members.

Inter-group conflict Strong, cohesive groups may develop a critical or even hostile attitude towards people outside the group or members of other groups. This can be the case, for example, when group cohesiveness is based on common status, qualifications, technical expertise or professional standing. Group cohesiveness may result in lack of co-operation with, or opposition to, non-members. As a result, resentment and intergroup conflict may arise to the detriment of the organisation as a whole. In order to help prevent, or overcome, unconstructive intergroup conflict, the manager should attempt to stimulate a high level of communication and interaction between the groups and to maintain harmony. Rotation of members among different groups should be encouraged.

Yet, intergroup rivalry may be deliberately encouraged as a means of building stronger within-group cohesiveness. The idea is that a competitive element may help to promote unity within a group. However, intergroup rivalry and competition need to be handled carefully. The manager should attempt to avoid the development of 'win–lose' situations. Emphasis should be placed on overall objectives of the organisation and on superordinate goals. These are goals over and above the issues at conflict and which, if they are to be achieved, require the co-operation of the competing groups.

CHARACTERISTICS OF AN EFFECTIVE WORK GROUP

The characteristics of an effective work group are not always easy to isolate clearly. The underlying feature is a spirit of co-operation in which members work well together as a united team and with harmonious and supportive relationships. This may be evidenced when members of a group exhibit:

- a belief in shared aims and objectives;
- a sense of commitment to the group;
- acceptance of group values and norms;
- a feeling of mutual trust and dependency;
- full participation by all members and decision-making by consensus;
- a free flow of information and communications;
- the open expression of feelings and disagreements;
- the resolution of conflict by the members themselves;
- a lower level of staff turnover, absenteeism, accidents, errors and complaints.

However, as *Brooks* points out, as teams operate at the higher order of group dynamics this list is arguably more reflective of 'effective **work teams** rather than work groups and this is how it should be – these are teams not groups'.[20]

The effects of technology

Technology is clearly a major influence on the pattern of group operation and behaviour. The work organisation may limit the opportunities for social interaction and the extent to which individuals are able to identify themselves as members of a cohesive work group.

more people as individuals even though their roles may be defined clearly and understood fully. In practice, the manner in which a person actually behaves may not be consistent with their expected pattern of behaviours. This inconsistency may be a result of role conflict. Role conflict as a generic term can include:

- role incompatibility
- role ambiguity
- role overload
- role underload.

These are all problem areas associated with the creation of role expectations (*see* Figure 8.6).

Figure 8.6	**Role relationships and conflicts**

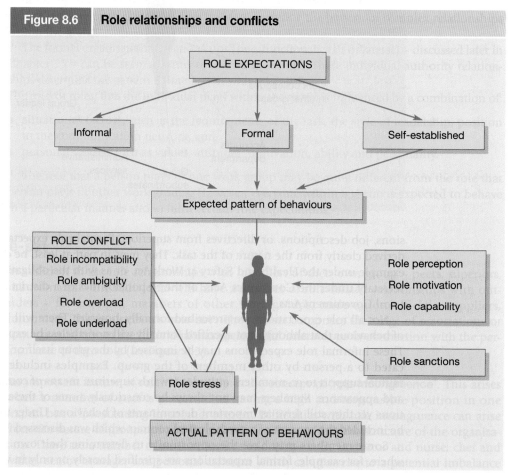

Source: Adapted from Miner, J. B., *Management Theory*, Macmillan (1971) p. 47.

- **Role incompatibility** arises when a person faces a situation in which simultaneous different or contradictory expectations create inconsistency. Compliance with one set of expectations makes it difficult or impossible to comply with other expectations. The two role expectations are in conflict. A typical example concerns the person 'in the middle', such as the supervisor or section head, who faces opposing expectations from workers and from management. Another example might be the situation of a manager who believes in a relaxed, participative style of behaviour more in keeping with a Theory Y approach, but whose superior believes in a Theory X approach and expects the manager to adopt a more formal and directive style of behaviour.

- **Role ambiguity** occurs when there is lack of clarity as to the precise requirements of the role and the person is unsure what to do. The person's perception of their role may differ from the expectations of others. This implies that insufficient information is available for the adequate performance of the role. Role ambiguity may result from a lack of formally prescribed expectations. It is likely to arise in large, diverse groups or at times of constant change. Uncertainty often relates to such matters as the method of performing tasks, the extent of the person's authority and responsibility, standards of work, and the evaluation and appraisal of performance.

- **Role overload** is when a person faces too many separate roles or too great a variety of expectations. The person is unable to meet satisfactorily all expectations and some must be neglected in order to satisfy others. This leads to a conflict of priority. Some writers distinguish between role overload and work overload. Role overload is seen in terms of the total role-set and implies that the person has too many separate roles to handle. Where there are too many expectations of a single role – that is, a problem of quantity – this is work overload.

- **Role underload** can arise when the prescribed role expectations fall short of the person's perception of their role. The person may feel their role is not demanding enough and that they have the capacity to undertake a larger or more varied role, or an increased number of roles. Role underload may arise, for example, when a new member of staff is first appointed or from the initial effects of empowerment.

Role conflict and matrix organisation

Problems of role conflict can often arise from the matrix form of organisation (which is discussed in Chapter 15) and, for example, from the use of flexible project teams. Where staff are assigned temporarily, and perhaps on a part-time basis, from other groups this creates a two-way flow of authority and responsibility.

Unless role differentiations are defined clearly this can result in conflicting expectations from the manager of the person's own functional grouping and from the manager of the project team (role incompatibility). It can also lead to uncertainty about the exact requirements of the part the person is expected to play as a member of the project team (role ambiguity). The combinations of expectations from both managers may also result in role overload.

Role stress

Role conflict can result in role stress. As discussed in Chapter 3, although a certain amount of stress may **arguably** be seen as a good thing, and especially at managerial level helps to bring out a high level of performance, it is also potentially very harmful. Stress is a source of tension, frustration and dissatisfaction. It can lead to difficulties in communication and interpersonal relationships and can affect morale, effectiveness at work and health. There are a number of ways in which management might attempt to avoid or reduce role conflict and the possibilities of role stress.

- Increase specification and clarity of prescribed role expectations, for example through written statements on objectives and policy, use of manuals and set procedures, introduction of appropriate rules, and detailed job descriptions. However, such measures may be resented by staff. They may restrict the opportunity for independent action and personal development, giving rise to even more role conflict.

- Improved recruitment and selection and the careful matching of abilities, motivation, interests and personalities to the demands of a particular role.

- Attention to induction and socialisation programmes, job training and retraining, staff development and career progression plans.

- Medical examinations and health screening to give early indications of potential stress-related problems.

- The creation of new roles or assimilation of existing roles. The reallocation or restructuring of tasks and responsibilities. The clarification of priorities, and the elimination or downgrading of minor roles.
- Giving advance notice and explanation of what is likely to happen, for example of an expected, additional heavy workload which must be completed urgently. Where possible and appropriate provide an opportunity for practice or experience.
- Attention to factors which may help improve group structure and group cohesiveness, and help overcome intergroup conflict.
- Review of organisation structure, information flow and communication networks, for example members of staff being answerable to more than one superior.

Other influences on behaviour

Even if there is an absence of role conflict and role stress, a person's actual behaviour may still be inconsistent with their expected pattern of behaviours. *Miner* gives three reasons that may account for this disparity.[32]

- The person does not perceive their job in the way the role prescriptions specify. This is a form of role ambiguity but may arise not because the role prescriptions themselves are unclear but because the person misunderstands or distorts them.
- Motivation is lacking and the person does not want to behave in the way prescribed.
- The person does not have the capabilities – knowledge, mental ability or physical skills – required to behave in the way the role prescriptions specify.

Application of sanctions Organisations apply a number of both positive and negative sanctions as inducements for members to contribute and behave in accordance with their prescribed roles. Typical examples are: an increase in salary or wages; promotion; a sideways or downwards move in the organisation structure; the threat of dismissal.

There are also a number of less direct sanctions that may be adopted. These include the size of office or work area, the allocation of unpopular tasks, giving opportunities for paid overtime work, level of supervision or empowerment, the amount of information given or the extent of consultation, granting or withholding privileges.

Role sanctions may also be applied through the operation of the informal organisation. Members of the group may impose their own sanctions and discipline individuals who contravene the norms of the group or expected standards of behaviour.

THE IMPORTANCE OF TEAMWORK

How people behave and perform as members of a group is as important as their behaviour or performance as individuals. Harmonious working relationships and good teamwork help make for a high level of staff morale and work performance. Effective teamwork is an essential element of modern management practices such as empowerment, quality circles and total quality management, and how groups manage change. Teamwork is important in any organisation but may be especially significant in service industries, such as hospitality organisations where there is a direct effect on customer satisfaction.[33]

According to ACAS, teams have been around for as long as anyone can remember and there can be few organisations that have not used the term in one sense or another. In a general sense, people talk of teamwork when they want to emphasise the virtues of co-operation and the need to make use of the various strengths of employees. Using the term more specifically, teamworking involves a reorganisation of the way work is carried out. Teamwork can increase competitiveness by:

- improving productivity;
- improving quality and encouraging innovation;
- taking advantage of the opportunities provided by technological advances;
- improving employee motivation and commitment.[34]

The general movement towards flatter structures of organisation, wider spans of control and reducing layers of middle management, together with increasing empowerment of employees, all involve greater emphasis on the importance of teamworking. 'There's no doubt that effective teamwork is crucial to an organisation's efforts to perform better, faster and more profitably than their competitors.'[35]

Skills of effective teamworking

From a recent study of Europe's top companies, *Heller* refers to the need for new managers and new methods, and includes as a key strategy for a new breed of managers in a dramatically changed environment: 'making team-working work – the new, indispensable skill'. Heller refers to the happy teams at Heineken. Part of the cultural strength of Heineken is a realisation that 'the best culture for an organisation is a team culture' and that 'any large organisation is a team of teams – and people who have to work together as a team must also think together as a team'.[36] Heller also lists Heineken's manifesto for 'professional team-thinking' and maintains that 'arguing with any of these eleven points is absurd'.

1 The aim is to reach the best decision, not just a hasty conclusion or an easy consensus. The team leader always has the ultimate responsibility for the quality of the decision taken – and, therefore, for the quality of the team-thinking effort that has led up to the decision.

2 To produce the best professional team-thinking, the team leader must ensure that ego-trips, petty office politics and not-invented-here rigidity are explicitly avoided. There should be competition between ideas – not between individual members of the team.

3 The team-thinking effort must first ensure that the best question to be answered is clearly and completely formulated.

4 The team-thinking process is iterative – not linear. Therefore, the question may have to be altered later and the process repeated.

5 The team leader is responsible for seeing that sufficient alternatives and their predicted consequences have been developed for evaluation by the team.

6 The team leader will thus ask, 'What are our alternatives?' – and not just, 'What is the answer?'

7 The team leader also recognizes that it is wiser to seek and listen to the ideas of the team before expressing his or her own ideas and preferences.

8 In any professional team-thinking effort, more ideas will have to be created than used. But any idea that is rejected will be rejected with courtesy and with a clear explanation as to why it is being rejected. To behave in this way is not naive, it is just decent and smart.

9 A risk/reward equation and a probability of success calculation will be made explicitly before any important decision is taken.

10 Once a decision is made professionally, the team must implement it professionally.

11 When you think, think. When you act, act.

Source: From Robert Heller, *In Search of European Excellence*, Profile Books (1997), p. 231. Reproduced with permission.

According to *Guirdham*, the growth of teamwork has led to the increased interest in interface skills at work.

> *More and more tasks of contemporary organisations, particularly those in high technology and service businesses, require teamwork. Taskforces, project teams and committees are key elements in the modern workplace. Teamwork depends not just on technical competence of the individuals composing the team, but on their ability to 'gel'. To work well together, the team members must have more than just team spirit. They also need collaborative skills – they must be able to support one another and to handle conflict in such a way that it becomes constructive rather than destructive.*[37]

A similar point is made by *Ashmos and Nathan*: 'The use of teams has expanded dramatically in response to competitive challenges. In fact, one of the most common skills required by new work practices is the ability to work as a team.'[38]

The nature and importance of teamwork is discussed further in Chapter 9.

Refresh your understanding

Activity 8D
www.pearsoned.co.uk/
mullins

Critical reflection

Groups and teamworking are an essential and integral part of the work organisation, but people value their individuality and own identity and enjoy the right of self-expression. The real skill of management should therefore be to make full use of people's individuality for the mutual benefit of the group as a whole. Do you agree? How do you think managers might best be trained to enhance the contribution and performance of groups?

MANAGEMENT IN THE NEWS

The Pink Ladies mean business
No men please, we're cabbies

Robert Watts

While government reports and official statistics seem to suggest that women are still lagging behind men in terms of pay and status, and many commentators focus on making existing organisations more female friendly, there may also be other solutions. The story of the Pink Ladies Cabs service is one example of an organisation which shows how women can take successful business initiatives and run their own show.

'Pink Ladies Cabs' was founded by Tina Dutton and Andrea Winders in Warrington, Cheshire, in June 2005. The idea was simple and had been lurking in Tina's mind for some time when a family conversation triggered her to take action. Leanna, Tina's daughter, mentioned that she was anxious about being the last person in a taxi after a night out with friends. There were many taxi companies to choose from, but not all were operating legally and there were a number of reported attacks on women by taxi drivers, especially in London. Here was a small but significant market

Is it 'a man's world?' The successful Pink Ladies Cab service run for women by women suggests that it doesn't have to be.

niche. Together Tina and Andrea did some market research and came up with a distinctive package to fit the gap.

The basic idea is to provide safe transport for women. The drivers are all women and Pink Ladies makes sure they are trained in self-defence and first aid. All their cabs (conspicuously bright pink Renault Kangoos) are fitted with satellite navigation and tracking devices, and have extra safety features such

as gel-filled tyres to minimise the risk of the cab being stranded with a puncture. Bookings are made for specific times and customers receive text or telephone messages when the cabs are two minutes away, so that they don't have to wait around outside to be picked up. When a client is dropped off, the Pink Ladies driver will wait until they can see that she is safely inside her destination before driving away. Further security measures include a no-cash policy which means that the cabs never have money on board; instead clients have a pre-payment card which can be recharged over the internet or by phone.

But is it legal? At first glance a business which serves and employs only women (for the most part; they do have a male mechanic) might seem to be in contravention of the Sex Discrimination Act. However, Tina and Andrea know that by operating as a club, not a taxi company, they are able to run this women-only service. If you want to use a Pink Cab you pay a small membership fee to have access to the service and your membership card is also the pre-pay card you use to book and pay for the ride. As for employment, the EOC agreed with their interpretation of one part of

the law on sex discrimination which allows a 'women only' policy if the holder of the job provides individuals with personal services promoting their welfare.

And it's not just Warrington; they have developed an operation in London, and their service is already featuring in foreign tourist guides for visitors to London. They are planning further expansion through franchise operations. Pink Ladies are certainly going places!

Source: Watts, R., 'No men please, we're cabbies', *Daily Telegraph*, 5 January 2006. © Copyright of Telegraph Group Limited 2006, reproduced with permission.

Discussion questions

1 'Pink Ladies' have created a women's organisation rather than seeking to feminise an existing one. Critically evaluate the ways in which this factor might affect the group values and norms of the company.

2 How does modern technology (such as satellite navigation) affect the roles that individuals can play within this organisation? Does the organisation challenge or reinforce stereotypes of women's roles?

SYNOPSIS

● Work is a group-based activity, and groups and teams are a major feature of human behaviour and work organisation. Members must co-operate for work to be carried out. Harmonious working relationships and good teamwork help make for a high level of staff morale and organisational performance. There is a tendency for the terms 'groups' and teams' to be used interchangeably. Whereas all teams are groups, it does not necessarily follow that all groups are teams. Groups develop their own pattern of values and norms of behaviour.

● Groups are formed as a consequence of the pattern of organisation structure and arrangements for the division of work. There are two main types of groups at work, formal and informal. Formal groups are deliberately planned and created by management as part of the organisation structure and to achieve specific organisational objectives. Informal groups are based on personal relationships and develop irrespective of the formal structure. Informal groups serve to satisfy members' psychological and social needs. Groups are formed, therefore, for a number of reasons relating to both work performance and social processes.

● Individuals will form into groups or teams, both formal and informal, for a number of reasons relating to both work performance and social processes. The

manager's main concern is that members co-operate. Factors that affect group cohesiveness can be considered under the broad headings of membership, work environment, organisational and group development and maturity. Membership of strong and cohesive groups can be a rewarding experience for the individual and have beneficial effects for the organisation.

● There are, however, potential disadvantages of strong, cohesive groups and the manager should attempt to prevent unconstructive intergroup conflict. However, intergroup rivalry may be deliberately encouraged as a means of building stronger within-group cohesiveness. Individuals make a contribution to the work of the organisation in different ways. The effective management of work groups requires an understanding of the psychological and social influences on behaviour within organisations.

● The characteristics of an effective work group are not always easy to isolate. The underlying feature is a spirit of co-operation in which members work well together as a united team, and with harmonious and supportive relationships. The combination of increasing globalisation and widespread developments in information communications and technology has given greater emphasis to the opportunities for, and

need of, virtual teams. Members are geographically separated but still work together closely.

● The concept of 'role' is important to the functioning of groups and for an understanding of group processes and behaviour. It is through role differentiation that the structure of work groups and relationships among members is established. Role expectations may be established formally, they may be informal or they may be self-established. Inadequate or inappropriate role definition can result in role conflict, including role incompatibility, role ambiguity, role overload and role underload. It is important that the manager makes every effort to minimise role conflict and the causes of role stress.

 Refresh your understanding, assess your progress and begin your research with online resources at **www.pearsoned.co.uk/mullins**

REVIEW AND DISCUSSION QUESTIONS

1 What is a group? Explain the importance and influence of group values and norms and give practical examples from within your own organisation.

2 How would you distinguish between a 'group' and a 'team'? To what extent do you believe the distinction has practical significance for managers?

3 Distinguish between formal and informal groups and provide your own supporting examples. What functions do groups serve in an organisation?

4 Identify different stages in group development and maturity. What other factors influence the cohesiveness of work groups? Give examples by reference to a work group to which you belong.

5 Discuss critically the advantages and disadvantages of virtual teams and how you believe they are likely to develop in the future.

6 What is meant by the role structure of an organisation? Construct a diagram that shows your own role-set within a work situation. Give examples of informal role expectations to which you are, or have been, a party.

7 Explain different forms of role conflict that can result in role stress. Give an account of a work situation in which you have experienced role conflict/role stress. As a manager, what action would you have taken in an attempt to rectify the situation?

8 Detail fully what you believe are the essential characteristics of a successful work group or team. As a manager, explain how you would attempt to develop effective group/team relationships and performance.

ASSIGNMENT 1

Recall your experience of a work group or team with which you are familiar and comment critically on:

1 the extent to which members were clear about the goals of the group, what they were expected to achieve, and how their performance would be evaluated;

2 the diversity of group membership, and significances of diversity for the operations and success of the group;

3 and what *exactly* made the group effective or fall apart?

ASSIGNMENT 2

Obtain, or prepare, a chart depicting the formal groupings within your organisation or a large department of the organisation.

1 Using this chart, identify clearly the informal groups that exist within the formal structure.

2 Discuss ways in which these informal groups aid, and/or conflict with, the work of the organisation/department.

3 Explain the extent to which management recognises the influence of the informal groups.

4 What conclusions do you draw from this assignment?

PERSONAL AWARENESS AND SKILLS EXERCISE

Objectives

Completing this exercise should help you to enhance the following skills:

● Observe and record the development and maturity of a small work group.

● Analyse the behaviour of individual members of the group.

● Identify those factors that most influence the cohesiveness of the group.

Exercise

You are required to observe a small group or project team at work; *alternatively*, recall the working of any small group of which you have recently been a member.

1 Complete the following grid by giving a tick in the appropriate box to denote each contribution by individual members.

	Names of group members (or reference numbers)				
Forming					
Storming					
Norming					
Performing					
Adjourning (if appropriate)					

2 Give specific examples of the group values or norms that constituted 'proper' behaviour of group members.

3 Detail sanctions applied to those members who did not conform to the group norms and the apparent effectiveness of these sanctions.

4 Comment critically on the effectiveness of the group as a whole.

Discussion

● To what extent do you believe groups develop clearly through the five main successive stages of forming, storming, norming, performing and adjourning?

● Which in your opinion is the most crucial stage?

● Give your views, with supporting reasons, on the apparent satisfaction derived by individuals from membership of the group.

CASE STUDY

Mumbai's Dabbawalahs a world-class quality service

Those studying organisational behaviour often find themselves reading about the issues faced by global businesses, whose managerial excellence is supported by cutting-edge technology and major financial investment. The organisation in this case study has neither cutting-edge technology nor major investment and never has had. However, it has become famous in recent years, as the world's business schools have beaten a path to its door to study the extraordinary organisation of Mumbai's dabbawalahs.

Dabbawalahs (or 'tiffinwalahs') run a service in Mumbai whose purpose is easy enough to describe: each working day, they arrange the collection and delivery from Bombay's suburbs of about 175,000 lunches in the traditional tiffin boxes. These meals are prepared by wives or mothers (or sometimes local restaurants) for individual workers in central Mumbai: obviously, the contents of each box are unique, which is the central appeal of the service. A little later in the day, the dabbawalahs collect the empties and return them to the workers' homes.

In some ways, the design of the system resembles that of a modern international courier service. It is based on local collection of the tiffin boxes, which are then loaded on to local trains for bulk transportation into the centre of Mumbai (special compartments are reserved for the boxes). At each of the central stations, other members of the team unload the boxes for destinations near the station and sort them for hand delivery to the offices and workshops where the individual recipients work. They also load any boxes for delivery further down the line. The train stops for about 20 seconds at these stations, resulting in a turnaround time that would make many of Europe's low-cost airlines look up in surprise. Delivery to the hungry workers is achieved by 12.45 sharp, following which the process is reversed to return the boxes to the homes.[39] The service costs Rs300–350 per month ($US6–7) and the dabbawalahs earn about Rs5,000 (about $US115) a month. Customers pay one month's bonus to the organisation for the Diwali festival. This intricate, precisely co-ordinated operation takes place in a city famous for its bustle, traffic delays and occasional chaos – the dabbawalahs negotiate the traffic on foot and by bicycle at a cracking pace, whatever the weather: the tiffin must get through. The error rate is said to be vanishingly small: one box may go astray every two months.

Source: Nick Hanna/Alamy

The amazing dabbawallahs deliver 175,000 lunchtime tiffin boxes a day in Bombay in a well co-ordinated and highly effective team operation.

A team to beat the best

There is no IT support for this daily miracle – no track and trace, no computers, no bar codes, just a handwritten code on each box that allows the dabbawalah to recognise which station the box has to be sent to and unloaded, its ultimate destination and its return address. Many of the dabbawalahs have low levels of literacy, but their ability to decode and correctly route the 40 or so boxes that they each carry through the crowded streets is key to the whole system. The very high levels of effectiveness and efficiency achieved in this service have attracted the attention of business schools from many countries. As the dabbawalahs proudly proclaim, the reliability of the system is at Six Sigma levels (one error in 1 million), a performance that is comparable to that of the world's leading corporations.[40] Business strategy expert C.K. Prahalad was struck by the performance level of this system as well as by its very low levels of capital-intensiveness:

That's a good thing by itself because you can dramatically reduce the capital intensity of a business. A lot of the float there is between points of production and consumption can be reduced dramatically around the world.[41]

However, the interest in this case is not so much in the technical details of the logistics but in the team that makes the service happen. The dabbawalah service is said to have originated in 1890,[42] and to have been invented by Indian entrepreneur Mahadeo Havaji Bacchex.[43] At the same time, a then much smaller Mumbai was starting to experience a strong growth of daily commuting into the centre. From the outset, the

design of the service was much the same as today – the local trains were hauled by steam engines and the traffic jams on the streets were animal rather than automotive, but the challenge was essentially the same. There has always been strong cultural preference for home cooking among workers in India: in Mumbai, which has always drawn its working population from all over India, 'home cooking' means a kaleidoscope of different regional styles and traditions. Clearly, a service that can bring this diverse range of home-prepared meals reliably to the individual in the workplace is going to be in demand. The service grew to its present levels by the 1950s.

There are about 5,000 dabbawalahs in Mumbai today, organised into teams of 20–25 under an experienced group leader. Ragunath Medge is President of Nutan Mumbai Tiffin Box Suppliers Charity Trust (and a regular guest speaker these days at business school conferences). As he explains, those who work for the organisation are mostly shareholders, rather than employees:

> If you have employees, then you have unions and strikes. We are all shareholders in the Trust and thus we share in the earnings.

He explains that the dabbawalahs mainly come from the same region, the Pune district and that most are related to each other:

> We all come from the region east of the Sahyadri (Western Ghats), and everyone who joins us, is known to us. If an outsider does join in, we initially employ him on a fixed salary, and if in a couple of years he wins our trust, we may make him a shareholder.[44]

These sentiments are echoed in the comments of one of the dabbawalahs in an article published in *The Guardian* in 2002:

> It's a very sociable job,' Sapan Mare, a tiffin-wallah since 1970 explained, as we rattled into central Bombay [Mumbai].'I like the fact that I meet so many people every day. Between 100 to 110 members of my family are in the tiffin business. I come from a family where four generations have been tiffin-wallahs,' he added proudly.[45]

Mr Medge explains that the job for Trust shareholders lasts for as long as the member is strong enough to do the work. Notes on a blogspot (weblog) of a talk given by Mr Medge provide further detail of the discipline that characterises the dabbawalah team: members are mainly vegetarians and most don't drink alcohol.[46] Drinking at work is against the rules: the first and second offence will result in a fine and the third will result in removal from the service. There is also a dress code for team members, presumably to show pride and confidence in the high standards of the service and also perhaps to secure public co-operation with the smooth daily running of the operation. The organisation sets great store by the integrity and trustworthiness of its members: dabbawalahs just do not have police records.

The future of the service

As any services marketing textbook will confirm, customers often take part in the production of services. In this case, the expertise and hard work of the dabbawalahs will come to nothing if the meals are not ready for collection on time: those who prepare the meals in homes and local restaurants can also be seen as part of the team. Sometimes, it is suggested that customers also use the network as an informal communications medium, sending each other little notes in the tiffin boxes.

The city of Mumbai is at the forefront of the huge economic and social changes that are sweeping through India. The dabbawalah system is still a mainstay of the working day in the city, but is starting to experience and respond to change. The growth of fast food is a global phenomenon that has been relatively slow to penetrate the Indian market but is now starting to make its mark. Mr Medge's operation is still resolutely uncomputerised (what good would gigabytes and parallel processors be in the traffic in Mumbai?), but it does have a website and is now able to accept orders via the site or by SMS. Its website also seeks to re-assert the traditional core values of the organisation in the face of the tide of global fast food.[47] Among the 'top ten reasons for using the Dabbawalahs' services' are the following appeals to the good sense of Mumbai workers:

1 Home made food is best for health … Outside junk foods may take your life and makes you sick…
2 Home made food is cheaper … It's simple maths.
3 Do you not love your mother or wife and like to eat food made by her?

The dabbawalahs have fed thousands of people for more than a century. Their astonishingly effective logistics continue to deliver reliable, low-priced service every working day. As can be seen on their website, they have admirers all around the world – Prince Charles (who invited the two dabbahwalahs quoted in this case to his wedding to Camilla), Richard Branson (of course) and – perhaps paradoxically – the Slow Food movement. For generations, the cohesion, dedication and discipline of this team have been the main guarantees of their legendary service and it seems likely to retain a place in the hearts of Mumbai residents as modernisation proceeds.

Your tasks

1 If a team can be defined as a group of people working towards a common goal, discuss the advantages and disadvantages of the dabbawalah practice of making team members shareholders rather than employees. Would the same arguments apply to other logistically similar operations?

2 Use the framework in Figure 8.4 to analyse the cohesiveness and performance of the dabbawalah team. To what extent does the dabbawalah service display the characteristics of an effective work group?

3 Why has technology played such a small part in the development of the dabbawalah service so far? Is this likely to change in future? Identify ways in which this might affect the team spirit of the organisation.

Notes and references

1 Schein, E. H. *Organizational Psychology*, Third edition, Prentice-Hall (1988), p. 145.

2 Adair, J. *Effective Teambuilding*, Gower (1986).

3 Guzzo, R. A. and Dickson, M. W. 'Teams in Organizations: recent research on performance and effectiveness', *Annual Review of Psychology*, vol. 47, (1996), pp. 307–38.

4 Holpp, L. 'Teams: It's All in the Planning', *Training & Development*, vol. 51, no. 4, April 1997, pp. 44–7.

5 Crainer, S. *Key Management Ideas: Thinkers that changed the management world*, Third edition, Financial Times Prentice Hall (1998), p. 237.

6 Cane, S. *Kaizen Strategies for Winning Through People*, Pitman Publishing (1996), p. 116.

7 Belbin, R. M. *Beyond the Team*, Butterworth-Heinemann (2000).

8 Riches, A. 'Emotionally Intelligent Teams', Organisational Change & Leadership Development, www.anneriches.com.au, accessed 11 March 2003.

9 Huck, S., Kubler, D. and Weibull, J. 'Social Norms and Economic Incentives in Firms', *Economic & Social Research Council*, 5 March 2003.

10 Boynton, A. and Fischer B. *Virtuoso Teams: Lessons from teams that changed their worlds*, Financial Times Prentice Hall (2005).

11 Lysons, K. 'Organisational Analysis', *Supplement to The British Journal of Administrative Management*, no. 18, March/April 1997.

12 Law, S. 'Beyond the Water Cooler', *Professional Manager*, January 2005, pp. 26–8.

13 See, for example: Jay, A. *Corporation Man*, Penguin (1975). In an amusing historical account of the development of different forms of groups, Jay suggests that ten is the basic size of human grouping.

14 Cane, S. *Kaizen Strategies for Winning Through People*, Pitman Publishing (1996), p. 131.

15 McKenna, P. J. and Maister, D. H. 'Building Team Trust', *Consulting to Management*, vol. 13, no. 4, December 2002, pp. 51–3.

16 Bass, B. M. and Ryterband, E. C. *Organizational Psychology*, Second edition, Allyn and Bacon (1979).

17 Tuckman, B. W. 'Development Sequence in Small Groups', *Psychological Bulletin*, vol. 63, 1965, pp. 384–99; and Tuckman, B. W. and Jensen, M. C. 'Stages of Small Group Development Revised', *Group and Organizational Studies*, vol. 2, no. 3, 1977, pp. 419–27.

18 Cited in Green, J. 'Are your teams and groups at work successful?', *Administrator*, December 1993, p. 12.

19 Argyle, M. *The Social Psychology of Work*, Second edition, Penguin (1989).

20 Brooks, I. *Organisational Behaviour: Individuals, Groups and Organisation*, Third edition, Financial Times Prentice Hall (2006) p. 99.

21 Teamwork: Success Through People', Advisory Booklet, ACAS, April 2003, p. 9.

22 See, for example: Kinsman, F. 'The Virtual Office and The Flexible Organisation', *Administrator*, April 1994, pp. 31–2; and Chowdhury, S. *Management 21C*. Financial Times Prentice Hall (2000).

23 See, for example: Johnson, P., Heimann, V. and O'Neill, K. 'The "Wonderland" of Virtual Teams', *The Journal of Workplace Learning*, vol. 13, no. 1, 2001, pp. 24–30.

24 Hall, P. 'Team Solutions Need Not Be the Organisational Norm', *Professional Manager*, July 2001, p. 45.

25 Parker, C. 'Remote Control – a Case Study', *Manager, The British Journal of Administrative Management*, March/April 2002, p. 30.

26 Norval, D. in conversation with Law, S. 'Beyond the Water Cooler', *Professional Manager*, January 2005, pp. 26–8.

27 Symons, J. 'Taking Virtual Team Control', *Professional Manager*, vol. 12, no. 2, March 2003, p. 37.

28 Francesco, A. M. and Gold, B. A. *International Organizational Behavior*, Second edition, Pearson Prentice Hall (2005), p. 118.

29 Murray, S. 'Virtual teams: Global harmony is their dream', *Financial Times*, May 11, 2005.

30 Reproduced with permission from *Manager, The British Journal of Administrative Management*, March/April 2002, pp. 30–31 and with the permission of Murray Blair, Chameleon Training and Consulting, Surrey.

31 See, for example: Lerner, P. M. 'Beware the Gatekeeper', *Amtrak Express*, July/August 1994, pp. 14–17.

32 Miner, J. B. *Management Theory*, Macmillan (1971).

33 See, for example: Mullins, L. J. *Hospitality Management and Organisational Behaviour*, Fourth edition, Longman (2001).

34 *Teamwork: Success Through People*, Advisory Booklet, ACAS, April 2003.

35 Lucas, E. 'And the Winner is Everyone', *Professional Manager*, January 2001, p. 10.

36 Heller, R. *In Search of European Excellence*, HarperCollins Business (1997), p. 229.

37 Guirdham, M. *Interactive Behaviour at Work*, Third edition, Financial Times Prentice Hall (2002), p. 12.

38 Ashmos, D. P. and Nathan, M. L. 'Team Sense-Making: A mental model for navigating uncharted territories', *Journal of Managerial Issues*, vol. 14, no. 2, Summer 2002, p. 198.

39 Harding, L. 'A Bombay Lunchbox', *The Guardian* on-line 24 June 2002.

40 The Dabbawalah website http://www.mydabbawala.com/ [accessed 4 August 2006].

41 Anderson, B. Fast food delivers lunchtime lesson 17 August 2004 CNN.com website http://www.cnn.com/2004/ BUSINESS/ 08/16/ mumbai.dabbawallahs/index.html [accessed 4 August 2006].

42 The Dabbawalah website http://www.mydabbawala.com/ [accessed 4 August 2006].

43 Harding, L. *A Bombay Lunchbox*, The Guardian on-line, 24 June 2002 http://www.guardian.co.uk/elsewhere/ journalist/story/0,7792,743042,00.html [accessed 4 August 2006].

44 The Dabbawalah website http://www.mydabbawala.com/ [accessed 4 August 2006].

45 Harding, L. 'A Bombay Lunchbox', *The Guardian* on-line 24 June 2002. http://www.guardian.co.uk/ elsewhere/journalist/ story/0,7792,743042,00.html [accessed 4 August 2006].

46 Nomad(i) Blogspot of an unknown Indian http:// nomad-i.blogspot.com.

47 The Dabbawalah website http://www.mydabbawala.com/ [accessed 4 August 2006].

9

WORKING IN GROUPS AND TEAMS

If the manager is to make the most effective use of staff, it is important to have an understanding of working in groups and teams. It is necessary to recognise the nature of human relationships and the functions, roles and factors that influence team performance and effectiveness. Attention should be given to the analysis of behaviour of individuals in group situations and to their effective performance. The manager needs to be aware of the interactions and operation of work groups and teams.

> We know everyone is different. When selecting people for your team, the most important thing to look for is ones who are decent, honest, bright and capable. You will find that good people will naturally work together as a team, will interrelate well and will want each other to succeed. And while I'm on the subject of teams, don't send people off on those terrible outward-bound weekends. Have a party instead.

(Sir) Gerry Robinson – one of the UK's most powerful businessmen
I'll Show Them Who's Boss, BBC Books (2004), p. 183

Learning outcomes

After completing this chapter you should be able to:

- explain interactions among members of a group and membership of successful teams;
- detail main types of contributions or team roles;
- contrast patterns of communication networks within small work groups;
- examine methods of analysing the behaviour of individual members;
- distinguish different group functions and member roles, and explain the use of frameworks of behavioural analysis;
- evaluate the nature of individual or group or team performance;
- review the importance of, and influences on, successful teamworking.

Critical reflection

????

Much is written and talked about the nature of groups and teams, but how well do you think all this theory works in practice? Despite all the hype and myths, is it simply a question of ensuring the right mix of skills and that all the members of the group co-operate with each other? Or is this an over-simplification?

INTERACTIONS AMONG MEMBERS

In the previous chapter we mentioned that how people behave and perform as members of a group is as important as their behaviour or performance as individuals, and drew attention to the importance of effective teamwork. The main focus of attention in this chapter is the actual roles, behaviours and performance of people working in groups or teams. Once again, however, we should be aware of the tendency for the terms 'groups' and 'teams' to be used interchangeably. If groups are to be successful and perform effectively, there must be a spirit of unity and co-operation. Members of a group must work well together as a team. As *Crainer* reminds us, in most teams people will contribute individual skills, many of which will be different. However, referring to the work of *Obeng*,[1] Crainer points out that it is not enough to have a rag-bag collection of individual skills.

> *The various behaviors of the team members must mesh together in order to achieve objectives. For people to work successfully in teams, you need people to behave in certain ways. You need some people to concentrate on the task at hand (doers). You need some people to provide specialist knowledge (knowers) and some to solve problems as they arise (solvers). You need some people to make sure that it is going as well as it can and that the whole team is contributing fully (checkers). And you need some people to make sure that the team is operating as a cohesive social unit (carers).*[2]

As ACAS points out: 'To remain competitive organisations need to make optimum use of equipment and people if they are to thrive or even survive … In a general sense people talk of teamwork when they want to emphasise the virtues of co-operation and the need to make use of the various strengths of employees.'[3]

In order to understand the functions and processes of a group, it is necessary to understand what happens when people meet; the actions and behaviour of individual members; the parts people play; the patterns of interactions and forces within the group; and influences on individual and group performance. According to *Guirdham*, for example:

> *Many of the concepts that have helped us understand interactive behaviour in work relationships are also needed for understanding it in groups, including role behaviour, norms and co-operation, competition, conflict and conflict resolution. Most of what there is to understand about group work applies equally to both decision-making groups and teams but there are some further issues particular to the two different kinds of groups. There is, however, no suggestion that teams do not have to solve problems!*[4]

BELBIN'S TEAM-ROLES

One of the most popular and widely used analyses of individual roles within a work group or team is that developed by *Meredith Belbin*. Following years of research and empirical study, Belbin concludes that groups composed entirely of clever people, or of people with similar personalities, display a number of negative results and lack creativity. The most consistently successful groups comprise a range of roles undertaken by various members. The

constitution of the group itself is an important variable in its success.[5] Initially, Belbin identified eight useful types of contribution – or team-roles.

A **team-role** is described as a pattern of behaviour, characteristic of the way in which one team member interacts with another whose performance serves to facilitate the progress of the team as a whole. In a follow-up publication, Belbin discusses the continual evolution of team-roles, which differ in a few respects from those originally identified and adds a ninth role.[6] Strength of contribution in any one role is commonly associated with particular weaknesses. These are called allowable weaknesses. Members are seldom strong in all nine team-roles. A description of the evolved nine team-roles is given in Table 9.1.

The types of people identified are useful team members and form a comprehensive list. These are the key team-roles and the primary characters for successful teams. Creative teams require a balance of all these roles and comprise members who have characteristics complementary to each other. 'No one's perfect, but a team can be.' Belbin claims that good examples of each type would prove adequate for any challenge, although not all types are necessarily needed. Other members may be welcome for their personal qualities, for example a sense of humour, but experience suggests there is no other team-role that it would be useful to add.

Table 9.1	Belbin's evolved nine team-roles	
Roles and descriptions – team-role contribution		**Allowable weaknesses**
Plant	Creative, imaginative, unorthodox. Solves difficult problems.	Ignores details. Too preoccupied to communicate effectively.
Resource investigator	Extrovert, enthusiastic, communicative. Explores opportunities. Develops contacts.	Over-optimistic. Loses interest once initial enthusiasm has passed.
Co-ordinator	Mature, confident, a good chairperson. Clarifies goals, promotes decision-making. Delegates well.	Can be seen as manipulative. Offloads personal work.
Shaper	Challenging, dynamic, thrives on pressure. Has the drive and courage to overcome obstacles.	Can provoke others. Hurts people's feelings.
Monitor-Evaluator	Sober, strategic and discerning. Sees all options. Judges accurately.	Lacks drive and ability to inspire others.
Teamworker	Co-operative, mild, perceptive and diplomatic. Listens, builds, averts friction.	Indecisive in crunch situations.
Implementer	Disciplined, reliable, conservative and efficient. Turns ideas into practical actions.	Somewhat inflexible. Slow to respond to new possibilities.
Completer	Painstaking, conscientious, anxious. Searches out errors and omissions. Delivers on time.	Inclined to worry unduly. Reluctant to delegate.
Specialist	Single-minded, self-sharing, dedicated. Provides knowledge and skills in rare supply.	Contributes on only a narrow front. Dwells on technicalities.

Source: Belbin, R. M., *Team Roles at Work*, Butterworth-Heinemann (a division of Reed Elsevier UK Ltd) and Belbin Associates (1993) p. 23. Reproduced with permission.

Back-up team-roles and functional roles The most consistently successful teams were 'mixed' with a balance of team-roles. The role that a person undertakes in a group is not fixed and may change according to circumstances. Individuals may have a 'back-up team-role' with which they have some affinity other than their primary team-role. If certain roles were missing members would call upon their back-up roles. Team-roles differ from what Belbin calls 'functional-roles'. These are the roles that members of a team perform in terms of the specifically technical demands placed upon them. Team members are typically chosen for functional roles on the basis of experience and not personal characteristics or aptitudes.

Belbin has developed a Self-Perception Inventory designed to provide members of a group with a simple means of assessing their best team-roles.

The value of Belbin's team-roles inventory

Despite possible doubts about the value of Belbin's Self-Perception Inventory, it remains a popular means of examining and comparing team-roles. For example, in order to explore whether local government managers were distinctively different from the model of private sector management, *Arroba and Wedgwood-Oppenheim* compared samples of the two groups of managers and Belbin's key team-roles. There were noticeable similarities between the two groups, with the noticeable exception of the marked difference between private sector managers and local government officers in the score for teamworkers and the team-roles they preferred to adopt. The individual characteristics of managers in the two sectors differed. The data implied that local government officers were committed to organisational objectives and dedicated to task achievement, but the low score for teamworkers suggested the high commitment to organisational tasks was not supplemented by a concern for interpersonal processes. In local government, the drive and enthusiasm and emphasis on task were exaggerated, while attention to idea generation and productive interpersonal relationships was less marked.[7]

Distribution of team roles among UK managers Using Belbin's model, *Fisher et al.* undertook a study of the distribution of team roles among managers. Over the past 15 years many layers of management have been removed and the gap in people to lead and motivate has increasingly been filled by the creation of multitudes of teams. The participants of the study were 1441 male and 355 female managers, all with some management experience. All had completed a personality questionnaire and were candidates short-listed for a range of management positions in both the private and public sectors. The study analysed data supplied by ASE/NFER Publishing Company and results were then compared with the Belbin model. The data broadly agreed with the Belbin model. The authors conclude that as much is still unknown about teams, it is reassuring that further support has been found for the popular Belbin team-role model. There are several unresolved problems with teamworking but these might lie more with practices in staff recruitment than in team theory.[8]

Refresh your understanding

Activity 9A
www.pearsoned.co.uk/mullins

PATTERNS OF COMMUNICATION

The level of interaction among members of a group or team is influenced by the structuring of channels of communication. Laboratory research by *Bavelas*[9] and subsequent studies by other researchers such as *Leavitt*[10] have resulted in the design of a series of communication networks. These networks were based on groups of five members engaged in a number of problem-solving tasks. Members were permitted to communicate with each other by written notes only and not everyone was always free to communicate with everyone else.

There are five main types of communication networks – wheel, circle, all-channel, Y and chains (*see* Figure 9.1).

Figure 9.1	Communication networks

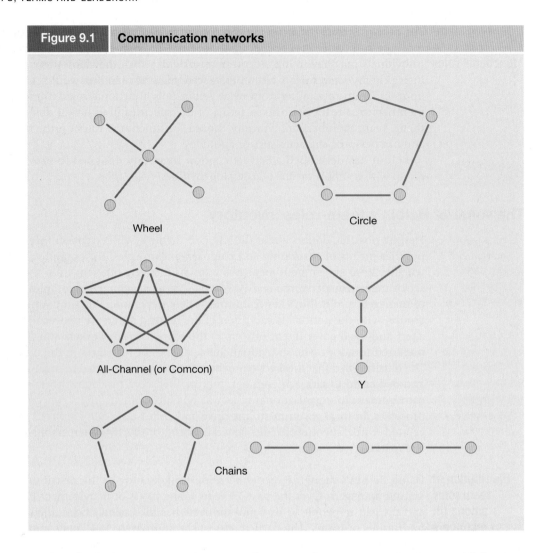

- **The wheel**, also sometimes known as the star, is the most **centralised network**. This network is most efficient for simple tasks. Problems are solved more quickly with fewer mistakes and with fewer information flows. However, as the problems become more complex and demands on the link person increase, effectiveness suffers. The link person is at the centre of the network and acts as the focus of activities and information flows and the co-ordinator of group tasks. The central person is perceived as leader of the group and experiences a high level of satisfaction. However, for members on the periphery, the wheel is the least satisfying network.
- **The circle** is a more **decentralised network**. Overall it is less efficient. The group is unorganised, with low leadership predictability. Performance tends to be slow and erratic. However, the circle is quicker than the wheel in solving complex problems and also copes more efficiently with change or new tasks. The circle network is most satisfying for all the members. Decision-making is likely to involve some degree of participation.
- **The all-channel (or comcon) network** is a decentralised network that involves full discussion and participation. This network appears to work best where a high level of interaction is required among all the members in order to solve complex problems. Leadership predictability is very low. There is a fairly high level of satisfaction for members. The all-channel network may not stand up well under pressure, in which case it will either disintegrate or reform into a wheel network.

- **A 'Y' or chain network** might be appropriate for more simple problem-solving tasks, requiring little interaction among members. These networks are more centralised, with information flows along a predetermined channel. Leadership predictability is high to moderate. There is a low to moderate level of satisfaction for members.

The relationship between centralised and decentralised networks and performance of the group is outlined in Figure 9.2.

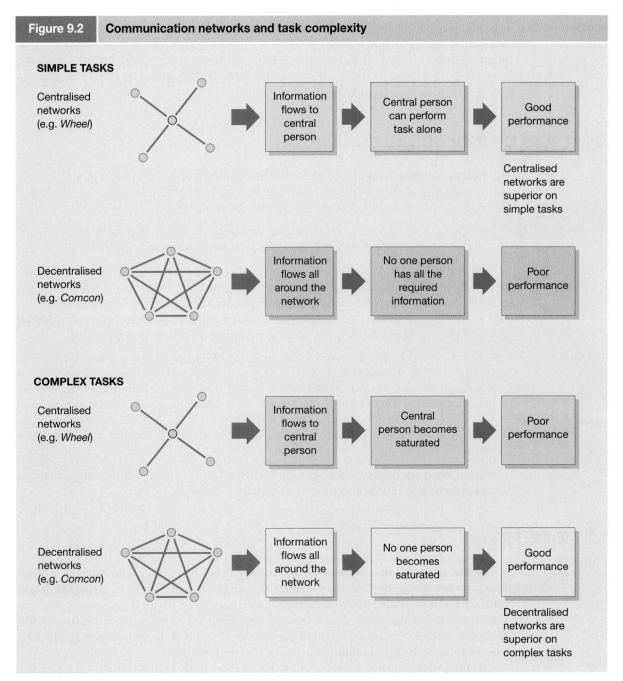

Figure 9.2 | **Communication networks and task complexity**

SIMPLE TASKS

Centralised networks (e.g. *Wheel*) → Information flows to central person → Central person can perform task alone → Good performance

Centralised networks are superior on simple tasks

Decentralised networks (e.g. *Comcon*) → Information flows all around the network → No one person has all the required information → Poor performance

COMPLEX TASKS

Centralised networks (e.g. *Wheel*) → Information flows to central person → Central person becomes saturated → Poor performance

Decentralised networks (e.g. *Comcon*) → Information flows all around the network → No one person becomes saturated → Good performance

Decentralised networks are superior on complex tasks

Source: Greenberg, J. and Baron, R. A., *Behavior in Organizations,* Sixth Edition, Prentice-Hall Inc. (1995), p. 306. Reproduced with permission from Pearson Education, Inc.

Implications for the manager Despite the obvious artificiality and limitations of these communication network studies, they do have certain implications for the manager. Knowledge of the findings may be applied to influence the patterns of communication in meetings and committees. They also provide a reasonable representation of the situations that might apply in large organisations. It will be interesting for the manager to observe the patterns of communication adopted by different groups in different situations. The manager can also note how communication networks change over time and how they relate to the performance of the group.

No one network is likely to be effective for a range of given problems. The studies draw attention to the part of the manager's job that is to ensure the most appropriate communication network for the performance of a given task. Problems which require a high level of interaction among members of the group may not be handled efficiently if there are inadequate channels of communication or sharing of information. The choice of a particular communication network may involve trade-offs between the performance of the work group and the satisfaction of its members.

ANALYSIS OF INDIVIDUAL BEHAVIOUR

In order to understand and to influence the functioning and operation of a group or team, it is necessary to study patterns of interaction and the parts played by individual members. For example, in a more recent publication *Belbin* acknowledges:

> Teamwork does not, of course, guarantee in itself good results. As in sport, there can be good teams and poor teams. And as in sport, it all depends on how the players play together.[11]

It is necessary to balance the requirement for effective performance of the team with respect for the individuality of its members and to achieve the right mix. Not all skilled and capable individuals are necessarily good team players and it may sometimes be an advantage to have someone who will have a more sceptical attitude and be more open to change. For example, *Stanley* refers to the challenge of managing a high-performance team.

> When assembling a high-performance team, you are gathering together energy-packed employees, who are a lot like thoroughbreds. Keep in mind, they have an innate drive to excel. Their thoughts run outside the mundane and familiar. With a flare for the unique, they are extraordinary and can generate new ideas that will keep the organisation ahead of the competition … Along with assigning each member appropriate tasks, the manager must monitor individual performance. By encouraging members to maximise their individual effort, the team will greatly increase the probability of success.[12]

Two of the main methods of analysing the behaviour of individuals in group situations are **sociometry** and **interaction process analysis**.

SOCIOMETRY

Originally developed by *Moreno* in 1953, **sociometry** is a method of indicating the feelings of acceptance or rejection among members of a group.[13] A sociogram is a diagrammatical illustration of the pattern of interpersonal relationships derived from sociometry. The sociogram depicts the choices, preferences, likes or dislikes and interactions between individual members. It can also be used to display the structure of the group and to record the observed frequency and/or duration of contacts among members.

The basis of sociometry, however, is usually 'buddy rating' or 'peer rating'. Each member is asked to nominate or to rate, privately, other members in terms of some given context or characteristic – for example, with whom they communicate, or how influential or how likeable they are. Questions may relate to either work or social activities. For example:

- Who would you most prefer or least prefer as a workmate?
- Who would make a good leader?
- With whom would you choose and not choose to go on holiday?

Positive and negative choices may be recorded for each person, although sometimes positive choices only are required. The choices may be limited to a given number or they may be unlimited. Sometimes individuals may be asked to rank their choices.

Sociograms Members' choices could be shown in tabular form. For example, Table 9.2 shows first and second choices for a group of final-year degree students. Members were asked to indicate, in confidence, those whom they would most prefer to talk to about: (i) a major work-related problem, and (ii) a difficult personal problem. Positive choices only were requested.

An advantage of the diagrammatical illustration, however, is that the sociogram provides a visual description of the sociometric structure of a group. It can indicate cliques and sub-groups, compatibility, and members who are popular, isolated or who act as links. Figure 9.3 gives a simple illustration of an actual sociogram for a group of 15 members with single, positive choices only.

1 G and M are popular (the stars) and most often chosen by members.
2 M is the link between two overlapping cliques, KML and MNO.
3 H and P are unpopular (isolated) and chosen least by members.
4 JKMO is a chain.
5 ABCD is a sub-group and separated from the rest of the members.

It should be noted, however, that there are several methods of compiling and drawing sociograms, and a number of potential criticisms and limitations. Problems also arise over *how* to draw the sociogram and how to interpret the roles of individual members. In the experience of the author, less concern should be given to the concept of sociometry itself. It

Table 9.2	Example of a 'tabulated' sociogram (positive choices only)				

Work-related problem				Personal problem	
Second choice	First choice			First choice	Second choice
		A			///
		B		/	//
///	/	C		//	/
/		D		//	
		E		/	
		F		/	//
	/	G		//	
/////	//	H		//	
		J		/	/
	//	K			
////	///////	L			//
	/	M		/	/
		N			//
/		O		/	
14	14			14	14

Figure 9.3	A simple illustration of a sociogram

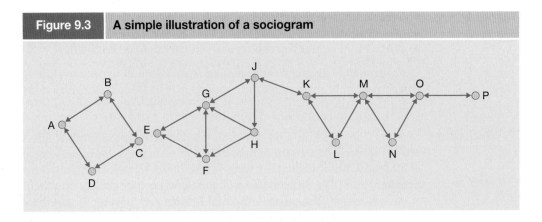

is better seen as a useful vehicle that, if handled sensitively, can serve to encourage meaningful discussions on patterns of social interactions, group behaviour and the perceptions of individual members towards each other.

Critical reflection

How would you argue that all first-year students should be encouraged to participate in a sociometry exercise with members of their class? What possible difficulties or opposition would you foresee?

INTERACTION ANALYSIS

The basic assumption behind **interaction analysis** is that behaviour in groups may be analysed from the viewpoint of its function. This approach has developed largely from the work of *Bales* on methods for the study of small groups. This aim is to provide ways of describing group process and indications of factors influencing the process.[14] In Bales' 'Interaction Process Analysis' every act of behaviour is categorised, as it occurs, under twelve headings. These differentiate between 'task' functions and 'socio-emotional' functions. The categories apply to both verbal interaction and non-verbal interaction.

A Socio-emotional: positive reactions
 1 **Shows solidarity**, raises others' status, gives help, reward.
 2 **Shows tension release**, jokes, laughs, shows satisfaction.
 3 **Agrees**, shows passive acceptance, understands, concurs, complies.
B Task: attempted answers
 4 **Gives suggestion**, direction, implying autonomy for others.
 5 **Gives opinion**, evaluation, analysis, expresses feeling, wish.
 6 **Gives orientation**, information, repeats, clarifies, confirms.
C Task: questions
 7 **Asks for orientation**, information, repetition, confirmation.
 8 **Asks for opinion**, evaluation, analysis, expression of feeling.
 9 **Asks for suggestion**, direction, possible ways of action.
D Socio-emotional: negative reactions
 10 **Disagrees**, shows passive rejection, formality, withholds help.
 11 **Shows tension**, asks for help, withdraws out of field.
 12 **Shows antagonism**, deflates others' status, defends or asserts self.

Task and maintenance functions

If the group is to be effective, then, whatever its structure or the pattern of interrelationships among members, there are two main sets of functions or processes that must be undertaken – task functions and maintenance functions.

● **Task functions** are directed towards problem-solving, the accomplishment of the tasks of the group and the achievement of its goals. Most of the task-oriented behaviour will be concerned with 'production' activities or the exchange and evaluation of ideas and information.
● **Maintenance functions** are concerned with the emotional life of the group and directed towards building and maintaining the group as an effective working unit. Most of the maintenance-oriented behaviour will be concerned with relationships among members, giving encouragement and support, maintaining cohesiveness and the resolution of conflict.

Task and maintenance functions may be performed either by the group leader or by members. Ultimately it is the leader's responsibility to ensure that both sets of functions are carried out and the right balance is achieved between them. The appropriate combination of task-oriented behaviour and maintenance-oriented behaviour is essential to the success and continuity of the group.

In addition to these two types of behaviour, members of a group may say or do something in attempting to satisfy some personal need or goal. The display of behaviour in this way is termed **self-oriented behaviour**. This gives a classification of three main types of functional behaviour that can be exhibited by individual members of a group: **task-oriented, maintenance-oriented** and **self-oriented**.

Classification of member roles
A popular system for the classification of member roles in the study of group behaviour is that devised originally by *Benne and Sheats*.[15] The description of member roles performed in well-functioning groups is classified into three broad headings: **group task roles, group building and maintenance roles** and **individual roles**.

● **Group task roles**. These assume that the task of the group is to select, define and solve common problems. For example, initiator-contributor, opinion seeker, co-ordinator, evaluator, recorder. Any of the roles may be performed by the various members or the group leader.
● **Group building and maintenance roles**. The analysis of member functions is oriented towards activities which build group-centred attitudes or maintain group-centred behaviour. For example, encourager, gatekeeper, standard setter, group commentator. Contributions may involve a number of roles and members or the leader may perform each of these.
● **Individual roles**. These are directed towards the satisfaction of personal needs. Their purpose is not related either to group task or to the group functioning. For example, aggressor, blocker, dominator, help-seeker.

Refresh your understanding
Activity 9B
www.pearsoned.co.uk/ mullins

FRAMEWORKS OF BEHAVIOURAL ANALYSIS

Several frameworks have been designed for observers to categorise patterns of verbal and non-verbal behaviour of group or team members. Observers chart members' behaviour on specially designed forms. These forms may be used to focus on single individuals or to record the total interaction with no indication of individual behaviour. The system of categorisation may distinguish between different behaviours in terms of the functions they are performing. The completed observation forms can be used as a basis for discussion of individual or group performance in terms of the strengths/weaknesses of different functional behaviour.

Use of different frameworks

Different frameworks use a different number of categories for studying behaviour in groups. The interaction analysis method can become complex, especially if non-verbal behaviour is included. Many of the categories in different frameworks may at first sight appear to be very similar. It is important, therefore, to keep the framework simple and easy to understand and complete. The observer's personality, values and attitudes can influence the categorisation of behaviour. For these reasons it is preferable to use trained observers, and wherever possible and appropriate to use more than one observer for each group. The observers can then compare the level of consistency between their categorisations. Observation sheets can be designed to suit the particular requirements of the group situation and the nature of the activity involved. An example of a reasonably simple, ten-point observation sheet used by the author is given in Figure 9.4.

Completing the observation sheet Where appropriate, it may be helpful to note the initial seating, or standing, arrangements of the group. This will help in the identification of group members. Depending on the nature of the activity involved, it might also be possible to indicate main channels of interaction among individuals – for example, to whom eye contact, hand movements or ideas and questions are most frequently directed. A note could also be made of changes in arrangements during, and at the end of, the activity. Headings on the observation sheet are not necessarily exclusive. For example, leadership could be included under Taking Initiative, or under Performing Group Roles. Similarly, the role of humorist could be included under Performing Group Roles, but might also appropriately be included under the heading of Harmonising.

Observers will tend to use their own methods for completing the sheet: for example, a simple stroke or tick for each contribution and perhaps a thick stroke for a particularly significant contribution. Some observers might use some other distinguishing mark to indicate non-verbal behaviour such as body movements, smiles or eye contact. The most important point, however, is that the charting should not become too complex. The observer should feel happy with the framework and be capable of explaining the entries in a meaningful way. Where more than one observer is present there should be some degree of consistency between them.

BALANCE BETWEEN THE TEAM AND THE INDIVIDUAL

Groups and teams are an essential feature in the life of work organisations. Individuals on teams interact extensively with each other and with other teams in the organisation. Team-based management is used to improve communication, co-ordination and co-operation within the organisation.[16] For example, as *Green* maintains:

> *The generally perceived advantages of working in teams are the release of creativity and energy, much more interaction between people satisfying the need to belong … teamworking can improve efficiency by people planning activities together with cooperation and communication. Team members together should be able to identify many ways to improve work organisation; how information, ideas and outputs flow and how team-working can reduce costs and improve productivity.*[17]

We mentioned previously the need to balance effective team performance with respect for the individual members. Although everyone operates fundamentally as a loner at work, *James* draws attention to the need in most jobs for the eponymous teamworking. 'Effective teams need equilibrium, no matter how uneasy. The perfect team will have balance, with each member aware of their role and happy to add that value to the task. The natural leaders for any given job will be in charge and their leadership will be cherished by mutual consent.

Figure 9.4 | **Observation sheet for behaviour in groups**

Nature of group

Nature of activity

Date | *Name of observer(s)*

Initial
arrangement
of group

				C D		
			B			E
	A				F	

Name of group members
(or reference letters)

	A	B	C	D	E	F
Taking initiative – e.g. attempted leadership, seeking suggestions, offering directions						
Brainstorming – e.g. offering ideas or suggestions, however valid						
Offering positive ideas – e.g. making helpful suggestions, attempting to problem-solve						
Drawing in others – e.g. encouraging contributions, seeking ideas and opinions						
Being responsive to others – e.g. giving encouragement and support, building on ideas						
Harmonising – e.g. acting as peacemaker, calming things down, compromising						
Challenging – e.g. seeking justification, showing disagreement in constructive way						
Being obstructive – e.g. criticising, putting others down, blocking contributions						
Clarifying/summarising – e.g. linking ideas, checking progress, clarifying objectives/proposals						
Performing group roles – e.g. spokesperson, recorder, time keeper, humorist						
Other comments						

Being a perfect team member means commitment to the task and overrides personal ambition and glory. Unfortunately this is rarely achieved in the workplace.'[18]

> Successful organisations are good at building teams and exploiting teamwork. People need to be able to work in teams; they need to subordinate their own agenda to the wellbeing of the group. Further, organisations need to foster diversity, which entails respect for the individual and makes group decision making more creative.
>
> M. Kets de Vries, 'Beyond Sloan: Trust is at the Core of Corporate Values'.[19]

In order to help improve the performance of the organisation it is necessary to understand the nature of human relationships and what goes on when groups of people meet. Working in a group is likely to be both a psychologically rewarding, and a potentially demanding experience for the individual. Group performance and the satisfaction derived by individuals are influenced by the interactions among members of the group. As an example of this, Figure 9.5 gives an unsolicited commentary from five final-year business studies degree students after completing a group-based assignment.

Figure 9.5	Unsolicited commentary from students after completing a group-based assignment

WHAT WE FEEL WE HAVE LEARNED FROM WORKING IN A GROUP

1 'We learned that we had to listen to everybody's points of view and take these into consideration.'

2 'We found that we had to be prepared to make certain sacrifices and adopted a democratic decision process. However, if an individual felt very strongly about a specific point and persisted with a valid argument then this had to be included.'

3 'We often felt frustrated.'

4 'It was time-consuming and difficult to schedule meetings due to differences in timetables and preferences in working hours.'

5 'We learned that it is good to pool resources because this increased the overall standard of the piece of work. We feel this was only because we all set high personal standards and expected these from our fellow group members. We learned that it is possible to work in other less productive groups where individual levels of achievement may decrease.'

6 'We learned that it is better to work in a smaller and not a larger group, as there is a tendency for individual ideas to be diluted.'

7 'Groups formed on the basis of friendship alone are not as effective as groups formed with work as the major influence. The former tend to be unproductive.'

8 'We found that it was good to get positive response, encouragement and feedback from team members. Likewise, it was demotivating to receive a negative response.'

9 'We learned a lot about our individual personalities.'

10 'We benefited from sharing personal experiences from our industrial placements.'

11 'It is important to separate work and personal relationships.'

Critical reflection ?????

'The nature of the hierarchical structure and the inevitable role conflicts, power struggles, politics and personality clashes means that individuals will usually complete a task more quickly and effectively than a group or team.' To what extent do you think this is fair comment? What has been your experience?

INDIVIDUAL COMPARED WITH GROUP OR TEAM PERFORMANCE

It is, however, difficult to draw any firm conclusions from a comparison between individual and group or team performance. An example of this can be seen from a consideration of decision-making. Certain groups, such as committees, may be concerned more specifically with decision-making, but all groups must make some decisions. Group decision-making can be costly and time-consuming.

One particular feature of group versus individual performance is the concept of social loafing and the 'Ringelmann effect', which is the tendency for individuals to expend less effort when working as a member of a group than as an individual. A German psychologist, *Ringelmann*, compared the results of individual and group performance on a rope-pulling task. Workers were asked to pull as hard as they could on a rope, performing the task first individually and then with others in groups of varying size. A meter measured the strength of each pull. Although the total amount of force did increase with the size of the work group, the effort expended by each individual member decreased with the result that the total group effort was less than the expected sum of the individual contributions.[20] Replications of the Ringelmann effect have generally been supportive of the original findings.[21]

According to *Hall*, there is a danger of elevating teams into a 'silver bullet' – a magic solution to all business problems. 'It is not that I don't think teams work. They clearly do and it would be difficult to run an organisation of any size if you couldn't create and manage a team … The truth is that teams are not always the right answer to a problem. Often a well-briefed and well-managed group of individuals will do a task fine … A further point is that some very skilled individuals are not good team players.'[22]

However, the general feeling appears to be that the collective power of a group outshines individual performance.[23] 'Even though individuals working on their own are capable of phenomenal ingenuity, working together as a team can produce astounding results and a better decision.'[24] *Guirdham* believes that: 'Compared with individuals, groups can make objectively better decisions to which people feel more commitment, while teams can perform functions and carry out projects better and more efficiently. This can only happen, however, if the people have the special skills and abilities needed.'[25]

One might expect, therefore, a higher standard of decision-making to result from group discussion. However, on the one hand, there is the danger of compromise and decisions being made in line with the 'highest common view' and, on the other hand, there is the phenomenon of the so-called risky-shift.

The risky-shift phenomenon

This suggests that instead of the group taking fewer risks and making safer or more conservative decisions, the reverse is often the case. Pressures for conformity means there is a tendency for groups to make more risky decisions than would individual members of the group on their own. Studies suggest that people working in groups generally advocate more risky alternatives than if they were making an individual decision on the same problem.[26]

Presumably, this is because members do not feel the same sense of responsibility for group decisions or their outcomes. 'A decision which is everyone's is the responsibility of no one.' Other explanations offered for the risky-shift phenomenon include:

1 People inclined to take risks are more influential in group discussions than more conservative people.
2 Risk-taking is regarded as a desirable cultural characteristic that is more likely to be expressed in a social situation such as group working.[27]

However, groups do appear to work well in the evaluation of ideas and to be more effective than individuals for problem-solving tasks requiring a range of knowledge and

Figure 9.7	Advantages of brainstorming

BRAINSTORMING

Brainstorming is a problem-solving/solution-finding technique which can be used by individuals, groups or teams. Its full benefit is gained by sharing ideas and possibilities with others.

The first step is to define the problem or situation to which the group or team wants solutions or ideas. Ideally one person should act as scribe and write up ideas on a flipchart. He or she can contribute, but should not comment on others' suggestions. Every idea should be written up, however far-fetched or silly it might seem, without challenge from others.

Everyone should be encouraged to participate.

When all possibilities have been exhausted, suggestions can be examined, clarified, amended, accepted or rejected.

It may be that several options are accepted as possible ways forward. Reverse brainstorming looks at the possibilities and then brainstorms all the *problems* associated with the ideas. This helps give an objective view of ideas or solutions.

If performed correctly, brainstorming is an excellent, non-threatening way to include all members of a team in the problem-solving/decision-making process. It has the added benefit of producing many and various ideas, some of which will be of no value but others which may be of immediate or future benefit. Creativity is contagious and one idea will spark off another. Often, it is one of the most apparently silly ideas that points the way to a solution.

Brainstorming:

- involves everyone;
- focuses the mind;
- encourages creativity;
- meets individual needs for team inclusion;
- encourages communication – listening, information sharing;
- maximises ideas/possible solutions to problems;
- minimises risk of overlooking elements of the problem or issue under question.

Source: Bishop, S. and Taylor, D., *Developing Your Staff*, Pitman Publishing/Longman Training (1994). Reproduced with permission from Pearson Education Ltd.

Aid to creativity Any procedure which aids the process of creativity should be welcomed and there are a number of potential positive achievements in terms of related structural techniques for stimulating innovation. These include the Delphi technique and quality circles.

The **Delphi technique** is based on multiple, anonymous inputs from individual members of the group. Ideas and suggestions are recorded by a central manager and then recirculated to other members for their feedback. The central manager collates the responses and continues the circulation process again until consensus is reached. Although a time-consuming process, the Delphi technique helps to overcome the limitations of face-to-face brainstorming and symptoms of groupthink.

QUALITY CIRCLES

A **quality circle** is a group of people within an organisation who meet on a regular basis to identify, analyse and solve problems relating to quality, productivity or other aspects of day-to-day working arrangements using problem-solving techniques. Although quality circles actually originated in America they were exported to Japan and are more usually associated with their wide applications (since 1962) in Japanese manufacturing industries, as well as in some white-collar operations. Since the refinement of the quality circle process in Japan there has been increasing interest in their use in America and Britain as well as in many other countries. In America, quality circles appear to have been first implemented in 1974.[35]

The essential features of a quality circle group include the following:

- membership is voluntary;
- the group usually numbers between five and ten members;
- membership is normally drawn from people undertaking similar work or from the same work station;
- the group selects the problems to be tackled and the methods of operation;
- a leader can be chosen from within the group but is usually the immediate supervisor;
- the group members receive training in communication and problem-solving skills, quality control techniques and group processes;
- the group recommends solutions to management and, where possible, has authority to implement agreed solutions.

Potential limitations There are a number of potential limitations on the effectiveness of quality circles:

- Any attempt at solving organisational problems cannot be considered as a single dimension. The promotion of quality circles needs to be approached in terms of possible effects on related sub-systems of the organisation, for example human resource management and industrial relations procedures.
- Quality circles can rely too heavily on intrinsic motivation and the assumption that involvement and recognition are sufficient rewards in themselves. This reflects a major difference between the operation of quality circles in the West and in Japan. Workers in Japan appear, for example, to accept that financial gains will go to the organisation.
- The greater involvement of members in problem-solving and decision-making may be resented by some groups, for example quality control departments, or by managers or trade union officials who may be suspicious of possible challenges to their traditional authority.

The application of quality circles does appear simple and straightforward, but early experience must be viewed in the context of Japanese culture and management systems. However, quality circles offer a number of potential benefits. They provide problem-solving at a more local level and the participation of employees in work-related decisions which concern them. Quality circles do work and have been used successfully by a number of British organisations. There are some doubts, however, as to the extent to which the hopes for, or potential benefits of, quality circles are realised fully in organisations.[36]

GROUP DYNAMICS

Interest in the study of group process and behaviour has led to the development of group dynamics and a range of group training methods aimed at increasing group effectiveness through improving social interaction skills. A central feature of group dynamics is **sensitivity training**, in which members of a group direct attention to the understanding of their own behaviour and to perceiving themselves as others see them. The objectives are usually stated as:

- to increase sensitivity (the ability to perceive accurately how others react to oneself);
- diagnostic ability (the skill of assessing behavioural relationships between others and reasons for such behaviour); and
- behavioural flexibility or action skill (the ability to relate one's behaviour to the requirements of the situation).

T-groups

A usual method of sensitivity training (which is increasingly used as a generic term) is the T-group (training group), sometimes called laboratory training. A **T-group** has been defined as:

*an approach to human relations training which, broadly speaking, provides participants with an oppor-
tunity to learn more about themselves and their impact on others, and in particular to learn how to
function more effectively in face-to-face situations.*[37]

The original form of a T-group is a small, leaderless, unstructured, face-to-face grouping.
The group normally numbers between eight and twelve members who may be strangers to
each other or who may come from the same organisation (a family group). A deliberate
attempt is made to minimise any status differentials among members. There is no agenda or
planned activities. Trainers are present to help guide the group, but do not usually take an
active role or act as formal leader. The agenda becomes the group's own behaviour in
attempting to cope with the lack of structure or planned activities. Training is intended to
concentrate on process rather than content, that is on the feeling level of communication
rather than the informational value of communication.

Faced with confusion and lack of direction, individuals will act in characteristic ways.
With the guidance of the trainers these patterns of behaviour become the focus of attention
for the group. Participants are encouraged to examine their self-concepts and to be more
receptive to the feelings and behaviours of others. Feedback received by individuals from
other members of the group is the main mechanism for learning. This feedback creates a
feeling of anxiety and tension, and the individual's self-examination leads to consideration
of new values, attitudes and behaviour. Typically, the group meets for a 1–2 hour session
each day for up to a fortnight. The sessions are supported by related lectures, study groups,
case studies and other exercises.

**The Johari
window**
A simple framework for looking at self-insight, which is used frequently to help individuals
in the T-group process, is the 'Johari window' (*see* Figure 9.8). This classifies behaviour in
matrix form between what is known–unknown to self and what is known–unknown to
others.[38] A central feature of the T-group is reduction of the individual's 'hidden' behaviour
through self-disclosure and reduction of the 'blind' behaviour through feedback from others.

- **Hidden behaviour** is that which the individual wishes to conceal from, or not to com-
 municate to, other group members. It is part of the private self. An important role of the
 group is to establish whether members conceal too much, or too little, about themselves
 from other members.
- **The blind area** (that is behaviour known to others but unknown to self) includes man-
 nerisms, gestures and tone of voice and represents behaviour of the impact of which on
 others the individual is unaware. This is sometimes referred to as the 'bad breath' area.

Members must establish an atmosphere of openness and trust in order that hidden and
blind behaviours are reduced and the public behaviour enhanced.

Figure 9.8	The Johari window

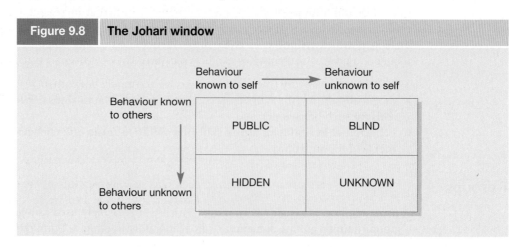

Value and effectiveness of T-groups

Reactions to the value and effectiveness of T-group training are very mixed. The experience can be disturbing and unpleasant, at least for some members. T-group training is difficult to evaluate objectively and there is still a main problem of the extent to which training is transferred 'back home' to practical work situations. However, a number of studies do suggest that participation as a member of a T-group does increase interpersonal skills, induce change and lead to open communications and more flexible behaviour. T-groups probably do result in a change of behaviour but it is not always clear whether such change is positive or related to improved organisational performance.[39]

T-groups now take a number of forms. Some place emphasis on the understanding of group processes, others place more emphasis on the development of the individual's self-awareness and feelings towards the behaviour of other people. They are now used frequently as a means of attempting to improve managerial development and organisational performance. The *Blake and Mouton* managerial grid seminars, discussed in Chapter 12, can be seen as an applied, and refined, form of T-group. A number of training packages have been designed, often under the broad heading of interpersonal skills, which are less confrontational and less disturbing for participants.

Critical reflection

'Sensitivity training programmes are an unnecessary activity that have no practical value as a means of increasing the long-term standard of group performance, and for many people they are an embarrassing and demeaning experience.' Do you think this is fair comment or under what circumstances can such programmes be justified? How do you feel about participating in such a programme?

SELF-MANAGED WORK GROUPS

An important development in work redesign and job enrichment is a form of work organisation based on self-managed work groups (or autonomous work groups). This involves a socio-technical approach with technological processes, production methods and the way in which work is carried out integrated with the social system of the organisation, including the informal group structure. Members of the group assume greater autonomy and responsibility for the effective performance of the work. With greater empowerment the belief is that members will feel more committed to the objectives and operations of the group. Key features of the self-managed work group include the following:

- specific goals are set for the group but members decide the best means by which these goals are to be achieved;
- group members have greater freedom and choice and wider discretion over the planning, execution and control of their work;
- collectively members of the group have the necessary variety of expertise and skills to successfully undertake the tasks of the group;
- the level of external supervision is reduced and the role of supervisor becomes more one of giving advice and support to the group;
- feedback and evaluation are related to the performance of the group as a whole.

There is, however, a potential danger that a self-managed group is more likely to establish its own values and norms (discussed in Chapter 8) that may be at variance with those of the organisation.

Popularity and applications

Wilson points out that self-directed teams feature high in the list of most popular management tools in a study by the Institute of Management with Bain & Company. 'Once people are fully committed to teamworking and enthusiastic about getting on with it, training can be a rewarding experience for everyone involved and also great fun.'[40] However, despite the apparent potential advantages, to date self-managed teams appear to have only limited applications. For example, *Torrington, Hall and Taylor* suggest that teamwork has evolved from autonomous working groups and although it is still used as a means of empowering employees and facilitating their development, there is of late a more critical perspective. 'There remain many strong supporters of teamwork and many organisations are committed to this approach, although it is also criticised as management control by another means and has often failed to improve performance.'[41]

Autonomy and control

A strong supporter of the idea of the autonomous work group is *Waterman*. In order to build spirit, morale and commitment in any organisation Waterman believes that people should be in control of at least some part of their lives and that they should be given some influence over things that affect them. The quintessence of this belief is the self-managing team – groups of three to ten people who work without any direct supervision. Employees should be organised into teams that cut across old boundaries, trained and placed in jobs that challenge their abilities, given the information they need, informed of what they need to accomplish and then turned loose.[42]

ACAS also strongly supports autonomous work groups for both increased competitiveness and for the quality of working life.

> The concept of autonomous teams may be misleading as teams will always be answerable to management and rely on the provision of resources and other support. Nevertheless, one of the best ways to ensure that teams continue to develop is to move towards self-regulation – an important way of monitoring the progress of teams is to assess the level of dependence on management. It is for management to encourage progress by helping the teams develop greater independence.
>
> Reorganising the workforce into teams is not easy but when successfully developed, teamworking has been shown to be a way of improving competitiveness and at the same time enhancing the quality of working life for employees.[43]

BUILDING SUCCESSFUL TEAMS

Whatever the debate about a comparison between individual and group or team performance, or self-managed groups, effective teamworking is of increasing importance in modern organisations. This demands that the manager must be aware of, and pay attention to, a number of interrelated factors, including:

- clarification of objectives and available resources;
- organisational processes and the clarification of roles;
- empowerment, decision-making and channels of communication;
- patterns of interaction, and attention to both task and maintenance functions;
- social processes and the informal organisation;
- management systems and style of leadership;
- training and development.

The effectiveness of the team will also be influenced by the tasks to be undertaken, the nature of technology and the organisational environment. Ultimately, however, the performance of the team will be determined very largely by the characteristics of its members. The nature of group personality means that what works well for one team may not work well for an apparently similar team in the organisation.

As *Wilson* points out, for example, although teamworking, like most management ideas, is very simple, nevertheless this simplicity conceals a great challenge.

> *The principles of teamworking may be easily understood, but the task of installing it can be quite daunting. Introducing teamworking is not a straightforward grafting job, the simple matter of adding a new idea to those already in place. It is about making a fundamental change in the way people work. Every teamworking application is different. Each organisation, department and individual group is faced with unique problems and in some situations it is more about getting rid of old ways of doing things than injecting new ones.*
>
> J. Wilson, 'Building Teams – with Attitude'[44]

A concept map of effective work groups is set out in Figure 9.9.

Skills for successful teamwork The increasing need for collaboration and teamwork together with recognition for the individual has highlighted the need for attention to social skills and effectively relationships among people. If people are not working together they are essentially a collection of individuals. *Douglas* refers to the importance of helping people to master the so-called 'soft' skills:

> *Organisations in most sectors – and especially in ones that are particularly demanding from a scientific or technical point of view – are operating in environments where collaboration, teamwork, and an awareness of the commercial consequences and implications of technical research are as important as scientific and technical skills themselves. Personnel with scientific and technical skills significantly disproportionate to their 'people' skills – by which I primarily mean people management capabilities and the knowledge of how to work with maximum effectiveness as part of a team – are increasingly unlikely to be as much of an asset to their organisation as they ought to be.[45]*

However, Douglas points out that as we all interact with people to a greater or lesser extent in our everyday lives, there is a tendency to assume that people management skills are merely an extension of our natural abilities. In fact, people management skills are the more difficult and rare type of skill but to a large extent they can be learned.

Cloke and Goldsmith refer to the special skills required for successful teamwork and list ten skills team members can develop in order to build innovative self-managing teams. All of these skills are interrelated, mutually reinforcing and dependent upon each of the others.[46]

- **Skill of self-management** – overcoming obstacles together and in the process building a sense of ownership, responsibility, commitment and efficiency within each team member.
- **Skill of communication** – collaboratively developing their skills in becoming better listeners, commiserating with others, reframing communications so they can be heard, and communicating honestly about things that really matter.
- **Skill of leadership** – creating opportunities for each member to serve as leader. Employees need to be skilled in linking, organising, co-ordinating, collaborating, planning, facilitating, coaching and mentoring.
- **Skill of responsibility** – everyone is personally responsible not only for their own work but for the work of every other member of the team. Team members have to exercise responsibility in order to become self-managing.
- **Skill of supportive diversity** – collaborative experiences allow team members to overcome prejudices and biases and not create winners and losers, reject outsiders or mistrust people who are different.
- **Skills of feedback and evaluation** – essential to improving learning, team communication and the quality of products, processes and relationships. In a true team environment, self-critical perspectives are expected, welcomed, acknowledged and rewarded.

Figure 9.9 Concept map of effective work groups

EFFECTIVE WORK GROUPS

- GROUP EFFECTIVENESS
- FACTORS INFLUENCING GROUP EFFECTIVENESS
- BENEFITS OF EFFECTIVE WORKGROUPS

ORGANISATION

- Individual contributions when taken together can result in a greater level of achievement (synergy).
- Groups can often work better at problem solving than can individuals.
- The employees can see more clearly that they are undertaking a process of employee involvement in the organisation.
- Decisions become collectively shared, leading to easier implementation.
- Communication channels become less fragmented and more efficient.
- Conflict resolution is more often handled at the workgroup level.

BENEFITS
- INDIVIDUAL
- ORGANISATION

MANAGEMENT
- TEAM COMPOSITION

OVERALL MANAGEMENT

Management needs to deal with the following aspects:
- Setting appropriate team tasks
- Choosing team members carefully, having regard to:
 - individual skills
 - personality
 - availability, if a potential team member works on more than one project
 - the correct balance of skills
- Providing appropriate support
 - information
 - resources
 - such training as may be needed
 - opportunities for the team to build itself before & during the project
 - arrangements to monitor & inform the team over the project period.

GROUP EFFECTIVENESS

Groups are effective when:
- The group achieves the target set
 - on time
 - to acceptable quality standards
 - within budget

 AND
- the group members achieve personal rewards including
 - recognition of effort by other group members
 - recognition by the organisation
 - encouragement in their efforts.

IT IS ONLY IN LARGE TEAMS THAT EACH ROLE IS CARRIED BY ONE PERSON – MORE USUALLY, MORE THAN ONE ROLE IS HELD BY EACH INDIVIDUAL. CARE SHOULD BE TAKEN THAT ROLES DO NOT CONFLICT.

INDIVIDUAL

Individual needs can be satisfied by:
- providing support;
- maintaining morale;
- having a small group to identify with;
- efforts being more easily recognised;
- enhanced mental security;
- a feeling of protection.

NOTE THAT NOT ALL EMPLOYEES WORK HAPPILY AS MEMBERS OF TEAMS. ORGANISATIONS NEWLY ADOPTING A PROJECT TEAM-BASED APPROACH NEED TO TAKE INTO ACCOUNT WORKING PREFERENCES OF EXISTING EMPLOYEES.

TEAM COMPOSITION AND ROLES (after BELBIN)

LEADER................................ Co-ordinates the team activity
SHAPER................................ Ensures the team attends to the task
PLANT................................... Source of ideas
EVALUATOR......................... Examines and dissects ideas
RESOURCE INVESTIGATOR...... Seeks resources inside and outside the team
COMPANY WORKER.............. Schedules tasks and activities
FINISHER............................. Ties up loose ends
TEAM WORKER.................... Backs up the team and maintains social relationships

Source: Training Learning Consultancy Ltd, Bristol, England. Reproduced with permission.

- **Skill of strategic planning** – to identify challenges and opportunities collaboratively and influence the environment in which problems emerge. Strategic planning encourages employees to think long term, be proactive and preventative and focus on solutions rather than problems.
- **Skill of shaping successful meetings** – team meetings can be streamlined and made shorter, more satisfying and more productive, and result in expanded consensus.
- **Skill of resolving conflicts** – encouraging team members to improve skills in problem solving, collaborative negotiation, responding to difficult behaviour and conflict resolution.
- **Skill of enjoyment** – most team members enjoy working together to accomplish difficult tasks. Their pleasure derives from meeting high-performance challenges and producing results that benefits themselves and their teams, organisations and communities.

The role of team leader Building successful teams also requires effective leadership with an emphasis on trust, clear communications, full participation and self-management. 'The influence and usefulness of team leaders comes, not from their delivery of traditional supervisory and control methods, but from their ability to lead from the front and in training, coaching and counselling their team members to high standards of performance.'[47]

In her discussion of the 'democratic enterprise' (organisations which can flourish economically and can also be places of excitement and stimulation, fulfilment and tranquillity), *Gratton* maintains that it is the leaders of the teams across the organisation who make the company vision a reality on a day-to-day basis. The team leaders are the creator of space in which choice and freedom can be exercised; they delineate the obligations and accountabilities contained within the business goals; they become a role model for how members should behave; and they bring the philosophy of autonomy and personal development to realisation by the manner in which they act as mentor and coach.[48]

Continuous process of improvement and innovation

The requirement for continual development and improvement is a necessary part of effective teamwork. However, as *Riches* points out: 'Understandably, teams are pre-occupied with getting the job done. Few teams regularly take time out to reflect on how the team itself is working and what it needs to do to improve the way its modus operandi ... Even fewer set measurable objectives for team functioning and/or get feedback from internal and external customers about the team's effectiveness.'[49]

The ACAS advisory booklet concludes that although self-regulation is necessary if the potential of teamworking is to be realised, teams will always need some degree of management direction. The task of management is to oversee the development of teams and provide the necessary support and training. Even when in place, teams will need constant monitoring and development. Teamworking is not a finite project but a process of continuous improvement and innovation.

The introduction of teamworking is a major step for an organisation to take. It is important that management, trade unions and employees ensure they know how teamworking will contribute to their business strategy and that it is likely to involve a long-term transformation ... The early challenge and excitement of establishing teams may fade and it is easy for organisations to accept a level of performance which is short of optimum ... In order to achieve high performance, teams require regular changes and challenges. These may include: changes to team personnel; new tasks; re-examining the contribution the team makes to the overall business aims; and ensuring that the team has regular dealings with other teams.[50]

Refresh your understanding
Activity 9D
www.pearsoned.co.uk/
mullins

Critical reflection

All this discussion about group membership and building successful teams is very interesting and sounds fine in the classroom. But how far do you think it works in practice, for example with managing groups of workers in a restaurant kitchen, on a production assembly line, in a gay pub, or with professionals such as lecturers, doctors or lawyers?

MANAGEMENT IN THE NEWS

Winning teams

Football's example can help companies score

John Kay

Like many lecturers, I have a library of presentation slides. The most frequently used is 15 years old and relates the performance of English soccer league clubs to their expenditure on players. Both wages and transfer fees over a 25-year period are included. The message is that you get what you pay for. There is a strong relationship between cash spent and average league position. There were some outliers, but the outstanding story was Liverpool. Liverpool and Manchester United had invested more than others. But while the performance of Manchester United was exactly what our equations predicted, Liverpool had done much better. Manchester United had assembled a group of outstanding players. Liverpool had assembled an outstanding team.

The story of the 2006 World Cup is that outstanding teams defeated groups of outstanding players. All players in top sides are very good. The reason the countries in the final four were not the ones pundits expected was that their predictions were based on the quality of individual players. But the trophy goes not to the best players but to the best team.

My slide is popular because references to football bring back to life audiences battered into somnolence by harangues on transformational change. The serious purpose is to illustrate that business success is not simply a matter of acquiring the best people, technology or resources. Businesses create value by establishing a difference between the cost of their input and the effectiveness of their output. The Italian team was more than the sum of its parts, the Brazilian team was not.

The difference between output and value added is relevant to every type of business, but especially important for the professional services company – whether it is a football team or an investment. Goldman Sachs and McKinsey do not simply attract exceptional people – so did Manchester United and

Is a team more than the sum of its parts? Would another group of equally talented players have had Liverpool's successes?

Brazil. Like Liverpool and Italy, these businesses achieve more than would be predicted from the quality of the people alone. That makes these companies very profitable. By sharing that excess profitability with their talented employees they keep them in post and maintain their leadership position.

But what are the characteristics that distinguish a great team from a group of great players? Organisational knowledge belongs to the business rather than the individuals who make up the business. My group was impressed by the systematic way in which Liverpool assembled through post-match debriefing and disseminated through pre-match briefing extensive information about other players, clubs and pitches. But their main explanation of Liverpool's relative success came from a simple economic model of the game of football. A player can kick for goal or pass the ball to a better situated player. His choice will depend on the degree to which his incentives relate to the performance of the team rather than his performance as an individual and on his

expectations about whether the next player will shoot or pass in turn. Because an individual's behaviour depends on expectations of the behaviour of others, teams will become locked into particular states. Individuals joining a team will find it best to conform to the local style, so these equilibria are stable.

That is why transformational change cannot be achieved by talking about it and my audiences were right to be more interested in the footballing metaphor than in the guff that had gone before.

Source: Kay, J., 'Football's example can help companies score', *Financial Times*, 10 July 2006. Copyright © 2006 The Financial Times Limited, reproduced with permission.

Discussion questions

1 Analyse the commentary on teamwork in this article using the concept map outline of effective work groups given in Figure 9.9. Which features of the model appear to be present and which are missing?

2 Critically evaluate the comments about Liverpool football club in terms of communication patterns. What skills and activities might help managers to achieve effective communication between the members of their team?

SYNOPSIS

● Organisational performance and the satisfaction derived by individuals are influenced by the interactions among members of the group. Members must work well together as a team and there must be a spirit of unity and co-operation. One of the most popular analyses of individual roles is that developed by *Belbin*, who suggests nine key contributions or team-roles for successful groups. The level of interaction is influenced by the channels of communication. There are five main types of communication networks – wheel, circle, all-channel, Y and chains.

● In order to understand and influence the functioning and operation of a group, it is necessary to study the behaviour of individual members. Two main methods are: (i) sociometry, and (ii) interaction analysis. Sociometry is usually based on 'buddy rating' or 'peer rating'. It is a method of indicating feelings of acceptance and/or rejection among members of a group. A sociogram gives a diagrammatical illustration of the pattern of interpersonal relationships derived from sociometry.

● Interaction analysis is based on the assumption that the behaviour of individuals may be analysed from the viewpoint of its function or process. Two essential functions necessary for the success and continuity of a group are: (i) task-oriented behaviour, and (ii) maintenance-oriented behaviour. In addition, members may display self-oriented behaviour. Several frameworks have been designed for observers to categorise patterns of verbal and non-verbal behaviour of members. It is important, however, that the frameworks do not become too complex.

● Groups and teams are an essential feature in the life of the organisation but there must be a balance with respect for the individual members. Working in a group is likely to be a rewarding but also potentially demanding experience for the individual. In order to help improve the performance of the organisation it is necessary to understand the nature of human relationships and what goes on when groups of people meet. It is difficult to draw any firm comparison with individual performance. Group decision-making would appear to offer a number of advantages but can be adversely affected by the 'risky-shift' phenomenon and by 'groupthink'.

● Brainstorming (or thought showers) is an attempt to help a group produce more creative problem-solving ideas. However, there appears to be some doubt about the effectiveness of brainstorming over an individual working under the same conditions. Interest in the study of groups and teams has led to the development of training methods aimed at improving social interaction skills and self-insight. Attention is also given to self-managed (or autonomous) work groups. Quality circles are another potential aid to group problem-solving, innovation and creativity.

● Building successful teams is of increasing importance in modern organisations. It is necessary to take into account a variety of interrelated factors, including the characteristics and behaviour of their members, social skills and relationships among people and effective leadership with an emphasis on trust and clear communications. The task of management is to oversee the development of teams and provide the necessary support and training. Although self-regulation is necessary if the potential of teamworking is to be realised, teams will always need some degree of management direction. The requirement for continual development and improvement is a necessary part of effective teamwork.

Your tasks

1 Critically review Reed's account of Innocent's approach to its staff in relation to the difference between 'task' functions and 'maintenance' functions as described on p. 339.

2 Do you think Innocent is vulnerable to 'groupthink'? What measures could the management team put in place to avoid such a risk?

3 Discuss way in which the Belbin model of team roles might be applied to the recruitment and selection of new team members in growing organisations like Innocent. Consider and outline both its strengths and its limitations.

NOTES AND REFERENCES

1 Obeng, E. *All Change*, Pitman Publishing (1994).

2 Crainer, S. *Key Management Ideas: Thinkers that changed the management world*, Third edition, Financial Times Prentice Hall (1998), p. 238.

3 'Teamwork: Success Through People', Advisory Booklet, ACAS, April 2003, pp. 6–7.

4 Guirdham, M. *Interactive Behaviour at Work*, Third edition, Financial Times Prentice Hall (2002), p. 463.

5 Belbin, R. M. *Management Teams: Why They Succeed or Fail*, Butterworth-Heinemann (1981).

6 Belbin, R. M. *Team Roles at Work*, Butterworth-Heinemann (1993).

7 Arroba, T. and Wedgwood-Oppenheim, F. 'Do Senior Managers Differ in The Public and Private Sector? An Examination of Team-Role Preferences', *Journal of Managerial Psychology*, vol. 9, no.1, 1994, pp. 13–16.

8 Fisher, S. G., Hunter, T. A. and Macrosson, W. D. K. 'The Distribution of Belbin Team Roles among UK Managers', *Personnel Review*, vol. 29, no. 2, 2000, pp. 124–40.

9 Bavelas, A. 'A Mathematical Model for Group Structures', *Applied Anthropology*, vol. 7, 1948, pp. 19–30, and Bavelas, A. 'Communication Patterns in Task-Oriented Groups', in Lasswell, H. N. and Lerner, D. (eds) *The Policy Sciences*, Stanford University Press (1951).

10 Leavitt, H. J. 'Some Effects of Certain Communication Patterns on Group Performance', *Journal of Abnormal and Social Psychology*, vol. 46, 1951, pp. 38–50. See also: Leavitt, H. J. *Managerial Psychology*, Fourth edition, University of Chicago Press (1978).

11 Belbin, R. M. *Changing The Way We Work*, Butterworth-Heinemann (1997), p. 13.

12 Stanley. T. J. 'The Challenge of Managing a High-Performance Team', *SuperVision*, vol. 63, no. 7, July 2002, pp. 10–12.

13 Moreno, J. L. *Who Shall Survive?* Beacon House (1953). See also: Moreno, J. L. and Jennings, H. H. *The Sociometry Reader*, Free Press of Glencoe (1960).

14 Bales, R. F. 'A Set of Categories for the Analysis of Small Group Interaction', *American Sociological Review*, vol. 15, April 1950, pp. 257–63.

15 Benne, K. D. and Sheats, P. 'Functional Roles of Group Members', *Journal of Social Issues*, vol. 4, 1948, pp. 41–9.

16 Whitfield, J. M., Anthony, W. P. and Kacmar, K. M. 'Evaluation of Team-Based Management: A Case Study', *Journal of Organizational Change Management*, vol. 8, no. 2, 1995, pp. 17–28.

17 Green, J. R. 'Team Building in Practice', *Chartered Secretary*, November 1997, pp. 34–5.

18 James, J. *Body Talk at Work*, Judy Piatkus (2001), p. 212.

19 Kets de Vries, M. 'Beyond Sloan: Trust is at the Core of Corporate Values', in Pickford, J. (ed.), *Financial Times Mastering Management 2.0*, Financial Times Prentice Hall (2001), p. 268.

20 Kravitz, D. A. and Martin, B. 'Ringelmann Rediscovered: The Original Article', *Journal of Personality and Social Psychology*, May 1986, pp. 936–41.

21 See, for example: Karau, S. J. and Williams, K. D. 'Social Loafing: A Meta-Analysis Review and Theoretical Integration', *Journal of Personality and Social Psychology*, October 1993, pp. 681–706.

22 Hall, P. 'Team Solutions Need Not Be the Organisational Norm', *Professional Manager*, July 2001, p. 45.

23 See, for example: Blanchard, K. and Bowles, S. *High Five: None of Us Is As Smart As All of Us*, HarperCollins Business (2001).

24 Stanley, T. J. 'The Challenge of Managing a High-Performance Team', *SuperVision*, vol. 63, no. 7, July 2002, pp. 10–12.

25 Guirdham, M. *Interactive Behaviour at Work*, Third edition, Financial Times Prentice Hall (2002), p. 498.

26 Kogan, N. and Wallach, M. A. 'Risk-Taking as a Function of the Situation, the Person and the Group', in Newcomb, T. M. (ed.) *New Directions in Psychology III*, Holt, Rinehart and Winston (1967).

27 For a comprehensive review of the 'risky-shift' phenomenon, see, for example: Clarke, R. D. 'Group Induced Shift Towards Risk: A Critical Appraisal', *Psychological Bulletin*, vol. 76, 1971, pp. 251–70. See also: Vecchio, R. P. *Organizational Behavior*, Third edition, Harcourt Brace and Company (1995).

28 Shaw, M. E. *Group Dynamics*, McGraw-Hill (1976).

29 Janis, J. L. *Victims of Groupthink*, Houghton Mifflin (1972) and Janis, J. L. *Groupthink*, Second edition, Houghton Mifflin (1982).

30 Hambrick, D. 'Putting the Team into Top Management', in Pickford, J. (ed.), *Financial Times Mastering Management 2.0*, Financial Times Prentice Hall (2001), p. 289.

31 Misselhorn, H, *Understanding and Managing Your Organization*, Third edition M.O.D. Consulting (2001).

32 Osborn, A.F. *Applied Imagination: Principles and Procedures of Creative Thinking*, Scribner's (1963).

33 See, for example: Bishop, S. and Taylor, D. *Developing Your Staff*, Pitman Publishing/Longman Training, (1994).

34 See, for example: Waterman, R. *The Frontiers of Excellence*, Nicholas Brearley (1994).

35 Meyer, G. W. and Scott, R. G. 'Quality Circles: Panacea or Pandora's Box', *Organizational Dynamics*, Spring 1985, pp. 34–50.

36 See, for example: Hill, S. 'Why Quality Circles Failed But Total Quality Management Might Succeed', *British Journal of Industrial Relations*, vol. 29, no. 4, 1991, pp. 541–68.

37 Cooper, C. L. and Mangham, I. L. (eds) *T-Groups: A Survey of Research*, Wiley (1971), p. v.

38 Luft, J. *Group Processes: An Introduction to Group Dynamics*, Second edition, National Press (1970). (The term 'Johari Window' was derived from a combination of the first names of the original authors, Joseph Luft and Harry Ingham.)

39 See, for example: McKenna, E. Business *Psychology and Organisational Behaviour*, Lawrence Erlbaum (1994).

40 Wilson, J. 'Building Teams – with Attitude', *Professional Manager*, September 1998, pp. 12–13.

41 Torrington, D., Hall, L. and Taylor, S. *Human Resource Management*, Sixth edition, Financial Times Prentice Hall, (2005), p. 280.

42 Waterman, R. *The Frontiers of Excellence*, Nicholas Brearley (1994).

43 *Teamwork: Success Through People*, Advisory Booklet, ACAS, April 2003, p. 34.

44 Wilson, J. 'Building Teams – with Attitude', *Professional Manager*, September 1998, p. 13.

45 Douglas, M. 'Why Soft Skills Are an Essential Part of the Hard World of Business', *Manager, The British Journal of Administrative Management*, New Year 2003, pp. 34–5.

46 Cloke, K. and Goldsmith, J. *The End of Management and the Rise of Organizational Democracy*, Jossey-Bass (2002).

47 'Teamwork: *Success Through People*', Advisory Booklet, ACAS, April 2003, p. 31.

48 Gratton, L. *The Democratic Enterprise*, Financial Times Prentice Hall (2004).

49 Riches, A. 'Emotionally Intelligent Teams', Organisational Change & Leadership Development, www.anneriches.com.au [accessed 28 January 2006].

50 *Teamwork: Success Through People*. Advisory Booklet, ACAS, April 2003, p. 34.

51 *The Independent*, 'Innocent Drinks wins "company of the year" award', 4 July 2006.

52 A list of its awards under various categories can be located on the company website, www.innocentdrinks.co.uk

53 Richard Reed, 4 February 2005. Speech to the Advancing Enterprise 2005 Conference, available at HM Treasury website: www.hm-treasury.gov.uk

54 Not only at Innocent's own website, but also by in a major article by Rowan Gibson at www.rethinkinggroup.com.

55 Girton Newsletter Spring 2006; Alumni Interview with Dan Germain, pp. 22–3.

56 Richard Reed 'Diary of an Entrepreneur', *The Guardian*, 15 October 2005.

57 Richard Reed 'Diary of an Entrepreneur', *The Guardian*, 17 November 2005.

THE NATURE OF LEADERSHIP

> **Leadership is not about the leader, it is about how he or she builds the confidence of everyone else. Leaders are responsible for both the big structures that serve as the cornerstone of confidence, and for the human touches that shape a positive emotional climate to inspire and motivate people ... Leaders deliver confidence by espousing high standards in their messages, exemplifying these standards in the conduct they model and establishing formal mechanisms to provide a structure for acting on those standards.**

Rosabeth Moss Kanter – prominent business thought leader and award-winning author

Confidence: Leadership and the Psychology of Turnarounds, Random House (2004), pp. 325–6

An essential part of management is co-ordinating the activities of people and guiding their efforts towards the goals and objectives of the organisation. This involves the process of leadership and the choice of an appropriate form of action and behaviour. Leadership is a central feature of organisational performance. The manager needs to understand the nature of leadership influence, factors that determine relationships with other people and the effectiveness of the leadership relationship.

Learning outcomes

After completing this chapter you should be able to:

- explain the meaning and importance of leadership in work organisations;
- contrast main approaches to, and studies of, leadership;
- examine leadership as an aspect of behaviour, and different styles of leadership;
- explore contingency theories of leadership;
- evaluate the nature and main components of transformational leadership and inspirational leadership;
- explain the leadership relationship and the exercise of leadership power and influence;
- review the variables which determine effective leadership and development.

Critical reflection

Leadership is all about determination, personality and innate ability at the right time for a particular competitive situation. Many business leaders have no formal academic qualifications and each has their own individual leadership style. Does this suggest that great leaders are born to be so? Or do you think it is possible to train a person to be an effective leader?

THE MEANING OF LEADERSHIP

There are many ways of looking at **leadership** and many interpretations of its meaning. Leadership might be interpreted in simple terms, such as 'getting others to follow' or 'getting people to do things willingly', or interpreted more specifically, for example as 'the use of authority in decision-making'. It may be exercised as an attribute of position or because of personal knowledge or wisdom. Leadership might be based on a function of personality or it can be seen as a behavioural category. It may also be viewed in terms of the role of the leaders and their ability to achieve effective performance from others. According to *Crainer* there are over 400 definitions of leadership and 'it is a veritable minefield of misunderstanding and difference through which theorists and practitioners must tread warily'.[1]

It is difficult, therefore, to generalise about leadership, but essentially it is a **relationship through which one person influences the behaviour or actions of other people**. This means that the process of leadership cannot be separated from the activities of groups and effective teambuilding.

According to *Useem*, leadership is a matter of making a difference. It entails changing an organisation and making active choices among plausible alternatives, and depends on the development of others and mobilising them to get the job done.

> *Leadership is at its best when the vision is strategic, the voice persuasive and the results tangible. In the study of leadership, an exact definition is not essential but guiding concepts are needed. The concepts should be general enough to apply to many situations, but specific enough to have tangible implications for what we do.*[2]

However, Useem suggests vision and strategy have been joined by new critical capabilities – leading out and leading up. With the increasing use of outsourcing, managers need the skill to lead out: not just to send work downwards to subordinates but also to have a talent for lateral leadership in arranging work with colleagues. And as organisations decentralise authority, managers must be able to lead their own bosses, to have the capacity to lead up and muster support from above as well as below.

Inspiring and influencing other people

Today, leadership is increasingly associated not with command and control but with the concept of inspiration, of getting along with other people and creating a vision with which others can identify. According to a recent CBI report: 'Effective leaders, who can inspire their people to realise their personal and collective potential, are often the deciding factor between a company being good at what it does and achieving greatness.'[3]

> *The vision is absolutely key to getting your troops together. It has to be qualitative, daring and grab the imagination. The test of it should be how quickly people will latch on to where you are going; you can entrust them with the how. You only get a company going where you want it to go by leadership by example and by honest and endless communication. Everyone in the business has to buy into your vision.*
>
> Sir John Harvey-Jones [4]

According to *Levine*, leaders need to focus on moving people and organisations forward by increasing the competency of staff and the co-operation of teams in order to improve the organisation. A leader's job is to constantly challenge the bureaucracy that smothers individual enthusiasm and the desire to contribute to an organisation. Leaders in the new millennium will create an environment that encourages the development of skills, learning and openness so that those on their team can participate in the deployment of financial and human resources. [5]

Inspirational leadership is discussed more fully later in this chapter.

The importance of leadership

The changing nature of work organisations, including flatter structures and recognition of the efficient use of human resources, coupled with advances in social democracy, have combined to place growing importance on leadership. The nature of management is moving away from an emphasis on getting results by the close control of the workforce and towards an environment of coaching, support and empowerment.

Leadership is related to motivation, interpersonal behaviour and the process of communication. According to *Sir Paul Judge*: 'Thirty years ago it was very much about what you knew, the technicalities of things. Managers now are leaders of their groups, their departments. Although they may well need some specialist knowledge, the human relations part of the management job is more important than ever. People have more flexibility and more choice in their careers, which are themselves more fluid, so keeping people motivated is very important.'[6]

Good leadership involves the effective process of delegation and empowerment. The leadership relationship is not limited to leader behaviour resulting in subordinate behaviour. Leadership is a dynamic process. The leader–follower relationship is reciprocal and effective leadership is a two-way process that influences both individual and organisational performance. A major report from the Advanced Institute of Management Research refers to the dual role of leadership. 'Leaders both motivate employees and design effective organisations. There are two broad conceptions of what leaders do – they motivate their followers and they design organisational contexts to enable their followers to function effectively.'[7]

Fullan discusses leadership in a culture of change and points out that leadership is key to large-scale improvement. It is essential for leaders to understand the change process and moral purpose without change will lead to moral martyrdom. Leaders must be able to operate under complex, uncertain circumstances. [8]

Leadership development in the public sector A research report by the Chartered Management Institute highlights the attitudes and opinions of managers working in the public sector on the key issues of leadership and performance. The report indicates a strong positive relationship between the organisational priority given to leadership development and the level of employee motivation and satisfaction. [9]

LEADERSHIP AND MANAGEMENT

What is the relationship between leadership and management? Although the two terms are often used interchangeably, management is more usually viewed as getting things done through other people in order to achieve stated organisational objectives. The manager may

react to specific situations and be more concerned with solving short-term problems. Management is regarded as relating to people working within a structured organisation and with prescribed roles. To people outside the organisation the manager might not necessarily be seen in a leadership role. The emphasis of leadership is on interpersonal behaviour in a broader context. It is often associated with the willing and enthusiastic behaviour of followers. **Leadership does not necessarily take place within the hierarchical structure of the organisation**. Many people operate as leaders without their role ever being clearly established or defined. *Belbin* suggests that:

> *there is a clear implication that leadership is not part of the job but a quality that can be brought to a job ... The work that leadership encompasses in the context clearly is not assigned but comes about spontaneously.*[10]

The 7-S organisational framework The differences between leadership and management have been applied by Watson to the 7-S organisational framework. Watson suggests that whereas managers tend towards reliance on strategy, structure and systems, leaders have an inherent inclination for utilisation of the 'soft' Ss of style, staff, skills and superordinate (or shared) goals. Watson also suggests, although cautiously, that 7-S management could be seen as the province of leaders. Managers will not ordinarily be capable of achieving sufficient mastery of all seven factors to attain a consistently high level of organisational performance.[11]

Differences in attitudes and relations with others

There are other differences between leadership and management. *Zaleznik* explores difference in attitudes towards goals, conceptions of work, relations with others, self-perception and development.

- Managers tend to adopt impersonal or passive attitudes towards goals. Leaders adopt a more personal and active attitude towards goals.
- In order to get people to accept solutions, the manager needs continually to co-ordinate and balance in order to compromise conflicting values. The leader creates excitement in work and develops choices that give substance to images that excite people.
- In their relationships with other people, managers maintain a low level of emotional involvement. Leaders have empathy with other people and give attention to what events and actions mean.
- Managers see themselves more as conservators and regulators of the existing order of affairs with which they identify and from which they gain rewards. Leaders work in, but do not belong to, the organisation. Their sense of identity does not depend upon membership or work roles and they search out opportunities for change.[12]

Close relationship between management and leadership

Despite a continuing debate on differences between management and leadership, there is a close relationship between them and it is not easy to separate them as distinct activities. Today, there appears an increasing tendency to emphasise the interrelationship between management and leadership and to see them more as synonymous.

> *I have never been fond of distinguishing between leadership and management: they overlap and you need both qualities.*[13]

> *Increasingly, management and leadership are being seen as inextricably linked. It is one thing for a leader to propound a grand vision, but this is redundant unless the vision is managed so it becomes real achievement.*[14]

Many methods of management training can also be used as a means of measuring leadership style. For example, the Leadership Grid (discussed in Chapter 12) was until recently

known as the Managerial Grid. Note also that the new framework of effective leadership introduced by Investors in People is called the 'Leadership and Management Model'.[15]

Figure 10.1	A framework for the study of managerial leadership

QUALITIES OR TRAITS APPROACH

Assumes leaders are born and not made. Leadership consists of certain inherited characteristics or personality traits. Focuses attention on the person in the job and not on the job itself.

THE FUNCTIONAL or GROUP APPROACH

Attention is focused on the functions and responsibilities of leadership, what the leader actually does and the nature of the group. Assumes leadership skills can be learned and developed.

LEADERSHIP AS A BEHAVIOURAL CATEGORY

The kinds of behaviour of people in leadership positions and the influence on group performance. Draws attention to range of possible managerial behaviour and importance of leadership style.

STYLES OF LEADERSHIP

The way in which the functions of leadership are carried out and the behaviour adopted by managers towards subordinate staff. Concerned with the effects of leadership on those being led.

THE SITUATIONAL APPROACH AND CONTINGENCY MODELS

The importance of the situation. Interactions between the variables involved in the leadership situation and patterns of behaviour. Belief that there is no single style of leadership appropriate to all situations.

TRANSFORMATIONAL LEADERSHIP

A process of engendering motivation and commitment, creating a vision for transforming the performance of the organisation, and appealing to the higher ideals and values of followers.

INSPIRATIONAL LEADERSHIP

Based on the personal qualities or charisma of the leader and the manner in which the leadership influence is exercised.

The debate between Leadership and Management is well rehearsed, and usually produces shades of two perspectives, presented here as extremes: A hierarchical relationship with Leadership at the top; Leadership and Management equal in status, but at opposite ends of a continuum. Frankly, there is little evidence to support one view over the other. But there is overwhelming evidence that people like the idea of being a 'leader'. Indeed this may be the reason why the debate still rages, as it fulfils a need for differentiation.

Ray Moorcroft, 'To lead or to manage? That is the question'[16]

Critical reflection

In universities, many lecturers inspire students and are viewed as leaders but not usually as managers. In sport, we frequently hear talk about great leaders who are not managers of the team. There appears to be a clear and accepted distinction between leadership and management. Why do you think this distinction does not appear to apply in the same way within business organisations?

APPROACHES TO LEADERSHIP

Due to its complex and variable nature there are many alternative ways of analysing leadership. It is helpful, therefore, to have some framework in which to consider different approaches to study of the subject.

One way is to examine managerial leadership in terms of:

Refresh your understanding

Activity 10A

www.pearsoned.co.uk/mullins

- the qualities or traits approach;
- the functional or group approach, including action-centred leadership;
- leadership as a behavioural category;
- styles of leadership;
- contingency theories;
- transitional or transformational leadership; and
- inspirational or visionary leadership.

(*See* Figure 10.1.)

THE QUALITIES OR TRAITS APPROACH

The first approach assumes that leaders are born and not made. Leadership consists of certain inherited characteristics, or personality traits, which distinguish leaders from their followers: the so-called Great Person theory of leadership. The **qualities approach** focuses attention on the man or woman in the job and not on the job itself. It suggests that attention is given to the selection of leaders rather than to training for leadership.

Drucker (writing originally in 1955) makes the point that:

> *Leadership is of utmost importance. Indeed there is no substitute for it. But leadership cannot be created or promoted. It cannot be taught or learned.*[17]

There have been many research studies into the common traits of leadership. However, attempts at identifying common personality, or physical and mental, characteristics of different 'good' or 'successful' leaders have met with little success.[18] Investigations have identified lists of traits that tend to be overlapping, contradictory or with little correlation for most features. It is noticeable that 'individuality' or 'originality' usually features in the

list. This itself suggests that there is little in common between specific personality traits of different leaders. It is perhaps possible therefore to identify general characteristics of leadership ability, such as self-confidence, initiative, intelligence and belief in one's actions, but research into this area has revealed little more than this.

Limitations of the traits approach

There are three further limitations with this approach.

- First, there is bound to be some subjective judgement in determining who is regarded as a 'good' or 'successful' leader.
- Second, the lists of possible traits tend to be very long and there is not always agreement on the most important.
- Third, it ignores the situational factors.

Even if it were possible to identify an agreed list of more specific qualities, this would provide little explanation of the nature of leadership. It would do little to help in the development and training of future leaders. Although there is still limited interest in the qualities, or traits, approach, attention has been directed more to other approaches to leadership. The qualities or traits approach gives rise to the questions of whether leaders are born or made and whether leadership is an art or a science, The important point, however, is that **these are not mutually exclusive alternatives**. Even if there are certain inborn qualities that make for a good leader, these natural talents need encouragement and development. Even if leadership is something of an art, it still requires the application of special skills and techniques.

THE FUNCTIONAL (OR GROUP) APPROACH

This approach to leadership focuses attention not on the personality of the leader, nor on the man or woman in the job, *per se*, but on the **functions of leadership**. Leadership is always present in any group engaged in a task. The functional approach views leadership in terms of how the leader's behaviour affects, and is affected by, the group of followers. This approach concentrates on the nature of the group, the followers or subordinates. It focuses on the content of leadership. Greater attention can be given to the successful training of leaders and to the means of improving the leaders' performance by concentrating on the functions which will lead to effective performance by the work group.

The functional approach believes that the skills of leadership can be learned, developed and perfected. In contrast to the view of Drucker (referred to above), *Kotter* makes the point that successful companies do not wait for leaders to come along. 'They actively seek out people with leadership potential and expose them to career experiences designed to develop that potential. Indeed, with careful selection, nurturing and encouragement, dozens of people can play important leadership roles in a business organisation.'[19] A similar point is made by *Whitehead*: 'There has been a dramatic change in how management thinkers regard leadership today. Leaders are not born, they say, but made. And the good news is everyone can do it. You don't have to be promoted to a management position. You can be a leader whatever job you do. You don't have to be the boss to be a leader.'[20]

Action-centred leadership

A general theory on the functional approach is associated with the work of *John Adair* and his ideas on **action-centred leadership** which focuses on what leaders actually *do*.[21] The effectiveness of the leader is dependent upon meeting three areas of need within the work group: the need to achieve the common **task**, the need for **team maintenance**, and the **individual needs** of group members. Adair symbolises these needs by three overlapping circles (*see* Figure 10.2).

Figure 10.2	Interaction of needs within the group

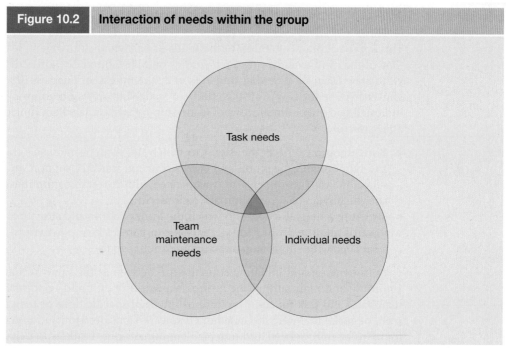

Source: Adair, J., *Action-Centred Leadership*, Gower Press (1979), p. 10. Reproduced with permission from Gower Publishing Ltd.

Task functions involve:

- achieving the objectives of the work group;
- defining group tasks;
- planning the work;
- allocation of resources;
- organisation of duties and responsibilities;
- controlling quality and checking performance;
- reviewing progress.

Team functions involve:

- maintaining morale and building team spirit;
- the cohesiveness of the group as a working unit;
- setting standards and maintaining discipline;
- systems of communication within the group;
- training the group;
- appointment of sub-leaders.

Individual functions involve:

- meeting the needs of the individual members of the group;
- attending to personal problems;
- giving praise and status;
- reconciling conflicts between group needs and needs of the individual;
- training the individual.

The action by the leader in any one area of need will affect one or both of the other areas of need. The ideal position is where complete integration of the three areas of need is achieved. The three-circle approach used by Adair also serves to illustrate the close relationship between leadership and management. Building the team and satisfying individual needs would include leadership. Achieving the common task clearly involves the process of management.

LEADERSHIP AS A BEHAVIOURAL CATEGORY

This approach draws attention to the kinds of behaviour of people in leadership situations. One of the most extensive research studies on behavioural categories of leadership was the Ohio State Leadership Studies undertaken by the Bureau of Business Research at Ohio State University. The focus was on the effects of leadership styles on group performance. Results indicated two major dimensions of leadership behaviour, labelled 'consideration' and 'initiating structure'.[22]

- **Consideration** reflects the extent to which the leader establishes trust, mutual respect and rapport with the group and shows concern, warmth, support and consideration for subordinates. This dimension is associated with two-way communication, participation and the human relations approach to leadership.
- **Structure** reflects the extent to which the leader defines and structures group interactions towards attainment of formal goals and organises group activities. This dimension is associated with efforts to achieve organisational goals.

Consideration and initiating structure can be seen as the same as maintenance function (building and maintaining the group as a working unit and relationships among group members) and task function (accomplishment of specific tasks of the groups and achievement of goals) that were discussed in Chapter 9. Consideration and initiating structure were found to be uncorrelated and independent dimensions. Leadership behaviour could, therefore, be shown on two separate axes. A high-consideration, high-structure style appears to be generally more effective in terms of subordinate satisfaction and group performance, but the evidence is not conclusive and much seems to depend upon situational factors. However, later findings suggest that the best leadership style entails high levels of both people-centred and task-centred dimensions.[23]

Employee-centred and production-centred supervisors

Another major research study was carried out at the University of Michigan Institute for Social Research at the same time as the Ohio State studies. Effective supervisors (measured along dimensions of group morale, productivity and cost reduction) appeared to display four common characteristics:

- delegation of authority and avoidance of close supervision;
- an interest and concern in their subordinates as individuals;
- participative problem-solving; and
- high standards of performance.

Likert, who has summarised the findings of the University of Michigan studies, used the terms **employee-centred** and **production-centred** supervisors.[24] These terms are similar to the dimensions of consideration and structure. The first three of these supervisory characteristics are examples of consideration. The fourth characteristic exemplifies structure. Like consideration and structure, employee-centred and production-centred supervision need to be balanced. Likert concluded that employee-centred supervisors who get best results tend to recognise that one of their main responsibilities is production. Both the Ohio State and the University of Michigan studies appear to support the idea that there is no single behavioural category of leadership that is superior. There are many types of leadership behaviour and their effectiveness depends upon the variables in any given situation.

Major dimensions of managerial leadership

Despite the many types of actual leadership behaviour, we have seen that there appears to be general agreement on two major dimensions of managerial leadership. This can be extended to include the works of McGregor and of Blake and McCanse, discussed as part of managerial behaviour in Chapter 12 (*see* Figure 10.3).

Figure 10.3	Two major dimensions of managerial leadership

Group interaction analysis	Task functions	Maintenance functions
Ohio State leadership study	Initiating structure	Consideration
University of Michigan study	Production-centred supervision	Employee-centred supervision
McGregor, assumptions about people and work	Theory X	Theory Y
Blake and McCanse, Leadership Grid	Concern for production	Concern for people

STYLES OF LEADERSHIP

Attention to leadership as a behavioural category has drawn attention to the importance of leadership style. In the work situation it has become increasingly clear that managers can no longer rely solely on the use of their position in the hierarchical structure as a means of exercising the functions of leadership. In order to get the best results from subordinates the manager must also have regard for the need to encourage high morale, a spirit of involvement and co-operation, and a willingness to work. This gives rise to consideration of the style of leadership and provides another heading under which to analyse leadership behaviour.

Leadership style is the way in which the functions of leadership are carried out, the way in which the manager typically behaves towards members of the group.

The attention given to leadership style is based on the assumption that subordinates are more likely to work effectively for managers who adopt a certain style of leadership than they will for managers who adopt alternative styles.

Broad classification of leadership style

There are many dimensions to leadership and many possible ways of describing leadership style, such as dictatorial, unitary, bureaucratic, benevolent, charismatic, consultative, participative and abdicatorial. The style of managerial leadership towards subordinate staff and the focus of power can, however, be classified, broadly, within a simplified three-fold heading.

- The **authoritarian (or autocratic) style** is where the focus of power is with the manager and all interactions within the group move towards the manager. The manager alone exercises decision-making and authority for determining policy, procedures for achieving goals, work tasks and relationships, control of rewards or punishments.
- The **democratic style** is where the focus of power is more with the group as a whole and there is greater interaction within the group. The leadership functions are shared with members of the group and the manager is more part of a team. The group members have a greater say in decision-making, determination of policy, implementation of systems and procedures.
- A *laissez-faire* (genuine) **style** is where the manager observes that members of the group are working well on their own. The manager consciously makes a decision to pass the focus of power to members, to allow them freedom of action 'to do as they think best', and not to interfere; but is readily available if help is needed. There is often confusion over this style of leadership behaviour. The word 'genuine' is emphasised because this is

to be contrasted with the manager who could not care, who deliberately keeps away from the trouble spots and does not want to get involved. The manager just lets members of the group get on with the work in hand. Members are left to face decisions that rightly belong with the manager. This is more a non-style of leadership or it could perhaps be labelled as abdication.

Attention to style of leadership Attention to the manager's style of leadership has come about because of a greater understanding of the needs and expectations of people at work. It has also been influenced by such factors as:

- increasing business competitiveness and recognition of efficient use of human resources;
- changes in the value system of society;
- broader standards of education and training;
- advances in scientific and technical knowledge;
- changes in the nature of work organisation;
- pressure for a greater social responsibility towards employees, for example through schemes of participation in decision-making and work/life balance; and
- government legislation, for example in the areas of employment protection, and the influence of the European Union.

All of these factors have combined to create resistance against purely autocratic styles of leadership.

CONTINUUM OF LEADERSHIP BEHAVIOUR

One of the best-known works on leadership style is that by *Tannenbaum and Schmidt* (Figure 10.4).[25] Originally written in 1958 and updated in 1973, their work suggests a continuum of possible leadership behaviour available to a manager and along which various styles of leadership may be placed. The continuum presents a range of action related to the degree of authority used by the manager and to the area of freedom available to non-managers in arriving at decisions. The Tannenbaum and Schmidt continuum can be related to McGregor's supposition of Theory X and Theory Y. Boss-centred leadership is towards Theory X and subordinate-centred leadership is towards Theory Y.

Four main styles of leadership Moving along the continuum, the manager may be characterised according to the degree of control that is maintained. Neither extreme of the continuum is absolute as there is always some limitation on authority and on freedom. This approach can be seen as identifying four main styles of leadership by the manager: tells, sells, consults, joins.

- **Tells.** The manager identifies a problem, makes a decision and announces this to subordinates, expecting them to implement it without an opportunity for participation.
- **Sells.** The manager still makes a decision but recognises the possibility of some resistance from those faced with the decision and attempts to persuade subordinates to accept it.
- **Consults.** The manager identifies the problem but does not make a decision until the problem is presented to the group, and the manager has listened to the advice and solutions suggested by subordinates.
- **Joins.** The manager defines the problem and the limits within which the decision must be made and then passes to the group, with the manager as a member, the right to make decisions.

Figure 10.4	Continuum of manager–non-manager behaviour

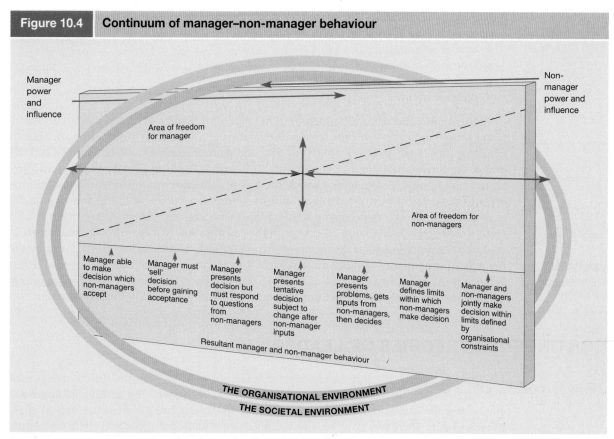

Main forces in deciding type of leadership Tannenbaum and Schmidt suggest that there are three factors, or forces, of particular importance in deciding what types of leadership are practicable and desirable. These are: forces in the manager, forces in the subordinate and forces in the situation.

1 **Forces in the manager.** The manager's behaviour will be influenced by their personality, background, knowledge and experiences. These internal forces will include:
 - value systems;
 - confidence in subordinates;
 - leadership inclinations; and
 - feelings of security in an uncertain situation.

2 **Forces in the subordinate**. Subordinates are influenced by many personality variables and their individual set of expectations about their relationship with the manager. Characteristics of the subordinate are:
 - the strength of the need for independence;
 - the readiness to assume responsibility for decision-making;
 - the degree of tolerance for ambiguity;
 - interest in the problem and feelings as to its importance;
 - understanding and identification with the goals of the organisation;
 - necessary knowledge and experience to deal with the problem; and
 - the extent of learning to expect to share in decision-making.

The greater the positive response to these characteristics, the greater freedom of action can be allowed by the manager.

3 Forces in the situation. The manager's behaviour will be influenced by the general situation and environmental pressures. Characteristics in the situation include:

- type of organisation;
- group effectiveness;
- nature of the problem; and
- pressure of time.

Tannenbaum and Schmidt conclude that successful leaders are keenly aware of those forces which are most relevant to their behaviour at a particular time. They are able to behave appropriately in terms of their understanding of themselves, the individuals and the group, the organisation, and environmental influences. Successful managers are both perceptive and flexible. Forces lying outside the organisation are also included. Recognition is given to the possibility of the manager and/or subordinates taking initiatives to change the boundaries of the rectangle through interaction with external forces. Recognition is also given to the power available to all parties in the organisation (for example individual workers and trade unions) and to the factors which underlie decisions on the use of power by the manager. Tannenbaum and Schmidt suggest a new continuum of patterns of leadership behaviour in which the total area of freedom shared between managers and non-managers is redefined constantly by interactions between them and the forces in the environment.

Refresh your understanding

Activity 10B
www.pearsoned.co.uk/mullins

CONTINGENCY THEORIES OF LEADERSHIP

The continuum of leadership behaviour draws attention to forces in the situation as one of the main forces influencing the nature of managerial behaviour. The situational approach emphasises the situation as the dominant feature in considering the characteristics of effective leadership. There are, however, limitations to the situational approach. There are people who possess the appropriate knowledge and skills and appear to be the most suitable leaders in a given situation, but who do not emerge as effective leaders. Another limitation is that it does not explain fully the interpersonal behaviour or the different styles of leadership and their effect on members of the group. Finally, in the work organisation, it is not usually practicable to allow the situation continually to determine who should act as the leader.

Despite the limitations of the situational approach, situational factors are important in considering the characteristics of leadership. More recent studies focus on the interactions between the variables involved in a leadership situation and patterns of leadership behaviour, and provide another general approach to the study of leadership – contingency theory. Contingency theories are based on the belief that there is no single style of leadership appropriate to all situations. Major contingency models of leadership include:

- **Favourability of leadership situation** – *Fiedler*
- **Quality and acceptance of leader's decision** – *Vroom and Yetton* and *Vroom and Jago*
- **Path–goal theory** – *House*, and *House and Dessler*
- **Readiness level of followers** – *Hersey and Blanchard*.

FIEDLER'S CONTINGENCY MODEL

One of the first leader–situation models was developed by *Fiedler* in his contingency theory of leadership effectiveness.[26] Fiedler's contingency model was based on studies of a wide range of group situations and concentrated on the relationship between leadership and organisational performance. In order to measure the attitudes of the leader, Fiedler developed a 'least preferred co-worker' (LPC) scale. This measures the rating given by leaders about the person with whom they could work least well. The questionnaire contains up to 20 items. Examples of items in the LPC scale are pleasant/unpleasant, friendly/unfriendly,

helpful/frustrating, distant/close, co-operative/unco-operative, boring/interesting, self-assured/hesitant, open/guarded.

Each item is given a single ranking of between one and eight points, with eight points indicating the most favourable rating. For example:

Pleasant	:	:	:	:	:	:	:	:	Unpleasant
	8	7	6	5	4	3	2	1	

The LPC score is the sum of the numerical ratings on all the items for the 'least preferred co-worker'. The original interpretation of the LPC scale was that the leader with a high LPC score derived most satisfaction from interpersonal relationships and, when relationships with subordinates need to be improved, is motivated to act in a supportive, considerate manner. The leader with a low LPC score derived most satisfaction from performance of the task and achieving objectives. Establishing good relationships with subordinates is a secondary motivation. It was thought that high LPC scores would be associated with effective performance by the group. However, the interpretation of LPC has changed a number of times and there is still uncertainty about its actual meaning.

Favourability of leadership situation

Fiedler suggests that leadership behaviour is dependent upon the favourability of the leadership situation. There are three major variables which determine the favourability of the situation and which affect the leader's role and influence:

- **Leader–member relations** – the degree to which the leader is trusted and liked by group members, and their willingness to follow the leader's guidance.
- **The task structure** – the degree to which the task is clearly defined for the group and the extent to which it can be carried out by detailed instructions or standard procedures.
- **Position power** – the power of the leader by virtue of position in the organisation, and the degree to which the leader can exercise authority to influence (for example) rewards and punishments, or promotions and demotions.

From these three variables, Fiedler constructed eight combinations of group–task situations through which to relate leadership style (*see* Figure 10.5).

When the situation is

- **very favourable** (good leader–member relations, structured task, strong position power), or
- **very unfavourable** (poor leader–member relations, unstructured task, weak position power),
- then a **task-oriented leader** (low LPC score) with a directive, controlling style will be more effective.

When the situation is

- **moderately favourable** and the variables are mixed, then the leader with an interpersonal relationship orientation (high LPC score) and a **participative approach** will be more effective.

Fiedler is suggesting, therefore, that leadership style will vary as the favourability of the leadership situation varies.

Organisational variables Fiedler's work has been subject to much debate and criticism but it does provide a further dimension to the study of leadership.[27] It brings into consideration the organisational variables that affect leadership effectiveness and suggests that in given situations a task-oriented, or structured, style of leadership is most appropriate. The 'best' styles of leadership will be dependent upon the variable factors in the leadership situation.

Figure 10.5	**Correlations between leader's LPC scores and group effectiveness**

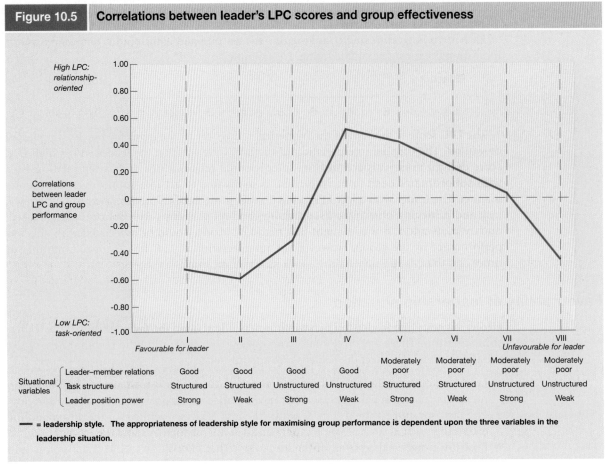

Situational variables		I	II	III	IV	V	VI	VII	VIII
	Leader–member relations	Good	Good	Good	Good	Moderately poor	Moderately poor	Moderately poor	Moderately poor
	Task structure	Structured	Structured	Unstructured	Unstructured	Structured	Structured	Unstructured	Unstructured
	Leader position power	Strong	Weak	Strong	Weak	Strong	Weak	Strong	Weak

─── = leadership style. **The appropriateness of leadership style for maximising group performance is dependent upon the three variables in the leadership situation.**

Source: Adapted from Fielder, F .E., *A Theory of Leadership Effectiveness*. McGraw-Hill (1967), p. 146. Reproduced with permission from The McGraw-Hill Companies, Inc.

Fiedler argues that leadership effectiveness may be improved by changing the leadership situation. Position power, task structure and leader–member relations can be changed to make the situation more compatible with the characteristics of the leader. Leaders with a low LPC score could be placed in a leadership situation that is very favourable or very unfavourable. Leaders with a high LPC score could be placed in a leadership situation that is of moderate favourability.

VROOM AND YETTON CONTINGENCY MODEL

Another contingency model of leadership is provided by *Vroom and Yetton*.[28] They base their analysis on two main aspects of a leader's decision: its quality and its acceptance.

- **Decision quality**, or rationality, is the effect that the decision has on group performance.
- **Decision acceptance** refers to the motivation and commitment of group members in implementing the decision.

 A third consideration is

- the amount of **time required** to make the decision.

The Vroom and Yetton model suggests five main management decision styles:

- **Autocratic**
 A.I: Leader solves the problem or makes the decision alone using information available at the time.
 A.II: Leader obtains information from subordinates but then decides on solution alone.

- **Consultative**
 C.I: The problem is shared with relevant subordinates, individually. The leader then makes the decision that may or may not reflect the influence of subordinates.
 C.II: The problem is shared with subordinates as a group. The leader then makes the decision that may or may not reflect the influence of subordinates.

- **Group**
 G.II: The problem is shared with subordinates as a group. The leader acts as chairperson rather than an advocate. Together the leader and subordinates generate and evaluate alternatives and attempt to reach group consensus on a solution.

Decision rules Vroom and Yetton suggest seven decision rules to help the manager discover the most appropriate leadership style in a given situation. The first three rules protect the **quality of decisions.**

1 Is there a quality requirement such that one solution is likely to be more rational than another?
2 Is there sufficient information to make a high-quality decision?
3 Is the problem structured? The last four rules protect the **acceptance of decisions**.
4 Is acceptance of the decision by subordinates critical to effective implementation?
5 If you were to make the decision yourself, is it reasonably certain that it would be accepted by subordinates?
6 Do subordinates share the organisational goals to be obtained in solving the problem?
7 Is conflict among subordinates likely in preferred solutions?

These rules indicate decision styles that the manager should **avoid** in a given situation and indicate the use of others. Decision tree charts can be produced to help in the application of the rules and to relate the situation to the appropriate leadership style.

THE VROOM AND JAGO REVISED DECISION MODEL

In a revised version of the original model, *Vroom and Jago* retain the five main decision-making styles but incorporate a larger number – 12 – of contingency variables.[29] The new model specifies that any of the five decision styles may be effective in given situations. The contingency variables relate to:

- quality requirement;
- commitment requirement;
- leader information;
- problem structure;
- commitment probability;
- goal congruence;
- subordinate conflict;
- subordinate information;
- time constraint;
- geographical dispersion;
- motivation time; and
- motivation development.

Unlike the Vroom and Yetton model that requires a definite yes/no answer, ten of these situational variables are answered on a five-point scale. For example, to the question 'How important is subordinate commitment to the decision?', the manager selects one of the following responses: no importance; low importance; average importance; high importance; critical importance.

Use of decision trees
Vroom and Jago developed four decision trees relating to a generic type of managerial problem:

- an individual-level problem with time constraints;
- an individual-level problem in which the manager wishes to develop an employee's decision-making ability;
- a group-level problem in which the manager wishes to develop employees' decision-making abilities; and
- a time-driven group problem.

Refresh your understanding
Activity 10C
www.pearsoned.co.uk/mullins

The manager selects one of the trees and moves along the branches by answering the questions at each decision point. This leads to one of the five described decision-making styles.

PATH–GOAL THEORY

A third contingency model of leadership is the path–goal theory, the main work on which has been undertaken by *House*,[30] and by *House and Dessler*.[31] The model is based on the belief that the individual's motivation is dependent upon expectations that increased effort to achieve an improved level of performance will be successful, and expectations that improved performance will be instrumental in obtaining positive rewards and avoiding negative outcomes. This is the 'expectancy' theory of motivation, which is discussed in Chapter 7.

Four main types of leadership behaviour
The path–goal theory of leadership suggests that the performance of subordinates is affected by the extent to which the manager satisfies their expectations. Path–goal theory holds that subordinates will see leadership behaviour as a motivating influence to the extent that it means:

- satisfaction of their needs is dependent upon effective performance; and
- the necessary direction, guidance, training and support, which would otherwise be lacking, is provided.

House identifies four main types of leadership behaviour:

- **Directive leadership** involves letting subordinates know exactly what is expected of them and giving specific directions. Subordinates are expected to follow rules and regulations. This type of behaviour is similar to 'initiating structure' in the Ohio State Leadership Studies.
- **Supportive leadership** involves a friendly and approachable manner and displaying concern for the needs and welfare of subordinates. This type of behaviour is similar to 'consideration' in the Ohio State Leadership Studies.
- **Participative leadership** involves consulting with subordinates and the evaluation of their opinions and suggestions before the manager makes the decision.
- **Achievement-oriented leadership** involves setting challenging goals for subordinates, seeking improvement in their performance and showing confidence in subordinates' ability to perform well.

Path–goal theory suggests that the different types of behaviour can be practised by the same person at different times in varying situations. By using one of the four styles of leadership behaviour the manager attempts to influence subordinates' perceptions and motivation, and smooth the path to their goals (*see* Figure 10.6).

| Figure 10.6 | Representation of the path–goal theory of leadership |

Two main situational factors Leadership behaviour is determined by two main situational factors: the personal characteristics of subordinates and the nature of the task.

- **The personal characteristics of subordinates** determine how they will react to the manager's behaviour and the extent to which they see such behaviour as an immediate or potential source of need satisfaction.
- **The nature of the task** relates to the extent that it is routine and structured or non-routine and unstructured.

For example, when a task is highly structured, the goals readily apparent and subordinates are confident, then attempts to further explain the job or to give directions are likely to be viewed as unacceptable behaviour. However, when a task is highly unstructured, the nature of the goals is not clear and subordinates lack experience, then a more directive style of leadership behaviour is likely to be welcomed by subordinates. Effective leadership behaviour is based, therefore, on both the willingness of the manager to help subordinates and the needs of subordinates for help. Leadership behaviour will be motivational to the extent that it provides necessary direction, guidance and support, helps clarify path–goal relationships and removes any obstacles which hinder attainment of goals.

READINESS OF THE FOLLOWERS OR GROUP

A major variable in the style of leadership adopted by the manager is the nature of subordinate staff. This view is developed by *Hersey and Blanchard* who present a form of situational leadership based on the 'readiness' level of the people the leader is attempting to influence. Readiness is the extent to which followers have the ability and willingness to accomplish a specific task. It is not a personal characteristic of the individual but how ready the individual is to perform a particular task.[32]

Readiness (R) is divided into a continuum of four levels: R1 (low), R2 and R3 (moderate) and R4 (high).

- **R1 – low follower readiness** – refers to followers who are both *unable and unwilling* and who lack commitment and motivation; or who are *unable and insecure.*
- **R2 – low to moderate follower readiness** – refers to followers who are *unable but willing* and who lack ability but are motivated to make an effort; or who are *unable but confident.*
- **R3 – moderate to high follower readiness** – refers to followers who are *able but unwilling,* and who have the ability to perform but are unwilling to apply their ability; or who are *able but insecure.*

theory of transformational leadership that argues that the leader transforms and motivates followers by:

1 generating greater awareness of the importance of the purpose of the organisation and task outcomes;
2 inducing them to transcend their own self-interests for the sake of the organisation or team; and
3 activating their higher-level needs.[34]

Transformational leadership is comprised of four basic components:

- **idealised influence** – the charisma of the leader, and the respect and admiration of the followers;
- **inspirational motivation** – the behaviour of the leader which provides meaning and challenge to the work of the followers;
- **intellectual stimulation** – leaders who solicit new and novel approaches for the performance of work and creative problem solutions from followers; and
- **individualised consideration** – leaders who listen and give special concern to the growth and developmental needs of the followers.[35]

Yukl provides a set of guidelines for transformational leadership:

- **Articulate a clear and appealing vision** of what the organisation could accomplish or become to help people understand the purpose, objectives and priorities of the organisation, and to help guide the actions and decisions of members.
- **Explain how the vision can be attained** and establish a clear link between the vision and a credible conventional yet straightforward strategy for attaining it.
- **Act confident and optimistic** about likely success, demonstrate self-confidence and conviction, and emphasise positive aspects of the vision rather than the obstacles and dangers.
- **Express confidence in followers** and their ability to carry out the strategy for accomplishing the vision, especially when the task is difficult or dangerous, or when members lack confidence in themselves.
- **Use dramatic, symbolic actions to emphasise key values** and demonstrate leadership behaviour through dramatic, highly visible actions including risking personal loss, self-sacrifice or acting unconventionally.
- **Lead by example** by recognising actions speak louder than words, through exemplary behaviour in day-to-day interactions with subordinates and by demonstrating consistency in daily behaviour.[36]

INSPIRATIONAL OR VISIONARY LEADERSHIP

Many writers see transformational leadership as the same thing as charismatic, visionary or inspirational leadership. *Kreitner et al.* refer to charismatic leadership as transforming employees to pursue organisational goals over self-interests: 'Charismatic leaders transform followers by creating changes in their goals, values, needs, beliefs, and aspirations. They accomplish this transformation by appealing to followers' self-concepts – namely, their values and personal identity.'[37] Writers such as *Burns* and *Bass* identified leaders by their actions and the impact those actions have on other people.

Successful transformational leaders are usually identified in terms of providing a strong vision and sense of mission, arousing strong emotions in followers and a sense of identification with the leader. As mentioned at the start of this chapter, leadership today is increasingly associated with the concept of creating a vision with which others can identify, getting along with other people and the concept of inspiration. This might be considered as part of transfor-

mational leadership or arguably it has given rise to a new approach to leadership – that of inspirational or visionary leadership. Inspirational leadership is not concerned so much with the theory of leadership but more with the skills of motivating and inspiring people.

Personal qualities or charisma

Leadership may be based on the personal qualities, or charisma, of the leader and the manner in which influence is exercised. The importance of charisma for effective leadership is emphasised by *Conger*, who also believes that many of the traits that make a successful leader can be taught, including charisma.

> Now the big question is whether you are born with charisma or whether you can develop it. I believe you can develop elements of it. For example, you can take courses to improve your speaking skills. You can learn to stage events that send powerful messages. You can learn to think more critically about the status quo and its shortcomings. You can do more on a daily basis to motivate your team. What you simply cannot learn is how to be passionate about what you do. You have to discover that for yourself, and passion is a big part of what drives a charismatic leader. It is also what motivates and inspires those who work for the charismatic leader.[38]

Is charisma enough? However, the extent to which charismatic or inspirational leadership helps bring about improvement in organisational performance is open to much debate. Conger also draws attention to the danger that the leader's vision, dynamism and inspirational nature are highly attractive to followers, which leads to a natural dependence. Staff see this extraordinary figure as a model to be emulated and the leader's abilities become the yardstick by which they measure their own performance. This is a potential source of leadership derailment. Dependence makes the followers more susceptible to deception.[39]

Dearlove draws attention to the increasing focus on leaders as real people managing in a consensus-seeking manner. 'While traditional views of leadership tend eventually to concentrate on vision and charisma, the message now seems to be that charisma is no longer enough to carry leaders through.'[40] *Bloomfield* also refers to the cult of the individual, supposedly charismatic leader and the danger that this leads businesses into deep water far more often than the application of rational leadership. Too often the charismatic leader, aided and abetted by the language of current management fashion, attempts to 'inspire', to delight with their vision and to produce a mission statement of where the business might be – at the expense of real substance.[41]

Adair argues that to be a truly inspirational leader one must understand the spirit within. All people have the potential for greatness. The inspirational leader connects with the led, appreciates the capabilities of others and through trust will unlock the powers in others. Adair refers to 'the inspired moment' – a recognition and seizure of a brief window of opportunity that can act as a powerful catalyst that inspires both the leader and the led.[42]

The importance of vision

Effective transformational leaders are those who inspire people and create a vision for the organisation and its future direction. According to *Whitehead*:

> The big word now associated with leadership is vision. The ability to see the bigger picture. To take the long-term view. What the ultimate objectives of the organisation are and how people can work together to achieve them … Perhaps the most important attribute is that a good leader inspires people by creating a climate where it is OK for people to make mistakes and learn from them, rather than what happened in the past which was to blame and punish them. Leading from this position, they gain a higher level of commitment from their people than mere compliance.[43]

Kahan sees visionary leadership as transformative. It involves greatness, penetrating the ordinary, and requires total involvement. Among the qualities visionary leaders cultivate are imagination, engagement, tangible results and penetrating self-reflection. They engage society with its competitive, divergent viewpoints. Visionary leadership is ultimately about increasing performance but also with the rewards of tangible results to your membership and deep personal satisfaction.[44]

Need for visionary leadership In her discussion of the creation of the democratic enterprise (organisations that can flourish economically and can also be places of excitement and stimulation, fulfilment and tranquillity), *Gratton* maintains that it is the creation of a shared purpose and the role of the leadership team that are most vital. The role of the leader as visionary is fundamental to creating the broad philosophical context of democracy and as the architect of shared purpose.[45]

Referring to the work of Goffee and Jones, *Witzel* suggests: 'Leadership is one of the most vital and yet elusive ingredients in modern business. Leaders provide vision, direction, inspiration, give the business a sense of purpose and at the same time act as a moral compass.'[46] *Goffee and Jones* point out that the need for visionary leadership is becoming increasingly important. Traditional business hierarchies gave managers and workers a sense of their own position and what was expected of them. Now, as these hierarchies break down, it is leaders themselves who must fill the void, helping subordinates to understand their place and purpose. Personal leadership is beginning to replace organisational structure.[47]

> *What sets great leaders apart is their ability to engage those around them in a shared vision of the future. By making the right decisions, they demonstrate their commitment to turning that vision into reality; and by doing so successfully, they instil in others the confidence to trust in their leadership.*
>
> Sir Bryan Nicholson[48]

The inspirational gap

According to a survey by the Chartered Management Institute, the power to inspire is rated highest among desirable leadership qualities. A detailed survey of almost 1500 practising managers in a broad cross-section of organisations found that the key characteristic that leaders should ideally possess, inspiration, was identified by 55 per cent of managers. However, most leaders appeared to lack this characteristic, with only 11 per cent of respondents saying they experienced this in reality.[49]

The survey from the Chartered Management Institute highlighted a significant 'inspirational gap' in leadership across UK organisations. The Department of Trade and Industry undertook a research project to explore how to start closing this critical leadership inspiration gap.[50] 'It is now accepted that for the UK to maintain its competitiveness there is a growing need for companies to adopt strategies that will enable a greater level of innovation and the provision of higher value and services.' The report is based on a study of 568 followers at different management levels working in a wide variety of organisations. It confirms that today's workforce is more diverse, informed and sophisticated than ever before. Ultimately people are still looking for something different and better in organisational leadership.

Key conclusions of the report include:

- For the past 30 years there have been increasing amounts of data to suggest that leadership has a lot more to do with inspiration and vision than with straightforward technical competence. Leadership is now recognised as a transferable skill, it can be developed by continued learning and development throughout a person's career.
- Managers demand visionary leaders who win not only results but also the trust and respect of their teams. It is the relationship between people that results in action.

Figure 10.8 Concept map of leadership and management

LEADERSHIP AND MANAGEMENT

- MANAGEMENT
- LEADERSHIP

MANAGERS have to ensure their subordinates collectively or separately reach their goals

- Leadership by function
- Leadership by personality

No single trait or group of characteristics has been isolated which sets off the leader from members of groups (Jenkins)

MANAGERS have the authority to direct work and behaviour
LEADERS have influence through example, persuading, motivating, teaching

Leadership may be situationally governed
– arising due to a set of circumstances
Some managers are more suitable to operate in one set of situations than others

LEADERSHIP
– the ability to ensure subordinates perform their tasks and duties up to the standards required, by inspiration or inducement

Leaders cannot achieve the goals by themselves
Subordinates require direction to obtain the goals

Therefore co-operation or coercion required
– Leaders are those individuals who are perceived most frequently to perform those roles and functions which initiate or control behaviour of others towards the achievement of group goals or sub goals (Gibb)

Charisma ↔ Technocrat

- Group tasks usually complex
- Organisations require stability not continuous change in leader

- Situational Theory Leadership is specific to the situation under investigation, i.e. a leader emerges in response to the problem or challenge

- Personnel with highly technical skills possessing wide sapiential (knowledge) gives authority/ leadership

LEADERSHIP TRAITS
- Intelligence
- Self Confidence
- Initiative talking
- Empathy
- Self-awareness
- Objectivity (human relationships)

FOUR VARIABLES
1 Characteristics/traits of the leader
2 Attitudes of the folllowers
3 Organisation purpose, technology, ethos, values, structure
4 Social economic and political milieu (McGregor) between countries between cultures

THE ESSENTIALS OF LEADERSHIP
- Social skills
- Ability to communicate
- Flexibility/judgement as to which management style to adopt

ACTION-CENTRED LEADERSHIP (ADAIR)

INDIVIDUAL NEEDS
- Concern for the individual
- fairness and consistency in disciplinary matters
- help with training, career prospects with …
 preparation for retirement
 recognition of performance
- good or adequate with …
 commendation or helpful criticism
- Job enrichment
- Giving status

GROUP NEEDS
Defence of the group needs
– laterally and vertically
Building up teamwork, recognising informal groups
Protection of interests which may lead to disruption e.g. relocation to another site; uneven work loads; accomodation; pay differentials

TASK NEEDS
Task definition
Planning
Allocating work and resources
Controlling quality, pace of work
Monitoring
Amending the plans
Co-ordinating with other groups
Obtaining resources required

Group Needs / Task Needs / Individual Needs

Use of authority by manager

Area of freedom by subordinate

tell | sell | consult | share | delegate | abdicate
1 | 2 | 3 | 4 | 5 | 6 | 7

1 Tell them
2 Tell them and sell it to them
3 Tell them and talk about it
4 Tentative decision and talk
5 Problem – talk and manager decides
6 Manager gives limits; all discuss, group decides
7 Manager gives limits; group discusses and decides

- Organisational leadership
- Personal leadership …
 contribution by the individual in the post showing – charisma/energy/vision

Authoritarian ↔ Democratic

KINDS OF LEADERSHIP
Formal
– appointed in the hierarchy by the management
Informal
– exercises influence but is not in formal position; can initiate or block actions; can be in conflict with the formal leader; can set the group norms

Source: Training Learning Consultancy Ltd., Bristol, England. Reproduced with permission.

● In order to keep followers motivated and committed in an era of unrelenting change, leaders must be able to create organisation cultures that foster not only performance but also a sense of pride and fun.

Critical reflection

????

There is a great deal of support today for the idea that effective leaders need to demonstrate the qualities of commitment and vision, and to inspire loyal followers to higher levels of performance. However, it is also clear that identifying the profile of such leaders, and defining their distinctive characteristics and skills, is still subject to uncertainty and debate. So do you think we are any further forward in establishing what makes a good leader?

A summary of leadership and management is set out in the concept map in Figure 10.8.

LEADERSHIP AND INNOVATION

A 2005 report by the Advanced Institute of Management Research in co-operation with the Chartered Management Institute draws attention to the impact of leadership on innovation.[51] The report refers to the dual role of leaders, first as motivators, inspiring people to transcend the ordinary, and second as architects, designing an organisational environment that enables employees to be innovative. 'The impact of leadership on innovation goes well beyond the motivating effect of the inspirational or charismatic leader. Leaders also affect innovation through organisational design and must create appropriate organisational environments to suit the different innovation processes.' The primary challenges for organisational leaders in promoting innovation are to:

● recognise and develop appropriate leadership for the different stages of the innovation process; and
● create organisational contexts that support complete innovation processes of different degrees of novelty.

Conceptual framework

The report distinguishes between leaders who primarily motivate through transformational actions – a 'motivational' perspective – and those take a more transactional approach and emphasise the co-ordination of organisational tasks – a 'structuralist' perspective. In order to address the question of how leadership affects innovation within organisations, the report proposes a conceptual framework that reflects the complex interaction among leadership, the organisational context and innovation (Figure 10. 9).

There is, however, a need for being mindful that leadership:

● can manifest itself at all levels in the organisation, not just the top;
● need not be concentrated in the person of a single leader but may act through distributed leadership systems; and
● sets the organisational context for followers' activities both through motivation and the administrative co-ordination of systems that support innovation.

Figure 10.9	The 'leadership for innovation' conceptual framework

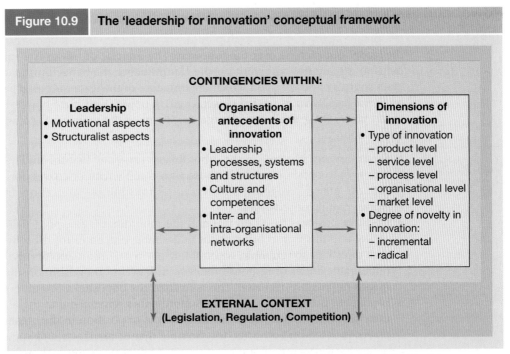

Source: From Munshi, N. *et al.*, *Leadership for Innovation: The Impact of Leadership on Innovation*, Advanced Institute of Management Research (AIM) (2005), Figure 5, p.18. Reproduced with permission from the Advanced Institute of Management Research.

THE LEADERSHIP RELATIONSHIP

Whatever the perceived approach to leadership, the most important point is the nature of the leadership relationship and the manner in which the leader influences the behaviour and actions of other people.

Leadership is a dynamic form of behaviour and there are a number of variables that affect the leadership relationship. Four major variables are identified by *McGregor* as:

- the characteristics of the leader;
- the attitude, needs and other personal characteristics of the followers;
- the nature of the organisation, such as its purpose, its structure, the tasks to be performed; and
- the social, economic and political environment.

McGregor concludes that 'leadership is not a property of the individual, but a complex relationship among these variables'.[52]

According to *Kouzes and Posner*, 'credibility is the foundation of leadership'. From extensive research in over 30 countries and response to the question of what people 'look for and admire in a leader, in a person whose direction they would willingly follow', people have consistently replied that they want:

> *leaders who exemplify four qualities: they want them to be honest, forward-looking, inspiring and competent. In our research our respondents strongly agree that they want leaders with integrity and trustworthiness, with vision and a sense of direction, with enthusiasm and passion, and with expertise and a track record for getting things done.*[53]

Fullan refers to the importance of relationship building as a basic component of the change process and effective leadership: 'Leaders must be consummate relationship builders with diverse people and groups – especially with people different from themselves. Effective leaders constantly foster purposeful interaction and problem solving, and are wary of easy consensus.'[54]

Power and leadership influence

Within an organisation, leadership influence will be dependent upon the type of power that the leader can exercise over the followers. The exercise of power is a social process which helps to explain how different people can influence the behaviour/actions of others. Five main sources of power upon which the influence of the leader is based have been identified by *French and Raven* as reward power, coercive power, legitimate power, referent power and expert power.[55] We shall consider these in terms of the manager (as a leader) and subordinate relationship.

- **Reward power** is based on the subordinate's *perception* that the leader has the ability and resources to obtain rewards for those who comply with directives; for example, pay, promotion, praise, recognition, increased responsibilities, allocation and arrangement of work, granting of privileges.
- **Coercive power** is based on fear and the subordinate's *perception* that the leader has the ability to punish or to bring about undesirable outcomes for those who do not comply with directives; for example, withholding pay rises, promotion or privileges; allocation of undesirable duties or responsibilities; withdrawal of friendship or support; formal reprimands or possibly dismissal. This is in effect the opposite of reward power.
- **Legitimate power** is based on the subordinate's *perception* that the leader has a right to exercise influence because of the leader's role or position in the organisation. Legitimate power is based on authority, for example that of managers and supervisors within the hierarchical structure of an organisation. Legitimate power is therefore 'position' power because it is based on the role of the leader in the organisation, and not on the nature of the personal relationship with others.
- **Referent power** is based on the subordinate's *identification* with the leader. The leader exercises influence because of perceived attractiveness, personal characteristics, reputation or what is called 'charisma'. For example, a particular manager may not be in a position to reward or punish certain subordinates, but may still exercise power over the subordinates because the manager commands their respect or esteem.
- **Expert power** is based on the subordinate's *perception* of the leader as someone who is competent and who has some special knowledge or expertise in a given area. Expert power is based on credibility and clear evidence of knowledge or expertise; for example, the expert knowledge of 'functional' specialists such as the personnel manager, management accountant or systems analyst. The expert power is usually limited to narrow, well-defined areas or specialisms.

Finlay suggests that in addition to the five sources of power identified by French and Raven can be added:

- personal power, supported and trusted by their colleagues and subordinates; and
- connection power, which results from personal and professional access to key people and information.[56]

Subordinates' perception of influence It is important to note that these sources of power are based on the subordinate's *perception* of the influence of the leader, whether it is real or not. For example, if a leader has the ability to control rewards and punishments but subordinates *do not believe this*, then in effect the leader has no reward or coercive power. Similarly, if subordinates in a line department *believe* a manager in a (different) staff department has executive authority over them then even if, *de facto*, that manager has no such authority there is still a *perceived* legitimate power.

French and Raven point out that the five sources of power are interrelated and the use of one type of power (for example, coercive) may affect the ability to use another type of power (for example, referent). Furthermore, the same person may exercise different types of power, in particular circumstances and at different times.

> *You have to look at leadership through the eyes of the followers and you have to live the message. What I have learned is that people become motivated when you guide them to the source of their own power and when you make heroes out of employees who personify what you want to see in the organisation.*
>
> Anita Roddick[57]

NO ONE BEST FORM OF LEADERSHIP

We have seen that there are many alternative forms and styles of managerial leadership. Within an organisation different individuals may fulfil the functions of leadership and there are many different styles of leadership. A potential danger with the contingency approach is that the manager may appear to lack consistency in leadership style. However, although subordinates may reasonably expect some degree of consistency from the manager in approaching the same type of problem with the same style, this is not to say that different types of problems should be approached in the same manner. Subordinates would ordinarily expect a different style of managerial leadership according to the contingencies of the situation.

The right leader for the right situation As *Rajan* also points out: 'Of course, different leadership styles are needed to cope with different situations: for example, the autocratic style makes sense when an organisation is in deep trouble and needs to achieve a rapid turn-around. That style would be counter-productive when the organisation is in a growth situation.'[58] And *Stern* maintains that although in more carefree times business gurus exalted leaders who admitted to frailty, not any more. The task of sustaining growth in a sluggish market calls for driven, leather-skinned bosses. Instead of touchy-feely management the quality of 'mental toughness' is needed to help elite performers to prevail.[59]

Different styles at different stages of a business Different types of leadership may also be most appropriate at different stages in the development of a business organisation. Leadership can also vary between public and private sectors and depend upon the size of the organisation. According to the DTI, a primary challenge for organisational leaders in promoting innovation is:

> *Recognise and develop appropriate leadership for the different stages of the innovation process. How leaders are selected, supported, evaluated, motivated and developed is likely to differ depending upon the stage of the innovation process they are responsible for. For instance, transformational leadership skills may be more useful in early-stage innovation activity, such as R & D and product development, but transactional leadership skills are also essential to the smooth functioning of commercialisation.*[60]

National cultural dimensions

Another major variable influencing choice of leadership style may be national culture. *McGregor* concluded that the social, economic and political environment affected the leadership relationship, together with the attitudes and needs of 'followers'.[61] *Tannenbaum and Schmidt* identify leaders' own value systems as factors that influence their chosen style. They also highlight subordinates' – or non-managers' – needs for independence and tolerance of ambiguity as relevant variables in the choice of style.[62] These factors vary according to the cultural context in which the leadership relationship takes place. One should be wary of stereotyping the behaviour of leaders or subordinates, and many myths appear to have grown around notions of 'orderly' German, 'undisciplined' Italian and even 'obstructive' British workers. However, there are reasons to suggest that there may indeed be national cultural differences that are relevant to an understanding of leadership.

Refresh your understanding

Activity 10D
www.pearsoned.co.uk/
mullins

Culture as a contingent factor in leadership? The contribution of contingency approaches to understanding leadership suggest that contrasting types and styles of leadership may be more or less appropriate in different situations. *Tayeb* draws attention to cross-cultural leadership and points out that in a global business landscape, national culture affects leadership styles and behaviours. It is clear that people living in different parts of the world have different expectations from those in a leadership position. The way in which employees perceive their leaders, as employee-oriented or task-oriented, appears to vary from culture to culture.[63]

LEADERSHIP EFFECTIVENESS

Research undertaken by the consulting firm Hay/McBer, as reported by Goleman, has studied which precise leadership behaviours yield positive results. The research drew on a sample of 3871 executives worldwide and identified six, well-known different styles of leadership, each springing from different components of emotional intelligence:

- coercive leaders – who demand immediate compliance;
- authoritative leaders – who mobilise people towards a vision;
- affiliative leaders – who create emotional bonds and harmony;
- democratic leaders – who build consensus through participation;
- pacesetting leaders – who expect excellence and self-direction;
- coaching leaders – who develop people for the future.

However, only four of these leadership styles had a positive effect. The coercive style demanded immediate compliance, lacked flexibility and motivation, and was the least effective style. The pacesetting style set high standards of performance but led to a drop in morale and had a largely negative impact.

Reliance on more than one style *Goleman* reports that the most effective executives use a collection of distinct leadership styles, each in the right measure, at just the right time. Although the authoritative style of leadership can be occasionally overbearing, it was found to be most effective and can motivate and inspire commitment to the goals of the organisation. The affiliative style has potential to create harmony within teams and can be used in conjunction with the authoritative style. The democratic approach was seen as positive, and encourages input from staff and helps build consensus through participation. The coaching style, although the least frequently used, can help staff identify their strengths and encourage long-term development goals. The study concludes that the most effective leaders rely on more than one leadership style, and were able to master a mixture of authoritative, democratic, affiliative and coaching styles. Leaders with the best results use most of the styles in a given week – seamlessly and in different measure – depending on the business situation.[64]

Variables affecting leadership effectiveness

Clearly, there is no one 'best' form of leadership that will result in the maintenance of morale among group members and high work performance. Three main aspects to be considered in determining the most appropriate style of leadership are: the manager, the group and the work environment.

However, there are many variables that underlie the effectiveness of leadership in work organisations. More specifically, these include the following:

- the characteristics of the manager, personality, attitudes, abilities, value system, and the personal credibility of the manager;
- the type of power of the manager and the basis of the leadership relationship;

- the characteristics of the followers: diversity, their needs and expectations, attitudes, knowledge, confidence and experience, and their motivation and commitment;
- the relationship between the manager and the group, and among members of the group;
- the type and nature of the organisation, organisation culture, and different stages in innovation and development;
- the nature of the tasks to be achieved, the extent to which structured or routine;
- the technology, systems of communication and methods of work organisation;
- organisation structure and systems of management;
- the type of problem and the nature of the manager's decisions;
- the nature and influence of the external environment;
- the social structure and informal organisation, and the psychological contract;
- the influence of national culture.

The shadow of leadership *McCabe* suggests that leaders who want to transform their performance and the effectiveness of the team should look at how their own shadow could be getting in the way. Leaders focus on what they see as important and they are typically quite unconscious of the unintended but massive impact they are having on their colleagues, teams and clients. All leaders cast a shadow and whatever a particular leadership style, the shadow will affect others and can compromise people's engagement at work and business effectiveness. Leaders need to be fully aware of the shadow they cast and the impact they have on others.

> To be successful, leaders today have to find ways to engage people's ideas, energy and inspiration and this means they will have to build much stronger relationships – and what will prevent such relationships from occurring is their shadow.[65]

Leadership attributes *Valenti* suggests that by whatever means a person attains a leadership position, there are five essential qualities that he or she must possess to be a successful leader over time. A leader must have:

- **courage** – to do what is right and to overcome obstacles;
- **confidence** – the unshakeable belief in yourself to make happen what you want to happen;
- **concentration** – persistence and the unwillingness to quit, and focus to stay on track;
- **passion** – for what they do and what they believe in with enthusiasm and commitment;
- **values** – a strong sense of enduring standards of behaviour.[66]

The DTI found that the three most frequently identified leadership attributes are vision (79 per cent), trust (77 per cent), and respect (73 per cent). However, less than four in ten followers see these behaviours demonstrated within their own company.[67]

LEADERSHIP DEVELOPMENT

Education and training in management needs to emphasise not only interpersonal skills but also a flexibility of approach, diagnostic ability and the realisation that the most effective form of leadership behaviour is a product of the total leadership situation.

According to Investors in People, leadership development is not just a corporate issue: 'The ability to create and communicate a clear vision, and motivate people to deliver it, is as important to the small entrepreneur as to the leader of 1000 people. All organisations should be identifying the managers they will need in a few years' time and developing them. All top managers should be planning their succession and supporting the people who will step into their shoes when it's time to move on.'[68] (The Investors in People 'Leadership and Management Model' is discussed in Chapter 20.)

Leadership development in the public sector

Extensive research undertaken by the Chartered Management Institute reveals that consistently poor ratings accorded to public sector leaders is a key cause for concern during a period of major reform. The survey of 1900 public sector managers, mostly at middle and junior level, reveals that only 33 per cent of managers rate the leadership demonstrated by their most senior management team as high quality. Although a wide and varied range of training activities is taking place, the majority of managers perceive a low priority placed on leadership development. Only a quarter of respondents claimed their organisational budget for developing leaders is adequate and organisations are still tending to rely on traditional and formalised methods of developing their leaders.[69]

Seven principles for developing leaders

Referring to his action-centred leadership model (discussed earlier in this chapter), *Adair* identifies seven key principles of leadership development that can be applied successfully in different kinds of organisations in both the public and private sectors.

1 **Development of a strategy for leadership development** for each of the three levels of leadership – operational, strategic and team.
2 **Selection** of those with high potential for becoming effective leaders.
3 **Training for leadership** that implies instruction with a specific end in view. Identify your business training needs in the leadership context and assign them priorities.
4 **Career development** through giving a person the right job at the right time. People grow as leaders through the actual practice of leading.
5 **Line managers as leadership developers** by developing the individual's potential and sharing their knowledge of leadership.
6 **Corporate culture** that is valued at all levels and should encourage a climate of self-development in leadership.
7 **The chief executive** who should be leading from the front and who owns the problem of growing leaders.

The seven principles are complementary and are likely to have a synergetic effect if applied as a whole. Although a simple framework, Adair maintains the seven principles form the first coherent and effective approach for growing leaders.[70]

The leadership jigsaw

The DTI report referred to previously found that around a third of employees surveyed had never worked for, or been motivated by, an exceptional leader. In order that aspiring leaders can find out if they have the necessary skills, *Cutler* has designed a 'jigsaw' of best practice. There are six interlinking pieces: vision, example, relationships, motivation, empowerment and communications as a guide to the measurement and development of leadership skills. Cutler believes that leadership is not such a difficult role if condensed to these essential elements and has devised a set of questions to help aspiring leaders to find out if they have all the necessary pieces of the jigsaw (*see* Figure 10.10).[71]

LEADERS OF THE FUTURE

Gratton points out that while we are part of organisations shaped by technology that created the patents, ideas and innovations that brought success, the past will not bring sustainable competitive advantage for the future. To do this we have to build the potential of people in our organisations, the knowledge they bring and their commitment and enthusiasm.

Figure 10.10 | **The leadership 'jigsaw'**

VISION – Do you:
1 Work hard at communicating your vision for the organisation to all staff at all levels?
2 Understand that your vision must appeal to your staff at both an emotional and practical level if they are to join you on your journey?
3 Understand the culture and values of your organisation and their impact on its future development?
4 Recognise blind alleys!

MOTIVATION – Do you:
1 Understand that every member has a different set of motivational stimuli?
2 Explain your decisions in terms of their benefit to the organisation and its members?
3 Celebrate and reward individual and team achievements?
4 Prefer to offer carrots, rather than weird sticks!

EXAMPLE – Do you:
1 Match your words with your actions?
2 Take full responsibility for organisational problems, even if you were not directly responsible?
3 Occasionally muck in when your staff are under pressure at work?
4 Regularly consider what you see in the bathroom mirror!

EMPOWERMENT – Do you:
1 Believe that people generally respond well when given greater responsibility for their own performance?
2 Allocate sufficient resources to training and development?
3 Get a buzz when staff set and achieve their own goals?
4 Realise that the organisation would still function if you were not there!

RELATIONSHIPS – Do you:
1 Work hard at countering a them and u s' culture within your organisation?
2 Set clear codes of acceptable conduct and take action against breaches of them?
3 Stress that everyone contributes to the success of the team(s) they belong to?
4 Admit when you make a mistake!

COMMUNICATIONS – Do you:
1 Use your influence to encourage two-way communications at all levels in your organisation?
2 Encourage personal contact rather than written, mechanical or technological alternatives?
3 Encourage a diversity of opinion and constructive criticism?
4 Walk the talk!

Source: Adapted from Cutler, A., 'A good fit is essential', *Professional Manager*, vol. 15, no. 3, May 2005, p. 38. Reproduced with permission from Chartered Management Institute and the author.

Building human potential demands a new agenda, a new set of challenges for leaders and a redefined set of managerial capabilities. This new agenda creates a set of expectations of the leaders. Gratton sets out four expectations as the message for leaders.

- **Expectation 1: dream collectively** – create a time and a process for you and your colleagues to dream about the future; create enthusiasm and excitement and a vision for the future; view the present as a pathway to the future; allow people to work independently but within the frame of the general direction; and work to identify and co-ordinate the major themes for action.
- **Expectation 2: balance the short term with the longer term** – think in the past, the present and the future; be aware of the human scale of change and create plans of action that reflect human time scales and a capacity in human potential; build a vision for the future that engages people and allows them to understand their future role.
- **Expectation 3: build an organisation that values people** – treat people with respect and have their ideas taken seriously and allow them to believe they can make a difference; be aware of the need to create communication channels with employees; demonstrate a commitment to people; treat people with politeness, respect and dignity and create a strong role model for others to follow.

- **Expectation 4: understand the reality of the organisation** – create a deep, shared understanding of the current state of the business, and examine the metaphor of the organisation; put the building of a highly committed workforce at the centre of strategy; build a model of your organisation around high levels of trust, commitment and inspiration; develop an understanding of process fairness and justice, and understand employees' perceptions of integrity, consistency and pride.[72]

Leaders as architects of collectives According to *Hill*, world-class companies in the 21st century will be ever-evolving collectives of talented, passionate and diverse individuals. Leaders will be the architects of these collectives. With more companies having access to the same technology, markets, production method and channels of distribution, the competitive element has fundamentally changed. The strategic management of talent has become the key to competitive advantage. Leadership is about providing the moral and strategic vision that defines the collective's identity and binds the individuals together. A significant portion of leaders' time will be spent on locating, assessing, attracting and, when necessary, developing the needed talent. Once leaders have clarified the vision and collected the talent, they have to execute the vision. This entails shaping the collective, the culture, processes and the structure.[73]

New skills and competencies

Bennis hails the arrival of new leadership and suggests that 'the leaders of the future will have to cast off the heavy burden of command and control, hierarchically based leadership'. Leaders will have to learn an entirely new set of skills and that four competencies will determine the success of new leadership.

1 **The new leader understands and practises the power of appreciation** – as a generalisation most organisations are woefully neglectful of bestowing acknowledgement or appreciation, yet it is one of the most powerful motivators, especially for knowledge workers.
2 **The new leader keeps reminding people of what is important** – organisations drift into entropy and bureaucratisation of imagination when they forget what's important. Reminding people of what is important can give meaning and value to work, and collective focused energy.
3 **The new leader generates and sustains trust** – the terms of the new social contract of work have changed and no one can depend on lifelong loyalty or commitment to any organisation. Trust has powerful connotations and the ingredients are a combination of competencies, constancy, caring, fairness, candour and, most of all, authenticity.
4 **The new leader and the led are intimate allies** – new leadership is all about great leaders being made by great groups and by organisations that create the social architecture of respect and dignity, and great leadership brings that about. Without each other, the leader and the led are culturally impoverished.

Refresh your understanding

Activity 10E
www.pearsoned.co.uk/
mullins

The post-bureaucratic organization requires a new kind of alliance between leaders and the led. Today's organizations are evolving into federations, networks, clusters, cross-functional teams, temporary systems, ad hoc task forces, lattices, modules, matrices – almost anything but pyramids with their obsolete top–down leadership. The new leader will encourage healthy dissent and value those followers courageous enough to say no. It will go to the leader who exults in cultural differences and knows that diversity is the best hope for long-term survival and success. This does not mark the end of leadership. Rather the need for a new, far more subtle and indirect form of influence for leaders to be effective.[74]

Critical reflection

??????

Despite the vast amount of writing on the subject by both academics and practising managers, it is extremely difficult to give a precise and agreed definition of leadership. Do you find this confusing and a hindrance to your studies? Nor is there agreement on one best model or style of leadership, or how leadership potential can best be developed. What do you believe are the essential characteristics that make for an effective leader?

MANAGEMENT IN THE NEWS

Learning to lead

Leadership: ways to instil those elusive qualities

Richard Donkin

Leadership studies have become a multi-million-pound earner for business schools and consultants on both sides of the Atlantic, as companies clamour to imbue their executives with the qualities needed to create, transform and sustain successful businesses. Underpinning this 'market' are scores of leadership books, all adding a particular view or facet to the genre. Leadership is the number one topic in the *Harvard Business Review* and few large companies have neglected to develop their own leadership or talent management programmes.

Like art, leadership tends to defy attempts at framing precise definitions. Warren Bennis, the world's leading exponent of leadership theory, has described it as 'the capacity to create a compelling vision and translate it into action and sustain it'. But, also like art, leadership is subject to competing influences and popular movements that are constantly changing the way it is perceived.

Harvard-based Ronald Heifetz, one of the most influential of the modern generation of theorists, says leadership is about 'mobilising people to make progress on the hardest of problems'. Debate still rages on the extent to which leadership must be a quality not only of a recognised leader but of managers and other employees throughout a business. The vast majority of leadership programmes, however, are designed to prepare people for senior positions at the head of organisations, divisions or departments in roles that have become invested with authority.

One of the biggest challenges facing companies is preparing people for leadership positions who may have excelled in their specialist role but have little experience of managing or leading. Here, some of the latest thinking is directed not at creating leadership positions but towards investing specialists with influencing and interventionist behaviours that equip them to lead without designated authority.

'New research we have undertaken among clients points to an identified need for more of the so-called soft skills of leadership such as emotional intelligence, rather than concerns with position and function,' says Kim Lafferty, country director, UK and Ireland, at the Center for Creative Leadership (Europe). 'Interdependent decision-making is coming to be valued more than independent decision making and companies are becoming far more interested in collaboration than used to be the case,' she says.

While some leadership issues may be universal, there is also a growing recognition among business schools that companies may have specific leadership issues. Some companies, including IBM in a recent exercise, seek to identify leadership competencies based on traits, behaviours and skills identified in high performers. Future leaders are then selected or developed against the competency base.

According to Prof Heifetz, most students of leadership turn up to class with a list of what he calls 'technical problems' that have ready solutions. His task, he believes, is to confront his classes less with issues of power, persuasion and personality – what might be classed as traditional concerns of leadership – and more with their capacity to deal with competing values, changing attitudes and new learning.

'We used to talk about the 'knowing–doing' gap. Now we are talking about the 'knowing–being' gap,' says Ms Lafferty. 'It's a subtle difference but it makes

Management in the news – continued

leadership something more inclusive than exclusive and that's important.'

Source: Donkin, R., 'Leadership: ways to instil those elusive qualitites'. *Financial Times*, 13 November 2005. Copyright © Richard Donkin, reproduced with permission.

Discussion questions

1 What different skills do you think might be necessary for organisational leaders who hold positions of authority, and those who do not? How far do the requirements overlap?

2 Review and discuss the implications of this trend away from leadership on the basis of designated authority for both the design and structure of organisations, and the selection and training of managers.

SYNOPSIS

● There are many ways of looking at leadership and many interpretations of its meaning, but essentially it is a relationship through which one person influences the behaviour or actions of other people. The leader–follower relationship is reciprocal and effective leadership is a two-way process. Leadership is related to motivation, the process of communication, the activities of groups and the process of empowerment. The changing nature of business organisations has placed increasing importance on leadership.

● There is a close relationship between leadership and management, especially in work organisations, and an increasing tendency to see them as synonymous. However, arguably there are differences between the two and it does not follow that every leader is a manager. Leadership may be viewed in more general terms, with emphasis on interpersonal behaviour in a broader context.

● Due to its complex nature there are many alternative ways of analysing leadership. Leadership may be examined in terms of the qualities or traits approach, in terms of the functional or group approach, as a behavioural category, in terms of styles of leadership, through the situational approach and contingency models, and in terms of the distinction between transactional or transformational leadership.

● Contingency theories draw attention to the interactions between the variables involved in a leadership situation and patterns of leadership behaviour. The most appropriate form of leadership is dependent upon the variables in a particular leadership situation. Different contingency theories have concentrated on different situational variables. These include favourability of the leadership situation, decision acceptance and decision quality, path–goal theory, and the 'readiness' of followers.

● The attention given to transformational leadership and the importance of charisma has given rise to an increasing focus on the concept of leaders creating a vision with which others can identify and inspiring followers to improve organisational performance. There is, however, doubt about the extent to which leaders possess these personal qualities. Attention is also given to the impact of leadership on innovation and to the dual role of leaders as both motivators and organisational architects.

● Leadership is a dynamic form of behaviour and the leader's influence is dependent upon the type of power exercised over other people. However, there is no one best form or style of leadership. There are many variables that underlie the effectiveness of leadership, including dimensions of national culture. The most successful form of leadership behaviour is a product of the total leadership situation. Attention needs to be given to leadership development. Leaders of the future will face new expectations and will need to learn new sets of skills.

Refresh your understanding, assess your progress and begin your research with online resources at **www.pearsoned.co.uk/mullins**

REVIEW AND DISCUSSION QUESTIONS

1 Explain clearly what you understand by the meaning of leadership. How would you distinguish leadership from management?

2 Distinguish between different approaches to the study of leadership and discuss critically what you see as the relevance today of each of these approaches.

3 Using the Tannenbaum and Schmidt continuum, identify, with reasons, your preferred style of leadership. Give an example of a situation in which you might need to adopt an alternative style of leadership.

4 What do you understand by leader–situation models of leadership? Assess the practical value to the manager of: (i) Fiedler's contingency model of leadership effectiveness, and (ii) Hersey and Blanchard's model of situational leadership.

5 Discuss the main sources of power and leadership influence. Give a practical example of each of these main sources of power and influence within your own organisation.

6 Explain clearly the nature and main features of transformational leadership. Give your own examples of people you would regard as transformational leaders. Discuss critically the relevance of personal qualities or charisma for effective leadership.

7 Discuss the main situational variables that are likely to influence the most appropriate form of managerial leadership behaviour. Detail three work situations in which a different style of leadership is likely to be most effective.

8 If you were a consultant on leadership, what areas of needs would you include in designing a leadership development programme for managers in a large work organisation? Justify your ideas.

ASSIGNMENT 1

a Think of:
 (i) one of the 'best' leaders, *and*
 (ii) one of the 'worst' leaders that you have experienced, preferably in a work situation.

b Identify and list those specific qualities, or lack of them, which were characteristic of *each* leader. Where possible, draw up your list under three broad headings of:
 (i) personal attributes – for example, intelligence, appearance;
 (ii) social relationships – for example, approachability, interests;
 (iii) task performance – for example, delegation, discipline.

c Give a brief description of an actual situation that illustrates the behaviour/actions of *each* leader and the results of such behaviour/action. Keep your answer balanced. Try to be as objective as possible and avoid personal bias.

d Draw up your *own* list, with brief supporting descriptions, of the main characteristics you would expect to be exhibited by a successful leader. Be prepared to justify your lists and descriptions in class discussion.

ASSIGNMENT 2

Your leadership style

For each of the following ten pairs of statements, divide five points between the two according to your beliefs, perceptions of yourself, or according to which of the two statements characterises you better. The five points may be divided between the A and B statements in any way you wish with the constraint that only whole positive

Assignment – continued

integers may be used (i.e. you may not split 2.5 points equally between the two). Weigh your choices between the two according to the one that better characterises you or your beliefs.

1 A As leader I have a primary mission of maintaining stability. _____

 B As leader I have a primary mission of change. _____

2 A As leader I must cause events. _____

 B As leader I must facilitate events. _____

3 A I am concerned that my followers are rewarded equitably for their work. _____

 B I am concerned about what my followers want in life. _____

4 A My preference is to think long range: What might be. _____

 B My preference is to think short range: What is realistic. _____

5 A As a leader I spend considerable energy in managing separate but related goals. _____

 B As a leader I spend considerable energy in arousing hopes, expectations, and aspiration among my followers. _____

6 A While not in a formal classroom sense, I believe that a significant part of my leadership is that of a teacher. _____

 B I believe that a significant part of my leadership is that of a facilitator. _____

7 A As leader I must engage with followers at an equal level of morality. _____

 B As leader I must represent a higher morality. _____

8 A I enjoy stimulating followers to want to do more. _____

 B I enjoy rewarding followers for a job well done. _____

9 A Leadership should be practical. _____

 B Leadership should be inspirational. _____

10 A What power I have to influence others comes primarily from my ability to get people to identify with me and my ideas. _____

 B What power I have to influence others comes primarily from my status and position. _____

Details of scoring and interpretation will be provided by your tutor.

Source: From Schermerhorn, J. R., Jr., *et al*. *Managing Organizational Behaviour*, Fourth Edition, John Wiley & Sons (1991), p. 484. Reproduced with permission from John Wiley & Sons Inc.

PERSONAL AWARENESS AND SKILLS EXERCISE

Evaluate your skills

Self-knowledge is crucial for evaluating achievements and potential. Below is a list of attributes associated with leadership. Read through these statements and evaluate the leadership skills demonstrated by your team and those that you display. Score yourself from one to ten for each attribute or put ticks or crosses in the boxes. Use this information to consider areas where you or your team could develop.

1 **Demonstrating initiative, delivering operational excellence, implementing decisions and delivering results.**

 I reinforce people's determination to do the right thing. ☐

 I have a strong work ethic. ☐

I do things right for the first time.

I stay focused on priorities and recognise when to delegate tasks.

I stretch myself to meet the values of others and myself simultaneously.

I demonstrate values by tangible and visible actions.

I choose service over self-interest.

I act with integrity.

2 Drawing groups together, enjoying team management and placing importance on the development of others.

I reward and recognise team members daily.

I use analogy to simplify conceptual ideas.

I connect and integrate values into the working operation of the organisation.

I clarify future direction in terms that make sense.

I reduce strategic plans to simple ideas which can be easily communicated.

I communicate effectively with internal and external stakeholders.

I target communication to the needs of the audience in pace, level and method of delivery.

I break complex targets down into digestible pieces.

3 Offering support, demonstrating active listening and encouraging others to achieve objectives.

I demonstrate trust in others to perform effectively.

I recognise that leadership is a process of upward as well as downward influence.

I inspire excitement with my communication style.

I encourage hard-hitting debate and dialogue.

I display stature and presence to gain commitment and loyalty.

I put aside personal ambition for the sake of the whole.

I take time to connect with each team member.

I set clear goals and success criteria, allowing people to use their initiative.

4 Demonstrating decisiveness, offering inspiration and eliciting respect by touching hearts, not just minds.

I take pride in winning as a team, not just individually.

I foster the development of a common vision.

I appear consistently enthusiastic and inspirational about the vision.

I build the capacity of the next generation of leaders by investing in the team

I hold myself accountable, without blaming others.

I hold myself accountable with the clear understanding that ethical standards must never be comprised.

I manage the ambiguity of leadership and power.

I find a sense of continuity through others.

Source: *The Path to Leadership: Developing a Sustainable Model within Organisations*, CBI (in association with Harvey Nash), September 2005. Reproduced with permission from CBI.

Your tasks

1 How and to what extent does Steve Jobs' career illuminate the difference between management and leadership?

2 How can Steve Jobs' leadership style be analysed? To what extent does the evidence so far conform to the Burns model of transformational leadership?

3 Jobs' career has been in two industries that are characterised by rapid market change, fast technological development and considerable turbulence. Critically examine the extent to which these situational factors bear upon the leadership style that Jobs has shown over the years.

Notes and references

1 Crainer, S. 'Have the Corporate Superheroes had their Day?', *Professional Manager*, March 1995, pp. 8–12.

2 Useem, M. 'How to Groom Leaders of the Future', in Pickford, J. (ed.) *Financial Times Mastering Management 2.0*, Financial Times Prentice Hall (2001), p. 297.

3 CBI, 'The Path to Leadership: Developing a sustainable model within organisations', Caspian Publishing, September 2005, p. 4.

4 Havey-Jones, J. (Sir) in Mann, S. 'Top Guru', *Professional Manager*, September 2002, p. 17.

5 Levine, S. R. 'The Value-Based Edu-Leader', in Chowdhury, S. *Management 21C*, Financial Times Prentice Hall (2000), p. 90.

6 Judge, P. (Sir), 'Standard-bearer', *Professional Manager*, vol. 12, no. 1, January 2003, p. 19.

7 'Leadership for Innovation', Advanced Institute of Management Research, 2005.

8 Fullan, M. *Leading in a Culture of Change*, Jossey-Bass (2001).

9 Charlesworth, K. Cook, P. and Crozier, G. *Leading Change in the Public Sector: Making the Difference*, Chartered Management Institute, May 2003.

10 Belbin, R.M. *Changing the Way We Work*, Butterworth-Heinemann (1997), p. 98.

11 Watson, C. M. 'Leadership, Management and the Seven Keys', *Business Horizons*, March–April 1983, pp. 8–13.

12 Zaleznik, A. 'Managers and Leaders: Are They Different?' *Harvard Business Review*, May–June 1977, pp. 67–78.

13 Fullan, M. *Leading in a Culture of Change*, Jossey-Bass (2001), p. 2.

14 Dearlove, D. 'Reinventing Leadership', in Crainer, S. and Dearlove, D. (eds) *Financial Times Handbook of Management*, Second edition, Financial Times Prentice Hall (2001), p. 538.

15 'The Leadership and Management Model', Investors in People UK, 2003.

16 Moorcroft, R. 'To lead or to manage? That is the question'. *Manager, The British Journal of Administrative Management*, November 2005, p. 4.

17 Drucker, P. F. *The Practice of Management*, Heinemann Professional (1989), p. 156.

18 See for example Bryman, A. 'Leadership in Organisations' in Clegg, S. Hardy, C. and Nord, W. (eds), *Managing Organsations: Current Issues*, Sage (1999), pp. 26–62.

19 Kotter, J. P. 'What Leaders Really Do', *Harvard Business Review*, May–June 1990, p. 103.

20 Whitehead, M. 'Everyone's a Leader Now', *Supply Management*, 25 April 2002, pp. 22–4.

21 Adair, J. *Action-Centred Leadership*, Gower (1979). See also: Adair, J. *The Skills of Leadership*, Gower (1984).

22 Fleishman, E. A. 'Leadership Climate, Human Relations Training and Supervisory Behavior', in Fleishman, E. A. and Bass, A. R. *Studies in Personnel and Industrial Psychology*, Third edition, Dorsey (1974).

23 Bryman, A. 'Leadership in Organisations', in Clegg, S. Hardy, C. and Nord, W. (eds), *Managing Organsations: Current Issues*, Sage (1999), pp. 26–62.

24 Likert, R. *New Patterns of Management*, McGraw-Hill (1961).

25 Tannenbaum, R. and Schmidt, W. H. 'How to Choose a Leadership Pattern', *Harvard Business Review*, May–June 1973, pp. 162–75, 178–80.

26 Fiedler, F.E. *A Theory of Leadership Effectiveness*, McGraw-Hill (1967).

27 See, for example: Yukl, G. *Leadership in Organizations*, Fifth edition, Prentice Hall (2002).

28 Vroom, V. H. and Yetton, P. W. *Leadership and Decision-Making*, University of Pittsburgh Press (1973).

29 Vroom, V. H. and Jago, A. G. *The New Leadership: Managing Participation in Organizations*, Prentice-Hall (1988).

30 House, R. J. 'A Path–Goal Theory of Leadership Effectiveness', *Administrative Science Quarterly*, vol. 16, September 1971, pp. 321–38.

31 House, R. J. and Dessler, G. 'The Path–Goal Theory of Leadership', in Hunt, J. G. and Larson, L. L. (eds) *Contingency Approaches to Leadership*, Southern Illinois University Press (1974).

32 Hersey, P. and Blanchard, K. H. *Management of Organizational Behavior: Utilizing Human Resources*, Sixth edition, Prentice-Hall (1993).

33 Burns, J. M. *Leadership*, Harper & Row (1978).

34 Bass, B. M. *Leadership and Performance Beyond Expectations*, Free Press (1985).

35 Bass, B. M. and Avolio, B. J. *Improving Organizational Performance Through Transformational Leadership*, Sage Publications (1994).

36 Yukl, G. *Leadership in Organizations*, Sixth edition, Pearson Prentice-Hall (2006).

37 Kreitner, R., Kinicki, A. and Buelens, M. *Organizational Behaviour*, First European edition, McGraw-Hill (1999), p. 487.

38 Conger, J. 'Charisma and How to Grow It', *Management Today*, December 1999, pp. 78–81.

39 Conger, J. 'Danger of Delusion. The qualities that make leaders great can also cause their downfall. Success and self-confidence often breed narcissism and a sense of infallibility', *Financial Times*, 29 November 2002.

40 Dearlove, D. 'Reinventing Leadership', in Crainer, S. and Dearlove, D. (eds) *Financial Times Handbook of Management*, Second edition, Financial Times Prentice Hall (2001), p. 538.

41 Bloomfield, S. 'Charismatic Leaders are Passé', *Professional Manager*, vol. 12, no. 1, January 2003, p. 37.

42 Adair, J. *The Inspirational Leader: How to Motivate, Encourage and Achieve Success*, Kogan Page (2003).

43 Whitehead, M. 'Everyone's a Leader Now', *Supply Management*, 25, April 2002, pp. 22–4.

44 Kahan, S. 'Visionary Leadership' *The Great Washington Society of Association Executives*, www.leader-values.com [accessed 28 January 2006].

45 Gratton, L. *The Democratic Enterprise*, Financial Times Prentice Hall (2004).

46 Witzel, M. 'Book review: A rewarding read if you want to lead' www.ft.com [accessed 31 January 2006].

47 Goffee, R. and Jones, G. *Why Should Anyone Be Led By You?* Harvard Business School Press (2006).

48 Nicholson, Bryan (Sir), 'In my opinion', *Management Today*, January 2006, p. 10.

49 Horne, M. and Jones, D. S. *Leadership: the Challenge for All?*, Chartered Management Institute, December 2001.

50 'Inspired Leadership: Insights into people who inspire exceptional performance', Department of Trade and Industry, August 2004.

51 'Leadership for Innovation', Advanced Institute of Management Research, March 2005.

52 McGregor, D. *The Human Side of Enterprise*, Penguin (1987), p. 182.

53 Kouzes, J. M. and Posner, B. Z. 'The Janusian Leader', in Chowdhury, S. *Management 21C*, Financial Times Prentice Hall (2000), p. 18.

54 Fullan, M. *Leading in a Culture of Change*, Jossey-Bass (2001), p. 5.

55 French, J. R. P. and Raven, B. 'The Bases of Social Power', in Cartwright, D. and Zander, A. F. (eds) *Group Dynamics: Research and Theory*, Third edition, Harper and Row (1968).

56 Finlay, P. *Strategic Management: An Introduction to Business and Corporate Strategy*, Financial Times Prentice Hall (2000), p. 103.

57 Roddick, A. *Body and Soul*, Ebury Press (1991), p. 214.

58 Rajan, A. 'Meaning of Leadership in 2002', *Professional Manager*, March 2002, p. 33.

59 Stern, S. 'If You Think You're Hard Enough', *Management Today*, March 2003, pp. 46–51.

60 'Leadership for Innovation', Advanced Institute of Management Research, March 2005.

61 McGregor, D, *The Human Side of Enterprise*, Penguin (1987).

62 Tannenbaum, R. and Schmidt, W. H. 'How to Choose a Leadership Pattern', *Harvard Business Review*, May–June 1973, pp. 162–75, 178–80.

63 Tayeb, M. 'Cross-cultural leadership' in CBI, *The Path to Leadership: Developing a sustainable model within organisations*, Caspian Publishing, September 2005, pp. 14–20.

64 Goleman, D. 'Leadership That Gets Results', *Harvard Business Review*, vol. 78, no. 2, March–April 2000, pp. 78–90.

65 McCabe, B. 'The disabling shadow of leadership', *Manager, British Journal of Administrative Management*, April/May 2005, pp. 16–17.

66 Valenti, A. 'Five Essential Qualities of Leadership' www.leader-values.com [accessed 28 January 2006].

67 'Inspired Leadership: Insights into people who inspire exceptional performance', Department of Trade and Industry, August 2004.

68 *The Leadership and Management Model*, Investors in People UK, 2003, p. 3.

69 Charlesworth, K., Cook, P. and Crozier, G. *Leading Change in the Public Sector: Making the Difference*, Chartered Management Institute, May 2003.

70 Adair, J. *How to Grow Leaders*, Kogan Page (2005).

71 Cutler, A. 'A good fit is essential', *Professional Manager*, vol.14, no. 3 May 2005, p. 38.

72 Gratton, L. *Living Strategy: Putting People at the Heart of Corporate Purpose*, Financial Times Prentice Hall (2000).

73 Hill, L. 'Leadership as Collective Genius', in Chowdhury, S. *Management 21C*, Financial Times Prentice Hall (2000), pp. 45–65.

74 Bennis, W. 'The New Leadership', in Crainer, S. and Dearlove, D. (eds) *Financial Times Handbook of Management*, Second edition, Financial Times Prentice Hall (2001), pp. 546–50.

75 See, for example, the selection at http://www.answers.com/topic/steve-jobs.

76 Those around in that year may recall the iconic Orwellian '1984' television advert which cost $1.5m, was directed by Ridley Scott, aired only once in the USA during the 1984 Superbowl, and made advertising history with its implied critique of IBM. If you missed it, then you can view it at www.apple-history.com.

77 Waters, R (2005), 'Apple Bites Back', *Financial Times*, 10 June 2005.

78 Naughton, J and Mathiason, N (2005), Will Jobs' departure cut Apple to the core?' Observer Business and Media, 30 July 2006.

79 Waters, R (2005), 'Apple Bites Back', *Financial Times*, 10 June 2005.

80 http://americanhistory.si.edu/collections/comphist/sj1.html 'Oral and Video Histories: Steve Jobs', interview dated 20 April 1995.

81 http://www.quotationsbook.com/quotes/215/view and many others.

82 Hawn, C. (2004), 'If he's so smart … Steve Jobs, Apple and the Limits to Innovation', *Fast Company Magazine*, January 2004, at http://www.fastcompany.com/magazine/78/jobs.html.

83 http://www.forbes.com/lists/2006/10/Rank_1.html.

84 Naughton, J and Mathiason, N (2005), Will Jobs' departure cut Apple to the core?' *Observer Business and Media*, 30 July 2006.

85 Quoted in: Waters, R (2005), 'Apple Bites Back', *Financial Times*, 10 June 2005.

If a single word can be used to sum up the achievements of Tim Smit, that word might be 'regeneration'. To turn one derelict, neglected corner of southwest England into a successful tourist business attracting millions of visitors is a remarkable achievement; but to do it twice is simply astonishing. Yet this is precisely what Smit has done; and in the Eden Project we can see the nature of this achievement through a blend of visionary and innovative leadership combined with a strong sense of the value of teamwork.

Before Eden
Cornwall is one of several parts of the UK which suffered economic decline during the later 20th century. Its industrial heritage has all but disappeared in the wake of globalisation and the shifting nature of the industrial world landscape. The last tin mine closed in 1998, and the ruined mine towers are witness to what was once the largest tin mining industry in the world. The production of china clay remains one of Cornwall's oldest current industries, but that too is in decline and job losses in this sector continue to be announced. The fishing business is contracting, and traditional agricultural and horticultural production, mainly vegetables and flower bulbs, is being challenged by similar, year-round levels of production in developing countries. Cornwall as a county has, for some years, been in receipt of European Union Objective One funding destined to assist with economic regeneration in Europe's poorest regions. This level of relative poverty is probably something which many of the tourists who visit Cornwall's beautiful landscapes, historic properties and wild coastland do not generally see; and indeed tourism has become one of the largest single income-generating business sectors in the area. While there are some strong indications that the Cornish economy might be revitalised by the arrival of new, knowledge-based industries which are supported by technological developments, tourism remains at the heart of the county's economy.[1]

In 1990, in a project which would contribute substantially to Cornwall's reputation as a tourist destination, John Willis, Tim Smit and John Nelson began to restore the long derelict gardens surrounding the stately home and seat of the Tremayne family at Heligan, near Mevagissey. The story of this garden, its dereliction after the start of the Great War of 1914, its

The Eden Project is the realisation of one man's extraordinary vision through powerful teamwork and global co-operation.

rediscovery following a storm in 1990 and its restoration, in part as a memorial to the gardeners who would have died in the war, is one of enormous poignancy and beauty.[2] For Smit, an archaeology and anthropology graduate who had also developed a love of gardens, it was a project which enabled him to use many of his professional skills, and the garden itself has become one of England's most loved, and a major attraction for Cornwall.[3]

However, while Heligan is horticultural archaeology and the gardens today are, in essence, a living museum of 19th-century estate gardening, the Eden Project was a very different type of restoration, and one which drew upon Smit's additional skills as a rock music producer and showman. What Smit was restoring in his second major project was land; and the vision and purpose behind the Eden Project looks to the future rather than the past.

Ten things to do with a disused clay pit …
Photographs of what was to become the Eden Project prior to the arrival of Tim and his team reveal the extent of the transformation. In the mid 1990s the worked-out Bodelva china clay pit near St Austell looked very much like what many believed it to be; a derelict, polluted and worthless piece of land stripped of fertile soil – essentially a 34–acre puddle. The statistics behind its transformation into one of the most spectacular tourist attractions in the country are mind-boggling. The first task, in 1998 when the project began, was to landscape

the site, and shift 1.8 million tons of earth to reduce the pit side gradients; a task which took 12 dumper trucks and eight bulldozers six months. During the first few months of work, it rained almost continuously which resulted in 43 million gallons of water draining into the clay-lined pit.[4] This was both a problem and an opportunity; the problem was to design a drainage system which would prevent the whole site turning into a soggy bog during the average English summer; but the opportunity was to demonstrate one of the founding principles of sustainability, and use the run-off water to service the site. The system designed to meet this purpose collects, on average, 22 litres a second, and 74 per cent of the water needed to run the project (including plant watering, a 22 metre waterfall in the tropical biome and the numerous toilets!) is 'grey' water, in other words that which can be harvested from the site itself. Over 85 000 tonnes of soil, made from waste products and other organic material, were needed to turn the clay-lined puddle into the fertile ground in which over 1 000 000 plants of 5 000 and more species could grow, to create a series of global gardens.

The two original 'biomes', spectacular greenhouses which recreate a humid tropical environment and warm temperate climate respectively, are perhaps what most visitors remember about the project, although more than half the site is actually open air. The Humid Tropics biome was confirmed, in 2004, by the *Guinness Book of Records* as the largest conservatory in the world at 240 metres by 100 metres by 55 metres high, enclosing 15 590 square metres. It houses 'the biggest jungle in captivity' and contains plants native to the tropical areas of the world including Malaysia, West Africa and South America as well as islands like the Seychelles. The Warm Temperate biome covers 6540 square metres, and replicates a mediterranean climate housing plants which represent those which grow between 30–40° north and south of the equator. A recent addition to the buildings on site is 'The Core', the Project's education centre, the roof of which is constructed on the same mathematical principle (the Fibonacci sequence of interwoven spirals) which appears in nature in many plant formations, and which appears to be the way in which some plants pack the maximum number of seeds, spines or leaves into the smallest possible area.[5] The next planned development is that of an additional biome to house a Dry Tropics area.

If you build it, they will come

The Annual Report of 2005 stated that, to date, the Eden Project (which is a wholly owned subsidiary of the Eden Trust, a registered charity) had cost £120 million to build.[6] The money has been raised from a variety of sources including grant funding such as that from the UK government's millennium project fund; and further funding is being sought from the National Lottery to finance additional building. Together with commercial loans, the grant money is used for capital investment on the site and educational or conservation projects in other parts of the world. Revenues come from both the commercial activities of the Project and gifts or donations, and these are used to run the operation, maintain the asset base and service the commercial loans; so although as a charity it does not make a profit, it does have to run at commercially successful levels. Visitors are the major source of revenue. In its first year of operation it attracted twice the number of visitors estimated in the business plan, and over 7 million in its first five years of operation. Visitor numbers appear to be stabilising at about 1.2 million a year. But what exactly do people come to see?

Tim Smit's vision for Eden is far from being that of just another garden. He is, as we have noted, not a horticulturalist, but an archaeologist, anthropologist and former rock show organiser. The purpose of Eden is essentially to educate people about the environment and man's relationship with the plant world, but to do so in such a way as to set a conservation and sustainability example which is, above all things, spectacular fun. The 2005 Annual Report explains this purpose thus:

> *The Trust exists to explain how the natural world works and our dependence on it; telling the story of how plants support our social, economic and environmental well-being. We also explore how people might best organise themselves in the face of this knowledge and thereby reach an understanding of what sustainability can mean in practice. Meanwhile we are creating an organisation that is sustainable and will act as a model for others through best application of these principles.[7]*

The Project identifies three essential elements in its approach to this task:

- its educational activities and associated programmes; this includes the design of the site, and all the events which happen there, many of which are connected with schools and colleges or seek to convey important social messages. Eden, for instance, ran an 'Africa Calling' concert during the 2005 'Live8' day which featured a host of bands and internationally known artists from many parts of Africa;
- its operational practice and the way it runs the site should be an inspiration and example to both commercial corporations and public bodies; this is part of its aim to develop the notion of Social Enterprise, 'where the twin needs of good citizenship and the rigour of sound commerce meet'.[8] A good illustration of this is its 'waste neutral' initiative; and
- its outreach initiatives which seek to engage far-flung communities in related projects, most of which are about sustainability; for example, the 'Gardens for Life' initiative, the aim of which is to involve 70

schools from the UK, India and Kenya in developing shared educational resources about sustainable agriculture and horticulture.

The educational purpose which underlies the Project shows that this is, indeed, far more than just another garden.

> The underlying concept of the Eden educational programmes is to present the need for environmental care to the widest possible audience through celebrating what nature gives us – the focus is unashamedly on love and awe rather than guilt and fear. Eden weaves expertise in arts, media, science, technology, education and commerce to create a vehicle for raising awareness and inspiring people to action, to create a more sustainable future. Eden uses plants and products derived from them with the aim of making the visitor experience personal, relevant, thought-provoking; in short, a voyage of discovery.[9]

The achievement of this objective requires both focused and decisive leadership, but also powerful teamwork.

Taking a lead

The television series 'Gardeners of Eden' which presented a year in the life of the Eden Project gives some insight into both the nature of Tim Smit's leadership style and the range of activities undertaken by the different teams required to run the Project.[10] It also shows some of the very human problems associated with such an enterprise, including conflicts of interest between the Project's main purpose and some of the professional teams whose tasks are to contribute to that objective.

Smit generally dresses casually and has the slightly scruffy air of someone who is not accustomed to spending much of his working day in an office or behind a desk. He is comfortable talking to small groups or making formal presentations, such as his lecture at the RSA's 2004 'Day of Inspiration' to an audience of 3000 at the Albert Hall on the subject of Global Citizenship.[11] In a *Guardian* interview shortly before this lecture, the interviewer noted some of Smit's key qualities.

> Smit's secret, if there is one, seems to be that he can bring people of very different disciplines and skills together, get them to brainstorm and collaborate, and come up with the extraordinary. The Eden Project, he says, has attracted locals by the score, but also high-flying artists, businessmen, architects, scientists, engineers, educationalists, horticulturalists and ecologists from all over Britain. 'It feels like a renaissance organisation,' says one woman who left a senior management job to work there as a director and has been amazed both at what gets done and the way it works. 'It's attracted a critical mass of people, and there's this passionate belief, right through the project, that it belongs to everyone who works there, that it's a team thing. I guess it demonstrates that you can

> have an organisation that is highly effective financially, environmentally and socially. It's a kind of experiment to show that you can work in different ways.' A local woman who has been with Eden since the start is more succinct. 'It's the most equal place I've known,' she says.
>
> This is a stage for change,' says Smit, who admits that Eden can seem like a sect to outsiders. 'Many people have made life choices to come here. Most could earn five times as much elsewhere. But I'm aware that if you want to effect real change, and we do, that you must not own it. You have got to make sure that it's owned by more than one person.'[12]

Smit is described as optimistic and positive, with a mission to make people think differently. He is concerned to challenge dogma from all sides and is happy to question the views of committed environmentalists like José Bové as well as those of traditionalists. Although educational, he is convinced that the Eden Project need not be stuffy or seek to preach; above all, fun, excitement and spectacle are integral to the educational process. This lays him open to the accusation that it is no more than a 'green theme park', and indeed his desire to make the project a centre for spectacle and display brings him into conflict with the horticulturalists on the site. In the year of filming, it is clear that the two managers of the biomes deeply resent the disturbance and damage done to their plants by teams of electricians hired to lay lighting cables in and around the buildings to support some of the spectacles and events which are planned. A third curator-in-waiting is frustrated that the project to build the dry tropics biome which is planned to house his extensive cactus and succulent collection has been put back by several years, leapfrogged by the project to build the 'Core' education centre.

Smit is also very 'hands on' in the sense that he is both integral to many of the special events (for instance, the Rainforest Conference organised in September 2005) but is equally prepared to help sell tickets and guide visitors on the peak season 'tricky days' – peak visitor days on which staff who do not normally work with visitors are encouraged to follow his example and pitch in to help keep the operation moving.[13]

Working in paradise

By 2006, the Project had grown to be a major local employer with 500 staff on the payroll, and 70 or more additional regular volunteer workers who are drafted in to help with (mostly) peak seasonal activities such as horticulture and visitor operations. The workforce is focused into a number of 'Eden Teams', the main one being **The Destination Team**. This team includes the Green Team of horticultural curators and other experts who manage the biomes and the planting, but in addition the people who run events and exhibitions as well as the retail and catering operations. This team is

very much the 'front of house', as the gardeners work in the public eye during the day. However, as the programme shows, they also work outside opening hours, often at night, to carry out certain potentially hazardous activities, such as lopping unstable branches from trees in the rainforest. It is also clear from the series that there can be significant differences of opinion and interest between the Green Team and Smit. This came to the fore when Smit planned the first major winter event, the 'Time of Gifts' festival. This was partly an attempt to increase winter visitor numbers to the site, but required special construction (of an ice rink) and lighting in order to accommodate a variety of story-telling activities in the biomes, as well as 'light-and-magic' processions and shows. The whole event clearly opened something of a rift between members of the Green Team and Smit since many felt that their values were being compromised and the whole Project was becoming a sort of Disneyland. One curator told the BBC crew that the events not only did physical damage, but also damaged the morale of staff. Not only were curators upset, but the catering and housekeeping staff were also very concerned by the heavy demands (not least of which was having to learn to skate!) which would be made, and Smit is seen running a fairly fraught staff meeting with Destination personnel in an attempt to encourage them and gain extra commitment. When the event was successful, the staff were thrown a celebratory party, but nevertheless some of the Green Team were absent in protest. Smit explains his view about this conflict of interests:

I'm not into horticulture; my role isn't horticulture. My job is to fizz people into getting excited about horticulture, which is a very, very different activity. And actually, the

certainties that horticulturalists want are exactly the sort of thing I want to shake up.[14]

While the Destination Team is clearly the face of the Eden Project, other teams include the **Foundation Team** who work with supporters of the Project and also look outwards to develop education and other scientific and technological projects; **The Marketing Team** and the **Communications Team** who run an in-house publishing company as well as more traditional communications activities including the website; **The Development Team** which is involved with major projects such as building and includes people from partner organisations such as architects and construction companies; **The Finance Team**, who ensure the project is economically viable and fully accountable to its various stakeholders; **The Creative Team** which develops and produces events, including the regular concerts, many of which feature major pop and rock artists; and **The Organisational Development Team** who 'look after our people' and are essentially concerned to link the processes and operations and build the Eden culture. Eden also includes the public as their **Visiting Team**, in other words the paying customers whose interaction with the project is vital to its continuation.

Between them Tim Smit and the Eden Project teams have been tremendously successful in both business and educational terms. Not only has a vision been realised in terms of the physical development of the site, but the benefits to the Cornish economy have been estimated at increased local income of approximately £700 million during its first five years of operation.[15] It has created over 500 jobs, and the majority of staff were recruited locally. But above all, it has provided millions of people with a memorable and exciting experience which almost all would recommend to others.

Your tasks

- In the television programme, Smit explains part of his management philosophy thus:

 It is essential for me to like everybody I work with, which is not a very professional thing if you were doing an MBA; you employ people on their merits and their CVs. Bugger that for a game of darts! If I'm going to get out of bed in the morning to do something like this, I want to walk through that door really looking forward to seeing everybody that's there. And you know what? I have the tremendous privilege of that being so.

- Using frameworks and concepts from the chapters on work groups and teams, critically review this approach to the creation of work teams and organisations. What are the strengths and the risks of taking such a view about the people who work for you?

- Analyse Tim Smit's leadership style in the light of appropriate theories. Does it help or hinder his leadership that, as chief executive of a project about plants, he is 'not a horticulturalist'?

- To what extent do you think that the non-profit-making nature of this organisation enhances the sense of collaboration and teamwork between various groups of the workforce?

- Tim Smit now lectures to all sorts of both commercial and non-commercial organisational leaders about management. Analyse the extent to which his approach might be transferable to both profit-making organisations and public sector ones, whose stakeholder groups are very different from those at The Eden Project.

THE ROLE OF THE MANAGER

> **Management is about human beings. Its task is to make people capable of joint performance, to make their strengths effective and their weaknesses irrelevant. This is what organization is all about, and it is the reason that management is the critical, determining factor ... We depend on management for our livelihoods and our ability to contribute and achieve.**

Peter F. Drucker – internationally renowned author and consultant
Classic Drucker, Harvard Business School (2006), p. 194

Organisations can achieve their goals and objectives only through the co-ordinated efforts of their members and it is the task of management to get work done through other people. Management is fundamental to the effective operation of work organisations. It is by the process of management and execution of work that the activities of the organisation are carried out. Management is an integral part of the people–organisation relationship. It is essentially an integrating activity that permeates every facet of the operations of an organisation.

Learning outcomes

After completing this chapter you should be able to:

- explain the meaning of management and main activities, or functions, of management;
- analyse the essential nature of managerial work;
- contrast management in private enterprise and public sector organisations;
- outline empirical studies on the nature of managerial work and behaviour;
- debate the attributes and qualities of a successful manager;
- review the nature of management and the changing role of managers;
- evaluate the importance of management for effective organisational performance.

THE MEANING OF MANAGEMENT

Management is a generic term and subject to many interpretations. A number of different ideas are attributed to the meaning of management and to the work of a manager.[1] In certain respects everyone can be regarded as a manager, at least to some extent. We all manage our own time and everyone has some choice whether or not to do something, and some control, however slight, over the planning and organisation of their work. *Knights and Willmott* refer to managing as an everyday activity that involves interactions between people that are not unrelated or entirely dissimilar to other spheres of life, except perhaps in the rhetoric and hype that surround management. They contend that most established textbooks about management and organisation provide little that enables practising managers to make sense of their particular problem or dilemma, and in order to appreciate the living of management draw on a number of contemporary novels.[2]

However, we are concerned with management as involving people looking beyond themselves and exercising formal authority over the activities and performance of other people. For our purposes, therefore, we can regard management as:

- taking place within a structured organisational setting with prescribed roles;
- directed towards the attainment of aims and objectives;
- achieved through the efforts of other people; and
- using systems and procedures.

At its most basic, management may be viewed as 'making things happen'.

> *Management is active, not theoretical. It is about changing behaviour and making things happen. It is about developing people, working with them, reaching objectives and achieving results. Indeed, all the research into how managers spend their time reveals that they are creatures of the moment, perpetually immersed in the nitty-gritty of making things happen.*[3]

Significance of cultural influences

Schneider and Barsoux contend that trying to define the meaning of management shows up differences in beliefs and values. Cultural influences are a significant feature of management. Managers in some countries might have more concern for the 'spiritual' aspects of management, while in others there would be greater concern for the business sense. Developing people through work could be seen as an intrusion of privacy, and others may perceive empowerment as another name for manipulation.[4] According to *Francesco and Gold*, if international managers are to perform successfully in the global economy they need to understand the affects of different cultures on organisational behaviour. Reliance on theories developed in one culture is not sufficient.[5]

The emergence *Peter Drucker*, who is widely regarded as the guru of management gurus, has written about
of management the significance in social history of the emergence of management:

> *The emergence of management as an essential, a distinct and a leading institution is a pivotal event in*
> *social history. Rarely, if ever, has a new basic institution, a new leading group, emerged as fast as has*
> *management since the turn of this* [20th] *century. Rarely in human history has a new institution*
> *proven indispensable so quickly; and even less often has a new institution arrived with so little opposi-*
> *tion, so little disturbance, so little controversy.*[6]

Drucker sees management as denoting a function as well as the people who discharge it,
a social position and authority, and also a discipline and field of study. 'Management is
tasks. Management is a discipline. But management is also people. Every achievement of
management is the achievement of a manager. Every failure is a failure of a manager.'[7] Other
writers, however, take the view that management is not a separate discipline. The problem is
identifying a single discipline that encompasses the work of a manager, or agreeing the dis-
ciplines that a manager needs in order effectively to carry out this work. Note, however, the
discussion on 'The Changing Role of Managers' at the end of this chapter.

Manager as a Even within a work organisation you cannot identify a manager necessarily by what a
job title person is called or by their job title. In some organisations there is a liberal use of the title
'manager' in an apparent attempt to enhance the status and morale of staff. As a result there
are a number of people whose job title includes the term manager but who, in reality, are
not performing the full activities of a manager. Yet there are many people whose job title
does not include the term manager (for example, group accountant, head chef, chief inspec-
tor, captain, headteacher, production controller, district nursing officer, company secretary)
but who, in terms of the activities they undertake and the authority and responsibility they
exercise, may be very much a manager.

Managers born There is frequent debate about whether managers are born or made or whether management
or made? is an art or a science. Briefly, the important point is that neither of these is a mutually
Management an exclusive alternative. The answer to either question is surely a combination of both. Even if
art or science? there are certain innate qualities that make for a potentially good manager, these natural tal-
ents must be encouraged and developed through proper guidance, education and training,
and planned experience.

Clearly, management must always be something of an art, especially in so far as it involves
practice, personal judgement and dealing with people. However, it still requires knowledge of
the fundamentals of management, and competence in the application of specific skills and
techniques – as illustrated, for example, with developments in information technology.

> *The trouble is that, for all the techniques at their disposal, managers generally act at a very intuitive*
> *level. Managers may have absorbed the latest thinking on core competencies, but are more likely to base*
> *a decision on prejudice or personal opinion rather than a neat theory.*[8]

The discussion of management as an art or a science is developed by *Watson* who suggests
that in order to make sense of the complex and highly ambiguous situations in which man-
agers find themselves, management can be viewed as both art and science but also magic
and politics (*see* Figure 11.1).[9]

Management and administration

There is often confusion over different interpretations of the two terms **'management'** and
'administration'. One of the main reasons for this confusion would seem to result from the
translation of *Fayol's* book *Administration industrielle et générale* from the French into English.
In the original (1929) English edition there was a direct translation of 'administration', but
in the wider republication of the book in 1949 the term 'management' replaced 'administra-

| Figure 11.1 | Management as art, science, magic and politics |

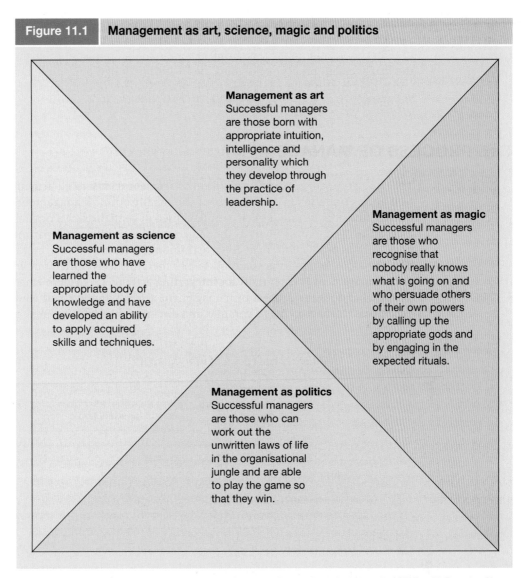

Management as art
Successful managers are those born with appropriate intuition, intelligence and personality which they develop through the practice of leadership.

Management as magic
Successful managers are those who recognise that nobody really knows what is going on and who persuade others of their own powers by calling up the appropriate gods and by engaging in the expected rituals.

Management as science
Successful managers are those who have learned the appropriate body of knowledge and have developed an ability to apply acquired skills and techniques.

Management as politics
Successful managers are those who can work out the unwritten laws of life in the organisational jungle and are able to play the game so that they win.

Source: From Watson, T. J., *Management, Organisation and Employment Strategy*, Routledge & Kegan Paul (1986), p. 29. Reproduced by permission of the publisher, Routledge, a division of Taylor & Francis, Ltd.

tion' in the title. In the introduction to the revised edition, Urwick indicates regret at this change and also expresses concern at the possible division between management being seen to apply only to business organisations, and (public) administration as applying to the same functions in public service organisations.[10]

Dictionary definitions tend to see the two words as synonymous. Management is sometimes referred to as 'administration of business concerns' and administration as 'management of public affairs'. However, the term 'management' is now used far more widely within the public sector. There is clearly an overlap between the two terms and they tend to be used, therefore, in accordance with the convenience of individual writers. This confirms the feeling that although most people perceive a difference between the two terms, this difference is not easy to describe. (A comparison of management in private enterprise and public sector organisations is to be found later in this chapter.)

Administration part of management
There appears, therefore, to be growing acceptance of the term management as the general descriptive label and **administration** as relating to the more specific function of the implementation of systems and procedures instigated by management. Administration can be seen

as taking place in accordance with some form of rules or procedures, whereas management implies a greater degree of discretion. For our purposes, management is viewed as applying to both private and public sector organisations; and administration is interpreted as part of the management process, and concerned with the design and implementation of systems and procedures to help meet stated objectives. Systems of communication and procedures relating to information technology are particularly important today.

THE PROCESS OF MANAGEMENT

The nature of management is variable. Management relates to all activities of the organisation and is undertaken at all levels of the organisation. Management is not a separate, discrete function. It cannot be departmentalised or centralised. An organisation cannot have a department of management in the same way as it can have a department for other functions, such as production, marketing, accounting, or human resources. Management is seen best, therefore, as a process common to all other functions carried out within the organisation. **Management is essentially an integrating activity.** (*See* Figure 11.2.)

But what does the process of management actually involve and what activities does it encompass? Management is a complex and discursive subject. Despite the widespread use of

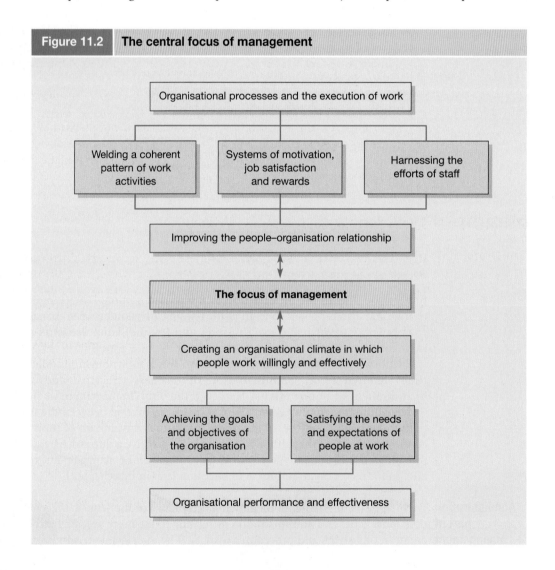

Figure 11.2 The central focus of management

414

the term and the large amount written about the subject, it is not easy to find agreement on a simple yet comprehensive definition of management or of a manager. Moreover, **'management' is not homogeneous. It takes place in different ways and at different levels of the organisation**. One approach, especially favoured by classical writers, is to analyse the nature of management and to search for common activities (or functions, or elements) applicable to managers in all organisations.

Common activities of management

One of the first, and most widely quoted, analyses is that given by *Henri Fayol*, who analysed the activities of industrial undertakings into six groups:

- technical (production, manufacture and adaptation);
- commercial (buying, selling, exchange and market information);
- financial (obtaining capital and making optimum use of available funds);
- security (safeguarding property and persons);
- accounting (information on the economic position, stocktaking, balance sheet, costs, statistics); and
- managerial. (The term 'management' is a translation of the French term 'administration'.)[11]

The managerial activity is divided into five elements of management, which are defined as: 'to forecast and plan, to organise, to command, to co-ordinate and to control'. Fayol describes these elements as:

- **Planning** (translated from the French *prevoyer* = to foresee, and taken to include forecasting) – examining the future, deciding what needs to be achieved and developing a plan of action.
- **Organising** – providing the material and human resources and building the structure to carry out the activities of the organisation.
- **Command** – maintaining activity among personnel, getting the optimum return from all employees in the interests of the whole organisation.
- **Co-ordination** – unifying and harmonising all activities and effort of the organisation to facilitate its working and success.
- **Control** – verifying that everything occurs in accordance with plans, instructions, established principles and expressed command.

PRINCIPLES OF MANAGEMENT

Fayol also suggests that a set of well-established principles would help concentrate general discussion on management theory. He emphasises, however, that these principles must be flexible and adaptable to changing circumstances. Fayol recognised that there was no limit to the principles of management but in his writing advocated 14 of them.

1 **Division of work**. The object is to produce more and better work from the same effort, and the advantages of specialisation. However, there are limits to division of work which experience and a sense of proportion tell us should not be exceeded.
2 **Authority and responsibility**. Responsibility is the corollary of authority. Wherever authority is exercised responsibility arises. The application of sanctions is essential to good management, and is needed to encourage useful actions and to discourage their opposite. The best safeguard against abuse of authority is the personal integrity of the manager.
3 **Discipline** is essential for the efficient operation of the organisation. Discipline is in essence the outward mark of respect for agreements between the organisation and its members. The manager must decide on the most appropriate form of sanction in cases of offences against discipline.
4 **Unity of command**. In any action an employee should receive orders from one superior only; if not, authority is undermined and discipline, order and stability threatened. Dual command is a perpetual source of conflicts.

5 **Unity of direction.** In order to provide for unity of action, co-ordination and focusing of effort, there should be one head and one plan for any group of activities with the same objective.

6 **Subordination of individual interest to general interest.** The interest of the organisation should dominate individual or group interests.

7 **Remuneration of personnel.** Remuneration should as far as possible satisfy both employee and employer. Methods of payment can influence organisational performance and the method should be fair and should encourage keenness by rewarding well-directed effort, but not lead to overpayment.

8 **Centralisation** is always present to some extent in any organisation. The degree of centralisation is a question of proportion and will vary in particular organisations.

9 **Scalar chain.** The chain of superiors from the ultimate authority to the lowest ranks. Respect for line authority must be reconciled with activities which require urgent action, and with the need to provide for some measure of initiative at all levels of authority.

10 **Order.** This includes material order and social order. The object of material order is avoidance of loss. There should be an appointed place for each thing, and each thing in its appointed place. Social order involves an appointed place for each employee, and each employee in his or her appointed place. Social order requires good organisation and good selection.

11 **Equity.** The desire for equity and for equality of treatment are aspirations to be taken into account in dealing with employees throughout all levels of the scalar chain.

12 **Stability of tenure of personnel.** Generally, prosperous organisations have a stable managerial personnel, but changes of personnel are inevitable and stability of tenure is a question of proportion.

13 **Initiative.** This represents a source of strength for the organisation and should be encouraged and developed. Tact and integrity are required to promote initiative and to retain respect for authority and discipline.

14 **Esprit de corps** should be fostered, as harmony and unity among members of the organisation is a great strength in the organisation. The principle of unity of command should be observed. It is necessary to avoid the dangers of divide and rule of one's own team, and the abuse of written communication. Wherever possible verbal contacts should be used.

Figure 11.3	Ten new principles for effective administrative management

1	Manage information through people.
2	Change is a constant, and must be managed.
3	Technology is the future.
4	Relationships matter.
5	Investment in training and development is important.
6	Measure only against the best.
7	The market is global.
8	Unity of direction is important.
9	Equity is expected.
10	Initiative is important.

Source: From Moorcroft, R., 'Managing in the 21st century', *Manager, The British Journal of Administrative Management*, January/February 2000, p. 10. Reproduced with permission from The Institute of Administrative Management.

A number of these principles relate directly to, or are influenced by, the organisation structure in which the process of management takes place. Fayol's set of principles can be compared therefore with those given by Urwick and discussed in Chapter 15.

Relevance for the 21st century

In an article bringing together the thinking of senior members of the Institute of Administrative Management, *Moorcroft* suggests that Fayol's five elements of management are still recognised as relevant and appropriate for the managers of today and tomorrow. However, although some of the principles of management remain fresh and relevant, at the start of a new millennium a new set of principles is needed to guide a manager's everyday actions. These 'principles' are not offered as an exclusive or authoritative list but are proposed as a thought-provoking starting point to address the management problems awaiting us in the new millennium (*see* Figure 11.3, page 416).[12]

MANAGEMENT AS A SOCIAL PROCESS

Another well-known analysis is given by *Brech* who defines management as:

> A social process entailing responsibility for the effective and economical planning and regulation of the operations of an enterprise, in fulfilment of given purposes or tasks, such responsibility involving:
> (a) judgement and decision in determining plans and in using data to control performance and progress against plans;
> (b) the guidance, integration, motivation and supervision of the personnel composing the enterprise and carrying out its operations.[13]

Brech identifies four main elements of management:

- **Planning** – determining the broad lines for carrying out operations, preparing methods by which they are carried out and setting standards of performance.
- **Control** – checking actual performance against standards to ensure satisfactory progress and performance, and recording as a guide to possible future operations.
- **Co-ordination** – balancing and maintaining the team by ensuring a suitable division of work and seeing that tasks are performed in harmony.
- **Motivation** – or inspiring morale. Getting members of the team to work effectively, to give loyalty to the group and to the task, to carry out their tasks properly, and to play an effective part in the activities of the organisation. This general inspiration is accompanied by a process of supervision or leadership to ensure the teams are carrying out their activities properly.

Other analyses Many other writers have provided an analysis of the elements of management. At first sight these analyses may appear to differ in certain aspects, but on closer study they show a basic similarity. Debate on the inclusion or exclusion of a particular element of management tends to revolve round the use and interpretation of different terms, and the emphasis which is placed upon them.

For example, what *Fayol* calls **command** – maintaining activity among personnel and getting optimum return from employees – might be taken to mean what *Brech* refers to as **motivation** – getting members of the team to work effectively and to carry out properly the activities allocated to them. Brech does not use the term **organising** but this appears to be covered under the headings of **planning** and **co-ordination**.

Refresh your understanding

Activity 11A
www.pearsoned.co.uk/
mullins

Critical reflection

?????

'It is difficult to think of any aspect of the functioning of the organisation, or behaviour of people, which does not concern, or relate back to, management in some way. For example, personality clashes could be traced back to management procedures for recruitment and selection, socialisation and training, delegation or the level and style of supervision. And personality clashes are likely to affect the attitudes and work performance of the members concerned, and also affect the morale of other staff.' Can you give an example which contradicts this assertion?

THE TASKS AND CONTRIBUTION OF A MANAGER

Yet another approach to describing management is given by *Drucker* who identifies three tasks, equally important but essentially different, that have to be performed:

1 fulfilling the specific purpose and mission of the institution, whether business enterprise, hospital, or university;
2 making work productive and the worker achieving;
3 managing social impacts and social responsibilities.[14]

Drucker then goes on to identify five basic operations in the work of the manager:

- **Sets objectives** – determines objectives and the goals for each area of objectives, and describes what needs to be done to achieve these objectives.
- **Organises** – analyses the activities, decisions and relations required, classifies and divides work, creates organisation structure and selects staff.
- **Motivates and communicates** – creates a team out of people responsible for various jobs.
- **Measures** – establishes targets and measurements of performance which focus on both the individual and the organisation as a whole.
- **Develops people** – directs, encourages and trains. How well subordinates develop themselves depends on the way a manager manages.

These categories require a combination of analytical ability, synthesising ability, integrity, human perception and insight and social skill.

Responsibility for the work of other people Drucker argues that the traditional definition of management based on the responsibility for the work of other people is unsatisfactory and too narrow, and emphasises a secondary rather than a primary characteristic. There are people, often in responsible positions, who are clearly 'management' but who do not have responsibility for the work of other people.

A person's function and contribution may be unaffected by the number of subordinate staff. A 'manager' is someone who performs the tasks of management whether or not they have power over others.

Who is a manager can be defined only by that person's function and by the contribution he or she is expected to make. And the function that distinguishes the manager above all others is the function no one but the manager can perform. The one contribution a manager is uniquely expected to make is to give others vision and ability to perform. It is vision and moral responsibility that, in the last analysis, define the manager.[15]

ESSENTIAL NATURE OF MANAGERIAL WORK

Despite the view expressed by Drucker on the tasks and contribution of a manager, one of the most popular ways of defining management is that it involves getting work done second-hand, that is through the efforts of other people. Managers are judged not just on their own performance but on the results achieved by subordinate staff. If we look at how people at work actually spend their time, we should be able to distinguish between those whose main occupation is the carrying out of discrete tasks and the actual doing of work themselves, and those who spend proportionally more of their time in determining the nature of work to be undertaken by other people, the planning and organising of their work, issuing them with instructions and giving advice, and checking on their performance.

'Managing' and 'doing'

By distinguishing 'managing' from 'doing' in this way we can see management as clarifying objectives and the planning of work, organising the distribution of activities and tasks to other people, direction of subordinate staff and controlling the performance of other people's work. **This provides us with a convenient description and summary of managerial work as clarification of objectives, planning, organising, directing and controlling** (*see* Figure 11.4).

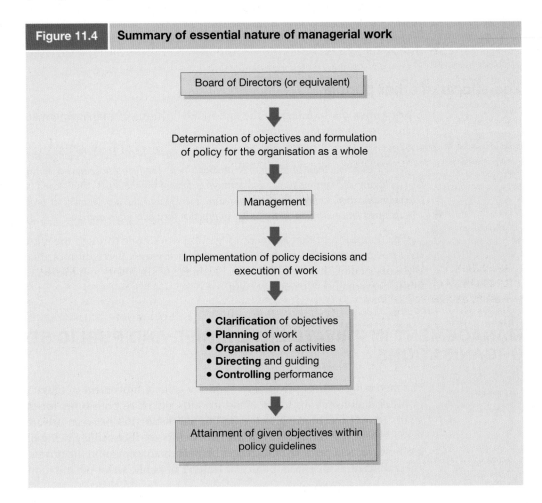

Figure 11.4	Summary of essential nature of managerial work

Board of Directors (or equivalent)

⬇

Determination of objectives and formulation
of policy for the organisation as a whole

⬇

Management

⬇

Implementation of policy decisions and
execution of work

⬇

- **Clarification** of objectives
- **Planning** of work
- **Organisation** of activities
- **Directing** and guiding
- **Controlling** performance

⬇

Attainment of given objectives within
policy guidelines

The degree of emphasis given to these different activities may vary widely, however, from one manager to another. Some managers are likely to spend more time on certain activities than other managers. The application of these activities reflects a wide range of management practice and managerial style.

Direction, motivation and control

Having already identified direction, of the organisation as a whole, as a responsibility of the board of directors (or equivalent body), it is tempting to use the term 'motivating' instead of 'directing' in our definition of the activities of management. This would avoid possible confusion over terminology: and motivation is perhaps a less emotive word. But is motivating an adequate description? It is certainly part of the manager's job to motivate staff but it involves more than this. Subordinate staff also need development and guidance. They need to be motivated **to perform well in the right areas**. The manager has a responsibility to see that subordinate staff are effective as well as efficient. Their efforts must be **directed** towards the achievement of given objectives in accordance with stated policy. This involves the process of control. It is acknowledged that control is another emotive word and some writers prefer alternatives such as monitoring, inspecting or checking – although whatever the wording the functions that it embraces are usually very similar. The real importance is not the particular term itself but what it is intended to achieve and the manner in which 'control' is exercised (*see* Chapter 18).

> Management is all about control. Success gives you control and control gives you longevity as a manager. In football very few managers achieve a position of complete control over their teams.
>
> Sir Alex Ferguson[16]

The efforts of other people

Stewart attempts to integrate the various definitions of management and summarises the manager's job, broadly defined as:

> *deciding what should be done and then getting other people to do it. A longer definition would be concerned with how these tasks are to be accomplished. The first task comprises setting objectives, planning (including decision-making), and setting up formal organization. The second consists of motivation, communication, control (including measurement), and the development of people. The two tasks are separated for convenient analysis, but in practice they may often overlap.[17]*

The definition of management as 'getting work done through the efforts of other people' may not perhaps meet all criteria or satisfy everyone's perception of the nature of managerial work. It does, however, have the advantage of simplicity and focuses on what in reality is at the heart of effective management.

MANAGEMENT IN PRIVATE ENTERPRISE AND PUBLIC SECTOR ORGANISATIONS

The increasing scale of privatisation and the general movement of major organisations away from local authority jurisdiction and towards greater responsibility for managing their own affairs have led to blurring of the traditional distinction between private and public sector management. Divisions between the two sectors are increasingly being broken down. There are, however, still perceived differences between management in the private and public sectors. These differences arise from particular features of public sector organisations. For example:

- aims concerned with providing a service for, and for the well-being of, the community rather than just of a commercial nature;

- the scale, variety and complexity of their operations;
- the tendency for them to be subject more to press reports on their activities;
- the political environment in which they operate, and in the case of local government, for example, the relationship between elected members and permanent officers;
- high levels of statutory controls, legislation and ministerial guidance;
- the generally high level of trade union involvement;
- the difficulties in measuring standards of performance of services provided compared with profitability;
- the demand for uniformity of treatment and public accountability for their operations; and
- the tendency towards more rigid HR policies, for example specific limitations on levels of authority and responsibility, fixed salary gradings based on general pay scales, long-term career structures and set promotion procedures.

A number of these features frequently combine to result in increased bureaucracy within public sector organisations.

The same general problems of management

Both private enterprise and public sector organisations, however, face the same general problems of management. Both are concerned with, for example:

- the efficiency and effectiveness of their operations;
- the clarification of aims and objectives;
- the design of a suitable structure; and
- carrying out essential administrative functions.

Basic principles of management apply in any series of activities in any organisation. Although actual methods and procedures will of necessity differ, the common activities and concerns of management apply to a greater or lesser extent in both private enterprise and public sector organisations. As *Robinson* points out:

> *Innovation in industry and commerce is a given. In local government organisations some may find it a more curious concept. But this simplistic, stereotypical view of management is wrong. Managers must manage professionally in whatever sector they function – or leave themselves vulnerable to the threats in an increasingly global and competitive environment. This applies to managers of public sector organisations as well as to private sector managers – and survival for many will be dependent upon the effective management of change and innovation.*[18]

Common challenges for all management

Fenlon suggests that 'public and private leadership are fundamentally alike and different in important respects'. Although public sector executives also confront unique challenges in every aspect of their leadership, the essentials of leadership and management in the public sector are the same as those in the private sector. In both sectors classical managerial activities are required such as designing organisational structures and processes that support strategies, building systems for staffing, budgeting and planning, and measuring results. While public sector executives must also develop strategies that create benefits, as opposed to profits, at an acceptable rate of return on political capital employed, the skills of leading and managing are fundamentally alike.[19]

Hannagan refers to the need to continuously improve productivity faster than the competition as the challenge for all management in both the private and public sectors. Management theories apply to all managers and both sectors face a central factor of the management of change.

> *In the public sector the challenge may be measured in different ways to those used in the private sector. Profit may not play a part, but measurement of activity against costs may replace monitoring of the*

return on capital invested. Income is now often linked to output and outcomes, while expenditure is firmly controlled and audited. Public sector managers are increasingly being asked to manage their organisations in a more commercial and effective way, exposed to competition without any guarantee of survival. In many areas, public sector management is little different from that in the private sector, with the same urgencies and pressures. This is exemplified by the increasing frequency of movement between the two sectors.[20]

The importance of task and context

However, according to Stewart, the belief that one should manage the public sector in the same way as the private sector is an illusion of our times. Within all categories of work there are critical differences in the nature of management depending on the tasks to be undertaken and their context. The good manager will be one who recognises the need to relate their management style and approach to context and task, and this is as important in the public sector as in the private sector. The management of difference can be seen at work in local government, where the sheer diversity of services means that different services are managed in different ways. Stewart maintains that many of the dominant management approaches advocated for local government assume a uniformity of approach which promises to ignore difference. The belief in a generic type of management for all situations can be misleading in that it conceals the need for the hard analysis of the nature of task and context.[21]

Management in service industries

Refresh your understanding

Activity 11B

www.pearsoned.co.uk/mullins

In Chapter 3 we discussed the distinction between production and service organisations. In order to operate effectively, service industries need management like any other industry. Both require attention to the same general problems of management in the same way as management in public and private sector organisations. The open systems model applies in exactly the same way to service organisations as to any other business organisation. Increasing attention is being given to the applications of general management theory within the service industry and to the links between management in service and other industries.[22]

THE WORK OF A MANAGER

Despite similarities in the general activities of management, the jobs of individual managers will differ widely. The work of the manager is varied and fragmented. In practice, it will be influenced by such factors as:

● the nature of the organisation, its philosophy, objectives and size;
● the type of structure;
● activities and tasks involved;
● technology and methods of performing work;
● the nature of people employed; and
● the level in the organisation at which the manager is working.

These differences do not just exist between organisations in the private and public sectors; they are often more a matter of degree. For example, many large business organisations may have more in common in their management and operations with public sector organisations than with small private firms.

The environmental setting

A major determinant of the work of the manager is the nature of the environment, both internal and external, in which the manager is working. Managers have to perform their jobs in the situation in which they find themselves (*see* Figure 11.5).

The **internal environment** relates to the culture and climate of the organisation – 'how things are done around here' – and to the prevailing atmosphere surrounding the organisation.

| **Figure 11.5** | **The work of a manager – the environmental setting** |

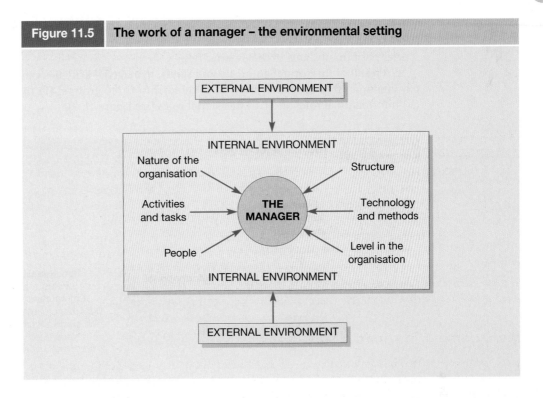

Organisational culture and climate are discussed in Chapter 19. The **external environment** relates to the organisation as an open system, as discussed in Chapter 3. Managers must be responsive to the changing opportunities and challenges, and risks and limitations facing the organisation. External environmental factors are largely outside the control of management.

The diversity of management More recent studies on the nature of management have been based on wider observation and research, and have concentrated on the diversity of management and differences in the jobs of managers. Among the best-known empirical studies on the nature of managers' jobs, and how managers actually spend their time, are those by *Mintzberg, Kotter, Luthans* and *Stewart*.[23]

Critical reflection ??????

There are many ways of looking at the meaning of management. The essential nature of managerial work is not easy to describe as aspects that are common in many applications escape us in others. How do you view the role of the manager? All managers have their individual way of working. The basic criteria must therefore be no more than a compromise between the ideas of some of the more lucid writers on the subject. Do you agree therefore that the study of management is of only limited value?

MANAGERIAL ROLES

Based on the study of the work of five chief executives of medium-sized to large organisations, *Mintzberg* classifies the activities which constitute the essential functions of a top manager's job.[24] What managers do cannot be related to the classical view of the activities of management. The manager's job can be described more meaningfully in terms of various

'roles' or organised sets of behaviour associated with a position.[25] Mintzberg recognises that people who 'manage' have formal authority over the unit they command and this leads to a special position of status in the organisation.

As a result of this formal authority and status, managerial activities can be seen as a set of ten managerial roles which may be divided into three groups: (i) interpersonal roles, (ii) informational roles and (iii) decisional roles (*see* Figure 11.6).

Figure 11.6	**The manager's roles**

Interpersonal roles The **interpersonal roles** are relations with other people arising from the manager's status and authority.

1 **Figurehead role** is the most basic and simple of managerial roles. The manager is a symbol and represents the organisation in matters of formality. The manager is involved in matters of a ceremonial nature, such as the signing of documents, participation as a social necessity, and being available for people who insist on access to the 'top'.

2 **Leader role** is among the most significant of roles and it permeates all activities of a manager. By virtue of the authority vested in the manager there is a responsibility for staffing, and for the motivation and guidance of subordinates.

3 **Liaison role** involves the manager in horizontal relationships with individuals and groups outside their own unit, or outside the organisation. An important part of the manager's job is the linking between the organisation and the environment.

Informational roles The informational roles relate to the sources and communication of information arising from the manager's interpersonal roles.

4 **Monitor role** identifies the manager in seeking and receiving information. This information enables the manager to develop an understanding of the working of the organisation and its environment. Information may be received from internal or external sources, and may be formal or informal.

5 **Disseminator role** involves the manager in transmitting external information through the liaison role into the organisation, and internal information through leader role between the subordinates. The information may be largely factual or may contain value judgements. The manager is the nerve centre of information. If the manager feels unable, or chooses not, to pass on information this can present difficulties for delegation.

6 **Spokesperson role** involves the manager as formal authority in transmitting information to people outside the unit, such as the board of directors or other superiors, and the general public such as suppliers, customers, government departments and the press.

Decisional roles The decisional roles involve the making of strategic organisational decisions on the basis of the manager's status and authority, and access to information.

7 **Entrepreneurial role** is the manager's function to initiate and plan controlled (that is, voluntary) change through exploiting opportunities or solving problems, and taking action to improve the existing situation. The manager may play a major part, personally, in seeking improvement, or may delegate responsibility to subordinates.

8 **Disturbance handler role** involves the manager in reacting to involuntary situations and unpredictable events. When an unexpected disturbance occurs the manager must take action to correct the situation.

9 **Resource allocator role** involves the manager in using formal authority to decide where effort will be expended, and making choices on the allocation of resources such as money, time, materials and staff. The manager decides the programming of work and maintains control by authorising important decisions before implementation.

10 **Negotiator role** is participation in negotiation activity with other individuals or organisations, for example a new agreement with a trade union. Because of the manager's authority, credibility, access to information, and responsibility for resource allocation, negotiation is an important part of the job.

Mintzberg emphasises that this set of ten roles is a somewhat arbitrary division of the manager's activities. It presents one of many possible ways of categorising the view of managerial roles. The ten roles are not easily isolated in practice but form an integrated whole. If any role is removed, this affects the effectiveness of the manager's overall performance.

Why organisations need managers As a result of describing the nature of managerial work in terms of a set of ten roles, *Mintzberg* suggests six basic purposes of the manager, or reasons why organisations need managers:

- to ensure the organisation serves its basic purpose – the efficient production of goods or services;
- to design and maintain the stability of the operations of the organisation;
- to take charge of strategy-making and adapt the organisation in a controlled way to changes in its environment;
- to ensure the organisation serves the ends of those people who control it;
- to serve as the key informational link between the organisation and the environment; and
- as formal authority to operate the organisation's status system.

BEHAVIOUR PATTERN OF GENERAL MANAGERS

From a detailed study of 15 successful American general managers involved in a broad range of industries, *Kotter* found that although their jobs differed and the managers undertook their jobs in a different manner, they all had two significant activities in common: **agenda-setting** and **network-building**.[26]

- **Agenda-setting** is a constant activity of managers. This is a set of items, or series of agendas involving aims and objectives, plans, strategies, ideas, decisions to be made and priorities of action in order to bring about desired end-results. This requires individual managers responsible for achieving targets to have a continual and changing series of agendas to help bring intentions into reality.
- **Network-building** involves the managers interacting with other people and establishing a network of co-operative relations. These networks are outside the formal structure. They have often included a very large number of people, many of whom were in addition to their boss or direct subordinates, and also included individuals and groups outside the organisation. Meetings provided exchanges of information over a wide range of topics in

a short period of time. A major feature of network-building was to establish and maintain contacts that could assist in the successful achievement of agenda items.

Typical pattern of behaviour

On the basis of interviews, observations, questionnaires and relevant documents, *Kotter* found the following features of a typical pattern of daily behaviour for a general manager (GM).[27]

1 They spent most of their time with others.
2 The people they spent time with included many in addition to their superior and direct subordinates.
3 The breadth of topics covered in discussions was very wide.
4 In these conversations GMs typically asked a lot of questions.
5 During these conversations GMs rarely seemed to make 'big' decisions.
6 Discussions usually contained a considerable amount of joking, kidding and non-work-related issues.
7 In not a small number of these encounters, the substantive issue discussed was relatively unimportant to the business or organisation.
8 In such encounters, the GMs rarely gave 'orders' in a traditional sense.
9 Nevertheless, GMs frequently attempted to influence others.
10 In allocation of time with other people, GMs often reacted to the initiatives of others.
11 Most of their time with others was spent in short, disjointed conversations.
12 They worked long hours. (The average GM studied worked just under 60 hours per week. Although some work was done at home and while commuting or travelling, they spent most of their time at work.)

Refresh your understanding

Activity 11C
www.pearsoned.co.uk/ mullins

DETERMINING WHAT REAL MANAGERS DO

Developing the work of Mintzberg and Kotter, *Luthans* and associates undertook a major investigation into the true nature of managerial work through the observation of 44 'real' managers.[28] A detailed record was maintained of the behaviours and actions of managers from all levels and many types of organisations, mostly in the service sector and a few manufacturing companies. The data collected were reduced into 12 descriptive behavioural categories under four managerial activities of real managers:

- **communication** – exchanging information, paperwork;
- **traditional management** – planning, decision-making, controlling;
- **networking** – interacting with outsiders, socialising/politicking;
- **human resource management** – motivating/reinforcing, disciplining/punishing, managing conflict, staffing, training/developing.

Frequency of activities Following determination of the nature of managerial activity, Luthans then went on to study a further, different set of 248 real managers in order to document the relative frequency of the four main activities. Trained observers completed a checklist at random times once every hour over a two-week period. The time and effort spent on the four activities varied among different managers. The 'average' manager, however, spent 32 per cent of time and effort on traditional management activities, 29 per cent on communication activities, 20 per cent on human resource management activities and 19 per cent on networking activities.

PATTERNS OF MANAGERIAL WORK AND BEHAVIOUR

Based on earlier studies of managerial jobs,[29] *Stewart* has developed a model for understanding managerial work and behaviour.[30] The model directs attention to the generalisations that can be made about managerial work, and differences that exist among managerial jobs. It acknowledges the wide variety, found from previous studies, among different managers in similar jobs in terms of how they view their jobs and the work they do.

Demands, constraints and choices

The three main categories of the model are **demands**, **constraints** and **choices**. These identify the flexibility in a managerial job.

- **Demands** are what anyone in the job has to do. They are not what the manager ought to do, but only what must be done: for example, meeting minimum criteria of performance, work which requires personal involvement, complying with bureaucratic procedures which cannot be avoided, meetings that must be attended.
- **Constraints** are internal or external factors which limit what the manager can do: for example, resource limitations, legal or trade union constraints, the nature of technology, physical location, organisational constraints, attitudes of other people.
- **Choices** are the activities that the manager is free to do, but does not have to do. They are opportunities for one job-holder to undertake different work from another, or to do the work in a different way: for example, what work is done within a defined area, to change the area of work, the sharing of work, participation in organisational or public activities.

The flexibility of managerial jobs Stewart suggests that the model provides a framework for thinking about the nature of managerial jobs, and about the manner in which managers undertake them. To understand what managerial jobs are really like it is necessary to understand the nature of their flexibility. Account should be taken of variations in behaviour and differences in jobs before attempting to generalise about managerial work. Study of managers in similar jobs indicates that their focus of attention differs. Opportunities for individual managers to do what they believe to be most important exist to a greater or lesser extent in all managerial jobs. Stewart also concludes that the model has implications for organisational design, job design, management effectiveness, selection, education and training, and career decisions.

How managers really behave From a review of research into managerial behaviour, Stewart concludes that the picture built up gives a very different impression from the traditional description of a manager as one who plans, organises, co-ordinates, motivates, and controls in a logical, ordered process. Management is very much a human activity.

The picture that emerges from studies of what managers do is of someone who lives in a whirl of activity, in which attention must be switched every few minutes from one subject, problem, and person to another; of an uncertain world where relevant information includes gossip and speculation about how other people are thinking and what they are likely to do; and where it is necessary, particularly in senior posts, to develop a network of people who can fill one in on what is going on and what is likely to happen. It is a picture, too, not of a manager who sits quietly controlling but who is dependent upon many people, other than subordinates, with whom reciprocating relationships should be created; who needs to learn how to trade, bargain, and compromise; and a picture of managers who, increasingly as they ascend the management ladder, live in a political world where they must learn how to influence people other than sub-ordinates, how to manoeuvre, and how to enlist support for what they want to do. In short, it is a much more human activity than that commonly suggested in management textbooks.[31]

WHAT GREAT MANAGERS DO

According to *Buckingham*, an average manager sees employees as workers who fill roles; an exceptional manager sees them as individuals to build roles around. Great managers perform their magic by discovering developing and celebrating what is different about each person who works for them. 'While there are as many styles of management as there are managers, there is one quality that sets truly great managers apart from the rest: They discover what is unique about each person and then capitalize on it ... Great managers know and value the unique abilities and even the eccentricities of their employees, and learn how best to integrate them into a coordinated plan of attack.'

Identifying and capitalising on each person's uniqueness is a powerful tool because it saves time in the allocation of roles; makes each person more accountable; builds a stronger sense of team through creating interdependency; and introduces a healthy degree of disruption by shuffling existing hierarchies and existing assumptions about who is allowed to do what. Managers need to know to collate what they know about each person and put their idiosyncrasies to use. In order to manage people well, this demands that the manager knows:

- their strengths;
- the triggers that activate those strengths; and
- how they learn.

Great managers do not try to change a person's style. The majority of differences in traits and talents are enduring and resistant to change.

> A manager's most precious resource is time, and great managers know that the most effective way to invest their time is to identify exactly how each employee is different and then to figure out how best to incorporate those enduring idiosyncrasies into the overall plan.[32]

THE ATTRIBUTES AND QUALITIES OF A MANAGER

The 'Quality of Management' is one of nine ingredients of success by which *Management Today* rates performance in its annual survey of Britain's Most Admired Companies. In 2003 The Investors in People introduced a 'Leadership and Management Model' that focuses on the development of organisational leadership and management capability. The model is discussed in Chapter 20. Whatever the role of the manager or whether in the private or public sector, in order to carry out the process of management and the execution of work, the manager requires a combination of technical competence, social and human skills, and conceptual ability.[33]

As the manager advances through the organisational hierarchy, greater emphasis is likely to be placed on conceptual ability, and proportionately less on technical competence (*see* Figure 11.7). (*See also* the discussion on levels of organisation in Chapter 15.)

- **Technical competence** relates to the application of specific knowledge, methods and skills to discrete tasks. Technical competence is likely to be required more at the supervisory level and for the training of subordinate staff, and with day-to-day operations concerned in the actual production of goods or services.

Figure 11.7	The combination of attributes of a manager

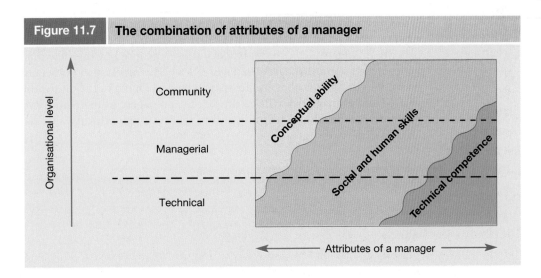

- **Social and human skills** refer to interpersonal relationships in working with and through other people, and the exercise of judgement. A distinctive feature of management is the ability to secure the effective use of the human resources of the organisation. This involves effective teamwork and the direction and leadership of staff to achieve co-ordinated effort. Under this heading can be included sensitivity to particular situations, and flexibility in adopting the most appropriate style of management.
- **Conceptual ability** is required in order to view the complexities of the operations of the organisation as a whole, including environmental influences. It also involves decision-making skills. The manager's personal contribution should be related to the overall objectives of the organisation and to its strategic planning.

Although a simplistic approach, this framework provides a useful basis from which to examine the combination and balance of the attributes of an effective manager. For example the extent of technical competence or conceptual ability will vary according to the level of the organisation at which the manager is working. However, major technological change means that managers at all levels of the organisation increasingly require technical competence in the skills of information communications technology.

Balance of 'hard' and 'soft' skills

Management has become more about managing people than managing operations, however, and social and human skills which reflect the ability to get along with other people are increasingly important attributes at all levels of management. *Green* suggests that most managers will spend most time operating between the spectrum of 'hard' skills such as conducting disciplinary matters or fighting one's corner in a debate about allocation of budgets; and 'soft' skills such as counselling, or giving support and advice to a member of staff. The most successful managers are those able to adjust their approach and response to an appropriate part of the spectrum.[34]

And as *Douglas* also reminds us, although there is a clear need for mastery of technical expertise, 'soft skills' are also an essential part of the world of business.

Living as we do in a society that is technologically and scientifically extremely advanced, most kinds of professional advancement are close to impossible without the mastery of one or more specialised branches of systematic technical knowledge … What is the downside? Organisations in most sectors – and especially in ones that are particularly demanding from a scientific or technical point of view – are operating in environments where collaboration, teamwork, and an awareness of the commercial implications of technical research are as important as scientific and technical skills themselves. Personnel with scientific and technical skills significantly disproportionate to their 'people' skills – by which I primarily mean people management capabilities and knowledge of how to work with maximum effectiveness as part of a team – are increasingly unlikely to be as much of an asset to their organisation as they ought to be.[35]

Importance of job experience A recent report from the Chartered Management Institute found changing perceptions of what makes a good manager. For the first time since the question was asked in 1986, the belief that 'leaders are born not made' has been eclipsed by the view that relevant job experience makes good managers (*see* Figure 11.8). The report also points out that a clear trend emerges in those skills that employers will be developing in the future: the ability to manage change and manage risk will be the key for managers in the coming years. The ability to facilitate organisational learning and to lead through ethical/value-based behaviour are identified as priority areas.[36]

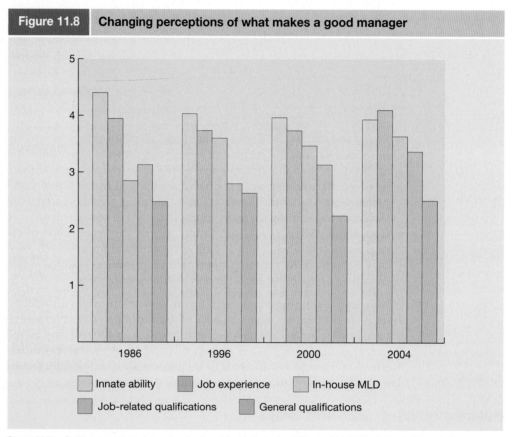

Figure 11.8 Changing perceptions of what makes a good manager

Source: Mabey, C., 'Management development works: the evidence', *Professional Manager*, Vol. 14, No. 2, March 2005, p. 4. Reproduced with permission from Chartered Management Institute.

Situational management

According to *Misslehorn*, the challenge for managers is to sharpen their ability to **perceive** more accurately, **process** the information more wisely, **respond** more appropriately and examine the **feedback** from the actions taken in order to learn and keep things on track. Managers need to **think** through situations, bringing their rational and creative brainpower to bear on them. They also need to involve others through appropriate **interaction** and communication. The way managers think about the situation and interact with others has a direct bearing on their **perceptions** of the situation – helping to curb some of the distortions from their past experience, values, bias, fears, feelings and prejudices. And the way managers think about a situation and interact with others also has a direct bearing on their **responses** and the results produced and outcomes of their actions. This interplay between thinking and interacting takes place in complex strategic organisational situations. This process of **situational management** is illustrated in Figure 11.9.[37]

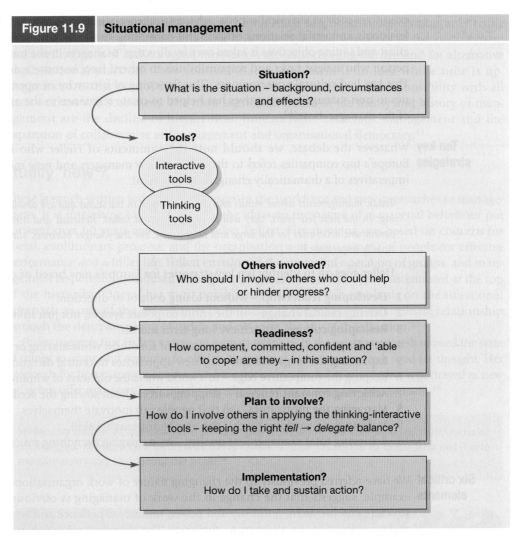

Figure 11.9 Situational management

Situation?
What is the situation – background, circumstances and effects?

Tools?
Interactive tools
Thinking tools

Others involved?
Who should I involve – others who could help or hinder progress?

Readiness?
How competent, committed, confident and 'able to cope' are they – in this situation?

Plan to involve?
How do I involve others in applying the thinking-interactive tools – keeping the right *tell* → *delegate* balance?

Implementation?
How do I take and sustain action?

Source: Adapted from Misselhorn, H., *The Head and Heart of Management*, Management and Organization Development Consultants (2003), p. 13.

> The fact is that management ultimately depends on an understanding of human nature. I suggest it goes much further than that. In the first place, good management depends on the acceptance of certain basic values. It cannot be achieved without honesty and integrity, or without consideration for the interests of others. Secondly, it is the understanding of human foibles that we all share, such as jealousy, envy, status, prejudice, perception, temperament, motivation and talent, which provides the greatest challenge to managers.
>
> HRH The Duke of Edinburgh[38]

THE CHANGING ROLE OF MANAGERS

Billsberry points out that the number of people who are managers has been growing rapidly and also that the scope and variety of what managers are required to do has been continually expanding.[39] By contrast, *Belbin* contends that many of the quintessential managerial activities that fell within the everyday domain of the manager, such as communicating, motivating and organising, have now become shared with an assortment of well-educated

Management in the news – continued

person, it would surely be a personal matter. Yet last week I found that two large organisations were boldly placing their employees' personal and parental success at the heart of company policy.

The first is Goldman Sachs, which has set up a Wellness Exchange for all its busy workers. The very name gives a hint that all is not well. Wellness is an annoying new word that is spreading across the corporate world like some lethal virus. Gyms are now called wellness centres and even respectable companies such as Nestlé have a wellness division. But what does it mean? I cannot find it in my dictionary, and the online definition goes like this: 'Wellness as defined by the National Wellness Association is an active process of becoming aware of and making choices toward a more successful existence.' Which does not leave you any the wiser. The idea of a wellness *exchange* is positively sinister. Goldman gives wellness to its employees but, in return, what do they give back? Their working lives, with their souls thrown in, one fears.

'The driving force behind the Wellness Exchange is to recognise Goldman Sachs employees in all aspects of their lives, personally and professionally,' it says on the company website. So there are wellness fairs you can go to, seminars and lectures on personal growth and, more prosaically (and usefully), gyms and doctors. The bank offers everything you need to combat the non-wellness of working so hard. It even gives adoption assistance, infertility treatment and manages 'fitness activities' that 'allow for interaction outside the work environment'. One of the offerings at the Wellness Exchange is one-on-one counselling for employees, 'empowering them with the tools to make positive lifestyle choices'. Quite a few Goldman

employees do seem to have made a positive lifestyle choice recently: they have left the bank.

The other policy I studied last week was from Ernst & Young and is all about helping 'parents manage their personal and professional goals' (in other words, stopping mothers from quitting). The policy is called My JournEY, which raises the question: journey to where? To and from work via the daycare centre, one assumes. This policy is about 'new moms' and 'veteran moms' networking and sharing best practice. There is a lot of reaching out and talk of 'connectivity' but there is something more practical on offer, too: a new lactation programme, which includes a 'hospital-grade pump'.

The only thing that one might be able to borrow from My JournEY is the clever way that the Ernst & Young brand is reflected in the name. There are surely possibilities for the Financial Times here and I have just spent an enjoyable and creative hour or so brainstorming and have come up with this: aFTer childbirth you oFTen go soFT and daFT. That might be true but it is not really a good name for a policy for new moms.

Source: Kellaway, L. 'Managers who want to get up close and personal', *Financial Times*, 25 June 2006. Copyright © 2006 The Financial Times Limited, reproduced with permission.

Discussion questions

1 Outline and evaluate the reasons why organisations might set up programmes like these to support the personal lives of their employees.

2 What role conflicts might this concern with people's domestic and personal lives cause for individual managers and members of their staff? Can such conflicts be successfully reconciled?

SYNOPSIS

● 'Management' is a generic term and subject to many interpretations. Our concern is with management within a structured organisational setting and involving the exercise of formal authority over the work of other people. The nature of management is variable. It relates to all activities of the organisation and is undertaken at all levels. Management is essentially an integrating activity that permeates all other aspects of the organisation.

● It is not easy to find agreement on the definition of management, or of a manager. Management is not homogeneous but takes place in different ways. One approach is to analyse the nature of management and

to identify common activities and principles. By distinguishing 'managing' from 'doing' we can summarise the nature of managerial work as clarification of objectives, planning, organising, directing and controlling. The degree of emphasis given to these different activities may vary widely from one manager to another. There are, however, many other approaches to the analysis of management.

● There are important differences between management in private enterprise and public sector organisations. However, all organisations face the same general problems of management. Although there are perceived differences between management

in the private and public sectors, increasing attention is being given to applications of general management theory and the adoption of business practices in the public sector. There are common challenges for all managers. Management theories apply to all managers and the skills of managing are fundamentally alike.

● Despite similarities in the general activities of management, the jobs of individual managers differ widely. Empirical studies have concentrated on the diversity of management and differences in the nature of managerial work. These studies have drawn attention to such features as managerial roles, agenda-setting and network-building, what real managers do, and demands, constraints and choices in a managerial job.

● In order to carry out the process of management and execution of work, the manager requires a combination of technical competence, social and human skills, and conceptual ability. Growing attention is attached to managerial competencies including skills in information communication technology. Despite the increasing emphasis on technical expertise, it is important that managers have a balance of both 'hard' and 'soft' skills, including people skills.

● While the importance and responsibility of management is still widely recognised there is a need for a changed role for managers. Europe's new breed of managers need to focus attention on key strategies including the importance of values and behaviours. Important issues for the future include managing change, leadership and motivation of staff, managing diversity, the development of human resources, and demands for alternative organisational practices. One can, however, question what is really new about managerial behaviour.

Refresh your understanding, assess your progress and begin your research with online resources at **www.pearsoned.co.uk/mullins**

REVIEW AND DISCUSSION QUESTIONS

1 How would you summarise the essential nature of managerial work? In what ways does the job of a manager differ from any other job in a work organisation?

2 Explain fully and with supporting reasons what you see as the most important attribute(s) or quality(ies) required of a successful manager.

3 To what extent is it possible to establish rules or principles of good management? Assess critically the practical applications of these rules or principles.

4 Contrast critically the nature of management in (i) service and production industries, and (ii) private enterprise and public sector organisations.

5 Why do organisations need managers? Suggest how the flexibility in managerial jobs might be identified and compare and contrast any two different managerial jobs.

6 Suggest which *one* writer has in your opinion made the greatest contribution to our understanding of the nature of management. Justify your answer.

7 Discuss critically the suggestion that management is a much more human activity than is commonly suggested in management textbooks. Support your discussion with practical examples.

8 Explain fully how you see the nature of managerial activities and the likely role of the manager in ten years' time.

ASSIGNMENT 1

Select a particular managerial job and observe the manager in action, preferably over an extended period of time.

a Make notes, with supporting examples, of the proportion of the manager's work and time which is spent on:

1 the carrying out of discrete tasks and the actual 'doing' of work personally, and

2 deciding what work is to be done and planning, organising, directing or controlling the work of other people.

Notes and References

1 See, for example: Margretta, J. *What Management Is: How it Works and Why it's Everyone's Business*, HarperCollins (2002).

2 Knights, D. and Willmott, H. *Management Lives: Power and Identity in Work Organizations*, Sage Publications (1999), p. iix.

3 Crainer, S. *Key Management Ideas: Thinkers that Changed the Management World*, Third edition, Financial Times Prentice Hall (1998), p. xi.

4 Schneider, S. C. and Barsoux, J. *Managing Across Cultures*, Second edition, Financial Times Prentice Hall (2003).

5 Francesco, A. M. and Gold, B. A. *International Organizational Behavior*, Second edition, Prentice Hall (2005).

6 Drucker, P. F. *The Practice of Management*, Heinemann Professional (1989), p. 3.

7 Drucker, P. F. *Management*, Pan Books (1979), p. 14.

8 Crainer, S. 'The Rise of Guru Scepticism', *Management Today*, March 1996, p. 51.

9 Watson, T. J. *Management, Organisation and Employment Strategy*, Routledge & Kegan Paul (1986).

10 Fayol, H. *General and Industrial Management*, Pitman (1949). See also: Gray, I. *Henri Fayol's General and Industrial Management*, Pitman Publishing (1988).

11 Fayol, H. *General and Industrial Management*, Pitman (1949).

12 Moorcroft, R. 'Managing in the 21st Century', *The British Journal of Administrative Management*, January/ February 2000, pp. 8–10.

13 Brech, E. F. L. *Principles and Practice of Management*, Third edition, Longman (1975), p. 19.

14 Drucker, P. F. *People and Performance*, Heinemann (1977), p. 28.

15 Ibid., p. 59.

16 Ferguson, A. (Sir) in Gwyther M. and Saunders, A. 'United they stand?' *Management Today*, April 2005, p. 41.

17 Stewart, R. *The Reality of Management*, Third edition, Butterworth Heinemann (1999), p. 6.

18 Robinson, G. 'Improving Performance through People', *The British Journal of Administrative Management*, September/ October 1999, p. 4.

19 Fenlon, M. 'The Public Spirit', Mastering Leadership, *Financial Times*, 22 November 2002, pp. 4–5.

20 Hannagan, T. *Management: Concepts and Practices*, Fourth edition, Financial Times Prentice Hall (2005), p. 32.

21 Stewart, J. 'Managing Difference', *Chartered Secretary*, October 2003, p. 31.

22 See, for example: Mullins, L. J. *Hospitality Management and Organisational Behaviour* Fourth edition, Longman (2001).

23 For a useful summary of the work of the manager, see for example: Birchall, D. W. 'What Managers Do', in Crainer, S. and Dearlove, D. (eds) *Financial Times Handbook of Management*, Second edition, Financial Times Prentice Hall (2001), pp. 110–31.

24 Mintzberg, H. *The Nature of Managerial Work*, Harper and Row (1973).

25 Mintzberg, H. 'The Manager's Job: Folklore and Fact', *Harvard Business Review Classic*, March–April 1990, pp. 163–76.

26 Kotter, J. P. *The General Managers*, The Free Press (1982).

27 Kotter, J. P. 'What Effective General Managers Really Do', *Harvard Business Review*, vol. 60, no. 6, November–December 1982, pp. 156–67.

28 Luthans, F. 'Successful vs. Effective Real Managers', *The Academy of Management Executive*, vol. 11, no. 2, May 1988, pp. 127–32.

29 Stewart, R. *Contrasts in Management*, McGraw-Hill (1976).

30 Stewart, R. *Choices for the Manager*, McGraw-Hill (1982). See also, Stewart, R. *Managing Today and Tomorrow*, Macmillan (1991).

31 Stewart, R. 'Managerial Behaviour: How Research has Changed the Traditional Picture', in Earl, M. J. (ed.) *Perspectives on Management: A Multidisciplinary Analysis*, Oxford University Press (1983), pp. 96–7.

32 Buckingham, M. 'What Great Managers Do', *Harvard Business Review*, vol. 83, no. 3, March 2005, pp. 70–9.

33 Katz, R. L. 'Skills of an Effective Administrator', *Harvard Business Review*, September–October 1974, pp. 90–102.

34 Green, J. 'When Was Your Management Style Last Applauded?', *Chartered Secretary*, December 1998, pp. 28–9.

35 Douglas, M. 'Why "Soft Skills" Are an Essential Part of the Hard World of Business', *Manager, The British Journal of Administrative Management*, No. 34, Christmas 2002/New Year 2003, p. 34.

36 Mabey, C. 'Management Development Works: The Evidence' Chartered Management Institute, January 2005.

37 Misselhorn, H. *The Head and Heart of Management*, Management and Organization Development Consultants, South Africa (2003), pp. 12–13.

38 'In Celebration of the Feel-good Factor', *Professional Manager*, March 1998, p. 6.

39 Billsberry, J. (ed.) *The Effective Manager: Perspectives and Illustrations*, Sage Publications (1996).

40 Belbin, R. M. *Changing the Way we Work*, Butterworth-Heinemann (1997), p. 95.

41 Heller, R. *In Search of European Excellence*, HarperCollins Business (1997), p. xvi.

42 Prahalad, C. K. 'Emerging Work of Managers', in Chowdhury, S. *Management 21C*, Financial Times Prentice Hall (2000) pp. 141–50.

43 Poole, M. and Mansfield, R. *Two Decades of Management*, Chartered Management Institute, June 2001.

44 Cloke, K. and Goldsmith, J. *The End of Management; and the Rise of Organizational Democracy*, Jossey-Bass (2002).

45 Metcalfe, H. and Urwick, L (eds), *Dynamic Administration – The Collected Papers of Mary Parker Follett*, Harper (1941).

46 Parker, L. E. 'Shock of the New a Century on', *Professional Manager*, vol. 14, no. 6, November 2005, pp. 34–5.

47 Crainer, S. *Key Management Ideas*, Third edition, Financial Times Prentice Hall (1998), p. xvi.

48 BBC news website, 'Staff brand colleagues as "lazy"' 12 August 2006 [accessed 12 August 2006].

49 BBC news website, 'Workers want bosses to "get lost"' 12 August 2006 [accessed 12 August 2006].

50 Thomas, D. 'Middle managers face mass lay-offs' *Personnel Today* available from www.personneltoday.com 2 June 2005 [accessed 12 August 2006].

51 Kennett, M. 'View from the Middle' *Management Today* March 2006 pp. 35–42.

52 Rigby, R. 2006 Employee Absence; Sick Notes, *HR Magazine* 1 January 2006 available at www.hrmagazine.co.uk [accessed 12 August 2006].

53 DDI 2003 'Leading on the Fault Line' Research report published by DDI and available from www.ddiworld.com [accessed 12 August 2006].

54 *Personnel Today* 2006 'How to Lead from the Middle' 9 May 2006 and available from www.personneltoday.com [accessed 12 August 2006].

55 IIP Press Release 19.08.05 available at www.investorsinpeople.co.uk [accessed 12 August 2006].

56 Rigby, R. 2006 'The best bit is in the middle', *HR Magazine* 6 July 2006 available at www.hrmagazine.co.uk [accessed 12 August 2006].

57 Kennett, M. 'View from the Middle', *Management Today* March 2006 pp. 35–42.

MANAGERIAL BEHAVIOUR AND EFFECTIVENESS

> **Very often, your resources are greater than you might think. I don't like it when people underestimate me, and I try not to underestimate anyone else, either. People are multifaceted, and its important to let them function in a way that will allow them to shine. Most people would rather succeed than fail, but sometimes the leader has to be the catalyst for putting 'success' into their personal vocabulary.**

Donald J. Trump – Head of the Trump Organisation
How to Get Rich, BBC Books (2004), p. 27

It is the responsibility of managers to achieve results through the utilisation of human resources and the efforts of other people. The way in which managers exercise their responsibilities and duties is important. The behaviour of managers and their style of management will influence the effort expended and level of performance achieved by subordinate staff. Attention must be given to the skills of management and to influences on managerial effectiveness.

Learning outcomes

After completing this chapter you should be able to:

- contrast different attitudes and assumptions of managers about human nature and behaviour at work;
- examine managerial styles in terms of concern for production and concern for people;
- assess different systems of management;
- debate suggested philosophies for the successful management of people;
- analyse criteria for evaluating the effectiveness of managers;
- explain the importance of the management of time and distinguish activity from effectiveness;
- recognise the importance of adopting an appropriate style of managerial behaviour.

Critical reflection

??????

People respond according to the manner in which they are treated. 'The majority of people come to work eager to do a good job and to perform to the best of their abilities. Therefore if individual performance fails to match the ideal, this is a result of poor management.'
What is your response to this view? What is your experience of the workplace?

MANAGERIAL STYLE AND BEHAVIOUR

The changing nature of the work environment and the association between organisations and individuals draws attention to the traditional boss–subordinate relationship. There appears to be a growing recognition that managers can no longer rely solely on their perceived formal authority as a result of a hierarchical position in the structure of the organisation. For example, according to *ACAS*, much of the emphasis in employee relations today has to be on the individual and their position in the workplace.[1] This changing relationship suggests that more than ever an essential ingredient of any successful manager is the ability to handle people successfully. There is therefore a heavy responsibility on managers and on the styles and systems of management adopted.

It is, however, interesting to note the views of *Watson* who, while acknowledging that to create the goods, services and quality of life that people look for in the modern world, rather complex patterns of co-operative behaviour have to be orchestrated and 'managed', identifies three major problems in thinking about organising and managing work in terms of 'managing people'. First, in a modern democratic society, is it realistic even to contemplate the possibility of managing people and that there are people willing to be managed? Second, can it be argued that a manager has no moral right to direct, manage or boss any individual? Third, does the focus on people management tend to blur the part played by structures, systems, cultures, processes and the rest?[2]

Nevertheless, whatever the veracity of these problems or the importance attached to the management of systems, the organising and management of work depends ultimately on the people who make up the organisation. Without people, systems and procedures and indeed organisations themselves are meaningless. And people need to be managed. What, of course, are of increasing importance are the style of managerial behaviour and its effectiveness for *both* organisational performance and the satisfaction of its members. As *Austin* points out, good people management produces financial success. Companies which look after their staff on average out-perform the stock market by two or three times and there is no moral dilemma in either choosing to make money or look after people. If employees feel valued, they give more of themselves and are more productive.[3]

With the general movement towards flatter organisation structures, flexible working and greater employee empowerment, there is more emphasis on an integrating rather than a traditional controlling style of management. Management style and behaviour can be as important as management competence. As *Greenhalgh* points out, it is clear that managers today face a new era for business and need to face up to the new opportunities and constraints. Successful management involves adapting to the new order.

> Gone is the notion of the corporate leader as the person who supplied the vision, decided on the appropriate strategy and tactics to achieve that vision, then assigned tasks of implementation to a hierarchy of subordinates. Also gone is the notion of worker-as-robot, someone who didn't think but merely performed as instructed … The new generation of knowledge workers don't think of themselves as 'subordinates': they consider themselves independent professionals who can be given a general goal and be left to accomplish it without 'micromanagement'. They look to managers to facilitate their achievement rather than to direct and control their work.[4]

Human capital management (HCM) Increasingly, attention is drawn to the concept of human capital management (discussed in Chapter 13) as a key indicator of a company's success and to good people management. *Lloyd* raises the question of the similarities and differences between a good people manager and human capital management. It could be argued that HCM is frequently identified with a more formalised, technical and manipulative approach, although despite the language of words such as 'capital' and 'assets' it is not inherently incompatible with a good people manager. However: 'In the end, management is not about more manipulation – people quickly see through this and hence the high levels of cynicism in many organisations. It is about helping people really to believe in what they are doing (pure McGregor Theory Y?).'[5] McGregor's Theory X and Theory Y are discussed below.

MANAGERS' ATTITUDES TOWARDS PEOPLE

The way in which managers approach the performance of their jobs and the behaviour they display towards subordinate staff is likely to be conditioned by predispositions about people, and human nature and work. Drawing on Maslow's hierarchy of needs model (which is discussed in Chapter 7), *McGregor*, in 1960, put forward two suppositions about human nature and behaviour at work. He argued that the style of management adopted is a function of the manager's attitudes towards people and assumptions about human nature and behaviour. The two suppositions are called Theory X and Theory Y and are based on polar assumptions about people and work.[6]

Theory X assumptions about human nature Theory X represents the carrot-and-stick assumptions on which traditional organisations are based. Its assumptions are that:

- the average person is lazy and has an inherent dislike of work;
- most people must be coerced, controlled, directed and threatened with punishment if the organisation is to achieve its objectives;
- the average person avoids responsibility, prefers to be directed, lacks ambition and values security most of all; and
- motivation occurs only at the physiological and security levels.

The central principle of Theory X is direction and control through a centralised system of organisation and the exercise of authority. McGregor questioned whether the Theory X approach to human nature is correct and the relevance of management practices which are based upon it. Assumptions based on a Theory X approach, and the traditional use of rewards and sanctions exercised by the nature of the manager's position and authority, are likely to result in an exploitative or authoritarian style of management.

Theory Y assumptions about human nature At the other extreme to Theory X is Theory Y which represents the assumptions consistent with current research knowledge. **The central principle of Theory Y is the integration of individual and organisational goals**. Its assumptions are:

- for most people work is as natural as play or rest;
- people will exercise self-direction and self-control in the service of objectives to which they are committed;
- commitment to objectives is a function of rewards associated with their achievement;
- given the right conditions, the average worker can learn to accept and to seek responsibility;
- the capacity for creativity in solving organisational problems is distributed widely in the population;
- the intellectual potential of the average person is only partially utilised; and
- motivation occurs at the affiliation, esteem and self-actualisation levels as well as at the physiological and security levels.

McGregor implies that a Theory Y approach is the best way to elicit co-operation from members of an organisation. It is the task of management to create the conditions in which individuals may satisfy their motivational needs and in which they achieve their own goals through meeting the goals of the organisation. McGregor develops an analysis of the implications of accepting Theory Y in regard to performance appraisal, administration of salaries and promotions, participation, staff–line relationships, leadership, management development and the managerial team.

Managerial strategies

Although Theory X and Theory Y are based on polar extremes and are an over-simplification, they do represent identifiable philosophies that influence managerial behaviour and strategies. Most people have the potential to be self-motivating. They can best achieve their personal goals through self-direction of their efforts towards meeting the goals of the organisation. Broadening educational standards and changing social values mean that people today have wider expectations of the quality of working life, including opportunities for consultation and participation in decisions that affect them. Managers should develop practices based more on an accurate understanding of human behaviour and motivation.

The Theory Y approach, however, is not a 'soft' option. In practice it is often difficult to achieve successfully. It can be frustrating and time-consuming, and mistakes will occur.

> *Since 1952 I've been stumbling around buildings and running primitive Theory Y departments, divisions, and finally one whole Theory Y company: Avis. In 1962, after thirteen years, Avis had never made a profit (except one year when they jiggled their depreciation rates). Three years later the company had grown internationally (not by acquisitions) from $30 million in sales to $75 million in sales, and had made successive annual profits of $1 million, $3 million, and $5 million. If I had anything to do with this, I ascribe it all to my application of Theory Y. And a faltering, stumbling, groping, mistake-ridden application it was.*
>
> Robert Townsend, *Further Up the Organisation* [7]

Demands of the situation The two views of Theory X and Theory Y tend to represent extremes of the natural inclination of managers towards a particular style of behaviour. In practice, however, the actual style of management behaviour adopted will be influenced by the demands of the situation.[8] Where the job offers a high degree of intrinsic satisfaction or involves a variety of tasks, an element of problem-solving and the exercise of initiative, or where output is difficult to measure in quantitative terms, an informal, participative approach would seem to be more effective. It is more likely to lead to a higher level of staff morale. In many cases this would apply to work of a scientific, technical or professional nature. Where commitment to the goals of the organisation is almost a prerequisite of membership, such as in certain voluntary or charity organisations, for example, then a Theory Y approach would clearly seem to be most appropriate.

Use of a Theory X approach

However, even if a manager has a basic belief in Theory Y assumptions, there may be occasions when it is necessary, or more appropriate, to adopt a Theory X approach. When the nature of the job itself offers little intrinsic reward or limited opportunities to satisfy higher-level needs, a more dictatorial style of management might work best. Some jobs are designed narrowly, with highly predictable tasks and output measured precisely. This is the case, for example, with many complex production processes in manufacturing firms. With these types of jobs a Theory X approach may be needed if an adequate level of performance is to be maintained.

A Theory X approach may also be indicated in emergency situations, or where shortage of time or other overriding factors demand the use of authority in directing actions to the tasks in hand. For example, in the hustle, heat and noise of a busy hotel kitchen preparing fresh meals for a large banquet, with many tasks to be co-ordinated over very short time scales, it seems to be recognised that a Theory X style of management is most appropriate. In such circumstances this style of management appears to be accepted by the kitchen staff.

If subordinates match the Theory Y assumptions of the manager, then this style of management may well be effective. However, there are many staff who, whatever the nature of their job, do not wish to accept responsibility at work. They seem to prefer, and respond better to, a more directed and controlled style of management. There are times, therefore, when the manager may be justified in adopting Theory X assumptions about staff.

JAPANESE 'THEORY Z' ENVIRONMENT

Developing the work of *McGregor*, a comparison of management style and practice in different cultural settings is provided by *Ouchi* (1981). In contrast to the traditional, more bureaucratic American organisational environment, Ouchi recommends a Japanese-style **'Theory Z'** environment.

> *The problem of productivity in the United States will not be solved with monetary policy nor through more investment in research and development. It will only be remedied when we learn how to manage people in such a way that they can work together more effectively. Theory Z offers several such ways.*[9]

The characteristics of a Theory Z organisation are described by Ouchi as:

* long-term employment, often for a lifetime;
* relatively slow process of evaluation and promotion;
* development of company-specific skills, and moderately specialised career path;
* implicit, informal control mechanisms supported by explicit, formal measures;
* participative decision-making by consensus;
* collective decision-making but individual ultimate responsibility;
* broad concern for the welfare of subordinates and co-workers as a natural part of a working relationship, and informal relationships among people.

Japanese industry and management According to Ouchi, type Z organisations would be more effective as a result of an emphasis on trust, which goes hand in hand with productivity; a less hierarchical and bureaucratic structure; and higher levels of worker involvement – all of which would create a distinctive company style and culture. His ideas generated considerable debate about the nature of Japanese industry and Japanese managers that to some extent continues today.

Note also that while many British and US organisations once attempted to emulate Japanese methods and styles of management, with mixed results, there is now evidence of a reversal of this trend, with Japanese corporations moving away from a Theory Z environment and restructuring along the lines of Western organisations.[10]

> *The cynic might describe efforts to turn Theory Y into practice as doing with difficulty what comes naturally to the Japanese. There, excellent managers apply principles of behaviour which translate perfectly into western language – and which have long been echoed in the progressive areas of the west. Yet you still encounter the old ostrich attitudes that caused western companies so much damage in the past: for instance, the argument that to emulate Japan is impossible because of its peculiar culture. But the famous national enthusiasm for good business and effective management isn't simply a product of Japan's culture. After all, sloppy western habits, like investing too little in productive capacity, new products, training, quality and marketing are hardly cultural – not unless bad business economics are built into the western mentality.*
>
> Robert Heller, *In Search of European Excellence*[11]

Refresh your understanding

Activity 12A

www.pearsoned.co.uk/mullins

Critical reflection

?????

A first step in the effective management of other people is confidence in your own ability and awareness of your own strengths and weaknesses. It might follow that acknowledgement of '*mea culpa*' and responsibility for failings should be part of the philosophy and language of successful managers. Why, then, do you think that many managers find it difficult to admit, or apologise publicly for, their mistakes?

THE MANAGERIAL/LEADERSHIP GRID®

One means of describing and evaluating different styles of management is the *Blake and Mouton* Managerial Grid® (*see* Figure 12.1). First published as the **Managerial Grid** in 1964, restated in 1978 and 1985[12] and republished in 1991 as the **Leadership Grid**,[13] the Grid provides a basis for comparison of managerial styles in terms of two principal dimensions:

- concern for production; and
- concern for people.

Concern for production is the amount of emphasis that the manager places on accomplishing the tasks in hand, achieving a high level of production and getting results or profits. This is represented along the horizontal axis of the Grid.

Concern for people is the amount of emphasis that the manager gives to subordinates and colleagues as individuals and to their needs and expectations. This is represented along the vertical axis of the Grid.

Five basic combinations

'Concern for' is not how much concern, but indicates the character and strength of assumptions which underlie the manager's basic attitudes and style of management. The significant point is 'how' the manager expresses concern about production or about people. The four corners and the centre of the Grid provide five basic combinations of degree of concern for production coupled with degree of concern for people (*see* Figure 12.1(a)):

- the **impoverished manager** (1,1 rating), low concern for production and low concern for people;
- the **authority–compliance manager** (9,1 rating), high concern for production and low concern for people;
- the **country club manager** (1,9 rating), low concern for production and high concern for people;
- the **middle-of-the-road manager** (5,5 rating), moderate concern for production and moderate concern for people; and
- the **team manager** (9,9 rating), high concern for production and high concern for people.

Managers with a 1,1 rating tend to be remote from their subordinates and believe in the minimum movement from their present position. They do as little as they can with production or with people. Too much attention to production will cause difficulties with staff and too much attention to the needs of staff will cause problems with production.

Managers with a 9,1 rating are autocratic. They tend to rely on a centralised system and the use of authority. Staff are regarded as a means of production and motivation is based on competition between people in order to get work done. If staff challenge an instruction or standard procedure they are likely to be viewed as unco-operative.

Figure 12.1	The Leadership Grid®

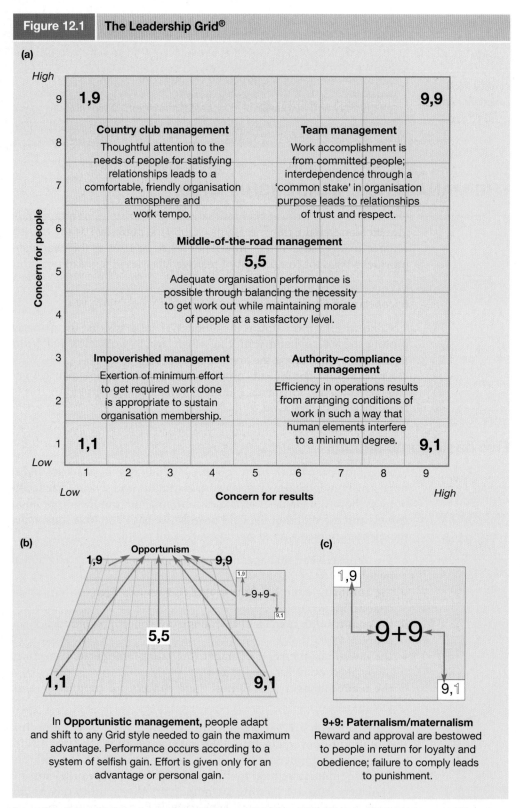

Source: Blake, R. R. and McCanse, A. A., *Leadership Dilemmas – Grid Solutions*, Gulf Publishing Co. (1991), Grid Figure, p. 29, Paternalism Figure, p. 30, Opportunism Figure, p. 31. Reproduced by permission of Grid International, Inc., Houston, Texas.

The 1,9 rating managers believe that a contented staff will undertake what is required of them and achieve a reasonable level of output. Production is secondary to the avoidance of conflict and maintenance of harmony among the staff. Managers will seek to find compromises between staff and solutions acceptable to everyone. Although innovation may be encouraged, they tend to reject good ideas if likely to cause difficulties among the staff.

The 5,5 rating is the middle-of-the-road management with the approach of 'live and let live' and a tendency to avoid the real issues. This style of management is the 'dampened pendulum' with managers swinging between concern for production and concern for people. Under pressure, this style of management tends to become task management (9,1). Where this strains relations and causes resentment from staff, however, pressure is eased and managers adopt a compromise approach. If there is a swing too much the other way (towards 1,9), managers are likely to take a tighter and more hardened approach.

Managers with a 9,9 rating believe in the integrating of the task needs and concern for people. They believe in creating a situation whereby people can satisfy their own needs by commitment to the objectives of the organisation. Managers will discuss problems with the staff, seek their ideas and give them freedom of action. Difficulties in working relationships will be handled by confronting staff directly and attempting to work out solutions with them.

These five styles of management represent the extremes of the Grid. With a nine-point scale on each axis there is a total of 81 different 'mixtures' of concern for production and concern for people. Most people would come up with a score somewhere in an intermediary position on the Grid.

Two additional grid styles The 1991 edition of the Grid covers two additional styles: opportunism and 9+9 paternalism/maternalism, which take account of the reaction of subordinates.

- In **opportunistic management**, organisational performance occurs according to a system of exchanges, whereby effort is given only for an equivalent measure of the same. People adapt to the situation to gain maximum advantage of it (*see* Figure 12.1(b)).
- In **9+9 paternalistic/maternalistic management**, reward and approval are granted to people in return for loyalty and obedience; and punishment is threatened for failure to comply (*see* Figure 12.1(c)).

A summary of the seven basic combinations of the Grid is given in Table 12.1.

Framework for patterns of behaviour

The Managerial Grid provides a framework in which managers can identify, study and review their patterns of behaviour. Instead of viewing management styles as a dichotomy of 'either/or', Blake and Mouton claim that the Managerial Grid illustrates that the manager can gain the benefits of maximising, simultaneously, methods which are both production-oriented and people-oriented. The 9,9 position, although an ideal, is worth working for. Based on their experience of using the original Grid, Blake and Mouton give three reasons why it is important to consider which style of management is used to achieve production through people:

- the 9,9 style of management correlates positively with bottom line productivity;
- 9,9 oriented managers enjoy maximum career success;
- there is now greater knowledge about the correlation between extreme grid styles of management and mental and physical health.

Dominant style of management From their research, Blake and Mouton emphasise that managers may switch from one style to another or combine elements of different styles. However, they also found that managers tend to have one dominant style of management that they use more often than any other. In

Table 12.1	Leadership Grid® style definitions
9,1 Authority– compliance management	Managers in this position have great concern for production and little concern for people. People are seen as 'tools' for production. They demand tight, uni-lateral control in order to complete tasks efficiently. They consider creativity and human relations to be unnecessary.
1,9 Country club management	Managers in this position have great concern for people and little concern for production. They try to avoid conflicts and concentrate on being liked, even at the expense of production. To them the task is less important than good inter-personal relations. Their goal is to keep people happy. (This is a soft Theory X and not a sound human relations approach.)
1,1 Impoverished management	This style is often referred to as *laissez-faire*. Leaders in this position have little concern for people or productivity. They avoid taking sides and stay out of conflicts. They do just enough to maintain group membership.
5,5 Middle-of- the-road management	Leaders in this position have medium concern for both people and production. They rely on tried and true techniques and avoid taking untested risks. They attempt to balance their concern for both people and production, but are not committed strongly to either. Conflict is dealt with by avoiding extremes and seeking compromise rather than sound resolution.
9+9 Paternalistic 'father knows best' management	This leader takes the high 9 level of concern from 9,1 and 1,9 to create a com-bined style of controlling paternalism. The paternalist strives for high results (high 9 from 9,1) and uses reward and punishment to gain compliance (high 9 from 1,9). The paternalist uses a high level of concern for people to reward for compliance or punish for rejection.
Opportunistic 'what's in it for me' management	The opportunist uses whatever Grid style is needed to obtain selfish interest and self promotion. They adapt to situations to gain the maximum advantage. They may use 9,1 to push their own goals with one person, and 1,9 to gain trust and confidence with another. Performance occurs according to a system of exchanges. Effort is given only for an equivalent measure of the same.
9,9 Team management	These managers demonstrate high concern for both people and production. They work to motivate employees to reach their highest levels of accomplish-ment. They explore alternatives openly and aggressively. They are flexible and responsive to change. This style is considered ideal.

Source: Blake, R. R. and McCanse, A. A., *Leadership Dilemmas – Grid Solutions*, Gulf Publishing Company (1991), p. 29. Reproduced with permission from Grid International, Inc., Houston, Texas.

addition, they found that many managers have a 'back-up' style that they adopt if their dominant style does not work in a particular situation.

The dominant style of management is influenced in any particular situation by any of four conditions:

- **organisation** – the nature of the organisation in which the manager is employed, and the extent to which there are rigid rules and regulations;
- **values** – the personal values, beliefs or ideals that the manager holds concerning how to treat people or to manage results;
- **personal history** – the deep-rooted personal history of the manager may be an important factor and may lead to a preference for a particular approach because that style may have been experienced frequently in the past;

Figure 12.3 | **The cycle of MBO activities**

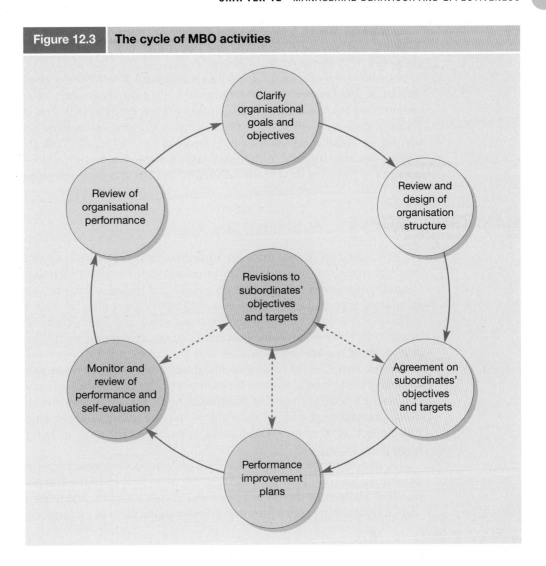

Relevance today

MBO is potentially an attractive system. It provides an opportunity for staff to accept greater responsibility and to make a higher level of personal contribution. There is much to recommend it to both the organisation and individual managers. MBO, however, is not a panacea and it is subject to a number of criticisms and potential limitations. It is not always easy to set specific targets or figures for certain more senior jobs or where the work involves a high degree of self-established role prescriptions (discussed in Chapter 8). The same might apply to jobs that require a high level of interpersonal relationships, especially where this involves confidential matters, such as counselling. There is a potential danger that where objectives and targets are more difficult to specify and measure in precise terms, these are neglected and greater emphasis is placed on objectives that are more easily monitored.

MBO appears to have suffered a decline in popularity. However, there are still differences in opinion. *Heller* paints a far less optimistic picture. He suggests:

MBO had only one defect: it didn't work. No matter how much care had been taken in formulating the objectives, drawing up the plans and involving all the managers, the corporate targets were invariably missed. So the technique passed away as one of the more fashionable management theories, defeated by the refusal of reality to conform to the plan.[20]

By contrast, however, *Gratton* refers to a quote from David Packard (founder of Hewlett-Packard) that 'no operating policy has contributed more to Hewlett-Packard's success than the policy of management by objective'.[21]

Arguably, a major reason for the apparent demise of MBO is that the basic idea and fundamental features are now incorporated into modern systems of staff appraisal and performance management systems. Greater attention to the setting of clear objectives and levels of expected performance, flexible organisation structures and self-managed teams, and empowerment and self-regulating feedback can be related to the essential elements of MBO. *Hannagan* suggests: 'Although it [MBO] has fallen out of fashion as a system, many present day methods are very similar to MBO in their approach and results.'[22]

MANAGING PEOPLE

We have stated previously that, although there are many aspects to management, the one essential ingredient of any successful manager is the ability to handle people effectively. Recall the discussion in Chapter 1 on people and organisational behaviour. An increasing number of organisations take apparent delight in expounding (in their mission statements, corporate objectives, annual reports and the such) that their employees are their greatest assets. It is, however, arguable how much an understanding, people-centred approach to management is exercised in practice and the extent to which there still appears to be an emphasis on the use of rules, systems, procedures and paperwork rather than **with and through people**. And as *Gratton*, for example, points out on the basis of six years of study in conjunction with the London Business School, there has been no uniform progress in people management and 'yet for many people the reality of life in an organisation is that they do not feel they are treated as the most important asset, or that their knowledge is understood or used'.[23]

It is important that managers have a highly developed sense of **people perception** and understand the feelings of staff, and their needs and expectations. It is people who are being managed and people should be considered in human terms. A genuine concern for people and for their welfare goes a long way in encouraging them to perform well.

Basic managerial philosophies

A positive policy of investment in people and an interpersonal relationship approach to management is, in the longer term, worth the effort. For example, the UK government-sponsored initiative Investors in People is based on a commitment to the benefits organisations can gain through their people and on the vital role of managers. (Investors in People is discussed in Chapter 13.)

It is possible to put forward a number of underlying philosophies that *arguably* are likely to make for the successful management of people, and lead to both improved work performance and more contented staff (*see* Figure 12.4). **These philosophies are not intended to be prescriptive but to encourage discussion on the extent to which you agree with the points of view.**

Consideration, respect and trust People generally respond according to the way they are treated. If you give a little, you will invariably get a lot back. Make people feel important and give them a sense of personal worth. The majority of staff will respond constructively if treated with consideration and respect, and as responsible individuals who wish to serve the organisation well. *Gratton* makes the point: 'Treat people with politeness, respect and dignity and in doing so create a strong role model for others to follow. Building a reputation of fairness gives you a buffer against the times when the policy is wrong, or you behave badly.'[24] A similar point is made by *Lloyd*:

| Figure 12.4 | The effective management of people |

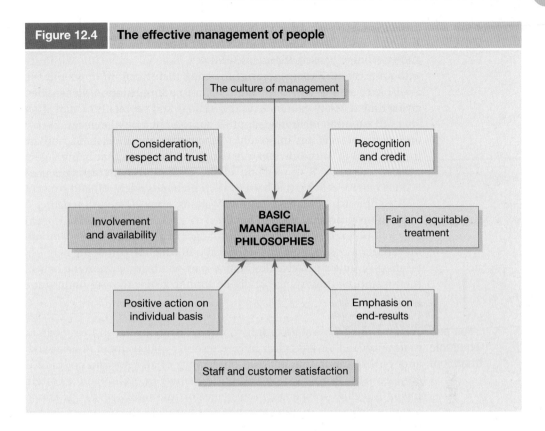

A good people manager believes in the value of people, treats them fairly and with respect: hence that vital element of trust is established and grown. But how often does this happen in practice? Management, of course, involves a combination of what you do and the way that it is done.[25]

However, how can members of staff show that they can be trusted unless trust is first placed in them? **The initiative must come from management**. 'Lack of trust is probably one of the greatest time and resource wasters in the workplace. Managers who do not trust their employees are probably wasting hours every week checking up on them at every turn and failing to utilise the resources at their disposal.'[26]

Recognition and credit People can be praised to success. Give full recognition and credit when it is due and let people know you appreciate them. Too often managers are unresponsive to good performance, which may occur the vast majority of the time, and appear to take this for granted, but are quick to criticise on the few occasions when performance falls below expectations. **However, it should not be assumed that staff would necessarily take a lack of response as a sign of positive recognition rather than just the absence of criticism.** So often you hear the comment: 'Well nobody has complained so I suppose everything is all right.' What a poor indictment of management style! Positive feedback on good performance is a strong motivator *and* staff are then more likely to accept and respond to constructive criticism. If staff are to take a pride in their work they need to know when they are performing well and to receive appropriate recognition for their efforts.

A sincere word of thanks from the right person at the right time can mean more to an employee than a formal award ... What is important is that someone takes the time to notice an achievement, seeks out the employee responsible and personally gives praise in a timely way.

Federico Castellanos, Vice President, Human Resources, IBM (EMEA)[27]

Involvement and availability Involve yourself with the work of the staff and make sure you fully understand the difficulties and distastes of their duties and responsibilities. Ensure an open flow of communications and encourage participation and feedback. Take an active interest in the work of staff but without excessive supervision or inhibiting their freedom of action. Wherever possible be available to staff as a priority, rather than to administration. Remember the importance of giving time to listen genuinely to the feelings and problems of staff. This means giving staff your full attention including adopting appropriate body language. Even if you disagree with their point of view it is important to show that you understand, and are sensitive to, what they are saying. It is, however, also important to note that being a good listener is a skill which needs to be developed and as *Fletcher* reminds us: 'Hearing is not listening. Listening is not a passive activity. It is hard work. It demands attention and concentration.'[28]

The approach of Management By Walking About (MBWA), together with informal communication processes, is often heralded as a positive management practice – and indeed it may well be so. However, there is the danger of arousing mistrust among staff, the suspicion of management snooping and doubts about 'what are you doing here?'. MBWA is unlikely to be effective unless perceived by staff as part of a broader, genuine belief by management in the continuing importance of giving time to listen to, and understand, the feelings and problems of staff.

Fair and equitable treatment Treat people fairly but according to merit. Ensure justice in treatment, equitable systems of motivation and rewards, clear human resource management policies and procedures, avoidance of discrimination, and full observance of all laws and codes of conduct relating to employment. People expect certain outcomes in exchange for certain contributions or inputs. A feeling of inequality causes tension and motivates the person to indulge in certain forms of behaviour in order to remove or to reduce the perceived inequity.[29] Recall also the discussion on the psychological contract in Chapter 1.

Positive action on an individual basis Treat members of staff as individuals. Deal with individual situations on an individual basis and avoid the 'blanket' approach. For example, it has come to the manager's attention that a couple of members of staff have failed to provide some urgently requested information on time. The manager's reaction is to send a circular to *all* members of the department reminding them of the need for, and importance of, meeting deadlines. This may appear to be an easy way out to the manager. But what are likely to be the reactions of staff?

The two members concerned might shield behind the generality of the circular and persuade themselves that it doesn't apply particularly to them. They might even choose to believe that the manager must be referring to other members of staff, perhaps in a different section, and take little notice of the circular. In contrast, the majority of staff in the department who do have a good record of providing requested information on time may well be annoyed or upset by the circular.

There could be some staff who despite pressing personal difficulties have taken great pride in their work and made a special effort to maintain an excellent record of co-operation – quite possibly without any previous positive recognition from management. **It would be understandable if the reaction of these staff was one of resentment and disillusionment, and with a possible adverse effect on their future attitude to work**. The manager has more to lose than to gain from adopting a 'blanket' approach to a particular problem and by the failure to take selective, positive action on an individual basis.

Emphasis on end-results Place emphasis on end-results and levels of actual performance and achievement rather than on compliance with detailed instructions, rules or regulations. For example, where set attendance times are *clearly* seen as a necessary requirement of the job, it is right that managers should ensure that time-keeping is adhered to and enforced as appropriate. But in many cases rigid times of attendance are not an essential requirement for effective performance.

Who makes the greatest contribution to the work of the organisation? Person A who is always on time, keeps to the exact lunch break and never leaves early (or late), but spends much of the day in idle conversation and gossip, shuffling papers and looking at the work, and achieves only adequate performance? Or Person B who may 'not be seen about the place so much', but always gives maximum effort, makes full use of time and is never idle, is flexible, delivers whatever is expected on time and achieves a consistently high level of performance?

Good time-keeping can be an important part of the job. However, if 'always being there' is not a requirement, *per se*, for effective performance, what is to be gained by insisting on rigid times of attendance? Such a requirement is likely to be perceived by Person B-type staff as an unwarranted bureaucratic style of management. Furthermore, it could turn a Person B into a Person A – with an adverse effect on the level of effective performance. The increasing movement to flexible working patterns and teleworking coupled with demands to boost productivity are placing growing emphasis on what staff actually achieve rather than the time spent at work. The important criteria are the level and quality of performance.

Staff and customer satisfaction The starting point for customer, or consumer, satisfaction is good manager–subordinate relationships. Supportive and harmonious working relationships are more likely to create a working environment that results in high levels of both staff *and* consumer satisfaction. Managers need to adopt a positive attitude towards staff and to develop a spirit of mutual co-operation. Staff should feel that they are working *with* the manager rather than *for* the manager.

Make all staff part of the management team

- *Virgin pays some of the lowest salaries in the industry yet its staff are very talented and loyal – paradox?*
- *The company's success in this field is down to Sir Richard's (Branson) management philosophy where all staff feel valued and Branson is just as interested in a flight stewardess's opinion as he is in his marketing director's.*
- *Successful people management is about inclusion and Branson works on making all his staff like a team where each is valued not only for fulfilling their job remit but for contributing to the development of the business as a whole.*

The Virgin Factor[30]

Critical reflection ????

In your interactions with people at work, as in life more generally, there will always be some people you just cannot seem to please. Give them a bag of gold and they will complain that the bag is the wrong colour, or it is too heavy to carry, or why could you not give them a cheque instead! How would you behave towards a 'bag of gold' person?

CHOICE OF MANAGERIAL STYLE

Some might well consider that these philosophies are too idealistic and that given the harsh realities of the working environment managers need to adopt a more dominant stance. However, it is not suggested that managers should in any way give up the right to manage: it is a question of *how* they manage and how they use their authority – for example, a 'Theory X' style with emphasis on direction and control, and the use of rewards and sanctions exercised by nature of the manager's position and authority; or a 'Theory Y' style in which individuals may satisfy their motivational needs through integration with meeting the goals of the organisation.

Management may also be based on 'organisational power' derived from status or position within the hierarchical structure, and the use of formal authority; or 'personal power' derived from competence and expertise, identification with subordinates, commanding respect, and urging and encouraging people in the performance of their tasks.[31] *Green* contends that most successful managers are able to adjust their approach and response between a continuum of hard skills and soft skills, and react appropriately to different situations.[32]

The nature of people at work

Galunic and Weeks refer to the changing nature of the employment relationship and that developing people, not just managing them, has become a necessary yet tricky task. Fortunately, however, some things have not changed.

> *Human nature remains remarkably stable. People want to feel competent and secure, they are consistent in reciprocating good or bad deeds; and they are influenced by, and often imitate, behaviours that surround them. Nothing changes from the sandpit to the boardroom, so managers should revisit these truths as they think about investing in people.*[33]

Golden rule management One example of an interesting and enlightened people approach is put forward by *Mary Kay Ash*, founder of the huge, multi-million-dollar company Mary Kay Cosmetics in the USA.[34] Ash writes about the intentional development of a management concept that allows fairness to flourish in business, the belief that people will shine if given a chance, and methods that are applicable to any organisation. Her concept of the management of people is based on the Golden Rule 'Do unto others as you would have them do unto you', with emphasis on being a 'people company'. (Again, this is a philosophy very much in line with the views of the author.)

> *People come first at Mary Kay Cosmetics – our beauty consultants, sales directors and employees, our customers, and our suppliers. We pride ourselves as a 'company known for the people it keeps'. Our belief in caring for people, however, does not conflict with our need as a corporation to generate a profit.*[35]

The philosophy of 'Golden Rule Management' is applied in such ways as, for example:

- **Treat people fairly but according to merit.** In order to balance responsibilities to the company, the employee, and all other employees, every manager must be able to say 'no'. But employees should be encouraged to turn a 'no' into the motivation to accomplish more.
- However busy you are, **make the other person feel important** and let people know you appreciate them.
- **Motivate people through giving praise.** A good manager must understand the value of praising people to success.
- **Encourage feedback** and don't undervalue the ability to listen.
- **Sandwich every bit of criticism between two layers of heavy praise.**
- **An open-door philosophy.**
- **Help other people get what they want** – and you will get what you want. Good managers' success is reflected in the success of their people.
- **Never hide behind policy or pomposity**.

Refresh your understanding

Activity 12B
www.pearsoned.co.uk/
mullins

MANAGERIAL EFFECTIVENESS

The importance of managerial performance and effectiveness has long been recognised by major writers such as *Drucker* who, originally in 1955, propounded that:

> *The manager is the dynamic, life-giving element in every business. Without their leadership 'the resources of production' remain resources and never become production. In a competitive economy,*

above all, the quality and performance of the managers determine the success of a business; indeed they determine its survival. For the quality and performance of its managers is the only effective advantage an enterprise in a competitive economy can have.[36]

The importance of management performance has also been more recently emphasised by *Foppen*:

Management is of pivotal importance for modern society. It is for this reason that, no matter what, thinking about management, certainly at university level, is of great relevance to management practice. So apart from the question of whether management's claim that it is indispensable is really valid or not, the fact that practically everyone believes it is, is what counts.[37]

The overall responsibility of management can be seen as the attainment of the given objectives of the organisation. Upon the attainment of its aims and objectives will rest the success and ultimate survival of the organisation. There is therefore a clear and important need for effective management. And this need is just as strong in public sector organisations as in private enterprise organisations. Indeed, it could be argued that in local government, for example, the accountability of public servants to elected members for their actions means that professional standards of management of the highest order are even more essential. Whether in private or public sector organisations, however, managerial effectiveness is a difficult concept both to define and to measure.

Efficiency and effectiveness

Managerial efficiency can be distinguished from **managerial effectiveness**. **Efficiency** is concerned with 'doing things right' and relates to inputs and what the manager does. **Effectiveness** is concerned with 'doing the right things' and relates to outputs of the job and what the manager actually achieves.

To be efficient the manager must attend therefore to the **input requirements of the job** – to clarification of objectives, planning, organisation, direction and control. But in order to be effective, the manager must give attention to **outputs of the job** – to performance in terms of such factors as obtaining best possible results in the important areas of the organisation, optimising use of resources, increasing profitability, and attainment of the aims and objectives of the organisation.

Effectiveness must be related to the achievement of some purpose, objective or task – to the performance of the process of management and the execution of work. Criteria for assessing the effectiveness of a manager should be considered in terms of measuring the results that the manager is intended to achieve. But **what is also important is the manner in which the manager achieves results and the effects on other people**. This may well influence effectiveness in the longer term. Managerial effectiveness results from a combination of personal attributes and dimensions of the manager's job in meeting the demands of the situation, and satisfying the requirements of the organisation.

Stewart suggests that effectiveness is more important than efficiency.

> *Managers who want to improve should review both their effectiveness and their efficiency. Effectiveness is doing the right things. Efficiency is making the most economic use of the resources. Effectiveness is more important than efficiency because one must be doing the right kind of work. Only then does it matter whether the work is done efficiently.*[38]

Effective and successful managers

From a study of what real managers do (discussed in Chapter 10), *Luthans* attempted to distinguish between effective and successful managers.

- **Effective managers** are defined in terms of the quantity and quality of standards of performance, and the satisfaction and commitment of subordinates.
- **Successful managers** are defined operationally in terms of the speed of their promotion within an organisation.

Effective managers had a different emphasis from successful managers and do almost the opposite activities, and Luthans found few real managers who were both effective and successful. The biggest contribution to **effectiveness** came from first, communicating and second, human resource management; with the least relative contribution from the networking activity. By contrast, for a significant number of managers by far the strongest key to success came from the networking activity, with the weakest contribution from the human resource management activity.[39]

MEASURES OF EFFECTIVENESS

Management involves getting work done through the co-ordinated efforts of other people. **Managers are most likely to be judged not just on their own performance but also on the results achieved by other staff.** The manager's effectiveness may be assessed *in part*, therefore, by such factors as:

● the strength of motivation and morale of staff;
● the success of their training and development; and
● the creation of an organisational environment in which staff work willingly and effectively.

The difficulty is determining objective measurement of such factors. Some possible indication might be given by, for example:

● the level of staff turnover;
● the incidence of sickness;
● absenteeism;
● poor time-keeping; and
● accidents at work.

However, such figures are likely to be influenced also by broader organisational or environmental considerations, for example poor job security due to the economic climate, which are outside the direct control of the individual manager. In any case, there is the general question of the extent to which such figures bear a direct relationship to the actual performance of subordinate staff.

Other criteria of effectiveness Other criteria that may give some indication of managerial effectiveness include the efficiency of systems and procedures, and the standard of services afforded to other departments. Again, however, there is the question of how to determine objective measurement of such criteria.

For some management jobs it might be possible to identify more quantitative factors which *may* give an indication of managerial effectiveness, including:

● meeting important deadlines;
● accuracy of work carried out by the department, perhaps measured by the number of recorded errors;
● level of complaints received from superiors, other departments, customers or clients, suppliers, the public;
● adherence to quality standards, for example, the amount of scrap or waste material;
● keeping within agreed cost or budgetary control limits; and
● levels of output and productivity (*see* Figure 12.5).

Another broad, qualitative criterion of increasing significance today is in terms of perceived social accountability, and the ethical behaviour of individual managers and the organisation as a whole (discussed in Chapter 14).

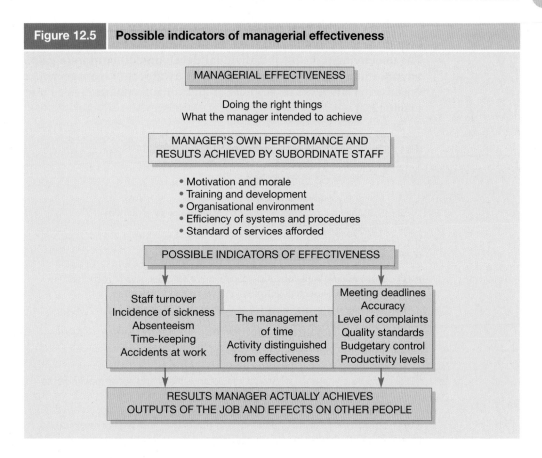

Figure 12.5 Possible indicators of managerial effectiveness

MANAGEMENT STANDARDS CENTRE

The Management Standards Centre (MSC) is the government-recognised standards-setting body for the management and leadership areas. Upgrading the skills of managers is fundamental to the government's aim to raise UK productivity and competitiveness. The MSC was responsible for developing a new set of National Occupational Standards (NOS) for management and leadership in May 2004. They describe the level of performance expected in employment for a range of management and leadership functions/activities.

As an employer-led organisation which champions management and leadership, the MSC is working with the Skills for Business Network to identify and address the skills gaps and shortages on a sector-by-sector basis, thereby contributing to the profitability of the UK.

> *Our vision* – *To create a UK partnership of employers and other key stakeholders to lead the professional development of all those working in the field of management and leadership.*

> *Our mission* – *To fulfil the needs of employers by developing a skilled management workforce through promoting our nationally recognised set of standards and qualifications which have full employer relevance and 'ownership'.*[40]

Components of the Management and Leadership Standards

The MSC undertook a review of World Class National Occupational Standards for Management and Leadership during 2004 with the aim of producing a new set of standards which:

- identify the full range of management and leadership functions/activities typically undertaken in organisations; and
- describe what individuals need to know, understand and be able to do in undertaking the identified functions/activities to the level or 'standard' expected in employment.

The new Management and Leadership Standards were approved in May as benchmarks to help managers – and the organisations in which they work – improve their performance. The underlying principle is **individual development, corporate gain**. The standards are arranged in a logical sequence to cover every aspect of management at every level in an organisation. There are six key roles or functional groupings divided into a total of 47 units (Table 12.2).

Table 12.2	New Management Standards 2004

A Managing self and personal skills

A1	Manage your own resources
A2	Manage your own resources and professional development
A3	Develop your personal networks

B Providing direction

B1	Develop and implement operational plans for your area of responsibility
B2	Map the environment in which your organisation operates
B3	Develop a strategic business plan for your organisation
B4	Put the strategic business plan into action
B5	Provide leadership for your team
B6	Provide leadership in your area of responsibility
B7	Provide leadership for your organisation
B8	Ensure compliance with legal, regulatory, ethical and social requirements
B9	Develop the culture of your organisation
B10	Manage risk
B11	Promote equality of opportunity and diversity in your area of responsibility
B12	Promote equality of opportunity and diversity in your organisation

C Facilitating change

C1	Encourage innovation in your team
C2	Encourage innovation in your area of responsibility
C3	Encourage innovation in your organisation
C4	Lead change
C5	Plan change
C6	Implement change

D Working with people

D1	Develop productive working relationships with colleagues
D2	Develop productive working relationships with colleagues and stakeholders
D3	Recruit, select and keep colleagues
D4	Plan the workforce
D5	Allocate and check work in your team
D6	Allocate and monitor the progress and quality of work in your area of responsibility
D7	Provide learning opportunities for colleagues

E Using resources

E1	Manage a budget
E2	Manage finance for your area of responsibility
E3	Obtain additional finance for the organisation
E4	Promote the use of technology within your organisation
E5	Ensure your own actions reduce risks to health and safety
E6	Ensure health and safety requirements are met in your area of responsibility
E7	Ensure an effective organisational approach to health and safety

Table 12.2	*Continued*
F	**Achieving results**
F1	Manage a project
F2	Manage programme of complimentary projects
F3	Manage business processes
F4	Develop and review a framework for marketing
F5	Resolve customer service problems
F6	Monitor and solve customer service problems
F7	Support customer service improvements
F8	Work with others to improve customer service
F9	Build your organisation's understanding of its market and customers
F10	Develop a customer focused organisation
F11	Manage the achievement of customer satisfaction
F12	Improve organisational performance

Source: From the Management Standards Centre (www.management-standards.org). I am grateful to Dr Kion Ahadi, Policy and Projects Manager, Management Standards Centre for providing this information.

3-D MODEL OF MANAGERIAL BEHAVIOUR

However effectiveness is measured, managers are likely to be effective only if they adopt the most appropriate style of behaviour.

A development of the Blake and Mouton Managerial Grid, discussed earlier, is the three-dimensional (3-D) model of managerial behaviour suggested by *Reddin*.[41] By adding a third dimension of managerial effectiveness to task orientation and relationship orientation, the 3-D model identifies eight possible styles of managerial behaviour.

- **Task orientation (TO)** is the extent to which the manager directs both personal and sub-ordinates' efforts through planning, organisation and control.
- **Relationship orientation (RO)** is dependent upon the manager's personal job relationships. This is characterised by consideration for subordinates' feelings, mutual trust and encouragement.

The combination of TO and RO determines the manager's basic style of behaviour. The four possible basic styles (*see* Figure 12.6) are similar to those identified by Blake and Mouton in the Managerial Grid.

Figure 12.6	The four basic styles of managerial behaviour

Apparent effectiveness and personal effectiveness

Each of these four basic styles of management can be effective or ineffective depending on the situation in which they are applied. Effectiveness is defined by Reddin as:

> the extent to which a manager achieves the output requirements of his position ... Managerial effectiveness has to be defined in terms of output rather than input, by what a manager achieves rather than by what he does.

Reddin distinguishes managerial effectiveness from (i) apparent effectiveness, and (ii) personal effectiveness.

- **Apparent effectiveness** is the extent to which the behaviour of the manager – for example punctuality, giving prompt answers, tidiness, making quick decisions and good public relations – gives the appearance of effectiveness. Such qualities may or may not be relevant to effectiveness.
- **Personal effectiveness** is the extent to which the manager achieves personal objectives – for example power and prestige – rather than the objectives of the organisation.

Eight styles of managerial behaviour

Applying the third dimension of managerial effectiveness provides eight styles of managerial behaviour – four effective styles, which achieve output requirements, and four ineffective styles (*see* Figure 12.7). For each of the basic styles – separated, dedicated, related or integrated – there is a more effective or less effective version. Effectiveness results from the appropriateness of a particular style of management to the demands of the situation in which it is applied. When one of the basic styles (for example 'separated') is adopted in an appropriate situation, a more effective style ('bureaucrat') results. When the basic style is adopted in an inappropriate situation, the result is a less effective style ('deserter').

Figure 12.7	The 3-D model of managerial effectiveness

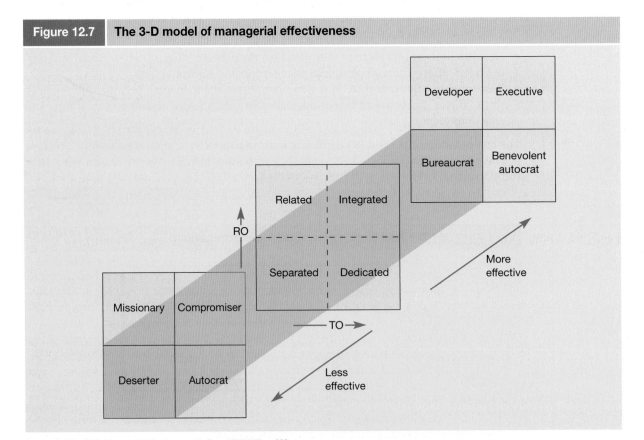

Source: Reddin, W.J., *Managerial Effectiveness*, McGraw-Hill (1970), p. 206.

The eight styles of management may be described briefly as follows.

More effective styles

1 **Bureaucrat** – a low concern for both task and relationships. The manager adopting this style is seen as being interested mainly in rules and procedures to control the situation, and as conscientious.

2 **Benevolent autocrat** – a high concern for task and a low concern for relationships. Managers adopting this style know what they want and how to achieve it without causing resentment.

3 **Developer** – a high concern for relationships and a low concern for task. The manager adopting this style is seen as having implicit trust in people and concerned mainly with developing them as individuals.

4 **Executive** – a high concern for both task and relationships. The manager adopting this style is seen as a good motivator, sets high standards, treats people as individuals, and favours team management.

Less effective styles

5 **Deserter** – low concern for both task and relationships in a situation where such behaviour is inappropriate. The manager lacks involvement and is passive or negative.

6 **Autocrat** – a high concern for task and a low concern for relationships in a situation where such behaviour is not appropriate. The manager is seen as lacking confidence in others, unpleasant and interested only in the task in hand.

7 **Missionary** – a high concern for relationships and a low concern for task where such behaviour is inappropriate. The manager is seen as interested mainly in preserving harmony.

8 **Compromiser** – a high concern for both task and relationships in a situation requiring high concern for neither, or for only one orientation. The manager is seen as a poor decision-maker, too easily influenced by the pressures of the situation, and as avoiding immediate pressures and problems at the expense of maximising long-term output.

Appropriate style of behaviour

According to Reddin's 3-D theory, managerial effectiveness cannot be measured simply in terms of achieving production or relationships with other people. The manager must also be adaptable in adopting the appropriate style of behaviour that will determine effectiveness in achieving the output requirements of the job. Reddin has developed a 'management-style-diagnosis' test to identify styles of management and of organisations. The test comprises 64 paired statements which compare one style of management with another. From each pair of statements is selected the one statement which describes best the manager's behaviour in their present job. Analysis of the answers can help the manager to evaluate their own perceived style of management.

THE MANAGEMENT OF TIME

Whatever the attributes or qualities of a successful manager, one essential underlying criterion is the effective use of time. With many managers who complain that they do not have sufficient time it may be more a case that they have failed to organise themselves or their work properly. The most important members of staff to be managed are themselves. Although it is currently a popular topic of attention, the importance of time management has long been recognised as an inherent feature of management. *Drucker*, writing in 1988, refers to time as the limiting factor for effective executives. Time is a unique resource – you cannot rent, hire, buy or otherwise obtain more time. The supply of time is totally inelastic; time is totally irreplaceable and everything requires time.[42]

There are a number of suggested procedures and techniques for managing time but the essential requirements of good time management include:

- clear objectives;
- careful forward planning;
- the definition of priorities and action;
- the ability to delegate successfully; and
- flexible working.

A 'concept map' of the management of time is presented in Figure 12.8.

Effectiveness and activity

For many managers, appearing always to be busy, a cluttered desk and a continual flurry of activity are outward signs of their effectiveness. The trouble is that such managers may be too busy 'doing' rather than **thinking about what they, and their staff, should be doing and how they should be doing it**. Activity may be a substitute for actual achievement. It is important therefore to distinguish effectiveness from activity. *Rees and Porter* suggest that:

> *Activity-centred behaviour is in any case much more likely to spring from incompetence and/or insecurity rather than adroit political behaviour. Activity-centred behaviour is likely to aggravate the position of the manager in the long run rather than ameliorate it.* [43]

Beware the busy manager A recent study by *Bruch and Ghoshal* suggesting that we should beware of the busy manager raises the question: 'Are the least effective executives the ones who look like they are doing the most?' They refer to unproductive busyness and what they call 'active non-action'. After ten years of studying the behaviour of busy managers in nearly a dozen large companies, Bruch and Ghoshal claim that fully 90 per cent of managers squander their time in all sorts of ineffective activities.

> *No doubt, executives are under incredible pressure to perform, and have far too much to do, even when they work 12-hour days. But the fact is, very few managers use their time as effectively as they could. They think they're attending to pressing matters, but they're really just spinning their wheels ... A mere 10 per cent of managers are purposeful – that is, both highly energetic and highly focused. They use their time effectively by carefully choosing goals and then taking deliberate actions to reach them. Managers that fall into the other groups, by contrast, are usually just spinning their wheels; some procrastinate, others feel no emotional connection to their work, and still others are easily distracted from the task at hand. Although they look busy, they lack either the focus or the energy required for making any sort of meaningful change.* [44]

Manager's checklist

Stewart suggests that it is often salutary for managers to compare what they think they do against what happens in practice. Answers to the following questions will help managers decide what, if anything, they should check, and to review their effective management of time. [45]

1. Am I giving adequate attention to current activities, to reviewing the past and to planning for the future? In particular, am I giving enough thought to the future?
2. Am I dividing my time correctly between different aspects of my job? Is there, perhaps, one part of my job on which I spend too much of my time?
3. Have I changed what I am trying to do, and how I work to allow for the effects of changes in my work?
4. Am I certain that I am not doing any work that I ought to have delegated?
5. Who are the people that I ought to be seeing? Am I spending too much or too little time with any of them?

Figure 12.8 **Concept map of the management of time**

THE MANAGEMENT OF TIME

- **WHY MUST MANAGERS MANAGE THEIR OWN TIME?**
- **THEIR STAFF'S TIME**

MANAGING YOUR TIME
- Importance of time management
- Where does time go?
- Conserving time
- Time management tools

IMPROVING DEADLINE TIMES
PRODUCTION COMPLETION
DELIVERY DEADLINES
- Changing working practices
- Using better equipment
- Training staff
- Collecting more/better information

Careful network planning will assist the manager to reorganise and reduce time pressures, eliminate wasted time and maximise time usage

MANAGING DEPARTMENTAL TIME
Requires:
- Responding to external time pressures
- Maximising the time capacity available
- Analysing the components of total job time
- Using time planning techniques
- Recording time spent

RECORDING TIME
- for future reference – record and keep times for specific jobs
- for estimating and quoting
- for buying in replacement labour – sub-contracting/ out-sourcing

METHODS/TECHNIQUES FOR TIME PLANNING
- Network planning for long jobs (and Critical Path Analysis) – explore benefits of project management computer software
- GANTT charts
- Plan priority sequences
- Ordered sequences
- Short-term scheduling – consider value/costs of setting up specific 'jobbing' capacity for quick repeat order, or
- Fill-in jobs for waiting time between longer or larger jobs

TIME MANAGEMENT
A systematic step approach to using time effectively
1 – Analysis of time usage in the past.
2 – The time budget in the future
3 – Allocate time to specific tasks
- Plan and adhere to a weekly time schedule
4 – Record activities
4 – Classify activities

MANAGING TIME USAGE
- Work sampling and time study techniques may be applicable
- Set time standards for jobs with realistic (+/–) allowances
- Use standard data catalogues for estimating job durations
- Give time allowances for an end-of-day activity to prepare for tomorrow

WHY IS IT IMPORTANT?
- There is more jobs to be done than there is time to do them
- Managers usually face more jobs than there is time to do them
- Jobs have different priorities
- Some jobs have to be done and some delegated – which?

WHERE DOES PRODUCTIVE TIME GO?
- Routine jobs (minor jobs but important)
- Regular duties
- Maintenance role as part of the organisation
 e.g. – meetings
 – selection/recruitment
 – seeing visitors
- Special assignments (unpredictable)
- Creative work (requires time)

PARKINSON'S LAW
- Work expands in such a way as to fill the time available

PARETO PRINCIPLE
In any series of events which you do
e.g. your job, 80% of the output arises from 20% of your input
(the %s may vary but the principle remains)
e.g. 20% of the customer base leads to 80% of the income

COSTING TIME
- What is your total cost?
- How much productive time do you achieve?
- What utilisation do you obtain?
- How much would a consultant/teleworker /subcontractor charge?

CONSERVING TIME
- Learn to communicate effectively
- Train subordinates to listen by Question & Answer techniques
- Organise meetings effectively – don't just hold them
- Reduce paperwork (form filling is slow, is it all necessary?)
- Control interruptions
- Set time objectives for tasks

COMPONENTS OF TOTAL JOB TIME
- Inherent time – sum of labour time, machine time and handling time
- Set-up time – time to prepare or tear-down after work; % time wastage reduced by scheduling longer runs
- Lost time – personal time for breaks, toilet, sickness, holidays, etc.
- Technical time – machinery failure or component shortage
- Learning time – familiarisation with the job. Can only be estimated and is often inaccurate

WHERE DOES THE REMAINDER GO?
Wasted and lost time due to–
- Lack of focus on task (Poor directions/lack of understanding)
- Failure to delegate (Assumes there is someone to delegate to)
- Interruptions (Should you have an 'open door'?)
- Fatigue – losing concentration (Take the breaks especially lunch)
- Failure to communicate – instructions not clear – failure to listen
- Failure to anticipate ('I never thought')
- Advance planning can – avoid problems later – anticipate trouble in different situations – allow an overview of the task

FOR EFFECTIVE TIME MANAGEMENT YOU SHOULD–
- Establish the KEY TASKS (the six most important tasks you do)
- Set your OBJECTIVES (the achievements you are trying to attain in the key post)
- Identify PERFORMANCE STANDARDS (the quantifiable measure of the objectives)
- Identify CONSTRAINTS (things standing in the way of your objectives)
- Decide on ACTION PLANS (ways of removing the constraints)

Source: Training Learning Consultancy Ltd, Bristol, England. Reproduced with permission.

6 Do I organise my working day and week, as far as possible, according to priorities, or do I tend to deal with each problem as it turns up, or even as I think of it, without stopping to think whether there is something more important that I should be working on?

7 Am I able to complete a task, or am I constantly interrupted? If the latter, are all these interruptions an essential part of my work?

There are three questions that managers should ask of each of their activities:

- Should it be done at all?
- If so, when should it be done?
- Should it be delegated?

The Chartered Management Institute has published a checklist which explains that:

Good time management has always been an important skill, but it is now essential. Factors such as widespread corporate restructuring, accelerating change, information overload and the need to balance private and working lives have put the squeeze on managers to get more from their working day.[46]

Presenteeism and output

Despite growing interest in time management, it should not be viewed in isolation from related activities of management such as leadership and delegation. For example, a key aspect of managerial leadership (discussed in Chapter 10) is visibility. Time management needs to be balanced against potential benefits from maintaining an open-door policy or the MBWA approach. When making a conscious effort to find more time for themselves, managers need to take account of their availability for consultation with subordinates, superiors or colleagues and for ensuring effective processes of communication.

Clegg suggests that working more flexibly can be managed in a variety of ways but essentially it is about using our time, and the time of other people, more intelligently.

Traditionally we managed input. The time that an individual spent at his or her desk (or wherever) was a measure of their contribution. But there is a snag with this approach because there is no linkage between presenteeism and value to the company. Some staff could sit at their desk from 7am to 9pm keeping intensely busy all the time and never do anything to improve the bottom line. Others could, in minutes, boost revenue or slash costs by thousands or even millions of pounds. To cope with this paradox we need to change the focus to outputs – measuring what an individual produces, particularly the value of that output.[47]

Critical reflection ?????

'Many of the 'newer' pronouncements on managerial behaviour are no more than the repetition of well-established concepts in a more contemporary context. In fact, management thinking has advanced little since the work of original authors such as Peter Drucker in 1955 or Douglas McGregor in 1960. How much truth do you think there is in this statement?

Refresh your understanding

Activity 12C
www.pearsoned.co.uk/mullins

MANAGEMENT IN THE NEWS

Bad Manners and Bad Managers

Bosses with 'no time to be nice'

Alison Maitland

Lucy quit her job in university administration after finding herself routinely ignored and undermined by a manager. On one occasion, the female boss returned from leave and sent everyone in the department except Lucy an email thanking them for their work during her absence. On another, she told some of Lucy's peers that she could not be trusted. Lucy, whose name has been changed, says things rapidly went downhill. 'I found it exceptionally rude,' she says. 'It made me extremely negative towards her. It shut me down. I felt she was someone I didn't really want to get to know or work with. Communication became very poor, which made the job difficult.'

Her experience is echoed in a survey of workplace behaviour in the UK which shows that people in positions of power are often the worst perpetrators of incivility. Respondents accuse their bosses of dressing down employees in front of colleagues or customers, delivering unpleasant messages by email, ignoring the contribution of more junior staff and even tearing up someone's work in public.

'I have been shouted at in front of 20 people by the MD who said that the work I had done was 'crap' and I was to do it again,' says an employee in her 30s. In a similar vein, a 30-year-old female employee of an accountancy firm recalls 'one of the partners clicking his fingers at a senior manager to get his attention and calling him down the office, as though he were a puppy'. In a case of eye-popping discourtesy, a 29-year-old employee reports that 'a director who has since left asked me to go out in the pouring rain for his sandwich when I was eight months pregnant'.

'The lesson in manners must be taught from the top,' says Colette Hill, chief executive of CHA, the consultancy that commissioned the survey, Business Behaving Badly. 'In an organisation whose leaders are selectively courteous, fail to attend scheduled meetings, are cavalier about deadlines or casually bully their direct reports, others will inevitably follow the unspoken rules of engagement.'

While some of the 1,100 respondents to the online survey say that the only rude people they encounter at work are customers and that their colleagues are scrupulously polite, others report endemic incivility. email abuse is a particular bugbear, especially when people use it to avoid face-to-face contact. A respondent in his 40s says: 'One so-called member of the local management team regularly makes snide comments by email and presses the 'send' button as he puts on his coat and heads for home, knowing he won't see the people he's targeting for several days because of their shift pattern.'

The erosion of hierarchy and authority, and the growing pluralism of society, has left people less clear about how to behave at work, says Nigel Nicholson, professor of organisational behaviour at London Business School. 'We used to know where we stood a bit better. Now everybody has different standards, so there is much more room to perceive these [uncivil] things as happening.'

Despite persisting cases of rudeness and bullying by managers, Prof Nicholson sees some cause for optimism. Employees are speaking out more, he says. 'Bosses have always indulged themselves. In the old days, people used to knuckle under. Now they won't accept it.'

Source: Maitland, A., 'Bosses with "no time to be nice"', *Financial Times*, 11 May 2006. Copyright © 2006 The Financial Times Limited, reproduced with permission.

Discussion Questions

1 Critically review what this article reveals about the changing nature of managerial authority.

2 Discuss the extent to which 'good manners' are simply a matter of individual perception and personal standards, and the implications this might have for managerial behaviour.

SYNOPSIS

● It is the responsibility of managers to achieve results through the efforts of other people. This involves the effective management of human resources. The way in which managers exercise their authority and carry out their responsibilities is important. The changing nature of the work environment is reflected in changes in the traditional boss–subordinate relationship. The style of management adopted, and the behaviour displayed towards subordinate staff, is likely to be conditioned by predispositions about people, human nature and work.

● One means of describing different styles of management is the Managerial Grid, now republished as the Leadership Grid®, and the combination of concern for production and concern for people. There are five basic combinations with a total of 81 different 'mixtures' of concern for production and concern for people. Managers tend to have one dominant style of management but may switch from one style to another. The Grid provides a framework in which managers can identify, study and review their patterns of behaviour, and aid training and development.

● An organisation is arguably more likely to harness its staffing resources effectively if there is a participative style of management. Likert identifies a four-fold model of management systems that can be related to a profile of organisational characteristics. System 4 is based on the principle of supportive relationships and group processes. One particular style or system of management is management by objectives (MBO). There are, however, a number of limitations and criticisms and, arguably, MBO has now been incorporated into modern systems of staff appraisal and performance management.

● There are many aspects to management but one essential ingredient of any successful manager is the ability to handle people effectively. It is important that managers have a highly developed sense of 'people perception' and understand the feelings of staff, and their needs and expectations. It is people who are being managed, and people should be considered in human terms. There are a number of views on what is likely to make for the successful management of people and lead to improved work performance.

● There is a clear and important need for managerial effectiveness, which can be distinguished from managerial efficiency and from activity. Effectiveness is concerned with doing the right things and relates to outputs of the job and to what the manager actually achieves. Managers are likely to be judged not just on their own performance but also on results achieved by other staff. The concept of managerial effectiveness is, however, difficult both to define and to measure. The Management Standards Centre provides a list of standards as benchmarks to help managers and their organisations improve performance.

● The combination of task orientation and relationship orientation results in four basic styles of managerial behaviour. Each of these styles can be effective or ineffective depending on the situation in which it is applied. One essential underlying criterion is the management of time. With the changing nature of the work organisation, good time management is arguably more essential than ever. However, studies suggest that activity may be a substitute for actual achievement and that busy managers are not necessarily effective managers.

 Refresh your understanding, assess your progress and begin your research with online resources at **www.pearsoned.co.uk/mullins**

REVIEW AND DISCUSSION QUESTIONS

1 Distinguish between different sets of attitudes and assumptions about people at work that managers might hold. Suggest how these different attitudes and assumptions might influence actual managerial behaviour.

2 Critically assess the value and relevance today of management by objectives (MBO) as a means of improving organisational performance.

3 From your experience, explain fully a situation that you believe demonstrates a successful way of dealing with subordinate staff. To what extent can you relate this situation to the application of theories or principles of management?

4 Discuss what you see as the most important considerations in adopting a people-centred approach to management.

5 How would you, as a senior manager, attempt to manage your staff effectively as knowledge workers rather than subordinates?

6 How would you attempt to distinguish between an effective and an ineffective manager? Give specific examples of the criteria you would apply to assess the effectiveness of a particular managerial job of your choice.

7 Explain Reddin's 3-D model of managerial behaviour. Give a practical example of situations that demonstrate (i) a more effective style, and (ii) a less effective style.

8 Debate critically what you believe are the essential features relating to the effective management of time.

ASSIGNMENT

Complete the 'Your Management Style' questionnaire. Move quickly and do not think too deeply about each question but give your first immediate response.

Your Management Style Questionnaire

There are ten pairs of statements. Assign a weight from 0 to 10 to each statement to show the relative strength of your belief in the statements in each pair. The points assigned for each pair must total 10 in each case. Be as honest with yourself as you can and resist the natural tendency to respond as you would 'like to think things are'. This instrument is not a test. There are no right or wrong answers. It is designed to be a stimulus for personal reflection and discussion.

1 It's only human nature for people to do as little work as they can get away with. _____ (A)

 When people avoid work, it's usually because their work has been deprived of its meaning. _____ (B)

 10

2 If employees have access to any information they want, they tend to have better attitudes and behave more responsibly. _____ (C)

 If employees have access to more information than they need to do their immediate tasks, they will usually misuse it. _____ (D)

 10

3 One problem in asking for employees' ideas is that their perspective is too limited for their suggestions to be of much value. _____ (E)

 Asking employees for their ideas broadens their perspective and results in the development of useful suggestions. _____ (F)

 10

4 If people don't use much imagination and ingenuity on the job, it's probably because relatively few people have much of either. _____ (G)

 Most people are imaginative and creative but may not show it because of limitations imposed by supervision and the job. _____ (H)

 10

5 People tend to raise their stakes if they are accountable for their own behaviour and for correcting their own mistakes. _____ (I)

 People tend to lower their stakes if they are not punished for their misbehaviour and mistakes. _____ (J)

 10

Assignment – continued

6 It's better to give people both good and bad news because most employees want the whole story, no matter how painful. _____ (K)

It's better to withhold unfavourable news about business because most employees really want to hear only the good news. _____ (L)
10

7 Because a supervisor is entitled to more respect than those below him or her in the organisation, it weakens the supervisor's prestige to admit that a subordinate was right and he or she was wrong. _____ (M)

Because people at all levels are entitled to equal respect, a supervisor's prestige is increased when he or she supports this principle by admitting that a subordinate was right and he or she was wrong. _____ (N)
10

8 If you give people enough money, they are less likely to be concerned with such intangibles as responsibility and recognition. _____ (O)

If you give people interesting and challenging work, they are less likely to complain about such things as pay and supplemental benefits. _____ (P)
10

9 If people are to set their own goals and standards of performance, they tend to set them higher than the boss would. _____ (Q)

If people are allowed to set their own goals and standards of performance, they tend to set them lower than the boss would. _____ (R)
10

10 The more knowledge and freedom people have regarding their jobs, the more controls are needed to keep them in line. _____ (S)

The more knowledge and freedom people have regarding their jobs, the fewer controls are needed to ensure satisfactory job performance. _____ (T)
10

Source: Adapted from Myers, M. S., *Every Employee a Manager*, McGraw-Hill (1970). Reproduced with permission from the McGraw-Hill Companies, Inc.

PERSONAL AWARENESS AND SKILLS EXERCISE

Objectives

Completing this exercise should help you to enhance the following skills:

- Discover the level of trust that people have in you.
- Gain a deep appreciation of factors influencing interpersonal relationships.
- Examine and review those factors that influence your management style.

Exercise

You are required to ask yourself the following 11 questions:

1 Do people tend to open up to you and tell you things about themselves that they don't tell many others?
2 Are you generally accepting and non-judgemental of others?
3 Do people freely offer you help and support?
4 Do people come and seek your advice?

5 Do people feel comfortable being vulnerable around you?

6 Do you readily admit when you are wrong or have made a mistake?

7 Do you tend to use sarcasm and make putdown comments about people?

8 Do you gossip about others more than just occasionally?

9 Do you tell lies if it will benefit you to do so?

10 Do you like to make yourself look good even if it is at the expense of others?

11 Do you take credit for things that others have done?

Source: From Bibb, S. and Kourdi, J., 'Do people trust you?' *Professional Manager*, vol. 14, July 2004, p. 32. A Chartered Management Institute publication, reproduced with permission.

Discussion

● How important is trust to the success of an organisation?

● What do you believe are the characteristics of a trusted leader?

● How can managers develop and retain trust?

CASE STUDY

Effective management: a question of context?

As this chapter has illustrated, the nature of management effectiveness is to some degree dependent upon context. There may be a number of skills, personal qualities and behaviours which are central to effective management in any context, but the need for a contingency approach based upon the nature and environment of an organisation is highlighted by many of the authors whose work is discussed here.

Talented people with successful careers can sometimes fail to fulfil expectations in new roles or changed circumstances; for instance, the problems surrounding the Morrison's supermarket company illustrates the way in which a major organisational change (the acquisition of Safeway) resulted in the under-performance of a previously very successful company chairman, Sir Ken Morrison. At many levels of organisational life, management training and development programmes can help to smooth out individual transitions, for example as the result of promotion, but experience and performance remain key to the assessment of managerial effectiveness. An increasing amount of academic research is revealing that the *perceived* effectiveness of managers may also be of significance in relation to both the evaluation of an individual's success in a managerial role and with regard to decisions about their future promotion. This mix of fact and perception can sometimes have a

damaging effect on the careers of both specific individuals and others in the group to which they might be seen to belong. In particular, we might consider the long-running debate about the effectiveness of women as managers.

Part of this debate has centred on the difficulty which some women have experienced in performing effectively in organisations and sectors of the economy which have traditionally been a male preserve. The evolutionary result of traditional work patterns is often seen in organisational structures and cultures which can be viewed as highly male-oriented, both in their overt features – aggressive language, open, personal competitiveness between colleagues, and loud banter in the workplace – and in their systems and practices – long working hours, the assumption of 24/7 availability and performance measures which seem to lock individuals into long working hours as a means to success. This naturally has an impact in defining and institutionalising behaviours which are both *regarded* as effective and which are likely to *be* effective (the term patriarchal is often used to describe such institutionalised 'maleness'). As more and more women gain professional expertise through improved opportunities and access to education, their expectations of having a working life and a career outside the family are likely to become the norm. This naturally raises

Critical reflection

Until HR professionals can produce hard and clear measures of their value to improved performance, it is perhaps no surprise that they are perceived as making only a marginal contribution to organisational effectiveness. Do you think HR professionals lack creditability among line managers? How would you attempt to measure the contribution of the HR department?

THE NATURE OF HUMAN RESOURCE MANAGEMENT

However the activities of management are identified, and whatever the nature of organisational processes, an essential part of the process of management is that proper attention be given to the efficient use of resources, in particular human resources. The human element plays a major part in the overall success of the organisation. There must be effective management of human resources.

The significance of human resources and people as the most important asset of any organisation is emphasised by *Gratton*. As the basis of her 'Living Strategy', Gratton puts forward four basic propositions:

1 there are fundamental differences between people as an asset and the traditional assets of finance or technology;
2 an understanding of these fundamental differences creates a whole new way of thinking and working in organisations, a shift in mind-set;
3 business strategies can only be realised through people;
4 creating a strategic approach to people necessitates a strong dialogue across the organisation.[1]

The personnel management/HRM debate

You will be aware that in recent years there has been a noticeable popularity in the use of the term 'human resource management' to replace the term 'personnel management'. The personnel management/HRM debate is now a well-trodden path and much has been written about the subject. Discussion generally centres on the extent to which either: HRM is a new and distinctive philosophy with a paradigm shift towards a more strategic approach to people management; or simply' new wine in old bottles' and in reality no more than a different term for what good personnel managers have always been doing.[2]

There seems little to be gained by proliferating this debate except perhaps in summary to suggest that it is difficult to escape the thought that the increasing use of the term HRM has been associated with those engaged in personnel work seeking to enhance their status and influence. Not, however, that there is anything **necessarily** to criticise about this. The essential point is that it does not follow that HRM however it is described will, *per se*, result in a higher level of motivation and job satisfaction or organisational performance than would be achieved with a traditional personnel management approach. It is, however, recognised that developments in communications information technology, new forms of work organisation and structure, and increasing attention to empowerment, flexible working arrangements and new psychological contracts (discussed in Chapter 1) certainly provide a challenge to traditional personnel management (or HRM) theories and practices.

Definitions of HRM

HRM is often defined in very general and broad terms. For example, according to *Fisher et al.*: '**Human resource management (HRM)** involves all management decisions and practices that directly affect or influence the people, or **human resources**, who work for the organisation.'[3]

The Chartered Institute of Personnel and Development is a professional body for all those concerned with the management and development of people. The Institute provides the following definition:'The design, implementation and maintenance of strategies to manage people for optimum business performance including the development of policies and processes to support these strategies and the evaluation of the contribution of people to the business.'[4]

Interestingly, apart from a change in title from personnel management to human resource management, a more detailed definition given by *Torrington et al.* in 1995 remains unchanged today.

> *Human resource management is a series of activities which: first enables working people and the organisation which uses their skills to agree about the objectives and nature of their working relationship, and secondly, ensures that the agreement is fulfilled.*[5]

A strategic approach

It seems reasonable to conclude that there is no clear distinction between personnel management and human resource management. However, the increasing emphasis on effective employee relations and the importance of securing the involvement and commitment of staff to the aims of the organisation may, at least in part, be argued as justification for the change in title. *Crainer* refers to the change from personnel management to human resource management.

> *With hierarchies decreasing and the growing emphasis on becoming leaner and fitter, the onus is increasingly on corporations extracting the best possible performance from all employees. In (best) practice this means recruiting well-qualified and highly skilled people and developing the skills of everyone in the organisation. With increased acceptance of its importance, personnel management has become human resource management. The emerging role of human resource management is radically different from that of the past when it dealt with the bureaucracy of employing people and little else. From being a caring role, human resources is being realigned as a strategic role, focused on the business needs and strategic plans of the corporation.*[6]

Competencies-based human resources management

The strategic use of human resources will help managers to contribute to the release of true value by the optimum use of people's competencies. A strategic HR approach requires that the needs and talents of employees become matched with the organisation's goals. People's competencies should become the building blocks of successful organisations in the future. To sustain and develop the required people's competencies for future success, an organisation needs to have a system with which it can discriminate good to superior from poor to average performance by means of critical observance or measurement.

Organisations in the future will be different from today. Traditional hierarchical relations will be replaced by networks of empowered workgroups. Information will be at everyone's fingertips. Careers will become a sequence of assignments rather than a logical sequence of different jobs representing a climb to the top. In this context, employees will work more in teams, where they are not tied to a management level by traditional hierarchical lines. Performance of teams is measured on the accomplishment of the mission to contribute to the business' future success.

To benefit from the opportunities this new type of organisation provides, a new type of human resource management is needed, which is based on a clear notion of required competencies for future success in individual and team-roles. This will require a sharper image of the real strengths and weaknesses of people, and their possible contribution to the organisation and to teamwork. If the effort to transform human resources practices is done well, HR practitioners can play a strategic role as managers that can leverage human capital and expert knowledge for competitive advantages. If HR practitioners cannot meet this challenge, they will play a more limited role in the future organisation.[7]

HUMAN CAPITAL MANAGEMENT

Recent attention to a more strategic approach to HRM has given rise to the idea of **human capital management**. However, according to a DTI report, although the expression 'human capital management' is now widely used, there is no generally agreed definition. In the report the term is used to denote a strategic approach to people management that focuses on the issues that are critical to an organisation's success. The report maintains that greater transparency on how value is created through effective people policies and practices will benefit organisations and their stakeholders.

> *The Accounting for People Task Force believes that the way organisations manage their people affects their performance. Human Capital Management (HCM) – an approach to people management that treats it as a high level strategic issue and seeks systematically to analyse, measure and evaluate how people policies and practices create value – is winning recognition as a way of creating long-term sustainable performance in an increasingly competitive world.[8]*

Gratton refers to three elements of human capital – intellectual capital, emotional capital and social capital – which have implications for both individuals and organisations:

- **Intellectual capital** is at the heart of individual development and the creation of knowledge and personal value. This enables the exercise of choice.
- **Emotional capital** enables the continual growth and fulfilment of ambition. It is maintained through self-awareness and insight.
- **Social capital** arises from the forging of relationships. Traditional hierarchical roles and responsibilities are now being replaced by integrated structures and relationships of trust and reciprocity.

The three elements, or personal assets, are highly interrelated. It is through their combination, the feedback-loops and connectivity, that they bring advantage to the organisation and to the individual. Taken together the three elements form the basis for strong and supportive relationships and for developing the courage and grit necessary for entrepreneurship and taking action.[9]

People, strategy and performance

According to *Coppin*, 'human capital' is simply the knowledge, skills and competencies of people, which generates wealth for organisations. However, despite increasing evidence to show that HCM can and does improve business performance, UK companies appear to be slow in putting it into practice. There is a need for: (i) further training and development of board members in HR management with the aim of seeing people as balance sheet assets rather than costs, and (ii) devising relevant measures as human capital is somewhat intangible and more difficult to measure than financial key performance indicators.

Coppin suggests that HR professionals within an organisation should be more than staffing, training and remuneration helpers, and need to contribute on matters that show real bottom line impact. 'Of course, human capital measurement is not enough in itself. If it and HR management that underpins it are to be key to competitive advantages they need to be embedded in the holistic management of a business, linking people, strategy and performance.'[10]

A similar point is made by *Reeves*, who suggests that although organisations have bought the notion that people are a vital asset, the trouble is they have precious little idea how to invest in them. Organisations, and the HR profession in particular, still need a clearer idea on what they should actually be doing. To stand any chance of being seen as a strategic business partner, HR professionals need to be more thoughtful about the interaction between people and other investments, and more consistent in the application of existing policies.[11]

The management of people Whatever the debate on comparative meanings, terms such as 'human resource management' or 'human capital', despite their (present) popularity, have overtones of a cold, impersonal approach. Referring to people as resources, assets or capital is an instrumental approach implying a means to an end. Human resources are clearly the most important asset of any organisation and a resource that needs to be managed, but it is important to remind ourselves that, unlike physical resources, people are not owned by the organisation. People are individuals who bring their own perceptions, feelings and attitudes towards the organisation, systems and styles of management, their duties and responsibilities, and the conditions under which they are working. It is people who make the organisation. Without its members, an organisation is nothing. It is pleasing, therefore, to see what appears to be the increasing use of the terminology 'people management' or the 'management of people'.

HRM POLICIES, ACTIVITIES AND FUNCTIONS

Recognition of the needs and wants of staff and of the nature of their grievances is a positive step in motivating them to perform well. The efficiency of staff, their commitment to the aims of the organisation, and the skills and attitudes they bring to bear on the quality of service offered are fostered by good human relationships and effective HRM policy and practice. The effective management of people is influenced by the philosophy of top management and the attitudes they bring to bear on relationships with staff, and the problems which affect them. HRM policies therefore should emanate from the top of the organisation. They should be defined clearly and communicated through managers and supervisors to staff at all levels. An example is the need for a clearly stated policy on the use of ICT resources (including email and the Internet) that is clear about prohibited activities and consequences of failure to adhere to the policy such as disciplinary action and potential sanctions.

Underlying philosophies

The formulation of HRM policies, and the implementation of practices and procedures, should be based on underlying philosophies of managerial behaviour and employee relationships. Such philosophies should embrace:

- the recognition of people's needs and expectations at work;
- respect for the individual;
- justice in treatment and equitable reward systems;
- stability of employment;
- good working environment and conditions of service;
- opportunities for personal development and career progression;
- democratic functioning of the organisation; and
- full observance of all laws and codes of conduct relating to employment.

In overall terms, HRM policies can be seen to embrace:

● designing an effective organisation structure;
● staffing the structure with suitable people;
● defining work roles and relationships; and
● securing optimum working arrangements.

The objective is to develop and maintain a level of morale and human relationships that evoke willing and full co-operation of all people in the organisation in order to attain optimum operational performance. This is the total concept of the HRM function. It is important to remember, however, that no matter how genuine and well intended are HRM policies, they must also be practically and effectively implemented, and integrated vertically and horizontally throughout the organisation.

Ethical dimensions of HRM *Winstanley and Woodall* also draw attention to the ethical dimension of HRM. They suggest that ethical frameworks and principles can be applied through action on three levels:

● **academic debate** – including incorporation of ethical aspects into HRM and organisational behaviour curricula at both undergraduate and postgraduate level;
● **academic research** – including evidence-based research to identify the full range of ethical concerns and practices, and to explore relationships between humanism and employee performance; and
● **professional HR practice** – including a role for the CIPD in promoting ethical debate, and for HR professionals to become a champion, architect and steward of ethical management of people.[12]

ORGANISATION OF THE HRM FUNCTION

Smaller organisations may not justify a specialist human resource manager or a separate department. But **it is still necessary to have an effective HRM function**, whether it is the responsibility of the owner or of a manager or an administrative assistant. Even in the smallest organisations, or in organisations where a specialist department has not been established, there will be a need to recruit staff, to train them, to motivate and reward them, and to comply with the law relating to employment. HR work must still be carried out even if an organisation is too small to justify a separate department or chooses not to establish one.

In the larger concerns, where more time is taken up with problems of organisation and the management of people, there is greater need for a specialist member of staff to whom are delegated full-time responsibilities for advising top management on human resource matters and for the development and implementation of clearly defined policies which permit consistent HRM practices. For example, high staffing costs together with increasing employment legislation and the changing nature of the work organisation (discussed in previous chapters) combine to suggest that personnel activities and employee relations are areas of increasing specialisation. There continues to be much debate about the value of the HR function to the bottom line. This has inevitably contributed to the changing nature of the personnel function and increasing specialisation of the role.[13]

The human resources manager Even where personnel work is established as a separate, specialist function, it is not easy to define closely the activities of the HRM department. The range of responsibilities varies from one organisation to another, as do the title and status of the head of the department and position in the management structure. In the larger organisations activities might be divided between two or more specialists, so that it would be possible to have, for example, a human resources manager, training officer and employee relations advisor. Whatever the range of responsibilities, the manager operates by consent, by delegated authority. How much con-

sent is dependent upon the attitudes of top management, the role they see the personnel specialist(s) performing and formal organisational relationships with 'line' managers.

Line managers are departmental or unit managers with responsibility for the 'production' process – for the operational functions directly related to the purpose and aims of the organisation. They form a hierarchical level in the chain of command throughout the organisation structure and are responsible for the management of their own staff. However, although line managers are specialists in their own area of work, they are not necessarily specialists in human resource management. Just as line managers turn to specialists on legal and accounting matters and the use of technology, so they will need help, guidance and specialist advice on personnel activities.

Many organisations, especially in the public sector, are working towards a service level agreement approach where a service is defined along with costs, and departments purchase full or parts of the service according to needs. This encourages HR to focus on customer service.

HRM: A SHARED RESPONSIBILITY

The HRM function is part of the generality of management and the responsibility of all managers and supervisors. The HR manager, as a separate entity, operates in terms of a 'functional' relationship; that is, as a specialist advisor on matters and on the implementation of policies through all departments of the organisation. It is the job of the HR manager to provide specialist knowledge and services for line managers, and to support them in the performance of their jobs. In all other respects the HR manager's relationship with other managers, supervisors and staff is indirect: it is an advisory relationship. It is the line managers who have authority and control over staff in their departments and who have the immediate responsibility for personnel activities, although there will be times when they need specialist help and advice. **If the HRM function is to be effective there has to be good teamwork, and co-operation and consultation between line managers and the HR manager.**

This is made easier when top management take an active part in fostering goodwill and harmonious working relationships among departments. It is important to have clear role relationships and to attempt to avoid difficulties with role incongruence or role conflict (discussed in Chapter 8). Top management should agree clear terms of reference for the HR manager within a framework of sound personnel policies. The effective management of people involves a partnership between managers and HR specialists. Within this framework the HRM function can be seen as operating at two levels: the organisational level and the departmental level (*see* Figure 13.1).

The organisational level At the organisational level the detailed involvement of the work activities of several departments, available time and the need for specialisation suggest that the HR manager has a prominent role to play and is the main executor of policies but acting in consultation with, and taking advice from, line managers. On this basis the HR manager would be concerned mainly with broader aspects of procedures that affect the organisation as a whole or staff generally. This could include such activities as human resource planning, procedures for recruitment and selection, induction and training, consultations with trade unions or staff representatives, employee development, compliance with the law relating to employment, maintaining records and statistics, and liaison with outside bodies such as ACAS, employers' organisations, government agencies, the Criminal Records Bureau, training organisations and professional associations.

The department level At the departmental or unit level line managers might assume a prominent role for day-to-day personnel matters, with the HR manager as advisor and if necessary as arbitrator. Line managers would be more concerned, at least in the first instance, with the operational

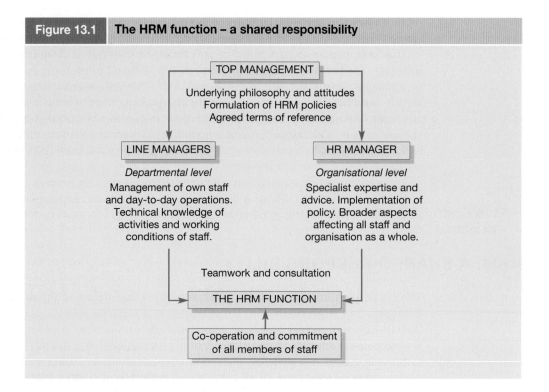

Figure 13.1 The HRM function – a shared responsibility

aspects of HR activities within their own departments, for example the organisation of work and allocation of duties, minor disciplinary matters, standards of work performance, safety, on-the-job training, communication of information, and grievances from staff. In this respect it could be said that **all line managers are their own human resource** managers. Line managers are on hand to observe directly the performance of their staff. They will actually see, and be directly affected by, for example, lateness of staff, unsatisfactory work, insufficient training, low morale, staff unrest, or poor planning of work duties and responsibilities.

Whatever the respective roles of the HR manager and line managers, the HRM function can be effective only if it is based and implemented on sound policies and procedures. It also requires the co-operation and commitment of all members of staff, whatever their duties or positions within the organisation. The HRM function cannot be housed within one discrete department or as the sole responsibility of selected members of staff. It permeates all levels of the organisation and all phases of its operations.

Critical reflection

HRM is an integral part of any managerial activity. Do you think line managers should act as their own human resource manager? Line managers have the right and the duty to be concerned with the effective operation of their own department, including the well-being of their staff. Do you believe that having a separate HR department leads only to poor line managers abdicating responsibility for their people?

Decision by top management The extent to which authority and responsibility for the personnel function is devolved to line managers is a decision for top management and is likely to be influenced by the nature, culture, structure and characteristic features of the particular industry or organisation. For example, in the hospitality industry, *Rocco Forte* has emphasised the importance of a caring

and efficient personnel function to assist line managers in what is one of their primary responsibilities. The nature of the hospitality business, with many separate units of differing size, location and mix of skills, means of necessity the personnel function is decentralised and prime responsibility has to be with line management.

'However, even if we have had a choice, I believe we would elect to put the prime responsibility for personnel on line management rather than on specialists. The nature of our work calls for active participation by management in day-to-day operations and they need to know that line management has the authority and responsibility for taking actions which vitally affect them in their work and in their working environment. The link therefore must be a direct one.'[14] This philosophy is still very much part of the structure of many hospitality organisations.

The concern of all managers It is clear, then, that the human resource managementl function is a shared responsibility among top management, line managers and supervisors, and the HR manager.

Johnson et al. also maintain that people-related issues are a central concern and responsibility of most managers in organisations and not confined to a specialist human resource function.

> *Indeed, although formal HR systems and structures may be vitally important in supporting successful strategies, it is quite possible that they may hinder strategy if they are not tailored to the types of strategies being pursued. Also the relationship between people and successful strategies goes beyond the traditional agenda of the HR function and is concerned with behaviours as much as competencies. The ability to change behaviours may be the key ingredient for success. Creating a climate where people strive to achieve success and the motivation of individuals are crucial roles of any manager and are a central part of their involvement in their organisation's strategy.*[15]

THE IMPORTANCE OF HRM

Whatever the choice of terminology or decisions on organisation, effective HRM and the successful implementation of personnel activities are essential ingredients for improved organisational performance. *Lynch* refers to the importance of people as a vital resource for sustainable competitive advantage. 'For most organisations, people are a vital resource. There are some industries where people are not just important but are the *key factor* for successful performance.'[16]

Ulrich refers to serious and widespread doubts about HR's contribution to organisational performance but suggests that it has never been more necessary. The question for senior managers is not, should we do away with HR, but, what should we do with HR? Companies today face five critical business challenges: globalisation, profitability through growth, technology, intellectual capital, and change, change and more change. These challenges provide HR with an opportunity to play a leadership role in the development of new capabilities to meet the challenges. However, Ulrich maintains that HR cannot transform itself alone and the primary responsibility belongs to the CEO and every line manager who must achieve business goals.

The five challenges present a new mandate for human resource management in order to help deliver organisational excellence in the following four ways. It should become:

- a partner with senior and line managers in strategy execution;
- an expert in the way work is organised and executed to ensure costs are reduced and quality maintained;
- a champion for employees, vigorously representing their concerns to senior management and working to increase employee contribution and commitment; and
- an agent of continuous transformation, shaping processes and a culture to improve an organisation's capacity for change.[17]

challenging; it offers us choice, because it opens our eyes and our minds. Training works outside-in; education works inside-out … Training will only help if organisations learn to be wise in how they use an individual's capability, marrying talent with healthy cultures, systems and processes, serving well conceived business goals.[27]

THE MANAGEMENT OF TRAINING

Training should be viewed as an investment in people. This is important at any time, but particularly so with the increasing pace of technological, structural and social change. But training for its own sake achieves little. It must be real, operational and rewarding. Training requires the co-operation of line managers, adequate finance and resources, time, skilled staff and a supporting appraisal system. There has to be a genuine commitment – from top management and throughout all levels of the organisation.

Stern argues that 'staff training and development have become matters of vital strategic importance'. It is, however, necessary to take an individual approach based on competencies and development needs.

> *In selecting training and development programmes, one size will not fit all. Nor can one course or degree be expected to do the whole development job. It is the menu of options that is offered, a complementary range of learning opportunities that will make sure new skills and learning are properly embedded, helping managers to raise their game and fulfil their potential. Practical, interpersonal or presentational skills training may fill the gaps left by more formal or more academic work.*[28]

A planned and systematic approach

In order to secure the full benefits of successful training there must, therefore, be a planned and systematic approach to the effective **management of training**.

- There must be a **clear commitment to training throughout all levels of the organisation**. This should include seeking the co-operation of line managers and, where appropriate, trade unions or staff representatives. Top management should set the scene by giving active support and encouragement to the training process, and through the provision of adequate finance, resources, time and skilled staff.
- There should be **an objective assessment of training needs** related to: (i) a vision of where the organisation is going; (ii) the need to be responsive to changes in external environmental influences; (iii) a comprehensive system of human resource planning; and (iv) a process of job analysis leading to the preparation of job descriptions and person specifications.
- It is important that **staff themselves should also feel a sense of involvement** and know how they can play their part in achieving the goals and objectives of the organisation. They should be given 'ownership and partnership' in the training process.
- There should be **a clear set of objectives and a defined policy for training**. This will enable the design of a carefully planned programme of training. The programme should address such questions as: Who is to be trained and why? What should they be taught? How and where should the training be undertaken, and by whom? How will the training be assessed and evaluated? The expected results of training should be understood clearly and realistically and be seen as reasonably attainable. Wherever possible, desired objectives should be stated in behavioural terms such as: Exactly what, after training, should the trainee now be able to do?
- People cannot absorb properly a large amount of information at one time. **The training programme should therefore be planned carefully** and staggered over a reasonable period of time. Consideration should be given to the priority, loading and pacing of information; timing and sequence, common or related items; variety of subject matter and methods of presentation; review and consolidation.

- Consideration must be given **to the choice of the most appropriate methods of training**. These can include internal courses, external courses and distance learning. The methods must be selected carefully according to the particular needs of the organisation and the employees. Guidance should be given on how to prepare for training and how to deal with the various material or situations presented.

- Consideration should also be given to **external courses and training opportunities linked to the educational system**. These include programmes designed to provide improved employment opportunities and centred on standards of occupational competence; those that are essentially vocational in nature; and relevant professional, diploma and degree courses.

- Full regard should be given **to the training needs of those groups who are not currently active in the workforce**, including married women, ethnic minorities, older members of staff, and people with disabilities. Special consideration should be given to the most appropriate methods of training for these groups of people and to observance of all relevant legislation.

- There should be **an effective system of review and evaluation** including the ongoing monitoring of progress, a supporting performance management system and the maintenance of suitable training records. Evaluation should involve assessment by the trainers, line managers and supervisors, and the trainees. The review process should include identification of those areas to which greater attention should be given in future training programmes.

- Wherever possible **evaluation should be related to objective, measurable factors,** for example: increased output or sales; reduced scrap or wastage; fewer accidents at work; fewer errors or customer complaints. Other measurable factors may include reduced staff turnover, absenteeism or sickness. However, such measures are difficult to isolate in terms of a single cause and effect. The ultimate evaluation of training is, of course, the extent to which it contributes to improved organisational performance and effectiveness; and to the quality, job satisfaction and prospects of employees. As an example, Hampshire County Council ask for three learning outcomes and then 6–8 weeks after the training course individuals discuss with their managers reinforcement of the learning and how their working practices have changed as a result of their training.

Training in people skills With the rapidly changing nature of the business world and the need to maintain competitive advantage, organisations need to ensure that staff are fully trained not only in knowledge of their products and/or services and technical skills, but also in their human relations skills. *Douglas* draws attention to the need for companies in all industrial and commercial sectors to be more serious about helping their technical people to master the so-called 'soft skills' and for training in their people skills and how to work with maximum effectiveness as part of a team.

> *Indeed, it is an accepted truism that some people who are truly gifted from a scientific and technical point of view find their career progress checked by their fundamental difficulties with managing people. They cannot be blamed for their lack of facility in this area: their entire training has been based around acquiring the rigorous knowledge they need to succeed at a technical level in their profession or industry. Expecting them automatically to excel at managing people is at best naïve, and at worst quite unreasonable.*[29]

E-LEARNING

Learning via technology – **e-learning** – is now a global phenomenon and is central to many organisations. It is not difficult to see why online learning is growing in popularity. It offers the opportunity to provide a standard message to a large number of widely geographically

dispersed people with the minimum disruption to their working and private lives. And, where large numbers of learners are involved, learning materials delivered online can bring the cost per learner to negligible proportions. Thus, learning becomes more accessible than ever before.

While e-learning is making progress as far as learners are concerned, the other key group that needs to be convinced of its efficacy are the trainers and lecturers. These people can fear for their jobs on the introduction of e-learning. Traditionally, trainers gave knowledge to a group of people. The challenge involved in online learning is not simply teaching in a different way. Rather, it means rethinking the whole nature of the learning/teaching process.

Benefits and limitations

According to *Sweeten*, however, the success rate for implementations of technology-based training over the past 20 years has not been high and large numbers of companies have spent countless millions on failed initiatives of what is now called e-learning. In order to make investment in technology work, those responsible for training need to be clear on the difference between learning and reference, the difference between training and education, and understanding what e-learning is good at and not so good at. Sweeten suggests that there are skills that you cannot impart through an e-learning course, for example to e-learn how to ride a bicycle.

> *However, you can deliver knowledge and understanding more effectively by computer than by any other way, and all the skills are underpinned and enhanced by knowledge and understanding. Achieving this through e-learning frees you to put more life into your live training with practical exercises, role-playing, etc.*[30]

It also appears that e-learning is most commonly used by IT staff. It is more appropriate for the acquisition of knowledge and there are doubts about its application to training in social skills. Despite such reservations, as communications technology develops and as people want to learn exactly what they need to know, with the minimum disruption to their lives, e-learning will become an increasingly significant part of training. For example, *Burns* suggests this method can be a powerful addition to conventional training, review and project support, saving both time and money, and has particular relevance for quality training. 'E-learning can be applied to three major aspects of quality: training, reviewing already learned material or communicating with employees to help them learn about quality, and supporting improvement teams.'[31]

Critical reflection ?????

The concept of e-learning may have popular appeal, especially as it is associated with modern technology, but it arguably has only limited potential and is no more than 'flavour of the month'. What do you think? In reality effective training can be achieved only through individual or small group, face-to-face interactions and personal feedback. Do you agree?

INVESTORS IN PEOPLE

Designed to advance the performance of organisations through their people, **Investors in People** now offers two directly linked leading business improvement tools, the Investors in People Standard and Profile. Adopted widely throughout the UK and internationally, the Standard and Profile are flexible frameworks that organisations of any size or sector can work with.

The Standard is a business improvement tool designed to advance an organisation's performance through the training and development of its people. The Standard includes a strong emphasis on improvement, the review of people, development plans and using success to inform future plans, and also on the vital role of managers in the development of employees. Since it was developed the Standard has been reviewed every three years. The Standard involves a set of ten key indicators of good practice each with a central theme and against which organisations wishing to be recognised as an 'Investor in People' will be assessed. **Details of the Investors in People Standard are given in the appendix to this chapter.**

Like the Standard, Profile is a powerful tool for business improvement. Based on the same principles, it builds on the breadth and depth of the Standard, but goes further to embrace a wider range of people management issues, exploring them in considerable depth. Through Profile, organisations have a deeper understanding of how well an organisation is working and how it can continue to improve going forward and also allows organisations to benchmark their performance against other organisations using the framework. A highly valuable tool in an increasingly competitive environment.

Both the Standard and Profile are based on a 'plan, do and review' model, which means that they can be aligned with existing business planning models easily.

- **Plan** – developing strategies to improve organisation performance, from business goals to leadership strategies.
- **Do** – implementing those strategies, taking action to improve the performance of the organisation.
- **Review** – evaluating and adjusting those strategies, through measuring their impact on the performance of the organisation.

Through this model, organisations are encouraged to work to a continuous improvement approach.

Refresh your understanding

Activity 13B

www.pearsoned.co.uk/mullins

PERFORMANCE MANAGEMENT (PM)

The process of management involves a continuous judgement on the behaviour and activities of staff. It is important that members of the organisation know exactly what is expected of them and the yardsticks by which their performance and results will be measured. One way in which to review the performance and potential of staff is through a formal system of **performance management**. (In some organisations this is still referred to as 'performance appraisal'.) A formalised and systematic PM scheme will enable regular reviews of the individual's performance, highlight potential, and identify training and development needs. The focus is on the continuous monitoring of performance to prevent any surprises at the annual development review. The PM scheme can also form the basis of a review of financial rewards and planned career progression.

Performance management and career plans

Performance management is therefore a crucial activity of the management of human resources. A comprehensive system can provide the basis for key managerial decisions such as those relating to allocation of duties and responsibilities, pay, empowerment and levels of supervision, promotions, training and development needs, and career progression. According to *ACAS*, the identification of individual training needs will best be supported by a performance review system that focuses on future development needs. The system should be used by managers and workers to:

- create career plans which encompass not only training proposals but also areas of work experience, job goals and personal development;
- consider career tracks which may be as much about lateral moves designed to expand learning and competence as upward promotion.

This policy will, in particular, highlight the need for greater use within organisations of open learning facilities and formalised human resource development programmes. With the support of the organisation emphasis should be placed on individuals taking responsibility for their own personal development. The manager's role in this process is predominantly that of counsellor.[32]

Design and implementation

The design and implementation of a successful PM system requires attention to a number of basic questions, including who should undertake the review, the frequency of reviews, and whether there should be an 'open' system.

The traditional practice is for reviews to be carried out by the immediate manager or supervisor – as the person who allocates work and has the closest knowledge of the individual's duties and performance. There is, however, an argument in favour of review at a higher level. This would extend the lines of communication and feedback. This may also help to demonstrate 'fair play' and to overcome problems of individual managers or supervisors applying different standards. A third approach is for the immediate manager/supervisor to conduct the review and write the report. Senior management are then asked to comment, to monitor the system, to review the consistency of reporting and to countersign as confirmation of approval. The review can also be undertaken by a member of the HR department, or by assessment centres. The removal of middle levels of management, flatter structures and greater empowerment of self-managed teams also have possible implications for who should undertake the PM process.

With the majority of schemes, staff receive an annual review, and for many organisations this may be sufficient. However, the frequency of reviews should be related to the nature of the organisation, the purpose and objectives of the scheme, and the characteristics of the staff employed. For some organisations, for example those operating in a dynamic, changing environment, more frequent reviews may be called for. More frequent reviews may also be appropriate for new members of staff, those recently promoted or appointed to a new position or for those whose past performance has not been up to the required standard.

There is an argument that suggests that open reporting restricts managers from giving a completely honest and frank review. However, the more staff see of their report – that is the more 'open' the system – the more they are likely to accept the process of performance management. Staff are better able to check the consistency of the report with verbal feedback from the manager. With an open system of reporting, staff should be given the opportunity to sign the completed form and to add any comments on their perception of the accuracy of the review. When decisions such as salary are based on the report there is greater demand for a transparent system so that individuals understand clearly the basis for decisions.

Establishing the system

In order to establish a successful performance management system, careful attention needs to be given to a number of important matters concerning its introduction and implementation. The system should not be viewed in isolation but in relation to the corporate objectives of the organisation, and designed to suit its culture and particular requirements The purpose and nature of the system should be made clear. Top management should be seen to own the system and be fully committed to the concept of performance management. They should ensure full consultation with trade unions, staff representatives, and all managers and members of staff. The system should not be perceived as something that is the prerogative of the HR department or introduced for its benefit. An effective administration system should aim to keep form-filling and paperwork to a minimum.

Monitoring and follow-up action The system needs to be monitored regularly to ensure that reviews are carried out properly and to obtain feedback from managers. The system should be kept under continual review and, where necessary, modified to meet changing environmental influences or the needs of the organisation. It is important to ensure that operation of the system and the criteria used for assessment satisfy equal opportunities, diversity and all legal requirements. The system must be supported by appropriate follow-up action, for example seeing that work plans or changes in duties and responsibilities actually take place and that suitable arrangements are made to meet identified training or development needs.

Appeals procedure In order to help establish the credibility of the system and to maintain goodwill, it is necessary to establish a formal appeals procedure which is clearly understood by all members of staff. Appeals should be made to a manager in a more senior position than the reviewer or sometimes, where appropriate, to the HR department or a representative committee. The appeals procedure should include provision for staff to be assisted, if requested, by a union or staff representative.

Performance management at Autoglass Limited

KEY PRINCIPLES

- Autoglass has a performance management system which is fair and equitable, and in line with the company's values: it encourages people to give their best.
- Individual output is a critical component of the overall product of the business and personal contribution counts towards remuneration.
- Performance management is an ongoing process with the annual review representing a summary of the year's work.
- The starting point for performance process should be the goals/outputs required from the individual (the WHAT), which in themselves should be stretching but achievable objectives.
- HOW the goals are achieved (e.g. teamwork), represents a critical part of the overall performance mix.
- Performance management is about dialogue, review and learning – not paperwork!
- Performance management matters.

PLANNING PERFORMANCE BY SETTING OBJECTIVES

Purpose

As well as reviewing past performance a key part of the performance management process is the setting of personal objectives. These objectives are set so that the person can effectively demonstrate their contribution to Autoglass' success, either individually or as part of a team. These objectives should always be aligned to the function/department's business plan.

Actions

1 Prior to the review establish what the targets of the branch/department in the coming months are to enable an effective contribution to the Autoglass business plan. If a non-operational department, consider what your department will do to maximise support for Autoglass and its customers.
2 Having established your department/branch targets consider what actions need to be maintained and what areas need to improve. Consider how those who report to you will contribute to these actions.
3 Taking into account the areas of improvement highlighted in the previous sections, determine the number of personal objectives for the reviewee. These should be agreed with the reviewee. The number depends on the complexity of the objectives, and to the weighting allocated to them.
4 Cross-reference to the rating performance matrix when setting objectives.
5 Ensure that the reviewee understands that the objectives set are a key part of planning performance and that achievement is key. It is best practice to review objectives at least quarterly.
6 Balance objectives to reflect areas in which the reviewee already excels (which you want to maintain) and areas that are in need of improvement.

Performance management at Autoglass Limited – continued

FEEDBACK FROM COLLEAGUES

The purpose of gathering feedback from colleagues is to produce a rounded view of performance over time, and to help the reviewee to recognise their strengths and development needs.

The emphasis should therefore be on highlighting good performance and helping reviewees to improve.

Select a number of colleagues who have direct dealings with the individual, e.g. work mates, staff who report to them, etc.

Process

To avoid a paper chase, gather feedback face to face or on the phone. You should not attempt to gather feedback via email or ask for written reports.

- Ask for constructive answers to three simple questions:

 What has the individual done well and how has this helped?

 What could the individual do better?

 How could the individual develop to be even more effective?

- Ask colleagues to be specific with their examples and follow up their answers by asking questions like:'Why was that?', 'What did they do then?'
- Make notes to refer back to.
- Relate the feedback to the leadership success factors/relevant competencies.

Confidentiality

It is important that you offer confidentiality when asking for feedback and that this is maintained.

Feedback should therefore be given in general terms without direct reference to the people concerned, and linked to performance against objectives and leadership success factors.

SELF-REVIEW

In preparation for the final review meeting, the reviewee should be asked to reflect on their performance by asking themselves the following questions:

'What have I achieved?'

(Refer to personal objectives and the job description. Refer to scorecard results where these are available.)

'How have I achieved this?'

(Refer to Leadership Success Factors or other relevant competencies.)

'What are my development needs?'

'What have I not achieved and why?'

'What action have I taken following my last review?'

Issue the reviewee with a self-review form at least one week before the event.

Make reference to the self-review at the review meeting, exploring differences between your views, colleagues' feedback and self-perception.

Encourage the reviewee to track their performance throughout the year.

Source: Reproduced with the permission of Simon Fitzgerald, Development and Training Manager, Autoglass Limited, the UK's leading vehicle glass repair and replacement business.

METHODS OF MEASUREMENT AND REVIEW

PM systems can be used to measure attitudes, behaviour and performance. Measurement may be a combination of:

- 'quantitative' measures using some form of rating scale, such as, for example, (1) excellent, (2) exceeds expectations or requirements of the job, (3) meets the expectations or requirements, (4) some weaknesses in meeting expectations or requirements, (5) unsatisfactory performance;
- 'qualitative' measures involving an unstructured, narrative report on specific factors and/or overall level of behaviour and work performance.

Behaviourally anchored rating scales (BARS) The use of behaviourally anchored rating scales (BARS) is an attempt to overcome difficulties with conventional rating scales and provide measurement scales that are directly related to the job being reviewed. A sample group of managers/supervisors is asked to identify, independently, several key behavioural aspects of the job in question. The responses are then collated and returned to the same or a different group to agree examples of good, average or poor performance and to allocate a scale point for each example. Those examples which are consistently rated at the same point on the scale can then act as 'anchors' and provide behavioural examples for each point on the scale.[33] Reviewers can then use the BARS as guidance against which to assess the expected behaviour of each person being rated. The disadvantages with BARS are that they can be time-consuming and costly to construct, and require careful and detailed training in their correct use. They are also more likely to be appropriate only in larger organisations.

Achieving objectives With this system, the manager agrees with members of staff set objectives at the beginning of the appraisal period. The 'SMART' approach to objectives setting is based on Specific, Measurable, Achievable, Realistic and Timebound examples. The appraisal is then based on the extent to which these stated objectives have been achieved. This method provides for participation by staff and also allows for at least some degree of self-appraisal. This method can be related therefore to a system of management by objectives (discussed in Chapter 12). A major consideration with this method is the extent to which circumstances beyond the control of the individual, such as changes in environmental influences, make the achievement of objectives unrealistic. Objectives need to be continually reviewed and revised in accordance with changing circumstances. Comparison with achieving objectives may not, by itself, provide a detailed assessment of performance. Therefore, some schemes combine this method with the use of rating scales.

Performance 'agreement' or 'contract' A variant of the 'meeting objectives' method is proposed by *Stein*. A good review system could be the key by which companies get the most out of all their staff without making them feel exploited.[34] Stein puts forward an approach based on the use of a performance 'agreement' or 'contract'. Members of staff create a succinct document, agreed with their superior, which sets out the individual's proposed contribution to the business plan of the organisation. This document provides an agenda that can be referred to during the review period and modified as necessary. This agenda serves as the basis of the appraisal judgement. Instead of rating performance in terms of a traditional five-box scale, as A, B, C, D or E, the question is simply: 'Has the plan been met?' This approach turns the appraisal system into a dialogue. The extent to which staff meet their contract also gives an indication of whether the business plan is realistic.

360° FEEDBACK AND UPWARD FEEDBACK

The concept of performance management has progressed into systems of '**360° feedback**' and 'upward feedback'. The idea of 360° feedback involves feedback from different groups within the work situation – peers and subordinates as well as bosses, and possibly internal and external customers. The idea is to provide a broader review covering good working relationship, teamwork, leadership, decision-making and quality of service provided.

An **upward feedback** review system involves subordinates' appraisal of managers. This can help to judge, among other things, managers' ability to accept constructive criticism. This initially can be a daunting experience for managers and also for individuals asked for feedback as they may fear antagonising their manager. To be effective, upward feedback requires an appropriate organisation culture and open management style. It is also necessary to involve an independent third person who can supply confidential feedback and comment.

Crainer refers to the need for the appraisal process to embrace the goals of the organisation and those of the individual in the short and long term, and the process must be managed effectively. A vast number of companies have abandoned the traditional approach in favour of a new model that tends to be flexible, continuous, revolves around feedback, involves many more people than one manager and a boss, and seeks to minimise bureaucracy.

> *As methods of appraisal go, 360-degree feedback is undoubtedly robust and rigorous … The attraction of 360-degree feedback is that it gives a more complete picture of an individual's performance. Different groups see an individual in a variety of circumstances and situations and can, as a result, give a broader perspective than that of a single boss. This, of course, relies on a high degree of openness and trust.*[35]

Potential drawbacks

Despite the apparent support for 360° feedback, *Pfau et al.* claim that this is a perfect example of how too many organisations base their human resources investment decisions on tradition, fads or competitors' practices, instead of on sound financial measures. Although adopted by a growing number of organisations, Pfau *et al.* report on research studies which show that 360° feedback may hurt more than it helps and that companies using 360° feedback have a 10.6 per cent decrease in shareholder value; while the concept delivers valuable feedback there are serious problems relating to privacy, validity and effectiveness. However, despite the drawbacks, Pfau *et al.* suggest that this does not mean 360° feedback programmes should be abandoned but that they should be implemented for the right reasons. Companies should ask themselves what they want to gain from the reviews. HR managers should revisit their programmes and take the necessary steps to implement the concept in order to transform 360° feedback into a value creator, not destroyer.[36]

Butcher also reports that 360° feedback is increasingly common in appraisals and makes sense. However, making peers review one another's strengths and weaknesses often leads to political tensions, particularly if bonuses or promotions are at stake. 'People can also feel a conflict between their role as a supportive colleague and their responsibility as a hard-nosed judge. What's more, close-knit teams may see the process as too focused on individual achievements – basically a popularity contest in disguise.'[37]

An example of a 360-degree feedback is provided by Gary Kusin, CEO of Kinko who received a low score in the area of rewards and recognition.

> *We adopted 360-degree feedback about a year after I came to Kinko's (this was before Kinko's partnered with FedEx). It was my first experience with having my performance reviewed by people who reported to me … I know that as a CEO, I'm not getting honest feedback a lot of the time, but I took these results as dead-on honest feedback. Also, I've got an ego, and that low score was a good motivator to change. If I were going to be an effective manager, a response was required … Every organisation at some point in its life will hit a rough patch. When this happens, whether it's belt-tightening or a reverse of direction, you'd like to have that foundation of trust to fall back on. Recognition is one of the things that builds trust over time. And I'd be way behind in this area had I not been slapped by that 360.*[38]

BENEFITS OF PERFORMANCE MANAGEMENT

The underlying objective of performance management is to improve the performance of individuals leading to improvement in the performance of the organisation as a whole. An effective scheme, therefore, offers a number of potential benefits to both the individual and the organisation:

- It can identify an individual's strengths and areas of development and indicate how such strengths may best be utilised and weaknesses overcome.
- It can help to reveal problems that may be restricting progress and causing inefficient work practices.
- It can develop a greater degree of consistency through regular feedback on performance and discussion about potential. This encourages better performance from staff.
- It can provide information for human resource planning, to assist succession planning, to determine suitability for promotion and for particular types of employment and training.
- It can improve communications by giving staff the opportunity to talk about their ideas and expectations, and how well they are progressing.

Potential problem areas

Despite the benefits of PM, the effectiveness of any system relies heavily on the quality and reliability of assessment. Variations in the consistency of reporting standards can quickly lead to a feeling of dissatisfaction and injustice. There are many potential sources of rating errors including, for example, perceptual distortions such as stereotyping and the halo effect, discussed in Chapter 5. Where a senior manager has the opportunity to confirm the ratings and countersign the report, this may help to identify inconsistencies and those appraisers who appear to be too generous or too critical in their assessments.

However well-designed the PM system, it is not possible to apply a completely objective approach to every unique situation. The system should therefore always allow for at least a degree of discretion and personal judgement. The reporting system should give the reviewer an opportunity to record formally any necessary qualifications to the given ratings.

The elimination of bias *Tackey* refers to the importance of eliminating bias in performance management. 'The evaluation of the performance of individuals in the workplace is fraught with difficulties even at the best of times. The difficulties are compounded when there are allegations of bias in such evaluation; and magnified out of recognition when the alleged bias has racial undertones.' Many problems with performance management systems arise from the application of the systems rather than inherent deficiencies in the systems themselves. For example it is important to understand whether certain behavioural descriptions are used more frequently to describe different groups. Questions also arise about issues of assessing actual, as opposed to perceived, performance and whether there are differences in perceptions of organisational and managerial support, career progression, etc. that may help explain 'poor' performance of minority ethnic employees. Success in general career development programmes for different organisational groups is more likely only when there is immense commitment in the top echelons of the organisation to equality of opportunity.[39]

Regular review of performance It is particularly important that a formal PM system does not result in managers failing in their responsibilities for reviewing performance on a day-to-day basis. Reviews should not be limited to a formal event occurring once or twice a year but should be a continuous process of monitoring, feedback and review. There should be regular communications and contacts between managers and staff, and discussions of problem areas and plans for the future.

According to *Kermally*, many organisations still do not fully understand the importance of measuring employee performance effectively. 'Managers need to value and measure the contribution of those that work them for in order to understand how people contribute to

Figure 13.3 Concept map of understanding the appraisal system

UNDERSTANDING THE APPRAISAL SYSTEM

- THE APPRAISAL SYSTEM
- FOR THOSE BEING APPRAISED
- FOR THOSE CARRYING OUT THE APPRAISAL

- SETTING THE STANDARDS
- ASSESSING THE PERFORMANCE
- PLANNING THE ACTIONS

APPRAISAL SYSTEM
This consists of several elements, as follows
– Setting targets
– Frequent reviews of progress
– Annual (or as appropriate) appraisal interview

CLARIFY JOB
SET TARGETS
ANNUAL APPRAISAL
REVIEW

ANNUAL APPRAISAL
– A formal system in which performance is compared with targets once a year to help both the organisation and the individual

ADVANTAGES
– To the organisation
– To the individual

WHY SET TARGETS?
– What is a target?
– Why set targets?
– How should targets be set?

TARGET SETTING
– To help the organisation achieve its objectives
 communicate
 appraise its staff
 plan and control
– To help the individual
 have direction/commitment
 communicate
 know how well he/she is doing
 manage time better

ORGANISATIONAL BENEFITS
– Human resource planning
– Recruitment and selection
– Lateral transfers
– Management succession
– Staff training and development
– Staff motivation
– Clarified priorities
– Improved perception of the organisation
– Greater commitment
– Organisational development
– Job evaluation
– Team building

INDIVIDUAL BENEFITS
– Self management
– Set priorities/planning
– Problem recognition easier
– Motivation can improve
– Feeling of involvement
– Better communication
– Better relationships
– Training and development

FEATURES
– Measureable and quantifiable
– Definable
– Dated and updated
– Challenging
– Realistic and achieveable

JOB CLARIFICATION
– How do I see my job?
– What does my boss expect of me?
– Where does my job fit into the organisation?

LIST CONTRAINTS
– Rules and regulations
– Security problems
– Resource constraints
– Time constraints
– Influences of people

SOME IDEAS FOR CLARIFYING
– List the 'purposes' of the job
– 4 to 6 key tasks
– The most important jobs done
– What is the department here for?
– What are the main divisions of work?
– What makes it a success or failure?
– What are most important tasks?
– What major contributions can it make?

THE MOST WORKABLE STANDARDS ARE THOSE SET IN AGREEMENT WITH THE EMPLOYEE

- JOB CLARIFICATION
- IDENTIFYING CONSTRAINTS
- REVIEWING

REVIEWING
– How well am I getting on?
– How do I know?
– Can I measure progress?
– What gets in the way?
– Would my manager agree with me?

SET STANDARDS
– A continuing yardstick for judging acceptable progress
– Leaving room for improvement
– Quality standard
– Quantity standard
– Time standards
– Cost standards

PERFORMANCE ASSESSMENT
- Has the performance reached the desired standard?
- How do you know?
- What has helped/hindered reaching the performance standard?
- Given the circumstances, are you satisfied with the performance?
- Were the measures you agreed with the employee
 – appropriate?
 – measuring the relevant targets?
 – appropriate for the future?
- Do you think the employee is satisfied with his/her performance?

ACTION PLANNING
- What needs to change?
- How can you help?
 – training
 – coaching
 – providing assignments to develop staff
- Should the statements be altered?
- Are the old standards still appropriate?

Source: Training Learning Consultancy Ltd, Bristol, England. Reproduced with permission.

New kind of employee relations

According to an ESRC publication in the Future of Work Programme, we could be witnessing the appearance of a genuinely new kind of employee relations across a widening range of private sector companies based on principles of industrial partnership. Research evidence suggests that there is a clear change taking place in employer attitudes with a greater willingness among many companies to at least tolerate the prospect of having to deal with trade unions. In part, this reflects a growing belief among a number of employers that trade unions are much more sensitive to the business needs of enterprises than they ever were in the past and are more willing to co-operate with management in developing and helping to enforce workplace reform.

In any analysis of the transformation of Britain's employee relations we cannot neglect the changing nature of work. The influence of technological innovation, work restructuring and job redesign are all helping to reshape shopfloor attitudes among managers, unions and workers. The underlying shifts in labour markets with the modest but important relative growth in the number of those employed in part-time, temporary and contract work are also helping to determine the evolution of our employee relations in new ways.[46]

UNITARY AND PLURALISTIC PERSPECTIVES

In the search for effective employee relations and a common commitment to the goals of the organisation, consideration should be given to contrasting approaches which present two major ways of perceiving work organisations; the unitary perspective and the pluralistic perspective. While neither of the approaches can be seen as 'right' or 'wrong', these contrasting views will influence the nature of employee relations and the management of human resources.

The unitary perspective With the unitary perspective the organisation is viewed as an integrated and harmonious whole with managers and other staff sharing common interests and objectives. There is an image of the organisation as a team with a common source of loyalty, one focus of effort and one accepted leader. Conflict is perceived as disruptive and unnatural and can be explained by, for example, poor communications, personality clashes or the work of agitators. Trade unions are seen as an unnecessary evil and restrictive practices as outmoded or caused by trouble-makers.

HR policies and managerial development can be seen as reflecting a unitary ideology. *Horwitz* suggests that the unitary perspective views company and trade union loyalty as mutually exclusive. He raises the question of human resource management as a reformation of a unitarist managerial ideology. Developments in HRM, in seeking to optimise co-operation and organisational loyalty, can be seen as imposing new forms of control. A managerial approach to facilitating organisational goals and the direct involvement of employees furthers a unitary perspective and can mask an underlying distaste for unionism.[47]

The pluralistic perspective An alternative view suggested by *Fox* is the pluralistic perspective which views the organisation as made up of powerful and competing sub-groups with their own legitimate loyalties, objectives and leaders.[48] These competing sub-groups are almost certain to come into conflict. From the pluralist perspective, conflict in organisations is seen as inevitable and induced, in part, by the very structure of the organisation. Conflict is not necessarily a bad thing but can be an agent for evolution, and internal and external change.

Restrictive practices may be seen as a rational response from a group that regards itself as being threatened. The role of the manager would be less commanding and enforcing, and more persuading and co-ordinating. Fox suggests that the pluralistic perspective is a more realistic frame of reference. He argues the importance of viewing work situations through the different groups involved rather than attempting a wished-for unitary approach.

According to *Horn*, 'these views were widely acceptable, particularly to trade unions, who saw this as legitimising their intervention into an increasing range of managerial prerogative areas'.[49] There are, however, relative shades of unitary and pluralistic perspectives, and the two can co-exist within the same organisation.

REGULATING THE EMPLOYMENT CONTRACT

A central feature of effective employee relationships is managing through people and regulating the employment relationship.[50] Whether as individuals or members of a group, the actions and decisions of people are governed by a set of underlying rules. In the work organisation these rules are implemented within a structured hierarchy of authority and responsibility. But regulating behaviour between people at work is a complex process. Effective employment relations are founded on a combination of legal and behavioural dimensions. The legal dimension embodies observance of employment legislation, the formal contract of employment and codes of practice. The behavioural dimension embodies recognition of the individual, the social responsibilities of management and the psychological contract (discussed in Chapter 1) (*see* Figure 13.4). Social responsibilities extend beyond terms and conditions of the formal contract of employment, and give recognition to the social and human needs of people at work including greater emphasis on creating and integrating a work/life balance. The recognition of social responsibilities should form an integral part of corporate strategy and regulating the employment relationship.

Legal dimensions

The work organisation has to operate within a system of legal rules and regulations. Legal dimensions regulate the relationship between employers and employees, provide individual rights for employees and strengthen the position of trade unions. Legislation and codes of practice lay down rules that govern patterns of behaviour to ensure that 'managers act reasonably in the circumstances'. Some managers view these rules with trepidation and avoid taking necessary action to discipline employees. Others are unaware of the rules or choose to disregard them, terminating contracts without due cause.

| Figure 13.4 | Effective employment relations: combination of legal and behavioural dimensions |

Legal dimensions

The organisation operating within a system of legal rules and regulations. Observance of employment legislation, the contract of employment and codes of practice.

EFFECTIVE EMPLOYMENT RELATIONS

Behavioural dimensions

The creation of a harmonious working relationship between management and staff. Recognition of the individual, social responsibilities of management and the psychological contract.

Either strategy is likely to result in behavioural problems among employees who will perceive avoidance or over-reaction as dysfunctional. A proper knowledge, understanding and respect of the law, coupled with appropriate managerial action, can turn a potentially difficult situation into an opportunity to motivate staff and improve organisational effectiveness.

Although it is not the purpose of this book to consider detailed aspects of employment law, it is important to recognise the existence of the legal framework within which organisations function and which affects employee relations.

Traditionally, employee relations in Britain have been characterised by the concept of free collective bargaining between employees and employers. However, in recent years this philosophy has been underpinned by increasing amounts of employment law. The substance of British laws is also increasingly being influenced by the impact of EU legislation. Until the 1960s the law governing terms and conditions was based almost entirely on the concept of the contract of employment and attracted little statutory intervention. However, this area of law has been significantly extended, introducing new statutory rights for both those in employment and those seeking employment. Employees can seek redress through a tribunal system, and have rights concerning a range of issues from relatively minor matters such as time off for public duties, to the more important employment protection rights such as the right not to be unfairly dismissed.

Behavioural dimensions

While the observance of legal rules and regulations is clearly a necessary part of effective employment relations, this does not, by itself, make for a harmonious environment at work. Legal dimensions help to regulate the working relationships of people within the organisation. But rules and regulations do not by themselves ensure that disputes will be settled amicably. Human behaviour cannot be made to conform to prescribed rules and regulations just because such rules and regulations exist.

Harmonious employee relations can be effective only if sustained within a generally good relationship between management and staff, with a willing commitment from both sides.[51] Effective managers need to take note of both legal and behavioural perspectives, and to adopt a balanced view when making decisions that affect the employment relationship. Notwithstanding any legal obligations, the employer–employee relationship demands that attention be given to those factors that influence the behaviour of people at work, the psychological contract and the style of managerial behaviour. For example, there is a general duty placed on an employer to disclose, on request, to authorised representatives of independent trade unions information for the purposes of collective bargaining and which it would be good employee relations practice to disclose. However, many organisations now consider the broader behavioural considerations and choose as a matter of policy to report fully, and in non-technical terms, wider details of their financial results and performance direct to all employees.

Critical reflection

Many people would argue the problem with employee relations is that too great an emphasis is placed on attempting to regulate the nature of jobs and work through increased legal requirements rather than with concern for human behaviour, the people–organisation relationship and the effective management of people. To what extent do you support this point of view?

Responsibility for employee relations

Refresh your understanding

Activity 13D
www.pearsoned.co.uk/
mullins

It is sometimes suggested that in many organisations the responsibility for employee relations still lies with the line managers, who are often sceptical or even hostile towards HR ideas and techniques and who frequently reject the concept of an employee relations policy because it hampers their work and limits their flexibility. As with other aspects of the HRM function it is important that line managers are involved, at least to some extent, with employee relationships. But there must be good communications and close consultation with the HR department. There must be teamwork and a concerted organisational approach to the management of employee relations. This is made easier when top management take an active part in fostering goodwill and co-operation between departments and with official union representatives. Top management should agree clear terms of reference for both the HR manager and line managers within the framework of sound HRM policies.[52]

INTERNATIONAL DIMENSIONS OF HRM

The field of international human resource management comprises two distinct areas: (i) the management of employees in global businesses operating across national boundaries, and (ii) the comparison of human resource management activities and policies in different societies. *Budhwar* identifies four approaches to international staffing which may help to explain how businesses operating across national borders choose to co-ordinate their human resource management policies:[53]

1 **Ethnocentric approach.** Here managerial positions are normally filled by staff from the 'parent' country. It is likely that within this approach the home country's approach will be dominant with subsidiaries operating standardised HRM practices.
2 **Polycentric approach.** Under this heading local managers from the host country are more usually appointed. The approach may be useful when a global strategy is to be implemented on a regional basis. It can also be seen when a subsidiary develops local HRM practices.
3 **Geocentric approach.** In this approach managers are recruited from within the company or from outside with no importance attached to their nationality. It could be argued that such managers may possess greater cultural flexibility.
4 **Regiocentric approach.** Recruitment of managers is undertaken on a regional basis. This is more likely when subsidiaries operate as part of a regional strategy and HRM practices are, in turn, formulated regionally.

Increasingly, global corporations are both willing and able to adopt a flexible approach to staffing. For example, there are increasing examples of the shift of call centre operations from the UK and USA to new locations, in particular the Indian subcontinent, and press reports suggest that the transfer of jobs may prove to be a worldwide trend on a scale greater than previously envisaged. In indicating the powerful pressures to reconsider global employment patterns, the *Daily Telegraph* article cites the chairman of a British bank who summarises his perspective as follows: 'We have to relocate these functions to India. Not only are the running costs a fraction of what they would be here, but also the quality of the workforce is significantly better. Taking advantage of that is a no-brainer.'[54]

Comparison of HRM in different societies

Human resource management practices, it is suggested, are influenced by the culture of the society in which they take place, being affected by both specific culturally derived attitudes and institutional factors. To take the example of recruitment and selection, *Koen* proposes that: 'The methodology of recruitment and selection has never been uniform across the

world. Moreover, whether a specific personnel selection practice should be adopted universally remains an unresolved issue. However, given the crucial role played by this personnel function, especially in managing a multinational workforce, understanding the similarities and dissimilarities of existing practices in different nations ought to be the first step taken by human resource managers and researchers.'[55]

In examining recruitment and selection methods in the USA, *Francesco and Gold* note that 'when making a hiring decision, people in an achievement-oriented country consider skills, knowledge and talent'.[56] This individual orientation will influence the selection methods typically chosen in such a society. Recruitment and selection in the United States has also been significantly affected by the relatively extensive laws prohibiting discrimination in employment, which can, in turn, be seen as an expression of a culture which places particular value on individual characteristics. It is also possible to view the largely American-derived battery of psychometric measures within this overall cultural framework.

It may also be that culturally based perceptions take effect in recruitment and selection in individual cultures. An executive from the Swedish company IKEA, cited in *Schneider and Barsoux*, provides one example of a culturally specific preference in this regard in the following quote. 'The most important quality for an Ikean is *odmjukhet* – a Swedish word that implies humility, modesty and respect for one's fellow man. It may be hard to translate, but we know it when we see it.'[57]

Grahl and Teague attempt to explain differences in the area of human resource management between countries in Europe with reference to a model contrasting competitive and constructive flexibility along a continuum.[58]

Competitive flexibility as a concept states that national competitiveness may best be achieved by minimising restrictions on managerial prerogative – that is, implying a minimal level of legislation and the removal of barriers to workforce flexibility. This approach may be compared to some of the features of HRM as it evolved in the United States. In Europe, Grahl and Teague suggest that the UK is the country that is located furthest at the competitive end of their model.

Constructive flexibility in contrast, while acknowledging the need for greater flexibility in all its dimensions – numerical, temporal and functional – aims to move towards this desired aim without exacerbating divisions within society. Here work employees may enjoy extensive legal rights and protection, and social costs to employers may be greater than in countries more closely associated with competitive flexibility. Constructive flexibility also presumes a social partnership model of co-operation within the enterprise whereby managers are required to consult with employee representatives before making decisions or conceivably to act jointly in conjunction with these representatives. Grahl and Teague find Germany and Sweden to be the two European countries most closely corresponding to constructive flexibility.

INDUSTRIAL DEMOCRACY IN EUROPEAN COUNTRIES

One example of how different cultural values and institutional arrangements combine to form distinctive philosophies and practices in the field of human resource management is evident in the concept of statutory industrial democracy prevalent in many European countries. This relates to the degree of consultation – or even joint decision-making – prescribed by both national or pan-European law within individual workplaces. One illustration of how the concept can affect the management of people in practice is provided by the system operating in Germany.[59]

The German system

The German system of industrial democracy is the most comprehensive and has tended to be used by commentators as a model of its kind. The system comprises both the works council (*Betriebsrat*) and representation on boards of directors, the supervisory board (*Aufsichtsrat*) and the executive board (*Vorstand*).[60]

The works council Works councils exist in organisations covering all sectors of the economy including both the private and public sector. Works council representatives are elected by fellow workers. They do not, however, stand on behalf of trade unions, and in elections stress their individual qualities and experiences. The works council has three rights:

- **the right of information** – the works council has the right to be given information concerning the performance and future prospects of the organisation;
- **the right of consultation** – owners and managers must consult the works council over a range of strategic matters including investment, and the acquisition of new premises and the closure of existing units; and
- **the right of co-determination** – the works council has the power to formulate certain policies jointly with managers.

The third and most extensive power relates essentially to issues concerning the management of personnel including the working day, holiday arrangements, shift working, promotion, dismissal, and welfare and social facilities. As an example, the works council has the right to participate in the selection of new members of staff and can veto appointments. This power of veto is constrained, however, since it can operate only in the light of criteria agreed in advance. Nevertheless, the works council does take an active part in personnel management in German organisations.

Representation on boards of directors The supervisory board may include employee representatives. In certain industries such as coal, iron and steel, workers make up 50 per cent of the membership of the board. In other sectors, one-third membership is common. The supervisory board has the power to appoint members of the executive board and can veto its decisions.

The composition of the executive board is most interesting in German organisations since it includes a labour director (*Arbeitsdirektor*). The labour director can be appointed only by a two-thirds majority of the worker representatives on the supervisory board. *French* shows how this director may be a worker representative, but equally may be a career personnel manager.[61] *Lawrence* suggests that increasingly personnel managers are labour directors and are thus represented on both boards of directors.[62]

Negotiation and discussion It can be seen that in Germany, personnel managers are constrained by law from acting unilaterally, and are required to work jointly with the workforce representatives. Lawrence concludes that the personnel function in Germany is marked by a high degree of both legalism and formalism with laws, documents and written agreements being more salient than in Britain. The same author gives us a sense of the flavour of personnel management in that country as follows:

> The works council is an important reference point for the German personnel manager and much of his time is spent in negotiation or discussion with the council.[63]

EFFECTIVENESS OF THE HRM FUNCTION

The ultimate measure of the effectiveness of the HRM function is the contribution it makes to meeting the objectives of the business and to improved organisational performance. But achievement in the area of HRM is difficult to measure and it is not easy to establish satis-

factory methods of assessment. There is also the more general problem of assessing managerial work where the end-product results from the efforts of other people. Cost is obviously a consideration but should not be viewed in isolation. Not every activity in the organisation can be identified clearly as making a direct contribution to profitability. A balance should be maintained between the more easily identified financial costs of the HRM function and the less readily apparent but very important long-term benefits which also make a positive contribution to the effectiveness of the organisation.

The contributions from an effective HRM function are not always readily apparent nor are they necessarily easy to identify. Account should be taken of intangible benefits such as the morale and job satisfaction of staff as well as their attitudes, behaviour and performance. Over a period of time, however, some quantified measures may serve to provide management with an indication of effectiveness. Possible examples include staffing costs, turnover and stability indexes; promotions and staff development; errors in work; levels of absenteeism and sickness, timekeeping, accidents at work; the number of discipline or grievance hearings, dismissals, labour disputes, employment tribunal cases; complaints from suppliers or customers.

According to *Lorange*, we will see many changes in the behavioural side of human resource processes. Instead of the typical hierarchical structure, executives will now largely be allowed to organise themselves in teams with a focus on realigning people to work together to find opportunities and learn how to exploit them. The strategic human resource process will therefore be drawn to support a mostly self-organised, virtual team process, attempting to guide people to find their productive places in such teams.[64]

Good HR policies and employment relations

According to *Slater*: 'Recognition that employees form the lifeblood of a company has highlighted the strategic role that the human resources department should now play.' For the first time HR professionals have the opportunity to add value to a business. There is a shift in emphasis in business and the bottom line is no longer all-important. Greater attention is placed on issues such as how well a company executes its business plan, employee morale, corporate culture and organisational structure. Although the customer is still king, companies realise that it is their employees who deliver the performance of value to the customer.

> Nowhere has this change impacted more greatly than in human resources. The need to focus more on internal 'customers' has put pressure on companies to release HR staff from a largely administrative role to a more strategic one that addresses increased productivity, employee commitment and career advancement. Only by addressing these issues will a company truly be able to leverage employee power ... Freed from many routine tasks, the HR department will be able to devote more time to adding value to the business.[65]

However the HRM function is organised or evaluated, proper attention to the establishment of good HR policies and employment relations will help to improve the efficiency of the workforce and standards of service to customers. Full use should be made of specialist HR staff, the involvement of line managers and modern methods and processes.

Browning lists ten ways to make HR effective:

1　Be the catalyst for making things happen.
2　Avoid being the corporate soft touch.
3　Understand the whole business.
4　Keep people-management systems simple.
5　Remember line managers manage people, not HR.

6 Work with, not above, line managers.
7 Be super-efficient in the transactional stuff.
8 Be leaders in the transformational stuff.
9 Help the business to manage change.
10 Accept that good 'people ideas' exist outside HR.[66]

Refresh your understanding

Activity 13E

www.pearsoned.co.uk/mullins

Critical reflection

It is the line or departmental managers who manage their own staff and are responsible for human resources and good employee relations. Do you agree? The human resource department provides only a support and administrative function to other managers and the title of 'human resource manager' is arguably a complete misnomer. What alternative title would you suggest?

MANAGEMENT IN THE NEWS

Fattism

Fattism is the last bastion of employee discrimination

Daniel Thomas

Personnel Today's exclusive survey of more than 2,000 HR professionals on obesity reveals some eye-opening statistics about the level of discrimination facing overweight employees in UK workplaces.

The issue of obesity has been in the headlines more than ever this year, whether it be Turkey Twizzlers in school meals, the amount of salt in breakfast cereals, or the growing waistline of the average Brit. While it has always been considered a matter for the individual, statistics showing that obese people cost the economy £2bn a year highlight the role employers have to play in improving staff health to boost productivity.

An exclusive *Personnel Today* survey of more than 2,000 UK-based HR professionals reveals that almost half believe that obesity negatively affects employee output, with more than a quarter believing that obesity is becoming a problem in their industry. Yet three-quarters of the respondents – from organisations of all sizes – admit their organisation is doing nothing actively to tackle staff obesity. Almost four in ten HR professionals say their organisation does not offer a medical check for employees, even at the initial stage of employment. When asked why their organisation was not tackling obesity, one respondent said:

Our organisation tackles most issues that restrict an individual's ability to do their job, but obesity seems to have a stigma that means it is not mentioned.

This seems to be the experience of most employers, with 69 per cent of respondents agreeing that 'obesity is a topic that is not discussed enough in our organisation'.

This taboo appears to be hiding, or perhaps feeding, a level of ingrained discrimination and resentment against obese workers. When asked which of two identically qualified applicants, but one of 'normal weight' and the other obese, would be hired, an astonishing 93 per cent would choose the former, purely on the basis of their weight.

Almost a third of the HR professionals consider obesity is a valid medical reason for not employing a person, while 11 per cent think that firms can fairly dismiss people just because they are obese. This discrimination is not limited to recruitment. Fifteen per cent of respondents admit their organisation would be less likely to promote an obese employee, and 12 per cent suggest they are not suitable for client-facing roles. This is where employers could get into legal hot water. Although there is no specific protection against so-called 'fattism' as there is for other forms of workplace discrimination, employers cannot simply dismiss people because of their size. Instead, they must prove their weight has had a negative impact on the business. And if someone becomes obese as a result of depression, diabetes or

arthritis, they could be protected under the Disability Discrimination Act.

With the government preparing a campaign to raise awareness of the steps both individuals and employers can take to prevent obesity, HR will come under increasing pressure to form policies for obese employees. Deliberately ignoring the larger members of society will no longer be an option.

Facts and figures

- 12 per cent suggest that obese workers are not suitable for client-facing roles.
- 93 per cent would employ the 'normal weight' person and only 7 per cent would employ the obese one.
- 30 per cent agree that 'obesity is a valid medical reason for not employing a person'.
- 47 per cent think obesity negatively affects employee output.

- 11 per cent think employers can fairly dismiss people just because they are obese.

Source: Thomas, D., 'Fattism is the last bastion of employee discrimination', *Personnel Today*, 25 October 2006. Copyright © 2006 Reed Business Information Limited. Reproduced with permission from Reed Business Information.

Discussion questions

1 The survey suggests that over 90 per cent of human resource management professionals would choose a 'normal weight' over an 'obese' candidate with the same qualifications. Discuss the extent to which this preference is justifiable. Should there be legislation to prevent 'fattism'?

2 Should employers adopt a policy to encourage or even require employees to maintain a healthy weight? What role could be played by a human resource or personnel manager in support of such a policy?

SYNOPSIS

- An essential part of the process of management is that proper attention be given to the efficient use of resources, in particular human resources. In recent years there has been increasing attention to a strategic approach to 'human resource management' (HRM) and also to the idea of 'human capital'. However, it is important to remember that it is people who are the most important asset of any organisation. Effective HRM and the successful implementation of activities are essential ingredients of improved organisation improvement.

- Success in the field of human relationships stems from good HRM policies and practices which should be based on underlying philosophies of managerial behaviour and employee relations. The range and scope of HRM activities are wide, and a shared responsibility among top management, line managers and supervisors, and the HR manager. As an element function, HRM is part of the generality of management and part of the responsibility of all managers and supervisors. The HRM function can be seen as operating at two levels, the organisational level and the departmental or unit level.

- One major area of HRM work of particular relevance to the effective management and use of people is training and development. Training is a key element of improved performance and offers a number of potential benefits for both the individual and the organisation. Too often, however, training is seen as a low-priority activity. In order to secure the full benefits of training there must be a planned and systematic approach to the effective management of training, and a continuous commitment to training standards. Investors in People provides a national framework for training and development of people to achieve business goals.

- One way to review the performance and potential of staff is through a formal performance management system. An effective system offers a number of potential benefits to both individuals and the organisation but there are a number of important questions to be addressed. Consideration must be given to the design and implementation of the system, methods of appraisals and potential problem areas. It is particularly important that a formal system does not detract from the manager's responsibility for reviewing performance on a day-to-day basis.

- Sound HRM policies help to foster good employment relations. It is necessary to take account of the institutions and parties involved, and their ideologies and motives. There are two major and contrasting perspectives of work organisations, and the explanation and outcomes of conflict – the unitary and the

pluralistic perspectives. These contrasting views influence the nature of employee relationships and the management of human resources. Good managerial strategies are important for effective employment relations that are founded on a combination of legal and behavioural dimensions.

● It is important that line managers are involved, at least to some extent, with the responsibility for employment relations. HRM practices are influenced by the culture of the society in which they take place. Increasingly the European Union is seeking to harmonise employment practices among member states. The ultimate measure of effectiveness of the HRM function is the contribution to good human relationship at work and improved organisational performance, but this is not always readily apparent or easy to identify.

Refresh your understanding, assess your progress and begin your research with online resources at **www.pearsoned.co.uk/mullins**

REVIEW AND DISCUSSION QUESTIONS

1 Discuss fully the range and scope of HRM activities within your organisation. Critically analyse the extent to which you believe that 'human resource management' differs from 'personnel management'.

2 'Every director an HR director, every line manager a HR manager.' In the light of this statement, discuss what you see as the role and functions of the human resource department in a large business organisation.

3 How would you justify to a group of sceptical line managers a high level of financial provision for training? Explain the steps you would take in order to ensure the effective management of training.

4 What are the potential benefits for both the individual and the organisation from a formal system of performance management?

5 Critically evaluate different methods of performance management and discuss fully the potential problem areas.

6 Explain those factors that are likely to influence the nature and contents of an employment relations policy, and give specific examples from your own organisation. What is meant by the legal and behavioural perspectives of employee relations?

7 Discuss critically the extent to which line managers should be involved with the responsibility for employment relations. What arrangements exist in your organisation?

8 Comment critically on the accountability and measurement of the functioning of the HR department.

ASSIGNMENT

Almost 50 years ago, Peter Drucker first raised the question:'Is personnel management bankrupt'? And answered: 'No, it is not bankrupt. Its liabilities do not exceed its assets. But it is certainly insolvent, certainly unable to honour, with the ready cash of performance, the promises of managing worker and work it so liberally makes.'[67]

In view of the work of more recent writers, the changing nature of work organisations and developments in human resource management, how would *you* attempt to answer this question today? Set your response out as fully as possible and give supporting reasons.

PERSONAL AWARENESS AND SKILLS EXERCISE

Objectives

Completing this exercise should help you to enhance the following skills:

● Review options in dealing with difficult work situations.

● Play the role of manager, employee or observer.

● Appreciate sensitivities when dealing with issues related to poor performance.

Exercise

Working in a team of three people, you are required to participate in the following role-play exercise.

Role play A: Manager/Kirsty

You are a line manager and Steve is an administrator who reports to you. The other members of the team, while liking him personally, complain about his disorganisation and the image he gives the department.

His last performance review was six months ago and he was rated as just meeting his performance objectives. Since then Steve's performance has slipped steadily.

● 80 per cent of work has to be returned for correction, indicating that it has not been proofread or spell-checked.

● Computer files and cupboards are a mess. Other administrators fear standing in for him because of his poor organisation.

● He does not prioritise workload or respond well to urgent requests.

● He has left a confidential document on his desk overnight twice in the last month.

● His work area is untidy, with papers and half-empty coffee beakers all over the desk.

You have done your research and have determined that his performance is entirely unsatisfactory. You have asked to see Steve formally in your office so that you can make it clear to him that if his performance does not improve in all areas, his continued employment with the organisation is in jeopardy.

Decide how you will approach this difficult situation.

→

Personal awareness and skills exercise – continued

Role play B: Employee/Steve

You are an administrator with eight years' experience. Your manager has asked to see you and you are pretty sure that it's about your performance. She had a chat with you a while ago and said your work was not up to scratch. You know this is true but you are a friendly person and most people get on well with you. You usually manage to come up with the goods in the end. If only some of the people you work for would plan ahead a bit, then you wouldn't have to rush things so much and therefore would make fewer mistakes. Your manager has complained about the way you file things, but you usually find things when they are needed. You enjoy your work and certainly need the money. You are pretty confident you will be able to get out of any kind of scrape with your manager, as you can be quite persuasive when you choose to be.

Role play C: Observer

The outcome here needs to be that Steve is absolutely clear that if his performance doesn't improve dramatically then the usual, formal disciplinary procedure will be instigated.

Watch out for the following from the manager:

- clear, assertive but unemotional communication to Steve throughout the meeting;
- keeping clear of attacking Steve as a person;
- not allowing Steve to take over and blame others;
- checking that Steve is clear on the implications of not improving;
- pointing out clearly where Steve is going wrong and what improvements are expected;
- giving Steve a deadline and review date.

Discussion

- What have you learned from this exercise about the nature and management of performance review?
- What do you think is the best way to manage poor performance? What options are available?
- What other conclusions do you draw from this exercise?

APPENDIX: THE INVESTORS IN PEOPLE STANDARD

Principles	Indicators	Evidence requirements
Developing strategies to improve the performance of the organisation An investor in people develops effective strategies to improve the performance of the organisation through its people.	**1 A strategy for improving the performance of the organisation is clearly defined and understood.**	1 Top managers make sure the organisation has a clear purpose and vision supported by a strategy for improving its performance. 2 Top managers make sure the organisation has a business plan with measurable performance objectives. 3 Top managers make sure there are constructive relationships with representative groups (where they exist) and the groups are consulted when developing the organisation's business plan. 4 Managers can descibe how they involve people when developing the organisation's business plan and when agreeing team and individual objectives. 5 People who are members of representative groups can confirm that top managers make sure there are constructive relationships with the groups and they are consulted when developing the organisation's business plan. 6 People can explain the objectives of their team and the organisation at a level that is appropriate to their role, and can describe how they are expected to contribute to developing and achieving them.
	2 Learning and development is planned to achieve the organisation's objectives.	1 Top managers can explain the organisation's learning and development needs, the plans and the resources in place to meet them, how these link to achieving specific objectives and how the impact will be evaluated. 2 Managers can explain team learning and devleopment needs, the activities planned to meet them, how these link to achieving specific team objectives and how the impact will be evaluated. 3 People can describe how they are involved in identifying their learning and development needs and the activities planned to meet them. 4 People can explain what their learning and development activities should achieve for them, their team and the organisation.
	3 Strategies for managing people are designed to promote equality of opportunity in the development of the organisation's people.*	1 Top managers can describe strategies they have in place to create an environment where everyone is encouraged to contribute ideas to improve their own and other people's performance. 2 Top managers recognise the different needs of people and can describe strategies they have in place to make sure everyone has appropriate and fair access to the support they need and there is equality of opportunity for people to learn and develop which will improve their performance. 3 Managers recognise the different needs of people and can describe how they make sure everyone has appropriate and fair access to the support they need and there is equality of opportunity for people to learn and develop which will improve their performance. 4 People believe managers are genuinely committed to making sure everyone has appropriate and fair access to the support they need and there is equality of opportunity for them to learn and develop which will improve their performance. 5 People can give examples of how they have been encouraged to contribute ideas to improve their own and other people's performance.
	4 The capabilities managers need to lead, manage and develop people effectively are clearly defined and understood.	1 Top managers can describe the knowledge, skills and behaviours managers need to lead, manage and develop people effectively, and the plans they have in place to make sure managers have these capabilities. 2 Managers can describe the knowledge, skills and behaviours they need to lead, manage and develop people effectively. 3 People can describe what their manager should be doing to lead, manage and develop them effectively.

*Plain English Campaign's Crystal Mark does not apply to Indicator 3.

20 Trompenaars, F. and Woolliams, P. ' When Two Worlds Collide', in Crainer, S. and Dearlove, D. (eds) *Financial Times Handbook of Management*, Second edition, Financial Times Prentice Hall (2001), pp. 745 and 750.

21 See, For example: Torrington, D., Hall, L. and Taylor S. *Human Resource Management*, Sixth edition, Financial Times Prentice Hall (2005).

22 Wolfson, B. (Sir), 'Train, retain and motivate staff', *Management Today*, March 1998, p. 5.

23 Drucker, P. F. *People and Performance*, Heinemann (1977).

24 Adair, J. 'Developing tomorrow's leaders', in CBI, *The Path to Leadership: developing a sustainable model within organisations*, Caspian Publishing, September 2005, p. 35.

25 'Training for Advantage', *Management Today*, May 1997, p. 89.

26 *Effective Organisations: the People Factor*, Advisory Booklet, ACAS, November 2001, p. 20.

27 Tate, W. 'Training – The Stuff of Legends', *Manager, The British Journal of Administrative Management*, September/ October 1996, pp. 22–3.

28 Stern, S. 'Firm Choice', *Management Today*, October 2002, p. 6.

29 Douglas, M. 'Why Soft Skills are an Essential Part of the Hard World of Business', *Manager, The British Journal of Administrative Management*, Issue 34, New Year 2003, p. 34.

30 Sweeten, G. 'E-learning: How to Move Forward', *Manager, The British Journal of Administrative Management*, Issue 36, Summer 2003, p. 25.

31 Burns, T. 'E-learning: The Future of Quality Training', *Quality Progress*, vol. 38, no. 2, February 2005, pp. 50–6.

32 *Effective Organisations: the People Factor*, Advisory Booklet, ACAS, November 2001, p. 21.

33 See, for example: *Employee Appraisal*, Advisory Booklet, ACAS, February 2003.

34 Stein, N. 'Remember, The Staff is the Bread of Life', *Management Today*, July 1991, pp. 58–60.

35 Crainer, S. *Key Management Ideas: Thinkers that Changed the Management World*, Third edition, Financial Times Prentice Hall (1998), pp. 134–7.

36 Pfau, B., Kay. I., Nowack, K. M. and Ghorpade, J. 'Does 360-degree Feedback Negatively Affect Company Performance?', *HR Magazine*, vol. 47, no. 6, June 2002, pp. 54–9.

37 Butcher, D. 'It Takes Two To Review', *Management Today*, November 2002, p. 57.

38 Kusin, G. 'A 360-Degree Spin', *Hemisphere Magazine*, United Airlines, October 2005, pp. 74–7.

39 Tackey, D. 'Eliminating Bias in Performance Management', *Manager, The British Journal of Administrative Management*, September/October 2001, pp. 12–13.

40 Kermally, S. 'Appraising Employee Performance', *Professional Manager*, July 2002, p. 19.

41 Butcher, D. 'It Takes Two To Review', *Management Today*, November 2002, p. 55.

42 Law, S. 'Appraisals fail to measure up', *Professional Manager*, vol. 13, no. 3, May 2004, pp. 24–6.

43 Shellabear, S. 'Performance Management: an art and a science?, *Training Journal*, January 2005, pp. 48–51.

44 ACAS, 'Employment Relations Matters', Issue 1, Autumn 2004, p. 2.

45 See, for example: 'Social Agenda', *European Commission Employment and Social Affairs*, Issue 6, July 2003, pp. 5–6.

46 Taylor, R. 'The Future of Employment Relations', Economic & Social Research Council, September 2001, pp. 7–8.

47 Horwitz, F. M. 'HRM: An Ideological Perspective', *International Journal of Manpower*, vol. 12, no. 6, 1991, pp. 4–9.

48 Fox, A. *Industrial Society and Industrial Relations*, HMSO (1966).

49 Horn, C. A. 'Management Style', *Administrator*, vol. 6, no. 4, April 1986, p. 14.

50 Mullins, L. J. and Peacock, A. 'Managing Through People: Regulating the Employment Relationship', *Administrator*, December 1991, pp. 32–3.

51 Mullins, L. J. and Peacock, A. 'Effective Employee Relations: Behavioural Dimensions', *Administrator*, April 1992, pp. 12–13.

52 For a fuller discussion on the part played by line managers and personnel specialists in the management of human resources, see, for example: Storey, J. *Developments in the Management of Human Resources*, Blackwell (1992).

53 Budhwar, P. S. Chapter 11, 'International Human Resource Management', in Tayeb, M. *International Management Theories and Practices*, Financial Times Prentice Hall (2003).

54 Ringshaw, G. 'Call Centres Take the Passage to India', *Daily Telegraph*, 25 May 2003.

55 Koen, K. *Comparative International Management*, McGraw-Hill (2005), p. 217.

56 Francesco, A. M. and Gold, B. A. *International Organizational Behavior: text, readings, cases and skills*, Second edition, Prentice Hall (2005), p. 149.

57 Schneider, S. C. and Barsoux, J. *Managing Across Cultures*, Second edition, Financial Times Prentice Hall (2003), pp. 155–3.

58 Grahl, J. and Teague, P. 'Industrial Relations Trajectories and European Human Resource Management', in Brewster, C. and Tyson, S. (eds), *International Comparisons in Human Resource Management*, Pitman Publishing (1991), pp. 67–91.

59 French, R. 'Employee Relations in the New Europe', *Administrator*, November 1992, pp. 25–6.

60 French, R. 'Employee Relations: The German Experience', *Administrator*, January 1993, pp. 29–30.

61 French, R. 'The Development and Structuring of Personnel Departments in Britain and West Germany', Unpublished PhD Thesis, Nottingham Polytechnic, 1985.

62 Lawrence, P. 'The Personnel Function: An Anglo-German Comparison', in Brewster, C. and Tyson, S. (eds) *International Comparisons in Human Resource Management*, Pitman (1991), pp. 131–44.

63 Ibid., p. 134.

64 Lorange, P. 'Ultra-Rapid Management Processes', in Chowdhury, S. *Management 21C*, Financial Times Prentice Hall (2000), pp. 153–4.

65 Slater, L. 'Realising Your Assets', *Digital Britain: Management Strategies for the 21st Century*, Issue 6, p. 13, Supplement to *Management Today*, June 2001.

66 Browning, G. 'Ten Ways to Measure HR', *Management Today*, July 2002, p. 18.

67 Drucker, P. F. *The Practice of Management*, Heinemann Professional (1955), pp. 267–82.

68 Clake, R. and Robinson, V. 2005 'Stay Tuned', *People Management*, vol. 11, no. 10 May 2005 pp. 30–4.

69 CIPD 2006 *The Guide to HR Outsourcing* issued in *People Management*, February 2006.

70 Accenture website; *Human Resources Outsourcing* www.accenture.com/Globa/Services/Client_Successes/By_Subject/Human_Resources_Mgmt/TheResult.htm [accessed 10 August 2006].

71 Broad, M. 2002 'BT's costs climb in outsourcing deal' *Personnel Today* 24 August 2002 available from www.personneltoday.com [accessed 10 August 2006].

72 Denis Reay, BT Wholesale's HR director quoted by Accenture; *BT: Human Resources Outsourcing 2001–2005* www.accenture.com/Globa/Services/Client_Successes/By_Subject/Human_Resources_Mgmt/BtOutsourcing.htm [accessed 10 August 2006].

73 CIPD 2006 *The Guide to HR Outsourcing* issued in *People Management*, February 2006.

74 Clake, R. and Robinson, V. 2005 'Stay Tuned', *People Management*, vol. 11, no. 10 May 2005, pp. 30–4.

75 CIPD 2005 *Outsourcing Human Resources; a framework for decisions* available from CIPD or in pdf format from www.cipd.co.uk.

76 Pickard, J. 2006 'Bridge the Divide', in CIPD *The Guide to HR outsourcing.*

PART 4 CASE STUDY
Jamie Oliver: the naked manager?

It would seem that the British are media food junkies. The last decade has seen an apparently unstoppable growth in the number and type of television shows (generally with accompanying recipe books) by and about celebrity chefs. Scarcely any weekend newspaper is complete without its food and cookery section, and almost every possible type of cuisine and food-related angle is covered from domestic goddess to obsessive restaurateur, from food technologist to wilderness survivalist. Websites abound, and there are heated discussions about the quality and ethical provenance of our food. And yet, despite this obsession with reading about it, the British generally don't seem to like cooking and show very limited concern about the quality of what they, and perhaps more importantly their children, actually eat.[1] The catering industry remains one dominated by low pay, stressful working conditions and very limited prestige.

Jamie Oliver, (christened the 'Naked Chef' in an early series), is a British celebrity chef, and one who has spent his whole career in kitchens, albeit occasionally kitchens full of camera crew. In 2005 he became a campaigner for the provision of better quality food in British schools after a startling series on Channel 4, 'Jamie's School Dinners'.[2] But his approach to the recruitment, training and motivation of 15 young people to work in his new London restaurant gives a lively example of effective, if sometimes unconventional, managerial behaviour.

Jamie's Kitchen; the project

Oliver himself went into the catering business at 16 after leaving school with no qualifications. His 2002 attempt to inspire some similarly unqualified young people to launch themselves into a career as chefs was followed by a Channel 4 documentary team.[3] The scheme itself was ambitious and required Oliver to fulfil several roles. First, the entrepreneur, as he was investing a substantial amount of his own money in the creation of a new restaurant (to be named 'Fifteen' for the 15 trainees who would work there). Second, he was the professional chef at the heart of the enterprise and his name, reputation and style of cooking would provide the basis of the business. And finally, he became a very public manager of people. The series shows his involvement in the recruitment and selection of the trainees, and his contributions to the design of the overall training

In the heat of the kitchen, managerial skills are seen in the raw. Jamie Oliver shows how good management can encourage personal achievement as well as business success.

Source: Kim Myung Jung Kim

programme which was in part sponsored by the UK government under the New Deal initiative, but also heavily reliant on Oliver's contacts in the industry to obtain access to work experience placements in some of London's top restaurants. It also shows him monitoring the trainees' development and follows his attempts to inspire and motivate them to achieve standards of performance which would match his own professional reputation and make the business successful. In other words, the series records a microcosm of management in a highly competitive and pressured business context.

Jamie's management style

The Oliver image is that of a tousled, cheeky but hugely enthusiastic cockney lad-made-good, and at a boyish 28 when the series was shot, not perhaps the stereotypical manager. The events of the series, however, show him very clearly in a managerial role, and some of the incidents illustrate significant managerial skill. Some of his trainees are what would generally be classed as 'difficult' staff; they are unskilled, at times some of them are seriously demotivated and disruptive, and none of them has had successful experience of holding down a permanent job. What are the key components of Oliver's managerial approach to the fifteen trainees?

Vision

There is no doubt that Oliver has a very clear vision of what the business itself should be. His particular style of cooking is based around fresh ingredients, and he has an

almost evangelical enthusiasm for the authenticity of produce and its 'traceability' (he emphasises the importance of knowing exactly where things come from, and building long-term relationships with growers and suppliers who share his values). He takes the trainees, many of whom have never really thought about the source of raw ingredients, on field visits to suppliers, farms and markets in order to communicate this vision. He has an equally clear goal, and one which is much harder to reach, of helping unemployed and unskilled people to launch themselves into a career as a chef. This is the people side of the vision:

> *It's about training unemployed people to a really professional level. I want them to be employable.*[4]

The early episodes of the series show the recruitment of the initial 15 potential trainees. A high-profile, media-friendly project such as this attracted large numbers of applicants, but the selection process could not be based on more usual criteria such as knowledge, skills or experience since the whole purpose of the project was to offer opportunities for training to young people without these things. Instead, the selectors had to gauge potential and trainability, so a series of tests was constructed as a form of assessment centre, each stage taking place within a few days.

At an open day, all applicants were asked to talk about food on camera; the purpose was to identify what Oliver considered an essential quality, enthusiasm or passion about food. The initial shortlist was largely based on these recordings. The next stage was an elimination day when the 60 chosen candidates were put through a 'taste test'. Oliver and three fellow chefs prepared two items for the candidates to taste; a butternut squash ravioli, and a tempura fried oyster. He deliberately chose items which he believed the candidates would not have tasted before, then challenged them to describe what they were eating in terms of textures and flavours. This was designed to find out how well candidates could use important sensory information. Very few were able to go beyond 'like' or 'don't like' and do what he asked, even when prompted. Students were then discussed and the four selectors finally agreed on 30 who would be put forward for a second test. This was a more detailed attempt to assess their ability to observe the method of preparing a simple dish of fried salmon and mixed vegetables, and then reproduce it in the kitchen. Having demonstrated and explained all the elements of the process, Oliver and the assessors were concerned to see how observant the candidates were, and also to watch the degree to which they took control of the process and reacted to the way the food was cooking. As they worked, the observers questioned them about what they were doing, often prompting them to remember the details of the process.

The final selection was made on the basis of their approach to the work as much as on the quality of the finished dish.

Having recruited the trainees, he participated in the training process. They received instruction in basic skills at college, but as they progressed he began the attempt to shape them to the needs of his particular style and the standards which would be necessary in the restaurant. This involved classes and demonstrations followed by practical activity (for instance, in bread making) which additionally gave him the opportunity to pay detailed attention to each individual's ability to do the job.

As the trainees began to realise the amount of work and mental effort which is involved in being a chef, some of them became demotivated and failed to attend college. His approach to the weaker students was personal and supportive; he talked to them individually, paid for travel expenses to ensure they could attend college on time, and even visited some of them at home to discuss their problems. But he expected them to respond and so he also gave them some tough assignments to check their commitment. At one stage he sent them to work the night shift in a bakery for a week, a shift which he shared with them and used as a way to observe their growing skill and determination. Additionally, he was concerned to create a strong team spirit because of the importance of co-operation in a commercial kitchen environment. He took the group to spend a week camping (and of course catering for themselves as a group) on a Cumbrian farm, where they got to know about the business of livestock farming and observe first hand how to evaluate the quality of meat. This, too, would be important in the restaurant – chefs are responsible for ordering, checking and assessing the quality of the goods being delivered. They also learned how to make sausages, including a chance to experiment and design their own.

Technical knowledge and understanding

As a chef, Oliver is both trained and experienced. His technical knowledge and ability is very important to the whole enterprise, as it provides him with part of his credibility among the young trainees as well as forming the basis for much of their training. The series shows him demonstrating basic techniques such as cutting and food preparation, as well as devising menus and improvising his way around the occasional disaster experienced by the trainees. The second half of episode five shows Oliver putting the trainees together in a kitchen for the first time, with the task of cooking a set menu for 50 guests. He watches them carefully during prep (the hours prior to service), coaching individuals in the application of simple techniques they are learning at college, but which they forget under pressure – which knife to use for vegetables, how to shave parmesan, not

14

ORGANISATIONAL STRATEGY, ETHICS AND RESPONSIBILITIES

The overall function and direction of a work organisation is determined by the nature of its corporate strategy. Strategy provides goals, objectives and guidelines for the structure and operations of the organisation. Organisations play a major and increasingly important role in the lives of us all. The power and influence of a business organisation must also be tempered by decisions relating to its broader social obligations and ethical responsibilities. Corporate strategy and responsibilities are important features in the study of management and organisational behaviour.

Learning outcomes

After completing this chapter you should be able to"

- explain the nature of, and functions served by, corporate strategy;
- assess the importance of organisational ideologies and principles;
- examine the need for objectives and policy, and the importance of the profit objective;
- assess the concept of corporate social responsibilities and organisational stakeholders;
- explore approaches to the consideration of values and ethics in organisations;
- evaluate the nature and scope of business ethics and codes of conduct;
- review the importance of corporate strategy and responsibilities for the effective management of a work organisation.

> The traditional perspective is that managers in business organizations are agents who represent the interests of the owners in achieving economic success for the organization. From this perspective, ethical leadership is satisfied by maximizing economic outcomes that benefit owners while not doing anything strictly prohibited by laws and moral standards.

Gary Yukl – State University of New York
Leadership in Organizations, Sixth Edition, Pearson Prentice Hall (2006), p. 423

THE IMPORTANCE OF STRATEGY

In Chapter 3 we saw that the context of the organisational setting is central to the application of organisational behaviour and the process of management. It is the interaction of people in order to achieve objectives that forms the basis of the particular organisation. If you do not know where you are going, you cannot tell whether you have arrived! Underlying the effective management of people, therefore, is the requirement for a clear understanding of the nature of the business that the organisation is in and how best to provide customer or consumer satisfaction.[1] In order to study organisational behaviour you need to understand the nature of corporate strategy for the formal organisation as a whole.

Johnson et al. define strategy as

The direction and scope of an organisation over the long term, which achieves advantage in a changing environment through its configuration of resources and competences with the aim of fulfilling stakeholders expectations.[2]

An alternative definition, cited in Lynch, is given by *Andrews*:

Corporate strategy is the pattern of major objectives, purposes or goals and essential policies or plans for achieving those goals, stated in such a way as to define what business the company is in or is to be in and the kind of company it is or is to be.[3]

Together, these definitions highlight the importance of the overall direction of the organisation, its goals and objectives and the expectations of stakeholders. Some writers distinguish different terms and various levels of 'strategy' but corporate strategy is seen here as a generic term embracing a link among organisation structure, the process of management and applications of organisational behaviour. All organisations have some function to perform, some contribution to make to the environment of which they are part. The function of the business organisation may be seen, for example, as the creation and/or supply of goods and services. This involves bringing together the factors of production and their successful mix and direction, to provide products or services in order to create value added. Others might see the function of business organisations as, for example, providing a source of employment and of income.

Explicit statement of strategy

Objectives and policy are formalised within the framework of a **corporate strategy**, which serves to describe an organisation's sense of purpose, and plans and actions for its implementation. *Tilles* has suggested that without an explicit statement of strategy it becomes more difficult for expanding organisations to reconcile co-ordinated action with entrepreneurial effort.[4] An explicit strategy for the business organisation is necessary for the following reasons. First, there is the need for people to co-operate together in order to achieve the benefits of mutual reinforcement. Second, there are the effects of changing environmental conditions.

The absence of an explicit concept of strategy may result in members of the organisation working at cross-purposes. The intentions of top management may not be communicated clearly to those at lower levels in the hierarchy who are expected to implement these intentions. Obsolete patterns of behaviour become very difficult to modify. Change comes about from either subjective or intuitive assessment, which become increasingly unreliable as the rate of change increases. Developing a statement of strategy demands a creative effort. If strategic planning is to be successful, it requires different methods of behaviour and often fundamental change in the nature of interactions among managers.

People and strategy

Johnson et al. draw attention to the importance of the relationship between people and successful strategies. This goes beyond the traditional HR agenda and is concerned with behaviours as well as competences. The people dimension of strategy is concerned with three related issues:

- people as a resource – personal and organisational competences, and performance management;
- people and behaviour – personal behaviours and collective behaviour;
- organising people – HR function, line managers, structures and processes.

> *The ability to change behaviours may be the key ingredient for success. Creating a climate where people strive to achieve success and the motivation of individuals are crucial roles of any manager and are a central part of their involvement in their organisation's strategy.*[5]

Allen and Helms suggest that different types of reward practices may more closely complement different generic strategies and are significantly related to higher levels of perceived organisational performance.[6]

Managers' skills and competencies Increased business competitiveness and the dynamic external environment have placed important emphasis on corporate strategy and the competencies of managers. For example, *Richardson and Thompson* argue that if organisations are to be effective in strategic terms they must be able to deal with the pressures and demands of change. Managers should be strategically aware and appreciate the origins and nature of change. They should possess a comprehensive set of skills and competencies and be able to deal effectively with the forces which represent opportunities and threats to the organisation. Effective strategic management creates a productive alliance between the nature and the demands of the environment, the organisation's culture and values, and the resources that the organisation has at its disposal.[7]

> *Strategy is about first asking questions, then improving the quality of those questions through listening to the answers and acting on the new knowledge. Any effective strategy requires the successful integration of thoughts about tomorrow's new business opportunities with both past experience and the pattern of today's behaviours.*[8]

Corporate approach in the public sector

Some form of corporate strategy or planning is necessary for all organisations, particularly large organisations and including service organisations and those in the public sector. In a discussion on strategy developments, *Lynch* suggests that many of the same considerations apply to both public and private organisations. The major difference has been the lack of the objective to deliver a profit in government-owned institutions. The trend in most parts of the world is now towards privatising large public companies in the utilities and telecommunications sectors. The principal impact of privatisation on strategy will depend on the form that privatisation takes. Some companies may remain monopolies even though in the private sector. Lynch sets out the following key strategic principles for public and non-profit organisations:

- Public organisations are unlikely to have a profit objective. Strategy is therefore governed by broader public policy issues such as politics, monopoly supply, bureaucracy and the battle for resources from the government to fund the activities of the organisation.
- Strategy in non-profit organisations needs to reflect the values held by the institutions concerned. Decision-making may be slower and more complex.
- Within the constraints outlined above, the basic strategic principles can then be applied.[9]

In the public sector, the establishment of objectives and policy requires clarification of the respective roles of both elected members and permanent officials. This dual nature of management requires harmonious relationships between the two parties and emphasises the need for a corporate approach.

The concept of synergy

An important aspect of corporate strategy and the growth and development of organisations is the **concept of synergy** that was developed in management applications by *Ansoff*.[10] **Synergy** results when the whole is greater than the sum of its component parts. It can be expressed, simply, in terms of the 2 + 2 = 5 effect. An example could be an organisation integrating its retail and online operations.

Synergy is often experienced in situations of expansion or where one organisation merges with another, such as an organisation responsible for the development and production of a product merging with an organisation that markets the product. The new organisation could benefit from the combined strengths and opportunities, skills and expertise, shared fixed overheads and technology, and from the streamlining and economy of its operations. An example could be the merger of a computer firm with expertise in the design and marketing of hardware, with a firm expert in software manufacture and systems design. In the search for synergy and increased productivity, a number of organisations are creating a more streamlined structure and concentrating on its key activities with the outsourcing of non-core activities. (The ethical issues that arise from outsourcing are discussed later in this chapter.)

It is possible, however, to experience negative synergy or the 2 + 2 = 3 situation. Such a situation might arise when a merger occurs between organisations operating in different fields, with different markets or with different methods, or where the new organisation becomes unwieldy or loses its cost-effectiveness. Another example could be customer and/or union resistance to the outsourcing of call centres to other countries.

ORGANISATIONAL GOALS

In addition to performing some function, all organisations have some incentive for their existence and for their operations. The goals of an organisation are the reason for its existence. The activities of the organisation are directed to the attainment of its goals. A goal is a future expectation, some desired future state. It is something the organisation is striving to accomplish. The meaning of a goal is, however, subject to a number of interpretations. It can be used in a very broad sense to refer to the overall purpose of an organisation – for example, to produce television sets. A goal may also be used to refer to more specific desired accomplishments – for example, to produce and sell a given number of a range of television sets within a given period of time.

Organisational goals are more specific than that of the function of an organisation. The goals of an organisation will determine the nature of its inputs and outputs, the series of activities through which the outputs are achieved, and interactions with its external environment. The extent to which an organisation is successful in attaining its goals is a basis for the evaluation of organisational performance and effectiveness.

Goals are therefore an important feature of work organisations. To be effective, goals should be emphasised, stated clearly and communicated to all members of the organisation. The movement towards greater delegation and empowerment down through the hierarchy means that staff at all levels must be aware of their key tasks and actions, and exactly what is expected of them and their department/section. For example, goal-setting theory is widely recognised as a successful means of increasing work motivation and performance.[11]

> In today's environment, old-style command and control structures no longer work. People want freedom, but it must be freedom within a framework. Organisations, like individuals, need goals. Ensuring that appropriate goals are set is every manager's responsibility. Although currently it is popular to encourage commitment by letting the organisation set its own goals, this approach frequently yields only modest results. More challenging goals, created top-down, can have far more dramatic effects on business performance ... Setting ambitious goals forces the organisation to dig deeper for creative solutions and to rethink how the business should be run.
>
> Sir Brian Pitman, Chairman of Lloyds TSB[12]

Balance of empowerment and control To be effective, organisational goals should encourage the use of empowerment but still incorporate an element of traditional management measurement and control.

Mills and Friesen suggest that to be effective, goals must exhibit several characteristics:

- **be understandable** – otherwise those who are given them seek further input before acting. If they cannot act on their own it follows they have not been empowered;
- **contain a time element** – in order that those being empowered will know when their progress will be measured. This helps them to accept empowerment and stop looking for direction;
- **be carefully drawn** – broad enough to support independent action but not so broad that confounding factors prevent their achievement. For example, asking a team to keep company stock price above target is too broad as factors influencing share prices are beyond the control of any one team;
- **be subject to alignment** – with other goals across the organisation in order to facilitate co-ordination among teams and to 'roll up' into collective company goals.[13]

The goal-setting process is of importance to all types of organisations and facilitates the attainment of objectives. In the public sector, for example, organisations such as hospitals, local authorities and universities have complex, diverse and competing goals. The clarification of goals and objectives is the basis for corporate planning, and a planning, programming, budgeting systems (PPBS) approach to decision-making.

An ambiguous concept However, the concept of organisational goals is ambiguous. Goals may be expressed very simply: in the case of business organisations, for example, to make a profit, or to increase productivity. Such broadly based goals might be taken for granted and they tell us little about the emphasis placed on the various activities of the organisation in meeting its goals. In any case, profit might more correctly be interpreted as a reward to the shareholders or providers of capital, and a means of ensuring the continued existence of the organisation and maintaining its growth and development. *Watson* questions whether it is necessary to have the notion of organisational goals as giving focus or direction to the idea of an organisation when such a purpose could readily and more simply be achieved using the notions of 'tasks'.[14]

INTEGRATION OF GOALS

Strictly, organisations have no goals; only people do. Organisational goals are established by people, either individually or, more usually, by a number of individuals co-operating. For example, a group of senior managers may collectively agree on a particular desired course of action that may then come to be referred to as an organisational goal. However, this is still the goal of those managers who initially determined it.

Success of the organisation is measured by the progress of people towards goals set by people. This gives rise to the questions:

- To what extent has the organisation one common set of goals, or is there diversity among the various goals of different departments or divisions of the organisation?
- How far are the goals of management compatible with the goals of the organisation?
- To what extent do individual members obtain satisfaction of their own goals through the attainment of organisational goals?

Informal goals

Members of the organisation have different, and often conflicting, goals. As a result, the goals which the organisation actually pursues (**informal goals**) may be distinguished from the officially stated goals (**formal goals**) that are set out in broad terms as the reasons for the purpose of the organisation. Informal goals may be inferred from the actual decisions made and actions taken within the organisation. Managers, and other members of the organisation, will have:

- their own perception of the goals of the organisation – for example, to produce high-quality television sets which satisfy requirements of the customers; and
- their personal goals – for example to earn high wages, to achieve promotion, to gain social satisfaction, to achieve status – which they expect to fulfil by participating in the activities of the organisation (*see* Figure 14.1).

Figure 14.1	**Compatibility of goals within an organisation**

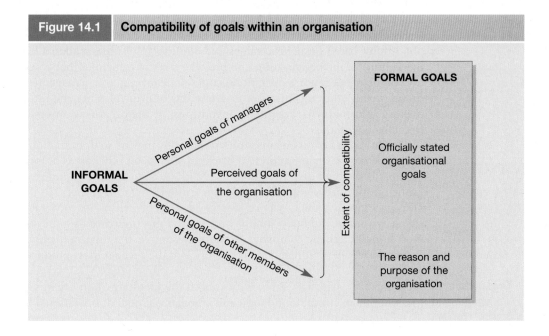

Compatibility of personal goals and organisational goals

If organisational goals and personal goals are pulling in different directions, conflict will arise and performance is likely to suffer. An organisation will be more effective when personal goals are compatible with organisational goals. Organisational performance will depend ultimately on the extent to which individuals are provided with the opportunity to satisfy their own goals by contributing to the goals of the organisation.

Management has a responsibility to clarify organisational goals and to attempt to integrate personal goals (including their own) with the overall objectives of the organisation. Only when organisational goals are shared by all members of the organisation will complete integration be achieved. In practice, this is unlikely. As McGregor points out:

> *Perfect integration of organizational requirements and individual goals and needs is, of course, not a realistic objective. In adopting this principle, we seek that degree of integration in which the individual can achieve his goals best by directing his efforts towards the success of the organisation.*[15]

Management should endeavour, therefore, to structure the organisation so that people may realise their own (personal) goals by helping the organisation to satisfy its goals. One attempt at integrating organisational goals with the needs of the individual members of the organisation is provided by the approach of Management by Objectives. This is discussed in Chapter 12.

Critical reflection ????

In large-scale organisations, the goals and objectives of the organisation, management and the workforce are never likely to be fully compatible. Do you think attempts at harmonisation are worth the effort? Or should one just accept the inevitability of organisational conflict?

ORGANISATIONAL IDEOLOGIES AND PRINCIPLES

The goals of the organisation may be pursued in accordance with an underlying ideology, or philosophy, based on beliefs, values and attitudes. This **organisational ideology** determines the 'culture' of the organisation and provides a set of principles that govern the overall conduct of the organisation's operations, codes of behaviour, the management of people and its dealings with other organisations.[16] These sets of principles may be recognised and implemented informally as 'accepted conventions' of the organisation or they may be stated formally in writing.

Certain aspects of an organisation's philosophy may be so dominant that they become the 'hallmark' of that organisation and place constraints on other areas or forms of activities. An example is the high quality standard of Marks & Spencer's merchandise and the company's explicit policy of buying primarily from United Kingdom sources. In the case of the Walt Disney Company, quality service is embedded deeply within its corporate culture. The overriding byword of The Body Shop is honesty and this underlies its policy of: 'We WILL be the most honest cosmetic company.' As another example, the highest-quality hallmark of Rolls-Royce cars would presumably prevent entry into the cheaper mass-production market.

Organisational values and beliefs

More than 30 years ago, *Brech* wrote about the ideology of an organisation related to the idea of both an ethical foundation and an organisational or operational foundation.

- **Ethical foundation** embodies the basic principles which govern the external and internal relations of the organisation. External relations concern standards of fair trading and relations with, for example, customers, suppliers and the general public. Internal relations

are concerned with fair standards of employment and relations with members of the organisation, including authorised union representatives.

- **Organisational or operational foundation** is concerned with the structure, operation, and conduct of the activities of the organisation. External aspects relate to, for example, methods of trading and channels of distribution. Internal aspects include methods of production, use of equipment and managerial practices relating to organisational performance, productivity and profitability.[17]

In more recent years organisations have given growing attention to a set of stated corporate values displayed prominently for all to see. *Lucas* questions whether such grand statements of corporate principles really mean anything and concludes that they actually have a point and values can be used with success. 'A set of values is obviously a nice thing for an organisation to have; something to pin on the notice board. But for those organisations that have learned to walk the talk, deeply embedded values can attract the right people, underpin the business in times of crisis and provide direction for the future.'[18]

Dainty and Anderson point out that values are the guidelines a person uses to make choices and within organisations, basic beliefs affect what decisions are made, how people interact, and the kind of work practices that are pursued and developed. They form the glue that binds an organisation's culture. 'Building an understanding of values that are shared within an organisation will be as important in the 21st century as it is today. In fact, many feel that organisations and people should be returning to more fundamental values, rather than moving away from them. Increasingly, organisations are spending time working out and agreeing the values by which they want their organisation to be managed.'[19]

Cloke and Goldsmith contend that organisations can increase their integrity, coherence, and integration and improve their performance by reaching consensus on shared values. They can bolster value-based relationships by recognising and encouraging behaviours that uphold their values; communicate and publicise their values, and encourage individual and team responsibility for implementing them; and develop methods for monitoring compliance with values, providing feedback and identifying potential conflicts of interest. Most importantly consensus on shared values means organisations can accomplish these goals without moralising, preaching, excusing or imposing their values on others.[20]

Refresh your understanding

Activity 14A
www.pearsoned.co.uk/
mullins

MISSION STATEMENTS

In recent years it has become increasing popular for an organisation to produce a **mission statement** and/or its 'vision' that sets out the purpose and general direction for the organisation. There is sometimes an apparent uncertainty of the distinction between the terms 'mission' and 'vision'. It seems to be generally accepted that the vision provides the overall frame of reference within which mission statements are written and goals selected. 'If vision is ill formed, mission statements will be vague and goal achievement hard to measure.'[21]

Mission statements vary in length, the extent of specific or general content, and according to the type of organisation. For example, the mission and vision of the Chartered Management Institute as set out in its Royal Charter is to: **'promote the art and science of management'**. Its vision is to be the **'authoritative and influential champion for professional management'**.

In fulfilling its mission, the Institute will:

- encourage and support the lifelong development of managers;
- raise the level of competence and qualification of management;
- initiate, develop, evaluate and disseminate management thinking, tools, techniques and practices;
- influence employers, policy makers and opinion formers on management.[22]

Value of mission statements

The desire to identify with as many stakeholders as possible means that many mission statements are all embracing with bland and abstract wording. The value of a mission statement is dependent, however, upon the extent to which it is understood and accepted throughout the organisation, and translated in meaningful terms to all members of staff including those at the operational level. *Perrin and Tavakoli* raise doubts over managers who have a naïve notion that the production and dissemination of a well-crafted statement will create a sense of mission:

> *The picture will remain gloomy while managers and consultants believe that creating a mission statement is synonymous with creating a sense of mission. You only create the latter if your mission statement is understood, believed and acted upon by a majority of organisation members.*[23]

A mission statement is only likely to be of any value if the organisation actually practices what it preaches. *Reeves* maintains that the problem with vision statements is that they are just that – statements, and typically they are disconnected from those they are meant to inspire. However, when values, mission and values are aligned to behaviour, this has an enormous impact on the productivity of organisations.[24]

A similar point is made by *Gratton*:

> *How often do corporate plans and mission statements remain simply that: senior executive rhetoric with little meaning to those people whose job it is to deliver customer satisfaction or bring complex products rapidly to the marketplace? Employees may hear corporate mission statements extolling the virtues of customer satisfaction or product innovation, but when the communication fanfare is over, the customer-focus workshops completed, and the lights dim on the business video, what is left? A group of employees trying to make sense and create meaning from the many messages and cues they have received.*[25]

OBJECTIVES AND POLICY

In accordance with its ideology or philosophy, the goals of the organisation are translated into objectives and policy. Terminology and use of the two terms varies but objectives are seen here as the 'what' and policy as the 'how', 'where' and 'when' – the means that follow the objectives.

- **Objectives** set out more specifically the goals of the organisation, the aims to be achieved and the desired end-results.
- **Policy** is developed within the framework of objectives. It provides the basis for decision-making and the course of action to follow in order to achieve objectives.

The establishment of objectives and policy is therefore an integral part of the process of management, and a necessary function in every organisation. In terms of a systems approach, the objectives of an organisation are related to the input–conversion–output cycle. In order to achieve its objectives and satisfy its goals the organisation takes inputs from the environment, through a series of activities transforms or converts these inputs into outputs and returns them to the environment as inputs to other systems. The organisation operates within a dynamic setting and success in achieving its goals will be influenced by a multiplicity of interactions with the environment (*see* Figure 14.2).

Objectives Clearly defined and agreed objectives are the first stage in the design of organisation structure and help facilitate systems of communication between different parts of the organisation. The choice of objectives is an essential part of corporate strategy and the

Figure 14.2 | **A systems view of organisational goals and objectives**

decision-making process involving future courses of action. Objectives may be set out either in general terms or in more specific terms. General objectives are determined by top management. Specific objectives are formulated within the scope of general objectives and usually have more defined areas of application and time limits.

Objectives may be just implicit but the formal, explicit definition of objectives will assist communications and reduce misunderstandings, and provide more meaningful criteria for evaluating organisational performance. However, objectives should not be stated in such a way that they detract from the recognition of possible new opportunities, potential danger areas, the initiative of staff or the need for innovation or change.

Policy A policy is a guideline for organisational action and the implementation of goals and objectives. Policy is translated into rules, plans and procedures; it relates to all activities of the organisation and to all levels of the organisation. Clearly stated policy can help reinforce the main functions of the organisation, make for consistency and reduce dependency on the actions of individual managers. Policy clarifies the roles and responsibilities of managers and other members of staff and provides guidelines for managerial behaviour. Some policy decisions are directly influenced by external factors – for example government legislation on equal opportunities and diversity.

Corporate guidelines

Whatever the type of organisation, there is a need for lines of direction through the establishment of objectives and determination of policy. Objectives and policy together provide corporate guidelines for the operations and management of the organisation. The activities of the organisation derive their significance from the contribution they make to achieving objectives in the manner directed. The formulation of objectives and policy, and the allocation of resources, provide the basis for strategic planning which is the first stage in the planning and control processes of business organisations. Clearly stated, good objectives help provide unity of direction and the basis for employee commitment and motivation. Recall, for example, the discussion on management by objectives in Chapter 12. A commonly used mnemonic is that objectives should be 'SMART':

<p align="center">**Specific Measurable Achievable Realistic Timebound**</p>

THE PROFIT OBJECTIVE

In order to be successful, the primary objectives of the business organisation may be seen as:

- to continue in existence – that is, to **survive**;
- to maintain **growth and development**; and
- to make a **profit**.

All three objectives are inextricably linked and it is a matter of debate whether the organisation survives and develops in order to provide a profit, or makes a profit by which it can survive and develop.

Summers and Nowicki suggest that using a Maslow-like hierarchy of needs (discussed in Chapter 7), the first concern for organisations is survival. After organisational survival is ensured, managers then have considerable latitude in what they want the organisation to be and do.[26]

If we accept survival as the ultimate objective of the business organisation, this involves the need for a steady and continuous profit. Organisations must be prepared to accept the possibility of a reduction in short-term profitability in order to provide for future investments. The profit goal is achieved through the process of management and the combined efforts of members of the organisation. In times of economic recession the survival objective takes on particular importance, especially for small businesses.

> *Managers today have a problem. They know their companies must grow. But growth is hard, especially given today's economic environment where investment capital is difficult to come by and firms are reluctant to take risks. Managers know innovation is the ticket to successful growth. But they just can't seem to get innovation right.[27]*

Not a sufficient criterion Although the objective of profit maximisation is undoubtedly of great importance, it is not, by itself, a sufficient criterion for the effective management of a business organisation. In practice, there are many other considerations and motivations which affect the desire for the greatest profit or maximum economic efficiency and the accompanying assumptions which underlie the economic theory of the firm.

The meaning of 'profit maximisation' is not, by itself, very clear. Consideration has to be given to the range and quality of an organisation's products or services, to the costs of its operations and to environmental influences. Reducing attention to longer-term 'investments' such as quality and after-sales service, research and development, sales promotion, management development, satisfaction of staff and their employment conditions may increase profitability in the short term, but is likely to jeopardise future growth and development, and possibly even the ultimate survival of the organisation.

A business organisation has to provide some commodity or service by which it contributes to the economic and/or social needs of the community. It also has broader social responsibilities to society. (Social responsibilities are discussed later in this chapter.) Profit can be seen as the incentive for an organisation to carry out its activities effectively. Profit does at least provide some broad measure of effectiveness and highlights the difficulty in evaluating the effectiveness of not-for-profit organisations, such as National Health Service hospitals, prisons or universities.

Furthermore, as discussed earlier, members of the organisation will have their own personal goals and their own perception of the goals of the organisation.

Fallacy of the single objective

The reality is that managers are usually faced with the challenge of several, often competing and/or conflicting objectives. *Drucker* has referred to the fallacy of the single objective of a business. The search for the one, right objective is not only unlikely to be productive, but is certain to harm and misdirect the business enterprise.

> *To emphasize only profit, for instance, misdirects managers to the point where they may endanger the survival of the business. To obtain profit today they tend to undermine the future ... To manage a business is to balance a variety of needs and goals ... the very nature of business enterprise requires multiple objectives which are needed in every area where performance and results directly and vitally affect the survival and prosperity of the business.* [28]

Drucker goes on to suggest eight key areas in which objectives should be set in terms of performance and results:

1 **Market standing** – for example: share of market standing; range of products and markets; distribution; pricing; customer loyalty and satisfaction.
2 **Innovation** – for example: innovations to reach marketing goals; developments arising from technological advancements; new processes and improvements in all major areas of organisational activity.
3 **Productivity** – for example: optimum use of resources; use of techniques such as operational research to help decide alternative courses of action; the ratio of 'contributed value' to total revenue.
4 **Physical and financial resources** – for example: physical facilities such as plant, machines, offices and replacement of facilities; supply of capital and budgeting; planning for the money needed; provision of supplies.
5 **Profitability** – for example: profitability forecasts and anticipated timescales; capital investment policy; yardsticks for measurement of profitability.
6 **Manager performance and development** – for example: the direction of managers and setting up their jobs; the structure of management; the development of future managers.
7 **Worker performance and attitude** – for example: union relations; the organisation of work; employee relations.
8 **Public responsibility** – for example: demands made upon the organisation, such as by law or public opinion; responsibilities to society and the public interest.

The balanced scorecard

The **balanced scorecard (BS)** is an attempt to combine a range of both qualitative and quantitative indicators of performance which recognise the expectations of various stakeholders and relates performance to a choice of strategy as a basis for evaluating organisational effectiveness. Citing the work of *Kaplan and Norton* in a year-long study of a dozen US companies,[29] Anita van de Vliet refers to the approach of a 'balanced scorecard' and the belief that

> *... relying primarily on financial accounting measures was leading to short-term decision-making, over-investment in easily valued assets (through mergers and acquisitions) with readily measurable returns, and under-investment in intangible assets, such as product and process innovation, employee skills or customer satisfaction, whose short-term returns are more difficult to measure.*

van de Vliet suggests that in the information era, there is a growing consensus that financial indicators on their own are not an adequate measure of company competitiveness or performance and there is a need to promote a broader view.

> *The balanced scorecard does still include the hard financial indicators, but it balances these with other, so-called soft measures, such as customer acquisition, retention, profitability and satisfaction; product development cycle times; employee satisfaction; intellectual assets and organisational learning.* [30]

The balanced scorecard can also be used in the public sector where there is an increasing need for organisations to improve their performance and to be seen as more businesslike in the delivery of services (including an employee perspective).

> *Given that the public sector has the difficult task of fulfilling a wide range of very different objectives, the BS could help in formal recognition and measurement of these objectives.* [31]

Critical reflection

'The single most important objective for the business organisation is profit maximisation; and for the workers high monetary rewards. These are the only realistic criteria by which organisational effectiveness can reasonably be judged.' To what extent do you think this is a realistic view or is it an oversimplification?

STRATEGY, OPPORTUNITIES AND RISKS

Every business needs to have a strategy and this strategy must be related to changing environmental conditions. In order to survive and maintain growth and expansion top management must protect the business from potentially harmful influences, and be ready to take maximum advantage of the challenges and opportunities presented. While top management must always accept the need for innovation, there is still the decision as to which opportunities it wishes to develop in relation to its resources and those it chooses not to pursue. An effective business strategy depends upon the successful management of opportunities and risks.

Drucker suggests that strategy should be based on the priority of maximising opportunities, and that risks should be viewed not as grounds of action but as limitations on action. He points out that while it is not possible to ensure that the right opportunities are chosen, it is certain that the right opportunities will not be selected unless:

● the focus is on maximising opportunities rather than on minimising risks;
● major opportunities are scrutinised collectively and in respect of their characteristics rather than singly and in isolation;
● opportunities and risks are understood in terms of the appropriateness of their fit to a particular business; and
● a balance is struck between immediate and easy opportunities for improvement, and more difficult, long-range opportunities for innovation and changing the character of the business.[32]

If the business is to be successful then its organisation structure must be related to its objectives and to its strategy. The structure must be designed so as to be appropriate to environmental influences, the continued development of the business, and the management of opportunities and risks. According to *Stern*, with the fast-changing world and competitive environment it becomes harder for leaders to distinguish between threats and opportunities, and between risks and rewards.[33]

E-business strategies

Advances in information technology and the Internet mean that organisations have to embrace successful e-commerce and **e-business** strategies. According to *Earl*:

Quite simply, IT affects business strategy. It is an input to business strategy as well as an output. The Internet, mobile communications, and future media present both threats and opportunities. So business strategy that ignores how technology is changing markets, competition, and processes is a process for the old economy, not the new economy. That is what 'e-everything' is about.[34]

Kermally points out that in order to operate within the new macro-economic environment, organisations have to seriously consider the arrival of the new economy and strategies. They have to embrace e-business in order to deal with the complexity of the new

business environment. Apart from scenario planning, e-businesses also have to focus special attention on recruiting and retaining staff. It is important to keep up with competitors and not to become complacent about adopting e-business. Kermally maintains that the e-business model is important because it:

- makes it possible for information to be shared more quickly and easily;
- facilitates human interaction;
- enables organisational resources and capabilities to be stretch strategically;
- provides global reach in marketing;
- allows consumers to shop 24 hours a day from any location; and
- promotes economic growth.[35]

SWOT ANALYSIS

In order to evaluate the nature of the business environment and its strategic capability, an organisation may undertake a **SWOT analysis** (sometimes also known as 'WOTS up'), which focuses on the Strengths, Weaknesses, Opportunities and Threats facing the organisation. The SWOT analysis provides convenient headings under which to study an organisation in its environmental setting and may provide a basis for decision-making and problem-solving. You may therefore find the analysis helpful in tackling case studies.

- **Strengths** are those positive aspects or distinctive attributes or competencies which provide a significant market advantage or upon which the organisation can build – for example, through the pursuit of diversification. These are characteristics of the organisation such as present market position, size, structure, managerial expertise, physical or financial resources, staffing, image or reputation. By searching out opportunities that match its strengths the organisation can optimise the effects of synergy.
- **Weaknesses** are those negative aspects or deficiencies in the present competencies or resources of the organisation, or its image or reputation, which limit its effectiveness and which need to be corrected or need action taken to minimise their effect. Examples of weaknesses could be operating within a particular narrow market, limited accommodation or outdated technology, a high proportion of fixed costs, a bureaucratic structure, a high level of customer complaints or a shortage of key managerial staff.
- **Opportunities** are favourable conditions and usually arise from the nature of changes in the external environment. The organisation needs to be sensitive to the problems of business strategy and responsive to changes in, for example, new markets, technology advances, improved economic factors, or failure of competitors. Opportunities provide the potential for the organisation to offer new, or to develop existing, products, facilities or services.
- **Threats** are the converse of opportunities and refer to unfavourable situations that arise from external developments likely to endanger the operations and effectiveness of the organisation. Examples could include changes in legislation, the introduction of a radically new product by competitors, political or economic unrest, changing social conditions and the actions of pressure groups. Organisations need to be responsive to changes that have already occurred and to plan for anticipated significant changes in the environment and to be prepared to meet them.

Although SWOT can offer a number of potential advantages for helping to evaluate corporate performance, care must be taken that the process does not lead to an over-simplified and misleading analysis. There are many ways of evaluating organisational performance and effectiveness, and varying criteria for success. *Levine* suggests that the new criteria for assessing the strength of an organisation will be in the area of quality results achieved through people.[36]

Refresh your understanding

Activity 14B
www.pearsoned.co.uk/mullins

CORPORATE SOCIAL RESPONSIBILITIES

Organisations play a major and increasingly important role in the lives of us all, especially with the growth of large-scale business and expanding globalisation. The decisions and actions of management in organisations have an increasing impact on individuals, other organisations and the community. The power and influence that many business organisations now exercise should be tempered, therefore, by an attitude of responsibility by management.

In striving to satisfy its goals and achieve its objectives, the organisation cannot operate in isolation from the environment of which it is part. The organisation requires the use of factors of production and other facilities of society. The economic efficiency of organisations is affected by governmental, social, technical and cultural variables. In return, society is in need of the goods and services created and supplied by organisations, including the creation and distribution of wealth. Organisations make a contribution to the quality of life and to the well-being of the community.

Organisational survival is dependent upon a series of exchanges between the organisation and its environment. These exchanges and the continual interaction with the environment give rise to a number of broader responsibilities to society in general. These broader responsibilities, which are both internal and external to the organisation, are usually referred to as **corporate social responsibilities** (CSR). These social responsibilities arise from the interdependence of organisations, society and the environment.

According to the All Party Parliamentary Group on Management, there are varying definitions of what CSR stands for, but in general terms, it refers to:

> *The comprehensive approach organisations take to meet or exceed the expectations of stakeholders beyond such measures as revenue, profit and legal obligations. It covers community investment, human rights and employee relations, environmental practices and ethical conduct.*[37]

The recognition of the importance of social responsibilities can be gauged in part by the extent of government action and legislation on such matters as employment protection, equal opportunities and diversity, companies acts, consumer law, product liability and safeguarding the environment. This has formalised certain areas of social responsibilities into a legal requirement. It is doubtful, however, whether legislation alone is sufficient to make management, or other members of an organisation, behave in what might be regarded as a 'proper' manner.

Growing attention to social responsibilities

There has been growing attention given to the subject of CSR and an increasing amount of literature on the subject and on a new work ethic. The importance of CSR can also be gauged by the extent of coverage included in the annual report of most major companies. Many businesses, both in the UK and in other parts of Europe, are attempting to provide a more open and transparent view of their operations.[38] The European Commission is encouraging firms to assess their performance not on profit margins alone but also on the welfare of their workforce and care for the environment.[39]

Ann Chant, Director General, HM Revenue & Customs, suggests that rather than worrying about exactly what it is, CSR might simply be one of those things where it is best to get on and try it. Chant argues that CSR should be a two-way partnership.

> *I believe the key to understanding CSR in the community is to recognise that when done properly, it is a partnership. Both parties – the organisation and the section of the community or group of individuals that the organisation is linking with – should have something to give and something to gain.*[40]

Global responsibilities Today there is also greater concern for business communities to accept their global responsibilities. This is recognised, for example, in the foreword to a book by Grayson and Hodges, by HRH The Prince of Wales.

> *For the business community of the twenty-first century, 'out of sight' is no longer 'out of mind'. Global communications and media operations can present every aspect of a company's operations directly to customers in stark, unflattering and immediate terms. Those customers increasingly believe that the role of large companies in our society must encompass more than the traditional functions of obeying the law, paying taxes and making a profit. Survey after survey reveals that they also want to see major corporations helping 'to make the world a better place'. That may be in some respects a naïve ambition, but it is, nevertheless, a clear expectation, and one that companies ignore at their peril ... It is immensely encouraging to find that there are business leaders who recognise the challenge of running their companies in ways that make a positive and sustainable contribution to the societies in which they operate. It is a huge task, not least in finding ways of reaching out to the thousands of managers at the 'sharp end' of the business who, every day, take the decisions that have real impact on employees, on whole communities and on the environment.*
>
> HRH The Prince of Wales[41]

ORGANISATIONAL STAKEHOLDERS

We have seen that social responsibilities are often viewed in terms of **organisational stakeholders** – that is, those individuals or groups who have an interest in and/or are affected by the goals, operations or activities of the organisation or the behaviour of its members.[42] Managers, for example, are likely to have a particular interest in, and concern for, the size and growth of the organisation and its profitability, job security, status, power and prestige. Stakeholders, meanwhile, include a wide variety of interests and may be considered, for example, under six main headings of:

- employees;
- providers of finance;
- consumers;
- community and environment;
- government; and
- other organisations or groups.

Employees People and organisations need each other. Responsibilities to employees extend beyond terms and conditions of the formal contract of employment and give recognition to the worker as a human being. People today have wider expectations of the quality of working life, including justice in treatment, democratic functioning of the organisation and opportunities for consultation and participation, training in new skills and technologies, effective HRM policies and practices, and provision of social and leisure facilities. Responsibilities to employees involve considerations of the new psychological contracts discussed in Chapter 1.

Providers of finance Joint stock companies are in need of the collective investments of shareholders in order to finance their operations. Shareholders are drawn from a wide range of the population. The conversion of a number of building societies and insurance companies from mutual societies to public companies extended significantly the range of share ownership and stakeholding among private individuals. Many people also subscribe indirectly as shareholders through pension funds and insurance companies. Shareholders expect a fair financial return as payment for risk bearing and the use of their capital. In addition, social responsibilities of management extend to include the safeguarding of investments, and the

opportunity for shareholders to exercise their responsibility as owners of the company, to participate in policy decisions and to question top management on the affairs of the company. In the case of public sector organisations, finance may be provided by government grants/subsidies – which are funded 'compulsorily' by the public through taxation and rates – as well as loans, and charges for services provided. There is, therefore, a similar range of responsibilities to the public as subscribers of capital.

Consumers To many people, responsibilities to consumers may be seen as no more than a natural outcome of good business. There are, however, broader social responsibilities including:

- providing good value for money;
- the safety and durability of products/services;
- standard of after-sales service;
- prompt and courteous attention to queries and complaints;
- long-term satisfaction – for example, serviceability, adequate supply of products/services, and spare and replacement parts;
- fair standards of advertising and trading;
- full and unambiguous information to potential consumers.

Increasing concern for social responsibilities to consumers can be seen by the activities of such bodies as the Consumers' Association, and the number of television and radio programmes devoted to this subject. In the case of public corporations there are Users' National Councils or consumers' regulatory bodies which are independent and look after the interests of customers. In the case of local government there is a system of Commissioners for Local Administration (popularly referred to as 'Ombudsmen'), designed to provide an independent investigation of citizens' complaints over alleged maladministration.

Community and environment It is in the area of concern for the community at large that social responsibilities can be seen most clearly. Organisations have a responsibility not to misuse the scarce factors of production upon which the wealth of the country depends. Organisations have a responsibility to society, to respect environmental considerations and take care of amenities. Some examples under this heading include:

- the effects and potential dangers of pollution, noise, disposal of waste;
- the siting and appearance of new buildings;
- transportation policies, such as the routing of heavy vehicles through narrow village roads; and
- avoidance of excessive packaging and more use of biodegradable materials.

Government Another important area of social responsibility could arguably be to the government. Organisations should, of course, respect and obey the law even where they regard it as not in their best interests. What is debatable, however, is the extent to which organisations should co-operate voluntarily with actions requested by the government. Some examples are restraint from trading with certain overseas countries, and the acceptance of controls over imports or exports, actions designed to combat inflation, such as limits on the level of wage settlements, assisting in the control of potential social problems – for example, the sale of tobacco or alcohol and the display of health warnings.

Other organisations or groups The potential range of social responsibilities is substantial. Other organisations or groups to whom organisations might be regarded as having a social responsibility, or obligation, are **suppliers, trade unions, business associates** and even **competitors**. Examples of social responsibilities might include fair standards of trading, honouring terms and conditions of

purchase or sale, and settlement dates (for example, payment of accounts), assistance to smaller organisations, engagement only in fair competition, respect for copyright and patents. Some organisations extend the range of social responsibilities even further – for example, by giving recognition to the needs of developing countries; limiting the extent of political involvement or campaigning; donations to, or sponsorship of, the arts, educational or research institutions, sporting organisations or charities.

A blurred distinction

It should be recognised, however, that the distinction is blurred between the exercise of a genuine social responsibility, on the one hand, and actions taken in pursuit of good business practice and the search for organisational efficiency on the other. One approach is that attention to social responsibilities arises out of a moral or ethical motivation and the dictates of conscience – that is, out of genuine philanthropic objectives. An alternative approach is that the motivation is through no more than enlightened self-interest and the belief that, in the long term, attention to social responsibilities is simply good business sense. In practice, it is a matter of degree and balance, of combining sound economic management with an appropriate concern for broader responsibilities to society.

Whatever the view of corporate social responsibility, management has as its priority the need to ensure the survival and effective performance of the organisation. As *Drucker* puts it:

> *The first responsibility to society is to operate at a profit, and only slightly less important is the necessity for growth. The business is the wealth-creating and wealth-producing organ of our society. Management must maintain its wealth-producing resources intact by making adequate profits to offset the risk of economic activity. And it must besides increase the wealth-creating and wealth-producing capacity of these resources and with them the wealth of society.*[43]

The attention given to social responsibilities must involve weighing the costs of meeting these responsibilities against the benefits derived. Provided the cost/benefit analysis is not detrimental to economic and/or competitive performance, management must then determine the extent to which, and the manner in which, the organisation will attempt to satisfy its social responsibilities. The recognition of social responsibilities should form an integral part of strategy and the establishment of objectives and policies of the organisation.

> It is inevitable that sometimes there will be a tension between a business' obligation to be ethical and its desire to be financially successful: the question is how these conflicts are dealt with ... In order for business leaders to win back the trust they have lost, ethics must be more than a quick bolt-on or a new-fangled job title. It has to go to the heart of the way in which they create wealth.
>
> R. Reeves, 'Do the right thing'[44]

Critical reflection ????

A National Health Service trust chairperson was heavily criticised for maintaining that the primary loyalty of doctors was owed to their employers and that their duty to patients came third, after themselves. When demands upon the health service are limitless and resources finite, do you believe the idea of owing first loyalty to the organisation for which you work is such a bad thing?

VALUES AND ETHICS

In the last few years, there have been more and more reports of UK and US service sector jobs being transferred to lower-cost Anglophone locations elsewhere in the world (India, Sri Lanka and others). Financial services organisations have provided notable examples of this 'offshoring', as have IT helpdesk services and many other customer service offices. It is now commonplace for customers in the UK to find themselves talking to someone thousands of miles away: stories circulate about how some call centre employees are briefed on UK weather conditions in order to appear more 'local'.

The availability of much cheaper, high-capacity international telecommunications is obviously a prime driver of this prominent feature of globalisation, as is the availability of educated English-speakers to perform these services. Like so many other aspects of globalisation, however, the development of offshoring also raises a range of *ethical* issues. For those who may be made redundant as jobs in the UK are moved offshore, for example, the news – at least in the short term – is mainly bad. For UK customers, the effects of lower costs in the new locations may be favourable, but there are some reports of customer dissatisfaction in some cases, with some companies choosing to bring this type of work back to the UK.[45] There have also been reports of security lapses in some financial services offshore operations[46] and of possibly serious errors in the transcription of medical notes carried out in offshore locations for UK NHS Trusts.[47]

In Indian cities, by contrast, the arrival of this type of work has had a mainly positive effect: for all that the pay rates may appear to be low by UK standards, many of these opportunities are very attractive in the local labour market, to the extent that concerns have been expressed about qualified professionals abandoning their work to seek call centre work. Shareholders in the offshoring companies will expect to benefit if the same quality of service can be delivered at lower cost, while there will also be indirect effects in both countries due to changes in things like demand for local services, tax revenues and social security payments.

Ethics is to do with good and bad (or right and wrong): it seeks to understand what makes good things good, for example, in ways that can be generalised to other similar cases. The example of offshoring shows how complex these questions can be – goodness or badness appears to depend on where you stand. But ethical questions are important because of their effect on people in organisations, as well as people outside organisations who are affected by the choices made by the people in organisations. Ethical complexity is probably the rule in real life, but the ethical aspects of organisational behaviour are too important to ignore. In this section, we outline the influence of ethical considerations in terms of the actions taken by the organisation in pursuit of its strategic objectives, together with the ethical implications of interpersonal interaction, both inside the organisation and between individuals across organisational boundaries.

Ethics and business

Ethics is concerned with the study of morality: practices and activities that are considered to be importantly right or wrong, together with the rules that govern those activities and the values to which those activities relate.[48] Business ethics can be seen as an example of applied ethics – just as medical ethics is about the application of general ethics to the human activity called medicine, business ethics seeks to explore the implications of general ethics for the conduct of business. This apparently obvious point is important: by taking this stance, one rejects the view that moral principles have no bearing on business, or that 'the business of business is business', as the common saying has it.

This is not to say that it is easy, or uncontroversial, to apply ethics to business: on the contrary, this fast-growing subject is characterised by a range of sharply contrasting views. Some of this controversy is inherent in ethics itself – as will be discussed below, there is no single clear view of how to judge good and bad, and this must impact on any application such as

business ethics. This particular application of ethics, however, is also complicated by the fact that ethics mainly deals with good or bad conduct on the part of individuals, resulting in possible difficulties in applying these ideas to impersonal corporate entities like companies. Is it appropriate to regard companies as if they were individual people and if not, what allowances should be made? Or, can the subject be satisfactorily seen as relating to the conduct of individuals as employees of businesses? Clearly, for very small businesses, the two views merge into one, but for larger, corporate entities, the position is more complex.

A discussion of ethics in business organisations has to take account of the purpose of the organisation, as well as its strategy (what it is trying to achieve, usually in competition with other similar businesses). These two factors are important because of their influence on what the organisation chooses to do and thus on the consequences for people inside and outside the organisation. A decision by an airline, for example, to pursue a low-cost strategy will have significant impacts on what is required of its staff and how well that business fares in the market. A successful implementation of such a strategy may mean fast growth, with attractive career development opportunities for some staff, but also more negative consequences for others. Yet, the failure of a strategy can lead to the end of the organisation as an independent entity, with more widespread adverse consequences for the organisation's people.

ETHICS AND CORPORATE SOCIAL RESPONSIBILITY

One illustration of the complexity of issues in business ethics is the diversity of opinion on the issue of corporate social responsibility (discussed above). On one side of the debate are those who would share *Milton Friedman's* view that the social responsibility of business is to make as much money as possible for the shareholders, within the rules of the game (fair competition, no deception or fraud, and so on).[49] This shareholder-centred view sees the directors of a company as agents of the owners, who are duty bound to act so as to maximise the interests of those owners, this being taken as the reason for owners having made the investment in the first place.

A more recent development of this general approach is that of *Sternberg* who proposes a teleological view of business ethics, based upon the pursuit of the business purpose – that of maximising long-term owner wealth by selling products and services.[50] Actions by a firm that are consistent with this aim and which satisfy the additional tests of common decency (for example refraining from stealing, cheating, coercion, and so on) and distributive justice (that is ensuring that rewards are proportional to contributions made) are ethical. Actions that fail any one of these three tests are, in this model, unethical.

At the other end of the spectrum are some forms of **stakeholder theory**, which emphasise a much broader set of social responsibilities for business. *Cannon* suggests that:

> There exists an implicit or explicit contract between business and the community in which it operates. Business is expected to create wealth; supply markets; generate employment; innovate and produce a sufficient surplus to sustain its activities and improve its competitiveness while contributing to the maintenance of the community in which it operates. Society is expected to provide an environment in which business can develop and prosper, allowing investors to earn returns while ensuring that the stakeholders and their dependants can enjoy the benefits of their involvement without fear of arbitrary or unjust action. The interdependence between society and business cannot be overstated.[51]

Differing assumptions about a business

The two perspectives provide very different views of how a business should act, because of their differing assumptions concerning what a business is *for*. In the shareholder-centred view, a business is principally for the shareholders and its actions should mainly be judged on the criterion of maximising their interests. In the stakeholder view quoted above, a busi-

ness is for its stakeholders (who are potentially a very large and diverse group) and its actions should be designed to balance stakeholder interests. From the point of view of business ethics – the study of good and bad conduct in business – this distinction is very important. The use of company resources to support a local community project, for example, might be seen as admirable in the stakeholder view but unethical in the shareholder-centred view, in that it would be a misapplication of funds that belong to the owners (unless, of course, such an investment could be shown to be consistent with the shareholders' best interests).

Each of the two approaches adopts a different yardstick for judging the 'goodness' of a proposed action by a company. In the shareholder-centred view, the action has to be shown to be consistent with the duty of maximising owner wealth, which is conceptually relatively simple, but which necessarily involves assumptions concerning the likely effect of the proposed action. In the stakeholder view (or, at least in those versions of the stakeholder view that emphasise an accountability to stakeholders), the task of management is to balance stakeholder interests. However, managers seeking to do this – often in the face of loud opposing claims from the various interests – will very quickly encounter the practical problem of how that 'balance' should be defined and recognised.

Although difficult to reconcile in practice, the two approaches are not completely incompatible: to a stakeholder theorist, shareholders count as one type of stakeholder, but not the only type to which duties are owed by the firm. Likewise, *Sternberg* acknowledges the importance of understanding and remaining aware of the various stakeholder groups and of actively managing relationships between the company and these groups, because doing so is likely to be consistent with maximising owner wealth. As she points out, however, 'taking account' of something is importantly different from 'being accountable' to it.[52]

Intelligent self-interest

It is also worth emphasising that a company seeking to maximise its owners' long-term wealth may well do very good things for its 'stakeholders', not necessarily through any direct intent but in pursuit of its main duty. Providing customers with excellent products and services is the central example, of course, but this form of intelligent self-interest may also – for example – drive a firm to build strong, trusting relationships with its suppliers and distributors (because it will be better off as a result), or an attractive working environment for its employees (because it wishes to recruit and keep the best, in order to be able to compete more effectively).

Even beyond its immediate commercial relationships, an intelligently self-interested company may deliberately set out to build strong relationships with other stakeholders, or to take a principled stance on an issue such as the use of child labour, because to do so is to maximise owner value. The 'value' in question is not just next year's dividends, but refers to the value of the investment as a whole and thus obliges the management to think long term as well as short term and to consider the impact of company actions as broadly as possible.

Offshoring example

In the 'offshoring' example at the beginning of this section, the shareholder-centred view would place emphasis on the unit cost savings to be achieved by moving the operation to a lower-cost area, provided that the required quality of service can be maintained. Other things being equal, lower unit costs obviously allow higher margins and improved rewards to shareholders. However, the assessment would also take into account the possibility of additional risks to be managed, such as security and quality control issues mentioned at the beginning of this section. Furthermore, this view would also consider the competitive implications of the decision: if other suppliers all outsource and reduce their prices to customers, a decision not to do the same could damage the company. Yet, being different could be a

viable competitive stance for one or more competitors, particularly if some customers are concerned about reduced quality of service from offshoring: NatWest in the UK seemed to take this stance in its advertising.

A stakeholder-centred company would place more emphasis on the impacts of the decision on the various stakeholder groups, notable including UK employees in this case. Although the decision to offshore might still be seen as competitively necessary by such a company, it might feel impelled to make more generous arrangements for those whose jobs are to be replaced, both out of a sense of long-term obligation and also to preserve its image in the UK labour market. The question as to whether the group defined as 'those that the company has not yet recruited in the offshore location' should also be considered to be a stakeholder group with a legitimate claim for attention is one of the numerous judgements to be made in this approach.

In the UK, the report of the RSA inquiry 'Tomorrow's Company' referred to the concept of an imaginary 'operating licence' granted to a company by the public, which can be effectively suspended or withdrawn if a company appears to be behaving badly.[53] Doing business effectively and well relies upon hundreds, sometimes thousands of transactions every day of the year. If some of these transactions become more difficult because trust has been squandered and co-operation has been withdrawn, then the firm will start to lose out to its better-behaved competitors and its owners' wealth will start to suffer.

Refresh your understanding

Activity 14C
www.pearsoned.co.uk/
mullins

BUSINESS ETHICS

The large-scale issues of corporate social responsibility are to do with how a company should conduct itself within society: these questions certainly have an ethical aspect, as has been discussed, but they are not the whole of business ethics. Day-to-day decisions made by individual managers are not usually made on the basis of some detailed calculation of the consequences for shareholder value (however theoretically desirable that might be) and more general ethical considerations must play a part in resolving the dilemmas that sometimes arise in practice.

The scope of **business ethics** is very broad, because anything done by a company or its employees can be done ethically or unethically. The following list is not intended to be exhaustive, but rather to illustrate the all-pervasive nature of ethical questions in business:

- behaviour towards customers, suppliers, distributors and competitors: for example, marketing and selling, fair competition, intelligence gathering, inducements and incentives;
- treatment of employees: for example, recruitment, rewards, training, promotion, dismissal, employee and employer rights and duties;
- treatment of other stakeholder groups: for example, local communities, governments, interest groups;
- effect on the natural environment: for example, pollution, recycling, sustainability;
- conduct in international operations: for example, use of power, respect for human rights, respect for local cultural values, offshoring, and so on.

No single view of right or wrong

These questions can be complex, since there is no single view in general ethics of what makes something right or wrong. One school of thought emphasises **duties**, things that must be done (or refrained from) irrespective of the consequences. This deontological point of view holds that goodness or badness is evident only in the action itself: that, for example, lying is bad because it is bad in itself. By contrast, a **consequentialist** view of ethics holds that the goodness or badness of a proposed action is evident only in the consequences of that action: whether a lie is good or bad depends upon the consequences of that particular

lie at the time. Utilitarianism, for example, is a consequentialist theory, in that it seeks to maximise the net happiness for everyone affected by a particular action ('the greatest good for the greatest number', as it is sometimes expressed). Both of the perspectives on corporate social responsibility discussed above are also to some extent consequentialist, in that they are mainly concerned with an assessment of the effects of a firm's actions.

Both duties and consequences (or 'means' and 'ends' in the familiar Machiavellian saying about the latter justifying the former) are plainly important in the way we deal with ethical issues in everyday life. Unfortunately, however, they are very different ways of reasoning, which can lead to contradictory outcomes in some cases. An exclusively duty-based view of ethics, for example, must sooner or later run into problems such as absolutism, or the difficulty of deciding which duty should take precedence over others in a particular situation. If, for example, both lying and killing are held to be inherently wrong, is it acceptable to lie in order to avoid a killing? And whatever answer is given, how do we know?

Nonetheless, duties and principles clearly do inform our views of how people should treat each other at work. An exclusively consequentialist view of ethics also entails methodological problems of forecasting reliably what the consequences of an action may be and of deciding how to measure those consequences. Some forms of utilitarianism can be very unjust to small minorities, by allowing their unhappiness (i.e. as a result of some proposed action) to be offset by the increased happiness of a much larger number. Again, however, we can hardly deny that our assessment of the likely consequences of different actions plays a part in our view of acceptable and unacceptable behaviour in an organisation.

By way of illustration, a deontological approach to the ethics of offshoring would focus on aspects of the proposal that might be in breach of clear principles and duties. While no business can reasonably accept a general duty to keep existing employees on the payroll for ever (or not ever to relocate operations), a contemplation of duties might cause a company to do as much as possible to soften the impact of the job losses, including the possibility of internal transfer, retraining, outplacement and more-than-minimum redundancy packages. A utilitarian analysis would seek to identify all who would be affected – anywhere in the world – by the proposed offshoring decision and then assess the impact (positive or negative) on each person (or, more realistically, groups).

This would allow a sort of 'trial balance' of the consequences to be drawn up and an evaluation of the net impact on aggregate happiness. Necessarily in this method, the reduction in happiness for others, such as those who are made involuntarily redundant is offset by the extra happiness created for some – those who get the offshore jobs, for example. Obviously, this is of little comfort to the former group, which illustrates one of the important criticisms of the utilitarian approach.

Further approaches Nor is the choice restricted to means and ends in ethics: several further approaches can be distinguished in Western thought, including the following:

- **Virtue** ethics, based upon an analysis of desirable human qualities that lie between undesirable extremes (the virtue of 'courage', for example, lies between the undesirable extremes of 'cowardice', at one end and 'foolhardiness' at the other). We might want to explore, for example, what virtues are found in good chief executives, and whether different virtues apply to good entrepreneurs.
- **Ethical relativism**, which holds that goodness and badness are largely or entirely determined by the prevailing values of the time in question and may thus change from one period to another, or one culture to another. Although it is clearly true that values and standards have changed over time (in the attitude towards child labour, for example), pure relativism is an uncomfortable stance for most people, who have intuitive conscience-based convictions that some things are just plain wrong.
- **Emotivism**, which suggests that statements about ethics are essentially statements about the speaker's attitudes, and that it is therefore futile to search for any ethical 'truths'. The statement 'lying is bad' is, from this point of view, saying little more than 'I don't like lying'.

Ethical decision-making at work

How, then, are ethical choices to be made by people working for organisations? No simple and universal answer is available – ethical awareness is something that can be cultivated and the different perspectives will often help to shed light on a particular dilemma. Some perspectives may appear to be better suited to particular situations: whereas, for example, it is difficult to avoid some sort of consequentialist component in thinking about how a company should act, it is also clear that duty-based arguments must also weigh heavily in thinking about the ethical treatment of people such as employees. The German philosopher Kant's view that we should always treat other people as ends in themselves and never simply as means is surely an important principle for decent human resource management and one that would often be seen as more important than the prospect of short-term gain.[54]

Personal integrity and individual values are important elements in ethical decision-making at work, but the increasingly common company, professional or industry codes of conduct may also provide support and guidance. This is not to say that these ethical 'resources' will always provide clear and comfortable guidance – sometimes, people in organisations will experience tension between the conflicting demands of, say, their own personal values and the demands placed on them by their organisation. If these conflicts become intolerable and cannot be resolved through normal means, then an individual may decide to become a 'whistleblower' in the public interest, by taking the high-risk approach of placing the problem in the public domain for resolution. Codes of conduct can help to reduce the risk of painful situations like this by providing a published set of values to which the individual can appeal, rather than taking the risk wholly personally.

(I am grateful to my colleague, Richard Christy, Department of Human Resource and Marketing Management, University of Portsmouth for providing the above information on Values and Ethics.)

A concept map outlining some issues of ethics at work is given in Figure 14.3.

CODES OF ETHICS

In American and Canadian organisations, codes of conducts are very common and in many cases members of the organisation are required to sign to indicate formally their acceptance. Codes may be updated on a regular basis and in some cases such as investment companies this may be at least once a year. In the UK an increasing number of organisations, of all types, are also now publishing a code of ethics (or code of conduct). For example, according to The Chartered Management Institute:

> *There is a growing belief that organisations can succeed only if they are seen to observe high ethical standards. As a result, more are choosing to make a public commitment to ethical business by formulating and publishing a code of operating principles. The key difficulty they face in doing so is translating high sounding principles into practical guidelines, and thence into actual practice.*

The Institute provide a checklist for codes of ethics that provides initial guidelines that apply equally to public, private and voluntary sectors.[55]

IBM publishes a document of business conduct relating to the ethical practices and values of the company. The document includes a comprehensive set of guidelines on:

- You and Your Job in IBM;
- Conducting IBM's Business; and
- On Your Own Time.

Figure 14.3 Concept map of ethics at work

ETHICS AT WORK

- WHO IS INVOLVED?
- SOME ETHICAL PROBLEMS

SOME ETHICAL PROBLEMS
- Should the business be just a little more than legal?
- Should we adhere to the spirit of legislation v actual legislation?
- Which is worse – stealing from employees or stealing from the employer?
- Is it OK to take things from a large employer but not a small organisation?
- What are the duties in looking after the customer?
- What, if any, is our duty of care to customers?
- Where does 'let the buyer beware' fit into our ethical approach?
- What do we mean by value for money?

GROUPS WHO HAVE AN ETHICAL CONCERN
- Customers existing and potential
- Internal customers
- Shareholders
- The environment (the general public)
- The government

- ORGANISATION: COMPANY AND EMPLOYER
- MANAGEMENT AND SUPERVISION
- EMPLOYEE

ETHICS AND YOURSELF
- Is it worse to steal from a colleague than from your organisation? If so why?
- If you meet what you consider to be unethical practices, do you
 - say nothing?
 - speak to the individuals?
 - tell your superior face to face?
 - write anonymously to senior management?
- Do you think your organisation behaves ethically to you?
- Where do you draw the line, does it depend:
 - on circumstances?
 - the individuals involved?
 - the amounts of money or the equivalent?

ETHICAL/ORGANISATIONAL CONTROL
through:–
- legal (statutory) requirements
- written procedures
- codes of conduct
- custom and practice
- management style
- person beliefs/conscience

EXAMPLES OF AREAS OF CONCERN
(SHOP FLOOR AND OFFICE STAFF)
- stealing from the employer
- using the telephone without permission
- taking pens, paper clips
- removing scrap/waste for personal use
- using employer's equipment for personal use
- falsifying expense claims
- manipulating bonus and incentive schemes
- falsifying information for internal and external customers

MANAGEMENT STYLE
- to create an open atmosphere where employees learn from their mistakes and are not subjected to ridicule/inappropriate admonishment

'WHISTLE BLOWING'
- Employers encouraging employees to report in suspected illegal/unacceptable practices of fellow employees including their managers

EXAMPLES OF AREAS OF CONCERN
(SUPERVISORS AND MANAGERS)
- not ensuring legal requirements
- health and safety obligations, e.g.
 - unsafe/dangerous equipment
 - worn electric cables and sockets
 - guards on equipment
- using bonus system to favour/bribe certain employees
- passing on confidential company information for personal gain or to damage the organisation
- using illegal copies of computer software

EXAMPLES OF AREAS OF CONCERN
(SENIOR MANAGEMENT)
- Are publicly stated corporate aims reflected in practice?, for example:
 - illegally dumping waste
 - polluting the atmosphere
 - Insider trading for personal profit
 - Personally profiting by creating advantageous financial measures to the detriment of other stakeholders
- Exploiting employees through
 - excessive hours
 - low levels of pay
 - poor working conditions

MANAGEMENT ISSUES
- Where do authority and responsibility rest?
- What should be the level of tolerance?
- Are there appropriate disciplinary systems in place?
- Are policies and procedures on ethical issues adequately communicated to all?

Source: Training Learning Consultancy Ltd, Bristol, England. Reproduced with permission.

At one level, the IBM Business Conduct Guidelines are a document of conduct we establish for ourselves to help us comply with laws and good ethical practices. We regularly review and update it as business and the world at large become more complex, and as the need for such guidelines becomes greater. But this is not just about compliance with the law and general standard of ethics. By establishing these guidelines and giving them the weight of a governing document, we are acknowledging that our choices and actions help define IBM for others. We are ensuring that our relationships – with clients, investors, colleagues and the communities in which we live and work – are built on trust. In other words, the Business Conduct Guidelines are a tangible example of our values and an expression of IBMer's personal responsibility to uphold them.[56]

In the public sector, the Local Government Act 2000 specifies the following principles to govern the conduct of members of relevant English authorities and Welsh police authorities: selflessness, honesty and integrity, objectivity, accountability, openness, personal judgement, respect for others, duty to uphold the law, stewardship and leadership. These principles are intended to underpin the mandatory provisions of the model codes of conduct for English local authorities.[57]

A matter of degree and balance

Allen, however, questions whether the emphasis on the caring sharing company of the new millennium and social responsibility is all going a bit far. There is scarcely a company without a loftily worded mission statement and high-minded references to shareholders. There are now numerous codes and standards and any company wishing to keep up to date with latest developments in social responsibility needs to look in many directions at once, and companies are talking of 'codemania'. While many codes offer voluntary guidelines, companies that fail to meet these can see themselves receiving a bad press or disinvestments. Nevertheless, the burden of social responsibilities can be seen as part of the response to ever-changing social conditions.[58] And, according to *Cook*, although it is easy to be cynical following the fall of big companies there are many organisations which are 'putting something back'. There is evidence about reversing the decline in public trusts and that in response to stakeholder and customer attitudes, corporate values are changing.[59]

According to *Philippa Foster Back*, OBE (Director, Institute of Business Ethics), the globalisation of business has raised questions of applying ethical values to the different cultures and societies in which organisations operate. The challenge for everyone concerned with ethics now is to ensure that values are embedded throughout an organisation. A code of ethics needs to be translated into reality through training and enforcement and driven from the top.[60]

Related legislation

As part of the growing attention to the concept of corporate social responsibilities there are a number of pieces of recent legislation that arguably relate to the concept of business ethics and organisational accountability. Although it is not in the scope of this book to provide detailed aspects of legal provisions, we should recognise the existence of such legislation, including the Human Rights Act 1998, the Public Interest Disclosure Act 1998, the Local Government Act 2000 and the Freedom of Information Act 2000.

The **Human Rights Act 1998** came into force on 2 October 2000 and incorporates into English law rights and liberties enshrined in the European Convention on Human Rights. The provisions apply to the acts of 'public authorities' and make it unlawful for them to act in a way incompatible with a right under the Convention. The Act is designed to provide greater protection for individuals, and to protect them from unlawful and unnecessary interference. Everyone has the right to respect for their private and family life, their home and their correspondence. The Act has a significant effect on people both as citizens and at work.

The **Public Interest Disclosure Act 1998**, which has become known widely as the 'Whistleblower's Act', is designed to protect people who expose wrongdoing at their work-

place, to provide reassurance that there is a safe alternative to silence and to provide a safe-guard against retaliation. Employers need to establish clear internal procedures by which members of staff can raise any matters of personal concern.

The **Local Government Act 2000**, the so-called 'New Ethical Framework', requires all local authorities to provide codes of conduct to promote high standards of behaviour. The government has distinguished between general principles of conduct in public service and the code of conduct containing specific actions and prohibitions that demonstrate the principles are being observed.

The **Freedom of Information Act 2000** gives the public one simple right to access information held by public authorities. Under the Act, the public have a 'right to know'.

An integrated approach

McEwan summarises the separate histories of corporate social responsibility, business ethics and corporate governance, and suggests a method of enquiry that attempts to integrate these different perspectives on business through three broad levels of enquiry:

- a **descriptive** approach that draws attention to the values and beliefs of people from different cultures and societies that influence their attitudes towards the various activities of business in their home countries and abroad;
- a **normative** approach that identifies sets of values and beliefs as a basis for making ethical decisions at the individual, group, or senior management level in an organisation;
- an **analytical** approach that attempts to explore the relationship between these normative values and beliefs and other value-systems or ideologies such as political or religious beliefs and culture or other social customs.[61]

Refresh your understanding

Activity 14D
www.pearsoned.co.uk/
mullins

Critical reflection

'Without EU intervention, government legislation and the threat of adverse press or television reports, the majority of business organisations would give little regard to their social responsibilities or to business ethics.' To what extent do you support this contention? What do you think is the single most important social responsibility of organisations?

MANAGEMENT IN THE NEWS

Power to the people
The cost of not caring for your customers

Tom Lester

If you have a complaint with the ferry service between Stranraer in Scotland and Belfast, employees are allowed to spend up to £1,000 to solve the problem for you – without having to obtain management approval. Stena Line, the Swedish operator, credits the 'satisfaction strategy' developed on the crossing with boosting its market share, and it has now been extended to all other Stena routes.

Such cases illustrate the growing commitment of companies to pay closer attention to their customers and help resolve complaints. Most consumers have personal horror stories of bank letters demanding payment of a non-existing account, helplines that can't or won't help and managers who cower behind expensive automated systems. Moreover, the problem is getting worse, surveys show. Research by

Good customer relations can boost market share. Stena Line employees are empowerd to spend up to £1,000 solving a customer's compaint.

Source: Neil Setchfield

Accenture, the management consultancy, found that when telephoning to complain, customers spent an average of six minutes on hold, and spoke to more than two service representatives. Researchers at Birmingham's Aston University found that the majority of chief executives regard complaining customers as a nuisance and too demanding. Yet most chief executives would swear their companies are 'customer-oriented'.

Research by Frederick Reichheld, director emeritus at Bain & Company, the strategy consultancy, provides a reality check. He has shown that over the past decade the only reliable guide to customer loyalty (and future purchases) is the answer to the question 'Would you recommend [company X] to a friend or colleague?'

Mere satisfaction is not enough to bring customers back, while those who come away vaguely dissatisfied won't complain, but next time simply vote with their credit cards – and quite probably, tell their friends. Chief executives must remember even when profits are tight that repeat purchases are several times cheaper than new business. Once the volume of complaints is reduced, the handling staff can concentrate on creating value for customers and company.

Alan Gordon, Stena Line's route director who came up with the scheme for ferry staff, says that he has never had to pay out the £1,000. Where five years ago they expected to receive four complaints for every compliment, now they find they get three compliments for every complaint. In what he believes is a direct consequence, 'We carry 60 per cent of foot passengers to Northern Ireland, and 56 per cent of cars.'

Whereas many companies are content merely to cut the rate of complaints, careful monitoring of the handling process reveals where products or services can be improved, and how they are best sold to customers. Charles Reed, customer services director at Nationwide, says that 40 per cent of complainants have been found to go on to consider other products. 'They're your best advocates,' he adds. For that reason, he strongly opposes any move to outsource the building society's four call centres. 'It is a core part of our business to talk to customers. Our directors regularly meet 100 or more customers in evening sessions, and we record and analyse their comments.' There will always be some mistakes, so ensure that staff nearest the customers are empowered to remedy them.

Source: Lester, T., 'The cost of not caring for your customers', *Financial Times*, 29 January 2006. Copyright © Tom Lester, reproduced with permission.

Discussion questions

1 Identify and discuss the implications for managers and supervisors of giving this type of decision-making power to front-line employees.

2 Analyse and explain how the implications of empowering front-line staff might differ if the organisation is a public sector one (for instance, a benefits agency or a hospital) rather than a business.

SYNOPSIS

● Underlying the study of organisational behaviour is the nature of corporate strategy for the organisation as a whole. The effective management of people requires a clear understanding of the business that the organisation is in. Corporate strategy highlights the importance of the overall direction of the organisation, its goals and objectives and the expectations of shareholders. All organisations have some function to perform and some incentive for their existence and for their operations. The goals of an organisation determine the nature of its outputs and the series of activities through which the outputs are achieved.

● The goals of the organisation may be pursued in accordance with an underlying ideology or philosophy that determines the culture of the organisation and governs the overall conduct of its operations. The concept of organisational goals serves a number of important functions, but there are potential disadvantages and limitations with this approach. Strictly, organisations have no goals, only people do.

Members of an organisation have different and often conflicting goals. Management has a responsibility to clarify organisational goals and to attempt to integrate personal goals with the overall objectives of the organisation.

● Organisational survival is dependent upon a series of exchanges between the organisation and its environment. In recent years it has become increasingly popular for organisations to produce a mission statement and/or vision of their purpose and general direction. However, such a statement is likely to be of value only if the organisation actually practises what it preaches. The goals of an organisation are translated into objectives and policy that provide corporate guidelines for the operation and management of the organisation.

● The choice of objectives is an essential part of the decision-making process involving future courses of action. Policy is developed within the framework of objectives. It provides the basis for decision-making and the course of action to follow in order to achieve objectives. Although the objective of profit maximisation is undoubtedly important, it is not by itself a sufficient criterion for the effective management of a business organisation. In practice, there are many other considerations and motivations which affect the desire

for the greatest profit or maximum economic efficiency.

● In striving to satisfy its goals and achieve its objectives, the organisation cannot operate in isolation from the environment of which it is part. The power and influence of business organisations should be tempered with its broad corporate social responsibilities (CSR). These responsibilities are often viewed in terms of organisational stakeholders. There is growing attention to the subject of CSR, including concerns for global responsibilities. There is, however, a blurred distinction between the exercise of genuine social responsibilities and actions taken in pursuit of organisational efficiency.

● The importance of CSR and how a company should conduct itself within society draws attention to values and ethics. There are differing assumptions about how a business should act, such as shareholder-centred or a stakeholder view. An example is the debate over the increasing number of organisations 'offshoring' activities to locations elsewhere in the world. The scope of business ethics is very broad and gives rise to a number of questions with no single view of what is right or wrong. An increasing number of organisations now publish a code of ethics (or code of conduct) but this needs to be embedded throughout the organisation and translated into reality.

Refresh your understanding, assess your progress and begin your research with online resources at **www.pearsoned.co.uk/mullins**

REVIEW AND DISCUSSION QUESTIONS

1 Discuss critically the purpose, nature and practical value of corporate strategy.

2 What do you see as the importance of organisational ideology or philosophy? Explain the extent to which there is a clear ideology or set of principles that govern the overall conduct of your organisation.

3 Distinguish between objectives and policy. Identify examples of objectives and policy in your organisation, and comment on how effectively you believe they have been implemented.

4 To what extent do you believe that profit maximisation is a sufficient criterion for the effective management of a business organisation? What other indicators might be applied in terms of organisational performance and results?

5 Assess the practical relevance of (i) the balanced scorecard and (ii) a SWOT analysis.

6 Discuss critically the extent to which you accept the concept of corporate social responsibilities.

7 How would you attempt to explain the meaning and significance of organisational values and business ethics?

8 Comment critically on the code of ethics (or code of conduct) for your organisation; or if one does not exist, draw up your own suggested code.

ASSIGNMENT 1

Obtain the mission/vision statements for three different organisations (including your university, college or work organisation).

Critically evaluate the extent to which each of these statements:

● gives a clear indication of the main purpose and general direction of the organisation;

● is written in clear, specific, substantial and meaningful language; and

● appears likely to inspire members of the organisation.

In the case of your own organisation, comment critically with supporting examples on the perceived value of the mission statement and the extent to which the wording is put into practice at the operational level. Explain what changes, if any, you would make to the mission statement.

What conclusions do you draw from this assignment?

ASSIGNMENT 2

a Detail fully what you believe are the social responsibilities or obligations of your own, or some other work organisation of your choice, and identify the major stakeholders.

b Give specific examples of the ways in which the organisation has attempted to satisfy, and/or has failed to satisfy, responsibilities or obligations to these stakeholders.

c Specify the extent to which attention has been given to values in the organisation, and to the principles, standards and expected practices or judgements of 'good' (ethical) behaviour.

d Compare your observations with those of your colleagues and summarise what conclusions you draw.

PERSONAL AWARENESS AND SKILLS EXERCISE

Objectives

Completing this exercise should help you to enhance the following skills:

● Clarify the work values and beliefs that are important to you.

● Examine your sensitivity to, and dealings with, other people.

● Debate and justify with colleagues the nature of your values and beliefs.

Exercise

You are required to:

a rate the following items: 5 (extremely important for me); 4 (very important for me); 3 (average importance for me); 2 (not important for me); 1 (I would oppose this). What is required are your genuine beliefs and feelings about each item, not what others think or believe, but what you personally and honestly believe and feel about each item.

1 There should be clear allocation of objectives and accountability for them _____

2 We should be open and honest in all our dealings with each other _____

3 People's talents should be recognised, developed and correctly utilised _____

Personal awareness and skills exercise – continued

4 One should give acknowledgement and praise to those in authority _____

5 There are clear rules about what we should and should not do in getting the job done _____

6 Conflicts should be surfaced and resolved rather than allowed to simmer _____

7 The causes of problems should be directed away from oneself _____

8 Encouragement and support should be placed above criticism _____

9 Problems should be tackled and resolved in co-operation with others _____

10 What is right should be placed above who is right _____

11 Clear standard procedures should be in place for all important jobs _____

12 One should become visible and build up one's personal image _____

13 Equity and fairness should be applied to all regardless of status or standing _____

14 Excellence should be our aim in all that we do professionally and administratively _____

15 We give close attention to codes of conduct since this is what builds character _____

16 We should keep each other informed and practise open and friendly communication _____

17 We know who should be making the decisions and refer decisions to the right person _____

18 Everyone and their contribution should be treated with respect and dignity _____

19 We should meet all our commitments to one another – we do what we say we will do _____

20 One should form networks of support among those with influence _____

21 There are clear reporting relationships – who reports to whom – and we stick to them _____

22 People should take responsibility for their own decisions and actions _____

23 Everyone should be committed to personal growth and life-long learning _____

24 Situations or events should be created so as to justify the advancement of one's goals _____

25 Performance should be assessed against objectives and standards declared up-front _____

26 Policies should be clear and not changed until there is proof that they need changing _____

27 Everyone's needs should be given equal standing regardless of their position or status _____

28 We should be committed to the service of others rather than ourselves _____

29 Positive relationships should be established with those who have influence _____

30 Warmth and affection should be demonstrated in our work relationships _____

31 Individual productivity and performance should be encouraged and actively promoted _____

32 We all know what our jobs are and we stick to our defined responsibilities _____

33 Those from disadvantaged backgrounds should be helped to catch up with others _____

34 One should expect to get support from those to whom we have given past support _____

35 Goals should be challenging and stretch people to higher levels of achievement _____

b In small groups, compare and discuss, frankly and openly, your ratings with those of your colleagues. Be prepared to justify your ratings but also listen with an open mind to the views of your colleagues.

Further information will be provided by your tutor.

Source: Misselhorn, A., *The Head and Heart of Management*, Organization Develeopment Consultants (SA) (2003), p. 36. Reproduced with permission from Organization Development Consultants.

Discussion

● How difficult was it for you to complete your ratings?

● How much agreement was there among members of your group? Did this surprise you?

● To what extent were you influenced to rethink your values or beliefs?

CASE STUDY

318 Mondays To Go … The London Olympics

There's no complacency here, because we will need every one of those 318 Mondays there are between now and the opening ceremony.[62]

All organisations have objectives, which may be expressed more or less formally. Sometimes, such objectives provide a very clear and very public statement of the whole purpose of the organisation, as well as a stark binary test of its effectiveness. The organisation established to make the London 2012 Olympics happen is one such case – as its website (with its real-time countdown graphic) explains, the games will run from Friday 27 July 2012, by which time everything has to be ready.[63] And being ready in 2012 will be the result of successfully co-ordinating the efforts of dozens of other independent organisations – 'only slightly late' is just not an option.

Recent experience of major UK sports facility development has often been mixed, with a number of very public delays to the redevelopment of the Wembley football ground for example, so it is unsurprising that media reports about the 2012 Olympics often focus on the potential for failure. At a different level, this critical time-dependence will be familiar to many organisations; specialist events management firms, for example, make a business from the effective co-ordination of a range of inputs towards a fixed target date. At a personal level we might even consider the organisation of a graduation ceremony, birthday party or wedding in the same way.

The quote at the top of this case is from a BBC radio interview with Lord Coe, Chairman of the London Organising Committee for the Olympic Games and Paralympic Games (LOCOG) on the first anniversary of the award of the 2012 games to London. In the preamble to the interview, the reporter recounted the apocryphal story of the International Olympic Committee official who visited Athens in early 2004 to check on the progress towards the summer Olympics in that year. 'All going well?' he asked the head building contractor. 'Sure, yes, we're making good progress', replied the contractor. 'So, it's all going to be ready for the Opening Ceremony, then?' enquired the official, a little tensely. 'Oh yes, that'll be OK … What date's that again?' said the contractor with practised assurance. 'Friday 13 August', said the official, expectantly. There was a pause' 'Err … would that be morning or afternoon?'

Organising, publicising and staging London 2012 is the responsibility of Lord Coe's LOCOG organisation, which will report to the International Olympic Committee. In the early stages, LOCOG will be a relatively small organisation, co-ordinating the efforts of many other bodies, but it is envisaged that around 100 000 people will be working on the games by 2012: 3 000 directly employed staff, 70 000 volunteers and a large number of contractors. Carrying out LOCOG's development programme will be the responsibility of a separate organisation – the Olympic Delivery Authority (ODA), which is co-located with LOCOG in Canary Wharf, East London.

The end product of London 2012 is diverse and complex – the Olympics will include 26 sports and the Paralympics 19. These events will require a total of 25 venues in five groups of centres, with the all-new Olympic Park in East London as the prime location. Operationally, 500 000 spectators are expected on each of the days of the games, with train facilities to be developed to the capacity to deliver 240 000 visitors per hour at peak. Stage-managing and co-ordinating these events efficiently and safely will be a task of immense complexity in itself, but perhaps less challenging than the co-ordination task in the preceding six years.

Source: Empics Sports Photo Agency

The London Organising Committee for the Olympic Games may have a clear objective, but that doesn't make the task easy for Chairman Sebastian Coe.

A marathon project

Funding London 2012 is also complex: a public sector funding of more than £2 billion for the infrastructure development has been agreed, comprising contributions from the National Lottery, London council tax (local tax paid by London residents) and the London

Development Agency (responsible for assisting economic development in the London area). The UK government is also funding a substantial programme of transport and other infrastructural improvement in East London. Running the Games themselves is expected to cost about £2 billion, which is expected to come from the private sector. In addition, LOCOG will receive a share of the International Olympic Committee's broadcasting revenues and the benefits of its own marketing programme.

Before 2012 the project led by the ODA must ensure the preparation of the Olympic Park infrastructure and surrounding site; this entails building new permanent venues, Olympic transport projects, the Olympic Village and a number of temporary facilities. Developing the facilities for this worldwide event was challenging from the outset. The land designated for the Olympic Park, for example, was already in use in one way or another when the Games were awarded to London, raising questions of ownership, compensation and regulation. The ODA has been equipped with statutory powers to enable it to deal with these issues before the substantial tendering process can begin. Some of the facilities to be provided will be temporary in nature, but the project as a whole also aims to provide a lasting legacy to the area and to London and the UK as a whole. Throughout the development, the theme of environmental sustainability must also be emphasised. ODA Chief Executive David Higgins commented in a recent interview[64] that long-term legacy development planning was likely to take the most time in developing the main planning application. The ODA identifies a number of key partners in this project, including Transport for London, the London Development Agency, the London Thames Gateway Development Corporation, as well as a number of other local government organisations. Working with this range of independent partners will require considerable skills of communication and co-ordination, and skill in balancing the range of interests that is likely to arise. ODA also needs to ensure that development contracts are awarded to the very best providers that can be attracted. Towards that end, ODA has been associated with the London 2012 Roadshow around the UK in 2006, the aim of which is to ensure that maximum awareness, interest and participation can be achieved and to make the Olympics a national, not just a London, event.

As mentioned above, London residents will be making a substantial contribution to the funding of the infrastructure development from their local tax payments. Not surprisingly, the Mayor of London's website goes to some lengths to explain the benefits to London of the 2012 Olympics.[65] For the Mayor, the benefits to London are in terms of economic development and regeneration, employment, infrastructure improvement, culture and sustainability.

Learning from experience

One year after the initial announcement, the International Olympic Committee reported itself to be pleased with progress in London. At the same time, Olympics Minister Tessa Jowell expressed confidence about budgetary management'

> We are carrying out a review of all the costs, and that will be a continuing discipline,' she said. 'We expect some costs to rise, but others will come down. We are right on top of that process.[66]

LOCOG is also taking the opportunity to learn from its counterparts in Italy, where the Winter Olympics took place in 2006, and China which hosts the Beijing 2008 Olympics. Its chief executive Paul Deighton commented that the Beijing experience had highlighted the importance of getting the long-term use of the facilities decided as early as possible, in order that construction could proceed continuously.[67]

After just one year, change and development could be seen on all fronts: the key appointments had been made and a strong team assembled. Eighty-six per cent of the land needed had been acquired, although some local resistance to the compulsory purchase orders remained. Fifty electricity pylons and transmission cables had been buried as a key preparatory task to redevelopment and work was under way on developments to the transport infrastructure. Problems such as contaminated land are likely to arise in some places, which will test the resilience of the plans. In commercial terms, already 60 per cent of the major sponsorship of the Games had been signed up and a new parliamentary bill passed to provide safeguards against ticket touts and 'ambush marketing' (the intrusion of unauthorised publicity).[68]

As the Mayor of London commented in a newspaper article in 2003, while the bid was being prepared

> The lessons of the Dome, Wembley and Picketts Lock will serve as cautionary tales for whoever heads the team for the Olympic bid, but they cannot be used as an excuse for avoiding ambitious projects. Our competitor cities too will have learned from previous failed sporting bids and less than successful projects. The expected battle between New York, London, Paris and Moscow will be a clash of the titans. Hosting the 2012 Olympics is one of the most ambitious projects we will have seen in Britain for many years, but as any sportsperson will tell you, you don't get anywhere without ambition.[69]

The organisation created to achieve that ambition has been careful to assign clear responsibilities for the many tasks involved. Some of the tasks will be carried out by direct employees of the LOCOG/ODA organisation, but the bulk of the work will be done by contractors to the ODA and by the co-ordinated efforts of independent partner organisations. The unique combination of scale,

complexity, prominence and complete inflexibility of the opening date make this an extraordinary organisational challenge. When asked whether the Olympic Park will be built in time, David Higgins, whose experience is based on the successful Sydney 2000 Olympics, replied simply:

Of course it will. Every Olympic city always builds it; they eventually finish it, some with more heartaches than others.[70]

Your tasks

1 The London 2012 project has a single overriding goal. How could the ideas of the goal model approach be applied to understand how that overriding goal might be achieved?

2 Make a list of stakeholders of the London 2012 project. Analyse the interest of each group in the project and identify the main issues that the London 2012 project will have to manage in balancing stakeholder interests.

3 Outline a SWOT analysis for the London 2012 project. What are the key organisational resources and skills that will need to be deployed in managing these opportunities and risks?

4 Identify ways in which the experience of managing a major project with a single goal differ from that of managing a regular process which does not have such a simple 'binary test' of success or failure. Suggest what different demands might be made of a manager in each of the two types of circumstance and what different skills might be required.

Notes and references

1 See, for example: Morley, M. 'What Business Are You In?', *Professional Manager*, March 1997, pp. 12–13.

2 Johnson, G., Scholes, K. and Whittington, R. *Exploring Corporate Strategy*, Seventh edition, Financial Times Prentice Hall (2005), p. 9.

3 Andrews, K. *The Concept of Corporate Strategy*, Irwin (1971), in Lynch, R. *Corporate Strategy*, Fourth edition, Financial Times Prentice Hall (2006), p. 6.

4 Tilles, S. 'Making Strategy Explicit', in Ansoff, H. I. (ed.) *Business Strategy*, Penguin (1969).

5 Johnson, G., Scholes, K. and Whittington, R. *Exploring Corporate Strategy*, Seventh edition, Financial Times Prentice Hall (2005), p. 448.

6 Allen, R. S. and Helms, M. M. 'Employee Perceptions of the Relationship Between Strategy, Rewards and Organizational Performance', *Journal of Business Strategies*, vol. 19, no. 2, Fall 2002, pp. 115–39.

7 Richardson, B. and Thompson, J. 'Strategic Competency in the 1990s', *Administrator*, July 1994, pp. 2–6.

8 Lloyd, B. 'In my Opinion', *Management Today*, August 2001, p. 8.

9 Lynch, R. *Corporate Strategy*, Fourth edition, Financial Times Prentice Hall (2006), p. 22.

10 Ansoff, H. I. (ed.) *Business Strategy*, Penguin (1969).

11 See, for example: Hannagan, T. *Management: Concepts & Practices*, Fourth edition, Financial Times Prentice Hall (2005), p. 363.

12 Pitman, B. (Sir) 'In my Opinion', *Management Today*, June 2000, p.14.

13 Mills, D. Q. and Friesen, G. B. 'Empowerment', in Crainer, S. and Dearlove, D. *Financial Times Handbook of Management*, Second edition, Financial Times Prentice Hall (2001), p. 335.

14 Watson, T. *Organising and Managing Work*, Second edition, Financial Times Prentice Hall (2006)

15 McGregor, D. *The Human Side of Enterprise*, Penguin (1987), p. 55.

16 See, for example: Brown, A. 'Organizational Culture: The Key to Effective Leadership and Organizational Development', *Leadership and Organization Development Journal*, vol. 13, no. 2, 1992, pp. 3–6.

17 Brech, E. F. L. (ed.) *The Principles and Practice of Management*, Third edition, Longman (1975).

18 Lucas, E. 'Believe It or Not, Values Can Make a Difference', *Professional Manager*, November 1999, pp. 10–12

19 Dainty, P. and Anderson, M. 'Mindsets For Managers', in Chowdhury, S. *Management 21C*, Financial Times Prentice Hall (2000), p. 110.

20 Cloke, K. and Goldsmith, J. The End of Management and the Rise of Organizational Democracy, Jossey-Bass (2002).

21 Mills, D. Q. and Friesen, G. B. 'Empowerment', in Crainer, S. and Dearlove, D. *Financial Times Handbook of Management*, Second edition, Financial Times Prentice Hall (2001), p. 334.

22 www.managers.org.uk (accessed 26 June 2006).

23 Perrin, L. and Tavakoli, I. 'Mission Impossible Without Commitment', *Professional Manager*, July 1997, pp. 14–15.

24 Reeves, C. 'Making vision statements meaningful', *Manager, British Journal of Administrative Management*, April/May 2006.

25 Gratton, L. *Living Strategy: Putting People at the Heart of Corporate Purpose*, Financial Times Prentice Hall (2000), p. 55.

26 Summers, J. and Nowicki, M. 'Achievement and Balance: What Do Managers Really Want?', *Healthcare Financial Management*, vol. 56, no. 3, March 2002, pp. 80–4.

27 Christensen, C. M., Raynor, M. E. and Anthony, S. D. 'Six Keys to Creating New-Growth Businesses', *Harvard Management Update*, 2003, p. 3.

28 Drucker, P. F. *The Practice of Management*, Heinemann Professional (1989), p. 59.

29 Kaplan, R. S. and Norton, D. P. *The Balanced Scorecard: Translating Strategy into Action*, Harvard Business School Press (1996).

30 van de Vliet, A. 'The New Balancing Act', *Management Today*, July 1997, pp. 78–80.

31 Tonge, R. and Callaghan, C. 'Using the Balanced Scorecard in the Public Sector', *Chartered Secretary*, October 1997, pp. 18–19.

32 Drucker, P. F. *Managing for Results*, Heinemann Professional (1989). See also: Drucker, P. F. *Managing in Turbulent Times*, Heinemann (1980).

33 Stern, S. 'Leading Lights', *Management Today*, June 2004, pp. 72–3.

34 Earl, M. 'IT Strategy in The New Economy', in Pickford, J. (ed) *Financial Times Mastering Management 2.0*, Financial Times Prentice Hall (2001), p. 109.

35 Kermally, S. 'E-strategy is Key to Future Success', *Professional Manager*, July 2001, pp. 28–9.

36 Levine, S. R. 'The Value-Based Edu-Leader', in Chowdhury, S. *Management 21C*, Financial Times Prentice Hall (2000), p. 90.

37 Cable, Vincent (MP) 'Hard-nosed case for CSR' *Professional Manager*, vol. 14, no. 3, May 2005, p. 11.

38 See, for example: Piggott, G. 'Open Relationships', *Holland Herald*, January 2003, pp. 54–64.

39 Harris, J. 'EU Acts to Promote More Socially Responsible Companies', *Social Agenda*, October 2002, pp. 3–4.

40 Chant, Ann 'In my opinion', *Management Today*, May 2005, p. 12.

41 HRH The Prince of Wales, Foreword to Grayson, D. and Hodges, A. *Everybody's Business: Managing Global Risks and Opportunities in Today's Global Society*, Financial Times (2001), pp. 8–9.

42 See, for example: Worthington, I. and Britton, C. *The Business Environment*, Fifth edition, Financial Times Prentice Hall (2006).

43 Drucker, P. F. *The Practice of Management*, Heinemann Professional (1989), p. 380.

44 Reeves, R. 'Do the right thing', *Management Today*, July 2005, pp. 549.

45 BBC News, 'Powergen shuts India call centres', 15 June 2006.

46 BBC News, 'Man held in HSBC India scam probe', 28 June 2006.

47 *The Guardian*, 'Overseas Transcription errors "putting patients' lives at risk"', 21 June 2006.

48 De George, R. T. *Business Ethics*, Fifth edition, Prentice Hall (1999).

49 Friedman, M. 'The Social Responsibility of Business is to Increase Its Profits', *New York Times Magazine*, 13 September 1970, pp. 32, 122–6.

50 Sternberg, E. *Just Business*, Little Brown (1994).

51 Cannon, T. *Corporate Responsibility*, Pitman (1994), pp. 32–3.

52 Sternberg, E. *Just Business*, Little Brown (1994).

53 RSA, *Tomorrow's Company – The Role of Business in a Changing World*, Royal Society for Arts, Manufactures and Commerce (1995).

54 For a discussion, see: De George, R. T. *Business Ethics*, Fifth edition, Prentice Hall (1999).

55 Chartered Management Institute, 'Codes of Ethics' Checklist 028, August 2005.

56 Palmisano, S. 'IBM Business Conduct Guidelines' IBM, December 2005. (With thanks to Lynn Thomson, First Line Manager, IBM (UK) Ltd.)

57 Dobson, N. 'Prejudicial Interests?', *Chartered Secretary*, May 2003, pp. 22–4.

58 Allen, A. 'Up the Moral Mountain', *Chartered Secretary*, May 2001, pp. 21–2.

59 Cook, S. 'Who Cares Wins', *Management Today*, January 2003, pp. 40–7.

60 Back, P. F. 'Taking a proactive approach to ethics' *Professional Manager*, vol. 15, no. 3, May 2006, p. 37.

61 McEwan, T. *Managing Values and Beliefs in Organisations*, Financial Times Prentice Hall (2001).

62 BBC Radio interview with Lord Coe, Radio 4 'The Today Programme', 2 July 2006.

63 The London 2012 website is at www.london2012.com.

64 *Daily Telegraph*, 20 July 2006.

65 Greater London Authority 'Mayor applauds procurement principles to create truly sustainable Games' press release 8 September 2005 www.london.gov.uk/mayor/olympics [accessed 22 July 2006].

66 BBC Sport website 2006 'IOC Pleased with London progress' 21 April 2006 http://news.bbc.co.uk/sport1 [accessed 22 July 2006].

67 London 2012 11 April 2006 'Masterclass in Olympic Planning' The London 2012 Website http://www.london2012.com [accessed 22 July 2006].

68 BBC news website 6 July 2006 'Preparing for 2012' accessed 22 July 2006 http://news.bbc.co.uk/sport1.

69 Livingstone, K. 2003 'We must go for gold with London's Olympic bid' *The Observer* 12 January 2003. http://observer.guardian.co.uk [accessed 24 July 2006].

70 *Daily Telegraph*, 20 July 2006.

ORGANISATION STRUCTURE AND DESIGN

"

The quality of the relationship between line and functional managers lies at the heart of achieving both compliance to rules and an ability to work with the principles behind them. If the relationship is good, and trust and respect high, then both sides understand the importance of each other's role ... Line management knows they will always be pressing to drive harder on performance, but understand the functional roles are there to help create, and strengthen, the boundaries they must not cross.

"

Carolyn Taylor – partner in the Mettle Group
Walking the Talk: building a culture for success,
Random House (2005), p. 290

In order to achieve its goals and objectives, the work of an organisation has to be divided among its members. Some structure is necessary to make possible the effective performance of key activities and to support the efforts of staff. Structure provides the framework of an organisation and its pattern of management. It is by means of structure that the purpose and work of the organisation are carried out. The manager needs to understand the importance and effects of organisation structure and design.

Learning outcomes

After completing this chapter you should be able to:

- explain the meaning and nature of organisation structure;
- identify levels of organisation and debate the importance of the hierarchy;
- explore the main factors to be considered in the design of organisation structure and different methods for the division of work;
- debate the relevance and applications of principles of organisation and organisational relationships;
- explain the importance of good structure and the consequences of a deficient structure;
- assess the importance of structure for organisational performance;
- review the relationship between the structure of an organisation and the people who work within it.

THE MEANING AND NATURE OF ORGANISATION STRUCTURE

The purpose of structure is the division of work among members of the organisation, and the co-ordination of their activities so they are directed towards the goals and objectives of the organisation. Structure is the pattern of relationships among positions in the organisation and among members of the organisation. Structure makes possible the application of the process of management and creates a framework of order and command through which the activities of the organisation can be planned, organised, directed and controlled. The structure defines tasks and responsibilities, work roles and relationships, and channels of communication.

Structure is clearly important for any organisation, whatever its size. However, in the smaller organisations there are likely to be fewer problems of structure. The distribution of tasks, the definition of authority and responsibility, and the relationship between members of the organisation can be established on a more personal and informal basis. With increasing size, however, there is greater need for a carefully designed and purposeful form of organisation. There is need for a formal **organisational structure**. There is also need for a continual review of structure to ensure that it is the most appropriate form for the particular organisation, and in keeping with its growth and development. This is likely to be of particular importance for the very large companies.

Birkinshaw discusses the structures behind global companies and the problem for international companies of balancing bureaucracy with the benefits of size.

> *There are many ways of addressing this balancing act. One way is to work on culture, to get people to think entrepreneurially. Another way is through systems – reward systems, career management and so on. A third way is through structure – the basic lines of reporting and accountability that are typically drawn on an organisation chart. The structure is never the whole story, it is just a way of dividing responsibilities among executives. It is meaningless unless supported by appropriate systems and a consistent culture. However, structure is still surprisingly informative about strategic priorities and the work going on, so it is as good a place to start as any.* [1]

Objectives of structure The objectives of structure may be summarised as to provide for:

- the economic and efficient performance of the organisation and the level of resource utilisation;
- monitoring the activities of the organisation;
- accountability for areas of work undertaken by groups and individual members of the organisation;
- co-ordination of different parts of the organisation and different areas of work;
- flexibility in order to respond to future demands and developments, and to adapt to changing environmental influences; and
- the social satisfaction of members working in the organisation. [2]

These objectives provide the criteria for structural effectiveness. Structure, though, is not an end in itself but a means of improving organisational performance. For example, as *Heller* points out:

> *No amount of reorganising and reshuffling will increase the long-term capability of a business unless you suit the organisation to the people and to a genuinely shared purpose.*[3]

Organisation structure and culture

In previous chapters we have made the point that the organisation does not exist independently but is open to, and in continual interaction with, the broader external environment of which it is part. A major determinant of an organisation's structure is its culture. The pervasive nature of culture in terms of both external influences and 'how things are done around here' and common values, beliefs and attitudes will have a significant effect on organisational processes including the design of structure. *Watson* suggests that we must be careful not to treat structures or cultures as if they were solid 'things' that exist separately from the processes and relationships that the two concepts are intended to help us make sense of. The structure of work organisations also involves the wider context of societal structures and cultures. 'Societal structures both contribute to and result from organisational structures.' *Watson* also refers to the closeness and overlap of structure and culture. 'Many of the processes and practices we observe in an organisation could as readily be said to be part of the structure of the organisation as part of its culture.'[4] (Culture as a contingency factor of structure is discussed in Chapter 16.)

THE IMPORTANCE OF GOOD STRUCTURE

According to *Drucker*, it is the correct design of structure that is of most significance in determining organisational performance.

> *Good organisation structure does not by itself produce good performance. But a poor organisation structure makes good performance impossible, no matter how good the individual managers may be. To improve organisation structure ... will therefore always improve performance.*[5]

The importance of good structure is also emphasised by *Child*:

> *A basic structure distributes responsibilities among the members of a company. Its purpose is to contribute to the successful implementation of objectives by allocating people and resources to necessary tasks and designing responsibility and authority for their control and coordination.*[6]

The structure of an organisation affects not only productivity and economic efficiency but also the morale and job satisfaction of the workforce. Getting the structure right is the first step in organisational change.[7] Structure should be designed, therefore, so as to encourage the willing participation of members of the organisation and effective organisational performance. There is also a close relationship between organisation structure and corporate strategy although the nature of this relationship, and whether structure follows strategy or strategy follows structure, is the subject of debate.[8]

The human element

The functions of the formal structure, and the activities and defined relationships within it, exist independently of the members of the organisation who carry out the work. However, personalities are an important part of the working of the organisation. In practice, the actual

operation of the organisation and success in meeting its objectives will depend upon the behaviour of people who work within the structure and who give shape and personality to the framework. *Lord Forte*, for example, has drawn attention to the importance of the human element in organisation structure:

> *The human aspect in a business is vital: you can keep drawing squares and lines, but within these squares you must have people and they must be deeply involved with the business. If this does not happen, then the lines and squares and the diagrams mean nothing.*[9]

In an IMD survey, the commitment and involvement of employees ranked second only to top management as a key success factor for restructuring. Yet the survey also showed that almost 40 per cent of restructuring obstacles related to the failure to achieve employee commitment.[10] According to *Hannagan*, softer corporate values are being emphasised now compared to the harder values by concentrating more on staff training, developing skills and ensuring that all employees understand the organisation's values. There is a shift from the harder values of strategy, structure and systems to the softer ones of staff, skills and style.[11]

The human relations writers are critical of the emphasis on the formal organisation. They favour a structure in which there is increased participation from people at all levels of the organisation, greater freedom for the individual, and more meaningful work organisation and relationships. One of the strongest critics of the formal organisation is *Argyris*.[12] He claims that the formal, bureaucratic organisation restricts individual growth and self-fulfilment and, in the psychologically healthy person, causes a feeling of failure, frustration and conflict. Argyris argues that the organisation should provide a more 'authentic' relationship for its members.

The view of the human relations writers represents more of an attitude towards organisation than specific proposals, but it reminds us of the importance of the human element in the design of structure. Managers need to consider how structural design and methods of work organisation influence the behaviour and performance of members of the organisation.

LEVELS OF ORGANISATION

Organisations are layered. The determination of policy and decision-making, the execution of work, and the exercise of authority and responsibility are carried out by different people at varying levels of seniority throughout the organisation structure. In small organisations, these activities tend to be less distinct but in the larger organisations it is possible to look at organisations in terms of three broad interrelated levels in the hierarchical structure: **the technical level, the managerial level** and **the community level**.[13] These last two levels are often referred to as middle management and senior management.

The **technical level** is concerned with specific operations and discrete tasks, with the actual job or tasks to be done, and with performance of the technical function. Examples are the physical production of goods in a manufacturing firm, administrative processes giving direct service to the public in government departments, and the actual process of teaching in an educational establishment.

The technical level interrelates with the **managerial level**, or organisational level, which is concerned with the co-ordination and integration of work at the technical level. Decisions at the managerial level relate to the resources necessary for performance of the technical function, and to the beneficiaries of the products or services provided. Decisions will be concerned with (i) mediating between the organisation and its external environment, such as the users of the organisation's products or services, and the procurement of resources, and (ii) the 'administration' of the internal affairs of the organisation including the control of the operations of the technical function.

In turn, the managerial level interrelates with the **community level** or institutional level, concerned with broad objectives and the work of the organisation as a whole. Decisions at

the community level will be concerned with the selection of operations, and the development of the organisation in relation to external agencies and the wider social environment. Examples of the community level within organisations are the board of directors of joint stock companies, governing bodies of educational establishments which include external representatives, and trustees of non-profit organisations. Such bodies provide a mediating link between the managerial organisation and co-ordination of work of the technical organisation, and the wider community interests.

Interrelationship of levels

In practice, there is not a clear division between determination of policy and decision-making, co-ordination of activities and the actual execution of work (see Figure 15.1). Most decisions are taken with reference to the execution of wider decisions, and most execution of work involves decision. Decisions taken at the institutional level determine objectives for the managerial level, and decisions at the managerial level set objectives for the technical level. Therefore, if the organisation as a whole is to perform effectively there must be clear objectives, a soundly designed structure and good communications, both upwards and downwards, among the different levels of the organisation.

The managerial level, for example, would be unable to plan and supervise the execution of work of the technical function without the knowledge, expertise, practical know-how and enthusiasm of people who are closest to the actual tasks to be undertaken. People operating at the technical level should, therefore, make known to higher levels the practical difficulties and operational problems concerning their work. It is the duty of the managerial level to take appropriate action on this information, and to consult with people at the community or institutional level.

Not all activities concerned with the management of an organisation can be considered, necessarily, in terms of these three levels of work. There will be certain activities that are analysed more meaningfully in terms of a greater, or possibly a smaller, number of levels. In many cases movements towards more democratic organisations, empowerment, an increase in knowledge workers and technological advances have contributed to a blurring of a clear differentiation between policy, management and the execution of work. However, the three broad levels provide a basis for a critical analysis of the interrelated activities of the organisation.

Figure 15.1	Interrelated levels of organisation

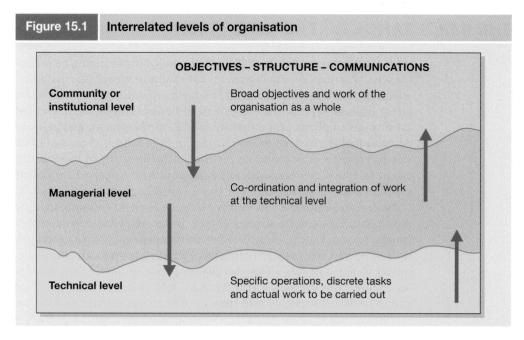

The management process in local government
An example of the interrelationship between the different levels of an organisation can be seen from the comments in the Bains Report on management in local government. The report recognises that elected members remain responsible for ultimate direction and control of the authority, key decisions on objectives and plans to attain them, and reviewing progress and performance of services. However, the report also refers to the dual nature of management and to the changing relationship between permanent officers and elected members at the different stages of the management process.

The report concludes:

> We doubt whether it is possible to divide the total management process into two separate halves, one for members and the other for officers ... That process itself can be seen as a scale, with the setting of objectives and allocation of major resources at one end, moving through the designing of programmes and plans, to the execution of those plans at the other end. As one moves through that management scale, the balance between the two elements changes from member control with officer advice at the 'objective' end to officer control with member advice at the 'execution' end.[14]

More recently, The Audit Commission has referred to the harmful gaps caused in local government and the National Health Service by the de-layering and the stripping out of middle managers which have been carried out without a full understanding of the impact on the council's management structures as a whole.[15]

Divide between senior and middle management
Rawson draws attention to the increasing absence of mutuality between senior and middle managers in both the public and private sector.

> Traditionally, senior managers have been concerned with setting the strategic direction and objectives for the organisation; middle managers with making it happen – resourcing and managing the changes. The corollary is that senior managers are concerned with results and middle managers with how these are achieved. The divide appears as middle levels complain that their seniors are solely concerned with short-term financial results and as seniors reply that the middle strata devote more effort to voicing problems than to finding solutions. In both sectors the delayering of organisations has dramatically reduced the resources available to middle managers. The divide deepens as each accuses the other of pursuing their own personal rather than organisational ends. Middle accuse senior of being concerned with their own career advancement: senior accuse middle of directing their efforts to protecting their positions.[16]

THE IMPORTANCE OF THE HIERARCHY

We have referred previously to the significance of the changing nature of the work organisation. Early writers on management, for example Weber (discussed in Chapter 2), drew attention to the importance of the hierarchy of authority. However, the increasing use of group or team approaches, the growth of flexible employment, increasing use of subcontracting, an emphasis on participation and empowerment, and many workers involved in decision-making have all led to changes in the traditional boss–subordinate relationship. This has lead to a discussion on the role of the hierarchy in modern organisations and the extent to which managers can rely solely on their perceived formal authority within the structure of the organisation.

Stewart maintains that: 'Authority is, and is likely to continue to be, less acceptable than in the past. This reflects a major change in society: what has been termed the end of the grateful society. Better educated and more independent people expect to be consulted rather than to be told what to do.'[17] However, according to *Jebb*: 'The hierarchy is not dead. It has merely changed its form. The trappings of power in the modern workplace may have been toned down but the boss is still the boss.' Jebb refers to Hampden Turner who maintains that to confuse informality with the end of the organisational pecking order is a mistake.

There is a lot of muddled thinking about hierarchies and the whole issue of how equally we treat people within companies. But treating someone as an equal does not mean they are equal. Any smart person wanting the best out of a person treats them as an equal. However informal the environment, you can't escape from a functional hierarchy although the more skilled the company's work, the fewer tiers of management and the fewer individual managers should be required.[18]

The importance of the hierarchy is also strongly emphasised by *Drucker* who asserts that: 'One hears a great deal today about "the end of the hierarchy". This is blatant nonsense. In any institution there has to be a final authority, that is, a "boss"– someone who can make the final decisions and who can expect them to be obeyed.'[19]

Is the hierarchy obsolete?

However, contrary to the views of writers such as Jebb and Drucker, *Butcher* maintains that hierarchy is in principle obsolete in the knowledge economy:

Intellectual capital possessed by knowledge workers implies management based on fragile coalition rather than control. The arguments for de-emphasizing hierarchical control are now well rehearsed. Hierarchical assignment of tasks worked well when central planning worked well, but those days are gone. Local autonomy and accountability are essential for creating organisational ability.[20]

A similar point is made by Cloke and Goldsmith who question whether we are accustomed to and have accepted that hierarchy, rules and managers are an essential part of organisational life. Have managers been seduced by the apparent power over others that a hierarchical organisation offers and by the disproportionate rewards it can provide to those at the top? If so, this is depriving individuals of the chance to develop themselves to their full potential and cluttering organisations with wasteful and counter-productive processes.[21]

According to *Gratton*, more than at any other point in time, there is now a chance to create the democratic enterprise.

Over the last decade it has become increasingly clear that through the forces of globalization, competition and more demanding customers, the structure of many companies has become flatter, less hierarchical, more fluid and virtual. The breakdown of hierarchies provides us with fertile ground on which to create a more democratic way of working.[22]

Refresh your understanding

Activity 15A
www.pearsoned.co.uk/
mullins

Critical reflection

'Organisations are a form of social stratification. Advancement through the hierarchy can reasonably be seen as an indication of merit and achievement, and a reward for hard work.' Do you think this statement has any relevance for modern work organisations? Is the idea of hierarchy still important as an indication of promotion and career progression?

THE DESIGN OF ORGANISATION STRUCTURE

It is important to bear in mind that there are many variables that influence the most appropriate organisation structure and system of management, including situational factors and the contingency approach. Changing patterns of work organisation, the demand for greater

flexibility and the multi-skilling challenge, and managerial processes such as delegation and empowerment also have a major interrelationship with structure and influence decisions on structural design, as discussed in Chapter 16.

Basic principles and considerations

While recognising that there is clearly no one right organisation, there is nevertheless, in the final analysis, an underlying need to establish a framework of order and system of command by which the work to be undertaken is accomplished successfully. This demands that attention be given to certain basic principles and considerations in the design of organisation structure, or in reviewing the effectiveness of an existing structure (*see* Figure 15.2).

These principles and considerations may perhaps appear prescriptive for the study of organisational behaviour, but they still present management with a series of important decision points.

> *Organisations are collections of people brought together for a purpose. To achieve this purpose successfully, people need to be organised within the best possible structure. Decisions on structure are primary strategic decisions. Structure can make or break an organisation.*[23]

Structure provides the framework for the activities of the organisation and must harmonise with its goals and objectives. The first step, therefore, is to examine the objectives of the organisation. Only when objectives have been clearly defined, can alternative forms of structure be analysed and compared.[24]

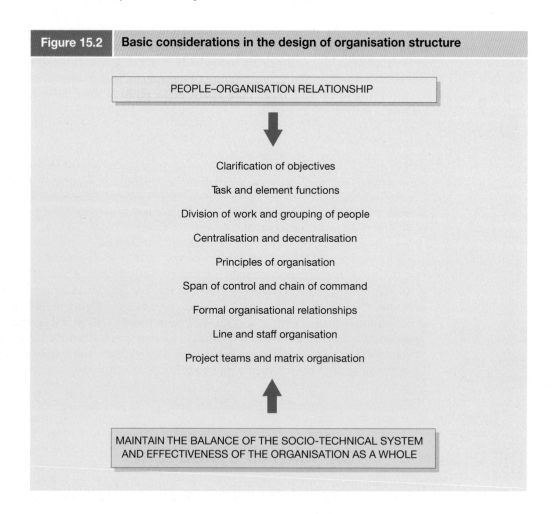

Figure 15.2 **Basic considerations in the design of organisation structure**

PEOPLE–ORGANISATION RELATIONSHIP

Clarification of objectives

Task and element functions

Division of work and grouping of people

Centralisation and decentralisation

Principles of organisation

Span of control and chain of command

Formal organisational relationships

Line and staff organisation

Project teams and matrix organisation

MAINTAIN THE BALANCE OF THE SOCIO-TECHNICAL SYSTEM AND EFFECTIVENESS OF THE ORGANISATION AS A WHOLE

CLARIFICATION OF OBJECTIVES

A clear definition of objectives is necessary in order to provide a basis for the division of work and grouping of duties into sub-units. The objectives for these sub-units must be related to the objectives of the organisation as a whole in order that an appropriate pattern of structure can be established. Clearly stated and agreed objectives (discussed in Chapter 14) will provide a framework for the design of structure, and a suitable pattern of organisation to achieve those objectives. The nature of the organisation and its strategy will indicate the most appropriate organisational levels for different functions and activities, and the formal relationships between them. Clearly defined objectives will help facilitate systems of communication between different parts of the organisation and the extent of decentralisation and delegation. The formal structure should help make possible the attainment of objectives. It should assist in the performance of the essential functions of the organisation and the major activities that it needs to undertake.

TASK AND ELEMENT FUNCTIONS

In order to produce some good, or provide some service, there are four essential functions that the organisation must perform.

1 The good or service must be developed.
2 Something of value must be created. In the case of the business organisation this might be the production or manufacture of a product; in the case of the public sector organisation the provision of a service.
3 The product or services must be marketed. They must be distributed or made available to those who are to use them.
4 Finance is needed in order to make available the resources used in the development, creation and distribution of the products or services provided.

These essential functions of developing the good or service, manufacturing the good or providing the service, marketing them, and financing the organisation, are what *Woodward* refers to as the **'task' functions**. These are the basic activities of the organisation that are related to the actual completion of the productive process and directed towards specific and definable end-results. To ensure the efficient achievement of overall objectives of the organisation, the results of the task functions must be co-ordinated.[25]

Other activities of the organisation are not directed towards specific and definable ends but are supportive of the task functions and an intrinsic part of the management process. These are referred to as **'element' functions** and include, for example, human resources, planning, management services, public relations, quality control and maintenance. In other organisations, noticeably in service industries involving direct customer contact, human resource management can be seen as closely associated with a task function.[26] In the majority of organisations, however, the personnel function does not normally have any direct accountability for the performance of a specific end-task.

Implications for organisation structure The two kinds of functions, task and element, differ in a number of ways and these differences have important implications for organisation. Failure to distinguish between the two types of functions can lead to confusion in the planning of structure and in the relationship between members of the organisation. For example, in her study of the management organisation of firms in this country, *Woodward* comments on the bad relationships between accountants and other managers referred to during the study. One reason for this hostility was the bringing together of two quite separate financial functions essential to the efficient operation of a business.

Nature of the work performed Division may be according to the nature of the work performed where there is some special common feature of the work such as the need for speedy decisions, accuracy, confidentiality/security, or where local conditions require first-hand knowledge not immediately available elsewhere. Another example may be the grouping of equipment or machinery which is noisy or which produces dust, fumes or unpleasant odours. When common processes are used in a range of different activities, this may also be used as the basis of division. This method of grouping includes, for example, the decision as to whether to establish a centralised resource centre for all departments of the organisation or to allow each department to have its own service. With manufacturing industries, a range of products may pass through a common production facility or configuration of machines that may be grouped together in a single unit – for example, a batch production engineering firm having departments based on like skills or methods of operation.

Common time scales Division may be according to time scales, for example shift working and the extent to which different tasks should be undertaken by different shifts. In a further education college there may be separate departments or groupings to deal with the different needs of full-time day students and part-time evening students. Another example of activities grouped according to time is in a hotel. Activities in the kitchen tend to be short term, especially when guests in the restaurant are waiting to be served, and a range of different tasks have to be co-ordinated very quickly. Other activities, for example market research and forecasting future room occupancy, are longer-term decisions and subject to different organisational requirements.

Staff employed The allocation of duties and responsibilities may be according to experience or where a particular technical skill or special qualification is required – for example, the division of work between surgeons, doctors and nurses, or between barristers, solicitors and legal executives. Another example is the sharing of routine work processes among members of a supervised group. In smaller organisations the allocation of work may be on an *ad hoc*, personal basis according to the knowledge and skills contributed by individuals. Work may also be planned deliberately to give a variety of tasks and responsibilities to provide improved job satisfaction or to assist in the training of staff.

Customer or people to be served Separate groups may be established to deal with different consumer requirements – for example, the division between trade or retail customers or between home or export sales. In hospitals there are different groupings dealing with, for example, patients in the gynaecology, geriatric and children's wards. In large clothes shops there may be separate departments for men's, women's and children's clothing. Government departments are often grouped by this method and work is divided according to for whom the services are provided – for example, the unemployed, low-pay families, students, young people or senior citizens. A further example is the provision of canteen services which may be grouped by customer demand according to price, range or standard of meals available, speed of service, or type of customer; this gives rise to separate facilities such as the directors' dining room, or for staff and students in educational establishments.

Combination of groupings

These different ways of dividing work can be combined in various forms and most organisations will contain examples of alternative combinations for grouping activities. Some activities might be grouped according to one method and other activities according to a different method. Decisions on the methods of grouping will include considerations of:

- the need for co-ordination;
- the identification of clearly defined divisions of work;
- economy;
- the process of managing the activities;

locking, or where responsibility is concerned more with the performance of specific tasks, the span of control may be larger.

influencing span of control

Practical studies of span of control, however, show that it varies widely in different organisations and that the average span is larger than suggested by Graicunas and Urwick. For example, in *Woodward*'s study of 100 manufacturing firms in south-east Essex (discussed in Chapter 16) she found that the size of span of control varied directly with technology and type of production system.[32]

In addition to the type of technology or production system there are a number of other factors that will influence the limit of span of control. These include:

- the nature of the organisation, the complexity of the work and the similarity of functions, and the range of responsibilities;
- the ability and personal qualities of the manager including the capacity to cope with interruptions;
- the amount of time the manager has available from other activities to spend with subordinates;
- the ability and training of subordinate staff, the strength of their motivation and commitment, and the extent of direction and guidance needed;
- the effectiveness of co-ordination and the nature of communication and control systems;
- the physical location or geographical spread of subordinates;
- the length of the scalar chain, discussed in the following section.

ince of If the span of control is **too wide**, it becomes difficult to supervise subordinates effectively
control and this places more stress on the manager. With larger groupings, informal leaders and sub-groups or cliques are more likely to develop and these may operate contrary to the policy of management. There may be lack of time to carry out all activities properly. Planning and development, training, inspection and control may suffer in particular, leading to poor job performance. A wide span of control may limit opportunities for promotion. Too wide a span of control may also result in a slowness to adapt to change or to the introduction of new methods or procedures.

If the span of control is **too narrow**, this may present a problem of co-ordination and consistency in decision-making and hinder effective communications across the organisation structure. Morale and initiative of subordinates may suffer as a result of too close a level of supervision. Narrow spans of control increase administrative costs and can prevent the best use being made of the limited resource of managerial talent. They can lead to additional levels of authority in the organisation creating an unnecessarily long chain of command.

HAIN OF COMMAND

This refers to the number of different levels in the structure of the organisation, the chain, or lines, of hierarchical command sometimes known as the 'scalar chain'. The **chain of command** establishes the vertical graduation of authority and responsibility, and the framework for superior–subordinate relationships in an unbroken line down from the top of the organisation (*see* Figure 15.7). Every person must know their position within the structure of the organisation. Most organisation charts demonstrate that this principle is used widely as a basis for organisational design. A clear line of authority and responsibility is necessary for the effective operation of the organisation.

- avoiding conflict; and
- the design of work organisation which takes account of the nature of staff employed, their interests and job satisfaction.

Management must decide upon the most significant factors that will determine the methods for division of work and linking of activities appropriate to the changing circumstances within the particular organisation.

CENTRALISATION AND DECENTRALISATION

A critical decision point that arises from division of work and grouping of activities is the extent of centralisation or **decentralisation**. Most organisations necessarily involve a degree of decentralisation arising from such features as an increase in size, the geographical separation of different parts of the organisation, or the need to extend activities or services to remote areas. Our main concern is with decentralisation or devolution in terms of specific delegation or empowerment to sub-units or groups within the organisation such that they enjoy a measure of autonomy or independence.

The advantages often claimed for centralisation tend to relate to economic and administrative considerations. However, such advantages frequently are not realised fully, and do not lead to an actual improvement in service. There are a number of contrary arguments against centralisation, including the criticism that it creates a more mechanistic structure and may result in lengthening the chain of command. There are also positive arguments, which tend to relate more to behavioural considerations, in favour of decentralisation (*see* Figure 15.6).

Extent of decentralisation

The balance between centralisation and decentralisation is one of the major debates in organisation structure. The advisability of decentralisation must be considered in terms of the nature

Figure 15.6	**Advantages of centralisation or decentralisation**

Advantages of centralisation

- the easier implementation of a common policy for the organisation as a whole;
- providing a consistent strategy across the organisation;
- preventing sub-units becoming too independent;
- making for easier co-ordination and management control;
- improved economies of scale and a reduction in overhead costs;
- greater use of specialisation, including better facilities and equipment;
- improved decision-making which might otherwise be slower and a result of compromise because of diffused authority.

Advantage of decentralisation

- enables decisions to be made closer to the operational level of work;
- increased responsiveness to local circumstances;
- improved level of personal customer service;
- more in keeping with developments in flatter and more flexible structures;
- support services, such as adminstration, are more likely to be effective if provided as close as possible to the activities they are intended to serve;
- provides opportunities for training and development in management;
- usually, it has an encouraging effect on the motivation and morale of staff.

of the product or service provided, policy-making, the day-to-day management of the organisation and the need for standardisation of procedures, or conditions or terms of employment of staff. Decentralisation generally tends to be easier to implement in private sector organisations than in the public sector organisations where there is a greater demand for the accountability of their operations, regularity of procedures and uniformity of treatment.

However, it is not always easy to gauge the true extent of decentralisation. With flatter organisation structures, managements may claim a greater degree of decentralisation but in reality this may not always be the case. The extent and nature of decentralisation will vary from organisation to organisation and also over time. The balance between centralisation and decentralisation will be affected by such factors as the importance of decision-making, the urgency of the situation and time scales and also by technological developments, changes in structure, the prevailing organisational climate and the nature of staff employed.

The growing emphasis on participation and empowerment suggests a focus of attention on the principles of decentralisation, yet senior management still needs to maintain effective co-ordination and overall control of the activities of the organisation as a whole. Ideally, business organisations should attempt to blend the benefits of decentralisation for customer orientation and increased responsiveness, with the advantages of size, common resources and economies of scale. In the case of the big company, *Barnevik*, for example, believes in both the vital importance of decentralisation for local entrepreneurship, and exploiting the advantages of a big company: 'We want to be global and local, big and small, radically decentralised with central reporting and control. If we can resolve those contradictions we can create real organisational advantage.'[28]

> **Critical reflection**
>
> ????
>
> 'The trend towards flatter structures, de-layering and virtual working leads to confusion and uncertainty, and can promote a climate of mistrust and low morale.' Do you think there is any truth in this statement? 'The reality is that most people would prefer to have a clearly established formal relationship with management and with their fellow workers.' To what extent do you agree with this contention?

PRINCIPLES OF ORGANISATION

The classical writers placed emphasis on the definition of structure in terms of division of work, chain of command, span of control and reporting relationships. Attention was focused on the requirements of the formal organisation and the search for a common set of principles applicable to all circumstances. Probably the leading authority in the UK was *Lyndall Urwick*, who originally specified eight principles of organisation, but revised these to ten in his later writing.[29]

1 **The principle of the objective**
'Every organisation and every part of the organisation must be an expression of the purpose of the undertaking concerned, or it is meaningless and therefore redundant.'

2 **The principle of specialisation**
'The activities of every member of any organised group should be confined, as far as possible, to the performance of a single function.'

3 **The principle of co-ordination**
'The purpose of organising *per se*, as distinguished from the purpose of the undertaking, is to facilitate co-ordination: unity of effort.'

4 **The principle of authority**
'In every organised group the supreme authority must r
a clear line of authority to every individual in the group

5 **The principle of responsibility**
'The responsibility of the superior for the acts of the sub

6 **The principle of definition**
'The content of each position, both the duties involved, t
contemplated and the relationships with other position
writing and published to all concerned.'

7 **The principle of correspondence**
'In every position, the responsibility and the authority shc

8 **The principle of span of control**
'No person should supervise more than five, or at the r
whose work interlocks.'

9 **The principle of balance**
'It is essential that the various units of an organisation shou

10 **The principle of continuity**
'Re-organisation is a continuous process: in every undertaki
be made for it.'

Relevance of principles As mentioned in Chapter 2, the idea of common sets of prin
management has been subject to much criticism. Many of the
ments expressed in non-operation terms and give little basis for
they tend to view people as a given rather than as a variable in th
such limitations, the principles do provide general guidance on t
tions and, as such, it is difficult to argue against them. It is als
much of the more recent writing on the subject appears to be base
inal statements.[30] The basic concept can be of value to the practica
suit the demands of the particular situation, including the nature
sation. The proper application of these principles is likely to help
performance.

Two of the more specific principles of general interest in the stru
are, (i) the span of control, and (ii) the chain of command.

SPAN OF CONTROL

The **span of control** arises in line authority and refers to the numbe
report directly to a given manager or supervisor. It does not refer to t
operating staff, that is those staff who report first to another person. F
responsibility' or 'span of supervision' is sometimes considered to be

V. A. Graicunas developed a mathematical formula for the span o
tion of the number of subordinates who can effectively be supervised
of direct and cross relationships,

$$R = n\left(\frac{2n}{n} + n - 1\right)$$

where n is the number of subordinates, and R is the number of inter
For example, with five subordinates the total number of interrelatic
attention of the manager is 100; with six subordinates the number of
222. Urwick supports the idea of Graicunas and, as we have seen from
states that the span of control should not exceed five or at the most six
whose work interlocks. At lower levels of the organisation, however, whe

It seems to be generally accepted, however, that for reasons of morale and to help decision-making and communications there should be as few levels as possible in the chain of command. There is the danger of adding to the structure in such a way that it results in increased hierarchical authority and control, leads to the risk of empire building and the creation of unnecessary work in justification of the new position. If efforts are made to reduce the number of levels, however, this may bring about an increase in the span of control with the resulting difficulties already discussed. The design of structure necessitates, therefore, maintaining an appropriate balance between span of control and chain of command.

Need for a balanced structure The combination of span of control and chain of command determines the overall pyramid shape of the organisation and whether the hierarchical structure is 'flat' or 'tall' (*see* Figure 15.7). The pyramid represents the structure of authority. Broader spans of control and few levels of authority result in a **flat hierarchical structure** as tends to be found, for example, in universities. Narrower spans of control and more levels of authority result in a **tall hierarchical structure** as tends to be found, for example, in the civil service or the armed forces. There is no one, ideal combination of span of control and scalar chain, which depends upon the particular situation for each organisation, but it is important to provide an appropriate, balanced structure.

Figure 15.7	How the span of control affects organisational structure

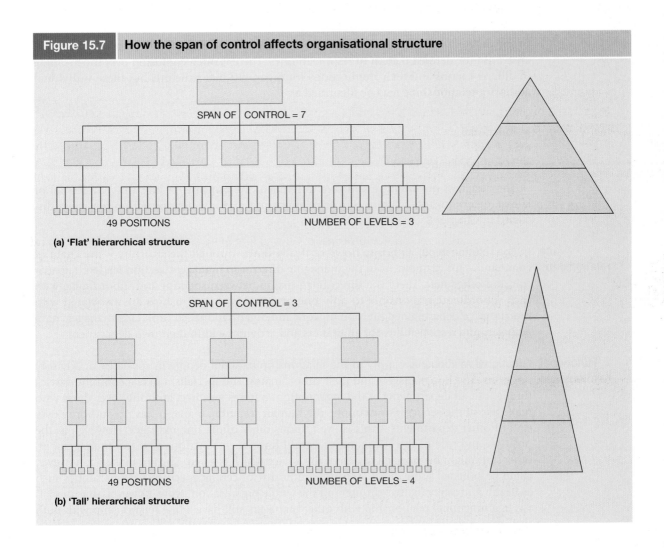

(a) 'Flat' hierarchical structure

(b) 'Tall' hierarchical structure

Information technology

An additional dimension of structural design is **information technology**. The impact of information technology will have significant effects on the structure, management and functioning of most organisations. It demands new patterns of work organisation and affects individual jobs, the formation and structure of groups, the nature of supervision and managerial roles. Information technology results in changes to lines of command and authority, and influences the need for restructuring the organisation and attention to job design. Computer-based information and decision-support systems influence choices in design of production or service activities, hierarchical structures and organisation of support staffs. Information technology may influence the centralisation/decentralisation of decision-making and control systems.

New technology has typically resulted in a 'flatter' organisational pyramid with fewer levels of management required. In the case of new office technology it allows the potential for staff at clerical/operator level to carry out a wider range of functions and to check their own work. The result is a change in the traditional supervisory function and a demand for fewer supervisors.

FORMAL ORGANISATIONAL RELATIONSHIPS

In any organisation structure certain formal relationships between individual positions will arise from the defined pattern of responsibilities. There is often confusion over the meaning of different terms and their implications for organisational structure, but these **individual authority relationships** may be identified as:

- line
- functional
- staff or
- lateral (*see* Figure 15.8).

The design of organisation structure in terms of the principle of line, functional, staff or lateral, determines the pattern of role relationships and interactions with other roles, discussed in Chapter 8.

Line relationships In line relationships, authority flows vertically down through the structure – the chain of command – for example, from the managing director to managers, section leaders, supervisors and other staff. There is a direct relationship between superior and subordinate, with each subordinate responsible to only one person. Line relationships are associated with functional or departmental division of work and organisational control. Line managers have authority and responsibility for all matters and activities within their own department.

Functional relationships Functional relationships apply to the relationship between people in specialist or advisory positions, and line managers and their subordinates. The specialist offers a common service throughout all departments of the organisation, but has no direct authority over those who make use of the service. For example, the human resources manager has no authority over staff in other departments – this is the responsibility of the line manager. However, as the position and role of the HR manager would have been sanctioned by top management, other staff might be expected to accept the advice which is given. The HR manager, however, could be assigned some direct, executive authority for certain specified responsibilities such as health and safety matters throughout the whole organisation. Note, however, that specialists in a functional relationship with other managers still have a line relationship with both their own superior and their own departmental subordinate staff.

Figure 15.8 **Illustration of formal organisational relationships**

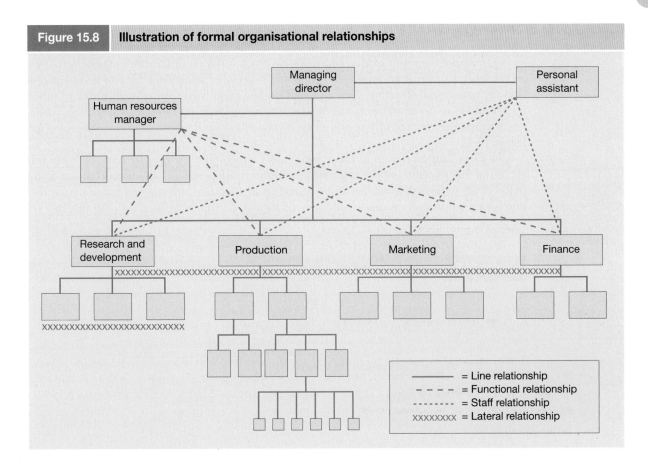

Staff relationships

Staff relationships arise from the appointment of personal assistants to senior members of staff. Persons in a staff position normally have little or no direct authority in their own right but act as an extension of their superior and exercise only 'representative' authority. They often act in a 'gatekeeper' role. There is no formal relationship between the personal assistant and other staff except where delegated authority and responsibility have been given for some specific activity. In practice, however, personal assistants often do have some influence over other staff, especially those in the same department or grouping. This may be partially because of the close relationship between the personal assistant and the superior, and partially dependent upon the knowledge and experience of the assistant, and the strength of the assistant's personality.

> In business and governmental agencies, from doctors' offices to licensing and regulatory boards, one may come face to face with people who have established themselves as gatekeeper to the boss. Gatekeepers aspire to and are rewarded with various titles, like administrative assistant, office manager or special assistant to such-and-such. But the essential role is usually that of secretary to the boss … Aspiring gatekeepers typically evoke polarised reactions among the office staff … Peers, unlike the boss, quickly recognise the individual's lack of integrity and willingness to step on all toes en route to the position of guardian and the gate.[33]

Lateral relationships

Lateral relationships exist between individuals in different departments or sections, especially individuals on the same level. These lateral relationships are based on contact and consultation and are necessary to maintain co-ordination and effective organisational performance. Lateral relationships may be specified formally but in practice they depend upon the co-operation of staff and in effect are a type of informal relationship.

LINE AND STAFF ORGANISATION

As organisations develop in size and work becomes more complex, the range of activities and functions undertaken increases. People with specialist knowledge have to be integrated into the managerial structure. Line and staff organisation is concerned with different functions that are to be undertaken. It provides a means of making full use of specialists while maintaining the concept of line authority. It creates a type of informal matrix structure (*see* Figure 15.9).

Line organisation relates to those functions concerned with specific responsibility for achieving the objectives of the organisation and to those people in the direct chain of command. **Staff organisation** relates to the provision of specialist and support functions for the line organisation and creates an advisory relationship. This is in keeping with the idea of

Figure 15.9	Representation of line and staff organisation

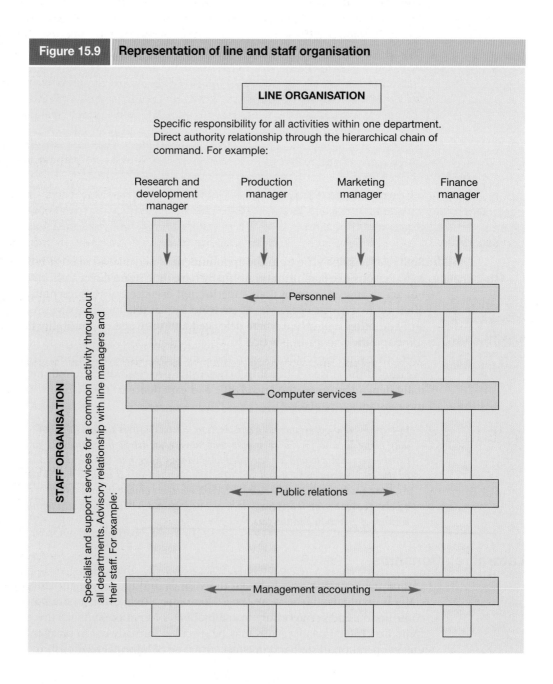

task and element functions discussed earlier. Again, confusion can arise from conflicting definitions of terminology. In the line and staff form of organisation, the individual authority relationship defined previously as 'functional' now becomes part of the actual structure under the heading of staff relationships.

Difficulties with line and staff relations The concept of line and staff relations presents a number of difficulties. With the increasing complexity of organisations and the rise of specialist services it becomes harder to distinguish clearly between what is directly essential to the operation of the organisation, and what might be regarded only as an auxiliary function. The distinction between a line manager and a staff manager is not absolute. There may be a fine division between offering professional advice and the giving of instructions. Friction inevitably seems to occur between line and staff managers. Neither side may fully understand or appreciate the purpose and role of the other. Staff managers are often criticised for unnecessary interference in the work of the line manager and for being out of touch with practical realities. Line managers may feel that the staff managers have an easier and less demanding job because they have no direct responsibility for producing a product or providing a service for the customer, and are free from day-to-day operational problems.

Staff managers may feel that their difficulties and work problems are not appreciated fully by the line manager. Staff managers often complain about resistance to their attempts to provide assistance and co-ordination, and the unnecessary demands for departmental independence by line managers. A major source of difficulty is to persuade line managers to accept, and act upon, the advice and recommendations which are offered. The line and staff relationship can also give rise to problems of 'role incongruence', discussed in Chapter 8.

Internal marketing of staff departments *Clutterbuck* suggests that a common feature of commercial life is staff departments, such as human resources and information technology, that have poor reputations with line managers. Even where line managers are clear what they want staff departments to do, they are rarely credited with initiative or much relevance to business objectives. In order to raise their profile, their perceived value and their contribution to the organisation there are a number of critical activities in the internal marketing of staff departments:

Refresh your understanding

Activity 15C
www.pearsoned.co.uk/
mullins

- understanding and responding effectively to the needs of internal customers;
- linking all the department's activities closely with the strategic objectives of the business;
- developing excellent communications and relationships with internal customers;
- ensuring internal customers' expectations are realistic; and
- continuously improving professionalism and capability in line with internal customers' needs.[34]

THE INVERTED ORGANISATION

Greater awareness of the importance of service delivery, total quality management and the continual search for competitive advantage has resulted in the concept of an inversion of the traditional hierarchical structure with customers at the summit and top management at the base. This will be accompanied by the devolution of power and delegation to the empowered, self-managing workers near the top of the inverted pyramid.[35]

> *In inverted organizations the line hierarchy becomes a support structure. The function of line managers becomes bottleneck breaking, culture development, consulting on request, expediting resource movements and providing service economies of scale. Generally, what was line management now performs essentially staff activities. The inverted organization poses certain unique challenges. The apparent loss of formal authority can be very traumatic for former line managers.[36]*

PROJECT TEAMS AND MATRIX ORGANISATION

The division of work and methods of grouping described earlier tend to be relatively permanent forms of structure. With the growth in newer, complex and technologically advanced systems it has become necessary for organisations to adapt traditional structures in order to provide greater integration of a wide range of functional activities. Although bureaucratic structures and hierarchies still exist in many organisations, increasing attention has been given to the creation of groupings based on project teams and matrix organisation. Members of staff from different departments or sections are assigned to the team for the duration of a particular project.

Project teams A project team may be set up as a separate unit on a temporary basis for the attainment of a particular task. When this task is completed the project team is disbanded or members of the unit are reassigned to a new task. Project teams may be used for people working together on a common task or to co-ordinate work on a specific project such as the design and development, production and testing of a new product; or the design and implementation of a new system or procedure. For example, project teams have been used in many military systems, aeronautics and space programmes. A project team is more likely to be effective when it has a clear objective, a well-defined task and a definite end-result to be achieved, and the composition of the team is chosen with care.

According to *Mann*, project-based working is as old as the pyramids but for increasing numbers of organisations it is very much the new way to do things. 'In today's leaner and meaner organisational set-up it seems that everything is a project and everyone a project worker.' Mann suggests two main drivers bringing about this change in the way work is managed. First, organisations have been stripped down to the core and resources are limited. Second, every area of the business has to contribute and be accountable as a cost centre. To be effective, projects require clarity at the outset, skills development, a supportive culture, managing communications and maintaining good working relationships.[37]

The matrix organisation

The matrix organisation is a combination of:

1 functional departments which provide a stable base for specialised activities and a permanent location for members of staff; and
2 units that integrate various activities of different functional departments on a project team, product, programme, geographical or systems basis. As an example, ICI is organised on matrix lines, by territory, function and business.

A matrix structure might be adopted in a university or college, for example, with grouping both by common subject specialism, and by association with particular courses or programmes of study. The matrix organisation therefore establishes a grid, or matrix, with a two-way flow of authority and responsibility (see Figure 15.10). Within the functional departments authority and responsibility flow vertically down the line, but the authority and responsibility of the 'project' manager (or course programme manager) flow horizontally across the organisation structure.

A matrix design might be adopted in the following circumstances:

1 **More than one critical orientation to the operations of the organisation**. For example, an insurance company has to respond simultaneously to both functional differentiation (such as life, fire, marine, motor) and to different geographical areas.
2 **A need to process simultaneously large amounts of information**. For example, a local authority social services department seeking help for an individual will need to know where to go for help from outside agencies (such as police, priest, community relations officer) and at the same time whom to contact from internal resources within the organisation (such as the appropriate social worker, health visitor or housing officer).

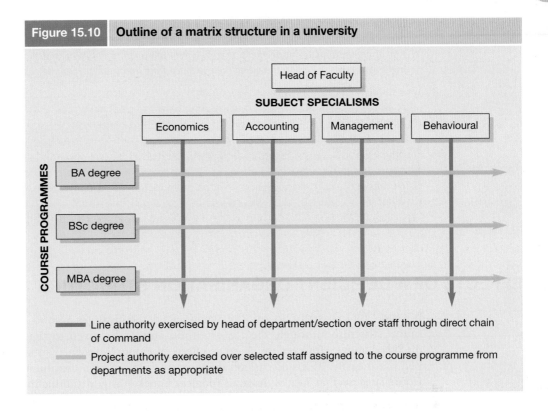

Figure 15.10 Outline of a matrix structure in a university

3 **The need for sharing of resources**. This could be justified only on a total organisational basis such as the occasional or part-time use by individual departments of specialist staff or services.

Developing an effective matrix organisation, however, takes time and a willingness to learn new roles and behaviour; this means that matrix structures are often difficult for management to implement effectively.[38]

Difficulties with matrix structures Matrix organisation offers the advantages of flexibility, greater security and control of project information, and opportunities for staff development. There are, however, a number of potential difficulties and problem areas:

- There may be a limited number of staff reporting directly to the project manager with extra staff assigned as required by departmental managers. This may result in a feeling of ambiguity. Staff may be reluctant to accept constant change and prefer the organisational stability from membership of their own functional grouping.
- Matrix organisation can result in a more complex structure. By using two methods of grouping it sacrifices the unity of command and can cause problems of co-ordination.
- There may be a problem in defining the extent of the project manager's authority over staff from other departments and in gaining the support of other functional managers.
- Functional groups may tend to neglect their normal duties and responsibilities.

An underlying difficulty with matrix structures is that of divided loyalties and role conflict with individuals reporting simultaneously to two managers; this highlights the importance of effective teamwork. According to *Bartlett and Ghoshal*, matrix structures have proved all but unmanageable. Dual reporting leads to conflict and confusion; the proliferation of channels of communication creates informational log-jams; and overlapping responsibilities result in a loss of accountability.[39] And *Senior* makes the point that:

Matrix structures rely heavily on teamwork for their success, with managers needing high-level behavioural and people management skills. The focus is on solving problems through team action ... This type of organisational arrangement, therefore, requires a culture of co-operation, with supportive training programmes to help staff develop their teamworking and conflict-resolution skills.[40]

Critical reflection

?????

'The idea of a matrix structure may appeal to those critical of a so-called prescriptive approach to organisational structure. But in reality a matrix structure is an unnecessary complication and creates more potential problems than it answers.' What do you think? What role do you believe the matrix structure serves?

EFFECTS OF A DEFICIENT ORGANISATION STRUCTURE

It is not easy to describe, in a positive manner, what constitutes a 'good' or effective organisation structure although, clearly, attention should be given to the design principles discussed above. However, the negative effects of a poorly designed structure can be identified more easily. In his discussion on the principles of organisation and co-ordination, *Urwick* suggests that 'lack of design is Illogical, Cruel, Wasteful and Inefficient'.

- It is **illogical** because in good social practice, as in good engineering practice, design should come first. No member of the organisation should be appointed to a senior position without identification of the responsibilities and relationships attached to that position and its role within the social pattern of the organisation.
- It is **cruel** because it is the individual members of the organisation who suffer most from lack of design. If members are appointed to the organisation without a clear definition of their duties or the qualifications required to perform those duties, it is these members who are likely to be blamed for poor results that do not match the vague ideas of what was expected of them.
- It is **wasteful** because if jobs are not put together along the lines of functional specialisation then new members of the organisation cannot be trained effectively to take over these jobs. If jobs have to be fitted to members of the organisation, rather than members of the organisation fitted to jobs, then every new member has to be trained in such a way as to aim to replace the special, personal experience of the previous job incumbent. Where both the requirements of the job and the member of the organisation are unknown quantities, this is likely to lead to indecision and much time wasted in ineffective discussion.
- It is **inefficient** because if the organisation is not founded on principles, managers are forced to fall back on personalities. Unless there are clearly established principles, which are understood by everyone in the organisation, managers will start 'playing politics' in matters of promotion and similar issues.

Urwick lays emphasis on the technical planning of the organisation and the importance of determining and laying out structure before giving any thought to the individual members of the organisation. Although Urwick acknowledges that the personal touch is important and part of the obvious duty of the manager, it is not a substitute for the need for definite planning of the structure.

In short, a very large proportion of the friction and confusion in current society, with its manifest consequences in human suffering, may be traced back directly to faulty organisation in the structural sense.[41]

Consequences of badly designed structure Urwick's emphasis on the logical design of organisation structure rather than the development around the personalities of its members is typical of the classical approach to organisation and management. Despite this rather narrow view, more recent writers have drawn similar conclusions as to the consequences of badly designed structure.

Child points out that:

> *Certain problems arise time and time again in struggling companies. Even at the best of times they can point to incipient dangers that have to be dealt with. Deficiencies in organisation can play a part in exacerbating each of these problems. High on the list are (1) low motivation and morale, (2) late and inappropriate decisions, (3) conflict and lack of co-ordination, (4) a generally poor response to new opportunities and external change, and (5) rising costs.* [42]

Child then goes on to explain the consequences of structural deficiencies.

- **Low motivation and morale** may result from: apparently inconsistent and arbitrary decisions; insufficient delegation of decision-making; lack of clarity in job definition and assessment of performance; competing pressures from different parts of the organisation; and managers and supervisors overloaded through inadequate support systems.
- **Late and inappropriate decisions** may result from: lack of relevant, timely information to the right people; poor co-ordination of decision-makers in different units; overloading of decision-makers due to insufficient delegation; and inadequate procedures for re-evaluation of past decisions.
- **Conflict and lack of co-ordination** may result from: conflicting goals and people working at cross-purposes because of lack of clarity on objectives and activities; failure to bring people together into teams or through lack of liaison; and lack of effective systems for communicating the modification of tasks.
- **Poor response to new opportunities and external change** may result from: failure to establish specialist jobs concerned with forecasting environmental change; failure to give adequate attention to innovation and planning of change as main management activities; inadequate use of teamwork and attention to relevant aspects of new projects.
- **Rising costs** may result from: a long hierarchy of authority with a high proportion of senior positions; an excess of rules, procedures and administrative work at the expense of productive work; and the presence of some, or all, of the other organisational problems.

Shortcomings in structure may also provide greater opportunities for the illicit activities of staff. For example, the collapse of Britain's oldest merchant bank, Barings, and the activities of 'rogue trader' Nick Leeson were made more straightforward by the major reorganisation and expanded structure of the Barings empire. [43]

ORGANISATION CHARTS

The structure of an organisation is usually depicted in the form of an organisation chart. This will show, at a given moment in time, how work is divided and the grouping together of activities, the levels of authority and formal organisational relationships. The organisation chart provides a pictorial representation of the overall shape and structural framework of an organisation. Some charts are very sketchy and give only a minimum amount of information. Other charts give varying amounts of additional detail such as an indication of the broad nature of duties and responsibilities of the various units.

Charts are usually displayed in a traditional, vertical form such as those already depicted in Figures 15.7 and 15.8 above. They can, however, be displayed either horizontally with the information reading from left to right, or concentrically with top management at the centre. The main advantage of both the horizontal and the concentric organisation charts is that they tend to reduce the indication of superior or subordinate status. They also offer the prac-

STRUCTURE AND ORGANISATIONAL BEHAVIOUR

It is clear, then, that it is essential to give full attention to the structure and design of an organisation. However, this is not always an easy task.

> *Designing structures which achieve a balance between co-operation and competition, which combine team behaviours and individual motivation, is one of the hardest parts of building organisations – or designing economic systems.*[46]

Structuring an organisation involves balancing a series of trade-offs.[47] In analysing the effectiveness of structure, consideration should be given to both the formal and technological requirements and principles of design and to social factors and the needs and demands of the human part of the organisation. Structure should be designed so as to maintain the balance of the socio-technical system and to encourage the willing participation of members and effective organisational performance.

> *An organisation can be separated into two parts or structures which can then be examined. One section is a definable structure that will be present in every company, the other is the structure caused by human intervention. The latter provides the company with its distinctive appearance, and may be regarded as the manager's particular response to the design requirements of organised behaviour. Essentially the effectiveness of an organisation depends on how accurately human design matches the structure of organised behaviour.*[48]

'Realities' of organisational behaviour The structure or charts do not describe what really happens in work organisations. For example, as *Watson* points out, a systems-control framing of organisations tends to take for granted that managerially designed structures and cultures more or less make organisations what they are. Account must be taken of both official and unofficial aspects of structure and culture.

> *An important element of the struggle for management control is one of the coming to terms with the fact that the formal or official arrangements that managers make when they 'design' organisations do not work out as expected, in practice.*[49]

To conclude our discussion we need to remind ourselves of the 'realities' of organisational behaviour and of points made in previous chapters. Rarely do all members of an organisation behave collectively in such a way as to represent the behaviour of the organisation as a whole. In practice, we are referring to the behaviour of individuals, or sections or groups of people, within the organisation. Human behaviour is capricious and prescriptive methods or principles cannot be applied with reliability. Individuals differ and people bring their own perceptions, feelings and attitudes towards the organisation, styles of management and their duties and responsibilities. The behaviour of people cannot be studied in isolation and we need to understand interrelationships with other variables that comprise the total organisation, including the social context of the work organisation and the importance of the informal organisation. The behaviour and actions of people at work will also be influenced by a complexity of motivations, needs and expectations.

Gray and Starke provide a humorous but perhaps realistic illustration of how an organisation actually works (*see* Figure 15.12).[50]

Heller also refers to:

> *the gap between the aims of big company organisations and what actually happens. Organisational form and organisational behaviour are not one and the same thing.*[51]

The changing world of organisations and management

Birchall refers to the changing world of organisations and its impact on management. As a consequence of factors such as global competition, the convergence of information and communications technology, the emergence of the digital economy, recession in most Western economies, the emergence of customer power and changing political philosophy, much of the work undertaken by middle management no longer requires the considerable layers of management. Tasks that used to take up a great deal of management time in hierar-

chical structures are now possible with minimal supervision or intervention. Much of the organisation's work is carried out in projects. Many managers will find themselves managing people who spend much of their time outside the office. There is a strong move towards the use of consultants. Managers will need to be familiar with electronic networks, the operation of dispersed teams and virtual organisations.[52]

Birchall draws attention to management as no longer the sole prerogative of an elite group called managers. The functions of management are being much more widely shared within an enterprise and possibly the greatest potential in managing complex organisations lies in releasing the organisation's creative capabilities. A similar point is made by *Cloke and Goldsmith* who maintain that management is an idea whose time is up and the days of military command structures are over.

> *Rather than building fixed structures with layers of middle management, many innovative organisations function as matrixed webs of association, networks, and fast-forming high-performance teams … The most significant trends we see in the theory and history of management are the decline of the hierarchical, bureaucratic, autocratic management and the expansion of collaborative self-management and organisational democracy.*[53]

Figure 15.12	How the organisation should be compared with how it actually works

Source: Gray. J. L. and Starke. F. A., *Organisational Behaviour: Concepts and Applications*, Fourth Edition. Merrill Publishing Company (1988), p. 431. Reproduced with permission from Pearson Education, Inc.

Refresh your understanding

Activity 15D
www.pearsoned.co.uk/mullins

Critical reflection

????

'Given the changing nature of organisations, the formal structure is unimportant. The only thing that really matters is whether individuals know what is expected of them, work well with other people and perform their tasks successfully.' Do you agree? What do you see as the purpose and importance of structural design for modern work organisations?

Freewheeling at Google

Can Google's random genius last?

Simon London

Googlemania has been in full swing for more than a year. Unless you devote your life to the subject, you have probably struggled to keep pace with the adventures of Sergey, Larry and their hoard of gifted geeks. You might even be asking yourself: do I really care? There are two important reasons why you should. The first has to do with Google's business model, the second with how the world's most written about company is run.

What does the original search engine have in common with Gmail, Google News, Google Earth and the myriad other services to have poured forth from Mountain View, California? They are all piped to your computer via the Internet and they are all free, in the sense of being funded by targeted advertising. Thus Google has found a way to turn almost anything you look at on your computer screen into advertising-supported media.

For traditional media companies, including the Financial Times, this is worrisome. Advertisers suddenly have a nifty new way to spend their money. For software companies – notably, but not only, Microsoft – the implications are super-scary: why should consumers pay for software if Google and its imitators can provide the basics (word processing, email, calendars, spreadsheets) for free? Perhaps even more significant than the business model, however, is the way Google is run. The company is reluctant to let management journalists roam freely around the Googleplex, but it seems to be engaged in nothing less than a giant experiment in 'emergence'.

Management gurus have for years been telling companies to abandon the traditional top–down, process-driven approach to strategy. Harness the imagination of employees, they exhort. Do not be afraid to experiment. Create an internal market for ideas. Place bets. Build a 'portfolio' of initiatives from which a winning strategy can emerge.

Yet old habits die hard. The strategic planning process remains an annual ritual. Chief executives talk about the need to experiment, then mete out punishment when experiments go wrong, or fail to champion unconventional projects when it matters most. Now compare that with Google, where software engineers can spend up to 20 per cent of their time on projects of their own choosing … since when did big companies allow such latitude? Imagine what delights might result if General Motors followed suit.

Giving employees freedom to choose their own projects has expanded Google from a search engine to a provider of countless services across the globe.

Command-and-control managers will respond that such practices are a recipe for slacking and wasted resources. A more enlightened interpretation is that Google is trying to harness the collective wisdom of employees about how resources should be allocated. Interesting projects attract talent, irrespective of whether they have been sanctioned by top management. While some initiatives at Google seem to be driven from the top, the company remains open to the possibility that internal market forces will come up with better decisions than committees.

None of this implies that Google is free from the normal headaches of project management. Froogle, its online shopping search service, has been in beta for so long that it is a standing Silicon Valley joke. Nor does its riotous run imply that the emergent approach will continue to deliver results. What works for a few dozen or even a few hundred programmers may not produce results in an international company of several thousand employees. The business model may have almost limitless potential, but will the organisation scale? This, as of the time of writing, is a $126bn (£71bn) question.

Source: London, S., 'Can Google's random genius last?', *Financial Times*, 31 January 2006. Copyright © 2006 The Financial Times Limited, reproduced with permission.

Discussion questions

1 Critically examine the extent to which Google's approach supports the idea that 'management is an idea whose time is up' as outlined in the final quote of the chapter.

2 Outline the implications for managers of adopting a 'freewheeling' approach that allows

organisational strategy to emerge from the workforce rather than being a choice made by organisational chiefs. Identify the benefits and problems that would occur in transferring such an approach to other types of organisation, for instance those in the public sector.

SYNOPSIS

● Structure provides the framework of an organisation and makes possible the application of the process of management. The structure of an organisation affects not only productivity and economic efficiency but also the morale and job satisfaction of its members. The overall effectiveness of the organisation will be influenced both by sound structural design, and by the behaviour of people who work within the structure. Attention must be given to integrating the structural and technological requirements of the organisation, and the needs and demands of the human part of the organisation.

● Some structure is necessary to make possible the effective performance of key activities and to support the efforts of staff. Organisations are layered and within the hierarchical structure there are three broad, interrelated levels: technical, managerial and community. The changing nature of the work organisation has led to discussion on the role of the hierarchy, the traditional boss–subordinate relationship and the extent to which managers can rely solely on their perceived formal authority within the structure of the organisation. However, although the hierarchy has changed its form, arguably it is not dead.

● There are many variables and situational factors which influence the most appropriate structure. However, there is an underlying need to establish a framework of order and system of command through which the activities of the organisation can be planned, organised, directed and controlled. This demands attention to certain basic considerations in the design of organisation structure. Although this may appear a prescriptive approach, it still presents management with a series of important decision points.

● The essence of structure is the division of work among members of the organisation, the co-ordination of activities and different jobs related to each other. Work can be divided and activities linked in a number of ways. Most organisations will contain examples of alternative combinations for grouping activities and relating different jobs to each other. A critical decision point arising from division of work and grouping of activities is the extent of centralisation and decentralisation.

● A particular form of relationship that can cause difficulty is the line and staff organisation, and the integration of people with specialist knowledge into the managerial structure. With the need to provide integration of a wide range of functional activities, greater attention has been given to more flexible forms of structure, such as project teams and matrix organisation. There are, however, a number of potential difficulties with matrix structures.

● A badly designed structure can have a number of negative effects and is likely to give rise to inefficiency, low motivation and morale, late and inappropriate decisions, conflict, rising costs and lack of development. The structure of an organisation is depicted usually in the form of a chart although there are a number of limitations with traditional organisation charts. It is important to remember relationships between structure and the realities of organisational behaviour. Some writers draw attention to the changing world of management and organisational democracy.

Refresh your understanding, assess your progress and begin your research with online resources at **www.pearsoned.co.uk/mullins**

REVIEW AND DISCUSSION QUESTIONS

1 What are the objectives of organising? To what extent do you think there are different levels in the hierarchical structure of an organisation?

2 What is the importance of good structure? How does structure relate to the overall effectiveness of an organisation? Discuss critically the continuing importance of the hierarchy.

3 Explain the main factors to be considered in the design of organisation structure. Debate critically the value of 'principles' of organisation.

4 Distinguish clearly between 'span of control' and 'chain of command'. Discuss the practical implications for the structure and effective operation of a large organisation.

5 Prepare your own diagrams to help explain: (i) line and staff organisation, and (ii) a matrix form of organisation structure. What are the reasons for adopting each of these forms of structure and what problem areas might arise?

6 To what extent would you agree with the contention that a logical structure for organisation is better for efficiency and morale than a structure allowed to develop around personalities? What are the likely consequences of a poorly designed structure?

7 Debate critically how the 'realities' of organisational behaviour influence organisation structure and design. Give your own examples.

8 What are *your* views on the idea of 'the end of management and the rise of organisational democracy'?

ASSIGNMENT 1

Examine closely arrangements for the division of work and linking together of activities in your own or some other organisation of your choice.

a Investigate and make notes on the variety of ways in which work is divided and combinations for grouping of activities within the organisation.

b Comment critically on the apparent effectiveness of different methods adopted for the division of work among members of the organisation.

c Give reasons, together with practical examples, in support of your comments.

d Explain fully changes you would recommend in order to help improve organisational performance. Where appropriate, prepare a revised, or a new, organisation chart.

ASSIGNMENT 2

Checklist for symtoms of organisational deficiencies

Read through the questionnaire and tick the questions (if any) for which you answer 'yes' for (1) your organisation as a whole and (2) your team or unit within it.

Symptoms	Your organisation	Your team or unit
Do morale and motivation seem noticeably low?	☐	☐
Do decisions seem inconsistent and arbitrary, without reference to rules or criteria?	☐	☐
Are people unclear about what is expected of them and how their contribution might be assessed?	☐	☐
Do people perceive they have too little responsibility and opportunity for achievement?	☐	☐
Are individuals subject to competing pressures from different parts of the organisation?	☐	☐
Are people overloaded?	☐	☐
Is decision-making delayed and lacking in quality?	☐	☐
Does vital information fail to reach decision-makers in time?	☐	☐
Are decision-makers segregated in separate units with insufficient co-ordination of their activities?	☐	☐
Are decision-makers overloaded because they have failed to delegate sufficiently?	☐	☐
Are there inadequate procedures for evaluating the results of similar decisions made in the past?	☐	☐
Is there noticeable conflict and lack of co-ordination?	☐	☐
Do individuals or groups have conflicting goals that are not in line with overall organisational objectives and priorities?	☐	☐
Have opportunities been missed for co-ordinating people's activities by forming teams or other ways of ensuring liaison between them?	☐	☐
Are systems lacking for ensuring that information on operational changes is communicated adequately to other parts of the company?	☐	☐
Does the organisation fail to respond innovatively to changing circumstances?	☐	☐
Is it no one's special responsibility to monitor change that is going on outside the organisation?	☐	☐
Do innovation and the planning of change get inadequate support from the top?	☐	☐
Is there inadequate co-ordination between the people who can identify new opportunites and those who might be able to develop ways of satisfying them (for example, between sales and R&D)?	☐	☐
Are costs rising (over and above inflation), especially in the administrative areas?	☐	☐
Does the organisation have too many managers and too few people carrying out the work?	☐	☐
Is there too much procedure and paperwork, distracting people from productive work and requiring additional administrative staff?	☐	☐

Source: From Child, J., *Organization: Contemporary Principles and Practice*, Blackwell Publishing (2005), p. 22. Reproduced with permission from Blackwell Publishing, Ltd.

a After completing the checklist compare your responses with colleagues.

b What conclusions did you draw from this exercise?

Every Tuesday and Saturday in SoHo, a big truck pulls to the curb on the east side of Broadway to have its cargo unloaded. From out of the truck emerge … stacks of dress shirts in soft colors, slim-cut black skirts, and elegant women's jackets that look – from a distance – like they just came off a Milan runway. All the pieces of clothing have two things in common. They come from a million-square-foot warehouse owned by a company called Zara, in the town of La Coruña … And, in all likelihood, three weeks before they were unloaded, they weren't even a glint in their designers' eyes.[58]

Managing a fashion laboratory

Unlike other companies which design and order their clothing ranges many months in advance, then stock up distribution centres with about three months' supply ahead of expected sales, Zara makes only what is selling at the moment. Its design team is based in La Coruña (other Inditex brand designers are based in Barcelona and Alicante) and with its hi-tech and highly integrated manufacturing centres close by, individual designers can see their creations turned into small batches of finished products within days and shipped out to stores within a few weeks. If the design sells well, more is produced and shipped out; if it flops, the company has lost very little as the volume of remaindered items is small and the design is scrapped. This small batch production process can enhance sales, as customers snap up eye-catching items quickly in case they aren't there tomorrow. As the recruitment page for fashion designers on the company website explains:

At Inditex collections are launched to enrich every week with new designs and proposals that improve our product offer. We re-invent trends because we adapt them to what our customers want, and win the battle of the very latest style.[59]

The close integration of design, production and logistics is only part of the story. The other crucial element in the company's design is the role of the stores, and in particular the store managers. Inditex describes its stores as 'fashion laboratories'.

They are where customers tell us what they want to wear. We listen to their opinions and tastes, and the store team passes it on to us. With this valuable information our fashion industry swings into action to offer our customers new items every week. Thanks to our store teams we have changed the rules of the fashion game … [they are] … teams of entrepreneurs with initiative, who take fashion into the streets every day.

Store assistants and managers constantly collect information about what is selling and how quickly it leaves the racks, meaning that local managers have a strong influence on the success of their stores and thus the company overall. If customers are asking for items in a different colour, or want certain styles that they can't find, their comments are recorded on hand-held computers, and a digest of both sales and customer feedback is transmitted daily to Zara HQ to alert the designers to trends. This degree of flexibility also allows Zara's store and regional product managers to adapt collections to local preferences – if Mexican customers want their strappy summer dresses in vivid reds and yellows but the Swiss prefer them in pastel pinks and blues, Zara can deliver.

With its flexible and integrated organisational structure, Inditex, and Zara in particular, has clearly rewritten many of the rules of the industry. The structure affects the nature of both the work (the work of a designer, for instance, becomes a blend of both long-range forecasting based on trends unveiled at catwalk shows and constant innovation based on day-by-day sales data) and the relationships within a global company which put individual store managers in direct and regular contact with design and production. It may have become a trendsetter in more ways than one.

Your tasks

1 Analyse Zara's structure in relation to the 'Interrelated levels of organisation' diagram at Figure 15.1. How does it match and how does it differ from the model?

2 Critically assess Zara's structure against each of Urwick's principles of organisation as outlined on pp. 576–7.

3 Organisations could be said to sit somewhere along a continuum between complete vertical integration, i.e. in-house control of all aspects of the operation, and complete outsourcing, i.e. externalisation of all operational aspects, with the core acting as a co-ordinating agent. What are the advantages and disadvantages of each structure in terms of responsiveness, resilience and efficiency?

4 How transferable is the Zara model to non-business sectors? Discuss this in relation to either a public sector operation (such as an NHS hospital) or a not-for-profit one.

Notes and references

1 Birkinshaw, J. 'The Structure behind Global Companies', in Pickford, J. (ed.), *Financial Times Mastering Management 2.0*, Financial Times Prentice Hall (2001), p. 75.

2 Adapted from Knight, K. (ed.) *Matrix Management: A Cross-functional Approach to GOrganization*, Gower (1977), pp. 114–15.

3 Heller, R. 'Resist That Urge to Reorganise', *Management Today*, January 1996, p. 21.

4 Watson, T. *Organising and Managing Work*, Second edition, Financial Times Prentice Hall (2006) pp. 254–62.

5 Drucker, P. F. *The Practice of Management*, Heinemann Professional (1989), p. 223.

6 Child, J. *Organization: Contemporary Principles and Practice*, Blackwell Publishing (2005), p. 6.

7 See, for example: Heller, R. *In Search of European Excellence*, HarperCollins Business (1997), p. 34.

8 See, for example: Lynch, R. *Corporate Strategy*, Fourth edition, Financial Times Prentice Hall (2003), Chapter 16.

9 Forte, C. (Lord Forte) *Forte: The Autobiography of Charles Forte*, Sidgwick and Jackson (1986), p. 122.

10 Vollmann, T. 'Restructuring: How to Improve your Success Ratio', *FT Mastering Management*, The Reader 2, Financial Times, June 1997.

11 Hannagan, T. *Management: Concepts and Practices*, Third edition, Financial Times Prentice Hall (2002).

12 Argyris, C. *Integrating the Individual and the Organization*, Wiley (1964).

13 Parsons, T. 'Some Ingredients of a General Theory of Formal Organization', in Litterer, J. A. *Organizations: Structure and Behaviour*, Third edition, Wiley (1980).

14 Department of the Environment, *The New Local Authorities: Management and Structure* (The Bains Report), HMSO (1972) pp. 10–11.

15 Audit Commission *Form Follows Function*, HMSO (1996).

16 Rawson, M. 'Whose Side Are You On?', *Professional Manager*, November 1997, p. 3.

17 Stewart, R. *The Reality of Management*, Third edition, Butterworth-Heinemann (1999), p. 190.

18 Jebb, F. 'Don't Call Me Sir (Everyone Knows I'm the Boss)', *Management Today*, August 1998, pp. 44–7.

19 Drucker, P. F. *Management Challenges for the 21st Century*, Butterworth-Heinemann (1999), p. 11.

20 Butcher, D. 'Breaking out of Organizational Mindsets', in Crainer, S. and Dearlove, D. (eds), *Financial Times Handbook of Management*, Second edition, Financial Times Prentice Hall (2001), p. 91.

21 Cloke, K. and Goldsmith, J. *The End of Management and the Rise of Organizational Democracy*, Jossey-Bass (2002).

22 Gratton, L. *The Democratic Enterprise*, Financial Times Prentice Hall (2004), pp. xii–xiv.

23 Lundy, O. and Cowling, A. *Strategic Human Resource Management* (1996), p. 141.

24 For a fuller discussion on strategy and structure see: Lynch, R. *Corporate Strategy*, Fourth edition, Financial Times Prentice Hall (2006), Chapter 16.

25 Woodward, J. *Industrial Organization: Theory and Practice*, Second edition, Oxford University Press (1980).

26 See, for example: Mullins, L. J. *Hospitality Management and Organisational Behaviour*, Fourth edition, Longman (2001).

27 Woodward, J. *Industrial Organization: Theory and Practice*, Second edition, Oxford University Press (1980), p. 113.

28 Barnevik, P. cited in Evans, P. A. L. 'The Dualistic Leader: Thriving On Paradox', in Chowdhury, S. *Management 21C*, Financial Times Prentice Hall (2000), p. 71.

29 Urwick, L. *Notes on the Theory of Organization*, American Management Association (1952).

30 See, for example: Moorcroft, R. 'Managing in the 21st Century', *The British Journal of Administrative Management*, January/February 2000, pp. 8–10.

31 Graicunas, V. A. 'Relationship in Organization', in *Papers on the Science of Administration*, University of Columbia (1937).

32 Woodward, J. *Industrial Organization: Theory and Practice*, Second edition, Oxford University Press (1980).

33 Learner, P. M. 'Beware the Gatekeeper', *Amtrak Express*, July/August 1994, pp. 14–17.

34 Clutterbuck, D. 'Marketing the Staff Departments', *Professional Manager*, January 1994, pp. 7–9.

35 Heller, R. 'The Manager's Dilemma', *Management Today*, January 1994, pp. 42–7.

36 Quinn, J. B., Anderson, P. and Finkelstein, S. 'Leveraging Intellect', in Crainer, S. and Dearlove, D. (eds), *Financial Times Handbook of Management*, Second edition, Financial Times Prentice Hall (2001), p. 592.

37 Mann, S. 'Working around Projects', *Professional Manager*, November 2002, pp. 29–32.

38 Adapted from Kolondy, H. F. 'Managing in a Matrix', *Business Horizons*, March/April 1981, pp. 17–24.

39 Bartlett, A. and Ghoshal, S. 'Matrix Management: Not a Structure, a Frame of Mind', *Harvard Business Review*, July–August 1990, pp. 138–45.

40 Senior, B. *Organisational Change*, Second edition, Financial Times Prentice Hall (2002), p. 87.

41 Urwick, L. *The Elements of Administration*, Second edition, Pitman (1947), pp. 38–9.

42 Child, J. *Organization: Contemporary Principles and Practice*, Blackwell Publishing (2005), p. 17.

43 Tibballs, G. *Business Blunders*, Robinson Publishers (1999), Chapter 2.

44 Rosenfeld, R. H. and Wilson, D. C., *Managing Organizations: Text, Readings & Cases*, Second edition, McGraw-Hill (1999), p. 255.

45 Townsend, R. *Further Up the Organisation*, Coronet Books (1985), p. 159.

46 Kay, J. *Financial Times*, 17 January 1997.

47 See for example, Galbraith, J. R. *Designing Organizations*, Jossey-Bass (1995).

48 Dunderdale, P. 'Analysing Effective Organisations', *Professional Manager*, September 1994, pp. 23–4.

49 Watson, T. *Organising and Managing Work*, Second edition, Financial Times Prentice Hall (2006), p. 259.

50 Gray, J. L. and Starke, F. A. *Organizational Behavior: Concepts and Applications*, Fourth edition, Merrill Publishing Company, an imprint of Macmillan Publishing (1988).

51 Heller, R. *In Search of European Excellence*, HarperCollins Business (1997), p. 4.

52 Birchall, D. W. 'What Managers Do', in Crainer, S. and Dearlove, D. (eds), *Financial Times Handbook of Management*, Second edition, Financial Times Prentice Hall (2001), pp. 110–31.

53 Cloke, K. and Goldsmith, J. *The End of Management and the Rise of Organizational Democracy*, Jossey-Bass (2002), p. 41.

54 D'Argy Smith, M. BBC News Website 'The Seaside Fashion Shows' 11 October 2002.

55 Elliott, B. 'What's really new in supply chains?' FT.com, 28 June 2006 [assessed 3 August 2006].

56 Revilla Bonnin, A. 'The Fashion Industry in Galicia: Understanding the "Zara" Phenomenon', *European Planning Studies*, vol. 10, no. 4, pp. 519–27.

57 Ibid.

58 Surowiecki, J. 'The Wisdom of Crowds', Abacus (2004), p. 192.

59 Inditex website; www.InditexJobs.com [accessed 3 August 2006].

PATTERNS OF STRUCTURE AND WORK ORGANISATION

There are no formal management structures in my companies – much to the disapproval of many. I know what is going on partly because I have told people what to do, and ensured the team is in place to deliver, and partly because I ask what's going on. It's not always easy to implement, but in theory it really is that simple.

(Sir) Alan Sugar – CEO and Chairman of Amstrad
The Apprentice, BBC Books (2005), p. 90

There are many variables that influence the most appropriate organisation structure and system of management. It is necessary to analyse structure in terms of the relationships among its components. Attention needs to be given to pressures for greater flexibility in patterns of organisation and the workforce, and the nature of the manager–subordinate relationship. The 'fit' between structure, systems of management and the behaviour of people will depend upon situational variables for each particular organisation.

Learning outcomes

After completing this chapter you should be able to:

- explain the meaning and nature of the contingency approach to organisation structure;
- examine main contingency models and assess their implication for management;
- assess the importance of changing external environments for the management and structure of organisations;
- evaluate the relevance and value of the contingency approach, and the importance of culture;
- recognise the changing face of the workplace and the demand for flexibility;
- explain the significance of the flexible firm, outsourcing and the shamrock organisation;
- review the importance of situational variables for patterns of structure and work organisation.

Critical reflection

????

'We trained very hard, but it seemed every time we were beginning to form up into teams we would be reorganised. I was to learn later in life that we tend to meet any new situation by reorganising and a wonderful method it can be for creating the illusion of progress while producing confusion, inefficiency and demoralisation' (Gaius Petronius, AD 66). To what extent do you think this is still true for modern work organisations?

VARIABLES INFLUENCING ORGANISATION STRUCTURE

In the previous chapter we looked at structure as providing the framework of management and at a number of basic principles and considerations that underlie the design of organisation structure. These principles and considerations suggest a prescriptive stance towards structure. There are, however, a number of variables and other factors which affect the most appropriate organisation structure and systems of management, the manner in which the work of the organisation is carried out and how people actually behave within the formal structure and system of the organisation.

Earlier approaches to organisation and management

Earlier approaches to organisation and management believed in one best form of structure and tended to concentrate on limited aspects of organisation. They also tended to study the organisation in isolation from its environment.

- The **classical approach** focused attention on the formal structure, technical requirements of the organisation and general sets of principles. There was an assumption of rational and logical behaviour. The identification of general objectives and the clarification of purposes and responsibilities at all levels of the organisation would lead to the most effective structure. Bureaucracy, as a sub-group of the classical approach, views the structure of the organisation in terms of specialisation, hierarchy of authority, system of rules and impersonality.

- The **human relations approach** focused attention on the informal organisation, and on the psychological and social needs of people at work. The neo-human relations writers concentrated on the personal adjustment of individuals within the structure of the organisation. Members were assumed to be committed to achieving the goals of the organisation. Attention was given to design of a structure that removed alienating aspects of work and restrictions on effective performance.

- The **systems view** of organisation and management placed emphasis on the socio-technical approach, the interrelationships of sub-systems and multiple channels of interaction, and recognised the importance of the external environment.

> Given the speed of technological change, an increasing rate of innovation, and growing demands by a more highly educated work force, many scholars suggest that the classical view of organizations will become outdated. In response to the resulting frustration, bureaucracies will begin to fade away and will be replaced by more creative forms of organization.
>
> R. P. Vecchio, *Organizational Behavior, Core Concepts*[1]

According to *Bouchikhi and Kimberly*, a feature that differentiates the 19th-, 20th- and 21st-century management paradigms is that as customers and shareholders have been more proactive, market-driven strategies and flexible organisations have developed as a conse-

quence.[2] The changing nature of the work environment, the increasing demands for flexibility and concerns with the contextual factors influencing structure have drawn attention to the contingency approach to organisational design.

THE CONTINGENCY APPROACH

The **contingency approach** can be seen as a development of the systems approach; it goes a stage further in relating the environment, and other variables, to specific structures of organisation. The contingency approach takes the view that there is no one best, universal structure. There are a large number of variables, or situational factors, which influence organisational design and performance. **The contingency approach emphasises the need for flexibility**.

As *Vecchio* puts it: 'The goal of the contingency view is to explain how differences in the contextual and structural dimensions are related. As the term *contingency* implies, this approach does not seek universal principles that can be used for every situation, but instead seeks to explain how one attribute or characteristic depends upon another.'[3]

The most appropriate structure is dependent, therefore, upon the contingencies of the situation for each individual organisation. These situational factors account for variations in the structure of different organisations.

Lynch points out: 'Every organisation is unique in size, products or services, people, leadership and culture' and provides helpful examples of some of the possible implications for organisation design (*see* Figure 16.1).[4]

Figure 16.1	Examples of the connection between purpose and organisation design
Purpose	**Implications for organisation design**
• 'Ideas factory' such as an advertising or promotions agency	• Loose, fluid structure with limited formalised relationships. As it grows in size, however, more formal structures are usually inevitable
• Multinational company in branded goods	• Major linkage and resource issues that need carefully co-ordinated structures, e.g. on common suppliers or common supermarket customers for separate product ranges
• Government civil service	• Strict controls on procedures and authorisations. Strong formal structures to handle major policy directions and legal issues
• Non-profit-making charity with a strong sense of mission	• Reliance on voluntary members and their voluntary contributions may require a flexible organisation with responsibility devolved to individuals
• Major service company such as a retail bank or electricity generating company	• Formal structures but supported by some flexibility so that variations in demand can be met quickly
• Small business attempting to survive and grow	• Informal, willingness to undertake several business functions such as selling or production, depending on the short-term circumstances
• Health service with strong professional service ethics, standards and quality	• Formalised structure that reflects the seniority and professional status of those involved while delivering the crucial complex service provisions
• Holding company with subsidiaries involved in diverse markets	• Small centralised headquarters acting largely as a banker, with the main strategic management being undertaken in individual companies

Source: Adapted from Lynch, R., *Corporate Strategy*, Fourth Edition, Financial Times Prentice Hall (2006), p. 582. Reprinted by permission of Pearson Education Ltd.

There is a continuing debate about the comparative advantages of large and small organisations, or whether 'bigger is best' or 'small is beautiful'. The conclusion appears to be that managers should attempt to follow a middle line in terms of the size of the organisations and that complexity rather than size may be a more influential variable.[8]

Structures of global companies

Refresh your understanding

Activity 16A

www.pearsoned.co.uk/mullins

Birkinshaw draws attention to size as a particular feature of the structures of global companies. 'The reality is that global companies end up being perceived as complex, slow-moving and bureaucratic. The challenge for top managers lies in minimizing these liabilities, while retaining the benefits of size.' The pure matrix (discussed in Chapter 15) with equal stress on two lines of accountability does not work. Attention must be given to strong but informal horizontal relationships and country managers in developing markets. The organisation of a global company depends on a host of factors including number of businesses and countries in which it operates, the type of industry, location of major customers, and its own heritage. Birkinshaw identifies four (simplified) models for the structure of a global company (*see* Figure 16.4).[9]

Figure 16.4	Four models for global company structure

Source: From Birkinshaw, J., 'The structures behind global companies', in Pickford, J. (ed.) *Mastering Management 2.0*, Financial Times Prentice Hall (2001), p. 76. Reproduced with permission from Pearson Education Ltd.

TECHNOLOGY

Two major studies concerning technology are:

● Woodward – patterns of organisation, production technology and business success; and
● Perrow – main dimensions of technology and organisation structure.

THE WOODWARD STUDY

A major study of the effects of technology on organisation structure was carried out by *Joan Woodward*.[10] Her pioneering work presents the results of empirical study of 100 manufacturing firms in south-east Essex and the relationships between the application of principles of organisation and business success. The main thesis was:

> *that industrial organisations which design their formal organisational structures to fit the type of production technology they employ are likely to be commercially successful.* [11]

Information was obtained from each of the firms under the four headings of:

1 history, background and objectives;
2 manufacturing processes and methods;
3 forms and routines used in the organisation and operation of the firm;
4 information relating to an assessment of commercial success.

The firms were divided into nine different types of production systems, from least to most technological complexity, with three main groupings of:

● unit and small batch production;
● large batch and mass production;
● process production.

The research showed that the firms varied considerably in their organisation structure and that many of the variations appeared to be linked closely with differences in manufacturing techniques.

Principles of organisation and business success

There appeared to be no direct link between principles of organisation and business success. As far as organisation was concerned, the 20 outstandingly successful firms had little in common. The classical approach appeared to fail in providing a direct and simple basis for relating organisational structure and business success. **There was, however, a stronger relationship between organisation structure and success within each of the three main groupings of production systems**.

Organisational patterns were found to be related more to similarity of objectives and production techniques than to size, type of industry or the business success of the firm. Among the organisational characteristics showing a direct relationship to technology were span of control and levels of management, percentage of total turnover allocated to wages and salaries, ratio of managers to total personnel, and ratio of clerical and administrative staff to manual workers. The more advanced the technology, the longer the length of the line.

Patterns of organisation and technology Woodward acknowledges that technology is not the only variable that affects organisation but is one that could be isolated more easily for study. She does, however, draw attention to the importance of technology, organisation and business success.

> *The figures relating to the span of control of the chief executive, the number of levels in the line of command, labour costs, and the various labour ratios showed a similar trend. The fact that*

organizational characteristics, technology and success were linked together in this way suggested that not only was the system of production an important variable in the determination of organizational structure, but also that one particular form of organization was most appropriate to each system of production. In unit production, for example, not only did short and relatively broad based pyramids predominate, but they also appeared to ensure success. Process production, on the other hand, would seem to require the taller and more narrowly based pyramid.[12]

Relationship between development, production and marketing

Another important finding of Woodward's study was the nature of the actual cycle of manufacturing and the relationship between three key 'task' functions of development, production and marketing. The most critical of these functions varied according to the type of production system (*see* Table 16.1).

- **Unit and small batch**. Production was based on firm orders only, with marketing the first activity. Greater stress was laid on technical expertise, and the quality and efficiency of the product. Research and development were the second, and most critical, activities. The need for flexibility, close integration of functions and frequent personal contacts meant that an organic structure was required.

- **Large batch and mass**. Production schedules were not dependent directly on firm orders. The first phase of manufacturing was product development, followed by production that was the most important function and third, marketing. The three functions were more independent and did not rely so much on close operational relationships among people responsible for development, production and sales.

- **Process**. The importance of securing a market meant that marketing was the central and critical activity. Products were either impossible or difficult to store, or capacity for storage was very limited. The flow of production was directly determined, therefore, by the market situation. The emphasis of technical knowledge was more on how products could be used than on how they could be made.

Table 16.1	Characteristics of production sytems		
Production systems	**Manufacturing cycle**		**Relationship between task functions**
Unit and small batch	Marketing	Development (Most critical function)	Production — Day-to-day operational relationship
Large batch and mass	Development	Production (Most critical function)	Marketing — Normally exchange of information only
Process	Development	Marketing (Most critical function)	Production — Normally exchange of information only

Source: Woodward, J., *Industrial Organization: Theory and Practice*, Second Edition, Oxford University Press (1980), p. 128. Reproduced with permission from Oxford University Press.

Subsequent studies A subsequent study by *Zwerman* supported, very largely, the findings of Woodward. Zwerman's study involved a slightly different sample of organisations and was carried out in Minneapolis in the USA.[13] In other respects, however, the study attempted to replicate Woodward's work. Zwerman reached a similar conclusion, that the type of production technology was related closely to variations in organisation structure. Another study in Japan also supported Woodward's findings and the relationship between technology and structure.[14]

However, a further study by *Collins and Hull* of 95 American manufacturing firms questioned the extent to which span of control is a by-product of main types of production technology. Variations in the span of control of production operations were attributed to the underlying effects of size, task complexity and automation. Collins and Hull suggest that the technology versus size debate has moved beyond an 'either–or' proposition to a 'both–and' proposition.[15]

MAJOR DIMENSIONS OF TECHNOLOGY: THE WORK OF PERROW

The work by Woodward was extended by *Perrow*, who drew attention to two major dimensions of technology:

● the extent to which the work task is predictable or variable; and
● the extent to which technology can be analysed.[16]

Variability refers to the number of exceptional or unpredictable cases and the extent to which problems are familiar. For example, a mass production factory is likely to have only a few exceptions but the manufacture of a designer range of clothing would have many exceptional and unpredictable cases. The **analysis of technology** refers to the extent to which the task functions are broken down and highly specified, and the extent to which problems can be solved in recognised ways or by the use of routine procedures.

Combining the two dimensions provides a continuum of technology from Routine → Non-routine. With non-routine technology there are a large number of exceptional cases involving difficult and varied problem-solving. The two dimensions of variability and the analysis of problems can also be represented as a matrix (*see* Figure 16.5).

Technology and structure The classification of each type of technology relates to a particular organisation structure. *Perrow* suggests that by classifying organisations according to their technology and predictability of work tasks, we should be able to predict the most effective form of structure. Variables such as the discretion and power of sub-groups, the basis of co-ordination and the interdependence of groups result from the use of different technologies.

Figure 16.5	**Matrix of technology variables**	
	FEW EXCEPTIONS	MANY EXCEPTIONS
PROBLEMS CANNOT BE ANALYSED	*Craft technology* Making a whole product probably in the same way each time, e.g. fine glassware	*Non-routine technology* e.g. psychiatric care in a mental hospital; manufacture of nuclear fuel systems
PROBLEMS CAN BE ANALYSED	*Routine technology* Manufacture of standard products; highly mechanised mass production	*Engineering technology* e.g. made-to-order machines such as electrical components; research consultancy

Source: Adapted from Perrow, C., *Organisational Analysis: A Sociological View*, Tavistock Publications (1970) p. 78; and Mitchell, T. R. *People in Organisations*, Second Edition. McGraw-Hill (1982) p. 32. Reproduced with permission from the McGraw-Hill Companies Inc.

In the **routine type of organisation** there is minimum discretion at both the technical and supervisory levels, but the power of the middle management level is high, co-ordination is based on planning and there is likely to be low interdependence between the two groups. This arrangement approaches a bureaucratic structure.

In the **non-routine type of organisation** there is a high level of discretion and power at both the technical and supervisory levels, co-ordination is through feedback and there is high group interdependence. This model resembles an organic structure.

ENVIRONMENT

Two important studies that focused not just on technology but also on the effects of uncertainty and a changing external environment on the organisation, and its management and structure, are those by:

● Burns and Stalker – divergent systems of management practice, 'mechanistic' and 'organic'; and
● Lawrence and Lorsch – the organisation of specific departments, and the extent of 'differentiation' and 'integration'.

THE BURNS AND STALKER STUDY

The study by Burns and Stalker was an analysis of 20 industrial firms in the UK and the effects of the external environment on their pattern of management and economic performance.[17] The firms were drawn from a number of industries: a rayon manufacturer, a large engineering company, Scottish firms attempting to enter the electronics field and English firms operating in varying sectors of the electronics industry.

Mechanistic and organic systems

From an examination of the settings in which the firms operated, Burns and Stalker distinguished five different kinds of environments ranging from 'stable' to 'least predictable'. They also identified two divergent systems of management practice and structure – the **'mechanistic' system** and the **'organic' system**. These represented the polar extremes of the form that such systems could take when adapted to technical and commercial change. Burns and Stalker suggested that both types of system represented a 'rational' form of organisation which could be created and maintained explicitly and deliberately to make full use of the human resources in the most efficient manner according to the circumstances of the organisation.

The mechanistic system is a more rigid structure and more appropriate to stable conditions. The characteristics of a mechanistic management system are similar to those of bureaucracy.

The organic system is a more fluid structure appropriate to changing conditions. It appears to be required when new problems and unforeseen circumstances arise constantly and require actions outside defined roles in the hierarchical structure.

A summary of the characteristics of mechanistic and organic organisations is provided by *Litterer* (*see* Table 16.2).[18] The mechanistic organisation is unable to deal adequately with rapid change; it is therefore more appropriate for stable environmental conditions. An example might be a traditional high-class and expensive hotel operating along classical lines with an established reputation and type of customer. However, major fast-food chains that tend to operate along the lines of scientific management (discussed in Chapter 3) also require a mechanistic structure. By contrast, a holiday or tourist hotel with an unpredictable demand, offering a range of functions and with many different types of customers, requires an organic structure.

Location of authority Although the organic system is not hierarchical in the same sense as the mechanistic system, Burns and Stalker emphasise that it is still stratified, with positions differentiated according to seniority and greater expertise. The location of authority, however, is by consensus and the lead is taken by the 'best authority', that is the person who is seen to be most informed and capable. Commitment to the goals of the organisation is greater in the organic system, and it becomes more difficult to distinguish the formal and informal organisation. The development of shared beliefs in the values and goals of the organisation in the organic system runs counter to the co-operation and monitoring of performance achieved through the chain of hierarchical command in the mechanistic system.

A study of 42 voluntary church organisations in the USA found that as the organisations became more mechanistic, the intrinsic motivation, sense of freedom and self-determination of their members decreased.[19]

Burns and Stalker point out that there are intermediate stages between the two extreme systems that represent not a dichotomy but a polarity. The relationship between the mechanistic and organic systems is not rigid. An organisation moving between a relatively stable and a relatively changing environment may also move between the two systems.

Organic cultures for high-technology organisations According to *Reigle*, knowledge workers in today's high-technology organisations require environments with organic characteristics. As technology continues to expand throughout the world, an organic organisational culture will become increasingly important. In order to retain highly skilled knowledge workers, managers should undertake investigations using an organisational culture assessment (OCA) to measure whether their organisations exhibit mechanistic or organic cultures. The OCA is based on five cultural elements of language, tangible artefacts and symbols, patterns of behaviour, rites and rituals, espoused values and beliefs and underlying assumptions.[20]

Table 16.2	Characteristics of mechanistic and organic organisations	
Mechanistic		**Organic**
High, many and sharp differentiations	SPECIALISATION	Low, no hard boundaries, relatively few different jobs
High, methods spelled out	STANDARDISATION	Low, individuals decide own methods
Means	ORIENTATION OF MEMBERS	Goals
By superior	CONFLICT RESOLUTION	Interaction
Hierarchical, based on implied contractual relation	PATTERN OF AUTHORITY CONTROL AND COMMUNICATION	Wide net based upon common commitment
At top of organisation	LOCUS OF SUPERIOR COMPETENCE	Wherever there is skill and competence
Vertical	INTERACTION	Lateral
Directions, orders	COMMUNICATION CONTENT	Advice, information
To organisation	LOYALTY	To project and group
From organisational position	PRESTIGE	From personal contribution

Source: Litterer, J. A., *The Analysis of Organisations*, Second Edition, John Wiley & Sons (1973), p. 339. Reproduced with permission from the estate of Joseph A. Litterer.

Different structures for individual departments
Given the possibility that different demands of the environment are characterised by different levels of uncertainty, it follows that individual departments may develop different structures. The study of the firms in the plastics industry supported this hypothesis and Lawrence and Lorsch found a clear differentiation between the major departments of research, production and sales.

- **Research** was more concerned with the long-run view and was confronted with pressures for new ideas and product innovation. The department operated in a dynamic, scientific environment and had the least bureaucratic structure.
- **Production** was more concerned with the here and now, short-term problems such as quality control and meeting delivery dates. The department operated in a fairly stable, technical environment and had the most bureaucratic structure.
- **Sales** was in the middle between research and production. The department was concerned with chasing production and had a moderately stable market environment.

The two most successful firms were those with the highest degree of integration and were also among the most highly differentiated.

Organisation structure and different environments

This view of differentiation and integration was confirmed in the subsequent study of firms in the container and consumer food industries. In this part of the study a comparison was made of both high- and low-performance firms operating in different environments. The aim was to discover what forms of organisation structure were required for different environments. It was concluded that the extent of differentiation and integration in effective organisations will vary according to the demands of the particular environment.

- The more diverse and dynamic the environment, the more the effective organisation will be differentiated and highly integrated.
- In more stable environments, less differentiation will be required but a high degree of integration is still required. Differences in the environment will require different methods of achieving integration.

Integrating mechanisms
The mechanisms used to achieve integration depend on the amount of integration required and the difficulty in achieving it.

- In mechanistic structures, integration may be attempted through the use of policies, rules and procedures.
- In organic structures, integration may be attempted through teamwork and mutual co-operation.
- As the requirements for the amount of integration increase, additional means may be adopted, such as formal lateral relations, committees and project teams.
- When there is a high degree of differentiation, the use of assigned 'integrators' or possibly a separate unit with a number of integrators were suggested. Because they are not dominated by any particular perspective, these integrators can help resolve problems of co-ordination and work programming between different departments.

Refresh your understanding

Activity 16B
www.pearsoned.co.uk/
mullins

It is important, however, to achieve the right balance of integration. Too high a level of integration may involve costs that are likely to exceed possible benefits. Too low a level of integration is likely to result in departments 'doing their own thing', poorer quality decisions and failure to make the best use of resources.[25]

Patterns of organisation and management
Lawrence and Lorsch do not see the classical and human relations approaches as being out of date but as part of a continuum of patterns of organisation and management related to the environment in which they operate. The work of Lawrence and Lorsch is an extension of this continuum and their case for 'a contingency theory of organisations' has provided a further insight into the relationship between organisation structure and the demands of the environment.

EVALUATION OF THE CONTINGENCY APPROACH

The contingency approach draws attention to the situational factors that account for variations in the structure of organisations. It is more concerned with differences among organisations than with similarities. It rejects a number of assumptions of the classical and human relations approaches, and the idea of one best form of structure. For its part, however, the contingency approach tends to assume that organisational performance is dependent upon the degree to which the structure of the organisation matches the prevailing contingencies.

Hunt explains the concept of contingency as follows:

The concept of contingency also implies that there is no one, absolute 'best' design; rather, there is a multitude of possibilities and the best or preferred choice will be contingent on the situation being analysed. Universal models designed to suit all situations are therefore rejected. This is consistent with the fact that most organizations are networks of a variety of bits of design rather than conforming, as one entity, to a particular model. So we might find units of bureaucracy, units of matrix structures, units with project teams, units with extremely loose, almost ad hoc structures – and all these within, say, the same oil company. In this sense, the contingency theorists merely reflected the findings of hundreds of researchers. There are common elements in the hierarchies of different organisations but there are also very many differences peculiar to the local situation.[26]

Criticisms/limitations

As with other approaches to organisation and management, contingency theory has been subject to a number of criticisms or doubts about its practical value to management. Among the writers who have assessed the contribution and relevance of the contingency approach are *Child*,[27] *Dawson*[28] and *Mintzberg*.[29]

The criticisms, difficulties and limitations of the contingency approach usually revolve around seven main issues.

1 **Causal relationship**. The nature of the causal relationship between organisation and performance is open to question. Most contingency models imply a causal relationship between structure, as an intervening variable, and performance as a dependent variable. It is probable, however, that certain factors such as the personal characteristics of management and staff, and changes in product markets and market conditions, influence performance independently of structure. It is also possible that organisational performance is an influence on structural design. Managers may be stimulated to make changes to structure as a result of feedback of information on performance.

2 **Organisational performance**. Implicit in contingency theory is the notion that the fit among components of the organisation and situation variables is related to maximising organisational performance. However, organisational performance is multifaceted and the measurement of performance applied in many of the contingency studies has not been precise. It is impossible to derive a single criterion for the appropriateness of the fit among various features of organisation and improved performance.

3 **Independent variables**. The supposed status of the independent 'contingent' variables as the 'given' and beyond the control of members of the organisation is open to question. Large organisations may be in a position to exercise control over certain aspects of their environment. For example, an organisation may be in a monopoly position or have its own protected niche in the environment. Organisations may also be able to influence their environment through, for example, advertising or political pressure groups. Some organisations, therefore, may be less dependent upon their environment and in a more secure position compared with other organisations. Any mismatch in contingency factors is likely to have less severe consequences for survival and level of performance.

4 **Multiple contingencies**. Different patterns of contingency factors have distinctive implications for organisational design. Organisations face multiple contingencies and there is potential for multi-way relationships among the range of organisational variables. Different contingencies may result in the need for different patterns of structure (as with a hybrid form of organisation discussed above) – for example, a department operating within a dynamic environment and demanding a more organic structure, within an organisation where other departments function within a more bureaucratic structure.

5 **Planned change**. Contingency models of organisation fail to give sufficient emphasis to unanticipated consequences of planned change – for example, the effects of the introduction of new technology on the internal working of the organisation or on the social interactions among groups of people engaged in certain activities.

6 **Power factors**. Organisation structure is not necessarily determined only by impersonal contingency conditions, but also by what are referred to as 'power' factors. The pressure of external control – such as government control of public sector organisations; the political context; the power needs of various members and managerial preferences; the culture of the organisation and the power of social norms – also enters into the design of structure.

7 **Timing of organisational change**. Most organisations operate under conditions of constant change, and this raises the question of the frequency and timing of organisational change. Developing organisations cannot, without difficulty, change their formal structure at too frequent an interval. There must be a significant change in contingency factors before an organisation will respond. Changes in structure tend to lag behind situational change. There is, therefore, a degree of luck about whether at any moment in time there is a good fit between structure and prevailing contingency factors.

> *Organization structure, like so many other aspects of business, is hostage to fads and fashions ... In looking at contemporary trends, we should note that many 'new' ideas have in fact been around in some form for decades.*
>
> J. Birkinshaw, *Mastering Management 2.0*[30]

CONTRIBUTION OF CONTINGENCY THEORY

Despite the criticisms and limitations of contingency theory, it has provided a further insight into our understanding of relationships among factors influencing the structure, management and operations of work organisations. An appropriate form of organisation will help prevent problems caused by unsuitable structures. The contingency approach has relevance in terms of, for example, division of work and co-ordination of activities, hierarchy and definition of responsibilities, methods of work, motivation and commitment of staff, and style and systems of management.

The basic concepts of the contingency approach help managers to develop a more thorough understanding of complex situations and to take appropriate action.[31] It also draws attention to the difficulties with mixed forms of organisation, and to the importance of different structures for different activities and situations – as illustrated in the example of M*A*S*H given earlier in the chapter.

Not every situation is unique According to *Robey*, modern contingency theory provides an increasing amount of empirical research, it defines variables ignored in earlier work, and it directs the attention of the manager to the contingencies to be considered in the design of organisation structure. However, the contingency approach runs the risk of concluding that 'it all depends on everything', and the greatest danger is the over-emphasis on differences between organisations and the exclusion of similarities. If the contingency approach is to be useful in guiding organisation design it should not treat every situation as being unique. 'Rather it must strike a balance between universal prescriptions and the statement that all situations are different

(which is really no theory at all). Thus, modern theory uses a limited number of contingencies to help explain structural differences between organizations.'[32]

Vecchio also refers to the contingency approach as 'it depends'. However, this is not meaning to be evasive but assuming that there are a number of important dependencies, and acknowledges:

> *the difficulty of offering simple general principles to explain or predict behavior in organizational settings ... If you ask a contingency researcher for a simple answer to a seemingly simple question, you should expect to be given a fairly complex and highly qualified answer. Because human behavior is itself complex, a statement of behavioral principles must also be complex.*[33]

CULTURE AS A CONTINGENT FACTOR

Several writers have sought to examine whether the principles of contingency theory hold true in different national contexts. For example, in Chapter 1 we drew attention to national culture as a feature of management and organisational behaviour including the contribution of *Hofstede*[34] and of *Trompenaars*.[35] *Hickson et al.* investigated 70 manufacturing units in Britain, the USA and Canada. They discovered that while there were differences in organisational arrangements, these could not be attributed to cultural effects. The relationship between variables, such as size, and the degree of specialisation and formality was found to be constant in all three countries, and the researchers suggested this would 'hold for work organisations in all societies'.[36]

Maurice, Sorge and Warner, however, concluded that 'matched' organisations in different societies grow in contrasting ways, which may be the result of distinctive patterns in the wider society. For example, their research showed that British organisations appeared to grow laterally – that is, to develop large numbers of specialised managers. This may be a reflection of the comparatively specialised nature of British education and the influential role played by the professions. In contrast, the smaller number of categories of workers found in the German organisations studied may be traced back to the notion of the company apprenticeship prevalent in that country. In this way culture can itself be seen as a contingent factor.[37]

Whatever the perspective, it is important for future managers to understand the effect of national culture on behaviour. This is of increasing significance with the growth of multicultural workforces and the effects of the European Union on organisational design.

Historical and societal context

Schneider and Barsoux suggest that while managers are ready to accept national culture as an influence on the way people relate to each other, they are less convinced of its real effect on the structure, systems and process of the organisation. However, the emerging approaches to management reflect different cultural assumptions and models of management have diffused across countries at different rates in different ways. Historical and societal context needs to be considered to understand the adoption of and diffusion of different forms of organisation across countries. Schneider and Barsoux discuss the multidimensional impact of culture on organisations and management and maintain that it would be a mistake to base a prediction regarding structure or process on a single cultural dimension.

> *Managers need to recognise that the relationship between cultural dimensions and structure (or processes) are not simple cause–effect links, but instead, are multidetermined. Similar approaches may exist for the same reason. Thus formalized rules and procedures or participative management approaches may have a different raison d'être on different sides of the national border.*
>
> S. C. Schneider and J. Barsoux, *Managing Across Cultures*[38]

An interesting set of caricatures for organisation charts of different countries is given in Figure 16.6.

Cultural variations and organisation structure

Francesco and Gold draw attention to cultural variations in the governance of business that affect organisational structure. For example, two forms of corporate governance substantially different from the West are the Japanese *keiretsu* and the Korean *chaebol*. The Japanese *keiretsu* are complex interfirm networks that combine market exchange and non-economic social relations. The group is usually in a large number of industries and often includes a bank at the core and a general trading company. Control and co-ordination is facilitated through each member firm of the *keiretsu* owning a small part, up to 20 per cent, of the

Figure 16.6 | **Caricatures of organisation charts for different countries**

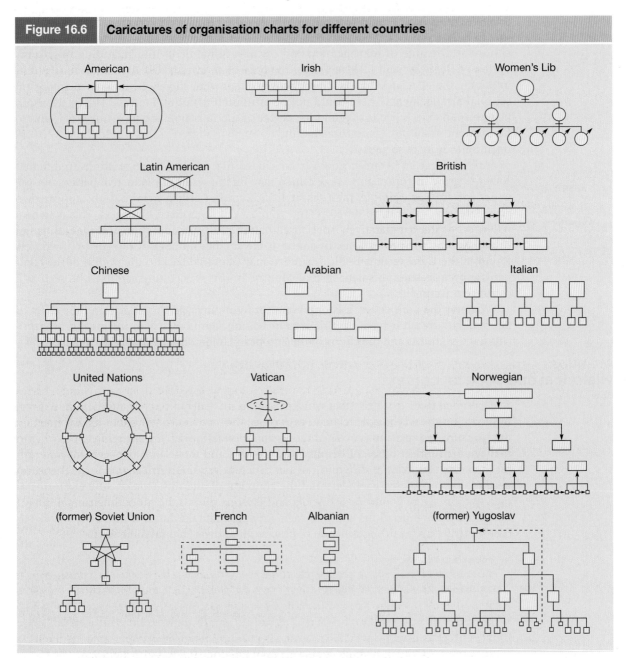

Source: Copyright © Reed Business Information Ltd, reprinted with permission.

stock of other firms in the group. *Chaebols* are large conglomerates or financial cliques that dominate the South Korean economy. The business group is owned and managed by family members or relatives. The founders are active in the operations of the *chaebols* and influence their business philosophy and management style. Most financial investment comes from government-controlled banks and in return the *chaebols* make political contributions for favourable treatment.[39]

THE CHANGING FACE OF THE WORKPLACE

The effects of increased economic pressures and demands for greater competitiveness have drawn attention to the importance of structural variables. The movement towards tighter and leaner organisations has emphasised the importance of alternative forms of structure and of the demand for flexibility. *Morgan* argues that we are leaving the age of organised structures and moving into an era where self-organisation will become a key competence. Looser organisations and different forms of control will entail a close examination of such issues as growth and size, teamwork, decentralisation, franchising and subcontracting.[40] And *Eden* maintains that:

> It is important to design at least parts of the organisation so that it can recognise early on the direction in which uncertain situations will unfold, and so respond to change and uncertainty in an opportunistic, flexible and effective manner.[41]

Seven habits of new organisations

Crainer suggests that the organisation is changing and the world of work is moving into a new age and lists 'seven habits of the new organisation':

1 flexible and free-flowing;
2 non-hierarchical;
3 based on participation;
4 creative and entrepreneurial;
5 based round networks;
6 driven by corporate goals;
7 utilising technology as a key resource.[42]

Relationship between the organisation and individuals

Management Consultancies Association (MCA) and *Management Today* carried out a survey of 1200 managers, from all types of organisations, in order to understand their attitudes to their employers and how these are likely to change in the future. The survey draws attention to the changing relationship between organisations and individuals and that ties to the workplace will increasingly cease to be a hindrance.

There are four interconnected forces that have brought about this changing relationship:

● changes in the shape of organisations themselves with outsourcing leading to a range of previously in-house processes and functions fulfilled elsewhere;
● changing pattern of people's working days with constant reference to flexibility. More than two-thirds of respondents spent a significant amount of time working outside the organisation;
● the pattern of people's working lives taking a very different shape with the ending of jobs for life and the active pursuit of career changes. Individuals increasingly choose employment that allows them to work from home or provides the latest technology;
● the impact of new technology enabling greater workforce mobility. However, although technology is usually an enabler, it can also be disabling. For example, email is the most important activity in helping people get their job done but it is also a burden.

flexibility. It enables companies to cope with workload fluctuations, and to use agencies when they need employees with specific skills.'[54]

However, despite the apparent popularity of flexible working, *Lucas* suggests that it is still causing organisations much anxiety.

> *It seems that for every organisation proactively embracing the many and varied forms of flexible working practices, there are those that are still tending to be reactive. Legislation and worries about the logistics appear to be putting some organisations and their management team on the back foot. They appear to view flexible working as just another problem or issue rather than an option which can be a motivational, performance enhancing and overhead cost-saving opportunity.*[55]

Telecommuting Recent advances in computerisation and telecommunications have had a further significant effect on the opportunities for flexible working. People can work from almost any geographic location: from head office, a satellite office, a shared access telecentre; or from their home, hotel room or car. An increasingly popular means of teleworking is **telecommuting** where staff work from home with a computer network telephone and fax.

From a discussion of the opportunities and challenges of telecommuters, *Manochehri and Pinkerton* conclude that telecommuting has come of age. The technological developments have made it possible, and economic and social factors have made it necessary. Managers have no choice but to learn how to take advantage of this new approach.

> *The advantages of telecommuting are already clear and distinct. Several trends such as further growth in information technology, the expanding role of the service sector, the emergence of virtual corporations and the diverse needs of the employees will guarantee a higher reliance on telecommuting as a viable alternative ... Managers have to appreciate the telecommuting management challenges and determine how to overcome them. If implemented and managed properly, telecommuting can be a valuable asset to an organization and to the people it employs.*[56]

A challenge for managers

The use of information communications technology and moves towards an increasingly flexible workforce call for attention to appropriate structures of organisation and systems of management. *Lucas* maintains that the big challenge for managers in the new millennium is: 'How do you create trust, communicate effectively, and foster teamwork with a group of people who could be working anywhere from their dining room table to an airport lounge?' Lucas suggests that this requires a sound performance management system, the effective management of virtual teams and managing communication. Flexible working calls for flexible managers who can cope with uncertainty, ambiguity and constant change, management development programmes, and a fundamental review of the role of a manager in the new world of work.[57]

Rigby suggests that for the first time, it is reasonable to say that the technological and financial barriers to some sort of mass home working have finally come down. 'The technology and communications infrastructure is now robust and fast enough – no, really – for a wide range of employees to do their job effectively without going past their front door.' There is, however, a downside. Home working flexibility blurs the boundaries between home and office. There are questions of measurement and the managerial fear that home workers do not actually work, and for whom this technology is most appropriate.[58]

Also, working from home does not appeal to everyone and it needs to be managed well, especially for full-time home workers. An increasing number of home workers report a feeling of detachment from the work situation and that they miss the interaction with colleagues.

Home Alone Stir Crazy

Unless managed well, the dream of working from home can turn into a nightmare, says former full-time home worker Rosemary Eatherden.

It's one o'clock, I've been at my laptop for five hours and I'm ready for a break. I need conversation. Across the office, I catch the eye of my only colleague. I walk over, fondly press his hand – well, paw actually – and he delivers my favourite conversational opener: 'Got any jelly babies?'

Even if you don't have a life-size talking Basil Brush to keep you company, if you work from home you'll know where I'm coming from. There are times for home workers when the exam-like intensity of your day leaves you desperate for human contact. Fox contact, even.

But surely home working is every weary commuter's dream? Well, no. Regular week-long home working can easily become a nightmare. I'm glad to have left it behind. On paper, I was the perfect home worker: disciplined, self-motivated and conscientious. But you also need to be happy working in isolation, able to survive without a daily fix of office chat.

I thought that was for me. After three years working at home, I knew it was not. It wasn't so much the gossip I missed, it was the interacting. I found I'd lost the knack. When you spend ten hours a day bonding with a laptop in a room on your own, you don't have a rich fund of stories with which to entertain your friends.

But why should all that matter to your employers? You're probably 25 per cent more productive, they're saving several grand a year on your desk space, and few of us are ever too sick to crawl across the hall to get to work.

I've heard the CIO of a big blue-chip company describe his utopia: a world where we can get information any time, any place, and where the office is redundant. We've pretty near got the technology cracked. So that leaves us with the hard bit: searching for a way to survive and thrive with almost zero interaction. Because if employers want creative, problem-solving team players, maybe solitary confinement, although it might boost the balance sheet, isn't the best answer.

You can have creative thoughts and solve problems on your own, but batting ideas around with colleagues in the same room is often so much better. Pressures that drag you down when you're on your own lighten or disappear when you laugh about them with others. Feeling part of a team helps you get through the day.

Occasional forays into the office don't give you the fix you need. You either hog the floor, delirious at the chance to speak, or wonder what everyone is talking about because you were sitting at home when the topic under discussion had an airing.

And many organisations find they have managers who are ill-equipped to cope with home workers. Trust is the hurdle, not technology. Yet trust is not the biggest challenge firms face. If home working is to be a success, they need to be smarter at understanding the long-term effects on people's health and well-being.

Working on your own, all day, every day, will wear down even the most resilient and spirited individual. Many full-time home workers say they feel forgotten and undervalued as a result of their isolation. Or could that be paranoia? That's another home-working hazard.

Rosemary Eatherden is a communications consultant[59]

Source: Eatherden, R., 'Home alone stir crazy', *Management Today*, March 2005, p. 75. Reproduced with permission from Haymarket Publishing Ltd.

THE SHAMROCK ORGANISATION

One particular approach to flexible structural design and the core and complementary model of employment is *Handy's* concept of the **'shamrock' organisation**.[60] The three leaves to each stem of the shamrock are symbolic of the organisation which is seen as made up of three distinct groups of people who are managed, organised and paid differently, and with different expectations: the professional core; the contractual fringe; and the flexible labour force (*see* Figure 16.7).

Figure 16.7	**Representation of Handy's shamrock organisation**

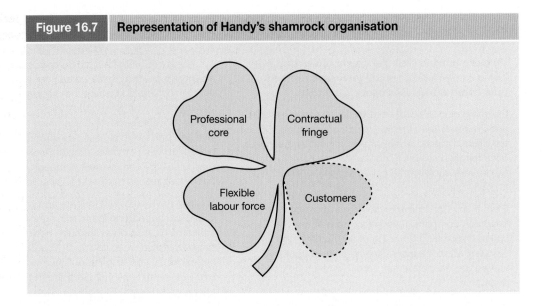

- **The professional core** comprises qualified professionals, technicians and managers essential to the existence and effective performance of the organisation. Collectively, these people own the knowledge that distinguishes the organisation. They get most of their identity and purpose from their work and are likely to be committed to it and dependent on it. The professional core are expensive and the tendency has been for organisations to restructure in order to reduce their numbers.
- **The contractual fringe** comprises those people, or other organisations, outside the organisation who provide specialist services and undertake all non-essential work which can be done by somebody else, and in theory are able to do it better for less. The organisational principle is that the contractual fringe are paid for results not for time, in fees and not wages. It is wise for the shamrock organisation to put boring and repetitive work out to contract, specifying the results expected and paying the fee.
- **The flexible labour force** represents all those part-time and temporary workers who make up the fastest growing group in the pattern of employment. It provides for flexibility in human resourcing. People are brought in as occasional extra part-time labour or temporary staff as changing work situations demand. Their commitment will be to a job and work group rather than to a career or organisation. Part-time or temporary work may be a matter of choice, not just a necessity.

Three significant workforces

According to Handy, organisations now have three significant workforces, each with a different kind of commitment to the organisation and a different set of expectations, and each workforce needs to be managed in different ways. The concept of the shamrock organisation can encourage managers to question the operations of their organisations. It gives rise to important decisions concerning what activities, and which people, should belong to the core, and concerning the management and control of subcontracting and of the flexible workforce. Managers could use the concept of the shamrock organisation and how this might best be adapted and utilised in a review of structure to suit the particular circumstances of the nature and operations of their organisation.

The increase in the flexible labour force is particularly noticeable with the growth of service industries. Services are created and consumed simultaneously. Unlike manufacturing, services are time-perishable and cannot be stored. The flexible labour force has increasingly

been used as a cheaper and more convenient means of dealing with the peaks and troughs of demands, and as a means of adjusting the level of service to match changing customer requirements. Although casual and part-time staff are unlikely to have the same degree of commitment or ambition as the core it is important that they are taken seriously and regarded as a valuable part of the organisation. If treated as casual labour such people respond casually. The flexible workforce should be treated with respect, given fair and equitable treatment, adequate training and status, and decent pay and conditions. If casual and part-time staff are to respond in a positive way and provide a high standard of service, they have to be managed in a considerate and effective manner.

Customers as the fourth leaf? Handy also refers to the growing practice of saving labour in the core by introducing another, informal and unpaid form of subcontracting – that of getting customers to do some of the work of the organisation. Examples include the collection rather than the delivery of goods, self-assembly furniture, automated banking facilities and self-serve petrol. In the hospitality industry, there are many examples of this 'serve yourself' philosophy. Examples include the provision of shoe-cleaning equipment or machines, hotel guests making their own tea and coffee in their rooms, restaurant self-service breakfast and buffet meals, and the provision of vending machines for snacks and beverages.

Challenges of the shamrock Handy suggests that although on the face of it the shamrock is logical, these are not easy organisations to run. Each leaf of the shamrock has to be managed differently, yet as part of the whole. The core is the critical hub of the organisational network and this raises important questions as to what activities belong in the core; and which people belong in the core, and for how long. Fixed-term contracts will be an increasing feature. Employing fewer people brings with it the need for better people, and pressure for alertness and quality will place greater demands on the core people.

EMPOWERMENT AND CONTROL

Whatever its structural design, the various operations of the organisation have to be distributed among its members. It is necessary to plan, organise, direct and control their activities. The demand for flexibility and greater freedom and autonomy for individuals raises questions about the location of decision-making within the organisation, the extent and nature of delegation and empowerment, the manager–subordinate relationship, and the maintenance of management control within the formal structure of the organisation. This is discussed more fully in Chapter 18.

Refresh your understanding

Activity 16D
www.pearsoned.co.uk/mullins

Critical reflection

'The potential problem with alternative patterns of structure and the changing nature of the work environment is the risk of undermining line of authority and clearly established management–subordinate relationships.' Do you believe there is a threat to the underlying basis of effective organisational control and performance? Or do you think the new patterns of structure benefit individuals and the organisation?

MANAGEMENT IN THE NEWS

Dead end or turning point?

Another side of a 'McJob'

Mc Job; colloq. derog., An unstimulating, low-paid job with few prospects, esp. one created by the expansion of the service sector.

Both the Oxford English and the Merriam-Webster Dictionaries ran into a regular 'McFlurry of trouble with US fast-food giant McDonald's when they included the word 'McJob'. McDonald's then Chief Executive, Jim Cantalupo, took exception to the Merriam-Webster definition of 'a low-paying job that requires little skill and provides little opportunity for advancement'[62] and argued, in an open letter of 2003, that

more than 1,000 of the men and women who own and operate McDonald's restaurants today got their start by serving customers behind the counter.[63]

In recent years, McDonald's has been working hard to overturn the image which affects the fast-food industry in particular. A number of initiatives, some very imaginative, have been launched in the UK by David Fairhurst, appointed vice-president of McDonald's UK in 2005 from Tesco.[64] Some key statistics about employment at McDonald's include the facts that for over a third of its UK staff it is their first job, and that the 90 day turnover for hourly-paid staff is on a steady course downwards. A high proportion (60 per cent) of staff (crew) is aged 16–21 years, and five of its board members together with 80 per cent of managers (average length of service a respectable 10 years) started out as crew.[65]

Fancy a career at McDonald? Far from being a low-paid, dead-end 'McJob', working at McDonalds can prove the gateway to a long-term, sucessful career for many young people.

The 'unskilled young worker' factor was perhaps behind one initiative, unveiled in September 2006, to help employees gain qualifications by both studying and taking exams at their place of work. A website, called 'Our Lounge', is available to all 67,000 staff, giving access to an online tutor who can help them towards NVQ or GCSE-equivalent qualifications in basic literacy and numeracy. Exams are taken at work using staff areas or training rooms, and Fairhurst expects that 1,000 employees would be taking up the initiative in its first year. He observed:

we recruit on qualities, not qualifications, but we want to ensure that no one is held back by not having the basics of numeracy and literacy.[66]

More unusually, McDonald's has launched an experimental form of shared contract to encourage flexibility by giving workers more personal control over their hours and shifts. The 'family contract' enables two people from the same family who work in the same restaurant to cover each other's shifts without having to notify the manager in advance. Fairhurst believes that pairings like this will help employees to manage their shift and family commitments more easily, thus increasing their job satisfaction and motivation.[67]

The company has also attempted to turn round its public image through a recruitment poster campaign 'Not Bad for a McJob' which draws on research carried out by Professor Adrian Furnham of University College London. Furnham's report suggests that a job at McDonald's can have a positive impact on workers' lives, especially younger low-skilled workers, who experience increased self-esteem, confidence and motivation. Amongst workers questioned, 90 per cent showed high levels of engagement, 85 per cent said the job was better than they'd expected, 83 per cent had seen positive change in themselves since starting work and 74 per cent saw a long-term career at McDonald's.

The youngsters we spoke to started work viewing a McJob like most other people. But there is an amazing change in perception once they start. They are happy, motivated and the work gives them confidence and self-esteem. The evidence indicates that these types of jobs are positive for young people.[68]

Furnham's report quotes Jason Hersey who left school at age 16 without any qualifications and little confidence. Nine years after getting a job at McDonald's he manages a store with an annual turnover of £1.7m.

Source: Empics/Associated Press

Management in the news – continued

'I went into the job so I could get a bit of money to have a laugh with my mates,' he says. 'My perception was the same as most other people – it was a means to an end and was not going to take me anywhere. My mum was just happy I'd got a job but me working for McDonald's wasn't something she was going to sing about to her mates. Now you can't shut her up. While other business wouldn't have given me a chance, I showed I was willing to work and they rewarded that. They realise it's not in their interest to hold someone back who wants to do well.'[69]

Discussion questions

1 What are generally considered to be the main characteristics of a McJob? How, and how far, do the initiatives described in the case, and the research by Adrian Furnham, challenge these assumptions?

2 Review the way in which the structure and technology of this type of organization determine the nature of the work itself. What are the implications for the management of people in such organizations?

SYNOPSIS

● There are a number of variables and other factors that affect organisation structures and systems of management. Earlier approaches to organisation and management believed in one best form of structure and tended to concentrate on limited aspects of organisation. The contingency approach, however, emphasises the need for flexibility and takes the view that there is no one best structure or system of management. If certain situational factors exist, **then** certain variables in organisation structure and systems of management are most appropriate.

● Situational factors may be identified in a number of ways and various studies have been carried out into the extent to which these contingency factors influence organisational design and effectiveness. Among the most important contingency factors are size of organisation, technology and environment. A particular concern for global companies is the need to balance the benefits of size with the liabilities of a complex, slow-moving and bureaucratic structure.

● Important studies concerning technology include those by Woodward, who draws attention to patterns of organisation and production systems, and business success, and Perrow on the variability and analysis of technology. Two important studies on the effects of the environment on the management and structure of organisations include work by Burns and Stalker, who have drawn attention to the significance of the distinction between the characteristics of mechanistic and organic structures, and Lawrence and Lorsch on the differentiation and integration of internal structures.

● As with other approaches to organisation and management, the contingency approach has been subject to a number of criticisms or doubts about its practical value to management. However, despite the criticisms and limitations it has provided a further insight into our understanding of relationships among factors influencing the structure, management and operations of organisations. The contingency approach also draws attention to the importance of different structures for different activities of the organisation.

● The effects of increased economic pressures and demands for greater competitiveness have drawn attention to the importance of structural variables. The movement towards tighter and leaner organisations has emphasised the importance of alternative forms of structure, of the demand for flexibility and greater freedom for the individual. There is a wide range of flexible working practices, which in many instances can be used in a variety of workplaces. In order to free management to concentrate on core activities, businesses are making increasing use of outsourcing and having a wider range of non-core services provided to them by specialist service providers.

● One particular approach to flexible structural design, and the core and complementary model of employment is Handy's concept of the 'shamrock' organisation which is seen as made up of three distinct groups of people who are managed, organised and paid differently, and with different expectations: the professional core, the contractual fringe and the flexible labour force. The demand for flexibility raises questions about the location of decision-making within the organisation, the extent and nature of delegation and empowerment, and the manager–subordinate relationship.

Your tasks

1 Using the Burns and Stalker model (Table 16.2) and the Handy model (Figure 16.7) as the basis for analysis, identify the degree to which the John Lewis Partnership, Waitrose and Ocado reflect mechanistic, organic and 'shamrock' structures of organisation.

2 Critically review the governing structure of the John Lewis partnership. What are the strengths and weaknesses of such a structure in a fast-moving competitive environment?

3 Discuss and evaluate the possible impact of this democratic style of organisation on the role and behaviour of managers. How is it likely to differ from the role and behaviour of managers in a more traditional, shareholder-owned company?

Notes and references

1 Vecchio, R. P. *Organizational Behavior, Core Concepts*, Fourth edition, Dryden Press (2000), p. 320.

2 Bouchikhi, H and Kimberly, J. R. 'The Customized Workplace', in Chowdhury, S. *Management 21C*, Financial Times Prentice Hall (2000), pp. 207–19.

3 Vecchio, R. P. *Organizational Behavior: Core Concepts*, Fourth edition, Dryden Press (2000), p. 338.

4 Lynch, R. *Corporate Strategy*, Fourth edition, Financial Times Prentice Hall (2006), p. 582.

5 See, for example: Luthans, F. *Organisational Behaviour*, Fourth edition, McGraw-Hill (1985).

6 See, for example: Miller, D. and Droge, C. 'Psychological and Traditional Determinants of Structure', *Administrative Science Quarterly*, 31 December 1986, pp. 539–60.

7 Child, J. *Organization: A Guide to Problems and Practice*, Second edition, Paul Chapman (1988), p. 221.

8 See, for example: McKinley, W. 'Decreasing Organisational Size: To Untangle or Not to Untangle?', *Academy of Management Review*, January 1992, pp. 112–23; and Shapiro, E. 'Power, Not Size Counts', *Management Review*, September 1996.

9 Birkinshaw, J. 'The Structures behind Global Companies', in Pickford, J. (ed.), *Financial Times Mastering Management 2.0*, Financial Times Prentice Hall (2001), pp. 75–80.

10 Woodward, J. *Industrial Organization: Theory and Practice*, Second edition, Oxford University Press (1980).

11 Dawson, S. and Wedderburn, D. 'Introduction' to Woodward, J. *Industrial Organisation: Theory and Practice*, Second edition, Oxford University Press (1980), p. xiii.

12 Woodward, J. *Industrial Organisation: Theory and Practice*, Second edition, Oxford University Press (1980), pp. 69, 71.

13 Zwerman, W. L. *New Perspectives on Organisation Theory*, Greenwood (1970).

14 Marsh, R. M. and Mannari, H. 'Technology and Size as Determinants of the Organisational Structure of Japanese Factories', *Administrative Science Quarterly*, 26, 1981, pp. 35–56.

15 Collins, P. D. and Hull, F. 'Technology and Span of Control: Woodward Revisited', *Journal of Management Studies*, vol. 23, no. 2, March 1986, pp. 143–64.

16 Perrow, C. *Organisational Analysis: A Sociological View*, Tavistock Publications (1970).

17 Burns, T. and Stalker, G. M. *The Management of Innovation*, Tavistock Publications (1966).

18 Litterer, J. A. *The Analysis of Organizations*, Second edition, Wiley (1973).

19 Sherman, J. D. and Smith, H. L. 'The Influence of Organisational Structure on Intrinsic Versus Extrinsic Motivation', *Academy of Management Journal*, December 1984, p. 883.

20 Reigle, R. F. 'Measuring Organic and Mechanistic Cultures', *Engineering Management Journal*, vol. 13, no. 4, December 2001, pp. 3–8.

21 Wilkins, R. 'The Management Challenge of Hybrid Organisations', *Administrator*, vol. 7, no. 8, September 1987, p. 3.

22 Mullins, L. J. *Hospitality Management and Organisational Behaviour*, Fourth edition, Longman (2001).

23 Parris, J. 'Designing your Organisation', *Management Services*, vol. 23, no. 10, October 1979, p. 14.

24 Lawrence, P. R. and Lorsch, J. W. *Organisation and Environment*, Irwin (1969).

25 Boschken, H. L. 'Strategy and Structure: Reconceiving the Relationship', *Journal of Management*, vol. 16, no. 1, March 1990, pp. 135–50.

26 Hunt, J. W. *Managing People at Work: A Manager's Guide to Behaviour in Organisations*, Third edition, McGraw-Hill (1992), p. 170.

27 Child, J. *Organisation: A Guide to Problems and Practice*, Second edition, Paul Chapman (1988).

28 Dawson, S. 'Organisational Analysis and the Study of Policy Formulation and Implementation', *Public Administration Bulletin*, 31, December 1979, pp. 52–68.

29 Mintzberg, H. *The Structuring of Organisations*, Prentice Hall (1979).

30 Birkinshaw, J, *Mastering Management 2.0*, Financial Times Prentice Hall (2001), p. 78.

31 See, for example: Fincham, R. and Rhodes, P. S. *The Individual, Work and Organisation*, Second edition, Weidenfeld and Nicolson (1992).

32 Robey, D. *Designing Organisations*, Irwin (1982), p. 59.

33 Vecchio, R. P., *Organisational Behavior: Core Concepts*, Fourth edition, Dryden Press (2000), pp. 11–12.

34 Hofstede, G. *Culture's Consequences: International Differences in Work-related Values'*, Sage Publications (1980).

35 Trompenaars, F. and Hampden-Turner, C. *Riding the Waves of Culture*, Second edition, Nicholas Brearley (1999).

36 Hickson, D., Hinings, C., McMillan, C. and Schwitter, J. 'The Culture Free Context of Organisation Structures: A Tri National Comparison', *Sociology*, vol. 8, 1974, pp. 59–80.

37 Maurice, M., Sorge, A. and Warner, M. 'Societal Differences in Organising Manufacturing Units: A Comparison of France, West Germany and Britain', *Organisational Studies*, vol. 1, no. 1, 1980, pp. 59–86.

38 Schneider, S. C. and Barsoux, J. *Managing Across Cultures*, Second edition, Financial Times Prentice Hall (2003), p. 101.

39 Francesco, A. M. and Gold, B. A. *International Organisational Behavior*, Second edition, Pearson Prentice Hall (2005).

40 Morgan, G. *Imaginisation: The Art of Creative Management*, Sage Publications (1993).

41 Eden, C. 'Coping with strategic risk', in Crainer, S. and Dearlove, D. (eds) *Handbook of Management*, Financial Times Prentice Hall (2001).

42 Crainer, S., *Key Management Ideas: Thinkers that Changed the Management World*, Third edition, Financial Times Prentice Hall (1998), p. 47.

43 Czerniawska, F. 'From bottlenecks to blackberries: How the relationship between organisations and individuals is changing', Management Consultancies Association, Executive Report, September 2005; and Vernon, M. 'The Changing Face of the Workplace' *Management Today*, September 2005, pp. 62–7.

44 See, for example: Hains, G. 'BPO: The Next Generation of Outsourcing', *Institute of Business Ideas and Solutions'*, December 2002, pp. 12–13.

45 Vernon, M. 'The Changing Face of the Workplace' *Management Today*, September 2005, pp. 62–7. See also Czerniawska, F. 'From bottlenecks to blackberries: How the relationship between organisations and individuals is changing', Management Consultancies Association, Executive Report, September 2005.

46 Bouchikhi, H. and Kimberly, J. R., 'The Customized Workplace', in Chowdhury, S., *Management 21C*, Financial Times Prentice Hall (2000), pp. 207–19.

47 'Advice Leaflet – Flexible Working' ACAS, November 2005. www.acas.org.uk [accessed 24 April 2006].

48 Pitman, B. (Sir) 'Flexibility is the Key to Competitiveness', *Professional Manager*, March 2000, p. 6.

49 Atkinson, J. 'Manpower Strategies for Flexible Organisations', *Personnel Management*, vol. 16, no. 8, August 1984, pp. 28–31.

50 'Work–Life Balance: The Business Case' Department of Trade and Industry, September 2001.

51 'Flexible Working – Case studies', Equal Opportunities Commission, www.eoc.org.uk, 24 June 2003.

52 'Flexible Working: The Implementation Challenge', CIPD, October 2005.

53 Cook, P. and Jackson, N. 'Motivation Matters', Chartered Management Institute, October 2005.

54 'Commission Proposal Supports Temporary Agency Work', *Social Agenda*, European Commission Employment and Social Affairs, Issue No. 2, July 2002.

55 Lucas, E. 'Riding the flexible working wave', *Professional Manager*, January 2006, pp. 22–4.

56 Manochehri, G. and Pinkerton, T. 'Managing Telecommuters: Opportunities and Challenges', *American Business Review*, vol. 21, no. 1, January 2003, pp. 9–16.

57 Lucas, E., 'Keep it Formal for Maximum Flexibility', *Professional Manager*, March 2000, pp. 10–12.

58 Rigby, R. 'Homing In', *Management Today*, March 2005, pp. 72–4.

59 Eatherden, R. 'Home Alone Stir Crazy' *Management Today*, March 2005, p. 75.

60 Handy, C. B. *The Age of Unreason*, Business Books (1989).

61 Oxford English Dictionary Online version

62 Merriam-Webster Dictionary, Online version

63 *McDonald's anger over McJob entry*, BBC online news, news.bbc.co.uk, 11 September 2003 [accessed 19 January 2006].

64 Thomas, D. 'HR challenges ... I'm lovin' it' *Personnel Today*, 6 September 2005, www.personneltoday.com [accessed 19 January 2006].

65 Ibid.

66 People Management, *Large on Learning*, www.peoplemanagement.co.uk [accessed 19 January 2006].

67 Thomas, D. 'McDonald's agrees shift swapping contract' *Personnel Today*, 25 January 2006, www.personneltoday.com [accessed 19 January 2006].

68 Winterman, D. 'The flip side of a McJob' BBC online news, news.bbc.co.uk, 6 August 2006 [accessed 19 January 2006].

69 Ibid

70 John Lewis Partnership website http://www.johnlewispartnership.co.uk/

71 John Spedan Lewis, quoted in the JLP corporate brochure.

72 John Lewis Partnership Annual Report and Accounts 2005–6.

73 Sir Stuart Hampson, Chairman of JLP.

74 Verdict, 2006 Consumer Satisfaction Index.

75 Wallop, H. 2006 'John Lewis Trumps M&S', *Daily Telegraph* 30 May 2006.

76 RSPCA Website www.rspca.org.uk [accessed 26 June 2006].

77 Day. P. 2005 'Right up Your Street'. BBC online news.bbc.co.uk, 9 August 2005 [accessed 26 June 2006].

17

> Just what is making work so hard? Technology has played a crucial role: firstly by increasing the mechanisms for accountability of one's work and thus depriving many of autonomy; and secondly by eroding the boundaries around work – the routines of set working hours, the spatial separation between work and home – which for the entire industrial era had given people privacy and rest.

Madeleine Bunting – Columnist on The *Guardian*

Willing Slaves: How the overwork culture is ruling our lives, HarperCollins (2004)

TECHNOLOGY AND ORGANISATIONS

Peter Scott[1]

Technology is pervasive within contemporary organisations. It is brought into organisations by people, is put to work by people and is discarded by people. This means that the ways technology is used and the purposes for which it is used are primarily a result of the decisions taken by members of the organisation and the contexts within which those decisions were taken. Managers need an understanding of the nature of technological change, its organisational and human resource dimensions, and its circumstances of use.

Learning outcomes

After completing this chapter you should be able to:

- detail the variety of perspectives used to theorise on the nature of technology;
- explain the relevance of technology for an increasing range of uses in organisations;
- analyse the significance of current generations of information and communication technology, and its potential to create complex networks;
- examine the nature and significance of the technology adoption and introduction phases;
- evaluate the involvement of non-technical specialists in technological change;
- assess how technology can influence ways in which work patterns are designed and controlled;
- explain how new technology can affect social interactions and stress at work.

TECHNOLOGY AS A SUBJECT OF STUDY

Technology is found and used in all organisations: in small and large businesses, educational establishments, multinational firms and the local corner shop. Since the industrial revolution it has been used to raise the productivity of workers; today, it is increasingly the source of new products, services and processes that were unrealisable only a few decades ago, and its effects are being felt more and more in the service sector and state institutions rather than in the traditional 'heartland' of manufacturing companies.

Interest by social scientists in technology as a variable and a source of change in organisations has waxed and waned since the 1950s. Some, such as *Hallier*, have observed that the study of technology and organisations is a relatively mature field, with current academic interest largely confined to a few innovations like telephone call centres and teleworking that are themselves dependent on recent technical advances.[2] Since approximately the mid-1990s it is true that organisational change techniques, such as lean production, business process re-engineering and other work reorganisation schemes, have attracted more academic attention than technical change. However, this chapter argues that the latter is still important, not least because some of the organisational change techniques mentioned are in fact underpinned by advances in information technology, but also because many of the 'classic' insights remain valid. Further, technical change programmes (as is also true of other types of change initiative) often fail in practice to deliver the anticipated benefits, with available research suggesting that neglect of the human dimension of technical change is often culpable in this failure.[3] Managers therefore need to be aware of the nature of technology and the technical change process.

THEORIES OF TECHNOLOGY

To begin, however, we need to address the question of what we actually mean by technology in some detail for a number of reasons. First of all, there is a variety of definitions and none is universally accepted. Second, the way in which a particular writer defines technology provides a significant clue as to the theoretical perspective that is informing their understanding of what technology actually means or consists of. Third, definitions can make a difference, as what one actually does or expects other people to do in relation to some technology flows in part from how one perceives that technology and its capabilities. One of the basic disagreements is where 'technology' begins and ends and the extent to which it can be separated from any surrounding social, political and organisational context in which it operates. Here, for example, *Orlikowski*[4] provides a useful basic distinction between what she calls the scope (what is defined as comprising technology itself) and the role of technology (how the interaction between technology and the organisation is defined).

We start here by briefly categorising the variety of conceptions into some of the key 'schools' or perspectives on technology in an organisational context. (It is important to note, however, that there is often a degree of overlap among the 'schools'.) The main approaches discussed are:

1 technological determinism;
2 socio-technical systems approaches;
3 radical/Marxist perspectives;
4 political/processual approaches;
5 the socio-economic shaping of technology (SST);
6 the social construction of technology (SCT);
7 Actor–Network Analysis (ANA);
8 technology as text and metaphor (TTM).

Technological determinism

In the opening paragraphs of their book, *MacKenzie and Wajcman* observe:

> *Technology is a vitally important aspect of the human condition. Technologies feed, clothe, and provide shelter for us; they transport, entertain, and heal us; they provide the bases of wealth and of leisure; they also pollute and kill. For good or ill, they are woven inextricably into the fabric of our lives ... [This] technological determinism contains a partial truth. Technology matters. It matters not just to the material condition of our lives and to our biological and physical environment ... but to the way we live together socially.*[5]

They refer to the view that technology alone causes certain things to happen or to be as they are as 'hard determinism' and go on to note that this can never provide an adequate or full explanation without additionally considering many other factors as well, such as political, social and economic. But 'the failure of hard technological determinism does not rule out a "soft" determinism, and to say that technology's social effects are complex and contingent is not to say that it has **no** social effects'.[6] Much of the influential early writing in organisation studies on the technology–organisation relationship in the 1950s also saw technology as a significant, and in some cases, determining variable on organisational behaviour. Typically here, the technology concerned was of a 'hard-wired' variety with an obvious physical presence, most usually and obviously in the form of mechanical manufacturing machinery.

As the area of study developed, the conceptualisation of what 'technology' was tended to broaden to incorporate, for example in *Woodward's* case, not just the machinery but also the associated knowledge and expertise for utilising that machinery.[7] Woodward has often been 'accused' of (hard) technological determinism (as in her conclusion that 'there is a particular form of organisation most appropriate to each technical situation'),[8] but, as *McLoughlin and Dawson* note, she

> *... also saw the role of 'technology' as being mediated to some extent by the interpretative action of management in realising the need to adapt organisational structures to the requirements of the production system. Indeed even in these early studies, often accused of a crude technological determinism, the notion of 'technology' being associated with variable 'organisational outcomes' was sometimes recognised ... However, the failure to explain such variations in terms other than problems of organisational adaptation to some form of technological requirements has meant that much of this early work has inevitably been labelled as 'technological determinist' and thereby [became] a critical reference point for nearly all subsequent organisational theory and research on the topic.*[9]

Hardness of technology While Woodward, then, can be argued to have adopted a 'softer' form of technological determinism, *Blauner*[10] in the USA in the early 1960s took up a harder version. Based on studies of four different industries, he argued that the type of technology used in an organisation's manufacturing process determined the level of job satisfaction (he used the term 'alienation', although not in the same sense as it was used by Marx) experienced by people working with and on the technology.

Perhaps one of the most concerted attempts to preserve a role for the 'hardness' of technology, while at the same time explicitly recognising that it is politically and socially created, chosen and deployed in organisations, is the work of *Thomas* in the USA.[11] His research is strongly based in longitudinal case studies of the use of technology in a range of organisations, and he argues for the study of organisational technology via what he terms a 'power-process' perspective. He draws upon both the technological determinist and social choice perspectives (see the discussion below), and makes two key assumptions: (i) the physical world constrains the range of alternative ways in which people can organise the production of social goods, and (ii) the social worlds which people create influence the way they understand and act on the social world. Thus, technology and organisation are engaged in a continual circular process whereby each helps to structure the other in turn:

> *The core argument of the book can be stated rather simply: to explain what new technology does to organisations ... we must also explain what people are trying to do to organisations and by extension, to themselves by means of new technology.*[12]

Thomas's work thus has some affinity with both the 'hard' and 'soft' technological determinist positions. It also has much in common with some of the theories of technology that we look at below, in particular the socio-economic shaping of technology, the social construction of technology, and processual approaches. But what perhaps most distinguishes his approach is the emphasis that he gives throughout the book to the political shaping and deployment of technology, illustrated by the following extracts:

> *If no one social group ... can lay claim to the 'truest' or the most 'real' understanding of the physical world, then we are forced to conceive of the relationship between technology and organisation as mediated by the exercise of power, that is, by a system of authority and domination that asserts the primacy of one understanding of the physical world, one prescription for social organisation, over others*[13] ... *Particular attention must be paid to the relative capacity of different organisational groups to influence the definition of organisational objectives and the technical means through which they are to be achieved ... Technology can appear to be determinant when its objective features become indistinguishable from the objectives of those who occupy positions of dominance.*[14]

Socio-technical systems approaches

The systems approach to the theorising and analysis of organisations has already been discussed in Chapters 2 and 3. Socio-technical approaches are located within this mode of analysis, and have a particular concern to find the 'best fit' in any given job/work design between the social elements (such as people's psychological and social needs) and technical elements (such as the apparatus and its physical location) of the organisational 'system'. *Trist*[15] has been an influential writer in this area. A characteristic of this school of systems design is that it anticipates that the 'best' overall socio-technical design is a compromise between what would constitute the ideal designs on 'technical' or 'social' grounds alone. In other words, 'joint optimisation' of the overall socio-technical system requires 'sub-optimisation' of its constituent technical and social sub-systems. For the socio-technical theorist, the eventual systems design is a matter for conscious organisational choice rather than any technical necessity (as a technical determinist would argue).

Radical/Marxist perspectives

Much writing and analysis about technical change within this tradition has been strongly influenced by the labour process perspective, developed from *Braverman's* work in the 1970s. This approach argues that the social and economic 'outcomes' of technical change must be understood through the location of events and decisions within the wider dynamics of capitalism, accumulation and the imperative of profitability for organisational survival. This is achieved through the intensification of management control over labour through a long-term trend towards rationalisation, deskilling and degradation of work.[16] Thus, technology is one of the means used by managers to retain and extend control and deskill work (the use of information technology for the monitoring and surveillance of work and employees being but one example). Braverman saw scientific management (discussed in Chapter 2) as the main means used by management to deskill work and extend their control over other employees.

The key point about the radical/Marxist perspective here is that it is not the technology *per se* which deskills jobs (as a technological determinist would claim), but the way it is used in the hands of (capitalist) management. Within the capitalist economic system, an inevitable deskilling trend is:

> *entirely a product of the need to control the labour process in order to increase profits. Under a different social system, advanced technology would open up the possibility of different forms of job design and work organisation which would benefit the workforce. This would involve workgroups possessing the engineering knowledge required to operate and maintain the technology, and a rotation of tasks to make sure everyone had opportunities to work on both highly complex and routine jobs. In other words, rather than being deskilled, they would retain autonomy and control over the labour process, and advanced technology would be used as a complement to, rather than a substitute for, human skills and abilities ... such a form of work organisation and control could not be brought about without a major political, economic and social transformation.*[17]

Social power issues There are some significant connections here with social power issues. *Zuboff*[18] has been a particularly influential writer on the topic of power. She distinguishes between the **'automating'** (the mere replacement of actions of the human body by the machine) and **'informating'** potential of IT (the simultaneous generation of new, additional information about organisational activities). It is this 'informating' capability, according to Zuboff, that presents a 'transformative' possibility to organisations through the increased organisational transparency that it offers. The problem is that this potential is rarely realised, because the necessary associated organisational changes do not occur (devolution of responsibility and influence to lower-level workers within the organisation, etc.) as pre-existing modes of organisation structuring and working practices continue.

Political/processual approaches

The focus of this perspective is much more strongly upon:

> *the assumption that the outcomes of technological change, rather than being determined by the logic of capitalist development, or external technical and product market imperatives, are in fact socially chosen and negotiated within organisations by organisational actors.*[19]

Processual approaches emphasise the interplay between three main elements that can be applied to technical change: what *Dawson* calls the substance of change (its actual technical content, its timeframe and perceived centrality to the organisation), the context of change (both within the organisation and in the outside environment, including the activities of competitors) and the politics of change (the actions and attitudes of actors having influence over the change process).[20] An influential early study was conducted by *Pettigrew*, who examined organisational politics and decision-making associated with the development and

structuring of computer applications. He showed, for example, how the head of a management services department was able to influence decisions in the computerisation domain through taking up a 'gatekeeper' role which allowed him to 'shape' the information reaching the key managerial decision-makers.[21]

Buchanan and Boddy argued that 'the capabilities of technology are enabling, rather than determining' and that it is 'decisions or choices concerning how the technology will be used' and not the technology itself, which leads to the organisational outcomes.[22]

Deployment of Lotus Notes A more recent example of authors adopting a political/processual perspective associated with the use of technology (in this case information and communication technology) comes from *Hayes and Walsham's* research into working practices and discourse around the deployment of Lotus Notes in a case study of a company selling medical products.[23] Lotus Notes were introduced in order to facilitate the collaborative working of employees across and within functional specialisms. Some shared databases proved to have more heightened political content than others, and this affected the quality of the interaction between employees and between employees and managers. To illustrate, the sharing of information and ideas was not as extensive in some cases as in others – Hayes and Walsham attribute this to such political factors as 'young careerists' trying to draw attention to themselves (showing how hard-working they are, for example) through the data they put up, and 'old-stagers'/non-careerists not being concerned with such matters, and hence not going to such trouble. What was communicated via the technology also appeared to be a function of who was known/suspected to be looking – for example, the statement of a senior manager that he was going to read and contribute to a particular site impacted upon what was subsequently placed on that site.

The socio-economic shaping of technology

With this perspective the dominant focus is upon the ways in which the technology is shaped by (rather than itself shaping, as with the technological determinist perspective) the economic, technical, political, gender and social circumstances in which it is designed, developed and utilised.[24] These non-'technical' factors are embodied in the emergent technology, and therefore technology alone does not have an 'impact'. SST often draws upon Marxian and gender analyses, and argues that:

> *Capitalism and patriarchy are primary contexts that influence the development and use of technologies. That is, the emergence of new technologies in some way responds to the expression of class and gender interests – whether through the industrial military, the domination of scientific and technological spheres of activity by men or through the activities of particular organisations in the economy.*[25]

It is important to note, however, as *McLoughlin and Harris* have argued, that from the SST perspective:

> *Technology is accorded a specific causal status: the idea that technology has 'causal effects' on society is rejected, but the idea of technological influences on the shaping of technology itself is not. A precondition of much technological innovation is in fact seen to be existing technology.*[26]

The social construction of technology

Rather than seeing technology emerging from a rational-linear process of invention, design, development and innovation, the SCT approach draws more upon the sociology of scientific knowledge. It examines the unfolding of technological change over time in its social and economic contexts to show that technology is created through a process that involves many actors and is multidirectional.[27] SCT argues that there is a range of technological options available or identifiable, which a variety of people, groups and organisations (such as sup-

pliers, designers, IT specialists, engineers) seeks to promote or challenge. These people's concerns are partly technical, but also social, moral and economic. These 'relevant' social groups define the 'problem' for which the artefact is intended to be a 'solution'. Technical change occurs where either sufficient consensus emerges for a particular design option or when a design option is imposed by a powerful actor or group. Search activity and debate is then closed, and the technology is 'stabilised' in a particular configuration. From this point on, it is possible to talk about 'impacts' or 'effects' on the organisation in general, working practices, skill requirements, etc., but, as with SST, these effects are not purely technical. It is important to note, however, that while

> *the social constructivist argument does not deny that material artefacts have constraining influences upon actors . . . it does hold a question-mark over what these constraints are. Such constraints – or enablers – do not acquire their significance without interpretative action on the part of humans, hence there can be no self-evident or transparent account of such 'material constraints'. There are, of course, more persuasive accounts and less persuasive accounts – but they remain accounts, not reflections.*[28]

Socio-technical ensembles An influential variant within the SCT perspective, associated particularly with the research of *Bijker*, is that relating to so-called 'socio-technical ensembles' (which have little, if any, connection with the socio-technical systems approaches discussed earlier).[29] Here, technology is seen as a key constituent element of the ensemble (defined below), which emerges within the social, economic and political contexts of the organisation. Bijker stresses the organisational politics dimension of the creation and maintenance of the ensemble:

> *Such an analysis stresses the malleability of technology and the possibility for choice, the basic insight **that things could have been otherwise**. But technology is not always malleable, it can also be obdurate, hard and very fixed. The second step is to analyse this obduracy of socio-technical ensembles, to see what limits it sets to our politics.*[30]

If an organisation is seen as a collection of groups, each of which has a particular technological 'frame', then political behaviour is seen as centring around attempts to achieve ascendancy for a particular frame, and often it is those groups which already have more power that are the most successful in this process. So, the socio-technical ensemble, then, embodies a web of relationships between individuals, groups, technology and internal and external organisational contexts. It is dynamic, and the exercise of power plays a key role in shaping and moulding it. The socio-technical ensemble, discussed below, illustrates how this particular perspective on technology and organisations can be used to analyse organisational behaviour.

Actor–Network Analysis

Actor–Network Analysis (ANA) is associated particularly with the work of *Callon, Latour and Law*.[31] ANA is admittedly a complex approach, which argues that actors define one another and their relationships through intermediaries such as literary inscriptions (e.g. books and magazines), technical artefacts (e.g. computers and machines), skills (e.g. the knowledge possessed by people) and money. They attempt to construct networks which will bring together a range of these human and non-human actants. The key to understanding ANA is its argument that:

> The relationship between the technological and the social cannot be understood by reductionist arguments which view either the technological or the social as ultimately determining. Whether it is the technological, social factors or other material or natural factors which determine the relationship between the technical is a complex empirical question the answer to which will vary from context to context. No definitive line can therefore be drawn between that which is 'technological' and that which is 'social'.[32]

A, if not the, key concern of ANA is to try to establish, in specific work and organisational contexts, 'the processes whereby relatively stable networks of aligned interests are created and maintained, or alternatively to examine why such networks fail to establish themselves'.[33]

From the ANA perspective, then, technology has a robustness and thus makes a difference in and of itself to organisational processes and 'outcomes'. As Coombs *et al.* have noted:

> Callon's treatment of non-humans ... in a similar way to humans ... is not intended to be anthropomorphic – the fact that they intervene in processes does not mean they have motives and intentions of their own. It is intended to underline ... the fact that technology is not infinitely plastic, to be shaped in any way whatsoever by social forces, any more than technology is driven solely by its own internal logic, independently of society.[34]

At the same time, however, ANA theorists are very reluctant to attach any major role or influence in their explanations and theories to pre-existing macro social structures, such as social classes and markets. They have been criticised for 'ceding too much power and autonomy to individual actors and eschewing existing social theory, leaving them poorly equipped to explain particular developments and beset by a tendency to offer mainly descriptions and post-hoc explanations'.[35]

Technology as text and metaphor

Like SCT, TTM draws on the sociology of scientific knowledge; however, TTM does not accept the proposition that technology becomes 'stabilised' – that is, that it comes to have some identifiable 'objective' implications, characteristics and capabilities.[36] Considerations such as what technologies are, what they can and cannot do, and what effects they have, are seen as always a socially negotiated phenomenon; technologies are only understood or 'read' in the particular social contexts in which they are found. Actor-networks of humans and non-humans create and sustain specific conceptualisations of what is 'social' and what is 'technical', and the relationship between them.

It follows, according to this perspective, that different representations of the nature of technologies/organisations can be created using different metaphors or 'readings', and thus the focus of interest turns to, not what a particular technology can or cannot do, but rather how such accounts (of what it can do) are derived.[37] *McLoughlin and Harris* have referred to TTM as an 'extreme' relativist position, arguing that its key problem is that:

> the influence of broader social structure and distributions of power, even organisational structure and the roles of competing stakeholder interests are viewed as superfluous to the analysis of technology and technological change. It is as if the 'lid' of the 'technological black box' has been 'opened' but then shut firmly tight behind the analyst.[38]

Let us make two final overall comments to end this section:

1 The chosen categorisation of perspectives on technology is inevitably somewhat arbitrary. It is quite possible to think of other ways in which this complex and heterogeneous field of study could be further divided or other perspectives included, etc.

2 Here we have merely defined and briefly described each perspective; space does not permit the inclusion of extended critiques of each perspective, of which a large number can be found elsewhere.[39]

Refresh your understanding

Activity 17A
www.pearsoned.co.uk/mullins

A SOCIO-TECHNICAL ENSEMBLE PERSPECTIVE

A socio-technical ensemble perspective can be used to aid the understanding of organisational structuring and practices that incorporate a strategic deployment of technology. *Blosch and Preece* provide a case study of a UK-based consumer goods company where the focus is on the configuration of the work and technology of sales representatives.[40] The company sells its

products into a mature and highly competitive market. It changed ownership twice during the 1990s and was 'de-layered' and rationalised, leading to a very flat organisation structure where the number of line managers between a sales representative and the CEO is only three. The reps work from home, thus they do not require any costly office space; their interaction with the organisation is strongly mediated by information technology. The sales team was charged with two key objectives: to increase market share and to gather marketing information.

The exercise of managerial power played a key part in shaping organisational action. Senior management played the key and determining role in designing, implementing and monitoring the socio-technical ensemble which both enabled and constrained the work and working practices of the sales reps. It was within this ensemble that the nature and quality of the relationships between the actors, and between the actors and the technology, were set out: senior management made the decisions, the reps carried out their instructions, and middle management (that is, the area managers) ensured that the reps complied.

TYPES AND CHARACTERISTICS OF TECHNOLOGY

What do we specifically mean by the word 'technology' in today's context? As already indicated, the concept of technology should be interpreted broadly to include both:

- the physical aspects of machines, equipment, processes and work layout (*machine technology*) involved in the transformation or conversion process; and
- the actual methods, systems and procedures involved (*knowledge technology*) in carrying out the work of the organisation and transforming or converting inputs into outputs.

By the physical side of technology we are mainly referring to microelectronics and microprocessors, information and communication technologies (ICTs) based on advances in telecommunications, which can be applied in manufacturing processes, information sharing and processing, service provision and in products themselves. These main forms or applications may be summarised as follows:

- Manufacturing/engineering/design technology – sometimes referred to as 'advanced manufacturing technology' (AMT) or 'computer-aided engineering' (CAE).
- Technology used for information capture, storage, transmission, analysis and retrieval. It may be linked to AMT/CAE or may be used separately in information-sharing and dissemination in administrative and managerial functions across a variety of organisations and in teleworking and telecommuting.
- Technology employed in the provision of services to customers, clients, patients, etc. in service sector applications.
- Technology as the product itself.

Figure 17.1 provides some examples of the different forms these technologies can take. There is in practice often overlap between the forms and applications of new technology and Figure 17.1 is by no means an exhaustive list.

It is worth noting that **some** of this technology has been in existence and available to organisations for varying periods of time (the extent to which it has been taken up by organisations or 'diffused' is, however, another matter). Numerically controlled and computer numerically controlled machine tools used in manufacturing industry, for example, have been in existence since the 1940s and 1950s. New developments and applications in hardware and software are coming onto the market all the time, and the take-up rate of the varieties of new technology is also continually expanding as more and more people in organisations become aware of its potential (and as its cost reduces in real terms).

Figure 17.1	Examples of technologies and technology applications

Advanced Manufacturing Technology

Computer numerical control machine tools (CNC)

Robotics

Computer-aided design/drafting (CAD)

Flexible manufacturing systems (FMS)

Computer-integrated manufacturing (CIM)

Computer-aided production planning and inventory control systems

Materials requirements planning (MRPI)

Manufacturing resource planning (MRPII)

Information technology

Word processing/personal computers

Intelligent knowledge-based systems

Mainframe, mini, microcomputers – used in a stand-alone mode or networked (LAN, WAN, WWW, etc.)

Teleconferencing

Videoconferencing

Teleworking/Telecommuting

Service Provision

Automated Teller Machines (ATMs)

Electronic Funds Transfer (EFT)

Electronic Data Interchange (EDI)

Electronic Point-of-Sale (EPOS)

Teletext

Patient monitoring systems

Products

Pocket calculators

Electronic games

Digital watches

Source: Adapted from Preece, D. A., *Organisations and Technical Change: Strategy, Objectives and Involvement*, Routledge/ITBP (1995), p. 3. Reprinted by permission of the publisher, Routledge, a division of Taylor & Francis, Ltd.

Advanced manufacturing technology

Computer numerical control machine tools (CNC)

Robotics computer-aided design/drafting (CAD)

Flexible manufacturing systems (FMS)

Computer-integrated manufacturing (CIM)

Computer-aided production planning and inventory control systems

Materials requirements planning (MRPI)

Manufacturing resource planning (MRPII)

nology, markets) are organized on a global scale ...';[48] and 'networked' because economic activity takes place through a global network of interaction between a variety of business networks. The emergence and development of new forms of technology made all this possible: 'This new economy emerged ... because the information technology revolution provided the indispensable material basis for its creation.'[49]

Newer new technology

As we saw earlier, a variety of forms of new technology embodying microelectronics and microprocessors, and often linked together through telecommunications, had emerged during the last quarter of the 20th century – not least, information and communication technology. This is the sort of technology Castells is thinking of above in his outline of the 'new economy'. However, further fundamental technological and related changes occurred during the very last years of the century, which led Castells to identify the opportunity for (and to some extent at least, subsequent realisation of, given his later discussion) more significant innovations in terms of the ways in which business and other activities can be undertaken across the world:

> *In the late 1990s, the communication power of the Internet, together with new developments in telecommunications and computing, induced another major technological shift, from decentralized, stand-alone microcomputers and mainframes to pervasive computing by interconnected information-processing devices, coming in multiple formats. In this new technological system computer power is distributed in a communicated network built around web servers using common Internet protocols, and enabled with access capability to mega-computer servers, usually differentiated between database servers and application servers ... users were accessing the network from a variety of single-purpose, specialized devices distributed in all spheres of life and activity, at home, at work, at shopping, at entertainment places, in transportation vehicles, and ultimately everywhere. These devices, many of them portable, can communicate among themselves, without needing their own operating system. Thus, computing power, applications, and data are stored in the servers of the network, and computing intelligence is placed in the network itself: web sites communicate with each other, and have at their disposal the necessary software to connect any appliance to a universal computer network.*[50]

Given the above analysis, it should come as no surprise that Castells sees networks as the core identifying feature not only of the 'new economy', but also increasingly of the businesses and infrastructure which interlink and support them and their activities.

The new enterprise (or organisation)

Castells tends to refer to the new 'enterprise', probably because this term does not so readily have the connotation of economic or social activity being carried out within a fixed and known geographic space or spaces, such as office buildings, which we often associate with the term 'organisation'. 'Enterprise' can perhaps more readily signal in this context economic activity which occurs across the world, between a variety of actors, some of whom might be located in an 'organisation' and work in/from a designated office, others working from home, as subcontractors, as 'outsourcers', or in a 'virtual' way, but all collaborating in some way or other in forms of economic activity, facilitated by technology.

Castells, then, talks about the 'network enterprise', which he defines as 'that specific form of enterprise whose system of means is constituted by the intersection of segments of autonomous systems of goals'.[51] That is, the components of the network are simultaneously both autonomous and dependent vis-à-vis the network, and may be part of other networks. The quality of the performance of a network depends upon (i) its 'connectedness', that is, its ability to facilitate noise-free communication between its component parts, and (ii) its 'consistency', that is, the overlap in the sharing of interests between the network's goals and the goals of its components.

This still leaves open the question 'what is a network?' in Castells' understanding. He provides a technical definition towards the end of the volume:

> *A network is a set of interconnected nodes. A node is the point at which a curve intersects itself. What a node is ... depends on the kind of concrete networks of which we speak. They are stock exchange markets, and their ancillary advanced services centres, in the network of global financial flows ... The topology defined by networks determines that the distance (or intensity and frequency of interaction) between two points (or social positions) is shorter (or more frequent, or more intense) if both points are nodes in a network than if they do not belong to the same network. On the other hand, within a given network, flows have no distance, or the same distance, between nodes. Thus, distance (physical, social, economic, political, cultural) for a given point or position varies between zero (for any node in the same network) and infinite (for any point external to the network). The inclusion/exclusion in networks, enacted by light-speed-operating information technologies, configure dominant processes and functions in our societies.*[52]

Types of networks It is recognised that there is a variety of types of networks. Earlier in this chapter we talked, for example, about 'actor-networks', and it is important to state here that the ways in which these are understood is quite different from the sort of network theorisation under discussion here. *Piore and Sabel* talked about 'industrial district' networks of collaborating (often small) firms, located in defined regions of the world.[53] Castells' 'network enterprise' was outlined above, and we will shortly refer to his 'network society', but before doing so let us look at some other possibilities. *Ernst*[54] identified the following types of networks:

- **supplier** – subcontracting and original equipment manufacturing arrangements between a client and its suppliers of intermediate inputs;
- **producer** – co-production arrangements which enable competing producers to pool their manufacturing facilities, financial and human resources with a view to extending their product offerings and geographic coverage;
- **customer** – the forward linkages of manufacturing companies with distributors, marketing channels, resellers and end-users;
- **standard coalitions** – initiated by would-be global standard setters with the objective of locking in as many companies as possible into their proprietary product/service or interface standards (for example, think of the ubiquity of Microsoft Windows as a computer operating system);
- **technology co-operation** – facilitate the acquisition of product design and production technology, enable joint production and process development, and allow generic scientific knowledge and R&D to be shared (for example, the European Airbus project).

In summary terms, then, the new enterprise paradigm consists of the following:

1 business networks;
2 technological tools;
3 global competition;
4 the state. For example, supporting the development of the new economy; helping nurture regionally based networks via local and/or regional government.

When all the above elements of the new economy, the new enterprise and the latest Internet and other new technologies are conflated across those parts of the world where they have taken hold, then, according to Castells, we can justifiably talk about the emergence of the new 'network society'.

The 'network society'

The 'material foundation' of the network society consists of the following:

1 **Information is the raw material**. Technologies act on information rather than information acting on technology, as in previous technological revolutions.

2 **Pervasiveness of effects of new technologies**. 'Because information is an integral part of all human activity, all processes of our individual and collective existence are directly shaped (although certainly not determined) by the new technological medium'.[55]

3 **Networking logic**. Using the new ICTs, the network can now be implemented in all kinds of processes and organisations:

> *Without them, the networking logic would be too cumbersome to implement. Yet this networking logic is needed to structure the unstructured while preserving flexibility, since the unstructured is the driving force of innovation in human activity. Moreover, when networks diffuse, their growth becomes exponential, as the benefits of being in the network grow exponentially, because of the greater number of connections ... [while] the penalty for being outside the network increases with the network's growth because of the declining number of opportunities in reaching other elements outside the network.*[56]

4 **The flexibility of IT**. This mainly concerns what was described in earlier sections of this chapter as the configuration and reconfiguration of organisations and institutions through IT. This 'reprogramming' of the material basis of the organisation through ICT can be liberating, but also repressive; only empirical research at the level of enterprises and economies will be able to tell us what is really occurring.

5 **The convergence of specific technologies into an integrated system**. 'Old, separate technological trajectories become literally indistinguishable. Thus, micro-electronics, telecommunications, opto-electronics, and computers are all now integrated into information systems.'[57]

> *In sum, the information technology paradigm does not evolve towards its closure as a system, but toward its openness as a multi-edged network. It is powerful and imposing in its materiality, but adaptive and open-ended in its historical development. Comprehensiveness, complexity, and networking are its decisive qualities.*[58]

And

> *... global networks of instrumental exchanges selectively switch on and off individuals, groups, regions, and even countries, according to their relevance in fulfilling the goals processed in the network, in a relentless flow of strategic decisions.*[59] *[Thus] For the first time in history, the basic unit of economic organization is not a subject, be it individual (such as the entrepreneur, or the entrepreneurial family) or collective (such as the capitalist class, the corporation, the state) ... the unit is the network, made up of a variety of subjects and organizations [emphasis in original]*[60] *... the power of flows takes precedence over the flows of power. Presence or absence in the network and the dynamics of each network vis-à-vis others are critical sources of domination and change in our society: a society that, therefore, we may properly call the network society ...*[61]

Conclusion

Castells recognises that networks do not lack structure, but argues that they flow according to logics of power (what he talks about as the 'power of flows'). To put it another way, '... some nodes are more powerful than others, exerting a greater gravitational force on the relations that stream around them'.[62] He talks of the 'switches' that connect up networks as being privileged instruments of power, i.e. 'global flows of financial capital, ensuring that the network society is a capitalist society of 'decentralized concentration'.[63] However, an important criticism of Castells is that he appears to see the 'power of flows' as having precedence over the 'flows of power', where the logic of the network supersedes all other logics – as can be seen in the extract above. Networks seem to have a life of their own – a concept that may leave some feeling rather uneasy. As *Fitzpatrick* has observed:

> *... as well as underestimating the power of capitalists, Castells enjoins us to abandon the ideological reference points and strategies that provide such struggles with long-term direction ... that ideology may actually motivate micro-political struggles, is a fact that he, like most postmodernists ... seems unable to accommodate.*[64]

Refresh your understanding

Activity 17B
www.pearsoned.co.uk/
mullins

Capitalist hierarchies of power and control have not been replaced by a new mode of social organisation, indeed 'the advent of informatics [ICTs, etc.] strengthens corporate capitalism'.[65] What is more, 'electronically generated information tends to act as information always acts in a market, i.e. it is information about the relatively powerless that flows to the relatively powerful'.[66] Thus, 'in short, the information revolution is a revolution *within* capitalism and not a revolution *of* capitalism'.[67]

Despite Castells' criticisms of technological determinism, he is also perhaps vulnerable to the same charge himself by putting so much emphasis on the technical changes since the last quarter of the 20th century as the drivers of his 'network society'.[68]

ADOPTING AND INTRODUCING NEW TECHNOLOGY

Let us now return in a more concrete way to the process whereby new technology is introduced into organisations. By 'new' technology we mean 'new' to its use by a particular organisation, regardless of for how long the technology concerned may have been available. In this section we will address two issues relating to that process which, between them, are likely to have far-reaching consequences for the eventual success and the acceptance of the change concerned. First, we consider the different phases of technical change. In each of these stages, a range of decisions needs to be made by various interested parties, although the range of those decisions is likely to get narrower and more detailed as the introduction process progresses. Second, it is important to ask just **who** are the 'interested parties' who actually tend to get involved in the various 'design spaces' that are opened up at the various stages of the process? Our primary concern here is with the impact of decision-making on human behaviour in organisations. Therefore, we need to ask whether the decision-making process is conceived as mainly the province of managers and technical 'experts' or whether personnel specialists or users of the new technology become involved and, if so, to what extent.

Phases and stages of technology introduction

Preece developed a useful detailed framework that identifies two phases and seven stages of new technology adoption and introduction (see Figure 17.2).[69]

The adoption phase consists of four stages: initiation, progression/feasibility, investment decision, and planning and systems design. It is only after this phase has been completed, in however cursory a manner, that it is possible to talk about the new technology coming to have a physical presence in the organisation – that is, it is at the first stage of being **introduced** into the organisation, which is the beginning of the second phase, consisting of Stages 5 to 7.

The existence of this schema is not meant to suggest that the adoption process is inherently rational and systematic, in the sense, for example, that all organisations have to go through all the stages mentioned here in the same order and manner. We know from case study research that the adoption and introduction of new technology is an iterative, contested and political process, with all that this implies.[70] Let us briefly look at each of these stages in turn.

Initiation

This stage is triggered by someone having the idea to introduce some form of new technology into the organisation. What is the nature of their job and expertise? Where did the idea come from – a business magazine, a conference, a competitor, or maybe a technology supplier? Who else, if anyone, was involved at this early stage? It is likely that employees' and managers' varying organisational backgrounds, training, qualifications, expertise and orientations will have an effect upon how the technology adoption process unfolds and is shaped from this point onwards – for instance, in terms of the objectives which are set for the introduction of the new technology, and the strategy of adoption and introduction which is deployed.

Figure 17.2 **Stages in new technology adoption and introduction**

Key: Stages 1–4 = Adoption phase
Stages 5–7 = Introduction phase

Source: Preece, D. A., *Organisations and Technical Change: Strategy, Objectives and Involvement*, Routledge/ITBP (1995), p. 7. Reprinted by permission of the publisher, Routledge, a divsion of Taylor & Francis, Ltd.

A wide range of strategies and objectives for new technology adoption and introduction can and have been pursued, aided by its inherent flexibility.[71] There is, therefore, a wide range of choice available with regard to how the technology is utilised in the organisation and the form(s) of working practices and job design adopted around the technology. Having said that, financial, economic and technical objectives often predominate.[72]

Child, talking more generally about company strategies and objectives, argued some time ago that social and organisational objectives are usually secondary to financial and economic ones, or are not strictly 'objectives' at all; rather, they can more accurately be classified as *consequences* of financial and economic objectives and strategies.[73] Inter- and intra-organisational political and social processes and structures exert an influence upon technical change and, while management strategies might not always be formulated with labour implications in mind, they can nonetheless have consequences for labour. What is more, having a strategy and objectives in place does not mean that they will be implemented and achieved as planned: they may be unspecific, poorly understood and subject to reinterpretation and opposition from managers and other employees. There may be disagreements and, indeed, conflicts among the actors involved about what these objectives and/or strategies are or *should* be. Different occupational specialisms may have different concerns, motives and priorities in the introduction of new technology and are likely to pursue their objectives using particular arguments, which may conflict with the views being put forward by other parties.

Given the range of different objectives, it is perhaps not surprising that they sometimes conflict, especially if they are held by different groups in the organisation. Thus, it can be concluded that technical change objectives will not always provide an unequivocal indication of whether to make an investment in IT (or whether such an investment has been an eventual 'success'). The opportunities for the exercise of power, negotiation and persuasion are apparent in a context of uncertainty, lack of information, competing perspectives, resource scarcity and continual change.

Progression and feasibility

This stage involves the more detailed work which follows initiation, assuming that the idea has sparked some interest in the organisation (not least, among people who have the power/authority to commit resources to the emergent project). It includes searching for further information inside and outside the company (possibly involving talking to hardware and software suppliers), looking at what competitors are doing and getting other people involved.

Investment decision

This is a crucial stage in the progression of the proposal, in that it is here that the **sponsors** (we now use this term rather than 'initiators', given that the idea has reached this stage) either get the agreement of senior managers to invest in the technology or have to resubmit or abandon the project. Argument in this stage revolves, in essence, around the estimation of costs and benefits and projections about rates of return (or some similar measure) from the investment over a certain time period.

This stage may be the first occasion on which the objectives for the introduction of new technology are **formally** articulated, if only for the simple reason that this has to be done for a presentation to the board. The meaningfulness and influence of this quantification and formalisation of technology benefits (and costs) are debatable, for, as observed above, technology adoption and introduction processes are inherently political and social, and therefore open to shaping by the various actors and groups involved.[74]

Planning and systems design

Planning and systems design follows the approval of the investment by senior managers, and involves a more detailed consideration and resolution of such matters as which supplier(s) should be used and their selection, preparation for introduction (training, communication, etc.), changes to working practices and job designs, payment and grading for working with the new technology, wiring and other technical and facilities preparation. If parties other than managers or engineers are involved during the adoption phase, this is likely to be the first occasion on which they get the opportunity to intervene (either directly or indirectly – that is, via representatives). have been involved in the adoption process. We will discuss the likelihood of this later in this chapter.

Introduction

It is at this stage that the technology first has any physical presence within the adopting organisation, and hence we move into the second main phase. In essence, the **introduction stage** involves working on the technology and the associated organisational changes with a view to making them effectively usable in an 'everyday' mode. When this is achieved, the stage shades into the next one – 'operationalisation'. Examples of the more strictly **technical** work include putting in the necessary wiring, locating the workstations, providing the necessary ambient conditions and facilities. With respect to the **organisational** aspects, these can include familiarisation training of users, pilots and trials of the technology, and supplier support and advice.

It should be noted that this is by no means necessarily a straightforward and uneventful stage. It might well take many months of effort and frustration before the technology is fully operational; indeed, there is a sense in which the technology may never become 'fully operational' due to continual and irresolvable problems. This is one of the main reasons why it is so important to spend time at the adoption phase trying to ensure that the organisation actually **does** need this technology and that, if it does, all relevant people understand why and have the necessary training and expertise to use and/or manage it (quite apart from all the other infrastructure requirements).

the role of personnel specialists appears to be one of late-in-the-day facilitators of implementation, constrained by technical and financial parameters over which they have little say and to which they can merely react.[81]

Legge suggests that there were three main reasons for this low level of involvement:

1 Employees have been secondary to other considerations in the choice and implementation of new technology, and thus personnel specialists' peripheral and reactive involvement is only to be expected.

2 As employees typically welcome rather than resist new technology, personnel specialists' involvement did not take off at implementation either (for example, they were rarely required to deal with tricky and complex issues relating to pay, gradings, employment, etc.).

3 Even on the odd occasion when resistance did occur, personnel's role was not seen as being crucial because of the weaknesses and divisions of the trade unions and employees more generally.

An additional factor is that personnel specialists are not directly present in the great majority of UK workplaces. For instance, the large-scale 2004 Fifth Workplace Employment Relations Survey classified only 28 per cent of its workplace-level management respondents as 'specialists' in employment relations issues, either by virtue of their job titles or by spending more than half their time on such tasks.[82]

Involvement with technical change What part, then, *did* personnel/HRM **considerations** (as distinct from specialists) play in technical change? By the early 1990s there was some evidence that personnel considerations had come to play a more important role, but 'as an executive and line management rather than personnel specialist concern'.[83] This, according to *Storey*, had been occurring in situations where managers had sought to develop employee commitment to, and effective utilisation of, new technology through consultation, team-building and training, and:

> *has often been in the context of devolved management and the revitalisation and legitimisation of line management transformed into 'manufacturing' or 'business' managers eager to experiment with non-proceduralised approaches to managing change.*[84]

On the basis of the above it would seem safe to conclude that personnel specialists typically had little, if any, involvement in the technology adoption phase.

Users of technology

Evidence also indicates that the users of technology are rarely involved in the process of technology **adoption**, although they are more likely to have input during the **operationalisation** stage, in terms of such aspects as working practices, tasks, decisions about methods, and tools and techniques. *Fröhlich, Gill and Krieger* conducted a major cross-national survey of workplace involvement in technical change, covering over 7000 management and employee representatives in 12 countries and 5 economic sectors. Overall, they found that only 20 per cent of respondents reported consultation or negotiation between management and employees in the adoption stages of technological change, but this rose to 33 per cent in the implementation stages.[85]

However, of these totals, it should be noted that the authors found that worker involvement was much more likely to occur in countries like Germany and Denmark than in countries with fewer established mechanisms for involving workers, such as the UK. The study identified a number of costs and benefits to the involvement of workers in the decision-making process. Ranking these, with those factors awarded the least positive net evaluations by the respondents first:

● the time needed to make decisions;
● the time needed to implement technological change;

- industrial relations within the firm;
- the quality of decision-making;
- the identification of the workforce with the company;
- attention to management's concerns;
- attention to employees' concerns;
- utilisation of skills.

Case study research by *Howcroft and Wilson* makes the point that user involvement is an inherently political process rather than simply 'good practice'. Managers are largely responsible for deciding on the extent of user involvement in technical change, how soon it will occur, the form it will take, and perhaps the selection of who will be consulted. Therefore in practice user involvement will be constrained by managerial agenda-setting and organisational politics.[86]

Involvement in socio-technical ensembles

While, then, employees may not be involved in the original design of the changed or new jobs around the technology, they are necessarily involved in the 'design-in-use', or 'valuing', or 'configuration' of the socio-technical 'ensemble'.[87] What is more, incremental changes such as these, taking place over an extended period of time, can lead to quite extensive changes in the nature of jobs and working practices – but there are constraints upon how far this can go. These include managers' (senior and middle) objectives, strategies and decision-making, linkages with other jobs and departments/sections/divisions across the organisation, the employment contract, and agreements which have been entered into between management and trade union(s) (for example with regard to working practices and work allocation).

While many of the key decisions may well have been taken by this stage, therefore, and, most likely, by managers or technical specialists, the day-to-day involvement and contribution of employees is necessary in order that the **potential** benefits of the new technology are realised in practice. Thus, managers can be said to have an interest in simultaneously controlling the work of employees and gaining their commitment to accepting and looking for new, more effective and efficient, ways of working.

TECHNOLOGY AND ORGANISATIONAL BEHAVIOUR

As we have already discussed, technological developments, and particularly those based on advancing information technology, are both essential for organisational effectiveness and powerful drivers of organisational change. We have shown how projects to adopt or update IT systems need to be assessed and evaluated in several ways. First, it is important that projects are assessed in terms of economic benefits to the organisation itself in terms of payback or return on investment. Investments of this type will certainly have implications for organisational cash flows, even if they are difficult to forecast. This assessment will come partly from financial measures, but it is equally important to consider other outcomes such as changes in levels of customer or client satisfaction and, of course, differences in the degree of job satisfaction experienced by the workforce, a set of relationships which comprises the organisational socio-technical ensemble. When we consider the issues surrounding the implementation of new web-based communication systems there are many social, managerial and organisational aspects to such projects.

The expectations of customers, clients or users of an organisation's services have become very demanding as IT systems are increasingly integrated into daily life both at work and at home. Developments such as broadband, wireless communication and ever more powerful and inexpensive computer technology mean that failure to adopt web-based technology is likely to be seriously detrimental to an organisation's future. Few businesses today can hope to survive without an Internet presence as their customers are increasingly likely to go with competitors who do.

However, those working in modern organisations might well have very different reactions to IT developments. For some, new systems and applications might be welcome as a means of becoming more effective; for others, perhaps those with less experience of IT, new systems might be viewed as threatening. While there might be fewer and fewer individuals in this latter category, their anxiety is likely to be very real as the ever rising tide of technological possibilities washes over them. For yet others, technological developments might be welcome, but their ability to make the most of what is on offer can be compromised by lack of time to learn about new systems or the lack of appropriate training. But there is also likely to be a fourth group, mostly younger workers, whose technological expertise is very sophisticated and who might find organisational systems archaic, frustrating and slow by comparison with those they encounter in their personal lives. Recent research has shown, for instance, that those under the age of 25 are using computers more than television as a source of entertainment and information, as well as a major means of social interaction.[88]

From an organisational perspective, websites are often split into 'public' and 'restricted' areas (the restricted areas being organisational intranets). The public website is concerned with image and for commercial organisations represents both a brand and a shop window. The intranet elements will often be sub-divided into restricted areas for specialist aspects of a business; an operational process (for instance the student records system of a university or college, or a personnel database) and more general areas which provide information for all authorised users (such as the institution's academic regulations, or the library catalogue). Individual users gain password-protected access to specified areas via different 'portals' for various categories of staff, students, etc. Many business organisations offer limited access for partner organisations, or even customers; for example when sending a letter by recorded delivery at a Post Office. The receipt contains a code which enables the customer to access a specific area of the Royal Mail website in order to track the progress of the letter or package to its destination.

As organisations become more IT 'rich' in their operations, the attitudes and behaviours of individual workers towards the use of technology must be considered in more ways than those relating to efficiency and job satisfaction already mentioned. Data protection and privacy legislation has implications for the use made by staff of stored data; many a manager might be tempted to set up a database or spreadsheet to record sickness absence without realising that they could be running up against the legislation. The prevalence of viruses and Trojans transmissible by email or associated with downloaded information is a systems security issue requiring firewalls and other forms of technical protection; but it equally requires a level of awareness among staff about what is and what is not safe to access. Hoax emails and 'spam', when disseminated via internal communications systems, can jam a system completely; even legitimate communications can cause chaos. (In May 2005 the UK Ministry of Defence Internet server was brought to its knees when serving troops in Iraq 'pinged' a humorous spoof video home to friends and family.)[89]

Finally, both individuals and organisations need to consider the way in which email is used. The 'informality' and speed of electronic communication systems, which are part of their attraction, can have embarrassing or compromising consequences. The term 'onosecond' has been coined for the millisecond between hitting the 'send' button and realising that your cheeky reply to a colleague also went to the chief executive who was on the original distribution list. A number of recent disciplinary and dismissal cases have centred on the abuse of email and distribution of inappropriate images.[90] Many organisations have developed email protocols, and automatic disclaimers which seek to prevent informal exchanges with external correspondents being used as the basis for a legal claim against the organisation of the individual sender. While the monitoring of staff computer use might seem intrusive and controlling, there is nevertheless a legitimate organisational interest in the way in which people are using email or access to the Internet during their working day not least in terms of hours spent working. Some organisations might in fact legitimise things like staff doing their Internet shopping, booking holidays or watching 'Big Brother' on an office computer, but this is likely to depend on the nature and circumstances of the organisation and its culture, and will certainly influence the role and task of the manager.

TECHNOLOGY AND THE EXPERIENCE OF WORK

Organisational research shows us that technology can influence the behaviour of people in work settings in many ways including, for example, the following:

1 It influences the specific design of each member's pattern of work including the skills exercisable, how work is organised and controlled.
2 It affects the nature of social interactions.
3 It can influence the pace and intensity of work.

These factors are likely to affect the experience of work, and therefore ultimately the levels of job satisfaction that individuals are able to attain. Let us look at each of these in turn.

Skill, work design and control

The impact of technological change on the nature and variety of job activities performed, the skills that workers can exercise and the amount of autonomy and control they have over their jobs have been among the most hotly contested areas in social science. We have already discussed, in the section on technological determinism above, how Blauner's studies demonstrated that different types of production technology can be a potent influence on the skills and control that workers are able to exercise, factors which Blauner linked to their levels of job satisfaction. The influential work of *Braverman*, also mentioned earlier in this chapter, questioned the assumption of the 'automation debates' of the 1960s that technical change would lead relatively unproblematically to rising levels of skills.[91] Instead, he argued that automation, in the hands of managers, comprised the second stage of a strategy to deskill and eliminate jobs that had started with the techniques of scientific management. An important insight in the debate that followed the publication of Braverman's work was that the exact effects of technical change on skill levels depend on how managers organise job design and the patterns of work organisation more broadly. Research indicates that this varies considerably between workplaces and that there are even differing patterns cross-nationally on how managers are likely to organise work.[92]

From the mid-1980s, the advent of more flexible forms of microprocessor-based automation led to separate predictions from *Piore and Sabel* in the USA and *Kern and Schumann* in Germany on the potential emergence of new multi-skilled workers capable of programming and overall system control.[93] Although such claims were influential for a while, statistical research by *Gallie* has argued convincingly that what we see is actually a pattern whereby skills are polarising: 'The polarisation of skills is also closely associated with technological change. Those that have been in a position to use advanced technology in their work have seen their skill increase; those that have not had this possibility, have been much more likely to see their skills remain unchanged.'[94]

The advent of the ICT revolution has reinvigorated concern with the use of technology as a means of workplace control, particularly in relation to the information-gathering potential

of ICTs and the use to which this could be put in technically monitoring or conducting surveillance on worker performance. The preoccupation with the labour surveillance and control issue can be seen in that research and writing on technological/organisational change which has deployed the metaphor of the 'electronic panopticon' – panopticon literally meaning 'all-seeing eye'. This literature draws attention to the insidious and not-so-insidious ways in which IT has been used by managers to monitor and record the work of employees, in some cases in such a way that they do not know exactly when they are being watched, but are aware that this could be at any time. Hence, it is argued, employees amend their behaviour to act as if they are under surveillance all the time.[95] As *Mason et al.* make clear, echoing previous debates on labour control, there is disagreement over whether the ability to collect such performance data necessarily means that managers always refer to, or act on it; whether technologies are actually capable of living up to their claimed surveillance potential; and to what extent employees can resist such techniques, rationalise their existence, or even turn them to their own advantage.[96]

Social interactions

Technology is likely to change the extent and manner in which managers and workers interact and workers interact with each other. It may affect the size and nature of work groups, the extent of physical mobility, and of contacts with other people. These factors will certainly be magnified with ICTs, where people working on linked tasks may be at a variety of locations, including at home (as discussed, for example, in the section on telecommuting in Chapter 16), and individuals may work more on their own, from personal work stations or work more with machines than with other people. There are clear dangers for organisations here that workers may become isolated, information about developing problems can be more easily hidden when workers are not interacting face-to-face, and that it becomes harder for the informal channels of information exchange on which organisations depend to flow freely. A comment from a knowledge management worker participating in a research study of virtual working sums up such problems: 'We try to have what we call virtual coffee sessions, which were dreadful ... all around the world we tried to get together and have a cup of coffee and sit down and look at each other, and you can't be spontaneous now, you can't do it, you can't force it.'[97]

The pace and intensity of work

Considerable evidence now exists that modern work patterns are becoming more intensive and, although organisational change more generally is one of the main causes of this, it is exacerbated by accompanying technical changes and the way in which technology is often utilised within organisations.[98] Technology can impose time dimensions on workers and affect the pace and intensity of work, such as in the mechanical pacing of work on a mass-production assembly line or the manner in which electronic control devices can be programmed to demand a human response within a given time frame. The introduction of information technology undoubtedly transforms, significantly, the nature of work and employment conditions for staff. Developments in the technical systems of communications such as international telephone connections and the increasing use of faxes, mobile telephones and email have generated a working climate in which there is a greater expectation of the immediacy of receipt and response, and have added to the dangers of information overload. For example, a report by management company Pitney Bowes claims that the ever-increasing use of email is a cause of rising stress levels in the workplace.[99]

Advances in sophisticated systems of information communications technology and greater opportunities for more and more people to work from home are helping to create and support the virtual office. The growth of information technology means that many individuals can undertake their work at any time and anywhere, and provides for greater mobility. *Lucas* maintains that 'the benefits to organizations, in terms of improved produc-

tivity, staff retention and employee motivation are well documented'.[100] However, *Thomas* suggests that it is impossible at this stage to draw conclusions about the impact of mobile working, which is a hugely varied experience. While for some people it is good news and may be clearly liberating, for others doing extra work and long hours of uninteresting work is less appealing.[101] Neither are the productivity benefits clear-cut. ICT, particularly in the form of high-speed Internet and email access in the workplace, can provide new opportunities for employees to use these advanced technologies for activities not directly related to work, such as Internet browsing and shopping, personal email, and so on. The distinction between what constitutes 'work' and what can be regarded as 'personal' use of such facilities can be very much a grey area within organisations.[102]

Personal area network

According to *Law*, the manager of the future, especially in larger organisations, will be someone who is a 'personal area network' wherever they may be, always connected to the Internet. Managers will be using personal digital assistants (PDAs) – handheld mobile devices that can access the Internet and act as a basic personal organiser by setting up a diary. However, if too many people are working remotely too often there is a risk of alienation and there is also the potential problem of pressures on staff who are permanently contactable.[103] *Reeves* maintains that IT is potentially the most progressive force for change in the workplace. It could free millions of workers from the drudgery of the nine-to-five and the absurdity of presenteeism. However, far from being liberating, IT feels enslaving. Email becomes a daily tyranny, the mobile phone a corporate electronic tagging device. Companies still expect their staff to work set hours even when IT makes this unnecessary.[104] Also, such innovations as electronic diary programs on office computer networks bring with them the danger that workers may lose control about how they organise their working day.

Refresh your understanding

Activity 17C
www.pearsoned.co.uk/
mullins

Critical reflection

????

'To make the best use of technology we must use it to support and develop the effectiveness of organisations, and not adapt business activities to the technology.' How would you go about making the best use of technology? Do you think technology is becoming too much our master rather than our servant?

MANAGEMENT IN THE NEWS

Clockwork radios: not all tech is hi-tech

Relaxing at his home on Eel Pie Island in 1991, Trevor Baylis turned on the TV. There was a harrowing report on the spread of HIV and AIDS across Africa, and how large numbers of people were totally ignorant of the risks because there was no easy way to get that sort of information to the vast majority of Africa's 600 million population. Radio would be an excellent way of doing that, but most people had no electricity, and even where batteries might be available they just couldn't afford them. A set of batteries could cost more than a week's food for a whole family.

The idea
Baylis started thinking about his old wind-up gramophone and how the energy to drive it was stored by a clockwork mechanism. In his home workshop he found a carpenter's brace, not unlike the winding handle of a gramophone, and started experimenting. He found he could use the brace to drive a small dynamo to generate enough power for a transistor radio. Adding some simple clockwork allowed the brace to wind up a spring, which would drive the dynamo by itself as it slowly unwound.

→

Management in the news – continued

Source: Hugh Threlfall/Alamy

The clockwork radio saves lives. The invention of clockwork radios has allowed thousands of villages in Africa to get important information about HIV and Aids.

Like many brilliant ideas, it was essentially that simple. After many hours' work he achieved his first working model, which ran a radio for 14 minutes on a two-minute wind. He had invented The Clockwork Radio. The design was later improved so that it could run a radio for an hour on a 25-second wind. Later enhancements included the addition of solar cells so that winding was needed only after dark.

Naturally, he did his best to promote the invention, but nobody took it seriously. One rejection note from an influential body said:

It is very unlikely that UK industry could enter profitably into a licensing agreement with this product. The major customers are third world countries which, with severe debts, would not be in a position to pay for this device.

Breakthrough

Baylis can well afford to laugh now as he recalls how he has seen whole villages of 400 to 500 people sitting around one of his radios, and how big business always seems to do its best to deter and suppress invention and originality.

It was the BBC that provided Baylis with his big break. In April 1994 his invention was featured on *Tomorrow's World*, a TV showcase for new ideas and inventions. The possibilities were seized on by a corporate accountant and a South African entrepreneur. Details of the invention were broadcast in South Africa on a Johannesburg radio station. Life Assurance boss Hylton Appelbaum, head of the Liberty Life Group, heard the broadcast, was impressed, and set about helping to fund production.

Production

A company called BayGen Power Industries was set up in Cape Town, South Africa, with Baylis owning the patents and trademarks. They wanted to employ disabled people to do the assembly work, and got various organisations for the disabled to become partners in the venture, with Liberty Life providing funds to begin production. Further technical development work was contributed in the UK by electronics engineers at Bristol University. Before long, some 250 disabled people in South Africa were producing thousands of clockwork radios per month.

Subsequently, to Baylis' disappointment, the production facility in South Africa was closed down, and production moved to China.

Source: Adapted from 'Clockwork Radios' from the h2g2 website run by the BBC (www.bbc.co.uk/dna/h2g2/A810154), 6 September 2002.

Discussion questions

1 Summarise and critically review what this article suggests about the value of 'low' technology as opposed to 'high technology' in the modern world.

2 In 2002 Freeplay Energy, the company run by Rory Stear, the South African entrepreneur mentioned in the article, began to produce clockwork mobile phone chargers, and in 2006 registered a patent on a foot-powered electricity generator. Outline and discuss both the possibilities and limitations of this type of low-technology for third world development in a high technology age.

SYNOPSIS

● In its various forms technology is found and used in all organisations. Technology has been theorised via a variety of perspectives. There are a number of definitions, none of them universally accepted. What one perceives as the nature of technology, what it can and cannot do, the degree of control which can be exercised over it, as against being controlled by it, its 'liberating' potential (and so on) largely depend on the theoretical perspective one adopts.

● Managers need to be aware of the nature of technology and the technical change process. Information and communication technology, telecommunications, the Internet and world wide web form the core material foundation of organisational networks, which operate on a global basis, and which are becoming increasingly pervasive during the early years of the 21st century.

● Much new technology, and particularly its newer manifestations, possesses characteristics that allow a wide degree of choice within organisations over how that technology is used, by whom, and for what purposes. The 'impacts' of the technological change process depend therefore, to a considerable extent, upon the nature and quality of the associated decision-making process. The quality of this process will be affected by whether personnel specialists and technology users are allowed to participate in it, and at which stage.

● To understand what technology can do, what it is and how it might be effectively managed, it is neces-sary to appreciate the social, economic and political contexts within which technology is created, devel-oped, produced and introduced. External and internal organisational contexts help to shape the evolving socio-technical ensemble and its use, potential and impact. In other words, technology is 'socially created and shaped', but is not infinitely malleable. Indeed, one 'constraint' upon evolving technology is existing technology and the way it has been applied and used.

● Once a particular technology has been developed and produced, it is available in the market place to organisations that can afford to buy it. From a manage-rial perspective, one can see how technology comes to have a presence within the organisation through a 'tech-nology adoption and introduction' framework, which attempts to capture the importance and influence of the social, political and economic contexts upon the emer-ging effectiveness and efficiency of the utilisation of that technology. Here, the role of politics, choice and deci-sion-making by different actors is central.

● Subsequent to introduction, technology can have major effects upon the ways in which work is experi-enced and upon job satisfaction. While use of advanced technology may improve job skills, experi-ences will also be profoundly affected by the social interactivity enabled by technology and the intensity of work. Technical change and the way technology is often utilised is a major feature of the increasing intense modern work patterns.

 Refresh your understanding, assess your progress and begin your research with online resources at **www.pearsoned.co.uk/mullins**

REVIEW AND DISCUSSION QUESTIONS

1 Outline and comment upon ways in which users can participate in the adoption and introduction of new technology.

2 Drawing upon the research evidence, discuss the suggestion that: 'nothing is to be gained by involving users in the adoption and introduction of technical change. It is far simpler and quicker to tell them what will happen and what they will have to do.'

3 It is not unusual for the outcomes of technical change not to match up to expectations. What can cause this gap and how might it have been prevented?

4 What sorts of objectives have and might managers set for the introduction of technological change? Draw upon case study research in answering this question.

5 Discuss critically the contention that 'decision-making with respect to technical change is an inherently political process'.

6 'New technology has resolved the control question, therefore managers can and will draw back from a Tayloristic approach to the supervision of employees.' Discuss.

Review and discussion questions – continued

7 'A theoretical or practical perspective which sees technology as having independent effects upon people and organisations is misguided.' Discuss.

8 Compare and contrast two approaches to theorising on the nature of technology. Which one do you prefer and why?

ASSIGNMENT

In self-selecting groups of three or four, each select an example of a job in your own organisation or some other organisation of your choice (you may find it easiest to use your own organisation, if possible). You should each draw up a list of the main duties of the chosen job and of the technical equipment that is available to assist in undertaking this job. Taking each job in turn, you should collectively discuss:

1 Which aspects of your chosen job do you think could, or should, be further automated, and why?

2 Which aspects of the job cannot, or should not, be further automated, and why?

3 How would the nature of the job change if your suggestions were followed? Would the job become more or less fulfilling for the occupant?

For the aspects you have discussed in the first two questions above, do you think senior managers would come to the same conclusions as yourselves, taking into account factors such as costs, product and service quality?

PERSONAL AWARENESS AND SKILLS EXERCISE

Objectives

Completing this exercise should help you to enhance the following skills:

● Understand better the impact of technical change on an organisation and its members and vice versa.

● Apply your theoretical knowledge to the analysis of organisational processes.

● Evaluate the benefits and drawbacks resulting from technical change.

Exercise

In an organisation with which you are familiar, you are required to:

1 Detail fully an example of technical change that has taken place or is taking place, comparing the work processes involved, and how they are carried out, both *before* and *after* the change.

2 Analyse the origins and development of that change, drawing upon the technological and organisational change literatures discussed in this text.

3 Assess the main implications of that change for both the organisation and its employees. For example, what have been the effects on job numbers, the nature of the work required, skill levels, training requirements; has the change solved the problems it was intended to address, or has it thrown up new issues; what have been the main costs and benefits, etc?

Discussion

● How might managers and other members of staff prepare for technical change? In the example you have studied, could organisation members have prepared themselves better and, if so, how?

● To what extent does theorising on the nature of technology help in analysing the nature of technical change?

● On the basis of the case you have studied, does it show that technical change results in more positive or more negative implications for individuals in an organisation? Would you come to same conclusion about technical change in general?

CASE STUDY

Accessible technology: Tesco's accessible website

The random impact of new technology

In 1998 the British Computer Society (BCS) and the Institute of Electrical Engineers (IEE) instigated an annual public lecture in memory of Alan Turing (1912–1954). Turing was one of the most influential early developers of computer technology, a member of the wartime UK code-breaking team at Bletchley Park, and proposer of the 'Turing Test' of machine intelligence.[105] The 2006 Turing Lecture, entitled 'Lifestyle Access for the Disabled – Adding Positive Drift to the Random Walk with Technology', was delivered by Chris Mairs, co-founder in 1981 of Metaswitch, part of the communications company Data Connection plc and chair of 'a-technic', a charity which develops assisted technology for people with disabilities, primarily those who (like Mairs) are blind or otherwise visually impaired.[106]

Mairs' theme was the way in which, as we become ever more sophisticated in our use of digital media and find ourselves in the midst of the 'information age', shifting technology can throw up both significant benefits and enormous barriers to those who live with a disability. This is the reason for his choice of phrase 'random walk', since the practical impact of the same technology can be both positive for some disabled people and negative for others. He gives one example of this by considering telephone technology. In the early days of call exchanges and phone operators, using a telephone was a simple matter of lifting the receiver, telling the operator the number you required and waiting for her (usually) to connect you; as easy for a blind person as for a sighted one. The advent of the circular dial telephone made operators redundant, but was a step back for visually impaired user, for whom a dial was tricky to use. Push-button phones were a step forward, as numbers on a keypad are easier to locate than holes in a dial; you may have noticed the centralising raised dot or bar on the number 5 on most modern keypads. Then along came mobile phones, which Mairs describes as a 'disaster' for the visually impaired, mainly because most of them require a menu system to enable the use of most of the features they now contain. Even where voice-activated dialling is available, the phone has to be programmed using a menu first. Associated with the growing use of mobile phones has come the development of the text message, something which is now an entirely new social model of communication, albeit one which generally excludes the visually impaired. Yet from a different perspective, while these developments might have made

Technological advances can change people's quality of life; Tesco's accessible website offers independence to blind and partially sighted shoppers as well as convenience to all its customers.

life harder for Mairs, text messaging opened up a whole new world of communication for deaf people. This is part of what he meant by the random impact; the differential and complex interplay of technology, social behaviour and disability.

Internet shopping

Mairs discusses several aspects of this interplay between technology, social behaviour and disability in his lecture. From an organisational point of view, the most relevant aspects are first, the way in which technology influences lifestyles and second, the way in which it can offer people with disability better access to existing lifestyles. There is perhaps no more obvious illustration than that of Internet shopping. The choice between trawling the supermarket aisles and ordering online for home delivery is open to both able bodied and disabled people, and has revolutionised life not only for busy workers but for anyone who finds this everyday chore physically difficult or even impossible. It has become a mainstay of many people's lives, created jobs and provided market opportunities where none existed. In the UK Tesco became an early and very successful player in this market. However, its first website was not at all suitable for people who use screen readers, i.e. 'user interface' devices which speak the content of computer screens, thus making it possible for those with visual impairments to use standard computer applications. The provisions of the Disability Discrimination Act (DDA) 1995 include a requirement that services must be provided in such a way as to be accessible to people with disabilities, but a Royal National Institute for the Blind (RNIB) survey of 17

28 Grint, K. and Woolgar, S. *The Machine at Work: Technology, Work and Organisation*, Polity Press (1997), pp. 23–4.

29 Bijker, W. *Of Bicycles, Bakelites and Bulbs, Towards a Theory of Socio-Technical Change*, MIT Press (1995); Pinch, T. and Bijker, W. 'The Social Construction of Facts and Artefacts: or How the Sociology of Science and the Sociology of Technology might Benefit Each Other', in Bijker, W., Hughes, T., and Pinch, T. (eds) *The Social Construction of Technological Systems: New Directions in the Sociology of History and Technology*, MIT Press (1987).

30 Bijker, W. (1995), op. cit., p. 280.

31 Callon, M. 'Some Elements of a Sociology of Translation: Domestication of the Scallops and the Fishermen of St Brieuc Bay', in Law, J. (ed.) *Power, Action and Belief. A New Sociology of Knowledge*, Routledge (1986); Callon, M., Law, J. and Rip, A. (eds) *Mapping the Dynamics of Science and Technology in the Real World*, Macmillan (1986); Latour, B. *Science in Action: How to Follow Scientists and Engineers through Society*, Harvard University Press (1987); Law, J. 'Technology and Heterogeneous Engineering: The Case of Portuguese Expansion', in Bijker, W., Hughes, T., and Pinch, T. (eds) *The Social Construction of Technological Systems*, MIT Press (1987).

32 McLoughlin, I. *Creative Technological Change: The Shaping of Technology and Organisations*, Routledge, (1999) p. 94.

33 Walsham, G. *Making a World of Difference: IT in a Global Context*, Wiley (2001), p. 46.

34 Coombs, R., Saviotti, P. and Walsh, V. 'Technology and the Firm: the Convergence of Economic and Sociological Approaches?', in Coombs, R., Saviotti, P. and Walsh, V. (eds) *Technological Change and Company Strategies*, Academic Press (1992), p. 17.

35 Williams, R. and Edge, D. 'The Social Shaping of Technology', in Dutton, W. (ed.) *Information and Communication Technologies: Visions and Realities*, Oxford University Press (1996), p. 65. See also: Doolin, B. and Lowe, A. 'To Reveal is to Critique: Actor–network theory and critical information systems research', *Journal of Information Technology*, vol. 17, no. 1, 2002, pp. 69–78.

36 See, for example: Grint, K. and Woolgar, S. *The Machine at Work*, Polity Press (1997).

37 Jackson, P. 'Information Systems as Metaphor: Innovation and the 3 Rs of Representation' in McLoughlin, I. and Harris, M. (eds), op. cit.

38 McLoughlin, I. and Harris, M. 'Understanding Innovation, Organisational Change and Technology', in McLoughlin, I. and Harris, M. (eds) *Innovation, Organisational Change and Technology*, International Thomson Business Press (1997), p. 17. See also: McLoughlin, I. 'Babies, Bathwater, Guns and Roses', in McLoughlin, I. and Harris, M. (eds), op. cit.

39 See, for example: McLoughlin, I. and Harris, M., op cit., Grint, K. and Woolgar, S., op cit., Woolgar, S., op. cit., McLoughlin, I. *Creative Technological Change: The Shaping of Technology and Organisations*, Routledge (1999); Preece, D., McLoughlin, I. and Dawson, P. (eds) *Technology, Organisations and Innovation: Critical Perspectives on Business and Management*, 4 vols, Routledge (2000); Laurila, J. and Preece, D. 'Looking Backwards and Sideways to See Forward: Some Notes on Technological Change and Organisational Action', in Preece, D. and Laurila, J. (eds) *Technological Change and Organisational Action*, Routledge (2003); McLoughlin, I. and Dawson, P. op. cit.

40 Blosch, M. and Preece, D. 'Framing Work through a Socio-technical Ensemble: The Case of Butler Co.', *Technology Analysis and Strategic Management*, vol. 12, no. 1, 2000, pp. 91–102.

41 Friedman, A. and Cornford, D. *Computer Systems Development: History, Organisation and Implementation*, Wiley (1989).

42 See, for example: Castells, M. *The Information Age: Economy, Society and Culture, Vol. 1: The Rise of the Network Society*, Blackwell (2000); Nohria, N. and Eccles, R. *Networks and Organisations*, Harvard Business School Press (1992); Snow, C., Miles, R. and Coleman, H. 'Managing 21st Century Network Organisations', *Organisational Dynamics*, 20, 3, 1992, pp. 5–21; Fulk, J. and DeSanctis, G. 'Electronic Communication and Changing Organisational Forms', *Organisation Science*, 6, 4, 1995, pp. 337–49; Jackson, P. and van der Wielen, J. *Teleworking: International Perspectives. From Telecommuting to the Virtual Organisation*, Routledge (1998); Stanworth, C. 'Telework and the Information Age', *New Technology, Work and Employment*, 13, 1, 1998, pp. 51–62. All these journal papers, and extracts from the books, are to be found in the following edited collection: Preece, D., McLoughlin, I. and Dawson, P. (eds) *Technology, Organisations and Innovation: Critical Perspectives on Business and Management*, Vol. 4, Routledge (2000).

43 Cairncross, F. *The Death of Distance: How the Communication Revolution will Change our Lives*. Orion (1997).

44 See, for example, Grimshaw, D., Cooke, F.-L., Grugulis, I and Vincent, S. 'New Technology and Changing Organisational Forms: Implications for Managerial Control and Skills', *New Technology, Work and Employment*, vol. 17, no. 3, 2002, pp. 186–203.

45 Taylor, P. and Bain, P. '"India Calling to the Far Away Towns": The Call Centre Labour Process and Globalization', *Work, Employment and Society*, vol. 19, no. 2, 2005, pp. 261–82.

46 Castells, M. *The Information Age: Economy, Society and Culture*. Volume I, *The Rise of the Network Society*; Vol. 2, *The Power of Identity*; Vol. 3, *End of Millennium*. Second edition, Blackwell (2000). See also Castells, M. *The Internet Galaxy*. Oxford University Press (2001).

47 Castells, Vol. 1, op. cit.

48 Ibid., p. 77.

49 Ibid.

50 Ibid., pp. 51–2.

51 Ibid., p. 187.

52 Ibid., p. 501.

53 Piore, M. and Sabel, C. *The Second Industrial Divide: Possibilities for Prosperity*, Basic Books (1984).

54 Ernst, D. 'Inter-firms Networks and Market Structure: Driving Forces, Barriers and Patterns of Control', University of California, Berkeley, BRIE research paper, cited in Castells, Vol. 1 (2000), op. cit.

55 Castells, op. cit., p.70.

56 Ibid., p. 71.

57 Ibid., pp. 71–2.

58 Ibid., pp. 75–6.

58 Ibid.

60 Ibid., p. 214.

61 Ibid., p. 500.

62 Ibid., p. 359.

63 Ibid.

64 Fitzpatrick, T. 'Critical Theory, Information Society and Surveillance Technologies', *Information, Communication and Society*, vol. 5, no. 3, 2002, p. 360. See also Noria, N. and Eccles, R. (eds) *Networks and Organisations*, Harvard Business School Press (1992); Snow, C., Miles, R. and Coleman, H. 'Managing 21st-century Network Organisations', *Organisational Dynamics*, vol. 20, no. 3, 1992, pp. 5–21; Fulk, J. and DeSanctis, G. 'Electronic Communication and Changing Organisational Forms', *Organisation Science*, vol. 6, no. 4, 1995, pp. 337–49; Agre, P. 'Real-Time Politics: The Internet and the Political Process', *Information Society*, vol. 18, 2002, pp. 311–31; McLoughlin, I., Preece, D., and Dawson, P. 'From Essex to Cyberspace: Virtual (Organisational) Reality and Real (Organisational) Virtuality', *Labour and Industry*, vol. 13, no. 3, 2003.

65 Fitzpatrick, ibid., p. 361.

66 Ibid., p. 363.

67 Ibid., p. 362.

68 Webster, F. *Theories of the Information Society*, Routledge (2000), p.123.

69 Preece, D. (1995), op. cit.

70 See, for example: Knights, D. and Murray, F. *Managers Divided: Organisation Politics and Information Technology Management*, Wiley (1994); Wilkinson, B. *The Shopfloor Politics of New Technology*, Heinemann (1983).

71 For a detailed outline and review, see Preece, D. A. *Organisations and Technical Change: Strategy, Objectives and Involvement*, Routledge (1995), Chapters 2 and 3.

72 Preece, D. (1995), op. cit.

73 Child, J. 'Managerial Strategies, New Technology and the Labour Process', in Knights, D., Willmott, H. and Collinson, D. (eds) *Job Redesign: Critical Perspectives on the Labour Process*, Gower (1985).

74 See, for example: Preece, D. A. *Organisations and Technical Change: Strategy, Objectives and Involvement*, Routledge (1995), Chapter 8.

75 Wilkinson, B. *The Shopfloor Politics of New Technology*, Heinemann (1983).

76 McLoughlin, I. and Clark, J. *Technological Change at Work*, Second edition, Open University Press (1994), p. 57.

77 McLaughlin, J, Rosen, P., Skinner, D. and Webster, A. *Valuing Technology: Organisations, Culture and Change*, Routledge (1999).

78 Preece, D. A., Steven, G. and Steven, V. *Work, Change and Competition: Managing for Bass*, Routledge (1999).

79 See: Daniel, W. W. and Millward, N. 'Findings from the Workplace Industrial Relations Surveys', and Legge, K. 'The Role of Personnel Specialists: Centrality or Marginalization?', in Clark, J. (ed.) *Human Resource Management and Technical Change*, Sage (1993).

80 Preece, D. A. and Harrison, M. 'The Contribution of Personnel Specialists to Technology-Related Organisational Change', *Personnel Review*, vol. 17, no. 1, 1988, pp. 13–19.

81 Legge, K. 'The Role of Personnel Specialists: Centrality or Marginalization?', in Clark, J. (ed.) *Human Resource Management and Technical Change*, Sage (1993).

82 Kersley, B., Alpin, C., Forth, J. Bryson, A., Bewley, H. Dix, G. and Oxenbridge, S. *Inside the Workplace: Findings from the 2004 Workplace Employment Relations Survey*, Routledge (2006), p. 39. Even so, it should be noted that the authors argue (p. 40) that the proportion of workplace-level employment relations specialists is actually increasing, especially in certain types of workplace.

83 Legge, K. (1993), op. cit.

84 Storey, J. *Developments in the Management of Human Resources*, Blackwell (1992), as expressed in Legge, K., op. cit., p. 41.

85 Fröhlich, D., Gill, C. and Krieger, H. *Workplace Involvement in Technological Innovation in the European Community* (2 volumes), Office for Official Publications of the European Communities (1993).

86 Howcroft, D. and Wilson, M., 'Participation: "Bounded Freedom" or Hidden Constraints on User Involvement', *New Technology, Work and Employment*, vol. 18, no. 1, 2003, pp. 2–19.

87 On 'valuing' technology, see McLaughlin *et al.*, op. cit. On 'configuring' technology, see Badham, R. 'Managing Socio-technical Change: a Configurational Approach to Technology Implementation', in Benders, J., de Haan, J. and Bennett, D. (eds) *The Symbiosis of Work and Technology*, Taylor & Francis (1995).

88 BBC news website Young drive radical media shift, 10 August 2006.

89 BBC news website 'Amarillo' video crashes *MoD PCs* 17 May 2005 at www.bbc.co.uk [accessed 17 August 2006].

90 See, for example: the case of 14 workers sacked for gross misconduct by the Driver and Vehicle Licensing Agency in Swansea for circulating downloaded pornographic images; Porn e-mail DVLA workers sacked 21 June 2006 at www.bbc.co.uk [accessed 18 August 2006].

91 Braverman, H. *Labour and Monopoly Capital: The Degradation of Work in the Twentieth Century*, Monthly Review Press (1974).

92 Jones, B. *Forcing the Factory of the Future*, Cambridge University Press (1997).

93 Piore, M. and Sabel, C. *The Second Industrial Divide: Possibilities for Prosperity*, Basic Books (1984); Kern, H. and Schumann, M. 'Limits of the Division of Labour: New Production and Employment Concepts in West German Industry', *Economic and Industrial Democracy*, vol. 8, no. 2, 1987, pp. 151–70.

94 Gallie, D. 'Patterns of Skill Change: Upskilling, Deskilling, or the Polarization of Skills', *Work, Employment and Society*, vol. 5, no. 3, 1991, p. 350.

95 See, for example: Sewell, G. and Wilkinson, B. 'Someone To Watch Over Me: Surveillance, Discipline and the Just-in-Time Labour Process', *Sociology*, vol. 26, no. 2, 1992, pp. 271–91; Lyon, D. *The Electronic Eye: The Rise of the Surveillance Society*, Polity Press (1994); Sewell, G. 'The Discipline of Teams: The Control of Team-based Industrial Work through Electronic and Peer Surveillance', *Administrative Science Quarterly*, vol. 43, no. 2, 1998, pp. 397–428; Taylor, P. and Bain, P. '"An Assembly Line in the Head": Work and Employee Relations in the Call Centre', *Industrial Relations Journal*, vol. 30, no. 2, 1999, pp. 101–16; Blosch, M. and Preece, D. 'Framing Work Through a Socio-technical Ensemble: The Case of Butler Co.', *Technology Analysis & Strategic Management*, vol. 12, no. 1, 2000, pp. 91–102.

96 Mason, D., Button, G., Lankshear, G. and Coates, S. 'Getting Real about Surveillance and Privacy at Work', in Woolgar, S. (ed.) *Virtual Society? Technology, Cyperbole, Reality*, Oxford University Press (2002), pp. 137–52.

97 Cited in Jackson, P. (ed.) *Virtual Working: Social and Organisational Dynamics*, Routledge (1999), p. 53.

Control can stand for reliability, order and stability. Whenever a person inquires 'I would like to know how well I am doing', this in effect can be seen as asking for control. Members of staff want to know what is expected of them and how well they are performing. This places emphasis on the exchange of information, and feedback and comparison of actual results against planned targets. Control is a basis for training needs, the motivation to achieve standards and for the development of individuals.[6]

According to *Tulgan*, 'control' (together with timing and customisation) is one of the three factors that should guide rewards and incentives in the workplace of the future. 'It is critical to make very clear to individual contributors exactly what performance – what results, within what guidelines, parameters and deadlines – the organisation needs, and will therefore reward.'[7]

However, as *Wilson* reminds us, individuals are not just passive objects of control: 'They may accept, deny, react, reshape, rethink, acquiesce, rebel, or conform and create themselves within constraints impose on them.'[8] And in a discussion of management processes in the new century, *Lorange* notes that the control process will also change dramatically:

> Perhaps the name 'control' will no longer exist, given the behaviourally dysfunctional overtones that tend to come with it. We shall, however, still use it here as a convenient term of reference, and remember that the content behind the phenomenon will be dramatically different.[9]

Organisational performance At the organisational level, management need to exercise '**control**' over the behaviour and actions of staff in order to ensure a satisfactory level of performance. Managerial control systems are a means of checking progress to determine whether the objectives of the organisation are being achieved. According to *Zimmermann* an organisation without control is impossible.

> Every organization has control systems that co-ordinate the exercise of decision rights that are dispersed among individuals. Control systems also serve another important function in the organization. They measure how effectively decisions have been translated into results. This second feature of control systems relates to the goal achievement of the company. In this perspective, control systems are about influencing the behaviour of individuals in the interest of the corporation. Both functions are closely interlinked.[10]

Control completes the cycle of managerial activities. It involves the planning and organisation of work functions, and guiding and regulating the activities of staff. Control provides a check on the execution of work and on the success or failure of the operations of the organisation. The whole purpose of management control is the improvement in performance at both the individual and organisational level (*see* Figure 18.1). Lack of adequate supervision and control, or of an effective risk-management system, are a major feature of poor organisational performance and can even lead to the collapse of a company.[11] A major international report undertaken by *Proudfoot Consulting* found that poor management in terms of inadequate planning and control, and insufficient day-to-day supervision of work is still the largest single reason for lost productivity.[12]

The ethical nature of control Concern for the regulation of behaviour and improvement in performance raises questions as to the ethical nature of control. For example, in discussing the goals of organisational behaviour (OB), *Robbins* makes the following observation:

> The most controversial goal is using OB knowledge to control behavior. When a manager asks, for instance: 'What can I do to make Dave put more effort on his job?' that manager is concerned with control. Why is control controversial? A democratic society is built upon the concept of personal freedom. Therefore, the idea that one person should attempt to get others to behave in some premeditated way, when the subjects of that control may be unaware that their behavior is being manipulated, has been viewed in some circles as unethical and/or repugnant ... However, you should be aware that the control objective is frequently seen by managers as the most valuable contribution that OB makes towards their effectiveness on the job.[13]

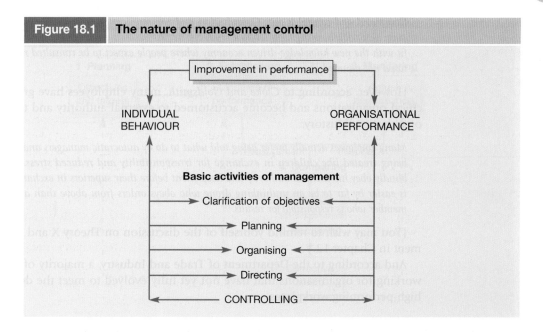

| Figure 18.1 | The nature of management control |

EXPRESSION OF MANAGEMENT BEHAVIOUR

While the need for some form of control is constant, the extent and manner of control is variable. The exercise of control is an expression of management systems and styles of behaviour.

One view of control is based on the classical approach and traditional assumptions of organisation and management. Control is viewed as an essential feature of formal organisation and a hierarchical structure of authority. It may also be recalled that the idea of 'Taylorism' and scientific management (discussed in Chapter 2) can be seen as representing a form of management control over workers and the actual process of work. As a consequence of their status and position within the hierarchical structure, managers have control over the flow of information that mainly moves down the organisation through vertical lines of communication.

By contrast, the human relations approach places emphasis on the social organisation, and the importance of groups and informal relationships. Control is seen more as a feature of interpersonal influence and takes place within a network of interaction and communications. Control should not be seen therefore only in the sense that it suggests close and constant supervision or as an organisational constraint on freedom of action by the individual.

The contingency approach takes the view that the most appropriate structure and system of management depend upon the particular situation. The nature of management control is an organisational variable. Recall the discussion on the organisational setting (Chapter 3) and consider likely variations in the extent and nature of management control among a range of diverse organisations.

Environment of consultation and communication

In previous chapters we have discussed the general movement towards flatter organisation structures and the increasing importance of an integrating rather than a hierarchical or controlling style of management. The message today appears to be that control must never outweigh leadership. 'Control is the hallmark of the Old World while leadership is a measure of the New'.[14] A similar point is made by *Lucas*:

Behavioural control and output control
Ouchi and Maguire suggest that the study of control in organisations includes selection and training, socialisation processes, bureaucracy, formalisation and the measurement of outputs.[19] From a study of retail department stores, they conclude that the control mechanism in an organisation is not a limited, single-purpose process. They refer to two independent forms of control that serve different functions:

- **Behavioural control** is based on direct personal supervision. This form of control appears more useful to the needs of individual managers in their attempts to control subordinates in one department or section. The use of behavioural control is responsive to the particular needs of the tasks, the abilities of the manager and the norms of the organisation.
- **Output control** is based on the measurement of outputs and the results achieved. This form of control serves the needs of the organisation as a whole and is used largely because of the demand for a quantifiable, simple measure of organisational performance.

Both types of control are important and they are not mutually exclusive. If controls over behaviour are applied without adequate attention to output controls this can lead to increased bureaucracy. An over-emphasis on formal rules and procedures may become more important in its own right rather than as a means to an end. People may behave as required by following the rules and regulations but important goals, such as, for example, providing effective customer service, may be overlooked.[20]

Control in the public sector
Public sector organisations have political purposes and are concerned with service to and the well-being of the community. However, in recent years there has been a vigorous policy of privatisation and creating freedom from direct state control and the transfer of business undertakings to private hands. At the same time, there has been increased government pressure to ensure cost-effectiveness, investment by private sector involvement, and efficiency and economy in their operations. The demand for uniformity of treatment and public accountability for their operations result in high levels of statutory controls, legislation and ministerial guidance. In the case of local government, for example, there is the added consideration of the relationship between elected members and permanent officers.

Despite the apparent relaxation of authority and transfer of power from central government there is evidence that public sector managers are under increasing political pressure. The demand for strategic management in the public sector has resulted in a greater emphasis on performance output measures with indicators of both a qualitative and quantitative nature.[21] For example, *Smith* suggests that:

the public sector poses particularly challenging problems of control and governments are increasingly relying on various types of performance indicator to inform the political process, and thereby secure control of public sector management.[22]

A similar view is expressed by *McKenna*, who maintains that:

The introduction into the public sector of managerialism – a form of management based on private sector economic and scientific management principles – introduced dramatic changes in the control systems used. The emphasis was switched from performance of jobs according to set routines and procedures to achievement of 'quantifiable' outputs.[23]

Shovelton draws attention to the increasing importance of accountability as one of the foundations of public services. Public sector organisations need to demonstrate shareholder value, fair treatment of employees and high environmental standards to a range of stakeholders, and public services face a difficult challenge in providing 'more' or 'better' or 'clearer' accountability.[24] In the case of local government there is also much publicity directed to the accountability of senior management and the effectiveness of control systems, especially, for example, with high-profile social services cases.[25]

CLASSIFICATION OF CONTROL SYSTEMS

Control therefore can take a number of forms and can be categorised in a number of different ways. *Reeves and Woodward* propose a classification of control systems based on seven case studies of differing industrial organisations.[26] They concluded that there was little likelihood of classifying control systems along a simple scale in one dimension, but from a large number of possible parameters they described two main aspects of control of particular relevance to the study of organisational behaviour:

● **personal or mechanical**; and
● **unitary or fragmented**.

Organisations might be positioned on a scale ranging from the extreme of completely personal hierarchical control to that of completely mechanical control, with administrative but impersonal control processes between the two extremes. This scale relates to how control is exercised within an organisation and the degree to which it is personal or impersonal. Impersonal control systems may be administrative or mechanical. Examples of administrative controls, which are based on formal standardised procedures, are production planning and cost control. An example of mechanical control is the automatic control system of machine tools or continuous flow production plant that is built into the production process and operates through mechanical or electronic devices.

A second characteristic of control systems, of importance in its behavioural effects, is the extent to which the various control systems are linked with each other and integrated into a single system of managerial control. Firms may be positioned on a scale ranging between the two extremes of a single integrated system of control and multi-system, fragmented control. Some firms attempt to relate the different control systems set for various departments into a unitary (integrated) system of managerial control. With multi-system control, standards of control are set independently by different functional specialists. People in the organisation are trying to satisfy a number of control criteria at the same time. For example, a particular task has to meet the demands of the production controller, the human resources manager, the supervisor and the cost accountant.

Technology and control systems

From a further analysis of the data collected from *Woodward's* south Essex study of 100 manufacturing firms (discussed in Chapter 16), clear links emerged between the original classification of technology and the above categorisation of managerial control systems (*see* Table 18.1).

Unit and small batch production firms tended to have unitary and mainly personal controls (A1). Process production firms tended to have unitary and mainly impersonal controls

Table 18.1	Relationship between control system and classification of technology

	Control system A1 (%)	Control system B1 (%)	Control system B2 (%)	Control system A2 (%)
Unit and small batch production	75	25	–	–
Large batch and mass production	15	35	40	10
Process production	–	–	5	95
Total firms	28	21	18	33

Source: Woodward, J., *Industrial Organisation: Theory and Practice*, Second Edition, Oxford University Press (1980), p. xxi. Reproduced with permission from Oxford University Press.

(A2). The similarities in some organisational characteristics between unit production firms and process firms identified in Woodward's south Essex study could be explained by the fact that in both groups unitary control systems predominated.

In the case of large batch and mass production firms, those with predominantly personal controls (B1) had similar organisational characteristics to unit firms and those with predominantly mechanical controls (B2) had an organisation structure similar to process firms.

> *From the analysis, Reeves and Woodward suggest that control systems may be the underlying variable that links organisational behaviour and technology. The classification of control systems they propose might provide a better means of predicting certain facets of organisational behaviour than the classification of technology.*

Wilson points out that technology is not just about devices and machines but also about social relations that encourage some form of interaction. Technology is a human, political and social activity. 'The locus of control cannot always be moved from workers to managers during technical change nor from managers to workers. Control ultimately does lie with management, though workers may resist it.'[27]

Information technology In previous chapters we have referred to the impact of developments in information technology and these developments will also have a significant impact on management control systems. Processes of communication are increasingly linked to computer systems with the rapid transmission of more information to more people including immediate access to other national or international offices. Information technology and office automation are changing the nature of the workplace and the way in which people work. For example, advances in telecommunications have resulted in a significant growth in teleworking, with staff working from home with a computer network, telephone and fax. This has many potential advantages but also raises questions of self-motivation, security and systems of management control.

Nordstrom and Ridderstrale suggest that with increasing use of IT, control will not disappear but become more indirect. Information systems will be used to increase control by measuring more things, new things at multiple levels, and at a greater frequency than before. To a certain extent this is a substitute for the loss of hierarchy control resulting from the introduction of new structures.[28] Another interesting situation arising from the increasing use of information technology is the legal position on organisations monitoring staff emails and Internet usage.[29]

Critical reflection

Some argue that a high level of management control is self-defeating as it is likely to produce a negative response, increase internal conflict and restrict the freedom and initiative of the individual. Others claim members of staff want to know how well they are performing, and control stands for reliability and good order. What do you think?

STRATEGIES OF CONTROL IN ORGANISATIONS

Six significant strategies of control in organisations are explained by *Child* (*see* Figure 18.3):

1 personal centralised control;
2 bureaucratic control;
3 output control;
4 control through electronic surveillance;
5 HRM control; and
6 cultural control.[30]

Personal centralised controls This approach is often found in small owner-managed organisations and is characterised by the centralisation of decision-making and initiative around a leadership figure. Control consists largely of personal inspection to see that decisions are carried out, and the leader may spend a high proportion of time supervising the work personally. Once the organisation grows large enough to employ someone to undertake detailed supervision of everyday tasks, the locus of decision-making and close supervision will tend to become separated. The authority of the leader will usually rest upon the rights of ownership, special personal qualities (charisma) or technical expertise.

Bureaucratic control This approach to control is familiar in public sector organisations and in many other types of large organisations. It is based on the specification of how members should behave and

Figure 18.3	Strategies of organisation control

1 Personal centralized control
 1.1 direct supervision of people's activities
 1.2 centralized decision taking
 1.3 personal leadership: founded upon ownership rights, charisma, and/or technical expertise
 1.4 reward and punishments reinforcing conformity to personal authority

2 Bureaucratic control
 2.1 breaking down of task into easily definable elements
 2.2 formally specified methods, procedures and rules applied to the conduct of tasks
 2.3 budgetary and standard cost-variance accounting controls
 2.4 technology designed to limit variation in conduct of tasks, with respect to pace, sequence and possibly physical methods*
 2.5 routine decision taking delegated within prescribed limits
 2.6 reward and punishment systems reinforcing conformity to procedures and rules

3 Output control
 3.1 jobs and units designed with responsibility for complete outputs
 3.2 specification of output standards and targets
 3.3 use of 'responsibility accounting' systems
 3.4 delegation of decisions on operational matters: semi-autonomy
 3.5 reward and punishment linked to attainment of output targets

4 Control through electronic surveillance
 4.1 speed and quality of work recorded and assessed remotely via information and communication technology (ICT)
 4.2 employee's performance assessed against that of other employees and trends
 4.3 such monitoring of performance used to reward and discipline employees

5 HRM control
 5.1 use of selection methods to ensure that new recruits 'fit' the profile of attitude, behaviour, and capabilities desired by management
 5.2 training and development designed to reinforce this desired profile
 5.3 assessment procedures and reward systems used to encourage conformity

6 Cultural control
 6.1 development of employees' personal identification with management goals
 6.2 strong emphasis on the collective and mutually supportive character of the organization – e.g. analogy with the 'family'
 6.3 employment characterized by security of tenure and progression within the organization
 6.4 semi-autonomous working: few formal controls

*Some authorities distinguish this as a separate control strategy. For example, Richard Edwards (1979), *Contested Terrain: The Transformation of the Workplace in the Twentieth Century*, New York, Basic Books.

Source: Child, J., *Organization: Contemporary Principles and Practice*, Blackwell Publishing (2005), p. 121. Reproduced with permission from Blackwell Publishing Ltd.

carry out their work. There is an attempt to ensure predictability through formal job descriptions and procedures, the breaking down of tasks into constituent elements, and the specification of standard methods for the performance of tasks. Reward and punishment systems can be designed to reinforce this control strategy. Compliance can be rewarded by upgrading, improved status, favourable employment benefits and job security. Bureaucratic control will make use of accounting control systems such as budgetary control and standard cost variances. The bureaucratic strategy also permits delegation without loss of control. Managers can delegate routine decision-making within formally prescribed limits of discretion.

Output control This approach relies upon the ability to identify specific tasks having a measurable output or criterion of overall achievement – for example, an end-product, a part manufactured to agreed standards, batch production or a sub-assembly. Rewards and sanctions can be related to performance levels expressed in output terms. Output control strategy is aimed at facilitating the delegation of operational decision-making without the need for bureaucratic controls or relying on close personal supervision. Once output standards have been agreed, subordinates can work with a 'semi-autonomous' relationship to management, free from detailed control over how tasks are carried out. Output control may be difficult to apply to certain activities, such as the legal department of a business organisation. Although it may be difficult to establish suitable and agreed measures of output, and it may be difficult for management to codify the activities involved, output control may be more appropriate than the application of a bureaucratic control strategy.

Control through electronic surveillance The essence of control is that the speed and quality of work is recorded and assessed remotely through the use of ICT without reliance on personal supervision. Control data are precise rather than impressionistic and subject to management bias. Monitoring of performance can be used readily as the basis for reward and discipline. Control through electronic surveillance is applied to many types and levels of activity. A common example is call centres although customer service representatives dislike the pressure from this form of control and the objectivity of relying on electronically produced statistics is subject to challenge.

HRM control HRM procedures can be used both to develop people at work and to control their behaviour and performance. They enhance the contribution to the achievement of organisational goals and objectives. Systematic selection techniques are designed to ensure new recruits fit the profile and technical competencies required by management. Performance evaluation and appraisal provide feedback to both management and employees. Appraisal should provide the basis for reward and for an assessment of the need for further training or development. If training and development programmes are attuned to the needs of employees and the requirements of their jobs this should contribute to better performance.

Cultural control This approach has been identified with moves away from conventional forms of organisation and is based on maintaining control through internalised compliance rather than external constraint. The basis of cultural control is the acceptance and willing compliance with the requirements of management and belief of the organisation. A major example is the cultural control of larger Japanese corporations tends to be exemplified by organisations although this is subject to criticism of compulsory sociability. Although a strong corporate culture is intended to provide an alternative to control, in practice strenuous efforts are usually made to ensure employees conform to the culture. Provided members have the necessary skills and ability they can be given wide freedom of action in deciding how to undertake their responsibilities. Cultural control, combined with personal autonomy, has long been associated with the professions. Despite criticisms of cultural control it is in tune with the increasing number of professional and knowledge workers, and is consistent with self-managing units or teams working with only limited formal controls.

- coercive power;
- legitimate power;
- referent power;
- expert power.

Power, however, arises not only from sources of structure or formal position within the organisation but from interpersonal sources such as the personality, characteristics and talents of individual members of the organisation. For example, in Chapter 10 we also discussed charisma, or personal power, as a feature of transformational leadership. We can also distinguish between **legitimate (organisational) power**, which derives from a person's position within the formal structure of the organisation and the managerial hierarchy of command, and **personal (informal) power**, which derives from the individual and is in the eye of the beholders who believe that person has the ability to influence other people or events and to make things happen.

The exercise of power is, then, a social process that derives from a multiplicity of sources and situations.[40] This suggests a more pluralistic approach and recognises power as a major organisational variable. Many different groups and individuals have the ability to influence the behaviour and actions of other people.

This is not a new concept, however. In the 1920s the renowned management writer *Mary Parker Follett* focused on a human behaviour aspect, rejected the notion of domination and the exercise of power other people, and argued for developing power with others in the organisation to make things happen. Effective control over work processes and social relationships would be achieved through group power and co-operative management. Follett advocated the replacement of personal power with the authority of task or function, and successful management based on the 'law of the situation'.[41]

Network of social relationships

Organisations function on the basis of networks of interdependent activities. Certain jobs or work relationships enable people to exercise a level of power in excess of their formal position within the structure of the organisation. A classic example is someone, perhaps a personal assistant or office manager, who fulfils the role of gatekeeper to the boss. There is an inherent danger with this type of role relationship that the boss may become too dependent upon the gatekeeper. Undertaking the responsibilities delegated by the boss and maintaining control can lead to the gatekeeper's misuse of their role and to an abuse of power.

Many people within organisations also have the ability to grant or withhold 'favours' within the formal or the informal interpretation of their job role – for example, secretaries, caretakers, security staff and telephonists. Staff may exercise negative power – that is, 'the capacity to stop things happening, to delay them, to distort or disrupt them'.[42] A common example could be the secretary who screens and intercepts messages to the boss, delays arranging appointments and filters mail. Negative power is not necessarily related proportionately to position and may often be exercised easily by people at lower levels of the hierarchical structure.

An example is given by *Green* who refers to the negative power that can be held by comparatively junior staff. The person who sorts and distributes the incoming mail has the opportunity to use negative power by the delay or disruption of items for reasons that may be entirely personal.[43] A reality of organisational life is the vagaries of social relationships including office politics, and also the grapevine and gossip. Although it is a difficult topic to pin down, *Mann* refers to the key role that gossip plays in power relationships and knowledge production in organisations and maintains that: 'There is an undeniable relationship between knowledge and power which lies at the root of gossiping.'[44]

Motivational Power can be a positive source of motivation for some people (see the discussion on
need for power achievement motivation in Chapter 7). There is often a fine line between the motivation to
achieve personal dominance and the use of social power. It has to be acknowledged, how-
ever, that there are clearly some managers who positively strive for and enjoy the exercise of
power over other people. They seek to maintain absolute control over subordinates and the
activities of their department/section, and welcome the feeling of being indispensable. The
possession of power is an ultimate ego satisfaction and such managers do not seem unduly
concerned if as a result they are unpopular with, or lack the respect of, their colleagues or
subordinate staff.

> ## Critical reflection
>
> 'It is a poor manager who relies on the exercise of formal power, position within the
> organisation structure and rules and procedures rather than on an understanding of
> human relationships, social influences and the exercise of personal power.' To what
> extent do you believe this is fair comment?

THE BALANCE BETWEEN ORDER AND FLEXIBILITY

Stewart refers to the classic dilemma that underlies the nature of control: finding the right
balance for present conditions between order and flexibility. This involves the trade-off
between trying to improve predictability of people's actions against the desirability of encour-
aging individual and local responsiveness to changing situations. The organisation may need
a 'tight–loose' structure with certain departments or areas of work closely controlled ('tight')
while other departments or areas of work should be left fluid and flexible ('loose').[45]

Three main forms of control

According to Stewart, 'control can – and should – be exercised in different ways'. She identi-
fies three main forms of control:

- **Direct control by orders, direct supervision and rules and regulations**. Direct controls
 may be necessary, and more readily acceptable, in a crisis situation and during training.
 But in organisations where people expect to participate in decision-making, such forms
 of control may be unacceptable. Rules and regulations which are not accepted as reason-
 able, or at least not unreasonable, will offer some people a challenge to use their
 ingenuity in finding ways round them.
- **Control through standardisation and specialisation**. This is achieved through clear def-
 inition of the inputs to a job, the methods to be used and the required outputs. Such
 bureaucratic control makes clear the parameters within which one can act and paradoxi-
 cally makes decentralisation easier. Provided the parameters are not unduly restrictive
 they can increase the sense of freedom. For example, within clearly defined limits which
 ensure that one retail chain store looks like another, individual managers may have free-
 dom to do the job as they wish.
- **Control through influencing the way that people think about what they should do**. This
 is often the most effective method of exercising control. It may be achieved through selec-
 tive recruitment of people who seem likely to share a similar approach, the training and
 socialisation of people into thinking the organisation's way, and through peer pressure.
 Where an organisation has a very strong culture, people who do not fit in, or learn to adapt,
 are likely to be pushed out, even though they may appear to leave of their own volition.

Stewart also refers to a second, related dilemma of finding the appropriate balance between centralisation, as a means of exercising control, and decentralisation. (Centralisation and decentralisation were discussed in Chapter 15.)

The question of control versus autonomy

From their study of top-performing companies in the 1990s, *Goldsmith and Clutterbuck* refer to the sharing of power, and to the balance between control and autonomy. They question how companies manage to balance giving people maximum freedom against exerting controls to ensure the benefits of size and a common sense of direction. The more managers share power, the more authority and resources they gain:

> *The way to exert the most effective control is to limit it to the few simple, readily understandable processes that have the greatest impact on group performance, and to maximise the freedom that managers at all levels have to achieve clear goals in their own way. And the more rigidly those core controls are enforced, the greater are the freedoms people need in order to compensate and to release their creativity, initiative and proactivity. Control and autonomy are therefore two sides of the same coin ... What do we mean by control and autonomy? Formal control seems to be exercised in three main ways: through setting or agreeing targets for performance (mainly but not exclusively financial); through measurement and reporting systems; and through certain decisions to be made centrally or corporately. Autonomy is, in essence, an absence of formal control: once clear goals are set, the individual manager has greater or lesser freedom to determine how they will be met. There are still controls in place, but they are much less obvious or intrusive.* [46]

Refresh your understanding
Activity 18C
www.pearsoned.co.uk/
mullins

DELEGATION AND EMPOWERMENT

Discussion on the balance between order and flexibility, and control versus autonomy, draws attention to the importance of delegation and empowerment. At the individual (or personal) level, delegation is the process of entrusting authority and responsibility to others throughout the various levels of the organisation. It is arguably possible to have delegation upwards – for example, when a manager temporarily takes over the work of a subordinate who is absent through illness or holiday. It is also possible to delegate laterally to another manager on the same level. However, delegation is usually interpreted as a movement down the organisation. It is the authorisation to undertake activities that would otherwise be carried out by someone in a more senior position. Downsizing and de-layering have arguably limited the opportunities for delegation, although this may be offset by demands for greater flexibility and empowerment. In any event, delegation is still an essential process of management.

As *Crainer* points out, in the age of empowerment, the ability to delegate effectively is critical.

> *Delegation has always been recognised as a key ingredient of successful management and leadership. But, in the 1980s delegation underwent a crisis of confidence ... The 1990s saw a shift in attitudes. No longer was delegation an occasional managerial indulgence. Instead it became a necessity. This has continued to be the case.* [47]

The concept of delegation may appear to be straightforward. However, anyone with experience of a work situation is likely to be aware of the importance of delegation and the consequences of badly managed delegation. Successful delegation is a social skill. Where managers lack this skill, or do not have a sufficient awareness of people-perception, there are two extreme forms of behaviour that can result.

● At one extreme is the almost total lack of meaningful delegation. Subordinate staff are only permitted to operate within closely defined and often routine areas of work, with detailed supervision. Staff are treated as if they are incapable of thinking for themselves and given little or no opportunity to exercise initiative or responsibility.

● At the other extreme there can be an excessive zeal for so-called delegation when a manager leaves subordinates to their own resources, often with only minimal guidance or training, and expects them to take the consequences for their own actions or decisions. These 'super-delegators' misuse the practice of delegation and are often like the Artful Dodger, and somehow contrive not to be around when difficult situations arise. Such a form of behaviour is not delegation; it is an abdication of the manager's responsibility.

Either of these two extreme forms of behaviour can be frustrating and potentially stressful for subordinate staff, and unlikely to lead to improved organisational effectiveness. The nature of delegation can have a significant effect on the morale, motivation and work performance of staff. In all but the smallest organisation the only way to get work done effectively is through delegation, but even such an important practice as delegation can be misused or over-applied.

THE MANAGER–SUBORDINATE RELATIONSHIP

Delegation is not just the arbitrary shedding of work. It is not just the issuing and following of orders or carrying out of specified tasks in accordance with detailed instructions. Within the formal structure of the organisation, delegation creates a special manager–subordinate relationship. It is founded on the concept of:

● authority;
● responsibility; and
● accountability (ultimate responsibility).

> *Delegation means the conferring of a specified authority by a higher authority. In its essence it involves a dual responsibility. The one to whom authority is delegated becomes responsible to the superior for doing the job, but the superior remains responsible for getting the job done. This principle of delegation is the centre of all processes in formal organization.*
>
> J. D. Mooney, *The Principles of Organsation*[48]

● **Authority** is the right to take action or make decisions that the manager would otherwise have done. Authority legitimises the exercise of power within the structure and rules of the organisation. It enables the subordinate to issue valid instructions for others to follow.
● **Responsibility** involves an obligation by the subordinate to perform certain duties or make certain decisions and having to accept possible reprimand from the manager for unsatisfactory performance. The meaning of the term 'responsibility' is, however, subject to possible confusion: although delegation embraces both authority and responsibility, effective delegation is not abdication of responsibility.
● **Accountability** is interpreted as meaning ultimate responsibility and cannot be delegated. Managers have to accept 'responsibility' for the control of their staff, for the performance of all duties allocated to their department/section within the structure of the organisation, and for the standard of results achieved. That is, 'the buck stops here'.

The manager is in turn responsible to higher management. This is the essence of the nature of the 'dual responsibility' of delegation. The manager is answerable to a superior and cannot shift responsibility back to subordinates. The responsibility of the superior for the acts of subordinates is absolute.[49] In order to help clarify the significance of 'dual responsibility' in delegation, it might be better expressed as:

*The subordinate is **responsible** to the manager for doing the job, while the manager is responsible for seeing that the job gets done. The manager is **accountable** to a superior for the actions of subordinates.*

Figure 18.5 The basis of delegation

Authority commensurate with responsibility

Delegation, therefore, embraces both authority and responsibility. It is not practical to delegate one without the other (*see* Figure 18.5).

Responsibility must be supported by authority and by the power to influence the areas of performance for which the subordinate is to be held responsible. Authority can be delegated readily, but many problems of delegation stem from failure to delegate sufficient authority to enable subordinates to fulfil their responsibilities. For example, if a section head is held responsible to a departmental manager for the performance of junior staff but does not have the organisational power (authority) to influence their selection and appointment, their motivation, the allocation of their duties, their training and development, or their sanctions and rewards, then the section leader can hardly be held responsible for unsatisfactory performance of the junior staff. To hold subordinates responsible for certain areas of performance without also conferring on them the necessary authority within the structure of the organisation to take action and make decisions within the limits of that responsibility is an abuse of delegation.

The manager should accept the blame as the person **accountable** for the performance of the department/section, and obligated to see that the task was completed satisfactorily. It is necessary to maintain the organisational hierarchy and structure of command. Managers should protect and support subordinate staff and accept, personally, any reprimand for unsatisfactory performance. It is then up to managers to sort out things in their own department/section, to counsel members of staff concerned and to review their system of delegation.

BENEFITS OF DELEGATION

It is a principle of delegation that decisions should be made at the lowest level in the organisation compatible with efficiency. It is a question of opportunity cost. If decisions are made at a higher level than necessary they are being made at greater cost than necessary. Delegation is therefore a matter of sound economics as well as good organisation. Properly handled, delegation offers many potential benefits to both managers and staff. Delegation should lead to the optimum use of human resources and improved organisational perform-

ance. Studies of successful organisations lend support to the advantages to be gained from effective delegation.[50]

Best use of time Time is one of the most valuable, but limited, resources and it is important that the manager utilises time to the maximum advantage. Delegation leaves the manager free to make profitable use of time, to concentrate on the more important tasks and to spend more time in managing and less in doing. This should enable the manager to be more accessible for consultation and improve the process of communications.

A means of training and development Delegation provides a means of training and development, and of testing the subordinate's suitability for promotion. It can be used as a means of assessing the likely performance of a subordinate at a higher level of authority and responsibility. Delegation thereby helps to avoid the 'Peter Principle' – that is, 'in a hierarchy every employee tends to rise to his level of incompetence' (discussed in Chapter 1). If managers have trained competent subordinates this will not only aid organisational progress but should also enhance their own prospects for further advancement.

Strength of the workforce Delegation should lead to an improvement in the strength of the workforce. It should give subordinates greater scope for action and opportunities to develop their aptitudes and abilities. Delegation can lead to improved morale by increasing motivation and job satisfaction. It can help satisfy the employee's higher-level needs. Delegation focuses attention on 'motivators' or 'growth' factors and creates a climate in which subordinates can become more involved in the planning and decision-making processes of the organisation. Delegation is a form of participation. Where subordinates are brought to accept and welcome delegation this will encourage a positive attitude to their work and a willingness to discharge their authority and responsibilities.

Critical reflection

If the benefits of delegation are to be believed, there is a strong case for the assessment of students' performance at degree or equivalent level to be transferred from staff to the students themselves. How would you feel about this? What form of assessment would you recommend?

REASONS FOR LACK OF DELEGATION

With so many good reasons for delegation, why is it that managers often fail to delegate or do not delegate successfully? Delegation is influenced by the manager's perception of subordinate staff. It is also influenced by the subordinate's perception of the manager's reasons for delegation. Failure to delegate often results from the manager's fear.

- The manager may fear that the subordinate is not capable of doing a sufficiently good job. Also, the manager may fear being blamed for the subordinate's mistakes.
- Conversely, the manager may fear that the subordinate will do too good a job and show the manager in a bad light.

An essential ingredient of effective management is the ability to put your trust in others and to let go some of the workload. As *Stewart* points out, managers who think about what can be done only in terms of what they can do, cannot be effective. Managing is not a solo activity.

> *Managers must learn to accept their dependence upon people. A key part of being a good manager is managing that dependence. Managers who say that they cannot delegate because they have poor staff may genuinely be unfortunate in the calibre of the staff that they have inherited or been given. More often this view is a criticism of themselves: a criticism either of their unwillingness to delegate when they could and should do so, or a criticism of their selection, training and development of their staff.*
>
> R. Stewart, *The Reality of Management*[51]

The manager should, of course, remember that the task of management is to get work done through the efforts of other people. If the subordinate does a particularly good job this should reflect favourably on the manager.

Assumptions about human nature A reluctance to delegate might arise from the manager's belief in, and set of assumptions about, human nature and behaviour (discussed in Chapter 12).[51] The Theory X manager believes that people have an inherent dislike of work, wish to avoid responsibility, and must be coerced, controlled, directed and threatened with punishment in order to achieve results. Such a manager is likely, therefore, to be interested in only limited schemes of delegation, within clearly defined limits and with an easy system of reward and punishment.

The Theory Y manager believes that people find work a natural and rewarding activity, they learn to accept and to seek responsibility, and they will respond positively to opportunities for personal growth and to sympathetic leadership. Such a manager is more likely to be interested in wider schemes of delegation based on consultation with subordinates, and with responsibility willingly accepted out of personal commitment.

Lack of training Managers may not have been 'trained' themselves in the skills and art of delegation. They may lack an awareness of the need for, and importance of, effective delegation or what it entails. Another reason for a reluctance to delegate may, in part, be due to the fact that throughout childhood and in college life delegation is usually discouraged. There are few opportunities to learn how to delegate. Hence when people first become managers they tend to display poor delegation skills.[53]

A systematic approach to delegation

In order to realise the full benefits of delegation without loss of control, it is necessary to adopt a planned and systematic approach. Setting up a successful system of delegation involves the manager examining four basic questions.

- What tasks could be performed better by other staff?
- What opportunities are there for staff to learn and develop by undertaking delegated tasks and responsibilities?
- How should the increased responsibilities be implemented and to whom should they be given?
- What forms of monitoring control system would be most appropriate?

In order to set up an effective system of delegation, subordinates should know exactly what is expected of them, what has to be achieved, the boundaries within which they have freedom of action, and how far they can exercise independent decision-making. It is possible to identify six main stages in a planned and systematic approach to delegation (*see* Figure 18.6).

- **Clarification of objectives and suitable patterns of organisation.** Policies and procedures must be established and defined in order to provide a framework for the exercise of authority and the acceptance of responsibility.

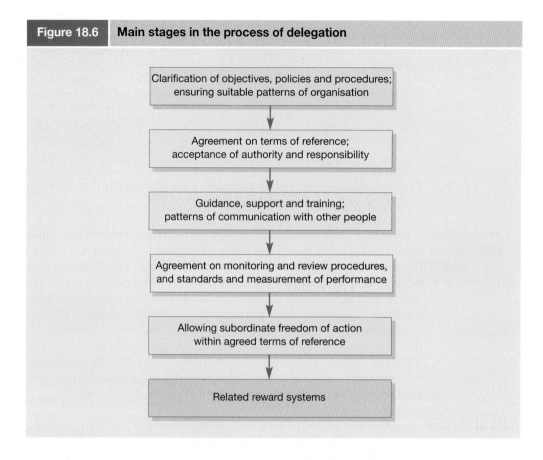

Figure 18.6	Main stages in the process of delegation

Clarification of objectives, policies and procedures; ensuring suitable patterns of organisation

Agreement on terms of reference; acceptance of authority and responsibility

Guidance, support and training; patterns of communication with other people

Agreement on monitoring and review procedures, and standards and measurement of performance

Allowing subordinate freedom of action within agreed terms of reference

Related reward systems

- **Agreement on terms of reference and acceptance of authority and responsibility.** The manager can then negotiate and agree the subordinate's role prescription and terms of reference. Those areas of work in which the subordinate is responsible for achieving results should be identified clearly. Emphasis should generally be placed on end-results rather than a set of detailed instructions.
- **Guidance, support and training and patterns of communication.** When subordinates have agreed and accepted the delegation, they should be properly briefed, given guidance and support and any necessary training. They should be advised where, and to whom, they could go for further advice or help.
- **Effective monitoring and review procedures.** The manager should agree time limits for delegation (such as a target date for completion of a specific task or a specified time period). It is necessary to agree the level and nature of supervision, and to establish a system to monitor progress and provide feedback. **Delegation is not an irrevocable act; it can always be withdrawn.** It is also important to make clear expected levels of achievement and agree on performance standards (wherever practically possible in quantitative terms), and how performance in each area is to be measured and evaluated.
- **Freedom of action within agreed terms of reference.** The subordinate should then be left alone to get on with the job. One of the most frustrating aspects of delegation is the manager who passes on authority but stays close behind the subordinates' shoulders keeping a constant watch over their actions. This is contrary to the nature of delegation. The true nature of successful delegation means that the subordinate is given freedom of action within the boundaries established and agreed in the previous stages.
- **Related reward system.** Wherever possible, the process of delegation should be related to some form of associated 'reward' system. Examples could include bonus payments, improved job satisfaction, reduction of work stress and enhanced opportunities for promotion or personal development, including further delegation.

A summary of delegation, authority, power and responsibility is given in the concept map set out in Figure 18.7.

A planned and systematic approach means that effective delegation can be achieved within the formal structure of the organisation and without loss of control. It is important, however, to make sure that subordinates accept the extent of, and any restrictions on, the authority and responsibility delegated to them. Subordinates should feel a sense of commitment to their new tasks or assignments and free to discuss any doubts or concerns. Delegation involves the acceptance theory of authority. *Davis and Newstrom* explain this as follows:

> *Although authority gives people power to act officially within the scope of their delegation, this power becomes somewhat meaningless unless those affected accept it and respond to it. In most cases when delegation is made, a subordinate is left free to choose a response within a certain range of behaviour. But even when an employee is told to perform one certain act, the employee still has the choice of doing it or not doing it and taking the consequences. It is, therefore, the subordinate who controls the response to authority. Managers cannot afford to overlook this human fact when they use authority.*[54]

THE ART OF DELEGATION

Delegation is not an easy task. It involves behavioural as well as organisational and economic considerations, and it is subject to a number of possible abuses. Effective delegation is a social skill. It requires a clear understanding of people-perception, reliance on other people, confidence and trust, and courage. It is important that the manager knows what to delegate, when and to whom. Matters of policy and disciplinary power, for example, usually rest with the manager and cannot legitimately be delegated. Delegation is a matter of judgement and involves the question of discretion.

Delegation is also a matter of confidence and trust – both in subordinates and the manager's own performance and system of delegation. In allowing freedom of action to subordinates within agreed terms of reference and the limits of authority, managers must accept that subordinates may undertake delegated activities in a different manner from themselves. This is at the basis of the true nature of delegation. However, learning to put trust in other people is one of the most difficult aspects of successful delegation for many managers, and some never learn it.

Training and learning experience Delegation involves subordinates making decisions. For example, as *Guirdham* points out: 'A strict separation of manager and subordinate roles sends the message to workers that they are only responsible for what they are specifically told to do. Managers who neglect to, or cannot, delegate are failing to develop the human resources for which they have responsibility.'[55]

Mistakes will inevitably occur and the subordinate will need to be supported by the manager, and protected against unwarranted criticism. The acceptance of ultimate responsibility highlights the educational aspect of the manager's job. The manager should view mistakes as part of the subordinate's training and learning experience, and an opportunity for further development. 'Even if mistakes occur, good managers are judged as much by their ability to manage them as by their successes.'[56]

Individual characteristics Notwithstanding any other consideration, the extent and nature of delegation will ultimately be affected by the nature of individual characteristics. The ages, ability, training, attitude, motivation and character of the subordinates concerned will, in practice, be major determinants of delegation. An example is where a strong and forceful personality overcomes the lack of formal delegation; or where an inadequate manager is supported by a more competent subordinate who effectively acts as the manager. Failure to delegate successfully to a more knowledgeable subordinate may mean that the subordinate emerges as an informal leader and this could have possible adverse consequences for the manager, and for the organisation. Another example, and potential difficulty, is when a manager is persuaded to

The meaning of empowerment

Empowerment is generally explained in terms of allowing employees greater freedom, autonomy and self-control over their work, and responsibility for decision-making. However, there are differences in the meaning and interpretation of the term. *Wilkinson* refers to problems with the existing prescriptive literature on empowerment. The term 'empowerment' can be seen as flexible and even elastic, and has been used very loosely by both practitioners and academics. Wilkinson suggests that it is important to see empowerment in a wider context. It needs to be recognised that it has different forms and should be analysed in the context of broader organisational practice.[59]

The concept of empowerment also gives rise to the number of questions and doubts. For example, how does it differ in any meaningful way from other earlier forms of employee involvement? Is the primary concern of empowerment getting the most out of the workforce? Is empowerment just another somewhat more fanciful term for delegation? Some writers see the two as quite separate concepts while other writers suggest empowerment is a more proactive form of delegation.

True empowerment

Stewart suggests that to support true empowerment there is a need for a new theory of management – Theory E – which states that managers are more effective as facilitators than as leaders, and that they must devolve power, not just responsibility, to individuals as well as groups.[60] *Morris, Willcocks and Knasel* believe, however, that to empower people is a real part of leadership as opposed to management and they give examples of the way empowerment can actually set people free to do the jobs they are capable of.[61] Both make the point, however, that true empowerment is much more than conventional delegation.

According to *Mills and Friesen*: 'Empowerment can be succinctly defined as the authority of subordinates to decide and act.'

> It describes a management style. The term is often confused with delegation but, if strictly defined, empowerment goes much further in granting subordinates authority to decide and act. Indeed, within a context of broad limits defined by executives, empowered individuals may even become self-managing.[62]

The Police Custody Officer and Empowerment

The Police Service has statutory responsibility for the treatment of persons detained by them (and other agencies such as Customs & Excise which brings people into a police station). These people must be treated in accordance with the Police & Criminal Evidence Act 1984 (PACE) that was enacted in January 1986 and any code of practice issued under the Act.

Section 39 of PACE specifies that these duties should be the duty of the custody officer at a police station. The same section goes on to declare where:

1. an officer of **higher** rank than the custody officer gives directions ... which are at variance with any **decision** or **action** taken by the custody officer in the performance of a duty imposed on him under this Act the matter **shall** be referred at once to an officer of the rank of Superintendent or above who is responsible for that police station.

There is statutory backing for the decisions and actions taken by custody officers in the performance of their duties.

- Organisational aims, objectives and targets are often expressed in financial terms and measured in terms of profitability. Results are measured and reported in financial terms.
- Money is quantifiable and is a precise unit of measurement. It is easily understood, and is often used as a common denominator and as a basis for comparison.
- Financial limits are easy to apply as a measure of control and easy to relate to. For example, the need for control is an integral part of the process of delegation or empowerment. This control may easily be applied where, for example, a manager gives a subordinate the authority, without prior reference, to incur expenditure on certain items up to a given financial cost limit.

It is understandable, therefore, that so much attention is given to financial and accounting systems of measurement and control. Managers rely on accurate information systems as a basis of control and this information is frequently expressed in financial terms. However, accounting statements focus on only a limited area of activity. 'Thanks to the need for objectivity, everything in accounting statements is inward looking, concentrating on costs and based on the concept of capital maintenance.'[75]

> Although many organisations claim that people are their greatest asset, when it comes to measuring performance, 80 per cent of organisations measure in financial terms. Employers also need to consider other less tangible criteria such as employee satisfaction levels and innovation/creativity. Only one in seven organisations takes employee satisfaction into account in this respect.
>
> Department of Trade and Industry[76]

Strategic control and financial control

Management control, however, embraces far more than just financial or accounting considerations. It is concerned with the whole process of management: with the extent to which organisational aims are achieved and with improvement in performance. Control includes considerations of such factors as production, inventory, quality, judgement, consumer satisfaction, market share, social responsibilities and the human factor and management of people. For example, *Goldsmith and Clutterbuck* point out that high-performance companies keep their operating businesses in line with a mixture of both strategic and financial control. Most high-performance companies give strategic control equal or near-equal priority to financial control.[77]

Gratton refers to a simple causal model that links business goals – people context – individual behaviour and attitudes – performance of the firm – financial performance.

> *High-performance companies are created by focusing on a number of appropriate business goals, which are translated into an appropriate context in which people work. Employees behave in a way that meets the business goals and this impacts on firm performance and ultimately financial performance.*[78]

Design and application of systems In their discussion of the role of accounting systems in organisational control, it is interesting to note the words of *Berry, Broadbent and Otley*:

> *Accounting systems provide a fundamental way of handling high levels of complexity by the imposition of a set of standard operating procedures; this provides a major strength of accounting as a control system. However, weaknesses also stem from the imposition of standard systems in complex situations because inventive human minds find ways of reporting desired results through the manipulation of the system rather than by behaving in expected ways.*[79]

This wording appears to imply that the accounting system is the arbiter of correct behaviour and that people are to 'blame' for their failure to act in the way imposed by accounting systems (and presumably by the accountants who designed them).

Budgetary control and human behaviour

Accounting control systems such as internal audit, management by exception and budgetary control tend to operate in a negative way and to report only on the unfavourable, or on favourable variances which may have adverse consequences, for example less spent than budgeted. 'Success' for the accounting staff may be equated with the 'failure' of other staff. As a result there is no specific recognition from management. There is only a limited sense of achievement or self-esteem for favourable performance or where no corrective action is required. There is little, if any, positive motivation.

There are, of course, potential benefits from a properly prepared budget. For example, *Perrin* acknowledges that as a company grows, the budget becomes more of a control point but suggests that budgeting doesn't have to be a tortuous experience. Involving relevant managers and opting for realism over fantasy help in achieving a reliable, focused budget and minimise the risk of unexpected deviations.[80]

As *Hannagan* points out, budgeting involves participation of managers and workforce representatives, and by its nature is the responsibility of people.

> *Budgeting by its nature necessitates the authorisation and delegation of budget activities between individual managers and other personnel. This principle is known as 'control by responsibility', i.e. it makes an individual responsible for the whole or part of a particular budget. It is designed so that the targets set can be achieved: if the machine groups achieve their targets the production department concerned achieves its target, and so on.[81]*

And *Watson* reminds us that, especially in bureaucratic work organisations, the means can get in the way of the ends for which they were designed.

> *Budgeting arrangements are a good example of this. It is not unusual to see budgeting procedures established to manage costs but where the system of annual budgets, in which money saved cannot be 'rolled over' into the next financial year, leads to frantic and even frivolous expenditure towards the end of the financial year. Why does this happen? It is again because human beings and human interests are involved in the procedure.[82]*

There is, of course, nothing wrong with the use of accounting systems of control such as internal auditing, management by exception and budgetary control. What needs to be considered is the manner in which these controls and techniques are applied and the differences in use as a result of the attitudes adopted and the motives felt to be important. Control systems can have positive as well as negative effects. Financial and accounting control systems, as with other forms of control, should be designed and implemented in a constructive and rewarding way. To do this, they must take account of individual, social and organisational factors that determine people's patterns of behaviour.

Refresh your understanding

Activity 18E
www.pearsoned.co.uk/mullins

Critical reflection ????

'Some form of power and order is an essential feature of effective organisational performance, so it is only a question of how much control is exercised.' Do you agree? Do you think the nature of modern organisations demands greater or less management control over the actions and behaviour of people at work?

MANAGEMENT IN THE NEWS

Vodafone's boardroom battles

Vodafone faces grilling at annual meeting

Kate Burgess and Andrew Parker

It seems that £9bn does not bring silence. Vodafone announced in May that it would give £9bn to shareholders during 2006–07. But some big investors continue to criticize the company. At Vodafone's annual meeting on Tuesday, shareholders will have their first chance to confront the company's board publicly since management warned of slowing revenue growth and lower profit margins last year.

Morley Fund Management, one of Vodafone's top-10 shareholders, has taken the unusual step of stating on the record that it will vote against the re-election of most of the company's longstanding directors, including Arun Sarin, the chief executive. It is a mark of the ongoing tensions between Vodafone and its investors. Relations with investors have become increasingly strained principally because of Vodafone's flagging financial performance. In May, the company reported a record pre tax loss of £14.9bn for its 2005–06 fiscal year after taking a £28bn write-down on its assets. The results were tempered by a £3.7bn dividend for 2005–06 and plans to return £9bn to shareholders during 2006–07 following the sale of Vodafone's Japanese business.

Standard Life, another top-10 investor, said immediately after the results that it remained 'sceptical of Vodafone's ability to realise its earnings potential', and warned it 'would consider its voting position carefully'. While other shareholders remain supportive, the AGM will provide the first numerical evidence of how deep investor discontent runs. Analysts and investors await more details of Vodafone's plans to improve its performance. Mr Sarin has outlined efforts to cut costs in Vodafone's European markets through outsourcing and to increase customers' use of mobiles in homes and offices.

He has also announced Vodafone would move beyond its mobile-centric past by supplying high speed internet access over landlines. Vodafone has underperformed the FTSE 100 index by 31 per cent since Mr Sarin became chief executive in July 2003 and some investors question whether Mr Sarin can revive the stock.

'We have concerns about whether he has a grip of the details and understanding of the group's operational issues,' said one top-ten investor.

However, another top-10 investor said Mr Sarin should not be blamed for dealing with the legacy of Sir Christopher Gent, his predecessor. The investor also said Vodafone's performance problems were no different from those at rivals striving to adjust to European markets that are saturated with mobiles. Vodafone said:

Flagging performance at Vodafone causes power struggles at the top.

If you look across the sector, you could very swiftly arrive at a view that Vodafone is performing either in line or ahead of its competitors.

Flagging performance is not the only investor concern. Some investors claim Vodafone's non-executive directors have not held management sufficiently to account. The board is in the middle of an overhaul. Some shareholders are particularly disappointed at the departure at the annual meeting of Penny Hughes, a non-executive director regarded as willing to challenge the company's management. Sir John Bond, who replaces Lord MacLaurin as Vodafone's chairman at the meeting, is to review the board in the coming weeks and months.

Source: Burgess, K. and Parker, A., 'Vodafone faces grilling at annual meeting', *Financial Times*, 22 July 2006. Copyright © 2006 The Financial Time Limited, reproduced with permission.

Discussion questions

1 Identify the different types of power exercised by the various actors in this case: the shareholders of Vodafone, Arun Sarin, the Chief Executive, and the managers of the company.

2 The board of Vodafone has been criticised for failing to hold the managers of the organisation to account properly for decisions and actions which have affected the overall performance of the company. Why and how might managers do things which are not in the interests of shareholders? (NB, this potential conflict of interests between the owners of a company and those who manage it on their behalf is sometimes known as the 'agency' problem.)

SYNOPSIS

● Control is an integral part of the process of management. There are, however, varying connotations of the meaning and exercise of control. It is often interpreted in a negative manner to suggest direction or command, the restriction of behaviour or even exploitation of employees. However, control is not only a function of the formal organisation, it is also a function of interpersonal influence. Control is a general concept that is applied both to individual behaviour and organisational performance.

● Control can serve many important functions and be manifested in a variety of forms. There are a number of important characteristics of an effective control system. The system should be understood, conform with the structure of the organisation, report deviations quickly, draw attention to critical activities of the organisation, be flexible, consistent with the activity to which it relates and subject to continual review. If control systems are to be successful in leading to improved performance, then attention must also be given to the factors which influence human behaviour.

● Work organisations are not only systems of hierarchical structure, they are also systems of social relationships, status and power. Power is an inherent feature of work organisations and an underlying reality behind the decision-making process. Organisations can be classified in terms of the relationship between power, involvement and the compliance of its members. The pluralistic approach, however, recognises power as a social process. Power is a major organisational variable that derives from a multiplicity of sources and situations. A dilemma that underlies the nature of control is finding the right balance between order and flexibility, or against autonomy.

● Control systems can help fulfil people's needs at work and their presence may be welcomed. Often, however, control over behaviour is resented and perceived as a threat. The manager should, therefore, enlist the co-operation and commitment of staff, and provide for participation in the operation of control systems. The effective functioning of control systems is also influenced by: the motivation of staff; organisation structure; the operation of groups and the informal organisation; leadership style and systems of management.

● It is a fundamental principle of management that for organisational effectiveness there must be delegation. At the individual level, delegation is the process of entrusting authority and responsibility to others but ultimate accountability cannot be delegated. A planned and systematic approach to delegation means that it can be achieved without the loss of management control. Increasing attention has been given to the concept of empowerment. Despite questions and doubts about whether empowerment actually delivers it does offer potential benefits for the individual and the organisation.

● Management control systems are frequently thought of in terms of accounting or financial systems. The reasons are easy to understand but accounting control systems tend to operate in a negative way, and to give little specific recognition from management and only a limited sense of achievement. What needs to be considered are behavioural factors and the manner in which control systems motivate people to improve their performance. To do this, they must take account of individual, social and organisational factors that determine people's patterns of behaviour.

 Refresh your understanding, assess your progress and begin your research with online resources at **www.pearsoned.co.uk/mullins**

REVIEW AND DISCUSSION QUESTIONS

1 What do you see as the purposes of management control in work organisations? What are the essential elements of a management control system?

2 Discuss the main factors that are likely to affect resistance to, and the successful implementation of, management control systems.

3 Explain fully the importance of the concept of power to management and organisational behaviour.

4 Discuss critically the nature of pluralistic approaches to power and give your own practical examples.

5 How would you explain the organisational and personal relationships between a manager and subordinate staff that is created by the process of delegation?

6 As a departmental manager explain fully how you would attempt to realise the full advantages of delegation without loss of control over subordinate staff.

7 Debate critically the potential limitations and benefits of empowerment. What factors need to be considered if empowerment is to be implemented successfully?

8 Discuss what you see as the likely consequences of a manager exercising close personal supervision as a means of maintaining control and power over the work of subordinate staff.

ASSIGNMENT

The Empowerment Questionnaire

The following questionnaire consists of managerial behaviours that promote empowerment. Think of any work experience you have had – even a short-term, vacation or part-time job. How frequently did your manager do each of the following? Please mark the response that best describes the manager's behaviour.

My Manager	Very Infrequently	Infrequently	Sometimes	Frequently	Very Frequently
1 Lets me do my job without interfering	☐	☐	☐	☐	☐
2 Makes an effort to locate and remove barriers that reduce efficiency	☐	☐	☐	☐	☐
3 Encourages all of us to work as a team	☐	☐	☐	☐	☐
4 Clearly defines what is expected of me	☐	☐	☐	☐	☐
5 Provides me with honest feedback on my performacne	☐	☐	☐	☐	☐
6 Openly recognises work well done	☐	☐	☐	☐	☐
7 Keeps me focused on customer needs	☐	☐	☐	☐	☐
8 Encourages me to monitor my own efforts	☐	☐	☐	☐	☐
9 Makes sure I have the training I need to do my job	☐	☐	☐	☐	☐
10 Allows me to make decisions about my own work	☐	☐	☐	☐	☐
11 Listens to me before making decisions affecting my area	☐	☐	☐	☐	☐
12 Provides me with an environment conducive to teamwork	☐	☐	☐	☐	☐
13 Rewards me for meeting company goals	☐	☐	☐	☐	☐
14 Informs me regularly about the state of business	☐	☐	☐	☐	☐
15 Encourages me to make suggestions	☐	☐	☐	☐	☐
16 Makes sure I have all the information I need to do my work	☐	☐	☐	☐	☐

Levels of culture *Schein* suggests a view of organisational culture based on distinguishing three levels of culture, from the shallowest to the deepest: artefacts and creations; values and basic assumptions.[14]

- **Level 1: Artefacts**. The most visible level of the culture is artefacts and creations – the constructed physical and social environment. This includes physical space and layout, the technological output, written and spoken language and the overt behaviour of group members.
- **Level 2: Espoused values**. Cultural learning reflects someone's original values. Solutions about how to deal with a new task, issue or problem are based on convictions of reality. If the solution works, the value can transform into a belief. Values and beliefs become part of the conceptual process by which group members justify actions and behaviour.
- **Level 3: Basic underlying assumptions**. When a solution to a problem works repeatedly it comes to be taken for granted. Basic assumptions are unconsciously held learned responses. They are implicit assumptions that actually guide behaviour and determine how group members perceive, think and feel about things.

Schein suggests that the basic assumptions are treated as the essence – what culture really is – and values and behaviours are treated as observed manifestations of the culture essence.

TYPES OF ORGANISATIONAL CULTURE

There are a number of ways in which to classify different types of organisational culture. Developing the ideas of *Harrison*,[15] *Handy* describes four main types of organisational cultures: power culture; role culture; task culture; and person culture.[16]

- **Power culture** depends on a central power source with rays of influence from the central figure throughout the organisation. A power culture is frequently found in small entrepreneurial organisations and relies on trust, empathy and personal communications for its effectiveness. Control is exercised from the centre by the selection of key individuals. There are few rules and procedures, and little bureaucracy. It is a political organisation with decisions taken largely on the balance of influence.
- **Role culture** is often stereotyped as a bureaucracy and works by logic and rationality. Role culture rests on the strength of strong organisational 'pillars' – the functions of specialists in, for example, finance, purchasing and production. The work of, and interaction between, the pillars is controlled by procedures and rules, and co-ordinated by the pediment of a small band of senior managers. Role or job description is often more important than the individual and position is the main source of power.
- **Task culture** is job-oriented or project-oriented. In terms of structure the task culture can be likened to a net, some strands of which are stronger than others, and with much of the power and influence at the interstices. An example is the matrix organisation. Task culture seeks to bring together the right resources and people, and utilises the unifying power of the group. Influence is widely spread and based more on expert power than on position or personal power.
- **Person culture** is where the individual is the central focus and any structure exists to serve the individuals within it. When a group of people decide that it is in their own interests to band together to do their own thing and share office space, equipment or clerical assistance then the resulting organisation would have a person culture. Examples are groups of barristers, architects, doctors or consultants. Although it is found in only a few organisations, many individuals have a preference for person culture, for example university professors and specialists. Management hierarchies and control mechanisms are possible only by mutual consent. Individuals have almost complete autonomy and any influence over them is likely to be on the basis of personal power.

Every organisation will have its own unique culture and most large businesses are likely to be something of a mix of cultures with examples for each of the four types in varying areas of the organisation. Different people enjoy working in different types of organisation culture and they are more likely to be happy and satisfied at work if their attributes and personalities are consistent with the culture of that part of the organisation in which they are employed.

Four generic types of culture

From an examination of hundreds of business organisations and their environments, *Deal and Kennedy* categorise corporate cultures according to two determining factors in the marketplace:

- the degree of risk associated with the organisation's activities; and
- the speed at which organisations and their employees receive feedback on the success of decisions or strategies.

These factors give rise to four generic types of culture: the tough-guy, macho culture; the work-hard/play-hard culture; the bet-your-company culture; and the process culture.[17]

- **Tough-guy, macho culture** – an organisation of individualists who frequently take high risks and receive quick feedback on the right or wrong of their actions. Examples cited include police departments, surgeons, construction, cosmetics, management consulting and the entertainment industry. Financial stakes are high and there is a focus on speed. The intense pressure and frenetic pace often results in early 'burn-out'. Internal competition and conflict are normal, stars are temperamental but tolerated. A high staff turnover can create difficulties in building a strong cohesive culture.
- **Work-hard/play-hard culture** – characterised by fun and action where employees take few risks, all with quick feedback. There is a high level of relatively low-risk activity. Examples include sales organisations such as estate agents and computer companies, mass consumer companies such as McDonald's, office equipment manufacturers and retail stores. Organisations tend to be highly dynamic and the primary value centres on customers and their needs. It is the team who produce the volume, and the culture encourages games, meetings, promotions and conventions to help maintain motivation. However, although a lot gets done, volume can be at the expense of quality.
- **Bet-your-company culture** – where there are large-stake decisions with a high risk but slow feedback so that it may be years before employees know if decisions were successful. Examples include oil companies, investment banks, architectural firms and the military. The focus is on the future and the importance of investing in it. There is a sense of deliberateness throughout the organisation typified by the ritual of the business meeting. There is a hierarchical system of authority with decision-making from the top down. The culture leads to high-quality inventions and scientific breakthroughs, but moves only very slowly and is vulnerable to short-term fluctuations.
- **Process culture** – a low-risk, slow-feedback culture where employees find difficulty in measuring what they do. Typical examples include banks, insurance companies, financial services and the civil service. The individual financial stakes are low and employees get very little feedback on their effectiveness. Their memos and reports seem to disappear into a void. Lack of feedback forces employees to focus on how they do something, not what they do. People tend to develop a 'cover your back' mentality. Bureaucracy results with attention to trivial events, minor detail, formality and technical perfection. Process cultures can be effective when there is a need for order and predictability.

Note, however that in a subsequent publication, *Deal and Kennedy* suggest revisions to the original typology. For example, under process cultures, banks might not yet fit into the work-hard/play-hard culture but have evolved more into sales-type organisations.[18]

P(copy)

Figure 19.1 The cultural web of an organisation

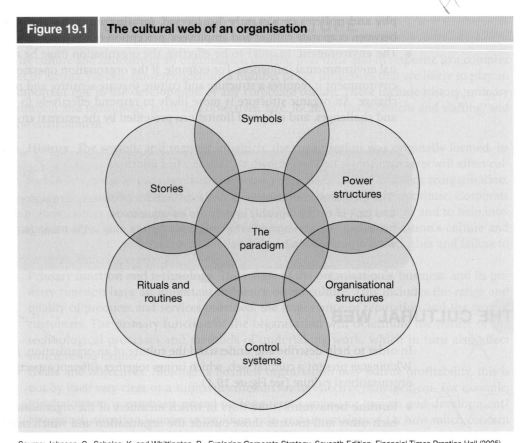

Source: Johnson, G., Scholes, K. and Whittington, R., *Exploring Corporate Strategy*, Seventh Edition, Financial Times Prentice Hall (2005), p. 202. Reproduced with permission from Pearson Eduction Ltd.

One way of examining the culture of an organization is to look at its corporate image to see what and who is valued in the organization. A corporate image is the mental picture the clients, customers, employees, and others have of an organization. The impression is the combination of unconscious, unintended, conscious, and intended factors that arise.[26]

ACAS distinguishes two different organisation cultures and different ways of doing things:

- **Control culture** with the emphasis on rules and procedures, control and compliance with precedent providing guidelines; and
- **Quality of working life culture** with the emphasis on core values, with mission statements providing guidance and commitment via shared goals, values and traditions.[27]

Naylor suggests that quite what forms organisational culture is a difficulty and to make a start we need to recognise both the visible and invisible layers. On the surface is the visible layer made up of elements such as artefacts, symbols, languages, stories and activities which can be collected, compared and assembled into a description of the organisation. Underpinning this 'visible culture' is the invisible layer of beliefs, values, norms, basic assumptions and understanding.[28]

Charters questions the extent to which the concept of 'folklore' offers the potential to explore the existence of company myths and legends. Dictionary definitions and discussions of the term in research papers, point to its close connection with culture.

Elements of folklore include myths and legends, and hence the concept of folklore appears to validate the exploration of organisational stories as part of cultural research ... If folklore really is an expression

Characteristics of a healthy organisational climate

Organisational climate is characterised, therefore, by the nature of the people–organisation relationship and the superior–subordinate relationship. These relationships are determined by interactions among goals and objectives, formal structure, the process of management, styles of leadership and the behaviour of people.

Although similar types of organisations will share certain common features and norms, each organisation will have its own different and distinctive features. In general terms, however, a healthy organisational climate might be expected to exhibit such characteristic features as:

- the integration of organisational goals and personal goals;
- the most appropriate organisation structure based on the demands of the socio-technical system;
- democratic functioning of the organisation with full opportunities for participation;
- justice in treatment with equitable HRM and employment relations policies and practices;
- mutual trust, consideration and support among different levels of the organisation;
- the open discussion of conflict with an attempt to avoid confrontation;
- managerial behaviour and styles of leadership appropriate to the particular work situations;
- acceptance of the psychological contract between the individual and the organisation;
- recognition of people's needs and expectations at work, and individual differences and attributes;
- concern for job design and the work/life balance;
- opportunities for personal development and career progression;
- a sense of identity with, and loyalty to, the organisation and a feeling of being a valued and important member.

If organisational climate is to be improved, then attention should be given to the above features. A healthy climate will not by itself guarantee improved organisational effectiveness. However, an organisation is most unlikely to attain optimum operational performance unless the climate evokes a spirit of support and co-operation throughout the organisation, and is conducive to motivating members to work willingly and effectively.

Whitmore suggests that two human drives rise above all others; the need for self-belief, and the need for a sense of meaning and purpose in our lives. They exist independent of race, creed and culture. These two needs are the fundamental bedrocks that underlie business performance, and the importance of generating a climate of creativity within an organisation stems from recognition of their significance.[52]

EMPLOYEE COMMITMENT

Among the factors that contribute to a healthy organisational climate is the extent to which members of staff have a sense of commitment to the organisation. The extent of their commitment will have a major influence on the level of work performance. *Walton* suggests that a significant change in approaches to the organisation and management of work is from organisational control to commitment in the workplace. The evidence is well grounded that underlying all the policies of commitment strategy is a management philosophy at the centre of which 'is a belief that eliciting employee commitment will lead to enhanced performance'.[53]

The concept of **employee commitment** itself, and the manner in which it is actually created, is not easy to describe. There does, however, appear to be a growing acceptance of the notion of attachment and loyalty. *O'Reilly* refers to the term 'organisational commitment' as 'typically conceived of as an individual's psychological bond to the organization, including a sense of job involvement, loyalty, and a belief in the values of the organization'.[54]

In order to help ensure its survival and future success the organisation must be readily adaptable to the external demands placed upon it. The organisation must be responsive to change. Other major forces of change include:

- increased demands for quality and high levels of customer service and satisfaction;
- greater flexibility in the structure of work organisations and patterns of management;
- the changing nature and composition of the workforce; and
- conflict from within the organisation.

According to a survey from Management Consultancies Associations, four interrelated forces are driving change, each of which brings organisations and individuals into conflict:

1 outsourcing and the continual redefinition of what constitutes an organisation's core business;
2 the distribution of work across different people, organisations and locations, and the extent to which this makes work fragmented;
3 changing demographics and expectations that create an employees', rather than employers', market;
4 the doubled-edge sword of technology, which enables people to do more but tempts organisations to do too much.[62]

Change within the organisation
Change also originates within the organisation itself. Much of this change is part of a natural process of ageing – for example, as material resources such as buildings, equipment or machinery deteriorate or lose efficiency; or as human resources get older, or as skills and abilities become outdated. Some of this change can be managed through careful planning – for example, regular repairs and maintenance, choice of introducing new technology or methods of work, effective human resource planning to prevent a large number of staff retiring at the same time, and management succession planning – training and staff development. However, the main pressure of change is from external forces. The organisation must be properly prepared to face the demands of a changing environment. It must give attention to its future development and success and this includes public sector organisations and the armed forces.[63]

Public sector executives face unique obstacles in leading organisational change, in part because of entrenched civil service bureaucracies, procedural constraints such as managing performance and firing employees, and dealing with many different stakeholders with competing priorities.[64]

A concept map of sources of change is presented in Figure 19.2.

Increasing pace of change
The latest 'Quality of Working Life' report published by the Chartered Management Institute draws attention to the intensifying pace, scale and complexity of organisational change.

What has emerged is a picture of managers coming under increasing pressure from the imposition of targets, performance management systems and league tables against a backdrop of global competition, technological change, the drive to maximise shareholder value and, in the public sector, a modernisation agenda.

Not surprisingly, managers in larger organisations in all sectors experienced most change. While a higher proportion of managers working in the public sector had experienced change initiatives compared to managers working in PLCs, those working in the private sector experienced a greater variety of change initiatives.[65]

Figure 19.2 Concept map of sources of change

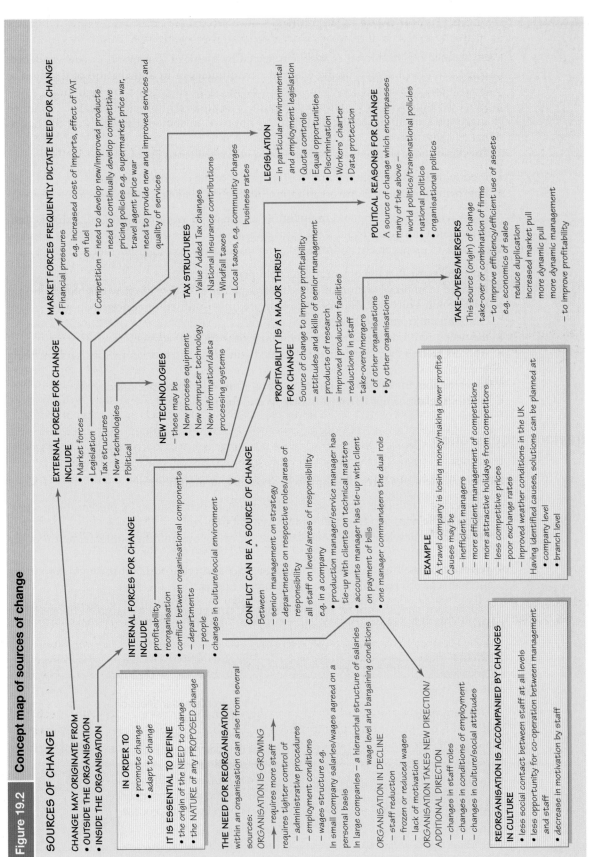

Source: Training Learning Consultancy Ltd, Bristol, England. Reproduced with permission.

PLANNED ORGANISATIONAL CHANGE

Most planned organisational change is triggered by the need to respond to new challenges or opportunities presented by the external environment, or in anticipation of the need to cope with potential future problems, for example, intended government legislation, a new product development by a major competitor or further technological advances. Planned change represents an intentional attempt to improve, in some important way, the operational effectiveness of the organisation.

The basic underlying objectives can be seen in general terms as:

- modifying the behavioural patterns of members of the organisation; and
- improving the ability of the organisation to cope with changes in its environment.

ACAS refers to initiating and maintaining a Quality of Working Life (QWL) change programme. Such initiatives could stem from a variety of issues that might provide 'a window for change' to management and/or worker representatives. Examples include:

- a general sense that the organisation could perform better;
- the need to improve organisation flexibility, quality or to develop new customer concern;
- a sense that skills and abilities of people are under-utilised or concerns about a lack of commitment from employees;
- the need to introduce changes in technology or working practices;
- workers feeling over-controlled by supervision or by the process or jobs seen as being boring;
- concerns about ineffective communications or poor performance indicators;
- fractious relationships between managers and the managed.[66]

Behaviour modification

A programme of planned change and improved performance developed by *Lewin* involves the management of a three-phase process of behaviour modification:

- **unfreezing** – reducing those forces which maintain behaviour in its present form, recognition of the need for change and improvement to occur;
- **movement** – development of new attitudes or behaviour and the implementation of the change;
- **refreezing** – stabilising change at the new level and reinforcement through supporting mechanisms, for example policies, structure or norms.[67]

French, Kast and Rosenzweig list eight specific components of a planned-change effort related to the above process (*see* Figure 19.3).[68]

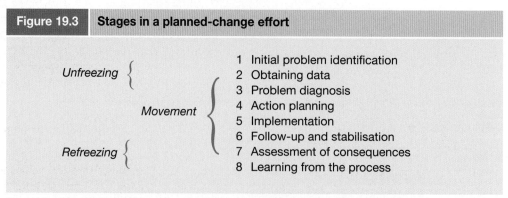

Figure 19.3	Stages in a planned-change effort

Unfreezing {
Movement {
Refreezing {

1 Initial problem identification
2 Obtaining data
3 Problem diagnosis
4 Action planning
5 Implementation
6 Follow-up and stabilisation
7 Assessment of consequences
8 Learning from the process

Source: Adapted from French, W. L., Kast, F. E. and Rosenweig, J. E., *Understanding Human Behaviour in Organizations*, Harper and Row (1985), p. 9. Reproduced with permission from Pearson Education, Inc.

Changes in managerial work Change is reciprocal and changing organisations will affect the nature of managerial work. *Stewart*, for example, describes how changes in organisations affect the kinds of jobs that managers have to do and the nature of their lives and careers. Older managers now work for very different kinds of organisations from those in which they first became managers. Although hierarchies of authority will continue to exist in large organisations they will be shorter and there will be wider networking. There will be a smaller number of middle managers but with more responsible roles. Managers' jobs are more complex and demanding, and managers' careers are much less predictable. But managers now have a greater choice in their work and careers.[69]

However, according to *Crainer*, many managers refuse to accept the necessity of change. Instead of being proactive, change is often reactive, the last resort.

> *Research repeatedly shows that it is managers who are the chief stumbling block to making change happen. Changing organizational structures and managerial thinking challenges and undercuts traditional power bases ... For the manager reared on the old functional certainties, the new world organization is very difficult to manage. Indeed, the vast majority of managers are neither trained nor equipped to manage in such an environment.*[70]

And, according to *Gratton*, 'understanding the soul of the organisation and building trust and commitment is crucial to ongoing adaptation and change'.[71]

The challenge of e-business It is impossible to know exactly what the future of e-business will bring but it will continue to bring tremendous change. One of the biggest changes for managers, especially within large organisations, is learning how to get to grips with an increasingly flexible workforce. As a result of the e-business environment many people can work at any time, anywhere and at any place. Many employees work at home but although the virtual office may help organisations to cut costs, it also poses many management challenges including the challenge to put structures in place to ensure regular meetings take place. Flexible working calls for flexible managers. This means that the traditional line managers need to become leaders, coaches and facilitators. Given the accelerating rate of change particularly with the intranet, it is essential that organisations invest in and develop their managers to succeed with this change.

RESISTANCE TO CHANGE

Despite the potential positive outcomes, change is often resisted at both the individual and the organisational level. Resistance to change – or the thought of the implications of the change – appears to be a common phenomenon. As long ago as 1970, *Toffler* wrote about the psychological dimension of 'future shock', and that people are naturally wary of change. 'Among many there is an uneasy mood – a suspicion that change is out of control.'[72]

Resistance to change can take many forms and it is often difficult to pinpoint the exact reasons. The forces against change in work organisations include: ignoring the needs and expectations of members; when members have insufficient information about the nature of the change; or if they do not perceive the need for change. Fears may be expressed over such matters as employment levels and job security, de-skilling of work, loss of job satisfaction, wage rate differentials, changes to social structures and working conditions, loss of individual control over work, and greater management control.

Individual resistance Some common reasons for individual resistance to change within organisations include the following:

- **Selective perception**. People's interpretation of stimuli presents a unique picture or image of the 'real' world and can result in selective perception. This can lead to a biased view of a particular situation, which fits most comfortably into a person's own perception of reality,

and can cause resistance to change. For example, trade unionists may have a stereotyped view of management as untrustworthy and therefore oppose any management change, however well founded might have been the intention. Managers exposed to different theories or ideas may tend to categorise these as either those they already practise and have no need to worry about or those that are of no practical value and which can be discarded as of no concern to them.

- **Habit**. People tend to respond to situations in an established and accustomed manner. Habits may serve as a means of comfort and security, and as a guide for easy decision-making. Proposed changes to habits, especially if the habits are well established and require little effort, may well be resisted. However, if there is a clearly perceived advantage, for example a reduction in working hours without loss of pay, there is likely to be less, if any, resistance to the change, although some people may, because of habit, still find it difficult to adjust to the new times.

- **Inconvenience or loss of freedom**. If the change is seen as likely to prove inconvenient, make life more difficult, reduce freedom of action or result in increased control, there will be resistance.

- **Economic implications**. People are likely to resist change that is perceived as reducing either directly or indirectly their pay or other rewards, requiring an increase in work for the same level of pay or acting as a threat to their job security. People tend to have established patterns of working and a vested interest in maintaining the status quo.

- **Security in the past**. There is a tendency for some people to find a sense of security in the past. In times of frustration or difficulty, or when faced with new or unfamiliar ideas or methods, people may reflect on the past. There is a wish to retain old and comfortable ways. For example, in bureaucratic organisations, officials often tend to place faith in well-established ('tried and trusted') procedures and cling to these as giving a feeling of security.

- **Fear of the unknown**. Changes which confront people with the unknown tend to cause anxiety or fear. Many major changes in a work organisation present a degree of uncertainty, for example the introduction of new technology or methods of working. A person may resist promotion because of uncertainty over changes in responsibilities or the increased social demands of the higher position.

Organisational resistance Although organisations have to adapt to their environment, they tend to feel comfortable operating within the structure, policies and procedures which have been formulated to deal with a range of present situations. To ensure operational effectiveness, organisations often set up defences against change and prefer to concentrate on the routine things they perform well. Some of the main reasons for organisational resistance against change are as follows.

- **Organisation culture**. Recall that the culture of an organisation develops over time and may not be easy to change. The pervasive nature of culture in terms of 'how things are done around here' also has a significant effect on organisational processes and the behaviour of staff. An ineffective culture may result in a lack of flexibility for, or acceptance of, change.

- **Maintaining stability**. Organisations, especially large-scale ones, pay much attention to maintaining stability and predictability. The need for formal organisation structure and the division of work, narrow definitions of assigned duties and responsibilities, established rules, procedures and methods of work, can result in resistance to change. The more mechanistic or bureaucratic the structure, the less likely it is that the organisation will be responsive to change.

- **Investment in resources**. Change often requires large resources that may already be committed to investments in other areas or strategies. Assets such as buildings, technology, equipment and people cannot easily be altered. For example, a car manufacturer may not find it easy to change to a socio-technical approach and the use of autonomous

work groups because it cannot afford the cost of a new purpose-built plant and specialised equipment.

- **Past contracts or agreements**. Organisations enter into contracts or agreements with other parties, such as the government, other organisations, trade unions, suppliers and customers. These contracts and agreements can limit changes in behaviour – for example, organisations operating under a special licence or permit, or a fixed-price contract to supply goods/services to a government agency. Another example might be an agreement with unions that limits the opportunity to introduce compulsory redundancies, or the introduction of certain new technology or working practices.

- **Threats to power or influence**. Change may be seen as a threat to the power or influence of certain groups within the organisation, such as their control over decisions, resources or information. For example, managers may resist the introduction of quality circles or worker-directors because they see this as increasing the role and influence of non-managerial staff, and a threat to the power in their own positions. Where a group of people have, over a period of time, established what they perceive as their 'territorial rights', they are likely to resist change.

Perceptions and change Although change is often resisted, *Cunningham* maintains that one of the greatest myths in management is the generalisation that people resist change. In fact people love change. The commonest reason for resistance is where people perceive a potential loss. For example because of negative rumour-mongering, people may perceive that they will be worse off from a proposed change even if the opposite is in fact true. In a different context, changes that result, for example in the loss of one's job, can create real, fact-based resistance. While people welcome change that they want, they have to be careful about the pace of change. In a more general context people may be enthusiastic for change, for example in large organisations where some people want to see changes and improvements in communication.

> What seems to get in the way is the continual chanting of the untrue generalisation that 'people resist change'. People resist some change – if they perceive that they are going to lose out. People welcome change that makes things better.[73]

Critical reflection ????

Change is nothing new and a simple fact of life. Some people actively thrive on new challenges and constant change, while others prefer the comfort of the status quo and strongly resist any change. Do you agree that it is all down to the personality of the individual? Do you accept that despite all the attention there is little management can do about resistance to change?

THE MANAGEMENT OF ORGANISATIONAL CHANGE

The successful management of change is clearly essential for continued economic performance and competitiveness. New ideas and innovations should not be perceived as threats by members of the organisation. The efforts made by management to maintain the balance of the socio-technical system will influence people's attitudes, the behaviour of individuals and groups, and thereby the level of organisational performance and effectiveness.

Stewart is among those writers who point out how changes in technology and in domestic government policies have had a radical impact on managers in many companies and in public service organisations.

- **Changes to the work organisation must maintain the balance of the socio-technical system.** Increased technology and automation may result in jobs becoming more repetitive and boring, and providing only a limited challenge and satisfaction to staff. It is important, therefore, to attempt to improve the quality of work, to remove frustration and stress from jobs, and to make them more responsible and interesting. Actual working arrangements rely heavily on the informal organisation and effective teamwork. Groups and teams are a major feature of organisational life and can have a significant influence on the successful implementation of change. New working practices should take account of how best to satisfy people's needs and expectations at work through the practical application of behavioural science.

- **Careful attention should be given to job design, methods of work organisation, the development of cohesive groups, and relationships between the nature and content of jobs and their task functions.** The introduction of new technology has also highlighted the need to give attention to the wider organisational context including the design of technology itself, broader approaches to improved job design, employee involvement and empowerment, the development of skills and problem-solving capacity, and the effective management of change.

Style of managerial behaviour One of the most important factors in the successful implementation of organisational change is the style of managerial behaviour. Some members may actually prefer, and respond better, to a directed and controlled style of management. (Recall, for example, the discussion on Theory X and Theory Y styles of managerial behaviour in Chapter 12.)

In most cases, however, the introduction of change is more likely to be effective with a participative style of managerial behaviour. If staff are kept fully informed of proposals, are encouraged to adopt a positive attitude and have personal involvement in the implementation of the change, there is a greater likelihood of their acceptance of the change. However, *Reis and Pena* maintain that too often, management ignores human resistance issues and the need to address them in the implementation plan.

> *The success of any change depends on the willingness of employees to accept it with enthusiasm and implement it with care. Yet, business changes at times are undertaken without understanding how the human element influences the success or failure of a project. Frequently, companies develop impressive technical plans and simply assume the change – technical or organizational – will occur. The difficult and often neglected part of such initiatives is leading and managing behavioural change with those persons who interface with the new technology or the new initiatives.* [78]

McHugh, O'Brien and Ramondt point out that many public sector organisations have embarked upon far-reaching programmes of unsettling strategic change. They argue that such change programmes initiated by senior management without involvement of organisational members are unlikely to be successful. Organisations are more likely to experience the desired metamorphosis where the change is led by relatively junior front line staff with senior management practitioners acting as facilitators of organisational transformation. [79]

OVERCOMING RESISTANCE TO CHANGE

The effective management of change must be based on a clear understanding of human behaviour at work. Most people are not detached from their work but experience a range of emotional involvements through their membership of the organisation, they feel threatened and disoriented by the challenge of change. Emotions such as uncertainty, frustration or fear are common reactions. It is understandable therefore that people often adopt a defensive and negative attitude, and demonstrate resistance to change. It is important to remember that change is a complex and powerful psychological experience, and that individuals react internally to change.

According to *Atkinson*, a major problem in driving change in organisations is dealing with and managing the resistance that will be encountered – but that resistance should be welcomed as a healthy response. Resistance is natural and should not be viewed only as a negative response to change. In the absence of really positive benefits from the proposed change, the 'default' response of resistance is acceptable.

> *It is unusual for any change not to attract some resistance. Even with foresight, pre-planning and all the apparent logic behind the need to change, you should expect some resistance as the norm. Recognise and welcome it as a healthy response and an opportunity to openly debate possibilities and treat resistance as a powerfully ally in facilitating the learning process.*
>
> Philip Atkinson, 'Managing resistance to change'[80]

People are the key factor The successful implementation of new work methods and practices is dependent upon the willing and effective co-operation of staff, managerial colleagues and unions. People are the key factor in the successful management of change. If change is to work, it must change the perceptions, attitudes and behaviour of people.

However, *Lucas* reminds us that a high proportion of change initiatives fail, derailed by the people factor.

> *Given that change has become such a fact of business life, it is worrying that so many change management programmes fail to fulfil their potential. The consensus among the experts is that it is often the people factor that derails the effort. Put simply, organisations know where they want to go – but they are not taking their people with them.*[81]

Responsibilities of top management

The successful management of change is a key factor of organisational performance and effectiveness and should emanate from the top of the organisation. Top management has a responsibility for the underlying philosophy and attitudes of the organisation, for creating and sustaining a healthy climate; and establishing appropriate and supportive organisational processes. The successful implementation of change demands positive action from top management and a style of transformational leadership in order to gain a commitment to change.[82]

However, *Champy* points out that one of the biggest challenges occurs not with middle management or deep in the organisation but at the level of senior managers.

> *I don't agree with the old song that people resist change. I think that people are fearful of change when they don't know where they're going, but they can get excited about these changes once they have a sense of where the whole operation is heading.*[83]

Change leaders From a study of 25 chief executives in the UK and abroad, *Hooper and Potter* investigated what were thought to be the crucial attributes for effective change leaders. They point out that effective change leadership is not easy but found the following key factors and behaviours that have been crucial to the success of top people:

- effective communication of the reasons for change and developing an open communications culture;
- releasing the potential of everyone involved in the change, and championing innovation and creativity;
- setting a good personal example; and
- self-pacing to avoid unnecessary stress.[84]

An interesting proposition is put forward by *Drucker*, who contends that 'one cannot manage change. One can only be ahead of it. We do not hear much anymore about "overcoming resistance to change"'. Everyone now accepts that change is unavoidable.

● Applications of organisational behaviour and the effective management of human resources are dependent upon the characteristic features of the individual organisation – and its culture. The pervasive nature of culture has an important effect on the behaviour and actions of individuals, the process of management and on organisational performance. It describes what the organisation is all about. Culture helps to account for variations among organisations and managers, both nationally and internationally.

● Organisational climate is based on the perception of members towards the organisation, and can be seen as the state of mutual trust and understanding among members of the organisation. Climate influences the attitudes that staff bring to bear on their work performance and personal relationships. Among the factors which contribute to a healthy climate is the extent to which employees have a sense of commitment to, and psychological bond with, the organisation.

● Organisations operate within an increasingly volatile environment and are in a state of constant change. Change is a pervasive influence and an inescapable part of social and organisational life. There is a wide range of forces acting upon organisations which make the need for change inevitable. Change can affect all aspects of the operation and functioning of the organisation. Planned organisation change involves a process of behaviour modification. Change is reciprocal and changing organisations may affect the nature of managerial work.

● Despite the potential positive outcomes, change is often resisted at both the individual and the organisational level. Resistance to change can take many forms and it is not always easy to pinpoint the exact reasons. It is important that management adopt a clearly defined strategy for the successful initiation of change, including attention to the style of managerial behaviour, and the human and social factors of change. The effective management of change is a key factor of organisational performance and competitiveness, and should emanate from the top of the organisation.

 Refresh your understanding, assess your progress and begin your research with online resources at **www.pearsoned.co.uk/mullins**

REVIEW AND DISCUSSION QUESTIONS

1 Explain fully what you understand by the meaning and nature of organisation development (OD).

2 Suggest how you would attempt to explain the concept of organisational culture. What factors might influence the development of culture?

3 Discuss critically the importance of culture for effective organisational performance. Give practical examples from your own organisation.

4 What do you understand by organisational climate and what do you think are its main characteristic features? From your own organisation, give examples of features that have contributed to and/or detracted from a healthy climate.

5 Explain the concept of employee commitment and suggest how it might actually be created. Give examples of factors that have contributed to your own strength of commitment in any work situation.

6 Give specific examples of major changes confronting management today and their probable implications for an organisation of your choice.

7 Why do individuals and organisations tend to resist change? To what extent do you believe such resistance can be effectively overcome?

8 Explain fully what *you* believe are the most important features in the successful implementation of organisational change.

ASSIGNMENT

Rate your readiness to change

A Quiz

The left-hand column lists 17 key elements of change readiness. Rate your organisation on each item. Give three points for high ranking ('We're good at this; I'm confident of our skills here'), two for medium score ('We're spotty here; we could use improvement or more experience') and one point for a low score ('We've had problems with this; this is new to our organisation'). Be honest. Don't trust only your own perspective; ask others in the organisation, at all levels, to rate the company too. The consultants at Symmetrix believe – no surprise – it helps to have an outsider do the assessment with you.

Readiness scoring

How to score: High = 3 Medium = 2 Low = 1

Category		Score
Sponsorship	The sponsor of change is not necessarily its day-to-day leader; her or she is the visionary, chief cheerleader, and bill payer – the person with the power to help the team change when it meets resistance. Give three points – change will be easier – if sponsorship comes at a senior level; for example, CEO, COO, or the head of an autonomous business unit. Weakest sponsors: midlevel executives or staff officers.	☐
Leadership	This means the day-to-day leadership – the people who call the meeting, set the goals, work till midnight. Successful change is more likely if leadership is high level, has 'ownership' (that is, direct responsibility for what's to be changed) and has clear business results in mind. Low-level leadership, or leadership that is not well connected throughout the organization (across departments) or that comes from the staff, is less likely to succeed and should be scored low.	☐
Motivation	High points for a strong sense of urgency from senior management, which is shared by the rest of the company, and for a corporate culture that already emphasizes continuous improvement. Negative: tradition-bound managers and workers, many of whom have been in their jobs for more than 15 years; a conservative culture that discourages risk taking.	☐
Direction	Does senior management strongly believe that the future should look different from the present? How clear is management's picture of the future? Can management mobilize all relevant parties – employees, the board, customers, etc. – for action? High points for positive answers to those questions. If senior management thinks only minor change is needed, the likely outcome is no change at all; score yourself low.	☐
Measurements	Or in consultant-speak, 'metrics'. Three points if you already use performance measures of the sort encouraged by total quality management (defect rates, time to market, etc.) and if these express the economics of the business. Two points if some measures exist but compensation and reward systems do not explicitly reinforce them. If you don't have measures in place or don't know what we're talking about, one point.	☐
Organizational context	How does the change effort connect to other major goings-on in context of the organization? (For example: Does it dovetail with a continuing total quality management process? Does it fit with strategic actions such as acquisitions or new product lines?) Trouble lies ahead for a change effort that is isolated or if there are multiple change efforts whose relationships are not linked strategically.	☐

→

Assignment – continued

Category		Score
Processes/ Functions	Major changes almost invariably require redesigning business processes that cut across functions such as purchasing, accounts payable, or marketing. If functional executives are rigidly turf conscious, change will be difficult. Give yourself more points the more willing they – and the organisation as a whole – are to change critical processes and sacrifice perks or power for the good of the group.	☐
Competitor benchmarking	Whether you are a leader in your industry or a laggard, give benchmarking yourself points for a continuing programme that objectively compares your company's performance with that of competitors and systematically examines changes in your market. Give yourself one point if knowledge of competitors' abilities is primarily anecdotal – what salesmen say at the bar.	☐
Customer focus	The more everyone in the company is imbued with knowledge of customers, the more likely that the organization can agree to change to serve them better. Three points if everyone in the work force knows who his or her customers are, knows their needs, and has had direct contact with them. Take away points if that knowledge is confined to pockets of the organization (sales and marketing, senior executives).	☐
Rewards	Change is easier if managers and employees are rewarded for taking risks, being innovative, and looking for new solutions. Team-based rewards are better than rewards based solely on individual achievement. Reduce points if your company, like most, rewards continuity over change. If managers become heroes for making budget, they won't take risks even if you say you want them to. Also: If employees believe failure will be punished, reduce points.	☐
Organizational structure	The best situation is a flexible organization with little churn – that structure is, reorganizations are rare and well received. Score yourself lower if you have a rigid structure that has been unchanged for more than five years or has undergone frequent reorganization with little success; that may signal a cynical company culture that fights change by waiting it out.	☐
Communication	A company will adapt to change most readily if it has many means of two-way communication that reach all levels of the organization and that all employees use and understand. If communications media are few, often trashed unread, and almost exclusively one-way and top-down, change will be more difficult.	☐
Organizational hierarchy	The fewer levels of hierarchy and the fewer employee grade hierarchy levels, the more likely an effort to change will succeed. A thick impasto of middle management and staff not only slows decision-making but also creates large numbers of people with the power to block change.	☐
Prior experience with change	Score three if the organization has successfully implemented major changes in the recent past. Score one if there is no prior experience with major change or if change efforts failed or left a legacy of anger or resentment. Most companies will score two, acknowledging equivocal success in previous attempts to change.	☐
Morale	Change is easier if employees enjoy working in the organization and the level of individual responsibility is high. Signs of unreadiness to change: low team spirit, little voluntary extra effort, and mistrust. Look for two types of mistrust: between management and employees, and between or among departments.	☐

Category		*Score*
Innovation	Best situation: The company is always experimenting; new ideas are implemented with seemingly little effort; employees work across internal boundaries without much trouble. Bad signs: lots of red tape, multiple signoffs required before new ideas are tried; employees must go through channels and are discouraged from working with colleagues from other departments or divisions.	☐
Decision-making	Rate yourself high if decisions are made quickly, taking into account a wide variety of suggestions; it is clear where decisions are made. Give yourself a low grade if decisions come slowly and are made by a mysterious 'them'; there is a lot of conflict during the process, and confusion and finger pointing after decisions are announced.	☐
	Total score	☐

After completing your total score, compare and discuss your response with those of your colleagues.

PERSONAL AWARENESS AND SKILLS EXERCISE

Objectives

Completing this exercise should help you to enhance the following skills:

- Relate classifications of culture to different types of organisations.
- Assess influences on the development of culture.
- Evaluate the appropriateness of culture for specific organisations.

Exercise

Using the classifications of organisational culture proposed by Handy, and by Deal and Kennedy, you are required to:

1 Compare and contrast the influences on the development of culture in any two different types of organisations. Your two organisations could be, *for example*:

 Private and public sector; For profit and not-for-profit; Service sector and manufacturing sector; Production and academic.

2 Suggest, with supporting reasons, which of **either** the Handy or the Deal and Kennedy typologies you would try to foster if you were appointed as a senior manager in any two of the following organisations:

 - wheel-clamping contractor;
 - research laboratory;
 - battleship;
 - private hospital;
 - second-hand car business;
 - high-fashion clothing store;
 - fast-food chain;
 - advertising agency.

→

Personal awareness and skills exercise – continued

Discussion

● How important is organisational culture? How would you attempt to foster a change in the prevailing culture of an organisation?

● To what extent do textbook classifications aid our practical understanding and analysis of organisational culture?

● Should there be/is there a most 'suitable' culture for specific organisations?

CASE STUDY

The Haier Corporation

Haier is one of the most remarkable success stories associated with the extraordinary growth of the Chinese economy over the last 20 years. Its story shows the importance of a strong culture, deliberate strategy and a successful focus on operational management and quality.

In 1984, Haier was a small, unsuccessful state-owned corporation in Qingdao, a city of about 7 million people in eastern China. It was losing $178,000 on annual revenues of $421,000 and had 600 employees.[86] Twenty years later, it was profitable, with an annual sales revenue of almost $10 billion. Over that period, it had built up export sales to more than 160 countries, together with a range of manufacturing and other alliances and investments around the world. Its product range – originally just refrigerators – had expanded massively to cover dozens of categories in the domestic electrical appliance market, with thousands of individual products. As an article in *Forbes* magazine in 2001 pointed out, Haier had achieved this growth by deploying a genuinely international approach, unlike many other Chinese manufacturers: it traded, for example, under its own brand rather than making products anonymously for other companies.[87] It also ran manufacturing operations in other countries and was always looking for opportunities to adapt its products to local tastes. In the United States, for example, a successful wine fridge was designed by Haier America's President. Unexpectedly for many in the West (given its origins in what is still a one-party communist state), Haier seemed to be growing into a fully fledged multinational corporation, competing successfully with longer-established rivals.

Source: Lou Linwei/Alamy

Zhang's hammer forged a successful organisational culture in China, but can it succeed in global markets?

Zhang's hammer

However, Haier is far from a standard faceless, stateless multinational: its culture, style and operational approach reflect its Chinese traditions and its successes are clearly identified with some of its key leaders. In *Fortune* magazine in 2005, Haier president Yang Mianmian was listed as the fifteenth most powerful businesswoman in the world: her strategy of 'one low (price), three high (value, growth and quality)' was cited as a key foundation of Haier's continuing success.[88] The corporation's superstar, however, must be CEO Zhang Ruimin, who took the company over at its low point in 1984 and whose drive, imagination and personal philosophy largely powered its transformation into a truly global player. One story that crops up again and again in reports about Haier concerns the day in 1985 that CEO Zhang took a sledgehammer to a row of 76

faulty Haier fridges, to the great distress of the workforce who were lined up to watch (a fridge cost about two years' wages in that year).[89] Explaining his dramatic action, Zhang said:

If we don't destroy these refrigerators today, what is to be shattered by the market in the future will be this enterprise![90]

The hammer is reportedly on display in Haier's exhibition hall, a symbol of Zhang's complete rejection of the previous company attitude that defective products could be tolerated and knocked out at a discount. Perhaps the story has been idealised a little over the years; the point, however, is that Haier is a corporation with a soul – one that creates and retells stories about itself, one with a strong and distinctive culture.

Some of that distinctive identity can be seen in the nature of its external relationships. As mentioned above, its international strategy seeks to make maximum use of local human resources and capital, an approach that also helps Haier to offer fast delivery and very good service to its customers and distribution partners. It is always open to opportunities to adapt its products to local preferences and habits (as with the wine fridge), a practice that could become costly in terms of complexity and logistics. Its international strategy has been to go for the difficult markets first on the basis that success in these markets would require the company to improve faster than seeking to dominate less fiercely contested markets.[91] Haier is, of course, very strong in its enormous and fast-growing home market and has built up an enviable distribution network in China. This has helped it to dominate the Chinese market, but Zhang has also sought to expand the network via multinational alliances, such as the 2002 agreement with Japan's Sanyo, through which Sanyo products are distributed by Haier in China and vice versa in Japan.[92]

Haier's strong culture can be seen most clearly in its internal relationships: for all of its willingness to adapt its output to local preferences and demands, Haier seems to be much less flexible about how things should be done within the corporation. As with so many organisations with strong cultures, there is a well-articulated Haier way of doing things, which new Haier employees must become used to. The company's philosophy and values are set out in some detail on its website and the sentiments include some fairly standard rallying cries about excellence and innovation:[93]

Haier spirit: we work diligently to serve the country and to pursue excellence through innovation.

Management accountability – the 80/20 principle: management is 80 per cent responsible for any subordinate's wrongdoing.

Quality focus: excellent employees produce high quality products.

Team spirit – 10/10 principle: The top 10 per cent of performers ought to help the bottom 10 per cent performers to improve the firm's competitive advantage.

Haier should be like the sea and make contributions to mankind 'sincerely and forever'. In so doing, it will exist forever for the good of all and Haier will be part of the whole society.[94]

The philosophy and values section also contains a series of gloriously off-the-wall metaphors and statements that would make a newly formed creative advertising agency proud (check the website for a discussion of the dietary and behavioural differences between 'shockfish' and 'sharks', for example).

These strangely (to Western ears) poetic sentiments do not intrude, however, into the Haier 'OEC' management control system. This is defined by Haier's HRM Director Wang Yingmin as follows:[95]

- O stands for Overall.
- E stands for Everyone, Everything, Everyday.
- C stands for Control and Clear.
- OEC means that every employee has to accomplish the target work every day. The OEC management-control system aims at overall control of everything that every employee finishes on his or her job every day, with a 1 per cent increase over what was done the previous day.

The OEC system is designed to ensure high levels of discipline in the company's operations, through a set of rewards and punishments, including detailed fines; for instance, failing to check or maintain equipment daily (5 yen), not cleaning up their work environment (2 yen), being late to work (2 yen) or 'gathering for fun or chat during work time' (2 yen). Rewards include a bonus for saving raw materials of 5 per cent of the value of the savings. This approach was developed as part of Zhang's turnaround strategy for Haier in the bad days of the 1980s and early 1990s, with the aim of getting the workforce to focus on creating quality products for customers and on the process of innovation, which is actively encouraged at the working level. The OEC approach has now become part of Haier's internationalisation strategy, to be applied in the company's many operations around the world. It is backed by a detailed target-setting and monitoring system, together with a series of incentive bonuses for the best performers.

Exporting the Haier culture

Remarkably, Haier built and opened a factory in South Carolina to serve the US market. Initially, its methods were strange to the new employees from the local labour market. However, according to a report in the *Chinese People's Daily*:

... both sides have harmonious exchanges, the difference of cultural background, instead of causing estrangement between the Chinese and American workers in their work, has increased their interest in mutual understanding.[96]

At first, the US workers were slow to volunteer for overtime to complete the day's target work, but (according to the report) all accept the importance of the Haier system and are even sometimes prepared to call into work on Independence Day to prepare for the next day's work. For all that one would expect an enthusiastic report from this particular source, Haier does seem to have established a reputation as a good employer in the area.

Haier has done spectacularly well during its brief life. It has established a strong international brand based upon high quality and value for money. It has internationalised on the basis of a strong culture, which sets out the company way of doing things but which also contains a commitment to local adaptation and content. Having become so big in such a short time, it

must now face new challenges as a global player. Longer-established Western brands are competing vigorously in Haier's rapidly developing home market as well as in the richer markets of Europe and North America. Many of today's superbrands started as local Japanese operations with successful export systems that managed to establish and consolidate their global position. Haier may manage to do the same, but it is not going to be easy. As CEO Zhang put it, with characteristic eloquence:[97]

Another challenge unique to China is we have started our brand development very late. So we have to catch up in a very short period of time. I will give you an analogy: It's like constructing a 10-story building. Our foreign competitors have already finished all the way up to the ninth floor. The Chinese market is their 10th floor. Once they have moved successfully into the China market, they will be finished with building this highrise. But in China, we have only built the first floor. There are still nine floors to be built.

Your tasks

1 What type of organisational culture appears to exist at Haier? To what extent can that be explained by the cultural influences (p. 724) discussed in this chapter? How can the ideas of national culture (discussed in Chapter 1) add to this explanation?

2 Using the components of Johnson *et al.*'s cultural web, Figure 19.1, critically review the cultural aspects of the Haier Corporation over the course of its development.

3 Given Haier's prominent position in global markets, what external influences on Haier's culture are likely to be important over the next few years? What challenges does this pose for Haier's management and what key management skills are likely to be needed in responding to these challenges?

Notes and references

1 French, W. L. and Bell, C. H. *Organization Development: Behavioral Science Interventions for Organization Improvement*, Sixth edition, Prentice-Hall (1999), pp. 25–6.

2 Ibid., p. 29.

3 Hamlin, B., Keep, J and Ash, K. *Organizational Change and Development*, Financial Times Prentice Hall (2001), p. 13.

4 Maier, D., Leban, B. and Orr-Alfeo, D. 'A values statement on OD: An interview with practitioner-scholar Dr Allan Church RODC', *Organization Development Journal*, vol. 19, no. 3, Fall 2001, pp. 69–74.

5 Patching, K. *Management and Organisation Development*, Macmillan Business (1999) p. 27.

6 Blake, R. R. and Mouton, J. S. *The Managerial Grid III*, Gulf Publishing Company (1985).

7 Naylor, J. *Management*, Second edition, Financial Times Prentice Hall 2004, pp. 645–6.

8 See, for example: Smircich, L. 'Concepts of Culture and Organizational Analysis', *Administrative Science Quarterly*, vol. 28, 1983, pp. 339–58.

9 See, for example: Brown, A. D. *Organisational Culture*, Second edition, Financial Times Management (1998).

10 Atkinson, P. E. 'Creating Cultural Change', *Management Services*, vol. 34, no. 7, 1990, pp. 6–10.

11 McLean, A. and Marshall, J. *Intervening in Cultures*, Working Paper, University of Bath, 1993.

12 See, for example: Oswick, C., Lowe, S. and Jones, P. 'Organisational Culture as Personality: Lessons from Psychology?', in Oswick, C. and Grant, D. (eds) *Organisation Development: Metaphorical Explorations*, Pitman Publishing (1996), pp. 106–20.

13 Cartwright, J. *Cultural Transformation*, Financial Times Prentice Hall (1999), p. 34.

14 Schein, E. H. *Organizational Culture and Leadership: A Dynamic View*, Third edition, Jossey-Bass (2004).

15 Harrison, R. 'Understanding Your Organization's Character', *Harvard Business Review*, vol. 50, May/June 1972, pp. 119–28.

16 Handy, C. B. *Understanding Organizations*, Fourth edition, Penguin (1993).

17 Deal, T. E. and Kennedy, A. A. *Corporate Cultures: The Rites and Rituals of Corporate Life*, Penguin (1982).

18 Deal, T. E. and Kennedy, A. A. *The New Corporate Cultures*, Perseus Books (2000).

19 See, for example: Handy, C. B. *Understanding Organizations*, Fourth edition, Penguin (1993); and McLean, A. and Marshall, J. *Cultures at Work*, Local Government Training Board, October 1988.

20 Kransdorff, A. 'History – A Powerful Management Tool', *Administrator*, October 1991, p. 23.

21 See for example: Beckett-Hughes, M. 'How to Integrate Two Cultures' , *People Management*, vol. 11, no. 5, 10 March 2005, pp. 50–1.

22 Roddick, A. *Body and Soul*, Ebury Press (1991) and Roddick, A. *Business As Usual*, Thorsons (2000).

23 Blackhurst, C. 'Up Front at Pearson', *Management Today*, May 1997, pp. 50–7.

24 Gerstner, L. V. Jr. *Who Says Elephants Can't Dance?: Inside IBM's historic turnabout*, HarperBusiness (2002).

25 Johnson, G., Scholes, K. and Whittington, R. *Exploring Corporate Strategy*, Seventh edition, Financial Times Prentice Hall (2005).

26 Wilson, F. *Organizational Behaviour and Work: A Critical Introduction*, Second edition, Oxford University Press (2004), p. 185.

27 'Effective Organisations: the People Factor', Advisory Booklet, ACAS, November 2001.

28 Naylor, J. *Management*, Second edition, Financial Times Prentice Hall (2004).

29 Charters, J. 'Are You a "Woodentop?"', *The British Journal of Administrative Science*, May/June 2000, p. 20.

30 Oliver, J. 'Losing Control', *Management Today*, June 1998, pp. 32–8.

31 Harrison, R. and Stokes, H. *Diagnosing Organizational Culture*, Pfeiffer & Company (1992), p. 1.

32 Reigle, R. F. 'Measuring organic and mechanistic cultures', *Engineering Management Journal*, vol. 13, no. 4, December 2001, pp. 3–8

33 Egan, G. 'The Shadow Side', *Management Today*, September 1993, p. 37.

34 Egan, G. 'Cultivate Your Culture', *Management Today*, April 1994, pp. 38–42.

35 Meudell, K. and Gadd, K. 'Culture and Climate in Short-Life Organizations: Sunny Spells or Thunder-storms?', *International Journal of Contemporary Hospitality Management*, vol. 6, no. 5, 1994, pp. 27–32.

36 Peters, T. J. and Waterman, R. H. *In Search of Excellence*, Harper and Row (1982), pp. 75–6.

37 Heller, R. *In Search of European Excellence*, HarperCollins Business (1997), p. 229.

38 Goldsmith, W. and Clutterbuck, D. *The Winning Streak Mark II*, Orion Business Books (1998).

39 Cummings, T. G. and Worley, C. G. *Organization Development and Change*, Eighth edition, Thompson South-Western (2005), p. 509.

40 Chatman, J. A. and Cha, S. E. 'Culture of Growth', Mastering Leadership, *Financial Times*, 22 November, 2002, pp. 2–3.

41 Stewart, R. *The Reality of Management*, Third edition, Butterworth Heinemann (1999), p. 123.

42 Naylor, J. *Management*, Second edition, Financial Times Prentice Hall (2004), p. 79.

43 'Inspired Leadership: Insights into people who inspire exceptional performance' DTI, August 2004.

44 Potter, C. C. 'What is Culture: And Can It Be Useful For Organisational Change Agents?', *Leadership and Organization Development Journal*, vol. 10, no. 3, 1989, pp. 17–24.

45 Siddall, P. 'Working With Cultural Differences', *Chartered Secretary*, February 1998, p. 30.

46 Schneider, S. C. and Barsoux, J. *Managing Across Cultures*, Second edition, Financial Times Prentice Hall (2003).

47 Cheng, T., Sculli, D. and Chan, F. 'Relationship dominance – Rethinking management theories from the perspective of methodological relationalism, *Journal of Managerial Psychology*, vol. 16, no. 2, 2001, pp. 97–105.

48 Francesco, A. M. and Gold, B. A. *International Organizational Behavior*, Second edition, Pearson Prentice Hall (2005).

49 Moran, E. T. and Volkwein, J. F. 'The Cultural Approach to the Formation of Organizational Climate', *Human Relations*, vol. 45, no. 1, 1992, p. 43.

50 Tagiuri, R. and Litwin, G. H. (eds) *Organizational Climate*, Graduate School of Business Administration, Harvard University (1968), p. 27.

51 Rentsch, J. R. 'Climate and Culture: Interaction and Qualitative Differences in Organizational Meanings', *Journal of Applied Psychology*, vol. 75, no. 6, 1990, p. 668.

52 Whitmore, Sir John 'Breaking Down the Barriers to Management Creativity', *The British Journal of Administrative Management*, September/October 2002, pp. 24–5.

53 Walton, R. E. 'From Control to Commitment in the Workplace', in Steers, R. M. and Porter, L. W. (eds), *Motivation and Work Behavior*, McGraw-Hill (1991), p. 448.

54 O'Reilly, C. 'Corporations, Culture and Commitment: Motivation and Social Control in Organizations', in Steers, R. M., Porter, L. W. and Bigley, G. A., *Motivation and Leadership at Work*, Sixth edition, McGraw-Hill (1996), p. 374.

55 See, for example: Thornhill, A., Saunders, N. K. and Stead, J. 'Downsizing, Delayering – But Where's the Commitment?', *Personnel Review*, vol. 26, no. 1/2, 1997, pp. 81–98.

56 Guirdham, M., *Interactive Behaviour at Work*, Third edition, Financial Times Prentice Hall (2002), p. 341.

57 Altman, W., Cooper, C. and Garner, A. 'New Deal Needed to Secure Commitment', *Professional Manager*, September 1999, p. 40.

58 Galunic, C. and Weeks, J. 'Survey – Mastering People Management', *Financial Times*, 12 November 2001.

59 Gratton, L. 'The Democratic Enterprise', Financial Times Prentice Hall (2004), p. 184.

60 Watson, T. J. *Organising and Managing Work*, Second edition, Financial Times Prentice Hall (2006).

61 For a discussion of change in relation to the complexities of organisational life, see: Senior, B. and Fleming, J. *Organizational Change*, Third edition, Financial Times Prentice Hall (2006).

62 Czerniawska, F. 'From Bottlenecks to Blackberries: How the relationships between organisations and individuals is changing' MCA/FT, September 2005.

63 See, for example: Henderson, H. (Squadron Leader) 'Flying High', *The British Journal of Administrative Management*, January/February 1998, pp. 10–13.

64 Fenlon, M. 'The Public Spirit', Mastering Leadership, *Financial Times*, 22 November 2002, p. 4.

65 Worrall, L. and Cooper, C. 'Managers just soldiering on', *Professional Manager*, vol. 15, no. 3, May 2006, pp. 30–2.

66 'Effective Organisations: the People Factor', Advisory Booklet, ACAS, November 2001.

67 Lewin, K. *Field Theory in Social Science*, Harper and Row (1951).

68 French, W. L., Kast, F. E. and Rosenzweig, J. E. *Understanding Human Behavior in Organizations*, Harper and Row (1985).

69 Stewart, R. *Managing Today and Tomorrow*, Macmillan (1991).

70 Crainer, S. *Key Management Ideas: Thinkers that Changed the Management World*, Third edition, Financial Times Prentice Hall (1998), pp. 144–5.

71 Gratton, L. *Living Strategy: Putting People at the Heart of Corporate Purpose*, Financial Times Prentice Hall (2000), p. 191.

72 Toffler, A. *Future Shock*, Pan Books (1970), p. 27.

73 Cunningham, I. 'Influencing people's attitudes to change', *Professional Manager*, vol. 14, no. 3, May 2005, p. 37.

74 Stewart, R. *The Reality of Management*, Third edition, Butterworth Heinemann (1999), p. 161.

75 Christensen, C. M. and Overdorf, M. 'Meeting the Challenge of Disruptive Change', *Harvard Business Review*, vol. 78, no. 2, March–April 2000, pp. 67–76.

76 See, for example: 'Mapping an Effective Change Programme', *Management Checklist 038*, Institute of Management, November 2001; and Covington, J. and Chase, M. L. 'Eight steps to sustainable change', *Industrial Management*, vol. 14, no. 6, November/December 2002, pp. 8–11.

77 Kotter, J. P. and Cohen, D. S. *The Heart of Change*, Harvard Business School Press (2002).

78 Reis, D. and Pena, L. 'Reengineering the Motivation to Work', *Management Decision*, vol. 39, no. 8, 2001, pp. 666–75.

79 McHugh, M., O'Brien, G. and Ramondt, J. 'Organizational Metamorphosis Led by Front Line Staff', *Employee Relations*, vol. 21, no. 6, 1999, pp. 556–76.

80 Atkinson, P. 'Managing resistance to change' *Management Services*, Spring 2005, p. 15.

81 Lucas, E. 'Riding the Change Roller-coaster', *Professional Manager*, September 2002, pp. 27–9.

82 See, for example: BBC, *Building Tomorrow's Company, Leadership – Supporting Notes*, BBC for Business; and The Centre for Tomorrow's Company and William Tate, 1999.

83 Champy, J. *Reengineering Management: The mandate for new leadership*, HarperBusiness (1996) p. xxi.

84 Hooper, A. and Potter, J. 'Take It from the Top', *People Management*, vol. 5, no. 16, August 1999, pp. 46–9.

85 Drucker, P. F. *Management Challenges for the 21st Century*, Butterworth Heinemann (1999), p. 73.

86 Lin, T.W. (2005) 'OEC Management-Control system helps China Haier group achieve competitive advantage', *Management Accounting Quarterly*, Spring 2005, retrieved from www.allbusiness.com.

87 Flannery, R (2001), China goes global, *Forbes* 6 August 2001.

88 'The 50 most powerful women in business', *Fortune*, 14 November 2005.

89 Other versions of the story suggest that Zhang had some help: those who made the faulty fridges were obliged to smash them in front of their colleagues.

90 *Chinese Peoples' Daily*, Opinion, 8 August 2001.

91 *Business Week*, 31 March 2003.

92 http://www.sanyo.co.jp/koho/hypertext4-eng/0201/0108-e.html.

93 http://www.haier.com/abouthaier/CorporateCulture/index.asp.

94 Lin, T.W. (2005) 'OEC Management-Control system helps China Haier group achieve competitive advantage', *Management Accounting Quarterly*, Spring 2005, retrieved from www.allbusiness.com.

95 Quoted in Lin, T.W. (2005) 'OEC Management-Control system helps China Haier group achieve competitive advantage', *Management Accounting Quarterly*, Spring 2005, retrieved from www.allbusiness.com.

96 *Chinese People's Daily*, 19 February 2002.

97 *Business Week*, 31 March 2003.

ORGANISATIONAL PERFORMANCE AND EFFECTIVENESS

Every work organisation is concerned with being effective. Upon the attainment of its aims and objectives rests the success and ultimate survival of the organisation. The quality of management is central to organisation development and improved performance. There is, however, a multiplicity of variables that impinge upon the successful organisation. The manager needs to understand the importance of improving the overall performance and effectiveness of the organisation.

Learning outcomes

After completing this chapter you should be able to:

- assess the nature of organisational effectiveness;
- examine the benefits of the learning organisation, TQM and business process re-engineering;
- explain the importance of effective management;
- evaluate the main features and requirements of the management development process;
- explore the importance and effectiveness of management education, training and development;
- provide criteria for assessing organisational performance and effectiveness;
- review the future of management and the nature of successful organisations.

> A symphony conductor is usually a good musician, but seldom a world-class performer. The most efficient university deans are often not the best professors. The ability to lead, to Engage Others and to Turn Them On, rarely coincides with being at the tip-top of Individual Performance Heaps ... In business, alas, it's all too common to promote the 'best' practitioner to the job of leading other practitioners.

Tom Peters – International management guru

Reimagine!, Dorling Kindersley, (2004), p. 321

Critical reflection

There are varying measures of organisational performance that can be viewed at different levels, over different time spans and in different ways by competing interest groups. What measures can you identify? Given the wide range of interrelated variables, do you think it possible to establish clear links between management processes and organisational effectiveness?

THE NATURE OF ORGANISATIONAL EFFECTIVENESS

The underlying theme of this book has been the need for organisational performance and effectiveness, and the role of management as an integrating activity. Organisational effectiveness, however, is affected by a multiplicity of variables. For example, *Handy* identifies over 60 factors that impinge on any one organisational situation and which illustrate the complicated nature of the study of organisational effectiveness (*see* Figure 20.1).[1]

Efficiency, effectiveness and innovation Organisations need to be **efficient** in doing the right things, in the optimum use of their resources and in the ratio of outputs to inputs. But organisations must also be **effective** in doing the right things and in their outputs related to some specific purpose, objective or task. **Performance** should be related to such factors as increasing profitability, improved service delivery or obtaining the best results in important areas of organisational activities. Organisations must also ensure that they meet satisfactorily, or exceed, the demands and requirements of customers, and are **adaptable** to specific requirements, changes in the external environment and the demands of the situation.[2]

Mann draws attention to **innovation** as the key to long-term success and what leaders of best practice organisations do that is different. They

- ensure they have a vision, mission and strategy that are known and understood;
- oversee the setting of demanding but realistic targets;
- set examples in generating an open, communicative management style;
- champion a culture conducive to learning and continuous improvement; and
- distribute leadership responsibilities with the necessary authority, training and resources.[3]

The Peters and Waterman study

In their 1982 study of 62 American companies with outstandingly successful performance, *Peters and Waterman* identify eight basic attributes of excellence which appear to account for success:[4]

- **a bias for action**; that is, being action-oriented and with a bias for getting things done;
- **close to the customer**; that is, listening and learning from the people they serve, and providing quality, service and reliability;
- **autonomy and entrepreneurship**; that is, innovation and risk-taking as an expected way of doing things;
- **productivity through people**; that is, treating members of staff as the source of quality and productivity;
- **hands-on, value driven**; that is, having well-defined basic philosophies and top management keeping in touch with the 'front lines';
- **stick to the knitting**; that is, in most cases, staying close to what you know and can do well;

Figure 20.1	Some factors affecting organisational effectivess

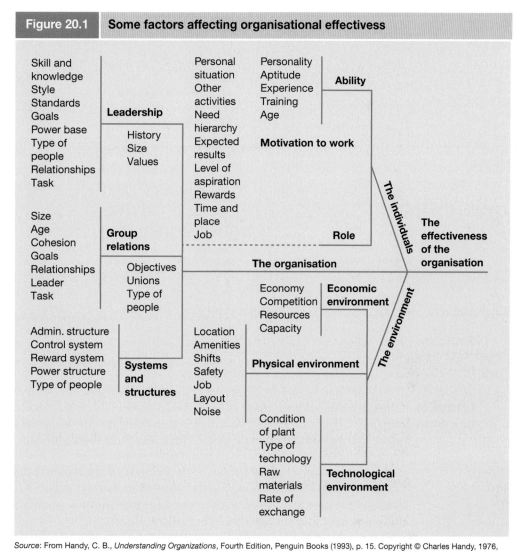

Source: From Handy, C. B., *Understanding Organizations*, Fourth Edition, Penguin Books (1993), p. 15. Copyright © Charles Handy, 1976, 1981, 1985, 1993, 1999. Reproduced by permission of Penguin Books Ltd.

- **simple form, lean staff**; that is, simple structural forms and systems, and few top-level staff;
- **simultaneous loose–tight properties**; that is, operational decentralisation but strong centralised control over the few, important core values.

The companies were marked, above all, by the 'intensity itself' which stemmed from their strongly held beliefs.

The McKinsey 7-S framework

From their research, *Peters and Waterman* report that:

any intelligent approach to organizing had to encompass, and treat as interdependent, at least seven variables: structure, strategy, people, management style, systems and procedures, guiding concepts and shared values (i.e. culture), and the present and hoped-for corporate strengths or skills. We defined this idea more precisely and elaborated what came to be known as the McKinsey 7-S Framework. With a bit of stretching, cutting and fitting, we made all seven variables start with the letter S and invented a logo to go with it.[5]

(*See* Figure 20.2.)

| Figure 20.2 | The McKinsey 7-S framework |

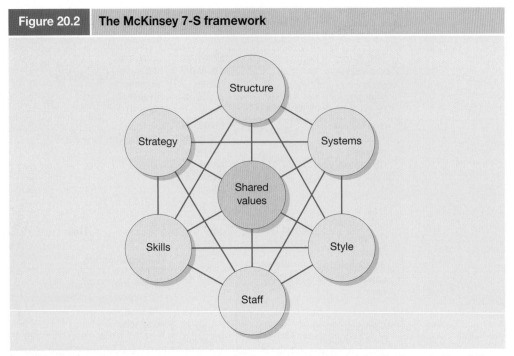

Source: From Peters, T. J. and Waterman, R. H., Jr. *In Search of Excellence: Lessons from America's Best Run Companies*, HarperCollins (1982). Copyright © 1982 by Thomas J. Peters and Robert H. Waterman Jr.

Lessons to be learned Although much has been made of the fact that many of the original 'excellent' organisations have since fallen from grace, it should be remembered that the formulas for their success did appear to have been appropriate in the 1980s. The study highlighted the importance of culture and organisational renewal. Important lessons can always be learned, and the 7-S model still provides a helpful framework as a basis for organisational analysis.

In a later (2003) publication, *Peters* acknowledges that a number of the featured companies ran into very rough sledding and some portion performed at levels short of 'excellence' but others have done reasonably well. Some of the exemplars of excellence have become routine elements of the business vocabulary and while some of the eight basic attributes now require revision all serve as salient points of reference for the 'New Mandate' of our disruptive age.[6]

THE DEMOCRATIC ENTERPRISE

According to *Gratton*, we have become accustomed to how contemporary organisations are structured, managed and run, but many more possibilities exist. Many people feel disconnected from their organisation and at times feel they have been treated unfairly and unjustly. Gratton refers to the 'democratic enterprise' that is organisations that are inspiring and meaningful, with the possibility for the individual and the organisation to create a win–win relationship and both benefiting but not at the expense of the other.

> We are witnessing the emergence of a new way of looking at people and their role in organizations ... More than at any other point in time, there is now a chance to create the Democratic Enterprise. Over the last decade it has become increasingly clear that through the forces of globalization, competition and more demanding customers, the structure of many companies has become flatter, less hierarchical, more fluid and virtual. The breakdown of hierarchies provides us with fertile ground on which to create a more democratic way of working.[7]

Figure 20.3	**The six tenets of the democratic enterprise**

1 The relationship between the organisation and the individual is adult-to-adult.

2 Individuals are seen primarily as investors actively building and deploying their human capital.

3 Indviduals are able to develop their natures and express their diverse qualities.

4 Individuals are able to participate in determining the conditions of their association.

5 The liberty of some individuals is not at the expense of others.

6 Individuals have accountbilities and obligations both to themselves and the organisation.

Source: Gratton, L., *The Democratic Enterprise*, Financial Times Prentice Hall (2004) p. 35. Reproduced with permission from Pearson Education Ltd.

In order to give clarity to a view of democracy that is viable within the scope of an economic enterprise, Gratton defines six tenets of democracy (Figure 20.3) and applies three litmus tests to each tenet:

Refresh your understanding

Activity 20A

www.pearsoned.co.uk/ mullins

- the capacity of the tenets to be mutually reinforcing and to create a consistent system of thinking about an organisation;
- to be economically viable and within the structure and goals of both commercial and not-for-profit organisations; and
- their practicality and capacity to be operationalised through a set of supporting practices and processes.

THE LEARNING ORGANISATION

A key factor in organisational effectiveness is the successful management of change and innovation, and corporate renewal. Increasing international competitiveness and the need for organisations to respond rapidly to constant change in their environment have drawn renewed attention in recent years to the concept of the **learning organisation** (discussed previously in Chapter 5 as part of the nature of learning and understanding individual differences). A central theme of the learning organisation is that learning is an essential ingredient of organisational performance and effectiveness. It is therefore often associated with organisation development. The original idea has been around for many years, however, and was popularised in the 1960s–1980s by major writers such as *Argyris*.[8]

Another significant contribution has been made by *Senge*, who maintains that organisations need to develop a culture of learning, and to instil 'people's commitment and capacity to learn at all levels in an organisation'. Senge suggests that there are five basic features of a learning organisation:

- **systems thinking** – the recognition that things are interconnected and organisations are complex systems;
- **personal mastery** – the competencies and skills associated with management including spiritual growth;
- **mental models** – the driving and fundamental values and principles of the organisation;
- **shared vision** – the importance of co-operation and a shared vision by team members;

Implementation If TQM is to be implemented successfully it must be seen as a total process involving all operations of the organisation and the active participation of top management. It demands a supportive organisational culture and a programme of management change. TQM places emphasis on the involvement of people as the key to improved quality. It involves changes to the traditional structure with greater emphasis on natural work groups, multi-discipline working and team-based management. Attention must be given to effective education and training, empowerment and the motivation to take ownership of quality, and systems of communications at all levels of the organisation.

A concept map setting out a summary of TQM, organisation and culture is set out in Figure 20.4.

The success of TQM

Almost inevitably, there are negative comments and criticisms about the concept of TQM and doubts about its value. *Thomas*, for example, suggests that the term total quality management is a bit of an oxymoron and that in all probability it would be advantageous if the 'M' were to be removed.

> *Total Quality cannot be 'managed' in the traditional, i.e. supervise and control, sense of the word because it involves factors such as commitment, purpose, vision and trust that are not amenable to mechanistic prescription. Quality can, and must be, managed. Total Quality, however, must be encouraged to evolve.*[19]

However, there are many success stories that give evidence of its benefits and effectiveness. *Heller* refers to the disillusion with, and backlash against, TQM that was bound to come. 'No technique has ever spread so far so fast – or so wide.' However, he makes the point:

> *The successes, and many other European cases, however, are emphatic evidence that Total Quality Management delivers – you can't argue with the results.*[20]

Drummond puts forward an interesting debate on comparing the philosophies and ideas of Deming with Taylor's Scientific Management, and questions whether Deming's ideas are as radical as they seem. Drummond suggests:

> *Clearly, 'total quality management' offers some new ideas. Whether these ideas have proved successful is unclear ... Moreover, much depends upon how success is measured. Different measures can suggest different conclusions. Another difficulty in assessing the effectiveness of 'total quality management programmes' is that organizations have implemented Deming's ideas selectively.*[21]

TQM and related reward practices *Allen and Kilmann* raise the question: why aren't TQM practices as effective as they could be? The rise of total quality management represents one of the biggest changes in the past two decades in the way companies are managed. However, while many studies have found that in general TQM has had positive effects on company performance, reports of failure are surprisingly common in the press. Allen and Kilmann suggest that the alignment of a company's system of rewards is a critical ingredient in successful organisational change and they investigate the relationship between reward practices and TQM. From a survey of managers, non-managerial and professional/technical staff in a wide variety of organisations they conclude that the commonly held wisdom of supporting TQM with only non-monetary rewards – such as certificates, letters of appreciation, merchandise or celebration events – is not enough. If managers want better performance from TQM they must implement supportive monetary reward practices. Firms with such practices in place report stronger organisational performance.[22]

Figure 20.4 Concept map of Total Quality Management organisation and culture

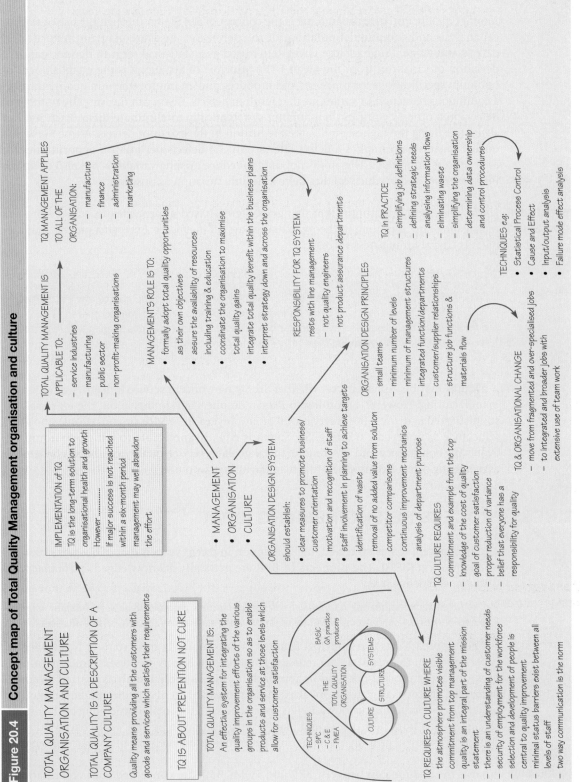

Source: Training Learning Consultancy Ltd, Bristol, England. Reproduced with permission.

Six Sigma

Another quality initiative programme is the concept of **Six Sigma** through the use of statistical analysis and computer simulation for the definition, measurement and reduction of defects and waste. (Sigma is the Greek letter used as a statistical term to denote standard deviation or variations from the mean.) The principle of Six Sigma is the establishment of optimum specifications for processes and products, and an improvement in quality through a continuous reduction of variations that result in defects. If you can measure the number of defects in a process you can then attempt systematically to eliminate them. Each level of sigma (six being the highest) indicates a reduction in the extent of defects. A true Six Sigma quality organisation implies a defect rate of only 3.4 defects per million opportunities for each process or product. The aim is not only to reduce existing variations but also to design new processes and products so that there is as little variation as possible.

Importance of Six Sigma *Hayler and Nichols* maintain that using Six Sigma-based approaches to achieve process management, so appealing in theory, actually pays off in *practice*. Six Sigma process management is crucial for business success.

> *Managing processes for optimal performance has always been important. Today's global business environment is characterised by increasingly extended supply chains across multiple organisational functions, third-party partners, and suppliers, in many cases operating across different cultures, time zones and geographies. Thus it is even more challenging and important for leaders to optimally manage their organisational processes.*[23]

Doubts may be expressed over whether Six Sigma works in service industries as well as in manufacturing. However, according to *Patton*, despite such doubts about the emphasis on sophisticated statistics, the reservations of employees in service organisations, and their reluctance to undertake training, Six Sigma is equally applicable to either environment. 'Achieving consistency and meeting financial goals in service quality can be as challenging as delivering defect free products to a manufacturing customer.'[24]

BUSINESS PROCESS RE-ENGINEERING (BPR)

Another concept to have received much attention in recent years is that of **business process re-engineering (BPR)**. The pioneers of BPR are generally acknowledged as *Hammer and Champy*, who define it as:

> *The fundamental rethinking and radical redesign of business processes to achieve dramatic improvements in critical, contemporary measures of performance, such as cost, quality, service and speed.*[25]

Their approach has two principal features: (i) a completely fresh start, or blank sheet of paper approach, to organisational redesign ignoring past history or present structure or practices, and (ii) a process-orientation approach to organisational analysis centred around a horizontal review of all activities involved in the process, or set of activities, in the delivery of a product or service to the customer. BPR is concerned with the total restructuring of the organisation. It starts from how one would like the organisation to be and works backward in an effort to achieve real gains in organisational performance, and delivery of products or services.

Relationship with TQM What is the relationship between BPR and TQM? Both are concerned with organisational processes that lead to customer satisfaction. However, while TQM tends to seek continuous incremental improvement within a specific framework, BPR seeks major advances in performance from a **horizontal**, cross-functional anatomy of performance perspective. It

involves a challenge to traditional structure, relationships, boundaries or barriers. TQM requires a supportive environment and relies on teamwork, participation and commitment. BPR takes a more strategic approach and needs to be driven, at least initially, by top management. Some commentators appear to suggest that TQM has been taken over by BPR, although others argue that it can be seen as complementary to and/or a forerunner for BPR.

From a postal survey of Northern Ireland's top 100 companies, *Hill and Collins* found that both TQM and BPR are quite widely perceived as being significant elements of organisational change strategies for the foreseeable future. The need for radical change seems to be well understood and TQM appears to have become more of a competitive necessity. The findings also found more widespread reported use and understanding of BPR than anticipated. Their survey revealed that factors such as cultural change and performance measurement are important elements of both TQM and BPR.

> *It also seems that when used in an integrated manner, BPR and TQM can produce a profile of organisational change characterised by periods of continuous improvement interrupted by episodes of radical innovation which serve to steepen the overall improvement/learning curve.*[26]

Decline of re-engineering In a discussion on outdated motivational patterns utilised to maintain role performance in organisations, *Reis and Pena* link this with what they maintain is a failure in re-engineering. Although the originators of re-engineering insisted it was about rethinking work, not eliminating jobs, managers equated re-engineering with downsizing. Despite early successes, with each passing year fewer and fewer projects appeared to be producing the desired results and doubts have surfaced about the effectiveness of re-engineering. Reis and Pena suggest that theories of motivation might offer an important observation and point to the decline in re-engineering based on its lack of concern for people and its takeover by managers wishing to downsize. The ultimate success of re-engineering, or other approaches such as TQM, depends on the people who do the work. The difficult and often neglected part of such initiatives is leading and managing behavioural change with those who interface with the new technology or new initiatives. Attention must be given to removing barriers to motivation and to a greater recognition of the human element including the resistance to, and fear of, change.[27]

However, in a subsequent publication, *Hammer* restates that BPR is just as valid today but acknowledges that in the light of experience re-engineering needs to be complemented with a range of other changes, a focus on a corporate objectives and building collaborative partnership with suppliers.[28]

Managing the white space

Based on the concept of business process re-engineering, *Rummler and Brache* propose a framework for the improvement of organisational performance. They contrast the traditional, functional view of the organisation as represented by the organisational chart with a more descriptive and useful systems approach, and put forward a methodology based on three levels of performance and the management of the white spaces between the boxes on the organisation chart.[29]

- **The organisational level** – the basic 'skeleton' of the major functions which comprise the organisation and its relationship with its market. Variables affecting performance at this level include strategies, corporate goals and measures, structure and deployment of resources.
- **The process level** – looking beyond the functional boundaries which make up the organisation chart, and examining the workflow and how work actually gets done. To manage performance variables at this level it is necessary to ensure processes are installed which satisfy customer needs.
- **The job/performer level** – involving performance variables such as recruitment, promotion, job responsibilities and standards, feedback, rewards and training. Rummler and

Brache suggest that overall performance of the organisation and how well it meets the expectations of its customers are the result of goals, structures and management at all three levels.

The three levels represent an anatomy of performance and Rummler and Brache draw attention to the importance of measuring performance and designing a performance management system. If performance is not being measured, it is not being managed.

Refresh your understanding

Activity 20B
www.pearsoned.co.uk/
mullins

Critical reflection

'Effective organisational performance is about a shared vision, inspired leadership and the quality of its managers. Concepts such as total quality management or techniques such as business process re-engineering have little real practical value to the business organisation.' How would you challenge this statement? How much attention do you think should be given to such concepts and techniques?

THE IMPORTANCE OF EFFECTIVE MANAGEMENT

Previous chapters of this book have emphasised the importance of management as an integrating activity that permeates every facet of the operations of the organisation. Management is the cornerstone of organisational effectiveness and the contribution to economic and social needs of society. This applies as much to public sector and service organisations as to any other industry. The quality of management is one of the most important factors in the success of any organisation. For example, a major global study of managers and workers undertaken by *Proudfoot Consulting* reports that inadequate management is a major cause of lost productivity, and among key factors noted in the report were absence of people skills and inadequate management training.[30]

Managers need a balance of technical, social and conceptual knowledge and skills, acquired through a blend of education and experience. There is, therefore, a continual need for managerial development. The organisation must ensure the development of both present and future managers. *Stern* draws attention to the importance of management education, training and development as a matter of vital strategic importance.

> *Competition and the pace of change in business require continuous improvement – and that means continuous learning ... Today, learning and development opportunities rank high among the concerns of talented employees. Support for management development, in whatever form, is perhaps the strongest weapon that a business can use in its struggle to retain the best employees.*[31]

The culture of the organisation is also important in determining the behaviour of managers and how well the organisation works. *Brodbeck* refers to a blame culture that exists in many organisations and where the brickbats fly more often than the bouquets. Such organisations are a very unhealthy environment in which to work. For example, an organisation may see low reports of errors as a healthy sign but in reality this is because individuals are worried about reporting mistakes. Improving the safety culture and a climate of proactive error management will encourage individuals to see the benefits when errors are pinpointed.[32]

Structure and people In analysing effective organisations, *Dunderdale* argues that an organisation can be separated into two parts or structures – one a definitive structure present in every company, the other caused by human intervention. Each part can then be examined. Essentially the effectiveness of an organisation depends on how accurately human design matches the structure of organised behaviour.[33] *ACAS* draws attention to the role of people as a key factor for improved organisational performance. The 'control' approach to people management is still

much in evidence but in a faster changing and more competitive environment organisations using such an approach will be at a disadvantage competing against more flexible organisations designed to develop people and generate commitment and not merely obedience.[34] *Allen and Helms* suggest that higher levels of perceived organisational performance may be closely related to strategy and reward systems. 'The use of reward practices which logically complement a specific organisational strategy should serve to motivate employees to help the organization perform at a higher level.'[35]

Are managers really necessary?

A major survey undertaken by the Management Consultancies Association and *Management Today* draws attention to the changing relationship between organisations and individuals. More and more work is outsourced, teams are dispersed across multiple locations, an increasing number of people work away from the organisations and greater empowerment has shifting responsibility to individuals. This shift of responsibility from the organisation to the individual begs the question: Are managers really necessary and what is the role of management? 'Ironically, a time when people appear to require less management is also a time when they want it more than ever. Half of all respondents to the MCA/MT survey felt their bosses spent insufficient time actually managing their staff, a figure that was highest among employees of large organisations and in the manufacturing, financial services and the public sector.'[36]

According to *Stephens*, if managers are to survive, they need to reinvent themselves.

Managers get caught up in a lot of organisational rubbish, but the underlying need for good managers is even more critical than before. Managers should be thinking about the five most important things they need to do in order to help the organisation achieve its overall strategy and how to measure those things. They should then be cascading this way of thinking throughout their team, helping people understand how they contribute to the overall objectives, especially if they're part of a complex, matrix structure, or if they're working remotely or on projects rather than on-going work. Managers will have to motivate people because employees will have more choice about where they work, so talent management needs to be embedded.[37]

THE MEANING AND NATURE OF MANAGEMENT DEVELOPMENT

There is no single, agreed definition of **management development**. A common view is that whereas training is concerned with the achievement of effective performance in the manager's present job, development is concerned with preparing the manager for expected changes in the job, or for an anticipated future job or role. Nevertheless, management development is likely to include at least an element of training.

However, according to *Lilley*, 'in truth, Management Development is a very inexact science'. The best method of developing effective managers continues to be a subject for debate and there are a number of competing models of those who seek to improve management performance.

- **There is nothing you can do** – management is an inherited talent driven by characteristic personality traits and charisma.
- **It's all down to experience and the needs of the moment** – better performance is achieved through pooling of minds and sharing experiences that focus on common issues and problems.
- **Become a better manager by taking a course** – formal structured programmes on knowledge and analysis such as MBAs, and business seminars.
- **Performance is the only criterion, and competence is of the essence** – the definition of generic performance standards such as NVQs, measured and assessed through evidence and observation.

opment is effective human resource planning coupled with procedures for recruitment and selection. Programmes of management development should be designed in accordance with the culture and specific requirements of the particular organisation, and the demands of particular managerial jobs. There should be a clear management development policy together with regular reviews of individual performance and a programme of career progression. The execution of management development activities should be part of a continuous, cumulative process and take place within the framework of a clear management development policy.

An essential feature of management development is performance review, which was discussed in Chapter 13. The systematic review of work performance provides an opportunity to highlight positive contributions from the application of acquired knowledge, skills, qualifications and experience. An effective system of performance review will help identify individual strengths and weaknesses, potential for promotion, and training and development needs. If performance appraisal is to be effective, there must be clearly stated objectives that help managers to achieve goals important to them, and allow them to take control of their own development and progression. Whatever the nature of a management development programme, one of the most important requirements of any learning process is the need for effective feedback. Without feedback there can be no learning. Feedback should be objective, specific and timely and give a clear indication of how other people perceive behaviour and performance. Wherever possible there should be supporting evidence and actual examples.

Succession planning and career progression

Management succession planning aims to ensure that a sufficient supply of appropriately qualified and capable men and women is available to meet the future needs of the organisation. Such people should be available readily to fill managerial or supervisory vacancies caused through retirement, death, resignation, promotion or transfer of staff, or through the establishment of new positions. Succession planning should be related to the overall corporate strategy. Despite the influence of de-layering, changes to the traditional hierarchical structures and fewer opportunities of jobs for life, there is still an important need for effective succession planning in order to develop internal talent and help maintain loyalty and commitment to the organisation.

Allied to management development and succession planning should be a programme of planned career progression. This should provide potential managers with:

● training and experience to equip them to assume a level of responsibility compatible with their ability; and
● practical guidance, encouragement and support so that they may realise their potential, satisfy their career ambition and wish to remain with the organisation.

Career progression should involve individual appraisal and counselling. However, care should be taken to avoid giving staff too long or over-ambitious career expectations. If these expectations cannot be fulfilled, staff may become disillusioned and frustrated.

Relevance today? Given the nature of today's business climate, *Altman* questions whether there is a strong case for management succession planning. For example, old-fashioned loyalty is becoming rarer, suitable candidates may not wish to stay the course, directors and senior managers have little time to coach potential successors, and the tenure of chief executives is getting shorter. However, while some organisations seem to prefer to shop around when top jobs become vacant, other successful organisations such as BP and Tesco make a virtue of growing their own managerial talent.[47] Nevertheless, now that people are less likely to stay with the same company for long periods of time there does appear to be some doubt about whether succession planning is really necessary.

But according to *Stern*, succession planning is not a dark art but a basic business necessity and there is no question that you must nurture and retain your own talent. It is important, however, not to upset or demotivate those members of staff not highlighted as high flyers. It is necessary to be straight with everybody, to be honest and objective, and to treat them with respect.[48]

Management development in Europe

A survey of European managers carried out by the European Commission, Leonardo da Vinci CVTS programme and the DTI has found that investment in management training and development can and does improve organisational performance. The survey canvassed the views of 1400 HR managers in 700 private sector organisations across seven European countries. The findings indicate that it is not enough just to have 'best practices'. Managers' development can make a substantial impact on firm performance but it needs to be linked to the business strategy. It is also important that line managers perceive their top team seeing this as a genuine and sustained commitment, and to be delivering on the promise of management development. Across Europe, an average of nine days per manager is given to training but with wide variations in the amount spent per head. Cost and practical difficulties of covering for staff were generally more a reason for constraints in development than lack of support from the top team or lack of enthusiasm from managers themselves.[49] A summary of findings across the seven European countries is given in Table 20.1.

Evidence for management development

The Chartered Institute of Management undertook a major study of management and leadership development (MLD) covering all activities that contribute towards improving the effectiveness and performance of managers and leaders. The study involved 1000 respondents of HR and line managers in 500 organisations. The key message from the study is that investing in MLD of employees really does pay dividends. Strategically driven MLD, implemented over time, makes a significant difference.

- Sustained management and leadership development can improve organisational performance.
- The need for MLD to be driven strategically if competitive advantages are to be realised through improved people management.
- Growing demand for development activities that improve people skills and change-management capabilities.
- That the most effective forms of development are those connected directly to managers' experiences in the workplace. The belief that 'leaders are born and not made' has finally been eclipsed by the importance of job experience.

The demand for people skills The study found that the skills most organisations are most concerned with are those associated with people management, leadership, customer care and motivation/teamwork. A clear trend emerges also in skills that employers will be developing for the future: the ability to manage change and manage risk. The ability to facilitate organisational learning and to lead through ethical/value-based behaviour are identified as priority areas. It appears that the most effective organisational learning takes place where there is a culture of managers learning from their colleagues and others in the workplace through the interpersonal dimension.[50]

Table 20.1	Developing Managers: Summary of country findings

Country	Type	Key features	Strong points	Challenges
United Kingdom (UK)	Generalist and reliant on externally accredited vocational training or education	Comparatively weak career structures. Training objectives clarified by use of competences and appraisals	Significant progress since mid-1980s in amount of development undertaken	Lack of continuity in national policy frameworks. Employer approach to development often short-term, tokenistic and non-strategic
France (Fr)	Decisive vocational educational institutions Formal internal career structures	Law requires firms to spend at least 1.2 per cent of wage bill on training	High standard of Grands Ecole education with origins and close proximity to business world	Training levy no guarantee of strategic approach to development
Germany (Ger)	In-house	High proportion of CEOs hold PhDs Emphasis on formal rather than informal structures for development	Strong emphasis on technical education and individual loyalty to their employer	Need to encourage greater flexibility and diversity of managerial skills
Spain (Sp)	Limited to large corporations	Large number of SMEs and family owned businesses has restricted growth of professional managerial class	Has become systematised in successful large corporations	Extending management development to the broader SME community
Denmark (Den)	Combines general, vocational and 'on-the-job' training	Experimental learning Emphasis on informal management development	Open to new practices Public training institutions with high status Combines egaliterianism with entrepreneuralism	Weak formal or systematic attempts to evaluate the impact of management development on performance
Norway (Nor)	Emphasis on company and vocational training	Eglitarian and communitarian ethos Limited individual rewards for performance	Widespread expectation by managers that they will receive training and development and positive view of its outcomes	Combining its egalitarianism with the need to encourage greater individual entrepreneurship, innovation and risk management
Romania (Rom)	External	Content heavily influenced by external organisations and agencies	Many managers benefiting from EU sponsored up-to-date know-how through management development	Complementing external training with indigenous training to build necessary competencies

Source: Mabey, C. and Ramirez, M., 'Developing managers: a European perspective', Chartered Management Institute report, May 2004, p. 6. Reproduced with permission from Chartered Management Institute.

CONTINUING PROFESSIONAL DEVELOPMENT (CPD)

Management development should be seen as a continuous process, including the preparation for and responsibilities of a new job, and the manager's subsequent career progression. In recent years, greater recognition has been given to the significance of life-long learning and to **continuing professional development** (CPD). A number of professional bodies have developed a competence-based CPD scheme for their members. For example, with the Chartered Management Institute CPD is linked to gaining the status of 'Chartered Manager'.

> CPD stands for Continuing Professional Development, although the 'P' could equally be for 'Personal' or 'Performance', depending on how you interpret and apply your learning and development. Continuing Professional Development is about planned self-development which embraces both personal and professional aims, and, in many cases, intended to impact on performance.[51]

Life-long learning should, however, be the concern of all employees in the organisation and (despite the title) it is arguable that the concept of CPD should not be seen as applying only to professionals or managers as opposed to all employees. Clearly, however, CPD does have particular significance for management development.

Self-development An important part of the process of improving the performance of managers is self-development. Part of being an effective manager is the responsibility to further one's own development. A significant factor affecting the success of self-development is the extent to which individual managers take advantage of development opportunities around them. This demands that the manager must be able to identify clearly real development needs and goals, to take responsibility for actions to reach these goals and recognise opportunities for learning. Self-development has to be self-initiated. But if this is to be a realistic aim it requires an organisational climate that will encourage managers to develop themselves and the active support of top management. Managers need sufficient authority and flexibility to take advantage of situations which are likely to extend their knowledge and skills. Superiors should be prepared to delegate new and challenging projects including problem-solving assignments.

Self-development is now widely accepted as an integral part of management development. *Farren* points out that complexity will continue to increase at every level of society in the 21st century and managers will need the depth and breadth that comes from mastery of a profession or trade. As the rate of change accelerates, business success will require the eye and ear of a master. Mastery requires time and practice but builds confidence as well as competence.

> People who are great at their profession or trade are always learning, questioning, tinkering, and taking the practice to a new level. These people don't have to worry about whether they are employable. They are desperately needed by organizations and industries to address the ever-changing needs they are drawn to serve. They become natural managers and coaches for those around them, both formally and informally.[52]

Refresh your understanding

Activity 20C
www.pearsoned.co.uk/
mullins

Critical reflection

Many top executives make the point that they never had any formal management education or training. Why do you think this is so? Yet, many organisations waste a fortune paying for the development of staff and then prevent them from using their new ideas in practice. How would you explain this?

LEADERSHIP AND MANAGEMENT MODEL

Following demand from employers and government, Investors in People UK created a supplementary Model to the Investors in People Standard dedicated to giving guidance on Leadership and Management. The new Leadership and Management Model was launched in February 2003 and is a blueprint for ensuring that UK organisations have the effective role model leadership that they need, now and in the future.[53]

The **Leadership and Management Model** is a development framework for ensuring that organisations create, manage and invest in effective leadership – now and in the long term. It helps companies to ensure that top managers are not only committed to effective leadership and management but that they know what it looks like, take the right steps to practise it themselves and, above all, use it to improve the organisation's performance. The Model works on four principles of commitment, planning, action and evaluation, and stands separately from the Investors in People Standard and Profile (discussed in Chapter 13). Organisations can be assessed and recognised against it independently. For organisations looking at leadership and management as part of a holistic approach to business improvement, the Investors in People Profile can be used.

Four key principles

The Leadership and Management Model is a cyclical process based on four key principles:

1 Top managers are committed to making sure that the organisation is successful through effective leadership and management.
2 The organisation knows what effective leadership and management is and how it can be achieved.
3 The organisation takes action to improve leadership and management.
4 The approach to effective leadership and management helps the organisation to succeed.

The four key principles are broken down into nine indicators against which the organisation has to produce evidence for assessment (*see* Figure 20.5). The Leadership and Management Model is based on the real-life good practices of successful organisations.

THE EFQM EXCELLENCE MODEL

Total quality is the goal for many organisations, but it has been difficult until relatively recently to find a universally acceptable definition of what this actually means. The European Foundation for Quality Management (EFQM) **Excellence Model** (also known in the UK as the Business Excellence Model) builds on the experience of previous models and was adopted by the British Quality Foundation as the basis for both self-assessment and for the UK Quality Award for Business Excellence.

The model is the most widely used organisational framework in Europe where it has become the basis for the majority of national and regional Quality Awards. The 'Model' is based on the concept that an organisation will achieve better results by involving all the people in the organisation in the continuous improvement of their processes; it provides a focus for integrating all contributors to the organisation's performance. It is a practical tool that facilitates measurement of where an organisation is on the path to excellence, helping it to understand where there are gaps and stimulating solutions. The 'Model' is designed to be non-prescriptive but is there to provide guidelines. Organisations are able to benchmark themselves against others both within and outside their sectors (*see* Figure 20.6). The basic assumption is that excellent results in terms of Performance, Customers, People and Society (the Results) are achieved through Leadership driving Policy and Strategy, People,

Figure 20.5	Leadership and Management Model

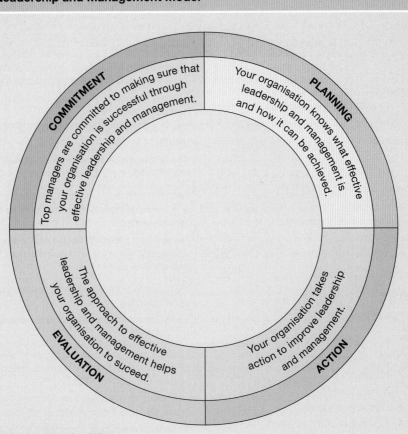

It is based on four basic principles

- The Leadership and Management Model is based on the real-life good practices of successful organisations.

- These practices are grouped in the same tried and tested four principles framework of the Investors in People Standard, which thousands of organisations have used to improve their performance through their people.

- So the same four principles of commitment, planning, action and evaluation apply here too, each with their indicators and evidence requirements.

The Leadership and Management Model

Principle	Indicators	Evidence
COMMITMENT Top managers are commited to making sure that your organisation is sucessful through effective leadership and management.	1 Top managers direct your organisation's approach to effective leadership and management.	Top managers can describe how effective leadership and management will contribute to achieving your organisation's aims and objectives. Top managers are actively involved in defining the knowledge, skills and behaviour that leaders and managers require. Top managers are actively involved in defining your organisation's approach to effective leadership and management.
	2 Top managers are role models for leadership and management development.	Top managers learn and develop. Leaders and managers can describe how top managers inspire them to learn and develop.

Figure 20.5 Continued

Principle	Indicators	Evidence
PLANNING Your organisation knows what effective leadership and management is and how it can be achieved.	3 Leadership and management requirements are defined and understood.	The requirements reflect your organisation's aims and objectives, and the culture you want to create. The requirements reflect relevant external standards and good practice. The requirements reflect relevant social-responsibility issues. The requirements are defined at all levels and are understood.
	4 Leadership and management development is planned.	Learning and development is planned to help current and potential leaders and managers to meet the requirements. Current and potential leaders and managers can describe the learning and development opportunities that are available to them.
ACTION Your organisation takes action to improve leadership and management.	5 Leader and manager section is effective.	Current and potential leaders and managers are selected in line with the requirements. The selection of current and potential leaders and managers is fair.
	6 Effective leadership and management is reviewed and encouraged.	Leaders and managers are regularly reviewed and recieve constructive feedback on their performance against the requirements. Leaders and managers can describe how effective leadership and management is recognised. A range of rewards is considered to recognise effective leadership and management.
	7 Leadership and managers continuously learn and develop.	Current and potential leaders and managers confirm that access to learning and development activities is fair. Current and potential leaders and managers can describe the learning and development activities they are currently taking part in, including work-based activities, to help them meet the requirements. Current and potential leaders and managers confirm that learning and development activities meet the needs of different individuals and groups.
EVALUATION The approach to effective leadership and management helps your organisation to succeed.	8 The approach to effective leadership and management improves your organisation's performance.	The approach helps to meet the leadership and management requirements. The approach helps your organisation to achieve its aim, objectives and desired culture. Top managers understand the costs and benefits of the approach.
	9 The approach to effective leadership and management is improved.	Relevant and timely improvements are made to the approach.

Source: From *The Leadership and Management Model*, Investors in People UK (2006), pp. 5–7. Copyright © 2006. Reproduced with permission from Investors in People UK (www.investorsinpeople.co.uk)

Partnership and Resources, and Processes (The Enablers). Innovation and Learning are key to improving enablers that in turn improve results.

> *The [Excellence] Model is based on the principle that the fundamentals of running a successful organisation in the public, private or voluntary sector are the same – no matter what type, or size, of organisation they are applied to. The Model distils these principles into a framework of assessment and analytical criteria which can be applied to a whole organisation, a department, division, or operational unit.*
>
> Joe Goasdoué, Chief Executive of the British Quality Foundation[54]

Nine criteria of the Model

Each of the nine criteria featured in the 'Model' are described by the British Quality Foundation as follows.

1 **Leadership**. How leaders develop and facilitate the achievement of the mission and vision, develop values for long-term success and implement these via appropriate actions and behaviours, and are personally involved in ensuring that the organisation's management system is developed and implemented.

2 **People**. How the organisation manages, develops and releases the knowledge and full potential of its people at an individual, team-based and organisation-wide level, and plans these activities in order to support its policy and strategy and the effective operation of its processes.

3 **Policy and strategy**. How the organisation implements its mission and vision via a clear stakeholder-focused strategy, supported by relevant policies, plans, objectives, targets and processes.

4 **Partnerships and resources**. How the organisation plans and manages its external partnerships and internal resources in order to support its policy and strategy and the effective operation of its processes.

Figure 20.6	EFQM Excellence Model

Source: EFQM. Copyright © 1999 EFQM. The Model is a registered trademark of the EFQM. Reproduced with permission.

5 **Processes**. How the organisation designs, manages and improves its processes in order to support its policy and strategy and fully satisfy, and generate increasing value for, its customers and other stakeholders.

6 **People results**. What the organisation is achieving in relation to its people.

7 **Customer results**. What the organisation is achieving in relation to its external customers.

8 **Society results**. What the organisation is achieving in relation to local, national and international society as appropriate.

9 **Key performance results**. What the organisation is achieving in relation to its planned performance.

Use of the Excellence Model The British Quality Foundation recommends the following methodology for using the EFQM Excellence Model:

- develop commitment to self-assessment;
- plan self-assessment;
- establish teams to perform self-assessment and educate;
- communicate the self-assessment plans;
- conduct self-assessment;
- establish action plan; and
- implement action plan.

Widely used, comprehensive, developmental, addressing the needs of all stakeholders the EFQM Excellence Model is already playing an important role in improving competitiveness, levels of service and shareholder value across Europe. Providing a common language with significant benchmarking opportunities and role model exmaples, it is set to be the defining model of the 21st century.

Mel Farrar, Associate Director, Public Sector Development Excellence North West [55]

ASSESSING ORGANISATIONAL PERFORMANCE

Based on experience in a broad range of organisations, *Steele* suggests nine questions to help managers assess the performance of their companies. These questions have been submitted to approximately 125 different groups of managers from all industries – manufacturing, banking, retail and general commerce. Although the questions are not exhaustive and not intended to be a panacea, there has been full agreement that they are a reasonable list of questions for assessing organisational effectiveness.

1 What is the attitude to change?

2 What is the degree of trust in the management's view of the workforce, is there a them and us mentality?

3 Really a manifestation of Question 2 – how much management information, especially financial, is communicated?

4 How visible and accessible is management, especially top management?

5 What is the atmosphere like in the organisation? Focusing on more specific areas to help identify the quality of an organisation's atmosphere:
 (a) What do people believe about the organisation?
 (b) How much control exists?
 (c) Is there a fear of failure?
 (d) Do people feel free to talk back?
 (e) Is there a fun atmosphere in the organisation?

6 How frequently are people rewarded and recognised?

7 What is the posture and prowess of the first point of customer contact?

8 Is customer service actively measured and the results communicated widely?

9 Do people have an appropriate purpose?[56]

Benchmarking

An increasingly popular management technique is that of 'benchmarking'. The premise behind benchmarking is simple. 'If you want to improve a particular aspect of your organization or service it provides, find someone else who is good at the activity and use them as a benchmark to raise your own standards.'[57] This can vary from an informal or casual look at how other companies are performing, gathering information about other company's best practices, to an in-depth investigation of a company's performance compared with that of its major competitors. With large organisations benchmarking may also be undertaken internally with a comparison between different divisions, units or locations. This is a common practice in universities, for example, with comparisons between different faculties or schools. From a review of benchmarking techniques, *Barnes* concludes that although external benchmarking has a role to play in raising business performance it should be used with care, and only after considering the circumstances and contingencies in the organisation involved.[58]

According to *Modena*, benchmarking is one of the key tools for learning and enables forward-looking organisations to measure their performance against the best in the business. It should cover a balanced portfolio of practices and capabilities to bring about both short- and long-term success.[59] *Bishop* suggests that although benchmarking remains a vital first step in evaluating and measuring performance, its real value comes when it is applied in a consistent and ongoing way, and that it is not only of value for large corporations. The Small Business Service, an agency of the DTI, has developed a Benchmarking Index specifically for small to medium-sized enterprises for which it can bring real, tangible benefits and overall business improvement.[60]

Management standards, the leadership and management model and the excellence model (discussed above) can all be used by organisations as a means of benchmarking.

Gap analysis

Gap analysis involves an investigation of the gap between the vision, objectives and goals of the organisation and actual levels of performance, and establishing the actions necessary to bring activities in line with that which is planned. *Ittner and Larcker* refer to the large quantity of non-financial measures that most companies track, and the extent to which such measures are aligned with the company's strategies and value drivers. One method for assessing this alignment is 'gap analysis' which requires managers to rank performance on at least two dimensions: their importance to strategic objectives and the importance currently placed upon them.[61]

Gratton refers to the importance of a collective understanding and vision of what the organisation is capable of achieving, expressed as short-term goals and as a long-term vision; and to creating superior performance through inspired and committed people.

> The short-term business goals and long-term vision create a broad strategic agenda and an understanding of where the organization should be heading. But to make these goals a reality there must be a more clearly defined awareness of what has to be achieved. The pathway of action comes from the second element, the gap analysis, which creates a deep understanding of the gap between current capability and the desired state. The extent of this gap is the basis for a shared understanding of what needs to be achieved, and potentially the energy for the journey.[62] (*See* Figure 20.7.)

Performance indicators in the public sector

In earlier chapters we have referred to the nature of management in public sector organisations, and to the increasing scale of privatisation and strategic developments. This has led to growing attention to public accountability for their operations and to the measurement of their performance and standards of service delivery, including a wide range of performance

social responsibilities, and ethical standards of behaviour. The effectiveness of an organisation might be assessed against Drucker's eight key areas in which objectives need to be set in terms of business performance and results: market standing, innovation, productivity, physical and financial resources, profitability, manager performance and development, worker performance and attitude, and public responsibility.

- **Design of organisation structure** – one of the most significant factors that determine effective organisational performance is the correct design of structure. Part of the attempt to gauge organisational effectiveness could involve a review of structure to assess the extent to which it aids the process of management and the execution of work. In particular, does the structure harmonise with organisational goals and objectives, and maintain the balance of the socio-technical system? How flexible is the structure and how effective is the 'fit' between structure, systems of management, the behaviour of people and situational variables?

- **Organisational control systems** – the effectiveness of organisational control systems can be gauged by the extent to which they draw attention to the critical activities that are important to the overall success of the organisation. To what extent do control systems provide an effective means of checking progress to determine whether the objectives of the organisation are being achieved, and help lead to an improvement in performance? Are structures of control congruent with power and involvement, and the means of ensuring compliance among members?

- **Planned organisation change** – the extent to which the organisation is ready to respond to new challenges and opportunities presented by the external environment, and able to overcome resistance to change. What is the organisational response to change, for example in relation to the behavioural considerations with new technological developments?

- **Organisation culture and climate** – the analysis of organisation culture could be related to the cultural web of *Johnson et al.* and aspects of routine behaviours, rituals, stories, symbols, power structures, control systems, organisation structure and paradigm. Organisational climate relates to the nature of the people–organisation relationship and the superior–subordinate relationship. A healthy organisation climate can be gauged by the extent to which it exhibits the characteristics that engender a spirit of support and co-operation throughout the organisation, and is conducive to motivating members to work willingly and effectively.

In more general terms, attention needs to be given throughout all levels of the organisation to the extent to which there is proper recognition and effective management of such factors as diversity, the psychological contract, the informal organisation, systems of communication, and underlying consideration and respect for the people who are the organisation.

Organisation audit

A programme of **organisation audit** (or management audit) involves a review of the operations of the organisation as a whole and an examination of the full range of management activities, including the effective use of human resources. Organisation audit is concerned with the identification of problems that are encountered in achieving organisational goals and disparities between strategy formulation and policy decisions, and actions necessary for their successful implementation.

Such a review may be undertaken by members of the organisation, external consultants on organisation and management, or a combination of both internal members and external consultants. Organisation audit tends to be concerned more with the current state of the organisation, and with what must be done now in order to meet set objectives and targets. But an organisation must also be properly prepared to face the demands of a changing environment. It must give attention to its future development and success.

A word of caution

As any student of management or reader of this book will have realised, there is no shortage of ideas on how to improve organisational performance. Understanding the latest concepts and pronouncements of leading management writers is a part of a manager's development, and there clearly are potential benefits to be gained both for the individual and the organisation. *Crainer* suggests, however, that there is a growing disillusionment with the pedlars of managerial wisdom. Perhaps they should be treated as sources not of solutions but of inspiration.

> *Instead of seeking out approaches which are appropriate to their businesses, managers appear in perpetual search of the holy grail of management. It is not that these various ideas – whether re-engineering, empowerment or TQM – are poor concepts. Many do work, but not if they are set in tablets of corporate stone. They have to be open to be flexible interpretations, and used when needed, rather than as all-encompassing 'solutions'. Becoming the slavish disciple of a particular managerial luminary is likely to end in commercial disaster.*[66]

SUCCESSFUL ORGANISATIONS AND PEOPLE

In his discussion of the future of management, Chowdhury maintains that the success of the 21st-century organisation will depend upon the effective use of talented people.

> *Talent-centered organizations will constantly search for the new talent, keep them by satisfying their needs, use them effectively, and create a challenging environment for them to work in. People create organizations and people can destroy them. The most valuable commodity in business is not technology or capital but people. The driving force behind a 21st century organization will be its people.*[67]

The importance of people for organisational effectiveness is reinforced by the survey undertaken by the MCA and Management Today.

> *Organisations and managers are heading for trouble. Although people believe they are more productive than five years ago, they attribute this gain to their own efforts rather than to their manager's help. This attitude points to a contradiction at the heart of today's organisations … Outsourcing and off-shoring have allowed organisations to shift from a fixed to a more variable cost basis, but at the expense of individuals who have to seek alternative employment. Empowerment has shifted responsibility to individuals. These trends raise fundamental questions about how long people will continue to believe it is worth working for an employer rather than themselves.*

The MCA survey emphasises that the role of the organisation is social as well as economic and points to the desperate need for the basic, softer skills of managers in leadership, coaching and mentoring. Organisations need individuals they can trust, who are engaged in and committed to their work. If they want to survive, organisations need to recognise that they have to add value to their employees, that their social capital is just as important as their financial capital.[68]

Refresh your understanding

Activity 20D

www.pearsoned.co.uk/ mullins

Critical reflection ?????

'Despite all my studies it is difficult to find simple answers on how best to improve organisational performance. And the effective management of people now seems to be more involved than I ever thought. So what's the point?'

'But don't you see – that is exactly the point. You now have a better understanding of the complex nature of management and organisational behaviour, and attempting to relate theory to practice.'

What do you think? How much benefit have you derived from your studies? Do you have a better understanding of the subject area?

MANAGEMENT IN THE NEWS

Writing the unwritten rules

Why most managers are plagiarists

Lucy Kellaway

A few years ago, William Swanson, head of the world's biggest missile maker, sat down to write a little book containing the secrets of his greatness. There is nothing unusual about this. The content was the usual mixture of platitude, wishful thinking and plain dullness but the style was lucid enough, and the jargon content low. His company, Raytheon, distributed more than one-quarter of a million copies of *Unwritten Rules of Management* and the great Warren Buffett apparently liked it enough to request a couple of dozen extras.

The story would have ended on this happy note were it not for a young engineer who spotted that 17 of the rules bore an uncanny resemblance to a book called *The Unwritten Laws of Engineering* published in 1944 by W.J. King. The young man wrote this up in his blog. From there, the story made it into newspapers. Mr. Swanson squirmed a bit and tried to laugh it off, but last week was told by his board that he had erred and was to be punished by forgoing his pay rise for the year. However, they said they still considered him to be a terrific leader and declared he could continue with his job regardless. Red face, small slap, but otherwise business as usual. So what do we learn from this odd tale? I dare say there are at least 33 managerial maxims that this touches, but observing rule six (below), I'm going to limit mine to seven.

1 There are no new management rules under the sun. Peter Drucker said most that was worth saying on how to manage a long time ago. Since then it has all been endless repetition.
2 Management itself is about plagiarism. This is the first great rule that anyone serious about making it as a manager must learn: make sure you take the credit for other people's actions and ideas. Not all of it perhaps, but a healthy slug.
3 An exception to rule one. If you have made a mistake, reverse plagiarism kicks in. The secret now is to try to make someone else the author of what you have done.
4 If you wish to copy out someone else's work, change the word order around a bit. King wrote: 'Be extremely careful of the accuracy of your

statements'. There were surely other ways of getting across the same view, but Mr. Swanson plumped for: 'Be extremely careful of the accuracy of your statements'.
5 If you have ignored rule four and got caught copying, do not give the excuse, as Mr. Swanson did, that he had absorbed the material unconsciously through a lifetime's reading. This does not wash at all. I have read dozens of management books in my life, and cannot recall a single thing from any of them.
6 If you insist on listing maxims, 33 is far too many. Ten were enough for God, but seven is better still.
7 Boards should not sit on fences. If the Raytheon board considered him to have done something badly wrong they should have sacked him.

In the booklet, Mr. Swanson expressed the hope that after reading it 'maybe you too can become a leader of a company'. In the – frankly inconceivable – case that anyone was helped in this way, I hope this little story may have taught them something even more useful. Writing a book of maxims is an exercise in vanity and a hostage to fortune. The real upshot is that Swanson now looks an idiot.

Which leads me to my final, breathtakingly obvious maxim: looking an absolute idiot is not the thing if you are trying to be a business leader.

Source: Kellaway, L. 'Why most managers are plagiarists', *Financial Times*, 7 May 2006. Copyright © 2006 The Financial Times Limited, reproduced with permission.

Discussion questions

1 Discuss the extent to which it is possible to have successful managers in unsuccessful organisations, and vice versa. What type of management development activity would you recommend to an organisation that needs to improve its overall levels of performance?
2 From your studies of management and organisational behaviour, what would you include in your list of seven 'golden rules' for managers?

SYNOPSIS

● There is a multiplicity of variables which impinge on any one organisational situation and which illustrate the complicated nature of the study of organisational effectiveness. Organisations need to be efficient, effective, adaptable and give attention to innovation. One significant approach to organising is the McKinsey 7-S framework of interdependent organisational variables – structure, strategy, skills, staff, style, systems and shared values. Gratton refers to the six tenets of the democratic organisation in which there is a win–win relationship for both the individual and the organisation.

● A key factor in organisational effectiveness is the successful management of change and innovation, and the concept of the learning organisation. One particular approach to improved organisational effectiveness is Total Quality Management (TQM). The successful organisation should as a matter of policy be constantly seeking opportunities to improve the quality of its products and/or services and processes. People are the key if TQM initiatives are to succeed. Another concept to have received much attention is Business Process Re-engineering. This involves a fundamental rethinking of business processes, and a radical approach to organisational change and restructuring.

● The quality of management is one of the most important factors in the success of any organisation. There is, therefore, a continual need for managerial development as an integral part of the process of organisation development. Attention needs to be given to performance review, training and learning, management succession planning and career progression. Management development should be seen as a continuous process and involves formal programmes of continuous professional development and managers accepting responsibility for self-development.

● Following demand from employers and government, Investors in People UK created a new Leadership and Management Model which is a development framework for ensuring organisations create, manage and invest in effective leadership. The model is based on the real-life good practices of successful organisations. The European Foundation for Quality Management (EFQM) proposes a model of excellence for leading to improved business results. The model is based on the concept that an organisation will achieve better results by involving all people in the continuous improvement of their processes.

● Based on experience in a broad range of organisations, Steele suggests nine questions to help assess organisational effectiveness. Popular management techniques include benchmarking and gap analysis. Growing attention has been given to measures of performance in the public sector but there is a potential difficulty in measurement of a service ethic. There is a wide range of interrelated individual, group, organisational and environmental influences on behaviour in work organisations. Accordingly there are many different criteria that might be applied in attempting to assess organisational performance and effectiveness.

● An organisation may be analysed in terms of an open systems framework; teamwork and leadership; the role of management; managerial style and effectiveness; profile of organisational characteristics; contribution of the HRM function; key areas of performance and results, design of organisation structure, organisational control systems; planned organisation change; and organisation culture and climate. A programme of organisation audit involves a review of the operations of the organisation as a whole. However, in addition to concern for the current state of the organisation, attention must be given to its future development and success. The driving force behind the successful twenty-first century organisation will be its people.

 Refresh your understanding, assess your progress and begin your research with online resources at **www.pearsoned.co.uk/mullins**

REVIEW AND DISCUSSION QUESTIONS

1 Summarise clearly what you believe are the main factors which affect organisational performance and effectiveness.

2 Discuss critically the relevance and applications to organisational effectiveness of:

 (i) total quality management; and

 (ii) business process re-engineering.

3 Discuss fully the importance of effective management to organisational effectiveness.

4 Explain fully what areas of need you would include in designing a management development programme for an organisation of your choice.

5 Comment critically on the apparent effectiveness of management education and training in your own organisation.

6 Debate what you believe are the relevance and applications of:

 (i) the learning organisation, and

 (ii) the leadership and management model.

7 Detail the questions you would ask, and the specific criteria you would apply, in attempting to evaluate the performance and effectiveness of your own organisation, or some other organisation of your choice.

8 Give your own views on how you see the future of management and the nature of successful organisations in the future.

ASSIGNMENT 1

Critically analyse your own (or some other chosen) organisation in terms of the McKinsey 7-S Framework (p. 758). Describe fully each of the seven components as they relate to the organisation, the fit among the components and the extent to which they are interconnected.

● Strategy

● Structure

● Systems

● Style

● Staff

● Skills, and

● Shared values.

What conclusions do you draw from your analysis?

ASSIGNMENT 2

Assessing your organisation

These questions are designed to help you reflect on how well your company is doing, and to generate ideas for improvement.

Terminology

The term 'company' relates to business here, but you can adapt and interpret the questionnaire for other forms of organisation such as firm, partnership, public service, non-profit-making, etc. 'Customers' include clients, consumers, end-users, intermediaries, wholesalers, distributors, subscribers, members and trustees. 'Employees' include staff, colleagues, associates, people, volunteer helpers, self-employed contractors and trade unions. 'Suppliers' include conventional suppliers as well as business partners and joint ventures. 'Investors' include private and institutional shareholders, lending banks, donors and funders. 'Community' encompasses local, national, worldwide and governmental; and from a social, philanthropic and environmental standpoint.

Questions

a Purpose and vision

1 Do the directors have a shared understanding of the company's purpose, one that is couched in other than purely financial or commercial terms, and do they believe in it?

2 Is the company embarked on a journey that is founded in a vision of the company's future, which is communicated and shared with the company's stakeholders?

3 How meaningful to the company's various stakeholder groups are the purpose and vision?

b Values and beliefs

4 Is there a clear set of shared values, standards, business ethics, etc., which form the basis for actions, decisions and behaviour by the company and those acting in its name?

5 Is there consistency from top to bottom between stated values and actual behaviours, i.e. are the espoused values being lived out in practice?

6 When did you last review your company's statement of philosophy, values and behaviour standards?

7 Has the leadership built a robust and sustainable culture that has the capacity to live on beyond the tenure of the present leader(s)?

c Leadership development

8 What leadership development provision is made for those with the potential for senior management positions?

9 Does the organisation offer:

– early opportunities to practise leadership;

– mentoring and feedback to develop self-awareness in current and potential leaders;

– opportunities to reflect on and develop a template of values to inform future leaders' decision-making?

d Leadership succession

10 How does the organisation help current leaders to be objective about their own life-cycle, recognising when they have become part of the problem rather than part of the solution, and knowing when it is in the company's best interest for them to step aside to make way for a successor?

11 How objective is the present leadership about the possibility of handing power over to those with a different approach (i.e. not selecting in one's own image).

e Sharing the fruits of success

12 Does the leadership have a clear rationale for remuneration and the sharing of the fruits of success in line with the company's stated values?

13 Is the rationale widely understood, communicated and respected throughout the company?

14 Do share-based bonus schemes or their equivalent apply to everyone in the company?

15 Does your company submit directors' remuneration to shareholders for their approval?

→

Assignment 2 – continued

f Your own leadership competence and development

16 Are you confident in your own ability to:

– engage stakeholders in the development of vision and strategy?

– maintain dialogue and manage the relationship with all stakeholders?

– identify and make provision for future leaders?

– surround yourself with people who will complement your own strengths?

– be open to challenge and to the opinions of others?

– coach and mentor others?

– engage in lifelong learning, and help others to learn?

– take appropriate risks?

– help people change?

– enable people to confront uncomfortable realities?

17 Where does most scope exist to improve capability and performance in terms of the tomorrow's company model of leadership, for you personally and for the wider leadership?

18 How clear are you concerning the kind of organisation you want to lead?

19 How aware are you of your own leadership style, alternative models of leadership and the range of options available, and the conscious choices you have made?

Source: From Building tomorrow's company – Supporting Notes and the Centre for Tommorow's company and William Tate 1999.

PERSONAL AWARENESS AND SKILLS EXERCISE

Objectives

Completing this exercise should help you to enhance the following skills:

● Analyse key aspects of effective structure, managerial staffing and organisational performance.

● Draw attention to priorities for review of the organisation.

● Evaluate practical management situations, either now or in the future.

Exercise

You are required to imagine you are the managing director or chief executive of your organisation, and complete the following checklist.

a Structure

Does your organisation have:	Yes	No	Maybe
1 an outdated structure – for example, geared to forgotten objectives, old markets, retired top managers;	☐	☐	☐
2 a structure that does not allow the organisation to respond to business growth, technical change or to the competition;	☐	☐	☐
3 changed organisational objectives, but structure and staffing basically unchanged;	☐	☐	☐
4 flexibility, adaptability and delegation impeded by bureaucracy or detailed built-in procedures;	☐	☐	☐
5 a structure that does not encourage people to readily identify how their role/position relates to the overall objectives and structure of the organisation?	☐	☐	☐

b Managerial staffing

Does your organisation have: Yes No Maybe

6 unclear top management succession; or does it offer only a 'Hobson's Choice' for
 several senior positions; ☐ ☐ ☐

7 a general and unduly heavy loss of managers, especially the younger or better ones; ☐ ☐ ☐

8 quite numerous examples of badly under-employed managers in 'non-jobs'; ☐ ☐ ☐

9 development of the organisation clearly held back by a lack of good people; ☐ ☐ ☐

10 fairly widespread managerial job dissatisfaction and frustration; ☐ ☐ ☐

11 managerial vacancies frequently difficult to fill, from either within or outside the
 organisation? ☐ ☐ ☐

c Performance

Does your organisation have:

12 poor organisational performance, due to ineffective management controls; ☐ ☐ ☐

13 poor performance because of a generally low level of managerial competence for
 present-day tasks; ☐ ☐ ☐

14 poor performance which arises from blurred or badly drawn managerial
 responsibilities; ☐ ☐ ☐

15 widespread overburdening of managers, which undermines performance; ☐ ☐ ☐

16 extensive waste of managerial time – for example, in board meetings, committees,
 working groups; ☐ ☐ ☐

17 widespread delays in obtaining either decisions, or the information needed to make
 decisions; ☐ ☐ ☐

18 frequent failure to seize opportunities, or to react speedily to new challenges? ☐ ☐ ☐

Use the completed checklist and your own analysis to highlight the priorities for reviewing your organisation.
Compare and discuss your responses with colleagues.

What overall conclusions do you draw about your organisation?

Source: John Bourn for a UNISON distance learning course and is used with permission of the education officer.

Discussion

● If you had to make a forced choice and in rank order, what **three** variables would you say ultimately determine
 the effectiveness of an organisation more than any others?

● What have you learned about effective organisational performance and your study of management and
 organisational behaviour?

CASE STUDY

Who says business is boring? M&S's rollercoaster ride

Marks and Spencer was a national institution in the UK at the end of the last century. The supplier of underwear to at least two prime ministers, M&S was the darling of the British middle classes – familiar, trusted and admired.[69] Those who teach in business schools may recall how M&S was a by-word for quality, managerial flair and all-round excellence throughout the 1990s – case studies described its close relationships with suppliers, its strong positioning and its qualities as a good employer.

But as the new millennium approached, it became clear that M&S was in serious trouble – falling sales, failed revamps and profit warnings in 1999 wiped a third off the company's share price.[70] The focus of this case study is on events at the company some five years later, but it is relevant to note that the main reason for M&S' millennial misery was that its management did not seem to have its eye on the ball while some key changes were happening in the sector. M&S' broad appeal left it vulnerable to attack by specialist competitors – fashionable designer labels at the top of the market and rapidly growing low-price, good quality market entrants at the bottom. Stuck in the middle, the M&S range started to look uninteresting, even dowdy, and was slow to move off the racks. Its international strategy looked over-stretched and risky.

As the crisis deepened, M&S appointed a new Chairman and Chief Executive in 2000: Belgian-born Luc Vandevelde, whose career experience included the French supermarket group Carrefour. The first year or so of his tenure was gruelling, with disappointing sales figures, a disastrous advertising campaign and some difficult retrenchment decisions, including pulling out of 39 of its European locations.[71] At the same time, M&S hired designer George Davies to develop and introduce the new Per Una range, in order to improve the company's image with the all-important women buyers. By the middle of 2002, things were looking up and Vandevelde was so confident in the recovery that he started to scale back his commitment to M&S, appointing Roger Holmes as a separate Chief Executive and announcing his intention to spend more time on other interests. Unfortunately, that confidence proved to be ill-founded. By early 2004, sales and profits were starting to slip again and later that year Vandevelde resigned, leaving M&S in a dangerously uncertain position.

Whose M&S?

Then things started to hot up. In May 2004 M&S suddenly replaced its Chief Executive Roger Holmes with Stuart Rose, former head of the clothes store group Arcadia. Why? The M&S board (and everyone else) was expecting a takeover bid from Phillip Green, a self-made entrepreneur and retail tycoon with a fearsome reputation for bold, aggressive moves, whose success had earned him a golden reputation on the financial markets. Rose's task was to create and implement a plan that would see off the expected Green bid.

Rose was in many ways the ideal candidate for the job. With 17 years at M&S before building up extensive retail experience elsewhere, he had achieved some impressive turnaround successes in a range of other appointments. He had encountered Green before, when Green bought out Arcadia in 2002. The two were said to be on generally friendly terms, although that friendship was placed under some strain during the fierce battle of summer 2004.[72] At the beginning of July, Green proposed to offer £4 per share for the company (a total of £9.1 billion), a major premium on the then £3 or so share price. A bid premium effectively sends a message that the would-be buyer expects to be able to work the assets more profitably than the present management, a competency that Green had very effectively demonstrated to the City with his Arcadia purchase. Rose's task was to convince the shareholders

By going back to core values and getting the details right, Stuart Rose achieved a turnaround in the performance of M&S.

that he could do even better and that Green's advances should be rejected.

This was high finance and high excitement: two powerful retailing heavyweights going head to head in full public view over the nation's favourite store. Rose published his three-year turnaround plan on 12 July. It was a commitment to refocus on core values and on the key segment of 35–55-year-old women, whom Rose believed had been neglected in the preceding years. The stores were to be simplified and modernised and expansion plans pruned. Money was to be handed back to shareholders, financed by the sale of the M&S Money business to HSBC.[73] The Rose plan also promised further efficiency gains in the supply chain. Immediate reaction was mixed – it seemed to focus on effective management of the core business, without any eye-catching initiatives. A few days later Green decided to abandon his campaign to take over M&S, following endorsement of Rose and his plan by shareholders at the company's annual meeting.[74]

The Rose recovery

What happened next? Two years later, Marks and Spencer was still very much present on the High Street and its shares trading at just under £6. Things can change very quickly in the retail world, but the Rose turnaround plan seemed to be working. Press comment was increasingly favourable, but the first year had been tough for M&S. In August 2004, one month after seeing off the Green bid, it suffered the humiliation of losing its position as the country's largest clothing retailer to Asda.[75] In November, the company announced a fall in profits and like-for-like sales, together with the news that four directors would be leaving.[76] Rose himself took charge of retailing, merchandising and buying, bringing the Per Una clothing label in house and commenting that the company needed to talk to its customers directly, to get a clearer grasp of what they wanted:

I don't think we have really had a full understanding of who our customers are, what turns them on and what they want from us. We have been relying too much on hearsay, too much on pure research and not enough on actually talking to them[77]

In the early stages, M&S also cleared all its slow-moving lines out of the distribution chain at an estimated cost of £1.3 billion to make way for the results of this improved dialogue with customers.[78] Christmas 2004 sales were disappointing, but Rose was able to claim that the company was already in a much leaner condition in preparation for the changes planned for 2005.

We've got costs under control. I believe we've got the foundations in place to drive the business forward.[79]

The takeover battle and the Rose recovery plan not only affected M&S' stock market position, but had a clear impact on levels of staff motivation. M&S had always been known for having some of the best terms and conditions in the retail sector, but during the crucial months between summer 2004 and the end of 2005, the Rose plan involved a major review and renegotiation of staff contracts. These would trade longer working hours to ensure good levels of cover at evenings and weekends – the busiest times for the company – for the offer of better financial rewards. M&S does not recognise a trade union and intended to renegotiate the deal via its internal consultation mechanism, the business involvement group (Big). The uncertainty amongst staff caused by this move led USDAW (the UK retail union) to launch a major recruitment drive within M&S at the start of 2005,[80] and to be able to claim a doubling of its membership within M&S by July of that year (if union membership within an organisation reaches 10% of the workforce, the union can use the UK's 1999 Employment Act to approach the Central Arbitration Committee to enforce union recognition and negotiation).[81] A sales training package, including the development of in-house coaching systems, was also included as part of the Rose plan to increase sales by enhancing staff confidence and sales skills. USDAW publicly criticised the company for 'wasting' what it estimated at £10 million to engage American retail sales guru Mary Gober to deliver a series of motivational training sessions to 60 000 of its store staff.[82]

Back on track

By autumn 2005 M&S had announced improved trading and the share price touched the £4 level of the Green bid. Commentators noted that M&S clothing ranges were back on form and that the efficiency gains of the previous year had also improved performance.[83] By the next spring, M&S was reporting stronger-than-expected results, and the effects of increasing sales and a clear turnaround in the fortunes of the business in early 2006 enabled Rose to recommend a 'thank-you' bonus to all staff (who were expected to share a dividend of £60 million).[84] USDAW had not hit the critical 10 per cent mark to force the company into union recognition. Additionally, M&S announced a recruitment drive in July 2006, as the financial recovery enabled it to approach expansion plans with confidence.[85] For the time being at least, both staff and stock market were able to have renewed confidence in the company and the management approach taken by Rose.

Your tasks

1 Some of the recent history of Marks and Spencer seems to revolve around the personalities of leaders and would-be leaders. Critically examine the importance of the character, actions and pronouncements of the leader to an organisation's performance.

2 In the mid to late 1990s, M&S seemed still to be doing well, although with hindsight it was starting to lose its way. What are the lessons of this episode for effective organisational leadership?

3 To what extent does business success appear to affect the motivation of staff? How far could you argue that increasing support for trade unions (such as that for USDAW in early 2005) indicates a failure of organisational management?

Notes and references

1 Handy, C. B. *Understanding Organizations*, Fourth edition, Penguin (1993).

2 For a fuller discussion see, for example: Baguley, P. *Improving Organizational Performance: A Handbook For Managers*, McGraw-Hill (1994).

3 Mann, S. 'Doing Things Differently', *Professional Manager*, vol. 12, no. 3, May 2003, pp. 34–5.

4 Peters, T. J. and Waterman, R. H. *In Search of Excellence*, Harper and Row (1982).

5 Ibid., p. 9.

6 Peters, T. *Re-imagine!*, Dorling Kindersley, (2003).

7 Gratton, L. *The Democratic Enterprise*, Financial Times Prentice Hall (2004), pp. xiii-xiv.

8 See, for example: Caulkin, S. 'Chris Argyris', *Management Today*, October 1997, pp. 58–9.

9 Senge, P. M. *The Fifth Discipline: The Art of Practice of the Learning Organization*, Doubleday (1990).

10 McKenna, E. *Business Psychology & Organisational Behaviour*, Lawrence Erlbaum (1994), p. 211.

11 Pedler, M., Burgoyne, J. and Boydell, T. (eds) *Applying Self-Development in Organizations*, Prentice-Hall (1988), p. 209.

12 Garratt, B. *The Fish Rots From The Head*, HarperCollins (1996). See also: Garratt, B. *The Learning Organization: Developing Democracy at Work*, HarperCollins Business (2000).

13 Modena, M. 'A Matter of Balance', *Professional Manager*, vol. 12, no. 4, July 2003, pp. 34–5.

14 Lane, T., Snow, D. and Labrow, P. 'Learning to Succeed with ICT', *The British Journal of Administrative Management*, May/June 2000, pp. 14–15.

15 Deming, W. E. *Out of Crisis*, Cambridge University Press (1986) and *The New Economies for Industry*, Cambridge University Press (1993).

16 'Total Quality: Getting TQM to Work', Checklist 030, *Chartered Management Institute*, June 2005.

17 Cane, S. *Kaizen Strategies for Winning Through People*, Pitman Publishing (1996), p. 8.

18 www.kaizen-institute.com [accessed 10 July 2006].

19 Thomas, B. *The Human Dimension of Quality*, McGraw-Hill (1995), p. 185.

20 Heller, R. *In Search of European Excellence*, HarperCollins Business (1997), p. 239.

21 Drummond, H. *Introduction to Organizational Behaviour*, Oxford University Press (2000), p. 112.

22 Allen, R. S. and Kilmann, R. H. 'Aligning Reward Practices in Support of Total Quality Management', *Business Horizons*, vol. 44, no. 3, May 2001.

23 Hayler, R and Nichols, M. *What is Six Sigma Process Management?* McGraw-Hill (2005), p. 5.

24 Patton, F. 'Does Six Sigma Work in Service Industries?' *Quality Progress*, vol. 38, no. 9, September 2005, pp. 55–60.

25 Hammer, M. and Champy, J. *Re-engineering the Corporation: A Manifesto For Business Revolution*, Second edition, Nicholas Brearley (2001), p. 32.

26 Hill, F. M. and Collins, L. K. 'The positioning of BPR and TQM in Long-term Organizational Change Strategies', *The TQM Magazine*, vol. 10, no. 6, 1998, p. 445.

27 Reis, D. and Pena, L. 'Reengineering the Motivation to Work', *Management Decision*, vol. 39, no. 8, 2001, pp. 666–75.

28 Hammer, M. *The Agenda: What Every Business Must Do to Dominate the Decade*, Three Rivers Press (2003).

29 Rummler, G. A. and Brache, A. P. *Improving Performance: How to Manage the White Space on the Organization Chart*, Second edition, Jossey-Bass (1995).

30 'Untapped Potential: The barriers to optimum corporate productivity', Proudfoot Consulting, October 2002. For a summary, see: 'News Update', *Manager, The British Journal of Administrative Management*, no. 34, New Year 2003, p. 6.

31 Stern, S. 'Enhancing Your Talent', *Management Today*, October 2002, pp. 2–3.

32 Brodbeck, F. 'The more we blame, the less we gain', *Professional Manager*, vol. 13, no. 6, November 2004, p. 37.

33 Dunderdale, P. 'Analysing Effective Organisations', *Professional Manager*, September 1994, pp. 23–5.

34 'Effective Organisations: the people factor', Advisory Booklet, ACAS, November 2001.

35 Allen, R. S. and Helms, M. M. 'Employee Perceptions of the Relationship between Strategy, Rewards and Organizational Performance', *Journal of Business Strategies*, vol. 19, no. 2, Fall 2002, pp. 115–39.

36 Czerniawska, F. 'From Bottlenecks to Blackberries: How the relationship between organisations and individuals is changing,' Management Consultancies Association, September 2005.

37 Stephens, D. cited in Czerniawska, F. Ibid.

38 Lilley, D. 'Managerial Development: Where do the Professions sit?', *The British Journal of Administrative Management*, 29, January/February 2002, pp. 22–3.

39 Stern, S. 'Someone To Talk To', *Management Today*, July 2002, pp. 56–9.

40 See, for example: Lucas, E. 'Workers' play time', *Professional Manager*, vol. 12, no. 5, September 2003, pp. 29–31. See also: De Vita, E. 'Training à la Mode', *Management Today*, January 2004, pp. 50–1.

41 Revans, R. *ABC of Action Learning*, Chartwell-Bratt (1983).

42 Crainer, S. *Key Management Ideas: Thinkers that Changed the Management World*, Third edition, Financial Times Prentice Hall (1998), p. 259.

43 Hazard, H. 'An Action Learning Teacher Reflects on Case Teaching', *ECCHO: The Newsletter of the European Case Clearing House*, Issue No. 22, Autumn/Fall 1999, pp. 6–7.

44 Lound, E. 'Transforming Management Development', *The British Journal of Administrative Management*, March/April 2002, pp. 34–5.

45 Weston, J. 'Room to Learn: training in the boardroom', *Chartered Secretary*, March 2002, p. 19.

46 Mullins, L. J. and Aldrich, P. 'An Integrated Model of Management and Managerial Development', *Journal of Management Development*, vol. 7, no. 3, 1988, pp. 29–39.

47 Altman, W. 'Dead Men's Shoes', *Professional Manager*, vol. 12, no. 4, July 2003, pp. 16–17.

48 Stern, S. 'High Flyers: Low Risers', *Management Today*, June 2005, pp. 56–61.

49 Mabey, C. and Ramirez, M. 'Developing Managers: A European Perspective', Chartered Management Institute , May 2004. For a summary, see: 'Training policies and practice across Europe revealed', *Professional Manager*, January 2004, p. 25.

50 Mabey, C. 'Management Development Works: The Evidence', Chartered Management Institute, January 2005: See also, Lucas, E. 'Good managers born or made?' *Profesional Manager*, July 2006, pp. 26–9.

51 www.managers.org.uk (accessed 10 July 2006).

52 Farren, C. 'Mastery: The Critical Advantage', in Chowdhury, S. '*Management 21C*, Financial Times Prentice Hall (2000), p. 98.

53 'The Leadership and Management Model', *Investors In People UK*, 2003.

54 Goasdoué, J. 'Is Quality Taken for Granted?', *The British Journal of Administrative Management*, February 2001, p. 10.

55 Farrar, M. 'The Excellent Organisation', *Manager, The British Journal of Administrative Management*, January/February 2004, pp. 24–5.

56 Steele, M. *Assessing Organisational Effectiveness*, Cranfield School of Management, Working Paper 5/88, 1987.

57 Crainer, S. and Dearlove, D. (eds), *Financial Times Handbook of Management*, Second edition, Financial Times Prentice Hall (2001), p. 405.

58 Barnes, P. 'Benchmarking – a technique of the 90s to be used with care', *Chartered Secretary*, May 1999, pp. 30–1.

59 Modena, M. 'A Matter of Balance', *Professional Manager*, vol. 12, no. 4, July 2003, pp. 34–5.

60 Bishop, P. 'Benchmarking – a Misconceived Business Asset', *The British Journal of Administrative Management*, February 2001, pp. 12–13.

61 Ittner, C. and Larcker, D. 'A Bigger Yardstick for Company Performance', in Pickford, J. (ed), *Financial Times Mastering Management 2.0*, Financial Times Prentice Hall (2001), pp. 385–9.

62 Gratton, L. *Living Strategy: Putting people at the heart of corporate purpose*, Financial Times Prentice Hall (2000), p. 99.

63 See, for example: 'Managing high performance in the public sector', *IRS Employment Trends*, 690, October 1999, pp. 5–16.

64 Prowle, M. 'Performance Indicators and Performance Management in the Public Sector', *Chartered Secretary*, February 2001, pp. 18–19.

65 Furnham, A. 'Pouring Money Down the Drain? '*Manager, The British Journal of Administrative Management*', June/July 2006.

66 Crainer, S. 'The Rise of Guru Scepticism', *Management Today*, March 1996, p. 50.

67 Chowdhury, S. *Management 21C*, Financial Times Prentice Hall (2000), p. 10.

68 Czerniawska, F. 'From Bottlenecks to Blackberries: How the relationship between organisations and individuals is changing', Management Consultancies Association, September 2005.

69 Q&Q: Is Marks and Spencer back in fashion? 10 July 2002 http://news.bbc.co.uk/1/hi/business/2119606.stm.

70 Whatever happened to Lucky Luc? bbc.co.uk 10 May 2004 http://news.bbc.co.uk/1/hi/business/3699899.stm.

71 Whatever happened to Lucky Luc? bbc.co.uk 10 May 2004 http://news.bbc.co.uk/1/hi/business/3699899.stm.

72 Profile; M&S boss Stuart Rose bbc.co.uk 1 June 2004 http://news.bbc.co.uk/1/hi/business/3766215.stm (1 June 2004).

73 Q&A: Rose's M&S revival plan bbc.co.uk 12 July 2004 http://news.bbc.co.uk/1/hi/business/3886161.stm.

74 Green pledges high street battle bbc.co.uk 15 July 2004 http://news.bbc.co.uk/1/hi/business/3895641.stm.

75 M&S Loses clothes crown to Asda bbc.co.uk 23 August 2004 http://news.bbc.co.uk/1/hi/business/3588010.stm.

76 One of these, HR manager Jean Tomlin, has since been appointed to lead the HR team at the London Organising Committee of the Olympic Games.

77 M&S unveils management shake-up bbc.co.uk 9 November 2004 http://news.bbc.co.uk/1/hi/business/3994713.stm.

78 Retail giants face investor scrutiny bbc.co.uk 13 July 2005 http://news.bbc.co.uk/1/hi/business/4671549.stm.

79 Comeback eludes retail icon M&S bbc.co.uk 24 May 2005 http://news.bbc.co.uk/1/hi/business/4575007.stm.

80 Usdaw targets M&S staff *Personnel Today* 28 February 2005 (available at www.personneltoday.com).

81 Usdaw launches national M&S recruitment campaign *Personnel Today* 28 February 2005 (available at www.personneltoday.com).

82 Marks and Spencer HR director defends £10m staff motivation exercise *Personnel Today* 6 October 2005 (available at www.personneltoday.com).

83 Is M&S ready to deliver? bbc.co.uk 11 October 2005 http://news.bbc.co.uk/1/hi/business/4325956.stm.

84 Cash bonus for Marks and Spencer staff *Personnel Today* 3 April 2006 (available at www.personneltoday.com).

85 M&S announces recruitment drive after another set of positive sales figures *Personnel Today* 12 July 2006. (available at www.personneltoday.com).

Notes and references

1 Fukuyama, F. 1992 *The End of History and the Last Man*, New York, The Free Press.
2 http://news.bbc.co.uk/1/hi/business/3398913.stm 'Q&A: The Enron Case', 5 July 2006.
3 McLean, B. and Elkind, P. (2004), *The Smartest Guys in the Room: the amazing rise and scandalous fall of Enron*, London, Penguin.
4 Ibid., p. 217.
5 Ibid., p. 68.
6 Ibid., p. 216.
7 Ibid., p. 120.
8 Ibid., p. 66.
9 http://news.bbc.co.uk/1/hi/business/5151140.stm 'Enron ex-chief Kenneth Lay dies', 5 July 2006.
10 http://money.cnn.com/2004/01/14/news/companies/enron_fastows 'Fastow and his wife plead guilty', 14 January 2004.
11 http://news.bbc.co.uk/1/hi/business/5151140.stm 'Enron ex-chief Kenneth Lay dies', 5 July 2006.
12 Surowiecki, J. (2005), *The Wisdom of Crowds*, London, Abacus.
13 Ibid., p. 255.
14 http://news.bbc.co.uk/1/hi/business/5010310.stm 'Lay 'too busy' to spot law break', 23 May 2006.
15 Shelley, P.B. *Ozymandias*, first published 1818 and can be found reproduced in full in Wikipedia at http://en.wikipedia.org/wiki/Ozymandias.

CONCLUSION

The main thrust of this book has been to present a managerial approach to the study of organisational behaviour.

We live in an organisational world. Organisations of one form or another are a necessary part of our society and serve many important needs. It is necessary therefore to understand how organisations function and the pervasive influences which they exercise over the behaviour of people. The nature of organisational behaviour, however, cannot be studied in isolation. It is necessary to understand the constantly changing network of interrelated dimensions – the individual, the group, the organisation and the environment – that collectively influence the behaviour of people and together comprise the total organisation. The behaviour and actions of people at work, and the activities of the organisation, are directed towards the achievement of certain goals. It is through the process of management that the efforts of members of the organisation are co-ordinated and guided. Management is an integrating activity and at the heart of the people–organisation relationship.

Any organisation is only as good as the people who are its members and who work within it. In an increasingly global and competitive business environment the management of people is central to organisational survival and success. Consideration should be given to developing an organisational climate in which people work willingly and effectively.

No single book could hope to cover adequately what is a wide and essentially multi-disciplinary field of enquiry, and it has not been the intention to cover all aspects of individual or social behaviour. Accordingly, the book has concentrated on selected topics of particular relevance to organisational behaviour and the management of people within work situations, and which meet the needs of the intended audience.

I hope that the book has helped you to formulate a critical appraisal of contrasting perspectives on the nature of management and organisational behaviour.

Thank you for looking at it.

Laurie J. Mullins

Management, I had discovered, is not something mysterious or conceptually difficult. Its difficulty lies in applying the ideas, not in the ideas themselves.

Charles Handy – Management writer and broadcaster
Myself and Other More Important Matters, William Heinemann (2006), p. 64

GLOSSARY

360° feedback (ch. 13, p. 498)
An appraisal and feedback regarding an individual from different groups within the work situation that may include peers, subordinates, bosses and possibly customers.

Accountability (ch. 18, p. 694)
This is the ultimate responsibility which managers cannot delegate. While managers may delegate authority, they remain accountable for the decisions and actions of their subordinates.

Achievement-oriented leadership (ch. 10, p. 378)
Involves setting challenging goals for subordinates, seeking improvement in their performance and showing confidence in subordinates' ability to perform well.

Action-centred leadership (ch. 10, p. 368)
A theory on leadership which focuses on what leaders do. It states that the effectiveness of a leader is dependent upon meeting three areas of need within the work group: the need to achieve the common task, the need for team maintenance and the individual needs of group members.

Action learning (ch. 20, p. 768)
An approach to management development which involves a small self-selecting team undertaking a practical, real-life and organisational-based project. The emphasis is on learning by doing with advice and support from tutors and other course members.

Actor–Network Analysis (ANA) (ch. 17, p. 640)
Networks which bring together a range of human and non-human actants. The relationship between technological and social intermediaries such as literary inscriptions, technical artefacts, skills of people and money.

Adjourning (ch.8, p. 310)
The adjourning or disbanding of a group because of, for example, completion of a task, members leaving the organisation or moving to other tasks.

Administration (ch.11, p. 412)
A part of management relating to the more specific function of the implementation of systems and procedures, and taking place in accordance with some form of rules or procedure.

Adoption phase (ch. 17, p. 649)
A range of choices relating to the introduction of new technology into organisations consisting of initiation; progression/feasibility, investment decision, and planning and systems design.

Agenda-setting (ch.11, p. 425)
A constant activity of managers involving a set of items, or series of agendas relating to aims and objectives, plans, strategies, ideas, decisions to be made and priorities of action in order to bring about desired end-results.

Alienation (ch. 7, p. 279)
Refers to the detachment of the person from his or her work.

Alienative involvement (ch. 18, p. 689)
Where members are involved against their wishes. There is a strong negative orientation towards the organisation.

Anthropology (ch. 1, p. 7)
The study of the cultural system, i.e. human behaviour as a whole and the science of mankind.

Attitudes (ch. 4, p. 142)
Attitudes can be defined as providing a state of 'readiness' or tendency to respond in a particular way. They are learned through life and are embodied within our socialisation process.

Attribution theory (ch. 6, p. 233)
The way in which individuals make sense of other people's behaviour through attributing characteristics to them by judging their behaviour and intentions on past knowledge and in comparison with other people they know.

Authoritarian style of leadership (ch. 10, p. 371)
Where the focus of power is with the manager. The manager alone exercises decision-making and authority for determining policy, procedures, the allocation of work and has control of rewards or punishments.

Authority (ch. 18, p. 694)
The right of subordinates to take action or make decisions that the manager would otherwise have done.

Automating technology (ch. 17, p. 638)
Replacement of the actions of the human body by the machine.

Balanced scorecard (ch. 14, p. 539)
An attempt to combine a range of both qualitative and quantitative measures of performance which recognise the expectations of various stakeholders.

Behavioural control (ch. 18, p. 682)
A form of control based on direct personal supervision which is responsive to the particular needs of the tasks, the abilities of the manager and the norms of the organisation.

Behaviourism (ch. 5, p. 182)
A school of psychology developed out of research studies into **learning** which is interested in the study of behaviour and those actions which could be observed, measured and controlled.

Benchmarking (ch. 20, p. 779)
An organisation's assessment of the performance and practices of other organisations and competitors in an effort to analyse and compare its own performance.

Brainstorming (ch. 9, p. 345)
Where a group adopts a 'freewheeling' attitude aimed at generating as many ideas as possible. The focus is on freedom of expression and the quantity of ideas rather than quality.

Bureaucracy (ch. 2, p. 47)
A form of structure found in many large-scale organisations. Bureaucracy is based on specialisation of tasks, hierarchy of authority and decision-making, systems of rules and regulations and an impersonal orientation from officials.

Bureaucratic orientation (ch. 1, p. 9)
An individual's orientation to work in which he or she regards it as a central life issue. There is a sense of obligation to the work of the organisation.

Business ethics (ch. 14, p. 549)
An example of applied ethics which seeks to explore the implications of general ethics to the conduct of business.

Business process re-engineering (BPR) (ch. 20, p. 764)
Concerned with the total restructuring of an organisation which involves a radical redesign of business processes to achieve dramatic improvements in organisational performance.

Calculative involvement (ch. 18, p. 689)
Where attachment to the organisation is motivated by extrinsic rewards.

Centralised network (ch. 9, p. 334)
A network of communication where a link person is at the centre of the network and acts as the focus of activities and information flows and is the co-ordinator of group tasks.

Chain of command (ch. 15, p. 578)
The number of different levels in the structure of the organisation, the chain of hierarchical command.

Charismatic organisation (ch. 3, p. 82)
An organisation in which authority is legitimised by belief in the personal qualities of the leader and their strength of personality and inspiration.

Classical approach to management (ch. 2, p. 41)
The organisation is thought of in terms of its purpose and formal structure and this approach aims to identify how methods of working can improve productivity.

Emphasis is placed on the planning of work, the technical requirements of the organisation, principles of management and the assumption of rational and logical behaviour.

Classical conditioning (ch. 5, p. 182)
A theory on **learning** developed by Pavlov, using dogs, who found that instinctive reflexes could be 'conditioned' to respond to a new situation and new stimulus.

Coaching (ch. 5, p. 196)
A supportive relationship aimed at creating understanding, direction and action. Coaching uses deductive techniques and the coach does not have to be an expert in the subject.

Coercive power (ch. 10, p. 388, ch. 18, p. 689)
Based on fear and the subordinate's perception that the leader has the ability to punish or bring about undesirable outcomes for those who do not comply with the directives (e.g. withholding promotion or privileges).

Cognitive theories of learning (ch. 5, p. 181)
Theories of learning that identify how and why people learn, taking individual factors into consideration, and not simply the behaviour demonstrated through the learning process.

Communities of practice (COP) (ch. 5, p. 174)
Groups of people who nurture new knowledge, stimulate innovation and share tacit knowledge.

Community (institutional) level (ch. 15, p. 566)
The level within an organisation that is concerned with broad objectives and the work of the organisation as a whole.

Conceptual ability (ch. 11, p. 429)
The ability to view the complexities of the operations of the organisation as a whole, including environmental influences, and the ability to make decisions.

Conflict (ch. 3, p. 94)
Conflict is present where there is an incompatibility of goals arising from opposing behaviours at the individual, group or organisational level. Particularly, conflict is behaviour intended to obstruct the achievement of some other person's goals.

Constructive behaviour (ch. 7, p. 253)
A positive reaction to the blockage of a desired goal through problem-solving or compromise.

Content theories of motivation (ch. 7, p. 256)
These theories attempt to explain those specific things which actually motivate the individual at work and are concerned with identifying people's needs, the strength of those needs and the goals they pursue in order to satisfy those needs.

Contingency approach (ch. 2, p. 57)
An extension of the systems approach to management that implies that the structure of an organisation and its success are dependent upon the nature of tasks which are undertaken and the nature of environmental influences. There is, therefore, no one best way to structure or manage organisations, rather it must be dependent upon the contingencies of the situation.

Continuing professional development (ch. 20, p. 773)
The process of planned, continuing development of individuals throughout their career.

Control (ch. 18, p. 678)
Within an organisation control is primarily a process for motivating and inspiring people to perform organisational activities and monitoring those activities to ensure that they will further the organisation's goals.

Corporate social responsibility (ch. 14, p. 542)
This concept gives rise to how a company should conduct itself within society, and different views on what a business is for and how it should act. Social responsibilities arise from the interdependence of organisations, society and the environment.

Corporate strategy (ch. 14, p. 429)
Corporate strategy formalises the objectives and policy of an organisation and serves to describe its sense of purpose together with its direction and scope over the long term.

Creativity (ch. 5, p. 192)
The application of imaginative thought which may lead to new ways of seeing things and result in innovative solutions to a problem or the initiation of change.

Decentralisation (ch. 15, p. 575)
Where specific delegation is given to sub-units or groups within an organisation such that they enjoy a measure of autonomy or independence.

Decentralised network (ch. 9, p. 334)
A network of communication where there is no link person at the centre of the network but communication takes place freely between all members of the network.

Decision-making approach (ch. 2, p. 57)
An approach to management that focuses on managerial decision-making and how organisations process and use information in making decisions.

Delegation (ch. 18, p. 693)
The process of entrusting authority and responsibility to others throughout the various levels of the organisation, and the creation of a special manager–subordinate relationship.

Delphi technique (ch. 9, p. 346)
A technique based on multiple, anonymous inputs from individual members of a group. Ideas and suggestions are recorded by a central manager and then recirculated to other members for their feedback.

Democratic style of leadership (ch. 10, p. 371)
Where the focus of power is more with the group as a whole than with the manager. Leadership functions are shared with members of the group and the manager is more part of a team.

Directive leadership (ch. 10, p. 378)
Involves letting subordinates know exactly what is expected of them and giving specific directions.

Displaced aggression (ch. 7, p. 254)
When aggression is displaced towards some other person or object than that which is perceived as the source of frustration, i.e. a 'scapegoat' is found for the outlet of frustration.

Diversity (ch.4, p. 145)
The recognition of individual differences and that people are not homogeneous. Focuses on the multiplicity of visible and non-visible differences among people.

E-business (ch.14, p. 540)
An organisation which connects critical business systems directly to their customers, employees, partners and suppliers via intranets, extranets and over the web.

E-learning (ch. 13, p. 491)
Learning via communications technology.

Electronic panopticon (ch. 17, p. 658)
Use of information technology to monitor and record the work of employees.

Element functions (ch. 15, p. 571)
Activities within an organisation which are not directed towards specific and definable ends but are supportive of the task functions and an intrinsic part of the management process.

Employee commitment (ch.19, p. 731)
Typically conceived as an individual's psychological bond to the organisation including a sense of job involvement, loyalty and a belief in the value of the organisation.

Employee relations (ch. 13, p. 501)
Concerned with the relationships between the policies and practices of the organisation and its staff, and the behaviour of work groups.

Empowerment (ch. 18, p. 702)
Where employees are allowed greater freedom, autonomy and self-control over their work, and the responsibility for decision-making.

Equity theory (ch. 7, p. 271)
A theory of motivation which focuses on people's feelings of how fairly they have been treated in comparison with the treatment received by others.

Ethics (ch. 14, p. 546)
The study of morality – practices and activities that are considered to be importantly right and wrong, together with the rules that govern those activities and the values to which those activities relate.

Excellence Model (European Foundation for Quality Management) (ch. 20, p. 774)
A model that is based on the concept that an organisation will achieve better results by involving all the people in the organisation in the continuous improvement of their processes.

Expectancy theory (ch. 7, p. 265)
A theory of **motivation** based on the idea that people prefer certain outcomes from their behaviour over others. Motivation is a function of the relationship between effort, level of performance and rewards related to performance.

Expert power (ch. 10, p. 388)
Based on the subordinate's perception of the leader as someone who is competent and who has some special knowledge or expertise in a given area. This power is based on credibility and clear evidence of knowledge or expertise.

Explicit knowledge (ch. 5, p. 173)
Knowledge which is easily communicated, quantified and systematic.

External environment (ch. 3, p. 85, ch. 11, p. 423)
The external factors outside of the organisation that can influence and affect the performance of it, the major environmental factors being technical, economic, social and governmental.

Extrinsic motivation (ch. 7, p. 251)
Related to tangible rewards such as salary, promotion, working conditions and fringe benefits. These tangible rewards are often determined at the organisational level and may be outside the control of individual managers.

Fixation (ch. 7, p. 254)
When an individual is frustrated but persists in a form of behaviour which has no adaptive value and actions are continued which have no positive results.

Flat hierarchical structure (ch. 15, p. 579)
An organisation that has broad spans of control and few levels of authority.

Flexible working arrangements (ch. 16, p. 621)
A range of flexible working practices designed to help employees balance work and home life.

Formal goals (ch. 14, p. 533)
Goals of an organisation set out in broad terms as the purpose of the organisation.

Formal group (ch. 8, p. 303)
Formal groups are created to achieve specific organisational objectives and are concerned with the co-ordination of work activities. Group members have defined roles and the nature of tasks to be undertaken is a predominant feature of the group.

Formal organisation (ch. 3, p. 77)
A planned co-ordination of the activities of a number of people for the achievement of some common, explicit purpose or goal, through the division of labour and function, and through a hierarchy of authority and responsibility.

Forming (ch. 8, p. 310)
The initial formation of a group and the first stage in group development.

Frustration (ch. 7, p. 254)
A negative response to the blockage of a desired goal resulting in a defensive form of behaviour.

Functional relationships (ch. 15, p. 580)
The formal relationships within an organisation between people in a specialist or advisory position, and line managers and their subordinates. This occurs when a person offers a common service throughout all departments of the organisation.

Functions of leadership (ch. 10, p. 368)
This focuses attention on the functions of leadership, rather than the personality of the leader, and how the leader's behaviour affects and is affected by the group of followers. This approach to leadership believes that the skills of leadership can be learned and developed.

Gap analysis (ch. 20, p. 779)
An investigation of the gap between the vision, objectives and goals of the organisation and actual levels of performance, and establishing the necessary actions to bring activities in line with that which is planned.

Globalisation (ch. 1, p. 21)
In broad terms, organisations integrating, operating and competing in a worldwide economy.

Goal theory (ch. 7, p. 273)
A theory of motivation that is based on the premise that people's goals or intentions play an important part in determining behaviour. Goals guide people's responses and actions and direct work behaviour and performance, leading to certain consequences or feedback.

Group (ch. 8, p. 299)
Any number of people who interact with one another, are psychologically aware of one another and who perceive themselves as being in a group.

Group cohesiveness (ch. 8, p. 307)
The extent to which members of a group interact, co-operate, are united and work together effectively. Generally, the greater the cohesiveness within a group, the more rewarding the experience is for the members and the higher the chances are of success.

Group norm (ch. 8, p. 303)
Codes and practices developed by a group which group members consider to constitute proper group behaviour.

Groupthink (ch. 9, p. 344)
The tendency within a group to 'drift along' towards decisions which may be inappropriate or unquestioned due to various in-group pressures.

Halo effect (ch. 6, p. 237)
When the perception of a person is formulated on the basis of a single favourable or unfavourable trait or characteristic and tends to shut out other relevant characteristics of that person.

Harassment (ch. 4, p. 135)
Conduct which is unreasonable, unwelcome and offensive and which creates an intimidating or humiliating working environment. Harassment is a direct type of discrimination if the victim can show that the behaviour caused injury to feelings.

Hierarchy of needs (ch. 7, p. 258)
A theory of motivation developed by Maslow which states that people's behaviour is determined by their desire to satisfy a progression of physiological, social and psychological needs.

Human capital management (ch. 13, p. 482)
The measurement and value of employees (human capital) to the organisation and as a key indicator of a company's success.

Human relations approach (ch. 2, p. 51)
A management approach based on the consideration of and attention to the social factors at work and the behaviour of employees within an organisation. Particular importance is paid to the informal organisation and the satisfaction of individual's needs through groups at work.

Human resource management (HRM) (ch. 13, p. 480)
The design, implementation and maintenance of strategies to manage people for optimum business performance including the development of policies and processes to support these strategies.

Hygiene (maintenance) factors (ch. 7, p. 262)
Factors within a job that serve to prevent dissatisfaction. They are related to the job environment, are extrinsic to the job itself and include job security, working conditions and salary.

Idiographic approaches (ch. 4, p. 125)
Approaches to the study of **personality** that focus on understanding the uniqueness of individuals. These approaches regard personality as a process which is open to change.

Informal goals (ch. 14, p. 533)
The goals which the organisation actually pursues as a result of the members of the organisation having different and conflicting goals to the officially stated (formal) goals of the organisation as a whole.

Informal groups (ch. 8, p. 304)
Informal groups serve to satisfy the psychological and social needs of the group members and are not necessarily related to tasks to be undertaken. Informal groups are based on personal relationships and membership can cut across the formal structure of an organisation.

Informal organisation (ch. 3, p. 91)
An organisation arising from the interaction of people, their psychological and social needs, and the development of groups with their own relationships and norms of behaviour, irrespective of those defined within the formal structure.

Informating technology (ch. 17, p. 638)
Generation of new information about organisational activities.

Information technology (ch. 15, p. 580)
The impact of information technology will involve changes to patterns of work organisation, the hierarchical structure, decision-making and control systems, and the nature of supervision.

Inspirational (or visionary) leadership (ch. 10, p. 383)
Leadership associated with the concept of creating a vision with which others can identify, getting along with others and inspiring through personal qualities or charisma.

Instrumental orientation (ch. 1, p. 9)
An individual's orientation to work in which they regard it as a means to an end and not as a central life issue.

Interaction analysis (ch. 9, p. 338)
The description of group process and indications of factors influencing the process through the categorisation of every act of behaviour within the group.

Interactionist perspective (ch. 3, p. 95)
A view that believes conflict is a positive force and necessary for effective performance. This approach encourages a minimum level of conflict within a group in order to encourage self-criticism, change and innovation.

Internal environment (ch. 11, p. 422)
Relates to the culture and climate of an organisation and to the prevailing atmosphere surrounding the organisation.

Intrinsic motivation (ch. 7, p. 251)
Related to psychological rewards such as achieving appreciation, positive recognition and being given the opportunity to use one's ability. These psychological rewards can usually be determined by the actions and behaviour of individual managers.

Introduction stage (ch. 17, p. 651)
The second main phase in the adoption and introduction of new technology into an organisation. This involves working on the technology and the associated organisational changes with a view to making them effective.

Investors in People (ch. 13, p. 492)
The Investors in People Standard is a business improvement tool designed to advance an organisation's performance through the training and development of its people. The standard is based on a set of ten key indicators of good practice.

Job satisfaction (ch. 7, p. 277)
An attitude or internal state that is associated with, for example, a personal feeling of achievement either quantitative or qualitative.

Kaizen (ch. 20, p. 761)
A Japanese concept of a total quality approach based on continual evolutionary change with considerable responsibility to employees within certain fixed boundaries.

Knowledge management (ch. 5, p. 173)
The promotion and formalisation of learning within the workplace with the aim of aligning training with the needs of the business.

Laissez-faire **(genuine) style of leadership** (ch. 10, p. 371)
Where the manager consciously makes a decision to pass the focus of power to members of the group allowing them freedom of action. The manager has observed that the members of the group work well on their own and does not interfere.

Lateral relationships (ch. 15, p. 581)
Formal relationships within an organisation which exist between individuals in different departments or sections, especially between individuals on the same level.

Leadership (ch. 10, p. 363)
A relationship through which one person influences the behaviour or actions of other people.

Leadership and Management Model (ch. 20, p. 774)
A developmental framework for ensuring that organisations create, manage and invest in effective leadership now and in the long term. The model is based on four key principles of commitment, planning, action and evaluation.

Leadership Grid (ch. 12, p. 447)
A grid which compares the varying styles of management based on the concern for production against the concern for people.

Learning (ch. 5, p. 168)
A change of a relatively permanent kind which may result in new behaviours and actions or new

understanding and knowledge gained through a formal process or spontaneously and incidentally through life experiences.

Learning organisation (ch. 20, p. 759)
An organisation that encourages and facilitates the learning and development of people at all levels of the organisation, values the learning and simultaneously transforms itself.

Legitimate (organisational) power (ch. 10, p. 388, ch. 18, p. 691)
Based on the subordinate's perception that the leader has a right to exercise influence because of the leader's role or position in the organisation. This power is based on authority and related to a person's position within an organisation.

Line organisation (ch. 15, p. 582)
Relates to those functions within an organisation concerned with specific responsibility for achieving the objectives of the organisation and to those people in the direct chain of command.

Line relationships (ch. 15, p. 580)
A formal relationship within an organisation between individual positions where authority flows vertically down through the structure.

Locus of control (ch. 6, p. 234)
The extent to which an individual perceives that his/her behaviour has a direct impact on the outcomes which result from that behaviour.

Maintenance function (ch. 9, p. 339)
Functions within a group that are concerned with the emotional life of the group and directed towards building and maintaining the group as an effective working unit.

Management (ch. 11, p. 412)
The process through which efforts of members of the organisation are co-ordinated, directed and guided towards the achievement of organisational goals.

Management by objectives (MBO) (ch. 12, p. 454)
A system or style of management which attempts to relate organisational goals to individual performance and development through the involvement of all levels of management.

Management development (ch. 20, p. 767)
Concerned with improving the effectiveness of individual managers but also with an improvement in management performance as a whole. It must be integrated with the development of the organisation and the associated improvement in organisational effectiveness.

Managerial effectiveness (ch. 12, p. 461)
Concerned with 'doing the right things' and relates to the outputs of the job and what the manager actually achieves.

Managerial efficiency (ch. 12, p. 461)
Concerned with 'doing things right' and relates to inputs and what the manager does.

Managerial Grid (ch. 12, p. 447)
See **Leadership Grid**.

Managerial level (ch. 15, p. 566)
The level within an organisation that is concerned with the co-ordination and integration of work at the technical level.

Managerial roles (ch. 11, p. 424)
Organised sets of behaviour associated with a manager. Arise as a result of the formal authority, status and activities of a manager.

Matrix structure (ch. 15, p. 584)
Where there is a two-way flow of authority and responsibility within an organisation due to the vertical flow of authority and responsibility from the functional departments and the horizontal flow of authority and responsibility from project teams.

Mechanistic system (ch. 16, p. 610)
A rigid system of management practice and structure which is characterised by a clear hierarchical structure, specialisation of task, defined duties and responsibilities and knowledge centred at the top of the hierarchy.

Mentoring (ch.5, p. 196)
A supportive and challenging relationship in which the mentor offers advice, guidance and support. The mentor is typically an expert in an area or a leader within an organisation.

Mission statement (ch. 14, p. 535)
Sets an organisation's purpose, guiding values and principles and the way in which it intends to achieve its objectives, while recognising the interests of other stakeholders.

Moral involvement (ch. 18, p. 689)
Based on the individual's belief in, and value placed on, the goals of the organisation.

Motivation (ch. 7, p. 250)
The driving force within individuals by which they attempt to achieve some goal in order to fulfil some need or expectation.

Motivators or growth factors (ch. 7, p. 262)
Factors within a job that, if present, serve to motivate the individual to superior effort and performance. These factors are related to the job content of the work itself and include recognition, personal growth and sense of achievement.

Myers–Briggs Type Indicator (MBTI) (ch. 4, p. 130)
A personality test which identifies 16 types of personality based on individuals' extroversion or introversion and their cognitive functions of thinking, feeling, sensation and intuition.

Neo-human relations (ch. 2, p. 54)
A management approach developed by such writers as Maslow, Herzberg and McGregor which adopts a more psychological orientation than that of the human relations approach. Particular attention is paid to the personal adjustment of individuals at work and the effects of group relationships and leadership styles.

Network-building (ch. 11, p. 425)
Involves individuals interacting with others and establishing a network of co-operative relations. These networks are outside of the formal structure and provide a means of exchanging information on a wide range of topics.

Neuro-linguistic programming (NLP) (ch. 6, p. 225)
The name originates from three disciplines which all have a part to play when people are communicating with others: neurology, language and programming. NLP emphasises the significance of the perceptual process, and ways in which information is subjectively filtered and interpreted.

Nomothetic approaches (ch. 4, p. 125)
Approaches to the study of **personality** that focus on people in general through the analysis of group data. These approaches claim that personality is largely inherited and resistant to change.

Normative power (ch. 18, p. 689)
A form of power which relies on the allocation and manipulation of symbolic rewards (e.g. esteem and prestige).

Norming (ch. 8, p. 310)
The third stage of group development during which members of the group establish guidelines and standards and develop their own norms of acceptable behaviour.

Objectives (organisational) (ch. 14, p. 536)
Objectives set out the specific goals of the organisation, the aims to be achieved and the desired end results.

Object-moulding organisations (ch. 3, p. 84)
Concerned with physical or material objects as the nature of work being carried out – for example, a manufacturing plant, a car plant or an oil company.

Open systems model (ch. 3, p. 84)
The organisation is viewed as an open system that takes input from the environment and through a series of activities transform or converts these into outputs to achieve some objective.

Operant conditioning (ch. 5, p. 183)
A theory of **learning** developed by Skinner showing the effects of reward and punishment and demonstrating that responses in behaviour are learned because of their outcomes.

Organic system (ch. 16, p. 610)
A fluid and flexible system of management practice and structure which is characterised by the adjustment and continual redefinition of tasks, a network structure of control, authority and communication and where superior knowledge does not necessarily coincide with positional authority.

Organisation audit (ch. 20, p. 782)
Involves a review of the operations of the organisation as a whole and an examination of the full range of management activities, including the effective use of human resources.

Organisation development (ch. 19, p. 719)
A generic term which embraces a wide range of intervention strategies which are aimed at the development of individuals, groups and the organisation as a total system.

Organisational behaviour (ch. 1, p. 3)
The study and understanding of individual and group behaviour and patterns of structure in order to help improve organisational performance and effectiveness.

Organisational climate (ch. 19, p. 730)
Relating to the prevailing atmosphere surrounding the organisation, to the level of morale, and to the strength of feelings or belonging, care and goodwill among members. Organisational climate is based on the perceptions of members towards the organisation.

Organisational culture (ch. 19, p. 721)
The collection of traditional values, policies, beliefs and attitudes that constitute a pervasive context for everything we do and think in an organisation.

Organisational goals (ch. 14, p. 531)
Something that the organisation is striving to achieve, a future expectation, a desired future state and something towards which the activities of the organisation are directed in an effort to attain this state.

Organisational ideology (ch.14, p. 534)
Based on the beliefs, values and attitudes of the individuals, determines the culture of the organisation and provides a set of principles which govern the overall conduct of the organisation.

Organisational structure (ch. 15, p. 564)
Structure is the pattern of relationships among positions in the organisation and among members of the organisation. It defines tasks and responsibilities, work roles and relationships and channels of communication.

Organisational sub-systems (ch. 3, p. 88)
The interrelated sub-systems of an organisation: tasks, technology, structure, people and management. These sub-systems need to be co-ordinated to ensure that the activities of an organisation are directed towards the achievement of aims and objectives.

Organisations (ch. 3, p. 75)
A consciously co-ordinated social unit created by groups in society to achieve specific purposes, common aims and objectives by means of planned and co-ordinated activities.

Output control (ch. 18, p. 682)
A form of control based on the measurement of outputs and the results achieved and that serves the needs of the organisation as a whole. Used largely because of the demand for a quantifiable, simple measure of organisational performance.

Parkinson's Law (ch. 1, p. 18)
The concept of the 'Rising Pyramid' and the idea that: 'work expands so as to fill the time available for its completion'.

Participative leadership (ch. 10, p. 378)
Involves consulting with subordinates and the evaluation of their opinions and suggestions before the manager makes the decision.

People-moulding organisations (ch.3, p. 84)
Concerned with human beings as the basis of work carried out – for example a school or leisure centre.

Perception (ch. 6, p. 209)
The dynamic and complex way in which individuals select information (stimuli) from the environment, interpret and translate it so that a meaning is assigned which will result in a pattern of behaviour or thought.

Perceptual defence (ch. 6, p. 237)
When people select information which is supportive of their own point of view and choose not to acknowledge contrary information. They avoid or screen out certain stimuli that are perceptually disturbing or threatening.

Performance management (ch. 13, p. 493)
A method of reviewing the performance and potential of employees that is usually undertaken formally and systematically at regular intervals.

Performing (ch. 8, p. 310)
The fourth stage of group development during which the group concentrates on the performance of the common task.

Personal (informal) power (ch. 18, p. 691)
Power that derives from the individual and is in the eye of the beholders who believe that person has the ability to influence other people or events to make things happen.

Personality (ch. 4, p. 125)
An individual's unique set of characteristics and tendencies which shape a sense of self, and what that person does and the behaviour they exhibit.

PESTEL analysis (ch. 3, p. 86)
A technique for analysing the general external environment of an organisation in terms of the political,

economic, socio-cultural, technological, environmental and legal aspects.

(The) Peter Principle (ch.1, p. 17)
Concerned with the study of occupational incompetence and hierarchies, and the idea that 'in a hierarchy every employee tends to rise to their level of incompetence'.

Pluralistic perspective (ch. 13, p. 503)
Where a work organisation is viewed as being made up of powerful and competing sub-groups with their own legitimate loyalties, objectives and leaders.

Policy (organisational) (ch. 14, p. 536)
Policy is developed within the frame of the objectives and details the 'how', 'where' and 'when' in terms of the course of action which must be followed to achieve the objectives.

Postmodernism (ch.2, p. 61)
A more recent view of organisations and management that rejects a rational, systems approach and accepted explanations of society and behaviour. Postmodernism places greater emphasis on the use of language and attempts to portray a particular set of assumptions or versions of the 'truth'.

Power (ch. 18, p. 688)
The level of control or influence a person holds over the behaviour of others with or without their consent.

Private enterprise organisations (ch. 3, p. 79)
Organisations owned and financed by individuals, partners or shareholders accountable to their owners or members. The main aim is of a commercial nature such as profit, return on capital employed, market standing or sales level.

Privatisation (ch. 3, p. 79)
The transfer of business undertakings from state (government) control to the private sector. The extent of state ownership, and the balance between commercial and social interests.

Process theories of motivation (ch. 7, p. 257)
Concerned with how behaviour is initiated, directed and sustained, i.e. the actual process of motivation.

Project team (ch.15, p. 584)
A team set up as a separate unit on a temporary basis for the attainment of a particular task. When the task is completed the team is banded or members reassigned to a new task.

Projection (ch. 6, p. 238)
Attributing or projecting one's own feelings, motives or characteristics to other people. Projection is a distortion which can occur in the perception of other people.

Psychological contract (ch. 1, p. 13)
An unwritten contract between employers and employees which covers a series of mutual expectations and satisfaction of needs arising from the people–organisation relationship.

Psychological (psychometric) tests (ch. 4, p. 140)
Tests which assess an individual's typical responses to given situations based on their choices and strength of feeling or which assess an individual's ability to perform effectively under standard conditions, including aptitude and ability.

Psychology (ch. 1, p. 7)
The study of the personality system, i.e. human behaviour, traits of the individual and membership of small social groups.

Public sector organisations (ch. 3, p. 79)
Organisations created by the government which do not generally have profit as their goal but have political purposes. They include municipal undertakings financed by rates, taxes, government grants and loans; and central government departments which are 'state owned' and financed by funds granted by Parliament.

Qualities (or traits) approach to leadership (ch. 10, p. 367)
This assumes that leaders are born and not made. Leadership consists of certain inherited characteristics, or personality traits, which distinguish leaders from their followers. Attention is focused on the person in the job and not the job itself.

Quality circles (ch. 9, p. 346)
A group of people within an organisation who meet together on a regular basis to identify, analyse and solve problems relating to quality, productivity or other aspects of day-to-day working arrangements using problem-solving techniques.

Radical perspective (ch. 3, p. 94)
A perspective on organisations that challenges the traditional view of conflict, and sees organisations in terms of disparity in power and control.

Rational–economic concept of motivation (ch. 7, p. 255)
Based on the belief of earlier writers such as F. W. Taylor that employees want, more than anything else from their employer, the highest possible wages for their work and are motivated by their economic needs.

Referent power (ch. 10, p. 388)
Based on the subordinate's identification with the leader. The leader exercises influence because of perceived attractiveness, personal characteristics, reputation or charisma.

Regression (ch. 7, p. 254)
When an individual is frustrated and reverts to a childish or primitive form of behaviour, e.g. sulking, crying or tantrums.

Remunerative power (ch. 18, p. 689)
A form of power that involves the manipulation of material resources and rewards (e.g. salaries and wages).

Responsibility (ch. 18, p. 694)
Involves an obligation by a subordinate to perform certain duties or make certain decisions and having to accept possible reprimand for unsatisfactory performance.

Reward power (ch. 10, p. 388)
Based on the subordinate's perception that the leader has the ability and resources to obtain rewards for those who comply with directives (e.g. pay or promotion).

Risky-shift (ch. 9, p. 343)
Where a group decides to take a riskier course of action rather than the more conservative or safer option.

Role (ch. 8, p. 316)
The expected pattern of behaviours associated with members occupying a particular position within the structure of the organisation.

Role ambiguity (ch. 8, p. 319)
This occurs when there is a lack of clarity as to the precise requirements of the role and the individual is unsure what to do.

Role conflict (ch. 8, p. 317)
Arises from inadequate or inappropriate role definition and results in a person behaving in a way which may not be consistent with their expected pattern of behaviour.

Role expectations (ch. 8, p. 316)
Indicate what the person is expected to do and their duties and obligations.

Role incompatibility (ch. 8, p. 318)
Arises when compliance with one set of expectations makes it difficult or impossible to comply with the other expectations. The two **role expectations** are in conflict.

Role incongruence (ch. 8, p. 316)
This arises when a member of staff is perceived as having a high and responsible position in one respect but a low standing in another respect.

Role overload (ch. 8, p. 319)
When an individual faces too many separate roles or too great a variety of expectations and is unable to satisfactorily meet all expectations.

Role-set (ch. 8, p. 316)
Comprises the range of associations or contacts with whom the individual has meaningful interactions in connection with the performance of their role.

Role underload (ch. 8, p. 319)
When the prescribed **role expectations** fall short of the individual's own perception of their role.

Rusty halo effect (ch. 6, p. 237)
Where general judgements about a person are formulated from the perception of a negative charactistic.

Scientific management (ch. 2, p. 43)
Developed by F. W. Taylor, this **classical approach to management** advocates the breaking down of work processes into discrete tasks to find the 'one best way' of performing each task in terms of scientific procedures. Increased productivity is rewarded by financial rewards.

Self-established roles (ch. 8, p. 317)
Where formal expectations are specified loosely or in very general terms, and members have the opportunity to determine their own role expectations.

Self-fulfilling prophecy (ch. 6, p. 238)
The essence of the prophecy is that simply because it has been made, this will cause it to happen. People strive to validate their perceptions irrespective of the actual reality.

Self-oriented behaviour (ch. 9, p. 339)
Where members of a group may say or do something in attempting to satisfy some personal need or goal.

Sensitivity training (ch. 9, p. 347)
A training method in which members of a group direct attention to an understanding of their own behaviour and to perceiving themselves as others see them.

Shamrock organisation (ch. 16, p. 623)
A concept developed by Handy which states that each leaf of the shamrock is symbolic of a different group of people within the organisation: the professional core; the contractual fringe; the flexible labour force; and customers.

Situational approach to leadership (ch. 10, p. 374)
Where the person who is best suited to lead in a particular situation takes on the role of leader. The importance of the situation is the focus and the person who is seen as the most suitable leader is appointed by the group.

Six Sigma (ch. 20, p. 764)
The use of statistical analysis and computer simulation for the definition, measurement and reduction of defects and waste.

Social action (ch. 2, p. 58)
A study of organisations in which the organisation is considered from the standpoint of the individual. Individual goals, interpretation of the work situation in terms of the satisfaction sought and the meaning that work has for them are used as a basis for explaining behaviour.

Social and human skills (ch. 11, p. 429)
Abilities related to interpersonal relationships in working with and through other people, and the exercise of judgement.

Sociology (ch. 1, p. 7)
The study of the social system, i.e. social behaviour, relationships among social groups and societies and the maintenance of order.

Sociometry (ch. 9, p. 336)
A method of indicating the feelings of acceptance or rejection among members of a group.

Socio-technical system (ch. 2, p. 56)
A sub-division of the systems approach which is concerned with the interactions between the psychological and social factors and the needs, demands of the human part of organisation and its structural and technological requirements.

Solidaristic orientation (ch. 1, p. 10)
An individual's orientation to work in which group activities are most important. There is an ego involvement with work groups rather than with the organisation itself.

Span of control (ch. 15, p. 577)
The number of subordinates who report directly to a given manager or supervisor.

Staff organisation (ch. 15, p. 582)
Relates to those functions within an organisation which provide specialist and support functions for the line organisation, creating an advisory relationship.

Staff relationships (ch. 15, p. 581)
These formal relationships within an organisation arise from the appointment of personal assistants to senior members of staff. Someone in a staff position usually has little or no direct authority in his or her own right but acts as an extension of his or her superior.

Stakeholder (organisational) (ch. 14, p. 543)
Any individual or group which has an interest in and/or is affected by the goals, operations or activities of the organisation or the behaviour of its members.

Stakeholder theory (ch. 14, p. 547)
A business is for its stakeholders and the actions of management should be designed to balance stakeholder interests.

Stereotyping (ch. 6, p. 236)
The tendency to ascribe positive or negative characteristics to a person on the basis of a general categorisation and perceived similarities. It occurs when an individual is judged on the basis of the group to which it is perceived that person belongs.

Storming (ch. 8, p. 310)
The second stage of group development which involves members of the group getting to know each other and putting forward their views.

Stress (ch. 3, p. 102)
A source of tension and frustration which tends to arise when an individual feels that a certain situation should not exist.

Structuralism (ch. 2, p. 51)
A management approach which combines elements of both the classical and human relations approaches.

Greater attention is given to the relationship between the formal and informal aspects of the organisation and, in particular, the study of conflict within the organisation.

Supportive leadership (ch. 10, p. 378)
Involves a friendly and approachable manner from the leader and displaying concern for the needs and welfare of subordinates.

SWOT analysis (ch. 14, p. 541)
The study of Strengths, Weaknesses, Opportunities and Threats facing an organisation that may provide a basis for decision-making and problem-solving.

Synergy (ch. 14, p. 531)
A concept developed in management applications by Ansoff. Synergy results when the whole is greater than the sum of its component parts, expressed for example as the 2 + 2 = 5 effect.

Systems approach (ch. 2, p. 55)
A management approach which attempts to reconcile the classical and human relations approaches. Attention is focused on the total work of the organisation and the interrelationships of structure and behaviour and the range of variables within the organisation. The organisation is viewed within its total environment and emphasises the importance of multiple channels in interaction.

Tacit knowledge (ch. 5, p. 173)
Knowledge and wisdom which is not easily communicated or quantified but is gained through experience and communicated on an informal basis.

Tall hierarchical structure (ch. 15, p. 579)
An organisation that has narrow spans of control and a relatively large number of levels of authority.

Task function (within groups) (ch. 9, p. 339)
Functions within a group that are directed towards problem-solving, the accomplishment of the tasks of the group and the achievement of its goals.

Task function (within organisations) (ch. 15, p. 571)
The basic activities of the organisation that are related to the actual completion of the productive process and directed towards specific and definable end-results.

Team-role (ch. 9, p. 332)
A pattern of behaviour, characteristic of the way in which one team member interacts with another, where performance facilitates the progress of the team as a whole.

Technical competence (ch. 11, p. 428)
Relates to the application of specific knowledge, methods and skills to discrete tasks.

Technical level (ch. 15, p. 566)
The level within an organisation which is concerned with specific operations and discrete tasks, with the

actual job or tasks to be done and with the performance of the technical function.

Technology approach (ch. 2, p. 56)
A sub-division of the systems approach which emphasises the effects of varying technologies on organisation structure, work groups and individual performance and job satisfaction.

Telecommuting (ch. 16, p. 622)
Where staff work from home with a computer network, telephone and fax.

T-groups (ch. 9, p. 347)
A leaderless and unstructured training group which is formed to provide participants with an opportunity to learn more about themselves and their impact on others.

Theory X (ch. 12, p. 444)
A theory towards human nature and behaviour at work that assumes that most people are lazy, have an inherent dislike of work and must be coerced, controlled and directed through a central system of organisation and the exercise of authority. Motivation occurs only at the lower level needs.

Theory Y (ch. 12, p. 444)
A theory towards human nature and behaviour at work that assumes that most people enjoy work, are creative, can exercise self-direction and control and want to accept responsibility. Motivation occurs at the higher level needs as well as lower levels.

Theory Z (ch. 12, p. 446)
A Japanese-style organisational environment where the characteristics include long-term employment, development of company-specific skills, participative and collective decision-making and a broad concern for the welfare of workers.

Total quality management (TQM) (ch. 20, p. 761)
An approach to quality within an organisation which is committed to total customer satisfaction through a continuous process of improvement, and the contribution and involvement of people.

Traditional organisations (ch. 3, p. 82)
An organisation in which authority is legitimised through tradition, custom and a longstanding belief in the natural right to rule or is possessed through the 'traditional' procedure.

Transactional analysis (ch. 6, p. 225)
Originally developed by Eric Berne, this is a popular way of explaining the dynamics of interpersonal communication which assumes that individuals store all events and feelings ever experienced and that the personality has three ego states: Child, Adult and Parent.

Transactional leadership (ch. 10, p. 381)
Based on legitimate authority within the bureaucratic structure of the organisation. The emphasis is on the clarification of goals and objectives, work task and outcomes, and organisational rewards and punishment.

Transformational leadership (ch. 10, p. 381)
Based on the objective of transforming the performance or fortunes of a business. The emphasis is on generating a vision for the organisation and the leader's ability to appeal to the values of followers in attempting to create a feeling of justice, loyalty and trust.

Type A personality (ch. 4, p. 135)
Individuals who thrive on hard work and long hours, and exhibit characteristics such as a high need for achievement, extreme competitiveness, impatience and aggressiveness. Type A personalities are more vulnerable to heart attacks.

Type B personality (ch. 4, p. 135)
Individuals who exhibit the opposite characteristics from Type A and who are less vulnerable to heart attacks.

Unitary perspective (ch. 3, p. 93)
Where a work organisation is viewed as an integrated and harmonious whole with managers and other staff sharing common interests and objectives.

Upward feedback (ch. 13, p. 498)
An upward review or appraisal system that involves subordinates' appraisal of managers.

Virtual teams (ch. 8, p. 312)
Teams where the primary interaction among members is by some electronic information and communication process.

Virtuoso teams (ch. 8, p. 304)
Teams that are formed specifically for a big change in the organisation and comprised of individual superstars or virtuosos.

Withdrawal (ch. 7, p. 254)
When an individual is frustrated and 'gives up' or resigns themself to the situation.

INDEX

Note: All references are to Britain, unless otherwise indicated. Page references in **bold** indicate glossary definitions and chapters.